PENGUIN BOOKS

THE COLLECTED STORIES OF COLETTE

Colette, the creator of Claudine, Chéri and Gigi, and one of France's outstanding writers, had a long, varied and active life. She was born in Burgundy in 1873, into a home overflowing with dogs, cats and children, and educated at the local village school. At the age of twenty she was brought to Paris by her first husband, the notorious Henry Gauthiers-Villars (Willy), writer and critic. By dint of locking her in her room, Willy forced Colette to write her first novels (the Claudine sequence), which he published under his name. They were an instant success. But their marriage (chronicled in *Mes Apprentissages*) was never happy and Colette left him in 1906. She spent the next six years on the stage – an experience, like that of her country childhood, which would provide many of the themes for her work. She remarried (*Julie de Carneilhan* 'is as close a reckoning with the elements of her second marriage as she ever allowed herself'), later divorcing her second husband, by whom she had a daughter. In 1935 she married Maurice Goudeket, with whom she lived until her death in 1954.

With the publication of *Chéri* (1920) Colette's place as one of France's prose masters was assured. Although she became increasingly crippled with arthritis, she never lost her intense preoccupation with everything around her. 'I cannot interest myself in anything that is not life,' she said; and, to a young writer, 'Look for a long time at what pleases you, and longer still at what pains you.' Her rich and supple prose, with its sensuous detail and sharp psychological insights, illustrates that personal philosophy.

Her writing runs to fifteen volumes, novels, portraits, essays, *chroniques* and a large body of autobiographical prose. She was the first woman President of the Académie Goncourt, and when she died was given a state funeral and buried in Père-Lachaise cemetery in Paris.

THE
COLLECTED STORIES
OF
Colette

EDITED, AND WITH AN INTRODUCTION, BY ROBERT PHELPS

TRANSLATED BY MATTHEW WARD, ANTONIA WHITE,

ANNE-MARIE CALLIMACHI, AND OTHERS

PENGUIN BOOKS

Penguin Books Ltd, Harmondsworth, Middlesex, England
Viking Penguin Inc., 40 West 23rd Street, New York, New York 10010, U.S.A.
Penguin Books Australia Ltd, Ringwood, Victoria, Australia
Penguin Books Canada Ltd, 2801 John Street, Markham, Ontario, Canada L3R 1B4
Penguin Books (N.Z.) Ltd, 182–190 Wairau Road, Auckland 10, New Zealand

First published in the U.S.A. by Farrar, Straus and Giroux 1983
Published by Secker and Warburg 1984
Published in Penguin Books 1985

Contents

❧❦❧

Introduction by Robert Phelps • x i
A Note on the Text • x v
Translator's Acknowledgments • x v i i

PART I

Early Stories

❧❦❧

CLOUK / CHÉRI
The Other Table • 3
The Screen • 6
Clouk Alone • 9
Clouk's Fling • 1 2
Chéri • 1 5
The Return • 1 8
The Pearls • 2 1

DIALOGUES FOR ONE VOICE

Literature · 2 5

My Goddaughter · 2 7

A Hairdresser · 3 1

A Masseuse · 3 3

My Corset Maker · 3 6

The Saleswoman · 3 9

An Interview · 4 2

MY FRIEND VALENTINE

A Letter · 4 5

The Sémiramis Bar · 5 1

"If I Had a Daughter . . ." · 5 6

Rites · 5 9

Newly Shorn · 6 1

Grape Harvest · 6 4

In the Boudoir · 6 9

The "Master" · 7 1

Morning Glories · 7 4

What Must We Look Like? · 7 9

The Cure · 8 5

Sleepless Nights · 9 1

Gray Days · 9 4

The Last Fire · 9 7

A Fable: The Tendrils of the Vine · 1 0 0

PART II

Backstage at the Music Hall

❧❦❧

ON TOUR
The Halt · 1 0 5
Arrival and Rehearsal · 1 0 8
A Bad Morning · 1 1 1
The Circus Horse · 1 1 3
The Workroom · 1 1 6
Matinee · 1 1 9
The Starveling · 1 2 2
Love · 1 2 6
The Hard Worker · 1 2 9
After Midnight · 1 3 1
"Lola" · 1 3 4
Moments of Stress · 1 3 7
Journey's End · 1 4 0
"The Strike, Oh, Lord, the Strike!" · 1 4 3

Bastienne's Child · 1 4 7

CHEAP-JACKS
The Accompanist · 1 5 4
The Cashier · 1 5 7
Nostalgia · 1 5 9

Clever Dogs · 1 6 3
The Child Prodigy · 1 6 6

The Misfit · 1 7 0

FROM THE FRONT
"La Fenice" · 1 8 0
"Gitanette" · 1 8 3

The Victim · 1 8 9
The Tenor · 1 9 4
The Quick-Change Artist · 1 9 6
Florie · 1 9 8
Gribiche · 2 0 5

PART III

Varieties of Human Nature

❦

The Hidden Woman · 2 3 5
Dawn · 2 3 9
One Evening · 2 4 2
The Hand · 2 4 6
A Dead End · 2 4 9
The Fox · 2 5 2
The Judge · 2 5 6
The Omelette · 2 5 9
The Other Wife · 2 6 3

Monsieur Maurice · 266
The Burglar · 270
The Advice · 274
The Murderer · 278
The Portrait · 281
The Landscape · 285
The Half-Crazy · 288
Secrets · 291
"Chả" · 294
The Bracelet · 297
The Find · 300
Mirror Games · 303
Habit · 306
Alix's Refusal · 309
The Seamstress · 311
The Watchman · 314
The Hollow Nut · 319
The Patriarch · 321
The Sick Child · 327
The Rainy Moon · 347
Green Sealing Wax · 387

PART IV

Love

In the Flower of Age · 401
The Rivals · 406

The Respite · 4 1 1

The Bitch · 4 1 7

The Tender Shoot · 4 2 1

Bygone Spring · 4 4 9

October · 4 5 2

Armande · 4 5 5

The Rendezvous · 4 6 9

The Kepi · 4 9 8

The Photographer's Wife · 5 3 2

Bella-Vista · 5 5 8

April · 6 0 1

Introduction

These one hundred stories are taken from some dozen volumes published during and after Colette's lifetime. Dating from 1908 to 1945, they vary in length and intensity, but even the slightest is *echt* Colette, and if the one called "The Kepi" is probably the least sentimental love story ever told, the one called "April," about a teenaged Adam and Eve, is probably the truest.

As always in Colette's world, the subject matter avoids any political or metaphysical themes and remains firmly implanted in the private life, in the joys and stresses of what Tolstoy once called "man's most tormenting tragedy—the tragedy of the bedroom." The backgrounds shift from Paris to the Mediterranean coast, from North African gardens to theater dressing rooms, from louche yet somehow wholesome bars to the fresh, sane countryside of the author's native Burgundy. The people we meet are lovers, loners, liberated women, sexual outsiders, acrobats and mimes, children and adolescents, old maids and divorcees, and to their needful lives Colette brings not only her classically trim art of storytelling but the canny, profoundly generous knowledge of all-too-human nature for which her name has become virtually a synonym.

These stories also represent Colette as an innovator, as well as a master, of the art of fiction. Most of our past century's experimentation with the novel has tried to impose omniscience on it, ignoring its primary reality as something being told by the voice whose name is on the title page (Valéry: "When all is said and done, a book is merely a selection from its author's monologue"). Like Proust, Colette declined anonymity and, in her most original work, establishes her own presence firmly in the foreground.

With closely observed action and dialogue, she mixes some of the intimacy and even irrelevancy (yet so keenly selected and arranged) of a good memoir. The result—imaginary autobiography, post-novel, what-

ever you want to call it—communicates that quality of truth Thoreau
had in mind when he said, "I desire to speak like a man in a waking
moment to men in their waking moments."

Hence any mere digest of the plots of the stories would be misleading. For even when, as in "The Rendezvous" or "Bella-Vista," there
is a surprise ending, this is the least of the matter. Even the supple and
wonderfully economic narrative line, even the lean precision of the prose
itself, are peripheral to, or contained in, what remains the most imposing
element in Colette's art: the use of herself.

This has nothing to do with her actual private life. It has simply to
do with art, the art of using her own first person, and creating on the
printed page a savory and magnetic presence (imaginary for all I know)
called Colette. She has created many memorable characters—Léa, Chéri,
Phil and Vinca, Julie de Carneilhan, Gigi. But Colette eclipses them all:
tart, moody, hardworking, she could take St. Benedict's "Laborare est
orare" as her motto. Capable of reckless lyricism on behalf of what moves
her, capable also of a superb contempt, she is essentially a born watcher,
fierce, dedicated, with an absolute vocation to behold. Listen to her at
her most characteristic, talking to herself on a late spring evening in
Provence:

*The night was murmurous and warmer than the day. Three or four
lighted windows, the clouded sky patched here and there with stars, the
cry of some night bird over this unfamiliar place made my throat tighten
with anguish. It was an anguish without depth; a longing to weep which
I could master as soon as I felt it rise. I was glad of it because it proved
that I could still savor the special taste of loneliness.*

Essentially Colette was a lyric poet, and her basic subject matter
was not the world she described so reverently but the drama of her
personal relation to the world. Her injunction to those around her was
always "Look!" and her own capacity to behold was acute and untiring.
But when she is writing at her best, it is not what she describes so much
as her own presence, the dramatic act of herself watching, say, a butterfly, which becomes so absorbing, morally exemplary, and memorable.
This is no accident, for the very delicate art of using the first person
without indulgence is one that Colette developed as thoroughly, and as
consciously, as Joyce explored the art of eschewing it.

At first she practiced it in only her non-fiction, and whether she
was writing a brochure for a perfume manufacturer, or a text to be read
over Paris Mondial Radio to American students, or marginal notes for an
almanac, she wove a deliberate thread of her personal life, her private
myth, into the fabric. Later she began to do the same thing in her

fiction. The result was a story in which the author sets aside Joyce's aloofness and brings the art of narration back to its origins, with Colette herself consciously in the foreground, intimately, unfearfully telling the reader what she has seen or heard, or maybe even imagined, and no longer pretending she is not there.

It is not, of course, a genre Colette invented. Prosper Mérimée probably suggested it to her, as much as anyone, in stories like "Carmen" and "The Venus of Ille." But it is certainly a genre which Colette perfected. In "Bella-Vista," for instance, she tells us about a middle-aged couple—both women—who keep a small offbeat hotel in the South of France. As a guest, Colette studies their relationship, its frailties, vulnerableness, risks; judges and revises her judgments; and then discovers the truth: which I shall not reveal here except to say that their secret is quite other than it seems. It is a strange, even beautiful story, but the character who is telling it, reconstructing it from day to day, is its greatest center of interest. It is the progression of *her* reactions that—in the best sense—instructs us in the morality of being a neighbor. And it is the qualitative greatness of her example that makes it just and unfulsome, exact and prescient, to think of her, as Glenway Wescott once did, as "a kind of female Montaigne," who wrote stories as well as essays.

Robert Phelps

A Note on the Text

❧

The Colette canon includes at least four categories of "short story" which overlap and mix genres:

1. *chroniques*: 1,800- to 3,500-word texts which include personal reportage, portraits of people, animals, flowers, theater reviews, etc.
2. autobiographical sketches, as *My Mother's House*
3. lyrical meditations whose mode is not narrative, such as "Gray Days" and "The Last Fire"
4. short stories proper, with characters, dialogue, a plot, conflict, and resolution.

In Colette's work, these texts tend to metamorphose into one another. An autobiographical sketch, such as "The Seamstress," is also a short story and a lyric monologue. "The Sémiramis Bar" is at once a letter, a self-portrait, and a cheerful aside on the Sapphic underground in Paris, 1910. "The Watchman" is part diary, part animal portraiture, part autobiography. The story called "Green Sealing Wax" might have been included in *My Mother's House*.

Therefore, in choosing one hundred texts to comprise *The Collected* (not *Complete*) *Short Stories of Colette*, I have tried to include all the stories that are patently fiction yet that have never before appeared in one volume (e.g., the early fable "The Tendrils of the Vine" and Colette's last story, "The Sick Child"); texts that have not been heretofore available in English (e.g., the early Chéri stories; the witty, sardonic "Dialogues for One Voice"); and to exclude the animal dialogues, which constitute a genre unto themselves, the purely autobiographical sketches such as appear in *My Mother's House*, and the reportage in which Colette deals with public rather than private matters.

Of the one hundred stories gathered here, it should perhaps be specified that the following appear in English for the first time: "The Other Table," "The Screen," "Clouk Alone," "Clouk's Fling," "Chéri," "The Return," "The Pearls," "Literature," "My Goddaughter," "A Hairdresser," "A Masseuse," "My Corset Maker," "The Saleswoman," "An Interview," "The 'Master,'" "Morning Glories," "What Must We Look Like?," "The Cure," "Gray Days," "The Last Fire," "The Quick-Change Artist," "The Tenor," "Florie," "Monsieur Maurice," "The Advice," "The Half-Crazy," "Alix's Refusal," "The Respite," "The Bitch," "Bygone Spring," and "April"; also the Preface to "Bella-Vista."

The remainder have appeared in American periodical or book form over the past fifty years, beginning with "The Fox" in *Harper's Bazaar* in May 1933. The following are newly translated for this edition: "A Letter," "The Sémiramis Bar," "'If I Had a Daughter,'" "Rites," "Newly Shorn," "Grape Harvest," "In the Boudoir," "The Victim," "The Hidden Woman," "Dawn," "One Evening," "The Hand," "A Dead End," "The Fox," "The Judge," "The Omelette," "The Other Wife," "The Burglar," "The Murderer," "The Portrait," "The Landscape," "Secrets," "Châ," "The Bracelet," "The Find," "Mirror Games," "Habit," "In the Flower of Age," and "The Rivals."

R.P.

Translator's Acknowledgments

Since my translations of Colette's stories appear here for the first time, I would like to thank Richard Howard for having brought Nancy Miller, Robert Phelps, Colette, and me together. My thanks also to Irene Ilton, Jean Audet, Jean-Jacques Sicard, Annie Gandon, and Ivan Kovacovic, all of whom helped bring me closer to Colette. My most special gratitude goes to Jean Alice Jacobson, who did far more than help me bring a faint reflection of Colette's genius into English.

Matthew Ward

PART I

Early Stories

&⬦&

*Born into an unmonied family, I never learned a
métier. I knew how to climb, whistle, and run,
but no one ever suggested that I earn my living
as a squirrel or a bird or a deer. The day
necessity put a pen in my hand, and in return for
my written pages I was given a little money, I
realized that every day thereafter I would slowly,
tractably, patiently have to write . . .*

CLOUK/CHÉRI

EARLY VERSIONS

OF *CHÉRI*

Chéri was first hatched as "Clouk." When I gave birth to this beautiful young man—who would believe it?—he was ugly, something of a runt, and sickly, suffering from swollen adenoids. But I had a vague feeling that I would not form any attachment to this quasi-scrofulous child. Spurned and thin-skinned, Clouk awoke from a few months' sleep, cast off his pale little slough like a molting snake, emerged gleaming, devilish, unrecognizable, and I wrote the first versions of Chéri without knowing at the time that a few succinct, casual stories would ripen and grow into two rather bitter novels.

Colette

Clouk

❧❧❧

THE OTHER TABLE

"And what if I do look at them? They're not going to eat me. Anyway, they really are characters. What happens to some women . . . it's not funny! The fattest one is . . . what's her name? Yes, I remember, I've seen pictures of her; even with hairstyles the way they were back then, she was very pretty. No, no champagne, it makes me bloated. Besides, we're not setting up shop here: when I think I have to be at my singing lesson at nine in the morning, it's not funny!"

Clouk says nothing. He wipes his monocle with the corner of his handkerchief and at the same time closes his bad eye, which the lights in the restaurant, so white they are mauve, sting to the point of tears.

It is only midnight, it is raining; the manager can tell there won't be many for supper and divides his attention between the corner where Clouk has just sat down opposite the dazzling Lulu and the table where four women are noisily eating away . . .

"Clouk, your nose!" prompts Lulu peremptorily. "I'm forever having to stop you from sniffling, and it's not funny!"

"I wonder what she does think is funny," muses Clouk. But he keeps quiet, like a good little boy, docile and loving, and sighs cautiously, through his mouth, so as to avoid the imperceptible, irritating nasal "clouk" to which he owes his nickname. He looks at Lulu. She is all black fire, dark sheen; she makes one think of jet, of deep-red rubies. She took the time, after leaving the stage, to take off her makeup and then reapply it outrageously, as if ashamed of the freshness of her twenty-four years. Her eyes, her rather thick hair, which she does not dye, her teeth, all shine with insolent strength.

Pearls and more pearls, a white dress which, in the style of the day, combines Louis XV panniers, a Directoire-style sash, Byzantine décolletage, and Japanese sleeves; on her head is a little black glengarry, which looks as if it is worth four sous, from which there rises an aigrette worth fifty louis. Her feet are not happy under the table because of two purple shoes with gold heels. But she no longer pays them any attention. Good heavens, one's feet are always what hurt most when, for three hours every night, one treads the boards of a raked stage, when one is subjected to spiked heels during the day and to unyielding ballet shoes in the morning.

For Lulu works. Four years have been enough to transform an undernourished dressmaker's assistant into a highly paid star of the music hall. In order to become rich she acquired the taste for money, and hard work gave her a sense of pride. Lulu is as proud as any locksmith or electrician. Like them she says in a tough voice and with mock simplicity, "I'm not afraid to work." She also says, "I didn't know how to do anything, but I learned how to do everything!" She in fact sings, dances, and acts with a cinematographic spirit and swiftness that is already being called "the Lulu style" . . .

"Now who's looking at those silly women! Clouk, you must have some old relative in the crowd!"

Clouk laughed stupidly into his glass and glanced at the neighboring table where there was some rather loud shouting going on over a broken glass. Two operetta singers, once notorious, were laughing through all their jovial wrinkles, across from a poor, graying bit player with a healthy appetite. The fourth woman is Léa de Lonval, overripe, enormous, and magnificent as a heavy fruit fallen beneath a tree . . . All four have given themselves over to the pleasure of eating a good supper unescorted, and drinking a champagne as celebrated as themselves. They form a well-heeled and cordial group of jewel-bedecked matrons. Clouk, listening to Lulu, turns his sickly little boy's smile toward them, without doing it on purpose . . .

"So, you see, Clouk, I'm not saying this play they're bringing out for me this winter isn't a marvelous play, not at all. But they're telling me that if I do it, I'll be considered a great actress overnight . . . As if I need them to be considered great . . . Which doesn't change the fact that it's a hopeless play."

"Yes?"

"Hopeless. I read it. For example, at one point it says that Linda—Linda, that's my role—Linda 'feverishly paces the living room with long strides,' and a little further on, 'She runs after him, panic-stricken,' and a little further than that, 'Linda, raising her arms to the sky in a wide, imploring gesture . . .' "

"Yes?"

"What do you mean, 'yes'? Oh, my poor dear, I can be talking to you about the theater, or literature, or anything serious, and you always have the same silly look on your face! You must understand that that scene, the way it is, can't be done! Can you see me, in a day dress, pacing the stage 'with long strides'? Can you see me, in that same dress, running after my lover 'panic-stricken'? And then try, just try raising your arms 'in a wide, imploring gesture' with sleeves nowadays not having any seams at the shoulders! So I told them, I said to the authors, 'I don't care if your play flops, but *I* do not want to fall flat on my face, nor do I want to dress like Raymond Duncan! There would have to be changes, a lot of changes!' "

"Yes . . ."

" 'Yes' . . . There's one thing no one can take away from you, you are a gifted conversationalist!"

Clouk keeps himself from sniffling and adjusts the monocle which he uses to hide a weak eye, smaller and paler than the other. He remains silent. What could he say? Lulu's metallic voice, her gemlike dazzle overwhelm him. That is how she is, vigilant, merciless, with a tough youthfulness nothing can penetrate. She is not a monster, she is one of those terrible young girls of today, hard and narrow-minded. He has seen her cry, but with rage, during her lessons. He has seen her laugh, to make fun of him or a friend. She is thought of as sensual, but he knows very well that she displays her beautiful skin, white and blue like milk in shadow, coldly, and that this too is part of her "job."

Clouk can hear, striking against the lace-covered windows, the hissing of a winter downpour which has almost turned to sleet. He is thinking about getting home, about Lulu's conjugal silence, the voice teacher coming at nine o'clock tomorrow morning, the masseuse who comes after him . . . As she does every day, Lulu will have that set, stern look on her face, darkened by important matters. As he does every day, he will wait until it is time for her to make her entrance, when her charming mouth flowers into fresh, aggressive laughter. He feels cold, a little ill. What he needs is . . .

Clouk stares at the other table, the table with the old ladies. They laugh constantly, and perhaps for no reason, with that lightheartedness which comes to a woman when the peril of men has at last left her. Léa de Lonval, a colorful woman beneath her white hair, looks like Louis XV, and the older of the operetta singers has the sauciness of a racy grandmother. If Clouk dared, he would slip over to their table, all frail and small, squeeze in between those fat gossips' arms, amid the rustling skirts and the doughy knees, and lean up against the ample shoulders, lost, drowned in that melting warmth of slightly senile nannies; he would warm himself, console himself for being the envied lover of Lulu, sparkling there in front of him like a frosty little tree . . .

THE SCREEN

When Lulu left him, Clouk did not give in right away to the stunned despair which dismays the very young. He went on with his life, going out to restaurants and bars, driving around in his car. His everyday little face seemed unchanged, clean and comical, his left eyebrow clamped down to hold his monocle in place, his fishlike mouth open slightly. As he was ordinarily quiet, no one noticed that he wasn't speaking at all and that he was sniffling more often. He was conducting himself quite well. But the "close" circle of friends who were looking after him finished him off with enough sympathy to kill an ox. One would clap him on the back with the crude cordiality of a sergeant. One melancholy and sisterly friend discreetly informed him as to Lulu's whereabouts and carryings-on, under the guise of "keeping things out in the open." Without saying a word, the least cruel would hand Clouk a full glass . . .

And so when his friends, gasping from self-sacrifice, wanted to return to their usual occupations, it was noticed that Clouk, drinking more, was not eating at all, and that his collars looked like hoops around the neck of a plucked bird.

Clouk was suffering, still stunned. He did not dare say it, and he began confronting his interrogators with the smile of one whose feet have been stepped on while waltzing. His headstrong, youthful sadness knew nothing of the confidences in which the lyricism of old incorrigible lovers takes comfort. He believed he was hardly thinking at all, did not delude himself, and did not repeatedly whisper her name: "Lulu . . . Lulu . . ." But without knowing it, he endured a twofold pain. At times he would reel, light-headed, floating, as if blank forever; at times he would run away, hoping to leave far behind him, in the place he was fleeing, the intolerable memory.

He ran into Lulu one night in the restaurant, accompanied by her new "friend," and was quite proud of himself for feeling neither shocked nor heartbroken. But the next day, sitting in a music hall, he broke down in tears watching a clown who couldn't free himself from a piece of flypaper; and his circle of friends, rising up as one, scorned Clouk to the point of dropping him altogether. Only the sisterly and melancholy friend named Eva stood by the sniffling, phlegmy Clouk, calling him "poor thing."

"You poor thing, I can't stand seeing you like this anymore. Let's go have a smoke."

"A smoke of what?"

"Opium."

"Oh, no . . . no opium."

Clouk still remembered, after one try—three pipes following a heavy dinner—a severe case of indigestion. But his consoler's authority left him no room to argue, and less than an hour later Clouk, undressed, shivering under a kimono, was lying down on a thin mattress covered with a white mat, cold and smooth to the touch like the skin of a lizard.

Across from him, on the other side of the lacquered tray, he could see Eva fussing about, stout and heavy in her Japanese dress, with her dyed hair hanging across her unpowdered cheek, suddenly affectionate with that bizarre motherliness of women opium smokers: "Wait, you're not comfortable . . . This cushion here under your head . . . Oh, he's so pale, a real Pierrot . . . You'll feel better in a minute . . . I'll turn off the ceiling light. As you can see, it's not set up as an opium den; most of the time, it's my little living room."

Clouk, lying on his side, clenched his teeth to keep himself from shivering, or crying, or talking. His eyes wandered from the ceiling hung with fabric to the cheap plaster Buddha, dark against the bright wall, then returned to the three luminous, living blazes formed by Eva's face and deft hands in the shadows. The little oil lamp, beneath its crystal hood, also caught his eye and he blinked, bothered by the short flame, without the strength to turn his head away . . .

"Wait," said Eva, "I'll cover the flame for you. Would you like the butterfly, or the spider, or the little moon?"

With the tips of her fingers, she turned the tiny screens of colored glass, jade, and horn around the globe of the lamp. Clouk was silent, intimidated, and tired, and the screens passed between him and the flame like the figures of a new and incomprehensible game . . .

Hearing the drop of opium sizzle, he leaned back on his elbows. His hands were shaking so badly as he took hold of the bamboo that he burned his first bowl somewhat, and his throat filled with acrid smoke.

"Very clever," said Eva without impatience. "Here, let me fix you another."

Clouk, having lain back down, breathed in the smell of the opium, surprised to find it agreeable, comestible, soothing.

"You understand . . ." he began despite himself.

Eva merely nodded and he ventured on. "You understand, don't you? I haven't been eating or sleeping much lately. When you're worrying yourself sick . . ."

She interrupted him by offering him a second pipe, which he exhausted with one long inhalation, without taking a breath, and his consoler, who knew the price of silence, whistled softly to express her admiration.

Lying back on the mat, Clouk repeated slowly: "You understand that since . . . since it happened, it's been as if I have nothing of my own. It's strange, I can't get it into my head that I still do have things of my own, even my money, since . . . well, since then. You see, I . . . I'm worried . . ."

Already intoxicated, Clouk spoke with childlike sweetness. Several more times he said, "I don't have anything of my own . . . of my own . . ." then was quiet, and stopped the pathetic shivering, the tightening of his stomach muscles, and the flexing of his toes. He sat up for a third pipe and lay back down once more, happy to be thinking again at last, lucidly assessing his lovelorn misery, assimilating it to his utter destitution. A mellifluous murmuring of rising water filled his ears, and his entire body, healed, experienced the sensation of a lukewarm bath, whose liquid density would lift him . . . He did not think of Lulu's apparition, and did not call it forth, but the successive settings of their life as lovers rose with singular and progressive strength. Clouk, motionless, his eyes half open and dead, was reveling in the heightened colors of Lulu's little living room, the deep greens of a garden at a spa. A gnarled old wisteria clung to the pitted wall of a tower; Clouk followed the tortured vine of the clambering trunk, counted the flowery clusters, inhaled their acacia-like fragrance . . .

Other landscapes appeared, without Lulu in them, but as if still fragrant with her passage, and all of them, vast or intimate, were inscribed in the nacreous little moon, in the tiny screen hooked on to the lamp . . .

"Clouk, are you asleep?"

Clouk heard but did not answer. Even if he had wanted to, he would not have been able to turn his eyes away from the transparent disk of lustrous mother-of-pearl. But Eva's hand, bumping the lamp, made the screen slip off and Clouk groaned, wounded by the naked light.

"There, there, shhhh . . . I didn't do it on purpose."

The pink penumbra once again veiled the flame, and Clouk's eyelids moistened, brimming with well-being. Borne along with the murmuring of the rising water, he was slipping off to a black and priceless sleep. "Nothing of my own?" he said to himself without moving his lips. "No more mistress, no more home?" He smiled, or thought he smiled, and took pity on himself for having cherished and regretted such perishable belongings, since now he possessed, beaming gently within reach of his eyes and his fingers, milky, iridescent, deliciously round, huge as a star, no bigger than a precious coin, the little mother-of-pearl moon, the opaline satellite of the opium lamp.

CLOUK ALONE

"You rats! You can't, you can't desert me like this!"

"We most certainly can! Stop, Clouk, you'll tear my coat . . . Make him stop, can't you see I can't raise my arms in these sleeves!"

The small woman struggles, and Clouk holds on to her with the sticky perseverance of a tipsy man. He is only a little drunk, and besides, the fine rain showers his damp forehead, the warm rims of his ears . . .

"*You're* not going to desert me too, are you? You're more loyal than that!"

The circle of friends dwindled despite Clouk's entreaties. He latched on to two "loyal" friends whom he succeeded in detaining for twenty minutes on the main staircase of his residence, then for a good quarter of an hour on the divan in the front hall. He still hopes to keep them awhile on the terrace, despite the damp night, the wind shaking the roasted chestnut trees . . .

All three stand around, black against the wide, illuminated hall, the muddy gravel of the garden. The small, imprisoned woman looks as if she is dancing in Clouk's arms. Her peaked hat meets a gray fox collar that muffles her neck and her ears; but the rest of her body shivers under a tight satin wrap glistening in the light like a blue fish.

"Lord," she exclaims, "this is August! I'm freezing! We'll see you tomorrow, Clouk. What am I saying, tomorrow? We'll see you today, it's already past two . . . My darling husband, are you asleep on your beautiful little feet?"

"Let Robert leave by himself," begs Clouk. "You can keep me company."

The woman bursts out laughing. "Robert? Leave by himself? No danger of that: he's much too afraid all alone at night! Aren't you, Robert?"

Robert only groans like a man shaken in his sleep, and Clouk doubles over with laughter and slaps his thigh. "He's afraid to be alone? That's too much . . . Come inside and tell me all about it, Eva!"

But, despite her tight coat, Eva gets away and manages to run, dragging Robert, drowsy and dignified, behind her. Her feet, in white shoes, skip with short hip-hops like two little rabbits. Clouk follows her like a puppy. He opens the gate regretfully, hoping that the car waiting at the curb won't start . . . But it does, on the first try, then glides off unctuously over the wet asphalt as Clouk shouts out one last time: "See you this afternoon! Hey, Robert . . . Robert! Leave Eva with me and I'll turn you over to my old nanny if you're so afraid of the dark!"

He leans forward to see the red light on the tail of the car pull off and fade away. Then, suddenly, his face freezes and he shuts the heavy gate. He walks back toward the brightly lit house, with long, gliding strides, forcing himself not to run, his arms pressed to his sides so as not to brush against the shrubs. The entrance hall dazzles and reassures him; he takes off his misty monocle, blinks his sensitive eyelids, and shrugs his shoulders.

"Afraid to be alone at night . . . Oh, brother . . ."

He was about to turn off the electricity before going up to his room, but stopped short: to get to the light switch he would have to walk past a long mirror, tinged green by the dampness, where he would have time to watch himself walking by, paler than normal, even more of the "poor child" than his fabulously wealthy mother had made him.

He does not like to walk past it at certain hours of the night. He prefers to go straight up to the second floor, letting the chandelier and the sconces burn on. Upon waking, he would open his fishlike mouth, which could feign astonishment quite easily, when his inexorable valet would say to him: "Monsieur realizes that Monsieur *again* left the lights on downstairs. Monsieur won't wonder why Monsieur's electric bill is seven hundred francs *again* this month, worse than a department store."

Clouk, born a millionaire, remained parsimonious by upbringing: a new car every year is a duty, turning off the electricity when one leaves a room is another.

He hurries noiselessly up the staircase, reaches his room, which he crosses double time, and rushes into his dressing room, turning on the light with a feverish hand before falling into an easy chair.

"Afraid to be alone at night . . ." Right now Robert must be undressing to the reassuring sound of feminine chatter; Eva humming, taking off her shoes, yawning with a moan, fluffing up the pillows . . . Since Lulu left him, Clouk, as weak as if he were being bled, would revert at night to the terrors of childhood. He is flabbergasted that, before Lulu, he had been able to live alone in this pretentious dungeon, erected near the gates of the Bois de Boulogne, "an edifice, Monsieur, to withstand a siege," the architect had declared.

"A siege," repeated Clouk. "Why did the idiot say that? Is it within the realm of possibility that it would ever come under siege?"

He reaches out a limp hand to touch the wall, to feel its deep resonance like that of a full wine cask, but the coldness of its varnish stings him like a burn.

"A siege . . . Who's stamping around down in the garden like that? Really now . . ."

For a brief instant, the combativeness of the proprietor in him struggles with an alcoholic cowardice.

"How many of them are there? My God, they're making a racket!" stammers Clouk, his head buzzing.

He wants to get up and run to the window, but would he even be able to raise the padlocked bar across the heavy iron doors? Clouk, immured in his citadel, panics behind the walls whose protection he had just invoked.

"Somebody could easily do me in here, the neighbors wouldn't even wake up . . ."

"Do me in . . ." The words struck Clouk's sad brain with the dull sound of doom. Whole pages from detective novels, illustrated with thugs in cars, masked men carrying bludgeons, came back to Clouk's memory like so many dire predictions. "Do me in . . . do me in . . ." and Clouk cursed his daily reading, which delighted him when the morning sunlight made the shadows of the leaves dance in the folds of the sheets. Oh, to believe in phantoms as when he was a little boy, to tremble at the mere rustling of an invisible, silky dress, to run from the harmless ghost abroad at midnight, how thrilling compared to the precise image which now has Clouk glued to his chair: a white hand wrapped around the black butt of a revolver moves slowly through the open door of the bedroom. Slowly, slowly, the muzzle of the gun turns its round eye toward Clouk . . . Afterward, there is nothing but chaos, horror, warm blood on the white rug, the smell of gunpowder and melted metal around the open safe . . . But this bloody confusion, still settling in Clouk's imagination, does not equal in shock the appearance of the white hand, there in the doorway of . . .

"No!" he screams despite himself.

The loudness of his scream makes him stand up, his back to the wall, hands groping. A bell button gives way beneath his fingers, and this involuntary gesture brings him back to his senses.

"Did I ring? Did I ring or not? I didn't hear the bell . . . But if I didn't ring, who's that coming up the stairs?"

Back against the wall, stiff, dripping with sweat, Clouk has time to appreciate the difference between the footsteps of an imaginary group of people and the sound of someone approaching slowly, heavily climbing the stairs, fumbling with the door, opening . . .

"Monsieur rang?" asked the valet.

Breath, movement, both came back to Clouk with life. And life is all vanity, reflection, the meaning of lies and frugality, his very soul . . .

"Yes . . . I'd like you to turn off the lights, downstairs, in the front hall."

CLOUK'S FLING

It is only half past midnight; they have arrived a little early, the bar is nearly empty. Clouk and his "companion" sit down side by side on the red banquette, haphazardly, with the vague feeling they would be better off at the table across from them, or in the corner at the back.

"You don't think we're too near the door?" his companion asks.

Clouk lifts one shoulder, sticks out a dubious lower lip, and his monocle falls. He wipes it, then applies it once again to his right eye, with a carefulness he knows is vain, for the monocle refuses to stay put for long on his soft little face, made, one might say, of pink butter.

"*Garçon!* Keep an eye on the door, will you, our legs are freezing!"

His companion gives the orders, with the authority of an old habitué, and lights a cigarette before even unbuttoning her coat.

"What are you having, Clouk?"

"Uh . . . I have no idea, really."

He too is smoking, his eyes on the entrance, and shivers each time the door is opened: what if, after her performance, Lulu had the idea to come have supper? . . . He barely gives it a thought, he doesn't think about it anymore, it's over, but each time the revolving door gleams and spins, he trembles imperceptibly.

"I think I'll have a nice little whiskey soda," says his companion. "And you?"

"I'll have . . . I don't know . . . a hot toddy."

He shivers at the thought of the steaming and spicy toddy. Opposite him the mirror reflects a stiff, pale little Clouk, next to his companion devoid of coquetry, somewhat heavy and squat in her moleskin coat. She is a brunette, dyed a redhead, whom one must meet several times before recognizing her, not ugly, not pretty, with big eyes and a hard mouth. She yawns nervously and, with a compulsive gesture, clicks the clasp of a long, dented gold case, bigger than a wallet, that can hold fifty cigarettes.

Neither she nor Clouk saw the color of this brief and bright winter day. They got home around five in the morning, after a dismal night in Montmartre. Suffused with tobacco and the smell of alcohol, they slept the uneasy sleep of those who drift off a little drunk, deprived of the warm spray of the shower and a scented bath.

They woke up stiff and unsightly around three in the afternoon, with the impression of having slept a very long time and being very old. The best time of their day was the interminable daily toilette, two hours of bath, hairdresser, manicurist, masseuse: the meticulous and listless toilette of cloistered women, the empty chatter, the perplexed fussing with ties and vests . . . Then the brief drive in the car around the already dark Bois, truly an old ladies' drive, cut short again by the desire, the need to return and sit down at the table of a bar. "Some port and herring sandwiches, right, Clouk? What dried us up like that last night was that nasty demi-sec champagne."

They tried to eat dinner around nine-thirty, both of them overtaken by a sudden concern for health: two *jus de viande* and pasta. Clouk, basically disgusted, gulped down the syrupy, peppery juices and twirled skeins of long noodles around two forks, broadening his narrow shoulders with the childish hope that his "diet" would endow him with new strength and muscles to amaze the universe, the entire universe—and Lulu too.

The hours after dinner, divided between the restaurant and box seats in a music hall, went by quickly—barely time for a dozen cigarettes —bringing back midnight and the moment to sit down, for the third time since waking, in front of a stiff tablecloth, glazed by the roller, and cold as oilcloth.

Each time he sits down at a table in some late-night bar, Clouk feels a warm, fleeting rush of exhilaration. He is beginning to believe, he the weak, he abandoned by Lulu whom he loved, he the poor little rich boy, miserable and friendless, that he was closing, joyfully and forever, the dark string of his errant days. There are nights when every reflection in the glass panes of the revolving door seems to announce a marvelous arrival, which he was no longer hoping for, nights when the soft handshake of his "friends" seemed warm to the touch and indicative of a vigorous friendship; nights when the bubbly alcohol, gulped down like medicine, numbs the cramps in his stomach and the migraine clamped around his head. So Clouk gives himself over to the pleasant, poisonous warmth dilating and deadening him; he leans his head on his sisterly companion's shoulder and speaks to her vaguely, in a low voice, while a familiar chorus of men and women eating their supper comment —some kindly, some ironically—on the tender pose of the two "lovers."

This same night, despite the emptiness of the room which creates an anxious idleness in the woman who owns the bar—yesterday's demi-mondaine, today's plump businesswoman dressed severely, like a minor town official's wife—Clouk does not despair and waits for his hour. From minute to minute, the glass door turns, flashes brightly, and Clouk shivers, not with hope, but by now it is a habit with him to jump at the sound of a door or the ringing of a bell.

"You can be such a bore," says his companion indolently. "I had a dog like you once, his left leg used to twitch all the time. The vet said it was worms . . ."

. . . It has been a long time, it has been months since Clouk stopped waiting for Lulu. He simply watches the door and counts the people who come in, the anonymous walk-ons vital to his happiness. There are the couples of petite women, regulation brunettes this year, hair all over the place and a little powdery, with lips as thick as a quadroon's. There, one by one, or in groups, are Clouk's "friends," who for the most part are juvenile, defiant, and brought up to hold women in respect. The fact of drinking in company does not incite them to generosity, for they are rich, and it took the worst misfortune of love to teach Clouk, if not prodigality and the disdain of money, at least the beginnings of a noblesse called casualness . . .

When the sky's no longer blue,
The hearts of lovers will be true . . .

The piano, the diuretic scratching of the mandolins, the thready voice of a short tenor all rose together, and Clouk nodded in time to the music as if greeting someone affectionately recognized. The time for the music has come; the bar, now packed, is thick with smoke. Clouk is no longer trembling, no longer waiting for anyone. His night is beginning according to ritual; he is warm, he is thirsty because he has been drinking; he will have all the songs he likes, all the chaste, melancholy songs which comprise the repertoire of disreputable establishments and Clouk's own poetic anthology: he will hum:

You swore you loved me only,
But you left me sad and lonely . . .

He will proclaim at the top of his voice:

I have a girl as blond as the sun,
In this wide world she's the only one . . .

He will be drunk, howling, and happy: nothing, except dawn, will disturb the reassuring and predictable course of his sleepless night. A few more drinks, a few more rhymes, and he will be drunk enough to abandon himself—his feet on the knees of a "friend" he doesn't know, his head leaning back against the warm shoulder of his sweet, insipid companion—to abandon himself to his most heartrending and purest memory, to his hidden, incurable love, still intact, for Lulu.

[*Translated by Matthew Ward*]

Chéri

❧

CHÉRI

"Léa! Give it to me, give me your necklace! Do you hear me, Léa? Give me your pearls!"

He moves, black and thin, back and forth across the sun-filled window. Because of the bright-pink curtains, slightly parted, he looks like a graceful demon dancing in front of a blazing fire. As he moves back into the center of the room, he turns white, dressed in silk pajamas and white babouches.

"Why won't you give me your necklace, Léa? It looks as good on me as it does on you . . . at least!"

He raises his hands, and around his neck he fastens a strand of pearls which iridesce and light up, radiant, next to the white silk . . .

At the faint snap of the clasp, the lace linens of a big bed ripple and two bare, strong arms, thin-wristed, raise two lovely, lazy hands. "Leave it alone, Chéri, you've played enough with that necklace."

"Why? It amuses me . . . Are you afraid I'll steal it from you?"

He had moved toward the bed, silent as a cat in his white slippers. He is a very handsome and very young man whose smooth black hair is worn like the tight cap of Pierrot. He leans his naughty chin over Léa, and the same pink spark, from the window, dances in his dark eyes, on his teeth, and on the pearls of the necklace . . .

The nonchalant hands draw a vague response in the air and Chéri insists, "Say it, go on! Are you afraid I'll take it?"

"No. But if I were to offer it to you, you're quite capable of accepting it."

He laughs softly, to himself, turns toward the warm light, and rolls the round pearls between his fingers.

"And why not? It's fine for a man to receive a set of studs and a tie pin, two or three pearls. But any more than that and the gift becomes a scandal. Really now . . . do I look ugly in a pearl necklace? Tell me."

He pirouettes nimbly and admires himself in the mirror, opening his pajama top with both hands and revealing a smooth, muscular neck and a tight, hard chest, curved like a shield.

"Go on, say it, say I'm ugly!"

Léa, leaning on her elbow, looks at him. In the merciful half-light, she shows what a pretty fifty-year-old woman, well cared for and in good health, can show: the bright complexion, somewhat ruddy and a bit weathered, of a natural blonde, shapely, solid shoulders, and celebrated blue eyes which have kept their thick chestnut lashes. But she is now a redhead, because of her hair, which is turning gray.

She loves to chat in bed, almost invisible, while her magnificent arms and expressive hands comment on her wise words. Nearing the end of a successful career as a sedate courtesan, she is neither sad nor spiteful. She keeps the date of her birth a secret, but willingly admits, as she settles her calm gaze on Chéri, that she is approaching the age when one is permitted little comforts . . .

"I'm not going to say you're ugly. In the first place, you wouldn't believe it. But can't you laugh without wrinkling up your nose like that? You won't be happy until you've got three wrinkles at the corners of your nose, will you?"

Chéri's handsome face suddenly freezes and he turns around to examine, with fierce closeness, the little lines marking Léa's cheeks from her nostrils to the corners of her mouth.

"Yes, yes, I know," she says without getting angry. "But I'm not twenty-four years old. Take off that necklace."

He obeys reluctantly and sulks. "I obviously wouldn't traipse around with this trinket on my neck, but if you were to give it to me, it would make an absolutely stunning wedding present!"

"Wedding present? For whom?"

"Why, for my fiancée!"

"Your fiancée?"

Léa sits up, showing above the covers. "Your fiancée! Are you serious?"

Chéri nods his head, malicious and self-important. "I'm afraid so. The poor child's crazy about me."

"Is it that same little girl? . . ."

"Yes, the same."

"And what about you, what do you have to say about it?"

Chéri raises his velvety eyes to the sky and opens his arms like a victim. "Take me . . ."

Conscious of his beauty, he strikes a pose, because Léa is staring at him intently.

"You're getting married . . . just like that? . . . You're getting married . . . Why?"

Chéri puts his finger to his lips, goes "Shhh!" mysteriously, and shrugs his shoulders. His charming liar's face grows sad, then smiles, then goes blank—he plays with all his features like an expert mime.

"Well, there you have it . . . Lofty motives, my dear. The kid's loaded. And pretty, too. And besides, the old girl—I mean my sainted mother—has spoken, and when my mother speaks . . . Besides . . . besides, what do I know?"

He leaps up, comes back down after a perfect *entrechat-six*, butts his way through the Persian door curtains, and disappears, shouting: "My bath—now! And send the masseuse to my dressing room, quick! I'm lunching at the old girl's!"

"Chéri! . . . Listen, Chéri!"

He does not hear or else does not want to come back.

Seated on the edge of the big bed, Léa thinks to herself: "What? He's getting married? It's impossible! The whole family's crazy! What can his mother be thinking? Marry Chéri!"

She looks at the Persian door curtains and raises her shoulders. "Marry that?"

Léa is neither pained nor jealous. She is shocked and is slowly becoming indignant.

"I swear, people are crazy! Here's a boy who's . . . well, who's Chéri! As far as reason goes, he's eight years old, except that he knows pearls like an old Jewess and speaks sharply to the help—at least to mine. What need is there for him to marry, I ask you. Doesn't he have everything he needs here, everything? A young girl . . . crazy about him . . . She's going to give this spoiled little brat her love, as if he needs it! He's too mean, he's too young. It doesn't matter to me. He can sharpen his nails on me, it doesn't leave any marks. But a young girl . . . who loves him! . . . . This one doesn't love anything. He doesn't know how. *They* don't know how, all the other Chéris just like him . . . People envy me because he's so young and so handsome, they envy me for being the nanny of one of these brainless boys, Chéri or some other one, brought up by lackeys, manicurists, and boxing instructors . . . Poor Chéri, people take him for a man because he has biceps. They're going to give him a wife—a young girl . . . a child . . . Oh, they can't do that! . . ."

Léa gives a start because Chéri has just come back, shivering and grumbling, in his bathrobe.

"You're not getting up today? But, Léa, you'll get so fat!"

She sizes him up and does not deign to respond.

"A young girl . . . a pretty, tender girl, a little dopey . . ."

"Is it my wedding that's bothering you, Léa?"

She hesitates, then decides to say it: "Yes . . . Listen, my dear, you shouldn't . . . I really wish . . ."

How can she say what she's thinking? Chéri files his nails; but beneath his distracted exterior he is waiting, he is listening for . . .

"They're going to make him the guardian, the support, the master," she thinks to herself, "of a child so young and so weak. It's terrible. She'll think she's marrying Prince Charming and the next day she'll find herself face to face with an old coquette. Because really, it's extraordinary, but of the two of us, he's the old coquette. He's the one who's always scrubbing himself, plucking hairs, and sleeping with cucumber cream on his face, and not one night of lovemaking goes by for him without a good facial massage afterward! An old coquette doubling as a rich and greedy petty bourgeois, who quibbles over tips, who yells if the bathwater is too hot, and counts the number of bottles of champagne in the cellar; a fussy, idle, petty bourgeois . . . With me, it didn't matter, because I've had so many of these naughty nurslings. I was the tree they blunted their nails on; I was the warm rug they curled up on to sleep. My God, the poor little girl! If only someone could stop it!"

Léa looks at Chéri almost with anguish—she forgets to raise the corners of her lovely, tired mouth. She makes one more effort: "Listen, child . . . I assure you, don't get married. You mustn't get married . . ."

It is exactly what Chéri was waiting for. He bursts out laughing and shakes Léa by the shoulders, with insulting hilarity. "Aha! You jealous . . ." he shouts at her.

THE RETURN

Half past midnight. Léa closes her book and thinks that it is time to sleep. She marks her place with a postcard from Chéri, which arrived the day before, in which he concisely expresses the boredom of being married. "I've had it! I've had it!"

Tomorrow she will file the card away with Chéri's other letters: a dozen telegrams, a few *pneumatiques,* two or three notes scribbled on hotel stationery . . . The telegrams composed pidgin-style, without needless tenderness or niceties: Chéri, like nearly all children of the rich, knows perfectly well that they cost by the word. His letters have a singular tone to them, sometimes that of one schoolboy to another, sometimes that of a child to an old and very dear nanny: "My darling Nounoune . . ." Léa smiles, thinking about it.

"Poor thing . . . He was so used to me . . . What an orphanage that must be, him and his child bride!"

She relaxes and reminisces, alone in her big bedroom of which, though it is somewhat *démodé,* she is quite fond. An elegant and tractable young woman up on the style of the day would like it to be more airy, with fewer cushions and fewer crimson curtains, but Léa holds on to her knickknacks and her big, heavy bed, made entirely of chased brass, which shines in the dark like a suit of armor.

The lace bed linen and the sheets heavy with embroidery also give away Léa's age, her fifty wise years, her bourgeois taste for fine, long-lasting linen. This sturdy luxury sits well on Léa, enthroned in its midst, plump and healthy, adorned only with cool, clean lawn, not the least tempted by the frills of soubrettes and the little bonnets described as "young-looking."

She looks approvingly at the order which reigns in the room: "It's easy to see that Chéri doesn't come around anymore," she thinks.

A serious ring of the bell in the courtyard gives her a start. She has just enough time to make out the sound of muffled footsteps and whispers; the door is pushed open roughly.

"It's me," says an angry voice.

There is Chéri standing under the chandelier. The overhead light chisels his high cheekbones and grazes his feminine chin. He knits his eyebrows over his eyes, which are too dark to be seen.

Léa does not cry out. She sits on the edge of the bed and, with instinctive modesty, merely arranges the short braids she has fixed her hair in for the night.

"I was afraid it was you," she says at last.

He looks thinner to her, he seems even more surly. He is wearing a suit beneath his open overcoat; his hands are thrust deep into the pockets of his trousers, and with his tousled hair and rumpled shirt he resembles a drunken best man.

"What do you want, my dear? Where did you come from? This is no way to make an entrance," she observes calmly.

He takes two or three sharp breaths and lets his stiff, raised shoulders fall, as if beginning to melt in the warmth of the room; he smiles vaguely, letting his extreme youthfulness show on his face, and sighs softly.

"Hello . . ."

"Hello . . ." says Léa in the same tone. "So, what brings you here? Has something happened? Where are you coming from?"

"From my wife's, of course."

He says "my wife's" awkwardly, with excessive vanity in his voice.

"It's late to be going out," remarks Léa discreetly.

"And it's too late to go back there!" shouts Chéri. "That's one place you'll never see me again!"

He throws off his overcoat as if ready to fight and falls dumbstruck into an armchair near the bed. "You know, Léa, I . . . don't you . . ." He says nothing more and shakes his head, sulking.

"Of course I know," says Léa indulgently.

She leans over and runs her hand over his tousled head, enhancing its disorder and his anger. She knows very well that Chéri does not speak easily and that he does not take great pains in choosing his words. She also knows that what he has to tell her could be summed up in three phrases: it is the story of his four months of marriage and travel in close quarters with a little girl, young like himself, rich like himself, and who perhaps resembles Chéri like one half-tame colt resembles another . . .

Under the familiar caress, Chéri leans his head back, closes his eyes, and his nostrils flare as if he was on the verge of crying.

"Nounoune . . ." he whispers despite himself.

He fights back his tears with the spiteful pride of a child, and Léa helps calm him. "There, there, Chéri."

Until his magnificent, moist eyes open again with a burst of laughter. "Can you imagine the look on their faces?"

"Whose?"

"Why, Mama's! This'll give the old girl a shock! And everybody else, too!"

"And . . . your wife?"

"Oh, this'll be the last straw for her!"

Léa shakes her head angrily. "But will she be upset?"

Chéri jumps furiously to his feet. "Upset? Of course she'll be upset! That's all she ever is—upset! For the last four months . . ."

He tears off his jacket and tie, which he throws on the dressing table. "You don't know what kind of life I've been living for the last four months! A child like that who isn't even twenty-one years old! Who doesn't know anything, doesn't do anything, doesn't understand anything! She's bored, she's afraid to be alone, she cries if I say anything, she hides under the table if I yell . . . I'm not a nursemaid!"

"Neither is she, unfortunately," thinks Léa.

"So, you see, it's not working out for me. And then always hanging on me, despite all that, saying I'm handsome and that she loves me! Do I even know her? I'm telling you, I've had it! Up to here!"

He kneels down beside the bed and rolls his head in the cool sheets. Seeing him, one would think it was the return of a smitten lover. But Léa does not fool herself. She understands the mysterious power of habit; she understands even better Chéri's closed heart, hard and belated like the buds of the oak . . . He had smiled at the fragrant bedroom; he had fallen, relieved, into the familiar armchair. A caress that was not in the least passionate had nearly opened the floodgates of his egotistical tears; what he longs for now is the bed in which he slept the long sleeps of his adolescence. But he had not yet kissed either Léa's hand or her face . . . He does not give a thought to the suffering of an abandoned child.

Pensively Léa brushes Chéri's clear cheek and his handsome, thankless forehead with the tips of her fingers. "Chéri . . ."

He groans lazily. "What?"

"You can't stay here, you know. You have to go back . . ."

He opens terrible, dark eyes. "Go back? You must be kidding! I'd rather die! I'm through with being married! Get me out of it, if you can!"

He has wrapped his strong arms around her . . . Léa shrugs her shoulders, powerless . . .

"Send Chéri back? Where will he go? He doesn't understand yet that the one waiting there for him is a woman . . ." He is too young, this child hanging on to his old friend, trying to heal a sickly love bruised by its own emergence . . . "Well, too bad, I'm keeping him!" Léa decides with calm fatalism. "Worse things could happen . . . Let him stay—in the meantime."

And loosening Chéri's grip, she makes a place for him in the hollow of her comforting side like a mother animal.

THE PEARLS

"We'll have the coffee in the lounge, won't we, Chéri?"

"Of course."

"And Turkish coffee, like yesterday?"

"Of course."

"You're so sweet here. You have a delightful disposition when you travel."

"Yes, but I don't want anyone telling me I do. It immediately makes me want to start acting up."

He laughs and his laughter arouses in his handsome face the ferocity of a wolf cub. His perfect mouth is nearly innocent of smiling; after brief outbursts of a stinging joke, it closes back up like a sullen flower. But today Chéri, languid and subdued, laughs lazily, turned toward the garden, which is blue with shadows and greenery.

Léa gazes at her young friend and admires him without servility or bitterness.

"You've never looked better than you have since we arrived in Tunis. What a face! And your eyes! Exactly like the eyes of the women here! You wouldn't happen to be part Tunisian by any chance?"

Blasé, Chéri does not deign to look at her with his dark eyes; but with a finger moist with saliva he shines his thrilling lashes and his gleaming eyebrows like plumage. They both fall silent, like satisfied lovers with nothing left to say to each other, like old friends resting together. A simple white dress and a white hat brighten Léa's healthy complexion and are not intended to make it look younger. With her beautiful, solid shoulders, her tranquil blue eyes, and without the dye in her hair, she might be taken for a very agreeable mother accompanying her son . . .

No one looks at them all that much at the Arabian Palace. In Paris they have been forgotten, and in any case, their running off together did not cause a big to-do. Chéri's attempt at marriage was so brief—four months!—he had barely had time to leave his more mature friend for his young wife.

And he has come back to her with the rage of a deceived child, impatient to rediscover in her, by turns obliging, calm, indifferent, and good, what for him takes the place of love. She took him back, peevish and wheedling, she looked after the ill-tempered, detestable little king, and they began living together again.

As before, he insults her, he strokes her naggingly; as before, she lets him play and destroy all around her with an indulgent disdain which dwarfs him. He wields a powerless spite against her. When he feels like shouting at her, "The least you could do is cry! That other one cries, that little girl I abandoned cries!" Léa smiles, strokes Chéri's forehead, and says only, "Poor baby."

Humiliated, bristling, he sometimes bites the appeasing hand, then little by little loosens his bite and stays there, eyes shut, lips closed around the skin he has bitten, as if slaking his thirst for her . . .

They came to Tunis as innocents, expecting to find on the other side of the sea a land without winter, a city with the whiteness of sugar, crisscrossed with blue shadows. With the first disappointment behind them, they gave in to their idleness, the one as unadventurous as the other, both incapable of any lasting curiosity but amused by a passing burnous or a veil worked with gold, and imagining that the entire Orient fits into a Jew's stall cluttered with rolled carpets and big silver jewelry.

Within a week this rather singular couple of lovers reverts to a Parisian use of time, mundane and inflexible. Before lunch, a stroll through the souks where Chéri fingers the gandurahs, the Bokharan embroidery. Léa takes her time picking out antique rugs, with a short pile, those whose red threads, worn with light, pale to a silvery pink. They make their way slowly toward the hotel and Chéri turns to look at the passing veiled women, sees his dark eyes in theirs, dark and magnificent like his.

After lunch, after the quiet hour of Turkish coffee and cigarettes, the car takes Léa and Chéri outside the city; they are going to Carthage for tea, or to some other Turkish café in Sidi-bou-Said, it being too far to the Pre-Catelan or the pavilion at Bellevue.

They can look at the mountains without their souls rushing toward the white sand, toward the desert they conceal; they can walk along the green and white sea without their hearts filling like a sail. Léa, growing older and wiser, has lost forever the thrill of travel, and Chéri, young, ardent, robust, carries with him, in him, something convalescent, belated, languid . . .

"It will be hard for you to go back to being married," says Léa, shaking her head.

They are alone in the hall, and Chéri can stretch out on the rattan chaise lounge. He inhales deeply the delicious aroma of the Turkish coffee prepared for him in a corner of the hall on the glowing coals of a tiny brazier. Léa leafs through the illustrated magazines and affectionately oversees the dozing Chéri, whose beautiful eyelashes flutter, heavy with sleep . . . Suddenly he opens his eyes with a start.

"Nounoune!"

Léa gets up, accustomed to the trepidation of a child wakened by a bad dream.

"There, there . . . Sleep, I'm right here next to you."

He rests his neck back down on the cushions, but his hand hangs on to the long strand of pearls that encircles Léa's neck three times before descending to her knees. Half asleep he plays with the luminous beads, whose slightest imperfections are detected by his sensitive fingers. He likes their roundness, their vibrant warmth, their soapy softness . . .

His heavy, thoughtless gaze moves from his friend to the bright bay window opening onto a garden of palm and orange trees. A dry hand, the color of toasted bread, has just set down on the low table two steaming cups, white and transparent like two halves of an eggshell. Onto the cushions next to Chéri, another hand, this one a black purple color, slips a bouquet of moist white carnations, which gives off the active fragrance of pepper and vanilla . . .

Chéri smiles with contentment and fingers the pearls as if saying the rosary. Each one harbors beneath its silky skin the glinting, veiled colors of an elusive rainbow. This one is the most beautiful . . . But this one is even more beautiful. And higher up those lying on the full, somewhat heavy breast . . . Oh, those . . . But the biggest, the purest, are wound into a triple strand around Léa's neck.

It is on this neck that Chéri's eyes settle, fixed, as if he were seeing it for the first time. His friend is reading, seated, her head tilted forward. Under her chin she has two folds of slightly yellow skin and her neck is covered with loose skin, also yellow, more yellow because of the pearls, and grainy below the ear . . . "The skin of an old hen," thinks Chéri fiercely. He cannot take his eyes off the neck or the pearls. He can sense an image, a memory taking shape, coming to him, still hazy, from the depths of his indolent memory. He suffers vaguely; something grows within him painfully. He would like to turn his eyes away or close them. This withered skin, these pearls . . . "What is it?" he asks himself impatiently.

His eyelids close suddenly and his entire body relaxes, as if allowed to rest. The dread image is coming to life, and in place of Léa's neck, in place of the triple, iridescent chain, Chéri can see a young, amber-colored neck, smooth, bent in sadness, adorned with a thin strand of pearls. And the nape of the neck, the necklace, the soft cascading hair, undone, all shudder to the rhythms of impassioned sobs . . .

The image, the whispering of the sobs accompany Chéri, descend with him to sleep, where a dream timid with tenderness and remorse sketches itself out, a dream in which his hand, protective for the first time, touches the necklace it has fastened there, on the silky young neck, the thin necklace of tiny little pearls . . .

[Translated by Matthew Ward]

DIALOGUES FOR
ONE VOICE

Literature

❧§❧

"Godmother?"

" . . . "

"What are you doing, Godmother? A story for the papers? Is it a sad story?"

" . . . ?"

"Because you look so unhappy!"

" . . . "

"Ah, it's because you're late? It's like a composition: you have to turn in your work on the day they tell you to? . . . What would they say if you turned in your notebook without anything in it?"

" . . . ?"

"The men who judge it at the paper!"

" . . . "

"They wouldn't pay you? That's so boring. It's the same thing for me; but Mama only gives me two sous for each composition. She says I'm mercenary. Well, work hard. Can I see your page? That's all you have? You'll never be ready!"

" . . . !"

"What! you don't have a subject? Don't they give you an outline, like us at school, for French composition? That way at least you have a chance!"

" . . . "

"What I'd like is for Mademoiselle to let us write whatever comes into our heads. Oh boy, if I was a writer!"

" . . . ?"

"What would I do? I'd write a hundred thousand million things, and stories for children."

" . . . "

"I *know* there's lots of them; but they're enough to make you sick of being a child. How many more am I going to get as presents? You know, too many people take us for idiots! When I see in a catalogue: 'For Young Readers,' I say to myself, 'Well, that's just great! more grownups knocking themselves out to come down to our level, as they say!' I don't know why grownups use a special tone to come down to our level. Do we children get to write books for grownups?"

"   . . .   "

"That's fair, isn't it? I'm for what's fair. For example, I want a book for teaching you things to be a book for teaching you things, and a book for fun, I want it to be fun. I don't want them mixed up. For years, you saw, in children's books, a car drive up, and there was always a man in the story to pass along to you his opinion about the progress of machines . . . Now you're sure to see a dashing aviator descend from the sky, but he talks about the conquest of the air . . . and of the . . . the glorious dead who lead the way. You see, there are constantly things breaking in on the story in children's books, things that smell of a grownup giving a lesson. It's no use for Papa to repeat, 'A child must understand everything he reads . . .' I think that's grotexque . . ."

"   . . .   "

"Grotesque? Are you sure? Grotexque is prettier."

"   . . . ?"

"I think it's grotexque because grownups never seem to remember about when they were little. I think things that I don't understand everything about are terrific. I like beautiful words that sound pretty, words you don't use in talking. I never ask what they mean, because I would rather think about them and look at them until they make me a little scared. And I like books without pictures too."

"   . . . ?"

"Yes, you see, Godmother, when they say, for example, in the history book I'm reading, 'There once was a beautiful young girl in a castle, on the edge of a lake . . .' I turn the page, and I see a drawing of the castle, and the young girl and the lake. Oh brother!"

"   . . . ?"

"I can't really explain, but it never, never looks like my young girl, or my castle or my lake . . . I can't put it in words. If I knew how to paint . . . That's why I prefer your books, your yellow books without any pictures. You understand me, Godmother?"

"   . . .   "

"You say 'yes' but I'm not sure . . . And also, they don't talk enough about love in books for children."

"   . . . !"

"What did I say now? Is love a bad word?"

" . . . "

"On top of that, I don't know what it is! I'm very much in love."

" . . . ?"

"Nobody. I know I'm only ten and that it would be ridiculous to be in love with somebody, at my age. But I am in love, that's all, just like that. I'm waiting. That's why I like love stories so much, terrifying stories, but that end happy."

" . . . "

"Because with stories that end sad, you go on feeling sad afterward, you're not hungry, you think about it for a long time, and when you look at the book's cover, you say to yourself, 'They just go on being unhappy in there . . .' You think about what you could do to make things right, you imagine writing the next story where everything would work out . . . I like it so much when people get married!"

" . . . ?"

"Yes, but only after they've been very unhappy before, each in his own way. It isn't that I like it, all the unhappiness, but it's necessary."

" . . . ?"

"For there to be a beginning, a middle, and an end. And also because love, the way I see it, is being very sad at first, and then very happy after."

" . . . "

"No, no, not at all, it's not often the opposite! Who's asking you that? Don't bother me with your grown-up opinions! And now try to write a beautiful story in your newspaper, a story for *me*, not for children. A story where people cry and adore each other and get married . . . And put words I like in it, too, yes, like 'foment,' 'surreptitious,' and 'pro rata' and 'corroborate' and 'premonitory' . . . And then when you start a new paragraph you'll say, 'At this juncture . . .'"

" . . . ?"

"I don't know exactly what it means, but I think it makes it very elegant."

My Goddaughter

❦

"Is it you who's calling me, Godmother? I'm here, under the stairs."

" . . . ?"

"No, Godmother, I'm not sulking."

" . . . ?"

"No, Godmother, I'm not crying anymore. I'm done now. But I'm very discouraged."

" . . . ?"

"Oh, it's always the same thing, for a change. I'm mad at Mama. And she's mad at me, too."

" . . . !"

"Why 'naturally'? No, not 'naturally' at all! There are times when she's mad without me being mad back—it depends on if she's right."

" . . . !"

"Oh, please, Godmother, not today! You can tell this to me another day. There are plenty of days when I'm in a good mood and when you can make me lay back my ears . . ."

" . . . "

"No, not lay *down*, lay *back*! When you scold the dog, what does he do? he lays back his ears. Me too, I've laid my ears back since lunch. So, I'll start over; you can lay back my ears about my parents, and the fairness of parents, and how a child shouldn't judge his parents, and this and that . . . But it's no use today."

" . . . ?"

"What's the matter? The matter is that Mama discourages me. Come here, so I can tell you about it. You're still the one I tell the most, because you don't have any children. You understand better."

" . . . !"

Yes, it does make sense! You don't have any children, you still have a mama, you get scolded, you storm, you rage, and you have the reputation of being unreasonable: Mama shrugs her shoulders when she talks about you, like with me . . . That pleases me. That gives me confidence."

" . . . "

"There's no need to apologize, I don't do it on purpose . . . Come on, we'll go sit by the fire: I've had enough of sitting under these stairs, too! There, now. Mama discourages me. I can't seem to make her understand certain things."

" . . . ?"

"Serious things, things about life. Can you believe she just bought me a hat to go to school in! . . . Oh, yes, it's true, you don't know, you're not from the country . . . In Montigny, the girls in the public school *never* wear hats, except in the summer for the sun, and I'm only telling you this under the ceiling of secrecy . . ."

" . . . !"

"The *ceiling*, I'm telling you! The proof is that you don't say it in another room . . . So, I'm telling you under the ceiling of secrecy that we go 'Boo!' in the street at the students of the nuns, because they wear hats to school. No repeating?"

" . . . !"

"Good. So then Mama buys me a hat. And so I make a face at the hat! Naturally, Mama starts a two-hour lecture, which has nothing to do with the point: that I'm more than ten years old, and that I'm almost a young lady, and that I should set the example of an irreproachable appearance . . . She finally ended up upsetting me. I lost my patience, I told her that it didn't concern her, that my life at school was a special life which parents don't understand anything about, et cetera . . . 'Tell me, Mama,' I said to her, 'do you tell Papa what he should do at his office? It's the same thing with me at school. I have a very noticeable position at school, a very delicate position, because I have personality, as Mademoiselle says. To hear you, Mama, I should only concern myself with my family! You send me to school, I spend half my life there. Well, that counts, half of my life . . . School's like another world, you don't talk about it the same: what's appropriate here isn't at school, and if I tell you I shouldn't go to class in the winter with a hat, it's because I shouldn't wear a hat! You see, Mama, there are things you sense, there are nuances!' I spelled this all out to her very calmly, all at once, so that she didn't have the time to get a word in edgewise, because you know how mamas are, don't you? They fly off the handle, and besides, they don't have a sense of proportion."

" . . . ?"

"I mean, they rant and rave over everything, as much for a broken glass as for something very, very bad. Mine especially. She's easily affected. Afterward, she was looking at me as if I fell from the moon, and she said in a soft voice, 'My God, this child . . . this child . . .' She looked so unhappy and so astonished, you would have thought I was the one who had scolded her. So much so that I put my arm around her like this and I rocked her up against me, saying, 'There . . . there . . . my little darling, there! . . . ' It ended very happy."

" . . . ?"

"Yes, we are! we *are* angry, but for a different reason. The story of the hat is from yesterday. Today . . . here, look at my finger."

" . . . !"

"Yes, a cut, a big one, and the nail is split. It has hydrogen peroxide and I don't know what else on it. And here, on my cheek, you can see a red burn; it stings. And my hair, can't you see, on my forehead? Smell it: It must still smell a little like when they singe the pig in the square. These are all today's ordeals, which got Mama and me angry with each other . . . I wanted curly bangs on my forehead; so, so I cut a few hairs— big deal! I know you always go further than you want with scissors . . .

And I burned my cheek trying to turn the curling iron, to cool it down, like the hairdresser, you know: it makes it so pretty . . ."

" . . . ?"

"The cut, that was the scissors. A little farther and I would have poked out my eye . . . So, here I am, right, with my hand covered with blood, my hair singed and cut like a staircase, my cheek burned . . . And naturally, right when Mama comes back! Boy, did I ever catch it!"

" . . . !"

"Yes, I was in the wrong, but she scolded me in a way that wasn't the way she usually does. I'm sure it wasn't a question of what's appropriate, or of dress, or of children who get into everything and are punished for it! It wasn't even a question of me—or barely!'

" . . . ?"

"Wait, I'm about to remember . . . She was like a fury. She said that I had ruined *her* daughter for her! She said, 'What have you done with *my* beautiful hair which I tended so patiently? You had no right to touch it! And that cheek, who gave you permission to spoil it! And this little hand? . . . How? . . . I've taken years, I've spent my days and my nights trembling over this masterpiece and all it takes is one of your exploits, you destructive little demon, to ruin the adorable result of so many pains! What you've done to it is cowardly, it's shameful! Your beauty is mine, you don't have the right to take away what I entrust to you!' What do you think of that, Godmother?"

" . . . "

"Me either, I couldn't think of anything to say. But it shook me up. I went under the stairs without saying a word. And I felt as sorry for myself as I could. I felt my hands, my legs, my head. 'Poor little things,' I said to myself, 'your hands, your legs, your head aren't even yours! You're like a slave, then! A lot of good it did for your mother to give you birth, since she's taken back all the rest! You wouldn't dare even lose a single baby tooth or break a nail, for fear that your mother will claim it back from you . . . ' Well, you know how you talk to yourself when you want to make yourself cry . . . Oh, I have a mother who torments me so much, Godmother!"

" . . . "

"You think I do the same to her! It's possible. So, if she's nice to me at dinner, I can forgive her, too?"

" . . . "

"I really want to. It's true, she did call me a destructive demon, but . . ."

" . . . ?"

"But she also called me an 'adorable result,' and I like that."

A Hairdresser

"Here, Madame, in the little salon at the back, we won't be bothered. Shampoo?"

" . . . "

"Naturally, I know the refrain: not enough time, just a rinse! And then afterward, they complain about having dry, split hair. I'll bet you're going to the preview at the Gymnase? I was sure of it! Did you like the one at the Ambigu?"

" . . . "

"It wasn't what I was expecting. Nothing really new, nothing audacious, no 'discovery.' Not one entrance which makes you cry out."

" . . . ?"

"Yes, cry out . . . 'There's one, at last!' "

" . . . ?"

"Well, a coiffure, naturally! There, like everywhere else, it was a mishmash, a mishmash of attempts; yes, that's the expression I was looking for! You saw the fright wigs, the sugar loaf, spit curls, the eternal turban, the *sac à mouches* made out of tulle wrapping the head . . . Watch your eyes, the fumes . . . Next time I'll give you a nice raw-egg shampoo."

" . . . ?"

"Is it good? It's excellent . . . for the egg sellers. Hah, hah!"

" . . . !"

"Sorry, the comb got stuck. You have dandruff."

" . . . !"

"No, I made a mistake. Don't pay any attention; it's just that we've reached the point where I always say that . . . to my regular clients. But I have so little business sense! You see, I don't insist. We've known each other a long time."

" . . . "

"Not at all, the pleasure's all mine. Besides, I have no malice whatsoever, and I leave to a certain colleague the bit about hair falling out after you have a baby."

" . . . ?"

"You don't know that one? It's simple. A client—I mean a woman

—loses her hair at the temples and hairline after having a baby, it never fails, but it grows back six months later. What does my colleague do? He says, 'You're losing your hair here, and here, and here, too . . .' —'Oh, my God!' the lady says —'Don't worry,' says the hairdresser, 'we have a tonic water which . . . a tonic water that . . .' Anyway, to make it short, three months later the lady sees her hair starting to grow back and sings long and hard the praises of the tonic which . . . the tonic that . . . Shall I wave you?"

" . . . ?"

"It'll take fifteen minutes. You ask me that every time, I'm not blaming you. And every time I tell you, 'It'll only take fifteen minutes,' like I'm supposed to for every operation that takes twenty-five minutes. Which dress are you wearing tonight?"

" . . . "

"Yes, yes, I know the one, the gold lamé on a midnight-blue background. People have already gotten a pretty good look at you in that one."

" . . . !"

"Certainly not, I have no intention of offering you another one like it. Because even if my means permitted me such whims, my clientele wouldn't allow it. Ah! . . . But we can give your blue dress a new look."

" . . . ?"

"With a pretty wig in the same shade."

" . . . !"

"Jump if it amuses you, but not too high, because I'm holding the hair on your neck. A pretty blue wig, I think. With two rows of little paste gems and a spray of paradise blue . . . Fine, fine, you'll come around!"

" . . . !"

"Maybe not you *personally*, but your best friend, your teatime acquaintances, your sister-in-law, your cousin, all the women to whom you say when talking about colored hair, 'What a horror! If I ever see you with dead, apple-green hair on your head, I'll never speak to you again!' Well, they will wear it, they're already wearing it, and you're still speaking to them. So I, your hairdresser, giggle in my little corner."

" . . . "

"No, that's not why. It's because I realize that I, as a hairdresser, a simple *wigmaker*, I nevertheless have more influence over your closest friends than you have over them yourself. I could die laughing. I'll be done in just a second."

" . . . !"

"Yes, I do, I think it's lovely. Look, a wig in a beautiful violet or midnight blue, like I'm suggesting to you, is ravishing with your complexion. It's flattering, it gives contour."

" . . . ?"

"Do *I* know what contour is? Well, I know what it is. Contour is . . . um . . . there, like that . . . something indefinable . . . I understand what I mean!'

" . . . ?"

"I'm with you a little less on the white wig. Mostly young women, very young, have gone for that one, and older women who were dyeing their hair."

" . . . ?"

"Because older women who had been dyeing their hair said to themselves, 'The day I no longer want to dye my hair, I'll want completely white hair, like a young woman!' "

" . . . ?"

"No, they went on dyeing it. The idea was enough for them. We're done. A little brilliantine?"

" . . . ?"

"It gives luster. It gives an extraordinary luster . . . to the lining of hats. Ah! Give a brief glance in the shop before you go, I have a small selection of colored wigs like none you've ever seen before . . . What's that, what did you say?"

" . . . !"

"No, you won't see them in Paris. You know where you will? In Germany. Berlin ordered thirty of them from me at the same time. *Fabriqué en France! Pariser Kunst!* So, did I ever give it to them—cabbage green, turnip yellow, Parma violet, and Prussian blue, which is only right. And do they ever pay—six, seven, eight hundred apiece; so there! One is patriotic in one's own way: it's just so much money coming in."

A Masseuse

❦

"Phew! . . . Bonjour, Madame. Phew! Am I ever tired! How's that knee?"

" . . . "

"So you say, so you say. Let's have a look. It's true, the swelling has gone down. But the area is still pretty black from the extravasated blood? Talk about a bad blow, that was a bad blow. Am I ever tired!"

" . . . ?"

"Why don't I sit down? Ah, yes! . . . Don't mind me, I say that every third thing—I'm tired. I say it because it's the truth; I can't help it anymore, I'm giving out. It's a real blessing."

" . . . ?"

"Think about it, Madame, it's a slaughterhouse with me. It's as if all these ladies are crazy. The one who wants to go to the south, another one who's just come back from the south, another who won't stop going out at night, and all the ones who've been thrashed dancing the tango—and worst of all, the ones who don't dance, who don't go out, who don't travel—they're the ones who get the most use out of my doormat . . . All of them in fact, I'm telling you! It's to the point where when I reach your house, a week after for your sprain, I shout, 'Oh, thank God, now for half an hour of relaxation, a nice quiet little sit-down massage!' Softer leg, completely relaxed, please."

" . . . ?"

"Don't be a tease! There is a world of difference between that and saying that it's a good thing that you sprained your knee! But I really am glad to have you between two big massages. When I leave your place, I go . . . clear into the wilds, to the end of Auteuil."

" . . . ?"

"You know perfectly well I never say whose house it is. The lady I told you about, the one who's so rich and so bad-tempered. You know, don't you? She receives me like a dog if I'm two minutes late, especially since for the moment she's without her head chambermaid; one that she had hired, a gem, was in the house for one hour . . . a story that would make you die laughing! The maid arrives, a very decent-looking girl; the lady, who had had a good lunch, cries out when she sees her, 'Why, she's so sweet, with the face of a real little soubrette! You'll be called Marton, and I'll use *tu* with you!' So the maid says, 'As for the name, it's all the same to me; but as for using *tu*, if Madame doesn't mind, I don't think we've known each other long enough, Madame and I.' "

" . . . "

"Of course it wasn't a bad way to put it. Only it cost her her job. To try and be witty at a hundred and twenty francs a month; at that rate, I'd just as soon be a dumb animal. Phew, am I tired!"

" . . . "

"Me, rest? You wouldn't want that! And in the first place, I don't like to rest. I'm made for working first and for complaining after. If I

don't complain, I'm not happy. Take days like the one I have tomorrow:
at five o'clock in the morning, my Greek lady . . ."

" . . ."

That's what I said: five o'clock in the morning. Well, if you're
looking for an easy job, I don't advise you to become a domestic in her
house. She never feels sleepy, and it annoys her that others are asleep.
At five o'clock in the morning she's leaning on all the bells, and while
she's waiting for the staff to come down, she runs around in her kimono,
hiding little wads of paper behind and under the furniture, to see if the
sweeping gets done. Right down to me, whom she keeps from sleeping!
She only wants her massage at five o'clock out of pure meanness; she
pays me an arm and a leg for it, just for the pleasure of saying to me
when I arrive, 'Oh, my poor Antoinette, it mustn't have been very warm
coming here this morning. My thermometer read twenty degrees, outside
the window!' And then I show off; I say, 'A little nippy, Madame, a
little nippy. It gets the blood circulating. If you were out on the street
at this hour, you wouldn't have legs the color of butter like you do,
probably.' "

" . . ."

"Look, I can get my digs in, too. Last winter, she almost had me
come at eight in the morning, but she decided against it. She must have
realized that the métro is running at that hour, and the buses, and that
would be too convenient for me. She's got one sharp tongue, I'm telling
you. She knows French every bit as well as any cabdriver. The blood's
risen in my face at the insults she's given me at times. Once, I got up my
courage and said to her, 'Madame, tomorrow it'll be fifty francs instead
of forty.' '—And why is that?' she says to me. —'Forty francs for the
massage and ten for the big words.' "

" . . ."

"You're so well behaved when you're being amused. You don't
move any more than my fat daddy, as I call him, my retired colonel,
when I massage his poor wrists. He's the one who comes after my Greek
lady. And all the rest of the day goes on like that, hour after hour, till
eight o'clock at night. And mind you, if one of my clients cancels, I feel
the earth go out from under my feet, I'm left ruined, I'm lost, do you
believe it? At night I finish up with my English lady, and when I get
to her place, I massage her, you might say, in a daze, I'm so worn out
with exhaustion. That's when you really hear me moaning that I'm
tired! A pretty blond lady, my English lady, and well built and everything. But she's got her touchy spots, too."

" . . ."

"She belongs to a special religion, and she wanted me to join too.
'Antoinette,' she says, 'you must become Christian Scientist.' —'It

sounds hard, just hearing the name,' I say. —'On the contrary,' says milady, 'it is a religion which guarantees all its adopts . . . adepts . . . perfect happiness. Look here, you who are forever tired, repeat vigorously: *I am not tired*, and by applying your mind firmly to convince yourself of it, you can suppress entirely the impression of tiredness. Just as, when you're sad, all you have to do is repeat vigorously—' 'Fine, Madame! fine, Madame,' I interrupt, 'I understand, I'll try it.' Why would I go and contradict a good client? . . . Last night, I get to my English lady's and I find her all upset. 'Oh, Antoinette,' she says to me, 'my barrette, my beautiful barrette with the two big diamonds and the gray pearl, I've lost it! You don't know how upset I am.' 'Well, Madame,' I say, 'now more than ever is the time to repeat vigorously to yourself, *I have not lost my barrette, I have not lost my barrette, I have not lost my barrette!*' "

" . . . ?"

"She didn't say anything, but she gave me the evil eye. Phew! We're done, blabbing all the while. You've got pins and needles, don't you? You're supposed to. And now I'm off . . . My bag! What did I do with my bag? Oh, my Lord! my bag, my iodine cream is in it! A client who waits for my iodine cream like the Mass! My bag, my iodine cream, my keys, my purse, my . . . Ah, here it is! Phew! That's better."

" . . . "

"No, not your knee—me! Good night, Madame, I'm in a hurry . . ."

My Corset Maker

❧❦❧

Characters: *My corset maker, a stout lady, asthmatic, who looks as if she's never worn a corset. Me, quasi-mute and revolted.*

The scene is a very small salon. Photographs on the mantelpiece, signed. On the wall, a chromolithograph of a vaguely feminine shape of wormlike thinness, with this caption: The Peri Corset 327 permits sitting and standing positions.

My corset maker: "Well, hello, Madame. I'd almost given up hope of seeing you this season! I was saying to myself, 'Will she be unfaithful to me again?' "

" . . . "

"Yes, I know you travel a lot. Travel is the death of the figure. Women buy corsets here and there, even in department stores, and that's how they lose their shape! You've come at a very bad time; with all these ladies leaving for the summer, I don't know which way to turn."

" . . . "

"Oh, my, you've gained weight since last year!"

" . . . "

"You certainly have gained weight! Look, here . . . and here . . . How could you let yourself get like this? And with fashions nowadays, you're not thinking about that!"

" . . . "

"Oh, I'm not pleased with you, not pleased at all! . . . Now get yourself undressed: I've prepared a linen pattern for you on my new model, my 327 . . ."

" . . . "

"Why, yes, it'll look good on you . . . And what is this? All you're wearing right now is two garter belts!"

" . . . "

'It probably *is* more convenient! But I wonder what you would do if you were like a lot of these ladies with fat lower stomachs. Fat stomachs don't just disappear like money!"

" . . . "

"Oh, how can you say that? Ah, you're just the same! You're going to make me blush . . . It's like these women who go on diets; they have to, for fashion's sake, don't they? They listened to me, they lost weight; only they have too much skin; it makes sense, doesn't it? They have too much skin on their stomach, especially on the stomach, and under the arms too, at the level of the breasts. It's a job, a real artist's job to arrange it all and put it back in order. Madame X, you know, that beautiful woman who has a 225,000-franc sable coat? She's a new client of mine. She is superb, you wouldn't recognize her anymore. A figure! hips! like this. Look. And she used to be so stout! Well, she has too much skin, it's perfectly natural. But with my 327, she's divine!"

" . . . ?"

"When she undresses? Ah, well, that's her business. Who isn't in that position, nowadays?"

" . . . "

"What do you mean, idiotic? But I'll tell you about fifty, I'll tell you about a hundred who are no more idiotic than you and me! You come here, with your bohemian ways, but you'll never change anything, with your little garter belts, which just leave you looking heavy and eccentric! I've had other clients who wanted to be unfashionable, but they came around in the end! They can't fight it . . . Say, you don't have varicose veins?"

" . . . "

"It's strange. I've never seen as many as I have this year."

" . . . "

"That's what you think, that it's our fault? Varicose veins come all by themselves. I'm not saying this for that poor Madame Z. You know her? She's ruined with varicose veins. Varicose veins like irrigation pipes! You won't repeat it? Good Lord! You've gotten so fat!"

" . . . "

"Not at all, it is not in my head! You don't fight it, you accept it calmly. You're not as energetic a woman as Madame P."

" . . . ?"

"What does she do? She *chases down* her fat. At first she had rather large hips, 'Madame Adele,' she says to me, 'I don't want my hips anymore! Do something!' So, I lengthen her corsets with a yank, and I tighten them at the bottom, hah! . . . Little by little the fat moves, descending down the thigh. But it was making a roll on the thigh. I lengthen the corset again with a yank and tighten, hah . . . So that Madame P. ended up having her rolls of fat way low, down where it can barely be seen. She is delighted . . . It's the same for the bust."

" . . . ?"

"A bust is no longer wanted. Princess gowns, flat furs, all this has dethroned the bust. These ladies have done everything they could: they've *distributed* it, to the left and to the right, they've sent it back a little under the arms. But is there anything as vile as a fold of skin at the armpit? We do better than that today!"

" . . . ?"

"Well, you grab hold of the breast, like this . . . Don't be afraid! I'll explain it to you with a bit of cloth. You grab hold of the breast, here, like this, and fold it, at the bottom, as you press it back as far as you can on the sides. Over that, you put a little brassiere: my 14A, gorgeous! Strictly speaking, it's not a brassiere, it's a small piece of elastic fabric for keeping the breast in position. And over all that, you put my corset, my large 327, the wonder of the day. And there you are, with a divine silhouette; no more hips, stomach, or rear than a bottle of Rhine wine, and especially, the chest of a youth. Having the chest of a youth, that's what matters. But it took some doing to get it that way. Well, Madame, I have competitors who've invented a lot of little things: a stretch fabric, an elastic band to compress and tighten the two halves of the rear end, the crotch clasp, but I can say that I was the first to make practical, and truly aesthetic, the arrangement of the 'folded breast'!"

The Saleswoman

❦

At the hat shop. With the arrival of a client, the saleswoman rushes up: twenty-five years old, with the eyes of a young tyrant, a tower of blond hair on the top of her head. Her hands, her figure, her mouth, her feet, all are thin to excess, witty, and aggressive.

"Ah, Madame! At last; you've come back to us! I had almost given up hope. I was saying to myself, 'That's it! She must have gone to Harry's to have some Berlin-style hats made for herself!' But . . . what is that you have on your head?"

" . . . ?"

"Yes, that thing with the blue wing on the side and the velour all around it?"

" . . . ?"

"What, you made it yourself? All by yourself. Why, that's incredible, it's miraculous! If I may indulge in a little joke, you have a future in fashion. Would you do our *maison* the honor of entering it as trimmer?'

" . . . ?"

"The trimmer? She's . . . well, heavens, she's the one who puts the linings inside the hats, who . . . well . . . who does a lot of little things. Give me your lovely little 'creation'; oh, I'll give it back to you! Here, I'll give it back . . . let's see . . . tomorrow. Yes, tomorrow. Exactly, the car is making a delivery tomorrow in your suburb."

" . . . ?"

"Yes, well, in your neighborhood, I meant. It's so far! I'm just a poor little Parisian girl who never has time to leave her post, you understand. The boulevard shop in winter, Deauville in the summer, the Biarritz shop in September, Monte Carlo in January . . . Oh, not everybody can live in Auteuil. Quick, come with me, I have a nice corner in the little fitting room facing the street. It's poorly lit? You don't like being with your back to the light? But it's the best place for trying on hats! Your silhouette is projected on the window, and with hats, it's primarily a question of silhouette, this season; one disregards the details. And, you see, you're between Mademoiselle X, the 'little diva,' who's trying on hats for her tour right now, and Princess Z, who's just back from the south."

" . . . "

"Yes, that one, the fat old lady. In the shop, we call her the 'Pink Pompon.' "

" . . . ?"

"Because whenever she doesn't like a hat, she always says, 'I think it's missing something, here, in the hollow . . . a little nothing, a little flower . . . a bouquet of pompon roses!' Mademoiselle X, that one there, to your left, she's not what you'd normally call pretty, but she has such a good heart!"

" . . . ?"

"Oh, a heart of gold. Look, the lady who's with her, yes, that sort of little shark in black, is a poor friend she's taken in. She takes her with her everywhere, to her couturier's, to her jeweler's; she stays here for hours trying on twenty-five different hats under her poor friend's nose—to distract her.

"Let's see now, how about if we talk a little more seriously now? I've gotten it into my head that I could really do a job on you today. It's days like this when my mind is set on business. Okay, for starters, pull this little cloche down over your beautiful hair for me! . . . You haven't changed color?"

" . . . "

"Excuse me, it's a reflection from the outside light. I was saying to myself: it has more gold in it than usual. You might have gotten the urge to change, just for a change. And then there are some people who go gray very early. On the side, on the side, completely covering one ear! There! . . . What do you think of it?"

" . . . !"

"I can see it's not a hit. Besides, you're right, it's not your style. On you, it looks a little . . . a little too ladylike. It's funny, I just sold the same hat to Mrs. W. She is ravishing in it, Mrs. W, with her long neck, and especially here, you see, her chin, her cheeks, so fresh and the ear . . . Let's say goodbye to this style here for a minute; one lost, ten found. Look at that, what was I telling you! This is what we're after. Way down, all right?"

" . . . "

"More than that, more than that! I can still see the hair on your temple, and on the back of your neck! I believe you're familiar with the 'great hat principle of the season,' as the owner herself says?"

" . . . ?"

"The great hat principle is that when you meet a woman on the street and her hat allows you to see whether she's a brunette, a blond, or a redhead, the woman in question is not wearing a chic hat. There! . . .

Notice I'm not saying anything, I'll let you make up your own mind. Well?"

"   . . . "

"You prefer the navy-blue one? That one there, on the mushroom? Yes? . . . Well, really!"

"   . . . "

"No, no, it's not sold."

"   . . . ?"

"Why no, Madame, I don't want to keep you from buying it! I wasn't suggesting it to you because I didn't think I was talented enough to sell hats like that one. But it's true, it does seem to go with your face. Ah, you really know what it is you want! Like I always say: there are only two categories of clients whose minds can't be changed: artists and lower-middle-class women."

"   . . . "

"You're not an artist, but you still have a very independent sense of judgment. Try on this one here, just for me. It's not at all excessive, but I think it's both rich and discreet, because of this polished cotton fantasia which gives it all its cachet . . . No? Ah, I'm not having any luck at all, you're just trying to mortify me. If your two sons have your personality, they'll be terrible men! Are those two big boys doing all right?"

"   . . . "

"Already? How time flies, my Lord! And still good-looking, I'm sure. Well, there's nothing surprising about that."

"   . . . !"

"No, Madame, there's no flattery intended at all; anyway, everybody in the shop agrees with me, it's just what everybody says about the presence, the charm, the intelligence of your husband . . . and everyone knows that your two gorgeous children also inherited your beautiful health! What a shame they're not daughters! I'd already be fitting them for hats, and spoiling them as much as you. So, nothing more today, except the little blue hat? Shall I have it sent down to you in your car?"

"   . . . "

"Yes, yes, don't worry, I give the description of the car to the messenger boy myself. You think I don't know the brown sedan you've had for six years? Goodbye, Madame, and thank you for your lovely visit, don't go so long without coming to see your faithful saleswoman; I enjoy seeing you so much . . . it gives me a rest from our American clientele: all I feel like telling those women are disagreeable things."

An Interview

❧❧❧

"I'm afraid so, dear lady, it's me! Curse fate, it's me again! You haven't forgotten our last interview, have you? You treated me so poorly! I can still see you at the conclusion of your talk, backstage at the public university. 'What's *he* doing here?' You muttered between your teeth. Oh, yes, don't deny it, I understood perfectly! The fact is, my evening clothes were singularly out of place in a working-class milieu . . ."

" . . ."

"You're right, it's not a working-class milieu, it's . . . help me out . . . it's . . . popular! That's it: a popular milieu! And now, let's talk seriously. This time I'm taking the chair you're not offering me, and settling in— oh, excuse me, digging in! Our old camaraderie gives me rights, and no one's going to have a nice little article about your new book before me. You understand that what I would like is something which would get us away from the eternal 'We found this unique artist at her worktable, between her police dog and her Siamese cat . . .' Just between you and me, people have had enough of your animals! I want to present our readers with the real 'you,' a more detailed 'you', more in depth, more . . . Notice, I have a pencil and a note pad! It amuses me quite a bit to play the reporter who chases down dogs who have been run over and potholes in the street. It's not like me at all to run around with the paraphernalia of a journaler . . ."

" . . ."

"Yes, yes, of a journaler, I like the word, whose discouraged ending bespeaks quite well the sadness, the meanness, the spinelessness of a profession which isn't a profession. That surprises you, admit it, to hear me melancholize in this way. But I've just gone through, I've barely managed to pull through a nasty period . . ."

" . . . ?"

"Bah! . . . everything and nothing . . . Neurasthenia. A vague word which contains so many precise miseries. It's at the point where I'm still asking myself: Let me see now, do I exile myself to the country, with the few sous left me by my father, so I can plant my cabbage, live obscurely and . . . how shall I say? monastically . . . ? There perhaps is where wisdom lies. And too bad for all the blackened pages, for the useless offspring of my thought!"

" . . . ?"

"Yes . . . I've undertaken a . . . how shall I say? a study, a fantastic 'study of man'—I rather like the title, which is a counterpart to Balzac's *Studies of Women* . . . I'm going to speak to you like a colleague, with perfect frankness: is my book finished—or isn't it? At each moment, I lean over my hero as over an abyss, and I cry out, 'But I didn't know him!—I only catch glimpses of him!' It is this exhausting task which has brought me to the point: neurasthenia, loss of sleep, fickle appetite, migraines, etc. And the profession, during this time, the terrible profession which does not wait, which forces itself on you, which pushes you: Go, the Queen of St. Marguerite's Market is calling you, the dramatist whose play is being performed tomorrow hopes for you! So the exasperated body rebels, your nerves get the better of you, you collapse in midstream! You know all this, you've suffered it all, naturally . . ."

" . . . "

"Go on, go on, there's no use denying it, we're talking heart to heart, to listen to you, it seems to me that your soul reflects mine somewhat, I am so happy, so honored that our impressions are so similar! What did you do to triumph over the crisis?"

" . . . "

"For me, at first, I was taken by a—how shall I say—by a phobia about noise and light, I was at the point of going through the childishness of doubling my shutters, of covering my walls with cork. I've been —it's laughably pitiful—at the point of proposing to my upstairs neighbors that I buy them a carpet . . . I lived a prisoner's life, illuminated by a single lamp: anemia—I take the word out of your mouth—wasting no time settling in; thus began the painstaking treatments intended as a tonic for an unfortunate organism, young and yet exhausted. I underwent cold hydrotherapy, raw horsemeat, the spa—ah, what a book, if I had had the strength for it, that season at the spa would have made!— and for illusory results, purely illusory . . . So, what do you think I did?"

" . . . "

"Yes, yes, you sensed it! I said to myself, You will forget your pain, by reaching out to the suffering of others, you will humbly see your reflection in their pettinesses, in their ambitions, you will confess what they hide: in a word, you will be a reporter! But a reporter in the way one is a doctor, somewhat, or a detective; you will not mingle with the masses of those who content themselves with the role of phonograph or camera, no! You'll turn an imprudent word into an anecdote; a smile or a gesture into a little novel. A peaceful novel, unquestionably, one which could take wing between the walls and beneath the foliage of this garden . . . don't you think? . . . Ah, it's wonderful. This provincial corner, this air which smells of lime trees. This is what my unfortunate nerves needed, but . . . I don't mean to be indiscreet, but how much is your rent?"

" . . . "

"Now! now! . . . Paradise is worth paying for. Paradise without heat? . . . No? with heat? Good. And do you think that in the neighborhood I could find . . ."

" . . . "

"Oh, you're just saying that. Deep down, you'd really like to entice your colleague and comrade to live nearby. Just the same, in a maisonette like this, one could create a charming place, done in nothing but horrible Restoration furniture, vanity dressers, overly small washbasins made of flowered porcelain . . . I have a genius for decorating, you know. Now that's all I'm going to think about! It's all your fault, but you'll pay for it!"

" . . . ?"

"Ah, hah! . . . who is it who's going to find herself in *L'Heure* tomorrow, sketched out from top to bottom, with her acute femininity and her hyperaestheticized sensibility? You, my dear friend, you!"

" . . . !"

"What do you mean, you haven't opened your mouth? Oh, that's just like a woman, that expression, just like a woman! Except that in that expression there are a hundred lines of psychology! Isn't a woman entirely in what she doesn't say? I'd better be off, you'd scratch out my eyes, for a woman forgives a man—even a reporter—everything except insight. And I'm stealing a rose from you—I have a passion for flowers. If today I had not been exclusively the slave of my profession—and of a sense of curiosity made up of sympathy and admiration—I would have told you how this cultish devotion to flowers came to me, it really is the strangest case . . . But today, first things first! Dear Madame and friend, the journaler kisses your hands and runs to his factory—but the friend remains in thought at your feet, on this lawn which they only skim . . ."

[*Translated by Matthew Ward*]

MY FRIEND VALENTINE

A Letter

❧❦❧

My Dear Valentine,

I received your postcard. I was able to make out—from the few lines covering the view of the Lac du Bourget like a network of fine hairs—what faithful friendliness and affectionate concern there is in it.

We parted somewhat coolly, and you write to me, circumspect: "Abominable weather, impossible excursions, we're thinking of going back home . . . And what about you, what are you doing?"

That's enough; it's not hard to translate: "I'm afraid I've made you very angry . . . Don't forget me, don't hold it against me; we don't share two ideas in common, but I'm very fond of you, I don't know why; I like you just as you are, with all your faults. I'm upset about you: put my mind at ease."

Don't blush, my friend Valentine—it'll make your face powder cake!—and understand right away that I am still your friend.

I've followed your travels in the newspapers. *Figaro* assured me of your presence in Trouville, and I don't know which fashionable women's paper it was that depicted you in the most surprising terms: you were attributed with an "impeccable navy-blue Louis XV suit, with a twisted Guayaquil pompadour . . ." A twisted Guayaquil pompadour! Really! As a friend by the name of Claudine used to say to me, "I don't know what it is, but it must be beautiful!"

Because I'm living in a desert of golden sand—sixty square kilometers of beach, without a single strand of greenery, without one bald pebble—I am surprised, honestly, that there still are ladies who wear hats, tight-fitting dresses, boned collars, long corsets, and perilously high heels. How can I admit to you that, for the season, I have put away my dresses and shoes, and that beneath the indifferent and calloused soles of my feet I walk on the varnished seaweed, the sharp-edged shells, and the gray, salty furze that breaks through the sand? How dare I paint myself to you, dark as I am, my nose peeling a little from too much sun, my arms gloved in a deep shade of reddish brown? Thank God, the gulls and the delightful curlews are the only ones frightened by my riding outfit: knickers which at one time were blue, and a coarse knitted jersey. Add to that blue cycling stockings, rubber shoes, a soft cap, and the whole thing perched on top of a big nag of a bay horse—and you'll have a little equestrian group you wouldn't want to run into in the Bois de Boulogne.

At least let me congratulate you! *Femina* prints a picture of you, in your tennis clothes, among those of the "best rackets" in Deauville . . . this Joan of Arc cuirass of white serge, which cuts across the pleated skirt at mid-thigh, is charming. You look like a little warrior in it, not the least bit athletic, but so endearing!

You see, we're not angry with each other at all. You're so unbearable, Valentine my friend! And I'm so impossible! I can still see us, very dignified, exchanging courteous and theatrical goodbyes. You had asked me what I was doing this summer and I'd answered, "Well . . . first of all I'm going to do 'Flesh' in Marseille." To which you said, "Again!"

Me: "What do you mean 'again'?"

You: "That horrid thing again!"

Me: "It's not horrid, it's a 'sensational mime-drama'!"

You: "It's perfectly horrid! Isn't that the one where you tear off your dress and appear . . ."

Me: "Undressed, precisely."

You: "And it doesn't matter to you?"

Me: "What do you mean, 'it'?"

You: "To show yourself off in public in an outfit, in a costume . . . well . . . It's beyond me! When I think that you stand there, in front of the whole world . . . oh . . . !"

Seized by an irresistible shudder of modesty, you covered your face with your hands and your whole body cringed, so that your dress, clinging to you, outlined you for an instant worse than naked: your little breasts crushed by the maillot corset, your stomach elongated and flat, ending in a mysterious fold, your round thighs pressed together, your delicate knees, bent slightly, every detail of your graceful body appeared to me so clearly beneath the crepe de Chine that it embarrassed me.

But you were already uncovering your incensed eyes.

"I have never seen . . . recklessness like yours, Colette!"

To which I responded, with witless rudeness, "My dear, you bore me. You're neither my mother nor my lover: therefore . . ."

An exasperated sigh, a stiff handshake, that's all there was to our goodbye. Now, alone, I laugh to myself when I think of your special modesty, which shelters a slight body beneath vast, high hats, a body whose every step reveals, underneath a short, tight tunic, the movement of the hips, the protruding and rolling of the tight buttocks, and even the pink and amber color of your arms, shoulders, and back beneath the lace of the sleeves and the bodice. I'd really like to give you a good dressing down . . . you who—not content to appear in the light of day in this getup that a little Tanagra nymph would have found just barely adequate—come out of the water at Trouville with your nipples showing under your tight silk bathing suit glistening like a wet fish . . .

There's one thing, Valentine my friend, that you will never teach me, and that is that the skin on my lower back or my hips can be more tempting and more secret than the skin on my hand or my calf, and it's this "recklessness," as you call it, this savage serenity, which makes all your indignation, your whole display of petty—do I dare say—local virtue, of your modesty by the square centimeter, pointless.

Do you remember the legal proceedings, still notorious, against nudity in the music hall? One little walk-on was cruelly upset at the time. She was playing two roles in a year-end review: in one she appeared nude, chaste, and silent, motionless on a cardboard cloud, with a bow in her hand. Two tableaux later, she came back onstage with "Feminine Undergarments," dressed in a lace teddy and a pair of half hose: her naked little knees would quiver, as she sang a little song with indistinct words, and the flowers of her breasts would show mauve beneath the sheer linen. She looked sweet in it, slightly ridiculous, and perfectly indecent; well, one of her roles was cut: you understand that that meant she gave up the bow of Artemis and kept her sheer lace.

Does that seem perfectly natural to you? I was sure it did.

O infernal little woman! There are still moments when I am weak enough to want to make you understand me, to grab that hard little head of yours by its golden hair—real or false—and give it a good hard knock, to shake loose all its prejudices, all the bits and pieces of ideas, the debris of principles which, all together, make such an immoral fuss inside it.

Yes, immoral, you little dolt! Immoral, you ninny! Immoral, you nitwit! (And I'm still using polite language!) I don't care about your wide eyes and gaping mouth. You will never know all the bad things I think of you, you who look at me because I broke off with my husband, as though I had contracted an embarrassing disease, hard to hide and hard to admit. You will laugh, as though it were an easy paradox, if I try to explain to you that the married state appears preposterous and quite abnormal to me, you who have a husband—a husband in automobiles!—and who forget, when you're in his arms, about infidelity and the flight of a first lover . . .

Haven't you ever thought long and hard about that man, your husband? Don't answer me wittily and evasively: "Yes, since I started cheating on him!" Remember back, without laughing, to the time when you didn't cheat on him. Wasn't there a day in your life when, faithful, loving, even in love, you suddenly looked at him and shrank back in astonishment: "What is this man doing in my house with me? Why, in fact, am I living with this man here in my bedroom? I married him, fine! I've gone to bed with him, fine!—all that doesn't change the fact that this is *a man*, a man like any other, who is here in my bedroom, in my bed, in my life. He comes in, into my bathroom, after asking, 'Am I bothering you, darling?' I reply, 'No, my love!' but that doesn't change the fact that *this man* is here, in my bedroom, and that his face, the shape of his back, the way he strokes his mustache, suddenly strike me as strange, shocking, out of place . . . All my life, then, I'll live like this *with a man*, who will have the right to see how awful I look in the morning, to walk in on me while I'm drinking my laxative tisane, who'll ask about awkward dates in my little lady's calendar, and walk around in his shorts in my bathroom! There he is in my life, for the rest of my life! Why? The fact is, I don't know why. I love him . . . but that's another matter. Love has nothing to do with living together—on the contrary, most of the time it dies from it."

Admit it, my friend: it is simply not possible that your married state has not appeared to you—for an hour, for an instant—in all its ludicrous crudeness! And who's to say that your husband, in his modesty, hasn't suffered from it too, with a man's modesty which is nearly always more delicate, more sincere than ours? I mean your husband, my husband, the husbands of all these ladies . . . One morning he'll wake up in a sullen mood, absorbed in his thoughts, hardly saying a word, eyes downcast. To your concerned "What's the matter, darling?," he'll reply, "Nothing . . . a little migraine . . ." And after swallowing the headache powder offered by your affectionate hand, he'll remain silent, with the look of a man to whom something has happened.

What has happened to him is the same thing that has happened to you! He doesn't recognize you. He steals glances at you, over his newspaper, stunned and revolted, to discover you suddenly, to examine, with a cold and lucid eye, *this woman* who is there in his home, who sings as she pushes the tortoiseshell hairpins into her chignon, rings for the maid, gives orders, makes decisions, arranges things . . . I swear to you, my friend, that in these fugitive moments there are looks, from lover to mistress, from wife to husband, which are frightening . . .

I remember a delightful remark my mother made one day, as she was being upbraided by my father.

"I forbid you," she said, "to speak to me that way: you're not even related to me!"

My childish ears remembered this singular remark and I have thought about it often since.

At this moment, you little pest, you're quite capable of reading this with a pretty, wicked little smile which means: "You can understand why she bad-mouths marriage, she who . . ." I who *what?* I who never had any reason to congratulate myself for it? What of it! I won't let you sidestep the question in a ladylike way. I will quote for you, as I remember it, the little sermon my mother gave me the night before I married the man I loved, and who loved me.

"So, my poor little *toutou*, you're going to go away and leave me? You're going away, and with who?"

"But, Mama, with the man I love!"

"I know perfectly well that you love him, and that's not the worst part of this whole business. Believe me, it would be much better if you loved him less. And afterward?"

"Afterward? Well, that's all!"

"That's all. A lot of good it'll do you! What I see most clearly is that you're going off with some man, and I don't find that very pretty, my daughter going off with some man."

"But, Mama, he'll be my husband!"

"Him being your husband doesn't mean a thing to me. I myself have had two husbands and I'm none the prouder for it . . . A man whom you don't even know!"

"Oh, but I do, Mama, I do know him!"

"You do not know him, you silly little thing, because you love him! You are going to go away, all alone, with a man, and we'll watch you leave, your brothers and I, with long, sad faces. It's disgusting that things like this are allowed."

"Oh really, Mama, you're extraordinary! What do you want me to do?"

"Whatever you want, naturally. But it's not right. The whole thing's set up so badly. Look at it for a minute! He tells you he loves you, and since you love him too, there you are in his arms, ready to follow him to the ends of the earth. But let him tell you all of a sudden, 'I don't love you anymore,' and he looks different to you! You discover he has the short nose of people who lack judgment and balance, the short, thick neck of those who kill in a fit of anger, the subtle and seductive voice of a liar, the weak and sensual chin of a woman . . . My darling little *toutou*, don't cry! I'm just an old killjoy. What can I do? I always say outrageous things, but the truth is that you'd have to marry your own brother if you wanted to marry with full knowledge of the facts, and even then! All this strange blood that comes into a family, and makes you look at your own son and say, 'Where does he get those eyes, and that forehead, and his wild fits of anger, and his talent for lying?' Ah, my poor darling *toutou*, I'm not trying to explain, or to make the world over, as they say, but the whole thing's set up so badly!"

Forgive me, my friend. I'm letting myself get carried away by memories which might be lacking in happiness. I'm not trying to change what exists any more than my charming, crazy mother. Solitude, an intoxicating sense of freedom, and the absence of corsets has, as you can see, quickly turned me into a preacher of the worst sort. I only wanted to moralize a little, in my turn, purely as a tease.

And I bring to the game a lamentable conviction. It seems as if I can see, ten years or so from now, an old, dried-up, quibbling Colette, with hair like a Russian schoolgirl, in a reformist dress, who'll go into the towns advocating free love, proud loneliness, and *patatipatata*, and a whole pile of nonsense! Brrrr! But what demon shows me the image, still more terrible, of a forty-year-old Colette, burning with a new love, ripe and soft beneath her makeup, combative and desperate? With both arms outstretched I push both phantoms away from me, and I look for a sheltered narrow path between the two of them, where a friendly hand guides me.

Goodbye, my dear Valentine. I am afraid you won't like this letter. We will never understand one another, my friend. And I hope each of us will search, all our lives, for the other, with aggressive, unselfish tenderness. You no longer hope to "bring me back to the fold"; I don't count on ever converting you. It provides our conversations with an artificial and inoffensive warmth, which gives us comfort and no illusions.

Goodbye! Go back to your tennis, in your Joan of Arc cuirass. I am going fishing for flatfish, which you find under your bare feet, in the deep holes left by the low tide. There's a strong wind up, the sand is blowing in long, swift streams which run parallel to the horizon, and their rippling locomotion is dizzying. Beneath the low sky, the beach is an endless desert, the color of ash, and the pale dunes smoke in the wind which scatters them. You would perish from desolation here, my dear, and yet it pleases me . . . I hug and kiss you; come back very beautiful and very happy.

Your friend,
Colette Willy

[*Translated by Matthew Ward*]

The Sémiramis Bar

What has to happen happens . . . Accused of every sin, I appeared before my friend Valentine, after having received from her this enigmatic communication by *pneumatique*: "I have a lot of things to scold you for. You grieve me . . ."

How could I, unworthy person, have distressed that lithe young woman, so very elegant, without a doubt sewed into her woolen dress, for it looked as though she could neither quite sit down nor quite bend over nor quite walk in it . . . What in the world had I done? My pretty judge collected her thoughts, searched in the depths of herself for an exceptional amount of courage, and finally spoke.

"Well, then, this is it. You dined at the Sémiramis bar day before yesterday."

"That's true. But so what?"

"So what? That's all. Isn't it enough for you?"

"Yes, it's enough, since I dine there two or three times a week. One eats well there."

The aigrette—what could it be made of? steel wool?—on the top of the bonnet of woven wood and American cloth shuddered, danced, saluted.

"Why, you unhappy creature, that is a place . . . a place . . ."

"With a bad reputation. Heavens, yes."

My friend Valentine abandons declamatory means and looks at me with sudden gentleness, a superior solicitude.

"Really, my poor dear, it looks as though you wanted to make your friends' task of defending you impossible."

"Who imposed that task on you? I certainly didn't."

"I mean, well, that . . . you know I'm very fond of you. What would you have me say when someone comes to tell me you were dining at the Sémiramis?"

"Tell them the plain truth—that it's none of your business."

My little judge blushes, hesitates. Dear me, how much easier is the role of the accused! I revel in the situation, I settle myself complacently, I sink into the most luxurious of my errors, and Valentine lacks the confidence needed to dislodge me from them.

"Of course, it's none of my business. It's in your interest. That sort of thing can do you harm. You seem to be doing it on purpose. And then, I will say, it's all right if you just drop in there by chance. But it's quite another thing to make a habit of it, to become as it were a subscriber to the place . . . If at least you went there with a group of people occasionally . . . But all alone in your corner there, with your newspaper and your dog, and all those people who speak to you, those odd little men in weird jackets, who wear rings and have bracelets on their ankles . . . And besides," she adds, plucking up courage, "they tell me that the suppers at that place are . . . frightful!"

"I don't know anything about that, my dear. I don't go there for supper."

"That's true, you don't eat supper. But you surely know that the suppers . . ."

"I know all about it. Sémiramis tells me."

"She tells . . ."

"Why, yes. She's a great person, Sémiramis. You don't know her? Haven't you ever seen her little snub nose, like a bulldog's, and her auburn chignon, and her fringe like the visor of a helmet, and her bosom like a Spanish balcony?"

"I haven't had the pleasure."

"Too bad. She exudes an air of impudence, good nature, patience, and ridiculous good health. She charges very little for her leek-and-potato soup, her roast chicken with sausages, and her loin of veal—she even gives it away to a crowd of hard-ups in weird jackets, poor little paupers all dolled up, and they can get at her place their plate of food and *la thune*—a *thune*, Valentine, is a five-franc piece . . ."

"Oh, I know that, everyone knows that, for goodness' sake."

"Excuse me. Well, you see, in her 'ill-famed' bar, Sémiramis reigns, helmeted, armored in an apron with pockets. And ill-famed it is, according to your way of seeing things, which is the way of everyone, moreover."

"I certainly hope so."

"Me, too. She knows all her customers by name, and knows the names of their friends. She doesn't like strangers and will bark at the people who drop in just by chance. 'There's no chow here for you!' I've heard her tell them. She knows all the scandals, all the gossip of all the bars, but is discreet, for one day, after telling me the sad and scandalous story of a brave little woman sitting there, Sémiramis added, 'I'm the only one in the world who knows her story, she'd be terribly upset if anyone else in Paris knew it!' "

"Charming."

"And I'll bet you do the same every day! At any rate, with Sémiramis it's only thoughtlessness. Then what can I do about it, my dear? I'm a homebody, I'm finicky, I like my quiet habits. I'm often obliged to dine out, before the theater, and I don't willingly go into a big restaurant in the boulevards or into a fashionable grill room where you hear the people at other tables being named in whispers and gossiped about, skinned alive. I go to the bar kept by Sémiramis, appropriately named—Sémiramis, warrior queen, helmeted in bronze, armed with the meat cleaver, who speaks a colorful language to her crowd of long-haired young lads and short-haired girls . . ."

"That's exactly what I reproach you for—associating with that low-class crowd!"

"Why?"

"Every night in that bar there are scenes: orgies, fistfights, even."

"I repeat, I know nothing about all that. What's it to me? The orgies at the Sémiramis bar must be, like all orgies, so banal they would convert the most far-gone to virtue. I'm only interested in the people who dine there. Valentine, it's about them I'd like to talk to you, since I goodheartedly consent to give you an explanation. True, you find there a majority of young men who are not at all interested in women. At dinnertime there they are, comfortably at home, enjoying a rest. They are recovering their strength for suppertime. They have no need to waggle their hips or cry out shrilly or flutter a handkerchief soaked in ether, or dance together, or call out their order in a loud voice: 'Sémiramis, another sherry for me, on Monsieur's bill!' They are gentle, weary, with their painted eyelids heavy with sleep. There's one who bestows upon himself the name of a genuine princess; he asks for Vittel mineral water, and a lot of leeks in the soup, because it's a depurative. Another one has the pathetic face of an anemic little girl, and he goes to the Sémiramis bar for his bouillon and his noodles, and the coarse ruler of the place fills his plate twice, crassly maternal. Then she exclaims, arms akimbo, standing in front of the lean and lanky young fellow with hallucinated blue eyes, who pushes aside his full plate: 'There you go! You've been hitting dope again, eh? What's your mother thinking about to let you destroy yourself like this? Doesn't she have a heart?' And there's another one who, with his dark blue eyes and his innocent little nose, looks like Suzanne Derval; he barely pecks at his food and says, 'Oh hell, don't give me any sauce. I don't want to ruin my stomach! And, Waiter! Once and for all, take away these pickles and bring me some *benzonaphthol* tablets.'

"Yes, there they are, not posing, but gentle and indolent and melancholy, like out-of-work prostitutes, but laughing easily and playing with the dog that Sémiramis found one night in the street. But if a stranger manages to get inside the bar for dinner, they become uneasy, with the sulky manners of shopkeepers wakened too early, exchanging from one table to another their shrill cries, forced laughs, obscene and trite remarks, the hanky-panky that attracts . . . Then, when the stranger or the group of thirsty and curious sightseers have emptied their beer steins, sipped their kümmels on ice, and left, as the door shuts upon them there is a whoop of relief, and afterward a settled calm and the murmured gossip, the thin chests bedizened with loud cravats and bright pocket handkerchiefs lean once more against the tables, relaxed and slothful, like circus animals after the exercise."

Valentine is not very fond of having people talk to her at great length. The animation, the brightness of her face dims after a few minutes of attention and is replaced by a rigidity, a drowsy effort to keep the eyes wide open. I notice this now and fall silent. But decidedly she has not said all she has to say.

"Yes, yes, that's all very nice. When you want to exonerate something you adorn it with literature and you tell yourself, 'If I talk very fast and insert some fancy words, Valentine won't see the fire for the smoke!' It's easier than telling me to go to the devil, isn't it?"

This kind of gentle feminine trickery always disarms me, and Valentine, who often exasperates and sometimes astounds me, as if I suddenly glimpsed through her coils of false hair or through her cloche hats or extravagantly big and gauzy hats the pointed tip of a sly little animal's ear. I cannot help laughing.

"But I'm not defending myself, you little beast! Defend myself for what and against whom? Against you? Would I condescend to that, megalomaniac that you are?"

She puts on her most seductive expression, as if responding to a man's overtures.

"You see, you see? Now I'm the one that's being attacked! Now, really! Because I allowed myself to say that the Sémiramis bar is not exactly a provincial branch of a convent and lacked respect when I spoke of that Queen of Babylon and other such places!"

"Sémiramis doesn't ask for respect. What would she do with it? Respect can't be eaten, can't be sold, and it takes up room. But she allots to me a portion of her grumpy motherliness, which transforms her regular customers into a progeny pampered, knocked about, and submissive. Besides, her capricious humor, both grasping and spendthrift, renders her in my eyes worthy of an authentic scepter. For example, take this exchange I overheard one night. 'What do I owe you, Sémiramis?' asked a wretched-looking regular customer with anxious eyes and in a low voice. 'No idea,' Sémiramis growled. 'I haven't made out your bill. Do you imagine I have no one but you to think about?' 'But I happen to have some money on me tonight, Sémiramis.' 'Money, money, money! You're not the only one who has money!' 'But, Sémiramis . . .' 'Oh, shut up, that's enough! I can always find money when I need it, you know. That yokel down there at the farthest table, he's just paid me a gold louis for his chicken-in-the-pot, that's one hundred sous more than he'd pay at Paillard's, just look at that bigmouth now, he's getting ready to leave. His lordship didn't want anything on my menu! His lordship had to order à la carte! His lordship thinks this is a restaurant!' As she spoke, she focused her brown eyes on the intimidated and fugitive back of the 'yokel,' and if looks could kill he'd have dropped dead. Just imagine! He thought that by paying a golden louis he could eat *poulet cocotte* at Sémiramis's bar . . . Am I boring you, Valentine?"

"Not at all. On the contrary."

"I didn't hope for so much! This is success! Well now, I can tell you that while dining at Sémiramis's bar I enjoy watching the girls dancing together, they waltz well. They're not paid for this, but dance for pleasure between the cabbage soup and the beef stew. They are young models, young scapegraces of the neighborhood, girls who take bit parts at the music hall but who are out of work. Under their big umbrella hats or cloches pulled down to their eyes, their faces are hidden, I have no idea what the waltzers' faces are like, so I can forget their no doubt dubious little fizzes, their slightly prognathous little fizzes, blue-white with powder. I see only two graceful bodies united, sculptured beneath thin dresses by the wind of the waltz, two long adolescent bodies, skinny, with narrow feet in fragile slippers that have come without a carriage through the snow and the mud . . . They waltz like the habitués of cheap dance halls, lewdly, sensuously, with that delicious inclination of a tall sail of a yacht . . . I can't help it! I really find that prettier than any ballet . . .

"And that, dear Valentine, is when I leave the Sémiramis bar, with Sémiramis herself sometimes detaining me with a friendly hand as I reach the doorway. 'Hush! don't say a word,' she whispered the other night, slipping over my finger the string of a bumpy parcel. 'Not a word! These are apples dug out for you, some old pippins the way you like them, wrinkled like the hind end of a pauper . . .' That makes you laugh, doesn't it? I thought it was very nice of her. You see, she'd found out that I like old wrinkled apples with that musky smell of the cellar where I used to line them up when I was a child . . ."

[*Translated by Herma Briffault*]

"If I Had a Daughter..."

❧

"In the first place, if I had a daughter . . ."

"But you don't have a daughter!"

My friend Valentine shrugs her shoulders, vexed. I've broken one of the rules of her favorite game: the game of If I Had. I already know how this peremptory young woman would behave *if* she had an automobile, *if* she had a yacht, *if* her husband were Minister of War, *if* she inherited ten million francs, *if* she were a great actress . . .

When she enters my home, it's as though the wind were rising, and I squint as I do at the seashore. She arrives, out of breath, and looks around her, sighing each time, "You can say what you like, my dear, but Passy is the middle of nowhere!"

Even if she asks me to, I won't say anything about what I want . . . but I let her spout off anything that comes into her head.

Since the Ballets Russes, my friend Valentine has been stiffly wearing fashions that the softest Oriental grace would barely excuse. She perfumes herself with jasmine and rose, swears by Teheran and Isfahan, and—wrapped in a Byzantine dress set off with a Marie Antoinette fichu, with a Cossack bonnet on her head and American shoes sharpened into sabots on her feet—is quick to exclaim: "How can anyone not be Persian!"

She is earnest, fickle, and spirited. Once in the door, she showers me with streams of words, endless strings of contradictory axioms. I am dear to her because I don't put up a struggle, and it pleases her to think I'm timid when I'm only flabbergasted. She talks while I read or write . . . Today, the warm and rainy autumn afternoon brings her to me very well behaved and stiff—she is playing the part of the bourgeoise and is despotically raising the children she doesn't have.

"If I had a daughter . . . Oh, my dear, I'd show people what I think of modern education and this mania for sports, and these Americanized young girls! It all makes for some very sorry wives, I can tell you, and absolutely pitiful mothers! What are you looking at in the garden?"

"Nothing . . ."

Nothing . . . I am silently asking the russet trees and the softened earth where my friend Valentine could have gotten her facts about modern education. I am not looking at anything, except my neighbors' narrow garden and their house, a brick and wooden chalet forgotten among the last gardens left in Passy.

"A return to family life, my dear, it's the only way! And family life like our grandmothers understood it! They didn't worry about baccalaureates for girls back then, and nobody was any the worse for it; on the contrary!"

I look up for a moment at my houri in the green caftan, searching in vain for the morbid trace of a poorly healed baccalaureate.

"Yes, you can be sure if I had a daughter, I'd make her a little provincial girl, healthy and quiet, the old-fashioned way. A little piano, not too much reading, but lots of sewing! She would know how to mend, embroider, and take care of the linen. My dear, I can see her as if she were right here—my daughter! Her smooth hair, with a flat collar . . . I swear to you, I can see her!"

I can see her, too. She has just sat down, as she does every afternoon, in the house next door, near the window: she is little more than a child, with sleek hair and a pale complexion, who lowers her eyes over some embroidery . . .

"I would dress her in those nice little fabrics, you know, with a somewhat subdued background and silly little patterns. Not to mention what a great hit she would be in them! And every day, every day, instead of classes at the Sorbonne or fashionable lectures, she would sit down by a window, or near a lamp—I have a little oil lamp, it's just the thing, made of tinted porcelain, it's gorgeous!—she would sit down with her embroidery or her crocheting. A young lady who plies her needle isn't looking for trouble, believe me!"

What is she thinking of, this diligent child, of whom, at this moment, all I can see is her smooth dark hair, tied at the back with a black ribbon? Her hand rises and falls, pulling on a long silk thread, and flutters like a bird on the end of a string . . .

In the middle of her attack of Platonic motherhood, my friend Valentine delivers a peroration: "Needlework, woman's work, oh, yes, my dear, needlework! People have joked about it enough, without realizing that, back then, it was responsible for the security of many a family, the moral well-being of many an adolescent!"

The child embroidering there in the little house has raised her head. She is looking out at the damp garden, where wet leaves are raining down, as if she doesn't even see it. She has deep-set and serious eyes, dark eyes, which are all that move in her motionless face . . .

"Don't you agree, deep down?"

. . . Big velvety eyes, which scan the garden, searching between the trees for a corner of sky, and turn back distrustfully toward the room drowned in shadow . . .

"Oh, when you're having one of your absentminded days, nobody can come near you! Well, I'm sorry, very sorry indeed! Good night!"

. . . and return to the embroidery she had begun, sheltered under the heavy eyelids. Every day this dark-haired little girl sits and embroiders until it is time to light the lamps.

If the weather's nice, her window is open, and as night falls, I can hear someone calling her.

"Lucy, come here now, you'll ruin your eyes!"

Reluctantly, she leaves her chair, and her light work—and I wait till the next day for the reappearance, against the obscure background of an old-fashioned room, of this pretty phantom from my own far-off adolescence . . .

A provincial girl with long, smooth hair, plying the needle . . . Very good, isn't she? and willingly silent, and not very curious . . . Do they call this girl "little dreamer" too? Does this girl go to her low chair, as to the threshold of the forbidden garden which she enters alone, each day, under the blind eyes of those around her? Between them and the dangerous lands she wanders through, does she spread out the handkerchief she is scalloping or the stiff toile, as if to bar all access?

Needlework, woman's work, the safety of confident mothers . . . For a solitary little girl, what immoral book can equal the long silence, the unbridled reverie over the openwork muslin or the rosewood loom? Overly precise, a bad book might frighten, or disappoint. But the bold daydream soars up, sly, impudent, varied, to the rhythm of the needle as it bites the silk; it grows, beats the silence with burning wings, inflames the pale little hand, the cheek where the shadow of the eyelashes flutters. It fades away, draws back, seems to dissolve when a word is spoken out loud, when a thread breaks, or a ball of thread rolls away— it becomes diaphanous in order to let the familiar furnishings, the passerby who brushes against the window, show through from time to time— but the newly threatened needle, the virgin canvas, the task resumed, assures its return, and it is that which always bends the necks of so many diligent girls, that which secretly dwells in so many "waking dreamers"—that which I recognize in the gaze of my little neighbor, the little girl-child leaning forward, the beautiful feminine gaze, astray, moving in a motionless face . . .

Rites

"You don't mind if I dress in front of you?"

"Not at all."

"You're so nice . . . I'm so glad to see you," adds my friend Valentine.

But I can see her reflection in the slanted mirror, her reflection with which she has just exchanged an anxious glance, an exasperated movement of her eyebrows . . . I'm annoying her . . . I've come at a bad time . . . She's telling me to go to the devil . . . Even farther: to the depths of Passy, where I live! She's wishing me there, she's getting me settled and locking me in, with a book on my knees, in front of a good summer fire.

"You see," she concludes aloud, not without ingenuity, "I'm dining out and our whole party will be going to the dress rehearsal of *The Wisteria Vine*, so . . ."

"Don't jabber, just get dressed as if I weren't here."

In fact, she tosses off her dress and her little underpants, her Valencia-lace brassiere, scratches her bare arms, and runs the palm of her hand over her rumpled chemise, with the shocking immodesty of a woman undressing in front of another woman. But she slips into the mystery of the shadows, to take off her shoes with her back turned. She recovers her self-assurance with a pair of purple tulle stockings and two glittering gold shoes, so beautiful that my friend smiles at them tenderly, as she walks around the room, graceful and lightly clad. A shooting pain pulls down the corners of her mouth and she lets out a very sincere and common "Ouch! my feet," as she collapses in front of the dressing table.

The work which is about to follow is quite familiar to me: it is the skillful, almost theatrical application of makeup, which completes and banalizes fashion-conscious young women-about-town. I say *young* women, because the others apply it with more discretion, leaving to their younger sisters the feverish taste for heavy makeup, the dabbling joy of children fingering the white, red, and blue paints, staining themselves with it up to the ears.

But I'm not going to open my mouth. There is a time for everything, and I know that one does not gossip while "doing" one's face. I have to settle for impatient little sounds and the tail ends of sentences which my friend Valentine drops, dry, in a heap, like the little wads of cotton she rubs over her cheeks and eyelids, and then throws away afterward . . .

"Everything's all right with you? . . . That's good . . . It really is very strange that I can't get my maid to fill my pot of cold cream when it's empty . . . Please, darling, tell me it isn't eight o'clock or I'll scream! . . . So, everything's all right with you? . . . Naturally, when I want to hurry, I mess up the tip of my nose . . . Why no, I don't have too much rouge on . . . Please, darling, don't talk to me right now, I'll end up with mascara in my eye . . ."

The activity and chatter of the theater, the nervousness of an actress about to miss her entrance . . . Except for the elegant boudoir, you couldn't tell the difference. I answer just enough so that my friend almost forgets my presence, so that she'll let me follow and record the transformations of her tilting reflection.

First there is her real face, completely naked, cleansed with Vaseline, the face her mother gave her. She shows it to her husband, to her maid, and to me, since I'm not important either. It's a little, fair-skinned face, with bright blue eyes and tired-looking eyelids, a little red in the cheekbones and the wings of the nose. The eyelashes are very blond and must shine in the sun like crushed glass—but when do they see the sun? They're just about to regain their artificial blackness and starch. A comb, which she has just stuck in place with a firm hand, holds my friend's delicately tinted, almost pink hair both up and back. Within the silver frame of the mirror, the whole effect is luminous, with a pretty neatness to it, anemic and distinguished. A neck that slender would need a white collar of fairly stiff, fresh-looking lace. The comb, stuck in sideways for this hasty toilette, would have to bite further into her beautiful hair, so as to draw it tighter, to smooth it back into a bold upsweep, high above the long graceful neck. I would like to see my friend Valentine keep the acid charm of a gleaming, genuine blonde, keen, sharp, and cambered like a vermeil fork. I would like . . .

But that is neither here nor there! Before my eyes, with imbecilic fervor, she is performing the rites ordained by Fashion. Her hair hangs down, lowering her forehead, hiding her little childish ears and the silvery nape of her neck. If it makes her chin look heavier, and her neck shorter, it's none of my business . . . A skillful "shading" of color, from white to crimson, covers her cheeks so richly that I feel the urge to write my name, with the tip of my fingernail, right in the powder.

Over the long elastic corset the maid slips the evening dress—a kind of complicated *zaïmph*, embroidered and re-embroidered, painted, slashed, torn to luxurious shreds, one of which restrains the breasts, another the knees, and a third which comes up the front of the skirt to fasten it, halfway up, in the most ludicrous and most indiscreetly precise manner.

A colorist's heated and barbaric imagination lavished this fabric with orange and purple, the green of Venetian necklaces, and the blue-black of sapphires, intermingled with gold; but a "master of fashion" tore it all up with the freakish imagination of an evil and illiterate gnome. Then a woman came along—my friend Valentine came along—and cried out, "I'm Scheherazade, too—like everybody else!"

She struts around in front of me, in knock-kneed rhythm. She has loaded down her light, blond beauty with everything befitting a sultana as pale and round as the moon. A precious and tear-shaped jewel from the Orient sparkles between her eyebrows, astonished that with its glimmering fires it should extinguish two Western eyes of a modest blue. What's more, my friend has just fixed a long aigrette sprinkled with stardust on her head . . .

The peris, in the Persian paradise, had both this star on their foreheads and this wispy cloud. But my friend's feet disappear under a very Greek petticoat, with regular and supple pleats, tightened at the knees by a Hindu drapery. Her hand teases and tucks the squared-off Byzantine sash with beaded Egyptian designs.

Satisfied and serious, she admires herself, without suspecting that something is happening to her . . . Well, for heaven's sake, it's the same thing that happens to so many young Parisiennes with light complexions, pointed noses and chins, poor skin, and thin eyelashes, as soon as they disguise themselves as Asian princesses: she looks like a little maid.

Newly Shorn

❧

My friend Valentine sat down, powdered the wings of her nose, the hollow of her chin and, after a friendly exchange of compliments, was silent. I viewed this with some surprise, for on days when we have nothing to say to each other, my friend Valentine embroiders with ease on the theme "Ah, subjects of conversation are becoming so rare!"—a good three-quarters of an hour of scintillating palaver . . .

She was quiet and I saw that she had changed something about the carriage of her head. With a slightly timid air, she had lowered her head and was looking at me from under her jutting brow.

"I've cut my hair," she confessed suddenly, and took off her hat.

The beautiful blond hair on the nape of her neck showed its fresh cut, still rebelling against the metal, and from a part on the left a big Chateaubriand-style wave swept down across her forehead.

"It doesn't look too bad on me, does it?" my friend asked with false daring.

"Surely not."

"I was just at the Hickses', they gave me hundreds of compliments, Monsieur Hicks told me I look like . . . guess."

"Like someone convalescing from typhoid fever?"

"Very funny, really . . . but that's not it."

"Like Dujardin-Beaumetz, only more shorn? Like Drummont, without his glasses?"

"Wrong again. Like an English peeress, my dear!"

"The Hickses know some English peeresses, do they?"

"You're sidestepping the question, as usual. Does it look good or bad on me?"

"Good. Very good, in fact. But I'm thinking about that long hair which is nothing but dead, golden grass now. Tell me, why did you have your hair cut too, like everybody else?"

My friend Valentine shrugged her shoulders. "How do I know? . . . Just an idea, that's all. I couldn't stand myself in long hair anymore . . . And then, it's the fashion. In England, it seems that . . ."

"Yes, yes, but why else?"

"Well, Charlotte Lysès cut hers," she says evasively. "And even Sorel. I haven't seen her, but I heard that she's wearing her hair 'like a Roman gladiator.' And Annie de Pène, and hundreds of other women of taste whose names I could mention, and . . ."

"And Polaire."

My friend paused in astonishment. "Polaire? She hasn't had her hair cut."

"I thought she had."

"She has very long short hair. That doesn't have anything to do with the current fashion. Polaire wears her hair like Polaire. I didn't think of Polaire for a minute when I was having my hair cut."

"What did you think of? I would like to try and understand, through you, why women are contagiously clipping their hair, level with the ear, so much hair which until now was pampered, waved, perfumed . . ."

She stood up impatiently, and walked around, tossing her romantic forelock.

"You're funny . . . I don't know. I couldn't stand my long hair anymore, I'm telling you. And besides it's hot. And at night that long braid would pull at the back of my neck, and it would get rolled up around my arm . . ."

"Thirty years wasn't long enough for you to get used to that thick, beautiful cable?"

"It seems that way. You question me, and I answer you, only because I'm so nice. Oh, yes, the other morning, my braid got caught in a dresser drawer I'd pushed shut. I hate that. And when we were having those air-raid alerts, it became a scourge; no one enjoys looking grotesque even in a cellar, now do they, with a chignon that's collapsing on one side and unraveling on the other. I could have died a thousand deaths because of that hair . . . And then, in the end, it can't be reasoned about. I cut my hair because I cut my hair."

In front of the mirror, she subdued her curls, and aired her 1830s wave, with newly acquired gestures. How many newly shorn women have already invoked, in order to excuse the same vandalism, reasons of coquetry, herd instinct, anglophilia—and even economy—before arriving at: "How do I know?"

One came up with "My neuralgia . . ."

"You understand, I had had it with bleaching, I just had to do something new with my hair . . ." explained another.

"It's cleaner," imagined a third. "You can wash your hair at the same time as the rest, in the bath . . ."

My friend Valentine did not add a novel lie of her own to this lot of modest verities. But her attitude, like theirs, is that of a prisoner who has just broken her chains. So I can assume myself—in the free coquetry of a head no longer weighed down by a pinned-up coil of hair, in the pride of a forehead on which the wind scatters a slightly masculine curliness—I can amuse myself by reading or imagining in it the joy of having shaken off an old fear that the war, the approach of the enemy, had roused from a long oblivion, and the barely conscious memory of the frantic flight of women before the barbarians when they ran naked and the flag of their hair, behind them, was suddenly knotted in the fist of their ravisher . . .

Grape Harvest

❧

I had written to my friend Valentine: "Come, they'll be harvesting the grapes." She came, wearing flat-heeled canvas shoes and an autumn-colored skirt; one bright-green sweater, and another pink one; one hat made of twill and another made of velvet, and both, as she said, "in-vertebrate." If she hadn't called a slug a snail, and asked if bats were the female of the screech owl, she wouldn't have been taken for 'someone from Paris."

"Harvesting the grapes?" she asked, astonished. "Really? Despite the war?"

And I understood that deep down she was finding fault with all that the pretty phrase "harvesting the grapes" seems to promise and call forth of rather licentious freedom, singing and dancing, risqué intentions, and overindulgence . . . Don't people traditionally refer to it as "the festival of the grape"?

"Despite the war, Valentine," I confessed. "What can you do? They haven't found a way of gathering the grapes without harvesting them. There are a lot of grapes. With the full-flavored grapes we'll make several casks of the wine that's drunk young and doesn't gain anything from aging, the wine that's as rough on the mouth as a swear word, and which the peasants celebrate the way people praise a boxer: 'Damn strong stuff,' being unable to find any other virtues in it."

The weather was so beautiful the day of the harvest, it was so enjoyable to dally along the way, that we didn't reach the hillside until around ten o'clock, the time when the low hedges and the shady meadows are still drenched in the blue and the cold of dripping dew, while the busy Limousin sun is already stinging your cheeks and the back of your neck, warming the late peaches under their cottony plush, the firmly hanging pears, and the apples, too heavy this year, which are picked off by a gust of wind. My friend Valentine stopped at the black-berries, the fuzzy teasel, even at the forgotten ears of maize whose dry husks she forced back and whose kernels she gobbled down like a little hen.

Like the guide, in the desert, walking ahead and promising the lagging traveler the oasis and the spring, I cried out to her from a distance, "Come on, hurry up, the grapes are better, and you'll drink the first juice from the vat, you'll have bacon and chicken in the pot!"

Our entry into the vineyard caused no commotion. The work pressed on, and moreover, our attire warranted neither curiosity nor even consideration. My friend had agreed, in order to sacrifice herself to the blood of the grape, that I lend her an old checked skirt, which since 1914 had seen many other such sacrifices, and my personal adornments didn't go beyond an apron-smock made of polka-dot sateen. A few weather-beaten heads were raised above the cordons of vines, hands held out two empty baskets toward us, and we set to work.

Since my friend Valentine was thinning her bunches of grapes like an embroideress, with delicate snips of her scissors, it pleased a jovial and mute old faun, popping up opposite her, to give her something of a fright, and then silently show her how the clusters of grapes come off the stock and drop into the basket, if one knows how to pinch a secret suspension point, revealed to the fingers by a little abscess, a swelling where the stem breaks like glass. A moment later, Valentine was gathering the grapes, *sans* scissors, as quickly as her instructor the faun, and I didn't want her doing better or more than I, so the eleven o'clock sun wasted no time in moistening our skin and parching our tongues.

Whoever said grapes quench one's thirst? These Limousin grapes, grafted from American stock, so ripe they had split, so sweet they were peppery, staining our skirts, and being crushed in our baskets, inflamed us with thirst and intoxicated the wasps. Was my friend Valentine searching, when she straightened up to rest from time to time, was she searching the hillside, amid the well-regulated comings and goings of the empty and full baskets, for the child cupbearer who might bring an earthen jar filled with cool water? But the children carried only bunch after bunch of grapes, and the men—three old caryatids with muscles bared—transported only purple-stained tubs toward the gaping storeroom of the farm at the bottom of the hill.

The exuberance of the pure morning had gone away. Noon, the austere hour when the birds are silent, when the shortened shadow crouches at the foot of the tree. A cope of heavy light crushed down on the slate roofs, flattened out the hillside, smoothed out the shady fold of the valley. I watched the sluggishness and melancholy of midday descend over my energetic friend. Was she looking around her, among the silent workers, for a gaiety she might find fault in perhaps? Some relief—which she didn't wait for long.

A village clock was answered by a joyful murmuring, the sound of clogs on the hardened paths, and a distant cry:

"Soup's on! soup's on! soup's on!"

Soup? Much more and much better than soup, in the shelter of a tent made of reed thatch draped with ecru sheets, pinned up by twigs with green acorns, blue convolvulus, and pumpkin flowers. Soup and all its vegetables, yes, but boiled chicken too, and short ribs of beef, and bacon as pink and white as a breast, and veal in its own juices. When the aroma of this feast reached my friend's nose, she smiled that unconscious, expansive smile one sees on nurslings who have had their fill of milk and women who have had their fill of pleasure.

She sat down like a queen, in the place of honor, folded her purple-stained skirt under her, rolled back her sleeves, and cavalierly held out her glass to her neighbor to the right, for him to fill, with a saucy laugh. I saw by the look on her face that she was about to call him "my good man" . . . but she looked at him, kept quiet, and turned toward her neighbor to the left, then toward me as though in need of help and advice . . . As it was, country protocol had seated her between two harvesters who between them carried, slightly bent under such a weight, a hundred and sixty-six years. One was thin, dried up, pellucid, with bluish eyes and impalpable hair, who lived in the silence of an aged sprite. The other, still a giant, with bones fit for making clubs, singlehandedly cultivated a piece of land, boasting ahead of time, in defiance of death, about the asparagus he'd get out of it "in four or five years"!

I saw the moment when Valentine, between her two old men, began losing her cheerfulness, and I had a liter of cider taken to her by a page who was just the sort to distract her, one of those beaming boys a little ungainly for their sixteen years—with a submissive and deceitful forehead, brown eyes, and a nose like an Arab—and every bit as handsome as the hundred-times-praised shepherds of Italy. She smiled at him, without paying him much attention, for she was in the grip of a statistical preoccupation. She asked the wispy old man, then the powerful octogenarian, their ages. She leaned forward to learn that of another frizzy-haired and wrinkled laborer who only admitted to seventy-three years. She gathered still other figures known to all from the far ends of the table—sixty-eight and seventy-one—began muttering to herself, adding up lustra and centuries, and was laughed at by a strapping young wench five times a mother, who shouted to her from where she sat: "Say, then, you like 'em like wine, huh, with cobwebs on the cork!"— provoking cracked laughter and young laughter, remarks in dialect and in very clear French as well, which made my friend blush and renewed her appetite. She wanted some more bacon, and cut into the peasant bread, made of pure wheat, brown but succulent, and demanded from the gnarled giant an account of the war of 1870. It was brief.

"What's to say? It wasn't a very pretty sight . . . I remember everybody falling all around me and dying in their own blood. Me, nothin' . . . not a bullet, not a bayonet. I was left standing, and them on the ground . . . who knows why?"

He fell into an indifferent silence, and the faces of the women around us darkened. Until then, no mother deprived of her sons, no sister accustomed to double work without her brother, had spoken of the war or those missing, or groaned under the weariness of three years . . . The farmer's wife, tight-lipped, busied herself by setting out thick glasses for the coffee, but she said nothing of her son, the artilleryman. One gray-haired farmer, very tired, his stomach cinched up with a truss, said nothing about his four sons: one was eating roots in Germany, two were fighting, the fourth was sleeping beneath a machine-gunned bit of earth . . .

From a very old woman, seated not far from the table on a bundle of straw, came this remark: "All this war, it's the barons' fault . . ."

"The barons?" inquired Valentine with great interest. "What barons?"

"The barons of France," said the cracked voice. "And them of Germany! All the wars are the fault of the barons."

"How's that?"

My friend gazed at her avidly, as if hoping that the black rags would fall, and that the woman would rise up, a hennin on her head, her body in vair, croaking, "I, I am the fourteenth century!" But nothing of the kind happened, the old woman merely shook her head, and all that could be heard were the drunken and confident wasps, the puffing of a little train off in the distance, and the mawing gums of the pellucid old man . . .

Meantime, I had broken the maize *galette* with my hands, and the tepid coffee stood in the glasses, which the harvesters were already turning away from, back toward the blazing hillside . . .

"What," said Valentine, astonished, "no siesta?"

"Yes, of course! But only for you and me. Come over under the hazelnut trees, we can let ourselves melt away, ever so gently, with heat and sleep. The grape harvest isn't allowed the siesta that goes with the wheat harvest. There they are already back at work, look . . ."

But it wasn't true, for the ascending column of men and women had just halted, attentive . . .

"What are they looking at?"

"Someone's coming through the field . . . two ladies. They're waving to the harvesters . . . They know them. Did you invite any of your country neighbors?"

"None. Wait, I think I know that blue dress. Why . . . Why, it's . . ."

"They're . . . Why, yes, certainly!"

Unhurried, coquettish, one beneath a straw hat, the other beneath a white parasol, our two maids moved toward us. Mine was swinging, above two little khaki-colored kid shoes, a blue serge skirt which set off the saffron-colored lawn of her blouse. My friend's soubrette, all in mauve, was showing her bare arms through her openwork sleeves, and her belt, made of white suede like her shoes, gripped a waist which fashion might perhaps have preferred less frail . . .

From our hideaway in the shade, we saw ten men run up to them, and twenty hands hail them on the steep slope, while envious little girls carried their parasols for them. The aged giant, suddenly animated, sat one of the maids down on an empty tub and hoisted the whole thing onto his shoulder; a handsome, suntanned adolescent smelled the handkerchief he had snatched from one of the two young women. The heavy air seemed light to them, now that two women's laughter, affected, deliberately prolonged, had set it in motion . . .

"They've gone to considerable expense, heavens!" murmured my friend Valentine. "That's my mauve Dinard dress from three years ago. She's redone the front of the bodice . . ."

"Really?" I said in a low voice. "Louise has on my serge skirt from two years ago. I would never have believed it could look so fresh. You could still find magnificent serge back then . . . The devil if I know why I ever gave her my yellow blouse! I could use it on Sundays this year . . ."

I glanced involuntarily at my polka-dot apron-smock, and I saw that Valentine was holding, between two contemptuous fingers, my old checked skirt, covered with purple stains. Above us, on the roasting hillside, the mauve young woman and the yellow one were walking amid flattering laughter and happy exclamations. The elegance, the Parisian touch, the chatelaine's dignity, of which we had deprived the grape harvest, were no longer missing, thanks to them, and the rough workers once again became gallant, youthful, audacious, for them . . .

A hand, that of a man kneeling, invisible, between the vine stocks, raised a branch laden with blue grapes up to our maids, and both of them, rather than fill any basket, plucked off what pleased them.

Then they sat down on their unfolded handkerchiefs on the edge of a slope, parasols open, to watch the harvesting of the grapes, and each harvester rivaled the other in ardor before their benevolent idleness.

Our silence had lasted a long time, when my friend Valentine broke it with these words, unworthy, to be sure, of the great thought they expressed: "What I say is . . . bring back feudalism!"

In the Boudoir

❧❦❧

In my friend Valentine's Restoration boudoir—for her the "Restoration" embraces, generously and anachronistically, the fifteenth century, the Directorate, the Second Empire, and on to the Grévy style—there is a little painting by Velvet Brueghel. Snow turned to smoky gold, a little house with a pointed roof from which stream miraculous beams of light, and, converging on the little house, theories of bourgeois gnomes in fur bonnets; in short, a *Nativity* by Velvet Brueghel, what an antique dealer might call a "pretty curio" or a "little wonder," depending on whether he's easygoing or distinguished.

At my friend Valentine's, I often drink tea I don't like, while looking at the Brueghel, which I do like. Yesterday, I asked my friend distractedly, "Valentine, how is it you came by this little painting?"

She blushed. "Why do you ask that?"

"I didn't think I was being indiscreet."

She blushed more. "What an idea! . . . It wasn't the least bit indiscreet, really . . . It's a family memento. It was given to me in 1913, by my Aunt Poittier."

"Your Aunt Poittier? Which one? You have as many aunts and uncles named Poittier as there are seeds in a watermelon!"

She fidgeted uneasily.

"Well, yes . . . it's quite true . . . Do you really have to remind me of that story, in which the role I played was . . . was . . ."

"Doubtful?"

"Almost. You won't leave me in peace until I've told you the story, will you? It was in 1913 that my Aunt Poittier . . ."

"Which one?"

"Aunt Olga. You don't know her. In 1913 my Aunt Olga lost her only son."

"A little boy, if I remember correctly?"

"Yes, a little boy of about forty-eight. So, since there was nothing keeping her at Chartres anymore, she came to live in Paris, with Uncle Poittier. They settled in the rue Raynouard, but since they felt very lonely, they spent almost all their time at my other Uncle Poittier's . . ."

"Which one?"

"The one in the Place d'Iéna, Paul Poittier, the brother . . . I'm telling you, you don't know him! And since at that time Aunt Marie was living in the Boulevard Delessert . . ."

"Who? Aunt Marie?"

"Oh! . . . Aunt Marie Poittier, really now, the wife of the third brother, you don't know her! If you insist on interrupting me all the time . . ."

"I'll shut up."

". . . So they were quite content to visit as they liked; it was convenient for me when I was making my monthly round of family visits. In 1913 I had gone to spend Easter vacation with Charles's family . . ."

"Charles who? Charles Poittier's family?"

"No, the Charles Loisillons."

"Oh, good, I like that better."

"Why?"

"I like having those Loisillons in there among all those nondescript Poittiers, like a poplar on a barren plain. Go on, please."

"What was I saying? Oh, yes . . . ! So, while I was at Charles's, I received a wire from Mama! UNCLE DIED YESTERDAY. FUNERAL TOMORROW. MEET PLACE D'IÉNA, TOMORROW MORNING, TEN O'CLOCK PRECISELY. So I borrow my cousin's crepe veil, black cape, and black gloves, and jump on the train, where I spend the night. I arrive at the house of the deceased, at my poor Aunt Olga's, half an hour late. A night on the rails, an empty stomach, my crepe veil . . . I could hardly see through it and I couldn't stand up, and then that odor of mortuary flowers as soon as I reached the staircase . . . In Aunt Olga's big drawing room there was a wall of seated women, veiled down to their feet in thick crepe. I started kissing all of them and was mumbling, 'Oh, poor uncle . . . Can you believe it . . .' You act so silly when you don't feel any grief, don't you . . .

"All the same, I recognized Mama's good, firm hand, and her violet perfume, and I clung to her skirt as I did when I was little. I said to her very softly, 'Well, how did it happen?' She didn't have time to answer, because another black wall, taller than the other, the men in full mourning, started moving toward us, and we stood up. Uncle Edme . . ."

"Who's Uncle Edme?"

"A distant uncle—you don't know him—came over to kiss me, and then another cousin, and then two schoolboys wearing woolen gloves, and other relatives, and finally a tall, dried-up old man, with red eyes, who kissed my hand and said to me: 'My dear niece, how good of you to have come back . . .'

"He straightened up: I let out a loud scream and fell back into I don't know whose arms."

"Why?"

"The dead man was standing in front of me, in a white tie, and was thanking me for having come back . . . Come back! And there *he* was! I was carried off, in a dead faint, and I only pulled myself together when I learned that I had gotten my uncles mixed up, that the real dead man had died of an embolism, at his brother's, he hadn't been brought to the rue Raynouard and . . ."

"I understand. But how does the little Brueghel painting fit in?"

My friend lowered her eyes. "Well . . . You can imagine what disorder the ceremony was thrown into by my attack of nerves and my fainting spell. As she was fanning me and making me breathe smelling salts, my mother said to Aunt Olga, the dead man's wife . . ."

"The wrong dead man?"

"No, the right one! Heavens, you are so annoying! . . . She said to my Aunt Olga, 'It's grief . . . shock . . . my poor little girl is so sensitive, so loving . . .' A month later, Aunt Olga sent me this Brueghel 'as a memento'—it still makes me feel ashamed—'as a memento of Uncle Poittier, whom his little Valentine loved so much.' What could I do? Admit I had gotten my uncles mixed up? I kept the Brueghel. It's so pretty . . ."

My friend picked up her tea napkin to gently wipe the gilded snow of the *Nativity*, and let out a sigh in which I tried to hear as much remorse as delight.

The "Master"

❧

Here? Yes, we have a hole here, yes, obviously, a hole . . . Think of a stone torn from a wall, huh? The couturier looks in my direction for a nod of approval. Shall I bow to this image, this bold new image? I feel detached: I slip him my best confraternal smile. He scares me a little—but less than he scares my friend Valentine, standing fervently before him. But then, I'm not the one he's dressing. I have no reason to assume that anxious and abandoned look, the look of the voluptuous victim . . .

My friend Valentine appalls me. She dangles her bare arms, and when the "master's" despotic forefinger points at her, she imperceptibly tightens her elbows against her sides. I feel like telling my friend, "Come now, pull yourself together, he's your dressmaker!" But she would answer back, still more vanquished, "Exactly!"

Moreover, the master shows an almost exaggerated, I was going to write: squeamish, discretion. It is with a distant, seemingly magnetic, index finger that he commands his client's revolutions. She turns, takes a step forward, and stops, mesmerized—he does not even graze the material of the dress. Perhaps this extreme reserve is not an affectation at all. Around us I hear an exclusively feminine hum; in the warm, dry air I breathe in mixed perfumes, and that of my friend Valentine, décolleté, is fresh and strong—and I think of a confession from my corset maker, who flees her apartment at night and goes out, sick to her stomach, to have her dinner in a restaurant. "After all those fittings, Madame, I can't bear to eat at home. It smells too strongly of women at the end of the day, it ruins my appetite."

This is the first time I've come here with my friend Valentine, who, of course, has her dresses made by a "master couturier." I study the "master," who returns the compliment. He busies himself with Valentine, but I am the one he wants to impress. He takes his time with her, he ignores his other impatient subjects—he poses, not quite knowing whether what I am making of him is a flattering portrait or a caricature . . .

He's a rather small man, well dressed, neither young nor old. His jacket is dark, his tie severe. Nothing aggressive about his clothes or his shoes, no jewelry. One doesn't think of looking for what there's too much of, but rather for what's missing. He's missing . . . a little of everything: three inches in height, as much in width, and then one would like more decisiveness in the nose, a more adventurous chin. He's arrogant without being authoritative, and his ferrety gaze deliberately loses all its expression when it fixes on something. I wonder why it is he seems disguised, from head to foot: his face looks as if it doesn't belong to him.

"A hole," repeats Valentine devoutly, "yes, a hole . . ."

She nervously fingers the small lace fichu pinned to her shoulders, crumpling it in her hand over the by-now-famous "hole," high on the waist, beneath the breast. The rest of the dress is a close-fitting shift, in a singular shade of mauve, which turns blue when the folds of transparent silk are gathered. There is also a small sprinkling of long pearls at the bottom of the tunic, and some sort of ragged piece of material, without any definite purpose, which trails off to the side onto the carpet. It is an "important" dinner dress.

"Wait! Why didn't I think of it sooner?"

The master steals off with a malicious little hop and reappears, preciously cradling what he needed to fill in the hole: a green flower, made of knitted wool, from which hangs a ludicrous cluster of blue cherries, made of knitted wool, topped by three black leaves—made of knitted wool.

"There!"

He plants the thing in the hollow of the décolleté bodice, and quickly pulls away his hand, like a cat that has burned its paw, and laughs an odious, theatrical laugh.

I look in the triple mirror at my friend Valentine. She has not batted an eyelash and, with the tips of her fingers, pushes up the knitted object, the horror, which is a disgrace to the mauve dress. Without hiding the sickness I feel, I also look at the master, who winks and leans his head to the side like a satisfied painter: I detest fools . . .

Very calmly, and in my honor, the master begins his recitation on the needlework so dear to our grandmothers, he sings the praises of naïve Tunisian crocheting and touchingly old-fashioned macramé— for these unsophisticated ornaments he claims a place of honor on our dresses of woven air and flowing water. Predictably, he uses words like "innovation," "amusing attempts" . . .

"We are a 'young house' but we are prepared to attack everything routine. No respect for our elders. You, Madame, who are an artist, don't you like this youthful enthusiasm which laughs while trampling on the established customs of austere couture—and which sometimes makes mistakes, heaven knows—but who else will jump into the breach and forge ahead?"

He slips away again, without waiting for an answer. And while silent young girls bustle about to get my passive and charmed friend dressed again, he calls out the procession of models for us—for me!

One after the other, in the dreary elegance of the white salon, the models dance the steps to the "mermaid on her tail fin" and the "upright serpent." They progress with difficulty, knees joined and bound, and cut through the air as though it were heavy water, helping themselves along with their hands, which paddle the air at hip level. These are lovely creatures, whose every deformity has its grace: they no longer have any rumps—the curve is gone from the small of their backs accentuating their length: where does the stomach begin? Where are the breasts hiding?

A sign from the master hurries them on or holds them back. Now and then I move involuntarily toward a particular dress, pink and alive like a glittering skin, toward this one, in a savage blue color which blots out everything around it, toward that one made of black velvet, deep and thick as a pelt.

But something holds my arm back and dampens my pleasure: every dress has its ludicrous flaw, the imbecilic and bizarre detail, the toad thrown there like a signature by the despotic and wicked dressmaker. I see knitted flowers on moonlight gauze and unseemly little white horse-hair fringe on royal Alençon lace. A delicate train hangs from a tapestry cabbage: a sheath of black plush, slender, curvacious, with a satanic elegance, tapers off, prisoner of the heaviest foundation of white cloth, twisted into a double skirt; a Greek tunic, pure white, moves forward, barred at the knees by a row of little taffeta flounces with chenille borders; finally, a spiral skirt of green Empire faille, tied up in all directions with Tom Thumb trimmings, unleashes my indignation.

"Monsieur," I say to the dressmaker, "Monsieur, will you please just look at that! Surely you must know how ugly that is. It's not simply a matter of bad taste; in every one of these dresses there is an *intention*: take any one of them, take this one here, which wipes the floor with this little square tail of gold linen embroidered with thick white cotton! Why, *why* do you do it?"

My unexpected vehemence makes the master stop short, and his beady eyes meet mine for a long moment. He hesitates; he lets me catch his true and mediocre face, the face of a small shopkeeper who had a hard time starting out—he hesitates between his urge to deceive me and a sudden need for confession, for cynicism . . .

"Would you please tell me, Monsieur, just me, why you do this?"

He smiles a loathsome, confidential smile, he looks around him, as if he wished we were alone: will he betray his appetite for domination, claim revenge for his past as an impoverished clerk, confess the disgusted misogyny that comes from dealing with too many females, the pleasure he takes in making them ugly, in humiliating them, in subjecting them to his half-crazed fantasies, in "branding" them . . .

He hesitates, he doesn't dare, and, finally, turning his eyes away from mine: "Just to see . . ." he says.

Morning Glories

❧

The wasp was eating away at the red-currant glaze of the tart. She set about it with methodical and gluttonous haste, head down, legs sticky, half disappearing into a little vat with pink transparent sides. I was surprised not to see her puff out, swell up, and become as round as a spider . . . And my friend hadn't arrived, my friend the gourmand, who faithfully comes to have her tea with me because I indulge her little idiosyncrasies, because I listen to her chatter, because I never agree with her about anything . . . She can relax with me; she is quick to tell me, in a tone of gratitude, that I'm hardly ever coquettish with her, and I don't scrutinize her hat or her dress with an aggressive, female eye. She keeps quiet if someone says anything bad about me at one of her other friend's; she goes as far as to exclaim, "Ladies, Colette may be a little crazy, but she is not as nasty as you make her out to be!" She is, you see, quite fond of me.

Whenever I think about her, I feel that pitying and ironic pleasure which is one of the forms which friendship takes. You have never seen a woman more blond, or more fair-skinned, or more dressy, or more carefully coiffed! The shade of her hair, of her real hair, hovers delicately between silver and gold; the ringlets of a little six-year-old Swedish girl had to be sent for when my friend wanted the prescribed *chichis* our hats require. Beneath this crown of so rare a metal, my friend's complexion, so as not to look yellow by comparison, is brightened up with pink powder, and her eyelashes, brushed brown, protect her mobile gaze, a gray-and-amber gaze, perhaps brown too, a gaze which knows how to settle, caressingly, imploringly, on a man's eyes, caressing and imploring.

That is my friend, about whom I will have said everything I know if I add that she flaunts the fact that her name is Valentine, in these days of short nicknames, when the little names women go by—Tote, Moute, Loche—sound like a hiccup that couldn't be held back.

"She forgot," I thought patiently. The wasp, asleep or dead from overindulgence, head down, had sunk into the vat of delights. I was about to open my book again when the doorbell shivered and my friend appeared. With a half twist, she spiraled her overlong dress around her legs and landed next to me, with her parasol across her knees—the skillful movement of an actress, or a model, almost an acrobat, which my friend executes so perfectly each time.

"This is a fine time for tea! What in the world have you been doing?"

"Why nothing, my dear! You are amazing, living here between your dog, your cat, and your book! Do you think Lelong could create all those gorgeous dresses without me trying them on?"

"Come on . . . just eat and be quiet. That? It's not dirty, it's a wasp. Can you believe she dug that little well all by herself! I watched her, she ate all that in twenty-five minutes."

"What? You watched her? Well, you really are a disgusting creature, after all. No, thank you, I'm not hungry. No, no tea either."

"Shall I ring for the toast, then?"

"If it's for me, don't bother . . . I'm not hungry, really,"

"Have you eaten somewhere else, you little beast?"

"Heavens, no! I just feel funny, I don't know what's wrong . . ."

Surprised, I looked up at my friend's face, which I had not yet isolated from her insane hat, as big as a parasol, topped with a bursting rocket of feathers, a hat like fireworks, like the fountains at Versailles, a hat made for a giantess which would have showered down my friend's little head all the way to her shoulders, if it weren't for the famous Swedish-blond *chichis* . . . The pink-powdered cheeks, the brightly rouged lips, and the stiff eyelashes made up her usual fresh little mask, but something underneath it all seemed changed to me, lackluster, missing. High up on the cheek with less powder, a mauve furrow held the mother-of-pearl glaze left by recent tears . . .

This made-up distress, the distress of a brave doll, suddenly moved me, and I couldn't keep myself from taking my friend by the shoulders in a gesture of concern, which was something that rarely occurred between us.

She sank back and blushed beneath her pink powder, but didn't have time to pull herself together and sniffed back her sobs in vain.

A minute later, she was crying, wiping the *inside* of her eyelids with the corner of a tea napkin. She cried freely, careful not to stain her crepe de Chine dress with her tears, not to ruin her face, she cried carefully, neatly, the little martyr to makeup.

"Is there anything I can do for you?" I asked her gently.

She shook her head "no," sighed, trembling, and held out her cup, which I filled with tea that had gone cold.

"Thank you," she murmured, "you're so nice . . . Please forgive me, I'm so nervous . . ."

"Poor thing! You don't want to tell me anything?"

"Oh, God, yes. It's not that complicated, really. He doesn't love me anymore."

He . . . her lover! I hadn't thought of that. A lover, her? when? and where? and who? this ideal mannequin was taking her clothes off in the middle of the afternoon for a lover? All sorts of ludicrous images rose up—spread themselves out—before me, which I dispelled, exclaiming, "He doesn't love you anymore? That's not possible!"

"Oh, yes, it is! It was a terrible scene . . ." She opened her gold mirror, powdered her face, and wiped her eyelids with a moist finger. "A terrible scene, yesterday . . ."

"Jealous?"

"Him, jealous? I'd be only too happy! He's mean. He scolds me for things . . . but there's nothing I can do about it!"

She sulked, her chin doubled up against her high collar.

"You be the judge, then! He's a delicious young man, and for six months there hasn't been a single cloud, not a hitch, never this! He got moody sometimes, but with an artist . . ."

"Oh, he's an artist?"

"A painter, my dear. And a very talented one. If I could tell you his name, you'd be very surprised. He has twenty red-pencil drawings he's done of me, some with my hat on, some with it off, in all my dresses! There's something soaring, something ethereal about them. The movement in the skirts is an absolute wonder . . ."

She was coming to life, a bit undone, the wings of her thin nose shining with carefully daubed tears and the beginnings of a faint blotchiness . . . her eyelashes had lost their black mascara, her lips their carmine . . . Beneath the big hat, both becoming and ridiculous, beneath the postiche *chichis*, I could make out for the first time a not very pretty woman, but not ugly either, a bland woman you might say, but touching, sincere, and sad.

Her eyelids suddenly reddened.

"And . . . what happened?" I asked, taking the risk.

"What happened? Why, nothing! We'll say *nothing*, my dear. Yesterday, he greeted me in a funny way . . . like a doctor . . . And then friendly all of a sudden: 'Take off your hat, darling!' he said to me. 'I'm keeping you for dinner, all right? I'll keep you for good if you want!' It was this very hat I had on, and you know what a terrible struggle it is to get it on and take it off again."

I didn't know, but I nodded my head, with great conviction.

". . . I sulk a little. He insists, I sacrifice myself and start taking out my pins and one of my *chichis* stays caught in the barrette of my hat, there, you see . . . It didn't matter to me, everybody knows I have hair, don't they, and he better than anyone! But he's the one who's blushing and trying to hide. I replanted my *chichi*, like a flower, put my arms around his neck, my lips up to his ear, and whispered to him that my husband was away in Dieppe on business, and that . . . Well, you understand! He didn't say anything. Then he threw down his cigarette and it all started. The things he said to me! The things he said to me . . . !"

With each exclamation she struck her knees with her open hands, with a common and disheartened gesture, like my maid when she tells me that her husband has beaten her again.

"He said the most unbelievable things to me, my dear! He controlled himself at first, but then he started walking around talking . . . 'I couldn't want anything more than to spend the night with you, darling . . .' (the nerve!) 'but I want . . . I want what you must give me, what you can't give me!' "

"Good Lord, what?"

"Wait, you'll see . . . 'I want the woman you are *at this moment,* the graceful, slim little fairy crowned with a gold so light and so abundant that her hair spills down to her brow like foam. I want this skin the color of fruit ripened in a hothouse, and these paradoxical lashes, all this beauty from the English School! I want you, just as you are now, and not how the cynical night will give you to me; I remember!—you'll come to me conjugal and tender, uncrowned and uncurled, with your hair untouched by the iron, straight and twisted into braids. You'll come small, without your high heels on, your eyelashes missing their velvety softness, your powder washed away; you'll come disarmed and self-assured, and I'll be left speechless in front of this other woman . . . !

" 'But you already knew that,' he cried, 'you knew it! The woman I desired, you, as you are now, has almost nothing in common with her poor and simple sister, who comes out of your bathroom every night! What gives you the right to change the woman I love? If you care about my love, how do you dare deflower the very thing I love?'

"The things he said, the things he said! I didn't budge, I looked at him, I was cold . . . And you know, I didn't cry! Not in front of him."

"It was very wise of you, my dear, and very brave."

"Very brave," she repeated, lowering her head. "As soon as I could move, I got out. I heard terrible things about women, about all women; about the 'prodigious unconsciousness of women, their improvident pride, their animal pride which, deep down, always thinks it will be enough for the man . . .' What would you have said?"

"Nothing."

Nothing, it's true. What is there to say? I'm not far from agreeing with him, a crude man pushed to the limit. He's almost right. It's always good enough for the man! Women have no excuses. They've given men every reason to run away, to cheat, to hate, to change. Ever since the world began, they've been inflicting men, behind the bed curtains, with a creature inferior to the one he desired. They rob him with effrontery nowadays, when reinforced hair and rigged corsets turn any ugly, saucy little woman into "a striking little lady."

I listen to my other friends talk, I look at them, and I sit there, embarrassed for them . . . Lily, the charmer, the page with short, frizzy hair, imposes on her lovers, from the first night on, the nakedness of her head, bumpy with brown snails, the fat and hideous hairpin snail! Clarissa preserves her complexion while she sleeps with a layer of cucumber cream, and Annie pulls all her hair back Chinese-style, tied with a ribbon! Suzanne coats her delicate neck with lanolin and swaddles it in old worn-out linen; Minna never goes to sleep without her chin strap on, the purpose of which is to stave off the fattening of her cheeks and chin, and she glues a little paraffin star on each temple.

If I get indignant, Suzanne raises her fat shoulders and says: "Do you think I'm going to ruin my skin for a man? I don't have a change of skin. If he doesn't like lanolin, he can leave. I'm not forcing anyone." And Lily declares impetuously: "In the first place, I am *not* ugly in my curlers! They make me look like a little frizzy-headed schoolgirl at an awards ceremony." When Minna's "friend" complains about her chin strap, her response is: "Darling, don't be a bore. You're quite happy at the races if someone behind you says: 'That Minna, she still has the oval face of a virgin!'" And Jeannine, who wears a reducing belt at night! And Marguerite, who . . . no, I can't write that . . . !

My little friend, grown plain and sad, was listening to my obscure thoughts, and her guess was that I did not pity her enough. She stood up . . .

"That's all you have to say to me?"

"My poor dear, what do you want me to say to you? What I think is that nothing is lost, and that your painter-lover will be scratching on your door tomorrow, maybe even this evening . . ."

"Do you think he might have telephoned? He's not basically a mean person. He's a little crazy, it's just a passing thing, isn't it?"

She was already on her feet, bright with hope.

I say "yes" to everything, full of goodwill and the desire to satisfy her . . . And I watch her hurry down the sidewalk, her steps shortened by her high heels. Maybe he really does love her. And if he does, the time will come again when, despite all the embellishments and all the frauds, she will once again become for him, with the shadows' help, the faun with freely flowing hair, the nymph with unblemished feet, the beautiful slave with flawless flanks, naked as love itself . . .

What Must We Look Like?

❧❦❧

"What are you doing Sunday, tomorrow?"
"Why do you ask?"
"Oh, no reason . . ."

My friend Valentine, in order to inquire as to how I will spend my Sunday, has assumed too indifferent an air.

I insist: "No reason? Are you sure? Come on, out with it . . . You need me!"

She slips away gracefully, the clever thing, and answers sweetly, "My dear, I always need you."

Oh, that smile! I am always left at a loss, whenever I'm taken in by her petty, sophisticated duplicity. I'd rather give in right away.

"Oh, Sunday, Valentine, I go to the concert, or else I go to bed. I've been going to bed quite a lot this year, because Chevillard has poor accommodations and because the Colonne concerts, which come after, are all alike."

"Oh! You think so?"

"Yes, I do. If you've gone to Bayreuth in the past, quite faithfully, if you've enjoyed Van Rooy as Wotan and suffered through Burgstaller as Siegfried, you get no pleasure, none whatsoever, in finding him at Colonne's, in civilian clothes, with the awkward gait of a frenetic sacristan crowned with childish ringlets, the knees of an old ballerina, and the mawkishness of a seminarian. An unkind coincidence brought us together, at the Châtelet, him on stage, me in the audience, a few weeks ago, and I had to listen to him bellow—twice—an *"Ich grolle nicht"* which Madame de Maupeou wouldn't dare serve to her relatives from the provinces! I fled before the concert was over, to the great relief of my neighbor to my right, the "lady companion" of a Paris city councillor, my dear!"

"Were you bothering her?"

"I was making her uncomfortable. She doesn't know me anymore, since our separation and division of property changed me so much. She trembled every time I batter an eyelash, for fear I might kiss her."

"Oh, I understand!"

She understands! Eyes lowered, my friend Valentine taps on the clasp of her gold purse. She is wearing—but I've already told you all about it—a huge, high hat, beneath which is an abundance of ruinously expensive blond hair. Her Japanese-style sleeves make her arms look like a penguin's, her skirt, long and heavy, covers her pointed feet, and it requires a terrible single-mindedness to appear charming under so many horrors.

She had just said, as if despite herself: "I understand . . ."

"Yes, you understand. I'm sure you do. You must understand that . . . My dear, shouldn't you be going home? It's late, and your husband . . ."

"Oh, that's not very nice of you . . ."

Her blue-gray-green-brown eyes beg me, humbly, and I repent immediately.

"I was only joking, silly! Come on now, what is it you wanted to do with my Sunday?"

My friend Valentine opens her little penguin arms comically and says, "Well, that's just it, it's almost as if it was on purpose . . . Imagine, tomorrow afternoon I'll be all alone, all alone . . ."

"And you're complaining."

The word just slipped out. I feel her almost sad, this young doll. Her husband away; her lover . . . busy; her friends—her real friends—celebrating the Lord behind closed doors, or going off in their cars . . .

"You wanted to come here tomorrow, my dear? Well then, come! It's a very good idea."

I don't believe a word of it, but she thanks me, with that little-lost-dog look, exactly the sort of thing I find touching, and off she goes, quickly, in a rush, as if she really did have something to do.

SUNDAY. My dear Sunday, day for idleness and my warm bed, my Sunday—for eating like a glutton, sleeping, reading—lost, ruined, and for whom? For an uncertain friend I feel vaguely sorry for.

Don't go to sleep, my gray contented pussycat, for my friend Valentine will soon ring the bell, make her entrance, swish about, and carry on. She will run her gloved hand over your back, and your spine will shudder as you look at her with murderous eyes. You know she really doesn't like you very much, my short-haired country girl; she goes into ecstasies over Angoras, which have capes like collies and whiskers like Chauchard. Ever since you scratched her that day, she keeps her distance; she knows nothing about your violent little soul, delicate and vindictive, the soul of a bohemian cat. As soon as she comes, turn your striped back to her, roll yourself up into a turban at my feet, on the satin scratched by your curved claws shaped like the thorns of a wild rosebush.

Shhh! she rang . . . here she is! She shivers and haphazardly plants her icy little nose on my face—she kisses so poorly!

"Lord, your nose has lost consciousness, my dear. Sit down *in* the fire, for heaven's sake."

"Don't laugh, it's terrible out there! All the same, you're lucky you're in bed! Twenty-five degrees; we'll all die."

In fact, my friend's face had turned lilac, the somewhat greenish lilac of plums just beginning to ripen.

A splendid tailored suit, made of mousy brown velvet, hugs her, clings to her, from collar to feet. Especially the jacket, oh, the jacket! tight at the top, flared at the bottom, the embroidered peplum hitting the knees, like a little overskirt . . . And thrown over that, in twenty-five-degree weather, a sable stole, an expensive scrap of useless fur—and here she is dying of cold with her nose turning purple.

"You little dodo! Couldn't you at least have put on your broadtail coat?"

She turns halfway around, hands on her hat, looking lost behind its veil.

"Well no, I couldn't! With this style of long jacket, the peplum shows under my broadtail coat, and I ask you now, what would that look like?"

"You should have lengthened the broadtail."

"Thank you! and what next! Max is very chic, and not all that expensive, but still . . ."

"You should have . . . bought a bigger sable . . ."

My friend turns on me, as if about to bite me. "A . . . a bigger sable!!! I'm not Rothschild!"

Me either. Or else . . . wait . . . you should have had a serious coat made of a less expensive fur, that wasn't sable . . ."

Disentangled from her veil, my friend lets her tired arms fall. "A different fur! There is no truly chic, no truly dressy fur, besides sable . . . A chic woman without sable, seriously, my dear, what must that look like?"

What, in fact, does it look like? I really don't know. I feel around with my toes, at the foot of the bed, for my hot-water bottle.

The fire crackles and hisses, a shameless country fire, which spits and shoots out little glowing embers.

"Valentine, be a sweetheart and take care of the chores. Pull the tea table up next to the bed. There's boiling water by the fire; the sandwiches, the wine, everything's there . . . you won't have to ring for Francine and I won't be forced to get up; we'll be quiet, lazy gluttons. Take off your hat, you can lean your head against the cushions . . . over there."

She looks sweet without her hat. A little like a hatmaker, a little like a mannequin, but sweet. A beautiful roll of golden hair billows down to her brown eyebrows and holds up a large, flowing wave; above it there is another, smaller wave, and still another above that, and in the back, curls, curls, curls . . . It's alluring, clean-looking, frothy and neat at the same time, as complicated as a side dish at a wedding feast.

The lamp—I've shut the blinds and drawn the curtains—casts a pink wash on my friend's face, but despite the even, velvety layer of face powder, despite the red lipstick, the drawn features, the stiff smile . . . she leans back against the cushions, with a long sigh of weariness . . .

"Dead?"

"Completely dead."

"Love . . . ?"

Movement in the shoulders. "Love? Oh, no . . . No time. With all the openings, the dinners, the suppers, driving here and there to lunch, the exhibitions and the teas . . . this is a terrible month!"

"So you get to bed late, huh?"

"Alas . . ."

"Get up late. Or you'll lose your beauty, my dear."

She looks at me, astonished. "Get up late? That's easy for you to say. What about the house? And the orders to give? And the bills to pay? And everything, everything! And the maid who knocks on my door twenty-five times!"

"Unlock the door and say you're not to be disturbed."

"But I can't! Nothing would get done; it would be a disaster, organized theft . . . unlock the door! I can imagine what kind of a face there'd be on the other side, on my fat headwaiter who looks like Jean de Bonnefin . . . Now what would I look like then?"

"I really don't know . . . Like a woman who's getting some rest . . ."

"Easy to say . . ." She sighs with a nervous yawn. "You can treat yourselves to it, you people who are . . . who are . . ."

"On the fringes of society . . ."

She laughs with all her heart, suddenly rejuvenated. Then melancholy: "Yes, you can. *We others* aren't allowed to."

We others . . . The mysterious plural, the strict imposing freemasonry of those whom the world hypnotizes, overworks, and disciplines. An abyss separates this young woman sitting there in her tailored brown suit from this other woman lying on her stomach, her chin resting on her fists. Silently, I savor my enviable inferiority.

To myself, I muse: "*You others* cannot live however you like . . . that is your torment, your pride, and your loss. You have husbands who take you out to supper after the theater—but you also have children and maids dragging you out of bed in the morning. You have supper at the Café de Paris, next to Mademoiselle Xaverine de Choisy, and you leave the restaurant at the same time she does, both of you a little tipsy, a little amorous, your nerves tingling . . . but once home, Mademoiselle de Choisy sleeps if she feels like it, loves if she feels up to it, and as she falls asleep she calls out to her faithful chambermaid: 'I'm going to sleep until two in the afternoon, and I don't want anyone bothering me before that or I'll send you all home for a week!' Having gotten nine hours of well-deserved rest, Mademoiselle de Choisy wakes refreshed, has her breakfast, and dashes down the rue de la Paix, where she runs into you, Valentine, all you Valentines, you my friend, on your feet since eight-thirty in the morning, already worn out, pale-looking, with dark circles under your eyes . . . And Mademoiselle de Choisy says aside to her fitter: 'Little Madame Valentine What's-her-name doesn't look well at all! She must be keeping late hours!' And your husband and your lover, at supper later, will also compare *in petto* Mademoiselle de Choisy's well-rested freshness to your obvious fatigue. You will think, furious and ill-considered: 'Women like that are made of steel!' Not at all, my friend! They get more rest than you. What demimondaine could withstand the daily hustle and bustle of certain women of the world or even of certain women with families?"

My young friend has brewed the tea, and is filling the cups with a deft hand. I admire her somewhat deliberate elegance, her precise gestures; I appreciate the fact that she is walking noiselessly as her long skirt both precedes and follows her, in an obedient, moiré stream . . . I appreciate the fact that she confides in me, that she comes back at the risk of compromising her position as a woman with a husband and a lover, for coming back here to see me with an affectionate persistence which verges on heroism.

When she hears the tinkling of the spoons, my gray cat opens her serpent-like eyes.

She is hungry. But she does not get up right away, out of pure cant. To beg, like a plaintive and wheedling Angora, in a minor threnody, bah! What would that look like, as Valentine says. I offer her a burned corner of toast, which crackles between her little teeth made of bluish-white silex, and her pearly purring doubles that of the kettle. For a long moment, a quasi-provincial silence settles on us. My friend is resting, arms at her sides . . .

"You can't hear a thing," she whispers cautiously.

I answer with my eyes, without speaking, glowing with warmth and idleness. It feels so nice . . . But wouldn't it be even nicer if my friend weren't here? She's going to start talking, it's inevitable. She's going to say, "What must we look like?" It's not her fault she was raised that way. If she had children, she would forbid them to eat their meat without bread, or to hold their spoon with their left hand: "John, behave yourself! What must you look like?"

Shhh! She isn't talking. Her eyelids are drooping and her eyes look as if they're fading away. I have in front of me an almost unknown face, the face of a young woman drunk with drowsiness who falls asleep before her eyelids are closed. The studied smile fades away, the lip pouts, and the little round chin crushes down on the collar of silver embroidery.

She's sleeping soundly now. When she wakes with a start, she'll apologize and exclaim: "Falling asleep during a visit, in an armchair! What must that look like?"

My friend Valentine, you look like a young woman left there like a poor but graceful rag. Sleep between me and the fire, to the purring of the cat and the faint rustling of the pages of the book I'm going to read now. No one will come in before you wake up; no one will cry out, staring at your sulky sleep and my unmade bed: "Oh, what must this look like!," for you might die of chagrin. I am keeping watch over you, with a mild, a kindly pity; I am keeping watch over your vigilant and virtuous concern for what it is we *must* look like . . .

The Cure

❦❦❦

The gray cat is delighted that I am on the stage. Theater or music hall, she shows no preference. What matters is that I disappear every evening, after swallowing down my cutlet, in order to reappear around half past midnight, and that once again we sit ourselves down at the table, in front of a chicken leg or some pink ham . . . Three meals a day instead of two! She no longer thinks of concealing her elation past midnight. Seated on the tablecloth, she smiles without dissimulation, the corners of her mouth turned up, and her eyes, spangled with scintillating sand, fixed wide open and confident on mine. She has waited all night for this precious hour, she savors it with a triumphant and egoistic joy which brings her closer to me.

O cat of ashen coat! To the uninitiated you look like every other gray cat on earth, lazy, oblivious, morose, somewhat listless, neuter, bored . . . but I know you to be wildly tender, and whimsical, jealous to the point of starving yourself, talkative, paradoxically awkward, and, on occasion, as tough as a young mastiff.

Now it is June and I am no longer in *Flesh* and my run in *Claudine* is over. Over, too, our late-night suppers together! Do you miss the quiet hour when, ravenous and somewhat dazed, I used to scratch that flat little skull of yours, the skull of a cruel beast, thinking vaguely, "It went well tonight . . ." Here we are alone, homebodies once again, unsociable, strangers to almost everything, indifferent to almost everyone. We are going to see our friend Valentine again, our "respectable acquaintance," and listen to her hold forth about a world of people, strange, little known to us, full of pitfalls, duties, prohibitions, a formidable world, or so she says, but so far from me that I can scarcely conceive of it.

During my training in pantomime and acting, my friend Valentine disappeared from my life, discreet, alarmed, modest. This is her polite way of showing her disapproval of my sort of existence. I'm not offended by it. I tell myself that she has a husband in automobiles, a society-painter lover, a salon, weekly teas, and twice-monthly dinners. Can you just see me, performing *Flesh* or *The Faun* at one of Valentine's soirees or dancing *The Blue Serpent* for her guests? I put up with it. I wait. I know that my more respectable friend will come back, sweet and embarrassed, one of these days. A little or a lot, she cares about me and proves it to me, and that is enough to make me indebted to her.

Here she is. I recognize the short and precise way she rings the bell, the ring of well-bred company.

"At last, Valentine! It's been such a long time . . ."

Something in her eyes, in her entire face, stops me. I cannot say just how my friend has changed. Is she sick? No, she never looks sick, under the evenly spread, velvety powder and the pink smear on her cheeks. She always has the air of an elegant mannequin, small-waisted, slim-hipped beneath her skirt of pale gold tussore. She has fresh blue-gray-green-brown eyes blossoming between the double fringe of her blackened lashes, and a mass, a beautiful mass of Swedish blond hair . . . What's wrong? A tarnish on all that, a new fixity in her gaze, a moral discoloration, if I may put it that way, which disconcerts, which stops the banalities of welcome on my lips. Nevertheless, she sits down, turning deftly in her long dress, smoothing out her linen jabot with a pat, and smiles and talks and talks until I undiplomatically interrupt her.

"Valentine, what's the matter?"

She is not surprised and answers simply: "Nothing. Almost nothing, really. He's left me."

"What? Henri . . . your . . . your lover's left you?"

"Yes," she says. "Exactly three weeks ago today."

Her voice is so soft, so cool, that I am reassured.

"Oh! Was it . . . was it painful?"

"No," she says, with the same softness. "It *was* not; it is."

Her eyes grow wider and wider, questioning mine with sudden rawness.

"Yes, I'm in pain. Oh, I am! Tell me, is it going to go on like this? How long am I going to suffer? Don't you know of any way . . . I can't get used to it . . . What am I going to do?"

The poor child! She is stunned by suffering, she who didn't believe herself capable of it.

"What about your husband, Valentine . . . he didn't know anything?"

"No," she says impatiently, "he didn't know anything. It's not a question of that. What can I do? Don't you have any ideas? For two weeks I've been asking myself what I should do."

"Do you still love him?"

She hesitates: "I don't know . . . I'm terribly angry with him, because he doesn't love me anymore and because he's left me . . . I don't know. All I know is that this is unbearable, unbearable, this loneliness, this giving up of everything you've loved, this emptiness, this . . ."

She has stood up at the word "unbearable" and is walking around the room as if a burn caused her to run off, to find the coolest place . . .

"You don't seem to understand. You don't know what it is . . ."

I shut my eyes, I hold back a pitying smile, in the presence of the naïve vanity of suffering, of suffering more and better than others'.

"Child, you'll wear yourself out. Don't walk around like that. Come sit down. Would you like to take your hat off and have a little cry?"

With an outraged denial, she sets the smoke-colored plumes on her head dancing.

"Certainly not. I would get no pleasure whatsoever out of crying, thank you! So I can ruin my entire face? And where would it get me, I ask you now. I have no desire to cry, my dear, it makes my blood boil, that's all."

She sits back down, and throws her parasol on the table. Her little, hardened face is not without real beauty at this moment. I think of the fact that every day for three weeks she has been putting on all her finery as usual, meticulously constructing her fragile castle of hair . . . for three weeks—twenty-one days!—she has been holding back accusatory tears, blackening her blond eyelashes with a steady hand, going out, receiving guests, gossiping, eating . . . The heroism of a doll, but heroism just the same.

Maybe I should seize her, with a great sisterly rush, wrap her in my arms, and melt this hardened, unbending little creature, enraged against her own grief, in my warm embrace. She would break down and sob, she would calm her nerves, which must not have relaxed for the past three weeks . . . I do not dare. Valentine and I are not that intimate, and her sudden confidence is not enough to make up for two months of separation.

Besides, what need is there to soften, with the coddling of a wet-nurse, this haughty strength which sustains my friend? "Tears will do you good," yes, yes, I know the old cliché. I also know the danger, the intoxication of lonely, endless tears—you cry because you've just cried, and you start in again—you continue by force of habit, to the point of choking, to the point of nervous exhaustion and drunken sleep from which you wake puffy, blotched, distraught, ashamed of yourself, and sadder than before. No tears, no tears! I feel like applauding, like congratulating my friend, who is still sitting there in front of me, wide-eyed and tearless, crowned with hair and feathers, with the stiff grace of young women who wear corsets that are too long.

"You're right, my dear," I say at last.

I am careful to speak without warmth, as if I were complimenting her on her choice of hat.

"You're right. Go on just as you are, if there isn't any remedy, any reconciliation possible . . ."

"There isn't," she says coldly, like me.

"No? . . . Then you just have to wait . . ."

"Wait? Wait for what?"

What a sudden awakening, what mad hope!

"Wait for the cure, for the love to end. You're suffering a lot, but worse is on the way. There will come a time—a month from now, three months, I don't know when—when you'll start to suffer intermittently. There will be respites, moments of animal oblivion which occur, for whatever reason, because it's beautiful outside, because you've slept well, or because you're a little ill . . . Oh, my dear! The recurrent pain is so terrible! It strikes you down without warning, without sparing anything. At some innocent and frivolous moment, some sweet, light moment, in the middle of a gesture or a burst of laughter, the *idea*, the crushing memory of the terrible loss silences your laughter, stops the hand bringing the teacup to your lips, and you sit there, terrified, wishing you were dead with the naïve conviction that you cannot suffer so much without dying . . . but you won't die! . . . not you either. Relief will come, irregularly, unpredictably, capriciously . . . it will be awful . . . truly awful . . . But . . ."

"But?"

My friend is listening to me, less defiant now, less hostile . . .

"But it gets even worse!"

I wasn't watching my voice carefully enough . . . With a movement from my friend, I lower my tone.

"Even worse. The time will come when you will hardly be suffering at all. Yes! Nearly cured, and that is when you become 'a lost soul,' one who wanders about, seeking she knows not what, she doesn't want to tell herself what . . . By that time, the recurrent pain is benign, and through a strange form of compensation, the periods of respite become abominable, with a dizzying, sickly emptiness which overwhelms the heart. That's the period of stupefaction and imbalance. Your heart feels drained, shriveled, adrift in a breast swollen at times with tremulous sighs which are not even sad. You go out with no place to go, you walk without purpose, you stop to rest without being tired . . . You dig at the place of your recent suffering with an animal's avidity, without being able to draw a single drop of living, fresh blood—you dig away at a half-dried scar, you miss—I swear!—you miss the sharp, searing pain. That's the arid, aimless period made more bitter still by regret. Oh, yes, regret! Regret over having lost the impassioned, trembling, despotic beauty of desperation . . . You feel diminished, blighted, inferior to the most mediocre creatures. You too will say to yourself, 'What? That's all I was, all I am? Not even the equal of some lovesick errand girl who throws herself into the Seine?' Oh, Valentine! You will blush at yourself in secret, until . . ."

"Until?"

God, what hope she has! I will never see her amber-colored eyes as beautiful or as big, her mouth as anguished.

"Until the cure, my friend, the real cure. It comes . . . mysteriously. You don't feel it right away. But it is like the gradual reward for so much pain. Believe me! It will come, I don't know when. One sweet spring day, or one wet autumn morning, maybe one moonlit night, you'll feel something inexpressible and alive expanding voluptuously in your heart—a happy snake growing longer and longer—a velvet caterpillar unrolling itself—a releasing, an opening, silky and salutary, like an iris unfurling. At that moment, without knowing why, you will put your hands behind your head, with an inexplicable smile . . . You will discover, with recaptured wonder, that the light coming through the lace curtains is pink, and that under your feet the rug is soft—that the fragrance of the flowers and the smell of the ripe fruit is exhilarating instead of stifling. You will experience a timid happiness, free of all desire, delicate, a little bashful, self-centered and self-concerned . . ."

My friend grabs me by the hands. "More! More! Tell me more!"

Alas, what more does she want? Haven't I promised enough by promising her the cure? I smile as I stroke her warm little hands.

"More! But that's all there is, my dear. What more do you want?"

"What more do I want? Why . . . love, of course, love!"

My hands let go of hers. "Ah, yes! Another love . . . You want another love . . ."

It's true . . . I hadn't thought of another love . . . I look at her pretty, anxious face up close, at her graceful body, studied and tidy, her stubborn, plain-looking forehead . . . She is already hoping for another love, one better, or worse, or no different than the one that has just killed her . . .

Without irony, but without pity either, I reassure her: "Yes, my dear, yes. You will have another love . . . I promise you."

[Translated by Matthew Ward]

Sleepless Nights

❧§❧

In our house there is only one bed, too big for you, a little narrow for us both. It is chaste, white, completely exposed; no drapery veils its honest candor in the light of day. People who come to see us survey it calmly and do not tactfully look aside, for it is marked, in the middle, with but one soft valley, like the bed of a young girl who sleeps alone.

They do not know, those who enter here, that every night the weight of our two united bodies hollows out a little more, beneath its voluptuous winding sheet, that valley no wider than a tomb.

O our bed, completely bare! A dazzling lamp, slanted above it, denudes it even more. We do not find there, at twilight, the well-devised shade of a lace canopy or the rosy shell-like glow of a night lamp. Fixed star, never rising or setting, our bed never ceases to gleam except when submerged in the velvety depths of night.

Rigid and white, like the body of a dear departed, it is haloed with a perfume, a complicated scent that astounds, that one inhales attentively, in an effort to distinguish the blond essence of your favorite tobacco from the still lighter aroma of your extraordinarily white skin, and the scent of sandalwood that I give off; but that wild odor of crushed grasses, who can tell if it is mine or thine?

Receive us tonight, O our bed, and let your fresh valley deepen a little more beneath the feverish torpor caused by a thrilling spring day spent in the garden and in the woods.

I lie motionless, my head on your gentle shoulder. Surely, until tomorrow, I will sink into the depths of a dark sleep, a sleep so stubborn, so shut off from the world, that the wings of dream will come to beat in vain. I am going to sleep . . . Wait only until I find, for the soles of my feet that are tingling and burning, a cool place . . . You have not budged. You draw in long drafts of air, but I feel your shoulder still awake and careful to provide a hollow for my cheek . . . Let us sleep. . . . The nights of May are so brief. Despite the blue obscurity that bathes us, my eyelids are still full of sunshine, and I contemplate the day that has passed with closed eyes, as one peers, from behind the shelter of a Persian blind, into a dazzling summer garden . . .

How my heart throbs! I can also hear yours throb beneath my ear. You're not asleep? I raise my head slightly and sense rather than see the pallor of your upturned face, the tawny shadow of your short hair. Your knees are like two cool oranges . . . Turn toward me, so that mine can steal some of that smooth freshness.

Oh, let us sleep! . . . My skin is tingling, there is a throbbing in the muscles of my calves and in my ears, and surely our soft bed, tonight, is strewn with pine needles! Let us sleep! I command sleep to come.

I cannot sleep. My insomnia is a kind of gay and lively palpitation, and I sense in your immobility the same quivering exhaustion. You do not budge. You hope I am asleep. Your arm tightens at times around me, out of tender habit, and your charming feet clasp mine between them . . . Sleep approaches, grazes me, and flees . . . I can see it! Sleep is exactly like that heavy velvety butterfly I pursued in the garden aflame with iris. Do you remember? What youthful impatience glorified this entire sunlit day! A keen and insistent breeze flung over the sun a smoke screen of rapid clouds and withered the too-tender leaves of the linden trees; the flowers of the butternut tree fell like brownish caterpillars upon our hair, with the flowers of the catalpas, their color the rainy mauve of the Parisian sky. The shoots of the black-currant bush that you brushed against, the wild sorrel dotting the grass with its rosettes, the fresh young mint, still brown, the sage as downy as a hare's ear— everything overflowed with a powerful and spicy sap which became on my lips mingled with the taste of alcohol and citronella.

I could only shout and laugh, as I trod the long juicy grass that stained my frock . . . With tranquil pleasure you regarded my wild behavior, and when I stretched out my hand to reach those wild roses— you remember, the ones of such a tender pink—your hand broke the branch before I could, and you took off, one by one, the curved little thorns, coral-hued, claw-shaped . . . And then you gave me the flowers, disarmed . . .

You gave me the flowers, disarmed . . . You gave me, so I could rest my panting self, the best place in the shade, under the Persian lilacs with their ripe bunches of flowers. You picked the big cornflowers in the round flower beds, enchanted flowers whose hairy centers smell of apricot . . . You gave me the cream in the small jug of milk, at teatime, when my ravenous appetite made you smile . . . You gave me the bread with the most golden crust, and I can still see your translucent hand in the sunshine raised to shoo away the wasp that sizzled, entangled in my curls . . . You threw over my shoulders a light mantle when a cloud longer than usual slowly passed, toward the end of the day, when I shivered, in a cold sweat, intoxicated with the pleasure that is nameless among mankind, the innocent pleasure of happy animals in the spring-time . . . You told me: "Come back . . . Stop . . . We must go in!" You told me . . .

Oh, if I think of you, then it's goodbye to sleep. What hour struck just then? Now the windows are growing blue. I hear a murmuring in my blood, or else it is the murmur of the gardens down there . . . Are you asleep? No. If I put my cheek against yours, I feel your eyelashes flutter like the wings of a captive fly . . . You are not asleep. You are spying on my excitement. You protect me against bad dreams; you are thinking of me as I am thinking of you, and we both feign, out of a strange sentimental shyness, a peaceful sleep. All my body yields itself up to sleep, relaxed, and my neck weighs heavily on your gentle shoulder; but our thoughts unite in love discreetly across this blue dawn, so soon increasing.

In a short while the luminous bar between the curtains will brighten, redden . . . In a few more minutes I will be able to read, on your lovely forehead, your delicate chin, your sad mouth, and closed eyelids, the determination to appear to be sleeping . . . It is the hour when my fatigue, my nervous insomnia can no longer remain mute, when I will throw my arms outside this feverish bed, and my naughty heels are already preparing to give a mischievous kick.

Then you will pretend to wake up! Then I shall be able to take refuge in you, with confused and unjust complaints, exasperated sighs, with clenched hands cursing the daylight that has already come, the night so soon over, the noises in the street . . . For I know quite well that you will then tighten your arms about me and that, if the cradling of your arms is not enough to soothe me, your kiss will become more clinging, your hands more amorous, and that you will accord me the sensual satisfaction that is the surcease of love, like a sovereign exorcism that will drive out of me the demons of fever, anger, restlessness . . . You will accord me sensual pleasure, bending over me voluptuously, maternally, you who seek in your impassioned loved one the child you never had.

[*Translated by Herma Briffault*]

Gray Days

❧❦❧

Leave me alone. I'm sick and cranky, like the sea. Tuck this tartan around my legs, but take away this steaming cup, with its bouquet of wet hay, lime blossom, stale violet . . . I don't want anything, I just want to turn my head away, and not see the sea anymore, nor the wind which runs, visible, in flurries on the sand, in spray on the sea. Sometimes it hums, patient and restrained, crouched down behind the dune, hidden beyond the horizon . . . Then it rushes out with a war cry, humanly rattling the shutters, pushing in under the door, in an impalpable fringe, the dust of its eternal tread . . .

Oh, how it hurts me! I no longer have one secret place left in me, not one sheltered corner, and my hands pressed flat against my ears do not keep the wind from getting through and chilling my brain . . . Naked, swept aside, routed, I tighten the tatters of my thoughts in vain; they escape me, beating, like a coat torn halfway off, like a gull held by its feet which frees itself by flapping its wings . . .

Leave me alone, you who come gently, pitiably, to place your hands on my forehead. I hate everything, and most of all the sea! Go and look at it, you who like it! It thrashes the terrace, it ferments, it shoots up in yellow foam, it glistens, the color of dead fish, it fills the air with a smell of iodine and fertile decay. Below the leaden waves, I can make out the abominable populace of feetless beasts, flat, slippery, icy . . . So you don't smell the flood and the wind carrying, as far as this room, the odor of rotting shellfish? . . . Oh, come back, you who can do almost everything for me! Don't leave me alone! Hold, beneath my nostrils, pinched and discolored by disgust, hold your perfumed hands, hold your fingers, dry and warm and delicate as mountain lavender . . . Come back! Stay close to me, order the sea to go away, make a sign to the wind, so that it will lie down on the sand, and play there in circles with the shells

. . . Make a sign: it will sit down on the dune, gently, and amuse itself, with a puff, by changing the shape of the moving . . .

Ah, you're shaking your head . . . You don't want to—you can't. Well then, go away, leave me helpless in the tempest, and let it knock down the wall and come and carry me off! Leave the room, so that I don't hear the useless sound of your footsteps anymore. Oh no, no caresses! Your magician's hands and your overwhelming gaze, and your mouth, which dissolves the memory of other mouths, would be powerless today. Today I long for someone who possessed me before all others, before you, before I was a woman.

I belong to a country which I have left. You cannot change the fact that there, at this moment, a whole canopy fragrant with forests is opening up to the sun. Nothing can change the fact that at this moment the deep grass there laps the foot of the trees, with a delicious and soothing green for which my soul thirsts . . . Come, you who do not know it, come let me tell you in a whisper: the fragrance of the woods in my country equals the strawberry and the rose! You would swear, when the bramble patches there are in bloom, that a fruit is ripening somewhere, over there, here, close by, an elusive fruit one inhales through wide-open nostrils. You would swear, when autumn penetrates and bruises the fallen foliage, that an overripe apple had just fallen, and you search for it and you smell it, here, over there, close by . . .

And if, in June, you passed between the new-mowed meadows, at the hour when the moon streams down on the round haystacks which are my country's dunes, you would feel, with the first whiff of that fragrance, your heart unfold. You would close your eyes, with that grave pride with which you veil your sensuousness, and you would let your head fall, with a muted sigh . . .

And if, one summer's day, you were to arrive in my country, at the back of a garden I know, a garden black with greenery and without flowers, and if you would see, off in the distance, a round mountain turn blue where the rocks, the butterflies, and the thistles are tinted with the same mauve and dusty azure, you would forget me, and you would sit down, never to move from there again till the end of your days.

There is also, in my country, a valley narrow as a cradle where in the evenings there stretches out and floats a stream of mist, a fine, white, living mist, a graceful specter of fog lying on the humid air . . . Enlivened by a gentle undulation, it melts into itself and becomes, by turns, a cloud, a sleeping woman, a languorous snake, a horse with a neck like a chimera's . . . If you stay too late, leaning toward it over the narrow valley, to drink in the cold air which carries this loving mist like a soul, a shudder will seize you, and all night your dreams will be mad . . .

One thing more, put your hand in mine: if you were to follow, in my country, a little path I know of, yellow and bordered with burning pink foxglove, you would think you were climbing the enchanted path which leads away from life . . . The bounding song of the velvet-furred hornets leads you to it and beat in your ears like the very blood of your heart, as far as the forest, up there, where the world ends . . . It is an ancient forest, forgotten by men, and exactly like paradise, listen now, for . . .

How pale you are and with such big eyes! What did I say to you? I don't know anymore . . . I was speaking, I was speaking about my country, in order to forget the sea and the wind . . . And here you are pale, with jealous eyes . . . You call me back to you, you can feel how far away I am . . . I must retrace my steps, I must once more tear up, all my roots, which bleed . . .

Here I am! Once again I belong to you. I wanted only to forget the wind and the sea. I spoke in a dream . . . What did I say to you? Don't believe it! No doubt I told you of a country of wonders, where the savor of the air intoxicates? . . . Don't believe it! Don't go there: you would search for it in vain. You would see only a rather sad countryside, darkened by the forests, a poor and peaceful village, a humid valley, a bluish and bare mountain which cannot feed even the goats . . .

Take me back! I've come back. Where did the wind go, while I was away? In what hollow of the dunes is it sulking, wearily? A sharp ray of light, squeezed between two clouds, pricks the sea and ricochets off here, into this flask where it does its cramped dance . . .

Throw aside this tartan, it's suffocating me; look! the sea is already turning green . . . Open the window and the door, and let us run toward the gilded end of this gray day, for I want to gather on the beach the flowers of your country brought here by the waves, imperishable flowers strewn about like petals of pink mother-of-pearl, O shells . . .

[Translated by Matthew Ward]

The Last Fire

❧❦❧

Kindle, in the hearth, the last fire of the year! The sun and the flame together will illuminate your face. Beneath your gesture, an ardent bouquet shoots up, ribboned with smoke, but I no longer recognize our winter fire, our arrogant and chatty fire, fed with bundles of dry wood and splendid stumps. That is because a more powerful star, having entered with a flash through the open window, has been living as master of our room since this morning . . .

Look, the sun cannot possibly favor other gardens as much as ours! Look closely! For nothing here compares to our garden of last year, and this year, still young and shivering, is already busy changing the decor of our sweet, secluded life . . . It is lengthening each branch of our pear trees with a horned and glossy bud, each lilac bush with a tuft of pointed leaves . . .

Oh, look how big they're getting, especially the lilacs! Come May, you will not be able to smell their flowers, which last year you kissed as you passed, except by rising up on the tips of your toes, you will have to lift your hands to lower their clusters toward your mouth . . . Look closely at the shadow, on the sand of the path, drawn by the delicate skeleton of the tamarisk: next year, you will not recognize it anymore . . .

And the violets themselves, budding as if by magic tonight, do you recognize them? You lean over, and like me, you are astonished; aren't they bluer this spring? No, no, you're mistaken, last year they looked less dark to me, an azured mauve, don't you remember? . . . You protest, you shake your head with your serious laughter, the green of the new grass lightens the lustrous bronze water of your gaze . . . More mauves . . . no, more blues . . . Stop this teasing! Rather carry to your nose the unchanging fragrance of these changing violets and watch, while inhaling the philter which dispels the years, watch like me the springs of your childhood rise up and quicken before you . . .

More mauves . . . no, more blues . . . I can see meadows, deep woods, which the first outburst of buds mists over with an elusive green, cold streams, forgotten springs drunk up by the sand as soon as they are born, Easter primroses, daffodils with the saffron-colored heart, and violets, violets, violets . . . I can see a silent little girl whom spring had already enchanted with a wild happiness, with a bittersweet and mysterious joy . . . A little girl imprisoned by day in a schoolhouse, and who exchanged toys and pictures for the first bouquets of violets from the woods, tied with a red cotton thread, brought by the little shepherdesses from the surrounding farms . . . Short-stemmed violets, white violets and blue violets, and white-blue violets veined with mauve mother-of-pearl, big anemic cowslip violets, which raise their pale, odorless corollas on long stems . . . February violets, blooming beneath the snow, ragged-edged, burned with frost, ugly, poor fragrant little things . . . O violets of my childhood! You rise up before me, all of you, you lattice the milky April sky, and the quivering of your countless little faces intoxicates me . . .

What are you thinking about, with your head tilted back? Your tranquil eyes are lifted toward the sun which they brave . . . Why, it is only to follow the flight of the first bee, sluggish, lost, in search of a honeyed peach-tree blossom . . . Chase it away! it will get stuck in the sap of that bud on the chestnut tree! No, it is lost in the blue air, the color of periwinkle milk, in this misty yet pure sky, which dazzles you . . . O you, who perhaps were satisfied with this little strip of azure, this rag of sky hemmed in by the walls of our narrow garden, dream that, somewhere in the world, there is an envied place where one discovers the whole sky! Dream, as you would dream of an unreachable kingdom, dream of the borders of the horizon, of how exquisitely pale the sky grows as it meets the earth . . . On this hesitant spring day, I can make out, over there, beyond the walls, the poignant line, slightly wavy, of what, as a child, I named land's end. It turns pink, then blue, in a gold sweeter at the heart than the sweet juice of a fruit . . . Do not feel sorry for me, beautiful pathetic eyes, for evoking so vividly what I long for! My voracious longing creates what it is missing and feeds on it. I am the one who smiles kindly at your idle hands, empty of flowers. Too soon, too soon! We and the bee and the peach-tree blossom are looking for spring too soon . . .

The iris is sleeping, furled into a little cornet under a triple greenish silk, the peony pierces the earth with a stiff branch of bright coral pink, and the rosebush still dares put out only suckers of a pink maroon, the bright color of an earthworm. Nevertheless, gather the brown gillyflower, ruddy, uncouth, and clad in solid velvet like a digger wasp, presaging the tulip . . . Do not look for the lily of the valley yet; between two valves of leaves, shaped like elongated mussel shells from which the sovereign odor will soon flow, its green Orient pearls mysteriously grow round . . .

The sun has walked on the sand. An icy breath, which feels like hail, is rising from the purple-and-blue east. The peach blossoms fly off horizontally. I'm so cold! The Siamese cat, a few minutes ago dead with ease on the mild warmth of the wall, suddenly opens her sapphire eyes set in her dark velvet mask . . . Crouched down, belly to the ground, she creeps off toward the house, her sensitive ears folded back on her head against the cold. Let's go now! I'm afraid of that violet, copper-edged cloud menacing the setting sun . . . The fire you lit a few minutes ago is dancing in the room, like a joyful, imprisoned animal watching for our return.

O last fire of the year! The last, the most lovely! Your peony pink, disheveled, fills the hearth with an endlessly blossoming shower of sparks. Let us lean toward it, offer it our hands, which its glow penetrates and bloodies. There is not one flower in our garden more beautiful than it, a tree more complicated, a grass more full of motion, a creeper so treacherous, so imperious! Let us stay here, let us cherish this changing god who makes a smile dance in your melancholy eyes . . . Later on, when I take off my dress, you will see me all pink like a painted statue. I will stand motionless before it, and in the panting glow my skin will seem to quicken, to tremble and move as in the hours when love, with an inevitable wing, swoops down on me . . . Let's stay! The last fire of the year invites us to silence, idleness, and tender repose. With my head on your breast, I can hear the wind, the flames, and your heart all beating, while at the black windowpane a branch of the pink peach tree taps incessantly, half unleaved, terrified, and undone like a bird in a storm . . .

[Translated by Matthew Ward]

A Fable:

The Tendrils of the Vine

In bygone times the nightingale did not sing at night. He had a sweet little thread of voice that he skillfully employed from morn to night with the coming of spring. He awoke with his comrades in the blue-gray dawn, and their flustered awakening startled the cockchafers sleeping on the underside of the lilac leaves.

He went to bed promptly at seven o'clock or half past seven, no matter where, often in the flowering grapevines that smelled of mignonette, and slept solidly until morning.

One night in the springtime he went to sleep while perched on a young vine shoot, his jabot fluffed up and his head bowed, as if afflicted with a graceful torticollis. While he slept, the vine's gimlet feelers—those imperious and clinging tendrils whose sharp taste, like that of fresh sorrel, acts as a stimulant and slakes the thirst—began to grow so thickly during the night that the bird woke up to find himself bound fast, his feet hobbled in strong withes, his wings powerless . . .

He thought he would die, but by struggling he managed after a great effort to liberate himself, and throughout the spring he swore never to sleep again, not until the tendrils of the vine had stopped growing.

From the next night onward he sang, to keep himself awake:

> *As long as the vine shoots grow, grow, grow,*
> *I will sleep no more!*

> *As long as the vine shoots grow, grow, grow,*
> *I will sleep no more!*

He varied his theme, embellishing it with vocalizations, became infatuated with his voice, became that wildly passionate and palpitating songster that one listens to with the unbearable longing to *see* him sing.

I have seen a nightingale singing in the moonlight, a free nightingale that did not know he was being spied upon. He interrupts himself at times, his head inclined, as if listening within himself to the prolongation of a note that has died down . . . Then, swelling his throat, he takes up his song again with all his might, his head thrown back, the picture of amorous despair. He sings just to sing, he sings such lovely things that he does not know anymore what they were meant to say. But I, I can still hear, through the golden notes, the melancholy piping of a flute, the quivering and crystalline trills, the clear and vigorous cries, I can still hear the first innocent and frightened song of the nightingale caught in the tendrils of the vine:

As long as the vine shoots grow, grow, grow . . .

Imperious, clinging, the tendrils of a bitter vine shackled me in my springtime while I slept a happy sleep, without misgivings. But with a frightened lunge I broke all those twisted threads that were already imbedded in my flesh, and I fled . . . When the torpor of a new night of honey weighed on my eyelids, I feared the tendrils of the vine and I uttered a loud lament that revealed my voice to me.

All alone, after a wakeful night, I now observe the morose and voluptuous morning star rise before me . . . And to keep from falling again into a happy sleep, in the treacherous springtime when blossoms the gnarled vine, I listen to the sound of my voice. Sometimes I feverishly cry out what one customarily suppresses or whispers very low—then my voice dies down to a murmur, because I dare not go on . . .

I want to tell, tell, tell everything I know, all my thoughts, all my surmises, everything that enchants or hurts or astounds me; but always, toward the dawn of this resonant night, a wise cool hand is laid across my mouth, and my cry, which had been passionately raised, subsides into moderate verbiage, the loquacity of the child who talks aloud to reassure himself and allay his fears.

I no longer enjoy a happy sleep, but I no longer fear the tendrils of the vine . . .

[*Translated by Herma Briffault*]

PART II

Backstage
at the Music Hall

*Was I, in those days, too susceptible to the
convention of work, glittering display, empty-
headedness, punctuality, and rigid probity which
reigns over the music hall? Did it inspire me
to describe it over and over again with a
violent and superficial love with all its
accompaniment of commonplace poetry?
Very possibly.*

ON TOUR

The Halt

❦≪⧬≫❦

Here we are at Flers . . . A bumpy, sluggish train has just deposited our sleepy troupe and abandoned us, yawning and disgruntled, on a fine spring afternoon, the air sharpened by a breeze blowing from the east, across a blue sky streaked with light cloud and scented with lilac just bursting into bloom.

Its freshness stings our cheeks, and we screw up our smarting eyes like convalescents prematurely allowed out. We have a two-and-a-half-hour wait before the train that is to take us on.

"Two and a half hours! What shall we do with ourselves?"

"We can send off picture postcards . . ."

"We can have some coffee . . ."

"We might play a game of piquet . . ."

"We could look at the town . . ."

The manager of our Touring Company suggests a visit to the park. That will give him time for forty winks in the buffet, nose buried in his turned-up collar, heedless of his peevish flock bleating around him.

"Let's go and see the park!"

Now we are outside the station, and the hostile curiosity of this small town escorts us on our way.

"These people here have never seen a thing," mutters the ingenue, in aggressive mood. "Anyhow, the towns where we don't perform are always filled with 'bystanders.' "

"And so are those where we do," observes the disillusioned duenna.

We are an ugly lot, graceless and lacking humility: pale from too-hard work, or flushed after a hastily snatched lunch. The rain at Douai, the sun at Nîmes, the salty breezes at Biarritz have added a green or rusty tarnish to our lamentable touring "outer garments," ample misery-hiding cloaks which still pretentiously boast an "English style." Trailing over the length and breadth of France, we have slept in our crumpled bonnets, all of us except the *grande coquette*, above whose head wave pompously—stuck on the top of a dusty black velvet tray—three funereal ostrich plumes.

Today I gaze at these three feathers as if I had never seen them before; they look fit to adorn a hearse, and so does the woman beneath them.

She seems out of keeping in the "town where we don't perform," rather ludicrous, with her Bourbon profile and her recurrent "I don't know why everyone tells me I resemble Sarah! What do you think?"

A gay little squall tugs at our skirts as we turn the corner into a square, and the carefully waved tresses of the ingenue's peroxide hair stream out in the wind. She utters a shriek as she clutches her hat, and I can see across her forehead—between eyebrows and hair—a carelessly removed red line, the trace of last night's makeup!

Why have I not the strength to look away when the duenna's bloomers brave the light of day! They are tan-colored bloomers and fall in folds over her cloth booties! No mirage could distract my attention from the male star's shirt collar, grayish white, with a thin streak of "ocher foundation" along the neckline. No enchanted drop curtain of flowers and tremulous leafage could make me overlook the comic's pipe, that fat, old, juicy pipe; the fag end stuck to the undermanager's lip; the purple ribbon, turning black, in the makeup man's buttonhole; the senior lead's matted beard, ill dyed and in part discolored! They are all so crudely conspicuous in the "town where we don't perform"!

But what about myself? Alas, what made me dawdle in front of the watchmaker's shop, allowing the mirror there time to show me my shimmerless hair, the sad twin shadows under my eyes, lips parched with thirst, and my flabby figure in a chestnut-brown tailor-made whose limp flaps rise and fall with every step I take! I look like a discouraged beetle, battered by the rains of a spring night. I look like a molting bird. I look like a governess in distress. I look . . . Good Lord, I look like an actress on tour, and that speaks for itself.

At last, the promised park! The reward justifies our long walk, dragging our tired feet, exhausted from keeping on our boots for eighteen hours a day. A deep, shady park; a slumbering castle, its shutters closed, set in the midst of a lawn; avenues of trees, just beginning to unfurl their sparse tender foliage; bluebells and cowslips studding the grass.

How can one help shivering with delight when one's hot fingers close around the stem of a live flower, cool from the shade and stiff with newborn vigor! The filtered light, kind to raddled faces, imposes a relaxed silence. Suddenly a gust of keen air falls from the treetops, dashes off down the alley chasing stray twigs, then vanishes in front of us, like an impish ghost.

We are tongue-tied, not for long enough.

"Oh, the countryside!" sighs the ingenue.

"Yes. If only one could sit down," suggests the duenna, "my legs are pressing into my body."

At the foot of a satin-boled beech we take a rest, inglorious and unattractive strollers. The men smoke; the women turn their eyes toward the blue perspectives of the alley, toward a blazing bush of rhododendrons, the color of red-hot embers, spreading over a neighboring lawn.

"For my part, the country just drains me . . ." says the comic with an unconcealed yawn, "makes me damned sleepy!"

"Yes, but it's healthy tiredness," decrees the pompous duenna.

The ingenue shrugs her plump shoulders. "Healthy tiredness! You make me sweat! Nothing ages a woman like living in the country, it's a well-known fact."

Slowly the undermanager extracts his pipe from his mouth, spits, then starts quoting: "A *melancholy feeling, not devoid of grandeur, surges from . . .*"

"Oh, shut up!" grumbles the *jeune premier*, consulting his watch as if terrified of missing a stage entrance.

A lanky boy, tall and pale-faced, who plays odd-job parts, is watching the movements of a little "dung beetle" with steel-blue armor, teasing it with a long straw.

I take deep, exhaustive breaths, trying to detect and recapture forgotten smells that are wafted to me as from the depths of a clear well. Some elude me, and I am unable to remember their names.

None of us laughs, and if the *grande coquette* hums softly to herself, it is bound to be a broken, soulful little tune. We don't feel at ease here: we are surrounded by too much beauty.

At the end of the avenue a friendly peacock appears, and behind his widespread fan we notice that the sky is turning pink. Evening is upon us. Slowly the peacock advances in our direction, like a courteous park-keeper whose task it is to evict us. Oh, surely we must fly! My companions are by now almost on the run.

"What if we missed it, children!"

We all know well enough that we shall not miss our train. But we are fleeing the beautiful garden, its silence and its peace, the lovely leisure, the solitude of which we are unworthy. We hurry toward the hotel, to the stifling dressing rooms, the blinding footlights. We scurry along, pressed for time, talkative, screeching like chickens, hurrying toward the illusion of living at high speed, of keeping warm, working hard, shunning thought, and refusing to be burdened with regrets, remorse, or memories.

Arrival and Rehearsal

❧✦❧

Toward eleven o'clock we arrive at X, a large town (whose name is of no consequence), where we are fairly well paid and have to work hard; the pampered audiences demand "Star Numbers" straight from Paris. It is raining, one of those mild spring showers that induce drowsiness and reduce one's calves to pulp.

The heavy lunch and the smoky atmosphere of the tavern, after a long night on the train, have turned me into a sulky little creature, reluctant to face the afternoon's work. But Brague stands no trifling.

"Shuffle your guts, come on. The rehearsal's at two sharp."

"Bother! I'm going back to the hotel to get some sleep! Besides, I don't like you addressing me in that tone of voice."

"Apologies, Princess. I simply wanted to beg you to have the extreme kindness of stirring up your wits. Fresh plasters await us!"

"What plasters?"

"Those of the 'Establishment.' We're opening cold tonight."

I had forgotten. This evening we are to inaugurate a brand-new music hall, called the Atlantic, or the Gigantic, or the Olympic—in any case, the name of a liner. Three thousand seats, an American bar, attractions in the outer galleries during the intervals, and a gipsy band in the main hall! We'll read about all these glories in tomorrow's papers. In the meantime, it makes no difference to us, except that we are certain to cough in the dressing rooms, since new central heating never works, making the place either too hot or not warm enough.

I meekly follow Brague, who elbows his way along the North Avenue, cluttered with clerks and shopgirls, hurrying, like ourselves, to their factories. A nipping March sun makes the rainy air smoke, and my damp hair hangs limp, as in a steambath. Brague's too-long overcoat flaps over his heels, gathering mud at each step. Taken at our face value we are just worth ten francs per evening: Brague, speckled with dirt; myself, drunk with sleep, sporting a Skye terrier's hairdo!

I let my companion guide me, and half dozing, I run over in my mind a few comforting facts and figures. The rehearsal is fixed for two o'clock sharp; with delays, we can count on half past four. One and a

half to two hours' work with the orchestra and we should be back at
the hotel about seven o'clock, there to dress, and dine, and return to the
joint by nine; by a quarter to twelve I'll be in my own clothes again and
just in time for a lemonade in the tavern. Well! Let's be reasonable and
hope, God willing, that within ten little hours I shall once again be in
a bed, with the right to sleep in it until lunchtime the next day! A bed,
a nice fresh bed, with smoothly drawn sheets and a hot-water bottle at
the end of it, soft to the feet like a live animal's tummy.

Brague turns left—I turn left; he stops short—I stop short.

"Good Lord!" he exclaims, "it isn't possible!"

Wide awake, I too judge at a glance that it really is not possible.

Huge dust carts, laden with sacks of plaster, obstruct the street.
Scaffolding screens a light-colored building that looks blurred and barely
condensed into shape, on which masons are hastily molding laurel
wreaths, naked females, and Louis XVI garlands above a dark porch.
Beyond this can be heard a tumult of inarticulate shouts, a battery of
hammers, the screeching of saws, as though the whole assembly of the
Niebelungen were busy at their forges.

"Is that it?"

"That is it."

"Are you certain, Brague?"

In reply I receive a fulminating glance that should have been
reserved solely for the Olympic's improvident architect.

"I just meant, you're certain we rehearse here?"

The rehearsal takes place. It passes all comprehension, but the
rehearsal takes place. We go on through the dark porch under a sticky
shower of liquid plaster; we jump over rolls of carpet in the process of
being laid, its royal purple already bearing marks of muddy soles. We
climb a temporary ladder leading, behind the stage floor, to the artistes'
dressing rooms, and finally we emerge, scared and deafened, in front of
the orchestra.

About thirty performers are disporting themselves here. Bursts of
music reach us during lulls in the hammering. On the conductor's
rostrum a lean, hairy, bearded human being beats time with arms, hands,
and head, his eyes turned upward to the friezes with the ecstatic serenity
of a deaf-mute.

There we are, a good fifteen "Numbers," bewildered, and already
discouraged. We have never met before, yet we recognize each other.
Here is the *diseur*, paid eight francs a night, who doesn't care a hoot
what goes on.

"I don't care a damn. I'm engaged as from this evening, and cash in
as from this evening."

There is the comic, with a face like a sneaky solicitor's clerk, who talks of "going to law," and foresees "a very interesting case."

There is the German family, athletes of the flying trapeze, seven Herculean figures with childish features, affrighted, amazed, already worried by the fear of being thrown out of work.

There stands the little "songstress," who's always "out of luck," the one who's always in "trouble with the management," and is supposed to have been robbed of "twenty thousand francs' worth of jewelry" last month, Marseilles! Naturally she is also the one who's lost her costume trunk on her way here and has had "words" with the proprietor of her hotel.

There is even, out in front, an extraordinary little man, looking worn, his cheeks furrowed by two deep ravines, a "star tenor" in his fifties, grown old in goodness knows what outlandish places. Indifferent to the noise, he rehearses implacably.

Every other minute he flings his arms wide to stop the orchestra, rushing from the double bass to the kettledrums, bent in two over the footlights. He looks like a stormy petrel riding the tempest. When he sings, he emits long shrill notes, metallic and malevolent, in an attempt to bring to life an obsolete repertory in which he impersonates, in turn, Pedro the Bandit, the lighthearted cavalier who forsakes Manon, the crazed villain and his sinister cackling at night on the moors. He scares me, but delights Brague, who instinctively reverts to his nomad fatalism.

Risking his luck in the general confusion, my companion lights the forbidden "fag" and lends an amused ear to the "vocal phenomenon," a dark lady who spins out almost inaudible high C's.

"She's killing, isn't she? Makes me feel as if I were listening through the wrong end of my opera glasses."

His laughter is infectious. Mysteriously a comforting cheerfulness starts to spread among us. We feel the approach of night, of the hour when the lamps are lit, the hour of our real awakening, of our glory.

"ANANKE!" suddenly shouts the litigious comic, a highbrow in his way. "If we perform, we perform; and if we don't . . . well, we don't."

With a ballet dancer's leap he skims over the edge of the stage box, ready to give the electricians a helpful hand. The "out of luck" girl goes to crack an acid drop with the Herculean septet. My drowsiness has left me and I settle down on a roll of linoleum, side by side with the "vocal phenomenon," who is all set to tell my fortune! Still another carefree hour ahead, empty of thought or plans.

Happy in our obtuse way, devoid of intuition or foresight, we give no thought to the future, to misfortune, to old age—or to the impending failure of this altogether too new and luxurious "Establishment," which is due to go smash one month from today, precisely on "Saint-Pay-Day."

A Bad Morning

Not one of us four feels fit to face the harsh light that falls from the glass roof like a vertical cold shower. It is nine in the morning; that is, dawn for the likes of us who go to bed late. Is it really possible that there can still exist, within a mile or so, a warm bed and a breakfast cup still steaming with the dregs of scented tea? I feel as if I shall never again lay myself down in my bed. I find this rehearsal room, the scene of our reluctant and too-early foregatherings, utterly depressing.

"Aah . . ." the lovely Bastienne yawns expressively.

Brague, the mimic, throws her a fearsome glance, as much as to say, "Serves you right." He is pale and ill shaven, whereas the lovely Bastienne, battered and shrunk to nothing inside her sentry box of a coat, would wring the heart of anyone other than a good companion by the pink swelling under her eyes and her bloodless ears. Palestrier, the composer, his nose bright purple on a wan countenance, is the personification of a drunk who has spent the night unconscious in a police station. As for myself! Good God, a saber slash across one cheek, limp skeins of hair, and skin left dry by my lazy bloodstream! One might think we are showing off, exaggerating our disgrace, in a fit of witless sadism. "Serves you right," say Brague's eyes, probing my sunken cheeks; while mine retort, "You're just such another wreck yourself."

Instead of shortening the rehearsal of our mime, we fritter time away. Palestrier starts on a salacious story, which could be funny, were it not that the dead cigarette he keeps masticating imparts a most obnoxious smell to his every word. The stove roars yet does not heat the hall, and we peer into its small mica window, like chilled savages hoping for some miraculous sunrise.

"What do they burn in it? I wonder," Palestrier hazards. "Newspaper logs, maybe, bound together with wire thread. I know how to make that stuff. I learned how from an old lady, the year I won my prize at the Conservatoire. She used to cough up three francs to make me play waltzes for her. There were times when I'd turn up, and she'd just say, 'We'll have no music today; my little bitch is nervy, and the piano puts her on edge!' So she would invite me to help with the fuel provision—nothing but newspapers and wire. It was she, too, who taught me how to burnish brass. I certainly didn't waste my time with her. In those days, providing I could feed, I would have clipped dogs and doctored cats!"

In the now glowing square of mica he gazes at the vision of his needy youth, the period when his talent struggled within him like a splendid, famished beast. As he sits staring, his pale-faced hungry youth becomes so alive that he reverts to the juicy slang of the suburbs, the drawling accent and thick voice; and sticking both hands in his pockets, he allows a shudder to shake his frame.

On this harsh winter morning we lack courage, lack all incentive to face the future. There is nothing inside us to burst into flame or blossom amid the dirty snow. Crouched and fearful, we are driven back by the hour, the cold, our rude awakening, the momentary malevolence in the air, to the most miserable, most humiliating moments of our past.

"The same goes for me," Brague breaks out suddenly. "Just to be able to eat one's fill . . . People who've always had plenty can't imagine what that means. I remember a time when I still had some credit at the pub, but never a chance to make any dough. When I drank down my glass of red wine . . . Well, I could have cried just at the thought of a fresh little crust to dip into it."

"The same goes for me . . ." The lovely Bastienne takes her cue. "When I was a mere kid—fifteen or sixteen—I'd all but faint in the mornings at the dancing class, because I hadn't had enough to eat; but if the ballet mistress asked me whether I was ill, I'd brag and answer: 'It's my lover, Madame, he's exhausted me.' A lover indeed! As if I'd even known what it meant to have one! She'd throw her arms in the air. 'Ah, you won't keep your queenly beauty for long! But what on earth have you all got in those bodies of yours?' What I had *not* got in my body was a good plateful of soup, and that's a cert."

She speaks slowly, with assiduous care, as if she were spelling out her reminiscences. Sitting with her knees wide apart, the lovely Bastienne has sunk into the posture of a housewife watching her pot boil. Her "queenly beauty" and her brassy smile have been discarded as if they were mere stage props.

A few slammed chords, a run up the scale by stumbling numb fingers, excite a superficial thrill. I shall have to move out of the posture of a hibernating animal, head inclined on one shoulder, hands tightly clasped like cold-stricken paws. I was not asleep. I am only, like my companions, emerging from a bitter dream. Hunger, thirst . . . they should be a full-time torture, simple and complete, leaving no room for other torments. Privation prevents all thought, and substitutes for any other mental image that of a hot sweet-smelling dish, and reduces hope to the shape of a rounded loaf set in rays of glory.

Brague is the first to jump to his feet. Rough-and-ready advice and inevitable invective assume, as they flow from his lips, a most familiar sound. What a string of ugly words to accompany so graceful an action! How many traces of trial and error are to be seen on the faces of the three mimes, where effort sets a too quickly broken mask! Hands that we compel to speak our lines, arms for an instant eloquent, seem suddenly to be shattered, and by their strengthless collapse transform us into mutilated statues.

No matter. Our goal, though difficult to attain, is not inaccessible. Words, as we cease to feel their urgency, become detached from us, like graceless vein stones from a precious gem. Invested with a subtler task than those who speak classical verse or exchange witticisms in lively prose, we are eager to banish from our mute dialogues the earthbound word, the one obstacle between us and silence—perfect, limpid, rhythmic silence—proud to give expression to every emotion and every feeling, and accepting no other support, no other restraint than that of Music.

The Circus Horse

"Dressing room 17, shall I find it along here?"

" . . ."

"Thank you very much, Madame. Coming straight in out of the street, one is quite dazed by the darkness of this corridor . . . So, as things are, it looks like our being neighbors!"

" . . ."

"True, it's nothing to write home about, but I've seen worse, as artistes' dressing rooms go. Oh, please, don't bother, I can drag it alone; it's my costume trunk. Anyway, my husband won't be long now: he's engaged at present in speaking to the management. You've turned your dressing room into something quite pretty, Madame. Ah! and there's your poster. I caught sight of it on the walls on our way from the station. A full-length poster, and in three colors, that always spells class. So you're the lady with the detective dogs?"

" . . ."

"Oh, sorry, I was confusing you. Pantomime, that's it, and very interesting too. It was actually in that line I first worked, before I took up the weights! Come to think of it, I had a little pink apron with pockets, and patent-leather shoes, something after the *soubrette* style, you know. Pantomime's not much of a bind, when all's said and done. One hand on your heart, a finger to your lips, which goes for 'I love you,' and then you take your bow, that's all there is to it! But I very soon got married, and off I went, to serious work!"

" . . ."

"Yes, weights are my job. I don't look the part? Because I'm so small, you mean? That's just what deceives people, but you'll see for yourself tonight. We're billed as 'Ida and Hector,' you've heard of us, surely? We've just done Marseilles and Lyons, on our way up from Tunis."

" . . . !"

"Lucky? Because we've done a fortnight in Tunis? I don't see what's lucky about that. Far rather play Marseilles and Lyons, or even St.-Etienne. Hamburg! There's a proper town for you! Naturally I'm not talking of big capitals, like Berlin or Vienna, places one can call big cities, especially when it comes to real slap-up establishments."

" . . . ?"

"Why, of course, we've moved around, gone places! You make me laugh, speaking so envious-like! As far as traveling goes, I'd willingly let you have my share, and no tears shed!"

" . . . ? "

"Not that I've had enough of it, but that I've just never cared for travel. I'm the cozy sort. So's my husband, Hector. But, you see, there's just the two of us in our show and the best we can hope for is three weeks in the same town, or a month at most, in spite of our number being very good to look at, very well presented. Hector with his athletics, all very flexible and light, and me with my weights, and a very special whirlwind waltz, very new, very stylish, to finish off our number. So— what more d'you want? We get around quite a bit, the way things go!"

" . . . !"

"It's Tunis that gets you, that's clear enough! And I wonder why, considering the establishment there's no great shakes!"

" . . . !"

"Oh, it's to see the town? and the surroundings too? Well, if that's your idea, I'm hardly the one to inform you; I've not seen much of it."

" . . . ?"

"Yes, I've been a little bit here, a little bit there. It's a big enough town. There are lots of Arabs. Then there are the small booths—*souks* they call them—along the covered streets; but they're all badly kept, crammed one on top of the other, and downright lousy too. Why, it made me itch all over when I had to clean and throw away half the stuff! All that's sold there, I mean, rugs that are not even new, cracked pottery, everything secondhand, so to speak. And the children, Madame! Scores of them, crawling on the bare ground, and half naked too! And what about the men! Handsome fellows, Madame, who stroll along, never in a hurry—with a little bunch of roses, or violets, in their hand, or even tucked behind their ear, like a Spanish dancer! And nobody puts them to shame."

" . . . ?"

"The country round about? I don't know. It's like here. The land is cultivated. When the weather's good it's quite pretty."

" . . . ?"

"What sort of plants? Exotic? Oh, yes, like in Monte Carlo? Yes, yes there are palm trees. And also little flowers that I don't know the names of. And then, lots of thistles. The people over there pick them and stick them onto long thorns, pretending they smell like white carnations. White carnations may be all right for you, but for me, smells just give me a headache!"

" . . . ?"

"No. I've not seen nothing else. What do you take us for? We have our work, and that comes first. My routine in the morning, to start with, then a friction, then my complete toilet, and by then it's breakfast time. Coffee and the daily papers, then I get busy with my work. D'you think it's a joke to keep two people spotless, underwear and all, without mentioning our stage tights and costumes? I couldn't stand a stain or a missing stitch . . . that's how I am! Between St.-Etienne and Tunis I made myself six slips and six pairs of underpants, and I'd have completed the dozen, had Hector not fancied he needed flannel waistcoats! And then there's the dressing room to be kept clean, the hotel room has to be tidied up, expenses accounted for, money to be banked. I'm very particular, you see."

" . . . "

"Now you, who talk so much of travel, now you just take Bucharest! Never did a town bring me such trouble! The Establishment had recently been renovated and the damp plasterwork sweated. At night, what with the heating and the lights, the walls of our dressing room simply dripped water. I noticed that at once, and lucky I did, for imagine the mess it would have made of our stage costumes! You should have seen me every evening, at midnight, dragging about my two sequinned dresses, the ones I wear in the whirlwind waltz, one in each hand, on a couple of coat hangers! And every day at nine I had to bring them back. Now, please tell me if I could come away with happy memories of that town."

"...?"

"Oh, you just leave me alone with your travel mania! You won't make me change my mind on that subject, and I've visited enough countries, I can tell you. Towns, the world over, they're all the same! You'll always find, first, a music hall to work in; second, a tavern, Munich-style, to eat in; third, a bad hotel to sleep in. When you've been all around the world, you'll think like me. Over and above that, there are nasty people everywhere, so one has to learn to keep one's distance; and one can count oneself lucky when one comes into contact, like today, with people who are good company and have class."

"...!"

"But not at all! No flattery intended, believe me. *Au revoir*, Madame, until tonight. When you've finished your number, I'll have the pleasure of introducing you to my husband, who will be as delighted as I was myself to make your acquaintance."

The Workroom

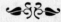

A small third-floor dressing room, little more than a cramped closet with a single window opening on a narrow side street. An overheated radiator dries up the air, and every time the door opens, the funnel of the spiral staircase belches up, like a chimney stack, all the heat from the lower floor, saturated with the human odor of some sixty performers and the even more potent stench of a certain little place, situated nearby.

Five girls are packed in here, with five rush-seated stools jammed between the makeup table and the recess in which are hung, hidden and protected by a grayish curtain, their costumes for the revue. Here they live every night from seven-thirty till twenty minutes after midnight and, twice a week, for matinees, from half past one till six. Anita is the first to come in, rather out of breath, but with cool cheeks and moist lips. She shrinks back and exclaims: "Lord above! It's not possible to stay in here, it turns you up!"

She soon becomes accustomed to it, coughs a little, then doesn't give it another thought, since she only just has time to undress and make up. Her frock and underslip are removed quicker than a pair of gloves and can be hung up anywhere. But there comes a moment when she curbs her haste and her face assumes a serious expression. Anita cautiously extracts two long pins from her hat, and carefully sticks them back through the same holes. Then, under the four turned-up corners of an outspread newspaper, she religiously protects that garish yet mingy edifice that contrives to look like a combination of a Red Indian headdress, a Phrygian cap, and a dressed salad. For everyone knows that grease powder, flying in clouds from shaken puffs, spells death to velvet and feathers.

Wilson, the second on the scene, enters with a vacant look, hardly awake.

"Listen! Hell! I'd got something to tell you . . . I must have swallowed it on the way."

She, too, takes off her hat according to established rites, then lifts a fringe of fair hair off her forehead, to disclose an incompletely healed scar.

"You can't imagine how my head still throbs from it!"

"Serves you right," interrupts Anita in a dry tone. "If you will go and get half the scenery on your 'nut,' and if this happens in a joint where the managers are mean enough to send you home with tuppence worth of ether on a handkerchief—without even paying the cab fare or the doctor's fee—so that you have to stay put, half dead, for a whole week, and if you haven't even the self-respect to sue the management, then you do not complain, you just shut up. Now, had it been me!"

Wilson does not reply, too busied—her features distorted by the effort—in trying to detach a long golden hair that is wickedly sticking to her wound. Besides, it is useless to answer back Anita, a born termagant and anarchist, always ready to "sue" or "get the story into the newspapers."

The three others arrive simultaneously: Régine Tallien, whose plump little housemaid's figure, abundantly furnished in front and behind, ironically casts her for page-boy parts, or "stylish male impersonations"; Marie Ancona, so dark she really believes herself a genuine Italian; and little Garcin, an obscure supernumerary, rather alarming, who flashes dark glances partly insincere, partly apprehensive, and is as thin as a starved cat.

They don't bother to pass the time of day, they meet too often. No rivalry exists between them because, with the exception of Maria Ancona, who has a small solo in the tarantella, they all vegetate in chorus routine. Nor is it Maria Ancona's "part" that little Garcin envies her, but much more the brand-new dyed fox fur around her neck. They are not friends either, yet from being thus thrown together, crowded and almost choked to death in their cribbed cabin, they have developed a sort of animal satisfaction, the cheerfulness of creatures in captivity. Maria Ancona sings as she unfastens her garters, held together by safety pins, and her stays with broken laces. She laughs to find that her slip is torn under the arm, and nettled by Régine Tallien, who wears the embroidered linen and stout cotton corsets of a well-behaved maidservant, she retorts: "Can't help it, my dear. I'm an artist by temperament! And d'you suppose I can keep my underwear clean with that horrible tin armor of mine!"

"Then do like me," whispers sly little Garcin; "don't wear any, any underslips, I mean."

She is clothed only in a pair of trellised tights, all gold and pearls, with two openwork metal discs stuck over her nonexistent breasts. The rough edges of her jeweled ornaments, the coarsely punched copper pendants, the clinking chain armor she wears, scratch and mark her lean and apparently insensitive bare skin without her even noticing.

"Just admit," shouts Anita, "that the management ought to provide the slips worn on the stage! But you're all so thin-skinned, you're not even capable of claiming your dues!"

She turns a half-made-up face toward her companions, a dead-white mask with bright red goggles, that makes her look like a Polynesian warrior, and without even interrupting her tirade, she ties around her head a filthy silk rag, all that remains of a "wig-kerchief," intended to protect the hair from the brilliantine on the stage wigs.

"It's like this tattered duster I've got on my nut," continues Anita. "Yes, yes, go on saying it disgusts you, but I-will-not-change-it! The management owes me one, and this *thing* can jolly well rot on my head, I will not replace it! My dues, that's all I care about."

Not one of them is carried away by her anarchic rage, knowing it to be merely verbal, and even little Wilson, wounded as she is, simply shrugs her shoulders.

The hour flies by, the unbreathable dryness of the air is now permeated by a hot dormitory smell. From time to time a dresser squeezes sideways into the room, somehow managing to move about, fastening a hook, tying the strings of stage tights or the ribbons of a Greek buskin. Régine Tallien and Wilson have already fled, halberd in hand, to their medieval parade. Anita hastens behind Maria Ancona, because a voice from the staircase is calling out: "Ladies of the Tarantella, have I to come in person to fetch you?"

Little Garcin, whose asexual graces are kept in store for a "Byzantine Festival," now remains alone. Out of her sordid handbag she extracts a thimble, a pair of scissors, a piece of needlework already begun, and, perched on her rush-seated stool, she begins to sew with avid concentration.

"Oh!" cries Maria Ancona, returning hot and out of breath. "So she's already settled down to it!"

"What d'you expect," jealously echoes Anita, "for all the work she has to do on the stage!"

The sound of a cavalcade on the stairs and a shrill distant bell announce the end of the first act, bringing back Wilson, still slightly dazed and with an aching forehead, and Régine Tallien with her red man-at-arms wig. The daily break for the intermission, instead of bringing relaxation, seems to excite the girls. Off fly bicolored tights and Neapolitan skirts, to be replaced by spongy dressing gowns or cotton kimonos, mottled with the stains of cosmetics. Bare feet, unexpectedly bashful, grope under the makeup table for shapeless old slippers, while hands, pale or red, suddenly become cautious in unrolling lengths of linen and bits of imitation lace. They all inquisitively bend over Maria Ancona's unfinished "combination," the cynical little garment of a poor prostitute, outrageously transparent, sewn with broad, clumsy stitches. Little Garcin smocks fine muslin with the patience of a persistent mouse. Régine fills in her time hemming white handkerchiefs.

The five of them, now seated on their high rush stools, are busy and quiet, as if they had at last reached their goal at the end of the day. This half hour is theirs. And during this half hour they allow themselves, as a respite, the candid illusion of being cloistered young women who sew.

They suddenly fall silent, pacified by some unknown spell, and even the rowdy Anita gives no thought to her "dues," and smiles mysteriously at a tablecloth embroidered in scarlet. In spite of their gaping wraps, of their high-pitched knees, of the insolent rouge still blossoming on their cheeks, they have the chaste attitude and bent backs of sedate seamstresses. And it is from the lips of little Garcin, naked in her beaded-net pants, that a childish little song, keeping time with her busy needle, involuntarily finds its way.

Matinee

"You see all those people in the char-à-bancs, don't you?—and those others in four-wheelers?—and again those in taxis? And you see the ones over there, in shirt sleeves on their doorsteps, and those sitting outside the cafés? Very well, then! All that crowd do not have to play in a matinee. D'you hear me?"

"... give a damn."

"But *you* are playing in a matinee!"

"Don't go on so, Brague!"

"I am playing in a matinee, too. We are playing in a matinee. On Thursdays, and on Sundays too, we have a matinee."

I could slap him—were it not for the effort of lifting my arm. He continues, relentlessly. "There are also those who are not here, those who decamped to the country yesterday evening and won't come back to town till Monday. They're out under the trees, or taking a dip in the Marne. Well, they're doing what they're doing, but . . . *they are not appearing in a matinee!*"

As our taxi jerks to an abrupt stop, the dry wind, which had been baking our faces, suddenly drops. I feel the pavement burning through the thin soles of my shoes. My cruel companion stops talking and purses his mouth, as much as to say: "Now it's becoming serious."

At the dark and narrow stage door there is still a trace of musty coolness. The doorman, dozing in his chair, wakes up as we pass to brandish a newspaper.

"Ninety-six in the shade, eh!"

He throws this figure at us, in triumph, yet scared, as if it were the death roll in some grand-scale catastrophe. But we pass in silence, sparing of speech and movement, in fact jealous of this old man who keeps watch in a shady paradise, a paradise invaded by stale cellar smells and ammonia, on the threshold of our own inferno. Anyhow, what do ninety-six degrees mean? Ninety-six, or ninety-six thousand, it's all the same. We have no thermometer up there on our second floor. Ninety-six degrees on the tower of St.-Jacques? And what will it rise to during this afternoon's matinee? How high will it be in my dressing room, with its two windows, two right royal windows facing due south and shutterless?

"There's no saying," sighs Brague, as he enters his cubicle, "we must jolly well be 'above normal' up here!"

After a dismal glance, devoid even of entreaty, at the panes set ablaze by the sun, I let my clothes drop off without any relief: my skin can no longer look forward to the biting little draft between door and window that only a month ago nipped my bare shoulders.

A strange silence reigns within our crowded cells. Opposite mine, a half-open door allows me a glimpse of the backs of two seated men, in dirty bathrobes, bending over their makeup table without a word passing. The electric bulb burns above their heads, anemically pink in the radiant light of three o'clock in the afternoon.

A shrill note, a prolonged piercing cry, rises up to us from the depths of the theater. This means that there really is at this very moment down there on the stage a rigidly corsetted woman, swathed in the long, tight-fitting dress so dear to lady novelists, who has achieved the miracle of smiling, singing, and reaching the gods with her high-pitched C, which makes my parched tongue thirst for slices of lemon, for unripe gooseberries, for all things acid, fresh, and green.

What a sigh answers mine from a nearby dressing room, such a tragic sigh, almost a sob! Surely it must come from that chit of a girl barely recovered from a bout of bronchial fever, the fragile little balladsinger, exhausted by this savage heat, who peps herself up by drinking iced absinthes.

My cold cream is unrecognizable, reduced to a cloudy oil that smells of gasoline. A melted paste, the color of rancid butter, is all that remains of my white grease foundation. The liquefied contents of my rouge jar might well be used "to color," as cooks say, a dish of *pêches Cardinal*.

For better or worse, here I am at last, anointed with these multicolored fats, and heavily powdered. I still have time, before our mimodrama, to survey a face on which glow, in the sunshine, the mixed hues of purple petunia, begonia, and the afternoon blue of a morning glory. But the energy to move, walk, dance, and mime, where can I hope to find that?

The sun has sunk a little, releasing one of my windows which I hasten to fling open; but the sill burns my hands, and the narrow mews below reeks of rotting melons and unwatered gutters. Two hatless women have pitched their chairs in the middle of the street and stare up at the powdery sky, like animals about to be drowned.

A hesitant step slowly mounts the stairs. I turn around at the moment when a frail little dancer dressed as a Red Indian reaches our landing: she is quite pale despite her makeup, and her temples are black with sweat. We look at each other without uttering a word. Then she lifts toward me the hem of her embroidered costume, weighted down with glass beads, strips of leather, metal, and pearls, and murmurs as she goes back to her dressing room, "And with all these trappings it must weigh eighteen pounds!"

The call bell is the only sound to break the silence. On my way down I pass stagehands, half stripped and mute. Girls of the Andalusian ballet cross the foyer in full costume, without any greeting other than a ferocious glance at the great mirror. Brague, suffering agonies under the black cloth of his short waistcoat and skin-tight Spanish trousers, whistles out of sheer vanity to show that he's "not going to snuff out like the others!" An enormously fat boy, round as a barrel in his innkeeper's clothes, looks about to suffocate and terrifies me: supposing he were to die on the stage!

Somehow or other, the mysterious forces of discipline and musical rhythm, together with an arrogant and childish desire to appear handsome, to appear strong, all combine to lead us on. To be truthful, we perform exactly as we always do! The prostrated public, invisible in the darkened auditorium, notices nothing that it should not, the short breaths that parch our lungs, the perspiration that soaks us and stains our silk costumes, the mustache of sweat and drying powder that so tactlessly gives me a virile upper lip. Nor must it notice the exhausted expression on its favorite comic's face, the wild glint in his eyes as though he were ready to bite. Above all, none must guess at the nervous repulsion that makes me shrink back at touching and feeling only damp hands, arms, cheeks, or necks! Damp sleeves, glued hair, sticky tumblers, handkerchiefs like sponges—everything is moist or ringing wet, myself included.

Once the curtain has fallen we separate hastily, somehow ashamed of being the wretched, steaming flock we are. We hurry on down to the street, yearning for the dry dusty evening, toward the illusion of coolness shed by the already high-riding moon, fully visible, yet warm and lusterless.

The Starveling

❧

In the first act of the play in which we are touring he takes the part of a profligate; whereas, in the third, he is transformed by a red wig and a neat white apron into a waiter.

When the time comes to catch our train, at dawn or late at night—for this is a strenuous tour, playing thirty-three towns in thirty-three days—he never fails to arrive late and in a rush, so that all I knew of him was a slim figure with his overcoat flying, agitated beyond measure by his race against time. The manager and my companions would wave their arms and shout at him.

"Come on, Gonzalez, for God's sake! One of these days you'll miss it for good!"

He would float into the gaping second-class carriage as on the wings of a whirlwind, so that I never had time to see his face.

Then, the other day, at the station at Nîmes, when I suddenly exclaimed, "There's a scent of hyacinths! Who smells of hyacinths?," with a polite, restrained little gesture he turned to offer me the nosegay that adorned his buttonhole.

Since that day I have taken more notice of him, and like the others, I raise my arms in despair when he arrives late, shouting in chorus: "Come on, Gonzalez, for God's sake!" and I even recognize his face.

A sallow little face, so biliously pale that one imagines his foundation makeup has penetrated his skin. A face all bumps and hollows, cheekbones protruding above deep-sunk cheeks, the eyebrows too thick, the mouth thin above an obstinate chin.

But why, I wonder, does he never remove his overcoat, which is faded near the shoulders from last year's sun and rain? A glance at his shoes provides the answer. Gonzalez exposes to the daylight, and my inspection, unspeakably shoddy footwear, the cracks and crevices of their once-gleaming patent leather only aggravated by the cheap polish of third-rate inns. His shoes lead my thoughts to his trousers, ever mysterious under the ample folds of his overcoat, and to his shirt collar, mercifully all but hidden behind an amazing black cravat wound thrice around his neck.

His clumsily mended cotton gloves refute any illusion I may have that this little comedian affects the "showing-off indifference" of a young bohemian, for they spell destitution. Once again I am confronted with genuine poverty. When, if ever, shall I cease to find it? Now I pay real attention to this boy, wait for his breathless arrival, notice that he does not smoke, carries no umbrella, that his suitcase is falling to pieces, and that he discreetly watches for the moment when he can pick up the daily paper after I have read it through and dropped it.

Warned by some bashful instinct, he in his turn now takes notice of me. He openly smiles at me, and presses in his warm skinny hand the fingers I extend toward him; yet he is careful, a moment later, to vanish and make himself as scarce as possible. He never joins us when we lunch in station buffets, and I cannot remember having seen Gonzalez at the same table as the less moneyed of our good companions for the "light meal at one franc fifty." Once, he performed his disappearing act at Tarascon, while we were devouring an omelet cooked in oil, tepid veal, and colorless chicken. He came back when the acorn-flavored coffee was being served; he came back spare, gay, carefree—"I've been to have a look at the neighborhood"—a pink carnation in his mouth and croissant crumbs in the folds of his clothes.

I confess I'm worried about this boy; I don't dare to make further inquiries. I set childish traps for him.

"Will you have some coffee, Gonzalez?"

"Thanks, but it's forbidden me. Nerves . . . you know."

"That's not nice of you! The round's on me today. You surely won't be the only one to refuse?"

"Oh, well, if you make it a question of comradeship . . ."

Another day, at Lourdes, I bought two dozen little hot sausages.

"Come on, children, don't let them get cold! Buck up, Gonzalez, or you'll miss the lot! Snatch those two quickly, before Hautefeuille pounces on them: he's quite fat enough as it is."

I watched him eat, with the sneaking curiosity of one expecting that some movement on his part, a famished sigh, might betray his ill-satisfied hunger. Finally, I decided to put a casual question to our manager.

"How much is Martineau getting nowadays? And that thinggummy over there, young Gonzalez?"

"Martineau is paid fifteen francs, because he plays in the curtain raiser as well as the main piece. Gonzalez gets only twelve francs a night—we're not on a Grand Duke's tour!"

Twelve francs . . . Let's see how I reckon his expenses! He sleeps in joints at one-fifty to two francs per night. Ten percent for valeting, a problematical *café-au-lait*, but count two meals at two-fifty for the price of one. Let's add another franc and a half for trams and buses . . . plus the gentleman's flowered buttonholes! Well then, this young man can live within it, he can exist quite comfortably. I felt relieved and in the evening, during the interval, I shook his hand as if he'd just inherited a fortune! Taking courage from the semidarkness and the fact that our faces were disguised by makeup, he allowed an anxious cry to escape his lips.

"It's drawing to a close, eh! Only thirteen more days! Oh, for a tour that would last a whole lifetime! How I dream of it!"

"You like your work as much as that?"

He shrugged his shoulders. "My work, my work! Naturally, I rather like it, but it's given me plenty of worries for my run . . . Besides, thirty-three days, it's short . . ."

"What d'you mean, short?"

"Short for what I want to do! Now, listen . . ."

He suddenly sat down beside me, on a dusty garden bench used for the last act, began to talk, began feverishly to tell me the story of his life.

"Now listen . . . I can really talk to you, can't I? You've been kind . . . a real good companion to me. I have to take back two hundred francs."

"Take back where?"

"To Paris . . . if I want to eat during the coming month, and the one after. I can't face going through all that I've endured a second time, my health won't stand it."

"You've been ill?"

"Ill, if you like. Being broke is a damned illness."

With a professional gesture he ran his forefingers along his false mustache, which is in the habit of getting unstuck, and averted his blue-rimmed sunken eyes.

"There's no shame in admitting it. I played the fool, left my father, who is a bookbinder, to get into the theater. That was two years ago. My father cursed me, then . . ."

"What d'you mean? Your father has . . ."

". . . Cursed me," Gonzalez repeated, with theatrical simplicity. "Cursed me, gave me a proper cursing. I found work with the Grenelle-les-Gobelins company. That's when I started not eating enough. When summer came, I hadn't a sou in my pocket. For six months I lived on the twenty-five francs a month an aunt of mine let me have . . . secretly."

"Good Lord! Twenty-five francs! How did you manage?"

He laughed, in a rather mad way, gazing straight in front of him.

"I don't know. It was plain murder, I don't know now how I got along. I no longer remember very clearly. My mind went blank. I remember I had a suit, one shirt, one collar, no change of anything . . . The rest I've forgotten."

He was silent for a moment while he extended both legs with care, to ease his already threadbare trousers over his knees.

"Then after that I had a few weeks in the *Fantaisies Parisiennes*, at the Comédie Mondaine. But the going was bad. You need a stomach for that and I no longer have one. The pay's so miserably small. I've got no name, no clothes, no craft outside the theater, no savings. I can't see myself making old bones!"

He laughed again, just as the spotlight came on, throwing into sharp relief his fleshless head, his hard cheekbones, the dark sockets of his eyes, and the too-wide slit of his mouth, for the lips were swallowed up by the contraction of his laughter.

"So, you see, then, I have to take back two hundred and twenty francs. With that sum I'm safe for two months at least. This tour was like winning a prize in a lottery, I can tell you . . . Have I bored you stiff with my stories?"

I had no time to answer him: the stage bell started to ring above our heads, and Gonzalez, incurably late, fluttered off to his dressing room with all the lightness of a dead leaf, with the airy macabre grace of a young skeleton, dancing.

Love

Because she is fair-haired and young, a rather skinny girl with huge blue eyes, she fulfills exactly all the requirements we expect of a "little English dancer." She speaks some French, with all the vigor of a young duckling, and to articulate these few words of our language she expends a useless energy which brings a flush to her cheeks and makes her eyes sparkle.

When she emerges from the dressing room she shares with her companions next to mine, and walks down toward the stage, ready made-up and in costume, I can't distinguish her from the other girls, for she strives, as is most fitting, to be just an impersonal and attractive little English dancer in a revue! When the first girl comes out, followed by the second, and the third, then the others up to the ninth, they all greet me, as they pass, with the same happy smile, a similar nod of the head that sets their pinkish-blond false curls bobbing in the same way. The nine faces are painted with identical makeup, cleverly tinted with mauve around the eyes, while the lids are burdened, on each of their lashes, with such a heavy touch of mascara that it is impossible to distinguish the true color of the pupil.

But when they leave, at ten past midnight, having hastily wiped their cheeks with the corner of a towel and repowdered them chalky white, their eyes still barbarously enlarged, or when they come to rehearse in the afternoon, punctually at one o'clock, I immediately recognize little Gloria, a genuine blonde, with two puffs of frizzy hair tied around the temples with a strip of black velvet inside her hideous hat like a bird nesting in an old basket. Her upper lip protrudes a little from two pointed canines, and this makes her look, in repose, as if she were sucking a white sugared almond.

I don't know why I noticed her. She is not as pretty as Daisy, that dark-haired demon, always in tears or in a rage, who dances with devilish gusto and then escapes to the top of the staircase, whence she spits out objectionable English expletives. She is less attractive than the awful Edith, who exaggerates her accent to raise a laugh and, with assumed innocence, utters French indecencies, well aware of their meaning.

Yet Gloria, who is dancing for the first time in France, compels my attention. She is sweet and touching, in an anonymous way. She has never called the ballet master "damned fool," and her name never appears on the board where the list of fines are posted. Admittedly, she shrieks when she runs up or down the two flights of steps leading to the stage; but she shrieks like the others, instinctively, and because a bunch of English girls, who change their costumes four times between nine o'clock and midnight, cannot run up and down staircases without yelling like Red Indians or singing inordinately loud. Gloria, therefore, lets her comically youthful falsetto mingle with the inevitable hubbub and she equally well holds her own in the girls' common dressing room, separated from mine by a rickety wooden partition.

These traveling showgirls have turned their rectangular closet into a real gipsy encampment. Red and black cosmetic pencils roll all over their makeup table, covered at one end with brown paper and at the other with a tattered old towel. The slightest draft would blow away the postcards fastened to the walls with pins stuck in at a slant. The jar of rouge, the Leichner eyebrow pencil, the woolen powder puff, could all be carried away in a knotted handkerchief, and these little girls, off and away in a couple of months, will leave fewer traces of their passage here than would a troop of wandering Romanies, whose halting place is marked by round patches of singed grass and the flaky ashes of fires kindled with stolen wood.

"——'k you," says Gloria in an educated voice.

"The pleasure is mine," our good companion Marcel politely replies. Though billed as a tenor, he may well be dancing this coming month or even performing in a drama at the Gobelins or in a revue at Montrouge.

As if by mere chance, Marcel waits on the landing for the return of the noisy flock of English showgirls. By apparent chance, too, Gloria comes up last and lingers for a moment, time enough to fumble with awkward grace in the paper bag of lemon drops our good companion offers her.

I take careful note of the slow progress of this idyll. He is young, famished, ardent, firmly determined not to "break down," and looks—in spite of his well-worn tails and artificial lily-of-the-valley buttonhole—like a handsome, crafty, working-class boy. But Gloria's strange foreign manners baffle him. With a French chum, a little Paris music-hall sparrow, he would already know where he stood—things work, or they don't—but he simply can't fathom this funny *anglishe*. She may rush off the stage, disheveled and yelling, hastily unhooking her dress, yet when she reaches the landing she pulls herself together, straightens her face to accept and acknowledge the proffered sweet with the dignified "——'k you" of a young lady in full evening dress.

She attracts him. She irritates him too. Sometimes he shrugs his shoulders as he watches her walk away, but I can feel that it is at himself he is poking fun. The other day he chucked into Gloria's large hat, held dangling by its ribbons, half a dozen tangerines, seized on at once by the horde of blond savages, who snatched at them with triumphant shrieks, loud laughter, and sharp nails.

This long flirtation exasperates the impatient French boy, lively and inconstant, whereas Gloria revels in its protraction. She now calls Marcel by his name, *Mâss'l*, and has given him a picture postcard of herself. Not the one in which she is dressed as a toddler with a hoop, or that on which she is disguised as a "Poulbot kid," with a hole in her pants—oh, no!—but the loveliest of all, presenting Gloria as a Medieval Lady wearing a high headdress, a quasi-regal Gloria.

They don't seem worried at being unable to talk to each other. With subtle shrewdness the boy sets out to be assiduous and unassuming. Have I not seen him kiss a thin little hand, one that was not withdrawn, a bony little paw, chapped by cold water and liquid white! But, on the sly, he looks at Gloria with indiscreet persistence, as if he were choosing in advance the proper place to implant a kiss. Once behind the closed door of the dressing room, she sings for him, then shouts his name, "*Mâss'l*," as if she were throwing him flowers.

In short, things go well: even too well . . . This quasi-mute idyll unfurls like a mimodrama, with no other music than Gloria's exuberant voice and no words but the name *Mâss'l*, diversified by love's number-less inflections. After the first radiant *Mâss'ls*, shouted on a slightly nasal note, I have heard lower *Mâss'ls*, provocative and tender, exacting too—and then, one fine day, came a tremulous *Mâss'l*, so low that it sounded like an entreaty.

Tonight, I fear, I am hearing it for the last time. At the head of the staircase, hovering on its top step, I find a forlorn little Gloria, with a distorted wig, crying humbly all over her makeup, and repeating under her breath, "*Mâss'l* . . . *Mâss'l* . . ."

The Hard Worker

❧≈❧

"Your arms, Hélène! Your arm control! That's the second time your hand has struck your head while you're dancing! I've told you again and again, my girl: the arms must curve like handles above your head, as if you were balancing a basket of flowers!"

Hélène answers with a sullen out-of-patience look only, and corrects the position of her arms. She's ready to launch forth again on the studio floor—a well-worn shiny parquet floor, battered by the raps of heels and the ballet master's wand—when she changes her mind, and cries out: "Are you still there, Robert?"

"Of course," replies a submissive voice from the other side of the door.

"Supposing you took the car and popped over to the furrier's and told him I won't be coming till tomorrow?"

No answer; but I hear the tap-tap of a walking stick and the sound of the front door being closed. "Robert" has gone.

"So much the better!" murmurs Hélène in a softened voice. "It exasperates me to feel he's there waiting for me and doing nothing."

Twice a week I sit through the last minutes of Hélène Gromet's dancing lesson: she is put through her paces from four to five, just before my own turn comes. She treats me more as a colleague than a friendly companion, much as if we were workers in the same factory; by which I mean that we talk little but seriously, and that sometimes she reveals her feelings with the same cool candor as when confiding in her masseuse or her pedicurist.

Hélène is not a real dancer, but a "little piece who dances." She made her music-hall debut last season, in a revue, and as her first attempt, she "flung" at her audience two scabrous little ditties, putting them across at the top of her brand-new, unsophisticated, brassy voice, without any of the simperings of false modesty, but with a perfectly straight face, and with an aggressive innocence that enchanted. Substantial offers of work, a no less substantial "friend," two motorcars, a string of pearls, and a mink coat were all showered on Hélène in one single stroke of luck—but her steady little head never wavered. She boasts of being a "hard worker," and sticks to her ungainly, plebeian name.

"Do you imagine I'm going to rechristen myself? A simple name, not too pretty, that's what puts you straight into the top class. Look at Badet and Bordin!"

All her entries amount to a miniature apotheosis. The subdued thunder of a motorcar heralds her approach, then she appears, weighed down under ermine and velvet, a trembling cloud of osprey feathers in her hat. A decisive and carefully devised makeup standardizes her youthful face under a mask of dead-white powder, with pink touches on the cheeks and chin. Her blued eyelids carry a heavy double fringe of lashes, stiff with mascara, and her teeth shine almost woundingly against the purplish lipstick that outlines her mouth.

"I know I'm young enough to do without all that muck," Hélène explains, "but it's now part of my array, and it's useful too. For like this I am made up for life. I'll have nothing to add when I'm twenty years older. Under this coating I can afford to look ill or to have tired eyes; it's as practical as a disguise. For you'd better know, I do nothing without good reason."

This young utilitarian scares me. She takes her lesson as she would swallow a glass of cod-liver oil: conscientiously, and to the bitter end. Nevertheless, it is a pleasure to watch her exercise, flexible and well balanced on her clever legs. She is pretty, and touchingly young. What then does she lack? For she does lack something.

"Your smile, Hélène, your smile!" exclaims the ballet mistress. "Don't put on your cashier's face. You don't seem to realize that you're dancing, my child."

The former ballerina's broad and blotched face endeavors in vain to teach Hélène that the lips must part to disclose the teeth, while the corners of the mouth must curve upward like the horns of a crescent moon. And I can't help laughing at the commercial composure of the pupil, as she faces her grinning teacher with a thoughtful brow and a rigid, painted mouth.

What are the thoughts of this obstinate child, this insensitive bee? She often repeats: "When one wants to get *somewhere* . . ." Get somewhere, but where? What suspended mirage keeps her eyes uplifted when she seems to look through me, through the walls, through the submissive features of her admiring young "friend"?

She is tense, and appears to aim relentlessly at some concealed goal. Glory? no . . . Those who seek glory admit it, and I have never heard Hélène Gromet express a desire for glamorous parts or proudly say, "When I can rival Simone . . ." Money! That sounds more likely. At the finish of a lively lesson, like today's, it is from her fatigue that I best discover in Hélène the solid little "child of the people," eager to earn and to hoard.

She bears her fatigue with the air of graceful fulfillment, the happily satisfied expression of a young washerwoman who has just put down her load of freshly laundered linen. Scantily clothed in a damp underslip and a tiny pair of silk knickers, she comes to sit beside me on the side bench. She has crossed her legs and remains silent, one shoulder hunched, while her bare arms hang limp.

As the twilight deepens, the black undulations of her hair seem tinged with a deeper blue.

My imagination conjures up somewhere, in some poor place, Hélène's mama, who, returning at this same hour from the trough by the river, lets her reddened arms hang loose in just the same way: or a sister, or a brother, who has just left a workshop or a stuffy office. They too are punctual, and bent, and temporarily weary, like Hélène.

She rests a while before redoing her face, with the aid of a fat powder puff and a small pad of rouged cotton wool. With the trusting calm of a drowsy animal she allows me to see on her dark-skinned undressed face the tawniness and slightly coarse grain that most common mortals ignore. In a moment or two a surfeit of powder will blur the sharply arched curve of her imperious nose, not unlike that of a bird of prey.

The return of "Robert" brings her to her feet, and immediately puts her on the defensive. Yet he is only a fair-haired, rather humble boy, eager to wait on her and help her to dress, fastening the shiny straps of her little shoes, and pulling the long pink lace of her stays. The pair of them together barely miss making an enchanting picture.

I can see she does not hate him, but I cannot see that she loves him either. The attention she grants him shows no subservience. When they leave together, she takes full stock of him with that penetrating, antagonistic look of hers, as if he were yet another lesson to be learned. And I feel, at times, very much like seizing this avaricious child's arm and asking her: "But, Hélène, what about Love?"

After Midnight

"How nice it is here."

The little dancer rubs her bare arms, the rather red, coarse-skinned arms of an undernourished blonde, and breathes in the hot dry air of the restaurant as if it were ozone.

On a polished strip of linoleum in the center of the big dining room a few couples are already revolving, among them a girl from Normandy in the lace headdress of the Caux district, a painted hussy with a red silk scarf, an Egyptian dancing girl, and a curly-headed baby wearing a tartan sash. This establishment, highly rated on the Riviera, employs some dozen dance hostesses and as many singers.

Little Maud comes here from the Eldorado, where she croons and gambols through an "English Number." She has just arrived, after running all the way through an icy wind, to earn her twenty francs' pittance at the Restaurant of the Good Hostess, from midnight till six in the morning.

She flexes her knees a little as she leans against the wall, and, after a rough calculation of her dancing at both performances at the Eldorado, and now waltzing here till dawn, finds it amounts to seven hours of valse and cakewalk, not counting dressing and undressing, rubbing on and removing her makeup. She was hungry enough when she arrived, but her appetite has been stayed by a glass of beer gulped down in the artistes' room. "So much the better," she reflects. "I've not got to get fat."

Maud's attraction lies in her angular girlish slimness; she is labeled English because of her fair hair, reddish elbows, and her funny little tippler's nose, blotchy around the nostrils. She has acquired a vicious little smile, and learned to shake her schoolgirl locks and hide her face behind her square-fingered paws, chapped by liquid white, at any suggestion of a risqué joke. In private life she is simply a "caf' conc' " girl like any of the others, overworked, innocent of malice or coquetry, forever on the move from hotel to train, from station to theater, ever tormented by hunger, lack of sleep, and the morrow's insecurity.

For the time being she takes a rest on her feet, like a saleswoman in a big store, and keeps worrying a recent hole in her flesh-tinted tights with her big toe. "Five francs for invisible mending!"

One hand absentmindedly smoothes the creases in the hem of her babyish satin frock, once Nile green, now yellow. "Dry cleaning, ten francs. Hell, that eats up my night's earnings! If only that tipsy little lady would come back, the one who was here the night of the masked ball, and threw me the change from her bill!"

A violinist in an embroidered Rumanian shirt plays "You Once Vowed to Be Mine" with such amorous intensity that he is smothered in encores.

"So much the better," she says to herself once more. "How I wish he'd play all night long, for then I'd be living on unearned income!"

Her fond hopes are dashed. A wink from the manager orders her to waltz, clinging to the shoulders of a sham toreador, thin and willowy and far too tall for her. Maud is so tired by this time that she waltzes without being aware of it, hanging on to the youth, who clasps her to him with professional, almost indecent unconcern. Everything swirls about her. The head of a hatpin, the clasp of a necklace, the setting of a ring, pierce her eyes as she dances around. The polished floor glides under her feet, glistening, soapy, as if wet.

"If I go on waltzing for very long tonight," she muses in a daze, "I'll end up without a thought in my head."

She shuts her eyes and abandons herself to her partner's insensitive breast, throwing herself into the whirl with the trustful semiconsciousness of a child ready to drown. But the music stops suddenly, and the toreador lets his charge drop without a glance, without a word, like flotsam, on the nearest table.

Maud smiles, passes a hand across her forehead, and looks around. "Ah, there's my 'sympathetic couple.'" For every night she picks out among those supping at the Good Hostess a couple who catch her fancy —in all innocence—and on whom she lavishes her most childish smiles, occasionally blowing them a kiss, or throwing them a flower; a couple whose departure brings her a short pang of regret, when she watches the woman rise to go with the air of regal boredom befitting one who knows she is being followed by an enamored escort.

"How sweet they are this evening, my sympathetic couple!"

Sweet . . . in a way. Maud chooses to see things in that way. A restless, vindictive desire seems to possess the man, who is very young and can barely conceal his impatience. His eyes are bright and shifty, and so constantly changing in color that they turn pale more often than his tanned face. He eats hurriedly, as if he had a train to catch. When his glance catches his companion's, he throws his head back as if a bunch of too-fragrant flowers had touched his nostrils.

She had arrived looking happy and self-assured, stimulated by the cold outside and a hearty appetite. She had clasped her hands under her chin and then asked the violinist in the embroidered shirt to play waltzes, more waltzes, and still more waltzes. He played for her "You Once Vowed to Be Mine" . . . "Now You Will Never Know!" . . . "Your Heart Was Cruel."

"Oh, how I adore that music!" she had sighed aloud.

She had smiled at Maud as she whirled past. And then she had fallen silent, gazing intently at her companion. "Leave me alone," she told him, pulling away the hand he was stroking.

"They're sweet, but they seem to quarrel without a word passing," Maud observes. "They may be in love, but they're not true friends."

Now the woman is leaning back in her chair, never taking her eyes off the ferocious eater facing her. Maud is fascinated by the woman's slender, feverish face, as though something were soon about to happen. The manager clacks his tongue to no purpose, in his attempt to recall the little dancer to her duty; Maud lingers on, bound by some mysterious telepathy to the woman who sits there, speechless, separated from her friend by gulfs of music, drifting farther from him, perhaps, at every throbbing note of the violin, with despairing clairvoyance.

"They love each other, but they're ill at ease in each other's company." Such devotion wells up in the woman's dark glances, yet she remains obstinately silent as though fearful of bursting into tears or unburdening her heart in a flood of banal complaints. Her eyes are beautiful, eloquent, and frightened, and seem to be telling the man: "You're a clumsy lover . . . You don't begin to understand me . . . I don't really know you, and you scare me . . . You sneer at everything I like . . . You lie so well! . . . You possess me completely, yet I can't trust you . . . If you knew what limpid springs you wall up within me because I fear you! What am I doing here at your side? Would that this music could free me of you forever! Or else that this violin would stop before I find out any more about you! You yearn for my undoing, not my happiness, and what is worst in me assures you of your victory."

Maud sighs, "Oh, what an ill-assorted pair they are this evening! She ought to leave him, but . . ."

"Come along," the man murmurs as he stands up.

His companion rises to her feet, tall, black, and glittering, like an obedient serpent, under the threat of his two bright eyes, so caressing, so treacherous. Defenseless, she follows him, with no support other than the sisterly smile of a little blond dancer, who inwardly regrets the exit of her "sympathetic couple" and whose pout seems to indicate a reproachful "Already?"

"Lola"

❧

From my dressing room I could hear, every night, the tap-tap of heavy crutches on the iron steps leading up to the stage.

Yet there was no "Cripple's Number" on our program. I used to open my door to watch the midget pony climbing the stairs on its nimble unshod feet. The white donkey followed, clip-clopping behind, then the piebald Great Dane on its thick soft paws, then the beige poodle and the fox terriers.

Bringing up the rear, the plump Viennese lady in charge of the "Miniature Circus" would herself supervise the ascent of the tiny brown bear, always reluctant and somehow desperate, clutching at the banisters and moaning as he mounted, like a punished child being sent up to bed. Two monkeys followed, in flounced silk sprinkled with sequins, smelling like an ill-kept chicken run. All of them climbed with stifled sighs, subdued groans, and inaudible expletives; they were on their way up to wait their daily hour's work.

I never again wished to see them up there, under full control and tame; the sight of their submissiveness had become intolerable to me. I knew too well that the martingaled pony tried in vain to toss its head and constantly pawed with one of its front legs, in a sort of ataxic jerk. I knew that the ailing, melancholic monkey would close its eyes and let its head rest in childish despair on its companion's shoulder; that the stupid Great Dane would stare into vacancy, gloomy and rigid, while the old poodle would wag its tail with senile benevolence; above all, I knew that the pathetic little brown bear would seize its head in both paws, whimpering and almost in tears, because a very narrow strap fastened around its muzzle cut into its lip.

I should have liked to forget the entire misery-stricken group, in their white leather harness hung with jingle bells and adorned with ribbons and bows, forget their slavering jaws, the rasping breath of these starved animals; I never again wanted to witness, and pity, this dumb animal distress I could do nothing to alleviate. So I remained down below, with Lola.

Lola did not come to visit me straightaway. She waited until the sounds of the laborious ascent had died away, till the last fox terrier had whisked its rump, white as a rabbit's scut, around the angle of the stairs. Only then did she push my half-open door with her long insinuating nose.

She was so white that her presence lit up my sordid dressing room. A slim, elongated greyhound body, white as snow; her neck, her leg joints, her flanks and tail, bristled with fine silver; her fleecy coat shone like spun glass. She walked in and looked up at me with eyes of orange melting into brown, a color so rare that it alone was enough to touch my heart. Her tongue hung out a little, pink and dry, and she panted gently from thirst . . . "Give me a drink. Give me a drink, though I know it's forbidden. My companions up there are thirsty too, none of us is allowed to drink before working time. But you'll give me a drink."

She lapped up the lukewarm water I poured into an enameled basin I had first rinsed out for her. She lapped it with an elegance that appeared, as did all her movements, to be an affectation, and in front of her, I felt ashamed of the chipped rim of the basin, of the dented jug, of the greasy walls she took good care to avoid.

While she drank I looked at her little winglike ears, at her legs, slender and firm as a hind's; at her fleshless ribs and beautiful nails, white as her coat.

Her thirst quenched, she turned away her coy tapering muzzle from the basin, and for a little while longer gazed at me with a look in which I could read nothing but vague anxiety, a sort of wild animal prayer. After that she went up by herself to the stage, where her performance was limited, it must be added, to an honorary appearance, to jumping a few obstacles which she took with accomplished grace, with a lazy, concealed strength. The footlights heightened the gold in her eyes, and she answered each crack of the whip with a nervous grimace, a menacing smile which disclosed the pink of her gums and her faultless teeth.

For nearly a month she begged no more of me than lukewarm, insipid water from a chipped basin. Every evening I used to say to her, but not in words, "Take it, though I am pining to give you all that is your due. For you have recognized me and deemed me worthy of quenching your thirst, you, who speak to no one, not even to the Viennese lady whose podgy, masterful hands fasten a blue collar around your serpent neck."

On the twenty-ninth day, sorrowfully, I kissed her flat silky forehead, and on the thirtieth . . . I bought her.

"Beautiful, but not a brain in her head," the Viennese lady confided to me. By way of a farewell, she chirped a few Austro-Hungarian endearments into Lola's ear, while the bitch stood beside me, serious, gazing straight in front of her, a hard look on her face, and squinting slightly. Whereupon I picked up her dangling leash and walked away, and the long brittle spindles, armed with ivory claws, fell into step behind me.

She escorted rather than followed me, and I held her chain high, so as not to inflict its weight on my captive princess. Would the ransom I had paid for her make her really mine?

Lola did not eat that day, and refused to drink the fresh water I offered her in a white bowl bought specially for her. But she languidly turned her undulating neck, her delicate feverish nose, toward the old chipped basin. Out of this she consented to drink, and then looked up at me with her luminous eyes, sparkling with gold like some dazzling liqueur.

"I am not a fettered princess, but a bitch, a genuine bitch, with an honest bitch's heart. I'm not responsible for my too conspicuous beauty, which has aroused your possessive instincts. Is that the sole reason for your buying me? Is it for my silver coat, my prow-shaped chest, the curved arc of my body which seems to drink in the air, my taut brittle bones barely covered by my light sparse flesh? My gait delights you, and also the harmonious leap in which I appear both to jump over and crown an invisible portico, and you call me chained princess, chimera, lovely serpent, fairy steed . . . Yet here you stand dumbfounded! I am only a bitch, with the heart of bitch, proud, ill with suppressed tenderness and trembling for fear I may give myself too quickly. Yes, I am trembling, because you now have me, past redemption, forever, in exchange for those few drops of water poured by your hand, every night, into the bottom of a chipped basin."

Moments of Stress

ༀ❦ༀ

Is it today he'll kill himself?

There he goes, bunched on his bicycle, back humped like a snail, nose between his knees, swaying as he pedals on the revolving platform, struggling as though in the teeth of a gale, against its centrifugal force.

The rimless tray spins beneath him, slowly at first, then faster, till it becomes at full speed a polished shimmering disk of watered silk, scored with concentric circles, like ripples when a pebble is dropped in a fountain. Upon its surface the small black figure astride two wheels pits his strength against the unceasing repulsion of the invisible force, and when he begins to falter, each lapse wrings from us one and all a similar strangled gasp.

The whole contraption sweeps around to the muffled roar of its motor; the deadly edges of the turntable crackle with electric sparks, green and red; a siren maintains a shrill, agonizing wail throughout the race.

Despite the spiraling blast that sweeps over the stage, we stay there, all of us, hidden in the wings; mute, competent mechanics in boiler suits; acrobats with their hair greased, their faces the pink of artificial flowers; small-part actresses in hastily flung-on faded kimonos, hair scraped back Chinese fashion under their filthy rubber "makeup bands." We stay there, all of us, glued to the spot by the hideous excitement of the unspoken query, "Is it today he'll ride to his death?"

No. It's all over now. The chromatic keening of the siren is silenced the moment the dizzy speed slackens to a standstill, and the black insect, after battling against odds gripped to the handlebars, alights with an elastic leap onto the now motionless disk.

No, it won't be today he'll kill himself. Unless, of course, this evening . . . For today is Sunday, and this is only the first house. Clearly, therefore, he still has time to kill himself at the evening performance.

I would like to get out of this place. But outside, rain is falling, the depressing, black, and desolate rain of the south, which has turned a whole town—white in the sun yesterday the length of its seafront—into a yellow quagmire. Outside this place there is only the rain and the hotel bedroom. Those who travel without respite, those who wander in isolation, those who sit down in a small restaurant at a table laid with a single plate, a single glass, and prop their folded newspaper against the water jug, such persons know the periodic, regular recurrence of fits of mental despair, the disease bred of loneliness.

I would like to get away from here, but for the moment I lack the strength to carry out my wish or to imagine any place that might bring me comfort. To create such a place, or revive it in my memory, to liven it with a beloved face, with flowers, streams, domestic animals, is for the present too great an effort, but it may be granted me a little later, perhaps in an hour's time. My mental inertia adapts itself to the physical lassitude which holds me here, fainthearted and with sagging legs, querulously repeating to myself, "I would like to get away . . ."

I fear, I expect some unknown tragedy, I am alarmed that the management has assembled here, for the perverse pleasure of an alien audience accustomed to view with indifference the spilling of the dark blood of bulls, so many dangerous or macabre "acts." A slight fever makes my temples throb—journey fatigue, change of climate, saline humidity?—transmogrifying, perhaps, familiar, almost friendly scenery into the trappings of a romantic nightmare. Tonight my peculiar mood isolates me from my bespangled and needy brethren who bustle about all around me; myself invisible, I watch their act from a sort of elevated quay, around which runs an iron balcony connecting the dressing rooms and overlooking the stage.

A red demon has just this moment sprung from a trapdoor and I can hear the laughs he raises among the distant public by his little pointed red beard and forked eyebrows, indeed by his entire mask, modeled in thick plaster and heavily black-penciled.

But the man has begun his labors as a contortionist, a slow, serpentine dislocation, the unscrewing of each articulation, a double-jointed entanglement of every limb knit into an involved, uncanny pattern, and from up here I can see why it is he hides his features beneath those of a laughable demon: his self-inflicted tortures are such that at times his face refuses to obey him and really does become that of a man condemned to everlasting flames. Will he succumb, like a reptile strangled by its own coils? What is more, he is on my side of the orchestra, and the music fails to drown his frequent moans, the brief involuntary moans of a man being slowly crushed to death.

When at last he goes off and passes, limping, below me, dragging his long body that looks half drained of its strength, I expand my constricted chest, I want to breathe. I trust this is the last of those brief horrors, I long for some insipid flowery ballet . . . but already the rifles are being leveled at their target, an ace of clubs held aloft in the hand of a trusting child.

I cannot endure the sight of this small hand, and in my morbid state I imagine its palm pierced by a red hole. Yet even so I remain, I even approach a little closer, returning to cower behind a stay, fascinated by a flight of navaja blades hurled at lightning speed by a knife thrower. The man seems hardly to move, a flash of blue steel darts from his fist to penetrate, vibrating, a vertical board and is to be seen planted close against the temples of a youth, who wears a fixed smile and never bats an eyelid.

I myself blink as each blade passes, and each time, I lower my head. A scream from the audience, the cry of a frightened woman, finally shatters my nerves, but the youth is still there, and alive, smiling and petrified. Nothing has happened; he is alive, alive! Nothing has happened but the suspension, no doubt, the temporary indecision—for an immeasurably short instant—of whatever was hovering over this theater. A sovereign wing, one that did not deign to descend today, has spared the man on the revolving table, spared the tortured neck of the red demon. It has not chosen to divert from their mark the bullets aimed at the ace of clubs held on high by a frail hand. Yet for a split second, it remained poised, capriciously, above the head of the youthful St. Sebastian, who is smiling, down there, his brow haloed with knives.

Now it has resumed its flight. Will it fly far from us, this Fate whose invisible presence has so painfully oppressed me and left me with so trembling a soul, pusillanimous and greedy for horrors, the soul of a theater addict?

Journey's End

❧❦❧

"Well I never! Who'd'ave thought our paths would ever cross again! How long is it now since I last set eyes on you! Why, Marseilles of course, remember? You were on tour with the Pitard Company, and I with the Dubois. We both played the same night. It was up to our group not to be outdone by yours, and vice versa. That didn't stop us going out to have a bite together that night, shellfish, eh! on the terrace, at Basso's.

". . . No, you've not changed much, I must say. You've looked after number one, all right; you're lucky! Your digestion's been your saving, but if you'd got thirteen years of touring in your system, like me, you wouldn't be looking so nifty!

"Yes, go ahead, you can tell me I've changed! At forty-six, it's a bit hard having to play duenna parts, when there are so many skittish youngsters of fifty and sixty to be seen footling about in juvenile leads on the Grands Boulevards, who'll throw up their parts, as likely as not, if there's a brat of over twelve in the cast! It was Saigon knocked me out, and long before my time too. I sang in operetta at Saigon, I did, in a theater lit by eight hundred oil lamps!

". . . And what else? Well, apart from that, there's not much to tell. I go on 'touring,' like so many others. I keep saying I've had enough of it, and this'll be the last time I'll do it; I go on saying to all who'll listen that I'd rather be a theater attendant or travel in perfumery. So what? Here I am back again with Pitard, and you're back with Pitard too. We came back to find work, and it's noses to the grindstone once again.

". . . I don't need you to tell me that prices have dropped all around. If it got about what I'm working for this time, my reputation would be gone. It really seems as if they think we don't need to eat when on tour.

"Not to mention that I've got my sister with me, you know. It may make two on the payroll but it means two mouths to feed. Oh, she's taken to the life right enough, the poor kid; she's got guts! More guts than health, if you ask me! She'll tackle any part. Take the time when we had a fifty-day contract with the Miral Touring Company, in a mixed bill of three plays nightly: the child took the part of the maid who lays the table in the first—ten lines; then an old peasant woman who tells everyone a few home truths—two hundred lines; and to end up, a girl of seventeen married off against her will who never stops crying throughout. Just think of the poor thing having to cope with all those changes of makeup!

"And for starvation fees, too, I'll have you know! On top of that we had the doctor's and chemist's bills to pay—it was the winter my bronchitis was so bad—not to mention the nurse's charge for cupping, thirty-seven francs' worth! I went on rehearsing with forty cups on my back and so hid the fact I was suffering. When I was seized by a fit of coughing, I rushed off to the lav, otherwise they'd have replaced me within the hour, you bet!

"I was able to get away, but doctors and their drugs had ruined me in advance. It was then the child began to knit woolen garments, you know, those loose coatees that are fashionable just now, with a little woolen jumper to match. She works when we're traveling, on the train; she's got the knack of it. When we're in for a journey, eight or nine hours by rail, she'll reel off a coatee in four days and post it off at once to a firm in Paris.

". . . Yes, yes, I know, you've got the music hall to keep you going. There's still a living to be made in the halls; but what d'you suppose there's left for me? They'll bury my bones on one of these tours, and believe me, I'm not the only one . . . Oh, I'm not trying to plead constant illness, you know. I still have my good moments; I was happy-go-lucky enough when young! If only my liver let me alone for three weeks, or if my cough left off for a fortnight, or the blessed varicose veins didn't make my left leg weigh so heavy, then I'd be my old self again!

"If, granted that, I chanced on a few good companions, not too mangy a lot, but sporty, who don't spend their lives harping on their woes and retailing their maladies and confinements, then I promise you I'd soon get my fair share of fun again.

"Provided, of course, I'm not laid out like Marizot . . . didn't you know? It wasn't in the papers, but the story might have come your way. We were . . . now, where were we? . . . in Belgium, in pouring rain. We'd just finished a passable dinner, that is, my sister and I, Marizot and Jacquard. Marizot goes out first, while we stay behind to settle the bill. You know how shortsighted he is. He misses his way, and off he goes down a dark narrow street, and there at the end was a stream, a river, I don't know, the Scheldt, or something: to be brief, he falls into the water and gets carried away. They only found him two days later.

It all happened so quick that the first night after, we hadn't even begun to feel sad, believe me! It wasn't till the next night, when the under-manager played Marizot's part, that we all began to get weepy and cried on the stage . . .

"Anyhow, people don't drown every day, thank God! We did find some consolation at the time of the railway strike. Yes, and it played us a most unusual trick. Listen to this: we ended up the tour with *Fiasco* —the devil of a title—and the night before we'd played it in Rouen. When we reach Mantes, the train stops. 'All change! Everyone to leave the train! We go no farther!' The strike was on! Off I went to have a good moan. I had acute liver trouble, rheumatism in my left leg, a high temperature, the whole boiling. I sat down on a bench in the waiting room, saying to myself, 'After a knock like this nothing will get me to budge again, my luck's right out, I'd rather die on the spot!' Jacquard was there, same as ever, with his big overcoat and his pipe, and he comes up to me and says, 'Why don't you just go home. You'd better take the Pigalle-Halle-aux-vins bus, which drops you on your doorstep.'

" 'Oh, leave me in peace!' I give him for answer. 'Have you no heart at all? Here we are, stuck for Lord knows how long by this filthy strike? D'you think I get much fun out of spending my miserable salary on drugs and digs, eh! I'd like you to be standing in my shoes and then see what you'd do in my place!'

" 'In your place?' he says. 'In your place I'd take the Pigalle-Halle-aux-vins bus.'

"I could have cried with rage, dearie. I could have struck him, that Jacquard, with his pipe and his wooden mug! I flayed him alive with my tongue! When I'm finished, he takes me by the arm and forcibly leads me to the glass door. And what d'you suppose I see in the station-yard? *Pigalle-Halle-aux-vins*, dearie! *Pigalle*, in so many words! Three Pigalle buses, which had been used to bring along another troupe that very morning! And there they were, having a soft drink, right in front of that station at Mantes!

"I started to giggle, not but what my liver was killing me, and on I giggled till I thought I never would stop. And the best of it was that we went back to Paris in *Pigalle-Halle-aux-vins*, dearie, by the special authority of the subprefect. It cost us a bit more than two and a half francs, but what a time we all had! Jacquard and Marval sat on the top deck and threw down sausage skins to us inside, and you should have seen the faces of the 'bystanders'! That alone was worth the whole trip!

"And what a shaking we had, I felt as if my liver were being torn from my body at every jolt! It might well have been worse, for I laughed the whole length of the way, and that's always something to the good!

"And when all's said and done, as Jacquard put it, 'What are speed and altitude records to the likes of us? Give me a nice little bus ride *Mantes-Paris* on a *Pigalle-Halle-aux-vins* every time! There's an endurance test quite out of the ordinary!' "

"The Strike, Oh, Lord, the Strike!"

❧❦❧

Through half-closed eyes I follow the "Pavane" as danced by the "Great Concubines of History." Previous to wearing the pearly veiled hennin, the starched ruff, the farthingale, the hooped panniers and knotted kerchief, they have, for the rehearsal, pinned up their skirts like loincloths about their hips, some even discarding their narrow dresses to work in black knickers, bare arms emerging from their brassieres, furry mobcaps on their heads.

They are led by the Roi Soleil, in the guise of a ballet master in shirt sleeves. Gabrielle d'Estrées and the Marquise de Pompadour persist in making mistake after mistake, and inwardly I bless them. They start over again from the beginning. If only they would go on making mistakes!

Seated in the orchestra stalls on a strip of gray dust sheet, I am waiting in the darkened auditorium till the revue rehearsal is over. It is now a quarter to six, my comrades have held the stage since twelve-thirty. There'll only be three-quarters of an hour left to rehearse our mimo-drama piece. But I long for Gabrielle d'Estrées and the Marquise de Pompadour to blunder again: I do so hate the thought of having to move.

The niggard gleam of a two-way "service lamp" acts as substitute for the footlights. These two points of light, hanging in the blackness, prick my eyes and induce sleep. Beside me, invisible, a fellow mime staves off his craving to smoke by chewing an unlit cigarette. "Another day's work ruined for the rest of us! I should like to see all revue promoters deep in a hundred feet of . . . Just take a look at those 'Great Concubines,' I ask you! And to think that they're toiling away there for the price of air . . . The strike, oh, Lord, the strike!"

The word arouses me. Is the strike, then, a reality? We've been talking about it so much among ourselves. There's been some change of atmosphere in this hard-worked café concert of ours, one of the happiest establishments in the district, always warm and packed to capacity, where, every night, the stormy laughter of the crowd rollicks around the house amid catcalls, whistling, and stamping of feet.

"The strike, oh, Lord, the strike!"

It's in the thoughts of all, it's mooted in corners. The chorus girls of the forthcoming revue, the little singing girls on tour, have this word only on their lips, each in her own manner. Some there are who shout in a whisper, "The strike—for paid matinees, and paid rehearsals!" their faces afire, brandishing a muff like a flag and a reticule like a sling.

Once again the "Great Concubines" have gone agley. Splendid, a further ten good minutes in my seat! My Ladies de Pompadour and d'Estrées are "getting it in the neck"! Bending over them, the ballet master lets fly a string of not very strong oaths which the Vert-Galant's mistress, a short, well-rounded brunette, receives with impatience, facing in our direction, her eyes on the exit.

The other, the Marquise, hangs her head like a child who has broken a vase. She stares at the floor, without saying a word; her breath lifts the heavy lock of blond hair that falls across her cheek. The dismal light beating down from above sculpts her head into that of a thin, hollow-cheeked boy-martyr, and this Pompadour, in her black knickers with bare knees showing above her rolled stockings, bears a strange resemblance to a young drummer boy of the Revolution. Her whole stubborn little hurt person spells rebellion and seems to cry aloud, "Long live the strike!"

At a standstill for the moment, the Pavane has regrouped around her twenty silent young women at the end of their tether. In the dark their eyes try to pick out the seat from which the manager supervises their movements, while they wait eagerly for the liberating words "That will be all for today" to surge up from some dim spot in the stalls. But they also appear tonight to be waiting for something else: "The strike, oh, Lord, the strike!" Tonight there is something aggressive about their fatigue.

In direct contrast to the men—singers and mimes, dancers and acrobats—who strive to preserve a serious man-to-man tone, courteous and calm in discussion, when they further their claims, the little "caf' conc'" girls, my comrades, have caught fire immediately. Being emotional Parisiennes, the mention of the single word "strike" makes them imagine confusedly mobs out in the streets, riots, barricades.

The girls don't make a practice of it. The strict and simple discipline by which we are ruled brooks no infringement. Under the bluish sun of two projectors has been evolved, up till these troubled days, the most rigorous and hard-worked routine for small communities, alleviated in a trice by a word from the manager, "Take it easy, ladies. Do you think you're in a theater?" or "I don't like people who bawl at me." Yes, they don't make a habit of "refractoriness" or going on strike. That Agnes Sorel over yonder, who stands so tall on her long legs, yawning with hunger, will soon be off and away to her pigeon house, at the back of beyond on the other side of the Butte de Montmartre. She never has the time for a hot meal, she lives too far away, she's always on the trot.

"It's not per performance she earns her monthly hundred and eighty francs, but per mile!" says Diane de Poitiers, who wears thin summer blouses in mid-December.

As for the handsome Montespan of the heavy bosom, is it for a moment likely that she acquired her habitual complaints from her husband, a consumptive bookbinder! She has more than enough on her hands looking after her man and two kids far out near the Château-d'Eau district.

They are so easily regimented, these poor honeyless bees! Any milliner's apprentice in the rue de la Paix could put them wise on the question of claims. They said in the past, "Great! We strike!" as they would have said, "We're going to win the big lottery!"—without any conviction. Now that they do believe in it, they are beginning to tremble, with hope.

Will they receive full pay for those terrible twice-nightly performances on Sunday and Thursday, and for the fête days sprinkled throughout the calendar? Even better: will they be compensated for the long prison hours, midday to six, while a revue is in production? Would the snack of croissants, bock, and banana they bolt in rehearsal time be buckshee? And Old Mother Louis, our rheumaticky duenna, who plays comic mothers-in-law and Negresses, will her bus fare on Sundays and Thursdays be drawn from some other source than the miserable pin money she earns by her knitting, she who knits, everywhere and every minute, for a knitted garment shop?

As for those rush-hour nights, dreaded above all when the full-dress rehearsal for a revue goes on till dawn, would it no longer be solely "for the honor of the house" that fifty or so "walkers" from the chorus have to go back home in the freezing early hours . . . swollen feet and weak ankles, yawning themselves to death?

It sounds good. It is disquieting. Our little community is at fever pitch. At night, in the wings, someone seizes me by the sleeves, and questions me.

"You're for the strike, aren't you?" and someone else adds, in a voice of assurance but with fluttering gestures, "In the first place, it's only fair."

Not everybody shares the bitter skepticism of this blond, hollow-cheeked child, Madame de Pompadour, a philosopher of nineteen, whom I have nicknamed Cassandra and who resents it without exactly knowing why. "If we strike, where will it get us? It will only help to fatten the cinema crowd. And while it lasts, what are the two of us going to feed on, Moman and me?"

It must be at least a quarter past six. I am almost asleep, my arms pushed deep in my muff, my chin in my fur. I feel warm on the shoulders and cold in the feet, due to the fact that the central heating is not lit for rehearsals. What am I doing here? It is too late for work today. I have gone on waiting with the fatalistic patience learned in the music hall. I may as well wait on a little longer and then leave at the same time as the tired swarm of day girls who will disperse over the face of Paris.

The ones in the greatest hurry, and those whose job brings them back here at eight, will not go far afield: the slice of pale veal on its bed of sorrel, or the dubious lamb stew, await them in the brasserie around the corner. The others make off at the run as soon as their feet touch the pavement. "I've just time to rush home for a minute."

Rush home to a grumbling "Moman," for a wash and clean, to retie the ribbon that binds hair and forehead, to make sure that the kid has not fallen from the window or burned himself on the stove, and hoopla! the return journey. They jump on a bus, a tram, the underground, pell-mell with all the other employees—milliners, seamstresses, cashiers, typists—for whom the day's work is over.

[*Translated by Anne-Marie Callimachi*]

Bastienne's Child

❦⟡❧

1

"Run, Bastienne, run!"

The ballerinas scurry the whole length of the corridor, brushing the petals of their skirts against the wall, leaving behind them the smell of rice powder, hair still warm from the curling tongs, new tarlatan gauze. Bastienne runs, not quite so fast, both hands encircling her waist. They have been "rung" rather late, and were she to arrive on the stage out of breath, might she not fumble, perhaps, the end of her variation, that lengthy spin during which nothing is seen of her but the fully extended, creamy swirl of a ballet skirt and two slim pink legs moving apart and coming together again with a mechanical precision already appreciated by connoisseurs?

She is not, as yet, anything more than a very young dancer, under a year's contract to the Grand-Théâtre at X; a poor girl, of radiant beauty, tall, "expensive to feed," as she says of herself, and underfed, because she is already five months pregnant.

Of the child's father, there is no news.

"He's a bad lot, that man!" says Bastienne.

But she speaks of him without tearing out her dark hair, so silky against her clear white skin, and her "misfortune" has not driven her either to the river or to the gas oven. She dances as before and recognizes three powerful deities: the manager of the Grand-Théâtre, the ballet mistress, and the proprietor of the hotel where live, besides Bastienne herself, a dozen of her comrades. However, since the morning when Bastienne, turning deathly pale during the dancing lesson, confessed with a peasant's simplicity, "Madame, it's because I'm expecting!" the ballet mistress has spared her. But she does not wish to be spared, and dismisses any special attention with an indignant jerk of the elbow and a "Why, I'm not ailing!"

The weight that swells her waistline she calmly accepts, apart from passing a few rude remarks on it with the inconsequence of her seventeen years. "As for you, I'm going to put some sense in you!" And she pulls in her belt, loath not to display for as long as possible, and above all on the stage, the flexibility of her slim, broad-shouldered figure. She laughingly insults her burden, slapping it with the flat of her hands, then adding, "How hungry it makes me!" Unthinkingly she commits the heroic imprudence of all penniless girls: having paid her weekly hotel bill, she often goes to bed without dinner or supper, and keeps her stays on all night to "cut her appetite."

Bastienne, in fact, leads the indigent, happy-go-lucky but hard-working life of the little motherless ballerinas who have no lover. Between the morning lesson, starting at nine, the afternoon rehearsal, and the nightly performance, they have next to no time left for thought. Their wretched phalanstery does not know the meaning of despair, since solitude and insomnia never afflict its members.

Impudent and crafty after their fashion, driven to extremes by the ragings of an empty stomach, Bastienne and her roommate—a dumpy little blonde—sometimes spend their last pennies in the Grand-Théâtre Brasserie, after midnight, on a bottle of beer.

Seated opposite one another, they shrilly exchange the remarks of a prearranged dialogue.

"Now, if I had the money, I'd treat myself to a fat ham sandwich!"

"Yes, but you've not got a sou. I've got none neither, but supposing I had, I'd certainly order myself a nice grilled black pudding, with lots of mustard and a hunk of bread . . ."

"Oh, I'd far rather have sauerkraut, with plenty of sausage . . ."

It so happens that the sauerkraut and the grilled black pudding, so feverishly evoked, providentially descend between the two little ballerinas, escorted by the generous donor, whom they welcome with thanks, with a joke and a smile, and then leave in the lurch, all before the half hour has struck.

This innocent method of begging is the invention of Bastienne, whose "interesting condition" earns her a curiosity not so far removed from consideration. Her comrades count the weeks and consult the cards concerning the child's fortune. They make a fuss over her, helping to tighten her dancing stays with a heave-ho as they pull on the lace, one knee pressed against her robust thighs. They freely bestow on her preposterous advice, recommending her to take witch's potions, ever helpful. and shouting after her, as tonight, down the long dark corridors, "Run, Bastienne, run!"

They keep an anxious eye on her imprudent dancing, insist above all on escorting her back to her dressing room, to be there at the moment when, unhooking her torturous breastplate, she laughingly threatens the youngest, silliest, and most inquisitive with "Take care, or he'll pop out and perch on your nose!"

Today, in the warmest corner of the big dressing room, there stands, supported on two chairs, the tray of an old traveling trunk with a canopy of flowered wallpaper. It is the piteous crib of a tiny little Bastienne, hardy as a weed. She is brought to the theater by her mother at eight, and is removed at midnight under her cloak. This much-dandled, merry little mite, this babe with scarcely a stitch of clothing, who is dressed by small clumsy hands that knit for it, awkwardly, pilches and bonnets, enjoys, despite her environment, the gorgeous childhood of a fairy-tale princess. Ethiopian slaves in coffee-colored tights, Egyptian girls hung with blue jewelry, houris stripped to the waist, bend over her cot and let her play with their necklaces, their feather fans, their veils that change the color of the light. The tiny little Bastienne falls asleep and wakes in scented young arms, while peris, with faces the rose-pink of fuchsias, croon her songs to the rhythm of a far-distant orchestra.

A dusky Asian maid, keeping watch by the door, shouts down the corridor, "Run, Bastienne, run! Your daughter is thirsty!"

In comes Bastienne, breathless, smoothing her tense billowing skirts with the tips of her fingers, and runs straight to the tray of the old traveling trunk. Without waiting to sit down or unfasten her low-cut bodice, she uses both hands to free from its pressure a swollen breast, blue in color from its generous veins. Leaning over, one foot lifted in the dancer's classical pose, her flared skirts like a luminous wheel around her, she suckles her daughter.

2

"Look, Bastienne, the Serbs are here, and over here is Greece. This part streaked with thin lines is Bulgaria. All this bit marked in black shows the advance made by the Allies, while the Turks have been forced to retreat as far as here. Now d'you understand?"

Bastienne's huge eyes, the color of light tobacco, are wide open and she nods her head politely, muttering, "Mmm . . . mmm . . ." She takes a long look at the map over which her companion Peloux is running a thin, hardened finger, and finally exclaims, "Lord, how small it is, how very small!"

Peloux, who was hardly expecting this conclusion, bursts out laughing, and it is on her now that Bastienne focuses in astonishment her huge orbs, always a little slow in registering any change of thought.

The complicated map, covered with dotted lines and hatching, represents to Bastienne nothing but a confused design for embroidery. Fortunately Constantinople is there, printed in capitals. She knows of its existence, it's a town. Peloux has a sister, an older sister of twenty-eight, who once played in a comedy at Constantinople, in the presence of . . .

"In whose presence was it, Peloux, your sister played in Constantinople?"

"In front of the Sultan, of course!" comes the lie direct from Peloux.

Bastienne, incredulous and deferential, spends another moment or two deciphering the newspaper. What a lot of unreadable names! What a lot of unknown countries! For, after all, she did once dance in a divertissement which brought together the five parts of the world. Very well, those five parts were: America, which had meant a foundation makeup of terra-cotta; Africa, brown tights; Spain, fringed shawls; France, a snow-white tutu, and for Russia, red leather boots. If the map of the world had now to be cut up like a jigsaw puzzle, and from each small section had to be conjured up a fully armed, wicked little nation nobody had ever heard of, then it made life far too complicated . . . Bastienne casts a hostile glance at the nebulous photographs around the edge of the map and declares, "To start with, all those fellows there look like the cycle cops in their flat caps! Now, Peloux, supposing you give the child a good slap, just to teach her not to eat your thread!"

Tired of staring so long at "small print," Bastienne gets to her feet, sighs, and winds around her ear, like a ribbon, a strand of her long black hair. She deigns to cast a majestic animal glance upon her daughter, crawling on all fours at her feet, then bends down and, lifting a corner of the petticoat and chemise, administers by the count, on a round rosy little behind, a good half dozen resounding slaps.

"Oh!" protests Peloux, in rather a frightened whisper.

"Don't you worry," Bastienne retorts, "I'm not killing her. Besides, she minds pain so little, it's unbelievable."

Indeed, there's no sound to be heard either of the dramatic tears or the piercing shrieks of very young children when they sob to the point of suffocation: nothing but the furious drubbing of two small shoes against the floorboards, where the tiny little Bastienne rolls herself into a ball like a caterpillar knocked off a gooseberry bush, and no more.

. . . Bastienne is today a truly magnificent creature, due to her premature motherhood, and to having recovered the habit of regular meals now that she has a warm lodging. A gallant tradesman, as much out of pity as dazzled by her beauty, had brought home mother and child on Christmas Eve when Bastienne was reveling on tuppence worth of hot roasted chestnuts.

His reward is to come back every evening to the small apartment from which can be seen a gray flowing river and find there a tall, friendly Bastienne, gay, a little standoffish but faithful, busied over her career and her daughter. She thrives in a home of her own, at ease in one of those aprons such as are worn by girls who deliver bread, and tied, as it is today, over her kimono, her hair hanging over her shoulders with that newly washed but still uncombed look that enhances her nineteen years.

This is a lovely holiday afternoon for Bastienne and her friend Peloux. No ballet is in rehearsal at the Grand-Théâtre, the dry December weather makes the stove roar, and ahead of them lie four good hours of freedom, while drop by drop the coffee fills the tinplate filter. Peloux is puckering the "underskirts" of a workaday costume in coarse bluish-white tarlatan, and without pricking her finger or making a mistake, she contrives to keep an eye on the war news, the deserted street, and a catalogue of novelties.

"You know, Bastienne, we won't have any more roasted pistachio nuts, on account of the war: that old Turk who sells them told me as much . . . That's the third time that lieutenant down there has repassed the house . . . Bastienne, what about an astrakhan cloak like this one here, when you're rich? You'd look stunning in it!"

But Bastienne's placid soul, her stay-at-home, domesticated little dancer's soul, yearns for no furs. When she goes window-shopping, her eye lingers on unbleached linen rather than on velvets, and she lets her fingers run over rough scarlet-bordered dusters . . . At present she is smiling in an honestly sensuous way over her favorite chore: standing over a small basin, her lovely arms covered in lukewarm froth, looking as beautiful as a queen in a washhouse, she is soaping her daughter's underwear, without spilling a drop around her . . . Why could not life, her future, that is, and even her duty, be contained within the four gaily papered walls of this small dining room, scented with coffee, white soap, and orris root? Life, for a now flourishing though once misery-racked Bastienne, means dancing in the first place, then working, in the humble and domestic sense of the word given it by the race of thrifty females. Jewelry, money, fine clothes . . . these are things not so much rejected by stern choice as postponed by Bastienne. They lie somewhere far away in her thoughts, and she does not call them forth. One day they may just happen, like a legacy, like a chimney pot falling on your head, or like the arrival of the mysterious little daughter now playing on the rug, whose healthy growth still gives Bastienne a daily increasing awareness of the miraculous and unforeseen.

A year ago everything in life had seemed simple: to suffer hunger and cold, to have leaky shoes, to feel lonely and miserable and heavily burdened in body, "all that might well happen to anyone," Bastienne had blandly remarked. All was simple then, and still is, except for the existence of her fifteen-month-old child, except for the blond little angel, curly-headed and up to every trick, now in a silent rage on the rug. To so young and inexperienced a mother, a child is a lovely warm little creature, dependent, according to its age, on milk, soup, kisses, and slaps. So things go on and on until . . . good heavens, until the time comes for the first dancing class. But it so happens that before her very eyes, under her warm kisses and stinging smacks, a small being is fast developing an independent personality, thinking, struggling, and arguing even before knowing how to talk! And that Bastienne had not foreseen. "A chit of fifteen months, who already has ideas of her own!"

Peloux shakes her head with the earnest, pinched expression that gives her at twenty an old-maidish look, and starts to tell stories of infant prodigies and criminal children. The truth is that the surprising little Bastienne, aged fifteen months, already knows how to captivate, fib, make pretense of tummyache, or, sobbing loudly, stretch out a plump hand nobody has trodden on; knows, too, the power of obstinate silence, and above all knows how to pretend to be listening to the grownups' conversation, eyes wide open, mouth tight shut, so much so that Peloux and Bastienne sometimes behave like frightened schoolgirls and suddenly stop talking, because this disturbing witness, with its mop of fair curls, looks less like a baby than a mischievous little Eros.

It is on the face of the tiny little Bastienne, far more than on her mother's lovely tranquil face or Peloux's already faded features, that are mirrored all the worldly passions: uncontrolled covetousness, dissimulation, beguiling seductiveness.

"Oh, how peaceful we should be," sighs Peloux, "were it not for this magpie of a child gobbling up all my needles."

"Catch her, if you can leave your stitching," Bastienne answers. "My hands are covered with suds."

But the "magpie of a child" has parked itself behind the sewing machine, and all that can be seen, between the treadle and the platform, is a pair of deep blue eyes, which, in their isolation, might be fifteen months, or fifteen years, or older still.

"Come here, you delicious lump of poison!" Peloux begs.

"Will you come here, you fiend incarnate!" Bastienne scolds.

No answer. The blue eyes move only an instant to cast their insolent light on Bastienne. And if Peloux redoubles her entreaties and Bastienne her invective, it will not be from fear that the fair chubby-cheeked Eros ambushed behind the sewing machine may devour a gross of needles; it will be rather to hide the constraint, the embarrassment imposed on outspoken grownups when under scrutiny from a small unfathomable child.

[*Translated by Anne-Marie Callimachi*]

The Accompanist

❦

"Madame Barucchi is on her way, Madame, please don't be impatient with her: she's just telephoned to say she can't help being a little late for your lesson, on account of the dress rehearsal of the ballet at the Empyrée. You have a few minutes to spare, I'm sure."

" . . . "

"In any case, we're a little fast in here, it's only ten to . . . When I say 'we,' well, I'm always on time myself. I hardly ever move from here the whole day long."

" . . . ?"

"No, it's not that the work is really hard; but it is sometimes a little dreary in this large, bare studio. And then, in the evening, I must say I do feel a bit tired in the back from sitting on the piano stool."

" . . . "

"So young? But I'm not so young, I'm twenty-six! Sometimes I feel old, from doing the same thing day after day! Twenty-six, a little boy of five, and no husband."

" . . . ?"

"Yes, he was mine, that little boy you saw yesterday. When he comes out from his nursery school, Madame Barucchi is kind enough to let me have him here, so that I don't have to fret about what's become of him. He's sweet. He watches all these ladies here at their lesson, he's learned a few steps already. He's an observant child."

" . . . "

"Yes, I know. I'm always being told that I'm doing an old woman's job and that I can well afford the time to wait until I'm gray-haired before settling down as an accompanist, but I'd rather stick where I am. And then I've already suffered a good many hard knocks in my life, so all I ask is to be left to sit quietly on my piano stool . . . You're looking at the time? Be patient for a little longer! Madame Barucchi can't be long now. I know you're wasting precious minutes, whereas I'm earning my income, at the moment, by twiddling my thumbs. That doesn't happen to me very often!"

" . . . ?"

"Because I'm paid by the hour. Two francs fifty."

" . . . !"

"You don't think that a lot? But just consider, Madame, everyone plays the piano, there's a neighbor of mine who gives lessons in town at a franc a time: out of that she has to pay her bus fare, plus the wear and tear of her shoe leather and umbrella. And here am I under cover all day, and warm, even too warm: the studio stove sometimes makes me feel dizzy. But then I have the satisfaction of being among artistes; that makes up for a lot."

" . . . ?"

"No, I've never been on the stage. I was a model once, before I had my little boy. That left me with certain tastes, certain habits. I could never again live a common or garden life. There was a moment, three years ago, when Madame Barucchi advised me to try the music hall, as a dancer . . . 'But,' I said to her, 'I don't know how to dance.'—'That makes no difference,' she answered, 'you could go on as a "dancer in the nude": then you wouldn't tire yourself out by dancing.' I had no wish to do that."

" . . . ?"

"Oh, that wasn't the only reason. A dancer in the nude, as the saying goes, displays no more than any of the others. A dancer in the nude always means something in the Egyptian style, and that entails a good ten pounds' weight of beaten-metal straps and belts and ornaments, beaded latticework on the legs, necklaces from here to there, and no end of veils. No, it wasn't merely the question of decency that made me decline. It's my nature to stay in my corner and watch the others.

"People are passing through here all day long, not only the ladies of the music hall, but actresses, real stage actresses, who play in the boulevard theaters, especially now that there is so much dancing in straight plays. I must admit they are like fish out of water at the start. They're not accustomed to taking their clothes off for their lesson. They arrive wearing the latest fashion models, they begin by lifting up their dress and fastening it with safety pins, then they become exasperated, the heat mounts higher, they unhook their collar, and then they get rid of their skirt and next thing it's the blouse . . . Finally, their stays come off, hairpins start falling out and some of their hair, too, on occasion, and their face powder turns moist. At the end of an hour's work you would be in fits to see, in the place of a smart lady, an ordinary little woman, running with sweat, who pants and rages, swears a little, dabs her cheeks with a handkerchief, and doesn't care a button if her nose is shining: in fact, just an ordinary woman! There's no malice in what I've been saying, believe me, but it does amuse me. I enjoy my little observations."

"...?"

"Oh, certainly not, it gives me no wish to exchange my lot for theirs. The mere thought of such a thing makes me feel tired. Dancing lessons apart, they still go rushing around outside, at least that's how I see it. You should hear them retailing their grievances. 'Oh, heavens above, I have to be at such and such a place at five, and at my masseuse's at five-thirty, then back home for an appointment at six! Then there's my three stage dresses to try on! Oh, heavens above, I'll never get through it all!'

"It's terrifying. I have to close my eyes, they make me feel sleepy. The other day, for example, Madame Dorziat—yes, Madame Dorziat, in person—very kindly said to Madame Barucchi, referring to me, 'That poor girl, who's been grinding away at my dance music for the last hour and a quarter, I shouldn't care to be in her place!' My place, my place, why, it's the one that suits me best! All I ask is to be left alone in it. I fooled about a bit in my younger days, and I've been well punished for it! But it's left me apprehensive. The more I see of the way others fling themselves into the swirl of life, the more I want to remain seated. For here I see little else but the fuss and bother in which people become involved. Bright lights, spangles, costumes, painted faces, smiles, that spectacular sort of life is not for me. I see nothing but careers, sweat, skins that are yellow by the light of day, and despondency . . . I'm not much good at expressing myself, but those are the lines along which my mind works. It seems as though I were the only person with a working knowledge of the sidelights that others view from the front of the stage."

"...?"

"Get married, me? Oh, no, I should be afraid, now. As I was saying, it's left me apprehensive. No, no, things are all right as they are, I wish to remain just as I am. Just as I am, with my little boy clinging to my skirts, both of us well sheltered behind my piano."

The Cashier

❧◦❧

Watchdogs, in a kennel with its back turned to the west wind, are better housed. She has her lair, from eight in the evening till midnight, and from two till five for matinees, in a damp recess under the stairs leading down to the artistes' dressing rooms, and the battered little deal pay desk is her sole protection against the brutal draft directed at her whenever the constantly opened and shut iron door swings back into place. Alternate hot and cold gusts, from the radiator on one side and the stairs on the other, slightly ruffle the curls around her head and her little knitted tippet, whose every stitch carries an imitation jet bead.

For the past twenty-four years she has been entering in a cash book the number of soft drinks consumed in the stalls of the Folies-Gobelins, as well as those in the Café-Gobelins annexed to the theater: bocks, mazagran coffees, brandied cherries. An electric bulb hangs above her head like a pear on a string, petticoated in green paper, and at first all that can be distinguished is a small yellow hand emerging from a starched cuff. A small yellow hand, clean, but with the thumb and forefinger blackened from counting coins and copper tallies.

After a short while of attentive scrutiny, the features of the cashier can easily be discerned, among the many green shadows cast by the lamp, on the shriveled face of a pleasant, timorous old lizard, devoid of all color. Supposing her cheek were pricked, would there spurt from it, instead of blood, pale globules of the anemic juice used in bottling brandied cherries?

When I go down to my dressing room, she hands me my key from on top of the five-shelved row of those special cherries for which the establishment is far famed: five cherries per portion in a glass cupel, arranged pyramidally, so that they look like the boxed shrubs in a French formal garden, with the inkwell, in this instance, a substitute for the glass-surfaced water.

I know nothing of the cashier except her bust, always bent forward from her habit of writing and her desire to please . . . She arrives at the Folies-Gobelins long before me and leaves at midnight. Does she walk? has she legs and feet, a woman's body? All that must have melted away, after twenty-four years behind her battered little pay desk!

A lizard, yes, a nice little wrinkled lizard, old and frail, but not so timorous after all: her tart voice has a shrill ring of authority, and to one and all alike she exhibits the equable kindliness of one whose power is undisputed. She treats the waiters like unruly children, tut-tutting like a governess, and the artistes like irresponsible or sick children, past correction. The chief stagehand, gray-haired, blue-boiler-suited, speaks to her as would a small boy: he has been on the house staff for a mere eighteen years!

In some obscure way, the cashier feels herself to be as fixed and weather-beaten as the building itself, and the panel of her hutch, never whitewashed, never repainted, is thickly coated with a shiny black, with an indelible varnish of dirt: I can't help being reminded of other smoky traces left untouched by the centuries, the smoky traces of a lamp—forever extinguished—at Cumae, in the Sibyl's cave.

It is from the lips of our benign Sibyl that I learn, in three words, whether the audience is dense or sparse, whether the trade in soft drinks is slack or flowing abundantly. She also informs me of how my face looks, of the temper of the upper gallery, and of the reception accorded to the evening's "first appearance."

I learn, into the bargain, that it is cold outside or that rain can be expected. What can she know of the weather, this cashier who, to reach her windswept hovel, must quit some other murky basement, far distant, and make her way by métro, under the ground, always under the ground.

Only smothered strains of the orchestra reach her, sometimes carrying on a wave of music the shrill high note of a popular soprano . . . The applause crackles like a distant fall of rubble.

The cashier lends it her ear and says to me, "You hear them? All that is for little Jady! She's made quite a hit here. She's got a way of putting it across that is all her own, and she . . ."

Her voice sounds discreet, amiable; it remains for me to detect the underlying censure, the compassionate scorn for all things and creatures connected with the music hall.

The cashier has great affection for the dirt and gloom of the Folies-Gobelins, for her hovel, her lamp with its green petticoat, and her flower borders of brandied cherries. What takes place on the stage is no concern of hers. When I rush off, out of breath, quite beside myself, and shout to her as I pass, "How splendidly it's gone tonight, a first-rate audience! They made us take four curtain calls!" she smiles in response, and says, "Now's the moment for you to rush to your dressing room and give yourself a hard rub with eau de Cologne, or you'll catch a chill." She adds nothing but a superficial flicker of her keen eyes over my unfastened dress and my bare sandaled feet.

It is in the warmth and darkness of the Folies-Gobelins incubator that the insufferable little Jady was hatched out: two quivering legs, as clever and responsive as antennae, a pointed, fragile voice that breaks every other instant—like the legs of an insect, no sooner snapped than they've grown together again—and, the other day, when standing by the pay desk, I happened to expatiate on the peculiar gifts of this singer born to be a dancer.

"Yes," the cashier concurred, "I'm bound to admit that she's won universal applause. They tell me she's got pep, she's got dash, she's got 'it,' in other words, she's got everything, but how can I tell? But do you know her little girl? No? A darling, Madame, a real beauty! And so sweet and well mannered! Only two, but she knows how to say please and thank you, and can even blow kisses! And amenable, too! You can leave her by herself at home the whole livelong day, just think of that!"

I do think of that. And I come to think that a despondent moralist, a discriminating if captious critic, is hidden away in this gloomy hovel under the stairs of the Folies-Gobelins. Our wrinkled Sibyl does not cry after us, "Unhappy, erring folk like you are, have the words 'family,' 'morals,' 'hygiene' no meaning for you?" She smiles, rather, and murmurs at the end of a sentence which has no conclusion, "Think of that! . . ." And it needed no more than that for me to visualize, in some suburban tenement, a baby of two, *amenable*, left alone by itself all day, waiting contentedly until such time as its mother should finish her act.

Nostalgia

"It's me, Madame, it's the dresser. Has Madame everything she requires?"

"...!"

"Well! If this isn't something more than a surprise! I felt sure it would bowl you over to see me again! Yes, yes, it's me all right! You never expected to find your old Jeanne of the Empyrée-Clichy down here! Yes, I'm spending the winter in Nice, like the English. And how are things with you? All going well?"

"..."

"Same goes for me, not but what there's a deal I could say on the subject . . ."

"..."

"Yes, yes, I'll get you dressed, never you worry. Now, for your first scene, is it this blue dress, or that tea gown affair in pink?"

" . . . "

"Good! Once I know, I don't need telling a second time. Now, that is really something, that muslin with nothing under it. Very becoming. Why, it's the very spit of the costume little Miriam wore at the Empyrée, you remember?"

" . . . ?"

"Little Miriam, you surely remember, in the 'Apotheosis of Aviation,' in this year's Spring Revue! And this one here does make a difference, as you might say, with the dress you wore at the Empyrée, don't it?"

" . . . ?"

"Why, the other winter. The peasant skirt, with the kerchief tied over your head, and clogs. My heart gave a jump when I read your name on the posters here! I saw you again as you were in your piece at the Empyrée; it seemed like I was still there!"

" . . . ?"

"Me? Perish the thought! You have to have time on your hands to feel proper fed up. My work's cut out for me here, for it's me that has the cleaning of the dressing rooms. They've got no man to do the job, the theater here being so small! And matinee twice a week! And those conferences, when I've got to be on the spot in case the audition ladies need a stitch putting in here or a pin there . . . During the acts, yes, I must say it does get a bit lonely-like in the corridor; I get chilly, sitting there on my chair. I doze off, and wake up thinking I'm still at the Empyrée-Clichy . . . Just think, when one's been dresser for fifteen years in the same establishment! And fifteen years of good service, I may say. Never a harsh word did I have from Madame Barney, 'the boss,' as you used to say. There's an able woman for you, Madame! Hard on slackers, maybe, but above all fair. Naturally, one spared oneself no pains when working for her. In the last revue, if you remember, I had sixteen ladies to dress, eight on my passage and eight on the landing, the landing, you know, they had to convert into a dressing room for want of space. I'm not saying it turned out the most suitable place: persons undressing don't much care to see whoever it may be passing through at any moment as they rush up and down the stairs . . . Not to mention the drafts . . . Sixteen, I ask you! My fingers were worn to the bone with all those hooks and eyes. But there you are, Madame, never an entrance missed!"

" . . . ?"

"But of course, I'm very happy here. What makes you think I'm not? Monsieur Lafougère is a very nice man. He's engaged my son, as from tonight."

"...?"

"Oh, no, not as an actor, you couldn't expect that! He starts as a stagehand. That makes a pair of you making your debut together like. It's for his health that I'm here. The doctor says to me, he says: 'What he needs is the south for his bronchial tubes.' Monsieur Lafougère has taken on the two of us."

"...?"

"Oh, no, you won't be late. Precious little chance of you ever being late here! A show billed for eight-thirty may well start at nine, more or less. Ah, we're not with Madame Barney no more! The music hall, I always say, is founded on punctuality."

"...?"

"What's that noise you can hear? That's the actors in the second piece, the one with the dancing. Listen to them, just listen! And we shout, and we sing, tra-la-la, and we pick quarrels! They've no manners, no self-respect. No, but I ask you, do you hear them? With a row like that, there's no more believing myself at the Empyrée-Clichy. You've worked there yourself, so you can tell me whether you ever heard one word spoken louder than another in that house! The theater and the café concert, it's not the same thing, whatever people may say!"

"..."

"Oh, you can sigh, I don't blame you! Many's the time I have to bite back my words not to give the ladies here a piece of my mind. Only the other day one of them yelled in my face, 'Keep the door shut, Jeanne, can't you, when people are stark naked in their dressing room. It's plain to see you come from the music hall!' Another word, and I'd have answered back: 'And it's plain to see that's where you don't come from. They've got no time for the likes of you! In the music hall, we've no use for a skimpy cricket like you; what we want are persons who have the wherewithal to fill out their tights and their stays . . .' Such words are best left unspoken: home truths are never popular . . . Your little bronze shoes and stockings to match, do you want me to have them ready for the second play?"

"...!"

"Could be it's a Greek play; but you'll never find anything that sets off your legs to better advantage than bronze stockings and a pair of little shoes like these here. The main point about dancing is to set off one's legs. However, let us say I've never said a word . . . You've never been back there again, to the old place?"

"...?"

"But to the Empyrée-Clichy, of course! You don't know if my old colleague Ma Martin is still there?"

" . . . "

"So much the worse. I'd very much like to have news of her. She'd promised me faithfully to write, but envy must have turned her heart green. My engagement here has made many envious of me, you know. 'To Nice!' is what Ma Martin said to me, 'you're going to Nice! You are among the honored! You'll be able to go over to Monte Carlo and win a fortune!' "

" . . . ?"

"No, I've not been there yet. But I'll go there, all right! I'll go, if only to be able to tell them all at the old place that I have been there. I'll first tell Ma Martin, then I'll tell Madame Cavellier . . ."

" . . . ?"

"Madame Cavellier, the romantic ballad singer, Rachel's sister!"

" . . . ?"

"Oh, yes, surely you do! Madame Cavellier, with a husband in the claque, her sister, an American dancer, and her son a program seller in the lobby. Good Lord, aren't you forgetful now! I'd never have thought it of you! And Rita, don't you remember her? I knew it. Well, she's there no more."

" . . . ?"

"Where but at the Empyrée-Clichy, what do you expect?"

" . . . ?"

"What! Haven't I been talking to you of nothing but the Empyrée-Clichy? But what else would you have me talk of? Ah, but you're still a proper tease, I can see that! Don't chaff me unkindly, I have a real liking for you, because we were there together. And I can say this to you, for I know you won't laugh at me, but I read through, in yesterday's *Comœdia*, the full account of the Christmas Revue at the Empyrée-Clichy. Well, at the idea that they'd managed the whole thing without me—the rush and bustle of the dress rehearsal, the critics' preview, and the first night—why the paper dropped from my hands, and I began to cry like a silly old fool."

Clever Dogs

❧❦❧

"Hold her! Hold her! Oh, the bitch, she's nipped her again!"

Manette has just eluded the stagehand's grip and hurled herself on Cora, who was half expecting it. But the little fox terrier is endowed with the speed of a projectile and her teeth have bitten right through the collie's thick fur and into the flesh of the neck. Cora does not retaliate at once; her ears intent on the curtain bell, her pendulous lips drawn back as far as her eyes, she offers no other threat to her comrade than a grimace as fierce as a vixen's mask and a strangled rattle, soft as the purring of a large cat.

Back in her master's arms, with the hair all down her back on end like pig's bristles, Manette is choking to say something offensive.

"They'd like to gobble each other up!" the stagehand remarks.

"The idea!" Harry retorts. "They're too conscientious for that. Quick, the collars."

While he is tying around Cora's neck the blue ribbon which sets off to advantage her fair coat, the color of ripe wheat, the stagehand fastens on Manette's back a pug's harness of green velvet studded with gold, heavy with plaques and jingle bells.

"Hold her tight, just long enough for me to get into my dolman . . ."

Harry's snuff-colored cardigan, brown with sweat, disappears beneath his sapphire-blue dolman, padded around the shoulders and almost skintight. Cora, restrained by the stagehand, gasps ever more loudly, keeping her eyes trained upward on Manette's posterior, on a Manette almost in convulsions and quite terrifying, with her bloodshot eyes and backward cockled ears.

"Wouldn't a good dressing down quiet 'em?" ventures the boy in the blue jacket.

"Never before their act," Harry snaps categorically.

Behind the lowered curtain, he tests the equilibrium of the railings which enclose the track of miniature obstacles, makes certain the platform and hurdle are secure, and polishes with a woolen rag the nickel-plated bars of the springboards on which the yellow collie will rebound. It is he too who goes to fetch from his dressing room a set of paper hoops still damp from hasty resticking.

"I do everything myself!" he declares. "The master's eye . . ."

Behind his back the stagehand shrugs his shoulders. "The master's eye, my foot! That means no tip for the team!"

The two-man "team" bears Harry no grudge on his fifteen francs a day takings. "Fifteen francs for three mouths and ten paws, that's not much!" the stagehand concedes.

Three mouths, ten paws, and two hundred kilos of luggage. The whole concern tours throughout the year with the aid of special third-class half-fare rates. The year before there was an extra "mouth," that of the white poodle now defunct; an overage old campaigner, a dog that had had his day, well known in every French and foreign establishment, and much regretted by Harry, who loves to sing the praises of poor old Charlot.

"He knew how to do everything, Madame: waltz, somersault, springboard work, all the tricks of a canine calculator, he knew the lot. He could have taught me a few, I'm telling you, and I've trained a good few circus dogs in my time! He loved his job, and nothing else, as for the rest, he was a duffer. Toward the end you wouldn't have given a bob for him had you seen him by day, he looked so old, fourteen he must have been, at least, and that stiff from the rheumatics, with his eyes running and his black muzzle going all gray. He only began to wake up when the time for his act came around; it was then that he was well worth seeing! I used to doll him up like a movie star, with black cosmetic on his nose, thick pencil around his poor old rheumy eyes, I'd starch-powder him all over to make him white as snow, then add the blue ribbons! My word, Madame, he soon came alive again! Hardly had I finished his makeup when off he went, walking on his hind legs, sneezing, and carrying on no end till the curtain rose. Back in the wings again, I used to wrap him in a blanket and then give him a spirit rub. I certainly prolonged his life, but no performing poodle can last forever!

"My two bitches there, they do their work all right, but it's not the same thing at all. They love their master, they fear the whip, they use their heads and are conscientious, but there's no professional pride in their makeup. They go through their routine as though they were pulling a cart, no more, no less. They're hard workers, but they're not true artistes. It's easy to see from their faces that they'd like to be through with the whole performance, and the public don't like that. Either they think the animals are playing them up, or else they make no bones about saying, 'Poor beasts, how sad they look! What tortures they must have endured to learn all those monkey tricks!' I'd just like to watch 'em, all those ladies and gentlemen of the Protection for Animals, trying to put the dogs through their paces. Why, they'd do exactly like me and my sort. Sugar, hunting crop; hunting crop, sugar; with a good dose of patience added: there's no other way that I know of."

At this very moment the "hard workers" are eyeing each other with hostile intent. Manette, perched on a block of multicolored wood, is nervously trembling; while, facing her, Cora has laid her ears back flat like a sorry cat.

At the shrill of the bell, the orchestra interrupts the heavy polka, intended to calm the public's impatience, with the opening bars of a slow valse; as if obeying a signal, the two dogs adjust their position: they have recognized *their* valse. Cora gently swishes her tail, pricks her ears, and takes on the neutral expression, amiable and bored, which makes her resemble the portraits of Empress Eugénie. Manette, insolent, alert, rather too fat, awaits the painfully slow rise of the curtain and Harry's arrival on the scene, yawns, and starts panting at once, from exasperation and thirst.

The act begins, without incident, without rebellion. Cora, forewarned by a flick of the whip under her belly, does not cheat while taking her jumps. Manette walks on her front legs, valses, barks, and jumps a few obstacles erect on the back of the yellow collie. Their performance is commonplace, but correct; there is nothing to be said against it.

Inveterate grumblers may find fault, perhaps, with Cora's queenly aloofness, or with the small terrier's artificial zest. It's easy to see that such grouchers have not got months of touring in their paws, and know nothing of the horrors of guard's vans, hostels, bread-and-meat mash that distends but does not nourish, the long hours of waiting in railway stations, the too-short constitutional walks, the iron collar, the muzzle, and above all the eternal waiting, the nerve-racking wait for exercise, for starting out, for food, for a thrashing. These exacting spectators ignore the fact that the life of performing animals is spent in waiting, and that this wears them out.

Tonight both dogs are waiting for nothing but the end of their turn. No sooner is the curtain down than a pitched battle ensues. Harry returns to the scene just in time to part the pair of them, flecked with pink nips, their ribbons in tatters.

"It's something quite new for them, Madame, something they've picked up while they've been here," he cries in a fury. "As a rule they're very good friends, they sleep together in my hotel bedroom. But here, why it's only a small town, you see. You can't pick and choose here. The innkeeper's wife said to me, 'I'll put up with one dog, but I'll not take two!' So, as I like to deal fair, I let first one, then the other of my two bitches spend the night in the theater, in a padlocked basket. They cottoned on to the rotation right away. And now, every night, they go through the high jinks you've just witnessed. All through the day they're as meek as lambs; as the hour approaches to buckle one in, it's a fight to decide which won't be the one to stay behind in the locked basket; they'd tear each other to shreds, they're so jealous! And you've not seen the half of it! It's a proper show to watch the performance of the one I'm taking back with me, when she starts yapping her head off and scampering around the basket as I shut the lid on the other! I don't like to be unfair to animals, not me! I'd do anything rather than what I have to do here, but since there is nothing else for it, how can I?"

I did not see Manette tonight, as she took her leave, arrogant and radiating joy; but I did see the imprisoned Cora, rigid with repressed despair. Her lovely golden fleece was crumpled against the wicker sides of the basket, and through the bars at the top poked her long, gentle, fox-like nose.

She listened to the receding sounds of her master's footsteps and Manette's tinkling bell. When the iron door finally closed behind them, she drew in a long breath to let out a howl; but she remembered that I was still there, and all I heard was a deep human sigh. Then she proudly closed her eyes and settled down for the night.

The Child Prodigy

"Really, there are a great many children in this show, I find; do you not agree, Madame?"

This remark is flung at me, in supercilious and superior tones, by a large blond lady—*Spécialité, Valses lentes*—who for the moment is bundled in a crepon kimono costing seven francs fifty, the sort of kimono invariably found in all music hall dressing rooms. Hers is pink, with storks printed on it; mine is blue, sprinkled with small red and green fans; and that of the dove trainer is mauve, with black flowers.

The stout, discontented lady has just been jostled by three kids no taller than fox hounds, dressed as Red Indians, who were rushing off to remove their makeup. But her bitter words were directed at a silent creature, a sort of unhappy governess dressed all in black, slowly pacing up and down the corridor.

Having spoken, the stout lady gives a slight cough, in a most distinguished manner, and retires to her dressing room, but not before throwing a last contemptuous glance at the governess, who shrugs her shoulders and smiles vaguely at me.

"She intended that remark for me. She finds there are too many children in the show! Very well, what about me in that case, I'm to start by removing my own child, I suppose!"

"What, you can't mean that you're dissatisfied? 'Princess Lily' is surely a success?"

"Yes, and don't I know it! My daughter is quite devastating, isn't she? Yes, she's my daughter, my real daughter . . . Wait a second and I'll button you up at the back, you can't possibly manage it yourself! Besides, I'm in no hurry myself. My daughter's gone to the hairdresser to have her ringlets set. I'd so much like to stay with you for a while. All the more, on account of her and me having had words just now."

In the mirror behind me I can see a plain humble face with moist eyes.

"She certainly answered me back just now! I tell you, Madame, that child fair takes me to pieces, for all that she's only thirteen. Oh, she don't look her age, I know, but then she's dressed to look so much younger on the stage. I'm not telling you all this to deny her, or to say anything against her.

"No flattery intended, but I'd be the first to agree that nothing could look sweeter or prettier than she does when she plays her piece on the violin in that white baby frock of hers. Or when she sings her Italian song—you've seen her, have you, in that little Neapolitan boy's costume? And her American dance, have you seen that, too?

"The public can soon tell the difference between a dainty number like my girl's and one like those three little miseries who've just gone rushing off. They're so scraggy, Madame, and they look so scared, too. Those frightened eyes they roll at the smallest mistake they make in their work! As I was saying only the other day to my Lily, 'They make a pitiful sight!' 'Phooey!' she gives me for answer, 'they're not interesting.' I know well enough it's that competitive spirit in her that makes her say things like that, but all the same she comes out with remarks that knock the stuffing out of me.

"I'm telling you all this, but you'll keep it to yourself, you won't let it go any farther, will you? I feel a bit nervy today because she's answered me back just now, me, her mother!

"Oh, I can't say I bless the man who put Lily on the stage! Fine gentleman though he is, and a good writer of plays. I used to work for his lady, by the day, embroidering fine linen. His lady was very kind to me, and allowed Lily to come and wait for me there when she came out of school.

"One day, it must be nearly four years since, the gentleman I was speaking of was on the lookout for a clever child to take a little girl's part in one of his plays, and for a lark he asked me for my Lily . . . It was soon settled, Madame. My little girl had them all flabbergasted from the start. Poise, memory, proper intonation, she'd got all that and more. I didn't take it too serious at first till I heard they'd pay Lily up to eight francs a day. There was nothing you could say against that, was there?

"After that play came another, and then another. And every time I'd say, 'After success like that, it's the last time Lily will act,' they all got after me. 'Now stop all this nonsense! Just drop that damned embroidery job of yours! Can't you see you've got a gold mine in that child! Not to mention you've no right to stifle a talent like hers.' And so on and so forth, till I hardly dared breathe . . .

"And during that time, you should have seen the progress my little one made! Hobnobbing with the celebrities, and saying 'My dear' to the manager himself! And grave as a judge with it all, which made everyone split their sides.

"Then came the time, two years ago, when my daughter found herself out of a job. 'Thank the Lord,' I says to myself, 'now we can have a rest, and settle down on the nice little sum we've put by from the theater.' I consult Lily, as was my duty; she'd already made a big impression on me with her knowing ways. Can you guess what she answered? 'My poor mamma, you must be crazy! I shan't always be eleven, unfortunately. This is not the time to go to sleep. There's nothing doing in the theater this season, but the music hall's there, all right, for me to have a go!'

"As you may imagine, Madame, she didn't lack encouragement from these, and those, and especially the others, none of whose business it was! Gifted as she is, it didn't take her long to learn to dance and sing. Her chief worry is that she's growing up. I have to measure her every fortnight: she'd like so much to stay small! Only last month she flew into a rage because she'd put on two centimeters in the last year, and reproached me for not having made her a dwarf from birth.

"It's terrible, the manner of speaking she's picked up backstage, and her bossiness, too! She soon gets the upper hand, I being so weak. She argued back at me again today. She'd been that la-di-da in her answers that for a moment I saw red and got on my high horse. 'And so what! I'm your mother, I'd have you know! And supposing I took you by the arm and put a stop to you going on with the theater!'

"She was busy making up her eyes; she didn't even turn around, she just started to laugh. 'Stop me going on with the theater? Ha! ha! ha! And I suppose you'd go on in my place and sing them "Chiribibibi" to pay the rent!'

"Tears came to my eyes, Madame: it's hard when one is humiliated by one's own flesh and blood. But it's not altogether that I feel so bad about. It's . . . I'm not sure how to explain what it is. There are times when I look at her and think, 'She's my little daughter, and she's thirteen. She's been four years in show business. Rehearsals, backstage tittle-tattle, unfair treatment on the part of the manager, rivalry between the stars, jealousy of her comrades, her posters, the bandleader who bears her a grudge, the call boy who was too late—or too soon—with her bell, the claque, her costume maker . . . That's all she's had in her head and on her lips for the last four years. All these past four years I've never once heard her talk like a child . . . And never, never, never again shall I hear her talk like a child—like a real child . . ."

[*Translated by Anne-Marie Callimachi*]

The Misfit

1

The stagehands called her "a choice piece"; but the Schmetz family—eight acrobats, their mother, wives, and "young ladies"—never mentioned her; Ida and Hector, "Duo Dancers," said severely, "She brings shame on the house." Jady, the *diseuse* from Montmartre, made use of her most rasping contralto to exclaim, on seeing her, "Well, what d'you know about that number!" and was quizzed in reply with imperious disdain, and the flashy deployment of a long ermine stole.

For the public this outcast was billed as "La Roussalka"; but for the entire caf'-conc' personnel she became, on the spot, "Poison Ivy." Within the span of a mere six days the austere backstage staff of the Élysée-Pigalle were at their wits' end, and deplored her superfluous presence. Dancer? Singer? Pah! Neither the one, nor t'other . . .

"She displaces air, that's all!" Brague assured everyone.

She sang Russian songs and danced the *jota*, the *sevillana*, and the tango, revised and corrected by an Italian ballet master—Spanish *olé!* with a Frenchified flavor!

No sooner was Friday's band call over than the whole house was eyeing her askance. La Roussalka chose to rehearse in a carefully considered Liberty gown and hat, hands in muff, indicating the *jota* with discreet little jerks of her hobble-skirted posterior, stopping abruptly to shout, "That's not it, Jesus! That's not it," stamping and screaming "Brutes!" at the members of the band.

Mutter Schmetz, who sat mending her sons' tights in the circle, could hardly be kept in her seat. "That, an *ardisde*! That, a *tanzer*! Ach! she is nozzings but a *dard*, yes?"

And La Roussalka continued, "with enough brazen cheek to gobble up her parents," to employ Brague's energetic metaphor, bullying the property man, cursing the electrician, demanding a blue flood on her entrance and a red spot on her exit, and goodness knows what else!

"I've played all the big houses in Europe," she yelled, "and I've neverrr seen a joint so disgrrracefully rrrun!"

She rolled her *r*'s in a most insulting manner, as if she were chucking a handful of pebbles straight in your face.

During this rehearsal one saw nothing but La Roussalka, and heard nothing but La Roussalka. In the evening, however, it was discovered that there were two of them: opposite La Roussalka, dark, ablaze with purple spangles and imitation topazes, danced a soft, fair-haired child, graceful, light as air. "This is my sisterrr," La Roussalka declared, though no one had asked for enlightenment. Further, she had an offensive way of clinching matters, on her "worrrd of honorrr," that shocked even her most candid listener.

Whether sister, servile poor relation, or a little dancer hired for a pittance—nobody knew or cared. She appeared, a mere chit of a girl, to be dancing in her sleep, docile as a lamb, pretty, with huge, vacant, brown eyes. At the end of the *sevillana*, she rested a moment against a flat, mouth agape, then noiselessly returned to the cellar, while La Roussalka started on her tango.

"What's more," Brague said for all to hear, "she dances with her hands!"

Hands, arms, hips, eyes, eyebrows, hair—her feet, being unskilled, did not know what they were up to. What saved the day for her was the cocksure flamboyance, the assured insolence of her least gesture. She congratulated herself if she made a false step, seemed highly delighted if she fluffed an entrechat, and, back in the wings, gave herself no time to draw breath before starting to talk, talk, talk, and lie with all the abandon of a southerner born in Russia.

She addressed herself to the world in general with the familiarity of a tipsy princess. She stopped one of the blond Schmetz boys, in his pale mauve tights, by laying both hands on his shoulders, so that with lowered eyes and blushing, he dared not make good his escape; she forcibly drove Mutter Schmetz into a corner, only to be met with a volley of *Ja, ja, ja*'s as stinging as smacks in the face; the facetious stage manager got more than he bargained for in the way of abuse, as did Brague, who kept whistling throughout her tirade.

"My family . . . My native land . . . I'm a Russian . . . I speak fourteen languages, like all my compatriots . . . I've gotten myself six thousand francs' worth of stage costumes for this wretched little number worth nothing at all . . . But you should see, my dearrr, all the town clothes I have! Money means nothing to me! . . . I can't tell you my real name: there's no knowing what might happen if I did! My father holds the most important position in Moscow. He's married, you know. Only he's not married to my mother . . . He gives me everything I want . . . You've seen my sister? She's a good-for-nothing. I beat her a lot, she won't work. All I can say is, she's pure! On my life, she's that! . . . You none of you saw me last year in Berlin? Oh, that's where you should have seen me! A thirty-two-thousand-franc act, my dearrr! With that blackguard Castillo, the dancer. He robbed me, on my worrrd of honorr, he stole from me! But once across the Russian border and I told my father everything. Castillo was jugged! In Russia, we show no mercy to thieves. Jugged, I tell you, jugged! Like this!"

She went through the motions of turning a key in its lock, and her heavily violet-penciled eyes sparkled with cruelty. Then, played out, she went down to her dressing room, where she relieved her nervous tension by giving her "sister" more than one good clout on the ears. Genuine stage slaps they were, resounding right enough, but they rang true on those young cheeks. They could be heard up on the stage. Mutter Schmetz, outraged, spoke of "gomblaining to de bolice" and pressed to her bosom two flaxen-haired lads of seven and eight, the youngest born of her flaxen-haired brood, as if "Poison Ivy" were about to give them a spanking.

By what noxious flames was this fiend of a woman consumed? Before the week was out, she had hurled a satin slipper at the band-leader's head, referred to the secretary-general, in his hearing, as a "pimp," and, by accusing her dresser of stealing her jewelry, reduced the poor creature to tears. Gone were the quiet evenings of the Élysée-Pigalle and the peaceful slumbers of its cells behind closed doors! Gone for good! "Poison Ivy" had ruined everything.

"She's out for my blood, is she!" was Jady's bold threat. "Let me hear one single word from that one, no, not even that, let her so much as brush against me in the doorway, and I'll get her fired!"

Brague, for once, might well have supported Jady, for he could not stomach the unwarrantable success of La Roussalka, and the way she glittered among the mended tights, home-cleaned dresses and smoke-blackened scenery, like a sham jewel in an imitation setting.

"I enjoy my rest," Ida whispered to Brague. "There's never been so much as a word uttered against my husband and me, you know that! Well then, I can assure you, that *when* I leave the stage, you know, *when* I carry Hector off standing on my hands, and I catch sight of 'Poison Ivy' sniggering at the two of us, it wouldn't need much for me to drop Hector plonk on her head!"

Nobody bothered anymore about the little blond "sister," who never uttered a word and danced like a sleepwalker between one stinging blow and the next. She was to be met with in the corridors, her shoulder weighed down by a slop pail or a pitcher full of water, shuffling along in bedraggled old slippers, her petticoats trailing behind her.

But after the show, La Roussalka rigged her out in a loosely belted dress, too voluminous for her flat-chested figure, and a hat that came halfway down her back, and whisked her off, red-cheeked from her drubbing and gummy-eyed, to the night haunts on the Butte de Montmartre. There she made her sit down, docile and half asleep, with cocktails in front of her, and once again, to the cynical amazement of chance "friends," she started to talk and talk and tell lies.

"My father . . . the most influential man in Moscow . . . I speak fourteen languages . . . I myself never tell lies; but my compatriots, the Russians, are one and all liars . . . I've sailed twice around the world on a princely yacht . . . My jewels are all in Moscow, for my family forbids me to wear them on the stage, because of the ducal coronets on every piece . . ."

Meanwhile, the little sister dozed on half awake. From time to time she almost took a somersault when one of the "friends" tried to squeeze her thin waist or stroke her bare neck, pale mauve with pearl powder. Her surprise unloosed the rage of La Roussalka.

"Wake up, you, where do you think you are? Jesus, what a life, having to drag this child around with me!"

Calling to witness not only the "friends" but the restaurant at large, she shouted, "Look at her there, that good-for-nothing! This table couldn't hold the piles of dough I've spent on her! I'm reduced to tears the whole day long because she will do nothing, nothing, nothing!"

The slapped child never batted an eyelid. Of what youthful past, or of what escape, was she dreaming behind her mysteriously vacant, huge brown eyes?

2

"This child," Brague decrees, "is a kid we'll stick in the chorus. One more, one less, it makes little difference. She'll always earn her forty sous . . . though I don't much like having to deal with misfits . . . I say this now so's it's known another time."

Brague speaks pontifically, in his dark kingdom of the Élysée-Pigalle, where his double function of mime and producer assure him undisputed authority.

The "misfit," or so it would seem, pays no heed to his words. Her vague thanks are expressed in a meaningless smile that does not spread to her large eyes, the color of clouded coffee, and she lingers on, arms limp, twiddling the handle of a faded bag.

She has just this moment been christened by Brague: henceforth she will be known as "Misfit." A week ago she was the "good-for-nothing little sister"; she gains by the change.

Little matter, for she discourages malice, and even attention, this foundling who has just been dumped down here, without a sound, by "La Roussalka, her sister," who went off leaving her with three torn silk underslips, a couple of "latest models" sizes too big for her, a pair of evening shoes with paste buckles, not to mention a hat, and the key to the room they occupied together in the rue Fontaine.

La Roussalka, alias "Poison Ivy," that human hurricane, that storm-cloud charged with hail ready to burst at the least shock, has shown in her flight a strange discretion, by removing her four large trunks, her "family papers," the portrait of her *fatherrr* "who controls rain and sunshine in Moscow," while forgetting the little sister who danced with her, docile, half asleep, and somehow weighed down by blows.

Misfit neither wept nor wailed. She stated her case to the lady manager in a few words and with a Flemish accent exactly suited to her blond sheep-like appearance. Madame did not overflow with maternal protestations or pitying indignation, any more than did Jady, the *diseuse*, or Brague himself. Misfit has attained the age of eighteen, and is therefore old enough to go out alone and look after her own affairs.

"Eighteen!" Jady grumbled, suffering from a hangover and bronchitis. "Eighteen, and she expects me to take pity on her!"

Brague, a good fellow at heart, felt more kindly disposed. "Forty sous, did I say? We'll bloody well give three francs, so's to give her time to look around."

Since then Misfit comes every day, at one, to sit in one of the canvas-covered stalls of the Élysée-Pigalle, and wait. When Brague calls out, "On stage, the great hetaerae!" she climbs onto the gangway that spans the orchestra pit and sits down at a sticky zinc table such as is used in low pubs. In the pantomime now in rehearsal she will take the part, wearing a reconditioned pink gown, of an "elegant customer" at a Montmartre cabaret.

She can hardly be seen from the auditorium, since she has been placed at the very back of the stage, behind the huge seedy-looking hats of the other ladies of the chorus. The stagehand sets in front of her an empty glass and a spoon, and there she poses, her childish chin resting on a dubiously gloved hand.

She is a thoroughly safe customer. She doesn't jabber on the stage, never complains of the icy draft whistling around her legs, nor has she either the unhappy look of young Miriam, so furiously hungry that it seems to demand food, or Vanda's feverish activity, Vanda the Cluck, forever producing from her pocket a baby's sock in need of darning, or a flannelette brassiere that she mends while trying to hide it.

Misfit has fallen into oblivion again, apparently thankful at last to be able to roll up into a ball, as though the general indifference has spared her the trouble of existing. She speaks even less than the star dancer from Milan, a heavy woman, pitted with smallpox and plastered with holy medals and coral callosities. Her silence, at any rate, is born of contempt, she being interested solely in the "five points," the *entrechats-six*, the whole graceless and laborious range of acrobatics that exercise the sailor's muscles on her calves.

Upstage, Brague is doing his level best not to husband an ounce of his energy. "Isn't he lucky to sweat like that!" sighs the wretched brat Miriam, white with cold under her rouge. Brague sweats in vain at his miming. He wears himself out trying to communicate his faith, his feverish enthusiasm, to the little tart in her hairless fur, to the stubborn mender of baby socks, to the arrogant ballerina. He insists—oh, the folly of it!—that Miriam, Vanda, and the Italian should at least appear to take an interest in the action of his piece.

"I'm telling you . . . Good God! I'm trying to tell you this is the moment when these two characters are starting to fight! When two chaps start a fight close beside you, doesn't it affect you more than that? Good God, do stir your stumps! At least say Ah! as you would when there's a brawl in a pub and you pick up your skirts ready to fly!"

After the sound and the fury of an hour's effort, Brague takes a rest, finding some compensation in running through his big scene, the scene where he reads the letter from his mother. Joy and surprise, then terror, and finally despair, are depicted on features seamed with such intensity of expression, such excess of pathos, that Vanda stops sewing, Miriam slapping the soles of her feet, and the Italian dancer, swathed in a gray woolen shawl, deigns to leave the framework of a flat to watch Brague's tears flow. A minor daily triumph, delectable all the same.

On each such occasion, however, a faint chortle like a smothered laugh has spoiled this affecting moment. Brague's sharp ear caught it from the very first day.

The second day: "Which of you ladies is the chucklehead that's convulsed with laughter?" he shouts. No answer, and the dismal faces of the "great hetaerae" reveal nothing.

The third day: "There's a fine of forty sous about to fall on somebody's nut—and I know very well who it is—for causing a disturbance during rehearsal!" But Brague does not know who it is.

The fourth day: "You there, Misfit, are you trying to get a rise out of me?" Brague storms. "You wear yourself to a shadow, yes, you strive to put into what you're doing a little . . . of the tragic side of life, of . . . simple truth and beauty, you try to pull the mimodrama out of the common rut, only to succeed in what? In reducing misfits like you to a state of hopeless giggles!"

A chair falls, and the pale trembling form of Misfit rises from out of the Stygian gloom, bleating like a goat. "But Mon . . . Monsieur Brague, I . . . I'm not laughing, I'm crying!"

3

I'm really a wonderful guy,
So fond of the kiddies am I,
The nice sweet little dears . . .
Garn, the little perishers!

Misfit leans against an iron strut, swaying like a small chained bear as she automatically rubs her powdered shoulder blades to and fro against the cold metal. She listens, while gazing from a distance at the character whom the Compère is about to introduce to the Commère as a choice titbit, by gently pressing forefinger to thumb as if he held between them a folded butterfly.

"Plebiscites are all the fashion, my dear friend: I am happy to present to you tonight the man who, by an impressive majority, has been newly elected the Prince of Mirth—our joyous friend, adventurer, and companion—Sarracq!"

"The frock coat don't fit him half as well as Raffort," thinks Misfit. "And you could see even then it hadn't been made to fit Raffort."

She notes the difference between the pearl gray frock coat that hangs too long and loose on Sarracq and the violet silk tail coat that trusses the stout body of the Compère, who does his best, by rounding his arms and shoulders, to conceal the shortness of his sleeves. As he steps up onto the stage again, his back to the public, he turns sideways and draws in his waist, to ease the tightness of the knee breeches that are squeezing the life out of him.

An ominous heat hangs heavy on the close of the evening performance. The exasperation is due not so much to the storm that is about to break into a torrential downpour as to the fact that it is one more August night in a succession of cloudless days and nights without a drop of rain. It is a merciless summer heat that has slowly penetrated through the dim recesses of the wings down to the musty lower regions of the

Empyrée-Palace. The performers know it well. Shouts of laughter are no longer heard; even the chorus girls' dressing rooms, wide open to the corridors, no longer resound with the tumult of invigorating slanging matches. From the Commère to the grips and flymen, all creep about cautiously, with the economy of movement of shipwrecked people determined to harbor the last ounce of their strength.

"Matinee tomorrow!" thinks Misfit. She droops her head like a cab horse and, without seeing them, gazes down at her satin shoes already agape where the big toes poke through. She is revived by the refreshing whiff of ether and smelling salts. "Yes, of course, for Elsie, who's a bit off-color. She's struck lucky, as you might say! She's through with it for the evening!"

Four skinny little creatures, in embroidered linen frocks, put in an appearance one after the other on the iron stairs. Their silent passage seems to attract Misfit like a magnet, and she follows them as if sleep-walking. With the same uncertain step, they file onto the stage one after the other, sing an indistinct little ditty about the games little girls get up to, at the same time kicking up their legs and baby-frock skirts, and then return breathless to the wings.

When Misfit, leaning against her iron stay, exhales an almost inaudible, desperate "Oh, this heat!" one of the four Babies breaks into a nervous laugh, as if Misfit had said something terribly funny.

The Summer Revue, condemned to survive until the first of September, is in the throes of its last agony. It plays to pitiful second houses where some two hundred spectators, dispersed over the echoing auditorium, eye one another with embarrassment and disappear before the Grand Finale. It comes to life again on certain Saturdays, or a rainy Sunday, when the galleries are crammed with a malodorous crowd.

With prudence verging on the cynical, the management has removed one by one from the cast all the expensive stars of the original production. The English male dancer turned up his nose at the Parisian summer; the operetta star now gives Trouville the benefit of her soprano; a hundred performances have exhausted relays of Commères. Sarracq, idol of the Left Bank, has stepped into the frock coat of Raffort, who himself had succeeded the English dancer, and thus elevated to top of the bill a name quite honestly unknown on this side of the bridges.

Only the costumes have not been renewed, the costumes and Misfit. Ever since the day when her temperamental sister, the *danseuse*, deposited her on the theater doorstep three years since, Mitfit has been part of the house, appearing in the chorus of all the revues, pantomimes, and ballets. Luck had it one day that the manager took notice of her to the extent of inquiring, "And what's that little girl over there?"

"She's one of the three francs thirty-threes," the stage manager replied.

As from the day following, a dazzled Misfit had her salary raised from a hundred to a hundred and sixty francs a month. This change entailed putting in an appearance for endless hours spent in bovine rumination, or in work more stultifying than abject idleness—parades, chorus routine, or plastic poses. Summer and winter alike come and go without releasing her, and her soft young eyelids are already swollen by fatigue into two lymphatic pouches. She is sweet and gentle, with large submissive eyes, so much so that the stage manager refers to her by turns as "the cream of the regulars," or "the dumbbell of the duds."

Tonight she is feeling the heat like the rest of the world, and even more than the others, because she has eaten next to nothing. The mere thought of her dinner makes her feel sick; she imagines she is still sitting at an outside table with an untouched plate of hot beef going cold in front of her. There are also the green peas that smell of wet dog. She shakes the curls of her thick wig against her cheeks and slowly starts toward the iron stairs. She is in no haste to quit the spot where she is slowly, peacefully, fading away in a sort of funereal security. Before going down below, she risks a peep through the curtain slit and murmurs apprehensively, "Oh, it's packed full of savages again tonight!"

The fact is, Misfit is afraid of summer audiences. She knows that the regular quiet shopkeepers who frequent the Empyrée-Palace relinquish their seats in August to strange hordes of foreigners whose raucous hubbub during the intervals she finds disquieting. She has an equal horror of rough Teutonic beards, Oriental hard blue-black hairpads and oily skins, and impenetrable Negro smiles . . . It must be the heat that brings them, with all the other scourges of these dog days.

Misfit is not ignorant of the fact that "savages," in the deserted streets after midnight, follow and solicit pale and anemic little chorus girls, whose theater salary is three francs thirty-three a day.

"One's got to live, of course," thinks Misfit, with her sorry nag's resignation. "But not with these, not with those, not those *savages!*"

She has quite made up her mind to go home alone, come what may. However worn out she may be, she will walk as far as Caulaincourt on the other side of the bridge. There her scorching small room awaits her, at the very top of a boarding house overlooking the Montmartre cemetery. The thin walls keep the heat all night long and what wind there is brings factory smoke only.

It is not a room to live in, let alone to sleep in. But Misfit has bought a half pound of plums, and these she will eat all alone, in her chemise, beside the window . . . This is her one summer luxury. She plays the game of squeezing the stones between finger and thumb and then seeing how far she can shoot them, even as far as the cemetery. When, in the silence before dawn, she hears a stone rebound from an iron crucifix and strike with a musical ring a glass pane of the chapel, she smiles as she says to herself, "I've won!"

[*Translated by Anne-Marie Callimachi*]

FROM THE FRONT

"La Fenice"

❧❧❧

"What is there to do tonight?"

Drenched throughout the day, Naples has been steaming like a dirty bath. The bay lies flattened by the continual rain, and Capri has melted away behind the rigid silvery downpour. A spectacular curtain of bluish-purple cloud veils and unveils Vesuvius from view and trails on down as far as the sea, where it finally shrouds the sky, crushing, as the sun sets, the living red rose that lay half open in its midst.

The tinkle of a bell echoes through the empty white hotel where we brave cholera and hail squalls. We could run or bowl a hoop down the interminable corridor under the dreary eye of the German waiters. We have the billiard room to ourselves and the bar—where the man in the white waistcoat is asleep—all the elevators and the crinkly-haired chambermaids with lovely eyes and fat shiny noses. We own the dining room—with places laid for two hundred guests—isolated from us by a three-paneled screen that prevents our seeing the half acre of polished parquet floor, dazzlingly bright . . . but . . .

"What is there to do tonight?"

In the first place, consult the barometer. Then, forehead pressed against the french window of the verandah, gaze out over the flooded quayside to watch, swaying in its iron gibbet, the electric globe big as a mauve moon as it swings in the wind.

Between one gusty squall and the next, a voice sings "Bella mia" and "Fa me dormi": a child's voice, shrill, metallic, nasal, sustained by mandolins. All of a sudden I am startled to see, on the other side of the windowpane, a forehead pressed against mine, two eyes trying to look into my eyes, a pair of dark eyes under the weather-beaten disorder of picturesque hair: the young girl who was singing has come up the terrace steps in search of her half-lira. I open the door a little way; the child has barely slipped in before she makes good her escape, after a confidingly suppliant gesture, a quick, utterly feminine, almost blush-making glance of appraisal. She glistens with raindrops under her stiff mantle with its pointed hood; a smell of ponds and soaking wet wool has come in with her.

"What is there to do tonight? Tell me, say something, what can we do tonight?"

Half an hour later we find ourselves stranded at La Fenice, a "caf' conc'" of moderate size, plastered all over—walls, drop curtain, passages—with posters glorifying a local liqueur in a riot of publicity. Insipid in design, the outmoded silhouettes of the women displayed, high-bosomed and high-waisted, suffice to make us feel suddenly very far from Paris, and a little lost.

Despite two glaring floodlights, the place as a whole remains dismal; there are exactly three women in the audience, two little countrified, shabbily dressed tarts and myself. But the men are there in their hordes! While waiting for the curtain to rise they laugh uproariously, hum to the rhythm of the band, shake hands with one another, and bandy quips across the house; here reigns the familiarity found in places of ill repute.

But, on the program, what a regiment of women! And what lovely Italian names, Gemma la Bellissima, Lorenza, Lina, Maria! Among this bevy I madly hope for red-haired Venetian beauties with pink-and-white skins, Roman goddesses pale under raven-black hair, Florentines with aristocratic chins . . . Alas! . . .

Against a crudely painted backcloth, on which I certainly never expected this scene of a French château mirrored in the Loire, file past Lina, Maria, Lorenza, and Gemma la Bellissima, and countless others. The frailest of them humiliates the caryatids that support the balcony. Here, the solid is patently preferred. So much so that I suspect Lorenza di Gloria of having supplied, with considerable aid from cotton wadding and rolled-up handkerchiefs, a suitable substitute for what is lacking in the still angular body of a young Jewess; for she waves a pair of skinny arms, yellow under the armpits, around an enormous bust and all along inflated hips draped in woven satin, violet, and gold.

A shattering storm of applause greets—but why?—Gemma la Bellissima, a flaccid dancing girl in green gauze. She is the "Dancer in the Nude," whose bashful antics are noisily acclaimed and accompanied, while her reserved smile acts as an apology for having to display so much! At one moment, turning her too-white back to the audience, she goes so far as to attempt a lascivious wriggle; but she quickly turns around again, as though wounded by the glances, to resume, eyes suitably lowered, her little game as a modest washerwoman, wringing and shaking out her spangled veil.

The local star performer is worth listening to, and looking at as well. She is Maria X, an Italian approaching her fifties, still beautiful, and cleverly pargeted. I cannot deny, nor do I reject, the appeal of her well-trained voice, already going, and of her overdemonstrative gestures. Nor will I dispute that she possesses a natural instinct for mime which enables her to "convey the meaning" with face, shoulders, curve of the waist, plump yet responsive legs, but above all with her hands; indefatigable hands that mold, weigh, and caressingly stroke the empty air, while her weary features, bright, seductive, express laughter or tears, or become creased with wrinkles regardless of the cracks they create in her heavy makeup, till with a single knife-edged glance, with a contraction of her proud velvety eyebrows, she compels the lustful attention of the entire audience.

"Lucette de Nice." . . . I have been looking forward to the appearance of the little French girl who bears such a pretty, childish name. Here she is. Slimness personified—at last! Rather misery-stricken in her short and heavily spangled dress, she sings hackneyed Parisian ditties. Where have I seen this slovenly yet graceful errand girl before, with no nose to speak of, and a sulky look as though she were afraid? At Olympia, perhaps? Or at the Gaîté-Rochechouart?

Lucette de Nice . . . She knows but one gesture, a curious scooping movement of the hand, not unlike a cat, preposterous but somehow pleasing. Where have I seen her? Her roving eyes encounter mine, and her smile leaves her lips to be transferred to her large blue-penciled eyes. She has recognized me too, and never again takes her eyes off me. She gives no further thought to her words. I can read on her poor-little-girl features the longing to join me, to talk to me. When she comes to the end of her song she gives me a fleeting smile, like someone about to cry, then hurriedly leaves the stage, knocking her arm against the entrance.

After that, there is yet another heavy, healthy girl, full of confidence but not fully awake, who scatters among the audience stalkless flowers attached to light pliable reeds. She is followed by a female acrobat, undisguisedly pregnant, who appears to find her act a torture and takes her bow with a distraught look on a face beaded with sweat.

Too many women, oh, far too many women! I could wish this flock enlivened by some fruity Neapolitan comic or the inevitable tenor with blue hair. Five or six poodles would not spoil the show, nor would a *cornet-à-piston* player who tries out his skill on a box of cigars.

Such a welter of females becomes depressing! One sees them at too-close range, one's thoughts go out to them. My eyes wander from the threadbare false hem to the tarnished gilt of a girdle, from the dim little ring to the pink-dipped white coral necklace. And then my eye lights on the red wrists under a coat of wet white, on hands hardened by cooking, washing, and sweeping; I surmise the laddered stockings and the leaf-thin soles; I imagine the grimy stairs leading up to the fireless room and the short-lived light of the candle . . . While gazing up at the present singer, I see the others, all the others . . .

"What do you say to our leaving?"

The deluge continues. A raging gale drives the downpour under the raised hood of our carriage as we go bouncing away, drawn by a devil-possessed crazy small black nag, that seems hell-bent under the encouragement of the frenzied bellowings of a humpbacked cabby.

"Gitanette"

Ten o'clock. There has been so much smoking in the Sémiramis bar tonight that my compote of apples has a vague flavor of Virginia cigarettes . . . It is Saturday night. A kind of holiday fever exists among the regulars in anticipation of the rest day tomorrow, that exceptional day so unlike all the others, with the long lie in bed in the morning, the drive out in a taxicab as far as the Pavillon-Bleu, the visit to relations, the outing for the kids shut up in some suburban boarding school who will be coming, on this lovely Sunday morning, to have a breath of the fresh invigorating air of Le Châtelet.

Sémiramis herself is up to her eyes in work, and has already put on a monster stockpot to serve as the main basis for her Sunday dinners. "Thirty pounds of beef, my dear, and the giblets of half a dozen chickens! That should keep them going for some time, I'm thinking, and allow me a few moments' peace, for I'll be able to serve it first as the main course for dinner, and then cold with salad for supper. And as for soup, just think of all the soup they'll be able to have!" She is by now much calmer, smoking her everlasting cigarette as she parades from table to table her good ogress smile and her whiskey-and-soda, from which unthinkingly she takes an occasional sip. The strong bitter coffee is getting cold in my cup; my bitch, her nose running from the cigarette smoke, urges me to leave.

"You don't recognize me?" says a voice close beside me.

A young woman, simply, almost poorly clad in black, is looking at me with inquiring eyes. It is hard to tell the true color of her hair under her matted-straw hat trimmed with quills; she is wearing a white collar with a neat tie, and her pearl-gray gloves are slightly soiled.

Her face is powdered, her lips are rouged, her eyelashes darkened with mascara: the indispensable makeup, but applied without due consideration, of necessity, from force of habit. I ransack my memory, when suddenly the lovely eyes, with huge pupils the shimmering dark brown of Sémiramis's coffee, bring me the answer.

"Why, of course, you're Gitanette!"

Her name, her absurd music-hall name, has come back to me, and with it the memory of where we met.

It must have been three or four years ago, at the time I was playing in the Empyrée Pantomime, that Gitanette occupied the dressing room next to mine. Gitanette and her girlfriend, "A Duo in Cosmopolitan Dances," used to dress with their door open onto the passage to get more air. Gitanette took the male parts and her girlfriend—Rita, Lina, Nina?— appeared, turn by turn, as a drab, as an Italian, then in red leather Cossack boots, and finally draped in a Manila shawl, a carnation behind her ear. A nice little pair, or should I say "little couple," for there are certain ways and looks that tell their own story and, in addition, the authority assumed by Gitanette, the tender, almost maternal care with which she would wrap a thick woolen scarf round her girlfriend's neck. As for the friend, Nina, Rita, or Lina, I have rather forgotten her. Peroxided hair, light-colored eyes, white teeth, something about her of an appetizing but slightly vulgar young washerwoman.

They danced neither very well nor very badly, and their act was borrowed from other "Dance Numbers." Provided they are both young and agile, with a mutual distaste for the *"bar à femmes"* and the *"promenoir,"* then's the time for them to collect their few pennies together to pay the ballet master so much a week to arrange a special dance routine, and the dressmaker . . . Then, if they are very, very lucky, the couple starts on the round of the various establishments in Paris, the provinces, and abroad.

Gitanette and her girlfriend were "playing" the Empyrée that month. For thirty nights running they bestowed on me all the discreet, disinterested attentions, the shy, reserved courtesy which seem to thrive exclusively among music-hall people. I would be dabbing on the last touch of rouge under my eyes when they came up, lips still trembling from lack of breath and temples moist, and stopped to smile at me without at first speaking, both panting like circus ponies. When recovered a little, they gave me politely, by way of greeting, some brief and useful piece of information: "An eighteen-carat audience tonight!" or else, "They're a lousy lot today!"

Then Gitanette, before taking off her clothes, would unlace her friend's bodice and Nina, or Lina, at once began to laugh and swear and jabber. "You'll have to watch your step," she'd shout across to me, "those roller skaters have gone and cut the boards to pieces again tonight, and you'll be darned lucky if you don't come a cropper!" The voice of Gitanette took up the tale, more soberly. "It's a sure sign of luck if you fall flat on your face on the stage. It means you'll come back to the same place before three years are out. That happened to me at Les Bouffes in Bordeaux, when I caught my foot in one of the cuts . . ."

They lived out loud, quite simply, in the next room to mine with their door left wide open. They twittered like busy, affectionate birds, happy to be working together and to have the shelter of each other's arms and their love as a protection against the barren life of the prostitute and the occasional tough customer.

My thoughts went back to those old days as Gitanette stood before me, alone and sad, and so changed . . .

"Sit down a minute, Gitanette, we'll have a coffee together . . . And . . . where is your friend?"

She shakes her head as she sits down. "We're not together anymore, my friend and me. You never heard what happened to me?"

"No, I've heard nothing. Would it be impertinent to ask?"

"Oh, good gracious, no. You see, you're an artiste like me . . . like I was, that is, for at present I'm not even a woman anymore."

"Are things as bad as that?"

"Things are bad, if you like to put it that way. It all depends what sort of person you are. I'm by nature the sort who becomes terribly attached, you see. I became terribly attached to Rita, she meant everything to me. It never entered my head that things could change between us . . . The year it all happened, we'd just had a real stroke of luck. We'd hardly finished dancing at the Apollo when up popped Saloman, our agent, who sent us word that we were to have a dance routine in the Empyrée Revue, a gorgeous revue, twelve hundred costumes, English girls, everything. For my part, I wasn't so mad keen to dance in it. I've always been a bit afraid of these big shows with so many females in them, for it always leads to rivalries, quarrels, or mischief of some sort. At the end of a fortnight in that revue, I wanted nothing so much as to be back in the quiet little number we'd been doing before. All the more because little Rita was no longer the same with me; she'd go visiting around here and there, palling up with this girl or that, till it was the bubbly she went for in the dressing room of Lucie Desrosiers, that great roan mare, who was poisoning herself with the drink and whose stays had all their whalebones broken. Champagne at twenty-three sous a bottle! Does anyone suppose you can get hold of any decent stuff at that price? The little one was going all la-di-da; there was no holding her. Then she came back to our dressing room one evening bragging that the Commère had given her the glad eye! Now, I ask you, was that very bright on her part, or very proper to me? I got ever so low-spirited and began seeing the bad side in everything. I'd have given I don't know how much for a good date in Hamburg, or at the Wintergarten in Berlin, or almost any place to get us out of the big revue that seemed never to be going to finish!"

Gitanette turns to look at me with her dark coffee-colored eyes, which seem to have lost all their keenness and vitality.

"I'm telling things just as they happened, you know. Don't run away with the idea I've made up this or that detail about anyone, or that there's any malice intended."

"No, of course not, Gitanette."

"That's good to hear. Well, came the day when my little bitch of a pal says to me: 'Listen, Gitanette,' she says, 'I need an underskirt' (we still wore underskirts in those days) 'and a natty one, too. I'm ashamed to put on the one I have!' As was only proper, I was the one who kept the key of the cash box, otherwise where would our meals have come from! I simply said to her: 'Now, about this underskirt, it will cost you how much?'—'How much, how much!' she shouts back at me in a rage. 'Why, you'd think I hadn't even the right to buy myself an underskirt!' After a start like that, I saw we were in for a scene. To cut it short, I just tell her: 'Here's the key, take what you want, but don't forget we've got the monthly rent to pay tomorrow.' She takes out a fifty-franc note, flings on her things helter-skelter, and off she rushes, to get to the Galeries Lafayette, supposedly, before the rush hour! Meanwhile, I stay behind to run over a couple of costumes just back from the dyers, and I stitch and I stitch, while waiting for her to come back . . . When all of a sudden I see I'll have to replace a whole ninon underflounce in Rita's dress, and I dash down to the nearest shop in the Place Blanche, it being already dark . . . Simply telling you the story brings it all back clear as the moment it took place! As I come out of the shop, I only just escape being squashed flat by a taxi that draws into the curb and comes to a stop, and then what do I see? Lo and behold, before my very eyes, that great Desrosiers getting out of the cab, her hair disheveled, her dress all undone, and waving goodbye to Rita, to my Rita, who is still sitting inside the taxi! I was that taken by surprise, I stood rooted to the spot, cut off at the legs, I couldn't budge. So much so that when I tried to make a sign to attract Rita's attention, the taxi was already far away, it was taking Rita back to our place in the rue Constance . . .

"I'm all in a daze when I get back home; and of course she was already there, Rita, that is. You should have seen the look on her face . . . no, you have to know her as well as I know her, to see what . . .

"There, let's leave it at that! So I act simple and I say to her: 'What about that underskirt of yours?'—'I never bought it.'—'And what about that fifty francs?'—'I lost it.' She fires this off point-blank, looking me straight in the eye! Oh, you can't imagine what it was like, you can't imagine . . ."

Gitanette lowers her eyes and nervously stirs the spoon in her cup.

"You can't imagine what a blow it was to me, when she came out with that. It was like I'd seen the whole thing with my own eyes: their meeting place, the taxi ride, that one's furnished room, the champagne on the night table, everything, everything."

She goes on repeating under her breath, "Everything, everything," till I interrupt her. "And then what did you do?"

"Nothing. I cried my eyes out over dinner, into my mutton and beans . . . And then, a week later, she left me. *Fortunately* I got so ill that I almost passed out, for if I had've though I loved her so much, I'd have killed her . . ."

She speaks calmly of killing, or of dying, all the time turning her spoon in the cup of cold coffee. This simple girl, who lives so close to nature, knows full well that all that is required to sever the threads of misery is one single act, so easy, hardly an act of violence. A person is dead, just as a person is alive, except that death is a state that can be chosen, whereas a person is not free to choose their own life.

"Did you really want to die, Gitanette?"

"Of course I did. Only I was so ill, you understand, I wasn't able to. And then, later, my granny came to look after me and nurse me through my convalescence. She's an old lady, you see, I didn't dare leave her."

"And now, at the present time, you are less sad than you were?"

"No," Gitanette answers, dropping her voice. "And I don't even want to be less sad. I should be ashamed of myself if I found consolation after loving my friend the way I did. You're sure to tell me, as so many others have told me, 'Do something to take your mind off it. Time is the great healer.' I'll not deny that time does straighten things out in the long run, but there again it all depends on what sort of person you are. You see, I've known nobody but Rita, it just happened that way. I never had a boyfriend, I know nothing about children, I lost my parents when I was quite young, but when I used to see lovers happy together, or parents with little children on their knees, I'd say to myself, 'I've got everything they've got, because I've my Rita.' No doubt about it, my life is finished in that respect, nothing can alter it. Each time I go back to my room at Granny's and see my pictures of Rita, the photos of us two in all our numbers, and the little dressing table we shared, it starts up all over again, the tears come . . . I cry, I call out to her . . . It does me no good, but I can't help it. It may sound funny, but . . . I don't believe I'd know what to do with myself if I didn't have my sorrow. It keeps me company."

[*Translated by Anne-Marie Callimachi*]

The Victim

❧❦❧

For the first twelve months of the war, it had been a daily *tour de force*, for her and for us, to keep her alive, a kind of bitter game, a challenge to unhappy fate. She was so pretty that all she would have had to do for a living, good heavens, was to sit back and do nothing . . . But it was precisely this beauty, and then her standing as a little lady whose boyfriend had been killed soon after the outbreak of the war in 1914, which moved us to pity. Our intention was to look after her thin halo for her, to provide her, during her widowhood, first with bread, and then with that luxury called chastity.

A more difficult task than it might seem, for we were dealing with the peculiar sensitivity of a sentimental, working-class suburban girl and an honest businesswoman. Josette admitted that everything can be bought and sold, even a revolted breast, even an unfeeling mouth. But a gift pure and simple made her suddenly embarrassed and flushed with wounded pride.

"No, thank you, really, I don't need . . . No, we disagree about the little bill for the jacket, I still owed you fifty sous from last week."

To keep her from wasting away or turning gloomily back to a traffic for which she felt nothing but disgust beforehand, we were forced to make her sew, iron, cover lampshades . . .

She did not want to work anywhere but home, in the middle of nowhere, in a "room with storage closet," furnished mainly with photographs, where, under the sad, hygienic smell of coarse soap, there hung the distinctive scent of a dark-haired, fair-skinned little girl.

During the winter of 1914, she would arrive gaily, bringing her work with her. "It's just me! Don't let me bother you!"

A toque, or I don't know what, a hobble skirt which clipped her impatient steps, narrow button boots—for her little feet danced ironically in our shoes—and the shabby fur neckpiece she preferred—more "chic" —to the coat one of us had offered her. And gloves!—but of course! but always!—gloves. Her smooth beauty humbled her poverty. I have never encountered anything smoother than this child, with her sleek black hair, never curled or waved, glued to her smooth temples with an artist's hand, and gleaming like a precious wood anointed with fine oil. Her pure and prominent eyes, her supple cheeks, her mouth and chin seemed to say to everyone: "See how, with almost no curliness, we're able to charm."

"I've brought you back the little skirt," explained Josette. "I didn't edge the bottom, it would have made it stronger, but it looks common. Just because there's a war on, that's no reason to look common, now, is it? And as for the blouse you wanted me to cut out of the evening coat, do you know what I found when I took the stitches out? A hem that big! Enough to make a big sailor collar to match!"

She would beam with joy to be kept busy and able to pay for herself, not to be a burden to anyone. She had always "had lunch before coming," and we had to resort to subterfuge to get her to take half a pound of chocolates.

"Josette, someone gave me these chocolates and I don't trust them. They must be drugged . . . Be an angel, try them and then tell me if they made you ill."

She accepted a sack of coal from Pierre Wolff, because I told her that the playwright had noticed her in a crowd scene at the Folies and still had a haunting memory of her.

She almost never spoke about her "young friend," an obscure actor killed by the enemy. But now and then she would pore over the pictures in the illustrated magazines from 1913.

"Remember that revue? It was well staged, no doubt about it . . . And can you believe my luck? The author was supposed to give me a small part in his next revue! Well, his next revue is still a long way off!"

One theater, however, half opened; then two theaters, ten theaters, and movie houses, too. Josette could not keep still any longer!

"There's the Gobelins-Montrouge-Montparnasse, which is going to do a season of plays, did you know? And then there's Moncey, which wants to put on a season of operettas, and Levallois too . . . Only, the problem is finding out if the artists will have the métro to take home afterward. At Levallois, there won't be a métro or a tram, natch . . ."

She disappeared, for three weeks, and reappeared thinner, with a cold, and quite proud.

"Madame, I got an engagement! *Miss Hellyett* three times a week, I'll play one of the guides and maybe even another small part, too! Three times during the week and twice on Sundays!"

"How much are you getting?"

She lowered her eyes. "Well, you know, *they're* taking advantage because of the war . . . I get three francs fifty for every day of performance. The other days, of course, we're not paid . . . And the show changes every two weeks, so we're rehearsing every day. I just wanted to explain to you why I haven't had time to finish the little bloomers for you."

"There's no hurry . . . And how are you getting home at night?"

She laughed. "Hoofing it, natch. An hour and a half's walk. I'll wear out more shoes than tires. But they told me I might get a part in *Les Mousquetaires au couvent* . . ."

How could we hold her back? She was aglow with the freedom, energy, fatigue, and fever of life in the theater . . . She went away, for months . . .

In August 1916, I was buying a child's toy in one of those charity bazaars where, along with bags of coffee, they sell necklaces made of dyed wooden beads, raffia baskets, and woolens, and I was waiting for an elegant customer to yield me her place at the counter.

"That there, and that one, yes, the blue sweater, and four packets of coffee, too," she said. "That makes four separate packages, military parcels; I'll write down the addresses for you, Mademoiselle. I'll be taking the little baskets with me in my car . . ."

"In your car, Josette!"

"Oh, Madame! . . . What a surprise! It's you I'm going to take with me in my car . . . Oh, yes, I am, just for a minute, just long enough to take you home."

She had not warned me that "her" car already contained a slightly graying and well-groomed man, to whom she issued the command to fold down one of the jump seats—for himself. She sat next to me and spoke with a forced air of having forgotten about the man. He looked at her like a slave, but Josette's black eyes did not fix on him even once. She took the glove off one of her hands, which sparkled with jeweled rings; the man trapped the fluttering hand as it passed by him and gave it a long kiss. She did not pull it away from him, but she closed her eyes and opened them again only when he had sat back up.

After a short silence, the car drove up to my house and Josette gave the man an order: "Get out, then, can't you see your seat is blocking the lady's way?"

He was quick to obey, excused himself, and Josette, as she left me, promised to come see me. "As soon as rehearsals at the Edouard VII are over, I'll come by."

She came a few days later, dressed all in lawn and "summer furs," with a single strand of pearls around her neck, and dangling a moiré handbag set with brilliants. But she hadn't changed her coiffure at all, and her hair, unwaved and uncurled, still clung to her temples like a Japanese child's.

"My little Josette, I don't need to ask what's happened to you."

She shook her head. "Every disaster possible! I've fallen into the ranks of the nouveaux riches."

"It looks that way. Are you in dried beans or projectiles?"

"Me? I'm not in anything—him . . . oh, he can buy and sell anything—what's it to me, he doesn't interest me."

"Listen, for a war supplier, he's very nice."

"Yes, he is very nice. Despite everything, he's very nice."

Without really seeing them, she was contemplating her beautiful white suede shoes, and her face, though lit up by pearls, snow-white lawn, pale fur, and silk, seemed to have lost its glow.

"If I understand you correctly, Josette, you miss the days when . . ."

"Not at all," she interrupted sharply. "You can't believe that! Why should I miss the days when I was cold, when I didn't have enough to eat, when I was running around in the filth and the snow, when without you and these ladies I'd've fallen ill or worse? Not at all. I'm no fool, I like what's good. Since I don't have anyone at the front anymore, except for a few young friends I'm looking after in Paul's memory, why shouldn't I be the lady with the car and the necklace, instead of the woman downstairs? Fair is fair. Doing as much of what I do, I think I'm worth all the blue foxes and tulle chemises . . . That's the least of it, since compared with that man, whom you've seen, I'm the victim!"

I said nothing. She sensed, acutely, that her words were driving me away from her and she burst out: "Madame, Madame, you don't know . . . You think bad of me . . . I swear to you, Madame . . ."

She was near tears but controlled herself. "You saw him, Madame. You don't have to be a genius to realize there's not a better man than him. He is a good man. He's refined and well-groomed, everything—which doesn't change the fact that I'm the victim."

"But why, my dear?"

"Why? Simply because I don't love him and I never will love him, Madame! If he were ugly and disgusting and stingy, I could console myself, I could tell myself, 'It's perfectly natural I can't stand the sight of him. He buys me, I loathe him—everything's out in the open.' But with this man, Madame, whom I don't love because I don't love him, my God, the things I could do to myself fretting over him . . ."

She was quiet a moment, searching for words, examples!

"Look, he gave me this ring the day before yesterday. And in such a nice way! So I started to cry . . . He called me 'My sensitive little girl!' and I cried thinking of the pleasure it would have given me to get a ring from a man I could love; it made me so furious I could have bitten him . . ."

"What a child you are, Josette."

She struck the arm of the chair in irritation. "No, Madame, I'm sorry, but you're wrong! One isn't that much of a child, in Paris, at twenty-five. I know what love is, I've been through it. I have a very loving nature, even if it doesn't show. That's what makes me think of myself as his victim, and I'm jealous of him, so jealous it makes me sick."

"Jealous?"

"Yes, envious, I envy everything he has, everything I can't have, since he's the one who's in love. The other day at rehearsal the little Peloux girl said to me, 'Your friend's got a nice mouth, he must kiss pretty well.' 'I wouldn't know,' I say to her. And it's true, I wouldn't know. It's not for me to know. It's for the woman who finds him to her liking. I'll die without ever knowing whether he kisses good or bad, if he makes love good or bad. When he kisses me, my mouth becomes like . . . like . . . nothing. It's dead, it doesn't feel anything. My body either. But him, with what little I give him—you should see his face, his eyes . . . Oh, it's a thousand times more than all I get! Ten thousand times more!

". . . So, of course, my nerves . . . I end up getting mean. I take my revenge, I'm cruel to him. I was so mean to him once that he cried. That was the last straw! I didn't say another word to him, I might have gone too far. Because I know what it's like to have someone in your life who only has to say one word to put you in heaven or hell! I'm that person for him. He has everything, Madame, he has everything. And there's nothing he can do for me, nothing—not even make me unhappy!"

She burst into sobs, mixing her vehement tears with, "Tell me, Madame, am I wrong? Tell me . . ." But I could find nothing—and I've found nothing since—to say to her.

[*Translated by Matthew Ward*]

The Tenor

He is beautiful. He dresses in the fashionable colors of the day: black and white. White shirtfront and black tuxedo, a gardenia in his lapel. A white face with regular features, Roman nose, black hair reflecting the stagelights, and large, tranquil black pupils set in the huge whites of his eyes. His mouth, set off by rich, dark makeup, his teeth, his hair, and his tremendous eyes, all shine with a slick flash, as if made lustrous by some rare oil. He is beautiful.

As he appears, introduced by the plaintive harmony of the violins, and stops directly in the center of the stage, only the claque applaud him. But I would swear that if the music and the bravos were silenced, one would hear a discreet, strictly feminine murmuring: sighs of pleasure and desire, a rustling of dresses as one settles down and leans forward, and whisperings which would be the hissing of the *s*'s in his name.

He sings the waltzes demanded by the current vogue and gives a precise rendition of a sentimental ballad in which a heroic gigolette dies to save the young man who has made her a mother—all in a lovely, easy voice, which he uses carefully, for the smoke and dust of the music hall make a tenor's glory brief. He is no less careful with his gestures and leaves it to his eyes to do the seducing. As he sings, his black-and-white eyes survey the boxes, slowly, confidently, veiled with sensual disdain, and then, in the same way, they caress the orchestra seats. Now and then, his gaze stops, fixes on a precise spot, where one is sure to see a woman lower her lorgnette and lean back suddenly in her seat, as if drawing away from an overly strong fire. It is only for an instant: the eyes have already resumed their professional stroll; regardless of any sentimental waltz, any love song, I would swear they seem oblivious to the fact that the tenor is singing . . .

Having acknowledged the applause, heels together, one hand resting on some bush made of flowering canvas and wood, he joins us in the wings and strolls around a bit. The clock has just struck ten, and the tenor yawns at the prospect of half an evening yet to kill. A chipped and frameless mirror hangs on the wall: the tenor looks at his teeth, at his clean-shaven chin powdered to mask the blue of his heavy beard. He checks the callboard, yawns again, and says out loud, to no one in particular: "Good house tonight."

He coughs and adds: "I don't know what this is I've had in my throat since this morning."

The prostrate comedian comes up with some trite response, or maybe it's the unappreciated *diseuse* who is about to distill the "Lovely Songs of France," or maybe it's me . . .

And still the tenor remains. He lingers in the sinister half-darkness, the strange silence, disturbed only by the orchestra, in the wings of a "caf' conc'." Occasionally, the young messenger boy hands him a letter, which he opens slowly with an indiscreet smile.

But I see no sign of haste, or excitement, and this "heartbreaker" never seems to behave like a man for whom someone is waiting . . . He is a very quiet colleague and I would swear him incapable of selling his charms except on stage. The thought never enters the tenor's mind. Each glance in the mirror repays him: no matter what is said by the duenna, who lovingly calls him "gorgeous," or by the puny comedian who mutters "pimp" as he passes by, I would call him neither Don Juan nor Alphonse, but Narcissus.

[*Translated by Matthew Ward*]

The Quick-Change Artist

I hear her dancing, I cannot see her from the wings, for she dances on a closed set, one of those strange sets found only in a music hall. This one represents a unique place, painted in a putrid pink color with gold highlights, bringing together a mantelpiece loaded with candelabra, a staircase of blue-veined marble imitating a bar of soap, a Persian portico entwined with rare flowers, and two large blue vases, both empty. A curtain of glass beads closes off the back of the stage; that is where the "cosmopolitan, dancing quick-change artist" disappears and reappears, dressed each time in a new costume.

I see only her in the wings, where each of her disappearances takes her. I remain in the background behind the long table on which her costumes are laid out in neat little piles. Dresses, hats, wigs, promise the audience a new idol every two minutes; I make myself inconspicuous, so as not to bother her, but she seems totally unaware of my presence anyway . . .

The end of a cakewalk hurls back at me, from between the tinkling beaded curtain, a slender Greenaway doll in blue tulle, breathing heavily. With a rough slap to her forehead, the English doll tears off her hat and wig, as the faded blue lampshade serving as a skirt falls. Before I can get a good look at her face—violet makeup under the lunar light from a row of blue electric bulbs—a silent, black, kneeling specter is fastening the hooks of a Spanish dress. In the orchestra, the pizzicati and the Sevillian tambourines are quivering, and the dancer groans with impatience: quick, the black wig with the red rose, shawl across the shoulders, the castanets . . . With a leap, she opens the beaded curtains and I hear, mingled with the sounds from the orchestra, the rhythmic language of her clever feet . . .

Two minutes: here she is again. She's breathing harder and she leans back for a moment against the wooden framework to take off her skirt with the chenille balls, head thrown back . . . The ritornell, longer than a tarantella, gives me time to look at her: it's an Italian face, with somewhat thick but regular features and heavy eyelids, looking drunk with exhaustion. My eyes, by now accustomed to the darkness, can make out the slight brown shoulders, the bare breasts, young and tired, not quite filled out enough, above a frayed corset belt of gray twill . . . A Neapolitan fisherman's castoffs—silk skirt, fringed sash, cap tilted over one ear—hide all that, as if by magic. The haggard face revives, and a Neapolitan fisherman shaking a tambourine steps out on stage.

During the tarantella, I count the number of costumes left on the table; the silent attendant, preparing the Egyptian dancing girl's veils, follows my gaze and shakes her head . . . Almost instantly, the Neapolitan fisherman falls into her arms, breathless. The dancer's forehead bears the sweat and pallor of someone being suffocated by his own heart. I want to say something, to help somehow, but there is something tragic about the two women's haste: one must, despite the trembling hands and the heaving sides, one must go on to the end . . .

Helpless, I witness the final "transformations": I see pass before me a Plains Indian, bristling with feathers, who has just had a lemon pressed into her mouth the way boxers do, then a reeling Egyptian dancing girl, who lets up an "ululu," then a muzhik in a red shirt, sobbing nervously, weeping big round tears because her legs are going to give out on her, then finally, finally, there is nothing more left in front of me, in that cold blue moonlight, at that inert hour, except the frame for all those costumes: the body of an exhausted young girl, half naked against the back of the set, who, seeking a breath of air, lifts her breast, as St. Sebastian offered his, to the arrows.

[Translated by Matthew Ward]

Florie

❧❀❧

"Why a juggler, Arsène? Will a juggler go over?"

"What can I do? You don't want a singer, do you? Or a dancer? I have an empty spot in my revue. I have to fill it."

"Yeh," said Florie thoughtfully, "yeh . . ."

When she was preoccupied, she would revert to the familiar accent of the working-class district she grew up in.

"How's that guy who fell, Arsène?"

"Jackie? He's all right, if you can believe what they say at the hospital. Fractured kneecap, occupational hazard. It happens . . ."

Florie stroked her knee, her own leg's precious joint, superstitiously.

"Well, I hope it never happens to me . . ."

"So," Sutter continued, "I'll give this juggler a try. His work is different. And he'll always bring women around, seeing as how he's a good-looking kid."

"Do what you want," said Florie indifferently.

Arsène Sutter and the ever-popular Florie, looking greenish and drowned beneath a blue running light, leaned against each other, squeezed between two flats in the wings. Director and star, shoulder to shoulder, exchanged few words, professionally accustomed as they were to resting on their feet and waiting. Sutter nevertheless turned toward Florie.

"You want to sit down?"

"On what?" asked Florie ironically.

Above them, atop a strange pyramid made of flounced skirts of rose muslin, sat a motionless figurante buried waist-deep in ruffles. She was waiting to portray the part of "Crinoline" in the tableau called "Fashions of the Second Empire." Because of the congestion in the wings, she was hoisted up every night twelve feet in the air and stayed planted up there, isolated from the world, for twenty-five minutes.

"I'm not tired," Florie added.

Sutter slipped her a look of affectionate and commercial regard. For close to thirty years, Florie had endured three hundred evening performances, two matinees on holidays, three months of rehearsals, costume changes, and sketches danced and sung without any lessening of either her vitality or her beauty.

"The juggler's on next," said Sutter.

"What's his name, anyway?" asked Florie.

"Lola."

"Lola? Another androgyne bit?"

"Hardly," said Sutter. "Lola is a man's name in Russian, or so he says."

Florie burst out laughing. A blue spark alighted on each of her flawless teeth, and two blue sparks danced in her periwinkle eyes.

"She's incredible," thought Sutter admiringly. Thick makeup, sticky and smooth, revealed little of the real Florie. She held her head high, out of habit, and so as to smooth out the wrinkles in her neck. But up close, Sutter could make out, beneath the star's ear and chin, the tendons lengthwise, the "necklaces" crosswise, a whole play of loosening skin and slackening muscles. The cheeks held up well, thanks to their high cheekbones and a magnificent rouge of gay, bright red, above which the eyelids were all lashes in diverging rays, a deftly muted purplish color, and the dark blue eyebrows, straight-edged and severely horizontal. Arsène Sutter placed a heavy and careful hand on Florie's bare shoulder, as if he were touching a costly and unbeatable racehorse. The stage crew revolved around them discreetly, on old, worn-out shoes and frayed espadrilles, with the respect due a couple from whom could rain a shower of abuse or praise.

"Here's Lola," prompted Sutter. "He enters stage right and exits stage left."

Florie followed the juggler through his act with serious scrutiny as he tossed a bizarre variety of light objects into the air, interspersed with heavy gold balls. Paper rose petals, plumes, little feathered arrows which soared up, then dived point first toward the ground, ribbons, and cellophane butterflies all floated slowly between the speeding balls and seemed tamed by the juggler's hands.

"That's really funny," Florie decided.

Lola finished with a release of boomerangs and withdrew as he had entered, nonchalantly. He seemed neither surprised nor moved to hear himself called back five times. While acknowledging the applause, his eyes swept the house, from left to right, from right to left, giving the audience a chance to appreciate the fact that Lola had bright eyes, gray or green, beneath a head of jet-black hair whose waves resisted all creams and waxes. Altogether a very handsome boy, narrow here, broad there, whose attractiveness would have appeared suspect if in the wide gray eyes there did not burn a watchful gravity, the infallibly steady gaze his profession demanded.

Sutter consulted Florie.

"O.K.?"

"O.K.," said Florie, stepping over the rubber-encased electric cables. "And good-looking too, which doesn't hurt any," she added.

During the next day's afternoon performance, the juggler made a mistake, and then exited stage left, almost knocking down Florie, who was standing behind the wing under the blue light.

"Oh, excuse me, Madame Florie . . . I just came from doing my act in Brussels, where I had to enter and exit on the same side, so . . ."

"They're calling for you," interrupted Florie. "Go take a bow."

When the curtains closed again, Florie had left her post. On the summit of the edifice of rose muslin, the stylistic figurante considered all things human with the serenity of a sad angel, and the assistant stage manager yelled out: "Madame Florie, you're on!" just as the juggler was walking off.

"Why did you send me flowers?" Florie asked Lola the following day. She was standing under the somber blue light, which streamed down over her, flowing from her raised chin onto her shoulder, moistening the slight outcurving of her hip and her sequined slippers.

"I wanted to thank you for having gotten me that curtain call," answered Lola.

He had almost no accent, only rolling his *r*'s like a Spaniard and saying "dhank you." But he spoke to the star-idol without a trace of shyness, and his gray-green eyes moved from Florie's eyes to her teeth, and from her teeth down to her famous legs, slowly and deliberately.

"That's an unusual act you've got," said Florie.

He did not acknowledge the compliment but merely pursed his lips with disdainful modesty, and Florie, who was looking straight at the man's dangerous mouth, pouting like a child's, felt herself shiver.

"Is Madame catching cold?"

"No," said Florie. "If I'm not used to it by now . . ."

She broke off with this "by now . . ." which evoked the length of her career, and started up again: "How did you come up with the idea of working with things that fly?"

"God knows," said Lola. "In my country, you know, the rosebushes are very big, you see them flying, the . . . the . . . petals."

He raised his arm and snapped his fingers in the air. Florie, following his gesture, searched overhead for a flight of wind-plucked roses, but all her eyes met with was the blank stare of little "Second Empire Crinoline," drained and motionless.

"See you tomorrow," she said mechanically, offering the juggler her hand.

Her calm and restful sleep, the sleep of a hardworking woman, was made fitful by dreams and memories, and by huge rosebushes whose petals were scattered by the wind.

The nights went by, marked for Florie by a passing word or a few seconds' banal exchange with the juggler. But the warmth that came to her from a tone of voice, from a look that had no rival was enough for her, gave her the strength to dance faultlessly, to change costumes feverishly, to incite "her" public in the second balcony, squeezed high up into the cupola like bees about to swarm.

"You amaze me, you know that?" said Sutter. "What's gotten into you lately?"

The night when Florie detected in Lola's clear gray-green eyes a kind of irresistible rancor, a menace that dispensed with words, a restlessness like that which troubled her own dreams, she trod the boards with the footsteps of a ballerina, abandoned herself to a gracefulness, to an ardor which seemed no more than twenty-five years old. Beneath the blue lantern she turned her beautiful, delirious face up toward Lola, and confessed everything.

"I'd be very happy if you'd stop by my dressing room later for a glass of champagne . . ."

"I only drink water," replied Lola, who suddenly resembled a man intoxicated, for Florie's knee was pressing against his for the first time. Weakened, Florie gave in and ran her finger over the delicious contour of the mouth she so desired, and murmured: "Well then, let's get through the Easter holidays and these six performances in three days. Monday at midnight, you can drink some ice water . . . in my room . . . if you want . . ."

He grabbed hold of her with artful strength, pressing to himself a long body which had not lost its enchanting proportions, and Florie closed her blue eyelids tragically.

The next night the juggler missed three of his most seductive miracles in a row and the audience, after murmuring some, decided to laugh instead and applauded just the same. Florie heard about the incident from Sutter, who always knew everything.

"Who the hell stuck me with a nut like that?" said Sutter, knitting his red eyebrows.

"I'm not the one who hired him," replied Florie, not without treachery.

"What was he saying to you last night in the wings?"

Florie feigned nearsightedness, pretending to look off into the distance stage right at the preparations for *"Les Jeunes Filles en Trapèze"*:

"Last night? . . . Oh, yeh. He told me he never drinks anything but water. Can you imagine?"

"That's very interesting," grumbled Sutter.

"Would you rather he'd pinched my ass?"

Sutter was about to respond, but he looked at Florie and kept quiet. In the past, when they had been lovers, he had seen that look before, the look of an insolent lioness, that flaring of the nostrils, those eyes that knew how to defy a man's raised fist . . .

Behind the wing Florie and Lola sized each other up, mute and seething like two enemies. "Day after tomorrow . . ." said Florie in a low voice, and Lola, who had let three gold balls roll into the orchestra and had fluffed a whole swarm of feathers and butterflies, exited to boos, impervious and superior.

"Strange house tonight," said Florie as she was leaving the stage after her sketch. "I can't get any feel from the audience, it's like walking on eggshells out there. What's wrong with them?"

Someone explained it to her. She knitted her aquamarine eyebrows, then counted the hours that separated her and the rendezvous, the supper of rare fruits, an orgy of ice water sparkling in the thin glasses, as intoxicating as champagne . . .

The next to last morning was devoted to a valiant and minute self-examination. She usually spent only a minimum of time on essentials and gave the more familiar ravages a rough once-over. "I treat myself like a piece of furniture," she said. But that morning, in a sort of laboratory wide open to the chaste and pitiless light of spring, Florie found it difficult to look at her reflection in the mirror. She scrutinized her face for a long time, confessing to it a late, great folly, and humbly vowed that this time would be no mere whim, not just pleasure, but the passion and pain she had long since kept from herself.

It had been a long time since she had seen tears well up, then fall over the edges of her eyelids with a little leap. She was unable to master them in time and all her features shipwrecked in the mirror . . .

She arrived in her dressing room a bit earlier than usual, and shut herself inside. When she recognized Lola's nonchalant footstep in the passageway, she held her breath and waited. Then she opened her door just enough to catch a glimpse of the figure moving away down the hall, the perfect nape, the shoulders that could easily have carried home the day's kill . . .

From within her closed dressing room, she heard the commotion in the audience exasperated by the clumsy juggler. What was needed to calm them down and to win them over was Florie's infallible humor, her taming influence. After her sketch her legs trembled slightly while she waited for Arsène to come by.

"Have you heard the latest, Arsène?"

"The juggler? Of course."

"Did you see it?"

"From my box."

"What does he say?"

"Him? He just laughs it off. Says he doesn't give a damn."

Florie leaned over toward her mirror and slipped a little roll of blotting paper between her lashes to drink up the tears.

"Is that right? Well, as for me, if there's one thing I do give a damn about, it's finding my audience in an uproar after that guy's act . . . Arsène, you want to do me a favor?"

"Switch the acts?"

Florie hesitated for only a second. "No. He's not worth it. No matter where you put him he's going to cause us trouble."

"Fire him?"

"Yes, Arsène. Right now. Will it cost a lot?"

"Next to nothing. Should we let him do tonight's show?"

"No . . . No, Arsène. Pay him off. Do it nicely . . . be generous. Arsène . . . Listen, Arsène . ''

"Fine, fine. You know perfectly well that all you have to do is say the word and it's yours. Don't let it bother you, darling. Hey, why don't you come have a little something to eat with my wife and me after the show tonight?"

"No . . . My stomach's all tied up in knots, Arsène . . ."

"Exactly. Six oysters and a little steak will untie it." He looked at her. "I have a feeling your sketch is going to be sensational today."

Florie raised her face, protected by makeup, toward Sutter. "Do you want me to be sensational, Arsène?"

"More than anything in the world."

She threw off her dressing gown, and across her shoulders her dresser hung an imponderable spray of rose plumes, which cascaded slowly and noiselessly to the ground; then came the high heels, and along with them the arrogant strut that was Florie's alone.

"Don't leave me, Arsène!"

"I won't leave you, darling."

"Walk me to the wings. Give me your arm, Arsène . . ."

Arm in arm, they reached the wings, through which escaped a loud gust of music.

Not until the moment when a ritornel lifted Florie up and onto the stage did the big, friendly hand of the director open its fingers. Hidden behind an azalea made of painted canvas, Sutter turned his keen ear to the noises coming from on stage. Between two flowers, his eye caught Florie's trademarks: Florie with her face awash in light, teeth flashing, Florie in profile, the narrow waist, a certain pawing of the foot, a certain waltz tempo that was Florie . . .

Relieved, he wiped his forehead, let out a long sigh, and retired to the director's office.

[*Translated by Matthew Ward*]

Gribiche

I never arrived before quarter past nine. By that time, the temperature and the smell of the basement of the theater had already acquired their full intensity. I shall not give the exact location of the music hall in which, some time between 1905 and 1910, I was playing a sketch in a revue. All I need say is that the underground dressing rooms had neither windows nor ventilators. In our women's quarters, the doors of the rows of identical cells remained innocently open; the men . . . far less numerous in revues than nowadays . . . dressed on the floor above, almost at street level. When I arrived, I found myself among women already acclimatized to the temperature, for they had been in their dressing rooms since eight o'clock. The steps of the iron staircase clanged musically under my feet; the last five steps each gave out their particular note like a xylophone—B, B flat, C, D, and then dropping a fifth to G. I shall never forget their inevitable refrain. But when fifty pairs of heels clattered up and down like hail for the big ensembles and dance numbers, the notes blended into a kind of shrill thunder which made the plaster walls between each dressing room tremble. Halfway up the staircase a ventilator marked the level of the street. When it was occasionally opened during the day, it let in the poisonous air of the street, and fluttering rags of paper, blown there by the wind, clung to its grating, which was coated with dried mud.

As soon as we reached the floor of our cellar, each of us made some ritual complaint about the suffocating atmosphere. My neighbor across the passage, a little green-eyed Basque, always panted for a moment before opening the door of her dressing room, put her hand on her heart, sighed: "Positively filthy!" and then thought no more about it. As she had short thighs and high insteps, she gummed a kiss-curl on her left cheek and called herself Carmen Brasero.

Mademoiselle Clara d'Estouteville, known as La Toutou, occupied the next dressing room. Tall, miraculously fair, slim as women only became twenty-five years later, she played the silent part of Commère during the first half of the second act. When she arrived, she would push back the pale gold swathes of hair on her temples with a transparent hand and murmur: "Oh, take me out of here or I'll burst!" Then, without bending down, she would kick off her shoes. Sometimes she would hold out her hand. The gesture was hardly one of cordiality; it was merely that she was amused by the involuntary start of surprise which an ordinary hand like my own would give at the touch of her extraordinarily delicate, almost melting fingers. A moment after her arrival, a chilly smell like toothpaste would inform us all that the frail actress was eating her half pound of peppermints. Mademoiselle d'Estouteville's voice was so loud and raucous that it prevented her from playing spoken parts, so that the music hall could only use her exceptional beauty; the beauty of a spun-glass angel. La Toutou had her own method of explaining the situation.

"You see, on the stage I can't say my *a*'s. And however small a part, there's nearly always an *a* in it. And as I can't say my *a*'s . . ."

"But you do say them!" Carmen pointed out.

La Toutou gave her colleague a blue glance, equally sublime in its stupidity, its indignation, and its deceitfulness. The anguish of her indigestion made it even more impressive.

"Look here, dear, you can't have the cheek to pretend you know more about it than Victor de Cottens, who tried me out for his revue at the Folies!"

Her stage costume consisted of strings of imitation diamonds, which occasionally parted to give glimpses of a rose-tinted knee and an adolescent thigh or the tip of a barely formed breast. When this vision, which suggested a dawn glittering with frost, was on her way up to the stage, she passed my other neighbor, Lise Damoiseau, on her way back from impersonating the Queen of Torments. Lise would be invariably holding up her long black velvet robe with both hands, candidly displaying her bow legs. On a long neck built like a tower and slightly widening at the base, Lise carried a head modeled in the richest tones and textures of black and white. The teeth between the sad voluptuous lips were flawless; the enormous dark eyes, whose whites were slightly blue, held and reflected back the light. Her black, oiled hair shone like a river under the moon. She was always given sinister parts to play. In revues, she held sway over the Hall of Poisons and the Paradise of Forbidden Pleasures. Satan, Gilles de Rais, the Nightmare of Opium, the Beheaded Woman, Delilah, and Messalina all took on the features of Lise. She was seldom given a line to speak and the dress designers cleverly disguised her meager and undistinguished little body. She was far from being vain about her appearance. One night when I was paying her a perfectly sincere compliment she shrugged her shoulders and turned the fixed glitter of her eyes on me.

"M'm, yes," said Lise. "My face is all right. And my neck. Down to here, but no farther."

She looked into the great cracked glass that every actress consulted before going up the staircase and judged herself with harsh lucidity.

"I can only get away with it in long skirts."

After the grand final tableau, Lise Damoiseau went into total eclipse. Shorn of her makeup and huddled into some old black dress, she would carry away her superb head, its long neck muffled in a rabbit-skin scarf, as if it were some object for which she had no further use till tomorrow. Standing under the gas lamp on the pavement outside the stage door, she would give a last smoldering glance before she disappeared down the steps of the métro.

Several other women inhabited the subterranean corridor. There was Liane de Parthenon, a tall big-boned blonde, and Fifi Soada, who boasted of her likeness to Polaire, and Zarzita, who emphasized her resemblance to the beautiful Otero. Zarzita did her hair like Otero, imitated her accent, and pinned up photographs of the famous ballerina on the walls of her dressing room. When she drew one's attention to these, she invariably added, "The only difference is that *I* can dance!" There was also a dried-up little Englishwoman of unguessable age, with a face like an old nurse's and fantastically agile limbs; there was an Algerian, Miss Ourika, who specialized in the *danse du ventre* and who was all hips; there was . . . there was . . . Their names, which I hardly knew, have long since vanished. All that I heard of them, beyond the dressing rooms near me, was a zoo-like noise composed of Anglo-Saxon grunting, the yawns and sighs of caged creatures, mechanical blasphemies, and a song, always the same song, sung over and over again by a Spanish voice:

> *Tou m'abais fait serment*
> *Dé m'aimer tendrement . . .*

Occasionally, a silence would dominate all the neighboring noises and give place to the distant hum of the stage; then one of the women would break out of this silence with a scream, a mechanical curse, a yawn, or a tag of song: *Tou m'abais fait serment . . .*

Was I, in those days, too susceptible to the convention of work, glittering display, empty-headedness, punctuality, and rigid probity which reigns in the music hall? Did it inspire me to describe it over and over again with a violent and superficial love and with all its accompaniment of commonplace poetry? Very possibly. The fact remains that during six years of my past life I was still capable of finding relaxation among its monsters and its marvels. In that past there still gleams the head of Lise Damoiseau and the bottomless, radiant imbecility of Mademoiselle d'Estouteville. I still remember with delight a certain Bouboule with beautiful breasts who wept offendedly if she had to play even a tiny part in a high dress and the magnificent, long, shallow-grooved back of some Lola or Pepa or Concha . . . Looking back, I can rediscover some particular acrobat swinging high up from bar to bar of a nickeled trapeze or some particular juggler in the center of an orbit of balls. It was a world in which fantasy and bureaucracy were oddly interwoven. And I can still plunge at will into that dense, limited element which bore up my inexperience and happily limited my vision and my cares for six whole years.

Everything in it was by no means as gay and as innocent as I have described it elsewhere. Today I want to speak of my debut in that world, of a time when I had neither learned nor forgotten anything of a theatrical milieu in which I had not the faintest chance of succeeding, that of the big spectacular revue. What an astonishing milieu it was! One sex practically eclipsed the other, dominating it, not only by numbers, but by its own particular smell and magnetic atmosphere. This crowd of women reacted like a barometer to any vagary of the weather. It needed only a change of wind or a wet day to send them all into the depths of depression; a depression which expressed itself in tears and curses, in talk of suicide and in irrational terrors and superstitions. I was not a prey to it myself, but having known very few women and been deeply hurt by one single man, I accepted it uncritically. I was even rather impressed by it although it was only latent hysteria; a kind of schoolgirl neurosis which afflicts women who are arbitrarily and pointlessly segregated from the other sex.

My contribution to the program was entitled "Maiou-Ouah-Ouah. Sketch." On the strength of my first "*Dialogues de Bêtes,*" the authors of the revue had commissioned me to bark and mew on the stage. The rest of my turn consisted mainly of performing a few dance steps in bronze-colored tights. On my way to and from the stage I had to pass by the star's dressing room. The leading lady was a remote personage whose door was only open to her personal friends. She never appeared in the corridors except attended by two dressers whose job was to carry her headdresses, powder, comb, and hand mirror and to hold up her trailing flounces. She plays no part in my story but I liked to follow her and smell the trail of amazingly strong scent she left in her wake.

It was a sweet, somber scent; a scent for a beautiful Negress. I was fascinated by it but I was never able to discover its name.

One night, attired in my decorous kimono, I was dressing as usual with my door open. I had finished making up my face and my neck and was heating my curling tongs on a spirit lamp. The quick, hurried little step of Carmen Brasero (I knew it was Carmen by the clatter of her heels) sounded on the stone floor and stopped opposite my dressing room. Without turning around, I wished her good evening and received a hasty warning in reply.

"Hide that! The fire inspectors. I saw those chaps upstairs. I know one of them."

"But we've all got spirit lamps in our dressing rooms!"

"Of course," said Carmen. "But for goodness' sake, hide it. That chap I know's a swine. He makes you open your suitcases."

I put out the flame, shut the lid, and looked helplessly around my bare cell.

"Where on earth can I hide it?"

"You're pretty green, aren't you? Do you have to be told every single thing? Listen . . . I can hear them coming."

She turned up her skirt, nipped the little lamp high up between her thighs, and walked off with an assured step.

The fire inspectors, two in number, appeared. They ferreted about and went off, touching their bowler hats. Carmen Brasero returned, fished out my lamp from between her thighs, and laid it down on my makeup shelf.

"Here's the object!"

"Marvelous," I said. "I'd never have thought of doing that."

She laughed like a child who is thoroughly pleased with itself.

"Cigarettes, my handbag, a box of sweets . . . I hide them all like that and nothing ever drops out. Even a loaf that I stole when I was a kid. The baker's wife didn't half shake me! She kept saying, 'Have you thrown it in the gutter?' But I held my loaf tight between my thighs and she had to give it up as a bad job. She wasn't half wild! It's these muscles *here* that I've got terrifically strong."

She was just going off when she changed her mind and said with immense dignity: "Don't make any mistakes! It's nothing to do with the filthy tricks those Eastern dancers get up to with a bottle! *My* muscles are all on the *outside!*"

I protested that I fully appreciated this and the three feathers, shading from fawn to chestnut, which adorned Carmen's enormous blue straw hat went waving away along the corridor.

The nightly ritual proceeded on its way. "The Miracle of the

Roses" trailed its garlands of dusty flowers. A squadron of eighteenth-century French soldiers galloped up the staircase, banging their arms against the walls with a noise like the clatter of tin cans.

I did my own turn after these female warriors and came down again with whiffs of the smoke of every tobacco in the world in my hair. Tired from sheer force of habit and from the contagion of the tiredness all around me, I sat down in front of the makeup shelf fixed to the wall. Someone came in behind me and sat down on the other cane-topped stool. It was one of the French soldiers. She was young and, to judge by the color of her eyes, dark. Her breeches were half undone and hanging down; she was breathing heavily through her mouth and not looking in my direction.

"Twenty francs!" she exclaimed suddenly. "Twenty francs' fine! I'm beyond twenty francs' fine, Monsieur Remondon! They make me laugh!"

But she did not laugh. She made an agonized grimace which showed gums almost as white as her teeth between her made-up lips.

"They fined you twenty francs? Why on earth?"

"Because I undid my breeches on the stairs."

"And why did you undo . . ."

The French soldier interrupted me: "Why? Why? You and your whys! Because when you can stick it, you stick it, and when you can't anymore, you can't!"

She leaned back against the wall and closed her eyes. I was afraid she was going to faint, but at the buzz of an electric bell, she leaped to her feet.

"Hell, that's us!"

She rushed away, holding up her breeches with both hands. I watched her down to the end of the passage.

"Whoever's that crazy creature?" asked Mademoiselle d'Estoute-ville languidly. She was entirely covered in pearls and wearing a breast-plate in the form of a heart made of sapphires.

I shrugged my shoulders to show that I had not the least idea. Lise Damoiseau, who was wiping her superb features with a dark rag thick with Vaseline and grease paint, appeared in her doorway.

"It's a girl called Gribiche who's in the chorus. At least that's who I think it is."

"And what was she doing in your dressing room, Colettevilli?" asked Carmen haughtily.

"She wasn't doing anything. She just came in. She said that Remondon had just let her in for a twenty-franc fine."

Lise Damoiseau gave a judicious whistle.

"Twenty francs! Lord! Whatever for?"

"Because she took her breeches down on the staircase when she came off the stage."

"Jolly expensive."

"We don't know for certain if it's true. Mightn't she just have had a drop too much?"

A woman's scream, shrill and protracted, froze the words on her lips. Lise stood stock-still, holding her makeup rag, with one hand on her hip like the servant in Manet's *Olympe*.

The loudness and the terrible urgency of that scream made all the women who were not up on the stage look out of their dressing rooms. Their sudden appearance gave an odd impression of being part of some stage spectacle. As it was near the end of the show, several of them had already exchanged their stork-printed kimonos for white embroidered camisoles threaded with pale blue ribbon. A great scarf of hair fell over the shoulder of one bent head and all the faces were looking the same way. Lise Damoiseau shut her door, tied a cord around her waist to keep her kimono in place, and went off to find out what had happened, with the key of her dressing room slipped over one finger.

A noise of dragging feet announced the procession which appeared at the end of the passage. Two stagehands were carrying a sagging body: a limp, white, made-up lay figure which kept slipping out of their grasp. They walked slowly, scraping their elbows against the walls.

"Who is it? Who is it?"

"She's dead!"

"She's bleeding from the mouth!"

"No, no, that's her rouge!"

"It's Marcelle Cuvelier! Ah, no, it isn't . . ."

Behind the bearers skipped a little woman wearing a headdress of glittering beads shaped like a crescent moon. She had lost her head a little but not enough to prevent her from enjoying her self-importance as an eyewitness. She kept panting: "I'm in the same dressing room with her. She fell right down to the bottom of the staircase . . . It came over her just like a stroke . . . Just fancy! Ten steps at least she fell."

"What's the matter with her, Firmin?" Carmen asked one of the men who was carrying her.

"Couldn't say, I'm sure," answered Firmin. "What a smash she went! But I haven't got time to be doing a nurse's job. There's my transparency for the Pierrots not set up yet!"

"Where are you taking her?"

"Putting her in a cab, I s'pose."

When they had gone by, Mademoiselle d'Estouteville laid her hand on her sapphire breastplate and half collapsed on her dressing stool.

Like Gribiche, the sound of the bell brought her to her feet, her eyes on the mirror.

"My rouge has gone and come off," she said in her loud schoolboy's voice.

She rubbed some bright pink on her blanched cheeks and went up to make her entrance. Lise Damoiseau, who had returned, had some definite information to give us.

"Her salary was two hundred and ten francs. It came over her like a giddy fit. They don't think she's broken anything. Firmin felt her over to see. So did the dresser. More likely something internal."

But Carmen pointed to something on the stone floor of the passage: a little star of fresh blood, then another, then still others at regular intervals. Lise tightened her mouth, with its deeply incised corners.

"Well, well!"

They exchanged a knowing look and made no further comment. The little "Crescent Moon" ran by us again, teetering on her high heels and talking as she went.

"That's all fixed. They've packed her into a taxi. Monsieur Bonnavent's driving it."

"Where's he driving her to?"

"Her home. I live in her street."

"Why not the hospital?"

"She didn't want to. At home she's got her mother. She came to when she got outside into the air. She said she didn't need a doctor. Has the bell gone for 'Up in the Moon'?"

"It certainly has. La Toutou went up ages ago."

The Crescent Moon swore violently and rushed away, obliterating the little regularly spaced spots with her glittering heels.

The next day nobody mentioned Gribiche. But at the beginning of the evening show, Crescent Moon appeared breathlessly and confided to Carmen that she had been to see her. Carmen passed the information on to me in a tone of apparent indifference.

"So she's better, then?" I insisted.

"If you like to call it better. She's feverish now."

She was speaking to the looking glass, concentrated on penciling a vertical line down the center of her rather flat upper lip to simulate what she called "the groove of chastity."

"Was that all Impéria said?"

"No. She said it's simply unbelievable, the size of their room."

"Whose room?"

"Gribiche and her mother's. Their Lordships the Management have sent forty-nine francs."

"What an odd sum."

In the mirror, Carmen's green eyes met mine harshly.

"It's exactly what's due to Gribiche. Seven days' salary. You heard them say she gets two hundred and ten francs a month."

My neighbor turned severe and suspicious whenever I gave some proof of inexperience which reminded her that I was an outsider and a novice.

"Won't they give her any more than that?"

"There's nothing to make them. Gribiche doesn't belong to the union."

"Neither do I."

"I should have been awfully surprised if you *did*," observed Carmen with chill formality.

The third evening, when I inquired, "How's Gribiche?" Lise Damoiseau raised her long eyebrows as if I had made a social gaffe.

"Colettevilli, I notice that when you have an idea in your head, it stays up in the top story. All other floors vacant and to let."

"Oh!" sneered Carmen. "You'll see her again, your precious Gribiche. She'll come back here, playing the interesting invalid."

"Well, *isn't* she interesting?"

"No more than any other girl who's done the same."

"You're young," said Lise Damoiseau. "Young in the profession I mean, of course."

"A blind baby could see *that*," agreed Carmen.

I said nothing. Their cruelty which seemed based on a convention left me with no retort. So did their perspicacity in sensing the bourgeois past that lay behind my inexperience and in guessing that my apparent youth was that of a woman of thirty-two who does not look her age.

It was on the fourth or fifth night that Impéria came rushing in at the end of the show and started whispering volubly to my roommates. Wanting to make a show of indifference in my turn, I stayed on my cane stool, polishing my cheap looking glass, dusting my makeup shelf, and trying to make it as maniacally tidy as my writing table at home.

Then I mended the hem of my skirt and brushed my short hair. Trying to keep my hair well groomed was a joyless and fruitless task, since I could never succeed in banishing the smell of stale tobacco which returned punctually after each shampoo.

Nevertheless, I was observing my neighbors. Whatever was preoccupying them and making them all so passionately eager to speak brought out all their various characters. Lise stood squarely, her hands on her hips, as if she were in the street market of the rue Lepic, throwing back her magnificent head with the authority of a housewife who will stand no nonsense. Little Impéria kept shifting from one leg to the other, twisting her stubby feet and suffering with the patience of an intelligent pony. Carmen was like all those lively energetic girls in Paris who cut out or finish or sell dresses; girls who instinctively know how to trade on their looks and who are frankly and avidly out for money. Only La Toutou belonged to no definite type, except that she embodied a literary infatuation of the time; the legendary princess, the fairy, the siren, or the perverted angel. Her beauty destined her to be perpetually wringing her hands at the top of a tower or shimmering palely in the depths of a dungeon or swooning on a rock in Liberty draperies dripping with jasper and agate. Suddenly Carmen planted herself in the frame of my open doorway and said all in one breath: "Well, so what are we going to do? That little Impéria says things are going pretty badly."

"What's going badly?"

Carmen looked slightly embarrassed.

"Oh! Colettevilli, don't be nasty, dear. Gribiche, of course. Not allowed to get up. Chemist, medicine, dressings, and all that . . ."

"Not to mention food," added Lise Damoiseau.

"Quite so. Well . . . you get the idea."

"But where's she been hurt, then?"

"It's her . . . back," said Lise.

"Stomach," said Carmen, at the same moment.

Seeing them exchange a conspiratorial look, I began to bristle.

"Trying to make a fool of me, aren't you?"

Lise laid her big, sensible hand on my arm.

"Now, now, don't get your claws out. We'll tell you the whole thing. Gribiche has had a miscarriage. A bad one, four and a half months."

All four of us fell silent. Mademoiselle d'Estouteville nervously pressed both her hands to her small flat stomach, probably by way of a spell to avert disaster.

"Couldn't we," I suggested, "get up a collection between us?"

"A collection, that's the idea," said Lise. "That's the word I was looking for and I couldn't get it. I kept saying a 'subscription.' Come on, La Toutou. How much'll you give for Gribiche?"

"Ten francs," declared Mademoiselle d'Estouteville without a second's hesitation. She ran to her dressing room with a clinking of sham diamonds and imitation sapphires and returned with two five-franc pieces.

"I'll give five francs," said Carmen Brasero.

"I'll give five too," said Lise. "Not more. I've got my people at home. Will you give something, Colettevilli?"

All I could find in my handbag was my key, my powder, some sous, and a twenty-franc piece. I was awkward enough to hesitate, though only for a fraction of a second.

"Want some change?" asked Lise with prompt tact.

I assured her that I didn't need any and handed the louis to Carmen, who hopped on one foot like a little girl.

"A louis . . . oh, goody, goody! Lise, go and extract some sous out of Madame ——" (she gave the name of the leading lady). "She's just come down."

"Not me," said Lise. "You or Impéria if you like. I don't go over big in my dressing gown."

"Impéria, trot around to Madame X. And bring back at least five hundred of the best."

The little actress straightened her spangled crescent in her mirror and went off to Madame X's dressing room. She did not stay there long.

"Got it?" Lise yelled to her from the distance.

"Got what?"

"The big wad."

The little actress came into my room and opened her closed fist.

"Ten francs!" said Carmen indignantly.

"Well, what she said was . . ." Impéria began.

Lise put out her big hand, chapped with wet white.

"Save your breath, dear. We know just what she said. That business was slack and her rents weren't coming in on time and things were rotten on the Bourse. That's what our celebrated leading actress said."

"No," Impéria corrected. "She said it was against the rules."

"What's against the rules?"

"To get up . . . subscriptions."

Lise whistled with amazement.

"First I've heard of it. Is it true, Toutou?"

Mademoiselle d'Estouteville was languidly undoing her chignon. Every time she pulled out one of the hideous iron hairpins, with their varnish all rubbed off, a twist of gold slid down and unraveled itself on her shoulders.

"I think," she said, "you're too clever by half to worry whether it's against the rules. Just don't mention it."

"You've hit it for once, dear," said Lise approvingly. She ended rashly: "Tonight, it's too late. But tomorrow I'll go around with the hat."

During the night, my imagination was busy with this unknown Gribiche. I had almost forgotten her face when she was conscious but I could remember it very clearly white, with the eyes closed, dangling over a stagehand's arm. The lids were blue and the tip of each separate lash beaded with a little blob of mascara . . . I had never seen a serious accident since I had been on the halls. People who risk their lives daily are extremely careful. The man who rides a bicycle around and around a rimless disk, pitting himself against centrifugal force, the girl whom a knife thrower surrounds with blades, the acrobat who swings from trapeze to trapeze high up in mid-air—I had imagined their possible end just as everyone does. I had imagined it with that vague, secret pleasure we all feel in what inspires us with horror. But I had never dreamed that someone like Gribiche, by falling down a staircase, would kill her secret and lie helpless and penniless.

The idea of the collection was enthusiastically received and everyone swore to secrecy. Nothing else was talked about in the dressing rooms. Our end of the corridor received various dazzling visitors. The "Sacred Scarab," glittering in purple and green ("*You* know," Carmen reminded me. "She's the one who was sick on the stage the night of the dress rehearsal"), and Julia Godard, the queen of male impersonators, who, close to, looked like an old Spanish waiter, came in person to present their ten francs. Their arrival aroused as much curiosity as it would in the street of a little town, for they came from a distant corridor which ran parallel to ours and they featured in tableaux we had never seen. Last of all Poupoute ("wonder quick-change child prodigy") deigned to bring us what she called her "mite." She owned to being eight and, dressed as a polo player ("Aristocratic Sports," Tableau 14), she strutted from force of habit, bowed with inveterate grace, and overdid the silvery laugh! When she left our peaceful regions, she made a careful exit backward, waving her little riding whip. Lise Damoiseau heaved an exasperated sigh.

"Has to be seen to be believed! The nerve of Her Majesty! Fourteen if she's a day, my dear! After all that, she coughed up ten francs."

By dint of one- and two-franc and five-franc pieces and the pretty little gold medals worth ten, the treasurer, Lise Damoiseau, amassed three hundred and eighty-seven francs, which she guarded fiercely in a barley-sugar box.

The troupe of "Girls" she left out of the affair. ("How on earth can I explain to them when they only talk English that Gribiche got herself in the family way and had a 'miss' and all the rest of it?") Nevertheless "Les Girls" produced twenty-five francs between them. At the last moment, a charming American who danced and sang (he still dances and he is still charming) slipped Carmen a hundred-franc note as he came off the stage, when we thought the "subscription" was closed.

We received some unexpected help. I won fifty francs for Gribiche playing bezique against a morose and elderly friend. Believe me, fifty francs meant something to him too and made their hole in the pension of a retired official in the Colonial Service. One way and another, we collected over five hundred francs.

"It's crazy," said Carmen, the night that we counted out five hundred and eighty-seven francs.

"Does Gribiche know?"

Lise shook her splendid head.

"*I'm* not crazy. Impéria's taken her sixty francs for the most pressing things. It's deducted on the account. Look, I've written it all down."

I leaned for some time over the paper, fascinated by the astonishing contrast between the large childish letters, sloping uncertainly now forward, now backward, and the fluent, assured, majestic figures, all proudly clear and even.

"I bet you're good at sums, Lise!"

She nodded. Her marble chin touched the base of her full, goddess-like neck.

"Quite. I like adding up figures. It's a pity I don't usually have many to add up. I like figures. Look, a 5's pretty, isn't it? So's a 7. Sometimes, at night, I sees 5's and 2's swimming on the water like swans . . . See what I mean? There's the swan's head . . . and there's its neck when it's swimming. And there, underneath, it's sitting on the water."

She brooded dreamily over the pretty 5's and the 2's shaped in the likeness of Leda's lover.

"Queer, isn't it? But that's not the whole story. We're going to take the five hundred and eighty-seven francs to Gribiche."

"Of course. I suppose Impéria will take care of that."

Lise proudly brushed aside my supposition with a jerk of her elbow.

"We'll do better than that, I hope. We're not going to fling it at her like a bundle of nonsense. You coming with us? We're going tomorrow at four."

"But I don't know Gribiche."

"Nor do we. But there's a right and a wrong way of doing things. Any particular reason for not wanting to come?"

Under such a direct question, reinforced by a severe look, I gave in, while blaming myself for giving in.

"No reason at all. How many of us are going?"

"Three. Impéria's busy. Meet us outside Number 3 —— Street."

I have always liked new faces, provided I can see them at a certain distance or through a thick pane of glass. During the loneliest years of my life, I lived on ground floors. Beyond the net curtain and the window-pane passed my dear human beings to whom I would not for the world have been the first to speak or hold out my hand. In those days I dedicated to them my passionate unsociability, my inexperience of human creatures, and my fundamental shyness, which had no relation to cowardice. I was not annoyed with myself because the thought of the visit to Gribiche kept me awake part of the night. But I was vexed that a certain peremptory tone could still produce an instinctive reflex of obedience, or at least of acquiescence.

The next day I bought a bunch of Parma violets and took the métro with as much bored resentment as if I were going to pay a ceremonial New Year's Day call. On the pavement of —— Street, Carmen and Lise Damoiseau watched me coming but made no welcoming sign from the distance. They were dressed as if for a funeral except for a lace jabot under Lise's chin and a feather curled like a question mark in Carmen's hat. It was the first time I had seen my comrades by daylight. Four o'clock on a fine May afternoon is ruthless to any defect. I saw with astonishment how young they were and how much their youth had already suffered.

They watched me coming, disappointed themselves perhaps by my everyday appearance. I felt that they were superior to me by a stoicism early and dearly acquired. Remembering what had brought me to this particular street, I felt that solidarity is easier for us than sympathy. And I decided to say "Good afternoon" to them.

"Isn't that the limit?" said Lise, by way of reply.

"What's the limit? Won't you tell me?"

"Why, that your eyes are blue. I thought they were brown. Grayish-brown or blackish-brown. Some sort of brown, anyway."

Carmen thrust out a finger gloved in suede and half pulled back the tissue paper which protected my flowers.

"It's Parmas. Looks a bit like a funeral, perhaps. But the moment Gibriche is better . . . Do we go in? It's on the ground floor."

"Looks out on the yard," said Lise contemptuously.

Gribiche's house, like many in the region of Batignolles, had been new around 1840. Under its eaves, it still preserved a niche for a statue, and in the courtyard there was a squat drinking fountain with a big brass tap. The whole building was disintegrating from damp and neglect.

"It's not bad," observed Lise, softening. "Carmen, did you see the statue holding the globe?"

But she caught the expression on my face and said no more. From a tiny invisible garden, a green branch poked out. I noted for future reference that the Japanese "Tree of Heaven" is remarkably tenacious of life. Following close behind Lise, we groped about in the darkness under the staircase. In the murk, we could see the faint gleam of a copper door handle.

"Well, aren't you ever going to ring?" whispered Carmen impatiently.

"Go on, ring yourself, then, if you can find the bell! This place is like a shoe cupboard. Here we are, I've found the thing. But it's not electric . . . it's a thing you pull."

A bell tinkled, crystal clear, and the door opened. By the light of a tiny oil lamp I could make out that a tall, broad woman stood before us.

"Mademoiselle Saure?"

"Yes. In here."

"Can we see her? We've come on behalf of the Eden Concert Company."

"Just a minute, ladies."

She left us alone in the semidarkness, through which gleamed Lise's inflexible face and enormous eyes. Carmen gave her a facetious dig in the ribs without her deigning to smile. She merely said under her breath: "Smells funny here."

A faint fragrance did indeed bring to my nostrils the memory of various scents which are at their strongest in autumn. I thought of the garden of the peaceful years of my life; of chrysanthemums and immortelles and the little wild geranium they call Herb Robert. The matron reappeared; her corpulence, outlined against a light background, filling the open frame of the second door.

"Be so good as to come in, ladies. The Couzot girl . . . Mademoiselle Impéria, I should say, told us you were coming."

"Ah," repeated Lise. "Impéria told you we were coming. She shouldn't have . . ."

"Why not?" asked the matron.

"For the surprise. We wanted to make it a surprise."

The word "surprise" on which we went through the door permanently linked up for me with the astonishing room inhabited by Gribiche and her mother. "It's unbelievable, the size of their room . . ." We passed with brutal suddenness from darkness to light. The enormous old room was lit by a single window which opened on the garden of a private house—the garden with the Japanese tree. Thirty years ago Paris possessed—and still possesses—any number of these little houses built to the requirements of unassuming, stay-at-home citizens and tucked away behind the big main buildings which almost stifle them. Three stone steps lead up to them from a yard with anemic lilacs and geraniums which have all run to leaf and look like vegetables. The one in this particular street was no more imposing than a stage set. Overloaded with blackened stone ornaments and crowned with a plaster pediment, it seemed designed to serve as a backcloth to Gribiche's heavily barred window.

The room seemed all the vaster because there was no furniture in the middle of it. A very narrow bed was squeezed against one wall, the wall farthest away from the light. Gribiche was lying on a divan-bed under the dazzling window. I was soon to know that it was dazzling for only two short hours in the day, the time it took the sun to cross the slice of sky between two five-story houses.

The three of us ventured across the central void toward Gribiche's bed. It was obvious that she neither recognized us nor knew who we were, so Carmen acted as spokesman.

"Mademoiselle Gribiche, we've all three come on behalf of your comrades at the Eden Concert. This is Madame Lise Damoiseau . . ."

"Of the 'Hell of Poisons' and Messalina in 'Orgy'," supplemented Lise.

"I'm Mademoiselle Brasero of the 'Corrida' and the 'Gardens of Murcia.' And this is Madame Colettevilli, who plays the sketch 'Miaou-Ouah-Ouah.' It was Madame Colettevilli who had the idea . . . the idea of the subscription among friends."

Suddenly embarrassed by her own eloquence, she accomplished her mission by laying a manila envelope, tied up with ribbon, in Gribiche's lap.

"Oh, really . . . I say, really. It's too much. Honestly, you shouldn't . . ." protested Gribiche.

Her voice was high and artificial, like that of a child acting a part. I felt no emotion as I looked at this young girl sitting up in bed. I was, in fact, seeing her for the first time, since she bore no resemblance either to the white, unconscious lay figure or to the French soldier who had incurred a fine of twenty francs. Her fair hair was tied back with a sky-blue ribbon, of that blue which is so unbecoming to most blondes, especially when, like Gribiche, they have thin cheeks, pallid under pink powder, and hollow temples and eye sockets. Her brown eyes ranged from Lise to Carmen, from Carmen to me, and from me to the envelope. I noticed that her breath was so short that I gave the matron a look which asked: "Isn't she going to die?"

I gave her my flowers, putting on the gay expression which the occasion demanded.

"I hope you like violets?"

"Of course. What an idea! Is there anyone who *doesn't* like violets? Thanks so much. How lovely they smell . . ."

She lifted the scentless bunch to her nostrils.

"It smells lovely here too. It reminds me of the smell of the country where I lived as a child. A bit like the everlastings you hang upside down to dry so as to have flowers in winter . . . What is it that smells so good?"

"All sorts of little odds and ends," came the matron's voice from behind me. "Biche, pull your legs up so as Madame Colettevilli can sit down. Do be seated, ladies. I'll bring you up our two chairs."

Lise accepted her seat with some hesitation, almost as if she had been asked to drink out of a doubtfully clean glass. For a moment that beautiful young woman looked extraordinarily like a prudish chair attendant. Then her slightly knitted eyebrows resumed their natural place on her forehead like two delicate clouds against a pure sky and she sat down, carefully smoothing her skirt over her buttocks.

"Well," said Carmen. "Getting better now?"

"Oh, I'll soon be all right," said Gribiche. "There's no reason now why I shouldn't get better, is there? Especially with what you've brought me. Everyone's been ever so kind . . ."

Shyly she picked up the envelope but did not open it.

"Will you put it away for me, Mamma?"

She held the envelope out to her mother, and my two companions looked decidedly worried as they saw the money pass from Gribiche's hands into the depths of a capacious apron pocket.

"Aren't you going to count it?" asked Lise.

"Oh!" said Gribiche delicately. "You wouldn't like me to do that."

To keep herself in countenance, she kept rolling and unrolling the ribbons of the sky-blue bed jacket, made of cheap thin wool, which hid her nightdress.

She had blushed and even this faint upsurge of blood was enough to start her coughing.

"Stop that coughing now," her mother urged her sharply. "You know quite well what I said."

"I'm not doing it on purpose," protested Gribiche.

"Why mustn't she cough?" inquired Carmen.

The tall, heavy woman blinked her prominent eyes. Though she was fat, she was neither old nor ugly and still had a ruddy complexion under hair that was turning silver.

"Because of her losses. She's lost a lot, you see. And all that isn't quite settled yet. As soon as she gets coughing, it all starts up again."

"Naturally," said Lise. "Her inside's still weak."

"It's like . . . It's like a girl I know," said Carmen eagerly. "She had an accident last year and things went all wrong."

"Whatever did she take, then?" asked Lise.

"Why, what does the least harm. A bowl of concentrated soap and after that you run as fast as you can for a quarter of an hour."

"Really, I can't believe my ears!" exclaimed Madame Gribiche. "My word, you'd think there was no such thing as progress. A bowl of soapy water and a run! Why, that goes back to the days of Charlemagne! Anyone'd think we lived among the savages!"

After this outburst, which she delivered loudly and impressively, Madame Saure, to give her her right name, relapsed into portentous silence.

Carmen asked with much interest: "Then she oughtn't to have taken soapy water? According to you, Madame, she'd have done better to have gone to one of those 'old wives'?"

"And have herself butchered?" said Madame Saure with biting contempt. "There's plenty have done that! No doubt they think it funny, being poked about with a curtain ring shoved up a rubber tube! Poor wretches! I don't blame them. I'm just sorry for them. After all, it's nature. A woman, or rather a child, lets a man talk her into it. You can't throw stones at her, can you?"

She flung up her hand pathetically and, in so doing, nearly touched the low ceiling. It was disfigured by concentric brown stains of damp, and cracked here and there in zigzags like streaks of lightning. The middle of it sagged slightly over the tiled floor whose tiles had come unstuck.

"When it rains outside, it rains inside," said Gribiche, who had seen what I was looking at.

Her mother rebuked her.

"That's not fair, Biche. It only rains in the middle. What d'you expect nowadays for a hundred and forty-five francs a year? It's the floors above that let in the water. The owner doesn't do any repairs. He's been expropriated. Something to do with the house being out of line. But we get over it by not putting any furniture in the middle."

"A hundred and forty-five francs!" exclaimed Lise enviously. "Well, that certainly won't ruin you!"

"Oh, no sir, no sir, no sir!" Gribiche said brightly.

I nearly laughed, for anything which disturbed Lise's serenity—envy, avarice, or rage—took away what little feminine softness her statuesque beauty possessed. I tried to catch Carmen's eye and make her smile too, but she was absorbed in some thought of her own and fidgeting with the kiss-curl on her left cheek.

"But, look," said Carmen, reverting to the other topic, "if the 'old wife' is no better than the soapy water, what's one to do? There isn't all that much choice."

"No," said Madame Saure professionally. "But there is such a thing as education and knowledge."

"Yes, people keep saying that. And talking about progress and all that . . . But listen, what about Miss Ourika? She went off to Cochin China, you know. Well, we've just heard she's dead."

"Miss Ourika? What's that you're saying?" said the high, breathless voice of Gribiche.

We turned simultaneously toward the bed as if we had forgotten her.

"She's dead? What did she die of, Miss Ourika?" asked Gribiche urgently.

"But she was . . . she tried to . . ."

To stop her from saying any more, Lise risked a gesture which gave everything away. Gribiche put her hands over her eyes and cried: "Oh, Mamma! You see, Mamma! You see."

The tears burst out between her clenched fingers. In three swift steps Madame Saure was at her daughter's side. I thought she was going to take her in her arms. But she pressed her two hands on her chest, just above her breasts, and pushed her down flat on her back. Gribiche made no resistance and slid gently down below the cheap Oriental cushion which supported her. In a broken voice, she kept on saying reproachfully: "You see, Mamma, you see. I told you so, Mamma . . ."

I could not take my eyes off those maternal hands which could so forcefully push down a small, emaciated body and persuade it to lie prone. Two big hands, red and chapped like a washerwoman's. They disappeared to investigate something under a little blue sateen quilt, under a cretonne sheet which had obviously been changed in our honor. I forced myself to fight down my nervous terror of blood, the terror of seeing it suddenly gush out and spread from its secret channels: blood set free, with its ferruginous smell and its talent for dyeing material bright pink or cheerful red or rusty brown. Lise's head was like a plaster cast; Carmen's rouge showed as two purple patches on her blanched cheeks as they both stared at the bed. I kept repeating to myself: "I'm not going to faint, I'm not going to faint." And I bit my tongue to distract from that pressure at the base of the spine so many women feel at the sight of blood or even when they hear a detailed account of an operation.

The two hands reappeared and Madame Saure heaved a sigh of relief: "Nothing wrong . . . nothing wrong."

She tossed her silvery hair back from her forehead, which was gleaming with sudden sweat. Her large majestic features which recalled so many portraits of Louis XVI did not succeed in making her face sympathetic. I did not like the way she handled her daughter. It seemed to me that she did so with an expertness and an apprehension which had nothing to do with a mother's anxiety. A great bovine creature, sagacious and agreeable but not in the least reassuring. Wiping her temples, she went off to a table pushed right up against the wall at the far end of the room. The sun had moved on and the room had grown somber: the imprisoned garden showed black under its "Tree of Heaven." In the distance Madame Saure was washing her hands and clattering with some glasses. Because of the distance and the darkness, her forehead seemed as if, any moment, it must touch the ceiling.

"Won't you ladies take a little of my cordial? Biche, you've earned a thimbleful too, ducky. I made it myself."

She came back to us and filled four little glasses which did not match. The one she offered me spilled over, so that I realized her hand was shaking. Lise took hers without a word, her mouth half open and her eyes fixed on the glass. For the first time, I saw a secret terror in those eyes. Carmen said "Thank you" mechanically and then seemed to come out of her trance.

"You know," she said hesitantly. "You know, I don't think she's awfully strong yet, your daughter . . . If I were you . . . What did the doctor say, Gribiche?"

Gribiche smiled at her with vague, still wet eyes and turned her head on the Oriental cushion. She pursed her lips to reach the greenish-gold oil of a kind of Chartreuse which was in the glass.

"Oh well, the doctor . . ."

She broke off and blushed. I saw how badly she blushed, in uneven patches.

"In the case of women," said Madame Saure, "doctors don't always know best."

Carmen waited for the rest of the answer but it did not come. She swallowed half her liqueur in one gulp and gave an exaggeratedly complimentary "mmm!"

"It's rather sweet, but very good all the same," said Lise.

The warmth returned to my stomach with the peppery taste of a kind of homemade Chartreuse that resembled a syrupy cough mixture. My colleagues were sufficiently revived to make conversation.

"Apart from that, is there any news at the theater?" inquired Gribiche.

She had pulled her plait of fair hair over one shoulder as young girls of those days used to do at bedtime.

"Absolutely not a scrap," answered Carmen. "Everything would be as dead as mutton if they weren't rehearsing the new numbers they're putting in for the Grand Prix every day."

"Are you in the new numbers?"

Lise and Carmen shook their heads serenely.

"We're only in the finale. We're not complaining. We've got quite enough to do as it is. I'm getting sick of this show, anyway. I'll be glad when they put on a new one. In the morning, they're rehearsing a sort of apache sketch."

"Who?"

Carmen shrugged her shoulders with supreme indifference.

"Some straight actors and actresses. A bitch they call . . . Oh, I can't remember. It'll come back to me. There are quite a lot of them but they're mainly comedians. The management wanted to get Otero but she's going into opera."

"Never!" said Gribiche excitedly. "Has she got enough voice?"

"She's got something better than voice, she's got *it*," said Lise. "It all goes by intrigue. She's marrying the director of the Opéra, so he can't refuse her anything."

"What's his name, the director of the Opéra?"

"Search me, dear."

I half closed my eyes to hear it better, this talk which took me back into a world unhampered by truth or even verisimilitude. A dazzling world, a fairy-like bureaucracy where, in the heart of Paris, "artistes" did not know the name of Julia Bartet, where it seemed perfectly natural that the great dancer Otero, dying to sing in *Faust* and *Les Huguenots*, should buy the director of the Opéra . . . I forgot the place and the reason which had drawn me back into it.

"Fierval's back from Russia," said Lise Damoiseau. "They're giving her the lead in the Winter Revue at the Eden Concert."

"Did she enjoy her tour in Russia?"

"Like anything. Just fancy, the Tsar rented a box for the whole season just to look in and see her number every night. And every single night, my dear, he sent her round presents by his own pope."

"His what?" asked Gribiche.

"His pope, dear. It's the same thing as a footman."

But of course! Naturally! Why not? Ah, go on . . . don't stop! How I loved them like that, swallowing the wildest improbabilities like children the moment they drop their outer shell of tough, hardworking wage earners with a shrewd eye on every sou . . . Let's forget everything except the absurd, the fantastic. Let's even forget this tortured little piece of reality lying flat on her bed beneath a barred window. I hope any moment to hear at the very least that President Loubet is going to elope with Alice de Tender . . . Go on, go on! Don't stop!

"Mamma . . . oh, quick, Mamma."

The whispered call barely ruffled a silence pregnant with other sensational revelations. But, faint as it was, Madame Saure found it reason enough to rush to the bedside. Gribiche's arm dropped slackly and the little glass which fell from her hand broke on the tiled floor.

"Oh, God!" muttered Madame Saure.

Her two hands dived once more under the sheets. She drew them out quickly, looked at them, and, seeing us on our feet, hid them in the pockets of her apron. Not one of us questioned her.

"You see, Mamma," moaned Gribiche. "I told you it was too strong. Why didn't you listen to me? Now, you see . . ."

Carmen made a brave suggestion: "Shall I call the concierge?"

The tall woman with the hidden hands took a step toward us and we all fell back.

"Quick, quick, get away from here . . . You mustn't call anyone . . . Don't be afraid, I'll look after her. I've got all that's needed. Don't say anything. You'll make bother for me. Get away, quick. Above all, not a word."

She pushed us back toward the door and I remember that we offered a faint resistance. But Madame Saure drew her hands out of her pockets, perhaps to drive us away. At the sight of them, Carmen started like a frightened horse, while I hustled Lise away, to avoid their contact. I don't know whether it was Lise who opened the door of the room and then the other door. We found ourselves in the mildewed hall under the statue holding the globe, we walked stiffly past the concierge's door, and as soon as we got outside on the pavement, Carmen shot ahead of us, almost at a run.

"Carmen! Wait for us!"

But Carmen did not stop till she was out of breath. Then she stood leaning her back against the wall. The green feather in her hat danced to the measure of her heartbeats. Whether from passionate desire for air, or from sheer gratitude, I turned my face up to the sky which twilight was just beginning to fill with pink clouds and twittering swallows. Carmen laid her hand on her breast, at the place where we believe our heart lies.

"Shall we take something to pull ourselves together?" I suggested. "Lise, a glass of brandy? Carmen, a pick-me-up?" We were just turning the corner of a street where the narrow terrace of a little wines and spirits bar displayed three iron tables. Carmen shook her head.

"Not there. There's a policeman."

"What does it matter if there is?"

She did not answer and walked quickly on ahead of us till we came to the Place Clichy, whose bustle seemed to reassure her. We sat down under the awning of a large brasserie.

"A coffee," said Carmen.

"A coffee," said Lise. "As for my dinner tonight . . . my stomach feels as if it were full of lead."

We stirred our spoons round and round our cups without saying a word. Inside, in the restaurant, the electric lights went on all at once, making us suddenly aware of the blue dusk of approaching evening flooding the square. Carmen let out a great sigh of relief.

"It's a bit stuffy," said Lise.

"You've got hot walking," said Carmen. "Just feel my hand. I know what I'm like. I'll have to put lots of rouge on tonight. I'll put on some 24."

"Now, I'd look a sight if I put on 24," retorted Lise. "I'd look like a beetroot. What *I* need is Creole 2½ and the same ground as a man."

Carmen leaned politely across the table.

"I think Colettevilli's awfully well made up on the stage, very *natural*. When you're not playing character parts, it's very important to look *natural*."

I listened to them as if I were only half awake and overhearing a conversation which had begun while I was asleep.

That coffee, though sugared till it was as thick as syrup, how bitter it tasted! Beside us, a flower seller was trying to get rid of her last bunch of lilacs: dark purple lilacs, cut while they were still in the bud, lying on sprays of yew.

" 'Les Girls,' " Carmen was saying, "they've got special stuff they use in England. Colors that make you look pink and white like a baby."

"But that's no good in character parts, is it, Colettevilli?"

I nodded, my lips on the rim of my cup and my eyes dazzled by an arrow from the setting sun.

Lise turned over the little watch which she pinned to the lapel of her jacket with a silver olive branch whose olives pretended to be jade.

"It's half past five," she announced.

"I don't give a damn," said Carmen. "I'm not going to have any dinner, anyway."

Half past five! What might have happened in half an hour to that girl on her soaking mattress? All we had done for her was to take her a handful of money. Lise held out her packet of cigarettes to me.

"No, thanks, I don't smoke. Tell me, Lise . . . isn't there anything we can do for Gribiche?"

"Absolutely nothing. Keep out of it. It's a filthy business. I've got my people at home who'd be more upset than me to see me mixed up in anything to do with abortion."

"Yes. But it was only falling downstairs at the theater that brought it on."

She shrugged her shoulders.

"You're an infant. The fall came *after*."

"After what?"

"After what she'd taken. She fell because she was nearly crazy with whatever it was she took. Colic, giddiness, and what have you. She told Impéria all about it in their dressing room. When she came into yours, she was so far gone, she was at her wits' end. She'd stuffed herself with cotton wool."

"Her old ma's an abortionist," said Carmen. "Gives you a dose to bring it on. She gave her daughter a lot more than a teaspoonful."

"Anyone can see that Ma Saure's already had some 'bothers,' as she calls them."

"How can you tell that?"

"Because she's so frightened. And also because they haven't a bean —no furniture, nothing. I wonder what she can have done to be as hard up as all that."

"Old murderess," muttered Carmen. "Clumsy old beast."

Neither of them showed any surprise. I saw that they were, both of them, thoroughly aware of and inured to such things. They could contemplate impartially certain risks and certain secret dealings of which I knew nothing. There was a type of criminality which they passively and discreetly acknowledged when confronted with the danger of having a child. They talked of the monstrous in a perfectly matter-of-fact way.

"But what about me?" I suggested rashly. "Couldn't *I* try? Leaving both of you right out of it, of course. If Gribiche could be got into a hospital! As to what people might say, I don't care a damn. I'm absolutely on my own."

Lise stared at me with her great eyes.

"'S true? As absolutely on your own as all that? You haven't anyone at all? No one who's close to you? Not even your family?"

"Oh, yes, there's my family," I agreed hastily.

"I thought as much," said Lise.

She stood up as if she considered the subject closed, put on her gloves, and snapped her fingers.

"Excuse me if I leave you now, Colettevilli. As I'm not going to have any dinner, I'm going to take my time getting down to the theater. I'll go by bus; it'll do me good."

"Me, too," said Carmen. "If we're hungry, we can buy a cheese sandwich off the stage doorkeeper."

She hesitated a moment before inviting me to join them.

"You coming too?"

"I'd love to, but I've promised to look in at my place first."

"See you later then. Bye-bye."

They went off arm in arm across the square, which was now all pink and blue: pink with the lit-up shops and bars, blue with the dusk of the late May afternoon.

My only longing was to get back to my little ground-floor room, to my odd scraps of salvaged furniture, to my books, to the smell of green leaves that sometimes drifted in from the Bois. Most of all I longed for the companion of my good and bad moments, my tabby cat. Once again she welcomed me, sniffing my hands and brooding thoughtfully over the hem of my skirt. Then she sat on the table and opened her golden eyes wide, staring into space at the invisible world which had no secrets for her. Neither of us ate more than a morsel or two and I went off punctually to the theater.

When I arrived at the Eden Concert, I found Mademoiselle d'Estouteville in a grubby bathrobe, with her feet as bare as an angel's and her cape of golden hair over her shoulders, trying to extract every detail of our visit to Gribiche from Lise and Carmen.

"Did it go off well?"

"Oh, yes, splendidly."

"Was she pleased?"

"I expected she thought it was better than a slap in the belly with a wet fish."

"And how is she? Is she coming back soon?"

Lise's face was impenetrable. She was occupied in making herself up for her first appearance as the demon Asmodeus.

"Oh, you know, I think it'll be some time yet. I don't think that girl's awfully strong."

"Got a decent sort of place?"

"Yes and no, as you might say. There's lots of space. At least, you can breathe there. I'd get the willies, myself, living in such a huge room."

"Her mother looks after her well?"

"Almost too well!"

"What did she say about the five hundred and eighty-seven francs?"

I took it on myself to answer so as to give Lise a little respite.

"She said we were to thank everyone ever so much . . . everyone who'd taken an interest in her. That she was so awfully touched."

"How did her face look? Quite normal again?"

"She's got a very babyish face, but you can see she's got much thinner. She'd got her hair tied back in a plait like a kid and a little blue bed jacket. She's very sweet."

The door of Carmen's dressing room banged, sharply pulled to from inside.

"Who's going to be late?" shouted Lise intelligently. "Colettevilli, of course. And who'll be to blame. That pain in the neck, Toutou d'Estouteville!"

The harsh voice of Mademoiselle d'Estouteville launched into a volley of insults, calmed down, and resolved into a laugh. Each of us went on to do what we always did: yawn, sing odd snatches of song, curse the stifling airlessness, cough, eat peppermints, and go and fill a tiny water jug at the tap in the passage.

Toward half past eleven, I was dressed again and ready to go home. It was the moment when the heat and lack of oxygen got the better of the dead-beat chorus girls and overworked dressers. As I left my dressing room, I noticed that the door of Carmen's dressing room was still shut and I raised my voice to call out my usual good night. The door opened and Carmen signed to me to come in. She was engaged in weeping as one weeps when one is wearing full stage makeup. Armed with a little tube of blotting paper the size of a pencil, she was pressing it first to her right eyeball, then to her left, between the lids.

"Pay no attention. I've got the . . . I'm unwell."

"Do you feel ill with it?"

"Oh, no. It's just that I'm so awfully relieved. Fancy, I was six days late. I was terrified of doing what Gribiche did . . . So, I'm so relieved."

She put her arm on my shoulder, then clasped it around my neck, and, just for the fraction of a second, laid her head on my breast.

I was just turning the corner of the long passage when she called out to me from the distance: "Good night! Don't have bad dreams!"

I had them all the same. I dreamed of anguished anxieties which had not hitherto fallen to my lot. My dream took place under the plant of ill-fame, wormwood. Unfolding its hairy, symbolic leaves one by one, the terrible age-old inducer of abortions grew in my nightmare to monstrous size, like the seed controlled by the fakir's will.

The next evening little Impéria came hobbling hurriedly up to us. I saw her whispering anxiously into Lise's ear. Balanced on one leg, she was clutching the foot that hurt her most with both hands. Lise listened to her, wearing her whitest, most statuesque mask and holding one hand over her mouth. Then she removed her hand and furtively made the sign of the cross.

I am perfectly aware that, in the music-hall world, people make the sign of the cross on the slightest provocation. Nevertheless, I knew at once and unerringly why Lise did so at that moment. Weakly, I made a point of avoiding her till the finale. It was easy and I think she deliberately made it easier still. Afterward, fate played into my hands. In honor of the Grand Prix, the management cut out the sketch "Miaou-

Ouah-Ouah," which did not, I admit, deserve any preferential treatment. Months and years went by during which I made a public spectacle of myself in various places but reserved the right to say nothing of my private life.

When I felt that I wanted to write the story of Gribiche, I controlled myself and replaced it by a "blank," a row of dots, an asterisk. Today, when I am allowing myself to describe her end, I naturally suppress her name, that of the music hall, and those of the girls we worked with. By such changes and concealments I can still surround Gribiche's memory with the emblems of silence. Among such emblems are those which, in musical notation, signify the breaking off of the melody. Three hieroglyphs can indicate that break: a mute swallow on the five black wires of the stave; a tiny hatchet cutting across them, and—for the longest pause of all—a fixed pupil under a huge, arched, panic-stricken eyebrow.

[*Translated by Antonia White*]

PART III
Varieties
of Human Nature

The human face was ever my great landscape.

The Hidden Woman

He had been looking at the swirl of masks in front of him for a long time, suffering vaguely from the intermingling of their colors and the synchronized sound of two orchestras too close together. His cowl pressed his temples; a nervous headache was building between his eyes. But he savored, without impatience, a mixture of malaise and pleasure which allowed the hours to fly by unnoticed. He had wandered down all the corridors of the Opéra, had drunk in the silvery dust of the dance floor, recognized bored friends, and wrapped around his neck the indifferent arms of a very fat girl humorously disguised as a sylph. Though embarrassed by his long domino, tripping over it like a man in skirts, the cowled doctor did not dare take off either the domino or the hood, because of his schoolboy lie.

"I'll be spending tomorrow night in Nogent," he had told his wife the evening before. "They just telephoned and I'm afraid that my patient, you know, that poor old lady . . . Can you imagine? And I was looking forward to this ball like a kid. It's ridiculous, isn't it, a man my age who's never been to the Opéra Ball?"

"Very, darling, very ridiculous! If I had known I might never have married you . . ."

She laughed, and he admired her narrow face, pink, matte, and long, like a thin sugared almond.

"But . . . don't you want to go to the Green and Purple Ball? You know you can go without me if you want, darling."

She trembled with one of those long shivers of disgust which made her hair, her delicate hands, and her chest in her white dress shudder at the sight of a slug or some filthy passer-by.

"Oh, no! Can you see me in a crowd, all those hands . . . What can I do? It's not that I'm a prude, it's . . . it makes my skin crawl. There's nothing I can do about it."

Leaning against the balustrade of the loggia, above the main staircase, he thought about this trembling hind, as he contemplated, directly in front of him, on the bare back of a sultana, the grasp of two enormous square hands with black nails. Bursting out of the braid-trimmed sleeves of a Venetian lord, they sank into the white female flesh as if it were dough. Because he was thinking about her, it gave him quite a start to hear, next to him, a little "ahem," a little cough typical of his wife. He turned around and saw someone in a long and impenetrable disguise, sitting sidesaddle on the balustrade, Pierrot by the looks of the huge-sleeved tunic, the loose-fitting pantaloons, the skullcap, the plaster-like whiteness coating the little bit of skin visible above the half-mask bearded with lace. The fabric of the costume and skullcap, woven of dark violet and silver, glistened like the conger eel fished for by night with iron hooks, in boats with resin lanterns. Overcome with surprise, he waited to hear the little "ahem," which did not come again. The Pierrot-Eel, seated, casual, tapped the marble balusters with a dangling heel, revealing only its two satin slippers and a black-gloved hand bent back against one hip. The two oblique slits in the mask, carefully covered over with a tulle mesh, allowed only a smothered fire of indeterminate color to pass through.

He almost called out, "Irene!" but held back, remembering his own lie. Not good at playacting, he also decided against disguising his voice. The Pierrot scratched its thigh, with a free and uninhibited gesture, and the anxious husband sighed in relief.

"Ah! It's not her."

But out of a pocket the Pierrot pulled a flat gold box, opened it to take out a lipstick, and the anxious husband recognized an antique snuffbox, fitted with a mirror inside, the last birthday present . . . He put his left hand on the pain in his chest with so brusque and so involuntarily theatrical a motion that the Pierrot-Eel noticed him.

"Is that a declaration, Purple Domino?"

He did not answer, half choked with surprise, anticipating, as in a bad dream, and listened for a long moment to the thinly disguised voice—the voice of his wife. The Eel, sitting there cavalierly, its head tilted like a bird's, looked at him; she shrugged her shoulders, hopped down, and walked away. Her movement freed the distraught husband, who, restored to an active and normal jealousy, started to think clearly again, and calmly rose to follow his wife.

"She's here for someone, with someone. In less than an hour I'll know everything."

A hundred other purple or green cowls guaranteed that he would be neither noticed nor recognized. Irene walked ahead of him nonchalantly. He was amazed to see her roll her hips softly and drag her feet a little as if she were wearing Turkish slippers. A Byzantine, in embroidered emerald green and gold, grabbed her as she passed, and she bent back, grown thinner in his arms, as if his grasp were going to cut her in half. Her husband ran a few steps forward and reached the couple as Irene cried out flatteringly, "You big brute, you!"

She walked away, with the same relaxed and calm step, stopping often, musing at the open doors of the boxes, almost never turning around. She hesitated at the bottom of a staircase, turned aside, came back toward the entrance to the orchestra stalls, slid into a noisy, dense group with slippery skillfulness, the exact movement of a knife blade sliding into its sheath. Ten arms imprisoned her, an almost naked wrestler roughly pinned her up against the edge of the boxes on the main floor and held her there. She yielded under the weight of the naked man, threw back her head with a laugh that was drowned out by other laughter, and the man in the purple cowl saw her teeth flash beneath the mask's lacy beard. Then she slipped away again with ease and sat down on the steps which led to the dance floor. Her husband, standing two steps behind, watched her. She readjusted her mask, and her crumpled tunic, and tightened the roll of her headband. She seemed calm, as though alone, and walked away again after a few minutes' rest. She went down the steps, put her arms on the shoulders of a warrior who invited her, without speaking, to dance, and she danced, clinging to him.

"That's him," the husband said to himself.

But she did not say a word to the dancer, clad in iron and moist skin, and left him quietly, when the dance ended. She went off to have a glass of champagne at the buffet, and then a second glass, paid, and then watched, motionless and curious, as two men began scuffling, surrounded by screaming women. Then she amused herself by placing her little satanic hands, all black, on the white throat of a Dutch girl with golden hair, who cried out nervously. At last the anxious man who was following her saw her stop as she bumped up against a young man collapsed on a banquette, out of breath, fanning himself with his mask. She leaned over, disdainfully took his handsome face, rugged and fresh, by the chin, and kissed the panting, half-open mouth . . .

But her husband, instead of rushing forward and tearing the two joined mouths away from each other, disappeared into the crowd. Dismayed, he no longer feared, he no longer hoped for betrayal. He was sure now that Irene did not know the adolescent, drunk with dancing, whom she was kissing, or the Hercules. He was sure that she was not waiting or looking for anyone, that the lips she held beneath her own like a crushed grape, she would abandon, leave again the next minute, then wander about again, gather up some other passer-by, forget him, until she felt tired and it was time to go back home, tasting only the monstrous pleasure of being alone, free, honest, in her native brutality, of being the one who is unknown, forever solitary and without shame, whom a little mask and a hermetic costume had restored to her irremediable solitude and her immodest innocence.

[*Translated by Matthew Ward*]

Dawn

❦

The surgical suddenness of their break left him stupefied. Alone in the house where they had lived as a quasi-conjugal couple for some twenty years, he was unable, a week later, to bring himself out of his stupor long enough to be sad. He struggled, comically, against the disappearance of ordinary objects, and berated his manservant in a childish manner: "Well, no one's eaten those collars! And don't tell me I don't have any more sticks of shaving soap; there were two of them, there, in the small cupboard in the bathroom! You're not going to make me believe that I don't have any shaving soap just because Madame isn't here!"

Bewildered at no longer feeling held accountable, he forgot meal-times, returned home for no apparent reason, went out just to get away, floundering about, half choked, at the end of a rope which the imperious hand of a woman no longer held.

He called his friends to witness, embarrassed them, offended their sense of reserve as men unfaithful or enslaved. "My good man, it's unbelievable! Cleverer men than I wouldn't understand it at all . . . Aline's gone. She's gone, that's it. And not alone, you can bet on that. She's gone. I could repeat it a hundred times and I still wouldn't find anything more to say. This sort of thing apparently happens every day to I don't know how many husbands . . . What can I say? I can't get over it. I just can't get over it."

His eyes would open wide, he'd raise his arms, and then drop them again. He seemed neither tragic nor humiliated, and his friends ridiculed him a little: "He's slipping, yes, he's slipping! At his age, it's hit him pretty hard." They talked about him as if he were an old man, secretly pleased at last to belittle this handsome, graying man who had never tasted disappointment in love.

"His beautiful Aline . . . He thought it was all perfectly natural that at forty-five she suddenly became a blonde, blond like an artificial flower, and that she changed her dressmaker, and her shoemaker. He wasn't suspicious . . ."

One day he took a train ride because his manservant had asked him for the week off. "Since there's less work with Madame not being here, I thought . . ." and also because he was losing more and more sleep, dozing off at daybreak after nights spent like a hunter on the lookout, motionless in the dark, jaws clenched, ears twitching. He left one evening, avoiding the country house he had bought fifteen years earlier and furnished for Aline. He bought a ticket for a large provincial town where he remembered having "spread the good word" and banqueted at the expense of *L'Extension Economique*.

"A good hotel," he told himself, "and a restaurant with good French cooking, and I'm in business. I don't want this thing to kill me now, do I? So then, off we go. Travel, good food . . ."

On the way, he saw reflected in the window of the compartment his still-erect figure and the gray brush which hid his relaxed mouth. "Not bad, not bad. I'm not going to let it kill me, by gum! The hussy!" He used no stronger word for the unfaithful woman than this mild, old-fashioned insult, which when spoken by older people is still meant to compliment the rashness of youth.

At the hotel he asked for the same room as last year. "The round corner room, you know, the one with a nice view of the square"; he dined on cold meat and beer and, as it was nightfall, went to bed. His weariness had led him to believe that sleep would soon reward his flight. Lying on his back, he felt the coolness of sheets which were not quite dry, and calculated in the darkness the half-forgotten place of the big round bay window, judging from two high shafts of bluish light between the drawn curtains. In fact, he was fast asleep in a matter of seconds, and then woke up for good by having unconsciously made room, with a movement of his legs, for her, who, absent now both day and night, returned faithfully under cover of sleep. He woke and bravely uttered the conjuring words: "Come on now, it'll be daylight soon, take it easy." The two shafts of blue light were turning rose, and from the square he heard the welcome, hoarse-sounding racket of the iron-hooped wooden buckets and the *clip-clop* of the horses' big, patient hooves. "Exactly the same sound as the stables at Fontainebleau, in that villa we'd rented near the hotel. At daybreak we would listen to . . ." He shivered, turned over, and once again sought sleep. The horses and the buckets were quiet now. Other sounds, more discreet, rose up through the open window. He could make out the dense, dull sound of flowerpots being unloaded from a truck, a light sprinkling of water on plants, and the soft thud of big armfuls of leaves thrown on the ground.

"A flower market," the sleepless man said to himself. "Oh, no doubt about it. It was in Strasbourg during that trip we made, sunrise brought us a charming flower market, under our windows, and she said she had never seen cinerarias as blue as . . ." He sat up, the better to withstand a despair which flowed over him in steady waves, a new despair, entirely fresh and unknown. Underneath the nearby bridge, oars slapped the sleepy river, and the flight of the first whistling swallows pierced the air. "It's early morning in Como, the swallows that followed the gardener's boat, loaded with fruits and vegetables whose smell came in through our window, at the Villa d'Este . . . My God, have some pity . . ." He was still strong enough to blush at the start of a prayer, although the pain of loneliness and memory had left him doubled over on his bed like a man struck in the chest. Twenty years . . . all the dawns of twenty years were pouring out their faint or brilliant rays, their bird cries, their raindrops, on the head of a companion asleep or awake at his side, twenty years . . .

"I don't want it to kill me, my God . . . twenty years means something . . . but I had other dawns, before her . . . Yes, let me see, when I was a very young man . . ."

But he could summon up only the twilights of a poor student, the gray mornings at law school, warmed by skimmed milk or alcohol, mornings in furnished rooms with narrow washbasins or zinc buckets. He turned away from them, called on his adolescence and dawns long past for help, but they came to him, mean and bitter, emerging from a rickety iron bed, prisoners of a wretched time, marked on his cheek with a stinging slap, dragging shoes with spongy soles . . . The abandoned man knew he had no refuge and that he would struggle in vain against the light's return, that the cruel and familiar harmony of the first hour of the day would sing only one name, reopening the same wound, fresh and new each time; so he lay back and broke down in tears.

[*Translated by Matthew Ward*]

One Evening

❧❧❧

The moment the gate closed behind us and we saw the lantern in the gardener's hand dancing in front of us, under a covering of clipped yews where the heavy downpour filtered through only in scattered drops, we felt that shelter was very near and agreed laughingly that the car trouble which had just left us stranded in the countryside clearly belonged in the category of "happy accidents."

It just so happened that Monsieur B., a country councillor and the owner of the château, who welcomed these two rain-soaked and unexpected women out on the terrace, knew my husband slightly, and his wife—a former student at the Schola Cantorum—remembered having met me at a Sunday concert.

Around the first wood fire of the season, there rose a talkative gaiety. My friend Valentine and I felt it only right to accept a potluck of cold meat washed down with champagne; our hosts had only just finished their dinner.

An old plum brandy and some still-steaming coffee made us feel almost intimate. The electric light, rare for the region, the smell of mild tobacco, fruits, the blazing, resinous wood—I savored these familiar delights like gifts from a newfound isle.

Monsieur B., square-shouldered, with just a hint of gray and the handsome, white-toothed smile of a man from the south, took my friend Valentine aside, and I chatted with Madame B. less than I observed her.

Blond, slim, and dressed as if for an elegant dinner and not for receiving stranded motorists, she surprised me with eyes so light that the least reflection robbed them of their pale blue. They became mauve like her dress, green like the silk of her chair, or disturbed, in the lamplight, by a fleeting red glimmer like the blue eyes of a Siamese cat.

I wondered if the entire face did not owe its vacant look, its empty amiability, its sometimes somnambulistic smile to these overlight eyes. A somnambulist, in any case, singularly attentive to everything that might please us and shorten the two or three hours it would take our chauffeur, with the help of Monsieur B.'s mechanic, to repair the car.

"We have a room you're welcome to use," Madame B. said to me. "Why not spend the night here?"

And her eyes, as though untenanted, expressed only an unlimited and almost unthinking solitude.

"It's not so bad here, really," she continued. "Look at my husband, he's getting on quite well with your friend!"

She laughed, while her wide-open, deserted eyes seemed not to hear what she said. Twice she made me repeat some phrase or other, starting slightly each time. Morphine? Opium? An addict would never have those rosy gums, that relaxed brow, that soft, warm hand, or that youthful flesh, firm and rounded beneath the low-cut dress.

Was I dealing with a silent conjugal victim? No. A tyrant, even a Machiavellian one, does not say "Simone" so tenderly, never bestows upon his slave so flattering a look . . .

"Why, yes, Madame, they do exist," Monsieur B. was saying to my friend Valentine. "There are couples who live in the country eight months out of the year, are never out of each other's sight, and don't complain about their fate! They do exist, don't they, Simone?"

"Yes, thank God!" replied Simone.

But in her eyes, just barely blue, there was nothing, nothing but a tiny yellow cinder, very far away—the lamp's reflection in a potbellied samovar. Then she stood up and poured us cups of steaming hot tea flavored with rum "for the dark road." It was ten o'clock. A young man came in, bareheaded, and before being introduced gave some opened letters to Monsieur B., who asked my friend to excuse him as he leafed quickly through his mail.

"He's my husband's secretary," Madame B. explained to me as she cut a lemon into thin slices.

I responded by saying exactly what I was thinking: "He's very good-looking."

"Do you think so?"

She raised her eyebrows like a woman surprised, saying, "I've never thought about it." However, what was striking about this svelte young man was his air of stubborn, completely unself-conscious persistence, a habit of lowering his eyelids which, when he raised them, made his brusque, wild, quickly masked glance all the more arresting, and more disdainful than shy. He accepted a cup of tea and sat in front of the fire, next to Madame B., thus occupying the other place on one of those horrid, handy, S-shaped settees which the style of the 1880s named love seats.

Suddenly everyone fell silent for a moment and I was afraid our amiable hosts had tired of us. In order to break the silence I said softly, "How cozy! I'm going to remember this charming house I will have been in without ever knowing what it looks like set in the countryside . . . This fire will warm us again, won't it, Valentine, if we close our eyes in the wind, a while from now."

"It will be your own fault," Madame B. cried out. "If it were me, I wouldn't need any sympathy. I love driving at night, with the rain streaking the air in front of the headlights and the drops of rain on my cheeks like tears. Oh, I love all that!"

I looked at her with surprise. She glowed all over with a delicious, human flame, which shyness had perhaps stifled for the first few hours. She no longer held herself back and the most attractive self-confidence showed her to be gay, sensible, well informed about local politics and her husband's ambitions, which she scoffed at by imitating him, the way little girls do when playacting. There was no lamp on the mantel, and only the crackling hearth, far from the central light, colored or left in shadow this young woman whose sudden animation made me think of the gaiety of canaries, awakened in their cage at the hour when the lamps are lit. The dark back of Monsieur B.'s secretary was angled against the S-shaped armrest which separated him from Madame B. While she was talking to her husband and my friend from a slight distance, turned toward them, I rose in order to set down my empty cup and I saw that the young man's concealed hand held Madame B.'s bare arm in a steady and perfectly motionless grip above the elbow. Neither one of them moved, the young man's visible hand held a cigarette he was not smoking, and Madame B.'s free arm waved a small fan. She was speaking happily, attentive to everyone, her eyes limpid, in a voice interrupted now and then by her quickened breathing, like the urge to laugh, and I could see the veins in one of her hands begin to swell, so amorous and strong had the hidden embrace become.

Like someone who feels another's glance weighing down on him, Monsieur B.'s secretary suddenly rose, bowed to everyone, and left.

"Isn't that our motor I hear?" I asked Madame B. a moment later. She did not answer. She was staring into the fire, inclining her head toward a sound beyond her hearing, and slightly slumped over, looked like a woman who had just taken a bad fall. I repeated my question; she gave a start.

"Yes, yes, I believe so . . ." she said hastily. She blinked her eyes and gave me a smile of frozen grace, her eyes overtaken by a cold emptiness.

"What a shame!"

We left, carrying with us autumn roses and black dahlias. Monsieur B. walked alongside the car, which started slowly, as far as the first turn in the drive. Madame B. stood on the lighted terrace, smiling at us from a face abandoned by the momentary certainty of being alive; one of her hands, rising up beneath a transparent scarf, clasped her bare arm above the elbow.

[Translated by Matthew Ward]

The Hand

❧§❨

He had fallen asleep on his young wife's shoulder, and she proudly bore the weight of the man's head, blond, ruddy-complexioned, eyes closed. He had slipped his big arm under the small of her slim, adolescent back, and his strong hand lay on the street next to the young woman's right elbow. She smiled to see the man's hand emerging there, all by itself and far away from its owner. Then she let her eyes wander over the half-lit room. A veiled conch shed a light across the bed the color of periwinkle.

"Too happy to sleep," she thought.

Too excited also, and often surprised by her new state. It had been only two weeks since she had begun to live the scandalous life of a newlywed who tastes the joys of living with someone unknown and with whom she is in love. To meet a handsome, blond young man, recently widowed, good at tennis and rowing, to marry him a month later: her conjugal adventure had been little more than a kidnapping. So that whenever she lay awake beside her husband, like tonight, she still kept her eyes closed for a long time, then opened them again in order to savor, with astonishment, the blue of the brand-new curtains, instead of the apricot-pink through which the first light of day filtered into the room where she had slept as a little girl.

A quiver ran through the sleeping body lying next to her, and she tightened her left arm around her husband's neck with the charming authority exercised by weak creatures. He did not wake up.

"His eyelashes are so long," she said to herself.

To herself she also praised his mouth, full and likable, his skin the color of pink brick, and even his forehead, neither noble nor broad, but still smooth and unwrinkled.

Her husband's right hand, lying beside her, quivered in turn, and beneath the curve of her back she felt the right arm, on which her whole weight was resting, come to life.

"I'm so heavy . . . I wish I could get up and turn the light off. But he's sleeping so well . . ."

The arm twisted again, feebly, and she arched her back to make herself lighter.

"It's as if I were lying on some animal," she thought.

She turned her head a little on the pillow and looked at the hand lying there next to her.

"It's so big! It really is bigger than my whole head."

The light, flowing out from under the edge of a parasol of bluish crystal, spilled up against the hand, and made every contour of the skin apparent, exaggerating the powerful knuckles and the veins engorged by the pressure on the arm. A few red hairs, at the base of the fingers, all curved in the same direction, like ears of wheat in the wind, and the flat nails, whose ridges the nail buffer had not smoothed out, gleamed, coated with pink varnish.

"I'll tell him not to varnish his nails," thought the young wife. "Varnish and pink polish don't go with a hand so . . . a hand that's so . . ."

An electric jolt ran through the hand and spared the young woman from having to find the right adjective. The thumb stiffened itself out, horribly long and spatulate, and pressed tightly against the index finger, so that the hand suddenly took on a vile, apelike appearance.

"Oh!" whispered the young woman, as though faced with something slightly indecent.

The sound of a passing car pierced the silence with a shrillness that seemed luminous. The sleeping man did not wake, but the hand, offended, reared back and tensed up in the shape of a crab and waited, ready for battle. The screeching sound died down and the hand, relaxing gradually, lowered its claws, and became a pliant beast, awkwardly bent, shaken by faint jerks which resembled some sort of agony. The flat, cruel nail of the overlong thumb glistened. A curve in the little finger, which the young woman had never noticed, appeared, and the wallowing hand revealed its fleshy palm like a red belly.

"And I've kissed that hand! . . . How horrible! Haven't I ever looked at it?"

The hand, disturbed by a bad dream, appeared to respond to this startling discovery, this disgust. It regrouped its forces, opened wide, and splayed its tendons, lumps, and red fur like battle dress, then slowly drawing itself in again, grabbed a fistful of the sheet, dug into it with its curved fingers, and squeezed, squeezed with the methodical pleasure of a strangler.

"Oh!" cried the young woman.

The hand disappeared and a moment later the big arm, relieved of its burden, became a protective belt, a warm bulwark against all the terrors of night. But the next morning, when it was time for breakfast in bed—hot chocolate and toast—she saw the hand again, with its red hair and red skin, and the ghastly thumb curving out over the handle of a knife.

"Do you want this slice, darling? I'll butter it for you."

She shuddered and felt her skin crawl on the back of her arms and down her back.

"Oh, no . . . no . . ."

Then she concealed her fear, bravely subdued herself, and, beginning her life of duplicity, of resignation, and of a lowly, delicate diplomacy, she leaned over and humbly kissed the monstrous hand.

[Translated by Matthew Ward]

A Dead End

◄⊰⊱►

He had taken her from another man, this slim magnificent blonde who looked like a greyhound on a leash. He had followed her everywhere, approached her romantically, and carried her off. They did not even know what had become of the other man and never bothered to find out. The other man conducted himself properly in defeat and ceased to exist for them. The victor—let us say he was called Armand and the woman Elsie—gave little thought to the other man, for Elsie loved *him*, and besides, his only concern was proving his love and his naïveté by organizing the jail called "life together." She helped him do it, flattered as she was, like all women who are told they are being sequestered in the name of love. The natural end to a few weeks of hotels and traveling was a villa on the edge of a lake where, in good faith, they believed they would make their happy home.

A certain laziness, her beauty care, the slowness of her gestures shortened the hours of the day for Elsie. Those of the night, given over to sleep or love, seemed all too brief. Having both agreed, in due time, that between lovers silence is golden, they were able to remain silent with impunity, for the time being. They never went out, returned home, or wandered through the woods unless they were together, leaning against one another, or he behind her, she trailing a ribbon, the tip of a veil, or the train of her dress at his feet, like a broken leash.

Away from Paris they had no difficulty ensuring their solitude; the spectacle of love is enough to drive away even the best of friends. One can seek out the company of a man or a woman in love—but being around a happy couple who show their happiness bores and shocks our taste for moderate diversions and healthy harmony.

So they lived together, alone, with the thoughtless and foolish bravura of lovers. She was not afraid, on certain days at twilight, with the sky closing in and the wind dying down, waiting for the storm when all nature seems to be brewing up some tragedy, she was not afraid to find herself with this strange man, with his broad shoulders, his fierce brow, and his swift movements. For deep within herself a woman places great trust in her ravisher.

Armand hardly thought about the woman's past, since he held her in his arms night and day, and since he knew nothing about the past of this woman whom he loved. For Armand, Elsie's past was some poor deceived man swallowed up by darkness and oblivion. Now and then he asked himself, as if out of duty, "and before that poor man . . . ?" and quickly returned to the present, where there were neither clouds nor secrets.

The suffering began one morning while he was looking out from behind a hedge, ablaze with crimson geraniums, at the lake and its mist the color of pink pewter, and Elsie was singing in a low voice, up on the second floor, as she dressed. He suddenly realized that he did not know the song, and that Elsie had never sung it before. It surprised him and he conjectured that she was thinking, as she sang, of a bygone time, of people with names he did not know, perhaps of some unknown man . . .

When his mistress rejoined him, he found her somehow different from the woman he was expecting, and told her so with tender solicitude. She replied, unsuspectingly, that the first rains of autumn made her feel cold, and she spoke about central heating, big wood fires, and fur coats, with an air of covetousness and coquettish fright. Then he stopped looking at her and, lowering his eyes, began to count the months they had now spent together, and he thought that maybe she felt like leaving again. The image he formed of Elsie's absence carried him back to when he lived without her, and he shuddered to think that during that time long past he had been capable of living another life.

He raised his eyes toward Elsie again and his heart did not melt with love, but pounded painfully, "because," he thought, "I've been a man like other men. Elsie's a woman like other women, except that she's more beautiful. No doubt the one I took her from has gone back to being a man like other men, a man stripped of happiness, an average, sad, fickle man. And the one who comes after me . . ."

He stumbled mentally, stopped reasoning, and felt himself, abject and broken, entering into that aimless jealousy which not even innocence can cure.

He did his best to hide his suffering, redoubling his amorous advances. But what he gained for all the pains he took to hide his misgivings was a mental exhaustion quickly perceived by the keen senses of his mistress. He struggled on, sure of the expression on his face and of the words he spoke, and it was Elsie who suffered from uneasiness, who yawned nervously and trembled, one moonlit night, when she saw Armand's shadow standing there, on the wall, as expressive and alive as a third person . . . He took note of her weaknesses, attributed them to regret, a desire to escape, and one day, he deeply insulted his mistress, who was reassured and filled with pride by his outburst.

"Like a prison . . . the harem door bolted shut . . ." he muttered angrily.

But at the same time he doubted that there was any remedy, and anxious over a few moments' separation, he nonetheless felt no gratitude at the reappearance of her whom he could not manage without. Now he looked for faults in her, and desperate for peace of mind, he wished the marks of age on her, but hated her when, less beautiful one day than the day before and the day after, she seemed to obey his hostile will.

He lived in the distraction which is the punishment for those whom love has abused by inspiring them to re-create the earthly paradise. He even tried to get away from Elsie, on idle pretexts, but came back more troubled and more vindictive each time, for he was never gone long enough to set foot on the firm ground of normal sorrow, the sorrow of privation, and his relief at having left his mistress would immediately give way to the intolerable supposition that she had run away during his absence.

One day when he had left Elsie at the villa, and was walking alone, by the edge of the lake, putting his distraction through a kind of hopeless discipline, he heard someone running behind him, turned around, and saw one of Elsie's servants coming toward him, extremely upset. She stopped, breathless, a few steps away.

"Oh, Monsieur . . . it's Madame . . ." And he cried out to her in a loud, artificial tone of voice, "Madame? . . . Yes? She's just left, hasn't she?"

The servant opened and closed her mouth, unable to speak immediately, then uttered a few words in which he understood her to say that there had been an accident . . . a fall on the stone steps . . . a fractured skull . . . died instantly . . . death . . . He sat down, relaxed, on the grassy bank.

"Oh," he said with a sigh, "I was afraid . . ."

[Translated by Matthew Ward]

The Fox

❦

The man who takes his fox for walks in the Bois de Boulogne is a good man indeed. He believes that it pleases the little fox, who was probably his companion in the trenches and whom he tamed to the horrible sound of exploding bombs. The man with the fox, whose captive follows him like a dog at the end of a chain, doesn't realize that, out in the open air in a setting which might recall the forest where he was born, the fox is merely a lost soul, filled with despair, a beast blinded by a forgotten light, drunk with smells, ready to rush out, to attack, or to flee—but one which has a collar around his neck . . . Apart from these details, the good little tame fox loves his master, and follows him, skimming the ground with his belly and his beautiful tail the color of lightly toasted bread. He is quick to laugh—a fox is forever laughing. He has beautiful, velvety eyes—like all foxes—and I don't see anything more to say about him.

The other good man, the man with the cock and the hen, would emerge around eleven-thirty from the Auteuil métro. He carried a sack made of dark cloth thrown over his shoulder, rather like the knapsacks of vagrants, and, walking briskly, reached the tranquil woods of Auteuil. The first time I saw him, he had set down his mysterious sack on a bench, and was waiting for my dogs and me to go away. I reassured him, and he delicately shook his sack, from which fell, lustrous, with red crests and plumage the color of autumn, a cock and a hen that pecked and scratched at the cool moss of the forest floor, without losing a second.

I asked no idle questions and the man with the chickens informed me simply: "I bring them out at noon whenever I can. It's only right, isn't it . . . Animals that live in apartments . . ."

I replied by complimenting him on the beauty of the cock and the liveliness of the hen; I added that I also knew the little girl who brings her big tortoise out to "play" in the afternoons, and the man with the fox . . .

"That's no one for me to meet," said the chicken man.

But chance was to bring the master of the fox and the master of the chickens together on one of those paths sought out by those who, in a solitary mood, are led there by fear of the park officials and the whim of a dog, a fox, or a hen. At first, the man with the fox did not come forth. Sitting in the thicket, he held his fox in a fatherly way, around the middle of his serpentine body, and felt sorry for him when he felt him stiffen to attention. The fox's nervous laugh bared his sharp canines, slightly yellow from soft living and soft food, and his white whiskers, pressed flat against his cheeks, had the look of makeup about them.

A few feet away, the cock and the hen, sated with grain, were taking their bath of sand and sun. The cock passed the feathers of his wings over the iron of his beak, and the hen, puffed out in the shape of an egg, feet invisible and neck ruffled, was powdering herself with dust as yellow as pollen. A faint and discordant cry, let out by the cock, roused her. She shook herself off and walked uncertainly over to her spouse as if to ask, "What did you say?"

He must have signaled a warning to her, for she did not argue and stood with him right next to the sack—the sack, a prison but not a trap . . .

However, the chicken man, astonished by this behavior, reassured his animals with "There, chick, chick, chick!" and familiar onomatopoeias.

A few days later, the fox man, who believed he was doing the right thing in giving his wild little animal this tantalizing pleasure, decided to be honest and reveal his presence and that of his fox.

"Oh, they're peculiar animals," said the chicken man.

"And intelligent," added the fox man. "And not an ounce of mischief in him. He wouldn't know what to do with your hen if you gave it to him."

But the little fox trembled, imperceptibly and passionately, under his fur, while the cock and the hen, reassured by the sound of friendly, low voices, pecked and clucked under the fox's velvet eye.

The two animal lovers became friendly, the way people become friendly in the Bois or at a spa. They meet, they chat, they tell their favorite story, they give away two or three secrets, not shared with their closest friends, to the unknown ear—and then they part near the No. 16

tram stop—having given neither the name of the street they live on nor the number of the house . . .

A little fox, even when tamed, cannot be near chickens without suffering serious upset. The fox grew thin, and dreamed aloud in his yelping language all night long. And his master, watching the fox's fine, feverish nose turn away from the saucer of milk, saw coming toward him, from the depths of a green thicket at Auteuil, a wicked thought, indistinct, its moving figure pale but already ugly . . . That day, he chatted good-naturedly with his friend the chicken man and absent-mindedly gave out a little play to the fox's chain. The fox took a step—shall I call this gliding, which neither showed the tips of his feet nor crushed a single blade of grass, a step?—toward the hen.

"Hey there!" cried the chicken man.

"Oh," said the fox man, "he wouldn't touch her."

"I know, I know," said the chicken man.

The fox said nothing. Jerked back, he wisely sat down, and his twinkling eyes betrayed no thought whatsoever.

The next day, the two friends exchanged opinions about fishing.

"If it was cheaper," said the chicken man, "I'd get a license for the upper lake. But it's expensive. It makes carp more expensive than it is at Les Halles."

"But it's worth it," replied the fox man. "You should have seen this one guy's catch the other morning, on the little lake. Twenty-one carp and a bream bigger than my hand."

"You don't say . . ."

"Especially since, without meaning to brag, I'm not so bad at it myself. You should see me cast . . . It's the way I flick my wrist . . . here, like this . . .'"

He stood up, let go of the fox's chain, and reeled his arm master-fully. Something red and frenzied streaked through the grass, in the direction of the yellow hen, but the chicken man's leg shot out sharply, blocking the swift red streak, and all one heard was a muffled little bark. The fox returned to his master's feet and lay down.

"Any closer . . ." said the chicken man.

"You can't imagine how surprised I am," said the fox man. "You little rascal, don't you want to say you're sorry to the man, right now? What is all this now?"

The chicken man looked his friend in the eye and there he read his secret, his dim, unformed, and wicked thought . . . He coughed, sud-denly choked with hot, angry blood, and nearly jumped on the fox man, who at that moment was saying to himself, "I'll knock his brains

out, him and his whole hen house . . ." Then both of them made the
same effort to return to everyday life, lowered their heads, and moved
away from each other, forever, with the common sense of good men who
have just come within a hair's breadth of turning into killers.

[*Translated by Matthew Ward*]

The Judge

❧

When Madame de la Hournerie returned home, after half a day devoted entirely to the hairdresser and the milliner, she quickly tossed aside her new hat to get a good look at her new hairstyle. Urged on by Anthelme, who declared himself to be the "last word" in hairdressing, she had just abandoned her 1910-style chignon, the bouffant waves of beautiful chestnut hair befitting a woman in her fifties, as well as the wave and curls which had covered her forehead and ears. She came home with her hair still brown, but pulled back and pressed down Chinese style, brilliantined, knotted into a varnished shell at the nape of her neck, and pierced through, like a heart, with a little arrow set with diamonds.

Looking into the mirror framed by two harsh lamps, she gave a little start at the sight of the sloping forehead, which she rarely saw and had concealed more carefully than a breast, and at the hard glare of her eyes, skillfully made up, but which the light reached and robbed of their mystery, like the sun on a forest spring after the woodcutter has been through. She picked up a hand mirror and admired the big knot of polished hair and the glinting arrow at the back of her neck.

"What is there to say? It's the style," she said out loud, to reassure herself. "Besides, Emilie de Sery just now swore to me that I was a real revelation . . ."

But faced with this lady with the lacquered skull, the broad and slightly sunken cheeks, thin lips, and thickening nose, she did not recognize herself and felt uneasy. With the art of a painter who enhances the color of a landscape suddenly inundated by unobstructed sunlight, she added some rouge to her bare ears, her temples, and underneath her eyebrows, and then covered her entire face with a shade of pink powder she hardly ever used.

"That's better," she decided. "It's obviously a daring hairstyle! After all, why shouldn't I wear my hair in a daring style?"

She rang, received the ambiguous compliments of her maid: "Everything that changes Madame enhances her!," took off her town clothes, and went downstairs to dine alone. Her elegant widowhood, dating back five years, was undaunted by a few hours' solitude, and Madame de la Hournerie frequently dined or lunched alone, as a form of hygienic and agreeable mortification, just as she would have eaten yogurt or gone to bed at five o'clock in the evening.

Marien, in evening dress, was waiting for her, arms at his side, in front of one of the sideboards. The pride of the *maison La Hournerie,* he stood six feet tall, with strong features, fair hair and fair skin, and the black eyes of a fanatical Breton. When he was thirteen, Madame de la Hournerie and her husband had taken him from the fifty cows he was tending in the fields. Promoted to "little servant" and provided with a sleeved vest and a white apron, Marien quickly earned his stripes. He overcame his fear of the telephone, demonstrated a flair for arranging the flowers in the vases and centerpieces, toned down his peasant voice, and learned to walk as quietly as a cat. Later, when he traded his footman's braided suit for the black tie and tails of the head butler, a sort of instinctive propriety taught him how not to overestimate by too much the cost of fruit, flowers, cleaning materials, and products for the care of all kinds of metals. In return for which Madame de la Hournerie prematurely awarded him the supreme rank of "treasure" usually reserved for servants who had grown white-haired and feeble. But Marien, an athletic statue of silence, could never extinguish the expressive fires of his severe black eyes, mirrors for soubrettes, stars in which this shopgirl or that saleswoman would be held burning . . .

Madame de la Hournerie entered the dining room briskly, sat down, and shivered.

"Serve me quickly, Marien. You wouldn't exactly say it's warm in here, would you? Well then, my dear, didn't I say something to you?" said Madame de la Hournerie familiarly, at times still openly treating Marien like a "little servant."

"But the oven isn't hot enough yet," replied an uncertain voice at last.

Madame de la Hournerie, who was feeling the cold in two recently exposed and sensitive places—her forehead and her ears—looked up at Marien, who seemed to lose his composure, poured a full ladle into the soup bowl, served Madame de la Hournerie, and resumed his traditional place, facing his mistress. The butler's dark eyes, wide with surprise, contemplated, with an indescribable expression of horror and shame, the huge naked forehead, white as marble, and the dome of waxed hair, which matched the red mahogany of the Empire furniture. Unsettled, Madame de la Hournerie pushed her soup away from her.

"Bring the next course, Marien. I'm not very hungry. I wouldn't be surprised if I had a touch of the flu."

Marien removed the soup, ran toward the kitchen as if in flight, and brought out a shrimp soufflé. As he was serving it, he chipped the edge of an old plate, spilled a few drops of red wine on the tablecloth, then returned to the sideboard and resumed his shocked contemplation.

"The flu's going around," continued Madame de la Hournerie uneasily . . . "You be careful in the kitchen . . . Henrietta was complaining of aches this morning. Take this soufflé away, the shrimp are dried up . . . You don't seem to have your mind on your work tonight . . ."

"It *is* flu season," said the same uncertain voice.

But Marien's black eyes, merciless and truthful, cried out between each course to Madame de la Hournerie: "No, it's not the flu! It's this shocking forehead, this pale steppe, this too-small skull, this heavy fruit: an old woman's head stripped of foliage where I was used to seeing it blossom! It's the indignation I feel as an honest thief of a servant, but one attached to the domicile I exploit and care for; it's the stupefaction of a former little valet who served a beautiful mistress, of a little cowherd devoted to a dazzling memory. It's just not done, good God, it's just not done!"

The chocolate trifle, swimming in its thick vanilla cream, was hardly more successful than the lamb chop or the artichoke hearts. Completely exasperated, Madame de la Hournerie wanted to lash out against the importunate and silent disapprobation; a trace of red powder left on the chasing of a fork, a lampshade singed at the edges, gave her the opportunity. But paralyzed by cowardice before she could utter the words of reprimand, she left the table, ordering sharply, "You will send Henrietta up to me," then ran to her bedroom and sat down in front of the triple mirror . . .

"Is that you, Henrietta? Tomorrow morning, as early as possible, you will telephone Anthelme, yes, the hairdresser . . . I want an appointment before lunch, do you hear? Before lunch."

[*Translated by Matthew Ward*]

The Omelette

The singing of a bird insinuated itself, with a grotesque sweetness, into the dream—trains in the night, revolving platforms, and red signal lights—which was bouncing Pierre Lasnier along on poorly tied rails. The pearly song contended with the whistling of locomotives and, victorious, woke the sleeper, lying on his back, in whose half-open eyes was the image, set against a background of dazzling sky, the inadmissible image of a slender branch on which a small bird was singing. Shocked, Pierre Lasnier closed his eyes again and covered them with his right forearm, which felt cold and damp. A bird . . . his cold, damp arm . . . He sat up and recognized his arm, the strong, tanned arm of a tennis player, bare to the elbow, coming out of a rolled-up shirt sleeve. Overhead, the slender branch which the bird had just left was still bobbing up and down . . . Then the delicious odor of half-dried hay caught his attention. Pierre Lasnier had just woken up, not at home in the rue d'Aumale, but up against a hedge in a meadow still marked by the soft parallel waves made at haymaking time. He yawned, stretched his arms out behind him according to the Muller method, peeled his shirt from his back, soaked with the abundant dew of the early June morning, ran his fingers through his hair, and smiled vaguely at the clouds, still pink, in a sky the color of bluish milk. A fiery red shaft pierced through the hedge, across the ground, the first sign of sunrise.

"How beautiful!"

Thoughtfully, he put his hand to his cheek and gave a start at the feel of his five-day-old beard . . . no, four . . . Monday, Tuesday, Wednesday, Thursday, Friday . . . his five-day-old beard. For five days, the body of a woman, knocked down on the rug and looking as if broken in the middle, had been lying there motionless, in his apartment, rue d'Aumale . . .

He stretched out his legs. His tennis shoes, stained with dirt, water marks, and cow dung, had grown old in four days, and one of the rubber soles had split. In just four days the light-gray flannel pants, the white socks and linen shirt, the whole sporting outfit, looked like old castoffs, splattered with stains and streaked a vegetable green. His jacket, rolled up in a ball and tied with a string, doubled as a pillow at night, and held several hundred francs—the money Pierre Lasnier had in his pocket at the time of the crime—and a watch.

Fettered horses jangled their leg chains and whinnied off toward some invisible farm. Swallows darted out from some hidden and inexhaustible place, draping the meadow with a curtain of long, whistling cries. The wind carried the mooing of cattle and another, steady, pleasant noise which must have been a waterfall; in the distance a little herdboy sang like a muezzin and the bright light of daybreak rose a shade toward yellow.

Pierre Lasnier, a city dweller, let himself be taken in by it all, indulging himself in it.

"Ah, the country . . . It's a beautiful life!"

He caught himself mentally and said, "It was a beautiful life . . ." and realized that he was speaking of everything in the past now.

"I could just as well have let the poor thing live, but in Paris you get so nervous . . . And the truth is, she'd been getting on my nerves for too long."

He lowered his head, the memory of his insufferable mistress casting a shadow over him, still deafened as he was by all the threats, all the jealousy, the insults and recriminations, by all the insectlike maliciousness which knew neither fear nor rest. It all came back to him, the gesture which had changed his frantic hands into criminal hands, the body doubled over on the rug; waiting there in the apartment with the shutters closed; escaping at just the right time, when the second-floor maid asked the concierge to open the front door and stole out with a handsome young man, going with him as far as the sidewalk across the street.

"I've been stupid," thought Pierre Lasnier. "I should have gone right to the police and told them, 'There she is. She had such a horrible temper . . . We fought for the thousandth time. I'm not guilty of premeditation, or of . . . of . . . I'm not a bad person. I gave her two thousand francs a month. And the day it happened we'd only come back from the country to look for some tennis rackets in my apartment' . . . That's what I should have done . . . but they've found her by now."

He thought back over his four days as a tramp, and no longer dared congratulate himself for not having run into any rural police, for four days. "What does that prove? Four days—it's nothing. Now what?" He forced himself to imagine some sort of future and could only make out a kind of pale speck, whose pallor made him physically nauseous.

"But I'm starving. That's what's wrong. That's what's getting me down."

He stood up, grabbed the staff he had cut the night before and which completed his vagabond's outfit. Last night's dinner—cold meat and bread, eaten on the road—left him with the wild hunger of a healthy man. He strode across the ditch, and set off down the white road, which cried out for rain and crunched under his feet like broken glass.

"Why did I eat that meat and bread on the road? Who was stopping me from going to an inn and ordering some meat and coffee and eggs?"

He shrugged his shoulders and lengthened his stride. The thought of hot coffee and an omelette sizzling in the pan made his mouth water. Nonetheless, he wisely passed up the isolated farmhouses, bright with chickens, the farmers' wives in white bonnets, and the red fireplaces where the cooking pot hung from the hook of the hearth crane. Around seven o'clock he passed through a large village and stopped at the last house where COEUVRE, RETAILER lodged travelers on foot or horseback and offered to cook "the best food in the world." On seeing him, a young woman, with her hair in a braided bun, set her child down on the ground and wiped her hands. Pierre Lasnier sat down.

"I suppose you want a bottle of wine. White or red?"

Pierre Lasnier pounded the table, as he had seen the peasants in the movies do.

"White! Do you have any bacon?"

"Bacon? Yes."

"And eggs?"

"I haven't been out to gather them yet," she said, annoyed. "And at the price . . ."

"Don't worry about it, I've got money. Enough to treat myself to a nice big omelette!"

The young woman brought a bottle of wine, a dull little glass with thick sides, and inspected Pierre Lasnier uncertainly. He was dirty, but refined, and his overall appearance lacked the aggressive mystery, the unbreachable indifference which marks the true vagabond.

"An omelette? How many eggs?"

Pierre Lasnier joked mockingly: "How many eggs . . . How should I know? An omelette of six, eight . . . Yes! A nice big omelette of six to eight eggs!"

The young woman opened her mouth and eyes wide in singular fashion, didn't say a word, took her child back up in her arms, and left the room. To kill time Pierre Lasnier filled and emptied his crude little glass three times, took a pack of cigarettes from his pocket, and struck a match. But for no apparent reason he let the flaming match fall, then turned around and saw standing in the doorway, behind the blue shoulders of two policemen, the suspicious face, white with fear, of the young woman with braided hair.

[*Translated by Matthew Ward*]

The Other Wife

"Table for two? This way, Monsieur, Madame, there is still a table next to the window, if Madame and Monsieur would like a view of the bay."

Alice followed the maître d'.

"Oh, yes. Come on, Marc, it'll be like having lunch on a boat on the water ..."

Her husband caught her by passing his arm under hers. "We'll be more comfortable over there."

"There? In the middle of all those people? I'd much rather ..."

"Alice, please."

He tightened his grip in such a meaningful way that she turned around. "What's the matter?"

"Shh ..." he said softly, looking at her intently, and led her toward the table in the middle.

"What is it, Marc?"

"I'll tell you, darling. Let me order lunch first. Would you like the shrimp? Or the eggs in aspic?"

"Whatever you like, you know that."

They smiled at one another, wasting the precious time of an overworked maître d', stricken with a kind of nervous dance, who was standing next to them, perspiring.

"The shrimp," said Marc. "Then the eggs and bacon. And the cold chicken with a romaine salad. *Fromage blanc?* The house specialty? We'll go with the specialty. Two strong coffees. My chauffeur will be having lunch also, we'll be leaving again at two o'clock. Some cider? No, I don't trust it ... Dry champagne."

He sighed as if he had just moved an armoire, gazed at the colorless midday sea, at the pearly white sky, then at his wife, whom he found lovely in her little Mercury hat with its large, hanging veil.

"You're looking well, darling. And all this blue water makes your eyes look green, imagine that! And you've put on weight since you've been traveling . . . It's nice up to a point, but only up to a point!"

Her firm, round breasts rose proudly as she leaned over the table.

"Why did you keep me from taking that place next to the window?"

Marc Seguy never considered lying. "Because you were about to sit next to someone I know."

"Someone I don't know?"

"My ex-wife."

She couldn't think of anything to say and opened her blue eyes wider.

"So what, darling? It'll happen again. It's not important."

The words came back to Alice and she asked, in order, the inevitable questions. "Did she see you? Could she see that you saw her? Will you point her out to me?"

"Don't look now, please, she must be watching us . . . The lady with brown hair, no hat, she must be staying in this hotel. By herself, behind those children in red . . ."

"Yes. I see."

Hidden behind some broad-brimmed beach hats, Alice was able to look at the woman who, fifteen months ago, had still been her husband's wife.

"Incompatibility," Marc said. "Oh, I mean . . . total incompatibility! We divorced like well-bred people, almost like friends, quietly, quickly. And then I fell in love with you, and you really wanted to be happy with me. How lucky we are that our happiness doesn't involve any guilty parties or victims!"

The woman in white, whose smooth, lustrous hair reflected the light from the sea in azure patches, was smoking a cigarette with her eyes half closed. Alice turned back toward her husband, took some shrimp and butter, and ate calmly. After a moment's silence she asked: "Why didn't you ever tell me that she had blue eyes, too?"

"Well, I never thought about it!"

He kissed the hand she was extending toward the bread basket and she blushed with pleasure. Dusky and ample, she might have seemed somewhat coarse, but the changeable blue of her eyes and her wavy, golden hair made her look like a frail and sentimental blonde. She vowed overwhelming gratitude to her husband. Immodest without knowing it, everything about her bore the overly conspicuous marks of extreme happiness.

They ate and drank heartily, and each thought the other had forgotten the woman in white. Now and then, however, Alice laughed too loudly, and Marc was careful about his posture, holding his shoulders back, his head up. They waited quite a long time for their coffee, in silence. An incandescent river, the straggled reflection of the invisible sun overhead, shifted slowly across the sea and shone with a blinding brilliance.

"She's still there, you know," Alice whispered.

"Is she making you uncomfortable? Would you like to have coffee somewhere else?"

"No, not at all! She's the one who must be uncomfortable! Besides, she doesn't exactly seem to be having a wild time, if you could see her . . ."

"I don't have to. I know that look of hers."

"Oh, was she like that?"

He exhaled his cigarette smoke through his nostrils and knitted his eyebrows. "Like that? No. To tell you honestly, she wasn't happy with me."

"Oh, really now!"

"The way you indulge me is so charming, darling . . . It's crazy . . . You're an angel . . . You love me . . . I'm so proud when I see those eyes of yours. Yes, those eyes . . . She . . . I just didn't know how to make her happy, that's all. I didn't know how."

"She's just difficult!"

Alice fanned herself irritably, and cast brief glances at the woman in white, who was smoking, her head resting against the back of the cane chair, her eyes closed with an air of satisfied lassitude.

Marc shrugged his shoulders modestly.

"That's the right word," he admitted. "What can you do? You have to feel sorry for people who are never satisfied. But we're satisfied . . . Aren't we, darling?"

She did not answer. She was looking furtively, and closely, at her husband's face, ruddy and regular; at his thick hair, threaded here and there with white silk; at his short, well-cared-for hands; and doubtful for the first time, she asked herself, "What more did she want from him?"

And as they were leaving, while Marc was paying the bill and asking for the chauffeur and about the route, she kept looking, with envy and curiosity, at the woman in white, this dissatisfied, this difficult, this superior . . .

[*Translated by Matthew Ward*]

Monsieur Maurice

❧⚜❧

Maurice Houssiaux beamed with a childlike contentment and a schoolboyish, bureaucratic exhilaration, which he had not felt a week earlier. It was then that the council president, calling on his experience in worldly matters and his regional influence as deputy county commissioner, had appointed him Minister of Tourism and Farm Mechanization. And he was thrilled by the large office at the ministry, its historic desk, and its Aubusson carpet. A small garden, green and flowerless, filled the tall French windows up to the arches; the window reflected the hollow back of a bewigged marble bust, and Maurice Houssiaux's private secretary added just the right touch of new deference to his friendly informality.

Houssiaux had just put his paraph to his first piece of correspondence in a bold hand.

"Is that all, Wattier?"

"All for today, Monsieur. You're free."

"Can I give you a lift?"

"No, thank you. I'm preparing your work for tomorrow. And there's that blasted grain circular . . . and your speech to the Hotel Industry, have you given it any thought?"

"Yes, but . . ."

"So have I. Your first speech must be a success . . . Don't you do a thing, though, I have my whole night for it. It's very important that you don't wear yourself out the first month. Oh! And those two women from the country are still here. They've been waiting for two hours . . ."

"Which women?"

"The stenotypists. Would you like me to just weed one out somehow? There's only one opening."

"Do you have their names?"

"Here they are. Mademoiselle Valentin and Mademoiselle Lajarisse. Both are from Cransac."

"Lajarisse, Lajarisse . . . there are three hundred people named Lajarisse in my district, sixty in the village alone. Which Lajarisse?"

"Shall I send for them? Shall I have them come in?"

Wattier danced with zeal, from one foot to the other, with the agility of a hairdresser or an acrobat, something he had suddenly acquired at the same time as his situation with Houssiaux. Houssiaux repeated the name with the distinctly southern ending, as he looked fondly at his green and melancholy garden. His once fair cheeks were covered with red blotches, and a little round belly, cinched up by a belt, moved ahead of him like a cushion for relics.

"I'll see them," he decided. "After all, they're from Cransac, the heart of my constituency. Has everyone else gone?"

"Everyone's gone. It's always the boss who stays late."

"I'll see them on my way out. They'll be telling me stories about Cransac for half an hour—first one, then the other—won't they? But I don't want anyone to go away upset."

Wattier slipped off with a cruel little laugh, and Houssiaux, in his overcoat, hat in hand, walked into an adjoining office whose ministerial indigence—faded plaster walls and yellow pine desks—no longer saddened him.

"Mademoiselle . . . You're from Cransac? Sit down, please."

"Oh, Monsieur . . ."

The tall girl stammered in confusion, but looked at him with the boldness of a slave who knows her price. A striking brunette indeed, her hair an amber brown, with a small, imperious nose, audacious underneath her feigned shyness.

"Ah, these girls from Cransac, what beauties!" Maurice Houssiaux said to himself as he asked Mademoiselle Valentin a few perfunctory questions.

"Yes, Monsieur . . . Oh, of course, Monsieur . . . I started out as a bookkeeper at Vanavan's, in the rue Grande, on the corner; does Monsieur know it? But I'm a good typist, on all models, and my steno is very good . . . My father's the one who put the banner across the rue Grande when we heard the news of your election two years ago. Does the Minister remember?"

She spoke about him in the third person, like a chambermaid, but with her eyes lowered like a smitten girl.

"She's trying her luck," Houssiaux said to himself. "She's right. She can have anything she wants. And she wouldn't be surprised to get it. She's from Cransac. What a jewel for the office, and that head on my shoulder!"

"One of my secretaries will notify you, Mademoiselle." She raised her eyes, which were big and tapered at the corner like a blood mare's.

"Can the Minister leave me with a little hope?"

"I think so!"

He offered her his hand, shook the cold hand of an excited damsel, and watched her with pleasure as she bumped into a chair and fumbled with the door as she was leaving. He was returning to his office when a long mirror confronted him with his own image, alas, that of a tall, fat, graying man. It distressed him more than usual.

"You can't have everything. There's a certain age when . . . but there's still Mademoiselle Lajarisse . . . What if I had Wattier send her away?"

But a short shadow already barred the door, and Mademoiselle Lajarisse, a woman in her fifties, a bit wrinkled, a bit slumped, wearing cotton gloves and a hat the color of cassis, stood before him, silently.

"You're from Cransac, Mademoiselle? That's quite a good recommendation. I'm so fond of Cransac and its people!"

"I moved to Paris seventeen years ago. Cashier, stenographer, typist, librarian . . ."

"Good, good. We'll look into that, we'll look into that . . . No, no papers. You can leave them with one of my secretaries, if there's any need. Lajarisse? Which Lajarisses? By the bridge?"

"No, on the hill, on the road to Casteix."

"Oh, I see, I see . . ."

He smiled, half closing his eyes. The hill on the road to Casteix . . . He used to go down to Cransac on that road, on horseback, greeted by everyone considered doubtful and seductive by that part of Cransac that wore skirts: factory girls, idle women leaning over wrought-iron balconies . . .

"I see . . . It's far . . ."

"Not that far, Monsieur Minister . . ."

Mademoiselle Lajarisse, faded under her nearly white hair, looked at him from head to toe.

"It was your favorite route, Monsieur. Everyone there remembers."

"So do I . . ."

. . . Handsome boy, never tired, hunter, runner, delighting in everything that flattered him, the tears and laughter of the women, spirited horses, fiery red wines . . . Houssiaux could hear the flint stones of the steep slope roll beneath the hooves of his saddle horse . . . He shook his head, half sincere.

"Oh, Mademoiselle Lajarisse, if only I could go back to the time when I used to come down that road on my horse . . ."

"Your horse Gamin, Monsieur Minister."

He made the joyous gesture of a young man.

"Yes!"

"And on summer days, you'd arrive without a jacket or vest, in a loose-fitting shirt, your sleeves rolled up . . ."

"Why, yes!"

"You would rein in your horse with one hand and wave to all the ladies with your hat . . . and even to the women who weren't ladies . . . to that Carmen up on her balcony, and that little woman at the tobacconist's, all of them."

Houssiaux took the cotton-gloved hand in his. "Why, yes! You remember all that?"

"Oh, Monsieur Maurice . . ."

The little lady did not turn her face away, or hide her tears, or her blue eyes, in which the unforgettable image of "Monsieur Maurice" on horseback still remained . . . Houssiaux sighed with regret and let go of the hands of Mademoiselle Lajarisse, who drew away from him slightly.

"So, Monsieur, you say that all the positions are filled?"

He ran his fingers through his gray hair, as he once did through his blond hair.

"Not yours, Mademoiselle Lajarisse. Do you have a minute? Here, take this steno pad. The pencils are right there . . . Ready? 'My dear friend and colleague, you have been so kind as to bring to my attention the facts which . . .' "

[*Translated by Matthew Ward*]

The Burglar

Getting into the little villa had been so easy that the burglar wondered why, held back by some excess of caution, he had waited so long. Once inside the entrance hall, he recognized the dreary dampness which permeates seaside villas during rainy summers. He found the drawing-room door open onto the front room, as was the dining room's, and the door to the cellar gaped beneath the staircase, testifying to the hasty flight, to a dance hall or some hollow in the dunes, of the little red-haired maid whose departure he had just witnessed. Only one servant, and she a mere slip of a thing: all that was required by Madame Cassart and her tiny villa of pink plaster and green mosaic, set in a sandy enclosure where the scrawy tamarisks all bowed at the same time and in the same direction, to the wind from the sea, like tall grass swaying in the current.

The burglar carefully closed off the open rooms; he didn't like banging doors and was counting on a quick visit to this ugly plaything, which Madame Cassart rented for the season. A quick glance into the drawing room—done in white lacquer and cotton print—the tenant wouldn't dare hide her savings in there.

The man walked about easily in the dark, helped by the faint light, a twilight gray, which forced its way through the lowered Venetian blinds. Only once did he risk the electric beam from his flashlight, which fell on the photograph of a very beautiful woman, wearing a long corset, her hair done up in a "figure eight," and evening gloves.

"Cassart in her better days. Some change."

For the past two weeks in this little fishing port with big ambitions and an overnight casino made of fibro-cement, he had been leading the austere life of an entomologist, studying the customs and habits of the bathers, especially the female bathers, noting their time of ar-

rival, their daily stations at the lotto tables and the dance hall. All
he had gained, since his arrival, was a gold purse, an ordinary ring left
on a washbasin, and a drawstring pouch with a hundred francs in it:
meager recompense for this scrupulous existence, which aspired to a
crystalline perfection. Properly attired, he frequented the casino, trying
to be as inconspicuous as possible, and made no acquaintances, for,
though confident in his appearance as a strikingly handsome man in his
forties with short hair, he knew the weaknesses of his syntax and the
colorful brevity of his vocabulary.

"Just enough," he thought, "to impress the girls in the candy store
—and old lady Cassart . . ."

He had been watching the woman whom he, like everyone else,
called the "old crazy lady," the tall septuagenarian whose figure was
still that of a young, if old-fashioned woman, straight-backed in her
stiff corset, with shoulders like a Prussian officer. Her organdy hats, her
dresses of *broderie anglaise*, and her long pink or orchid-colored veils
flapped on the jetty like flags, and the schoolboys behind her hurried
to see her face, a death's head in makeup, covered with balls of paraffin
sunk beneath the skin of her cheeks, above a neck tightly tucked into
boned tulle.

He had noticed her at the famous confectioner's, all a-jingle with
jewels, pink as a piece of cracked wax fruit; he had waited while she
greedily carried off a sack of chocolate "turtles." When she had gone,
scandalous and serene, he bought some almond cookies.

"Send them to the Hotel Beauséjour? For Monsieur . . ."

"Monsieur Paul Dagueret."

"D apostrophe?"

He gave the blond salesgirl a casual smile. "However you like,
Mademoiselle. It's of no importance to me."

Struck by this aristocratic insouciance, the girl allowed herself a
few remarks about Madame Cassart, deploring the fact that "diamonds
like those . . ."

"I hadn't noticed," interrupted Monsieur Dagueret coldly. "I'm
not an expert."

Now, in "old lady Cassart's" bedroom, he was searching not for the
diamonds which she hardly ever took off, but for the compensation due
his persevering and solitary work.

"Even if it's only a gold chain, or those big round bracelets she
threads her skinny arms through," he murmured as he quietly rum-
maged through the plain, bright room in which Madame Cassart had
shown her personal taste by pinning up bows made of ribbon and
flowers made of colored bread crumbs everywhere . . .

Rifling through a drawer with the butt of his flashlight, he passed up an aquamarine cross and took a gold locket worth at least fifty francs. At that precise moment, he heard the garden gate squeak musically, then a key in the lock. Heavy footsteps could already be heard mounting the stairs as he decided to seek refuge behind the unfastened curtains of the French windows.

Once behind them he immediately felt awkward and thwarted. This crazy old woman never came home from the casino before midnight, other days. Through the crack between the curtains he saw her walk back and forth and heard her mutter indistinctly. She no longer bothered to throw back her military shoulders, and walked hunched over, senilely mawing the air. She carefully took off her girlish hat, then took some pins out of her hair. The prisoner saw a pale little tonsure surrounded by an abundance of hair, still thick and dyed bright red. The low-cut dress fell to the floor, a beribboned negligee hid the grainy skin, with its red blotches caused by the salty air, and the dreadful dewlaps under the chin. Beneath the loose hair, the sour face, made up as though for some drama, added to Monsieur Paul Dagueret's uneasiness.

"What now?" he asked himself. "Obviously I have to do what I have to do, but . . . An old nag like that's no pushover! Damn!"

He didn't like either noise or blood, and with each second his discomfort increased. Madame Cassart spared him further agony. She turned her head sharply toward the curtains as if, all of a sudden, she had smelled him, opened them, letting out a cry hardly louder than a sigh and drew back three steps, hiding her face in her hands. He was just about to take advantage of this unexpected gesture to rush out and escape when she said to him, without uncovering her face, in an affectedly suppliant voice: "Why have you done this? Oh, why?"

He was standing between the parted curtains, bareheaded—a hat or a cap always gets lost—wearing gloves, his hair mussed.

She went on, in that high, crystalline voice certain old people have. "You should never have done this!"

She lowered her hands and it stunned him to see that she was looking at him without the slightest bit of fear, in a loving, vanquished way.

"Here we go. This is it," he thought.

"Was this violence necessary?" sighed Madame Cassart. "The most ordinary introduction, in the casino or on the jetty, would have been sufficient, wouldn't it? Could you believe that I hadn't noticed, hadn't guessed? It would have been very easy for you . . . But not like this, oh, not like this!"

She straightened her back, gathered her hair back up on the top of her head, and draped herself with a robe and the dignity of an old clown.

Astounded, the man stood there speechless, and then after a silence he said mechanically, "If anyone had ever . . ."

She interrupted him, quivering with emotion: "No, no, don't say anything, you will never know how deeply distressed I am . . . I am . . . My reputation is spotless . . . I've never been married . . . People address me as Madame, but . . . your being here . . . Oh, can't you see how upset . . . You will get nothing from me in this way, I assure you!"

Every gesture, every sigh, sparked the aggressive fires of her diamonds, but the burglar paid no attention to them, preoccupied as he was with the vexation of a sane and, moreover, modest man. He was ready to explode, to tell—and in what terms!—the impassioned old bag what she could do. He took a step forward and saw, there in front of him, his own image, reflected in a mirror, the flattering image of a handsome young man, dressed in black, and distinguished, yes . . .

"Tell me that I'll see you again, but it must be somewhere outside my home at first," the madwoman simpered. "Give me your word as a gentleman."

. . . Distinguished, yes, as long as he kept quiet. A kind of snobbery rid him of the desire to insult and brutalize, a snobbery which respected both the old woman's extravagant error and this moment in his own life which imitated that of a noble and romantic hero . . . He bowed as best he could and said in a deep voice, "Madame, I give you my word."

And left, red-faced and empty-handed.

[Translated by Matthew Ward]

The Advice

❦

Old Monsieur Mestre again poured one can of water on the bleeding hearts, one on the newly planted heliotropes, and two on the blue hydrangeas, which were always dying of thirst. He tied up the nasturtiums, eager to climb, and with the shears he clipped the last withered thyrsus of the lilacs with a little cry, "Ha!" and wiped the dirt from his hands. His little garden in Auteuil, densely planted, well watered, and neatly arranged like a too-small parlor, was overflowing with flowers and defying the dryness of June. Up until November, it astonished the eyes—those of the passers-by at least—for Monsieur Mestre, stooped over his walled-in rectangle of earth for hours, tended it from morning to night, with the doggedness of a truck farmer. He planted, grafted, and pruned; he hunted down slugs, small suspicious-looking spiders, the green flies, and the blight bug. When night came, he would clap his hands together, exclaim "Ha!" and instead of dreaming over the phlox, haunted by gray sphinx moths beneath the white wisteria entwined with purple wisteria, and spurning the fiery geraniums, he would turn away from his charming handiwork and go off for a smoke in his kitchen, or stroll along the boulevards of Auteuil.

The lovely May evening had prolonged his day as amateur gardener by an hour after dinner. The sky, the pale gravel path, the white flowers, and the white façades held a light which did not want to end, and mothers, standing in the doorways of the little open houses, called in vain to their children, who preferred the dusty warm sidewalk to their cool beds.

"Sweetheart," Monsieur Mestre called out, "I'm going out for a bit."

Their house, long owned by the modest old couple, still showed, beneath the Virginia creeper, its faded brick. Around it, rich villas had sprung up—Norman chalets, Louis XVI "follies," modern cubes painted China red or Egypt blue.

Old Monsieur Mestre knew every detail of the façades, every rare tree in the gardens. But his curiosity stopped there; he envied neither the towers nor the thick crystal of the bay windows, wide as the fish ponds. Covetous of his ignorance, he liked conjectures; he had named this thatched cottage, blinded by its long bignonia wig, "Guilty Love"; that turret the color of dried blood, "Japanese Torture." A proper white construction, with yellow silk curtains, was called "the Happy Family," and Monsieur Mestre, beaming with a sense of sweet irony in front of a kind of pink-and-blue confection made of cement, marble, and exotic wood, had christened it "First Adventure."

As a "native" of the sixteenth arrondissement, he cherished the strange provincial avenues, where a trusty old tree shelters new dwellings which a storm could wash away. He walked along, stopped, patted a little girl on the head, and clicked his tongue disapprovingly at a crying child. At night, his silver hair and beard reassured the women walking home alone and they slowed their pace in order to place themselves under the protection of "this nice old gentleman."

The pink and gold sky lingered late into the starless May night. But closer to the earth, the lights in the lamps came on, and the dauntless nightingales sang overhead, above the green benches and the stone kiosks. Monsieur Mestre greeted a little two-story house, laid out comfortably in its garden, with a friendly glance. He called it the "Brooding Hen." A light shone in a single window hung with pink curtains. At the same moment a young man, bareheaded in the fashion of the day, came out of the house, furiously slammed the door behind him, then the gate, and stood there motionless in the street, mulish, head down, eyes fixed on the lighted window in a black, dramatic stare. Monsieur Mestre smiled and gave his shoulders a little shrug.

"Another drama! And you can see right away what it's all about! We're eighteen, nineteen years old. We want to take a bite out of life with the teeth of a tiger. We want to be the master. We've had a scene with Mama and Papa, and we've run out, after some ugly words we already regret . . . And what we really want is to go back in. But our pride won't let us. Ah, youth!"

Carried along, he said in a low, fatherly voice, "Ah, youth!"

The young man spun around on his heels and looked none too kindly at the silver-haired old man, who looked at him from above, with the benevolent majesty of a fortune-teller, as he held out his arm toward the house.

"Young man, this isn't where you should be. That is."

The young man started and backed away a step.

"Oh . . . no . . ." he said dully.

"Oh, yes . . ." said Monsieur Mestre. "Will you deny the impulse you just had to go back in?"

The big dark eyes in the still-beardless face opened in disbelief. "How . . . how do you know?"

Monsieur Mestre placed a prophetic hand on the young man's shoulder. "I know quite a few things. I know . . . that you were wrong to resist the impulse that was urging you to go back in."

"Monsieur . . ." begged the pale young man, "Monsieur, I don't want, I don't ever want . . ."

"Yes, yes," scoffed the indulgent old man. "Rebellion, the flight to freedom . . ."

"Yes . . . oh, yes," sighed the adolescent. "You know everything . . . rebellion . . . escape . . . shouldn't I . . . can't I . . ."

Monsieur Mestre's hand rested on his shoulder. "Escape . . . freedom . . . It's all words! As unhappy as you are, when you get a hundred feet from here, won't you be seized again by that same force that made you stop in front of me, by the same voice crying out to you, 'Go back! I'm the truth, I'm happiness, I am where the secret to this freedom you're searching for lies, security . . .'"

The young man interrupted Monsieur Mestre's flowery speech with a look of unspeakable hope, smiled wildly, and ran back into the house.

"Bravo," exclaimed Monsieur Mestre in a low voice, congratulating himself.

After the door slammed shut, he heard the cry of a young voice, brief, as if muffled under a kiss. He nodded his head in thanks and was walking away, happy, discreet, when the door opened again and the young man, gasping, threw himself into his arms. He had a drunken look on his face, a pallor made green by the late light of day, which seemed wonderful to Monsieur Mestre; his eyes, brimming with tears, wandered from the rose sunset to Monsieur Mestre, to the cedar tree glistening with nightingales.

"Thanks to you . . . thanks to you," he stammered.

"I don't deserve it, young man."

"If . . . if . . ." the boy interrupted, grasping him by the hands. "It's done. Thanks to you. For days and days I didn't dare. I endured everything. I cared so much for her. I knew she was lying to me, and that all those nights . . . But I didn't dare. And then by some miracle I ran into you! You set me back on the track, you made me understand that running away wouldn't do me any good, that I would be carrying my torture with me . . . You told me that deliverance, peace . . . oh, at last, peace . . . depended on doing something . . . Thank you, thank you . . . I did it. Thank you."

He let go of Monsieur Mestre's hands, started to run as though on winged, silent feet, his black hair pushed back away from his pale face. Then Monsieur Mestre felt his heart sink; he took out his handkerchief to wipe his forehead and his hands, which the feverish grip had left feeling hot and moist, and saw on his handkerchief the red marks left by his fingers.

[*Translated by Matthew Ward*]

The Murderer

❧❦❧

After he had killed her, with a blow from the little lead weight
under which she kept her wrapping paper, Louis found himself at a
loss. She lay behind the counter, one leg bent back under her, her head
turned away, and her body turned toward him, in a ridiculous pose
which put the young man in a bad mood. He shrugged his shoulders
and almost said to her, "Get up now, you look ridiculous!" But at that
moment the bell on the shop door rang, and Louis saw a little girl
come in.

"A card of black mending wool, please."

"We don't have any more," he said politely. "We won't have any
until tomorrow."

She left, closing the door carefully, and he realized that he hadn't
even thought that she could have walked up to the counter, leaned
over, and seen . . .

Night was falling, darkening the little stationery-notions shop. One
could still make out the rows of white boxes with an ivory-nut button
or a knot of passementerie on the side. Louis struck a match mechanically on the sole of his shoe in order to light the gas jet, then caught
himself and put the match out under his foot. Across the street, the
wine merchant lit up his whole ground floor all at once, and in contrast
the little stationery-notions shop grew darker in a night streaked with
yellow light.

Once again Louis leaned over the counter. To his overwhelming
astonishment he saw his mistress still lying there, her leg bent back, her
neck turned to the side. And something black besides, a thread, as thin
as a wisp of hair, was trickling down her pale cheek. He grabbed the
forty-five francs in change and dirty bills that he had so furiously re-

fused earlier, went out, took off the door's lever handle, put it in his pocket, and walked away.

For two days he lived the way a child lives, amusing himself by watching the boats on the Seine and the schoolchildren in the squares. He amused himself like a child, and like a child, he grew bored with himself. He waited and could not decide whether to leave the city or to go back to street peddling like before. His room, paid for by the week, still harbored a stash of Paris monuments on stacks of postcards, mechanical jumping rabbits, and a product you squeezed from a tube to make your own fruit drinks. But Louis sold nothing for two days, while staying in another furnished room. He didn't feel afraid, and he slept well; the days flowed by smoothly, disturbed only by that pleasing impatience one feels in big port cities after booking passage on an ocean liner.

Two days after the crime he bought a newspaper, as on other days, and read: WOMAN SHOPKEEPER MURDERED IN THE RUE X. "Aha!" he said out loud like an expert, then read the article slowly and attentively, noted that the crime, because of the victim's "very retired" existence, was already being considered "mysterious," and folded the paper back up. In front of him his coffee was getting cold. The waiter behind the bar was whistling as he polished the zinc, and an old couple next to him were dipping croissants in hot milk. Louis sat there for several moments, dumbstruck, with his mouth half open, and wondered why all these familiar things had suddenly ceased to be close and intelligible to him. He had the impression that, if questioned, the old couple would answer in a strange language, and that, as he whistled, the waiter was looking right through Louis's body as if it weren't even there.

He got up, threw down some money, and headed off toward a train station, where he bought a ticket for a suburb whose name reminded him of the races and afternoons spent boating. During the ride it seemed to him that the train was making very little noise and that the other passengers were speaking in subdued voices.

"Maybe I'm going deaf!"

After getting off the train, Louis bought an evening paper, and reread the same account as in the morning paper, and yawned.

"Damn, they're not getting anywhere!"

He ate in a little restaurant near the station and inquired of the owner as to the possibility of finding a job in the area. But he accomplished this formality with great repugnance, and felt ill at ease when the man advised him to see a dentist in a neighboring villa who regrettably had just lost a young man, employed until the day before to care for his motorcycle and to sterilize his surgical instruments. Despite the late hour, he rang the dentist's doorbell, claimed he was a maker of mechanical toys, didn't argue about the pay—two hundred and fifty francs—and slept that same night in a small attic room, hung with that blue-and-gray-flowered wallpaper usually used for lining cheap trunks.

For a week he kept the job as laboratory assistant to the American dentist, a great horse of a man, big-boned and red-haired, who asked no questions and smoked with his feet up on the table, as he waited for his rare clients. Clad in a white linen lab coat and leaning against the open gate, Louis breathed the fresh air, and the maids from the villas would smile at his gentle, swarthy face.

He bought a paper every day. Banished from the front page, the "crime in rue . . ." now languished on page 2, amid colliding trains and swindling somnambulists. Five lines, two lines confirmed dispassionately that it remained "a complete mystery."

One spring afternoon, made fragrant by a brief shower and pierced with the cries of swallows, Louis asked the American dentist for a little money, "to buy himself some underwear," took off his white lab coat, and left for Paris. And since he was nothing but a simple little murderer, he went straight back to the stationery-notions shop. There were children playing in front of the lowered iron shutter and a week's worth of splashing had left the door caked with mud. Louis walked the hundred steps back and forth on the sidewalk across the street for a long time and did not leave the street till after nightfall.

The next day he went back again, a little later so as not to attract attention, and the following evenings he faithfully kept watch, after dinner, sometimes without dinner. He felt himself filled with a strange hope resembling the anguish of love. One evening, when he had halted to tilt his head back toward the stars and let out a deep sigh, a hand was placed gently on his shoulder. He closed his eyes and, without turning around, fell limply, blissfully into the arms of the policeman who was following him.

During the course of the interrogation, Louis confessed that, yes, he did regret his crime, but that a moment like the one when he felt the liberating hand on his shoulder was "worth it all" and that he could only compare it to the moment when he had, as he said, "known love."

[*Translated by Matthew Ward*]

The Portrait

Both women opened the windows of their adjoining rooms at the
same time, rattling the blinds, half closed against the sun, and smiled
at one another as they leaned over the wooden balcony.

"What weather!"

"And the sea doesn't have a wrinkle!"

"Just one lucky streak. Did you see how much the wisteria's grown
since last year?"

"And the honeysuckle! It's got its shoots caught in the blinds now."

"Are you going to rest, Lily?"

"I'm getting me a sweater and going down! I can't sit still the first
day . . . What are you going to do, Alice?"

"Arrange things in my linen closet. It still has the scent of last
year's lavender. Go on, I'll amuse myself like a madwoman. You go
about your little affairs!"

Lily's short, bleached hair bounced goodbye like a puppet's, and a
moment later Alice saw her, apple-green, going down into the sandy
garden, poorly protected against the wind from the sea.

Alice laughed good-naturedly. "She's so plump!"

She looked down contentedly at her long white hands and crossed
her thin forearms on the wooden rail, breathing in the salt and iodine
that enriched the air. The breeze did not disturb a single strand of her
hair, done in the "Spanish style," smoothed back, forehead and ears
uncovered, quite flattering to her fine, straight nose, but quite hard on
everything else that was showing the decline in her: horizontal wrinkles
above her eyebrows, hollow cheeks, the dark circles of an insomniac
around her eyes. Her friend Lily blamed the severe hairstyle. "What
can I say? I think that when fruit gets a little dry it needs some
greenery!"

To which Alice replied, "Not everybody forty-five can wear her hair like a girl in the Folies!"

They lived in perfect harmony, and this daily teasing was fuel for the fire of their friendship. Elegant and bony, Alice would voluntarily point out, "You might say my weight hasn't changed since the year my husband died. I've kept a blouse I had when I was a girl, out of curiosity: you'd think it was made for me yesterday!"

Lily did not mention any marriage, and for good reason. Her forties, after a dizzy youth, had endowed her with an irreducible plumpness.

"I'm plump, it's true," she would declare. "But you look at my face: not one wrinkle! And the same goes for the rest! Now, you must admit that's something."

And she would cast a malicious glance at Alice's hollow cheeks, at the scarf or fox meant to hide the tendons in her neck, or her collarbones forming the cross bar of the letter T . . .

But it was love, more than rivalry, that bound the two friends together: the same handsome man, famous long before he grew old, had rejected them both. For Alice, a few letters from the great man were evidence that for a few weeks he had found her jealous eyes, her irresistible elegance as a skinny, cleverly veiled brunette to his liking. All that Lily had from him was a telegram, one telegram, strangely terse and urgent. Shortly afterward he forgot both of them and the "What? You knew him too?" of the two friends was followed by nearly sincere confessions which they made tirelessly again and again.

"I never understood his sudden silence," admitted Alice. "But there was a moment in our life when I could have been, I'm sure of it, the friend, the spiritual guide to that fickle man, whom no one has been able to hold on to . . ."

"Well, my dear, I won't argue with you there," countered Lily. "The friend, the guide . . . I've never understood those big words. What I do know is that between him and me . . . Oh, heavens! What fire! We weren't thinking about pathos, take my word for it! I felt, right here, as clearly as I'm talking to you, that I could have ruled that man through the flesh. And then it fell apart . . . It always falls apart."

Content, in short, with their equal disappointments, having reached the age when women begin adorning little chapels, they had hung, in the drawing room of Lily's villa where they lived together, sharing expenses for two months, a portrait of the ingrate, the best portrait, the one used by all the daily papers and the illustrated magazines. A photographic enlargement, touched up, enhanced with only highlights like an impassioned etching, softened with some pink on the mouth, some blue on the eyes, like a watercolor . . .

"It's not what you'd call a work of art," Alice would say, "but when you knew him as I did—as we did, Lily, it's alive!"

For two years now they had happily resigned themselves to a kind of devout solitude, entertaining friends, inoffensive women and older well-bred men. Growing old? Well, heavens, yes, growing old, you have to get used to the idea . . . Growing old, under the eyes of that youthful portrait, in the glimmer of a beautiful memory . . . Growing old in good health, in the course of short, restful little trips, in the course of well-prepared little meals.

"Now, isn't this better than hanging around dance halls, masseuses, and gambling parlors?" Lily would say.

Alice would nod in agreement and add: "Everything is so pale, next to a memory like that . . ."

When she finished straightening the closet, Alice changed her dress, buckled a white leather belt around her waist, and smiled. "The same hole as last year! It really is amusing!"

But she scolded herself for not having greeted, downstairs in the drawing room, "their" portrait . . .

"Alice! Alice! Are you coming down?" called Lily's voice from below. Alice leaned out over the balcony.

"In a minute! What is it?"

"Come down . . . Something strange . . . Come on!"

Vaguely excited, always ready for some romantic encounter, she ran downstairs and found Lily standing in front of "their" portrait, taken down from its hook and set on an armchair in the light. The exceptionally humid weather, some combination of salt and paint, had, in ten months in the darkness of the closed villa, worked an intelligent disaster, an act of destruction in which chance had armed itself with an almost miraculous malevolence. Mold growing on the great man's Roman chin had drawn the whitish beard of an unkempt old man, the paper had blistered, puffing the cheeks up into two lymphatic pouches. A few grains of black charcoal, slipping down from the hair across the entire portrait, loaded the conqueror's face with wrinkles and years . . . Alice put her white hands over her eyes.

"It's . . . it's vandalism!"

Lily, ever prosaic, sighed out a long "Good God . . ." adding feverishly, "We're not going to leave it there, are we?"

"Lord, no! I'd be sick!"

They looked at each other. Lily found Alice's svelte figure young-looking, and Alice was unable to ward off a feeling of envy: "What a complexion Lily has! Like a peach!"

Their lunch rang with unusual chatter, during which there was talk of massages, diets, dresses, and the local casino. They spoke, as if incidentally, about the prolonged youth of certain artists and about their publicized love affairs. For no apparent reason, Lily exclaimed, "Hmph! Short and sweet? I prefer long and happy!" and Alice distractedly mentioned the same man's name four or five times, the name of one of their friends who would be spending—"or else I'm very much mistaken"—the summer in the neighborhood . . . A feverish desire to escape, a rush of wicked designs, made them eat, drink, smoke, and talk freely. But in the drawing room Alice turned her face away pityingly as she walked past the portrait, and it was the frivolous Lily, rubicund and a little tipsy, who exhaled the smoke through her nostrils at the great man with disdain.

"Poor old thing!"

[*Translated by Matthew Ward*]

The Landscape

❧§❧

The painter who wanted to die made the gesture, at once spontaneous and literary, of writing out a few lines before giving himself over to death. He reached for a large sheet of drawing paper and a pencil, and then, just as he was about to write, he changed his mind.

"A few lines? For whom? The concierge knows I live alone, that I have no family, that my mistress has left me. Let's give her the pleasure of telling the story of this meaningless accident, once to the police and twenty times to the neighbors. My paintings? Let somebody sell them. I'd just as soon burn them, but it would be such a strain . . . and the smell of burning oil and charred hemp, in this beautiful air . . . For my last earthly memory to be a nauseating stench, ugh! That's not what I want."

Yet he still hesitated, tormented by a childish restlessness, a kind of vanity and honesty that were very much alive: the need to leave behind him the mark of his passing, to note the hour of his dying; in short, a need which was equivalent to that of recounting his wretched life as a lover betrayed . . . He threw down the pencil.

"And after I'm dead, people will think I was looking for pity . . . Then die, without words! Is it so difficult to die simply?"

He grabbed his revolver, loaded it, and his right elbow felt instinctively for the familiar armrest of his big, stuffed chair; facing him, a blank canvas on the easel reflected back onto his face the soft yellow light of the spring afternoon. He set the weapon down on a small round table and then, slowly, he stood up.

"Yes . . . that's it, I can do that. I almost have to. I see a landscape, inside me, that resembles my life, that explains why it is I'm dying . . ."

He began to paint, rapidly, with a sweep and freedom to his strokes which was not typical of him. He barely paused to contemplate his model, the inner landscape composed of his stormy, youthful grief, sometimes sharp and clear, sometimes obscured by clouds which passed, only for him to restore its blinding clarity and somewhat conventional symbolism.

He painted a marshy plain and a desert where greenish-black reeds emerged, in scattered tufts, from pools the color of lead. From the foreground, where a few curled leaves floated like skiffs, to the horizon closed with a rigid barrier of cirrus, there was nothing but rushy marshes, flat desolation, and reflections, wrinkled by the wind, of a sky in which the low, swelling clouds moved forward in parallel banks.

In the foreground, a single, bare tree, bent beneath the gusting wind like river grass bowing in the current. The main branch, broken yet living, revealed the splintered white sapwood beneath the torn bark . . .

The feverishly working hand finally stopped, the stiff arm dropped to his side. A warm fatigue softened the last hour of life.

"It's good," the painter said to himself. "My portrait looks just like me. I'm satisfied. There's nothing holding me back now. I'm going to die."

The rectangular patch of sky, above the bay window, changed from yellow to pink, heralding a long spring twilight. A young woman's voice, very near, sang through the open window the first notes of so touching, so colorful a song that the painter, holding his breath, stared at the window as if waiting to see the sound pass by as copper spheres, round flowers, and fruit dripping with juice. Holding the revolver in his hand, he leaned out and looked down, curious, into the courtyard. He did not discover there the sweet mouth which was sending, toward his death, such a generous farewell. But across the courtyard, in a dark little apartment, the blond nape of a young girl's neck shone like a pile of golden straw in a dark loft.

The painter returned to his canvas, sat down, and rubbed his right elbow on the chair's armrest . . . In sympathy with a sustained B flat, a fragile crystal goblet close to him vibrated.

"Something is missing from the canvas . . . A link . . . an intelligible detail . . . A detail which would serve as the humble legend . . ."

He put down his revolver and began painting a gray bird on the main branch of the tree, a songbird which, filled with its song, head raised toward the closed sky, was singing.

He delighted in the lustrous plumage and the gleaming eye—a shining jet bead . . . When evening fell and a servant came up, bringing his meal, she found the painter standing in front of his canvas, next to the forgotten weapon. He had finished painting the bird. Now he was using the last lilac rays of day to sketch, at the foot of the bare tree, a still-rudimentary flower struggling to lift the sickly, obstinate petals of its face out of the marsh.

[Translated by Matthew Ward]

The Half-Crazy

❦

It is certain that we come in contact with the half-crazy every day. They cannot be confined like the insane; they cannot be punished like the sane. If certain people hesitate to admit the existence of the half-crazy, they have only to read the daily paper to be convinced.

My dear colleague, I too invite them in, and with the same end in mind, to write about them. In June, July, and August, the place where a daily paper takes shape is a snare which attracts the half-crazy, the way the baited mousetrap attracts the mouse. Is it the cool floor, the dark anteroom with padded doors, the pleasant humidity absorbed by the stacks of blank paper? Enticed, the half-crazy seeks out the shade of our factory, investigates the smell of the ink, slakes his hidden agitation at the very wellspring of the printed drama, the event which soon will stir the crowd gathered at the outside windows . . .

But above all, he brings with him, heavy, swollen with muddled language, the poor soul of a man already cut off from the normal world, his soul in danger at every moment of allowing his secret to escape. He knows he must keep quiet and the confession trembles on the tip of his tongue. Storms and sunshine increase these clever intrusions, so he plays with danger, risks the obsessive word in conversation, the nervous mannerism capable of giving away everything. He is almost always at the mercy of a few syllables, whose sound and pattern engender in him a frenzy of which he remains the master only as long as he resists the urge to utter them one more time . . . then again and then just once more . . . He resists, for his whole life is nothing but watching and mistrusting himself. His half-crazed conversation, the stubbornness with which he informs us of his discoveries, his political, literary, or financial genius, are not moments of abandon; on the contrary. He seeks these contacts out of a taste for risk, diversion, and boasting, to prove to himself that he can still chat with us without falling into the deadly intoxication of the repeated word, the forbidden phrase which sings in him like a flood still contained, or the gesture which, once unleashed, opens the sinister door to the house of the insane.

During the hot weather, three or four of these troubled souls roam around the room where I work, slipping in quietly or forcing the door by surprise. One, cordial and lively, full of a southern plumpness, empties his pockets filled with manuscripts, verse and prose neither good nor bad. He tells anecdotes, laughs loudly, then apologizes for babbling on. I know of nothing more reassuring than he—if it weren't for the way he lurks in the shadows for hours, and then springs out unexpectedly with a burst of gaiety which terrifies the less spirited. Yet I still prefer him to that gentle, well-bred, well-dressed young man, who the first time he came was called Vernier, the second time Lugard, and the third Wilder. He first inquired about ways of getting a quick divorce, because his freedom of mind, his ability to work depended on it. Under the name of Lugard, he decried the fact that family arguments thwarted his vocation as a painter; finally, the one named Wilder, with the charming, disenchanted smile of Lugard, spoke in restrained, well-chosen terms about imperious gifts—a unique voice, a personal understanding of the great works of music—which destined him to the opera and to light opera. His modesty forced him to admit, at the end of the conversation, that he didn't know a note of music . . . What scorching day brought to me, under the name of Durand or Bojidar Karageorgevitch, a young whispering Proteus? He was well-mannered and had the sweet face of adolescents who resemble a very pretty mother. No doubt he will return, spreading anxiety, himself well protected from it, having already found refuge in an incurable sense of security.

And will she be cured, the stout visitor with the downy upper lip who came, round as a bubble, carried here on the moaning wind of a sudden storm from the west? She arrived all talkative and communicative, embellished with the graces and attributes of a local muse. The dress the color of Greek olives, the large, somewhat precarious hat, the scarf that slips off, the ceremonial glove, and the manuscript rolled up and tied with a thin ribbon—she wasn't missing a thing! Only her black eyes, like a bird's which betray no thought, lit up this turret with an unstable and mysterious fire. The lady of letters began by complaining about the heat, then about the difficulty there is, for an unyieldingly honest woman, in guaranteeing the sale of her stories, novellas, and serials. A bitter and banal song, in short, delivered rather gaily.

"Nevertheless, Madame, I've no lack of references . . ."

She enunciated the last word with difficulty, in a harsh, high tone, and interrupted herself to laugh, for no apparent reason.

"Oh, I'm sure, Madame," I said to her. "Moreover, your name is far from unknown to me . . ."

My lie pleased her and she fiddled with her roll of paper.

"Is it? My name alone gives me a certain standing; it serves as its own . . . reference."

The sharp sound of the word made me start, but its loudly barked first syllable seemed to have more of an effect on her who had just pronounced it for the second time. She collected herself, then untied and unrolled her manuscript, which she placed in front of me.

"I only ask," she said, "for ten minutes of your time. That's exactly how long it takes to read my first chapter. My first chapter demonstrates the value of the entire work. It contains the plot of the novel, without giving it away, however . . ."

With a yellow-gloved hand, she spread out twenty little typed installments. "This one would suit the readership of a large daily. And this one, twelve short novellas . . . I have six hundred and twenty-four chapters at your disposal . . . The best, as you will see, is this first which . . . sets the . . . which is the . . . the point of . . ."

She hesitated at the edge of the word and her face was veiled with a confused and agonized expression, a kind of cloud which made me forget her coloring, her stoutness, even her build, a fog from the depths of which she cried out at me, as if drowning, " . . . of . . . reference . . . !

"I've always thought that the detective novel, once you dispense with the detective, is an inexhaustible source of drama and comedy. You'll see! With the help of just three characters—a young apprentice electrician, an English officer, and a young girl, not in the least neurotic, not in the least. A gay young girl, blond and full of . . . how shall I say? of . . . let me see . . . of . . ."

Despite myself, I blurted out, " . . . references . . ."

The lady of letters jerked her head back as though I had slapped her, and for a second I waited for the explosion, in my peaceful office with the Venetian blinds closed, of some unknown, monstrous force . . . Then she stood up, deftly gathered the papers scattered in front of me, rolled them up without ever taking her eyes off me, upright and circumspect for the moment, gave herself some room, and after a brief goodbye backed out mistrustfully, anxious to escape, like someone greatly afraid, in fact, of the half-crazy.

[Translated by Matthew Ward]

Secrets

"No, it's not an engagement party . . . But that doesn't fool anybody. Tomorrow I'll be forced to announce everywhere that Claudie Grey is engaged to André Donat, or else there'll be a scandal. The child hasn't danced with anyone else and they've found accomplices in all our friends. Charles himself . . ."

Madame Grey's eyes searched the room for her husband and found him seated at a poker table. "There he goes, he's running his thumbnail over his lip again. Again . . . again . . . and again . . . Last week I didn't catch him running his thumbnail over his lip once. It's this oppressive weather, the storm won't break." She sighed, and settled her gaze on her daughter and André Donat, who were dancing to the sound of the pianola. Claudie resembled her; she was just as tall, and blond like her at the same age.

"Blond . . . but not for very long. Blond hair like that turns white fast, I know what I'm talking about. But the child looks lovely tonight. Really lovely. Worthy of her mother. As for her face, the resemblance is disconcerting, despite a sort of shrinkage in her features. Smaller nose, smaller eyes unfortunately, smaller mouth than mine, thank God . . . She's just lovely. I can put my name to her, as they say. And a good girl . . . Oh, I can really feel that it's the end and that she's going to leave me! I'm singing her praises as if . . ."

She brought her train of thought to an abrupt halt and superstitiously knocked on the gilded wood of an armchair. Madame Grey felt an expert tenderness for her daughter, a tenderness incapable of blindness, the sort of critical devotion that ties the trainer to the champion. Her own health, her own mental and physical equilibrium had often made her uncompromising, and hard on womanly weaknesses she did not share.

"What? A migraine? You have a migraine? And where would you have dug up migraines, I never knew what they were! A chignon down low? You want to wear your hair in a chignon down low? You silly little thing, nothing looked worse on me at your age . . . What you want is your hair swept up on top of your head and the back of your neck left bare: look at the portrait Ferdinand Humbert did of me!"

What Madame Grey cherished in her daughter was a little girl in 1885, in a short dress, her legs bare and bathed in cold water; a young girl in 1895, on horseback in the Bois, her hair tied back with a bow under the black derby; a "good little girl," easy to bring up, a bit bold, as pure as a pedigree filly, a tall, lanky girl who never heard of a hysterical fit and who wouldn't wake up three doctors when she had her first baby . . .

Madame Grey turned a mother-in-law's vindictive eye toward her future son-in-law. "Oh, yes, he looks quite the pretty boy. And his bread's well buttered, he'll take over Daddy's business. Envious, this marriage will make everyone envious. But if I were to say what I think, deep down, I'd hear some fine shouting then!"

André Donat, interrupting the tango a moment for the buffet, bowed as he passed Madame Grey, kissed her hand lightly, snatched her little handkerchief from her sleeve, and ran off, laughing and flashing his white teeth. Madame Grey menaced him with her fan and smiled at him threateningly. She went out onto the terrace, sat down, and breathed in the dusty coolness of the Bois at night. Her fifty inflexible years bent somewhat in the solitude; she felt her stiff knees and the small of her proud back calling for bed, the smooth cambric sheets, the steaming hot-water bottle . . .

"That boy certainly is playing up to me. But for how long . . . ? When he laughed he showed me his big canines in his upper jaw and his little incisors on the bottom, too short, as if they'd been filed down; coarseness, quick physical responses . . . I pity my little girl if he has pretty chambermaids . . . And that nose of his, it's too short, shows a lack of judgment . . . And his earlobes joined to his neck at the bottom: degeneracy. What's more, when we visited him at his home, he was priding himself on being unable to live with disorder, on arranging his books according to the color of their spines, and on getting up at night to put his shoes in the shoe tree."

Madame Grey shuddered and stood up. She could see in her memory a young man in his shirttails, bare feet on a mosaic bathroom floor, standing in front of an absolutely astounded young woman; a young man in the midst of confessing, with horrible, unconscious candor, that he couldn't sleep if the fringes on the Turkish towels hung on the rack to dry were not lined up with each other. "It's funny, darling,

I'm pretty bohemian when it comes to everything else, but the fringe
on the Turkish towels . . ."

"But I can't tell Claudie that," thought Madame Grey agitatedly.
"No. I can't. If I tell her that, and that I nearly left her father because
of the way he runs his thumbnail over his lip, she'll laugh. She won't
understand. Besides, those are things you don't talk about. On her
wedding day you can whisper a few nervous, awkward things in a young
girl's ear . . . But I could never talk to her about towel fringe, or about
the thumbnail going back and forth across his lip a hundred times, or
about . . . Oh, enough! Enough! She, she'll hide things from me . . .
small, terrible things, the mold that grows on married life, the refuse
a man's character leaves behind at the border between childishness and
dementia . . .

"My poor little . . ." Madame Grey sighed, drew herself up to her
full height, which lost in suppleness and gained in majesty, and returned
to the drawing room. She gave only a little sigh to the two fiancés who
were doing a Boston two-step and hurried over to the poker table.

"Make room for me, Charles, there are only four of you."

She had no desire to play poker. But she sat down beside her husband, and her hand, that of a good wife, admonished, with a meaningful squeeze, the unconscious hand which had been running back and
forth, back and forth over his lip . . .

[Translated by Matthew Ward]

"Châ"

❧❦❧

His wife placed her hand on his shoulder as she passed by. "Aren't you glad you get to see the little dolls dance?"

He didn't much care for this trite way of referring to the Cambodian dancers, but he gave her a nod, and admired his wife as she walked away. She was wearing a silver dress, with sulphur-yellow roses at the waist, a large fan of sulphur-colored feathers, and her hair, skillfully bleached to a very pale yellow, looked like some sort of finery bought at the same time as the roses and the fan. A tall imposing woman, she impressed people with the somewhat rudimentary beauty of her features, and with her virile blue eyes, accustomed to judging all things from above.

"The beautiful Madame Issard looks superb this evening," said a man's voice behind a white silk curtain painted with a brown bamboo pattern.

"Battle dress," responded another voice. "Tonight's the night she intends to get the marshal to give her husband the assignment."

"That assignment is hardly any business of Issard's. A man of letters . . . a refined intellectual . . . a homebody . . ."

"But it *is* Madame Issard's business. In four months she'll have won the Legion's rosette for Issard and the ribbon for herself. Did you hear her at dinner? She was magnificent. What diplomacy! And unassailable with it . . . I don't feel sorry for Issard."

André Issard walked away from the bamboo-painted curtain. Not that he was afraid of hearing anything about his wife that might upset him. But he felt he needed a brief respite from all the admiration shown her throughout dinner. Moreover, announced by their timbals, each one of which separately dripped the liquid note which rings in the throats of toads, the Cambodian women were beginning their dance on a dais in front of Pierre Guesde's fifty guests, who were spread out around the hall. Looking rather blasé behind his monocle, Issard took extreme pleasure in seeing them. His notions of exoticism did not go beyond Algiers, and the only time he had seen Ith, Sarrouth, Trassoth, and their companions was in *L'Illustration*. He found them pretty; at the same time he regretted that their round cheeks were covered with white makeup. He blamed fashion, starting in Siam, which had them wearing their hair like little boys. But most of them carried their boyish heads on a neck like the shaft of a column, without crease or blemish, covered with firm, smooth, polished skin the color of fine stoneware, sometimes the color of cherry plums, ravishing to the eye. André Issard searched for words not too overused to describe these inscrutable, childlike faces, whose shallow carving—eyes slit with a fine chisel, nose barely raised above the cheek, small mouths whose full lips showed the red pulp inside . . . with the obstinacy of an artistic pen-pusher, he searched for a way to paint the curve of Sarrouth's hands, and the inverted fingers elongating a palm curving inward on the outside . . .

"A leaf seared by autumn? No . . . More like the twisting of a fish out of water . . . Or else . . . Yes, that's it: it's the heraldic curl of a panting dog's tongue . . ."

Then the music and the magic of the wavelike movements conspired, and André Issard hardly thought of anything else. "They're pretty . . . They're new . . . They're feminine, really feminine."

He looked up and caught sight of his wife in a deep embrasure, not paying attention to the dances, but talking with the governor of a large colony. She would speak, listen, speak again, and seemed to use as much energy listening as speaking. Her eyebrows, knit together, bore down on her blue eyes, whose gaze was contemplating a glorious and harsh future.

"She looks like a man," André said to himself. "How is it I hadn't noticed it before?"

At the same moment, the beautiful Madame Issard leaned forward, her chin in her hand, and turned and faced the audience, where her attention seemed to gather powerful acolytes, here, there, and there. Then she went on with her conversation in a low voice and André Issard noticed her chin working like a tribune's, her closed fist beating out the rhythm of her sentence on the back of chair.

"She's a man," Issard repeated to himself. "I was wondering what it was I had against her, unjustly . . . That's what it is, my wife is a man—and what a man! I only have what I deserve; I should have realized it sooner."

The dance was ending. A fatalist, he made his way toward the dais where the little dancers, scattered about, were being subjected at close range to the Europeans' wounding curiosity. He heard Pierre Guesde speaking in Cambodian with Soun, a singer in the chorus, not wearing makeup, but whose black eyes and white teeth sparkled; he allowed himself to be introduced to Ith, who was dressed as a Burmese prince— Ith, whose pure, innocent face a hundred photographs had glorified; he touched Sarrouth's melting, moving hands . . . André Issard held them in his, while Sarrouth listened to Pierre Guesde, hands as passive and cool as flesh-covered leaves. She responded with a short chirping sound, a little deferential greeting, a childish laugh, and particularly with a single syllable: "Châ . . . Châ . . ."

"Sha . . ." repeated Issard, imitating Sarrouth's liquid pronunciation. "What does it mean?"

"It means," explained Pierre Guesde, " 'very-respectfully-yes.' "

The dancers were leaving, and Issard made an interrogatory sign to his wife: "Are we leaving?" She responded in kind, a furious and barely visible "no." Ten minutes later, he caught her scent nearby and heard the swishing of her scaly dress.

"The marshal's leaving," she said.

He jumped up. "I'll run over . . ."

"No," she said. "Leave it. I've arranged a private meeting for you tomorrow."

"It's only proper that I . . ."

"No," she said. "Leave it, I'm telling you. Believe me. Everything's fine. I've planted the seed and planted it well."

She was shining with a mineral-like brightness, and led him off toward the exit. In the car, she shouted to the chauffeur, "Go back past the Prado!" and put her arm under her husband's with a kind of condescending cordiality, a despot's good humor. The full moon sprinkled her pale hair with silver, and the big yellow feathers of her fan rippled like waves in the wind. But André Issard was not looking at her. He was humming a little song imitating Oriental music and broke off to murmur under his breath, "Châ . . . Châ . . ."

"What did you say, Dede?"

He gave his wife a smile, with the look of a disloyal slave.

"Oh, nothing . . . It's a Cambodian word that doesn't really translate . . . A word that doesn't mean anything here."

[Translated by Matthew Ward]

The Bracelet

" . . . Twenty-seven, twenty-eight, twenty-nine . . . There really are twenty-nine . . ."

Madame Augelier mechanically counted and recounted the little *pavé* diamonds. Twenty-nine square brilliants, set in a bracelet, which slithered between her fingers like a cold and supple snake. Very white, not too big, admirably matched to each other—the pretty bijou of a connoisseur. She fastened it on her wrist, and shook it, throwing off blue sparks under the electric candles; a hundred tiny rainbows, blazing with color, danced on the white tablecloth. But Madame Augelier was looking more closely instead at the other bracelet, the three finely engraved creases encircling her wrist above the glittering snake.

"Poor François . . . what will he give me next year, if we're both still here?"

François Augelier, industrialist, was traveling in Algeria at the time, but, present or absent, his gift marked both the year's end and their wedding anniversary. Twenty-eight jade bowls, last year; twenty-seven old enamel plaques mounted on a belt, the year before . . .

"And the twenty-six little Royal Dresden plates . . . And the twenty-four meters of antique Alençon lace . . ." With a slight effort of memory Madame Augelier could have gone back as far as four modest silver place settings, as far as three pairs of silk stockings . . .

"We weren't rich back then. Poor François, he's always spoiled me so . . ." To herself, secretly, she called him "poor François," because she believed herself guilty of not loving him enough, underestimating the strength of affectionate habits and abiding fidelity.

Madame Augelier raised her hand, tucked her little finger under, extended her wrist to erase the bracelet of wrinkles, and repeated intently, "It's so pretty . . . the diamonds are so white . . . I'm so pleased . . ."

Then she let her hand fall back down and admitted to herself that she was already tired of her new bracelet.

"But I'm not ungrateful," she said naïvely with a sigh. Her weary eyes wandered from the flowered tablecloth to the gleaming window. The smell of some Calville apples in a silver bowl made her feel slightly sick and she left the dining room.

In her boudoir she opened the steel case which held her jewels, and adorned her left hand in honor of the new bracelet. Her ring had on it a black onyx band and a blue-tinted brilliant; onto her delicate, pale, and somewhat wrinkled little finger, Madame Augelier slipped a circle of dark sapphires. Her prematurely white hair, which she did not dye, appeared even whiter as she adjusted amid slightly frizzy curls a narrow fillet sprinkled with a dusting of diamonds, which she immediately untied and took off again.

"I don't know what's wrong with me. I'm not feeling all that well. Being fifty is a bore, basically . . ."

She felt restless, both terribly hungry and sick to her stomach, like a convalescent whose appetite the fresh air has yet to restore.

"Really now, is a diamond actually as pretty as all that?"

Madame Augelier craved a visual pleasure which would involve the sense of taste as well; the unexpected sight of a lemon, the unbearable squeaking of the knife cutting it in half, makes the mouth water with desire . . .

"But I don't want a lemon. Yet this nameless pleasure which escapes me does exist, I know it does, I remember it! Yes, the blue glass bracelet . . ."

A shudder made Madame Augelier's slack cheeks tighten. A vision, the duration of which she could not measure, granted her, for a second time, a moment lived forty years earlier, that incomparable moment as she looked, enraptured, at the color of the day, the iridescent, distorted image of objects seen through a blue glass bangle, moved around in a circle, which she had just been given. That piece of perhaps Oriental glass, broken a few hours later, had held in it a new universe, shapes not the inventions of dreams, slow, serpentine animals moving in pairs, lamps, rays of light congealed in an atmosphere of indescribable blue . . .

The vision ended and Madame Augelier fell back, bruised, into the present, into reality.

But the next day she began searching, from antique shops to flea markets, from flea markets to crystal shops, for a glass bracelet, a certain color of blue. She put the passion of a collector, the precaution, the dissimulation of a lunatic into her search. She ventured into what she called "impossible districts," left her car at the corner of strange streets, and in the end, for a few centimes, she found a circle of blue glass which she recognized in the darkness, stammered as she paid for it, and carried it away.

In the discreet light of her favorite lamp she set the bracelet on the dark field of an old piece of velvet, leaned forward, and waited for the shock . . . But all she saw was a round piece of bluish glass, the trinket of a child or a savage, hastily made and blistered with bubbles; an object whose color and material her memory and reason recognized; but the powerful and sensual genius who creates and nourishes the marvels of childhood, who gradually weakens, then dies mysteriously within us, did not even stir.

Resigned, Madame Augelier thus came to know how old she really was and measured the infinite plain over which there wandered, beyond her reach, a being detached from her forever, a stranger, turned away from her, rebellious and free even from the bidding of memory: a little ten-year-old girl wearing on her wrist a bracelet of blue glass.

[Translated by Matthew Ward]

The Find

The light from the declining sun struck the curtains, shone across the drawing room from one end to the other, and Irene's friends cried out in admiration.

"It's like a fairy tale!"

"What a find!"

"And the Seine is on fire!"

"The sky's turning pink . . ."

One of them, more honest, muttered vindictively, as she took it all in with a single glance—the Seine, the old drawing room lengthened by a rustic dining room, the purple-and-silver curtains, the orange cups, the wood fire—"There's no justice . . ."

And poor little Madame Auroux, who had gotten divorced so she could get married again and who couldn't get married because she couldn't find an apartment, had two such heartfelt tears in her blue eyes that Irene hugged her to her breast.

"And this one's in such a hurry to start some silliness all over again! You know, my dear, I believe that it was getting divorced that brought me luck. Because you could say to have found a marvel like this was pure luck."

She triumphed shamelessly and played up her lovely dwelling for all it was worth, she who had never dared flash a new ring in front of a poorer friend. She stretched in order to confess in the tone of a guilty confidence, "Ladies, ladies, if you knew what the mornings here are like! The boats, the reflection of the water dancing on the ceiling . . ."

But they had had enough. Green with envy and stuffed with cake, they all left together. Leaning on the wrought-iron banister, "an eighteenth-century gem, my dear," Irene called out to them, "Goodbye, goodbye," waving her hand like someone out in the country standing on the terrace of a château. She went back in and leaned her forehead on the windowpane. A brief winter twilight was rapidly extinguishing the pink-and-gold reflection of the sky in the water, and the night's first star twinkled brightly, foretelling a night of bitter cold.

Behind her, Irene heard the clattering of cups being gathered by an overly eager hand and the hurried footsteps of her maid. She turned around.

"Are you in a hurry, Pauline?"

"It's not that I'm in a hurry, Madame, but there's my husband . . . It's Saturday and Madame knows they have a five-day week."

"Go on, then, go on . . . You can leave the dishes for tomorrow. No, don't set a place for me, I ate so much I'll never be hungry tonight."

Since moving in she had put up with makeshift dinners, or cold meat from the local charcuterie, because Pauline was a general but not a "live-in" housemaid. On certain, particularly busy evenings, Irene would wrap the blue apron around her waist, grill herself some fresh ham, and break two eggs into the buttered skillet . . .

She heard the door slam and Pauline's clogs on the stairs. A tram sang on its rails along the quay opposite. The solid old house hardly shook at all as the cars passed, and its thick walls blocked out both the barking of the dog next door and the piano being played upstairs. Irene put another log on the fire, and arranged the little desk-table, the big armchair, the books, the screen around the fireplace—"period shell marble, my dear"—and stood there, contemplating the decor of her happiness . . . A clock outside tolled the hour in evenly measured strokes.

"Seven o'clock. Only seven o'clock. Thirteen more hours till tomorrow . . ."

She shivered humbly before her silent witnesses—the purple curtains, the monument which cut into the night sky like the prow of a ship, the useless armchair, and the book which had lost its magic—abdicating her condition as the happy woman about whom people say, "She has a quiet life" and "a unique apartment."

No more troublesome and squandering husband, no more scenes, no more unexpected entrances, departures that are more like flights, suspicious telegrams, no more invisible female intruders on the phone named "sir" or "my good man . . ."

No more husband, no child, no admirers, and no lover . . . "Free and sitting on top of the world!" her jealous friends would say.

"But did I ask to be free and sitting on top of the world?"

She had taken back her dowry, regained her independence, moved into a luxurious old apartment, sunny and secluded, made for a recluse or a passionate twosome, and lived in peace—ah, what peace . . .

"But did I want so much peace?"

She stood there, in front of the easy chair and the screen which were trying, beneath the ceiling, to enclose Irene in a refuge her own size. She felt a sudden need for light, and lit the little smoked-crystal chandelier, the antique bronze sconce, and the basket of electric fruit on the dining-room table. But she left the bedroom, which she had prided herself on earlier, and her Spanish bed from whose corners there rose, like heraldic pales, four gilded wooden flames, in darkness . . .

"Oh, yes, I have a lovely house," she said coldly. "I have nothing to do but wait till it's time to show it to other friends, other women. And afterward . . . ?"

She envisaged a series of days, with herself in the role of cicerone, praising the shell chimneypiece, the wrought-iron banister, the Seine, the woodwork with its fading gilt . . . All of a sudden, with desperate fierceness, she envied a little furnished apartment where for want of anything better one of her friends was living with a young painter, two dirty rooms with cigarette ashes and paint stains everywhere, but warm with the sounds of people quarreling, laughing, making up. At the same time she felt herself, almost physically ill and full of bitterness, being thrust into a studio which doubled as an apartment—you have to live somewhere!—for a whole family, the two parents, the three beautiful children, as much alike as three pure-bred puppies . . . The warmth of the narrow, sensual apartment, the high, vertical daylight from the studio windows on the three naked little bodies . . . Irene hit the light switch, suddenly cutting off the electricity, and sighed, somewhat relieved, as the beautiful antique order of the apartment disappeared. She moved the screen and the easy chair away from the fire, drew the curtains, put an old, warm overcoat across her shoulders, turned off the last lamp in the drawing room cautiously, and hastily left the room, taking with her a detective novel, the caviar sandwiches, and the pot of chocolate, to finish her evening in a straw chair wedged between the sink and the shower stall in the bathroom.

[Translated by Matthew Ward]

Mirror Games

It's not that I like it here, but it's so cold outside. As soon as you come in here, the air wraps you in eiderdown. When I was a child, during the winter I used to sleep under a thick cloud of fine goose down, enclosed in red marceline silk, choice, weightless down which gave off a mysterious warmth . . . But it's just plain stuffy in here. You breathe in all the smells of a tearoom: frangipane, warm pastry, the vegetable bitterness of scalding tea, the rum in the babas, burned toast crumbs that have fallen into the embers. And especially perfumes, women's perfumes . . . There are no sanctions against certain perfumers; the manufacture of essences is dangerously unrestricted and the female sense of smell, often rudimentary and poorly developed, confronts and tries out everything that's sold in little bottles. The faint lavender of angelica, the sticky rose of geranium, vanilla extract pointlessly braced with resin, tarry narcissus, prussic-acid lilac, creosoted carnation, benjamin disguised as amber, and all that vague flora, those distilled flower beds, inevitably giving off the poorly disguised, nauseating soul of wild parsnip!

I try to forget the cacophony of perfumes floating in the air. Besides, the two pretty women next to me smell nice. I would get tired of the brunette's sandalwood after a while, and I know that behind the "red rose" the blonde has sprayed on herself there hides, on the secondary olfactory plane, a vague, fetid smell of fresh ink. But so what? This brunette, this blonde, and I aren't going to spend the rest of our lives together.

The brunette is pretty and the blonde is charming—and bleached. But the brunette, dressed all in gray velvet with panels of flame-colored beads, a stole of silver foxes around her neck, shoes covered with sequins, feathers, and paste jewels, gloves that are embroidered and funnel-shaped, and a hat with a spray of aigrettes which hang, above two stars, like a threatening cloud, the brunette is resplendent with the somewhat harsh elegance people go for nowadays . . . The greedy, chattering women fall silent as she enters. They stare at her, and the envy in their eyes enhances her beauty the way a summer rain adds luster to the enameled feathers of a kingfisher. She is warm and drinks like a pigeon, her neck stretched out, her jabot hanging. She has two gestures which, though frequent as tics, are the result of a studied coquetry: with her forefinger she flicks a very light brown curl away from her eyebrow, displaying her almond-shaped fingernail, which glistens near her wide, tapering eye; she sticks a trident-shaped tortoiseshell comb into the hair at the nape of her neck, and as she raises her arm, the eye follows the roundness of her well-supported breast, which rises with the arm.

The blonde . . . the blonde is charming in her own way. She's merely a blonde in black Moroccan crepe and a plush cape, a blonde with a short neck and a carnivorous mouth. Her mannerisms do not make her more attractive. She thrusts out her chin the way a pug does, and wrinkles up her nose like a baby seal as it comes blinking up out of the water. It's not a pretty sight. I'd like to tell her so . . . another time. And now, beneath the fiery glances, she's imitating her friend's little game. She puffs out her chest and with one hand pats at her low, golden chignon. In the same way a younger sister unconsciously imitates an older sister already sure of her seductive power. What a delight to the eye it is to watch these two well-trained peahens! The more beautiful of the two is a bit contemptuous toward the more docile one, and the latter, not without a twinge of jealousy, imitates, conforms, corrects herself.

A man appears. Were they expecting him? I think so. For they both exclaim at the same time, "Well!" as if surprised. Which one has he come for? I don't know. One fills his cup, the other offers him cakes. Impartial, courteous, he leans toward the blonde, then gives his full attention to what the brunette is saying. The blonde seems to be getting nervous. She juts her chin out in little jerks, wrinkles up her nose, and laughs too much. Now she looks ugly next to her rival . . . The man will have eyes only for the brunette, her dress of ash and flame, her white skin, her pink forefinger, her round breast under her dress which has a vigor all its own. I bet on the brunette . . . and I lose. The man turns imperceptibly, irresistibly toward the blonde. First, his body shifts gradually. Then the chair, with little, impatient hitches. Now the blonde can stick out her chin, repeat that coarse gesture which shortens her neck, wrinkles her nose, and shows too much of her gums above her uneven teeth, because she's not risking anything anymore. The man prefers her. She wins and within a few seconds she blushes like a piece of fruit brushed by a streak of dawn.

And the brunette, upset and confused, intervenes, trying to discover the victorious blonde's secret, and risks, by way of imitation, the wrinkling of the nose, the batting of the eyelashes, the puppy-dog faces, chin out, teeth bared . . .

[Translated by Matthew Ward]

Habit

❦

They parted as they had come together, without knowing why. One thing, however, is certain. Jeannine did reveal to certain third parties, with far too much glee, that Andrée's real name, given to her by a grandmother at baptism, was Symphorienne. Another version had it that Andrée, clumsily overestimating her authority as the older and as a solidly built brunette, signaled Jeannine it was time to leave one afternoon, in front of twenty cups of tea and as many glasses of port, by whistling for her as she whistled for her dogs in the Bois. Uncertain friends, for once impartial, blamed both Andrée and Jeannine. "I don't know if Andrée whistled for Jeannine or not, but those truck-driver manners are just like her; and that silly Jeannine excels at arranging her own slavery for the sadistic pleasure of whining with humiliation afterward."

After their falling out, they bore with dignity and discretion the sorrow they felt for their great friendship, which had lasted through two seasons at Deauville, two at Chamonix, and three on the Riviera. Jeannine, the weaker, more impertinent, more frivolous of the two, changed dance halls, discovered a new tearoom-bistro in Belleville where she took her friends at three in the afternoon and then again at one o'clock in the morning for some potato salad and that strange fish, sea pike, prized in the open-air markets and snubbed by high-class fish markets because of its jade-green backbone. Without Jeannine, Andrée reverted to her rustic tastes and moved her walk in the Bois and her boat ride on the lake up an hour. Jeannine thought, "I'm drowning my sorrow," and Andrée, in her flat-heeled shoes, her balaclava around her neck, and her hands in her pockets, repeated, "I don't want to hear any more about intimate friends, men or women! I'm turning back into the wild nymph of the unexplored forest!" Deep down and with naïve astonishment, they accepted their shared indifference and the ease, the amazing benignity of their breakup.

Spring led Jeannine back toward the restaurants in the Bois. May found her shivering in a white crepe cape, dancing to stay warm, at eleven o'clock at night, on a dance floor whitened by electric moonlight, between the tables and the saplings lashing in the icy wind. She crossed the Bois whenever a day of shopping allowed her to parade beneath a false little sun, dressed in winter muslins, then summer furs. But neither by night nor by day did the Bois remind her of her friend, the nymph, for the Bois of the morning and pedestrians does not look like the Bois of cars and night.

It happened, however, that she was walking alone at the unlikely hour of fifteen minutes before noon, down one of the long paths which lead from the Entre-Deux-Lacs to the Cascade. She was walking fast, for her new friend, both intimate and athletic, had just chosen a game of tennis instead of her, and Jeannine, out of spite, had refused a ride. She was walking without enjoyment, and did not hear the nightingales, or the blackbirds and the orioles who were trying to imitate the nightingales. The acacias, which were losing their blossoms, snowed down in vain at Jeannine's feet, but her charming little nose, as imperious as a swift's beak, was closed to their fragrance, vanilla beignets and orange blossoms.

The sound of someone whistling stopped her, and she knew why she had stopped, listening through the trees to the voice calling, "Here, girl, here, girl, come on, come on!" A Belgian sheep dog appeared, just long enough to show its bearlike eyes and its thick tail, hanging down like a she-wolf's. A bulldog followed after her, snorting like an old taxi, white, and monocled with a black half-moon, then came a frantic griffon terrier, yellow and bristling like a bundle of straws . . .

"Mieke . . . Relaps . . . Joli-Blond . . ." counted Jeannine. Behind the dogs, Andrée crossed the path but did not see Jeannine, who recognized the chestnut-colored, all-weather suit, the muddy, flat-heeled boots, the red woolen scarf, and the whip with the big braided handle.

"Here, girls, here, girls, here . . . !"

The call faded away; one of the dogs barked in the distance. Jeannine stood there motionless, trembling. She hoped for the familiar cry to come again, heard nothing more, and set off on her way, hesitant, half-hearted, her face pale and her eyes brimming with two tears that refused to fall.

"I wonder . . . Really, I wonder what came over me . . . I wonder . . ."

For nothing in her heart leaped out toward Andrée. She calmly imagined her somewhat "haremesque" perfume and her virile hand in her big glove. But deep inside her a jealous tenderness, a regret, stinging like a child's hurt, demanded the three dogs eager for their daily walk, the pleasure of calling them by their names, the right to mark the damp path with two small sharp heels next to two flat rubber heels; the privilege of tossing off meaningless phrases into the mist of the lake, the canopy of the elder trees, or the branch alive with thrushes, phrases good only for the moment, a naïve and sweet custom, the security of saying them again the next day.

Her loneliness weakened her. She let herself moan softly as she walked along, mumbling childishly: "I want the dogs . . . I want the morning . . . I want to get up early . . . I want warm milk and rum at the refreshment stand near the lake, the day it rained so hard. I want . . ."

She turned around, waiting for some whim of Andrée's or for the dogs to bring back to the path the image of a time now forever out of reach, only to find, without seeking, the words for her longing, the expression of her anguish: "I want last year . . ."

[*Translated by Matthew Ward*]

Alix's Refusal

⋙⟐⋘

"Have you seen that poor Alix lately?"

"Yesterday, my dear, and it's frightening. She looks like she's a hundred years old."

"A hundred wouldn't be so bad. The worst thing is that she looks her age! What is all this . . . discouragement, this refusal to do anything to make herself attractive? Did she take a vow? She isn't in mourning for anyone, is she?"

"Yes, her second youth."

And they laughed. For even the most serious situations cannot keep women from picking at their fellow creatures, especially their fellow female creatures. It is a pastime as monotonous as sarcasm. When two women get together to disparage another woman, they first cite her vintage, then raise questions about her health, her marital fidelity, her monetary situation, fortunate or unfortunate . . .

It so happens that I knew not only these two women here but, better still, their victim, and it's the backbiters who, for once, I think are right.

As resistant as it is to every sort of shock, the precious and mysterious feminine constitution has had no lack of reasons to stagger and die out for quite some time. A woman is not destroyed by material wretchedness alone. She who endures despite near-poverty, despite hard work, disintegrates beneath the weight of an obsession. It will be enough, in order for her to consummate her own ruin, that a sort of false point of honor displace, in her mind, a hard-won sense of order. Such is the case of the person on whom these two women, in a moderately compassionate tone, had turned their attention.

A case which seemed curable, since "poor Alix" has neither fallen into the fire nor been ravaged by lupus, nor has she been wounded at the source of her livelihood. The crisis she is going through is merely one of discouragement, of whatgoodisitism—Rabelais has a beautiful word for it, one that creates an image, "*déflocquement*." Women who have suffered are afflicted by this sort of weakness less often than women who have not suffered enough. Having climbed to the half-century mark, a woman, hundreds of women, all women, are faced with another, more dizzying slope and begin to plan their defense. Most turn away from it, hiding their heads under their wings. There is hardly a woman who feels threatened by her age who does not know, after a period of trial and error, how first to try on, then how to give her face a characteristic look, a style which will defy the work of time for ten, fifteen years.

What a reprieve! I am careful not to speak lightly of these renovations, these twilight triumphs which Balzac denied. "Though already thirty-two years old," he writes, "she could still give the illusion of youth." What! At thirty, at the age of an old horse, the age of a tree in its most resplendent foliage, of a young elephant, of an adolescent crocodile, a woman should pack away her most ardent dreams and retire from the dance, for fear of being called an aged bacchante!

I give my indulgence—and I am not the only one—and approval to those who wear the colors of their survival, the signs of their activity, into the arena. Too much courage has shone among the female kind, and for too many years, for women, under the pretext of loyalty, to break the contract they signed with beauty. You all seem to have this new "Alix way" about you, a look of embarrassment and apology which is not yours. "But it's my real face!" No. Your real face is in the drawer of your dressing table, and sadly enough, you have left your good spirits in with it. Your real face is a warm, matte pink tending toward fawn, set off high on the cheeks by a glimmer of deep carmine, well blended and nearly translucent—which stops just under the lower eyelid, where it disappears deep into a bluish gray, barely visible, spread up to the brow; the thick eyebrow, carefully drawn out at the end, is brown like your thick, curling lashes between which your gray eyes look blue. I'm not forgetting the mouth whose design—equally well corrected—is a bold arc, its scarlet color making the teeth whiter. To work, my poor Alix! Show a little confidence in yourself, the inner smile you were known for will blossom all at once over the whole of you. One will only have to see you to be certain that the false Alix was that bland, retiring, discouraged, somewhat bletted woman . . . The true Alix is the one who always had a taste for adorning herself, defending herself, and pleasing others, for savoring the bitterness, the risk, and the sweetness of living—the true Alix, you see, is the young one.

[*Translated by Matthew Ward*]

The Seamstress

❧§❧

"Do you mean to say your daughter is *nine years old*," said a friend, "and she doesn't know how to sew? She really must learn to sew. In bad weather sewing is a better occupation for a child of that age than reading storybooks."

"Nine years old? And she can't sew?" said another friend. "When she was eight, my daughter embroidered this tray cloth for me, look at it . . . Oh, I don't say it's fine needlework, but it's nicely done all the same. Nowadays my daughter cuts out her own underclothes. I can't bear anyone in my house to mend holes with pins!"

I meekly poured all this domestic wisdom over Bel-Gazou.

"You're nine years old and you don't know how to sew? You really must learn to sew . . ."

Flouting truth, I even added: "When I was eight years old, I remember I embroidered a tray cloth . . . Oh, it wasn't fine needlework, I dare say . . . And then, in bad weather . . ."

She has therefore learned to sew. And although—with one bare sunburned leg tucked beneath her, and her body at ease in its bathing suit—she looks more like a fisherboy mending a net than an industrious little girl, she seems to experience no boyish repugnance. Her hands, stained the color of tobacco juice by sun and sea, hem in a way that seems against nature; their version of the simple running stitch resembles the zigzag dotted lines of a road map, but she buttonholes and scallops with elegance and is severely critical of the embroidery of others.

She sews and kindly keeps me company if rain blurs the horizon of the sea. She also sews during the torrid hour when the spindle bushes gather their circles of shadow directly under them. Moreover, it sometimes happens that a quarter of an hour before dinner, black in her white dress—"Bel-Gazou! your hands and frock are clean, and don't forget it!"—she sits solemnly down with a square of material between her fingers. Then my friends applaud: "Just look at her! Isn't she good? That's right! Your mother must be pleased!"

Her mother says nothing—great joys must be controlled. But ought one to feign them? I shall speak the truth: I don't much like my daughter sewing.

When she reads, she returns all bewildered and with flaming cheeks, from the island where the chest full of precious stones is hidden, from the dismal castle where a fair-haired orphan child is persecuted. She is soaking up a tested and time-honored poison, whose effects have long been familiar. If she draws, or colors pictures, a semiarticulate song issues from her, unceasing as the hum of bees around the privet. It is the same as the buzzing of flies as they work, the slow waltz of the house painter, the refrain of the spinner at her wheel. But Bel-Gazou is silent when she sews, silent for hours on end, with her mouth firmly closed, concealing her large, new-cut incisors that bite into the moist heart of a fruit like little saw-edged blades. She is silent, and she—why not write down the word that frightens me—she is thinking.

A new evil? A torment that I had not foreseen? Sitting in a grassy dell, or half buried in hot sand and gazing out to sea, she is thinking, as well I know. She thinks rapidly when she is listening, with a well-bred pretense of discretion, to remarks imprudently exchanged above her head. But it would seem that with this needleplay she has discovered the perfect means of adventuring, stitch by stitch, point by point, along a road of risks and temptations. Silence . . . the hand armed with the steel dart moves back and forth. Nothing will stop the unchecked little explorer. At what moment must I utter the "Halt!" that will brutally arrest her in full flight? Oh, for those young embroiderers of bygone days, sitting on a hard little stool in the shelter of their mother's ample skirts! Maternal authority kept them there for years and years, never rising except to change the skein of silk, or to elope with a stranger. Think of Philomène de Watteville and her canvas, on which she embroidered the loss and the despair of Albert Savarus . . .

"What are you thinking about, Bel-Gazou?"

"Nothing, Mother. I'm counting my stitches."

Silence. The needle pierces the material. A coarse trail of chain stitch follows very unevenly in its wake. Silence . . .

"Mother?"

"Darling?"

"Is it only when people are married that a man can put his arm around a lady's waist?"

"Yes ... No ... It depends. If they are very good friends and have known each other a long time, you understand ... As I said before: it depends. Why do you want to know?"

"For no particular reason, Mother."

Two stitches, ten misshapen chain stitches.

"Mother? Is Madame X married?"

"She has been. She is divorced."

"I see. And Monsieur F., is he married?"

"Why, of course he is; you know that."

"Oh! Yes ... Then it's all right if one of the two is married?"

"What is all right?"

"To depend."

"One doesn't say: 'to depend.'"

"But you said just now that it depended."

"But what has it got to do with you? Is it any concern of yours?"

"No, Mother."

I let it drop. I feel inadequate, self-conscious, displeased with myself. I should have answered differently and I could not think what to say.

Bel-Gazou also drops the subject; she sews. But she pays little attention to her sewing, overlaying it with pictures, associations of names and people, all the results of patient observation. A little later will come other curiosities, other questions, and especially other silences. Would to God that Bel-Gazou were the bewildered and simple child who questions crudely, open-eyed! But she is too near the truth, and too natural not to know, as a birthright, that all nature hesitates before that most majestic and most disturbing of instincts, and that it is wise to tremble, to be silent, and to lie when one draws near to it.

[*Translated by Una Vicenzo Troubridge and Enid McLeod*]

The Watchman

Sunday. This morning the children have an odd look on their faces. I've seen them look like this before, when they were organizing some theatrical production in the attic, with costumes, masks, shrouds, and dragging chains, that was their play, *Le Revenant de la commanderie*— a ghostly lucubration that cost them a week of fever, night frights, and furry tongues, so excited did they get with their own phantoms. But that is an old story. Bertrand is now eighteen and plans, as is suitable at his age, to reform the finances of Europe; Renaud, now over fourteen, has no other interest but to take apart and put together again motorcar engines; and Bel-Gazou, this year, asks me questions of desolating triteness: "When we go back to Paris, can I wear stockings? In Paris, can I have a hat? In Paris, will you curl my hair on Sundays?"

No matter, I find all three of them acting strange and disposed to go off in corners and talk in low voices.

Monday. The children don't look at all well this morning, and so I question them.

"What's wrong with you youngsters?"

"Nothing at all, Tante Colette!" exclaim my stepsons.

"Nothing at all, Mamma!" exclaims Bel-Gazou.

A fine chorus—and certainly a well-organized fib. The thing is becoming serious, all the more so since I overheard the two boys, at dusk, behind the tennis court, engaged in this bit of dialogue:

"I tell you, old man, it didn't stop from midnight to three in the morning."

"Who are you telling that to, for goodness' sake! I didn't shut an eye, it kept it up from midnight to four this morning. It went *poom* . . .

poom . . . poom! Like that, slowly, as if with bare feet, but heavy, heavy . . ."

They glimpsed me and rushed down upon me like two male falcons, with laughter, with white and red balls, with a studied and noisy thoughtlessness. I will learn nothing today.

Wednesday. When last night toward eleven o'clock I went through Bel-Gazou's bedroom to reach mine, she was not yet asleep. She was lying on her back, her arms at her side, and her dark eyes beneath the fringe of her hair were moving. A warm August moon, crescent, softly swayed the shadow of the magnolia on the parquet floor and the white bed gave off a bluish light.

"You're not asleep?"

"No, Mamma."

"What are you thinking about, all alone like this?"

"I'm listening."

"For goodness' sake, to what?"

"Nothing, Mamma."

At that very second I heard, distinctly, the sound of a heavy footstep, and not shod, on the upper floor. The upper floor is a long attic where no one sleeps, where no one, after nightfall, has occasion to go, and which leads to the top of the most ancient tower. My daughter's hand, which I squeezed, contracted in mine.

Two mice passed in the wall, playing and emitting birdlike cries.

"Are you afraid of mice now?"

"No, Mamma."

Above us, the footsteps sounded again, and in spite of myself I put the question "Why, who can be walking up there?"

Bel-Gazou did not reply, and this stubborn silence was unpleasant.

"So you hear something?"

"Yes, Mamma."

"'Yes, Mamma!' Is that all you can think of to say?"

The child suddenly burst into tears and sat up in bed.

"It's not my fault, Mamma. *He* walks like that every night."

"Who?"

"The footsteps."

"The footsteps of whom?"

"Of no one."

"Heavens, how stupid children are! Here you are again, making a fuss over nothing, you and your brothers! Is this the nonsense you hide in corners to discuss? Well now, I'm going upstairs. Yes, I'm going to let you hear some footsteps overhead!"

On the topmost landing, clusters of flies clinging to the beams whirred like a fire in the chimney as I passed with my lamp, which a gust of air put out the minute I opened the garret door. But there was no need of a lamp in these garret regions with their tall dormer windows where the moonlight entered by milky sheets spread out on the floor. The midnight countryside shimmered as far as the eye could see, the hills embossed with silver, the shallow valleys ashy-mauve, watered in the lowest of the meadows by a river of glittering fog which screened the moonlight . . . A little sparrow owl imitated the cat in a tree, and the cat replied to him. But nothing was walking in the garret beneath the forest of crisscrossed beams. I waited a long while, breathing in the fleeting nocturnal coolness, the odor of a granary which always hovers in a garret, then went downstairs again. Bel-Gazou, worn out, was sleeping.

Saturday. I have been listening every night since Wednesday. Someone does walk up there, sometimes at midnight, sometimes toward three o'clock. Tonight I climbed up and down the stairs four times. To no purpose. At lunchtime I forced the youngsters to speak out. Anyway, they have reached the limit with their hocus-pocus.

"Children, you must help me clear up a mystery. We're bound to be enormously amused—even Bertrand, who has lost all his illusions. Just imagine! I've been hearing, every night, someone walking above Bel-Gazou's room . . ."

They exploded, all at once.

"I know, I know!" Renaud exclaims. "It's the commander in armor, who came back to earth once before, in Grandfather's time. Page told me all about it and . . ."

"What a farce!" said Bertrand laconically. "The truth is that isolated and collective instances of hallucination have occurred here, ever since the Holy Virgin, in a blue sash and drawn by four white horses, suddenly appeared in front of Guitras and told him . . ."

"She didn't *tell* him anything!" squealed Bel-Gazou. "She *wrote* to him!"

"And sent the letter by the post?" sneered Renaud. "That's childish!"

"And your commander isn't childish?" said Bertrand.

"Excuse me!" retorted Renaud, flushing red. "The commander is a family tradition. Your Virgin, that's a piece of village folklore, the kind you hear everywhere . . ."

"Now, now, children, have you finished? Can I put in a word? I know just one thing and it's this: in the garret there are sounds, unexplainable, of footsteps. I'm going to stand watch tomorrow night. Beast or man, we'll find out who is walking. And those who want to stand watch with me . . . Good. Adopted by a count of hands!"

Sunday. Sleepless night. Full moon. Nothing to report except the sound of footsteps heard behind the half-open door to the garret, but interrupted by Renaud, who, trigged out in a Henri II breastplate and a red bandanna, dashed forward romantically shouting, "Stand back! Stand back!" We hoot at him and accuse him of having "spoiled everything."

"Strange," Bertrand remarks with crushing and reflective irony, "strange how anything fantastic can excite the mind of a boy, even though he grew up in British schools . . ."

"Eh, my lad," adds my girl in an unmistakably Limousin accent, "you must not say, 'Stand back!' You must say, 'I'm going to give you a wallop!' "

Tuesday. Last night the two boys and I stood watch, leaving Bel-Gazou asleep.

The moon at the full whitened from one end to the other a long track of light where the rats had left a few ears of nibbled maize. We kept ourselves in the darkness behind the half-open door and suffered boredom for a good half hour, watching the path of moonlight shift, become oblique, lick the lower part of the crisscrossed beams . . . Renaud touched my arm: someone was walking at the far end of the garret. A rat scampered off and climbed along a slanting beam, followed by its serpent tail. The footsteps, solemn-sounding, approached, and I tightened my arms around the necks of the two boys.

It approached, with a slow, muffled, yet incisive tread, which was echoed by the ancient floorboards. It entered, after a moment that seemed interminable, into the luminous path of moonlight. It was almost white, gigantic: the biggest nocturnal bird I have ever seen, a great horned owl, the kind we call "grand duke," taller than a wolf-hound. He walked emphatically, lifting his feathered feet, his hard bird's talons, which gave off the sound of a human footstep. The top of his wings gave him the shoulders of a man, and two little feather horns that he raised or lowered trembled like grass in the gust of air from the dormer window. He stopped, puffed out his chest, and all the feathers of his magnificent face swelled out around a fine beak and the two golden pools of his eyes, bathed in moonlight. He turned away from us, showing his speckled white and pale yellow back. He must be quite old, I thought, this solitary and powerful creature. He resumed his parade march and interrupted it to do a kind of war dance, shaking his head from right to left, making fierce right-about turns, which no doubt threatened the rat that had eluded him. For a moment he apparently thought he had his prey, and he jostled the skeleton of a chair, shaking it as if it were a dead twig. He jumped with fury, fell back again, scraped the floor with his fanned-out tail. He had the mien of one used to command, and the majesty of a sorcerer.

No doubt he sensed our presence, for he turned toward us as if outraged. Unhurriedly he went to the window, half opened his angel wings, let out a kind of cooing sound, very low, a short incantation, pressed against the air, and melted into the night, taking on its color of snow and silver.

Thursday. The younger of the boys, at his desk, writes a long travel story. Title: "My Experiences Hunting the Horned Owl in Eastern Africa." The older boy has left on my worktable the beginning of "Stanzas":

> *A fluttering, a ponderous vision in the night,*
> *Gray apparition, coming from the dark into the light.*

Things have returned to normal.

[*Translated by Herma Briffault*]

The Hollow Nut

Three shells like flower petals, white, nacreous, and transparent as the rosy snow that flutters down from the apple trees; two limpets, like Tonkinese hats with converging black rays on a yellow ground; something that looks like a lumpy, cartilaginous potato, inanimate but concealing a mysterious force that squirts, when it is squeezed, a crystal jet of salt water; a broken knife, a stump of pencil, a ring of blue beads, and a book of transfers soaked by the sea; a small pink handkerchief, very dirty . . . That is all. Bel-Gazou has completed the inventory of her left-hand pocket. She admires the mother-of-pearl petals, then drops them and crushes them under her espadrille. The hydraulic potato, the limpets, and the transfers earn no better fate. Bel-Gazou retains only the knife, the pencil, and the string of beads, all of which, like the handkerchief, are in constant use.

Her right-hand pocket contains fragments of that pinkish limestone that her parents, heaven knows why, name lithothamnion, when it is so simple to call it coral. "But it isn't coral, Bel-Gazou." Not coral? What do they know about it, poor wretches? Fragments, then, of lithothamnion, and a hollow nut, with a hole bored in it by the emerging maggot. There isn't a single nut tree within three miles along the coast. The hollow nut, found on the beach, came there on the crest of a wave, from where? "From the other side of the world," affirms Bel-Gazou. "And it's very ancient, you know. You can see that by its rare wood. It's a rosewood nut, like Mother's little desk."

With the nut glued to her ear, she listens. "It sings. It says: 'Hu-u-u . . .'"

She listens, her mouth slightly open, her lifted eyebrows touching her fringe of straight hair. Standing thus motionless, and as though alienated by her preoccupation, she seems almost ageless. She stares at the familiar horizon of her holidays without seeing it. From the ruins of a thatched hut, deserted by the customs officer, Bel-Gazou's view embraces, on her right hand the Pointe-du-Nez, yellow with lichens, streaked with the bluish purple of a belt of mussels which the low tide leaves exposed; in the center a wedge of sea, blue as new steel, thrust like an ax head into the coast. On the left, an untidy privet hedge in full bloom, whose oversweet almond scent fills the air, while the frenzied little feet of the bees destroy its flowers. The dry sea meadow runs up as far as the hut and its slope hides the shore where her parents and friends lie limply baking on the sand. Presently, the entire family will inquire of Bel-Gazou: "But where were you? Why didn't you come down to the shore?" Bel-Gazou cannot understand this bay mania. Why the shore, always the shore, and nothing but the shore? The hut is just as interesting as that insipid sand, and there is the damp spinney, and the soapy water of the washhouse, and the field of lucerne as well as the shade of the fig tree. Grown-up people are so constituted that one might spend a lifetime explaining to them—and all to no purpose. So it is with the hollow nut: "What's the use of that old nut?" Wiser far to hold one's tongue, and to hide, sometimes in a pocket, and sometimes in an empty vase or knotted in a handkerchief, the nut that a moment, impossible to foresee, will divest of all its virtue, but which meanwhile sings in Bel-Gazou's ear the song that holds her motionless as though she had taken root.

"I can see it! I can see the song! It's as thin as a hair, as thin as a blade of grass!"

Next year, Bel-Gazou will be past nine years old. She will have ceased to proclaim those inspired truths that confound her pedagogues. Each day carries her farther from that first stage of her life, so full, so wise, so perpetually mistrustful, so loftily disdainful of experience, of good advice, and humdrum wisdom. Next year, she will come back to the sands that gild her, to the salt butter and the foaming cider. She will find again her dilapidated hut, and her citified feet will once more acquire their natural horny soles, slowly toughened on the flints and ridges of the rough ground. But she may well fail to find again her childish subtlety and the keenness of her senses that can taste a scent, feel a color, and see—"thin as a hair, thin as a blade of grass"—the cadence of an imaginary song.

[*Translated by Una Vicenzo Troubridge and Enid McLeod*]

The Patriarch

Between the ages of sixteen and twenty-five, Achille, my half-brother by blood—but wholly and entirely my brother by affection, choice, and likeness—was extremely handsome. Little by little, he became less so as a result of leading the hard life of a country doctor in the old days; a life which lacked all comfort and repose. He wore out his boot soles as much as the shoes of his gray mare; he went out by day and he went out by night, going to bed too tired to want any supper. In the night he would be woken up by the call of a peasant banging his fists on the outer door and pulling the bell. Then he would get up, put on his woolen pants, and his great plaid-lined overcoat, and Charles, the man-of-all-work, would harness the gray mare, another remarkable creature.

I have never known anything so proud and so willing as that gray mare. In the stable, by the light of the lantern, my brother would always find her standing up and ready for the worst. Her short, lively, well-set ears would inquire: "Châteauvieux? Montrenard? The big climb up the hill? Seventeen kilometers to get there and as many on the way back?" She would set off a little stiffly, her head lowered. During the examination, the confinement, the amputation, or dressing, she leaned her little forehead against the farmhouse doors so as to hear better what *He* was saying. I could swear that she knew by heart the bits of *Le Roi d'Ys* and the Pastoral Symphony, the scraps of operas and the Schubert songs *He* sang to keep himself company.

Isolated, sacrificed to his profession, this twenty-six-year-old doctor of half a century ago had only one resource. Gradually he had to forge himself a spirit which hoped for nothing except to live and enable his family to live too. Happily, his professional curiosity never left him. Neither did that other curiosity which both of us inherited from our mother. When, in my teens, I used to accompany him on his rounds, the two of us would often stop and get out to pick a bunch of bluebells or to gather mushrooms. Sometimes we would watch a wheeling buzzard or upset the dignity of a little lizard by touching it with a finger: the lizard would draw up its neck like an offended lady and give a lisping hiss, rather like a child who has lost its first front teeth. We would carefully detach butterfly chrysalises from branches and holes in walls and put them in little boxes of fine sand to await the miracle of the metamorphosis.

The profession of country doctor demanded a great deal of a man about half a century ago. Fresh from medical school in Paris, my brother confronted his first patient: a well-sinker who had just had one leg blown off by an explosion of dynamite. The brand-new surgeon came out of this difficult ordeal with honor but white-lipped, trembling all over, and considerably thinner from the amount he had sweated. He pulled himself together by diving into the canal between the tall clumps of flowering rushes.

Achille taught me to fill and to stick together the two halves of antipyrine capsules, to use the delicate scales with the weights which were mere thin slips of copper. In those days, the country doctor had a license to sell certain pharmaceutical products outside a four-kilometer radius of the town. Meager profits, if one considers that a "consultation" cost the consultant three francs plus twenty sous a kilometer. From time to time, the doctor pulled out a tooth, also for three francs. And what little money there was came in slowly and sometimes not at all.

"Why not sue them?" demanded the chemist. "What's the law for?"

Whatever it was for, it was not for his patients. My brother made no reply but turned his greenish-blue eyes away toward the flat horizon. My eyes are the same color but not so beautiful and not so deeply set.

I was fifteen or sixteen; the age of great devotions, of vocations. I wanted to become a woman doctor. My brother would summon me for a split lip or a deep, bleeding cut and have recourse to my slender girl's fingers. Eagerly, I would set to work to knot the threads of the stitches in the blood which leaped so impetuously out of the vein. In the morning, Achille set off too early for me to be able to accompany him. But in the afternoon I would sit on his left in the trap and hold the mare's reins. Every month he had the duty of inspecting all the babies in the region and he tried to drop in unexpectedly on their wet or dry nurses. Those expeditions used to ruin his appetite. How many babies we found alone in an empty house, tied to their fetid cradles with handkerchiefs and safety pins, while their heedless guardians worked in the fields. Some of them would see the trap in the distance and come running up, out of breath.

"I was only away for a moment." "I was changing the goat's picket." "I was chasing the cow who'd broken loose."

Hard as his life was, Achille held out for more than twenty-five years, seeking rest for his spirit only in music. In his youth he was surprised when he first came up against the peaceful immorality of country life, the desire which is born and satisfied in the depths of the ripe grass or between the warm flanks of sleeping cattle. Paris and the Latin Quarter had not prepared him for so much amorous knowledge, secrecy, and variety. But impudence was not lacking either, at least in the case of the girls who came boldly to his weekly surgery declaring that they had not "seen" since they got their feet wet two months ago, pulling a drowned hen out of a pond.

"That's fine!" my brother would say, after his examination. "I'm going to give you a prescription."

He watched for the look of pleasure and contempt and the joyful reddening of the cheek and wrote out the prescription agreed between doctor and chemist: "*Mica panis*, two pills to be taken after each meal." The remedy might avert or, at least, delay the intervention of "the woman who knew about herbs."

One day, long before his marriage, he had an adventure which was only one of many. With a basket on one arm and an umbrella on the other, a young woman almost as tall as himself (he was nearly six foot two) walked into his consulting room. He found himself looking at someone like a living statue of the young Republic; a fresh, magnificently built girl with a low brow, statuesque features, and a calm, severe expression.

"Doctor," she said, without a smile or a shuffle, "I think I'm three months pregnant."

"Do you feel ill, Madame?"

"Mademoiselle. I'm eighteen. And I feel perfectly all right in every way."

"Well, then, Mademoiselle! You won't be needing me for another six months."

"Pardon, Doctor. I'd like to be sure. I don't want to do anything foolish. Will you please examine me?"

Throwing off the skirt, the shawl, and the cotton chemise that came down to her ankles, she displayed a body so majestic, so firm, so smoothly sheathed in its skin that my brother never saw another to compare with it. He saw too that this young girl, so eager to accuse herself, was a virgin. But she vehemently refused to remain one any longer and went off victorious, her head high, her basket on her arm, and her woolen shawl knotted once more over her breasts. The most she would admit was that, when she was digging potatoes on her father's land over by the Hardon road, she had waited often and often to see the gray mare and its driver go past and had said "Good day" with her hand to call him, but in vain.

She returned for "consultation." But far more often, my brother went and joined her in her field. She would watch him coming from afar, put down her hoe, and stooping, make her way under the branches of a little plantation of pine trees. From these almost silent encounters, a very beautiful child was born. And I admit that I should be glad to see, even now, what his face is like. For Sido confided to me, in very few words, one of those secrets in which she was so rich.

"You know the child of that beautiful girl over at Hardon?" she said.

"Yes."

"She boasts about him to everyone. She's crazy with pride. She's a most unusual girl. A character. I've seen the child. Just once."

"What's he like?"

She made the gesture of rumpling a child's hair.

"Beautiful, of course. Such curls, such eyes. And such a mouth."

She coughed and pushed away the invisible curly head with both hands.

"The mouth most of all. Ah! I just couldn't. I went away. Otherwise I should have taken him."

However, everything in our neighborhood was not so simple as this warm idyll, cradled on its bed of pine needles, and these silent lovers who took no notice of the autumn mists or a little rain, for the gray mare lent them her blanket.

There is another episode of which I have a vivid and less touching memory. We used to refer to it as "The Monsieur Binard Story." It goes without saying that I have changed the name of the robust, grizzled father of a family who came over on his bicycle at dusk, some forty-eight years ago, to ask my brother to go to his daughter's bedside.

"It's urgent," said the man, panting as he spoke. His breath reeked of red wine. "I am Monsieur Binard, of X."

He made a sham exit, then thrust his head around the half-shut door and declared: "In my opinion, it'll be a boy."

My brother took his instrument case and the servant harnessed the gray mare.

It turned out indeed to be a boy and a remarkably fine and well-made one. But my brother's care and attention were mainly for the far too young mother, a dark girl with eyes like an antelope. She was very brave and kept crying loudly, almost excitedly, like a child. Around the bed bustled three slightly older antelopes, while in the inglenook, the impassive Monsieur Binard superintended the mulling of some red wine flavored with cinnamon. In a dark corner of the clean, well-polished room, my brother noticed a wicker cradle with clean starched curtains. Monsieur Binard only left the fire and the copper basin to examine the newborn child as soon as it had been washed.

"It's a very fine child," Achille assured him.

"I've seen finer," said Monsieur Binard in a lordly way.

"Oh, Papa!" cried the three older antelopes.

"I know what I'm talking about," retorted Binard.

He raised a curtain of the cradle which my brother presumed empty but which was now shown to be entirely filled by a large child who had slept calmly through all the noise and bustle. One of the antelopes came over and tenderly drew the curtain down again.

His mission over, my brother drank the warm wine which he had well and truly earned and which the little newly confined mother was sipping too. Already she was gay and laughing. Then he bowed to the entire long-eyed troop and went out, puzzled and worried. The earth was steaming with damp, but above the low fog, the bright dancing fire of the first stars announced the coming frost.

"Your daughter seems extremely young," said my brother. "Luckily, she's come through it well."

"She's strong. You needn't be afraid," said Monsieur Binard.

"How old is she?"

"Fifteen in four months' time."

"Fifteen! She was taking a big risk. What girls are! Do you know the . . . the creature who . . ."

Monsieur Binard made no reply other than slapping the hindquarters of the gray mare with the flat of his hand, but he lifted his chin with such an obvious, such an intolerable expression of fatuity that my brother hastened his departure.

"If she has any fever, let me know."

"She won't," Monsieur Binard assured him with great dignity.

"So you know more about these things than I do?"

"No. But I know my daughters. I've four of them and you must have seen for yourself that there's not much wrong with them. I know them."

He said no more and ran his hand over his mustache. He waited till the gray mare had adroit' ·rned in the narrow courtyard, then he went back into his house.

Sido, my mother, did not like this story, which she often turned over in her mind. Sometimes she spoke violently about Monsieur Binard, calling him bitterly "the corrupt widower," sometimes she let herself go off into commentaries for which afterward she would blush.

"Their house is very well kept. The child of the youngest one has eyelashes as long as *that*. I saw her the other day, she was suckling her baby on the doorstep, it was enchanting. Whatever am I saying? It was abominable, of course, when one knows the facts."

She went off into a dream, impatiently untwisting the entangled steel chain and black cord from which hung her two pairs of spectacles.

"After all," she began again, "the ancient patriarchs . . ."

But she suddenly became aware that I was only fifteen and a half and she went no further.

[*Translated by Antonia White*]

The Sick Child

The child who was going to die wanted to hoist himself a little higher against his big pillow but he could not manage it. His mother heard his mute appeal and helped him. Once again the child promised to death had his mother's face very close to his own, the face he thought he would never look at again, with its light brown hair drawn back from the temples like an old-fashioned little girl's, the long, rather thin cheeks with hardly a trace of powder, the very wide-open brown eyes, so sure of controlling their anxiety that they often forgot to keep guard over themselves.

"You're rosy tonight, my little boy," she said gaily.

But her brown eyes remained fixed in a steady, frightened look that the little boy knew well.

So as not to have to raise his feeble head, the little boy slid his pupils, with their big sea-green irises, into the corners of his lids and corrected her gravely: "I'm rosy because of the lampshade."

Madame Mamma looked at her son sorrowfully, inwardly reproaching him for wiping out, with one word, that pink color she saw on his cheeks. He had shut his eyes again and the appearance of being asleep gave him back the face of a child of ten.

"She thinks I'm asleep." His mother turned away from the white-faced little boy, very gently, as if afraid he might feel the thread of her gaze break off. "He thinks I think he's asleep." Sometimes they played at deceiving each other like this. "She thinks I'm not in pain," Jean would think, though the pain would be making his lashes flicker on his cheekbones. Nevertheless, Madame Mamma would be thinking, "How well he can imitate a child who's not in pain! Any other mother would be taken in. But not me . . ."

"Do you like this smell of lavender I've sprayed about? Your room smells nice."

The child acquiesced without speaking; the habit and the necessity of preserving his strength had ended in his acquiring a repertoire of very tiny signs, a delicate and complicated mime like the language of animals. He excelled in making a magic and paradoxical use of his senses.

For him, the white muslin curtains gave out a pink sound when the sun struck them about ten in the morning and the scratched pale calf binding of an ancient *Journey on the Banks of the Amazon* smelled, to his mind, of hot pancakes. The desire to drink was expressed by three "claps" of the eyelids. To eat, oh, as to wanting to eat, he didn't think about that. The other needs of the small, limp, defeated body had their silent and modest telegraph code. But everything that, in the existence of a child under sentence of death, could still be called the capacity for pleasure and amusement retained a passionate interest in human speech. This faculty searched out exact and varied words to be employed by a musical voice, ripened, as it were, by the long illness and hardly shriller than a woman's. Jean had chosen the words employed in checkers, in "solitaire," with its glitter of glass marbles, in "nine holes," in a dozen other old-fashioned games that made use of ivory and lemonwood and were played on inlaid boards. Other words, mostly secret, applied to the Swiss patience pack, fifty-two little glazed cards, edged and picked out with gold like drawing-room paneling. The queens wore shepherdess hats, straw ones with a rose under the brim, and the shepherd-knaves carried crooks. On account of the bearded kings with rubicund faces and the small, hard eyes of mountain smallholders, Jean had invented a patience that excluded the four boorish monarchs.

"No," he thought, "my room doesn't really smell nice. It isn't the same lavender. It seems to me that, in the old days, when I was able to walk about . . . But I may have forgotten."

He mounted a cloud of fragrance that was passing within reach of his small, pinched, white nostrils and rode swiftly away. His life of being confined to bed provided him with all the pleasures of illness, including the spice of filial malice of which no child can bear to deprive himself, so he gave no hint of his secret delights.

Astride the scented cloud, he wandered through the air of the room; then he got bored and escaped through the frosted-glass fanlight and went along the passage, followed in his flight by a big silver clothes moth who sneezed in the trail of lavender behind him. To outdistance it, he pressed his knees into the sides of the cloud of fragrance, riding with an ease and vigor that his long, inert, half-paralyzed legs refused to display in the presence of human beings. When he escaped from his passive life, he knew how to ride, how to pass through walls; best of all, he knew how to fly. With his body inclined like a diver's plunging down through the waves, his forehead passed with careless ease through an element whose currents and resistances he understood. With his arms outstretched, he had only to slant one or the other of his shoulders to change the direction of his flight, and by a jerk of his loins, he could avoid the shock of landing. In any case, he rarely did land. Once he had rashly let himself come down too near the ground, over a meadow where cows were feeding.

So close to the ground that he had seen, right opposite his own face, the beautiful, astonished face of a cream-colored cow with crescent-shaped horns and eyes that mirrored the flying child like two magnifying glasses, while the dandelion flowers came up out of the grass to meet him, growing bigger and bigger, like little suns. He had only just had time to catch tight hold of the tall horns with both hands and thrust himself backward up into the air again; he could still remember the warmth of the smooth horns and their blunted, as it were friendly, points. The barking of a dew-drenched sheep dog who ran up to pro-tect his cow gradually faded away as the flying child soared up again into his familiar sky. Jean remembered very clearly that he had had to exert all the strength of his arm-wings that morning to make his way back through a periwinkle-colored dawn, glide over a sleeping town, and fall on his enameled iron bed, the contact of which had hurt him very much indeed. He had felt an agonizing pain burning his loins and tearing his thighs with red-hot pincers, a pain so bad that he had not been able to hide two pearly traces of tears from Madame Mamma's sharp-eyed tenderness.

"Has my little boy been crying?"

"In a dream, Madame Mamma, only in a dream . . ."

The cloud of pleasant scent suddenly reached the end of the pas-sage and butted its nose against the door leading to the kitchen.

"Whoa back! Whoa back! What a brute! Ah, these lavender half-breeds, with wild-thyme blood! They'd smash your face for you if you didn't hold them. Is *that* how you go through a kitchen door?"

He gripped the repentant cloud hard between his knees and guided it into the upper region of the kitchen, into the warmed air that was drying the washing near the ceiling. As he lowered his head to pass between two pieces of linen, Jean deftly broke off an apron string and slipped it into the cloud's mouth by way of a bit. A mouth is not always a mouth, but a bit is always a bit, and it matters little what it bridles.

"Where shall we go? We'll have to get back in time for dinner and it's late already. We must go faster, Lavender, faster . . ."

Having gone through the service door, he decided, for fun, to go down the staircase headfirst, then righted himself by a few slides on his back. The lavender cloud, frightened by what was being asked of it, jibbed a little. "Oh, you great goof of a mountain filly!" said the child, and this boy, who never laughed at all in his cloistered life, burst out laughing. As he rode wildly down, he grabbed hold, in passing, of the tangled hair of one of the house dogs, the one they told him was so clever he could go down the steps and out onto the pavement, "do his business all by himself," then return to his parents' house and scratch at the front door. Startled by Jean's hand he yelped and flattened himself against the banisters.

"Coming with us, Riki? I'll take you up behind me!"

With a small, powerful hand he caught up the dog and flung him onto the misty, ballooning rump of the lavender mare, who, spurred by two bare heels, galloped down the last two flights. But there the dog, panic-stricken, jumped down from the eiderdown pillion and fled upstairs to his basket, howling.

"You don't know what you're missing!" Jean shouted to him. "I was frightened too, at first, but now . . . Watch, Riki!"

Rider and mount hurled themselves against the heavy street door. To Jean's amazement, they encountered, not the malleable obstacle of yielding oak and melting ironwork and big bolts that said "Yes, yes" as they slid softly back, but the inflexible barrier of a firmly chiseled voice that was whispering: "See, he's fast asleep."

Numbed by the shock, anguished from head to foot, Jean was aware of the cruel harshness of the two words "See he's, Seehees, Seeheeze." They were sharper than a knife blade. Beside them lay three severed syllables, "fa-sta-sleep."

"Fa . . . sta . . . sleep," repeated Jean. "That's the end of the ride, here comes Fa . . . sta . . . sleep, curled up in a ball! Goodbye. Goodbye . . ."

He had no leisure to wonder to whom he was saying goodbye. Time was running out horribly fast. He dreaded the landing. The foundered cloud missed its footing with all the four legs it never had; before it dispersed in tiny cold drops, it threw its rider, with a heave of its nonexistent hindquarters, into the valley of the japanned bedstead, and once again, Jean groaned at the brutal contact.

"You were sleeping so well," said the voice of Madame Mamma.

A voice, thought her little boy, that was all a tangle of straight lines and curved lines—a curved one, a straight one—a dry line—a wet line. But never would he try to explain that to Madame Mamma.

"You woke up moaning, darling, were you in pain?"

He made a sign that he was not, waving his thin, white, well-groomed forefinger from right to left. Besides, the pain was calming down. Falling onto this rather harsh little bed, after all he was pretty used to it. And what could you expect of a big puffy cloud and its scented bumpkin's manners?

"The next time," thought Jean, "I'll ride the Big Skating Rink." In the hours when he lay with closed lids and they put a screen between the bright bulb and the lampshade, that was the name of the immmmmmmense nickel-plated paper knife, so big that, instead of two *m*'s, it needed three or often six in its qualifying adjective.

"Madame Mamma, would you bring the Big Skat . . . I mean the big paper knife, a little farther forward under the lampshade? Thanks awfully."

To prepare his next ride at leisure, Jean turned his head on the pillow. They had cut his fair hair very short at the back, to stop it from matting. The top of his head, his temples, and his ears were covered with curls of pale, faintly greenish gold, the gold of a winter moon, that harmonized well with his sea-green eyes and his face white as a petal.

"How exquisite he is!" murmured Madame Mamma's female friends. "He looks quite astonishingly like L'Aiglon." Whereupon Madame Mamma would smile with disdain, knowing well that the Duc de Reichstadt, slightly thick-lipped like his mother, the Empress, would have envied the firm, cupid's-bow mouth with its fine-drawn corners that was one of Jean's beauties. She would say haughtily: "Possibly there is something . . . yes, in the forehead. But, heaven be praised, *Jean* isn't tubercular!"

When, with a practiced hand, she had brought the lamp and big paper knife closer together, Jean saw what he was waiting to see on the long chromium blade, a pink reflection like snow at dawn, flecked here and there with blue, a glittering landscape that tasted of peppermint. Then he laid his left temple on the firm pillow, listened to the music of water drops and fountains played by the strands of white horsehair inside the cushion under the pressure of his head, and half closed his eyes.

"But, my little boy, it's almost your dinnertime . . ." said Madame Mamma hesitantly.

The sick child smiled indulgently at his mother. You have to forgive well people everything. Besides, he was still faintly concussed from his fall. "I've got plenty of time," he thought, and he accentuated his smile, at the risk of seeing Madame Mamma—as she did, faced with certain smiles, too perfect, too full of a serenity that, for her, could only have one meaning—lose countenance and rush out of the room, knocking herself against the doorpost.

"If you don't mind, darling, I'll have my dinner very quickly all by myself in the dining room, while you're having yours on your tray."

"Why, of course, of course," answered the white, graciously condescending small forefinger, crooking itself twice.

"We know, we know," also observed the two lash-bordered eyelids, blinking twice. "We know what an oversensitive lady Mamma is, and how a pair of tears suddenly comes into her eyes, like a pair of precious stones. There are lots of precious stones for ears . . . Eye rings, Madame Mamma has eye rings when she thinks about me. Won't she ever get used to me, then? How illogical she is."

As Madame Mamma was bending over him, he raised his unfettered arms and gave her a ritual hug. His mother's neck raised itself proudly under the weight suspended on it, pulling up the child's thin, overall body; the slim torso followed by the long legs, inert now yet capable of gripping and controlling the flanks of a shadowy cloud.

For a moment, Madame Mamma contemplated her gracious invalid son, propped up against a hard pillow that sloped like a desk; then she exclaimed: "I'll be back very soon! Your tray will be here in a minute. Besides, I must go and hurry up Mandora, she's never on time!"

Once again, she went out of the room.

"She goes out, she comes in. Above all, she goes out. She doesn't want to leave me but she keeps going out of my room all the time. She's going off to dry her pair of tears. She's got a hundred reasons for going out of my room; if by any chance she hadn't got one, I could give a thousand. Mandora's never late."

Turning his head with precaution, he watched Mandora come in. Wasn't it right and inevitable that this full-bodied, golden, potbellied maid, with her musical, resonant voice and her shining eyes that were like the precious wood of a lute, should answer to the name of Mandora? "If it weren't for me," thought Jean, "she'd still be calling herself Angelina."

Mandora crossed the room and her brown-and-yellow-striped skirt, as it brushed against the furniture, gave out rich cello notes that only Jean could perceive. She placed the little short-legged table across the bed; on its embroidered linen cloth stood a steaming bowl.

"Here's this dinner of yours."

"What is it?"

"First course, phosphatine: there, you know that. After . . . you'll see for yourself."

The sick child received all over his half-recumbent body the comfort of a wide brown gaze, thirst-quenching and exhilarating. "How good it is, that brown ale of Mandora's eyes! How kind to me she is, too! How kind everyone is to me! If only they could restrain themselves a little . . ." Exhausted under the burden of universal kindness, he shut his eyes and opened them again at the clink of spoons. Medicine spoons, soup spoons, dessert spoons. Jean did not like spoons, with the exception of a queer silver spoon with a long twisted stem, finished off at one end with a little engine-turned disc. "It's a sugar crusher," Madame

Mamma would say. "And the other end of the spoon, Madame Mamma?" —"I'm not quite sure. I think it used to be an absinthe spoon." And nearly always, at that moment, her gaze would wander to a photograph of Jean's father, the husband she had lost so young, "Your dear Papa, my own Jean," and whom Jean coldly and silently designated by the secret words: "That man hanging up in the drawing room."

Apart from the absinthe spoon—absinthe, absinthe, absent, apse saint—Jean only liked forks, four-horned demons on which things were impaled, a bit of mutton cutlet, a tiny fish curled up in its fried bread crumbs, a round slice of apple and its two pip eyes, a crescent of apricot in its first quarter, frosted with sugar.

"Jean, darling, open your beak."

He obeyed, closing his eyes, and swallowed a medicine that was almost tasteless except for a passing, hypocritical sickliness that disguised something worse. In his secret vocabulary, Jean called this potion "dead man's gully." But nothing would have wrenched such appalling syllables out of him and flung them gasping at the feet of Madame Mamma.

The phosphatized soup followed inevitably; a badly swept hayloft, with its chinks stuffed with mildewed flour. But you forgave it all that because of something that floated impalpably over its clear liquid; a flowery breath, the dusty fragrance of the cornflowers Mandora bought in little bunches in the street for Jean, in July.

A little cube of grilled lamb went down quickly. "Run, lamb, run, I'm putting a good face on you, but go right down into my stomach in a ball, I couldn't chew you for anything in the world. Your flesh is still bleating and I don't want to know that you're pink in the middle!"

"It seems to me you're eating very fast tonight, aren't you, Jean?"

The voice of Madame Mamma dropped from the height of the dusk, perhaps from the molded plaster cornice, perhaps from the big cupboard. By a special gracious concession, Jean granted his mother permission to ascend into the alpine world at the top of the cupboard, the world of the household linen. She reached it by means of the stepladder, became invisible behind the left-hand door, and came down again loaded with great solid slabs of snow, hewn straight out of the heights. This harvest was the limit of her ambition. Jean went farther and higher; he thrust up, alone, toward the white peaks, slipping through an odd pair of sheets, reappearing in the well-rounded fold of an even pair. And what giddy slides between the stiff damask table napkins or on some alp of starched curtains, slippery as glaciers, and edged with Greek-key pattern, what nibbling of stalks of dried lavender, of their scattered flowers, of the fat and creamy orris roots.

It was from there he would descend again into his bed at dawn, stiff all over with cold, pale, weak, and impish. "Jean! Oh, goodness, he must have uncovered himself again in his sleep! Mandora, quick, a hot-water bottle!" Silently, Jean congratulated himself on having got back just in time, as usual. Then he would note, on an invisible page of the notebook hidden in the active, beating nook in his side he called his "heartpocket," all the vicissitudes of his ascent, the fall of the stars and the orange tintinnabulation of the dawn-touched peaks.

"I'm eating fast, Madame Mamma, because I'm hungry."

For he was an old hand at all kinds of deception and didn't he know that the words "I'm hungry" made Madame Mamma flush with pleasure?

"If that's true, darling, I'm sorry I only gave you stewed apples for your pudding. But I told Mandora to add some zest of lemon peel and a little stick of vanilla to make it taste nice."

Jean resolutely faced up to the stewed apples, an acid provincial girl aged about fifteen who, like other girls of the same age, had nothing but haughty disdain for the boy of ten. But didn't he feel the same toward her? Wasn't he armed against her? Wasn't he an agile cripple, leaning on the stick of vanilla? "It's always too short, *always*, that little stick," he murmured in his elusive way.

Mandora returned, and her billowing skirt with the broad stripes swelled up with as many ribs as a melon. As she walked she sounded—*tzrromm, tzrromm*—for Jean alone—the inner strings that were the very soul, the gorgeous music of Mandora.

"Finished your dinner already? If you eat so fast, you'll bring it up again. It's not your usual way."

Madame Mamma on one side, Mandora on the other, were standing close by his bed. "How tall they are! Madame Mamma doesn't take up much room in width in her little claret-colored dress. But Mandora, over and above her great sounding box, makes herself bigger with two curved handles, standing with her arms akimbo." Jean resolutely defied the stewed apples, spread them all over the plate, pressed them down again in festoons on the gilded rim, and once again, the question of dinner was settled.

The winter evening had long ago fallen. As he savored his half glass of mineral water, the thin, light furtive water that he thought was green because he drank it out of a pale green mug, Jean reckoned he still needed a little courage to conclude his invalid's day. There was still his nightly toilet, the inevitable, scrupulous details that demanded the aid of Madame Mamma and even—*tzrromm, tzrromm*—the gay, sonorous assistance of Mandora; still the toothbrush, the washcloths and sponge, the good soap and warm water, the combined precautions for not getting the sheets the least bit wet; still the tender maternal inquiries.

"My little boy, you can't sleep like that, you've got the binding of the big Gustave Doré digging right into your side, and that litter of little books with sharp corners all over your bed. Wouldn't you like me to bring the table nearer?"

"No, thanks, Madame Mamma, I'm quite all right as I am."

When his toilet was finished, Jean struggled against the intoxication of tiredness. But he knew the limit of his strength and did not try to escape from the rites that ushered in the night and the marvels it might capriciously bring forth. His only fear was that Madame Mamma's solicitude might prolong the duration of day longer than he could bear, might ruin a material edifice of books and furniture, a balance of light and shadows that Jean knew and revered. Building that edifice cost him his final efforts and ten o'clock was the extreme limit of his endurance.

"If she stays, if she insists, if she still wants to go on watching over me when the big hand slants to the right of the XII, I'm going to feel myself turning white, whiter, whiter still, and my eyes will sink in and I shan't even be able to keep answering the no-thank-you—quite-all-right-Madame-Mamma—good nights that are absolutely necessary to her and . . . and . . . it'll be awful, she'll sob."

He smiled at his mother and the majesty that illness confers on children it strikes down wakened in the fiery glint of his hair, descended over his eyelids, and settled bitterly on his lips. It was the hour when Madame Mamma would have liked to lose herself in contemplation of her mangled and exquisite work.

"Good night, Madame Mamma," said the child, very low.

"Are you tired? Do you want me to leave you?"

He made one more effort, opened wide his eyes, the color of the sea off Brittany, manifested with his whole face the desire to be fit and bonny, and bravely lowered his high shoulders.

"Do I look like a tired boy? Madame Mamma, I ask you now!"

She replied only with a roguish shake of her head, kissed her son, and went away, taking with her her choked-back cries of love, her strangled adjurations, her litanies that implored the disease to go away, to undo the fetters on the long, weak legs and the emaciated but not deformed loins, to set the impoverished blood running freely again through the green network of the veins.

"I've put two oranges on the plate. You don't want me to put out your lamp?"

"I'll put it out myself, Madame Mamma."

"Good heavens, where's my head? We haven't taken your temperature tonight!"

A fog interposed itself between Madame Mamma's garnet dress and her son. That night Jean was burning with fever but taking a thousand precautions to conceal it. A little fire was smoldering in the hollow of his palms, there was a drumming *woo-woo-woo* in his outer ear, and fragments of a hot crown clinging to his temples.

"We'll take it tomorrow without fail, Madame Mamma."

"The bell is just under your wrist. You're quite sure you wouldn't rather have the company of a night light, during the hours you're alone, you know, one of those pretty night . . ."

The last syllable of the word stumbled into a pit of darkness and Jean collapsed with it. "Yet it was only a very tiny pit," he rebuked himself as he fell. "I must have a big bump at the back of my neck. I must look like a zebu. But I zeed, yes I zaw kvite vell that Madame Mamma didn't zee, no, didn't see anything fall. She was much too absorbed in all the things she takes away every night gathered up in her skirt, her little prayers, the reports she's got to give the doctor, the way I hurt her so much by not wanting anyone near me at night. She carries all that away in the lap of her skirt and it spills over and rolls on the carpet, poor Madame Mamma. How can I make her understand that I'm not unhappy? Apparently a boy of my age can either live in bed or be pale and deprived of his legs or be in pain without being unhappy. Unhappy . . . I *was* unhappy when they still used to wheel me about in a chair. I was drenched with a shower of stares. I used to shrink so as to get a bit less of it. I was the target for a hail of 'How pretty he is!' and 'What a dreadful pity!' Now the only miseries I have are the visits of my cousin Charlie, with his scratched knees and his nailed shoes and that phrase 'boy scout,' half steel, half India-rubber, he overwhelms me with . . . And that pretty little girl who was born the same day as me, whom they sometimes call my foster-sister and sometimes my fiancée. She's studying dancing. She sees me lying in bed and then she stands on the tips of her toes and says: 'Look, I'm on my points.' But all that's only teasing. There comes a time at night when the teases go to sleep. This is the time when everything's all right."

He put out the lamp and peacefully watched his nocturnal companions, the choir of shapes and colors, rising up around him. He was waiting for the symphony to burst out, for the crowd Madame Mamma called solitude. He drew the pear-shaped bell, an invalid's toy of moonlight-colored enamel, from under his arm and laid it on the bedside table. "Now, light up!" he commanded.

It did not obey at once. The night outside was not so black that you could not make out the end of a leafless branch of a chestnut tree in the street swaying outside one of the panes and asking for help. Its swollen tip assumed the shape of a feeble rosebud. "Yes, you're trying to soften my heart by telling me you're next season's bud. Yet you know how ruthless I am to everything that talks to me about next year. Stay outside. Disappear. Vanish! As my cousin would say: skedaddle."

His fastidiousness about words reared up to its full height and poured one more dose of withering scorn on that cousin with his scratched, purple knees and his vocabulary plastered with expressions such as "And how!" "I put a wrench in the works," "I'm not having any," and "Golly!" Worst of all, Charlie was always saying, "Just think!" and, "I do understand!" as if those immensely learned crickets, thought and penetration, would not have fled in terror on all their delicate legs from a boy like that, shod in hobnails and dried mud.

At the mere sight of his cousin Charlie, Jean wiped his fingers on his handkerchief as if to rid them of some kind of coarse sand. For Madame Mamma and Mandora, interposed between the child and ugliness, between the child and scurrilous words, between the child and the baser sorts of reading, had made it possible for him to know and cherish only two forms of luxury: fastidiousness and pain. Protected and precocious, he had quickly mastered the hieroglyphs of print, dashing as wildly through books as he galloped astride clouds. He could compel the landscapes to rise up before him from the smooth page or assemble around him all the things that, for those likewise privileged, secretly people the air.

He had never used the silver fountain pen, engraved with his initials, since the day when his rapid, mature writing had startled and, as it were, offended the doctor with the cold hands. "Is that really the handwriting of a young child, Madame?" —"Oh, yes, Doctor, my son has very definitely formed handwriting." And Madame Mamma's anxious eyes had asked apologetically: "It's not dangerous, Doctor, is it?"

He also refrained from drawing, fearing all the things the eloquence of a sketch might give away. After having drawn the portrait of Mandora, with all her inner keyboard of resounding notes, the profile of an alabaster clock galloping full speed on its four supporting pillars, the dog Riki in the hands of the barber, with his hair done, like Jean's own, "à L'Aiglon," he had been terrified by the truth to life of his efforts and had wisely torn up his first works.

"Wouldn't you like a sketchbook, my young friend, and some colored chalk? It's an amusing game and just the thing for a boy of your age." At the suggestion, which he considered outside the province of medicine, Jean had only replied by a look between half-closed lashes, a serious, manly look that summed up the doctor who was giving him advice. "My nice barber wouldn't dream of making such a suggestion!" He could not forgive the doctor for having dared to ask him one day when his mother was out of the room: "And why the devil do you call your mother Madame?" The angry masculine glance and the weak, musical voice had answered with one accord: "I didn't think that was any business of the devil's."

The nice haircutter performed his mission very differently and told Jean all about his Sunday life. Every Sunday he went fishing around Paris. With a dazzling sweep of his scissors, he would demonstrate the gesture that flings the float and the bait far out, and Jean would shut his eyes under the chill of the water drops, splashing out in wheels when the fisherman triumphantly hauled up his loaded line . . .

"When you're well again, Monsieur Jean, I'll take you with me to the riverbank."

"Yes, yes," agreed Jean, his eyes closed.

"Why do they all want me to be well again? I *am* on the riverbank. What should I do with a chub-as-big-as-my-hand-here and a pickerel-as-long-as-your-paper-knife-there?"

"Nice barber, tell me some more . . ."

And he would listen to the story of the hawkmoths clinging under the arch of a little bridge, impromptu bait that had caught a "wagon-load" of trout with a hazel twig cut from the hedge and three bits of string knotted together.

To the cool, grating accompaniment of the twittering scissors, the story would begin.

"You go as far as a tiny little creek no-broader-than-my-thigh that widens out as it crosses a meadow. You see two-three willows together and a bit of brushwood: that's the place."

On the very first day Jean had transplanted other things around the two-three willows: the tall spikes of common agrimony extracted from the big botany album and pink-flowered hemp that attracts butterflies and tired children and sends them to sleep. The monstrous pollarded head of the oldest willow, crowned with white convolvulus, pulled faces only for Jean. The leap of a fish burst the glittering skin of the river, then another fish leaped . . . The nice hairdresser, busy with his bait, had heard them and turned around.

"Makin' game o' me, those two! But I'll get 'em."

"No, no," Jean protested. "It was me. I threw two little pebbles into the water."

The tree frog was singing, the imaginary afternoon was passing.

"Singing invisible on his water-lily raft," mused Jean. "Why tree frog? Why not lily frog?"

The shearer of golden fleece, the river, and the meadow faded away like a dream, leaving behind on Jean's forehead a sweet, commonplace scent and a wavy crest of fair hair. Jean, waking up, heard a whispering coming from the drawing room, a long low colloquy between Madame Mamma and the doctor from which one word escaped, crisp and lively, and made a beeline for Jean, the word "crisis." Sometimes it entered ceremoniously, like a lady dressed up to give away prizes with an *h* behind its ear and a *y* tucked into its bodice: Chrysis, Chrysis Wilby-Sallatry. "Truly? Truly?" said the urgent voice of Madame Mamma. "I said: perhaps . . ." replied the doctor's voice, an unsteady voice that halted on one foot. "A crisis, salutary but severe . . . Chrysis Salutari Sevea, a young Creole from tropical America, lissome in her flounced white cotton dress."

The child's subtle ear also gathered the name of another person which no doubt it was expedient to keep secret. A name he couldn't quite catch, something like Polly O'Miley or Olly O'Miall, and he finally decided it must refer to some little girl, also stricken with painful immobility and possessed of two long, useless legs, whom they never mentioned in front of him in case he should be jealous.

Complying with the order it had received, the tip of the chestnut branch and its message of coming spring had foundered in the sea of night. Although Jean had a second time requested it to do so, the pear-shaped bell had not yet lit up. Its dim opal flame was not shining on the bedside table that bore the mineral water, the orange juice, the big nickel paper knife with the alpine dawn in its hidden depths, the myopic watch with its domed glass, and the thermometer . . . Not one book lay on the table, waiting for Jean to choose it. Printed texts, whatever their size and shape, slept inside and ready open in the same bed as the invalid child. At the foot of the bed, a great tile of binding sometimes weighed heavily on his almost lifeless legs without his making any complaint.

He groped about him with his still-active arms and fished up some paperbound books, tattered and warm. An ancient volume thrust out its friendly horn from under the pillow. The paperbacks, heaped in a cushion, took their place against one of the little boy's thin lips, and the soft childish cheek pressed against the light calf binding that was a century old. Under his armpit, Jean verified the presence of a tough favorite comrade, a volume as hard and squat as a paving stone, a grumpy, robust fellow who found the bed too soft and usually went off to finish his night on the floor on the white goatskin rug.

Angular pasteboard shapes and the sockets and sinuses and cavities of a fragile anatomy interlocked in the friendliest way. The temporary bruising made the chronic pain easier to bear patiently. Certain wayward little tortures, inflicted between the ear and the shoulder by the horned light brown calf, displaced and relieved the torments endured by that region and by the wretched little back with its wings of prominent shoulder blades.

"Whatever have you got there?" Madame Mamma would say. "It looks as if you'd had a blow. Really, I simply can't understand . . ." In perfect good faith, the bruised child would think for a moment, then inwardly reply to himself: "There . . . Why, yes, of course. It was that tree I couldn't avoid. It was that little roof I leaned on to watch the sheep going back into the fold. It was that big rake that fell on the back of my neck when I was drinking at the fountain. Still, what luck Madame Mamma didn't see the little nick at the corner of my eye, the mark of that swallow's beak I knocked up against in the air. I hadn't time to avoid it, it was as hard as a scythe. True, a sky is so small . . ."

The confused murmur of his nights began to rise, expected but not familiar. It varied according to his dreams, his degree of weakness, his temperature, and the fantasies of a day that Madame Mamma supposed depressingly like all the other days. This new night bore no resemblance whatever to yesterday's night. The darkness was rich in innumerable blacks. "The black is all purple tonight. I've got such a pain in . . . in what? In my forehead. No, whatever am I saying? It's always my back . . . But no, it's a weight, two weights that are hung on my hips, two weights shaped like pine cones like the ones on the kitchen clock. You there, for the last time, will you light up?"

To intimate his order to the enamel bell, he leaned his temple hard against the pale leather binding and shuddered to find it so cold. "If it's frozen, it means I'm burning." No light flowed from the enamel pear. "What's the matter with it? And what's the matter with me? Only this afternoon, the front door wouldn't let me go through it." He stretched out his hand into the inhabited night air and found the shadowy pear without groping for it. Capriciously changing its usual source, the light appeared on the fat, shortsighted face of the spherical watch. "What are you sticking your nose in for?" muttered Jean. "Mind your own business and be satisfied with knowing how to tell the time."

The mortified watch put out its light and Jean heaved a sigh of gratified power. But all he could get out of his rigid sides was a groan. All at once, a wind he recognized among all others, the wind that snaps the pine trees, dishevels the larches, and flattens and raises the sand dunes, began to roar. It filled his ears, and the images, forbidden to the more ordinary dream that does not pierce the curtain of closed eyelids, rose up and longed to run free, to take advantage of the limitless room. Some of them, queerly horizontal, checkered the vertical crowd who had reared straight up on end. "Scottish visions," thought Jean.

His bed trembled slightly, shaken by the vibrating ascent of High

Fever. He felt three or four years fall away from him, and fear, to which he was almost a stranger, clutched at him. He very nearly called out: "To the rescue, Madame Mamma! They're carrying off your little boy!"

Neither in his rides, nor in the rich kingdom of the very strangest sounds—humpbacked sounds carrying reverberating ampoules on their heads, on their cockchafer backs, pointed sounds with muzzles like mongooses—nowhere had Jean ever seen such a swarm suddenly appear. His hearing tasted it like a mouth; his eye laboriously spelled it out, fascinated. "Help, Madame Mamma! Help me! You *know* I can't walk! I can only fly, swim, roll from cloud to cloud . . ." At the same moment, something indescribable and forgotten stirred in his body, infinitely far away, right at the very end of his useless legs, a confused, scattered crowd of crazy ants. "To the rescue, Madame Mamma!"

But another person, whose decisions depended neither on impotence nor on motherly kindness, made a haughty sign that imposed silence. A magical constraint kept Madame Mamma on the other side of the wall, in the place where she waited, modest and anxious, to become as great as her little son.

So he did not scream. In any case, the unknown beings, the fabulous strangers, were already beginning to abduct him by force. Rising up on all sides, they poured burning heat and icy cold on him, racked him with melodious torture, swathed him in color like a bandage, swung him in a hammock of palpitations. With his face already turned to flee, motionless, to his mother, he suddenly changed his mind and launched himself in full flight, letting his own impetus carry him where it would, through meteors and mists and lightnings that softly opened to let him through, closed behind him, opened again . . . And just as he was on the very verge of being perfectly content, ungrateful and gay, exulting in his solitude as an only child, his privilege as an orphan and an invalid, he was aware that a sad little crystalline crash separated him from a bliss whose beautiful, soft, airy name he had yet to learn: death. A little, light, melancholy crash, coming perhaps from some planet deserted forever . . . The clear and sorrowful sound, clinging to the child who was going to die, held on so staunchly that the dazzling escape tried in vain to shake it off and outdistance it.

Perhaps his journey lasted a long time. But having lost all sense of duration, he could only judge of its variety. Often he thought he was following a guide, an indistinct guide who had lost his way too. Then he would groan at not being able to take on the pilot's responsibility and he would hear his own groan of humbled pride, or such weariness that he abandoned his voyage, left the wake of a spindle-shaped squall, and took refuge, dead-beat, in a corner.

There he was pounced on by the anguish of living in a country where there were no corners, no square, solid shapes; where there was only a dark current of icy air; a night in whose depths he was no longer anything but a small boy, lost and in tears. Then he would rear himself upright on a great many, suddenly multiplied legs, promoted to the rank of stilts, that a searing pain was slicing off in rattling bundles, like faggots. Then everything would go dark and only the blind wind told him how fast he was traveling. Passing from a familiar continent to an unfamiliar sea he caught a few words in a language he was surprised to find he understood.

"The sound of the glass mug breaking woke me up."

"Madame can see he's smacking his lips, doesn't Madame think he wants something to drink?"

He would have liked to know the name of that voice. "Madame . . . Madame . . . What Madame?" But already the speed at which he was going had swallowed up the words and the memory of them.

One pale night, thanks to a stop that jarred through his temples, he again gathered a few human syllables and would have liked to repeat them. The sudden stop had brought him painfully face to face with a harsh, solid object interposed between two noble and inhabited worlds. An object with no destination, finely striped, bristling with very tiny hairs and mysteriously associated—he discovered this afterward—with horrible "my-young-friends." "It's a . . . I know . . . a . . . sleeve . . ." Promptly he opened his wings and flung himself headfirst into reassuring chaos.

Another time, he saw a hand. Armed with slender fingers, with slightly chapped skin and white-spotted nails, it was pushing back a marvelous zebra-striped mass that was rushing up from the depths of the horizon. Jean began to laugh. "Poor little hand, the mass will make one mouthful of it, just imagine, a mass that's all striped in black and yellow and has such an intelligent expression!" The feeble little hand struggled with all its outspread fingers, and the parallel stripes began to broaden and bend and diverge like soft bars. A great gap opened between them and swallowed up the frail hand and Jean found himself regretting it. This regret was delaying his journey, and with an effort, he launched himself off again. But he carried the regret with him, just as once, very, very long ago, he had carried the tenacious tinkle of a broken mug. After that, through whatever whirlpools and troughs he swirled and dipped, drowsy and rather pleasantly giddy, his journey was disturbed by echoes, by sounds of tears, by an anxious attempt at something that resembled a thought, by an importunate feeling of pity.

A harsh barking suddenly rent the great spaces, and Jean murmured: "Riki . . ." In the distance, he heard a kind of sob that kept repeating: "Riki! Madame, he said Riki!" Another stammering reiterated: "He said Riki! He said Riki."

A little hard, quivering force, whose double grip he could feel under his armpits, seemed to want to hoist him up to the top of a peak. It was bruising him and he grumbled. If he had been able to transmit his instructions to the little force and its sharp corners, he would have taught it that this was no way to treat a famous traveler who only uses immaterial vehicles, unshod steeds, sledges that trace seven-colored tracks on the rainbow. That he only allowed himself to be molested by those . . . those elements whose power only the night can unleash and control. That, for example, the bird's belly that had just laid itself against the whole length of his cheek had no right at all. And moreover, it was not a bird's belly because it was not feathered but only edged with a strand of long hair. "That," he thought, "would be a cheek, if there were any other cheek in the universe except mine. I want to speak, I want to send away this . . . this sham cheek. I forbid anyone to touch me, I forbid . . ."

To acquire the strength to speak, he breathed the air in through his nostrils. With the air, there entered in the marvel, the magic of memory, the smell of certain hair, certain skin he had forgotten on the other side of the world and that started up a wild rush of recollections. He coughed, fighting against the rise of something that tightened his throat, staunched a thirst lurking in the parched corners of his lips, salted his overflowing eyelids, and mercifully veiled from him his return to the hard landing-bed. Over an endless stretch, a voice said, re-echoing to infinity: "He's crying, dear God, he's crying . . ." The voice foundered in a kind of storm from which there arose disjointed syllables, sobs, calls to someone present, but concealed. "Come quick, quick!"

"What a noise, what a noise," thought the child reproachfully. But more and more, he kept pressing his cheek unconsciously against the soft, smooth surface bordered by someone's hair, and drinking up a bitter dew on it that welled out, drop by drop. He turned away his head and, as he did so, encountered a narrow valley, a nest molded exactly to his measure. He had just time to name it to himself: "Madame Mamma's shoulder," before he lost consciousness or else fell asleep on it.

He came to himself to hear his own voice, light and faintly mocking, saying: "Wherever have you come from, Madame Mamma?"

There was no answer, but the deliciousness of a quarter orange, slipped between his lips, made him conscious of the return, of the presence of the person he was searching for. He knew that she was bending over him in that submissive attitude that flexed her waist and tired her back. Soon exhausted, he fell silent. But already a thousand questions were worrying him and he conquered his weakness to satisfy the most urgent one: "Did you change my pajamas while I was asleep, Madame Mamma? When I lay down last night, I had blue ones and these are pink."

"Madame, it's past believing! He remembers he had blue pajamas, the first night when . . ."

He did not listen to the rest of the sentence that a big, warm voice had just whispered and abandoned himself to the hands that were taking off his wet garments. Hands as deft as the waves between which he rocked, weightless and aimless . . .

"He's soaked. Wrap him up in the big dressing gown, Mandora, without putting his arms through the sleeves."

"The heat's on full, Madame, don't be afraid. And I've just put in a new hot-water bottle. Gracious me, he's positively drenched."

"If they knew where I've come from . . . Anyone would expect to be drenched," thought Jean. "I wish to goodness I could scratch my legs or that someone would take those ants off."

"Madame Mamma."

He received the muteness, the vigilant stillness that were Madame Mamma's answer when she was strained and on the alert.

"Would you please . . . scratch my calves a little because these ants . . ."

From the depths of silence, someone whispered, with a strange respectfulness: "He can feel ants . . . He said ants . . ."

Swathed in the dressing gown that was too big for him, he tried to shrug his shoulders. Why, yes, he had said ants. What was there astonishing about his having said Riki and ants? A reverie carried him away, relieved, to the margin between waking and sleeping; the rustle of some stuff brought him back again. Between his lashes, he recognized the hateful sleeve, the blue stripes, the little hairs of wool, and his resentment restored his strength. He refused to see any more of it, but a voice came and opened his closed lids, a voice that said: "Well, my-young-friend . . ."

"I abolish him, I abolish him!" shrieked Jean inside himself. "Him, his sleeve, his my-young-friend, his little eyes, I curse them, I abolish them!" Beside himself with irritation, he was panting.

"Well, well. What's the matter? You're very restless. There . . . there . . ."

A hand laid itself on Jean's head. Powerless to revolt, he hoped to strike the aggressor down with one thunderbolt from his eye. But all he could see, sitting on the bedside chair reserved for Madame Mamma, was a worthy, rather fat, rather bald man, whose eyes, as they met his own, filled with tears.

"Little one, little one. Is it true you've got ants in your legs? Is it true? That's splendid, my word, that's really splendid. Could you manage to drink half a glass of lemonade? Wouldn't you like to suck a spoonful of lemon ice? A mouthful of milk and water?"

Jean's hand yielded itself up to some thick, very soft fingers and a warm palm. He murmured a vague acquiescence, not quite sure himself whether he was apologizing or whether he wanted the lemon ice, the drink, the "watered" milk. His eyes, paled to a tired gray between the great black rings and the dark eyebrows, gazed amicably into two small eyes of a cheerful blue that were moist and blinking and tender.

The rest of the new era was nothing but a series of muddled moments; a medley of different kinds of sleep, now short, now long, now hermetically sealed, interspersed with sudden sharp awakenings and vague tremors. The worthy doctor indulged in an orgy of great satisfied coughs, ahem, ahem, and exclamations of "Dear lady, this is capital! We're safe now!" All this din was so cheerful that Jean, if he had not been sunk in apathy, would have asked himself what happy event had occurred in the house.

The hours passed inexplicably, signposted by fruits in jelly and milk flavored with vanilla. A boiled egg raised its little lid and revealed its buttercup yolk. The window, left ajar, let in a breath of spring, heady as wine.

The nice barber was not yet permitted to return. Jean's hair hung down over his forehead and neck like a little girl's and Madame Mamma risked tying it back with a pink ribbon, which Jean tore off with the gesture of an insulted boy.

Behind the pane, the chestnut branch's rose-like buds were swelling day by day and all up and down Jean's legs there ran ants armed with little nipping jaws. "This time, I've caught one, Madame Mamma!" But all he was pinching was his own transparent skin and the ant had fled inside a tree of veins the color of spring grass. On the eighth day of the new era, a great scarf of sunlight lying across his bed moved him more than he could bear and he decided that this very night the daily fever would bring him what he had been vainly awaiting for a whole week. Everything that profound weariness and sleep hewn out of a solid block of black repose had robbed him of would be restored: his faceless companions, his rides, the accessible skies, his security of an angel in full flight.

"Madame Mamma, I'd like my books, please."

"My darling, the doctor said that . . ."

"It's not to read them, Madame Mamma, it's so that they'll get used to me again."

She said nothing and, with some apprehension, brought back the tattered volumes, the big badly bound paving stone, the light calf soft as a human skin, a *Pomology* with colored plates of chubby fruits, the Guérin mottled with flat-faced lions and duck-billed platypuses with beetles big as islands flying over them.

When night came, having eaten his fill—food was now something magical and interesting that he ate with the avidity of children who have come back to life—he pretended to be overcome with sleep and murmured his good nights, and a vague, mischievous song he had recently improvised. Having secretly watched the departure of Madame Mamma and Mandora, he took command of his raft of in-folio and atlas and set sail. A young moon, behind the chestnut branch, showed that the buds, thanks to the warmer weather, were about to open in leafy fingers.

He sat up without assistance in bed, towing his still-heavy legs that were overrun with ants. In the depths of the window, in the celestial waters of night swam the curved moon and the dim reflection of a long-haired child, to whom he beckoned. He raised one arm, and the other child obediently copied his summoning gesture. Slightly intoxicated with the power to work marvels, he called up his boon companions of the cruel but privileged hours: the visible sounds; the tangible images; the breathable seas; the nourishing, navigable air; the wings that mocked feet; the laughing suns.

In particular, he called up a certain spirited little boy who chuckled with inward laughter as he left the earth, who took advantage of Madame Mamma and, lord of her sorrows and joys, kept her prisoner of a hundred loving lies.

Then he waited, but nothing came. Nothing came that night or the following ones, nothing ever again. The landscape of pink snow had vanished from the nickel paper knife and never again would Jean fly, in a periwinkle dawn, between the sharp horns and the beautiful bulging eyes of cattle azure with dew. Never again would brown-and-yellow Mandora reverberate with all the strings—*tzrromm, tzrromm*—humming beneath her vast, generous skirt. Was it possible that the damask alp, piled high in the big cupboard, would henceforth refuse to allow a child who was nearly well to perform the feats a small cripple had achieved on the slopes of imaginary glaciers?

A time comes when one is forced to concentrate on living. A time comes when one has to renounce dying in full flight. With a wave of his hand, Jean said farewell to his angel-haired reflection. The other returned his greeting from the depths of an earthly night shorn of all marvels, the only night allowed to children whom death lets go and who fall asleep, assenting, cured, and disappointed.

[*Translated by Antonia White*]

The Rainy Moon

"Oh, I can manage that," the withered young girl told me. "Yes certainly, I can bring you each set of pages as I type them, as you'd rather not trust them to the post."

"Can you? That would be kind of you. You needn't trouble to come and collect my manuscript, I'll bring it to you in batches as I go along. I go out for a walk every morning."

"It's so good for the health," said Mademoiselle Barberet.

She gave a superficial smile and pulled one of the two little sausages of gold hair, threaded with white, that she wore tied on the nape with a black ribbon bow, forward again into its proper place, over her right shoulder, just below the ear. This odd way of doing her hair did not prevent Mademoiselle Barberet from being perfectly correct and pleasant to look at from her pale blue eyes to her slender feet, from her delicate, prematurely aged mouth to her frail hands, whose small bones were visible under the transparent skin. Her freshly ironed linen collar and her plain black dress called for the accessories of a pair of those glazed cotton oversleeves that were once the badge of writers. But typists, who do not write, do not wear their sleeves out below the elbows.

"You're temporarily without your secretary, Madame?"

"No. The girl who used to type my manuscripts has just got married. But I don't possess a secretary. I shouldn't know what to do with a secretary, you see. I write everything by hand. And besides, my flat is small, I should hear the noise of the typewriter."

"Oh, I do understand, I do understand," said Mademoiselle Barberet. "There's a gentleman I work for who only writes on the right-hand half of the pages. For a little while, I took over the typing for Monsieur Henri Duvernois, who would never have anything but pale yellow paper."

She gave a knowing smile that lumped together and excused all the manias of scribblers and, producing a file—I noticed she matched the cardboard to the blue of my paper—she neatly put away the sixty or so pages I had brought.

"I used to live in this neighborhood once. But I can't recognize anything anymore. It's all straightened out and built up; even the street's disappeared or changed its name. I'm not wrong, am I, Mademoiselle?"

Mademoiselle Barberet removed her spectacles, out of politeness. Her blue eyes were then unable to see me and her aimless gaze was lost in the void.

"Yes, I believe so," she said, without conviction. "You must be right."

"Have you lived here long?"

"Oh, yes," she said emphatically.

She fluttered her lashes as if she were lying.

"I think that, in the old days, a row of houses opposite hid the rise."

I got up to go over to the window and passed out of the circle of light that the green-shaded lamp threw over the table. But I did not see much of the view outside. The lights of the town made no breaches in the blue dusk of evening that falls early, in February. I pushed up the coarse muslin curtain with my forehead and rested my hand on the window catch. Immediately, I was conscious of the faint, rather pleasant giddiness that accompanies dreams of falling and flying. For I was clutching in my hand the peculiar hasp, the little cast-iron mermaid, whose shape my palm had not forgotten after all these years. I could not prevent myself from turning around in an abrupt, questioning way.

Without her glasses, Mademoiselle Barberet noticed nothing. My inquiring gaze went from her civil, shortsighted face to the walls of the room, almost entirely covered with gloomy steel engravings framed in black, colored reproductions of Chaplin—the fair-haired woman in the black velvet collar—and Henner, and even, a handicraft rare nowadays, thatchwork frames which young girls have lost the art of fashioning out of tubes of golden straw. Between an enlarged photograph and a sheaf of bearded rye, a few square inches of wallpaper remained bare; on it I could make out roses whose color had almost gone, purple convolvulus faded to gray, and tendrils of bluish foliage; in short, the ghost of a bunch of flowers, repeated a hundred times all over the walls, that it was impossible for me not to recognize. The twin doors, to right and left of the blind fireplace where a stove was fitted, promptly became intelligible, and beyond their closed panels, I revisualized all I had long ago left.

Behind me, I became unpleasantly conscious that Mademoiselle Barberet must be getting bored, so I resumed our conversation.

"It's pretty, this outlook."

"Above all, it's light, for a first floor. You won't mind if I put your pages in order, Madame, I notice there's a mistake in the sequence of numbers. The three comes after the seven and I can't see the eighteen."

"I'm not in the least surprised, Mademoiselle Barberet. Yes, do sort them out, do . . ."

"Above all, it's light." Light, this mezzanine floor, where, at all times of the year, almost at all times of the day, I used to switch on a little chandelier under the ceiling rose? On that same ceiling there suddenly appeared a halo of yellow light. Mademoiselle Barberet had just turned on a glass bowl, marbled to look like onyx, that reflected the light up onto the ceiling rose, the same icing-sugar ceiling rose under which, in other days, a branch of gilded metal flowered into five opaline blue corollas.

"A lot of mistakes, Mademoiselle Barberet? Especially a lot of crossings out."

"Oh, I work from manuscripts much more heavily corrected than this. The carbon copy, shall I do it in purple or black?"

"In black. Tell me, Mademoiselle . . ."

"My name's Rosita, Madame. At least, it's nicer than Barberet."

"Mademoiselle Rosita, I'm going to abuse your kindness. I see that I've brought you the whole of my text up to date and I haven't a rough copy. If you could type page 62 for me, I could take it away with me so as to get my sequence right."

"Why, of course, Madame. I'll do it at once. It'll only take me seven minutes. I'm not boasting, but I type fast. Do please sit down."

All that I wanted to do was just that, to stay a few minutes longer and find in this room the traces, if any, of my having lived here; to make sure I was not mistaken, to marvel at the fact that a wallpaper, preserved by the shade, should not, after all these years, be in tatters. "Above all, it's light." Evidently the sanitary authorities or perhaps just some speculative builder had razed all the bank of houses that, in the old days, hid the slope of one of Paris's hills from my unwitting eyes.

To the right of the fireplace—in which a little wood stove, flanked by its provision of sticks, tarred roadblocks, and old packing-case staves, was snoring discreetly—I could see a door and, to the right, a door exactly like it. Through the one on the right, I used to enter my bedroom. The one on the left led into the little hall, which ended in a recess I had turned into a bathroom by installing a small tub and gas heater. Another room, very dark and fairly large, which I never used, served as a box room. As to the kitchen . . . That minute kitchen came back to my memory with extraordinary vividness; in winter, its old-fashioned blue-tiled range was touched by a ray of sun that glided as far as the equally Old World cooking stove, standing on very tall legs and faintly Louis XV in design. When I could not, as they say, stick it anymore, I used to go into the kitchen. I always found something to do there: polishing up the jointed gas pipe, running a wet cloth over the blue porcelain tiles, emptying out the water of faded flowers, and rubbing the vase clear again with a handful of coarse, damp salt.

Two good big cupboards, of the jam-cupboard type; a cellar that contained nothing but a bottle rack, empty of bottles.

"I'll have finished in one moment, Madame."

What I most longed to see again was the bedroom to the right of the fireplace, *my* room, with its solitary square window, and the old-fashioned bed-closet whose doors I had removed. That marvelous bedroom, dark on one side, light on the other! It would have suited a happy, clandestine couple, but it had fallen to my lot when I was alone and very far from happy.

"Thank you so much. I don't need an envelope, I'll fold up the page and put it in my bag."

The front door, slammed to by an impetuous hand, banged. A sound is always less evocative than a smell, yet I recognized that one and gave a start, as Mademoiselle Barberet did too. Then a second door, the door of my bathroom—was shut more gently.

"Mademoiselle Rosita, if I've got through enough work, you'll see me again on Monday morning around eleven."

Pretending to make a mistake, I went toward the right of the fireplace. But between the door and myself, I found Mademoiselle Barberet, infinitely attentive.

"Excuse me. It's the one on the other side."

Out in the street, I could not help smiling, realizing that I had run heedlessly down the stairs without making a single mistake and that my feet, if I may risk the expression, still knew the staircase by heart. From the pavement, I studied my house, unrecognizable under a heavy make-up of mortar. The hall, too, was well disguised and now, with its dado of pink and green tiles, reminded me of the baleful chilliness of those mass-produced villas on the Riviera. The old dairy on the right of the entrance now sold banjos and accordions. But, on the left, the Palace of Dainties remained intact, except for a coat of cream paint. Pink sugared almonds in bowls, red-currant balls in full glass jars, emerald pepper-mints, and beige caramels . . . And the slabs of coffee cream and the sharp-tasting orange crescents . . . And those lentil-shaped sweets, wrapped in silver paper, like worm pills, and flavored with aniseed. At the back of the shop I recognized too, under their coat of new paint, the hundred little drawers with protruding navels, the low-carved counter, and all the charming woodwork of shops that date from the Second Empire, the old-fashioned scales whose shining copper pans danced under the beam like swings.

I had a sudden desire to buy those squares of licorice called "Pontefract cakes," whose flavor is so full-bodied that, after them, nothing seems eatable. A mauve lady of sixty came forward to serve me. So this was all that survived of her former self, that handsome blond proprietress who had once been so fond of sky-blue. She did not recognize me, and in my confusion, I asked her for peppermint creams, which I cannot abide. The following Monday, I would have the opportunity of coming back for the little Pontefract cakes that give such a vile taste to fresh eggs, red wine, and every other comestible.

To my cost, I have proved from long experience that the past is a far more violent temptation to me than the craving to know the future. Breaking with the present, retracing my steps, the sudden apparition of a new, unpublished slice of the past is accompanied by a shock utterly unlike anything else and which I cannot lucidly describe. Marcel Proust, gasping with asthma amid the bluish haze of fumigations and the shower of pages dropping from him one by one, pursued a bygone and completed time. It is neither the true concern nor the natural inclination of writers to love the future. They have quite enough to do with being incessantly forced to invent their characters' future, which, in any case, they draw up from the well of their own past. Mine, whenever I plunge into it, turns me dizzy. And when it is the turn of the past to emerge unexpectedly, to raise its dripping mermaid's head into the lights of the present and look at me with delusive eyes long hidden in the depths, I clutch at it all the more fiercely. Besides the person I once was, it reveals to me the one I would have liked to be. What is the use of employing occult means and occult individuals in order to know that person better? Fortune-tellers and astrologers, readers of tarot cards and palmists are not interested in my past. Among the figures, the swords, the cups, and the coffee grounds, my past is written in three sentences. The seeress briskly sweeps away bygone "ups and downs" and a few vague "successes" that have had no marked results, then hurriedly plants on the whole the plaster rose of a today shorn of mystery and a tomorrow of which I expect nothing.

Among fortune-tellers, there are very few whom our presence momentarily endows with second sight. I have met some who went triumphantly backward in time, gathering definite, blindingly true pictures from my past, then leaving me shipwrecked amid a fascinating welter of dead people, children from the past, dates and places, leaped, with one bound, into my future: "In three years, in six years, your situation will be greatly improved." Three years! Six years! Exasperated, I forgot them and their promises too.

But the temptation persists, along with a definite itch, to which I do not yield, to climb three floors or work a shaky elevator, stop on a landing, and ring three times. You see, one day I might hear my own footsteps approaching on the other side of the door and my own voice asking rudely: "What is it?" I open the door to myself, and naturally, I am wearing what I used to wear in the old days, something in the nature of a dark pleated tartan skirt and a high-collared shirt. The bitch I had in 1900 puts up her hackles and shivers when she sees me double . . . The end is missing. But as good nightmares go, it's a good nightmare.

For the first time in my life, I had just, by going into Mademoiselle Barberet's flat, gone back into my own home. The coincidence obsessed me during the days that followed my visit. I looked into it and I discovered something ironically interesting about it. Who was it who had suggested Mademoiselle Barberet to me? None other than my young typist, who was leaving her job to get married. She was marrying a handsome boy who was "taking," as they say, a Gymnasium in the district of Grenelle and whom she had been anxious I should meet. While he was explaining to me, thoroughly convinced of my passionate interest, that, nowadays, a Gymnasium in a working-class district was a gold mine, I was listening to his slight provincial accent. "I come from B. like all my family," he mentioned, in passing. "And like the person who was responsible for certain searing disappointments in my life," I added mentally. Disappointments in love, naturally. They are the least worthy of being brought back to mind, but sometimes they behave just like a cut in which a fragment of hair is hidden; they heal badly.

This second man from B. had vanished, having fulfilled his obligations toward me, which consisted of flinging me back, for unknown ends, into a known place. He had struck me as gentle; as slightly heavy, like all young men made tired and drowsy by injudicious physical culture. He was dark, with beautiful southern eyes, as the natives of B. often are. And he carried off the passionate young girl, thin to the point of emaciation, who had been typing my manuscripts for three years and crying over them when my story ended sadly.

The following Monday, I brought Mademoiselle Rosita the meager fruit—twelve pages—of work that was anything but a labor of love.

There was no motive whatever for being in a hurry to have two typed copies of a bad first draft, none except the pleasure and the risk of braving the little flat of long ago. "Worth doing just this once more," I told myself, "then I'll put my mind on other things." Nevertheless, my remembering hand searched the length of the doorjamb for the pretty beaded braid, my pretentious bell pull of the old days, and found an electric button.

An unknown person promptly opened the door, answered me only with a nod, and showed me into the room with two windows, where Mademoiselle Barberet joined me.

"Have you worked well, Madame? The bad weather hasn't had too depressing an effect on you?"

Her small, cold hand had hurriedly withdrawn from mine and was pulling forward the two sausage curls tied with black ribbon and settling them in their proper place on her right shoulder, nestling in her neck.

She smiled at me with the tempered solicitude of a well-trained nurse or a fashionable dentist's receptionist or one of those women of uncertain age who do vague odd jobs in beauty parlors.

"It's been a bad week for me, Mademoiselle Rosita. What's more, you'll find my writing difficult to read."

"I don't think so, Madame. A round hand is seldom illegible."

She looked at me amiably; behind the thick glasses, the blue of her eyes seemed diluted.

"Just imagine, when I arrived, I thought I must have come to the wrong floor, the person who opened the door to me . . ."

"Yes. That's my sister," said Mademoiselle Barberet as if, by satisfying my indiscreet curiosity, she hoped to prevent it from going any further.

But when we are in the grip of curiosity, we have no shame.

"Ah! That's your sister. Do you work together?"

Mademoiselle Barberet's transparent skin quivered on her cheekbones.

"No, Madame. For some time now, my sister's health has needed looking after."

This time, I did not dare insist further. For a few moments more I lingered in my drawing room that was now an office, taking in how much lighter it was. I strained my ear in vain for anything that might echo in the heart of the house or in the depths of myself and I went away, carrying with me a romantic burden of conjectures. The sister who was ill—and why not melancholy mad? Or languishing over an unhappy love affair? Or struck with some monstrous deformity and kept in the shade? That is what I'm like when I let myself go.

During the following days, I had no leisure to indulge my wild fancies further. At that particular time F.-I. Mouthon had asked me to write a serial novelette for *Le Journal*. Was this intelligent, curly-haired man making his first mistake? In all honesty, I had protested that I should never be able to write the kind of serial that would have been suitable for the readers of a big daily paper. F.-I. Mouthon, who seemed to know more about it than I did myself, had winked his little elephant's eye, shaken his curly forehead, shrugged his heavy shoulders and—I had sat down to write a serial novelette for which you will look in vain among my works. Mademoiselle Barberet was the only person who saw the first chapters before I tore them up. For in the long run, I turned out to be right; I did not know how to write a serial novelette.

On my return from my second visit to Mademoiselle Barberet, I reread the forty typed pages.

And I swore to peg away at it, as they say, like the very devil, to deprive myself of the flea market and the cinema and even of lunch in the Bois . . . This, however, did not mean Armenonville or even the Cascade, but pleasant impromptu picnics on the grass, all the better if Annie de Pène, a precious friend, came with me. There is no lack of milder days, once we are in February. We would take our bicycles, a fresh loaf stuffed with butter and sardines, two "delicatessen" sausage rolls we bought at a pork butcher's near La Muette, and some apples, the whole secured with string to a water bottle in a wicker jacket, filled with white wine. As to coffee, we drank that at a place near the station at Auteuil, very black, very tasteless, but piping hot and syrupy with sugar.

Few memories have remained as dear to me as the memory of those meals without plates, cutlery, or cloth, of those expeditions on two wheels. The cool sky, the rain in drops, the snow in flakes, the sparse, rusty grass, the tameness of the birds. These idylls suited a certain state of mind, far removed from happiness, frightened yet obstinately hopeful. By means of them, I have succeeded in taking the sting out of an unhappiness that wept small, restrained tears, a sorrow without great storms, in short a love affair that began just badly enough to make it end still worse. Does one imagine those periods, during which anodynes conquer an illness one believed serious at the time, fade easily from one's memory? I have already compared them, elsewhere, to the "blanks" that introduce space and order between the chapters of a book. I should very much like—late in life, it is true—to call them "merciful blanks," those days in which work and sauntering and friendship played the major part, to the detriment of love. Blessed days, sensitive to the light of the external world, in which the relaxed and idle senses made chance discoveries. It was not very long after I had been enjoying this kind of holiday that I made the acquaintance of Mademoiselle Barberet.

It was—and for good reason—three weeks before I went to see her again. Conceiving a loathing for my serial novelette every time I tried to introduce "action," swift adventure, and a touch of the sinister into it, I had harnessed myself to short stories for *La Vie Parisienne*. It was therefore with a new heart and a light step that I climbed the slopes of her part of Paris, which shall be nameless. Not knowing whether Mademoiselle Barberet liked Pontefract cakes, I bought her several small bunches of snowdrops, which had not yet lost their very faint perfume of orange flowers, squeezed tight together in one big bunch.

Behind the door, I heard her little heels running forward over the uncarpeted wooden floor. I recognize a step more quickly than a shape, a shape more quickly than a face. It was bright outdoors and in the room with the two windows. Between the photographic enlargements, the "studies" of woodland landscapes, and the straw frames with red ribbon bows, the February sun was consuming the last faint outlines of my roses and blue convolvulus on the wallpaper.

"*This* time, Mademoiselle Rosita, I haven't come empty-handed! Here are some little flowers for you and here are two short stories, twenty-nine pages of manuscript."

"It's too much, Madame, it's too much . . ."

"It's the length they have to be. It takes thirteen closely written pages, a short story for *La Vie Parisienne*."

"I was talking of the flowers, Madame."

"They're not worth mentioning. And you know, on Monday, I've a feeling I'm going to bring you . . ."

Behind her spectacles, Mademoiselle Barberet's eyes fixed themselves on me, forgetting to dissemble the fact that they were red, bruised, filled with bitter water, and so sad that I broke off my sentence. She made a gesture with her hand, and murmured: "I apologize. I have worries . . ."

Few women keep their dignity when they are in tears. The withered young girl in distress wept simply, decently controlling the shaking of her hands and her voice. She wiped her eyes and her glasses and gave me a kind of smile with one side of her mouth.

"It's one of those days . . . it's because of the child, I mean, of my sister."

"She's ill, isn't she?"

"In one sense, yes. She has no disease," she said emphatically. "It's since she got married. It's changed her character. She's so rough with me. Of course all marriages can't turn out well, one knows that."

I am not very fond of other people's matrimonial troubles, they bear an inevitable resemblance to my own personal disappointments. So I was anxious to get away at once from the sorrowing Barberet and the unhappily married sister. But just as I was leaving her, a little blister in the coarse glass of one of the windowpanes caught a ray of sun and projected onto the opposite wall the little halo of rainbow colors I used once to call the "rainy moon." The apparition of that illusory planet shot me back so violently into the past that I remained standing where I was, transfixed and fascinated.

"Look, Mademoiselle Rosita. How pretty that is."

I put my finger on the wall, in the center of the little planet ringed with seven colors.

"Yes," she said. "We know that reflection well. Just fancy, my sister's frightened of it."

"Frightened? What do you mean, frightened? Why? What does she say about it?"

Mademoiselle smiled at my eagerness.

"Oh, you know . . . silly things, the sort that nervous children imagine. She says it's an omen. She calls it her sad little sun, she says it only shines to warn her something bad is going to happen. Goodness knows what else. As if the refractions of a prism really could influence . . ."

Mademoiselle Barberet gave a superior smile.

"You're right," I said weakly. "But those are charming poetic fancies. Your sister is a poet without realizing it."

Mademoiselle Barberet's blue eyes were fixed on the place where the rainbow-colored ghost had been before a passing cloud had just eclipsed it.

"The main thing is, she's a very unreasonable young woman."

"She lives in the other . . . in another part of the flat?"

Mademoiselle Barberet's gaze switched to the closed door on the right of the fireplace.

"Another part, you could hardly call it that. They chose . . . Her bedroom and dressing room are separate from my bedroom."

I nodded "Yes, yes," as my thorough acquaintance with the place gave me the right to do.

"Is your sister like you to look at?"

I made myself gentle and spoke tonelessly, as one does to people asleep so as to make them answer one from the depths of their slumber.

"Like me? Oh dear, no! To begin with, there's a certain difference of age between us, and she's dark. And then, as to character, we couldn't be less alike in every way."

"Ah! She's dark . . . One of these days you must let me meet her. There's no hurry! I'm leaving you my manuscript. If you don't see me on Monday . . . Would you like me to settle up with you for the typing you've already done?"

Mademoiselle Barberet blushed and refused, then blushed and accepted. And although I stopped in the hall to make some unnecessary suggestion, no sound came from my bedroom and nothing revealed the presence of the dark sister.

"She calls it her sad little sun. She says that it foretells something bad. Whatever can I have bequeathed to that reflection, that looks like a planet in a ring of haze, where the red is never anywhere but next to the purple? In the old days, when the wind was high and the sky cloudy, it would keep vanishing, reappearing, fading away again, and its caprices would distract me for a moment from my state of suspense, of perpetual waiting."

I admit that, as I descended the slope of the hill, I gave myself up to excitement. The play of coincidences shed a false, unhoped-for light on my life. Already I was promising myself that the "Barberet story" would figure in a prominent place in the fantastic gallery we secretly furnish and which we open more readily to strangers than to our near ones: the gallery reserved for premonitions, for the phenomena of mistaken identity, for visions and predictions. In it I had already lodged the story of the woman with the candle, the story of Jeanne D.; the story of the woman who read the tarot pack, and of the little boy who rode on horseback.

In any case, the Barberet story, barely even roughly sketched, was already acting for me as a "snipe's bandage." That is what I used to call, and still call, a particular kind of unremarkable and soothing event that I liken to the dressing of wet clay and bits of twig, the marvelous little splint the snipe binds around its foot when a shot has broken it. A visit to the cinema, provided the films are sufficiently mediocre, counts as a snipe's bandage. But, on the contrary, an evening in the company of intelligent friends who know what it is to be hurt and are courageous and disillusioned, undoes the bandage. Symphonic music generally tears it off, leaving me flayed. Poured out by a steady, indifferent voice, pronouncements and predictions are compresses and camomile tea to me.

"I'm going to tell the Barberet story to Annie de Pène," I mentally began. And then I told nothing at all. Would not Annie's subtle ear and lively bronze eyes have weighed and condemned everything in my narrative that revealed no more than the craving to go over old ground again, to deck out what was over and done with in a new coat of paint? "That window, Annie, where a young woman whose man has left her spends nearly all her time waiting, listening—just as I did long ago."

I said nothing to Annie. It is as well for a toy to be played with in solitude, if something or other about its color, about its acid varnish, about a chance distortion of its shadow, warns one it may be dangerous. But I went off and translated the "Barberet story" into commonplace language for the benefit of the woman who came by the day to "make and mend" for me, a stout brunette who was relaxing after singing in operetta in Oran by sewing and ironing for other people. In order to listen to me, Marie Mallier stopped crushing gathers under a cruel thumbnail, blew into her thimble, and waited, her needle poised.

"And then what happened?"

"That's the end."

"Oh," said Marie Mallier. "It seemed to me more like a beginning."

The words enchanted me. I read into them the most romantic omen and I swore to myself I would not delay another moment in making the acquaintance of the dark, unhappily married sister who lived in my gloomy bedroom and was frightened of my "rainy moon."

Those tugs on my sleeve, those little presents fate has offered me might have given me the power of escaping from myself, sloughing my skin, and emerging in new, variegated colors. I believe they might have succeeded, had I not lacked the society and influence of someone for whom there is hardly any difference between what really happens and what does not, between fact and possibility, between an event and the narration of it.

Much later on, when I came to know Francis Carco, I realized that he would, for example, have interpreted my stay at Bella-Vista and my meeting with the Barberets with an unbridled imagination. He would have plucked out of them the catastrophic truth, the element of something unfinished, something left suspended that spurs imagination and terror to a gallop; in short, their poetry. I saw, years afterward, how a poet makes use of tragic embellishment and lends a mere news item the fascination of some white, inanimate face behind a pane.

Lacking a companion with a fiery imagination, I clung to a rational view of things, notably of fear and hallucination. This was a real necessity, as I lived alone. On some nights, I would look very carefully around my little flat; I would open my shutters to let the nocturnal light play on the ceiling while I waited for the light of the day. The next morning, my concierge, when she brought me my coffee, would silently flourish the key she had found in the lock, on the outside. Most of the time I gave no thought to perils that might come from the unknown and I treated ghosts with scant respect.

That was how, the following Monday, I treated a window in the Barberet flat, which I had entered at the same moment as a March wind with great sea pinions that flung all the papers on the floor. Mademoiselle Rosita put both hands over her ears, and shrieked "Ah!" as she shut her eyes. I gripped the cast-iron mermaid with a familiar hand and closed the window with one turn of my wrist.

"At the very first go!" exclaimed Mademoiselle Barberet admiringly. "That's extraordinary! I hardly ever manage to . . . Oh, goodness, all these typed copies flying about! Monsieur Vandérem's novel! Monsieur Pierre Veber's short story! This wind! Luckily I'd put your text back in its folder . . . Here's the top copy, Madame, and the carbon. There are several traces of Indian-rubber. If you'd like me to redo some of the scratched pages, it'll be a pleasure to me, tonight after dinner."

"Find yourself more exciting pleasures, Mademoiselle Rosita. Go to the cinema. Do you like the cinema?"

The avidity of a small girl showed in her face, accentuating the fine wrinkles around the mouth.

"I adore it, Madame! We have a very good local cinema, five francs for quite good seats, that shows splendid films. But at this moment, I can't possibly . . ."

She broke off and fixed her gaze on the door to the right of the fireplace.

"Is it still your sister's health? Couldn't her husband take on the job of . . ."

In spite of myself, I imitated her prudish way of leaving her sentences unfinished. She flushed and said hastily: "Her husband doesn't live here, Madame."

"Ah, he doesn't live . . . And she, what does she do? Is she waiting for him to come back?"

"I . . . Yes, I think so."

"All the time?"

"Day and night."

I stood up abruptly and began to pace the room, from the window to the door, from the door to the far wall, from the far wall to the fireplace; the room where once *I* had waited—day and night.

"That's stupid!" I exclaimed. "That's the last thing to do. Do you hear me, the very last!"

Mademoiselle Barberet mechanically pulled out the spiral of hair that caressed her shoulder, and her withered angel's face followed my movements to and fro.

"If *I* knew her, that sister of yours, I'd tell her straight to her face that she's chosen the worst possible tactics. They couldn't be more . . . more idiotic."

"Ah, I'd be only too glad, Madame, if you'd tell her so! Coming from you, it would have far more weight than from me. She makes no bones about assuring me that old maids have no right to speak on certain topics. In which she may well be mistaken, moreover . . ." Mademoiselle Barberet lowered her eyes and gave a little resentful toss of her chin.

"A fixed idea isn't always a good idea. She's in there, with her fixed idea. When she can't stand it anymore, she goes downstairs. She says she wants to buy some sweets. She says: 'I'm going to telephone.' To other people! As if she thought I was deceived for a moment!"

"You're not on the telephone?"

I raised my eyes to the ceiling. A little hole in the molded cornice still showed where the telephone wire had passed through it. When I was in this place, I had the telephone. I could beg and implore without having to bother to go outside.

"Not yet, Madame. We're going to have it put in, of course."

She blushed, as she did whenever there was a question of money or of lack of money, and seemed to make a desperate resolve.

"Madame, since you think as I do that my sister is wrong to be so obstinate, if you have two minutes . . ."

"I have two minutes."

"I'll go and tell my sister."

She went out through the hall instead of opening the door on the right of the fireplace. She walked gracefully, carried on small, arched feet. Almost at once, she came back, agitated and with red rims to her eyelids.

"Oh, I don't know how to apologize! She's terrible. She says, 'Not on your life' and 'What are you sticking your nose in for?' and 'I wish to goodness everyone would shut up.' She says nothing but rude things."

Mademoiselle Barberet blew her distress into her handkerchief, rubbed her nose, and became ugly, as if on purpose. I had just time to think: "Really, I'm being unnecessarily tactful with these females," before I turned the handle of the right-hand door which recognized me and obeyed me without a sound. I did not cross the threshold of *my* room whose half-closed shutters filled it with a faintly green dusk. At the far end of the room, on a divan-bed that seemed not to have moved from the place I had chosen for it in the old days, a young woman, curled up like a gun dog, raised the dim oval of her face in my direction. For a second, I had that experience only dreams dare conjure up: I saw before me, hostile, hurt, stubbornly hoping, the young self I should never be again, whom I never ceased disowning and regretting.

But there is nothing lasting in any touch of the fabulous we experience outside sleep. The young me stood up, spoke, and was no longer anything more than a stranger, the sound of whose voice dissipated all my precious mystery.

"Madame . . . But I told my sister— Really, Rosita, whatever are you thinking of? My room's untidy, I'm not well. You must understand, Madame, why I couldn't ask you to come in."

She had only taken two or three steps toward me. In spite of the gloom, I could make out that she was rather short, but square-shouldered and self-assured. As a cloud outside uncovered the sun, the construction of her face was revealed to me: a straight, firm nose, strongly marked brows, a little Roman chin. It is a double attraction when well-modeled features are both youthful and severe.

I made myself thoroughly amiable to this young woman who was throwing me out.

"I understand perfectly, Madame. But do realize that your sister's only crime was to imagine I might be of some use to you. She made a mistake. Mademoiselle Rosita, it'll be all right, won't it, to fetch the typescript as usual, next Monday?"

The two sisters did not notice the ease with which I found the curtained door at the far end of the room, crossed the dark little hall, and shut myself out. Downstairs, I was joined by Rosita.

"Madame, Madame, you're not angry?"

"Not in the very least. Why should I be. She's pretty, your sister. By the way, what's her name?"

"Adèle. But she likes to be called Délia. Her married name is Essendier, Madame Essendier. Now she's heartbroken, she'd like to see you."

"Very well, then! She shall see me on Monday," I conceded with dignity.

As soon as I was alone, the temptation to be entrapped in this snare of resemblances lost its power; the strident glare of the rue des Martyrs at midday dissipated the spell of the bedroom and the young woman curled up "day and night." On the steep slope, what quantities of chickens with their necks hanging down, small legs of mutton displayed outside shops, fat sausages, enameled beer mugs with landscapes on them, oranges piled up in formation like cannon balls for ancient artillery, withered apples, unripe bananas, anemic chicory, glutinous wads of dates, daffodils, pink panties, bloomers encrusted with imitation Chantilly, little bags of ingredients for homemade stomach remedies, mercerized lisle stockings. What a number of *postiches*—they used to call them "chichés"—of ties sold in threes, of shapeless housewives, of blondes in down-at-heel shoes and brunettes in curlers, of mother-of-pearl smelts, of butcher boys with fat, cherubic faces. All this profusion, which had not changed in the least, awakened my appetite and vigorously restored me to reality.

Away with these Barberets! That chit of a girl with no manners was a sniveler, a lazy slut who must have driven her husband's patience beyond all bounds. Caught between a prim, fussy old maid and a jealous young wife, what a charming life for a man!

Thus, wandering along and gazing at the shops, did I indict Madame Délia Essendier, christened Adèle . . . "*Adèle . . . T'es belle . . .*" Standing in front of a sumptuous Universal Provision Store, I hummed the silly, already hoary song, as I admired the oranges between the tumbled rice and the sweating coffee, the red apples and the split green peas. Just as in Nice one longs to buy the entire flower market, here I would have liked to buy a whole stall of eatables, from the forced lettuces to the blue packets of semolina. "*Adèle . . . T'es belle . . .*" I hummed.

"If you ask *me*," said an insolent-eyed local girl, right under my nose, "I'd say *The Merry Widow* was a lot more up-to-date than that old thing."

I did not reply, for this strapping blonde with her hair curled to last a week, planted solidly on her feet and sugared with coarse powder, was, after all, speaking for the whole generation destined to devour my own.

All the same I was not old, and above all, I did not look my real age. But a private life that was clouded and uncertain, a solitude that bore no resemblance to peace had wiped all the life and charm out of my face. I have never had less notice taken of me by men than during those particular years whose date I dissemble here. It was much later on that they treated me again to the good honest offensive warmth of their looks, to that genial concupiscence which will make an admirer, when he ought to be kissing your hand, give you a friendly pinch on the buttock.

The following Monday, on a sultry March morning when the sky was a whitish blue and Paris, dusty and surprised, was spilling her overflow of jonquils and anemones into the streets, I walked limply up the steep slope of Montmartre. Already the wide-open entrances to the blocks of flats were ejecting the air that was colder inside than out, along with the carbonic smell of stoves that had been allowed to go out. I rang the bell of Mademoiselle Rosita's flat; she did not answer it and I joyfully welcomed the idea that she might be out, busy buying a pale escallop of veal or some ready-cooked sauerkraut . . . To salve my conscience, I rang a second time. Something brushed faintly against the door and the parquet creaked.

"Is that you, Eugène?" asked the voice of Mademoiselle Barberet.

She spoke almost in a whisper and I could hear her breathing at the level of the keyhole.

As if exculpating myself, I cried: "It's me, Mademoiselle Rosita! I'm bringing some pages of manuscript . . ."

Mademoiselle Barberet gave a little "Ah!" but did not open the door at once. Her voice changed and she said in mincing tones: "Oh, Madame, what can I have been thinking of. I'll be with you in a moment."

A safety bolt slid in its catch and the door was half opened.

"Be very careful, Madame, you might stumble . . . My sister's on the floor.'

She could not have spoken more politely and indifferently had she said: "My sister's gone out to the post." I did, in fact, stumble against a body lying prone, with its feet pointing skyward and its hands and face mere white blurs. The sight of it threw me into a state of cowardice which I intensely dislike. Drawing away from the body stretched out on the floor, I asked, to give the impression of being helpful, "What's the matter with her? Would you like me to call someone?"

Then I noticed that the sensitive Mademoiselle Rosita did not seem to be greatly perturbed.

"It's a fainting fit . . . a kind of dizziness that isn't serious. Just let me get the smelling salts and a wet towel."

She was already running off. I noticed she had forgotten to turn the light on and I had no trouble in finding the switch to the right of the front door. A ceiling light in the form of a plate with a crinkled border feebly lit up the hall and I bent down over the prostrate young woman. She was lying in an extremely decent attitude, with her skirt down to her ankles. One of her bent arms, whose hand lay palm upward, beside her ear, seemed to be commanding attention, and her head was slightly averted on her shoulders. Really, a very pretty young woman, taking refuge in a sulky swoon. I could hear Mademoiselle Rosita in the bedroom, opening and shutting a drawer, slamming the door of a cupboard.

And I found the seconds drag heavily as I stared at the tubular umbrella stand, at the cane table; in particular, at a door curtain of Algerian design that roused a regret in my heart for a rather pretty strip of leafy tapestry that used to hang there in the old days. As I looked down at the motionless young woman, I realized, from a narrow gleam between her eyelids, that she was secretly watching me. For some reason, I felt disagreeably surprised, as if by some practical joke. I bent over this creature who was shamming a faint and applied another approved remedy for swoons—a good, hard, stinging slap. She received it with an offended snarl and sat up with a jerk.

"Well! So you're better?" cried Rosita, who was arriving with a wet towel and a liter of salad vinegar.

"As you see, Madame slapped my hands," said Délia coldly. "You'd never have thought of that, would you? Help me to get up, please."

I could not avoid giving her my arm. And supporting her thus, I entered the bedroom she had practically asked me to leave.

The room reverberated with the noises of the street that came up through the open window. There was just the same contrast I remembered so well between the cheerful noises and the mournful light. I guided the young pretender to the divan-bed.

"Rosita, perhaps you'd have the charity to bring me a glass of water?"

I began to realize that the two sisters adopted a bitter, bantering tone whenever they spoke to each other. Rosita's small steps went off toward the kitchen and I prepared to leave her younger sister's bedside. But, with an unexpected movement, Délia caught hold of my hand, then clasped her arms around my knees and wildly pressed her head against them.

You must remember that, at that period of my life, I was still childless and that friendship, for me, wore the guise of undemonstrative, offhand, unemotional comradeliness. You must also take into account that, for many months, I had been starved of the coarse, invigorating bread of physical contact. A kiss, a good warm hug, the fresh touch of a child or anyone young had remained so long out of my reach that they had become distant, almost forgotten joys. So this unknown young woman's outburst, her surge of tears, and her sudden embrace stunned me. Rosita's return found me standing just where I was and the imploring arms unloosed their grip.

"I let the tap run for two minutes," explained the older sister. "Madame, how can I apologize . . ."

I suddenly resented Mademoiselle Barberet's air of business-like alacrity; her two ringlets bobbed on her right shoulder and she was slightly out of breath.

"Tomorrow morning," I interrupted, "I've got to buy some remnants in the St.-Pierre market. So I could come and collect the typed copies and you can give me news of . . . this . . . young person. No, stay where you are. I know the way."

What stirred just now in the thicket? No, it isn't a rabbit. Or a grass snake. Or a bird that travels in shorter spurts. Only lizards are so agile, so capable of covering a long distance fast, so reckless . . . It's a lizard. That large butterfly flying in the distance—I always had rather bad eyesight—you say it's a Swallowtail? No, it's a Large Tortoiseshell. Why? Because the one we're looking at glides magnificently as only the Large Tortoiseshell can, and the Swallowtail has a flapping flight. "My husband, such a placid man . . ." a friend of mine used to tell me. She did not see that he sucked his tongue all day long. She thought he was eating chewing gum, not differentiating between the chewing of gum and the nervous sucking of the tongue. Personally, I thought that this man had cares on his mind or else that the presence of his wife exasperated him.

Ever since I had made the acquaintance of Délia Essendier I had found myself "recapping" in this way lessons I had learned from my instinct, from animals, children, nature, and my disquieting fellow beings. It seemed to me that I needed more than ever to know of my own accord, without discussing it with anyone, that the lady going by has a left shoe that pinches her, that the person I am talking to is pretending to drink in my words but not even listening to me, that a certain woman who hides from herself the fact that she loves a certain man cannot stop herself from following him like a magnet whenever he is in the room, but always turns her back to him. A dog with evil intentions sometimes limps out of nervousness.

Children, and people who retain some ingenuous trait of childhood, are almost indecipherable, I realize that. Nevertheless, in a child's face, there is just one revealing, unstable area, a space comprised between the nostril, the eye, and the upper lip, where the waves of a secret delinquency break on the surface. It is as swift and devastating as lightning. Whatever the child's age, that little flash of guilt turns the child into a ravaged adult. I have seen a serious lie distort a little girl's nostril and upper lip like a harelip . . .

"Tell me, Délia . . ."

. . . but on Délia's features nothing explicit appeared. She took refuge in a smile—for me—or in bad temper directed against her older sister, or else she entered into a somber state of waiting, installing herself in it as if at the window of a watchtower. She would half sit, half lie on her divan-bed, which was covered with a green material printed with blue nasturtiums—the last gasps of the vogue for Liberty fabrics— clutching a big cushion against her, propping her chin on it, and scarcely ever moving. Perhaps she was aware that her attitude suited her often cantankerous beauty.

"But tell me, Délia, when you got married, didn't you have a presentiment that . . ."

Propped up like that, with her skirt pulled down to her ankles, she seemed to be meditating, rather than waiting. Since profound meditation is not concerned with being expressive, Délia Essendier never turned her eyes to me, even when she was speaking. More often than not, she looked at the half-open window, the reservoir of air, the source of sounds, a greenish aquarium in the shade of the green-and-blue curtains. Or else she stared fixedly at the little slippers with which her feet were shod. I, too, in the old days, used to buy those little heelless slippers of imitation silk brocade, adorned with a flossy pompon on the instep. In those days they cost thirteen francs seventy-five and their poor material soon tarnished. The young voluntary recluse I saw before me did not bother herself with shoes. She was only half a recluse, going out in the morning to buy a squirrel's provisions, a provender of fresh bread, dry nuts, eggs, and apples, and the little meat that sufficed for the appetite of the two sisters.

"Didn't you tell me, Délia . . ."

No. She had told me nothing. Her brief glance accused me of imagining things, of having no memory. What was I doing there, in a place which ought to have been forbidden ground for me, at the side of a woman young enough to give no indication of being a wife and who manifested neither virtues nor nobility of mind nor even as much intelligence as any lively, gentle animal? The answer, I insist, is that this was a period in my life which motherhood and happy love had not yet enriched with their marvelous commonplace.

People might already have taken me to task for my choice of associates—those who tried to got an extremely poor reception—and my friends might have been surprised, for example, to find me pacing up and down the avenue du Bois in the company of a shabby groom who brought and took away the horses hired out by a riding school. A former jockey who had been unlucky and come down in the world and who looked like an old glove. But he was a mine of information on everything to do with horses and dogs, diseases, remedies, fiery beverages that would kill or cure, and I liked his meaty conversation even though he did teach me too much about the way animals are "made up" to get a better price for them. For example, I would gladly have been dispensed from knowing that they pour sealing wax into a French bulldog's ears if it has slightly limp auricles . . . The rest of his expert knowledge was fascinating.

With less fundamental richness, Marie Mallier had considerable charm. If any of my circle had decided to be captious about all the things Marie Mallier did in the course of what she broadly described as "touring in operetta," I would not have stood for it. Reduced to accepting all and sundry, the only transgressions Marie Mallier really enjoyed were the unprofitable delights of sewing and ironing. For the spice of an occupation, generally considered innocent, can be more exciting than many a guilty act performed out of necessity.

"To make a darn so that the corners don't pucker and all the little loops on the wrong side stand out nice and even," Marie Mallier used to say. "It makes my mouth water like cutting a lemon!" Our vices are less a matter of yielding to temptation than of some obsessive love. Throwing oneself passionately into helping some unknown woman, founding hopes on her that would be discouraged by the wise affection of our friends, wildly adopting a child that is not ours, obstinately ruining ourselves for a man whom we probably hate, such are the strange manifestations of a struggle against ourselves that is sometimes called disinterestedness, sometimes perversity. When I was with Délia Essendier, I found myself once again as vulnerable, as prone to giving presents out of vanity as a schoolgirl who sells her books to buy a rosary, a ribbon, or a little ring and slips them, with a shy note, into the desk of a beloved classmate.

Nevertheless, I did not love Délia Essendier, and the beloved classmate I was seeking, who was she but my former self, that sad form stuck, like a petal between two pages, to the walls of an ill-starred refuge?

"Délia, haven't you got a photograph of your husband here?"

Since the day when her arms had clasped my knees, Délia had made no other mute appeal to me except, when I stood up to go, a gesture to hold me back by the hand, the gesture of an awkward young girl who has not learned how to grip or offer a palm frankly. All she did was to pull on my fingers and hurriedly let them go, as if out of sulkiness, then turn away toward the window that was nearly always open. Following the suggestion of her gaze, it was I who would go over to the window and stare at the passers-by, or rather at their lids, for in those days, all men wore hats. When the entrance down below swallowed up a man with a long stride, dressed in a blue overcoat, in spite of myself I would count the seconds and reckon the time it would take a visitor in a hurry to cross the hall, walk up to our floor, and ring the bell. But no one would ring and I would breathe freely again.

"Your husband, does he write to you, Délia?"

This time, the reticent young person whom I continued to ask tactless questions, whether she left them unanswered or not, scanned me with her insulting gaze. But I was long past the stage of taking any notice of her disdain, and I repeated: "Yes, I'm asking if your husband writes to you sometimes."

My question produced a great effect on Rosita, who was walking through the bedroom. She stopped short, as if waiting for her sister's reply.

"No," said Délia at last. "He doesn't write to me and it's just as well he doesn't. We've nothing to say to each other."

At this, Rosita opened her mouth and her eyes in astonishment. Then she continued her light-footed walk and, just before she disappeared, raised both her hands to her ears. This scandalized gesture revived my curiosity, which at times died down. I must also admit that, going back to the scene of my unhappy, fascinating past, I found it shocking that Délia—Délia and not myself—should be lying on the divan-bed, playing at taking off and putting on her little slippers, while

I, tired of an uncomfortable seat, got up to walk to and fro, to push the table closer to the window as if by accident, to measure the space once filled by a dark cupboard.

"Délia, was it you who chose this wallpaper?"

"Certainly not. I'd have liked a flowered paper, like the one in the living room."

"What living room?"

"The big room."

"Ah, yes. It isn't a living room, because you don't live in it. I should be more inclined to call it the workroom, because your sister works in it."

Now that the days were growing longer, I could make out the color of Délia's eyes—around her dilated pupils there was a ring of dark gray-green—and the whiteness of her skin, like the complexion of southern women who are uniformly pale from head to foot. She threw me a look of obstinate mistrust.

"My sister can work just as well in a living room if she chooses."

"The main thing is that she works, isn't it?" I retorted.

With a kick, she flung one of her slippers a long way away.

"I work too," she said stiffly. "Only nobody sees what I do. I wear myself out; oh, I wear myself out. In there . . . In there . . ."

She was touching her forehead and pressing her temples. With slight contempt, I looked at her idle woman's hands, her delicate fingers, long, slim, and turned up at the tips, and her fleshy palms. I shrugged my shoulders.

"Fine work, a fixed idea! You ought to be ashamed, Délia."

She gave way easily to tempers typical of an ill-bred schoolgirl with no self-control.

"I don't only just think!" she screamed. "I . . . I work in my own way! It's all in my head!"

"Are you planning a novel?"

I had spoken sarcastically but Délia, quite unaware of this, was flattered and calmed down.

"Oh! Well, not exactly so . . . it's a bit like a novel, only better."

"What is it you call better than a novel, my child?"

For I allowed myself to call her that when she seemed to be pitch-forked into a kind of brutal, irresponsible childishness. She always flinched at the word and rewarded me with an angry, lustrous glance, accompanied by an ill-tempered shrug.

"Ah, I can't tell you that," she said in a self-important voice.

She went back to fishing cherries out of a newspaper cornet. She pinched the stones between her fingers and aimed at the open window.

Rosita passed through the room, busy on some errand, and scolded her sister without pausing in her walk.

"Délia, you oughtn't to throw the stones out into the street."

What was I doing there, in that desert? One day, I brought some better cherries. Another day, having brought Rosita a manuscript full of erasures, I said: "Wait. Could I redo this page on . . . on a corner of a table, doesn't matter where. There, look, that'll do very well. Yes, yes, I can see well enough there. Yes, I've got my fountain pen."

Leaning on a rickety one-legged table, I received, from the left, the light of the solitary window and, from the right, the attention of Délia. To my amazement, she set to work with a needle. She was doing the fine beadwork that was all the rage at the moment for bags and trimmings.

"What a charming talent, Délia."

"It isn't a talent, it's a profession," said Délia in a tone of disgust.

But she was not displeased, I think, to devote herself under my eyes to work that was as graceful as a charming pastime. The needles, fine as steel hairs, the tiny multicolored beads, the canvas net, she manipulated them all with the deftness of a blind person, still half recumbent on a corner of the divan-bed. From the neighboring room came the choppy chatter of the typewriter, the jib of its little carriage at every line, and its crystalline bell. What was I doing in that desert? It was not a desert. I forsook my own three small, snug rooms, my books, the scent I sprayed about, my lamp. But one cannot live on a lamp, on perfume, on pages one has read and reread. I had moreover friends and good companions; I had Annie de Pène, who was better than the best of them. But just as delicate fare does not stop you from craving for saveloys, so tried and exquisite friendship does not take away your taste for something new and dubious.

With Rosita, with Délia, I was insured against the risk of making confidences. My hidden past climbed the familiar stairs with me, sat secretly beside Délia, rearranged furniture on its old plan, revived the colors of the "rainy moon," and sharpened a weapon once used against myself.

"Is it a profession you chose yourself, Délia?"

"Not exactly. In January, this year, I took it up again because it means I can work at home."

She opened the beak of her fine scissors.

"It's good for me to handle pointed things."

There was a gravity about her, like the gravity of a young madwoman, that oddly suited Délia. I thought it unwise to encourage her further than by a questioning glance.

"Pointed things," she reiterated. "Scissors, needles, pins . . . It's good."

"Would you like me to introduce you to a sword swallower, a knife thrower, and a porcupine?"

She deigned to laugh and that chromatic laugh made me sorry she was not happy more often. A powerful feminine voice in the street called out the greengrocer's cry.

"Oh, it's the cherry cart," murmured Délia.

Without taking time to put on my felt hat, I went down bareheaded and brought a kilo of white-heart cherries. Running to avoid a motorcar, I bumped into a man who had stopped outside *my* door.

"Another moment, Madame, and your cherries . . ."

I smiled at this passer-by, who was a typical Parisian, with a lively face, a few white threads in his black hair, and fine, tired eyes that suggested an engraver or a printer. He was lighting a cigarette, without taking his eyes off the first-floor window. The lighted match burned his fingers; he let it drop and turned away.

A cry of pleasure—the first I had ever heard from Délia's lips—greeted my entrance, and the young woman pressed the back of my hand against her cheek. Feeling oddly rewarded, I watched her eating the cherries and putting the stalks and stones into the lid of a box of pins. Her expression of greed and selfishness did not deprive her of the charm that makes us feel tender toward violent children, withdrawn into their own passions and refusing to condescend to be pleasant.

"Just imagine, Délia, down there on the pavement . . ."

She stopped eating, with a big cherry bulging inside her cheek.

"What, down there on the pavement?"

"There's a man looking up at your windows. A very charming man, too."

She swallowed her cherry and hastily spat out the stone.

"What's he like?"

"Dark, a face . . . well, pleasant . . . white hairs in his black hair. He's got red-brown stains on his fingertips, they're the fingers of a man who smokes too much."

As she tucked her slipperless feet under her again with a sudden movement, Délia scattered all her fragile needlework tools on the floor.

"What day is it today? Friday, isn't it? Yes, Friday."

"Is he your Friday lover? Have you got one for all the days of the week?"

She stared full in my face with the insulting glare adolescents reserve for anyone who treats them as "big babies."

"You know everything, don't you?"

She rose to pick up her embroidery equipment. As she flourished a delicate little antique purse she was copying against the light, I noticed her hands were trembling. She turned toward me with a forced playfulness.

"He's nice, isn't he, my Friday lover? D'you think he's attractive?"

"I think he's attractive, but I don't think he looks well. You ought to look after him."

"Oh, I look after him all right, you needn't worry about *him*."

She began to laugh crazily, so much so that she brought on a fit of coughing. When she had stopped laughing and coughing, she leaned against a piece of furniture as if overcome with giddiness, staggered, and sat down.

"It's exhaustion," she muttered.

Her black hair, which had come down, fell no lower than her shoulders. Combed up on her temples and revealing her ears, it looked like an untidy little girl's and accentuated the regularity of her profile and its childish, inexorable cast.

"It's exhaustion." But what exhaustion? Due to an unhealthy life? No unhealthier than my own, as healthy as that of all women and girls who live in Paris. A few days earlier Délia had touched her forehead and clutched her temples. "It's there I wear myself out . . . And there . . ." Yes, the fixed idea; the absent man, the faithless Essendier. No matter how much I studied that perfect beauty—if you scanned it carefully, there was not a flaw in Délia's face—I searched it in vain for any expression of suffering, in other words, of love.

She remained seated, a little out of breath, with her slender pointed scissors dangling over her black dress from a metal chain. My scrutiny did not embarrass her, but after a few moments, she stood up like someone getting her way again and reproaching herself for having lingered too long. The change in the light and in the street noises told me the afternoon was over and I got myself ready to leave. Behind me, irreproachably slim, with her muted fairness, stood Mademoiselle Rosita. For some time, I had lost the habit of looking at her; she struck me as having aged. It struck me too that, through the wide-open door, she had probably heard us joking about the Friday lover. At the same instant, I realized that, in frequenting the Barberet sisters for no reason, I left the older sister out in the cold. My intercourse with her was limited to our brief professional conversations and to polite nothings, observations about the weather, the high cost of living, and the cinema. For Mademoiselle Rosita would never have allowed herself to ask any question that touched on my personal life, on my obvious freedom of a woman who lived alone. But how many days was it since I had displayed the faintest interest in Rosita? I felt embarrassed by this, and as Délia was making her way to the bathroom, I considered being "nice" to Rosita. An exemplary worker, endowed with sterling virtues and even with natural distinction, who typed Vandérem's manuscripts and Arthur Bernède's novelettes and my own crossed-out and interlined pages deserved a little consideration.

With her hands clasped palm to palm, her two little ringlets on her right shoulder, she was waiting patiently for me to go. As I went up to her, I saw she was paying not the slightest heed to me. What she was staring at was Délia's back as she left the room. Her eyes, of a middling blue, were hardened; they never left the short, slightly Spanish figure of her sister and the black hair that she was putting up with a careless hand. And as we take our interior shocks and shudders for divination, I thought, as I walked down the hill, whose houses were already rosy at the top: "But it's in the depths of this prim, colorless Rosita that I must find the answer to this little enigma brooding between the divan and the solitary window of a bedroom where a young woman is pretending, out of sheer obstinacy and jealousy, to relive a moment of my own life. The stubborn young woman very likely has few clues to the little enigma. If she knew more about it, she would never tell me. Her mystery, or her appearance of mystery, is a gratuitous gift; she might just as well have a golden strand in her black hair or a mole on her cheek."

Nevertheless, I continued walking along the pavements where, now that it was June, the concierges sitting out on their chairs, the children's games, and the flight of balls obliged one to perform a kind of country dance, two steps forward, two steps back, swing to the right and turn . . . The smell of stopped-up sinks, in June, dominates the exquisite pink twilights. By contrast I quite loved my western district that echoed like an empty corridor. A surprise awaited me in the form of a telegram: Sido, my mother, was arriving on the morrow and was staying in Paris three days. After this particular one, she only made a single last journey away from her own surroundings.

While she was there, there was no question of the Barberet young ladies. I am not concerned here to describe her stay. But her exacting presence recalled my life to dignity and solicitude. In her company, I had to pretend to be almost as young as she was, to follow her impulsive flights. I was terrified to see her so very small and thin, feverish in her enchanting gaiety and as if hunted. But I was still far from admitting the idea that she might die. Did she not insist, the very day she arrived, on buying pansy seeds, hearing a comic opera, and seeing a collection bequeathed to the Louvre? Did she not arrive bearing three pots of raspberry-and-currant jam and the first roses in bud wrapped up in a damp handkerchief; had she not made me a barometer by sewing weather-predicting wild oats onto a square of cardboard?

She abstained, as always, from questioning me about my most intimate troubles. The sexual side of my life inspired her, I think, with great and motherly repugnance. But I had to keep guard over my words and my face and to beware of her look, which read right through the flesh she had created. She liked to hear the news of my men and women friends, and of any newly formed acquaintances. I omitted however to tell her the Barberet story.

Sitting opposite me at the table, pushing away the plate she had not emptied, she questioned me less about what I was writing than about what I wanted to write. I have never been subjected to any criticism that resembled Sido's, for while believing in my vocation as a writer, she was dubious about my career. "Don't forget that you have only one gift," she used to say. "But what is one gift? One gift has never been enough for anyone."

The air of Paris intoxicated her as if she had been a young girl from the provinces. When she left, I put her on her slow train, anxious about letting her travel alone, yet happy to know that, a few hours later, she would be in the haven of her little home, where there were no comforts but also no dangers.

After her departure, everything seemed to me unworthy of pursuit. The wholesome sadness, the pride, the other good qualities she had instilled in me could not be more than ephemeral, I had already lived away from her too long. Yet when she had gone, I took up my place again in the deep embrasure of my window and once more switched on my green-shaded daylight lamp. But I was impelled by necessity, rather than love, of doing a good piece of work. And I wrote until it was time to travel by métro up the hill whose slope I liked to descend on foot.

Mademoiselle Rosita opened the door to me. By chance, she exclaimed "Ah!" at the sight of me, which checked a similar exclamation of surprise on my own lips. In less than a fortnight, my withered young girl had become a withered old maid. A little charwoman's bun replaced the bow and the two ringlets; she was wearing a bibbed apron tied around her waist. She mechanically fingered her right shoulder and stammered, "You've caught me not properly dressed. I've been dreadfully rushed these last days."

I shook her dry, delicate hand, which melted away in mine. A rather common scent, mingled with the smell of a frying pan in which cooking oil is being heated, revived my old memory of the little flat and of the younger sister.

"Are you keeping well? And your sister too?"

She jerked her shoulders in a way that signified nothing definite.

I added, with involuntary pride: "You understand, I've had my mother with me for a few days. And how's Délia getting on? Still working hard? Can I go and say how d'you do to her?"

Mademoiselle Rosita lowered her head as sheep do when they are mustering up their courage to fight.

"No, you can't. That is to say, you can, but I don't see why you should go and say how d'you do to a murderess."

"What did you say?"

"To a murderess. *I* have to stay here. But you, what have *you* got to do with a murderess?"

Even her manner had changed. Mademoiselle Rosita remained polite but she used a tone of profound indifference to utter words that could have been considered monstrous. I could not even see her familiar little white collar; it was replaced by a piece of coarse, sky-blue machine embroidery.

"But, Mademoiselle, I couldn't possibly have guessed. I was bringing you . . ."

"Very good," she said promptly. "Will you come in here?"

I went into the big room, just as in the days when Mademoiselle Rosita used adroitly to bar one from entering Délia's bedroom. I unpacked my manuscript in the intolerable glare of the unshaded windows and gave instructions as if to a stranger. Like a stranger, Rosita listened, and said: "Very good . . . Exactly . . . One black and one purple . . . It'll be finished Wednesday." The frequent, unnecessary interjections—"Madame . . . Yes, Madame . . . Oh, Madame . . ." had vanished from her replies. In her conversation, too, she had cut out the ringlets.

As in the days of my first curiosity, I kept my patience at first, then suddenly lost it. I hardly lowered my voice, as I asked Mademoiselle Barberet point-blank: "Whom has she killed?"

The poor girl, taken by surprise, made a small despairing gesture and leaned against the table with both hands.

"Ah, Madame, it's not done yet, but he's going to die."

"Who?"

"Why, her husband, Eugène."

"Her husband? The man she was waiting for day and night? I thought he had left her?"

"Left her, that's easier said than done. They didn't get on but you mustn't think the fault was on his side, very far from it. He's a very nice boy indeed, Eugène is, Madame. And he's never stopped sending my sister something out of what he earns, you know. But she—*she's* taken it into her head to revenge herself."

In the increasing confusion that was overtaking Rosita Barberet, I thought I could detect the disorder of a mind in which the poison of an old love was at work. The commonplace, dangerous rivalry between the pretty sister and the faded sister. A strand of hair, escaped from Rosita's perfunctorily scraped-up bun, became, in my eyes, the symbol of a madwoman's vehemence. The "rainy moon" gleamed in its seven colors on the wall of my former refuge, now given over to enemies in the process of accusing each other, fighting each other.

"Mademoiselle Rosita, I do beg you. Aren't you exaggerating a little? This is a very serious accusation, you realize."

I did not speak roughly, for I am frightened of harmless lunatics, of people who deliver long monologues in the street without seeing us, of purple-faced drunks who shake their fists at empty space and walk zigzag. I wanted to take back my manuscript, but the roll of papers had been grabbed by Rosita and served to punctuate her sentences. She spoke violently, without raising her voice.

"I definitely mean revenge herself, Madame. When she realized he did not love her anymore, she said to herself: 'I'll get you.' So she cast a spell on him."

The word was so unexpected that it made me smile, and Rosita noticed it.

"Don't laugh, Madame. Anyone would think you really didn't know what you were laughing about."

A metallic object fell, on the other side of the door, and Rosita gave a start.

"Well, right, so it's the scissors now," she said, speaking to herself.

She must have read on my face something like a desire to be elsewhere, and tried to reassure me.

"Don't be afraid. She knows quite well that you're here, but if you don't go into her room, she won't come into this one."

"I'm not afraid," I said sharply. "What has she given him? A drug?"

"She's convoked him. Convoking, do you know what that is?"

"No . . . that's to say, I've got some vague idea, but I don't know all the . . . the details."

"Convoking is summoning a person by force. That poor Eugène . . ."

"Wait!" I exclaimed in a low voice. "What's he like, your brother-in-law? He's not a dark young man who's got white hairs among his black ones? He looks rather ill, he's got the complexion of people who have a cardiac lesion? Yes? Then it was him I saw about . . . say two weeks ago."

"Where?"

"Down there, in the street. He was looking up at the window of

my . . . the window of Délia's bedroom. He looked as if he were waiting. I even warned Délia she had a lover under her window . . ."

Rosita clasped her hands.

"Oh, Madame! And you didn't tell me! A whole fortnight!"

She let her arms fall and hang limp over her apron. Her light eyes
held a reproach, which, to me, seemed quite meaningless. She looked
at me without seeing me, her spectacles in her hand, with an intense,
unfocused gaze.

"Mademoiselle Rosita, you don't really mean to say you're accusing
Délia of witchcraft and black magic?"

"But indeed I am, Madame! What she is doing is what they call
convoking, but it's the same thing."

"Listen, Rosita, we're not living in the Middle Ages now . . . Think
calmly for a moment . . ."

"But I am thinking calmly, Madame. I've never done anything
else! This thing she's doing, she's not the only one who's doing it. It's
quite common. Mark you, I don't say it succeeds every time. Didn't
you know anything about it?"

I shook my head and the other faintly shrugged her shoulders, as
if to indicate that my education had been seriously lacking. A clock
somewhere struck midday and I rose to go. Absorbed in her own
thoughts, Rosita followed me to the door out of mechanical politeness.
In the dark hall, the plate-shaped ceiling light chiseled her features
into those of a haggard old lady.

"Rosita," I said, "if your sister's surprised I didn't ask to see
her . . ."

"She won't be surprised," she said, shaking her head. "She's far too
occupied in doing evil."

She looked at me with an irony of which I had not believed her
capable.

"And besides, you know, this is not a good moment to see her.
She's not at all pretty, these days. If she were, it really wouldn't be fair."

Suddenly I remembered Délia's extraordinary words: "It's good for
me to handle pointed things. Scissors . . . pins." Overcome by the excitement of passing on baleful news, I bent over and repeated them in
Rosita's ear. She seized the top of my arm, in a familiar way, and drew
me out onto the landing.

"I'll bring you back your typed pages tomorrow evening about half
past six or seven. Make your escape, *she'll* be asking me to get her
lunch."

I did not savor the pleasure I had anticipated, after leaving Rosita
Barberet. Yet when I thought over the extravagance, the ambitiousness
of this anecdote which aspired to be a sensational news item, I found

that it lacked only one thing, guilelessness. A want of innocence spoiled
its exciting color, all its suggestion of old women's gossip and brewings
of mysterious herbs and magic potions. For I do not care for the picturesque when it is based on feelings of black hatred. As I returned to
my own neighborhood, I compared the Barberet story with "the story
of the rue Truffaut" and found the latter infinitely pleasanter, with
its circle of worthy women in the Batignolles district who, touching
hands around a dinner table, conversed with the great beyond and
received news of their dead children and their departed husbands. They
never asked my name because I had been introduced by the local hairdresser and they slipped me a warning to mistrust a lady called X. It
so happened that the advice was excellent. But the principal attraction
of the meeting lay in the darkened room, in the tablecloth bordered
with a bobble fringe that matched the one on the curtains, in the spirit
of a young sailor, an invisible and mischievous ghost who haunted it on
regular days, and shut himself up in the cupboard in order to make all
the cups and saucers rattle. "Ah, *that* chap . . ." the stout mistress of
the house would sigh indulgently.

"You let him get away with anything, Mamma," her daughter
(the medium) would say reproachfully. "All the same, it would be a
pity if he broke the blue cup."

At the end of the séance, these ladies passed around cups of pale,
tepid tea. What peace, what charm there was in being entertained by
these hostesses, whose social circle relied entirely on an extraterrestrial
world! How agreeable I found her too, that female bonesetter, Mademoiselle Lévy, who undertook the care of bodies and souls and demanded so little money in exchange! She practiced massage and the
laying on of hands in the darkest depths of pallid concierges' lodges, in
variety artistes' digs in the rue Biot, and in dressing rooms in the music
halls of La Fauvette. She sewed beautiful Hebrew characters into
sachets and hung them around your neck: "You can be assured of its
efficaciousness, it is prepared by the hands of innocence." And she
would display her beautiful hands, softened by creams and unguents,
and add: "If things don't get better tomorrow, when I go away, I can
light a candle for you to Our Lady of Victories. *I'm* on good terms with
everyone."

Certainly, in the practices of innocent, popular magic, I was not
such a novice as I had wished to appear in the eyes of Mademoiselle
Barberet. But, in frequenting my ten- or twenty-franc sibyls, all I had
done was to amuse myself, to listen to the rich but limited music of old,
ritual words, to abandon my hands into hands so foreign to me, so worn
smooth by contact with other human hands, that I benefited from
them for a moment as I might have done from immersing myself in a

crowd or listening to some voluble, pointless story. In short, they acted on me like a pain-killing drug, warranted harmless to children . . .

Whereas these mutual enemies, the Barberets . . . A blind alley, haunted by evil designs; was this what had become of the little flat where once I had suffered without bitterness, watched over by my rainy moon?

And so I reckoned up everything in the realm of the inexplicable that I owed to some extent to obtuse go-betweens, to vacant creatures whose emptiness reflects fragments of destinies, to modest liars and vehement visionaries. Not one of these women had done me any harm, not one of them had frightened me. But these two sisters, so utterly unlike . . .

I had had so little for lunch that I was glad to go and dine at a modest restaurant whose proprietress was simply known as "that fat woman who knows how to cook." It was rare for me not to meet under its low ceilings one of those people one calls "friends" and who are sometimes, in fact, affectionate. I seem to remember that, with Count d'Adelsward de Fersen, I crowned my orgy—*bœuf à l'ancienne* and cider —by spending two hours at the cinema. Fersen, fair-haired and coated with brick-red suntan, wrote verses and did not like women. But he was so cut out to be attractive to all females that one of them exclaimed at the sight of him: "Ah, what waste of a good thing!" Intolerant and well-read, he had a quick temper and his exaggerated flamboyance hid a fundamental shyness. When we left the restaurant, Gustave Téry was just beginning his late dinner. But the founder of *L'Œuvre* gave me no other greeting than some buffalo-like glares, as was his habit whenever he was swollen with polemic fury and imagined he was being persecuted. Spherical, light on his feet, he entered like a bulky cloud driven by a gale. Either I am mistaken or else, that night, everyone I ran into, the moment I recognized them, showed an extraordinary tendency to move away and disappear. My last meeting was with a prostitute who was eyeing the pedestrians at the corner of the street, about a hundred steps from the house where I lived. I did not fail to say a word to her, as well as to the wandering cat who was keeping her company. A large, warm moon, a yellow June moon, lit up my homeward journey. The woman, standing on her short shadow, was talking to the cat Mimine. She was only interested in meteorology or, at least, so one would have imagined from her rare words. For six months I had seen her in a shapeless coat and a cloche hat with a little military plume that hid the top of her face.

"It's a mild night," she said, by way of greeting. "But you mustn't imagine it's going to last, the mist is all in one long sheet over the stream. When it's in big separate puffs like bonfires, that means fine weather. So you're back again, on foot, as usual?"

I offered her one of the cigarettes Fersen had given me. She remained faithful to the district longer than I did, with her shadow crouched like a dog at her feet, this shepherdess without a flock who talked about bonfires and thought of the Seine as a stream. I hope that she has long been sleeping, alone forever more, and dreaming of haylofts, of dawns crisp with frosted dew, of mists clinging to the running water that bears her along with it.

The little flat I occupied at that time was the envy of my rare visitors. But I soon knew that it would not hold me for long. Not that its three rooms—let's say two and a half rooms—were inconvenient, but they thrust into prominence single objects that, in other surroundings, had been one of a pair. Now I possessed only one of the two beautiful red porcelain vases, fitted up as a lamp. The second Louis XV armchair held out its slender arms elsewhere for someone else to rest in. My square bookcase waited in vain for another square bookcase, and is still waiting for it. This series of amputations suffered by my furniture distressed no one but myself, and Rosita Barberet did not fail to exclaim: "Why, it's a real nest!" as she clasped her gloved hands in admiration. A low shaft of sunlight—Honnorat had not yet finished serving his time as a page, and seven on the Charles X clock meant that it was a good seven hours since noon—reached my writing table, shone through a small carafe of wine, and touched, on its way, a little bunch of those June roses that are sold by the dozen, in Paris, in June.

I was pleased to see that she was once again the prim, neat Rosita, dressed in black with her touch of white lingerie at the neck. Fashion at that time favored little short capes held in place by tie ends that were crossed in front and fastened at the back of the waist. Mademoiselle Barberet knew how to wear a Paris hat, which means a very simple hat. But she seemed to have definitely repudiated the two little ringlets over one shoulder. The brim of her hat came down over the sad snail-shaped bun, symbol of all renouncements, on the thin, graying nape, and the face it shaded was wasted with care. As I poured out a glass of Lunel for Rosita, I wished I could also offer her lipstick and powder, some form of rejuvenating makeup.

She began by pushing away the burnt-topaz-colored wine and the biscuits.

"I'm not accustomed to it, Madame, I only drink water with a dash of wine in it or sometimes a little beer."

"Just a mouthful. It's a wine for children."

She drank a mouthful, expostulated, drank another mouthful and yet another, making little affected grimaces because she had not learned to be simple, except in her heart. Betweentimes, she admired everything her shortsightedness made it impossible for her to see clearly.

Soon she had one red cheek and one pale cheek and some little threads of blood in the whites of her eyes, around the brightened blue of the iris. All this would have made a middle-aged woman look younger, but Mademoiselle Barberet was only a girl, still young and withered before her time.

"It's a magic potion," she said, with her typical smile that seemed set in inverted commas.

Continuing, as if she were speaking a line in a play, she sighed: "Ah, if that poor Eugène . . ."

By this, I realized that her time was limited and I wanted to know how long she had.

"Has your sister gone out? She's not waiting for you?"

"I told her I was bringing you your typescript and that I was also going to look in on Monsieur Vandérem and Monsieur Lucien Muhl-feld so as to make only one journey of it. If she's in a hurry for her dinner, there's some vegetable soup left over from yesterday, a boiled artichoke, and some stewed rhubarb."

"In any case, the little restaurant on the right as you go down your street . . ."

Mademoiselle Barberet shook her head.

"No. She doesn't go out. She doesn't go out anymore." She swallowed a drop of wine left in the bottom of her glass, then folded her arms in a decided way on my worktable, just opposite me. The setting sun clung for a moment to all the features of her half-flushed, half-pale face, to a turquoise brooch that fastened her collar. I wanted to come to her aid and spare her the preamble.

"I have to admit, Rosita, that I didn't quite understand what you were saying to me yesterday."

"I realized that," she said, with a little whinny. "At first I thought you were making fun of me. A person as well-read as you are . . . To put it in two words instead of a hundred, Madame, my sister is in the process of making her husband die. On my mother's memory, Madame, she is killing him. Six moons have already gone by, the seventh is coming, that's the fatal moon; this unfortunate man knows that he's doomed, besides he's already had two accidents, from which he's entirely recovered, but all the same it's a handicap that puts him in a state of less resistance and makes the task easier for *her*."

She would have exceeded the hundred words in her first breath had not her haste and, no doubt, the warmth of the wine slightly choked her.

I profited by her fit of coughing to ask: "Mademoiselle Rosita, just one question. Why should Délia want to make her husband die?"

She threw up her hands in a disclaiming gesture of impotence.

"Ah, as to that . . . you may well hunt for the real reason! All the usual reasons between a man and a woman! And you don't love me anymore and I still love you, and you wish I were dead and come back I implore you, and I'd like to see you in hell."

She gave a brutal "Hah!" and grimaced.

"My poor Rosita, if all couples who don't get on resorted to murder . . ."

"But they do resort to it," she protested. "They make no bones about resorting to it!"

"You see very few cases reported in the papers."

"Because it's all done in private, it's a family affair. Nine times out of ten, no one gets arrested. It's talked about a little in the neighborhood. But just you see if you can find any traces! Firearms, poisons, that's all out-of-date stuff. My sister knows that, all right. What about the woman who keeps the sweet shop just below us, whatever's *she* done with her husband? And the milkman at Number 57, rather queer isn't it that he's gone and lost his second wife, too?"

Her refined, high-class saleslady's vocabulary had gone to pieces and she had thrust out her chin like a gargoyle. With a flip of her finger, she pushed back her hat, which was pinching her forehead. I was as shocked as if she had pulled up her skirt and fastened her suspenders without apologizing. She uncovered a high forehead, with sloping temples, which I had never seen so nakedly revealed, whence I imagined there was to be a burst of confidences and secrets that might or might not be dangerous. Behind Rosita, the window was turning pink with the last faint rose reflection of daylight. Yet I dared not switch on my lamp at once.

"Rosita," I said seriously, "are you in the habit of saying . . . what you've just said to me . . . to just anybody?"

Her eyes looked frankly straight into mine.

"You must be joking, Madame. Should I have come so far if I'd had anyone near me who deserved to be trusted?"

I held out my hand, which she grasped. She knew how to shake hands, curtly and warmly, without prolonging the pressure.

"If you believe that Délia is doing harm to her husband, why don't you try to counteract the harm? Because *you*, at least it seems so to me, wish nothing but good to Eugène Essendier."

She gazed at me dejectedly.

"But I can't, Madame! Love would have to have passed between Eugène and me. And it hasn't passed between us! It's never passed, never, never!"

She pulled a handkerchief out of her bag and wept, taking care not to wet her little starched collar. I thought I understood everything.

"Now we have it, jealousy of course." Promptly Rosita's accusations and she herself became suspect, and I turned on the switch of my lamp.

"That doesn't mean I must go, Madame?" she asked anxiously.

"Of course not, of course not," I said weakly.

The truth was that I could hardly bear the sight, under the strong rays of my lamp, of her red-eyed face and her hat tipped backward like a drunken woman's. But Rosita had hardly begun to talk.

"Eugène has never even thought of wanting me," she said humbly. "If he had wanted me, even just once, I'd be in a position to fight against her, you understand."

"No. I don't understand. I've everything to learn, as you see. Do you really attribute so much importance to the fact of having . . . having belonged to a man?"

"And you? Do you really attribute so little to it?"

I decided to laugh.

"No, no, Rosita, I'm not so frivolous, unfortunately. But all the same, I don't think it constitutes a bond, that it sets a seal on you."

"Well, you're mistaken, that's all. Possession gives you the power to summon, to convoke, as they say. Have you really never 'called' anyone?"

"Indeed I have," I said, laughing. "I must have hit on someone deaf. I didn't get an answer."

"Because you didn't call hard enough, for good or evil. My sister, she really does call. If you could see her. She's unrecognizable. Also, she's up to some pretty work, I can assure you."

She fell silent, and for a moment, it was quite obvious she had stopped thinking of me.

"But Eugène himself, couldn't you warn him?"

"I have warned him. But Eugène, he's a skeptic. He told me he'd had enough of one crack-brained woman and that the second crack-brained woman would do him a great favor if she'd shut up. He's got pockets under his eyes and he's the color of butter. From time to time he coughs, but not from the chest, he coughs because of palpitations of the heart. He said to me: 'All I can do for you is to lend you *Fantômas*. It's just your cup of tea.' That just shows," added Mademoiselle Barberet, with a bitter smile. "That just shows how the most intelligent men can argue like imbeciles, seeing no difference between fantastic made-up stories and things as real as this . . . as such deadly machinations."

"But what machinations, will you kindly tell me?" I exclaimed.

Mademoiselle Barberet unfolded her spectacles and put them on, wedging them firmly in the brown dints that marked either side of her transparent nose. Her gaze became focused, taking on new assurance and a searching expression.

"You know," she murmured, "that it is never too late to *summon*? You have quite understood that one can *summon* for good and for evil?"

"I know it now that you have told me."

She pushed my lamp a little to one side and leaned over closer to me. She was hot and nothing is so unbearable to me as the human smell except when—very rarely indeed—I find it intoxicating. Moreover, the wine to which she was not accustomed kept repeating and her breath smelled of it. I wanted to stand up but she was already talking.

There are things that are written down nowhere, except by clumsy hands in school exercise books, or on thin gray-squared paper, yellowed at the edges, folded and cut into pages and sewn together with red cotton; things that the witch bequeathed to the bonesetter, that the bonesetter sold to the love-obsessed woman, that the obsessed one passed on to another wretched creature. All that the credulity and the sullied memory of a pure girl can gather in the dens that an unfathomable city harbors between a brand-new cinema and an espresso bar, I heard from Rosita Barberet, who had learned it from the vaunts of widows who had willed the deaths of the husbands who had deserted them, from the frenzied fantasies of lonely women.

"You say a name, nothing but the name, the name of the particular person, a hundred times, a thousand times. No matter how far away they are, they will hear you in the end. Without eating or drinking, as long as you can possibly keep it up, you say the name, nothing else but the name. Don't you remember one day when Délia nearly fainted? I suspected at once. In our neighborhood there are heaps of them who repeated the name . . ."

Whisperings, an obtuse faith, even a local custom, were these the forces and the magic philters that procured love, decided life and death, removed that lofty mountain, an indifferent heart?

". . . One day when you rang the bell, and my sister was lying behind the door . . ."

"Yes, I remember . . . You asked me 'Is that you, Eugène?' "

"She'd said to me: 'Quick, quick, he's coming. I can feel it, quick, he must tread on me as he comes in, it's essential!' But it was you."

"It was only me."

"She'd been lying there, believe me or not, for over two hours. Soon after that, she took to pointed things again. Knives, scissors, embroidery needles. That's very well known, but it's dangerous. If you haven't enough strength, the points can turn against you. But do you imagine *that one* would ever lack strength? If I lived the life she does, I should have been dead by now. *I've* got nothing to sustain me."

"Has she, then?"

"Of course she has. She hates. That nourishes her."

That Délia, so young, with her rather arrogant beauty, her soft cheek that she laid against my hand. That was the same Délia who played with twenty little glittering thunderbolts that she intended to be deadly, and she used their sharp points to embroider beaded flowers.

". . . But she's given up embroidering bags now. She's taken to working with needles whose points she's contaminated."

"What did you say?"

"I said she's contaminated them by dipping them in a mixture."

And Rosita Barberet launched out into the path, strewn with nameless filth, into which the practice of base magic drags its faithful adherents. She pursued that path without blenching, without omitting a word, for fastidiousness is not a feminine virtue. She would not allow me to remain ignorant of one thing to which her young sister stooped in the hope of doing injury, that same sister who loved fresh cherries . . . So young, with one of those rather short bodies a man's arms clasp so easily and, beneath that black, curly hair, the pallor that a lover longs to crimson.

Luckily, the narrator branched off and took to talking only about death, and I breathed again. Death is not nauseating. She discoursed on the imminent death of this unfortunate Eugène, which so much resembled the death of the husband of the woman in the sweet shop. And then there was the chemist, who had died quite black.

"You must surely admit, Madame, that the fact of a chemist being fixed like that by his wife, that really is turning the world upside down!"

I certainly did admit it. I even derived a strange satisfaction from it. What did I care about the chemist and the unlucky husband of the woman who kept the sweet shop? All I was waiting for now from my detailed informant was one final picture: Délia arriving at the crossroads where, amid the vaporous clouds produced by each one's illusion, the female slaves of the cloven-footed one meet for the Sabbath.

"Yes, indeed. And where does the devil come in, Rosita?"

"What devil, Madame?"

"Why, the devil pure and simple, I presume. Does your sister give him a special name?"

An honest amazement was depicted on Rosita's face and her eyebrows flew up to the top of her high forehead.

"But, Madame, whatever trail are you off on now? The devil, that's just for imbeciles. The devil, just imagine . . ."

She shrugged her shoulders and, behind her glasses, threw a withering glance at discredited Satan.

"The devil! Admitting he existed, he'd be just the one to mess it all up!"

"Rosita, you remind me at this moment of the young woman who said: 'God, that's all hooey! . . . But no jokes in front of me about the Blessed Virgin!' "

"Everyone's got their own ideas, Madame. Good heavens! It's ten to eight! It was very kind of you to let me come," she sighed in a voice that did not disguise her disappointment.

For I had offered her neither help nor connivance. She pulled down her hat—at last—over her forehead. I remembered, just in time, that I had not paid her for her last lot of work.

"A drop of Lunel before you go, Mademoiselle Rosita?"

Involuntarily, by calling her "Mademoiselle" again, I was putting her at a distance. She swallowed the golden wine in one gulp and I complimented her.

"Oh, I've got a good head," she said.

But as she had folded up her spectacles again, she searched around for me with a vague eye, and as she went out, she bumped against the doorpost, to which she made a little apologetic bow.

As soon as she had gone, I opened the window to its fullest extent to let in the evening air. Mistaking the feeling of exhaustion her visit had given me for genuine tiredness, I made the error of going to bed early. My dreams showed the effects of it, and through them, I realized I was not yet rid of the two enemy sisters or of another memory. I kept relapsing into a nightmare in which I was now my real self, now identified with Délia. Half reclining like her on *our* divan-bed, in the dark part of our room, I "convoked" with a powerful summons, with a thousand repetitions of his name, a man who was not called Eugène . . .

Dawn found me drenched with those abundant tears we rain in sleep and that go on flowing after we are awake and can no longer track them to their source. The thousand-times repeated name grew dim and lost his nocturnal power. In my own mind, I said farewell to it and thrust its echo back into the little flat where I had taken pleasure in suffering. And I abandoned that flat to those other women, to their stifled, audacious, incantation-ridden lives, where witchcraft could be fitted in between the daily task and the Saturday cinema, between the little washtub and the frying steak.

When the short night was ended, I promised myself that never again would I climb the Paris hill with the steep, gay streets. Between one day and the next, I turned Rosita's furtive charm, her graceful way of putting down her slender feet when she walked, and the two little ringlets that fluttered on her shoulder into a memory. With that Délia who did not want to be called Adèle, I had a little more trouble. All the more so, as, after the lapse of a fortnight, I took to running into her by pure chance. Once, she was rummaging in a box of small remnants near the entrance of a big shop, and three days later she was buying spaghetti in an Italian grocer's. She looked pale and diminished, like a convalescent who is out too soon, pearly under the eyes, and extremely pretty. A thick, curled fringe covered her forehead to the eyebrows. Something indescribable stirred in the depths of me and spoke in her favor. But I did not answer.

Another time, I recognized only her walk, seeing her from the back. We were walking along the same pavement and I had to slow down my step so as not to overtake her. For she was advancing by little, short steps, then making a pause, as if out of breath, and going on again. Finally, one Sunday when I was returning with Annie de Pène from the flea market and, loaded with treasure such as milk-glass lamps and Rubelles plates, we were having a rest and drinking lemonade, I caught sight of Délia Essendier. She was wearing a dress whose black showed purplish in the sunlight, as happens with redyed fabrics. She stopped not far from us in front of a fried-potato stall, bought a large bag of chips, and ate them with gusto. After that, she stayed standing for a moment, with an air of having nothing to do. The shape of the hat she was wearing recalled a Renaissance "Beguine's," and cupping Délia's little Roman chin was the white crepe band of a widow.

[Translated by Antonia White]

Green Sealing Wax

❧❀❧

Around fifteen, I was at the height of a mania for "desk furniture." In this I was only imitating my father, whose mania for it lasted in full force all his life. At the age when every kind of vice gets its claws into adolescence, like the hundred little hooks of a burr sticking into one's hair, a girl of fifteen runs plenty of risks. My glorious freedom exposed me to all of them and I believed it to be unbounded, unaware that Sido's maternal instinct, which disdained any form of spying, worked by flashes of intuition and leaped telepathically to the danger point.

When I had just turned fifteen, Sido gave me a dazzling proof of her second sight. She guessed that a man above suspicion had designs on my little pointed face, the plaits that whipped against my calves, and my well-made body. Having entrusted me to this man's family during the holidays, she received a warning as clear and shattering as the gift of sudden faith and she cursed herself for having sent me away to strangers. Promptly she put on her little bonnet that tied under the chin, got into the clanking, jolting train—they were beginning to send antique coaches along a brand-new line—and found me in a garden, playing with two other little girls, under the eyes of a taciturn man, leaning on his elbow like the meditative Demon on the ledge of Notre-Dame.

Such a spectacle of peaceful family life could not deceive Sido. She noticed, moreover, that I looked prettier than I did at home. That is how girls blossom in the warmth of a man's desire, whether they are fifteen or thirty. There was no question of scolding me and Sido took me away with her without the irreproachably respectable man's having dared to ask the reason for her arrival or for our departure. In the train, she fell asleep before my eyes, worn out like someone who had won a battle. I remember that lunchtime went by and I complained of being hungry. Instead of flushing, looking at her watch, promising me my favorite delicacies—whole-meal bread, cream cheese, and pink onions—all she did was to shrug her shoulders. Little did she care about my hunger pangs, she had saved the most precious thing of all.

I had done nothing wrong, nor had I abetted this man, except by my torpor. But torpor is a far graver peril for a girl of fifteen than all the usual excited giggling and blushing and clumsy attempts at flirtation. Only a few men can induce that torpor from which girls awake to find themselves lost. That, so to speak, surgical intervention of Sido's cleared up all the confusion inside me and I had one of those relapses into childishness in which adolescence revels when it is simultaneously ashamed of itself and intoxicated by its own ego.

My father, a born writer, left few pages behind him. At the actual moment of writing, he dissipated his desire in material arrangements, setting out all the objects a writer needs and a number of superfluous ones as well. Because of him, I am not proof against this mania myself. As a result of having admired and coveted the perfect equipment of a writer's worktable, I am still exacting about the tools on my desk. Since adolescence does nothing by halves, I stole from my father's worktable, first a little mahogany set square that smelled like a cigar box, then a white metal ruler. Not to mention the scolding, I received full in my face the glare of a small, blazing gray eye, the eye of a rival, so fierce that I did not risk it a third time. I confined myself to prowling, hungrily, with my mind full of evil thoughts, around all these treasures of stationery. A pad of virgin blotting paper; an ebony ruler; one, two, four, six pencils, sharpened with a penknife and all of different colors; pens with medium nibs and fine nibs, pens with enormously broad nibs, drawing pens no thicker than a blackbird's quill; sealing wax, red, green, and violet; a hand blotter; a bottle of liquid glue, not to mention slabs of transparent amber-colored stuff known as "mouth glue"; the minute remains of a spahi's cloak reduced to the dimensions of a pen wiper with scalloped edges; a big ink pot flanked by a small ink pot, both in bronze; and a lacquer bowl filled with a golden powder to dry the wet page; another bowl containing sealing wafers of all colors (I used to eat the white ones); to right and left of the table, reams of paper, cream-laid, ruled, watermarked; and, of course, that little stamping machine that bit into the white sheet, and, with one snap of its jaws, adorned it with an embossed name: *J.–J. Colette*. There was also a glass of water for washing paintbrushes, a box of watercolors, an address book, the bottles of red, black, and violet ink, the mahogany set square, a pocket case of mathematical instruments, the tobacco jar, a pipe, the spirit lamp for melting the sealing wax.

A property owner tries to extend his domain; my father therefore tried to acclimatize adventitious subjects on his vast table. At one time there appeared on it a machine that could cut through a pile of a hundred sheets, and some frames filled with a white jelly on which you laid a written page face downward and then, from this looking-glass original, pulled off blurred, sticky, anemic copies. But my father soon wearied of such gadgets and the huge table returned to its serenity, to its classical style that was never disturbed by inspiration with its disorderly litter of crossed-out pages, cigarette butts, and "roughs" screwed up into paper balls. I have forgotten, heaven forgive me, the paper-knife section, three or four boxwood ones, one of imitation silver, and the last of yellowed ivory, cracked from end to end.

From the age of ten I had never stopped coveting those material goods, invented for the glory and convenience of a mental power, which come under the general heading of "desk furniture." Children only delight in things they can hide. For a long time I secured possession of one wing, the left one, of the great four-doored double bookcase (it was eventually sold by order of the court). The doors of the upper part were glass-fronted, those of the lower, solid and made of beautiful figured mahogany. When you opened the lower left-hand door at a right angle, the flap touched the side of the chest of drawers, and as the bookcase took up nearly the whole of one paneled wall, I would immure myself in a quadrangular nook formed by the side of the chest of drawers, the wall, the left section of the bookcase, and its wide-open door. Sitting on a little footstool, I could gaze at the three mahogany shelves in front of me, on which were displayed the objects of my worship, ranging from cream-laid paper to a little cup of the golden powder. "She's a chip off the old block," Sido would say teasingly to my father. It was ironical that, equipped with every conceivable tool for writing, my father rarely committed himself to putting pen to paper, whereas Sido—sitting at any old table, pushing aside an invading cat, a basket of plums, a pile of linen, or else just putting a dictionary on her lap by way of a desk— Sido really did write. A hundred enchanting letters prove that she did. To continue a letter or finish it off, she would tear a page out of her household account book or write on the back of a bill.

She therefore despised our useless altars. But she did not discourage me from lavishing care on my desk and adorning it to amuse myself. She even showed anxiety when I explained that my little house was becoming too small for me . . . "Too small. Yes, much too small," said the gray eyes. "Fifteen . . . Where is Pussy Darling going, bursting out of her nook like a hermit crab driven out of its borrowed shell by its own growth? Already, I've snatched her from the clutches of that man.

Already, I've had to forbid her to go dancing on the 'Ring' on Low Sunday. Already, she's escaping and I shan't be able to follow her. Already, she wants a long dress, and if I give her one, the blindest will notice that she's a young girl. And if I refuse, everyone will look below the too-short skirt and stare at her woman's legs. Fifteen . . . How can I stop her from being fifteen, then sixteen, then seventeen years old?"

Sometimes, during that period, she would come and lean over the mahogany half door that isolated me from the world. "What are you doing?" She could see perfectly well what I was doing but she could not understand it. I refused her the answer given her so generously by everything else she observed, the bee, the caterpillar, the hydrangea, the ice plant. But at least she could see I was there, sheltered from danger. She indulged my mania. The lovely pieces of shiny colored wrapping paper were given me to bind my books and I made the gold string into bookmarkers. I had the first penholder sheathed in a glazed turquoise-colored substance, with a moiré pattern on it, that appeared in Reumont's, the stationers.

One day my mother brought me a little stick of sealing wax and I recognized the stub of green wax, the prize jewel of my father's desk. No doubt I considered the gift too overwhelming, for I gave no sign of ecstatic joy. I clutched the sealing wax in my hand, and as it grew warm, it gave out a slightly Oriental fragrance of incense.

"It's very old sealing wax," Sido told me, "and as you can see, it's powdered with gold. Your father already had it when we were married; he'd been given it by his mother and his mother assured him that it was a stick of wax that had been used by Napoleon I. But you've got to remember that my mother-in-law lied every time she opened her mouth, so . . ."

"Is he giving it to me or have you taken it?"

Sido became impatient; she always turned irritable when she thought she was going to be forced to lie and was trying to avoid lying.

"When *will* you stop twisting a lock of hair around the end of your nose?" she cried. "You're doing your best to have a red nose with a blob at the tip like a cherry! That sealing wax? Let's say your father's lending it to you and leave it at that. Of course, if you don't want . . ."

My wild clutch of possession made Sido laugh again, and she said, with pretended lightness: "If he wanted it, he'd ask you to give it back, of course!"

But he did not ask me to give it back. For a few months, gold-flecked green sealing wax perfumed my narrow empire bounded by four mahogany walls; then my pleasure gradually diminished, as do all pleasures to which no one disputes our right. Besides, my devotion to stationery temporarily waned in favor of a craze to be glamorous. I asserted my right to wear a "bustle," that is to say, I enlarged my small, round behind with a horsehair cushion, which, of course, made my skirts much shorter at the back than in front. In our village, the frenzy of adolescence turned girls between thirteen and fifteen into madwomen who stole horsehair, cotton, and wool, stuffed rags in a bag, and tied on the hideous contraption known as a "false bottom" on dark staircases, out of their mother's sight. I also longed for a thick, frizzy fringe, leather belts so tight I could hardly breathe, high boned collars, violet scent on my handkerchief . . .

From that phase, I relapsed once more into childhood, for a feminine creature has to make several attempts before it finally hatches out. I reveled in being a Plain Jane, with my hair in pigtails and straight wisps straggling over my cheeks. I gladly renounced all my finery in favor of my old school pinafores with their pockets stuffed with nuts and string and chocolate. Paths edged with brambles, clumps of bullrushes, licorice "shoelaces," cats—in short, everything I still love to this day—became dear to me again. There are no words to hymn such times in one's life, no clear memories to illuminate them; looking back on them, I can only compare them to the depths of blissful sleep. The smell of haymaking sometimes brings them back to me, perhaps because, suddenly tired, as growing creatures are, I would drop for an hour into a dreamless sleep among the new-mown hay.

It was at this point there occurred the episode known for long afterward as "the Hervouët will affair." Old Monsieur Hervouët died and no will could be found. The provinces have always been rich in fantastic figures. Somewhere, under old tiled roofs, yellow with lichen, in icy drawing rooms and dining rooms dedicated to eternal shade, on waxed floors strewn with death traps of knitted rugs, in kitchen-garden paths between the hard-headed cabbages and the curly parsley, queer characters are always to be found. A little town or a village prides itself on possessing a mystery. My own village acknowledged placidly, even respectfully, the rights of young Gateau to rave unmolested. This admirable example of a romantic madman, a wooden cigar between his lips, was always wildly tossing his streaming black curls and staring fixedly at young girls with his long, Arab eyes. A voluntary recluse used to nod good morning through a windowpane and passers would say of her admiringly: "That makes twenty-two years since Madame Sibile left her room! My mother used to see her there, just as you see her now. And, you know, there's nothing the matter with her. In one way, it's a fine life!"

But Sido used to hurry her quick step and pull me along when we passed level with the aquarium that housed the lady who had not gone out for twenty-two years. Behind her clear glass pane the prisoner would be smiling. She always wore a linen cap; sometimes her little yellow hand held a cup. A sure instinct for what is horrible and prohibited made Sido turn away from that ground-floor window and that bobbing head. But the sadism of childhood made me ask her endless questions.

"How old do you think she is, Madame Sibile? At night does she sleep by the window in her armchair? Do they undress her? Do they wash her? And how does she go to the lavatory?"

Sido would start as if she had been stung.

"Be quiet. I forbid you to think about those things."

Monsieur Hervouët had never passed for one of those eccentrics to whom a market town extends its slightly derisive protection. For sixty years he had been well-off and ill dressed, first a "big catch" to marry, then a big catch married. Left a widower, he had remarried. His second wife was a former postmistress, thin and full of fire.

When she struck her breastbone, exclaiming, *"That's* where I can feel it burning!" her Spanish eyes seemed to make the person she was talking to responsible for this unquenchable ardor. "I am not easily frightened," my father used to say; "but heaven preserve me from being left alone with Mademoiselle Matheix!"

After his second marriage, Monsieur Hervouët no longer appeared in public. As he never left his home, no one knew exactly when he developed the gastric trouble that was to carry him off. He was a man dressed, in all weathers, in black, including a cap with earflaps. Smothered in fleecy white hair and a beard like cotton wool, he looked like an apple tree attacked by woolly aphis. High walls and a gateway that was nearly always closed protected his second season of conjugal bliss. In summer a single rosebush clothed three sides of his one-storied house and the thick fringe of wisteria on the crest of the wall provided food for the first bees. But we had never heard anyone say that Monsieur Hervouët was fond of flowers, and if we now and then caught sight of his black figure pacing to and fro under the pendants of the wisteria and the showering roses, he struck us as being neither responsible for nor interested in all this wealth of blossom.

When Mademoiselle Matheix became Madame Hervouët, the ex-postmistress lost none of her resemblance to a black-and-yellow wasp. With her sallow skin, her squeezed-in waist, her fine, inscrutable eyes, and her mass of dark hair, touched with white and restrained in a knot on the nape of her neck, she showed no surprise at being promoted to middle-class luxury. She appeared to be fond of gardening. Sido, the

impartial, thought it only fair to show some interest in her; she lent her
books, and in exchange accepted cuttings and also roots of tree violets
whose flowers were almost black and whose stem grew naked out of
the ground like the trunk of a tiny palm tree. To me, Madame Hervouët-
Matheix was an anything but sympathetic figure. I was vaguely scandalized that when making some assertions of irreproachable banality,
she did so in a tone of passionate and plaintive supplication.

"What do you expect?" said my mother. "She's an old maid."

"But, Mamma, she's married!"

"Do you really imagine," retorted Sido acidly, "people stop being
old maids for a little thing like that?"

One day, my father, returning from the daily "round of the town,"
by which this man who had lost one leg kept himself fit, said to my
mother: "A piece of news! The Hervouët relatives are attacking the
widow."

"No!"

"And going all out for her, too! People are saying the grounds of
the accusation are extremely serious."

"A new Lafarge case?"

"You're demanding a lot," said my father.

I thrust my sharp little mug between my two parents.

"What's that, the Lafarge case?"

"A horrible business between husband and wife. There's never been
a period without one. A famous poisoning case."

"Ah!" I exclaimed excitedly. "What a piece of luck!"

Sido gave me a look that utterly renounced me.

"There you are," she muttered. "That's what they're all like at that
age . . . A girl ought never to be fifteen."

"Sido, are you listening to me or not?" broke in my father. "The
relatives, put up to it by a niece of Hervouët's, are claiming that Hervouët didn't die intestate and that his wife has destroyed the will."

"In that case," observed Sido, "you could bring an action against
all widowers and all widows of intestates."

"No," retorted my father, "men who have children don't need to
make a will. The flames of Hervouët's lady can only have scorched
Hervouët from the waist up since . . ."

"Colette," my mother said to him severely, indicating me with a
look.

"Well," my father went on. "So there she is in a nice pickle. Hervouët's niece says she saw the will, yes, saw it with her very own eyes.
She can even describe it. A big envelope, five seals of green wax with
gold flecks in it . . ."

"Fancy that!" I said innocently.

". . . and on the front of it, the instructions: 'To be opened after my death in the presence of my solicitor, Monsieur Hourblin or his successor.' "

"And suppose the niece is lying?" I ventured to ask.

"And suppose Hervouët changed his mind and destroyed his will?" suggested Sido. "He was perfectly free to do so, I presume?"

"There you go, the two of you! Already siding with the bull against the bullfighter!" cried my father.

"Exactly," said my mother. "Bullfighters are usually men with fat buttocks and that's enough to put me against them!"

"Let's get back to the point," said my father. "Hervouët's niece has a husband, a decidedly sinister gentleman by the name of Pellepuits."

I soon got tired of listening. On the evidence of such words as "The relatives are attacking the widow!" I had hoped for bloodshed and foul play and all I heard was bits of gibberish such as "disposable portion of estate," "holograph will," "charge against X."

All the same, my curiosity was reawakened when Monsieur Hervouët's widow paid us a call. Her little mantle of imitation Chantilly lace worn over hock-bottle shoulders, her black mittens from which protruded unusually thick, almost opaque nails, the luxuriance of her black-and-white hair, a big black taffeta pocket suspended from her belt that dangled over the skirt of her mourning, her "houri eyes," as she called them; all these details, which I seemed to be seeing for the first time, took on a new, sinister significance.

Sido received the widow graciously, took her into the garden, and offered her a thimbleful of Frontignan and a wedge of homemade cake. The June afternoon buzzed over the garden, russet caterpillars dropped about us from the walnut tree, not a cloud floated in the sky. My mother's pretty voice and Madame Hervouët's imploring one exchanged tranquil remarks; as usual, they talked about nothing but salpiglossis, gladiolus, and the misdemeanors of servants. Then the visitor rose to go and my mother escorted her. "If you don't mind," said Madame Hervouët, "I'll come over in a day or two and borrow some books; I'm so lonely."

"Would you like to take them now?" suggested Sido.

"No, no, there's no hurry. Besides, I've noted down the titles of some adventure stories. Goodbye for the time being, and thank you."

As she said this, Madame Hervouët, instead of taking the path that led to the house, took the one that circled the lawn and walked twice around the plot of grass.

"Good gracious, whatever am I doing? Do forgive me."

She allowed herself a modest laugh and eventually reached the hall, where she groped too high and to the left of the two sides of the folding door for a latch she had twenty times found on the right. My mother opened the front door for her and, out of politeness, stood for a moment at the top of the steps. We watched Madame Hervouët go off, keeping at first very close to the house, then crossing the road very hurriedly, picking up her skirts as if she were fording a river.

My mother shut the door again and saw that I had followed her.

"She is lost," she said.

"Who? Madame Hervouët? Why do you say that? How d'you mean, lost?"

Sido shrugged her shoulders.

"I've no idea. It's just my impression. Keep that to yourself."

I kept silence faithfully. This was all the easier, as continuing my series of metamorphoses like a grub, I had entered a new phase—the "enlightened bibliophile"—and I forgot Madame Hervouët in a grand turnout of my stationery shop. A few days later, I was installing Jules Verne between *Les Fleurs animées* and a relief atlas when Madame Hervouët appeared on the scene without the bell having warned me. For we left the front door open nearly all day so that our dog Domino could go in and out.

"How nice of a big girl like you to tidy up the bookshelves," exclaimed the visitor. "What books are you going to lend me today?"

When Madame Hervouët raised her voice, I clenched my teeth and screwed up my eyes very small.

"Jules Verne," she read, in a plaintive voice. "You can't read him twice. Once you know the secret, it's finished."

"There's Balzac up there, on the big shelves," I said, pointing to them.

"He's very heavy going," said Madame Hervouët.

Balzac, heavy going? Balzac, my cradle, my enchanted forest, my voyage of discovery? Amazed, I looked up at the tall dark woman, a head taller than myself. She was toying with a cut rose and staring into space. Her features expressed nothing which could be remotely connected with opinions on literature. She became aware I was gazing at her and pretended to be interested in my writer's equipment.

"It's charming. What a splendid collection!"

Her mouth had grown older in the last week. She remained stooping over my relics, handling this one and that. Then she straightened herself up with a start.

"But isn't your dear mother anywhere about? I'd like to see her."

Only too glad to move, to get away from this "lost" lady, I rushed wildly out into the garden, calling "Mamma!" as if I were shouting "Fire!"

"She took a few books away with her," Sido told me when we were alone. "But I could positively swear she didn't even glance at their titles."

The rest of the "Hervouët affair" is linked, in my memory, with a vague general commotion, a kind of romantic blur. My clearest recollection of it comes to me through Sido, thanks to the extraordinary "presence" I still have of the sound of her voice. Her stories, her conversations with my father, the intolerant way she had of arguing and refuting, those are the things that riveted a sordid provincial drama in my mind.

One day, shortly after Madame Hervouët's last visit, the entire district was exclaiming "The will's been found!" and describing the big envelope with five seals that the widow had just deposited in Monsieur Hourblin's study. At once uneasy and triumphant, the Pellepuits-Hervouët couple and another lot, the Hervouët-Guillamats, appeared, along with the widow, at the lawyer's office. There, Madame Hervouët, all by herself, faced up to the solid, pitiless group, to what Sido called those "gaping, legacy-hunting sharks." "It seems," my mother said, telling the story, "that she smelled of brandy." At this point, my mother's voice is superseded by the hunchback's voice of Julia Vincent, a woman who went out ironing by the day and came to us once a week. For I don't know how many consecutive Fridays, I pressed Julia till I wrung out of her all she knew. The precise sound of that nasal voice, squeezed between the throat, the hump, and the hollow, deformed chest, was a delight to me.

"The man as was most afeared was the lawyer. To begin with, he's not a tall man, not half so tall as that woman. She, all dressed in black she was, and her veil falling down in front right to her feet. Then the lawyer picked up the envelope, big as that it was" (Julia unfolded one of my father's vast handkerchiefs) "and he passed it just as it was to the nephews so they could recognize the seals."

"But you weren't there, Julia, were you?"

"No, it was Monsieur Hourblin's junior clerk who was watching through the keyhole. One of the nephews said a word or two. Then Madame Hervouët stared at him like a duchess. The lawyer coughed, ahem, ahem, he broke the seals, and he read it out."

In my recollection, it is sometimes Sido talking, sometimes some scandalmonger eager to gossip about the Hervouët affair. Sometimes it seems too that some illustrator, such as Bertall or Tony Johannot, has actually etched a picture for me of the tall, thin woman who never withdrew her Spanish eyes from the group of heirs-at-law and kept licking her lip to taste the *marc* brandy she had gulped down to give herself courage.

So Monsieur Hourblin read out the will. But after the first lines, the document began to shake in his hands and he broke off, with an apology, to wipe his glasses. He resumed his reading and went right through to the end. Although the testator declared himself to be "sound in body and mind," the will was nothing but a tissue of absurdities, among others, the acknowledgment of a debt of two million francs contracted to Louise-Léonie-Alberte Matheix, beloved spouse of Clovis-Edme Hervouët.

The reading finished in silence and not one voice was raised from the block of silent heirs.

"It seems," said Sido, "that, after the reading, the silence was such you could hear the wasps buzzing in the vine arbor outside the window. The Pellepuits and the various Guillamats did nothing but stare at Madame Hervouët, without stirring a finger. Why aren't cupidity and avarice possessed of second sight? It was a female Guillamat, less stupid than the others, who said afterward that, before anyone had spoken, Madame Hervouët began to make peculiar movements with her neck, like a hen that's swallowed a hairy caterpillar.

The story of the last scene of that meeting spread like wildfire through the streets, through people's homes, through the cafés, through the fairgrounds. Monsieur Hourblin had been the first to speak above the vibrating hum of the wasps.

"On my soul and conscience, I find myself obliged to declare that the handwriting of the will does not correspond . . ."

A loud yelping interrupted him. Before him, before the heirs, there was no longer any Widow Hervouët but a somber Fury whirling around and stamping her feet, a kind of black dervish, lacerating herself, muttering, and shrieking. To her admissions of forgery, the crazy woman added others, so rich in the names of vegetable poisons, such as buckthorn and hemlock, that the lawyer, in consternation, exclaimed naïvely: "Stop, my poor good lady, you're telling us far more than anyone has asked you to!"

A lunatic asylum engulfed the madwoman, and if the Hervouët affair persisted in some memories, at least, there was no "Hervouët case" at the assizes.

"Why, Mamma?" I asked.

"Mad people aren't tried. Or else they'd have to have judges who were mad too. That wouldn't be a bad idea, when you come to think of it . . ."

To pursue her train of thought better, she dropped the task with which her hands were busy; graceful hands that she took no care of.

Perhaps, that particular day, she was shelling haricot beans. Or else, with her little finger stuck in the air, she was coating my father's crutch with black varnish . . .

"Yes, judges who would be able to assess the element of calculation in madness, who could sift out the hidden grain of lucidity, of deliberate fraud."

The moralist who was raining these unexpected conclusions on a fifteen-year-old head was encased in a blue gardener's apron, far too big for her, that made her look quite plump. Her gray gaze, terribly direct, fixed me now through her spectacles, now over the top of them. But in spite of the apron, the rolled-up sleeves, the sabots, and the haricot beans, she never looked humble or common.

"What I do blame Madame Hervouët for," Sido went on, "is her megalomania. *Folie de grandeur* is the source of any number of crimes. Nothing exasperates me more than the imbecile who imagines he's capable of planning and executing a crime without being punished for it. Don't you agree it's Madame Hervouët's stupidity that makes her case so sickening? Poisoning poor old Hervouët with extremely bitter herbal concoctions, right, that wasn't difficult. Inept murderer, stupid victim, it's tit for tat. But to try and imitate a handwriting without having the slightest gift for forgery, to trust to a special, rare kind of sealing wax, what petty ruses, great heavens, what fatuous conceit!"

"But why did she confess?"

"Ah," said Sido reflectively. "That's because a confession is almost inevitable. A confession is like . . . let's see . . . yes . . . it's like a stranger you carry inside you . . ."

"Like a child?"

"No, not a child. With a child, you know the exact date it's going to leave you. Whereas a confession bursts out quite suddenly, just when you weren't expecting it, it tastes its liberty, it stretches its limbs. It shouts, it cuts capers. She accompanied hers with a dance, that poor murderess who thought herself so clever."

It shouts, it cuts capers . . . Just like that, then and there, my own secret burst out into Sido's ear: on the very day of Madame Hervouët's last visit I had noticed the disappearance of the little stick of green sealing wax powdered with gold.

[*Translated by Antonia White*]

PART IV

Love

Love has never been a question of age.
I shall never be so old as to
forget what love is.

In the Flower of Age

❧❦❧

"Thursday . . . Thursday is the cocktail party at the Schlumbergers', a little six to nine affair . . . Friday we're taking a picnic to Thoronet. I'm preparing one of those warm breads for them, stuffed with crushed anchovies in oil and sweet red peppers, with a pinch of thyme . . ."

Madame Vasco pressed her lips together in greedy anticipation, half closing her eyes.

"Sunday, of course, we're giving the whole house the night off. Martine and Marinette want to go to the movies with the valet. Teobaldo will stay with the dogs . . . Oh, and about tonight . . . Shall we accept the invitation to the artists' impromptu? You know, everyone dresses up in costumes made exclusively out of whatever's lying around, old newspapers, kitchen aprons, wrapping paper, and towels . . . You already stood us up the day before yesterday, you bad boy. And last Wednesday it was the Simonis who brought me home. You don't have to worry about being bored tonight . . . Henri Simoni is making his costume out of discarded postal parcels, all corrugated cardboard and string, it'll be smashing!"

Paul Vasco did not answer right away. He lay stretched out on his back on the wide conjugal bed, his outspread arms bronze against the pink batiste and russet lace. A hand, whose firmness he knew well, ran like a stiff comb through the disorder of his damp, blond hair, and he decided it was time he opened his eyes.

"Ah, there you are, my two periwinkles!" said his wife in a softer voice.

Sitting up beside him, she held on her lap the small lemon-wood breakfast tray laden with pink china. The Paris morning papers were strewn across the pink bed, soiling it with their ink; a branch of pale blue plumbago, brought back by Paul from the path that led down to the sea, was being used by the white cat, which was deaf, as a toy. The sun had just entered the room and was making its way across the black rug. The bougainvillea hung slightly over the edge of the balcony. A pale sky, the sky of summer mornings on the Mediterranean, filled the window. Paul Vasco resigned himself, as he did every morning, to looking up at his wife, and every morning he was amazed.

Tall, careful of her weight, strong and healthy, she didn't hesitate to tie her hair, thrown back and dyed a golden chestnut, with a little ribbon whose color changed with that of her dressing gown, and in the summer she tanned like a young woman. But her tan refused to penetrate certain creases, fine as incisions, forming at the corners of her eyes and around her neck, despite surgical intervention. Madeleine Vasco smiled down at her young husband, showing her teeth looked after and corrected by a master. Between her ear and her hairline, between the hair at her temples and the corner of her eye, Paul could make out the thin, scarred folds, looking mauve beneath the ochered powder. "She's amazing," he thought. "Even I would never imagine she was sixty-two years old. Besides, even if I did, she'd tell me it was all in my imagination."

He closed his eyes again with the irresistible laziness that followed his morning swim and a run on the beach.

"You haven't answered me about tonight. Sleepyhead, oh, my beautiful sleepyhead . . ."

For him it was not a question of answering but of stalling for time, of holding out, by lying motionless, until the moment when his wife, summoned by the need to oblige her stubborn beauty, would leave him for an hour and a half.

"Whatever you like," he sighed at last.

With a snap of his fingers he called for a cigarette, which Madeleine put, already lit, between his lips.

"You could say," he joked, "that the only thing I brought here was a mouth to smoke with . . ."

"And who's asking you for anything else?" she countered.

With a penetrating and bold gaze, she caressed that mouth, whose smile and firm freshness had persuaded her into the foolishness of remarrying, ten months after the death of her first husband, thus snatching, from a minor office position, a poor, handsome, and by chance honest young man. For Paul Vasco she had given up her widow's weeds and her semi-mourning, dyed her gray hair, and from her widow's chrysalis had emerged a tall, strong woman in love, so set on happiness that she dazzled her young spouse, thirty years her junior. For two years now, from January to May, they had been coming "to the Riviera," as Paul naïvely put it, he as yet not having grown tired of the luxury of an estate in the south, with its paths of pink sand, its wisteria, and its marble terraces. The smiles around them were discreet, for Madame Paul Vasco, shaded by large hats, wearing simple makeup, had a rather flashy way of refusing her husband's arm when climbing the stairs of the casinos. He followed her, served her, and found her young. However, he could never overcome his apprehension when she was dancing with him. "I've got a strong heart, you know . . ." she would say. "I'll give you a few pointers when they play the hesitation waltz." In fact, she waltzed with long, gliding, somewhat masculine steps, and she never had to stop to catch her breath, holding her hand to her flat, jewel-clad breast. It was Paul who while dancing would experience a certain anguish, grow pale, and say softly, "Enough . . ." He could not hold up next to his wife's stamina, her bony and mechanical lightness. He had a childish fear of a sudden creaking of hinges, a squeaking of springs. She never seemed less alive than when she was proving her agility, and as they danced he would press his temple against hers, trying not to notice that as she waltzed she stared wildly, straight ahead, and breathed through her painted, half-open mouth.

But once he was back at the estate, life again became sweet and easy. He felt at home there, and quickly developed a taste for laying out gardens and plotting the best colors for the flower beds with the head gardener.

"Shall we go somewhere?" Madeleine asked him after their siesta.

"Yes!" exclaimed Paul enthusiastically. "Let's go to Fréjus. I need seven hundred geranium-ivy cuttings!"

"Teobaldo will pick them up in the station wagon, don't bother."

He pouted, and Madeleine looked at the pouting mouth.

"What a child! You really want to go? Have them bring the car around . . ."

For she gave in whenever she feared he might be getting bored. Somewhat distracted, and vain about his physical beauty, he was never bored when he was parading around half naked in the sun or tossing the medicine ball with the trainer who came down from Cannes.

One evening as Madeleine Vasco was calling her husband and fidgeting with impatience in a long black velvet dress trimmed with monkey fur, and shouting, "We'll be late! The ballet starts at nine in Monte Carlo!" she was stupefied to see Paul emerge from the cellar, whitened ever so slightly by spider webs and saltpeter, with a venerable old bottle under each arm.

"Where have you been?"

"Can't you tell?" he said. "We absolutely have to put the wine book back in order and the vintages in the racks have to be reclassified. It's a shambles down there!"

Madeleine raised her plucked eyebrows and the wrinkles on her forehead all the way up to her hairline.

"What can that possibly have to do with us, my darling?"

"Why," said Vasco, "it's the man's job to keep the cellar in order."

"Does it amuse you?"

He smiled a competent smile. "Very much."

"And that's why you're going to make us miss *Les Sylphides?*"

He seemed to wake up suddenly, looked at the dress, the woman, and the dazzling new jewel she was wearing on her bodice, next to skin which had lost its smoothness, its soft and supple mystery. He offered no protest and dashed off to get dressed.

"Give me five minutes!"

She remained alone, waiting for him on the lower terrace, walking in the wind which was ruffling the water and bringing the day to an end. She yawned and admitted to herself that she had no less of an appetite for delicate fish and champagne than for lights, music, new faces . . .

As soon as his wife had closed the door to her bathroom, Paul Vasco sat up on the rumpled bed and let out a gentle sigh. He was not a cynical man and he accepted kindness in a spirit of resignation. His wife's frivolous energy did not frighten him unduly, for she did not bring to her way of leading the life of a young socialite the insane bitterness of aged bacchantes, but rather the determination of an ex-bourgeoise who remembered what it was like to have a dotty old homebody for a first husband. Paul learned how to escape, every fifth time, then every third time, from the dinners, the suppers, the automobile races, and the rallies. "Banner of Honor to the red-and-white sedan of Madame Paul Vasco . . ."

He slid down to the foot of the pink bed and swore to himself that he would not go to the artists' costume party. "Those clowns of all ages can get themselves up in old newspapers, grocery bags, straw wigs, curtains, and straw mats without me." There was sure to be a painful moment when he would say to Madeleine, "I'm not going." There would be that look in his wife's eyes, as if they were lying in ambush between the lashes of a starlet, and the silent disdain inflicted on a stay-at-home young man by an indomitable sixty-year-old scatterbrain . . . But what a reward it was, afterward, to savor an evening devoted to filing away bills and reading a manual dealing with the rejuvenation of trees by frequent injections into the root cap!

He managed his day as carefully as an adolescent wanting to spend the night at a friend's, a soldier hoping to slip over the wall . . . While she was having a light dinner across from him, he asked his wife what sort of costume she was planning. Excitedly, she confided to him that, for herself, she was counting on using a crocheted bedspread lent her by

Luc-Albert Moreau, and for Paul, a big lampshade tied around his waist, or else a woven straw seat cover.

"But we go in evening clothes, and put our costumes on there," she added.

He made no objection, but as soon as he was alone, he put on a comfortable robe and his slippers, sat down in front of a blazing fire which made his cheeks glow, and, while waiting for the conjugal onslaught, read the evening edition of *L'Eclaireur de Nice et du Sud-Est*, over which he fell asleep.

Toward midnight, a sequined train slithered down the stairs with a delicate, snake-like sound. But the heavy tapping of heels, on each step, made it known that Madeleine's knees were struggling against the onset of anchylosis. She came to the bottom of the stairs followed by her obedient, steel-gray, and glittering train. A scarlet cape, thrown over her shoulders, left only her bedecked, golden, proud head showing. Walking toward a mirror, she caught sight of her young sleeping husband and stopped. He was asleep with his head drooping to one side, with the light from the fire caressing his plump, dimpled chin, and two clearly drawn frown marks framing his childishly pouting mouth. An empty cup was proof that he had had some verbena tea, and the deaf cat slept at his feet on the open newspaper. Leaning over, Madeleine Vasco pressed her bracelets to her side to keep them from jingling. Where had she seen that robe and those slippers before, and the hermetic cat, the medicinal cup, and above all this sudden sleepiness which betrays a man's weakness? . . . The image of the late Monsieur Perrin, her first husband, rose up between her and Paul Vasco, and she drew back. Facing her in the mirror, a tall woman, scarlet and gray, thin because she had to be, erect because she wanted to be, matched her glance for glance, and her mouth, smothered with lipstick, smiled. Madame Vasco took a last look at the sleeping man, muttered gruffly, "Just another old man!" and with two fingers picked up her train and left without looking back.

[Translated by Matthew Ward]

The Rivals

❧❧❧

"Nice dress," Clara thought. "But it seems to me Antoinette isn't looking very well. Maybe it's just because I don't want her to look very well . . . We'll see what he thinks. How can a man of taste be interested in a woman with such a high forehead?"

She leaned over the shoulder of a young woman sitting in the first row of gilded seats.

"Marise, do heights make you dizzy?"

"Heights? . . . Yes, very dizzy," Marise answered precipitously. "Don't even talk about it, it makes me weak in the knees."

"Then don't look at Antoinette's forehead. It's the steppes as far as the eye can see. Her hairline is all the way at the back of her head. It's . . . I don't know . . . it's indecent."

With a well-studied imitation of modesty, she lowered a large wave of curly auburn hair over her forehead. At the same time, alerted by the marvelous telepathy of enmity, Antoinette glared at her with luminous black eyes and guessed everything. She immediately began whispering urgently into the ear of a stout lady caparisoned in purple sequins, and tracing parallel lines with her fingernail on her pure, high forehead . . . Clara, who did not hide her forehead solely out of coquetry, clenched her jaws.

"So it's come to that," she thought. "If Antoinette and I were ever left alone, what wouldn't we be capable of? She would grab me by the throat, I'd drag her by her long hair, which she's never had cut, by those black braids of hers she used to wrap around my neck. I shudder to think . . ."

She gave a little shiver and threw a light scrap of ermine over her shoulders . . . In vain, the Capet Quartet outdid itself in the Brahms finale. In vain, two voices blended ravishingly in a mocking and lively

piece by Monteverdi. Clara, watching Antoinette, was waiting for a man
to arrive. "He won't get here until his play is over. Tonight's the second
night for the critics. God knows I know how to make allowances for
things; a dramatist can't lose interest in . . . There he is!"

She straightened her collar, adopted the attitude he preferred, a
myopic and impertinent air, with the crest of curly hair falling down
over her forehead between her eyebrows. As he greeted the mistress of
the house, then the large lady in purple, then Antoinette, Clara nearly
ceased thinking. She was all eyes and believed it could only be love.
She noticed that *he* lingered in front of Antoinette, taking advantage
of the slight commotion caused by the singers' success. She convinced
herself that it was not Antoinette's hand *he* had kissed, but her wrist,
one might as well say her arm. She observed, frozen with impatience,
that Antoinette had not gotten up, and that *he* remained standing, that
he was wallowing in an incomparable landscape of fleshy hills and
valleys, as white as the white velvet dress which was merely an extension
of it . . . Stinging tears of jealousy filled Clara's eyes and she feverishly
opened her gold compact . . .

"Would you like me to introduce you to the tenor?" asked her
friend seated in front of her.

"No!" she answered, a bit too loudly.

A short distance away, *he* heard, *he* recognized Clara's voice, and
walked toward her between two rows of empty seats. Whether out of
pleasure at seeing her or as a precaution, *he* smiled at her as he
approached, with that vague tenderness allowed him by the shape and
deep blue color of his eyes. He was not very young, but his wicked and
flattering reputation along with his success in the theater had not yet
given women of leisure the occasion to concern themselves with his age.
Ever since it began to appear as if he wanted to get married, ever since
one of his plays, which condemned celibacy, had given reserved young
girls and dauntless young women a ray of hope, Antoinette and Clara,
the one a widow, the other a divorcee, and former childhood friends,
were no longer on speaking terms.

"Good evening, Chiarissima!"

She was beside herself, but she kept thinking, "She's watching us,
she's watching us!" and looking up, she gave the bowing Bussy the
confident smile of a schoolgirl in love with her teacher.

"That pink dress!" he said.

"Do you like it?"

"Not at all."

"Oh . . ." she moaned. "Why not?"

"Too pink. Besides, a faun like you doesn't wear dresses with pink
ruffles. With that tuft of auburn curls, like a goat's or a nymph's, be-

tween those green eyes, no, you don't put on pink ruffles, you wear a garland, you drape yourself in an animal skin, a very small animal skin . . ."

Quickly, with calculated irreverence, he tugged at the bouquet of russet curls, sending them dancing over Clara's forehead. She could not hold back a little shriek, which must have pierced Antoinette's heart. Pale and watchful, her rival sat holding a glass of orangeade as if it were a poisoned cup, and did not drink.

"How did the play go tonight?"

"Fine."

"That's all . . . 'fine'?"

Bussy gave her a caressing and grateful smile. "No, better than fine, much better."

"How was the box office?"

"Twenty-two thousand, despite all the press comps. I tell you all my secrets."

"All of them, really?"

"All but one. But I expect you to pry that one out of me."

She stood up as if to dance, impulsively. That night she did not wish to hear any more. That night she would take with her what he had said, that ambiguous promise, its tone of amorous defeat and defiance.

"Are you leaving already?"

She replied with a nod of her head, held out the tips of her fingers, and Bussy prudently lowered his voice and asked: "Tomorrow, may I . . ."

"Tomorrow I'll phone you before eleven," she said. "As usual."

She reached the row of chairs, disarranged by the music lovers' departure toward the refreshment stand, where Antoinette stubbornly remained sitting alongside the purple lady. Treacherously, Clara brushed up against the white velvet dress as she passed, and murmured, "Pardon me . . ." while looking elsewhere.

Clara always woke at the same hour and all at once. Since she first felt herself in love with Robert Bussy, her clear mind's first thoughts were of the woman with whom she was vying for him. In her thoughts she would force open Antoinette's front door, climb a familiar staircase, slip into a bedroom she once knew quite well, hung everywhere with silk whose ivory color matched the ivory of dusky skin, and stopped only when she reached the bed where, protected by two long black braids, there slept her beautiful rival. "Wake up! Wake up!" ordered the early-morning phantom. "And let me wake your fears and suspicions; wake up for our daily task!"

On days when her jealousy was strongest, her phantom visit intoxicated her with a kind of hallucination, and then slowly, regretfully, she withdrew back into herself, from the white bedroom . . .

In the evening, after dreaming of Bussy and desiring Bussy, after measuring the small amount of security Bussy provided her, her last lucid moment drew her back to her former friend. She wished her "Bad night!" with a kind of gentleness, reviewed the use she had made of the day just ending, and laid plans for the next. When a party, an evening of music or dancing, promised her that she would run into her former friend, as well as Bussy, she would tremble with a little shock, feeling the blood rising to her cheeks, reddening them with anger, enhancing her . . . Her main concern had to do with attracting Bussy, of course. But at the same time—and sometimes even before—she had to outwit, by using her knowledge of Antoinette's habits, what was being planned for Bussy by the passionate and scheming Antoinette, the secretive Antoinette, the criminal and despised Antoinette . . . Unrelentingly, Clara aimed the weapon of persistent thought in her rival's direction. As it happened, Antoinette, forced on all occasions to concede and melt away, did in fact dissolve and disappear. It was the one thing that Clara, though she wished for it with all her might, had not foreseen. During the opening-night performance of Bussy's new play, *Bottomless Pits*, Clara, looking dazzling up in her box, leaned over the red velvet armrest and scanned the house with her keen eyes.

"Where is Antoinette, by the way?" she asked the author during the last intermission.

"I don't remember you making me her keeper," Bussy replied, wounded by the fact that Clara could be concerned with something other than his three acts.

She thought he was lying and did not insist. But Antoinette did not attend the "Venetian Night" given by the Fauchier-Magnans on the grounds of their château either, and so could not see Bussy as a lord in white and Clara as a doge's wife in red, being rocked on the black cushions of a gondola . . .

"What a party!" exclaimed Clara's friends the next day.

"Yes . . ." she said distractedly. "Lovely. But something was missing . . . I don't know what . . . Maybe I'm wrong . . . It was lovely . . ."

She was bored more often, she displayed an impatience that was unlike her, a desire for change. So she threw herself madly into Bussy's arms the day he confessed to her that his own solitude no longer made sense and that he was turning himself over, bound hand and foot, into Clara's power. At first she wanted a "Peasant Wedding," that is to say, a bunch of Parisians jammed into a small country church, and an out-

door reception, red roses on simple linen tablecloths . . . Then she renounced her rustic childishness when she realized that Antoinette could
not be present, even in disguise. "Just where is Antoinette?"

She decided to ask this question, which had been obsessing her
quietly, out loud to her friends, who laughed in her face.

"Where have you been, Clara? Antoinette married her most handsome cousin and the two of them are off traveling in the Indies. The
marriage took ten minutes, and the trip will take two years."

One day as she was lunching outdoors with Bussy, she noticed that
spring had arrived and that the petals of the apple tree were drifting
down into the pitcher of frothy cider. Bussy, noticing her silence, placed
his hand on hers. She raised her eyes and saw in her fiancé the dullness
women find in men they no longer love. He launched into an account
of the plot of his next play. Clara was seized by an attack of nervous
yawns so furious that she thought she was sick and asked to be taken
home.

"I'll call to see how you are before dinner," said Bussy, fussing over
her.

"No, no, don't. I'll phone you. It's nothing . . ."

He received no phone call, only a brief note, so cavalier that his
masculine pride could not believe it. "There's a man behind all this,"
he concluded. "She's made a fool out of me . . ." But he was mistaken. Clara, lying peacefully in bed, was giving herself over to the
benefits of aspirin, and on the backs of her closed eyelids Bussy's image
was growing more and more indistinct. Thanks to approaching sleep,
it disappeared entirely behind another image, which Clara welcomed
without rancor or distress, calling it as she once did by its nickname,
"Anto!" She cried, but softly. In the hope that a long friendship could
reunite two women, separated only by the passing of an ephemeral man,
Clara began calling, began waiting for the absent, the longed-for, the
irreplaceable Antoinette . . .

[*Translated by Matthew Ward*]

The Respite

"How's your arm tonight?"

"Not bad, not bad."

"Oh, you always say that. And your knee? I know, 'not bad, not bad' . . . The wind is blowing terribly outside. God only knows what I must have looked like on the Pont des Arts. Holding on to my hat like this; my pleated skirt—you'll never catch me in a pleated skirt again —blown up against my back, my purse without a handle, and me clutching it under my arm like this, no, no, women are just too foolish to dress in a way that's so . . . And as for my hair, just look at it!"

She exaggerated her disarray with a kind of artistry, raising one shoulder up to her ear, screwing up her mouth, wrinkling the skin on her forehead to help keep her hat in place, and squeezing her short skirt between her thighs. She had never been afraid of making faces; she indulged in extreme and grotesque mimicry and somehow remained beyond reproach. Already past thirty, she would imitate Chevalier, improvise an old general's mustache out of wads of cotton, stuff a pillow under her skirt, and exclaim: "Allow me to present to you the pregnant concierge!"

"Does she deliberately make herself ugly out of modesty or pride?" Brice wondered, watching his wife walk pigeon-toed, run into the corner of the table, and rub her thigh. "It's a kind of lie, too."

"You didn't pick up my medicine?"

She looked over her shoulder at her husband, and winked as if to say: "Child!"

"Yes, I did. Got you this time!"

"Oh, a phone call would have been enough to replenish my stock. I'm afraid about tonight . . ."

On his desk he set his big expert's magnifying glass, that venerable old tool dethroned by other newer methods of investigation. Antique, set in copper, it superimposed three lenses which could be used with one over the other or be opened out into a trefoil.

"Were you studying something?" asked Marcelle.

"Nothing," he sighed. "Who cares about painting these days, genuine or fake? Speaking of which, the Tiepolo drawings Myrtil Schwabe bought are fakes. Of course, I gave her ample warning."

> *Do you think it is that e-e-easy*
> *To fool an expert such as me-e-e . . .*

sang Marcelle.

"She's got her nerve . . ." thought Brice indignantly. With his left hand he grabbed his upper right arm, and smiled the way patients who flaunt a certain stoic aplomb smile. Marcelle's tall figure leaned over him.

"Is it very bad? Try to hold out for another thirty or forty minutes. Let's save the ammunition for tonight. Can you?"

"Can I? Come on, it's a game for me . . ."

He shut his eyes so that she would not read in them an overwhelming fact which he himself did not as yet believe: for the second time since that morning, the neuritis had just deserted his right shoulder and his arm as far as the elbow. So total was the reprieve becoming, so eager were the muscles to move, and so astonished were they to feel themselves free and light, that he nearly betrayed himself, nearly groaned with ease. "Not to suffer," thought Brice, "what pleasure can compare with this inner silence, this perfection of one's whole being? Do I even have a left arm? Where is my left arm, its burning right shoulder, the shooting pains of a probe being helped along with a stylet, replaced from time to time by a heavy roller which crushes half the forearm, leaving the other half bound down, in spasms, pulling on its chains?"

He stretched his leg out gingerly. "Nothing in the leg anymore. My knee is being a dear, like a young boy's knee, the knee of a runner . . ." Meanwhile, his wife, in the next room, was speaking to him.

"What did you say, Marcelle?" he shouted. "What square are you talking about?"

"St. Julien-le-Pauvre," she answered from the other bedroom. "What they've done with that little corner is just wonderful. I'm also going to go see the Jardins des Gobelins, apparently they've kept the old fruit trees. Can you imagine? Open-wind apricot trees in Paris . . ."

He heard her laugh.

"Talk about wind, they're getting plenty of it today!"

She reappeared in the doorway of his room. Brice had just enough time to draw in his arm, which he had been stretching, bending, stretching with underhanded exhilaration. Marcelle gave her husband a searching look.

"You're suffering like a poor little baby and hoping I won't be able to tell."

"It's impossible to hide anything from you," said Brice, taking on the jerky delivery, the smile of the discreet martyr.

She stopped twisting around her finger the ringlets of her hair tangled by the gusting wind, knelt down next to the armchair, put her big, careful arm around Brice's neck, and leaned over gently, cheek to cheek.

"Poor, poor baby."

"Marcelle," Brice said grimly, "you're wearing your hair too long, I've told you so a hundred times."

"Yes, darling."

"You should change that idiotic hairdo, those curly wood shavings, and that flat part on the back of your head!"

"Yes, darling."

"You say, 'Yes, darling,' but you're just making fun of me!"

"Yes, darling."

He freed his head with an exasperated gesture, and Marcelle stood up.

"Careful now, you silly goose," she said tenderly. "No acrobatics. What if I put a nice hot towel on your shoulder while you're waiting for your medicine?"

"Hot and useless . . ."

"So it will mix the pointless with the unpleasant. One more word and you'll get my Michel Simon imitation."

She stood in front of him, too tall, long-armed, but well proportioned, and built simply from head to feet. Maturity rested lightly on her, without excess weight, reddening her face a bit, heightening the clear blue of her eyes. Marcelle judged her nose, her mouth, the shape of her chin strictly: "It's not very finely made, but it's good and solid."

For the moment she felt useless and was trying not to show her pity. She pulled the little peplum of her dark green jacket down over her short green-, gray-and-brown-plaid skirt. "It's the same outfit she's wearing in the photograph," thought Brice. "The square buttons, the little Scotch trim on the pockets and collar, everything's the same . . . Photography really is a fine art!" He was overcome with rage, afraid of losing his composure, and asked to be left alone.

"I'd like to try to sleep a little before dinner, you understand."

Puzzled, Marcelle did not respond right away.

"I'd be happy if you slept, of course, but . . . what about tonight?"

"Tonight, tonight . . . One sleepless night more or less, for the last eight days . . ."

"Seven days, Georges . . ."

"Seven days, then! They obviously haven't seemed long to you!"

As he grew more upset, she was quick to give in.

"I'm going, I'm going. Something to drink? Are you comfortable like that? You don't want me to take away the big cushion?" His only response was a shake of his head, and before she left, he had still to endure the caress of a cool hand on his.

Left alone, he tested his arm and his leg, both feeling as new and impatient as himself. He closed his fist firmly around his bunch of keys to keep them from jingling. He took the page torn from the newspaper, the photograph he had studied twenty times, back out of the drawer, and placed the triple lens over it. Blurred faces came into focus and seemed to rise up toward him. *If you recognize yourself as the person in the circle, please stop by our offices; you will receive the sum of . . .* In the center of the white circle, the features of a fat lady peered questioningly at the photographer, as she was starting down the stairs to the métro. Above her, two lovers were bidding each other an avid goodbye, with a passionate kiss which bent the woman back over the iron railing; the man could barely be seen, behind a pleated plaid skirt, a dark jacket, and a pointed felt hat. Beneath the hat's wide brim Brice recognized the straight, somewhat large nose, the overly long ringlets of hair, and the religiously lowered eyelids. "I've never seen the shape of her jaw so clearly before. How long has she had that chin? It's like an animal's, really. She's like all women; once out of their usual companion's sight, they change . . ."

He felt keen, shrewd, filled with hatred. He started to undo, to take off his long, blue, flannel invalid's robe. "Too soon. She wouldn't believe the attack subsided so quickly. I'll take care of this dirty business tomorrow . . ."

At first he used the information provided by the newspaper itself: *Photograph taken in the Xth arrondissement,* and the name of the station, Château-Landon. He was proud of himself for not having asked his wife any questions, but he had her followed. In her presence, he had no trouble grasping his upper right arm with his left hand, as if overcome by a brief, sharp pain, and into his limping around the apartment he put all the casualness of the cripple reconciled to his lameness.

He experienced the strange vigor of the suspicious, their physical immunity, but also a jealous torment which at times made him tremble all over, especially at night, and against which he cowardly asked for help.

"Ask them to fix me a hot-water bottle, Marcelle. Would you hand me the vicuña blanket?"

He found out nothing, neither around the entrance to the métro nor in his wife's mail, and having called off the too-costly gumshoe after a week, he ventured a vague but direct inquiry: "What would make you really happy, Marcelle?"

She turned her prominent eyes toward him and answered without having to think: "Lots of money, to buy a house in the country with, a complete fishing outfit, and the best bootmaker for sport shoes. And another apartment that wouldn't be so close to the Seine."

"She's stupid," thought Brice. "Stupid or very clever."

"And another husband, Marcelle? What would you think of a brand-new husband? New, handsome, robust?"

He laughed, but Marcelle wrinkled up her nose.

"That, my dear, is what I call humor for men only. Little games that go over big in certain government offices. Take my Uncle Auguste, you know what he and his colleagues used to do in the offices for Air Purification? When they weren't telling stories about their wedding nights, they were staining pieces of paper with ink and folding them in half to make designs, or else they'd play at what-would-you-do-if-you-won-a-million."

"Customs of a bygone age," said Brice vexedly.

"Thank God! Ever since women started working in government offices, the men have been behaving a little better!"

In the end, Brice lost his patience. One day he even admitted to himself that his interrogation humiliated himself most of all. Surprised by an unexpected hug from Marcelle—"Do you still like my big monkey's arms around your neck?"—he was unable to hide his sudden emotion and his wet eyes.

"It's my nerves. You know, now that the worst is over . . . it's easing up . . ."

She kissed him, and boisterously celebrated the departure of the fickle pain. But when they were apart, he was once again seized with rage, became overexcited while out walking, rushed home, and did not wait any longer to thrust in front of his wife's eyes the crumpled page from the newspaper which never left him. He had considered accompanying his action with some accusatory remark, but all he could come up with was: "Can you see anything, here, in the way of a resemblance?"

Sitting down, Marcelle smoothed out the creases in the paper with the palm of her hand.

"Oh, well, yes," she said slowly. "Well, yes, yes . . ."

Brice suddenly felt very tired and sat down.

"I can see," Marcelle continued, "that a Scotch plaid is almost always prettier when it's worn on the bias than when it's worn straight. I can see that my saleslady is right when she says a design altered to a client's taste is always less pretty . . . This'll teach me . . . Compare the square shapes of my plaid to the diamonds on this woman here . . ."

She broke off to laugh. "Say, Georges, by the way, look at these two in the photograph, they're really putting their hearts into it, did you see? And *coram populo!*"

Speechless, Brice grabbed his upper right arm with his left hand.

"What is it, Georges? Hurting again?"

He tightened his lips, stricken from his shoulder to his elbow, called back to the burning, capricious, throbbing pain. His neuritis kept him awake till morning. Toward dawn, exhausted, he reached the point of surrender and vague prayers, and he begged: "My suspicions, let me have my suspicions back . . . Let me have last week's misery back, the torture that was easing my pain—a truce, a respite, that's all, a respite."

[Translated by Matthew Ward]

The Bitch

❧❦❧

When the sergeant arrived in Paris on leave, he found his mistress
not at home. He was nevertheless greeted with tremulous cries of surprise and joy, embraced and covered with wet kisses. His bitch, Vorace,
the sheep dog whom he had left with his young sweetheart, enveloped
him like a flame and licked him with a tongue pale with emotion.

Meanwhile, the charwoman was making as much noise as the dog
and kept exclaiming: "Of all the bad luck! Madame's just gone to
Marlotte for a couple of days to shut up her house there. Madame's
tenants have just left and she's going through the inventory of the
furniture. Fortunately, it isn't all that far away! Will Monsieur write
out a telegram for Madame? If it goes immediately, Madame will be
here tomorrow morning before lunch. Monsieur must sleep here. Shall
I turn on the water heater?"

"My good Lucie, I had a bath at home. Soldiers on leave are pretty
good at washing!"

He eyed his reflection in the glass; he was both bluish and ruddy,
like the granite rocks of Brittany. The Briard sheep dog, standing close
to him in a reverent silence, was trembling in every hair. He laughed
because she looked so like him, gray and blue and shaggy.

"Vorace!"

She raised her head and looked lovingly at her master, and the
sergeant's heart turned over as he suddenly thought of his mistress,
Jeannine, so young and so gay—a little too young and often too gay.

During dinner the dog faithfully observed all the ritual of their
former life, catching the pieces of bread he tossed for her and barking
at certain words. So ardent was the worship in which she was rooted
that the moment of return abolished for her the months of absence.

"I've missed you a lot," he told her in a low voice. "Yes, you too!"

He was smoking now, half lying on the divan. Crouching like a greyhound on a tombstone, the dog was pretending to be asleep, her ears quite still. Only her eyebrows, twitching at the slightest noise, revealed that she was on the alert.

Worn out as he was, the silence gradually lulled the man, until his hand which held the cigarette slid down the cushion, scorching the silk. He roused himself, opened a book, fingered a few new knickknacks and a photograph, which he had not seen before, of Jeannine in a short skirt, with bare arms, in the country.

"An amateur snapshot . . . How charming she looks!"

On the back of the unmounted print he read: "*June 5, 1916.* Where was I on June the fifth? . . . Oh, I know, over in the direction of Arras. June the fifth. I don't know the writing."

He sat down again and was overcome by a sleep which drove all thought away. Ten o'clock struck; he was still just sufficiently awake to smile at the rich and solemn sound of the little clock whose voice, Jeannine used to say, was bigger than its stomach. But as it struck ten the dog got up.

"Quiet!" said the sleepy sergeant. "Lie down!"

But Vorace did not lie down. She snorted and stretched her paws, which, for a dog, is the same as putting on a hat to go out. She went up to her master and her yellow eyes asked plainly: "Well?"

"Well," he answered, "what's the matter with you?"

Out of respect she dropped her ears while he was speaking, raising them again immediately.

"Oh, what a bore you are!" sighed the sergeant. "You're thirsty! D'you want to go out?"

At the words "go out," Vorace grinned and began to pant gently, showing her beautiful teeth and the fleshy petal of her tongue.

"All right, then, we'll go out. But not for long, because I'm absolutely dropping with sleep."

In the road Vorace was so excited that she barked like a wolf, jumped right up to her master's neck, charged a cat, and spun around playing "inner circle" with her tail. Her master scolded her tenderly and she did all her tricks for him. Finally, she sobered down again and walked along sedately. The sergeant suited his pace to hers, enjoying the warm night and making a little song out of two or three idle thoughts.

"I'll see Jeannine tomorrow morning . . . I'm going to sleep in a comfy bed . . . I've got seven more days to spend here . . ."

He became aware that his dog, which had trotted ahead, was waiting for him under a gas lamp with the same look of impatience. Her eyes, her wagging tail, and her whole body asked: "Well? Are you coming?"

As soon as he caught up with her, she turned the corner at a determined trot. It was then that he realized she was going somewhere.

"Perhaps," he thought to himself, "the charwoman usually . . . Or Jeannine . . ."

He stood still for a moment, then went on again, following the dog, without even noticing that he had, all at once, stopped feeling tired, and sleepy, and happy. He quickened his pace and the delighted dog went ahead, like a good guide.

"Go on, go on!" ordered the sergeant from time to time.

He looked at the name of a road, then went on again. They passed gardens with lodges at the gates; the road was dimly lit and they met no one. In her excitement, the dog pretended to bite the hand that hung at his side, and he had to restrain a brutal impulse, which he could not explain, in order not to beat her.

At last she stopped, as though saying: "Well, here we are!" before an old, broken-down railing, protecting the garden of a little low house smothered in vines and bignonia, a timid, shrouded little house.

"Well, why don't you open it?" said the dog, which had taken up a position before the wooden wicket gate.

The sergeant lifted his hand to the latch and let it fall again. He bent down to the dog, pointed with his finger to a thread of light along the closed shutters, and asked her in a low voice: "Who's there? . . . Jeannine?"

The dog gave a shrill "Hi!" and barked.

"Shhh!" breathed the sergeant, clapping his hands over her cool, wet mouth.

Once more he stretched out a hesitant arm toward the door and the dog bounded forward. But he held her back by her collar and led her to the opposite pavement, whence he gazed at the unknown house and the thread of rosy light. He sat down on the pavement beside the dog. He had not yet gathered together all those images and thoughts which spring up around a possible betrayal, but he felt singularly alone, and weak.

"Do you love me?" he murmured in the dog's ear.

She licked his cheek.

"Come on; let's go away."

They set off, he in front this time. And when they were once more in the little sitting room, she saw that he was putting his linen and slippers in a sack that she knew well. Desperate but respectful, she followed all his movements, while tears, the color of gold, trembled in her yellow eyes. He laid his hand on her neck to reassure her.

"You're coming too. I'm not going to leave you anymore. Next time you won't be able to tell me what happened 'after.' Perhaps I'm mistaken. Perhaps I haven't understood you properly. But you mustn't stay here. Your soul wasn't meant to guard any secrets but mine."

And while the dog shivered, still uncertain, he held her head in his hands, saying to her in a low voice: "Your soul . . . Your doggy soul . . . Your beautiful soul . . ."

[*Translated by Enid McLeod*]

The Tender Shoot

❦

"There's no reason for *you* to stay on in Paris," I said, in May 1940, to my old friend—what shall I call him? Let's say Chaveriat, yes, Albin Chaveriat; in France there are enough Chaveriats, Basque by origin, who have settled in Franche-Comté and all over the place to ensure that none of them will object to the use I make of his name. "As you'll only mope in Paris as long as the war goes on, find somewhere to live in the country for a bit. Why don't you go and join Curnonsky at Mélanie's place in Riec-sur-Belon?"

"I don't like sea breezes," said Chaveriat. "Also, I don't want to eat too well. I should lose my figure."

"The Midi? St.-Tropez? Cavalaire?"

Chaveriat bristled his short white mustache.

"Settings for the gay life . . . sinister, now it's dead and gone."

"Do you feel any inclination to be a paying guest? Go to Normandy, to the Hersents'. They won't budge from their estate unless they're dislodged by fire and sword. There's a river, a billiard room, a badly kept-up tennis court, a croquet lawn. The entire family is in excellent health and, with their daughters and nieces alone, the place teems with young girls . . ."

"Not another word! You've just said the very thing that would put me off."

"Neither the wind nor good food nor the South of France nor young girls. You're difficult to suit, Albin."

"I've always been difficult, my dear. That is what has made me end up as the pearl of bachelors."

Chaveriat walked across, without his stick, to one of my three windows. When he made a conscious effort, he limped hardly at all.

Last year an attack of gout that "ran up to the heart," as they used to say, laid him to rest before his martial figure, still slender at seventy, suffered the humiliation of being definitely crippled. White-haired, with lively black eyes and a clipped mustache, he was presumed to have broken many hearts in his youth. But I can definitely state that, in 1906, he was only a quite ordinary-looking dark man.

Being a good walker, he was as fond of long walks as hairdressers are of fishing. In the country, Albin, who did not shoot, would go off for hours with a gun. He would bring back, by way of game, a little pink peach tree snapped off by a hailstorm, a stray cat, a handkerchief full of flap mushrooms. Things like that endeared him to me. From time to time, I would search in vain for what was missing from our friendship, a friendship limited by the closely guarded secrets of Albin Chaveriat's love life. Before his death, he revealed only one to me and on that very day I suggested he should spend the war—we did not know, in May 1940, what those words implied—in a country house gay with young girls. For I reverted to his refusal which had been uttered with that marked reticence of voice and manner which provokes an inevitable retort from the other person: "My good man, you don't leave this house till you've told me the whole story!"

Albin did not leave the house. It was all the easier for me to make him stay because, for dinner, we had had deliciously fresh fish, mushrooms, taken off the fire before they were reduced to the condition of tasteless rags in which most French people serve them, and a semi-liquid *crème au chocolat* to satisfy those who like eating it with a spoon as well as those who prefer to drink it straight out of the little pot. In 1940, our Paris markets were still so well stocked that we walked through the neighborhood of Les Halles just to feast our eyes. In talking, we used such expressions as "the phony war" and "war in disguise" and we were, all of us, rather like animals without a sense of smell.

To break down my guest's inhibitions and loosen his tongue I offered him the last of my good *marc* brandy.

"Is it the Hersents themselves who put you off going to Normandy or their plethora of young girls, Colonel?"

Chaveriat had long ago given up laughing when one called him that. I think he rather liked having the tribute of an imaginary rank paid to his brush of white hair, his mustache, and his not unattractive limp.

"Neither one nor the other, my dear. There is nowhere in the world I like better than Normandy and I've always adored young girls, or rather the young girl as a species."

"Well, well, well!"

"Does that astonish you? Why? We've only known each other for twenty-five years and I'm sixty-eight. Do you suppose that for something like forty years I was entirely occupied in living up to your idea of me which, by the way, is certainly very different from my idea of yourself? Yes, my two ruling passions were young girls and shooting. Now I couldn't even take a shot at a jay and a young girl has, not cured me, but put young girls out of my life forever . . . You want a story and you shall have it. It isn't a pretty one, far from it. But it can no longer do any harm to anyone and by now I fear its heroine may well have sons of eighteen."

"How did I acquire a taste for young girls? I think it was through a masculine friendship. Between the ages of fifteen and twenty, I had a friend, one of those fellow adolescents to whom a normal boy is more faithfully devoted than to any mistress. Once turned twenty, a woman, or military service, or a profession breaks into one's life and ruins this beautiful mutual affection. Actually, our military service made hardly any difference to Eyrand and me: we went through the mill together. The first betrayal came from him, for that was what I called his marriage. Getting married at twenty-three and a half was, according to my family, an 'imprudence.' I have just told you the name I gave our separation. No, thanks, one glass of *marc* is enough for me. If I drank more, I would tell my story badly and not as impartially as I should.

"I remember I stubbornly refused to spend my holidays with Eyrand, the first year of his marriage, in a small country house standing in some seventy-odd acres which represented the best part of his wife's dowry and which he farmed himself. It was no good his writing to me over and over again and sending me snapshots of his young wife and his cattle and his farm, my back remained up. I sent him stupid letters in reply, because I thought his wife read them . . . And also because my friend's expressed nothing but a stolid happiness. Never a doubt or a worry or an anxiety, never anything at all about which I might have consoled him . . . Actually, I *would* like a drop of *marc*. Just a drop, no higher than the star engraved on the glass.

"In the end Eyrand got tired, as you can well imagine. When I saw that I had lost, and largely through my own fault, a friend I could never replace, I became unsociable with everyone except extremely young females. I was attracted by their sincere bluntness, by an interest that was usually sheer pretense, by beauty in embryo and character still unformed. They were seventeen, eighteen, a little more or a little less, while I was getting on for thirty. In their company, I felt the same age as themselves. In their company . . . It would be truer to say, in their arms. What is there in a young girl that is ripe and ready and eager to be exploited except her sensuality? No, don't let's argue about that, I know you don't agree with me. You won't prevent my having had—and for good reason—an almost terrified preference for that mixture of frenzy and determination, recklessness and prudence you find in a young girl who has—how shall I put it?—gone beyond certain limits. You have to have known a considerable number of young girls to realize that, compared to adult women, the majority of them are the inspired enthusiasts of the sex, ready to take the wildest risks. Also that, in dangerous situations, nothing can equal their complete calm. Public opinion has its set phrase: 'The coward who attacks young girls.' Good Lord! I can assure you that, on the contrary, one needs a very unusual temperament and remarkable self-control to resist them. Only don't get it into your head that my inclination became a monomania or a morbid obsession. In love, I've often been just like any other man, involved for a time in a liaison, attracted toward a sensible marriage, then no less sensibly escaping from it, irresolute . . . I assure you, a man just like other men.

"In 1923, I had already given up shooting but I accepted invitations from sportsmen. One of my friends, a retired chemist—there were parts of the country where, almost overnight, all the big estates had passed into the hands of the said chemists—had just bought such a beautiful property in Doubs that I planned my whole year so as to take a late summer holiday, between the fifteenth of August and the fifteenth of October. I did not enjoy it as much as I had hoped, on account of the rather boring collection of people staying there and the continual ostentatious gluttony. Food and drink alike, there was too much of everything, and it went on day after day. Things got to such a point that I had to pretend to be a dreamy recluse suffering from a liver complaint in order to have a right to solitude and sobriety. The owners of the big houses in the neighborhood used to tap me on the shoulders after meals, belching discreetly.

" 'So you're not quite up to the mark? You ought to see someone.' I abstained from replying that, on the contrary, I would far rather see no one, and I kept myself to myself. Except that I undertook to teach a quite good-looking woman, a cousin of the owner's, how one catalogues a library, and some other pleasant ways of spending a hot afternoon.

"What a country it is, my dear, all that region of Doubs! And what an estate! The new owner had not had time to make disastrous 'improvements' or to change that look—burning even more than burnt—that September has up there. The shortened days were still sweltering enough to take the skin off your hands when you lunched outdoors, and at night, just before dawn, a marvelous cold came in through the open windows, a cold that turned the leaves of the cherry trees all red—and the elms and chestnuts prematurely yellow. No season had ever been so yellow, including the grass in the fields which had not had enough rain to give a second hay crop. But, because the trees were so old and thick, the undergrowth remained and as mushroomy as you could wish. There are lots of 'violets' in Franche-Comté. The violet is a delicate kind of mushroom.

"Sparrow hawks—they were golden, too—would escort me a little way, circling very high above my head to find out my intentions, and as I was innocent of any evil design, they would abandon me.

"Being a good walker (I'm talking of twenty years ago) I wandered over hill and dale; I discovered a little lock in the park with its sluice gates rotted away and its pool dried up, the remains of a carved saint in her niche, an ancient 'belvedere,' from which it had long been impossible to see anything, full of rabbit dung and prickly broom. I left the park without realizing it because the chemist preferred to install bathrooms all over the house rather than rebuild the walls around his property. But a few hundred yards farther on, the landscape became tamer and was cut up into small cultivated squares bounded by low, mortarless walls that made warm shelters for vipers. Although the district was fairly thick with small hills, I did not lose my way. I never do get off my track, you know. What's making you smile? Ah, I see what you mean. No, thanks, no more brandy. I should love a glass of cold water.

"Perhaps you think I'm overdoing the landscape. But that season of long ago has left me a memory of being severely alone. On certain mornings, the dew was like a white frost, and then you baked for the rest of the day and the evening too, and the grapes—little black grapes in such tight clusters an ant couldn't have made its way into them—ripened ahead of time on the walls of the farm and the gatekeepers' lodges while the blue and mauve scabiosas announced that this blazing summer would soon be termed autumn. I was contented, contented without words and without many thoughts; I was getting tanned and beginning to look pleasingly like a country gentleman. One day . . . Yes, you see, I'm coming to the point.

"One day, I was outside the domain. I had shaken off all the fine-weather enthusiasts. I was on a hillside in the woods, climbing the fairly steep slope of a forest path, grassy but scored with wheel ruts. I was walking between birches; the wind was already blowing off their little golden leaves, so light that they fluttered a long time before they settled. Toward the top of the hill, I saw that the birches gave way to apple trees at the edge of a meadow. Behind the apple trees, a beautiful clump of rather melancholy firs more than half hid an ancient dwelling with a gable of old tiles, set very prettily sideways, as if intentionally, at the top of the slope. A great mantle of Virginia creeper, pink in places, covered its shoulder. An adjoining kitchen garden, a garden overgrown with weeds, a valley whose mist was the typical purple-blue of Franche-Comté. I thought, 'How charming it is—and how neglected,' and as a final touch, I could hear the ripple of water. Running water is a rare blessing in those little mountains. From the other side of the low, crumbling wall, the horned forehead of a goat touched my hand, a pair of spindle-shaped pupils stared me out of countenance. I put out my hand to scratch the pretty black forehead with a white star on it and it did not turn away.

" 'Don't touch her, don't touch her, she'll chase you!' cried a young voice.

"The accent of that part of the world drags out the vowels, as you know. 'Doön't touch her! She'll chaäse you!' Naturally, I stretched out my hand still farther, and with one bound, the goat was after me, pretty as a devil, pursued by a female child shouting, 'Stop it, you baäd girl, stop it!' A child . . . no. I don't call persons of around fifteen children. I should lose too much if I did. The young girl grabbed the she-goat by its horns and neatly threw it over on its side. The goat got up and bounded away in little leaps on all four feet.

" 'She's cross,' said the young girl.

"She was recovering her wind and breathing with her mouth half open. A blonde, even a little more than a blonde, verging on a redhead, with freckles on her cheeks and forehead and fiery eyelashes. But there was nothing of the albino redhead about her. On the contrary, her complexion was extraordinarily vivid under its bevy of freckles and her gray-green eyes, like her cheeks, were powdered with little chestnut freckles. One of the first things I noticed about her was the color of the little curly tendrils on her forehead and the nape of her neck (she wore her hair pretentiously piled up in a bun), they were almost pink with the midday sun shining through them. For it was noon, and scorching enough on this bare hilltop to peel the skin off your nose.

"I said to her: 'You've just definitely saved my life, Mademoiselle.'

"She laughed, wriggling her shoulders like a coquettish girl who has no idea of good manners. The inside of her mouth, as she laughed with her chin in the air, was lit up right to the back molars and I thought she was throwing her head back on purpose. You don't often find a flawless set of teeth in country girls. Country girls . . . My young girl had no apron and her clothes were dowdy, rather than rural. A cheap ready-made blue blouse with white spots, a badly cut skirt, and a leather belt—that was all as regards the outside. Underneath there was a young creature. The expression 'well-rounded,' so long out of fashion, describes a type of beauty which, believe me, is positively intoxicating when that beauty is adolescent. While I was making the little thing laugh at my simple jokes, I kept thinking, as I looked at that tautness and fullness and suppleness, of the drawings Boucher made of Louise O'Morphy, that girl who had not even finished growing before her entire dimpled body proclaimed its pressing need and cried aloud to lovers: 'Deliver me from myself or I shall burst!'

"My little O'Morphy ended by blushing, but only when she remembered that she had hung a necklace of 'square caps' around her neck, as all children do in autumn—you know, those bright pink wild euonymus berries with four lobes. I am stupid, as you have every reason to know.

"Furiously, she broke the thread and I remarked: 'That's a pity, it suited you very well. May I know the name of my protectress?'

" 'Louisette . . . Louise,' she corrected herself with dignity.

"I replied that my name was Albin and she signified with a little twitch of her mouth that she didn't care a rap. She was observing me surreptitiously, putting her hand over her eyes as if to keep the sun out of them. A voice called her and she answered with a shrill 'Yes.'

" 'I live there,' she said before leaving me. 'Over there, in the château.'

"She gave her home its name with a mannered haughtiness. Then she ran off toward her 'château' with long, boyish strides.

"I don't imagine I shall astonish you by telling you that . . . No, not the next day. The day after that, I braved the half-past-eleven sun, on the same spot. The day before, I had taken advantage of a car that went in to do the shopping to go into town and buy a little coral necklace whose beads were exactly the same bright pink as the 'square cap' berries . . . Excuse me, what were you saying, my dear? That it was a horrid proceeding, and a classic one? Allow me to defend myself. The lover of young girls is neither so simple nor so determined as to imagine the fulfillment of intentions he has not even had time to formulate clearly. But I admit that his method of approach is often of that commonplace kind Faust was taught by a demon whose tactics were far from subtle. Pretty trifles from the squire to the village maiden. So I ambushed myself at the edge of the wood, in that same scorching fine weather that seemed as if it would never end, in that same exacerbating eleven o'clock sun that was fast ripening the apples and the blackberries and those wall peaches known, for obvious reasons, as 'hardies.' And there I saw no sign of Louisette, but I could hear the ripple of the running water which marked its path on the other side of the slope by a track of greener herbage, some alders, a few willows. I had walked fast, I was dying to go and drink at it. Suddenly there was my young girl, a yard away, without the sound of a footstep or the rustle of a branch. She was staring at me with such fixed intensity that I can only convey it by brief ejaculations, such as: 'Well? So you've come? What do you want? I'm waiting. Say something. Do something!' I did not take the risk of using the same language and I greeted her politely as any man would, whether or not he had evil designs.

" 'Good morning, Mademoiselle Louisette.'

"She held out her hand like a young girl who does not know how to shake hands, an impersonal little paw.

" 'Good morning, Monsieur.'

" 'I've brought you back the necklace you broke the day before yesterday.'

"And I offered her my little necklace quite naked. Louisette tossed her chin and I observed she had the most delicious neck. An envelope of flesh so perfectly filled, a roundness that revealed not a hint of ligament or bone; never before or since have I seen a neck of such succulent perfection. And, besides, this was no bronzed beach girl I saw before me. Apart from the glorious coloring of her face and a little sunburned triangle in the opening of her blouse, the color of her body began at once at the base of the neck, a color so light, barely tinged with pink.

a lily under crimson skies . . .

. "Oh, you can laugh! Many a time I've felt that poem surging up in me above the purely physical feeling. In similar circumstances, that poem has often saved a young girl—and me—from myself.

"Well, I offered her my necklace, which had a little golden clasp. But Louisette refused it with a shake of the head, adding: 'No.'

" 'You don't want it? You think it's ugly?'

" 'No. But I can't take it.'

" 'It's an object of no value,' I said idiotically.

" 'That makes no difference. I can't take it because of Mamma. Whatever would Mamma say if she saw me with a necklace?'

" 'Mightn't you have . . . found it?'

"She gave a cynical little smile. She was still keeping her chestnut-flecked eyes fixed on mine. Spots of sunlight danced from her golden lashes to her chin. I have never seen a complexion like hers, such delicate chiseling of the mouth and nostrils. What's that? Was she pretty? It's true I haven't told you whether she was pretty. Actually, I don't think she was very pretty. Untidy, anyway. In her shining hair, I could see the ugly, battered, japanned hairpins that kept it in place. I could see that her stockings, beige lisle or cotton, were not very clean. For certain things, I have a remorseless eye.

"She was gazing at me so . . . how can I put it . . . so crudely that for a moment I was afraid there was something wrong with my appear-

ance. But only for a moment. My costume was so simple that it could
not make me look absurd: an open-necked shirt and trousers of some
smooth material that did not catch on brambles. I was carrying my
jacket over my arm—and nineteen less years than now. Long before it
became the fashion, I used to walk bareheaded, well thatched as I was
with my thick hair, alas! prematurely white. And I was lean, as you've
always known me.

"Naturally, I was also gazing at Louisette, but in a more cautious,
let us say a more civilized way. But even so, I saw that she had extended
the outer corners of her eyelids by means of two little penciled lines.
Such a preposterous, such an idiotic bit of coquetry made me burst out
laughing as one does at children who celebrate Shrove Tuesday by
solemnly wearing crepe-hair beards.

"You can imagine my young girl was not at all pleased. She understood perfectly well and rubbed her two forefingers over the corners of
her eyes. I took advantage of this to assert my authority.

" 'That's a nice thing,' I told her. 'At your age? You refuse a trifle
because you're afraid of your mother, and you don't hesitate to make up
your eyes!'

"She wriggled her shoulders, the way all badly brought-up girls do.
But no girl, badly brought-up or not, ever made such shoulders or such
a pair of young breasts tightly attached to them heave inside her blouse.
I hoped she was going to snivel a little so that I could console her.

" 'Do take this little necklace,' I said. 'Or else I shall throw it away.'

" 'Throw it away, then,' she said at once. 'I certainly shan't pick it
up. You'd better give it to someone else.'

" 'Are you so very frightened of your mother?'

"She shook her head again before she spoke, as she had done before.

" 'No. I'm afraid she'd think badly of me.'

" 'And your father, is he a rigid disciplinarian?'

" 'Is he a what?'

" 'Is he strict with you?'

" 'No. He's dead.'

" 'Forgive me. Was he very old?'

" 'Fifty-two.'

"It was within a month or two of my own age and I mechanically
stood up straighter.

" 'So you live alone with your mother?'

" 'And there are the Biguets too. They run the farm.'

" 'Is it yours, that water I can hear rippling?'

" 'Yes. It's the spring.'

" 'A spring! And a spring that gives so much water you can hear it
from here . . . Why, it's a fortune!'

" 'It's the most beautiful spring in the world,' said Louisette simply.

"Her expression changed and she shot me an angry look.

" 'You're not another of those people who want to buy it from us?'

" 'Who waänt to buy-ee it?' Her accent, stressed on certain words, did not displease me, on the contrary. I reassured her.

" 'No, no, Louisette. I'm on holiday at ——, staying with the new owner. I don't want to take your spring away from you. But I think I could drink it all up, I'm so thirsty.'

"She spread out her hands in a gesture of helpless regret.

" 'Oh dear, I can't take you there to drink. Mamma would think it queer for me to be talking to someone she doesn't know. Unless we went around outside by the back way.'

" 'And which is the back way?'

"She answered me by jerking her eyebrows, winking, and pursing her lips, a sign language of complicity I had not hoped for and that enchanted me. I saw she was ripe for dissimulation, for forbidden collusion, in other words, for sin. I replied as best I could by making the same sort of faces and we walked back, she in front and I following her, down the sheltered path at the edge of the wood, the whole length of the low, half-collapsed wall the goat had jumped to 'chaäse' me.

" 'Where's my enemy the goat, Mademoiselle Louisette?'

" 'She's out in the fields. We've got three. But that one's the nicest.'

"Louisette answered me without turning her head and I was more than content to have a good chance to study the nape of her neck revealed by her high-pinned bun, the small, ardently pink ears, the flat, well-placed shoulder blades, and the faint swell of the springy hips below the tight leather belt . . . I assure you, a work of art with no hint of angularity or awkwardness, but with nothing noble about it except its precocious perfection. A young creature so frankly inviting one definite thing that an imbecile might have thought her cynical. But I am not an imbecile, my dear. I need to tell you this in so many words because, very late in the day, I'm now introducing you to an unknown Chaveriat who for a long time made a point of remaining unknown. For I have never been vain about my vices, if vices they are.

"Well, I followed this little thing, admiring her. I was trying to find some definite classification for her based on her inborn effrontery, her craving to satisfy my curiosity and to deceive her mother's watchful eye. Already, I mentally called her 'the prettiest little servant girl in France.' Anyone can make a mistake.

"At the elbow of the crumbling wall, we left the undergrowth. The path was now no more than a track that descended fairly steeply, so that the wall loomed up higher and hid the 'château' from us. An old wall, as flowery as a herbaceous border. Scabiosas, the last foxgloves, valerians that I've noticed are always very red in Franche-Comté, and begonias slightly choked by ivy.

" 'What a beautiful wall!' I said to Louisette.

"She replied only by a sign and I presumed she preferred her voice not to be heard associated with a stranger's. The enclosing wall bent again at a right angle, revealing, at the same time, the other side of the hill and the entrance to the grounds of the house. The entrance, however, had been reduced to two pillars crowned with little stone lions, so worn by time that their faces looked more like those of sheep. An avenue of rowan trees, thick with berries and birds, led to the 'château,' whose coat of ivy disguised its dilapidation. If you've lived in Franche-Comté . . . yes, you have lived there. Then you know those solid country houses, built to withstand the weight of heavy snow in winter. But this one really was in a bad state. From a distance, it produced an illusion and dominated a valley that, even at midday, was still veiled in blue haze because the spring, now running underground, now enclosed in the bed it hollowed out for itself, filled it with mist.

"Louisette stopped abruptly before she reached the first pillar, so abruptly that I bumped up against her charming back, her red-gold nape, and her whole person, as plump and hard as a wall peach.

" 'We mustn't go any farther,' she said. 'Can you see the spring?'

"I could only half see it, that is to say, in a stone niche at the end of the rowan avenue, I caught a glimpse of a wild leaping. It was as if the niche, all overhung with plants that love shade and water, was frequented by great silver fish. I could also see that a liquid curtain flowed over the margin and probably ran down into a basin below . . . But I saw no means of quenching my thirst without crossing the barrier of the sheep-like lions. Louisette went in without saying a word and came back carrying a small, brimming watering can with a long spout.

" 'Drink before I do, Louisette.'

"And I added, without shame: 'Then I shall know your thoughts.'

"But she replied with a very curt refusal: 'I'm not thuürsty.' There's no drink to compare with water when it springs, mysteriously cold, straight out of the earth.

" 'Go down again the same way,' Louisette commanded me. 'This is the real entrance, but you might be seen from the house if you went down by the main road.'

"I obeyed without a word. At the spot where the wall overtopped the path by some twelve or fifteen feet, I received a small pebble on my head. Louisette, perched up there, was watching my departure. I waved my hand and blew her a kiss without her smiling or pretending to be embarrassed. The sight of a golden head, motionless and watchful between tufts of scabiosas and yellow stonecrop, that was all I got from her that day. I remember that, walking back down the hill toward the chemist's domain, I said to myself: 'All the same, she might have thrown me a flower instead of a pebble!' and in my heart of hearts, I reproached that little girl for her lack of poetry.

"I'm not going to bore you, my dear, with the details of our lovers' meetings that first week. In any case, Louisette and I didn't have any lovers' meetings, properly speaking. I used to climb the little hill around the really scorching hour, eleven or half past. The drought was making the leaves fall early. Up at the big house, my host's shooting guests brought bad reports of game grown lean and haggard. But I never listened to them. My own private game was always to be found, now here, now there, fresh, not in the least exhausted by the heat, and plump as ever. The strange thing was that my tentative affair, which was proving pleasant rather than amusing, was making no progress. Louisette, though she laughed easily, showed no fundamental gaiety. Being fifteen and a half and living in extreme and dangerous solitude, probably on the verge of poverty, is not, admittedly, conducive to a very gay life . . . Her answers to my questions never went beyond the strictly necessary.

"For example, when I asked her: 'Do you live very much alone?'

" 'Oh, yes,' she answered.

" 'Don't you find that rather dreary?'

" 'Oh, no. We have visitors on Sundays. People we know.' She added: 'Not every Sunday. That would be a lot.'

"Her little hands, dimpled at the base of each finger, told me more than she did about the heavy household chores imposed on them. Idle, they would have been very pretty and like Louisette herself: rather short, dimpled, with fingers that turned up at the tips. As she walked beside me, she picked a pointed twig and used it as an orange stick to clean her nails.

"Another time I said to her: 'Do you read a great deal?'

"She nodded twice, with the air of an expert.

" 'Papa left us a big library.'

" 'Are you fond of novels? Would you like me to give you some books?'

" 'No, thanks.'

"The refusal was always very definite. I could not make her accept either books or a bottle of scent or a suede belt or a trumpery bracelet or a lawn handkerchief . . . Nothing, do you understand? As she said herself: 'Not the leastest thing.' This inflexibility never yielded an inch. 'And what would Mamma say?' She invariably floored me with that one argument, produced in severe, triumphant tones. 'You must have a terrible mother,' I risked saying one day.

"Louisette shot me the same nasty look she had given me when she spoke of selling the spring.

" 'No, I haven't. She never does anything wrong, she doesn't. If she knew I talked to you, she'd be very upset. So, as I've got to keep it a secret from her that I do talk to you, I mustn't do *anything* to give it away. I think that's the least I can do for her, take pains to stop her knowing.'

"And in such a tone! The young lady was instructing me in her personal morality and it was I who was being given lessons! To mollify her and flatter her, I listened with an air of being much impressed. She was watching me covertly, as if she expected something from me and I did not know what it was she wanted or did not want. We men who fall in love with young girls, we don't take any risks till we're sure of success. The one thing that disconcerts us and holds us back is simplicity, firstly because we don't believe in it, secondly because our success depends on choosing the right moment. Those interviews, with the light beating down on us and Louisette always with one eye or one ear cocked in the direction of her mother, left me nervy and exhausted by so much sunshine. When I returned to —— I found a definite charm in playing bridge on a shady terrace, in reading the illustrated papers with the cool six o'clock wind ruffling their pages. Until the day, when that week had gone by, that I had the idea of telling Louisette, 'I've only got ten more days here.' The corners of her mouth quivered, but all she said was: 'Oh!'

" 'Yes, alas. And tomorrow the owner of —— is organizing a series of motor expeditions and picnics in the local beauty spots. I can't always go off on my own, and be unsociable. But if, instead of getting myself roasted up here, I came and took a breath of fresh air on this little mountain in the evening, mightn't I possibly happen to meet you?'

"I assure you I gave a quite marvelous imitation of shyness and I did not even hold her hand. I had the surprise of seeing her begin to fidget, biting one of her nails, and thrusting and rethrusting the hideous japanned hairpins into her bun from which the little tendrils escaped like a haze of fire. She looked all around her, then said hurriedly: 'I don't know, I don't know . . .' and as she raised her arms, I caught a drift of feminine odor. I pretended to hesitate, then to lose my head, and I seized Louisette by that slim waist so many plump little things have. I whispered into her hair, under her ear: 'This evening? . . . Six o'clock?' and I refrained from kissing her on the lips before going off with long, hurried strides. I went down quickly through the undergrowth so as to give her no time to think of calling me back, and when I had already left her far behind, I realized we had not uttered one word that implied tenderness, desire, or friendliness.

"My dear, it isn't only to drink up this glass of water that I'm breaking off. No, thank you, I'm not tired. When one's talking about oneself, one doesn't feel tired till one's finished. But I observe you're looking apprehensive, not to say disapproving. Why? Because my heroine is only aged sixteen minus three months? Because I've fastened my covetous gaze on too young a blossom? Don't be in too much of a hurry to judge me and, above all, to pity the tender ewe lamb. At fifteen, or even less, they threw a princess to an heir-apparent, probably an innocuous young man. Queens were married at thirteen. To search even higher than thrones for my justification, do I have to remind you what Juliet meant, at fifteen, by 'hearing the nightingale'? If my memory does not deceive me, didn't you tell me that, at sixteen, you yourself fell madly in love with a bald man of forty who looked twice that age? I think I'm using your very words. Old boughs for tender shoots, as our fathers used to say with genial lechery. I claim indulgence, at least *your* indulgence, considering that, with a few exceptions, I've been mad about tender shoots nearly all my life without withering one of them or making her produce another shoot. So I will now continue a story you brought on yourself and I shall lower neither my eyes nor my voice.

"Well, I had solicited a meeting at dusk, but because of my deliberate flight, I was not sure whether Louisette would turn up. I did find her there, however, and in a setting that seemed quite new at that late hour, among long shadows that marked the divisions between the little mountains and made them look higher. You know that country, you know how, as the light goes, valleys take on quite a different color from the blue of midday. That periwinkle, almost lilac blue, barred with pale yellow and dark green, the humpbacked, complex landscape, hitherto blotted out by the ferocious noonday sun, the smell of wood fires lit for the evening meal, it was all so enchanting that I was not in the least bored as I waited for Louisette. Frankly, I was already consoling myself for not seeing her when she arrived, running, and flung herself, as if in play, into my arms, where she was very well received. I admired her at once for having avoided, by an impetuous rush, the usual 'It's you at last!' or 'How sweet of you to come!' Whatever her social level, the female creature does not leave us a wide choice of phrases to greet her arrival. As I say, Louisette flung herself, breathless, into my arms as if she were playing Wolf and had reached 'home.' She laughed, unable to speak, or at least apparently unable to speak. Her ugly metal hairpins dropped out of her pretentious little bun and her hair hung about her head, not very long, but so frizzy that it stood out in a thick, fiery bush. As to her palpitation, I assured myself, with one cupped hand, that it was genuine. Our physical intimacy was established in one moment in an unhoped-for way and on entirely new ground. I say physical, because

I can't say plain intimacy. I think an ordinary man, I mean an ordinary lover, would have thought that, in Louisette, he'd met the most shameless of semi-peasant girls. But I was not an ordinary lover.

"I gave Louisette time to calm down before kissing her. When I did, she received my kisses so naturally, so eagerly . . . Don't raise your eyebrows like that, my dear, do I surprise you as much as all that? Yes, with an eagerness that would have been the ruin of a lover who was both careless and in a hurry, as they nearly all are. But I was not a careless lover. So Louisette gave herself up to the pleasure of being kissed, and in the intervals, she smiled at me and looked at me with wonderfully clear, radiant eyes, as if she were delighted to have found the real way to talk to me and not to have to be bored anymore with a stranger. The twilight had already fallen, and high in the sky, it was barred by a long cloud, still rosy with the setting sun. And, looking up from my supporting arm, I saw a happy face, exuberant hair, eyes no longer bashfully drooped but wide open, all echoing the color of the cloud. It was very lovely and, I assure you, I did not miss one iota of it. A cry broke out from the direction of the house and Louisette wrenched away from me everything I was holding fast; her hard little mouth, her slim, rounded torso, her feet I had gripped between mine. She listened, waited for a second cry, her eyes and ears on the alert to decide exactly where the cry came from, then fled full speed, with no goodbye beyond a little wave.

"That night, I made mistake after mistake at bridge. Away from Louisette, it was easier to admit that I was disconcerted. In her presence —as you can well imagine, I met her again the next day and every day after—I let myself be guided not only by my own experience but also by Louisette herself. Without going into a lot of details that would embarrass us both, I admit I have never met anyone like Louisette either in her simplicity or in her baffling mystery. To make myself clear, I believe that the sensuality of any grown-up woman who behaved like Louisette would have revolted me. Louisette was avid in the way children are, she was vicious with grace, with majesty. Physical confidence is always admirable. Louisette's preserved her from certain dangers, it is true, but it must also be said she was lucky to chance on me and not another man. She treated sensual pleasure as a lawful right, but nothing gave me reason to think that she had had any previous experience. This strange affair lasted longer than the fine weather and kept me staying on, rather inconveniently, with my friend the ostentatious retired chemist.

"At the end of a fortnight, I told myself quite sincerely: 'You've had enough of this. Any more would be too much.' Perhaps, in my heart, I was . . . how can I put it? I was shocked, I was . . . well . . . a little scandalized that this wild pony caught in the fields didn't show me a little . . . hang it all, a little affection, a little . . .

"What's that, my dear? Begging your pardon, I am *not* a brute—I proved that at least once every twenty-four hours—and I did not think it was asking too much to hope that Louisette, softened and satisfied, would come to treat her unselfish lover as a friend. So much so that, when my nerves were on edge, for very obvious reasons, it was I who said to Louisette, bending over her little shell-like ear: 'You won't quite forget your old friend when he's far away?' I was sitting on a granite boulder, coated with dry lichen that made it less hard. Louisette, sitting lower down, was leaning her head against my ribs. She turned up a face like a ripe peach—raised her eyes, which at that moment were very bright under their chestnut flecks, and I thought that, for the first time I was going to hear . . . a gentle word, a childish avowal, perhaps just a sigh. She merely said 'Oh, no!' exactly like a child answering an imbecile parent who has asked the imbecile question: 'You don't love Mamma more than Papa, do you?' And I left her that day earlier than usual without her appearing to notice it in the very slightest. We talked so little. She listened to me, certainly. But she was also listening to many other sounds I did not hear and now and then would sign to me, sometimes rather rudely, to be quiet. I was in the process of telling her something or other, goodness knows what, to make myself believe we enjoyed talking together, and seeing the fixed gaze of her beautiful flecked eyes, and her parted lips whose color I had just warmed to a rich glow, I felt flattered by her attentiveness. She was lying, leaning on her elbow, and we were in one of those tiny clearings that make bare patches among the tall heather. I was sitting, leaning over her, when she suddenly began to flutter her eyelids, overcome by a lassitude that pleased my vanity. One of Louisette's charms was to exclaim suddenly: 'I'm hungry' or 'I'm sleepy,' to yawn with hunger or suddenly to fall asleep for a few moments. As I say, she was fluttering her lids, and at every blink, her red eyelashes glinted like fire, when suddenly she opened her eyes wide, sat up, grabbed me by the shoulders, and pushed me over on the ground, where she held me down by main force. I tried to get up, but she threatened me with her fist, and her child's face became quite terrifying. All this lasted about the space of ten heartbeats. Then Louisette let me go, her cheeks and lips went white, and she collapsed, quite limp, on the grass.

"When her color returned, she explained: 'Your head was showing. There was someone on the path.'

" 'Who?' I asked.

" 'Someone who lives around here.'

"I think she had recognized her mother's footsteps. Without any embarrassment, she fastened her open blouse. Everything she allowed me to see of herself would have rejoiced what one calls a gay dog. Quite unlike a gay dog and a Don Juan, it made me feel solemn to see how much childhood and newly achieved womanhood can have in common. So much beauty, with no adornments except cotton underclothes, a little blue ribbon, and cheap, coarse stockings. No scent except the slightly russet fragrance of the hair. When she was violently excited I could breathe in the smell of that plant . . . what *is* its name? . . . one of the pea family, with pink flowers . . . that blondes give out when they sweat. Restharrow, that's right, thanks. When I was away from Louisette, I used to think what she might have been, which is always a stupid thing to do. I used to imagine her as a nymph, leaning over the spring, naked as she was worthy to be. We never rise to great heights when we try to mingle art and literature with the religious feeling inspired by a beautiful body.

"After a few days Louisette changed the time of our meetings, and for my host's benefit, I had to assume the role of poet and night walker, so as to be able to climb up to the 'château' around ten at night. 'Why so late?' I asked my little sweetheart.

" 'Because Mamma goes to bed at nine. She gets up before five all the year round. At half past eight, I've just finished washing up the supper things and putting them away. After that, I can do as I like, as long as I'm very careful.'

" 'You don't sleep near your mother, then?'

"She lowered her red-gold eyebrows.

" 'Fairly near. Look, I'll show you.'

"She led me as far as the lion-guarded entrance, walking along the narrow path as if it were broad daylight.

" 'That square tower, behind the spring. There's only one room on each floor. Mamma has the top one, she's given me the other one because it's nicer. But as soon as it gets cold, Mamma brings her bed down into my room where it's warmer. The cold weather comes early up here.'

"She fell silent. I could hear the spring and its imaginary fishes leaping in their basin.

" 'But, Louisette, darling,' I said, 'it's dangerous for you, going out at night.'

" 'Yes,' she said.

"That considered, almost gloomy 'yes' was so far removed from the cry of a girl in love flinging herself recklessly in the path of danger that I did not express my gratitude. A 'yes' that did not even seem to have any concern with me. She was staring vaguely at the square gable and the silver leaps of the spring at the end of the avenue. The moon was blurred that night, showing pink through its surrounding haze. So near the main gate, we might easily have been seen. But I trusted entirely to my little companion, who knew how to make us invisible at the right moment, making me walk in the dark at the foot of the garden wall, pushing me into the thick shadow of a laurel bush that left its fragrance on her hands. We only met stray ramblers she could trust not to betray us; a silent dog, guilty of going off hunting on his own; the white horse belonging to the 'château,' who was trailing his chain slackly behind him and taking advantage of the warmth of the night. The clouded moon threw few strong shadows, but from time to time, she emerged from her halo and I could see my long shadow welded to a shorter one, moving ahead of us.

"Don't you get the impression that I'm telling you rather a sad story? Curious, so do I. Yet the story of Louisette starts off as something rather charming, doesn't it? But tonight I'm feeling sentimental. In any case, it's the nature of affairs of this type to get tiresome very soon, to lose their freshness. Otherwise, the only thing that keeps the edge on them for those of us who are addicted to a particular type of woman is when we find ourselves coming to grips with young demons. Oh, they exist all right, there are more of them than you think. Louisette was nothing more than a young girl whose whole body had burst into blossom, a young girl whom I was relieving of her boredom, for I was not fatuous enough to think I was relieving her of her innocence. In country girls, there is no such thing as physical innocence. Louisette accepted, she even fixed the character of our relationship. She hardly ever used my Christian name; when she called me 'Albin,' she sounded self-conscious. I've always thought she had to restrain herself from calling me 'Monsieur,' and I should not have been offended if she had. On the contrary. This reserve redoubled the astonishment—I may also say the desire—that Louisette aroused in me.

"One day, I brought her a little ring, made of diamond chips, a jewel for a child, and taking her by surprise, I slipped it on her finger. She turned red as . . . as a nectarine, as a dahlia, as the most divinely red thing in the world. But it was with rage, you must understand. She tore the ring off her finger and brutally flung it back at me. 'I've already commanded you (she said *commanded*!) not to give me anything.' When I had sheepishly taken back my humble jewel, she made sure that the little cardboard box, the tissue paper, and the blue tinsel ribbon were not still lying about on our chair of rocks and lichen. Odd, wasn't it?

"But otherwise I had no cause but to rejoice in an idyll so exciting and so ideally suited to my natural bent. If Louisette's mutism was merely want of intelligence, I had met other stupid girls and less pleasing ones. All the same, at moments, I could feel something emanating from her that resembled sadness. I felt sorry for anyone whose destiny was as uncertain as Louisette's. And, besides, my holiday, what with consuming heat and consuming passion, was reducing me to something like exhaustion. I was getting impatient at being completely unable to understand a girl who roamed the woods at night, with me, but sprang up as if she had been shot, turned pale, and trembled at the knees if she heard the step or the voice of her mother.

"All that, my dear, belongs to the past. But to a past that has remained buried in silence. I am throwing fresh light on it by telling you about it because, looking back on it now, it seems, quite definitely, not to have been such a gay adventure as I thought. At the time, I used to wonder now and then whether Louisette was not exploiting me like a lecherous man who's found a willing girl. This ridiculous notion irritated me to such a point that I had a most unexpected little access of rage. No, not in front of her, but at bridge, in my host's house, one night when I had not arranged to meet Louisette. No one noticed anything, except that I played very badly. I was listening to the noise of the wind which, for the first time since my arrival, was sobbing under the doors and bringing us through the open windows—it was very mild— a poignant smell from the terrace outside—the smell of dampness before rain, of flowers when the season of flowers is over. The song of the wind, the scent of autumn, I knew that they both spoke of my return to Paris and I found myself quite astonishingly upset at the prospect. I thought of my departure, of what the life of two women must be like in winter, in the dilapidated 'château.' I forced myself to imagine the rowan trees without their leaves, green on one side and silvery on the other, without their umbels of red berries; the spring sealed up by the cold, its living water imprisoned between great bars of limpid ice.

"I went to bed early, and the rest, which I badly needed, put everything more or less right. The next morning I allowed myself a long lazy morning in a rocking chair on the terrace, making idle conversation with the other guests. I found I had got rid of that anxious, indiscreet feeling that made me want to know more about Louisette's private life. Indiscreet is the right word. Didn't she consider it so herself, since, after a whole month of daily meetings, I was still waiting for her to make me any sort of confidence? It gave me a definite pleasure to watch and listen to the people around me, and privately to regard my fellow quinquagenarians as old men because they were married and getting potbellied. The day passed quickly—it was warm, but free of the recent tremendous heat—and in such calm that I hardly thought at all about Louisette. But you know how dangerous the habit of making love is; it is exactly like being addicted to smoking or taking drugs. When the hand of the clock (a Louis XIV clock, I need hardly say) jerked its embossed point toward a tortoiseshell figure X, I could bear it no longer, and I got up from my chair.

" 'What, again, Chaveriat!' exclaimed my host. 'Even tomcats don't go out when their bellies are full.'

" 'I am not a tomcat,' I replied. 'I am a martyr to hygiene and vanity. If I didn't take at least an hour's exercise after my meals, I should ruin my waistline and my digestion.'

" 'Look out then, the weather's going to change any moment.'

" 'With a full moon? Nothing could be less likely. After my defeat last night, you can find another victim.'

"All the same, I took a mackintosh and my flashlight, which Louisette always forbade me to use as soon as I came anywhere near her 'château.' A Gustave Doré moon seemed to be leaping from cloud to cloud, plunging behind cumuli rimmed with fire and emerging naked, dazzling, and a little hunchbacked. These games of the moon and the flying clouds made me realize the wind had risen and I promised myself I would only spend a moment with Louisette. It was a wise resolution. Just as I had reached the spot where the garden wall overhung the path and gave it deepest shelter—that was where my sweetheart always waited for me—just as my arms had closed around an adored body, as lovely standing up as lying down, but never freely seen or enjoyed, just as the first kiss had assured me, in the darkness, that nothing had ever rivaled that elastic firmness, utterly surrendered to my honor, the wind rose in a fierce gust. I only held my companion all the tighter. From her invisible hair and her mouth that tasted of raspberries, from the smell that came from her already bared bosom which assured me I was crushing a woman, not a child, against me, I could have guessed all her rose and russet tints. My vague remorse for my day of indifference increased my ardor. Heaven knows where remorse of that kind may lead us! . . . Don't be alarmed, my dear, that last remark is not going to start me off on a digression. I only made it to indicate that, that night, I was on the very verge of behaving like a straightforward normal animal, like a man who knows only one way to possess the woman he desires. And I am not sure that Louisette, who was as frenzied as I was, would have stopped me.

"It was at that moment the rain, fast approaching through the scented darkness and the chirp of insects who thought summer had returned, suddenly burst down on us. A solid sheet of rain, like a ceiling collapsing on our heads, a crushing deluge of rain. I flung my waterproof cape over Louisette and she very deftly draped one half over my shoulders, but what stuff could have stood up to that drenching? The shower poured down in cascades below the bottom of the cape and soaked our feet. Louisette did not hesitate long, she ran, pulling me along with her. The diffused light of the hidden moon showed me we were passing the lions who guarded the nonexistent gate, the rowan trees, the spring lashed by rain that fell dead straight: I felt paving stones under my feet and bent my head down to Louisette's dripping ear to make myself heard in spite of the thunderous drumming of the raindrops: 'Till tomorrow, darling. Get inside quick!'

"But she did not let go my hand and led me on. I was aware of treading on dry stones, the noise of the rain became less deafening, and I realized, from the denser darkness, that I had crossed a threshold, the threshold of Louisette's 'château.'

"The fitful, stormy light only came in faintly through the open door. Forced inside by the solid curtain of rain, I could breathe the smell of those country-house lobbies where there are old straw hats hanging up and they keep the galoshes and the first windfalls.

" 'I mustn't make any light,' Louisette whispered to me. 'Give me your hand.'

"She pushed me, leaving the door wide open, toward one of those long, severely uncomfortable, cane-bottomed settees you find quite as often in Provence as in Breton country houses. A thin quilted mattress covers the seat without making it any less penitential. I remember you had one, in Brittany, around 1908. We sat down. Moving my hands cautiously over her, I made sure the rain had not soaked Louisette's thin clothes. And if she was shivering, it was not with cold. But my spirit of aggression was severely checked by this unfamiliar haven and the total darkness.

" 'As soon as it's raining less, you must go,' whispered Louisette.

"Mentally, I replied that I should not need to be told twice. And I settled Louisette against me, very respectably, with her feet stretched out on the vacant part of the settee and her head on my shoulder. She slipped her arm under mine and we stayed perfectly still. Little by little I made out the size of the room, and some of its features. A staircase with wooden banisters ran down into it just behind us. A bunch of pale flowers gradually grew clearer on a fairly large table that I could touch with my outstretched hand. On my right, an unshuttered window slowly began to show blue. I kept my eyes and ears strained and my jaws clenched. Obviously, what made me uneasy reassured Louisette, for I could feel her warm and relaxed against my arm and as still as a little hare in the hollow of a furrow.

" 'I think it's raining less,' I whispered in her ear.

"Hardly had I spoken when the deluge redoubled and the darkness thickened about us. My dear, I simply cannot tell you how I longed to get away from that place. I had just made up my mind to escape and was already looking forward with positive pleasure to being forced to run, guided by the halo of my flashlight, to a safe shelter when I realized, from the limpness of her little torso, that Louisette had dozed off. I've told you how promptly she obeyed, as robust temperaments do, the impulses of hunger, sleep, and other physical cravings. I was on the point of waking her up, but it was such a new sensation to hold her asleep in my arms that I wanted to wait just a little longer. You can understand what it meant to be, or at least to fancy myself, watching over her protectively for the first time . . . And I closed *my* eyes too, to give myself a brief illusion that we were sleeping like two lovers. But I opened my eyes at the slightest creak and heaven knows there was nothing that *didn't* creak in that barn of a place!

"A dim light shone down on us and I wanted to wake Louisette to tell her that the moon was out again and I must go. Then I realized that the light was coming neither from the open door nor from the window on the right. Far worse, the light began to move and lit up a landing higher up the staircase. There is a great difference between electric light and any other kind. It was the flame of a lamp, beyond all possibility of doubt, that was coming toward us, and the shadows of the banisters began to shift slowly around in the well of the staircase. I whispered urgently into the bush of damp hair that covered my shoulder: 'Louisette! Someone's coming!' The little thing gave a terrible start, and I leaped to my feet to . . . Oh, yes, quite frankly, to escape, but she clutched me with the same strength that had knocked me over that day among the brambles. All I succeeded in doing was to produce a tremendous clatter of sofa legs and chair legs and all that sprang to my lips was the beginning of a blasphemous oath. The shadows of the banisters swung full circle onto the walls and I saw a woman appear, holding the lamp—quite a small woman, in a mauve dressing gown tightly girdled around the waist. Her resemblance to Louisette left me no doubt, no hope. Same frizzy hair, but already almost completely white, and faded features that one day would be Louisette's. And the same eyes, but with a wide, magnificent gaze Louisette perhaps would never have, a gaze that was not upturned in anguish but that imperiously insisted on seeing everything, knowing everything. How interminable it seems, a moment like that, and how is it that boredom, yes, sheer boredom, a boredom that tempts one to yawn and chuck the whole thing, manages to intervene between the fractions of dramatic seconds? And that little idiot, clutching tight hold of me and refusing to let me go. With a violent shake, I tore my sleeve out of her fingers and stood up.

"I remember I said: 'Madame, don't be frightened . . .'

"And then, I found myself unable to go on. The little thing, still lying on the settee, was supporting herself on one arm like the *Dying Gladiator*. And with her other bent elbow, she flung back her hair. She did, poor girl, the only thing she could; she screamed for help: 'Mamma!'

"And then she began to cry. The astonishing thing is that I was not in the least touched, because, in spite of all my exasperation with everything, myself included, I was spellbound by the principal character who had just made her stage entrance, the mother. She set down her oil lamp, turned to Louisette, and asked her: 'So that's the man, is it, my girl?'

"The little thing raised her face, showing her streaming eyes and a mouth open square, like a crying baby's, and shrieked: 'No, Mamma, no, Mamma!'

" 'Not so much noise, my girl,' said the white-haired woman. 'Because it definitely is that man who's been leading you astray all this while. I've seen you, so it's no good lying. I saw you with him in the copse, in among the bushes. As to *him*, I'm not sorry to see his face, no, not at all sorry.'

"She turned to me with a quick movement. The unshaded lamp shone straight in her eyes but she did not blink. I could not prevent myself from noticing the difference between the expression of her face and the words on which she had broken off. I thought I ought to emerge from my silence. You can't imagine how immensely anxious one becomes, at such an unforeseen moment, about what is the proper thing to do or not to do. The decision I made was not the most fortunate one.

" 'Madame,' I said, 'in spite of appearances, which, I admit, are deplorable, I can assure you I have not behaved toward . . . toward Mademoiselle Louisette in a way that could . . .'

"The white-haired lady put her hands on her hips, thrusting her fists into the hollows of her waist. This gossip's attitude was not unbecoming to her; on the contrary.

" 'In a way that could . . .' she repeated.

" 'In a way that could put her into a certain situation . . .'

" 'I know what you're trying to say,' she broke in harshly. 'You think that's an excuse? *I* don't. Do you expect me to say thank you?'

"The little thing stopped sobbing. At the same moment, the rain stopped too and this double truce filled the room with a great silence that seemed to be awaiting my answer. It is extremely unusual for a man who is appearing at a disadvantage in the presence of two women not to be tempted to lose patience and make some stupid retort. That was what happened to me.

" 'Come now, Madame, it's true I'm not a saint, but in this case, I haven't forced anyone against their will, and your daughter's beauty . . .'

"The feet of the cane settee rasped on the flagstones as it was pushed backward and I was confronted with Louisette, her face red and inflamed with crying.

" 'I forbid you to talk to my mother in that tone,' she said in a low, harsh voice.

" 'Oh!' I said. 'If I've got the two of you against me, I prefer . . .'

"And I made an attempt to retreat, an attempt that was frustrated because the haughty little lady stood between me and the door and made no effort to get out of my way.

" 'You're not here to tell us about your preferences,' she said.

"She had really admirable eyes, and a sunburned, windburned face with a shiny glaze on the cheekbones and the bridge of the nose. And she was staring at me as if she were boring into my brain, so much so that it put my back up.

" 'Very well, Madame, if you will be good enough to tell me in what terms I may express my regrets . . .'

" 'Monsieur,' she interrupted me rudely, 'may one know your age?'

"If I had been expecting a question, it was most certainly not that one. Moreover, I was astonished that this strange mother, finding her daughter in the arms of a man, had not had recourse to any of the classical arguments and vituperations. She had a mouth made for vehemence, a freedom of manner that was half peasant, half middle class. Her preposterous question shattered me so much that I found myself making a series of idiotic gestures such as running my hand through my hair, pulling my leather belt down over my loins, and drawing myself up to my full height.

" 'I cannot see, Madame, what the precise number of my years has to do with all this. However, I am willing to confess to you that I am forty-nine.'

"For a moment, I thought she was going to laugh. Why not turn the scene into light comedy? The good woman seemed to me to have a sense of humor and she was anything but shy. A kind of laugh did, in fact, run over her features. She seized her daughter by the arm, pulled her close against her, mingling her white hair with the red hair, and whispered passionately: 'You hear him, child? You *see* that man there? Child, he's three times as much as your fifteen and a half, and even more! You've let yourself be led astray by a man of fifty, Louise! A young boy such as there are plenty of around here, *that* I could understand. But a man of fifty, Louise, of *fifty*! Ah! You may well be ashamed!'

"If I had not controlled myself, I assure you I should have gone for those two cows and knocked them down. Their two heads, close together and so terribly alike, stared me out of countenance. And that blinding, unshaded lamp. The older let go of the younger's arm, pointing the forefinger of her shriveled brown hand at me, and raised her voice: 'If your father were still alive, Louise, he'd be just the age of that man there!'

"Louisette gave a sharp little moan and hid her face in her mother's white mane. Her mother did not repulse her and went on talking.

" 'Yes, now you don't want to see him anymore, high time too, Louise! All the same, you've *got* to look at him! Yes, look at him, the man who was born the same year as your own father!'

"Plunging her hand into her daughter's hair, she forced her face around toward me. As if she were brandishing a decapitated head, she held her by her hair so tightly that the little thing's eyes were drawn up slantwise.

" 'That man who would have been fifty years older than his child, suppose you had been pregnant by him, Louise!'

"At that shriek, Louisette freed herself and did indeed begin to look at me. The screaming shrew had not finished with me and she no longer respected the silence of the night.

" 'Do you see what he's got on his temples? White hairs, Louise, white hairs, just like me! And those wrinkles he's got under his eyes! All over him, wherever you look, he's got the stamp of ancience, my girl, yes, ancience.'

"She screamed that peasant word with an air of murderous delight, with a gloating joy that shriveled me up. Louisette remained looking earnest and stupid as children do when they wake up, the flame of the lamp was reflected yellow in her eyes. She fastened her open blouse, smoothed down its pleats, buckled her belt again, and muttered to her mother: 'Do you want me to go for him, Mother? Us two'll "chaäse" him, shall we?'

"The mother had no time to answer before I had shot out of the house. Yes, right out of the house and the devil himself couldn't have stopped me. You don't understand? You can't understand that I'd rather do anything in the world than fight a woman—or two women. Any set-to between men, even war, is less alarming to us men, less alarming to our nerves, than the fury of a woman. We can never foresee what a woman may do when she loses all control. We never know whether she is going to call us a 'cad' with an air of tremendous dignity or whether she is going to try and tear our nails out or bite our nose off with one snap of her teeth. What's more, she herself hasn't the least idea either. It comes from too deep down in her. Goodness, I ran fast. And I kept my eyes open too, so as to dodge stones and ruts. If I've ever laughed about my misadventure, by gad, it certainly wasn't at that moment! The terrace, the spring, the avenue of rowans, the pillars with the lions, I fled past them as if in a nightmare. I outdistanced my two pursuers and I took the narrow path that skirted the outer wall. But the moon had moved across the sky and it now shone full on the path. When I came abreast of the scented laurels, I stopped. I could no longer hear footsteps behind me and I forced myself to recover my breath. To prove to myself I was perfectly calm, I deliberately gazed out over the valley, which was once again a clear blue, steaming with warm mists and dotted with delicate birches whose satiny trunks shimmered as if in broad daylight. I mopped my brow and the back of my neck, and as I searched for a cigarette, I noticed that my hands were trembling.

"A shiver of insecurity sharpened my uneasiness; I raised my head, and just above me, just behind the crest of the dilapidated wall, I saw the mother and the daughter. Only the top half of their bodies was visible and they were watching me like hawks. It cost me a tremendous effort not to start off again at full speed. I was firm with myself and walked on slowly and nonchalantly, as if absorbed in moonlight meditation. Two heads, close side by side, followed my movement; they must be starting off again in pursuit of me. I was only too right; the two heads reappeared farther on, waiting for me. White hairs and gold hairs fluttered in the air like poplar seeds.

"Seeing them there, perfectly still, I stopped. It was one of the hardest things I have done in my life. Then I started to walk on again slowly, down the increasing slope of the path. I passed underneath the two women. It was then that a large-sized stone fell from the top of the wall, grazed my shoulder, and rolled ahead of me down the steep path, just in front of my feet. I stepped over it and continued on my way. A little farther on, a second stone just like it took the skin off my ear as it fell before hitting my foot and quite severely bruising my big toe. I was only wearing canvas shoes. I came to a breach that lowered the level of the wall. My tormentresses were standing in the breach and waiting for me. A good honest rage, the rage of an injured man, seized me at last and inspired me to assault the breach and the two hussies. In three bounds, I was up there. No doubt they too suddenly recovered their reason and remembered that they were females, and I was a male, for after hesitating, they fled and disappeared into the neglected garden behind some pyramid fruit trees and a feathery clump of asparagus.

"I didn't care! I had regained control of myself. I shouted heaven knows what threats in the direction of my fugitives. I grabbed hold of a vine prop, which I brandished like a sword. It was ridiculous, but it did me no end of good. Afterward, I walked down to the path again and reached the undergrowth, spotted with moonlight like a leopard skin. Rabbits were already scurrying about and I frightened some birds. But I was much more startled than these timid small folk. However, my nerves did not entirely let me down; I dried my bleeding ear and I began to limp because of my crushed foot.

"The next day, I went down with what is called a 'first-class' bout of fever, due, I think, to the warm dampness and to the folly of not having taken a sweater. To emotion as well, I'm not idiotic enough to deny it. No encounter has ever staggered me as much as the one with that moralist, the little lady with the frizzy white hair. For an outraged mother to demand some form of compensation, right, that's logical enough. Even for her to insist on the supreme reparation—marriage— that's all right too. That sort of demand always ends by the lady softening down. But *that* mother, with that fleecy head, those eyes, that way of charging the enemy. She'd have stoned me to death if she could. Yes, yes, she really would have. What risk did she take? A wall that was crumbling of its own accord. The little thing, I think she was just an honest, straightforward, adorable idiot.

"Well, my bout of fever was long and violent, and accompanied by shivering fits that made the bed rattle, by nightmares, even a little delirium—I've always been highly strung. I saw ferocious yellow cats, twin heads on a single neck. My host looked after me admirably, and luckily found in his cupboard various medicaments compounded in his professional days. He made a hole in one of my slippers to make room for my swollen injured toe. And his agreeable female relative sewed a number of medals, all of proven efficacy, into my pajamas.

"No, I never saw Louisette again. I made no attempt to see her. At one fell swoop I had lost the taste for the twilights of Franche-Comté and satiny birch trees and clumps of heather. But for all too definite reason, there was no question of forgetting her. When I thought about her, I turned hot and cold and disgust came rushing over me, distorting and eclipsing her charms. Infinitely worse, my dear, the most hideous fear of my life unfortunately revived again, insinuating its little icy serpent, its drop of burning wax, between my shirt and my skin, between Louisette and myself, between me and other Louisettes. Henceforth, it was to deprive your old friend—look, the mere thought of it is making me sweat—of all the Louisettes in this world. What's that you say? A punishment for my sins? Just wait! I have been granted an unexpected kind of compensation. You know the theme, exploited hundreds of times in literature and funny stories: the enemies and the victims of Don Juan substitute the duenna or some overblown chambermaid in his bed for the beautiful quarry. And the next day, the gang of practical jokers assembles around the seducer and informs him, with loud laughter, what they have done . . . Inform him? Did he really know nothing about it? Wasn't the evidence of his own senses enough? Does that mean that, but for his tormentors, he might have been quite satisfied in the morning, when he emerged from the warm darkness of the bed? It's perfectly possible. So let's say, my dear, that instead of the Louisettes, I could still console myself with the chambermaid. And as I had no friends to shout it from the housetops, I did not complain too much of my lot."

[*Translated by Antonia White*]

Bygone Spring

❧❧❧

The beak of a pruning shears goes clicking all down the rose-bordered paths. Another clicks in answer from the orchard. Presently the soil in the rose garden will be strewn with tender shoots, dawn-red at the tips but green and juicy at the base. In the orchard the stiff, severed twigs of the apricot trees will keep their little flames of flower alight for another hour before they die, and the bees will see to it that none of them is wasted.

The hillside is dotted with white plum trees like puffs of smoke, each of them filmy and dappled as a round cloud. At half past five in the morning, under the dew and the slanting rays of sunrise, the young wheat is incontestably blue, the earth rust-red, and the white plum trees coppery pink. It is only for a moment, a magic delusion of light that fades with the first hour of day. Everything grows with miraculous speed. Even the tiniest plant thrusts upward with all its strength. The peony, in the flush of its first month's growth, shoots up at such a pace that its scapes and scarcely unfolded leaves, pushing through the earth, carry with them the upper covering of it so that it hangs suspended like a roof burst asunder.

The peasants shake their heads. "April will bring us plenty of surprises." They bend wise brows over this folly, this annual imprudence of leaf and flower. They grow old, borne helplessly along in the wake of a terrible pupil who learns nothing from their experience. In the tilled valley, still crisscrossed with parallel rivulets, lines of green emerge above the inundation. Nothing can now delay the mole-like ascent of the asparagus, or extinguish the torch of the purple iris. The furious breaking of bonds infects birds, lizards, and insects. Greenfinch, gold-finch, sparrow, and chaffinch behave in the morning like farmyard fowl gorged with brandy-soaked grain. Ritual dances and mock battles, to the accompaniment of exaggerated cries, are renewed perpetually under our eyes, almost under our very hands. Flocks of birds and mating gray lizards share the same sun-warmed flagstones, and when the children, wild with excitement, run aimlessly hither and thither, clouds of mayfly rise and hover around their heads.

Everything rushes onward, and I stay where I am. Do I not already feel more pleasure in comparing this spring with others that are past than in welcoming it? The torpor is blissful enough, but too aware of its own weight. And though my ecstasy is genuine and spontaneous, it no longer finds expression. "Oh, look at those yellow cowslips! And the soapwort! And the unicorn tips of the lords and ladies are showing! . . ." But the cowslip, that wild primula, is a humble flower, and how can the uncertain mauve of the watery soapwort compare with a glowing peach tree? Its value for me lies in the stream that watered it between my tenth and fifteenth years. The slender cowslip, all stalk and rudimentary in blossom, still clings by a frail root to the meadow where I used to gather hundreds to straddle them along a string and then tie them into round balls, cool projectiles that struck the cheek like a rough, wet kiss.

I take good care nowadays not to pick cowslips and crush them into a greenish ball. I know the risk I should run if I did. Poor rustic enchantment, almost evaporated now, I cannot even bequeath you to another me: "Look, Bel-Gazou, like this and then like that; first you straddle them on the string and then you draw it tight." "Yes, I see," says Bel-Gazou. "But it doesn't bounce; I'd rather have my India-rubber ball."

The shears click their beaks in the gardens. Shut me into a dark room and that sound will still bring in to me April sunshine, stinging the skin and treacherous as wine without a bouquet. With it comes the bee scent of the pruned apricot trees, and a certain anguish, the uneasiness of one of those slight preadolescent indispositions that develop, hang about for a time, improve, are cured one morning, and reappear at night. I was ten or eleven years old but, in the company of my foster-mother, who had become our cook, I still indulged in nursling whims. A grown girl in the dining room, I would run to the kitchen to lick the vinegar off the salad leaves on the plate of Mélie, my faithful watchdog, my fair-haired, fair-skinned slave. One April morning I called out to her, "Come along, Mélie, let's go and pick up the clippings from the apricot trees, Milien's at the espaliers."

She followed me, and the young housemaid, well named Marie-la-Rose, came too, though I had not invited her. Milien, the day laborer, a handsome, crafty youth, was finishing his job, silently and without haste.

"Mélie, hold out your apron and let me put the clippings in it."

I was on my knees collecting the shoots starred with blossom. As though in play, Mélie went "Hou!" at me and, flinging her apron over my head, folded me up in it and rolled me gently over. I laughed, thoroughly enjoying making myself small and silly. But I began to stifle and came out from under it so suddenly that Milien and Marie-la-Rose, in the act of kissing, had not time to spring apart, nor Mélie to hide her guilty face.

Click of the shears, harsh chatter of hard-billed birds! They tell of blossoming, of early sunshine, of sunburn on the forehead, of chilly shade, of uncomprehended repulsion, of childish trust betrayed, of suspicion, and of brooding sadness.

[*Translated by Una Vicenzo Troubridge and Enid McLeod*]

October

❦

On the wooden balcony this morning, all among the battered wisteria and the flattened flowers of a red salvia blown in there by last night's gale, there lay two pink and green butterflies, looking like the shed petals of a poppy. They were still just alive when I touched them, and a little spasm jerked their fragile feet up against the delicate fur of their thoraxes. One of them died very quickly; but the other continued for some minutes to quiver like an electrified flower, his antennae vibrating.

I leave them there on the wooden floor of the balcony. As soon as I turn my back, the sparrows will come and all I shall find will be eight wings deftly cut off. They must have been overcome by the sudden autumn, these sensitive silkworm moths with pink crescents on their wings; how many times have I seen them clinging to the warm chimney that runs the length of my house, trying to shelter from the baleful October dawn!

Every day from the balcony I watch all the gardens shrinking in this peaceful, threatened corner of Passy. Mine is losing its roof of leaves; and what remains now of the threefold arch of roses? Only the rusty iron, with a few bare branches tied to it. And what I call the "neighbor's park," where I used to hear invisible children laughing and running, was it nothing but that square enclosure, that clump of trees hemmed in by high, sad walls?

The pleasant provincial existence, which flourishes here in summer, deserts the gardens now and huddles as though abashed behind closed windows. Even on days when the sun returns, those young girls, whose pale frocks and shining hair I would glimpse between the branches, will no longer be there, lying back in their basket chairs.

I used to listen to them living close at hand behind a curtain of leaves. I would hear the embroidery scissors clattering on an iron table, the thimble rolling on the gravel, and the pages of a magazine rustling. A cheerful noise of spoons and cups told me that it was five o'clock and I would yawn with hunger. Now nothing remains all around me but the relics of a long summer: an empty hammock swings in the wind and a metal frog, belonging to some garden game, gulps the rain. Paths that have lost their mystery wind under the tattered trees, and walls stripped bare reveal the limits of our jealously measured paradises.

I am afraid now of discovering that the young girl in pink—a slim gardener who used to prune the rose bushes on the other side of the arbor—is ugly. I would like to remain uncertain, until the trees are green again, whether the united couple, whose leisurely sauntering I used to hear twice a day, is young or old.

The three children who sit singing on the terrace steps of the house that belongs to the lady in mourning stop abruptly if I look at them. I make them feel uncomfortable. All the same, they were aware this summer that I was here; but I didn't know which one it was who called out "Thank you" when I threw a lost ball back over the hedge of clipped acacias. Now I make them feel uncomfortable and they embarrass me. I shan't dare any longer to cross the garden wearing a dressing gown, with my hair still wet.

My thoughts turn to the house, to the fire and the lamp; there are books and cushions and a bunch of dahlias the color of dark blood; in these short afternoons, when the early evenings turn the bay window blue, decidedly it's time to be indoors. Already on the tops of the walls and on the still-warm slates of the roofs, there appear with tails like plumes, wary ears, cautious paws, and arrogant eyes, those new masters of our gardens, the cats.

A long black tom keeps continual watch on the roof of the empty kennel; and the gentle night, blue with motionless mist that smells of kitchen gardens and the smoke of green wood, is peopled with little velvety phantoms. Claws lacerate the barks of trees, and a feline voice, low and hoarse, begins a thrilling lament that never ends.

The Persian cat, draped like a feather boa along my windowsill, stretches and sings in honor of his mate dozing down below in front of the kitchen. He sings under his breath, as though in an aside, and seems to be awaking from a six months' sleep. He inhales the wind with little sniffs, his head thrown back, and the day is not far off when my house will lose its chief ornament, its two faithful and magnificent guests, my Angoras, silvery as the leaves of the hairy sage and the gray aspen, as the cobweb covered with dew or the budding flower of the willow.

Already they refuse to eat from the same plate. While waiting for the periodical and inevitable delirium, each plays a part before the other, just for the pleasure of making themselves unrecognizable to each other.

The male conceals his strength, walking with his loins low, so that the fluffy fringe of his flanks brushes the ground. The she-cat pretends to forget him, and when they are in the garden she no longer favors him with a single glance. In the house she becomes intolerant, and jealous of her prerogatives, grimacing with a look of bitter hatred if he hesitates to give way to her on the staircase. If he settles on the cushion that she wants, she explodes like a chestnut thrown on the fire, and scratches him in the face, like a true little cowardly female, going for his eyes and the tender velvet of his nose.

The male accepts the harsh rules of the game and serves his sentence, as its duration is secretly fixed. Scratched and humiliated, he waits. Some days yet must pass, the sun must sink lower toward the horizon, the acacia must decide to shed, one by one, the fluttering gold of its oval coins. Then there must come some dry nights, and an east wind to frighten the last leafy fingers off the chestnut trees.

Under a cold sickle of moon they will go off together, no longer a fraternal couple of sleeping and sparring partners, but passionate enemies transformed by love. He is compact of new cunning and bloodthirsty coquettishness, while she is all falsehood and tragic cries, equally ready for flight or for sly reprisals. The mysteriously appointed hour has but to sound, and old lovers and bored friends though they are, each will taste the intoxication of becoming for the other the Unknown.

[*Translated by Enid McLeod*]

Armande

❧❦❧

"That girl? But, good heavens, she adores you! What's more, she's never done anything else for ten whole years. All the time you were on active service, she kept finding excuses for dropping in at the pharmacy and asking if I'd had a letter."

"Did she?"

"She wouldn't leave the shop until she'd managed to slip in her 'How's your brother?' She used to wait. And while she was waiting, she'd buy aspirin, cough lozenges, tubes of lanolin, toilet water, tincture of iodine."

"So naturally, you saw to it she was kept waiting?"

"Well, after all, why not? When I finally did tell her I'd news of you, off she went. But never till I had. You know what she's like."

"Yes . . . No, to be honest, I *don't* know what she's like."

"What do you expect, my poor pet? You made everything so complicated for yourself, you're wearing yourself out with all these absurd scruples. Armande is a very well-educated girl, we all know that. She takes her position as a comfortably rich orphan a shade too seriously. I grant you it's none too easy a one in a subprefecture like this. But just because of that, to let her put it over on you to that extent, *you*, Maxime, of all people! Look out, this is the new pavement. At least one can walk without getting one's feet wet now."

The September sky, black and moonless, glittered with stars that twinkled large in the damp air. The invisible river lapped against the single arch of the bridge. Maxime stopped and leaned on the parapet.

"The parapet's new too," he said.

"Yes. It was put up by the local tradesmen, with the consent of the Town Council. You know they did tremendously well here out of food and clothing, what with all the troops going through and the exodus."

"Out of food, clothes, footwear, medical supplies, and everything else. I also know that people talk about 'the exodus' as they do about "the agricultural show' and 'the gala horse show and gymkhana.'""

"Anyway, they wanted to make a great sacrifice."

Madame Debove heard Maxime laugh under his breath at the word "sacrifice" and she prudently left her sentence unfinished to revert to Armande Fauconnier.

"In any case, she didn't let you down too badly during the war; she wrote to you, didn't she?"

"Postcards."

"She sent you food parcels and a marvelous pullover."

"To hell with her food parcels and her woollies," said Maxime Degouthe violently, "*and* her postcards! I've never begged charity from her, as far as I know."

"Good gracious, what a savage character you are . . . Don't spoil your last evening here, Maxime! Admit it was a charming party tonight. Armande is a very good hostess. All the Fauconniers have always been good hosts. Armande knows how to efface herself. There was no chance of the conversation getting on to that children's clinic that Armande supports entirely out of her own money."

"Who hasn't organized something in the way of a children's clinic during the war?" growled Maxime.

"Why, heaps of people, I assure you! In the first place, you've got to have the means. *She* really has got the means."

Maxime made no reply. He hated it when his sister talked of Armande's "means."

"The river's low," he said, after a moment or two.

"You've got good eyes!"

"It's not a question of eyes, it's a question of smell. When the water's low, it always smells of musk here. It's the mud, probably."

He suddenly remembered that, last year, he had said the very same words, on the very same spot, to Armande. She had wrinkled her nose in disgust and made an ugly grimace with her mouth. "As if *she* knew what mud was . . . Mud, that pearl-gray clay, so soft to the bare toes, so mysteriously musky, *she* imagines it's the same as excrement. She never misses an occasion of shrinking away from anything that can be tasted or touched or smelled."

Dancing owlet moths almost obscured the luminous globes at either end of the bridge. Maxime heard his sister yawn.

"Come on, let's go. What on earth are we doing here?"

"I'm asking *you!*" sighed Madame Debove. "Do you hear? Eleven o'clock! Hector's sure to have gone to bed without waiting up for me."

"Let him sleep. There's no need for us to hurry."

"Oh, yes, there is, old thing! I'm sleepy, I am."

He took his sister's arm under his own, as he used to in the old days when they were students, sharing the same illusions, in that halcyon period when a brother and sister believe, quite genuinely, that they are perfectly content with being a chaste imitation of a pair of lovers. "Then a big, ginger-headed youth comes along and the devoted little sister goes off with him, for the pleasure and the advantages of marrying the Grand Central Pharmacy. After all, she did the right thing."

A passer-by stepped off the pavement to make room for them and bowed to Jeanne.

"Good evening, Merle. Stopped having those pains of yours?"

"It's as if he'd said, Madame Debove. Good evening, Madame Debove."

"He's a customer," explained Jeanne.

"Good Lord, I might have guessed that," said her brother ironically. "When you put on your professional chemist's wife voice."

"What about you when you put on your professional quack's voice? Just listen, am I exaggerating one bit? 'Above all, dear lady, endeavor as far as possible to control your nerves. The improvement is noticeable, I will even go so far as to say remarkable, but for the time being, we must continue to be very firm about avoiding all forms of meat,' and I preach to you and instruct you and I drench you with awful warnings."

Maxime laughed wholeheartedly, the imitation of his slightly pontifical manner was so true to life.

"All women are monkeys, they're only interested in our absurdities and our love affairs and our illnesses. The other one can't be so very different from this one."

He could see her, the other one, as she had looked when he left her just now, standing at the top flight of steps that led up to the Fauconniers' house. The lighted chandelier in the hall behind her gave her a nimbus of blue glass convolvulus flowers and chromium hoops. "Goodbye, Armande." She had answered only with a nod. "You might call her a miser with words! If I had her in my arms, one day, between four walls or in the corner of a wood, I'd make her scream, and for good reason!" But he had never met Armande in the corner of a wood. As to his aggressive instincts, he lost all hope of gratifying them the moment he was in Armande's presence.

Eleven o'clock struck from the hospital, then from a small low church jostled by new buildings, last of all, in shrill, crystalline strokes from a dark ground-floor room whose window was open. As they crossed the Place d'Armes, Maxime sat down on one of the benches.

"Just for one minute, Jeanne! Let me relax my nerves. It's nice out of doors."

Jeanne Debove consented sulkily.

"You ought to have worked them off on Armande, those nerves of yours. But you haven't got the guts!"

He did not protest and she burst into a malicious laugh. He wondered why sexual shyness, which excites dissolute women, arouses the contempt of decent ones.

"She overawes you, that's it. Yes, she overawes you. I simply can't get over it!"

She elaborated her inability to get over it by inundating him with various scoffing remarks, accompanied now by a neighing laugh, now by a spurt of giggles.

"After all, you're not in your very, *very* first youth. You're not a greenhorn. Or a neurotic. Nor, thank heaven, physically deformed."

She enumerated all the things her brother was not and he was glad she omitted to mention the one quite simple thing he was—a man who had been in love for a very long time.

Maxime Degouthe's long-persisting love, though it preserved him from debauchery, turned into mere habit when he was away from Armande for a few months. When he was away from her, a kind of conjugal fidelity allowed him to amuse himself as much as he liked and even to forget her for a spell. So much so that, when he had finished his medical studies, he had been paralyzed to find himself faced with a grown-up Armande Fauconnier when the Armande he remembered was a gawky, sharp-shouldered, overgrown adolescent, at once clumsy and noble like a bony filly full of promise.

Every time he saw her again, she completely took possession of him. His feeling for her was violent and suppressed, like a gardener's son's for the "young lady up at the big house." He would have liked to be rather brutal to this beautiful tall girl whom he admired from head to foot, who was just sufficiently dark, just sufficiently white, and as smooth as a pear. "But I shouldn't dare. No, I daren't," he fumed to himself, every time he left.

"The back of the seat is all wet," said Madame Debove. "I'm going home. What are your plans for tomorrow? Are you going in to say goodbye to Armande? She's expecting you to, you know."

"She hasn't invited me."

"You mean you daren't go on your own? You may as well admit it, that girl's thoroughly got you down!"

"I do admit it," said Maxime, so mildly that his sister stopped cruelly teasing him.

They walked in silence till they reached the Grand Central Pharmacy.

"You'll lunch with us tomorrow, of course. Hector would have a fit if you didn't have your last meal with him. Your parcel of ampoules will be all ready. No one can say when we'll be able to get those particular serums again. Well, shall I ring up Armande and say you'll be coming over to say goodbye to her? But I needn't say definitely you're not coming?"

She was fumbling endlessly with a bunch of keys. Maxime lent her the aid of his flashlight and its beam fell full on Jeanne Debove's mischievous face and its expression of mixed satisfaction and disapproval.

"She wants me to marry Armande. She's thinking of the money, of the fine, rich house, of 'the excellent effect,' of my career, as she says. But she'd also like me to marry Armande without being overenthusiastic about her. Everything's perfectly normal. Everything except myself, because I can't endure the idea that *she*, Armande, could marry me without being in love with me."

He hurried back to his hotel. The town was asleep but the hotel, close by the station, resounded with all the noises that are hostile to sleep and blazed with lights that aggravate human tiredness. Hobnailed boots, shuddering ceiling lights, uncarpeted floors, the gates of the elevator, the whinnyings of hydraulic pressure, the rhythmic clatter of plates flung into a sink in the basement, the intermittent trilling of a bell never stopped outraging the need for silence that had driven Maxime to his bedroom. Unable to stand any more, he added his own contribution to the selfish human concert, dropped his shoes on the wooden floor, carried them out into the corridor, and shut his door with a loud slam.

He drenched himself with cold water, dried himself carelessly, and got into bed quite naked, after having studied himself in the looking glass. "Big bones, big muscles, and four complete limbs, after all, that's not too bad, in these days. A large nose, large eyes, a cap of hair as thick as a motorcyclist's helmet, girls who weren't Mademoiselle Fauconnier have found all that very much to their taste. I don't see Mademoiselle Fauconnier sleeping with this naked, black-haired chap . . ."

On the contrary, he saw her only too well. Irritated by fretful desire, he waited for the hotel to become quiet. When—save for a sound of barking, a garage door, the departure of a motorcar—silence was at last established, a breeze sprang up, swept away the last insults inflicted by man on the night, and came in through the open window like a reward.

"Tomorrow," Maxime vowed to himself. It was a muddled vow that concerned the conquest of Armande quite as much as the return to professional life and the daily, necessary triumph of forced activity over fundamental listlessness.

He reiterated "Tomorrow," flung away his pillow, rolled over on his stomach, and fell asleep with his head between his folded arms in the same attitude as a small intimidated boy of long ago who used to dream of an Armande with long black curls. Later on, another Maxime had slept like that, the adolescent who had plucked up courage to invite "those Fauconnier ladies," as they were coming out from High Mass, to have lemon ices at Peyrol's. "Really, Maxime, one doesn't eat lemon ices at quarter to twelve in the morning!" Armande had said. In that one word "really" what a number of reproofs she could convey! "Really, Maxime, you needn't *always* stand right in front of the window, you shut out the daylight. Maxime, really! You've gone and returned a ball *again* when it was 'out.' "

But when a particular period was over, there had been no more "reallys" and no more reproaches showered on his head. Still not properly asleep, Maxime Degouthe groped around a memory, around a moment that had restored a little confidence to his twenty-five-year-old self and had marked the end of Armande's gracious condescension. That day, he had arrived with Jeanne at the foot of the steps, just as Armande was opening the silvered wrought-iron door to go out. They had not seen each other for a very long time —"Hullo, fancy seeing! —Yes, my sister insisted on bringing me with her, perhaps you'd rather I hadn't come. —Now, really, you're joking. —A friend of mine in Paris gave me a lift in his car and dropped me here this morning. —How awfully nice! Are you going to be here for some time? —No, the same friend's picking me up tomorrow after lunch and driving me back. —Well, that *is* a short stay." In fact, such trivialities as to make either of them blush had either of them paid any attention to what they were saying. From the height of five or six steps, a wide, startled, offended gaze fell on Maxime. He also caught, at the level of his knees, the brush of a skirt hem and a handbag which Armande had dropped and which he retrieved.

After a gloomy game of ping-pong, a tea composed entirely of sugary things, a handshake—a strong, swift, but promptly withdrawn hand had clasped his own—he had left Armande once again, and on the way back, Jeanne had given her cynical opinion of the situation: "You know, you could have the fair Armande as easy as pie. And I know what I'm talking about." She added: "You don't know the right way to go about it." But those had been the remarks of a twenty-year-old, the infallibility of one girl judging another girl.

He thought he was only half asleep and fell into deep but restless dreams. A nightmare tortured him with the shaming illusion that he was dressing old Queny's incurable foot on the steps leading up to the Fauconniers' house and that Armande was enthroned, impassive, at the top of them. Didn't she owe part of her prestige to those eight broad steps, almost like a series of terraces, that were famous throughout the town? "The Fauconniers' flight of front steps is so impressive. Without these front steps, the Fauconniers' house wouldn't have nearly such a grand air . . ." As if insulted, the sleeper sat up with a start. "Grand air, indeed! That cube! That block with its cast-iron balconies and bands of tiles!" He woke up completely and once again the Fauconnier home inspired him with the old awed respect. The Fauconnier heliotropes, the Fauconnier polygonums, the Fauconnier lobelias recovered their status of flowers adorning the altar where he worshipped. So, to send himself to sleep again, Maxime soberly envisaged the duties that awaited him the next day, the day after, and all the rest of his life, in the guise of the faces of old Queny, of the elder Madame Cauvain, of her father Monsieur Enfert, of "young" Mademoiselle Philippon, the one who was only seventy-two . . . For old people do not die off in wartime. He swallowed half his bottle of mineral water at one gulp and fell heavily asleep again, insensible to the mosquitoes coming up from the shrunken river and the noises of the pale dawn.

"My last day of idle luxury." He had his breakfast in bed, feeling slightly ashamed, and ordered a bath, for which he had to wait a considerable time. "My last bath . . . I'm not going to get up till I've had my bath! I'm not leaving without my bath!" As a matter of fact, he preferred a very stiff shower or the chance plunges he had taken, straight into rivers and canals, these last months between April and August.

With some caution he made use of a toilet water invented by his brother-in-law, the red-haired chemist. "Hector's perfumes, when they don't smell of squashed ants, smell of bad cognac." He chose his bluest shirt and his spotted foulard tie. "I wish I were handsome. And all I am is just so-so. Ah, how I wish I were handsome!" he kept thinking over and over again as he plastered down his brilliantined hair. But it was coarse, intractable, wavy hair, a vigorous bush that preferred standing up to lying down. When Maxime laughed, he wrinkled his nose, crinkled up his yellow-brown eyes, and revealed his "lucky teeth," healthy and close-set except for a gap between the two upper front ones. Coatless and buckled into his best belt, he had, at nearly thirty, the free and easy charm and slightly plebeian elegance of many an errand boy you see darting through the crowd on his bicycle, nimble as a bird in a bush. "But, in a jacket, I just look common," Maxime decided, as he straightened the lapels of the hand-me-down jacket. "It's also the fault of the coat." He threw his reflection an angry glance. "Nevertheless, beautiful Armande, more than ten others have been quite satisfied with all that and have even said "Thank you." He sighed, and turned humble again. "But seeing that it's to no one but Armande I'm appealing when I conjure up my poor little girlfriends, what on earth does it matter whether they thanked me or even asked for more? It's not of them I'm thinking."

He packed his suitcase with the care and dexterity of a man accustomed to use his hands for manipulating living substance, stopping the flow of blood, applying and pinning bandages. The September morning, with its flies and its warm yellow light, came in fresh through the open window; at the end of a narrow street a dancing shimmer showed where the river lay. "I shan't go and say goodbye to Armande," Maxime Degouthe decided. "For one thing, lunch is always late at Jeanne's; for another, I've got my case of medical supplies to fill up at the last moment, and if I'm to have time to get a bite of food before the train goes, it'll be impossible, yes, physically impossible."

At four o'clock, he opened the front gate, marched up the gravel path of the Fauconniers' garden, climbed the flight of steps, and rang the bell. A second time, he pressed his finger long and vainly on the bell button, sunk in a rosette of white marble. No one came and the blood rushed up into Maxime's ears. "She's probably gone out. But where are her two lazy sluts of servants and the gardener who looks like a drunk?" He rang again, restraining himself with difficulty from giving the door a kick. At last he heard steps in the garden and saw Armande running toward him. She stopped in front of him, exclaiming "Ah!" and he smiled at seeing her wearing a big blue apron with a bib that completely enveloped her. She swiftly untied the apron and flung it on a rosebush.

"But it suited you very well," said Maxime.

Armande blushed and he blushed himself, thinking that perhaps he had hurt her feelings. "She would take it the wrong way, naturally. She's impossible, impossible! Pretty, those flecks of white soap in her black hair. I'd never noticed that the skin at the edge of her forehead, just under the hair, is slightly blue."

"I was at the end of the garden, in the washhouse," said Armande. "It's laundry day today, so . . . Léonie and Maria didn't even hear the bell."

"I shan't keep you from your work, I only looked in for a couple of minutes. As I'm leaving tomorrow morning."

He had followed her to the top of the steps, and Maxime waited for her to indicate which of the wicker chairs he should sit in. But she said: "From four to seven the sun just beats down on you here," and she ushered him into the drawing room, where they sat down opposite each other. Maxime seated himself in one of the armchairs tapestried with La Fontaine's fables—his was "The Cat, the Weasel, and the Little Rabbit"—and stared at the rest of the furniture. The baby-grand piano, the Revolution clock, the plants in pots, he gazed at them all with hostile reverence.

"It's nice in here, isn't it?" said Armande. "I keep the blinds down because it faces south. Jeanne wasn't able to come?"

"Goodness, is she frightened of me?" He was on the point of feeling flattered. But he looked at Armande and saw her sitting stiffly upright on "The Fox and the Stork," one elbow on the hard arm of the chair, the other on her lap, with her hands clasped together. In the dusk of the lowered blinds, her cheeks and her neck took on the color of very pale terra-cotta, and she was looking straight at him with the steady gaze of a well-brought-up girl who knows she must not blink or look sidelong, or pretend to be shy so as to show off the length of her lashes. "What the hell am I doing here?" thought Maxime furiously. "This is where I've got to, where we've both got to, after ten, fifteen years of what's called childhood friendship. This girl is made of wood. Or else she's choked with pride. You won't catch me again in the Fauconnier drawing room." Nevertheless, he replied to Armande's questions, he talked to her about his "practice" and the "inevitable difficulties" of this postwar period.

Nor did he fail to remark: "But you know better than anyone what these various difficulties are. Look at you, loaded with responsibilities, and all alone in the world!"

Armande's immobility was shattered by an unexpected movement; she unclasped her fingers and clutched the arms of her chair with both hands as if she were afraid of slipping off it.

"Oh, I'm used to it. You know my mother brought me up in a rather special way. At my age, one's no longer a child."

The sentence, begun with assurance, broke off on a childish note that belied the last words. She mastered herself and said, in a different voice: "Won't you have a glass of port? Or would you prefer orangeade?"

Maxime saw there was a loaded tray within easy reach of her hand and frowned.

"You're expecting guests? Then I'll be off!"

He had stood up; she remained seated and laid her hand on Maxime's arm.

"I never invite anyone on washing day. I assure you I don't. As you'd told me you were going away again tomorrow, I thought you might possibly . . ."

She broke off, with a little grimace that displeased Maxime. "Ah, no! She's not to ruin that mouth for me! That outline of the lips, so clear-cut, so full; those corners of the mouth that are so . . . so . . . What's the matter with her today? You'd think she'd just buried the devil for good and all!"

He realized he was staring at her with unpardonable severity and forced himself to be gay.

"So you're heavily occupied in domestic chores? What a lovely laundress you make! And all those children at your clinic, do you manage to keep them in order?"

He was laughing only with his lips. He knew very well that, when he was with Armande, love made him gloomy, jealous, self-conscious, unable to break down an obstacle between the two of them that perhaps did not exist. Armande took a deep breath, squared her shoulders, and commanded her whole face to be nothing but the calm regular countenance of a beautiful brunette. But three shadowy dimples, two at the corners of the mouth, one in the chin, appeared when she smiled and quivered at every hint of emotion.

"I've got twenty-eight children over at the clinic, did you know that?"

"Twenty-eight children? Don't you think that's a lot for a young unmarried girl?"

"I'm not frightened of children," said Armande seriously.

"Children. She loves children. She'd be magnificent, pregnant. Tall as she is, she would broaden at the hips without looking squat, like short women who are carrying babies. She'd take up an enormous amount of space in the garden, in bed, in my arms. At last she'd have trusting eyes, the lovely, dark-ringed eyes of a pregnant woman. But for that to happen, Mademoiselle has got to tolerate someone coming close to her, and a little closer than offering her a ball at arm's length on a tennis racket. She doesn't look as if the idea had ever occurred to her, that girl doesn't! In any case, *I'm* giving up all thought of it!"

He stood up, resolutely.

"This time, Armande, it's serious."

"What is?" she said, very low.

"Why, the fact that it's five o'clock, that I've two or three urgent things to do, a big parcel of medical supplies to get ready. My little village is right out of everything in the way of serums and pills."

"I know," said Armande at once.

"You know?"

"Oh, I just accidentally heard them say so, at your brother-in-law's."

He had leaned toward her a little; she drew away with such a fierce movement that she knocked her elbow against a monumental lamp-stand.

"Have you hurt yourself?" said Maxime coldly.

"No," she said, equally coldly. "Not in the least."

She passed in front of him to open the front door, with its wrought-iron lacework. It resisted her efforts.

"The woodwork's warped. I keep telling Charost to fix it."

"Haven't I always known it to stick like that? Don't destroy my childhood memories!"

Pursing her lips tight, she shook the door with a stubborn violence that made its panes rattle. There was a loud crash of glass and metal behind her, and turning around, she saw Maxime staggering among the splintered cups and chromium hoops of the chandelier that had just fallen from the ceiling. Then his knees went limp and he fell over on his side. Prone on the floor, he made an attempt to raise his hand to his ear, could not finish the gesture, and lay perfectly still. Armande, with her back against the front door she had not had time to open, stared at the man lying at her feet on his bed of broken glass. She said in a strangled, incredulous voice: "No!" The sight of a trickle of blood running down behind Maxime's left ear and stopping for a moment on the collar of the blue shirt, which it soaked, restored Armande's power of speech and movement. She squatted down, straightened up swiftly, opened the door that was half obstructed by the injured body, and screamed shrill summonses out into the garden.

"Maria! Léonie! Maria! Maria!"

The screams reached Maxime in the place where he reposed, unconscious. Along with the screams, he began to hear the buzzing of hives of bees and the clanging of hammers, and he half opened his eyes. But unconsciousness promptly swallowed him up again and he fell back among the swarms of bees and the hammering to some place where pain, in its turn, tracked him down. "The top of my head hurts. It hurts behind my ear and on my shoulder."

Once again, the loud screams disturbed him. "Léonie! Maria!" He came to, very unwillingly, opened his eyes, and received a sunbeam full in his face. The sunbeam appeared to be red; then it was cut off by a double moving shadow. All at once, he realized that Armande's two legs were passing to and fro across the light; he recognized Armande's feet, the white linen shoes trimmed with black leather. The feet were moving about in all directions on the carpet quite close to his head, sometimes open in a V and staggering, sometimes close together, and crushing bits of broken glass. He felt an urge to untie one of the white shoelaces for a joke, but at that very moment, he was shot through with agonizing pain, and without knowing it, he moaned.

"My darling, my darling," said a shaking voice.

"Her darling? What darling?" he asked himself. He raised his cheek, which was lying heavily on fragments of pale blue glass and the butt ends of electric light bulbs. The blood spread out in a pool and his cheek was sticky with it. At the pathetic sight of the precious red spilled all about him, he woke up completely and understood all. He took advantage of the fact that the two feet had turned their heels to him and were running toward the terrace to feel his aching head and bruised shoulder and to discover that the source of the blood was behind his ear. "Good, a big cut. Nothing broken. I might have had my ear sliced off. It's a good thing to have hair like mine. Lord, how my head does ache!"

"Maria! Léonie!"

The black-and-white shoes returned; two knees sheathed in silk went down on the splintered glass. "She'll cut herself!" He made a slight movement to raise himself, then decided instead to lie low and keep quiet, only turning his head over so as to show Armande where his wound was.

"Oh heavens, he's bleeding," said Armande's voice. "Maria! Léonie!"

There was no reply.

"Oh, the bitches," the same voice said violently.

Sheer astonishment made Maxime give a start.

"Speak to me, Maxime! Maxime, can you hear me? My darling, my darling . . ."

Sabots were heard running in the garden, then climbing the steps.

"Ah, there you are, Charost! Yes, the chandelier fell down. A person could die in this place without anyone's hearing! Where *are* those two wretched girls?"

"In the paddock, Mademoiselle, spreading out the sheets. Ah, the poor unfortunate young man! He had a hundred years of life ahead of him!"

"I'm quite sure he still has! Run around to Dr. Pommier, tell him . . . If he's not in, Dr. Tuloup. If *he's* not in, the chemist, yes, the ginger-haired one, Madame Jeanne's husband. Charost, go and get the towels from my bathroom, the little hand towel from the cloakroom, you can *see* I can't leave him. And the brown box in the cupboard! Hurry up, will you! Get someone to tell those two idiots to leave their washing, don't go yourself, send someone!"

The sabots clattered away.

"My darling, my darling," said the low, sweet voice.

"It really was me, the darling," Maxime told himself. Two hot hands feverishly massaged one of his, interrogating it. "There, there, my pulse is excellent! Don't get in a state! How beautiful she must be at this moment . . ." He groaned on purpose and slid the thread of a glance at Armande between his eyelids. She was ugly, with huge, terrified eyes and her mouth gaping stupidly. He closed his lids again, enraptured.

The hands pressed a wet towel over his wound, pushed away the hair. "That's not right, my pet, that's not right. Isn't there any iodine in the place, then? She'll make me bleed unnecessarily, but what the hell does that matter as long as she keeps busy on me?" The ferruginous smell of iodine rose in his nostrils, he was aware of the wholesome burning pain, and relaxed, content. "Well done! But when it comes to putting on an efficient bandage, my girl, I'm streets ahead of you. That one won't ever hold. You ought to have shaved off a bit of my hair." He heard the girl clucking her tongue against her teeth, "tst tst"; then she became despairing.

"Oh, I'm too stupid! A bloody fool, in fact!"

He very nearly laughed but turned it into a vague, pitiful mumbling.

"Maxime, Maxime!" she implored.

She untied his tie, opened his shirt, and, trying to find his heart, brushed the masculine nipple that swelled with pride. For a moment, the two of them were equally and completely motionless. As the hand withdrew, after receiving its reassuring answer from the heart, it slowly went over the same ground on its way back. "Oh, to take that hand that's stroking me in this startled way, to get up, to hug that grand, beautiful girl I love, to turn *her* into a wounded, moaning creature, and then to comfort her, to nurse her in my arms. It's so long I've waited for that. But suppose she defends herself?" He decided to go on with his ruse, stirred feebly, opened his arms, and fell back into pretended unconsciousness.

"Ah!" cried Armande, "he's fainted! Why don't those imbeciles come!"

She leaped to her feet and ran off to fetch a fiber cushion, which she tried to insert between Maxime's head and the splinters of glass. In doing so, the makeshift bandage came off. Maxime could hear Armande stamping her feet, walking away, and slapping her thighs with a forceful plebeian despair. She returned to him, sat down right in the litter of broken glass and the pool of bloodstained water, and half lay down against the wounded man. With exquisite pleasure he could feel she had lost her head and was crying. He squeezed his eyelids together so as not to look at her. But he could not shut out the smell of black hair and hot skin, the sandalwood smell that healthy brunettes exude. She raised one of his eyelids with her finger and he rolled up his eyeball as if in ecstasy or a swoon. With her sleeve, she wiped his forehead and his mouth; furtively, she opened his lips and bent over him to look at the white teeth with the gap between the front ones. "Another minute of this sort of thing and . . . and I shall devour her!" She bent a little lower, put her mouth against Maxime's, then drew back at once, frightened at the sound of hurried footsteps and breathless voices. But her whole body remained close to him, tamed and alert, and there was still time for her to whisper the hackneyed words girls new to love stammer out before the man has taught them others or they invent more beautiful, more secret ones: "Darling . . . My beloved boy. My very own Maxime."

When the rescue party arrived, she was still sitting on the ground in her soaked skirt and her torn stockings. Maxime was able to wake up, to complete his deception by a few, incoherent words, to smile in a bewildered way at Armande, and to protest at all the fuss going on around him. The Grand Central Pharmacy had provided its stretcher and its pharmacist, who constructed a turban of bandages on Maxime's head. Then the stretcher and its escort set forth like a procession incensed by a choir of voices.

"Open the other half of the door. Watch out, it won't go through. I tell you it will go through if you bear a bit to the right. There . . . just a bare millimeter to spare. You've got eight steps to go down."

At the top of the terrace, Armande remained alone, useless, and as if forgotten. But at the bottom of the steps, Maxime summoned her with a gesture and a look: "Come . . . I know you now. I've got you. Come, we'll finish that timid little kiss you began. Stay with me. Acknowledge me . . ." She walked down the steps and gave him her hand. Then she adapted her step to that of the stretcher-bearers and walked meekly beside him, all stained and disheveled, as if she had come straight from the hands of love.

[*Translated by Antonia White*]

The Rendezvous

A grasshopper jumped out of the beans and flew past with a metallic whir, interposing its fine canvas wings, its long dry thighs, and its horse's head between the orange pickers and the sun. It terrified Rose by brushing against her hair.

"Ee," Rose screamed.

"What's the matter? Oh, goodness!" said Odette, drawing back. "What on earth's that creature? Must be a scorpion, at least. Why, it's as big as a swallow. Bernard! I'm asking you what this monster is!"

But Bernard was looking at two frightened blue eyes, at hair that was too curly to be strictly fashionable, at a small hand outstretched to ward off the danger.

He shrugged his shoulders to indicate that he had no idea. The two girls, one dark, the other fair, were recklessly squandering the ripe, juicy fruit whose rind split easily under their nails. They tore them open savagely, sucked the best and easiest ones dry in two mouthfuls, and flung away the reddish skin of the Moroccan oranges whose sharp flavor does not cloy.

"I hope Cyril will be jealous," said Odette. "What on earth can he be doing at this hour? Asleep, of course. He's a dormouse. I've married a dormouse!"

Bernard stopped munching the green beans.

"Do you know what a dormouse looks like?"

"No," said Odette, always ready to give battle. "But I know that eating raw beans makes your breath smell horrid."

He spat out his bean so hastily that Odette burst into her malicious, insinuating laugh. That laugh made Rose blush.

"If I called out to Cyril from here, d'you think he'd hear?"

"Not a hope," said Bernard. "The hotel is . . . yes, about five hundred yards away."

Nevertheless Odette, who was never convinced by anyone's opinion, put her hands up to her mouth like a megaphone and shrieked: "Cyril! Cy-ri-i-il!"

She had a piercing shrill voice which must have carried far out to sea and Bernard winced with exasperation.

Being tyro travelers, they had let the best hours of the morning go by and the eleven o'clock sun was scorching their shoulders. But the April wind, before it reached the young barley, the orange grove, the well-kept kitchen gardens, the neglected park, and Tangiers itself, close by but invisible, had blown across a cool waste of salt water, pale and milky as a Breton sea.

"I believe," declared Odette, "Cyril's having a quiet cocktail on the hotel terrace."

"You forget there aren't any cocktails yet at the Mirador. The stuff's on the way."

"So that's what they meant when they warned us that they hadn't finished building it yet," said Odette. "I certainly wouldn't say no to a drink myself. Shall we go and have one at the Petit Socco?"

"Certainly," said Bernard in a gloomy voice.

"Oh, you're the limit as soon as one tries to get you off your orange-ades and your malted milks."

She bit into her orange as savagely as if she were biting Bernard himself. Her fierceness was possibly something of a pose. A brunette of the hard type, she exaggerated her cannibal laugh and made great display of crushing nuts and even plum stones between the two rows of teeth of which she was so vain.

A lizard or a tiny snake glided through the fresh grass and Odette lost all her haughtiness.

"Bernard! A viper! Oh, this awful country!"

"Why do you insist that it's a viper? There aren't any vipers here. Ask Ahmed."

"What's the good of asking him anything? He doesn't speak French!"

"I'm not so convinced as you that he doesn't . . ."

An infinite meekness, a gravity tempered by a vague, courteous smile, protected their guide from all suspicion. He was one of the servants of the absent pasha who allowed a few tourists to use his gardens.

"Who is Ahmed, anyway?"

"The oldest son of the bailiff who looks after the property and keeps it up," said Bernard.

"The concierge's kid, in fact," Odette translated.

"I prefer my description to yours," said Bernard. "It's more . . ."

"More polite, you mean?"

"Also more accurate. Ahmed's not in the least like a concierge."

Ahmed, who, whether from discretion or disdain, appeared to hear nothing, picked an orange from the tree and offered it on his brown palm to Odette.

"Thank you, blue-eyed boy. Allah have you in his holy keeping!"

She dropped Ahmed a comic curtsy, made some little clucking noises, and laid her hand on her heart, then on her forehead. Bernard blushed with shame for her. "After what she's just done, I'd leave them there flat. If it weren't for Rose, they wouldn't set eyes on me again. But there's Rose . . ."

There was indeed Rose, the pink-cheeked widow of the younger Bessier, who had been an architect. There was also her brother-in-law Cyril, Odette's husband, whom people still called Bessier Senior. Besides Cyril, there was the deed of partnership, not yet signed, which would substitute Bernard Bonnemains for the younger Bessier. "Bernard had better not count his chickens before they are hatched," Odette was in the habit of saying, whenever she thought it expedient to recall the fact that Bonnemains was exactly thirty, had no rich clients and not much money.

"I've had enough of this," declared Odette. "Let's do something else or I'm going in. Anyway, I'm tired."

"But . . . we haven't done anything tiring," Rose objected.

"Speak for yourself," snapped her sister-in-law.

She stretched, yawned uninhibitedly, then sighed: "Oh, that Cyril! I don't know what's the matter with him here . . ."

"That's her way of flaunting things under our noses," thought Bernard. "If I didn't control myself, I'd remind her there was such a thing as decency."

But he did control himself, wincing like a starving man reminded of food. "Eight days, eight nights since I've had nothing of Rose but little stolen kisses and allusions to our love in cryptic language . . ."

Rose's blue eyes asked him the reason for his sullen silence, and blinked moistly under the sun. Her eyes were a warm, generous blue, her cheeks almost too vividly pink, her naturally curly hair frankly and cheerfully golden. Looking at Rose's strong, bright coloring, at the red mouth engaged in sucking the dripping, almost scarlet orange, Bernard was furious that she had not yet given him all this glory of color. They had only been lovers a very short time and he had had to make love to her on hotel beds, in the dark, or under a pallid moon. "One of these days, I'll throw my scruples to the winds—and Rose's too. I'll say to Cyril: 'Look here, old man, Rose and I . . . well, that's the way things are. And I'm going to marry her.'" But he imagined Bessier Senior's faint, distant smile and Odette's spiteful laugh and ugly thoughts. "And, in any case, I don't call Bessier 'old man.'" He threw a bitterly resentful look at the "cannibal." Once again he recognized in Odette an ultra-feminine female, difficult to manage and always ready to pick a quarrel. Once again, his resentment weakened to respect.

A cloud darkened the green of the sea and the leaves: Bernard's desire and his good humor vanished at the same moment.

"Don't you think we might as well stay where we are? I can't help feeling that this pasha's been very amiable and that we're behaving like . . ."

"Like tourists," cut in Odette. "Look at the delightful little 'Bois de Boulogne' we're arranging for him, your pasha. Gold-tipped cigarette ends, cellophane wrappings, bean pods and orange peel. A few greasy newspapers and some métro tickets and the work of civilization will be complete."

Bernard slid a furtive glance of apology in Ahmed's direction. But Ahmed, facing toward the sea, was a perfect statue of youthful Arab indifference.

"Hi, Ahmed!" shrieked Odette. "We're going! Finish! *Macache!* Walk! Get a move on!"

"Don't muddle him," Rose implored. "What on earth do you expect him to make of all that?"

Odette went up to the youth of sixteen or so, stuck one of her Turkish cigarettes between his lips, and held out her lighter. Ahmed took two puffs, thanked her with a gesture, and continued to await the Europeans' good pleasure. He smoked nobly, holding the cigarette between two slender fingers and blowing the smoke out through his nostrils in a double jet, like a horse's warm breath.

"He's handsome," said Bernard in an undertone.

"She's quite aware of that," answered Rose in the same low voice.

He was shocked that Rose should have noticed the beauty of their young guide, even if only through the eyes of Odette.

"Well, Ahmed, shall we get going?" said Odette. "Which way?"

With his raised hand, Ahmed indicated the heights of the unknown park. The slopes above them were crowned with pines, gum cistus with limp petals, and trees imported at the whim of an American who had laid out the park and built his house there half a century earlier. The three French tourists left the orchard and vegetable garden and climbed up toward blue cascades of wisteria, roses festooned on thujas, broom over which danced butterflies of a similar yellow, and white transparent clematis grown weak through long neglect. Ahmed walked in front of them with a carefree stride.

"So he understood your question?" Bernard asked Odette.

"Telepathy," said Odette fatuously.

They emerged from the orange grove and took deep breaths, glad to be free of the overpowering scent of its fruit and flowers.

"I shan't go any farther this morning," declared Odette. "That blood-orange cocktail has gone to my legs. What'll we see up there, anyway? Only the same as here. Wisteria on trellises, clematis by the yard, and what else? On our right, a bottomless abyss. On our left, unexplored wilderness. It's almost midday. Shall we go back?"

"Quite a good idea," said Bernard blandly.

Ahmed came to a halt and they meekly followed suit. He had stopped in front of a little circle of level ground, an old pond half smothered in young grass and potentilla in flower. Its crumbling stone rim could no longer keep back the invasion of marsh marigolds and poppies. A trickle of water, deserting its dried-up spout in the mouth of a stone lion's head, ran free between the broken flags.

"Oh," cried Rose in delight.

"Rather snappy," declared Odette. "Bernard, what about something like that for a garden terrace at Auteuil?"

Bernard did not answer. He was measuring with his eye the flat space now overrun with wild grasses. He smiled to see that in the middle the slightly crushed grass seemed to indicate that someone had lain there. "One person, or two? Two bodies closely interlocked leave no more trace than one." Without raising his head he darted a covert glance at Rose. It was the look of a lascivious schoolboy which began at her knees and slid upward to her thighs and thence to her breasts. "*There*, it's firm, almost harsh to the touch, like a very downy peach and, I'm sure, slightly brindled. Real blondes are never all one color . . . *There*, it's probably bluish white, like milk, and there, oh, there it's as frankly rosy as her name. It was bad enough only being able to see with my eyes and my lips in the dark. But to see nothing at all, touch nothing at all for all these days and nights, no, no, it's unbearable . . . From that appalling hotel to this soft cushiony grass—let me see—it can't be more than five hundred yards."

He stared at Rose with such a harsh, explicit look that she blushed almost to tears, her face flooded with the burning color of the blonde at bay. "If I had her in my arms . . ." he thought. The power they had over each other was so new that they were defenseless against such shocks. Frightened, afraid to move, they were assaulted by identical pangs. And because they were both suffering the same thing, they felt themselves to be one.

"It's not only frightfully amusing," insisted Odette, "it's positively sexy."

Leaving Rose to her troubled feelings, Bernard turned away from her with a cowardice which he told himself was discretion.

"That bitch Odette, she's guessed everything! I'm sure she saw me blush." He mopped his forehead and the back of his strong neck. Rose, who was calming down, smiled as she recognized the blue handkerchief she had given him. "The darling, she's so silly when she loves me!"

Vaguely offended, obscurely jealous of a desire which was not fixed on herself, Odette went and sat down some distance away and put on her "Fiji Island face." The black fringe of her hair was etched sharply against her forehead under the white piqué hat and her hard eyes reviled the resplendent weather. When she sulked, she kept her prominent mouth shut. Usually it was open, showing the importunate whiteness of her teeth.

"She's ugly," Bernard decided on consideration. For he knew what a menace ugly women of that type can be when they decide to attract and infuriate. Bessier Senior, who was aging, must also know something on that subject!

With a savage heel, the woman he found ugly crushed a scarab beetle as it laboriously made its way across the clearing, and Bernard rushed up to her as if to ward off some danger. "Madame Odette . . ."

"Can't you call me Odette like everyone else? No, of course not!"

"But I should be only too delighted," he said promptly.

"Things are going badly," he thought. "Next week she's capable of insisting on even more intimate terms. But I haven't the least desire to go all out to make things easier." All the same, face to face with the enemy, he accentuated his smile, the smile which had conquered Rose.

"I wanted to make a suggestion, Odette—do you hear, Odette? Hodette?"

She leaned back and laughed, showing the interior of her mouth, the moist palate the color of a ripe fig, and all her even, flawless teeth.

"That's better. I'm not pretending that it's a very inspired suggestion. Still, why shouldn't we have some mint tea brought up here at teatime—Ahmed knows how to make it—or some sort of orange drink. And cadi's horns and gazelle's ears . . ."

"It's the other way around," said Rose with no malice.

"Well, those little cakes made of almonds and pistachio nuts, whatever they're called."

"One word more and I shall be sick," said Odette. "It only needs the vice-principal and the headmaster. And what's the grand climax?"

"I've thought of that," said Bernard in a malicious voice which made him loathe himself. "The grand climax is that we don't have any dinner and go to bed at ten. We go to bed and, thank God, we go to bed without the local cinema, without a forced march through that beastly steep town. We even go to bed at half past nine! It's all my own invention and I'm decidedly proud of it."

They did not answer immediately. Odette yawned. Rose waited for Odette to give her opinion. And Odette was never in a hurry to approve anyone else's suggestion.

"The fact is . . ." she began.

"Oh," put in Rose, "I'm the last person to stop anyone going to bed."

All three of them were thinking of their long evening of the day before, which had begun in a *café-chantant* under the canvas awning of a little courtyard that smelled of acetylene. They had been taken there by a young and voluble guide—who wore a dinner jacket but no hat on his sleek head—to mix with the local gentry as they sat sipping their *anis* and nibbling their nougat. On the platform there had been a Spanish woman in yellow stockings, who looked like a staved-in cask, and two Tunisian *commères*, pale as butter, who sang from time to time. Next they had stopped at a cleaner place with an arched roof, where they had watched another dancer, a slim, naked, competent little creature with well-set breasts, who stamped on the tiles with a lively business-like step. She displayed everything but her hair, which was tightly tied up in a silk handkerchief, and her eyes, which she kept downcast throughout. When her dance was over, she went and sat cross-legged on a leather cushion. She had no art other than that of moving modestly and keeping her sexual organs ingeniously concealed.

"It was pathetic, that little thing who danced naked," said Rose.

Bernard was grateful to her for having thought, at the same moment, just what he himself was thinking. Odette shrugged her shoulders.

"It's not pathetic. It's inevitable. In Madrid one goes to see the Goyas. Here, you mustn't miss native girls in the nude. But I admit the sight isn't worth the effort of staying up till half past three."

"But it is," thought Bernard. "Only not with her or Rose. You can't expect women to lay aside their own particular brand of indecency and their instinct for spontaneous comparison. Any pleasure in the world would be spoiled for me if Odette were looking on. I knew everything she was thinking: 'That Zorah . . . her breasts won't last three years. My back's longer than hers. My breasts are more like apples, not so much like lemons as hers. I'm made quite differently *there* . . .'"

He was embarrassed to find himself imagining the details of a woman's body over which he had no rights and he blushed as he met

Odette's look. "That female guesses everything. I'll never manage to do what I want to do tonight. Rose will never have the courage."

Ahmed seemed to be listening to the distant voice of the invisible Tangiers and pulled up his white sleeve to consult his wristwatch. He bent over the little circle of lush, trampled grass and picked a blue flower, which he slipped between his ear and his fez. Then he fell back into his immobility, his lids and lashes hiding his great dark eyes.

"Ahmed!"

Bernard had called him almost in an undertone. Ahmed started.

"We're going down again, Ahmed."

Ahmed turned toward Rose and Odette, questioning them with his smile. They both smiled back so promptly and with such obvious pleasure that Bernard was annoyed. Ahmed's slippers and lean, agile ankles led the way; Bernard took note of all the turnings and landmarks. "It's as easy as anything. The first turning that forks upward from the big avenue. Anyway, one can hear the trickling of the water almost at once." But he remained dissatisfied. He was languid under the assault of noon; the growing light and heat sapped his vitality. Nevertheless, he would like to have owned that vast domain, which struck him as peculiarly Oriental.

"I'll say goodbye to Odette and Bessier. I'll shut myself up with Rose. I'll keep Ahmed and that wild little Arab girl we saw down there."

On their way back down the slope they saw once again the pines and the blue cedars and, lower down, the white arums which Ahmed contemptuously beheaded as he passed.

Lower down still, a little girl, whose skin was almost black, crossed their path, followed by her white hens. Her hair was plaited into a horn, one shoulder was half bare, and her breasts, under the native muslin, were conical.

"Ah, that's the nice little thing we saw over by the kitchens," exclaimed Odette.

The nice little thing shot her an insulting look and disappeared.

"Success! Ahmed, what's she called? Yes, the little thing over there. Don't act the idiot! It doesn't take me in for a moment. What's her name?"

Ahmed hesitated and fluttered his lashes.

"Fatima," he said, at last.

"Fatima," echoed Rose, "Isn't that pretty! She had a smile for Ahmed. What a look she gave us!"

"She's got a marvelous mouth," said Bernard. "And those thick teeth that I adore."

"That I adore!" mocked Rose. "Merely that! Do you hear that, Odette?"

"I hear all right," said Odette. "But I don't care a damn what he says. My feet are hurting."

They reached the crumbling wall of the park. As he stopped a moment to thank the ever-speechless Ahmed with a handshake, Bernard noticed that a gate was missing and a rusty padlock hung at the end of a useless chain.

The three companions turned into the narrow, almost shadeless path, barbed with prickly pears. Odette walked ahead, her eyes almost closed between the black fringe of her hair and the white bar of her teeth. Rose twisted her ankle and groaned. Bernard, who was following her, took her by the elbow and mischievously squeezed her arm as he helped her along.

"So you've got the wrong sort of shoes on, too? Couldn't either of you come to Africa with any other sort of shoes except those absurd white buckskin things?"

"No, stop, that's the limit," Rose wailed. "As if I hadn't enough to put up with as it is, without your having to . . ."

"Oh, give over," broke in Odette, without turning around. "He's just another of those chaps who say, 'For goodness' sake, wear espadrilles!' and then they're furious with you because, with no heels, all your skirts droop at the back."

Bernard made no retort. The noonday hour, while depressing his two weary companions, was making him turn ferocious. He stared at the sea, which seemed to be going down along with them, sinking back into its depths behind the tufted hills, the empty spring fields, and the silent little gardens where everything was in flower. "This is no time to be trailing around outdoors! And these two women! One teeters along, stumbling over everything, and the other's limping. As to their conversation, one's is as idiotic as the other's. I wonder what the hell I'm doing here!"

Since he knew very well what he was doing there, he forced himself to be less cantankerous and managed to take a little pleasure in the swallows, which were scything the air just above the ground and turning short with a whistle of wings.

The plaster-strewn enclosure, which the Mirador Hotel intended shortly to convert into an Arab garden with formal pools, boasted no more than a yellow patio. Its squat archways threw back blinding reflections of various shades of yellow. A tuft of wild oats made one of these look almost green: some red geraniums turned another to the fleshy pink of watermelons. An Ali Baba jar of blue cinerarias threw a blue halo on the yellow wall, a kind of azure mirage. The strangled painter revived in the depths of Bernard Bonnemains.

"What light! Why not let myself be tempted by a long, uneventful life here . . . No, farther away than this . . . I'd have a little concubine, or two . . ." He pulled himself up out of decency. "Or Rose, of course. But with Rose it wouldn't be possible. And it wouldn't be the same."

A smell of *anis* whetted his desire for a drink. He turned his head and saw Bessier Senior sitting at one of the little tables, writing.

"So there you are, Cyril!" cried Odette. "I bet you've only just come down!"

But Bonnemains had already noticed that there were three glasses on the table and that on an adjoining one, among squeezed lemons, siphons, and tumblers, lay several bluish pages torn from the pad Bessier used for making notes. He took in all these details at one glance, with a professional jealousy as swift as a woman's suspicion and far more intelligent.

"You're wrong," answered Bessier laconically. "You three had a good walk?"

For a moment he raised his eyes toward the newcomers, the eyes of a fair man who had once been handsome. Then he went on writing. His hair was still thick, though its gold had faded. He affected a prewar coquetry. He liked clothes which were almost white, let one silver lock fall over his forehead, and made considerable play with his pale lashes and his shortsighted eyes.

"I find him as embarrassing as a faded beauty," thought Bernard. "I've nothing against him except that he's Rose's brother-in-law."

Accustomed to keeping quiet when Bessier was working, the two women sat down and waited, their hats on their knees. Rose slipped Bernard a faintly imploring smile, which revived his sense of the power he had over her. "After all, a real blonde, a hundred percent blonde, is pretty rare." As Odette so charmingly put it: "Pink cheeks at twenty-five; blotches and broken veins at forty-five." He followed the crimson play of light on Rose's bare neck and under her chin and in her nostrils, and felt an immense desire to paint her. Misunderstanding his look, she lowered her eyes.

"I've finished," said Bessier. "But there's a post out this afternoon . . . Have you three only come back to eat? Bonnemains, you look disappointed. Purple in the face, but disappointed. Wasn't it worth the effort?"

He dabbed his prominent, sensitive eyes with the tips of his fingers and smiled with automatic condescension.

"Oh, yes . . . quite," said Bernard uncertainly.

"Oh, *yes!*" cried Rose. "It's adorable. And we haven't seen more than a quarter of it! You should have come, Cyril. Such greenery everywhere! And the oranges! I've eaten twenty if I've eaten one! And the flowers! It's crazy!"

Bernard stared at her in surprise. His private Rose bore no resemblance to this pretty, voluble little bourgeoise. Then he remembered that the Rose who belonged to the Bessier brothers was expected to behave childishly, to blush frequently and drop an occasional brick to the accompaniment of tender, indulgent laughs. He clenched his jaws. "Spare us any more, Rose!"

"And the villa?" asked Bessier. "What's the villa like? As hideous as they say?"

"The villa?"

"There's no more a villa than there's a . . ." said Odette.

"Perhaps it was the way up to the villa," interrupted Bernard, "that Ahmed was pointing out near the top of the hill. These women weren't interested in finding out anything. And as Ahmed doesn't speak French . . ."

Bessier raised his eyebrows.

"He doesn't speak French?"

"So *he* says," insinuated Odette. "Personally, I've my own ideas about *that*."

Bessier turned to Bernard and spoke to him as if he were a child of eight. "My dear little Bonnemains, don't bother yourself about the villa. I've got it all here."

"You've got it all? All what?"

Bessier pushed two or three leaves of his notebook, a creased yellow plan, and an old photograph across the iron table.

"There!" he said theatrically. "While you were having a good time, I . . ."

Rose had stood up and her crisp, curly hair brushed Bernard's ear as she bent over the photograph. But Bernard, tense and absorbed, was not giving Rose a thought. The faded old photograph occupied his whole attention.

"The villa," explained Bessier, "here they call it the palace—that's this huge black smudge."

"Mh'm," nodded Bernard. "I see. I see. What else?"

"Well," said Bessier, "I've had some fellows here this morning. One called Dankali. One called Ben Salem, one called—eh—Farrhar with an 'h'—who's got power of attorney. Odette and Rose, let my *anis* alone, will you? If you want some, make it yourself, as Marius says. Farrhar even told me that he'd once started studying architecture in Paris, so he felt as if he were a sort of colleague of mine. Too honored! Architecture leads to everything, provided you get out of it. He's extremely elegant. A pearl tiepin and a blue diamond on his finger."

"Blue?" squealed Rose.

"How big?" asked Odette greedily.

"Big as my fist. Once and for all, have you finished sucking at my *anis*? I've a horror of people drinking through my straws. It absolutely revolts me. You know that perfectly well!"

"Me too," thought Bernard. The sight of Odette and Rose bending over Cyril's tumbler, each with a straw between her lips, made him pinch his lips wryly and swallow his saliva as he did every time anything showed him Rose in familiar intimacy with the two Bessiers. He loathed it when Bessier lit Rose's cigarette or lent her a handkerchief to wipe her lips or her fingers; when he put a spoon to her mouth with a lump of sugar soaked in coffee.

". . . those three chaps were well worth seeing," Bessier went on. "Dankali is the contractor . . ."

"I know," said Bernard.

Bessier did not conceal his surprise. "But how do you know?"

"All the trucks and timberyards and fences and houses under construction are plastered with DANKALI AND SONS," said Bernard. "Haven't you noticed?"

"I haven't, by Jove. But I'll certainly remember it in the future."

He paused awhile, gently tapping his prominent eyeballs.

"It's a big job. They're razing the villa to its foundations and starting all over again. The pasha's made up his mind."

"Bravo!" said Bernard. "Isn't that going to mean your staying out here longer?"

"On the contrary. Of course I shall have to come back in September with the plans of the whole thing on paper."

"Ah yes. Quite."

Bessier looked dreamy and appeared to have no more to say.

"He said, 'I shall come back.' He didn't say, 'We shall come back,'" thought Bernard. "So much for you, you thoroughgoing swine."

The two women, used to keeping silence while professional discussions were taking place, sat idle on a bench. "If I were to ask him how he got the job, he might tell me," thought Bernard. "But where would that get me?"

He reproached himself for the little shiver which dried his light sweat and for the terrible professional jealousy which was ruining his day.

"I'll swallow that like all the rest. But *shall* I swallow it? I've had my back up ever since I came out. The fact is that, except for Rose, I can't bear the sight of these people anymore." He looked about him and his eyes came to rest on two hard brown hands, two forearms the color of oak which, a few steps away, were turning over and pressing down the damp earth at the foot of the daturas under the arcade. On the kitchen doorstep, a small roly-poly child with a fez on its head tottered, fell on the ground, and laughed. Above the whistling of the gray swifts, which were drinking on the wing from the newly made fountain, rose a quavering song which trailed its long notes and its intervals of augmented seconds in the air and relaxed Bernard Bonnemains's contracted heart. "I'd like to live among them, among the people here. It's true that most of them don't belong here." His eyes returned to Rose. Her cheeks were scarlet and her hair tumbled: he could see that she was worried about him. "That girl's going to pay for the others! I swear that she's going through with it tonight, and how! And if she gets caught, if we both get caught, very well then! I can't see that it matters." He could not stop himself from admiring the attitude of the Fiji Islander. At the mention of the "big job," she had manifested her greed and delight only by a brief flicker in her eye. Now she was combing her fringe and her hair gleamed as blue as a Chinese girl's in the sun. "She keeps all the 'how, why, and when?' for when they're alone together. She's an admirable female in her own way." He turned again to Rose, who was disentangling her rough golden curls in imitation and humming as she did so. "As for her . . . The time it takes her to grasp anything! But she's entirely made—admirably made too—to be enjoyed." His desire gripped him again. It disturbed him yet, at the same time, it revived his awareness of the African spring, of his own strength, of the agreeable present moment. He leaped to his feet and cried: "Food! Food! Let's eat or I'll not be responsible for my actions!"

Then he rushed, gesticulating, up the steps. Behind him there burst out shrill cries of terror. He realized that they came from the little dimpled child in its miniature fez and he regretted having behaved like a maniac.

A few minutes later, the four of them sat at a table eating large, stringy shrimps, stuffed artichokes, and baby lamb. Bessier Senior, a rose in his buttonhole, tried vainly to steer the conversation back to the business of the villa.

"What's your opinion, Bonnemains? Farrhar made no secret of the fact that the pasha, after spending a summer at Deauville, has developed a passion for Norman buildings with crossbeams and all that. A Norman cottage in Tangiers, no, that's really too much! Bonnemains, my dear chap, I'm talking to you, d'you hear?"

Far less deferential than usual, Bonnemains laughed in his face, displaying his splendid teeth to tempt Rose.

"I hear perfectly, my dear fellow, I hear perfectly. But in the first place, I'm a little drunk with this sun and this country and this heavy white wine that glues one's tongue. And in the second place, I've a horror of meddling in other people's affairs. Didn't you know that?"

Bessier Senior raised his fair eyelashes and, for no apparent reason, laid his hand on Rose's forearm.

"No, dear boy, I didn't know anything of the kind. Rose, fish me a bit of ice out of the pail. Thank you. I prefer your hand to the Spanish waiter's."

He took his time to drink before adding, with too emphatic graciousness: "My affairs won't always be 'other people's affairs' to you, Bernard. At least, so I dare to hope."

"Yes, yes. Always these Old World courtesies," thought Bernard. "He doesn't give a damn for me, yet I still owe him some thanks. What can I say to him? He's obviously expecting some polite formula of gratitude."

"My dear Cyril, no one's clumsier than I am at showing a gratitude which . . . I should so much like, particularly for your sake, to prove myself before you give me your official confidence . . ."

At the word "official," Bessier once more unveiled his bluish eyes and fixed them for a moment on Bernard. He smiled into space, took the tea rose out of his buttonhole, and inhaled it at length, using the rose and the pale hand as a screen between himself and Bernard. Bernard had to be content with this coquettish gesture which implied: "All in good time," or "That's understood."

Odette, who was smoking discreetly, had allowed herself neither an allusive smile nor a meaningful look. "Well trained," thought Bernard. "I'll never get such good results with Rose. Unless by great kicks in the . . ." He laughed and became once more the Bernard Bonnemains whom he himself believed to be the authentic one. This Bernard was a strong, likable young man, rather an optimistic character, who used anger as a defense against his fundamental shyness and who was inclined to covet his neighbor's goods when they were flourished under his nose.

Some black, bitter coffee kept the two couples sitting on at the table. The hot air rose up from the gravel and a cool salt breeze smelling of cedarwood stirred over their heads. Caught by the sun which had moved around, Bessier folded a newspaper into a hat and put it on. It gave him an intolerable resemblance to a portrait of a middle-aged woman by Renoir. Suddenly Bernard could stand no more and he stood up, knocking his chair over on the gravel.

"If I die of heart failure," scolded Odette, "I know who'll be responsible."

"Oh, come now . . . come . . ." Rose began plaintively.

"A little touch of colic, dear friend?" simpered Bessier under his wide-brimmed printed hat.

"Oh, Cyril!" said Rose reproachfully.

"I might have replied," thought Bernard, as he reached his room, "that I actually was suffering from violent indigestion. Each one of those three said exactly what I knew they would say. Life is becoming impossible."

He locked his door, pulled down the blinds, and flung himself on his bed. The half-open window let in noises, not one of which was African: banging crockery, telephone bells, someone languidly dragging a rake. A ship's siren filled the air, drowning all other sounds, and Bernard, relaxed almost to the point of tears, shut his eyes and opened his clenched fists.

"What's the matter with me? What's the matter with me? The need to make love, obviously. My Rose, my little Rose . . . Rose of my life . . ."

He turned over with a leap like a fish. "Those names sound as silly for her as they do for me to say them. She's my Rose, my delicious little blond slavey, my pretty goldilocks of a washerwoman?" He broke off with a kind of sob of impatience, which he managed to choke down and which had nothing to do with tenderness. "Enough of all this gush! Tonight we're going for a walk, Rose and I."

On the wooden slats of the blinds, he conjured up the old pond in the deserted park, overgrown with delicate wild grasses, the trickle of water diverted from the dried-up lion's mouth, and Rose lying on her back. But a kind of ill will spoiled his pleasure and his hope, and he refused to be taken in by himself. "Yes, I know perfectly well that all this story would be much prettier if Rose were poor. But if she were poor, I shouldn't be thinking of marrying her."

Sleep fell on him so suddenly that he had no time to settle himself in a comfortable position. He slept, lying sprawled across the bed, one arm bent and the back of his neck pressing against the feather pillow. When he woke up, which was not till the sun had moved to another window, he was stiff all over. Before raising his perspiring head, he caught sight of the corner of an envelope under the door. "What's the trouble now?"

We're going out, Rose had written. *Dear Bernard, we didn't want to disturb your rest . . .*

"We, we . . . who the hell are 'we'? I'll give her a lesson in family solidarity!" In the glass, he saw his untidy image; his shirt rucked up, his trousers unbelted, and his hair on end, and thought he looked ugly.

Cyril has an awful migraine and asks us, as a favor, to have dinner at the hotel and go to bed early. As usual, Odette, as a model wife, entirely agrees with Cyril. But I admit that I myself . . .

Bernard ran to the window, pulled up the blinds, and leaned over the cooling patio. From now until tomorrow it would be bathed in shadow and spray from the fountain. The jet of water, shooting up straight from its basin, quivered in the breeze. Beyond the arcades lay the chalky African soil with its ubiquitous riot of pulpy white arum lilies.

He waited, naked, for his bath to fill. His young, slightly heavy body, without scar or blemish, pleased him. The thought of Rose gave him one of those moments of magical anguish such as he had felt when he was fifteen, moments when desire is so fierce that it almost consumes its object, then forgets it.

Freshly bathed and shaved, dressed in light clothes and smelling good, he went down and stood at the edge of the garden. He was rash enough to let his pleasure show on his face.

"You look like a First Communicant," said the voice of Bessier.

"I can smell you from here," said Odette. "You've put it on with rather a heavy hand. That Counterattack of yours . . . I've always said it wasn't a man's toilet water."

"On the other hand, I adore his white woolen socks," said Bessier.

"Personally," went on Odette, "I'd have preferred not *quite* such a blue tie. With a gray suit, a really blue tie looks as silly as a bunch of cornflowers in one's buttonhole."

She was sitting so close to her husband that their shoulders touched. United in their spite, they were summing him up as if he were a horse. It was their unity which struck Bernard as even more offensive than their insolence.

"Have you quite finished?" he said roughly.

"Now then, you! Come off it!" cried Odette.

Bessier restrained her by laying his heavy white hand on her arm. "We've quite finished," he said affectionately to Bernard. "Don't get annoyed because your friends are sensitive to all the outward signs that show you want to be handsome and gay."

"I'm not . . . I don't particularly want to . . ." Bernard clumsily protested.

The blood was singing in his ears and he ran a finger between his neck and his shirt collar. He was afraid he would not be able to stand Odette's little laugh, but Bessier had the situation well in hand and reproved his wife.

"You've touched him to the quick, otherwise to the tie! Insult my mother but don't dare suggest that I've chosen the wrong tie!"

He was speaking to her with a paternal mildness. Suddenly he grabbed the nape of her neck and kissed her on her peevish mouth, on her moist, shining teeth. "He's indecent, that fellow," thought Bernard. But all the same, it gave him a pang to imagine the chill, the perfect regularity of the teeth Bessier had kissed. He turned away, paced a few steps, and returned to the couple.

"For they certainly are a couple," he admitted. Bessier was stroking the shoulder of a silent and softened Odette, stroking it with the hand of an indifferent master. "It's unusual for a husband and wife to be a couple." He felt annoyed, in spite of the soft green twilight and the wind laden with the scent of mint tea.

"Here's our Rose," announced Bessier in a studied voice.

Bonnemains, who had recognized the little short step, carefully avoided turning around, but an exclamation from Odette made him forget his discretion.

"Whatever's the matter with you? What's gone wrong?"

He saw that Rose had thrown her dark blue raincoat over the rather crumpled dress she had kept on ever since the morning and that she was coming toward them with her head bent and wearing a brave little martyred smile.

"Have you lost a relation?" cried Odette.

"Oh, I've such a migraine. It's this afternoon. You dragged me through the bazaars, and I simply can't stand the smell of leather there is everywhere here. Forgive me, Cyril and Bernard, I just hadn't the energy. I've stayed just as I am without changing my frock. I know I look simply frightful."

"You look frightful, but you smell marvelous," observed Odette. "How you can stand scent when you've got a migraine! Doesn't she smell good, Bernard?"

"Delicious," said Bernard easily. "She smells of . . . wait a minute . . . marzipan tart . . . I adore that!"

He even went so far as to pretend to bite Rose's bare arm. Rose looked crosser than ever and went and sat very close to Cyril.

"Either we're the worst actors in the world," thought Bernard, "or else the Bessiers can sense a kind of atmosphere around me and Rose. Which doesn't stop the child being slyer than I supposed. Look at her now, got up in that dark thing over her light dress, a dress that's already been rumpled in full view of everyone. It's true that when it comes to deception, the stupidest of them has a genius for it."

After a thoughtful silence, Odette said in a resigned voice: "Well, we're all going to bed early."

They had a strange dinner, served in the patio under a naked electric bulb, which was soon covered with little moths in a hurry to die. Rose pretended at first that she could not eat; then devoured her food. Bernard insisted on champagne and pressed his three guests to drink. The two women held back at first, then Odette pushed her empty glass across the tablecloth to Bernard like a pawn on a chessboard and drank glass after glass, only giving herself time to take a deep breath between each refill. She gave great gasps and "ahs" as if she had been drinking under a tap, and the glitter of her teeth between her lips, the sight of her moist palate and tongue in her open mouth dazzled Bernard in spite of himself. "Yet Rose has a lovely, healthy, desirable mouth too. But Odette's great carnivorous mouth suggests something else." After a spasm of uncontrollable laughter, Odette had absurdly to wipe away tears. She clutched Rose's bare arm and Bernard saw the flat fingers, with the nails varnished dark red, print hollows in the flesh. Rose made no sound but seemed terror-stricken, and slowly and cautiously removed her arm from the fingers which gripped it, as if disentangling it from a briar. Bernard filled up the glasses and drained his own. "If I stop drinking, if I look at these people too close, I shall chuck everything and clear out."

He went on looking at them, however, and most of all, he looked at Rose. Her hair was standing out like the spokes of a wheel, her cheeks and ears were crimson, and there was a paler ring around her eyes. Her eyes were brilliant and vacant, but her quivering mouth had a majestic and dishonored expression as if she had just submitted to a long, passionate embrace. At the moment when all four of them stopped drinking and talking, she seemed so overcome that Bernard was afraid she would refuse to follow him.

But suddenly she got up stiffly and announced that she was going up to bed.

"You can't want to more than I do," said Bessier. "But permit me to drink a toast to the lady who's watching us and listening to us."

He grabbed his glass and raised his bluish eyes, clouded by the wine, to the sky. Bonnemains followed his gaze and was astonished to see a pink moon, halfway to being round, appearing in the square of sky above the patio.

"Well, of all things! I'd forgotten the moon. So much the worse. Anyway, what the hell! In its second quarter, and rather misty at that, the moon doesn't give much light. It's not the moon that'll stop us from . . ."

"Well," said Odette gloomily. "I'm going to bed, too. What about you, Bernard?"

"Aha!" said Bonnemains. "I'm not going to commit myself to anything. After all, I'm a bachelor. I haven't renounced the pleasures of Africa."

When he saw all three of them vanish up the staircase, which did not yet boast an elevator, he felt at the end of his strength and his patience. His last gesture of sociability cost him an immense effort. With voice and hand, he acknowledged Bessier's "Good night" as the latter went up the stairs behind Rose. "He climbs like an old man. He's got an old man's back." Before the trio disappeared, he thought he saw the hand of the "old man" deliberately touch Rose's buttocks. The second turn of the stairs, on the first landing, allowed him to see that both the women were well ahead of Bessier. "I made a mistake. I've had just one or two glasses too many." He looked questioningly at the half-moon, which was rapidly ascending the sky. "Not a cloud. Well, it can't be helped." He waited till the little Spaniards in dirty white jackets had cleared the table and ordered a glass of iced water. "I smell of wine and tobacco. After all, so does Rose. Anyway, thank God she's a woman who's not squeamish about the human body—a real woman."

He watched the light in Rose's room. "Now she's brushing her teeth with lots of scent in the toothglass. She does heaps of little odds and ends of beautifying—unnecessary in my opinion. Now she's gossiping with Odette through a closed door—or an open door. I've quite a bit of time to wait."

The light in the Bessiers' windows went out. Ten minutes later, Rose's window turned black. Then Bonnemains took cover under the arcades and made his way to a narrow door which opened out of the enclosure onto the waste ground beyond.

Crushing flakes of plaster and scraps of broken crockery under his shoe soles, caressing the white arums which stood stiff, drinking in the damp night air, he passed through this pallid purgatory.

Halfway along the rough little road which led to the pasha's park, the sea suddenly appeared in the distance like a misted looking glass. "How beautiful it is, that horizontal line and the sky gently pressing down on it, and that dim reflection in the shape of a boat. It needs that —and only that—for me to stop being unjust or envious or anything that I don't like being."

Leaning against the broken fence and reassured by the absence of dogs and barriers, he admired the black block of the cedars. Here and there the green showed less dark, softly massed in cloudy shapes which he knew were mimosas loaded with scent and flowers. Below him, the sleeping town gave out only a faint glimmer, and at moments, the silence was like a silence only known in dreams. During one of such moments, Bonnemains became aware of the sound of uneven footsteps and saw a wavering shadow on the broken road. "Amazing," he exclaimed to himself. "I'd stopped thinking about her."

He ran back and once again made contact with an unfettered body, a scent too lavishly applied, some wiry hair, and a panting breath.

"Here you are! Nothing broken?"

"No . . ."

"The Bessiers? You didn't make a noise?"

"No . . ."

"You weren't afraid?"

"Oh, yes . . ."

He held her firmly by the elbows, taking a peculiar pleasure in addressing her with a new sense of ownership. She lifted her face up to him, and in the nocturnal light, her lovely cheeks were tinged vivid blue and her painted mouth deep purple. "Am I never to have her all pink and white and red and golden?" He pulled open the silk raincoat to touch her dress, crumpled on purpose ever since the morning, and what the dress covered. Rose stood motionless, so as to lose nothing of the caress.

"Come along, I tell you!"

He passed his arm under her bare one and they crossed the confines of the park through a gap in the fence.

"You see—that path goes straight up and then it divides in two. It's the left one that takes us up to the lawn, to our bed walled in with stone and flowers. Rose, Rose . . . Come along! I'll hold you up."

She hung heavily on his arm, then stopped.

"It's dark."

"So I should hope! You can shut your eyes if you don't want to see the blackness. I'll guide you."

"Are you sure? Bernard, it's so dark."

He gave a low, patronizing laugh.

"Shut your eyes, silly! Little funk! I'll tell you when we get there."

Her confidence in him returned and she huddled close against him. But as they climbed the steep road full of ruts, Bonnemains could not recognize the path which had seemed so easy to find. He withdrew his supporting shoulder and guided Rose by her hand. His free hand fidgeted with the little flashlight in his pocket but he managed to refrain from using it. The forest darkness was impenetrable to the moonlight, and after a few moments, Bernard began to be aware of a rising tide of apprehension. He was beset by that nervous terror which afflicts any human being who braves the blackest hour of night in the redoubled darkness of a wooded place. He stumbled, swore, and switched on his flashlight. A round tunnel of light, edged with a rainbow, bored through the blackness.

"No!" shrieked Rose.

"You must really make up your mind, my child! You complain that it's dark and you refuse to see clearly . . ."

He switched it off, having seen that they were on the right road. Moreover, the vault of trees opened out above them, showing a river of sky in which stars twinkled.

"We're nearly there," went on Bernard, more gently, moved to pity by feeling Rose's hand grow damp in his without growing warm.

But she said nothing and concentrated on following him: he could hear nothing but her hurried breathing. Twice he shone his light on the path, just long enough to recognize the white clematis above their heads, then an arch of wisteria with long bunches of flowers.

"Do you smell their scent?" he asked very low.

He ventured a kiss in the dark and found her mouth. Rose's lips took fire from his. They set off again, going with as much difficulty as if they were hauling a load, helping themselves with occasional spurts of light. At last they found the fork of the avenue, the charming flowery margin of the pool, and the lion's mask. The diverted trickle of water sparkled under the white beam of the flashlight.

"Sit down there while I inspect our lawn."

Rose took off her raincoat and held it out to Bernard.

"There, spread that on the ground, with the lining on top."

"Whatever for?" he asked naïvely.

"But . . . for . . . well, after all."

She put her arm over her eyes to protect herself from the glare of the flashlight. He understood and was full of gratitude toward a Rose whom he scarcely knew yet, the Rose who was at once prudish and practical, a good companion in bed, entirely devoted to the material necessities of love.

"I'm putting the light on the edge, don't knock it over!" he whispered.

"I've got one in my bag, too," answered Rose. "Look carefully in case there are any creatures."

On its way, the vertical trickle of water, white against the background of greenery, encountered the remains of some mosaic which diverted it beyond the curb. The grass in the center was fine and concealed no mysteries. Small frightened wings fluttered from the branches, awakened by the electric beam. Bernard strode over the rim, bent down to feel the grass, and reared upright again with a start.

"What is it? Creatures? I'm sure there are creatures! Bernard!"

She went on imploring Bernard in a low voice as he stood there, staring fixedly at his feet.

"Don't be frightened," he said.

At that, Rose raised her hands to her temples and was on the verge of a scream, which Bernard checked by threatening her with his open hand. He bent down again and picked up, in the circle of light, a brown hand and a white sleeve which promptly slid out of his grasp and fell back again.

"He's not dead," he said. "The hand's warm, but . . ."

He held the light to his own hand, looked at it close to, then wiped his fingers in the grass. It was only then that he became conscious of Rose's silence. She did not run away, but in the rising shaft of light, he could see that her chin was trembling.

"Above all, don't turn faint," he said gently. "It's only a man who's bleeding."

Instinct made him glance questioningly into the darkness all about him.

"No . . . if there were other men here, the birds wouldn't have been asleep. I don't think there's anyone."

Under the crumpled dress, Rose's knees were trembling.

"Come, darling, give me a hand."

She took a step backward.

"He's not dead, Rose. We can't leave him like that."

As she remained obstinately silent, he became impatient.

"Give me your flashlight."

She took still another step back and vanished from the zone of light. He heard her clumsily groping in her bag.

"Hurry up."

Rose's hand and the cheap little flashlight appeared out of Bernard's reach. Squatting down, he lifted a white sleeve and felt carefully all the way up the wounded arm.

"Well, bring it here, can't you?"

"No," said a muffled voice, "I don't want to. I'm afraid."

"Idiot," growled Bonnemains. "At least, put the flashlight on the coping. And switch it on—if that's not too much to ask you. Don't you realize the man's wounded, Rose?"

With both arms he lifted a light, slender body which he propped up against the coping. The body emitted a moan as it let its head, with eyes closed, fall backward on the stone curb.

"But it's Ahmed!" cried Bonnemains.

The injured man opened his eyelids and moved his long lashes, promptly closing them again.

"Ahmed! Poor kid! Rose, it's Ahmed! Do you hear me, Rose?"

"Yes," said the voice. "So what?"

"What d'you mean, so what? He must have—oh, goodness knows— fallen down, hurt himself. What a bit of luck we're here."

"Luck!" repeated the hostile voice.

Bernard's eyes were dazzled so that he could barely make out where Rose was standing in the darkness. He lowered his eyes, saw that his hands and his sleeves were stained with blood, and fell silent. "He's lost a lot of blood. Where is he wounded?"

He arranged the two flashlights so as to give as much light as possible and carefully tapped Ahmed's body all over with his fingertips. The blood was coming neither from the chest nor from the loins nor from the stomach as hollow as a greyhound's. "His throat? No, he's breathing quietly." At last, on the shoulder, he discovered the source of the blood, and once again, Ahmed groaned and opened his eyes.

"Have you a penknife?" he asked without turning his head.

"A what?"

"A penknife or something of the sort. Doesn't matter what, as long as it cuts. Hurry up, for God's sake, hurry up!"

He listened exasperatedly to the jingle of small objects in the handbag.

"I've got some little scissors."

"Don't throw them to me or they'll get lost in the grass. Bring them here," he ordered.

She obeyed and then drew back into the shadow.

"Can I have my raincoat back?" she asked, after a moment.

Bernard, who was slitting Ahmed's white sleeve, did not raise his head.

"Your raincoat? No, you can't. I'm going to cut it up. I haven't anything else to bandage his shoulder with. The amount he must have bled, this boy."

Rose made no protest, but he heard her breathing in jerks and holding back tears.

"Really, that's too much! My raincoat! To make a bandage for a black boy. Couldn't you use his shirt—or yours?"

"Why not your bloomers?" broke in Bernard.

He felt strangely exalted, almost facetious even, as he worked coolly at baring the wounded shoulder. His ears were alert to every crackle in the undergrowth, every sigh in the boughs. A short blade which lay in the grass caught his eye with its glitter.

"Aha!" said Bernard. "You see that?"

He picked the knife up and, holding it by its point, laid it on the coping.

"Ahmed! Ahmed, can you hear me?"

The black lashes lifted and the eyes appeared, calm and severe, like those of a very young child. But the weight of the lids veiled them again almost at once. Bernard discovered the wound, quite a narrow one, but brutally inflicted. It's brown, swollen lips had still not stopped bleeding. With the palms of both hands, Bernard smoothed the bloodstained area around it so as to isolate the wound. "It's hellishly difficult," he said to himself.

"Ahmed! Who did this to you?"

Ahmed's mouth trembled and said nothing. Then it trembled again and murmured: "Ben Kacem."

"Quarrel?"

"Fatima."

"Fatima? Isn't that the pretty little girl down there?"

"Yes."

"Good. Now I think I see."

"What did he say?" asked Rose from far away.

"Nothing that would interest you. Ahmed, can you rest your weight on your hands for a moment? No? All right, don't move, then. I knew very well that you spoke French."

He pulled the slit sleeve toward him. Split into three, it made a bandage long enough for his purpose.

Seized with a sudden lightheartedness, he worked fast, repressing his desire to sing under his breath and whistle. He reckoned that the bandage, passing under the armpit and over the shoulder and tightly wound, would have a reasonable hope of staunching the flow of blood, which was already tending to stop of its own accord. Ahmed made no movement. Bernard could feel him watching his hands.

"The flashlight!" cried Rose.

The bulb of one of the flashlights was reddening, preparatory to fading. "Hmm, that's not so funny."

"Stay sitting down," he said to Ahmed. "Try to keep quite still while I put on the bandage. Am I hurting you? Sorry, old chap, it can't be helped. The girl might have helped us, but just you try and make her understand."

His sweat dripped down on his work, and in wiping his forehead, he smeared it with red.

"Talk of antisepsis! By Jove, was it for Fatima you've perfumed yourself so magnificently? You fairly reek of sandalwood. There . . . now you're fine."

He caught Ahmed around the waist, sat him up, and brought the light nearer to the faultless face. The lips, from which the crimson had vanished, the eyes circled with brown and olive, gave a ghost of a smile. Bonnemains, invisible behind the flashlight, answered with a smile which twisted into a grimace as he suddenly found himself wanting to cry.

"D'you want to drink? Just think, I'd forgotten all about this water."

"No, it's the water that comes from the oleanders. It's bad."

He spoke French without an accent, rolling his r's.

"Cigarette?"

The thumb and forefinger, yellow-stained with nicotine, came forward to accept. Bernard wiped his hands on his stained handkerchief, groped in his pocket without a thought that he was smearing his jacket with blood, and stuck a lighted cigarette between Ahmed's lips. The delight of the first puffs made them both silent. Neither of them moved except to make identical gestures. The smoke showed faintly iridescent, seeming to break off as it touched the edges of the halo of light and reappearing higher up in whorls under the spreading branches of the blue cedar.

A burst of coughing disturbed the repose of the two young men. Bernard turned his head.

"What's the matter?"

"I'm cold," said Rose plaintively.

"You wouldn't be cold if you'd helped us. Here, catch your coat, I didn't use it. Ahmed, my boy, we've got to get down from here somehow. What I've done in the way of a dressing is almost less than nothing. Let's see—what's the time?"

Bonnemains scratched away the blood that was drying on the face of his wristwatch and exclaimed in astonishment: "Quarter to three! Impossible."

"It was after one when we left the hotel," came the sulky voice.

He strode over the coping and ran up to Rose.

"Rose, look, here's what we're going to do . . ."

She shrank back.

"Don't touch me, you're covered with blood!"

"I'm quite aware of that! Rose, can you give him your shoulder to get down to the bottom? I'll hold him up on the other side. With stops, it'll take a good half hour. Or, wait a moment . . . Suppose you take the flashlight and go by yourself to the hotel or to the caretaker's house and send help? How about that?"

She did not answer at once and he became insistent.

"Tell me! Don't you think it would be better if you went down by yourself?"

"What do I think? I think you're mad," said Rose deliberately. "Whether I go down with you, with a wounded Arab between us, or whether I go by myself to rouse the entire population—it's as broad as it's long. Either way, the Bessiers will know I've been rambling about in the woods with you. Don't you see my point?"

"Yes, but I don't care a damn for the Bessiers."

"But I do. When one can avoid trouble with one's family . . ."

"Well? What solution do *you* propose?"

"Leave this—this wounded man here. Then we'll go down and you must wait till I've got back to my room to call for help. By then, the night will be over. A pretty night, I've had! So've you!"

"Don't pity me," he said shortly. "Mine's been all right."

"Charming!" snapped Rose in a low, savage voice. "If anyone had told me . . ."

"Shut up! Suppose I take Ahmed on my shoulders and that you light the path?"

". . . And that down there, they're already looking for him, and they see the light and come up, how do you expect me to explain?"

"Well? I presume you're of age, aren't you? Are you as ashamed of me as all that?"

He could sense her impatient gesture.

"But no, Bernard, there's no question of that. What's the good of putting people's backs up? You've no idea what the Bessiers have been to me ever since . . ."

"Hell!" Bernard interrupted. "You can go off. I'll manage alone."

"But, Bernard, look!"

"Get out. Go back and have your bottom pinched by Bessier. And drink out of his glass. And all the rest of it."

"What? What on earth? Whatever do you . . ."

"I know what I'm talking about. Be off with you! We're through. Pfft! None too soon, either."

He passed his hand over his wet face. With a quick glance, he made sure that Ahmed, who had not moved, had not fainted and was still smoking. His eyes were half closed and he seemed not even to hear the altercation.

"Bernard!" implored a small voice that had grown soft again. "You can't mean it! Bernard—I assure you . . ."

"What do you assure me? That Bessier has never pinched your behind? That Bessier is just a brother to you?"

"Bernard, if you've come to believe spiteful gossip—"

"No question of gossip!" he broke in violently. "No need for any gossip! Go back and make yourself charming to Bessier! Go back and sit on one of his knees! Go back to everything that suits a selfish little bourgeoise, not very clever but so hard that she's a positive marvel!"

She reacted to each attack with a little gasp of "Oh!" but could find no retort. When he paused for breath, she said at last: "But what are you driving at? Bernard, I'm certain that tomorrow . . ."

He sliced the air between them with his bloodstained hand. "Nothing! Tomorrow, I'll change my hotel. Or I take the boat. Unless I'm needed"—he indicated Ahmed—"as witness."

He drew back as if to let Rose pass.

"You can say exactly what you like to your Bessiers. That I'm the most loathsome of swine. And even that I've got disgusting manners. That I'm sick to death of the lot of you. Anything you like."

They were silent for a moment. Bonnemains's eyes, which were getting used to the darkness, made out Rose's face and her aureole of curly hair. He could see a strip of her light dress between the flaps of her open coat.

"And all for this black boy who's too tough to kill!" she flung at him furiously.

Bonnemains shrugged his shoulders.

"Oh, you know, if there hadn't been this little news item, there'd have been something else."

He picked up the one working flashlight and thrust it by force into Rose's hand. She clenched her fingers and pushed him away.

"What's the matter? It's blood, it's not dirty. I can't help it, it's blood. Blood that you didn't deign to stop flowing. And now, pleasant journey, Rose!"

As she did not move he put his finger on her shoulder and gave her a push.

"On your way. A bit quicker. Or, I promise you, I'll make you run."

She turned the little bull's-eye of the flashlight on him. His forehead and one cheek were smeared with blood and his eyes were almost yellow. The beam shone into his open mouth, lighting up both rows of his big teeth. She lowered the flashlight and went off hurriedly.

Bernard went back and sat down by Ahmed. He watched the tunnel of light going down the hill, slowly pushing back the darkness in the avenue. He laid his hand on Ahmed's unhurt shoulder.

"All right? You don't think you're bleeding?"

"No, Monsieur."

The voice was so much firmer that Bernard was delighted. But it surprised him that Ahmed should call him Monsieur. "Still, after all, what could he call me?"

A bird squawked discordantly. From the height of the cedars there fell, by degrees, a glimmer that was still nocturnal.

"But we can see!" exclaimed Bernard joyfully.

"It'll soon be day," said Ahmed.

"What luck! How are you feeling?"

"All right, thank you, Monsieur."

A slender icy hand slid against Bernard's and stayed there. "He's cold. All that blood he's lost . . ."

"Listen, my dear boy. If I try and take you on my back, that rotten dressing of mine will come unstuck. And if I fall while I'm carrying you, that's another big risk for you. On the other hand . . ."

"I can wait for the day, Monsieur. I know myself. If you'd just give me a cigarette. Aziz comes down every day with his donkey for the watering, he passes this way. He won't be long now."

Reassured, Bonnemains smoked to deaden the hunger and thirst which were beginning to torment him. A cock crowed, other cocks followed its example; the breeze rose, bringing out the accumulated scent of the cedars and the fragrance of the wisterias; gradually the color of the sky appeared between the trees. Bernard shivered in his shirt, which was cold with sweat. From time to time, he touched his companion's wrist, counting the pulse beats.

"Are you asleep, Ahmed? Don't go to sleep. That Kacem who did this, is he far away?"

He followed the progress of the dawning light on Ahmed's face. The black circles around the eyes, the cheeks shadowed by something other than the first beginnings of a beard, alarmed him.

"Tell me, has he gone? Did you see him run away?"

"Not far," said Ahmed. "I know . . ."

His free hand dropped, without letting go of the cigarette, and his eyes closed. Bernard had time to raise the head which had fallen forward: he felt the wounded shoulder. But no warm moisture came through the linen, and the deep breathing of sleep fell rhythmically and reassuringly on Bonnemains's straining ears. He pushed his knee forward to support the sleeping head, took away the fag end of the cigarette from the fingers which could no longer feel it, and stayed perfectly still. With his head raised, he watched the morning dawn and tasted a contentment, a surprise as fresh as love but less restricted and totally detached from sex. "He sleeps, I watch. He sleeps, I watch . . ."

The color and abundance of the spilled blood blackened the trampled grass. Ahmed was talking in his sleep in guttural Arabic and Bonnemains laid his hand on his head to drive away the nightmare.

"Rose has got back by now. She'll be in bed. Poor Rose . . ." That was over quickly. "She was my woman but this one here is my counterpart. It's queer that I had to come all the way to Tangiers to find my counterpart, the only person who could make me proud of him and proud of myself. With a woman it's so easy to be a little ashamed, either of her or of oneself. My wonderful counterpart! He only had to appear . . ."

Without the faintest sense of disgust, he contemplated his hands, his nails streaked with brown, the lines on his palms etched in red, his forearms marked with dried rivulets of blood.

"They say children and adolescents soon make up what they've lost. This boy must be an only son or the oldest one who'll be well looked after. A young male has his value in this country. He's handsome, he's already loved, he's already got a rival. The fact remains that, but for me . . ."

He swelled out his chest and smiled with pleasure at everything about him.

"Women! I know in advance pretty well what I'll do to them and they'll do to me. I'll find another Rose. A better Rose or a worse one. But one doesn't easily find a child in the shape of a man, hurt enough, unknown enough, precious enough to sacrifice some hours of one's life to him, not to mention the jacket of a suit and a night of love. Obviously it was decreed that I should never know whether Rose's breasts are rosier than her heels or her belly as pearly as her thighs. *Mektoub,* Ahmed would say!"

At the end of the long sloping avenue appeared a pink gleam which showed the place where the sun would rise over the sea: the shattering bray of a donkey and the tinkle of a little bell sounded from the top of the hill.

Before lifting Ahmed, Bonnemains tested the knots of his amateur dressing. Then he wrapped his arms around the sleeping boy, inhaled the sandalwood scent of his black hair, and clumsily kissed his cheek, which was already virile and rough. He estimated the young man's weight as he might have done that of a child of his own flesh or that of a quarry one kills only once in a lifetime.

"Wake up, dear boy. Here comes Aziz."

[*Translated by Antonia White*]

The Kepi

❧❧❧

If I remember rightly, I have now and then mentioned Paul Masson, known as Lemice-Térieux on account of his delight—and his dangerous efficiency—in creating mysteries. As ex-president of the Law Courts of Pondichéry, he was attached to the cataloguing section of the Bibliothèque Nationale. It was through him and through the library that I came to know the woman, the story of whose one and only romantic adventure I am about to tell.

This middle-aged man, Paul Masson, and the very young woman I then was, established a fairly solid friendship that lasted some eight years. Without being cheerful himself, Paul Masson devoted himself to cheering me up. I think, seeing how very lonely and housebound I was, he was sorry for me, though he concealed the fact. I think, too, that he was proud of being so easily able to make me laugh. The two of us often dined together in the little third-floor flat in the rue Jacob, myself in a dressing gown hopefully intended to suggest Botticelli draperies, he invariably in dusty, correct black. His little pointed beard, slightly reddish, his faded skin and drooping eyelids, his absence of any special distinguishing marks attracted attention like a deliberate disguise. Familiar as he was with me, he avoided using the intimate "*tu*," and every time he emerged from his guarded impersonality, he gave every sign of having been extremely well brought up. Never, when we were alone, did he sit down to write at the desk of the man whom I refer to as "Monsieur Willy" and I cannot remember, over a period of several years, his ever asking me one indiscreet question.

Moreover, I was fascinated by his caustic wit. I admired the way he attacked people on the least provocation, but always in extremely restrained language and without a trace of heat. And he brought up to my third story, not only all the latest Paris gossip, but a series of ingenious lies that I enjoyed as fantastic stories. If he ran into Marcel Schwob, my luck was really in! The two men pretended to hate each other and played a game of insulting each other politely under their breath. The *s*'s hissed between Schwob's clenched teeth; Masson gave little coughs and exuded venom like a malicious old lady. Then they would declare a truce and talk at immense length, and I was stimulated and excited by the battle of wits between those two subtle, insincere minds.

The time off that the Bibliothèque Nationale allowed Paul Masson assured me of an almost daily visit from him but the phosphorescent conversation of Marcel Schwob was a rarer treat. Alone with the cat and Masson, I did not have to talk and this prematurely aged man could relax in silence. He frequently made notes—heaven knows what about—on the pages of a notebook bound in black imitation leather. The fumes from the slow-burning stove lulled us into a torpor; we listened drowsily to the reverberating bang of the street door. Then I would rouse myself to eat sweets or salted nuts and I would order my guest, who, though he would not admit it to himself, was probably the most devoted of all my friends, to make me laugh. I was twenty-two, with a face like an anemic cat's, and more than a yard and a half of hair that, when I was at home, I let down in a wavy mass that reached to my feet.

"Paul, tell me some lies."

"Which particular ones?"

"Oh, any old lies. How's your family?"

"Madame, you forget that I'm a bachelor."

"But you told me . . ."

"Ah yes, I remember. My illegitimate daughter is well. I took her out to lunch on Sunday. In a suburban garden. The rain had plastered big yellow lime leaves on the iron table. She enjoyed herself enormously pulling them off and we ate tepid fried potatoes, with our feet on the soaked gravel . . ."

"No, no, not that, it's too sad. I like the lady of the library better."

"What lady? We don't employ any."

"The one who's working on a novel about India, according to you."

"She's still laboring over her novelette. Today I've been princely and generous. I've made her a present of baobabs and latonia palms painted from life and thrown in magical incantations, mahrattas, screaming monkeys, Sikhs, saris, and lakhs of rupees."

Rubbing his dry hands against each other, he added: "She gets a sou a line."

"A sou!" I exclaimed. "Why a sou?"

"Because she works for a chap who gets two sous a line who works for a chap who gets four sous a line, who works for a chap who gets ten sous a line."

"But what you're telling me isn't a lie, then?"

"All my stories can't be lies," sighed Masson.

"What's her name?"

"Her Christian name is Marco, as you might have guessed. Women of a certain age, when they belong to the artistic world, have only a few names to choose from, such as Marco, Léo, Ludo, Aldo. It's a legacy from the excellent Madame Sand."

"Of a certain age? So she's old, then?"

Paul Masson glanced at my face with an indefinable expression. Lost in my long hair, that face became childish again.

"Yes," he said.

Then he ceremoniously corrected himself: "Forgive me, I made a mistake. No was what I meant to say. No, she's not old."

I said triumphantly: "There, you see! You see it *is* a lie, because you haven't even chosen an age for her!"

"If you insist," said Masson.

"Or else you're using the name Marco to disguise a lady who's your mistress."

"I don't need Madame Marco. I have a mistress who is also, thank heaven, my housekeeper."

He consulted his watch and stood up.

"Do make my excuses to your husband. I must get back or I shall miss the last bus. Concerning the extremely real Madame Marco, I'll introduce you to her whenever you feel inclined."

He recited, very fast: "She is the wife of V., the painter, a school friend of mine who's made her abominably unhappy; she has fled from the conjugal establishment where her perfections had rendered her an impossible inmate; she is still beautiful, witty, and penniless; she lives in a boarding house in the rue Demours, where she pays eighty-five francs a month for bed and breakfast; she does writing jobs, anonymous feuilletons, newspaper snippets, addressing envelopes, gives English lessons at three francs an hour, and has never had a lover. You see that this particular lie is as disagreeable as the truth."

I handed him the little lighted lamp and accompanied him to the top of the stairs. As he walked down them, the tiny flame shone upward on his pointed beard, with its slightly turned-up end, and tinged it red.

When I had had enough of getting him to tell me about Marco, I asked Paul Masson to take me to be introduced to her, instead of bringing her to the rue Jacob. He had told me in confidence that she was about twice my age and I felt it was proper for a young woman to make the journey to meet a lady who was not so young. Naturally, Paul Masson accompanied me to the rue Demours.

The boarding house where Madame Marco V. lived has been pulled down. About 1897, all that this villa retained of its former garden was a euonymus hedge, a gravel path, and a flight of five steps leading up to the door. The moment I entered the hall I felt depressed. Certain smells, not properly speaking cooking smells, but odors escaped from a kitchen, are appalling revelations of poverty. On the first floor, Paul Masson knocked on a door and the voice of Madame Marco invited us to come in. A perfect voice, neither too high nor too low, but gay and well-pitched. What a surprise! Madame Marco looked young, Madame Marco was pretty and wore a silk dress, Madame Marco had pretty eyes, almost black, and wide-open like a deer's. She had a little cleft at the tip of her nose, hair touched with henna and worn in a tight, sponge-like mass on the forehead like Queen Alexandra's and curled short on the nape in the so-called eccentric fashion of certain women painters or musicians.

She called me "little Madame," indicated that Masson had talked so much about me and my long hair, apologized, without overdoing it, for having no port and no sweets to offer me. With an unaffected gesture, she indicated the kind of place she lived in, and following the sweep of her hand, I took in the piece of plush that hid the one-legged table, the shiny upholstery of the only armchair, and the two little threadbare pancake-cushions of Algerian design on the two other chairs. There was also a certain rug on the floor. The mantelpiece served as a bookshelf.

"I've imprisoned the clock in the cupboard," said Marco. "But I swear it deserved it. Luckily, there's another cupboard I can use for my washing things. Don't you smoke?"

I shook my head, and Marco stepped into the full light to put a match to her cigarette. Then I saw that the silk dress was splitting at every fold. What little linen showed at the neck was very white. Marco and Masson smoked and chatted together; Madame Marco had grasped at once that I preferred listening to talking. I forced myself not to look at the wallpaper, with its old-gold and garnet stripes, or at the bed and its cotton damask bedspread.

"Do look at the little painting, over there," Madame Marco said to me. "It was done by my husband. It's so pretty that I've kept it. It's that little corner of Hyères, *you* remember, Masson."

And I looked enviously at Marco, Masson, and the little picture, who had all three been in Hyères. Like most young things, I knew how to withdraw into myself, far away from people talking in the same room, then return to them with a sudden mental effort, then leave them again.

Throughout my visit to Marco, thanks to her delicate tact which let me off questions and answers, I was able to come and go without stirring from my chair; I could observe or I could shut my eyes at will. I saw her just as she was and what I saw both delighted and distressed me. Though her well-set features were fine, she had what is called a coarse skin, slightly leathery and masculine, with red patches on the neck and below the ears. But, at the same time, I was ravished by the lively intelligence of her smile, by the shape of her doe's eyes and the unusually proud, yet completely unaffected carriage of her head. She looked less like a pretty woman than like one of those chiseled, clear-cut aristocratic men who adorned the eighteenth century and were not ashamed of being handsome. Masson told me later she was extraordinarily like her grandfather, the Chevalier de St.-Georges, a brilliant forebear who has no place in my story.

We became great friends, Marco and I. And after she had finished her Indian novel—it was rather like *La Femme qui tue,* as specified by the man who got paid ten sous a line—Monsieur Willy soothed Marco's sensitive feelings by asking her to do some research on condition she accepted a small fee. He even consented, when I urgently asked him to, to put in an appearance when she and I had a meal together. I had only to watch her to learn the most impeccable table manners. Monsieur Willy was always professing his love of good breeding; he found something to satisfy it in Marco's charming manners and in her turn of mind, which was urbane but inflexible and slightly caustic. Had she been born twenty years later she would, I think, have made a good journalist. When the summer came, it was Monsieur Willy who proposed taking this extremely pleasant companion, so dignified in her poverty, along with us to a mountain village in Franche-Comté. The luggage she brought with her was heartrendingly light. But at that time, I myself had very little money at my disposal, and we settled ourselves very happily on the single upper floor of a noisy inn. The wooden balcony and a wicker armchair were all that Marco needed; she never went for walks. She never wearied of the restfulness, of the vivid purple that evening shed on the mountains, of the great bowls of raspberries. She had traveled and she compared the valleys hollowed out by the twilight with other landscapes. Up there I noticed that the only mail Marco received consisted of picture postcards from Masson and "Best wishes for a good holiday," also on a postcard, from a fellow ghostwriter at the Bibliothèque Nationale.

As we sat under the balcony awning on those hot afternoons, Marco mended her underclothes. She sewed badly, but conscientiously, and I flattered my vanity by giving her pieces of advice, such as: "You're using too coarse a thread for fine needles . . . You shouldn't put blue baby ribbon in chemises, pink is much prettier in lingerie and up against the skin." It was not long before I gave her others, concerning her face powder, the color of her lipstick, a hard line she penciled around the edge of her beautifully shaped eyelids. "D'you think so? D'you think so?" she would say. My youthful authority was adamant. I took the comb, I made a charming little gap in her tight, sponge-like fringe, I proved expert at softly shadowing her eyes and putting a faint pink glow high up on her cheekbones, near her temples. But I did not know what to do with the unattractive skin of her neck or with a long shadow that hollowed her cheek. That flattering glow I put on her face transformed it so much that I promptly wiped it off again. Taking to amber powder and being far better fed than in Paris had quite an animating effect. She told me about one of her former journeys when, like a good painter's wife, she had followed her husband from Greek village to Moroccan hamlet, washed his brushes, and fried aubergines and pimentos in his oil. She promptly left off sewing to have a cigarette, blowing the smoke out through nostrils as soft as some herbivorous animal's. But she only told me the names of places, not of friends, and spoke of discomforts, not of griefs, so I dared not ask her to tell more. The mornings she spent in writing the first chapters of a new novel, at one sou a line, which was being seriously held up by lack of documentation about the early Christians.

"When I've put in lions in the arena and a golden-haired virgin abandoned to the licentious soldiers and a band of Christians escaping in a storm," said Marco, "I shall come to the end of my personal erudition. So I shall wait for the rest till I get back to Paris."

I have said: we became great friends. That is true, if friendship is confined to a rare smoothness of intercourse, preserved by studiously veiled precautions that blunt all sharp points and angles. I could only gain by imitating Marco and her "well-bred" surface manner. Moreover, she aroused not the faintest distrust in me. I felt her to be straight as a die, disgusted by anything that could cause pain, utterly remote from all feminine rivalries. But though love laughs at difference in age, friendship, especially between two women, is more acutely conscious of it. This is particularly true when friendship is just beginning, and wants, like love, to have everything all at once. The country filled me with a terrible longing for running streams, wet fields, active idleness.

"Marco, don't you think it would be marvelous if we got up early tomorrow and spent the morning under the fir trees where there are wild cyclamens and purple mushrooms?"

Marco shuddered, and clasped her little hands together.

"Oh, no! Oh, no! Go off on your own and leave me out of it, you young mountain goat."

I have forgotten to mention that, after the first week, Monsieur Willy had returned to Paris "on business." He wrote me brief notes, spicing his prose, which derived from Mallarmé and Félix Fénéon, with onomatopoeic words in Greek letters, German quotations, and English terms of endearment.

So I climbed up alone to the firs and the cyclamens. There was something intoxicating to me in the contrast between burning sun and the still-nocturnal cold of the plants growing out of a carpet of moss. More than once, I thought I would not go back for the midday meal. But I did go back, on account of Marco, who was savoring the joy of rest as if she had twenty years' accumulation of weariness to work off. She used to rest with her eyes shut, her face pale beneath her powder, looking utterly exhausted, as if convalescing from an illness. At the end of the afternoon, she would take a little walk along the road that, in passing through the village, hardly left off being a delicious, twisting forest path that rang crisply under one's feet.

You must not imagine that the other "tourists" were much more active than we were. People of my age will remember that a summer in the country, around 1897, bore no resemblance to the gadabout holidays of today. The most energetic walked as far as a pure, icy, slate-colored stream, taking with them camp stools, needlework, a novel, a picnic lunch, and useless fishing rods. On moonlit nights, girls and young men would go off in groups after dinner, which was served at seven, wander along the road, then return, stopping to wish each other good night. "Are you thinking of bicycling as far as Saut-de-Giers tomorrow?" "Oh, we're not making any definite plans. It all depends on the weather." The men wore low-cut waistcoats like cummerbunds, with two rows of buttons and sham buttonholes, under a black or cream alpaca jacket, and check caps or straw hats. The girls and the young women were plump and well nourished, dressed in white linen or ecru tussore. When they turned up their sleeves, they displayed white arms, and under their big hats, their scarlet sunburn did not reach as high as their foreheads. Venturesome families went in for what was called "bathing" and set off in the afternoons to immerse themselves at a spot where the stream broadened out, barely two and a half miles from the village. At night, around the communal dining table, the children's wet hair smelled of ponds and wild peppermint.

One day, so that I could read my mail, which was rich with two letters, an article cut out of *Art et Critique,* and some other odds and ends, Marco tactfully assumed her convalescent pose, shutting her eyes and leaning her head back against the fiber cushion of the wicker chair. She was wearing the ecru linen dressing gown that she put on to save the rest of her wardrobe when we were alone in our bedrooms or out on the wooden balcony. It was when she had on that dressing gown that she truly showed her age and the period to which she naturally belonged. Certain definite details, pathetically designed to flatter, typed her indelibly, such as a certain deliberate wave in her hair that emphasized the narrowness of her temples, a certain short fringe that would never allow itself to be combed the other way, the carriage of the chin imposed by a high, boned collar, the knees that were never parted and never crossed. Even the shabby dressing gown itself gave her away. Instead of resigning itself to the simplicity of a working garment, it was adorned with ruffles of imitation lace at the neck and wrists and a little frill around the hips.

Those tokens of a particular period of feminine fashion and behavior were just the very ones my own generation was in process of rejecting. The new "angel" hairstyle and Cléo de Mérode's smooth swathes were designed to go with a boater worn like a halo, shirt blouses in the English style, and straight skirts. Bicycles and bloomers had swept victoriously through every class. I was beginning to be crazy about starched linen collars and rough woolens imported from England. The split between the two fashions, the recent one and the very latest, was too blatantly obvious not to humiliate penniless women who delayed in adopting the one and abandoning the other. Occasionally frustrated in my own bursts of clothes-consciousness, I suffered for Marco, heroic in two worn-out dresses and two light blouses.

Slowly, I folded up my letters again, without my attention straying from the woman who was pretending to be asleep, the pretty woman of 1870 or 1875, who, out of modesty and lack of money, was giving up the attempt to follow us into 1898. In the uncompromising way of young women, I said to myself: "If I were Marco, I'd do my hair like this, I'd dress like that." Then I would make excuses for her: "But she hasn't any money. If I had more money, I'd help her."

Marco heard me folding up my letters, opened her eyes, and smiled. "Nice mail?"

"Yes . . . Marco," I said daringly, "don't you have your letters sent on here?"

"Of course I do. All the correspondence I have is what you see me get."

As I said nothing, she added, all in one burst: "As you know, I'm separated from my husband. V.'s friends, thank heaven, have remained *his* friends and not mine. I had a child, twenty years ago, and I lost him when he was hardly more than a baby. And I've never had a lover. So you see, it's quite simple."

"Never had a lover . . ." I repeated.

Marco laughed at my expression of dismay.

"Is that the thing that strikes you most? Don't be so upset! That's the thing I've thought about least. In fact I've long ago given up thinking about it at all."

My gaze wandered from her lovely eyes, rested by the pure air and the green of the chestnut groves, to the little cleft at the tip of her witty nose, to her teeth, a trifle discolored, but admirably sound and well set.

"But you're very pretty, Marco!"

"Oh!" she said gaily. "I was even a charmer, once upon a time. Otherwise V. wouldn't have married me. To be perfectly frank with you, I'm convinced that fate has spared me one great trouble, the tiresome thing that's called a temperament. No, no, all that business of blood rushing into the cheeks, upturned eyeballs, palpitating nostrils, I admit I've never experienced it and never regretted it. You do believe me, don't you?"

"Yes," I said mechanically, looking at Marco's mobile nostrils.

She laid her narrow hand on mine, with an impulsiveness that did not, I knew, come easily for her.

"A great deal of poverty, my child, and before the poverty the job of being an artist's wife in the most down-to-earth way . . . hard manual labor, next door to being a maid-of-all-work. I wonder where I should have found the time to be idle and well groomed and elegant in secret— in other words, to be someone's romantic mistress."

She sighed, ran her hand over my hair, and brushed it back from my temples.

"Why don't you show the top part of your face a little? When I was young, I did my hair like that."

As I had a horror of having my alley cat's temples exposed naked, I dodged away from the little hand and interrupted Marco, crying: "No, you don't! No, you don't! I'm going to do your hair. I've got a marvelous idea!"

Brief confidences, the amusements of two women shut away from the world, hours that were now like those in a sewing room, now like the idle ones of convalescence—I do not remember that our pleasant holiday produced any genuine intimacy. I was inclined to feel deferent toward Marco, yet, paradoxically, to set hardly any store by her opinions on life and love. When she told me she might have been a mother, I realized that our friendly relationship would never be in the least like my passionate feeling for my real mother, nor would it ever approach the comradeship I should have had with a young woman. But at that time, I did not know any girl or woman of my own age with whom I could share a reckless gaiety, a mute complicity, a vitality that over-flowed in fits of wild laughter, or with whom I could enjoy physical rivalries and rather crude pleasures that Marco's age, her delicate constitution, and her whole personality put out of her range and mine.

We talked, and we also read. I had been an insatiable reader in my childhood. Marco had educated herself. At first, I thought I could delve into Marco's well-stored mind and memory. But I noticed that she replied with a certain lassitude, and as if mistrustful of her own words.

"Marco, why are you called Marco?"

"Because my name is Léonie," she answered. "Léonie wasn't the right sort of name for V.'s wife. When I was twenty, V. made me pose in a tasseled Greek cap perched over one ear and Turkish slippers with long turned-up points. While he was painting, he used to sing this old sentimental ballad:

> *Fair Marco, do you love to dance*
> *In brilliant ballrooms, gay with flowers?*
> *Do you love, in night's dark hours,*
> *Ta ra ra, ta ra ra ra . . .*

I have forgotten the rest."

I had never heard Marco sing before. Her voice was true and thin, clear as the voice of some old men.

"They were still singing that in my youth," she said. "Painters' studios did a great deal for the propagation of bad music."

She seemed to want to preserve nothing of her past but a superficial irony. I was too young to realize what this calmness of hers implied. I had not yet learned to recognize the modesty of renunciation.

Toward the end of our summer holiday in Franche-Comté, something astonishing did, however, happen to Marco. Her husband, who was painting in the United States, sent her, through his solicitor, a check for fifteen thousand francs. The only comment she made was to say, with a laugh: "So he's actually got a solicitor now? Wonders will never cease!"

Then she returned the check and the solicitor's letter to their envelope and paid no more attention to them. But at dinner, she gave signs of being a trifle excited, and asked the waitress in a whisper if it was possible to have champagne. We had some. It was sweet and tepid and slightly corked and we only drank half the bottle between us.

Before we shut the communicating door between our rooms, as we did every night, Marco asked me a few questions. She wore an absent-minded expression as she inquired: "Do you think people will be still wearing those wide-sleeved velvet coats next winter, you know the kind I mean? And where did you get that charming hat you had in the spring —with the brim sloping like a roof? I liked it immensely—on *you*, of course."

She spoke lightly, hardly seeming to listen to my replies, and I pretended not to guess how deeply she had hidden her famished craving for decent clothes and fresh underlinen.

The next morning, she had regained control of herself.

"When all's said and done," she said, "I don't see why I should accept this sum from that . . . in other words, from my husband. If it pleases him at the moment to offer me charity, like giving alms to a beggar, that's no reason for me to accept it."

As she spoke, she kept pulling out some threads the laundress had torn in the cheap lace that edged her dressing gown. Where it fell open, it revealed a chemise that was more than humble. I lost my temper and I scolded Marco as an older woman might have chided a small girl. So much so that I felt a little ashamed, but she only laughed.

"There, there, don't get cross! Since you want me to, I'll allow myself to be kept by his lordship V. It's certainly my turn."

I put my cheek against Marco's cheek. We stayed watching the harsh, reddish sun reaching the zenith and drinking up all the shadows that divided the mountains. The bend of the river quivered in the distance. Marco sighed.

"Would it be very expensive, a pretty little corset belt all made of ribbon, with rococo roses on the ends of the suspenders?"

The return to Paris drove Marco back to her novelette. Once again I saw her hat with the three blue thistles, her coat and skirt whose black was faded and pallid, her dark gray gloves, and her schoolgirl satchel of cardboard masquerading as leather. Before thinking of her personal elegance, she wanted to move to another place. She took a year's lease of a furnished flat; two rooms and a place where she could wash, plus a sort of cupboard-kitchen, on the ground floor. It was dark there in broad daylight but the red and white cretonne curtains and bedspread were not too hopelessly shabby. Marco nourished herself at midday in a little restaurant near the library and had tea and bread-and-butter at home at night except when I managed to keep her at my flat for a meal at which stuffed olives and rollmops replaced soup and roast meat. Sometimes Paul Masson brought along an excellent chocolate "Quillet" from Quillet's, the cake shop in the rue de Buci.

Completely resigned to her task, Marco had so far acquired nothing except, as October turned out rainy, a kind of rubberized hooded cloak that smelled of asphalt. One day she arrived, her eyes looking anxious and guilty.

"There," she said bravely, "I've come to be scolded. I think I bought this coat in too much of a hurry. I've got the feeling that . . . that it's not quite right."

I was amused by her being as shy as if she were my junior, but I stopped laughing when I had a good look at the coat. An unerring instinct led Marco, so discriminating in other ways, to choose bad material, deplorable cut, fussy braid.

The very next day, I took time off to go out with her and choose a wardrobe for her. Neither she nor I could aspire to the great dress houses, but I had the pleasure of seeing Marco looking slim and years younger in a dark tailor-made and in a navy serge dress with a white front. With the straight little caracul topcoat, two hats, and some underclothes, the bill, if you please, came to fifteen hundred francs: you can see that I was ruthless with the funds sent by the painter V.

I might well have had something to say against Marco's hairstyle. But just that very season, there was a changeover to shorter hair and a different way of doing it, so that Marco was able to look as if she was ahead of fashion. In this I sincerely envied her, for whether I twisted it around my head "à la Ceres" or let it hang to my skirt hem—"like a well cord" as Jules Renard said—my long hair blighted my existence.

At this point, the memory of a certain evening obtrudes itself. Monsieur Willy had gone out on business somewhere, leaving Marco, Paul Masson, and myself alone together after dinner. When the three of us were on our own, we automatically became clandestinely merry, slightly childish, and, as it were, reassured. Masson would sometimes read aloud the serial in a daily paper, a novelette inexhaustibly rich in haughty titled ladies, fancy-dress balls in winter gardens, chaises dashing along "at a triple gallop" drawn by pure-bred steeds, maidens pale but resolute, exposed to a thousand perils. And we used to laugh wholeheartedly.

"Ah!" Marco would sigh, "I shall never be able to do as well as that. In the novelette world, I shall never be more than a little amateur."

"Little amateur," said Masson one night, "here's just what you want. I've culled it from the Agony Column: 'Man of letters bearing well-known name would be willing to assist young writers both sexes in early stages career.'"

"Both sexes!" said Marco. "Go on, Masson! I've only got one sex and, even then, I think I'm exaggerating by half."

"Very well, I will go on," said Masson. "I will go on to lieutenant (regular army), garrisoned near Paris, warmhearted, cultured, wishes to maintain correspondence with intelligent, affectionate woman. Very good, but apparently, this soldier does not wish to maintain anything but correspondence. Nevertheless, do we write to him? Let us write. The best letter wins a box of Gianduja Kohler—the nutty kind."

"If it's a big box," I said, "I'm quite willing to compete. What about you, Marco?"

With her cleft nose bent over a scribbling block, Marco was writing already. Masson gave birth to twenty lines in which sly obscenity vied with humor. I stopped after the first page, out of laziness. But how charming Marco's letter was!

"First prize!" I exclaimed.

"Pearls before . . ." muttered Masson. "Do we send it? Poste Restante, Alex 2, Box 59. Give it to me. I'll see that it goes."

"After all, I'm not risking anything," said Marco.

When our diversions were over, she slipped on her mackintosh again and put on her narrow hat in front of the mirror. It was a hat I had chosen, which made her head look very small and her eyes very large under its turned-down brim.

"Look at her!" she exclaimed. "Look at her, the middle-aged lady who debauches warmhearted and cultured lieutenants!"

With the little oil lamp in her hand, she preceded Paul Masson.

"I shan't see you at all this week," she told me. "I've got two pieces of homework to do: the chariot race and the Christians in the lions' pit."

"Haven't I already read something of the kind somewhere?" put in Masson.

"I sincerely hope you have," retorted Marco. "If it hadn't been done over and over again, where should I get my documentation?"

The following week, Masson bought a copy of the paper and with his hard, corrugated nail pointed out three lines in the Agony Column: "Alex 2 implores author delicious letter beginning 'What presumption' to give address. Secrecy scrupulously honored."

"Marco," he said, "you've won not only the box of Gianduja but also a booby prize in the shape of a first-class mug."

Marco shrugged her shoulders.

"It's cruel, what you've made me do. He's sure to think he's been made fun of, poor boy."

Masson screwed up his eyes to their smallest and most inquisitorial.

"Sorry for him already, dear?"

These memories are distant, but precise. They rise out of the fog that inevitably drowns the long days of that particular time, the monotonous amusements of dress rehearsals and suppers at Pousset's, my alternations between animal gaiety and confused unhappiness, the split in my nature between a wild, frightened creature and one with a vast capacity for illusion. But it is a fog that leaves the faces of my friends intact and shining clear.

It was also on a rainy night, in late October or early November, that Marco came to keep me company one night; I remember the anthracite smell of the waterproof cape. She kissed me. Her soft nose was wet, she sighed with pleasure at the sight of the glowing stove. She opened her satchel.

"Here, read this," she said. "Don't you think he's got a charming turn of phrase, this . . . this ruffianly soldier?"

If, after reading it, I had allowed myself a criticism, I should have said: too charming. A letter worked over and recopied; one draft, two drafts thrown into the wastepaper basket. The letter of a shy man, with a touch of the poet, like everyone else.

"Marco, you mean you actually wrote to him?"

The virtuous Marco laughed in my face.

"One can't hide anything from you, charming daughter of Monsieur de La Palisse! Written? Written more than once, even! Crime gives me an appetite. You haven't got a cake? Or an apple?"

While she nibbled delicately, I showed off my ideas on the subject of graphology.

"Look, Marco, how carefully your 'ruffianly soldier' has covered up a word he's begun so as to make it illegible. Sign of gumption, also of touchiness. The writer, as Crépieux-Jamin says, doesn't like people to laugh at him."

Marco agreed, absentmindedly. I noticed she was looking pretty and animated. She studied herself in the glass, clenching her teeth and parting her lips, a grimace few women can resist making in front of a mirror when they have white teeth.

"Whatever's the name of that toothpaste that reddens the gums, Colette?"

"Cherry something or other."

"Thanks, I've got it now. Cherry Dentifrice. Will you do me a favor? Don't tell Paul Masson about my epistolary escapades. He'd never stop teasing me. I shan't keep up my relations with the regular army long enough to make myself ridiculous. Oh, I forgot to tell you. My husband has sent me another fifteen thousand francs."

"Mercy me, be I a-hearing right? as they say where I come from. And you just simply *forgot* that bit of news?"

"Yes, really," said Marco. "I just forgot."

She raised her eyebrows with an air of surprise to remind me delicately that money is always a subject of minor importance.

From that moment, it seemed to me that everything moved very fast for Marco. Perhaps that was due to distance. One of my moves—the first—took me from the rue Jacob to the top of the rue de Courcelles, from a dark little cubbyhole to a studio whose great window let in cold, heat, and an excess of light. I wanted to show my sophistication, to satisfy my newly born—and modest—cravings for luxury: I bought white goatskins, and a folding shower bath from Chaboche's.

Marco, who felt at home in dim rooms and in the atmosphere of the Left Bank and of libraries, blinked her lovely eyes under the studio skylight, stared at the white divans that suggested polar bears, and did not like the new way I did my hair. I wore it piled up above my forehead and twisted into a high chignon; this new "helmet" fashion had swept the hair up from the most modest and retiring napes.

Such a minor domestic upheaval would not have been worth mentioning, did it not make it understandable that, for some time, I only had rapid glimpses of Marco. My pictures of her succeeded each other jerkily like the pictures in those children's books that, as you turn the pages fast, give the illusion of continuous movement. When she brought me the second letter from the romantic lieutenant, I had crossed the intervening gulf. As Marco walked into my new, light flat, I saw that she was definitely prettier than she had been the year before. The slender foot she thrust out below the hem of her skirt rejoiced in the kind of shoe it deserved. Through the veil stretched taut over the little cleft at the tip of her nose she stared, now at her gloved hand, now at each unknown room, but she seemed to see neither the one nor the other clearly. With bright patience she endured my arranging and re-arranging the curtains: she admired the folding shower bath, which, when erected, vaguely suggested a vertical coffin.

She was so patient and so absentminded that in the end I noticed it and asked her crudely: "By the way, Marco, how's the ruffianly soldier?"

Her eyes, softened by makeup and shortsightedness, looked into mine.

"As it happens, he's very well. His letters are charming—decidedly so."

"Decidedly so? How many have you had?"

"Three in all. I'm beginning to think it's enough. Don't you agree?"

"No, since they're charming—and they amuse you."

"I don't care for the atmosphere of the *poste restante* . . . It's a horrid hole. Everyone there has a guilty look. Here, if you're interested . . ."

She threw a letter into my lap; it had been there ready all the time, folded up in her gloved hand. I read it rather slowly, I was so pre-occupied with its serious tone, devoid of the faintest trace of humor.

"What a remarkable lieutenant you've come across, Marco! I'm sure that if he weren't restrained by his shyness . . ."

"His shyness?" protested Marco. "He's already got to the point of hoping that we shall exchange less impersonal letters! What cheek! For a shy man . . ."

She broke off to raise her veil which was overheating her coarse-grained skin and flushing up those uneven red patches on her cheeks. But nowadays she knew how to apply her powder cleverly, how to brighten the color of her mouth. Instead of a discouraged woman of forty-five, I saw before me a smart woman of forty, her chin held high above the boned collar that hid the secrets of the neck. Once again, because of her very beautiful eyes, I forgot the deterioration of all the rest of her face and sighed inwardly: "What a pity . . ."

Our respective moves took us away from our old surroundings and I did not see Marco quite so often. But she was very much in my mind. The polarity of affection between two women friends that gives one authority and the other pleasure in being advised turned me into a peremptory young guide. I decided that Marco ought to wear shorter skirts and more nipped-in waistlines. I sternly rejected braid, which made her look old, colors that dated her, and, most of all, certain hats that, when Marco put them on, mysteriously sentenced her beyond hope of appeal. She allowed herself to be persuaded, though she would hesitate for a moment: "You think so? You're quite sure?" and glance at me out of the corner of her beautiful eye.

We liked meeting each other in a little tearoom at the corner of the rue de l'Échelle and the rue d'Argenteuil, a warm, poky "British," saturated with the bitter smell of Ceylon tea. We "partook of tea," like other sweet-toothed ladies of those far-off days, and hot buttered toast followed by quantities of cakes. I liked my tea very black, with a thick white layer of cream and plenty of sugar. I believed I was learning English when I asked the waitress: "Edith, please, a little more milk, and butter."

It was at the little "British" that I perceived such a change in Marco that I could not have been more startled if, since our last meeting, she had dyed her hair peroxide or taken to drugs. I feared some danger, I imagined that the wretch of a husband had frightened her into his clutches again. But if she was frightened, she would not have had that blank flickering gaze that wandered from the table to the walls and was profoundly indifferent to everything it glanced at.

"Marco? Marco?"

"Darling?"

"Marco, what on earth's happened? Have other treasure galleons arrived? Or what?"

She smiled at me as if I were a stranger.

"Galleons? Oh, no."

She emptied her cup in one gulp and said almost in a whisper: "Oh, how stupid of me, I've burned myself."

Consciousness and affection slowly returned to her gaze. She saw that mine was astonished and she blushed, clumsily and unevenly, as she always did.

"Forgive me," she said, laying her little hand on mine.

She sighed and relaxed.

"Oh!" she said. "What luck there isn't anyone here. I'm a little . . . how can I put it? . . . queasy."

"More tea? Drink it very hot."

"No, no. I think it's that glass of port I had before I came here. No, nothing, thanks."

She leaned back in her chair and closed her eyes. She was wearing her newest suit, a little oval brooch of the "family heirloom" type was pinned at the base of the high boned collar of her cream blouse. The next moment she had revived and was completely herself, consulting the mirror in her new handbag and feverishly anticipating my questions.

"Ah, I'm better now! It was that port, I'm sure it was. Yes, my dear, port! And in the company of Lieutenant Alexis Trallard, son of General Trallard."

"Ah!" I exclaimed with relief, "is *that* all? You quite frightened me. So you've actually seen the ruffianly soldier? What's he like? Is he like his letters? Does he stammer? Has he got a lisp? Is he bald? Has he a port-wine mark on his nose?"

These and similar idiotic suggestions were intended to make Marco laugh. But she listened to me with a dreamy, refined expression as she nibbled at a piece of buttered toast that had gone cold.

"My dear," she said at last. "If you'll let me get a word in edgewise, I might inform you that Lieutenant Trallard is neither an invalid nor a monster. Incidentally, I've known this ever since last week, because he enclosed a photograph in one of his letters."

She took my hand.

"Don't be cross. I didn't dare mention it to you. I was afraid."

"Afraid of what?"

"Of you, darling, of being teased a little. And . . . well . . . just simply afraid!"

"But why *afraid?*"

She made an apologetic gesture of ignorance, clutching her arms against her breast.

"Here's the Object," she said, opening her handbag. "Of course, it's a very bad snapshot."

"He's much better looking than the photo . . . of course?"

"Better looking . . . good heavens, he's totally *different*. Especially his expression."

As I bent over the photograph, she bent over it too, as if to protect it from too harsh a judgment.

"Lieutenant Trallard hasn't got that shadow like a saber cut on his cheek. Besides, his nose isn't so long. He's got light brown hair and his mustache is almost golden.

After a silence, Marco added shyly: "He's tall."

I realized it was my turn to say something.

"But he's very good-looking! But he looks exactly as a lieutenant should! But what an enchanting story, Marco! And his eyes? What are his eyes like?"

"Light brown like his hair," said Marco eagerly.

She pulled herself together.

"I mean, that was my general impression. I didn't look very closely."

I hid my astonishment at being confronted with a Marco whose words, whose embarrassment, whose naïveté surpassed the reactions of the greenest girl to being stood a glass of port by a lieutenant. I could never have believed that this middle-aged married woman, inured to living among bohemians, was at heart a timorous novice. I restrained myself from letting Marco see, but I think she guessed my thoughts, for she tried to turn her encounter, her "queasiness," and her lieutenant into a joke. I helped her as best I could.

"And when are you going to see Lieutenant Trallard again, Marco?"

"Not for a good while, I think."

"Why?"

"Why, because he must be left to wear his nerves to shreds in suspense! Left to simmer!" declared Marco, raising a learned forefinger. "Simmer! That's my principle!"

We laughed at last; laughed a great deal and rather idiotically. That hour seems to me, in retrospect, like the last halt, the last landing on which my friend Marco stopped to regain her breath. During the days that followed I have a vision of myself writing (I did not sign my work either) on the thin, crackly American paper I liked best of all, and Marco was busy working too, at one sou a line. One afternoon, she came to see me again.

"Good news of the ruffianly soldier, Marco?"

She archly indicated "*Yes*" with her chin and her eyes, because Monsieur Willy was on the other side of the glass-topped door. She submitted a sample of dress material which she would not dream of buying without my approval. She was buoyant and I thought that, like a sensible woman, she had reduced Lieutenant Alexis Trallard to his proper status. But when we were all alone in my bedroom, that refuge hung with rush matting that smelled of damp reeds, she held out a letter, without saying a word, and without saying a word, I read it and gave it back to her. For the accents of love inspire only silence and the letter I had read was full of love. Full of serious, vernal love. Why did one question, the very one I should have repressed, escape me? I asked— thinking of the freshness of the words I had just read, of the respect that permeated them—I asked indiscreetly: "How old is he?"

Marco put her two hands over her face, gave a sudden sob, and whispered: "Oh, heavens! It's appalling!"

Almost at once, she mastered herself, uncovered her face, and chided herself in a harsh voice: "Stop this nonsense. I'm dining with him tonight."

She was about to wipe her wet eyes but I stopped her.

"Let me do it, Marco."

With my two thumbs, I raised her upper eyelids so that the two tears about to fall should be reabsorbed and not smudge the mascara on her lashes by wetting them.

"There! Wait, I haven't finished."

I retouched all her features. Her mouth was trembling a little. She submitted patiently, sighing as if I were dressing a wound. To complete everything, I filled the puff in her handbag with a rosier shade of powder. Neither of us uttered a word meanwhile.

"Whatever happens," I told her, "don't cry. At all costs, don't let yourself give way to tears."

She jibbed at this, and laughed.

"All the same, we haven't got to the scene of the final parting yet!"

I took her over to the best-lighted looking glass. At the sight of her reflection, the corners of Marco's mouth quivered a little.

"Satisfied with the effect, Marco?"

"Too good to be true."

"Can't ever be too good. You'll tell me what happened? When?"

"As soon as I know myself," said Marco.

Two days later, she returned, in spite of stormy, almost warm weather that rattled the cowls on the chimney pots and beat back the smoke and fumes of the slow-combustion stove.

"Outdoors in this tempest, Marco?"

"It doesn't worry me a bit, I've got a four-wheeler waiting down there."

"Wouldn't you rather dine here with me?"

"I can't," she said, averting her head.

"Right. But you can send the growler away. It's only half past six, you've plenty of time."

"No, I haven't time. How does my face look?"

"Quite all right. In fact, very nice."

"Yes, but . . . Quick, be an angel! Do what you did for me the day before yesterday. And then, what's the best thing to receive Alex at home in? Outdoor clothes, don't you think? Anyway, I haven't got an indoor frock that would really do."

"Marco, you know just as well as I do . . ."

"No," she broke in, "I don't know. You might as well tell me I know India because I've written a novelette that takes place in the Punjab. Look, he's sent a kind of emergency supply around to my place—a cold chicken in aspic, champagne, some fruit. He says that, like me, he has a horror of restaurants. Ah, now I think of it, I *ought* to have . . ."

She pressed her hand to her forehead, under her fringe.

"I *ought* to have bought that black dress last Saturday—the one I saw in the secondhand shop. Just my size, with a Liberty silk skirt and a lace top. Tell me, could you possibly lend me some very fine stockings? I've left it too late now to . . ."

"Yes, yes, of course."

"Thank you. Don't you think a flower to brighten up my dress? No, *not* a flower on the bodice. Is it true that iris is a scent that's gone out of fashion? I'm sure I had heaps of other things to ask you . . . heaps of things."

Though she was in the shelter of my room, sitting by the roaring stove, Marco gave me the impression of a woman battling with the wind and the rain that lashed the glass panes. I seemed to be watching Marco set off on some kind of journey, embarking like an emigrant. It was as if I could see a flapping cape blowing around her, a plaid scarf streaming in the wind.

Besieged, soon to be invaded. There was no doubt in my mind that an attack was being launched against the most defenseless of creatures. Silent, as if we were committing a crime, we hurried through our beauty operations. Marco attempted to laugh.

"We're trampling the most rigorously established customs underfoot. Normally, it's the oldest witch who washes and decks the youngest for the Sabbath."

"Ssh, Marco, keep still—I've just about finished."

I rolled up the pair of silk stockings in a piece of paper, along with a little bottle of yellow Chartreuse.

"Have you got any cigarettes at home?"

"Yes. Whatever am I saying? No. But *he'll* have some on him, he smokes Egyptian ones."

"I'll put four amusing little napkins in the parcel, it'll make it more like a doll's dinner party. Would you like the cloth too?"

"No, thanks. I've got an embroidered one I bought ages ago in Brussels."

We were talking in low, rapid whispers, without ever smiling. In the doorway, Marco turned around to give me a long, distracted look out of moist, made-up eyes, a look in which I could read nothing resembling joy. My thoughts followed her in the cab that was carrying her through the dark and the rain, over the puddle-drenched road where the wind blew miniature squalls around the lampposts. I wanted to open the window to watch her drive away but the whole tempestuous night burst into the studio and I shut it again on this traveler who was setting off on a dangerous voyage, with no ballast but a pair of silk stockings, some pink makeup, some fruit, and a bottle of champagne.

Lieutenant Trallard was still only relatively real to me, although I had seen his photograph. A very French face, a rather long nose, a well-chiseled forehead, hair *en brosse* and the indispensable mustache. But the picture of Marco blotted out his—Marco all anxious apprehension, her beauty enhanced by my tricks, and breathing fast, as a deer pants when it hears the hooves and clamor of the distant hunt. I listened to the wind and rain and I reckoned up her chances of crossing the sea and reaching port in safety. "She was very pretty tonight. Provided her lamp with the pleated shade gives a becoming light. This young man preoccupies her, flatters her, peoples her solitude, in a word, rejuvenates her."

A gust of bad weather beat furiously against the pane. A little black snake that oozed from the bottom of the window began to creep slowly along. From this, I realized that the window did not shut properly and the water was beginning to soak the carpet. I went off to seek floor cloths and the aid of Maria, the girl from Aveyron who was my servant at that time. On my way, I opened the door to Masson, who had just rung three times.

While he was divesting himself of a limp mackintosh cape that fell dripping on the tiled floor, like a basketful of eels, I exclaimed: "Did you run into Marco? She's just this minute gone downstairs. She was so sorry not to see you."

A lie must give off a smell that is apparent to people with sensitive nostrils. Paul Masson sniffed the air in my direction, curtly wagged his short beard, and went off to join Monsieur Willy in his white study that, with its brief curtains, beaded moldings, and small windowpanes, vaguely resembled a converted cake shop.

After that, everything progressed fast for Marco. Nevertheless she came back, after that stormy night, but she made me no confidences. It is true that a third person prevented them. That particular day, my impatience to know was restrained by the fear that her confidence might yield something that would have slightly horrified me; there was an indefinable air of furtiveness and guilt about her whole person. At least, that is what I *think* I remember. My memories, after that, are much more definite. How could I have forgotten that Marco underwent a magical transformation, the kind of belated, embarrassing puberty that deceives no one? She reacted violently to the slightest stimulus. A thimbleful of Frontignac set her cheeks and her eyes ablaze. She laughed for no reason, stared blankly into space, was incessantly resorting to her powder puff and her mirror. Everything was going at a great rate. I could not long put off the "Well, Marco?" she must be waiting for.

One clear, biting winter night, Marco was with me. I was stoking up the stove. She kept her gaze fixed on its mica window and did not speak.

"Are you warm enough in your little flat, Marco? Does the coal grate give enough heat?"

She smiled vaguely, as if at a deaf person, and did not answer. So I said at last: "Well, Marco? Contented? Happy?"

It was the last, the most important word, I think, that she pushed away with her hand.

"I did not believe," she said, very low, "that such a thing could exist."

"What thing? Happiness?"

She flushed here and there, in dark, fiery patches. I asked her—it was my turn to be naïve: "Then why don't you look more pleased?"

"Can one rejoice over something terrible, something that's so . . . so like an evil spell?"

I secretly permitted myself the thought that to use such a grim and weighty expression was, as the saying goes, to clap a very large hat on a very small head, and I waited for her next words. But none came. At this point, there was a brief period of silence. I saw nothing wrong in Marco's keeping quiet about her love affair: it was rather the love affair itself that I resented. I thought—unjust as I was and unmindful of her past—that she had been very quick to reward a casual acquaintance, even if he were an officer, a general's son, and had light brown hair into the bargain.

The period of reserve was followed by the season of unrestricted joy. Happiness, once accepted, is seldom reticent; Marco's, as it took firm root, was not very vocal but expressed itself in the usual boring way. I knew that, like every other woman, she had met a man "absolutely unlike anyone else" and that everything he did was a source of abundant delight to his dazzled mistress. I was not allowed to remain ignorant that Alexis possessed a "lofty soul" in addition to a "cast-iron body." Marco did not, thank heaven, belong to that tribe who boastfully whisper precise details—the sort of female I call a Madame-how-many-times. Nevertheless, by looking confused or by spasms of perturbed reticence, she had a mute way of conveying things I would gladly have been dispensed from knowing.

This virtuous victim of belated love and suddenly awakened sensuality did not submit all at once to blissful immolation. But she could not escape the usual snares of her new condition, the most unavoidable of which is eloquence, both of speech and gesture.

The first few weeks made her thin and dry-lipped, with feverish, glittering eyes. "A Rops!" Paul Masson said behind her back. "Madame Dracula," said Monsieur Willy, going one better. "What the devil can our worthy Marco be up to, to make her look like that?"

Masson screwed up his little eyes and shrugged one shoulder. "Nothing," he said coldly. "These phenomena belong to neurotic simulation, like imaginary pregnancy. Probably, like many women, our worthy Marco imagines she is the bride of Satan. It's the phase of infernal joys."

I thought it detestable that either of her two friends should call Madame V. "our worthy Marco." Nor was I any more favorably impressed by the icily critical comments of these two disillusioned men, especially on anything concerning friendship, esteem, or love.

Then Marco's face became irradiated with a great serenity. As she regained her calm, she gradually lost the fevered glitter of a lost soul and put on a little flesh. Her skin seemed smoother, she had lost the breathlessness that betrayed her nervousness and her haste. Her slightly increased weight slowed down her walk and movements; she smoked cigarettes lazily.

"New phase," announced Masson. "Now she looks like the Marco of the old days, when she'd just got married to V. It's the phase of the odalisque."

I now come to a period when, because I was going about more and was also more loaded up with work, I saw Marco only at intervals. I dared not drop in on Marco without warning, for I dreaded I might encounter Lieutenant Trallard, only too literally in undress, in the minute flat that had nothing in the way of an entrance hall. What with teas put off and appointments broken, fate kept us apart, till at last it brought us together again in my studio, on a lovely June day that blew warm and cool breezes through the open window.

Marco smelled delicious. Marco was wearing a brand-new black dress with white stripes, Marco was all smiles. Her romantic love affair had already been going on for eight months. She looked so much fatter to me that the proud carriage of her head no longer preserved her chin line and her waist, visibly compressed, no longer moved flexibly inside the petersham belt, as it had done last year.

"Congratulations, Marco! You look marvelously well!"

Her long deer's eyes looked uneasy.

"You think I've got plump? Not too plump, I hope?"

She lowered her lids and smiled mysteriously. "A little extra flesh does make one's breasts so pretty."

I was not used to that kind of remark from her and I was the one who felt embarrassed, frankly, as embarrassed as if Marco—that very Marco who used to barricade herself in her room at the country inn, crying: "Don't come in, I'll slip on my dressing gown!"—had deliberately stripped naked in the middle of my studio drawing room.

The next second, I told myself I was being ungenerous and unfriendly, that I ought to rejoice wholeheartedly in Marco's happiness. To prove my goodwill, I said gaily: "I bet, one of these days, when I open the door to you, I'll find Lieutenant Trallard in your wake! I'm too magnanimous to refuse him a cup of tea and a slice of bread and cheese, Marco. So why not bring him along next time?"

Marco gave me a sharp look that was like a total stranger's. Quickly as she averted it, I could not miss the virulent, suspicious glance that swept over me, over my smile and my long hair, over everything that youth lavishes on a face and body of twenty-five.

"No," she said.

She recovered herself and looked back at me with her usual doe-like gentleness.

"It's too soon," she said gracefully. "Let's wait till the 'ruffianly soldier' deserves such an honor!"

But I remained appalled at having caught, in one look, a glimpse of a primitive female animal, black with suspicion, hostility, and possessive passion. For the first time, we were both aware of the difference in our ages as something sharp, cruel, and irremediable. It was the difference in age, revealed in the depths of a beautiful velvety eye, that falsified our relationship and disrupted our old bond. When I saw Marco again after the "day of the look" and I inquired after Lieutenant Trallard, the new-style Marco, plump, white, calm—almost matriarchal —answered me in a tone of false modesty, the tone of a greedy and sated proprietress. I stared at her, stupefied, looking for all the things of which voracious, unhoped-for love had robbed her. I looked in vain for her elegant thinness, for the firmness of her slender waist, for her rather bony, well-defined chin, for the deep hollows in which the velvety, almost black eyes used to shelter . . . Realizing that I was registering the change in her, she renounced the dignity of a well-fed sultana and became uneasy.

"What can I do about it? I'm putting on weight."

"It's only temporary," I said. "Do you eat a lot?"

She shrugged her thickened shoulders.

"I don't know. Yes. I *am* more greedy, that's a fact, than . . . than before. But I've often seen you eat enormously and *you* don't put on weight!"

To exonerate myself, I made a gesture to signify that I couldn't help this. Marco stood up, planted herself in front of the mirror, clutched her waist tightly with both hands, and kneaded it.

"Last year, when I did that, I could feel myself positively melting away between my two hands."

"Last year you weren't happy, Marco."

"Oh, so that's it!" she said bitterly.

She was studying her reflection at close quarters as if she were alone. The addition of some few pounds had turned her into another woman, or rather another type of woman. The flesh was awkwardly distributed on her lightly built frame. "She's got a behind like a cobbler's," I thought. In my part of the country, they say that the cobbler's behind gets flat from sitting so much but develops a square shape. "And, in addition, breasts like jellyfish, very broad and decidedly flabby." For even if she is fond of her, a woman always judges another woman harshly.

Marco turned around abruptly.

"What was that?" she asked.

"I didn't say anything, Marco."

"Sorry. I thought you did."

"If you really want to fight against a tendency to put on flesh . . ."

"*Tendency*," Marco echoed, between her teeth. "Tendency is putting it mildly."

". . . why don't you try Swedish gymnastics? People are talking a lot about them."

She interrupted me with a gesture of intolerant refusal.

"Or else cut out breakfast? In the morning don't have anything but unsweetened lemon juice in a glass of water."

"But I'm hungry in the morning!" cried Marco. "Everything's different, do realize that! I'm hungry, I wake up thinking of fresh butter —and thick cream—and coffee, and ham. I think that, after breakfast, there'll be luncheon to follow and I think of . . . of what will come after luncheon, the thing that kindles this hunger again—and all these cravings I have now that are so terribly fierce."

Dropping her hands that had been harshly pummeling her waist and bosom, she challenged me in the same querulous tone: "Candidly, could I ever have foreseen . . ."

Her voice changed. "He actually says that I make him so happy."

I could not resist putting my arms around her neck.

"Marco, don't worry about so many things! What you've just said explains everything, justifies everything. Be happy, Marco, make him happy and let everything else go hang!"

We kissed each other. She went away reassured, swaying on those unfamiliar broadened hips. Soon afterward, Monsieur Willy and I went off to Bayreuth and I did not fail to send Marco a great many picture postcards, covered with Wagnerian emblems entwined with leitmotifs. As soon as I returned, I asked Marco to meet me at our tearoom. She had not grown any thinner nor did she look any younger. Where others develop curves and rotundity, Marco's fleshiness tended to be square.

"And you haven't been away from Paris at all, Marco? Nothing's changed?"

"Nothing, thank God."

She touched the wood of the little table with the tip of her finger to avert ill luck. I needed nothing but that gesture to tell me that Marco still belonged, body and soul, to Lieutenant Trallard. Another, no less eloquent sign was that Marco only asked me questions of pure politeness about my stay in Bayreuth—moreover, I guessed she did not even listen to my answers.

She blushed when I asked her, in my turn: "What about work, Marco? Any novelettes on the stocks for next season?"

"Oh, nothing much," she said in a bored voice. "A publisher wants a novel for children of eight to fourteen. As if that was up my street! Anyway . . ."

A gentle, cowlike expression passed over her face like a cloud and she closed her eyes.

"Anyway, I feel so lazy . . . oh, *so* lazy!"

When Masson, informed of our return, announced himself with his usual three rings, he hastened to tell me he knew "all" from Marco's own lips. To my surprise, he spoke favorably of Lieutenant Trallard. He did not take the line that he was a tenth-rate gigolo or a drunkard destined to premature baldness or a garrison-town Casanova. On the other hand, I thought he was decidedly harsh about Marco and even more cold than harsh.

"But, come now, Paul, what are you blaming Marco for in this affair?"

"Pooh! nothing," said Paul Masson.

"And they're madly happy together, you know!"

"Madly strikes me as no exaggeration."

He gave a quiet little laugh that was echoed by Monsieur Willy. Detestable laughs that made fun of Marco and myself, and were accompanied by blunt opinions and pessimistic forecasts, formulated with complete assurance and indifference, as if the romance that lit up Marco's Indian summer were no more than some stale bit of gossip.

"Physically," Paul Masson said, "Marco *had* reached the phase known as the brewer's dray horse. When a gazelle turns into a brood mare, it's a bad lookout for her. Lieutenant Trallard was perfectly right. It was Marco who compromised Lieutenant Trallard."

"Compromised? You're crazy, Masson! Honestly, the things you say."

"My dear girl, a child of three would tell you, as I do, that Marco's first, most urgent duty was to remain slender, charming, elusive, a twilight creature beaded with raindrops, not to be bursting with health and frightening people in the streets by shouting: 'I've done it! I've done it! I've . . .'"

"Masson!"

My blood was boiling; I flogged Masson with my rope of hair. I understood nothing of that curious kind of severity only men display toward an innocence peculiar to women. I listened to the judgments of these two on the "Marco case," judgments that admitted not one extenuating circumstance, as if they were lecturing on higher mathematics.

"She *wasn't* up to it," decreed one of them. "She fondly supposed that being the forty-six-year-old mistress of a young man of twenty-five was a delightful adventure."

"Whereas it's a profession," said the other.

"Or rather, a highly skilled sport."

"No. Sport is an unpaid job. But she wouldn't even understand that her one and only hope is to break it off."

I had not yet become inured to the mixture of affected cynicism and literary paradox by which, around 1900, intelligent, bitter, frustrated men maintained their self-esteem.

September lay over Paris, a September of fine, dry days and crimson sunsets. I sulked over being in town and over my husband's decision to cut short my summer holiday. One day, I received an express letter that I stared at in surprise, for I did not know Marco's writing well. The handwriting was regular but the spaces between the letters betrayed emotional agitation. She wanted to talk to me. I was in, waiting for her, at the hour when the red light from the setting sun tinged the yellow-curtained windowpane with a vinous flush. I was pleased to see there was no outward trace of disturbance about her. As if there were no other possible subject of conversation, Marco announced at once: "Just imagine, Alex is going off on a mission."

"On a mission? Where to?"

"Morocco."

"When?"

"Almost at once. Perhaps in a week's time. Orders from the War Office."

"And there's no way out of it?"

"His father, General Trallard . . . yes, if his father intervened personally, he might be able . . . But he thinks this mission—incidentally, it's quite a dangerous one—is a great honor. So . . ."

She made a little, abortive gesture and fell silent, staring into vacancy. Her heavy body, her full, pale cheeks and stricken eyes made her look like a tragedy queen.

"Does a mission take a long time, Marco?"

"I don't know—I haven't the faintest idea. He talks of three or four months, possibly five."

"Now, now, Marco," I said gaily. "What's three or four months? You'll wait for him, that's all."

She did not seem to hear me. She seemed to be attentively studying a purple-ink cleaner's mark on the inside of her glove.

"Marco," I risked, "couldn't you go over there with him and live in the same district?"

The moment I spoke, I regretted it. Marco, with trunks full of dresses, Marco as the European favorite, or else Marco as the native wife going in for silver bangles, couscous, and fringed scarves. The pictures my imagination conjured up made me afraid—afraid for Marco.

"Of course," I hastily added, "that wouldn't be practical."

Night was falling and I got up to give us some light, but Marco restrained me.

"Wait," she said. "There's something else. I'd rather not talk to you about it here. Will you come to my place tomorrow? I've got some good China tea and some little salted cakes from the boulevard Malesherbes."

"Of course I'd love to, Marco! But . . ."

"I'm not expecting anyone tomorrow. Do come, you might be able to do me a great service. Don't put on the light, the light in the hall is all I need."

Marco's little "furnished suite" had changed too. An arrangement of curtains on a wooden frame behind the entrance door provided it with a substitute for a hall. The brass bedstead had become a divan-bed and various new pieces of furniture struck me quite favorably, as also did some Oriental rugs. A garlanded Venetian glass over the mantelpiece reflected some red and white dahlias. In the scent that pervaded it, I recognized Marco's married, if I can use the expression, to another, full-bodied fragrance.

The second, smaller room served as a bathroom; I caught sight of a zinc bathtub and a kind of shower arrangement fixed to the ceiling. I made, as I came in, some obvious remark such as: "How nice you've made it here, Marco!"

The stormy, precociously cold September day did not penetrate into this confined dwelling, whose thick walls and closed windows kept the air perfectly still. Marco was already busy getting tea, setting out our two cups and our two plates. "She's not expecting anyone," I thought. She offered me a saucer full of greengages while she warmed the teapot.

"What beautiful little hands you have, Marco!"

She suddenly knocked over a cup, as if the least unexpected sound upset the conscious control of her movements. We went through that pretense of a meal that covers and puts off the embarrassment of explanations, rifts, and silences; nevertheless, we reached the moment when Marco had to say what she wanted to say. It was indeed high time; I could see she was almost at the end of her tether. We instinctively find it odd, even comic, when a plump person shows signs of nervous exhaustion and I was surprised that Marco could be at once so buxom and in such a state of collapse. She pulled herself together; I saw her face, once again, look like a noble warrior's. The cigarette she avidly lit after tea completed her recovery. The glint of henna on her short hair suited her.

"Well," she began in a clear voice, "I think it's over."

No doubt she had not planned to open with those words, for she stopped, as if aghast.

"Over? Why, what's over?"

"You know perfectly well what I mean," she said. "If you're at all fond of me, as I think you are, you'll try and help me, but . . . All the same, I'm going to tell you."

Those were almost her last coherent words. In putting down the story that I heard, I am obliged to cut out all that made it, in Marco's version, so confused and so terribly clear.

She told it as many women do, going far back, and irrelevantly, into the past of what had been her single, dazzling love affair. She kept on repeating herself and correcting dates: "So it must have been Thursday, December 26. What *am* I saying? It was a Friday, because we'd been to Prunier's to have a fish dinner. He's a practicing Catholic and abstains on Fridays."

Then the detailed minuteness of the story went to pieces. Marco lost the thread and kept breaking off to say, "Oh well, we can skip that!" or "Goodness, I can't remember where I'd got to!" and interlarding every other sentence with "You know." Grief drove her to violent gesticulation: she kept smiting her knees with the palm of her hand and flinging her head back against the chair cushions.

All the time she was running on with the prolixity and banality that give all lovers' laments a family likeness, accompanying certain indecent innuendoes with a pantomime of lowering her long eyelids. I felt completely unmoved. I was conscious only of a longing to get away and even had to keep clenching my jaws to repress nervous yawns. I found Marco all too tiresomely like every other woman in love; she was also taking an unconscionably long time to tell me how all this raving about a handsome young soldier came to end in disaster—a disaster, of course, totally unlike anyone else's; they always are.

"Well, one day . . ." said Marco, at long last.

She put her elbows on the arms of her chair. I imitated her and we both leaned forward. Marco broke off her confused jeremiad and I saw a gleam of awareness come into her soft, sad eyes, a look capable of seeing the truth. The tone of her voice changed too, and I will try to summarize the dramatic part of her story.

In the verbosity of the early stage, she had not omitted to mention the "madness of passion," the fiery ardor of the young man who would impetuously rush through the half-open door, pull aside the curtain, and, from there, make one bound onto the divan where Marco lay awaiting him. He could not endure wasting time in preliminaries or speeches. Impetuosity has its own particular ritual. Marco gave me to understand that, more often than not, the lieutenant, his gloves, and his peaked cap were all flung down haphazardly on the divan. Poetry and sweet nothings only came afterward. At this point in her story, Marco made a prideful pause and turned her gaze toward a beveled, nickel-plated photograph frame. Her silence and her gaze invited me to various conjectures, and perhaps to a touch of envy.

"Well, so one day . . ." said Marco.

A day of license, definitely. One of those rainy Paris days when a mysterious damp that dulls the mirrors and a strange craving to fling off clothes incites lovers to shut themselves up and turn day into night, "one of those days," Marco said, "that are the perdition of body and soul . . ." I had to follow my friend and to imagine her—she forced me to—half naked on the divan bed, emerging from one of those ecstasies that were so crude and physical that she called them "evil spells." It was at that moment that her hand, straying over the bed, encountered the peaked forage cap known as a kepi and she yielded to one of those all-too-typical feminine reflexes; she sat up in her crumpled chemise, planted the kepi over one ear, gave it a roguish little tap to settle it, and hummed:

> *With bugle and fife and drum*
> *The soldiers are coming to town . . .*

"Never," Marco told me, "never have I seen anything like Alex's face. It was . . . incomprehensible. I'd say it was hideous, if he weren't so handsome . . . I can't tell you what my feelings were . . ."

She broke off and stared at the empty divan-bed.

"What happened then, Marco? What did he say?"

"Why, nothing. I took off the kepi, I got up, I tidied myself, we had some tea. In fact, everything passed off just as usual. But since that day I've two or three times caught Alex looking at me with that face again and with such a very odd expression in his eyes. I can't get rid of the idea that the kepi was fatal to me. Did it bring back some unpleasant memory? I'd like to know what *you* think. Tell me straight out, don't hedge."

Before replying, I took care to compose my face; I was so terrified it might express the same horror, disapproval, and disgust as Lieutenant Trallard's. Oh, Marco! In one moment I destroyed you, I wept for you— I saw you. I saw you just as Alexis Trallard had seen you. My contemptuous eyes took in the slack breasts and the slipped shoulder straps of the crumpled chemise. And the leathery, furrowed neck, the red patches on the skin below the ears, the chin left to its own devices and long past hope. . . . And that groove, like a dried-up river, that hollows the lower eyelid after making love, and that vinous, fiery flush that does not cool off quickly enough when it burns on an aging face. And crowning all that, the kepi! The kepi—with its stiff lining and its jaunty peak, slanted over one roguishly winked eye.

> *With bugle and fife and drum . . .*

"I know very well," went on Marco, "that between lovers, the slightest thing is enough to disturb a magnetic atmosphere . . . I know very well . . ."

Alas! What did she know?

"And after that, Marco? What was the end?"

"The end? But I've told you all there is to tell. Nothing else happened. The mission to Morocco turned up. The date's been put forward twice. But that isn't the only reason I've been losing sleep. Other signs . . ."

"What signs?"

She did not dare give a definite answer. She put out a hand as if to thrust away my question and averted her head.

"Oh, nothing, just . . . just differences."

She strained her ears in the direction of the door.

"I haven't seen him for three days," she said. "Obviously he has an enormous amount to do getting ready for this mission. All the same . . ."

She gave a sidelong smile.

"All the same, I'm not a child," she said in a detached voice. "In any case, he writes to me. Express letters."

"What are his letters like?"

"Oh, charming, of course, what else would they be? He may be very young but *he's* not quite a child either."

As I had stood up, Marco suddenly became anguished and humble and clutched my hands.

"What do you think I ought to do? What *does* one do in these circumstances?"

"How can I possibly know, Marco? I think there's absolutely nothing to be done but to wait. I think it's essential, for your own dignity."

She burst into an unexpected laugh.

"My dignity! Honestly, you make me laugh! My dignity! Oh, these young women."

I found her laugh and her look equally unbearable.

"But, Marco, you're asking my advice—I'm giving it to you straight from the heart."

She went on laughing and shrugging her shoulders. Still laughing, she brusquely opened the door in front of me. I thought that she was going to kiss me, that we should arrange another meeting, but I had hardly got outside before she shut the door behind me without saying anything beyond: "My dignity! No, really, that's *too* funny!"

If I stick to facts, the story of Marco is ended. Marco had had a lover; Marco no longer had a lover. Marco had brought down the sword of Damocles by putting on the fatal kepi, and at the worst possible moment. At the moment when the man is a melancholy, still-vibrating harp, an explorer returning from a promised land, half glimpsed but not attained, a lucid penitent swearing "I'll never do it again" on bruised and bended knees.

I stubbornly insisted on seeing Marco again a few days later. I knocked and rang at her door, which was not opened. I went on and on, for I was aware of Marco there behind it, solitary, stony, and fevered. With my mouth to the keyhole, I said: "It's Colette," and Marco opened the door. I saw at once that she regretted having let me in.

With an absentminded air, she kept stroking the loose skin of her small hands, smoothing it down toward the wrist like the cuff of a glove. I did not let myself be intimidated; I told her that I wanted her to come and dine with me at home that very night and that I wouldn't take no for an answer. And I took advantage of my authority to add: "I suppose Lieutenant Trallard has left?"

"Yes," said Marco.

"How long will it take him to get over there?"

"He isn't *over there*," said Marco. "He's at Ville d'Avray, staying with his father. It comes to the same thing."

When I had murmured "Ah!" I did not know what else to say.

"After all," Marco went on, "why shouldn't I come and have dinner with you?"

I made exclamations of delight, I thanked her. I behaved as effusively as a grateful fox terrier, without, I think, quite taking her in. When she was sitting in my room, in the warmth, under my lamp, in the glare of all that reflected whiteness, I could measure not only Marco's decline in looks but a kind of strange reduction in her. A diminution of weight—she was thinner—a diminution of resonance— she talked in a small, distinct voice. She must have forgotten to feed herself, and taken things to make herself sleep.

Masson came in after dinner. When he found Marco there, he showed as much apprehension as his illegible face could express. He gave her a crab-like, sidelong bow.

"Why, it's Masson," said Marco indifferently. "Hello, Paul."

They started up an old cronies' conversation, completely devoid of interest. I listened to them and I thought that such a string of bromides ought to be as good as a sleeping draught for Marco. She left early and Masson and I remained alone together.

"Paul, don't you think she looks ill, poor Marco?"

"Yes," said Masson. "It's the phase of the priest."

"Of the . . . *what*?"

"The priest. When a woman, hitherto extremely feminine, begins to look like a priest, it's the sign that she no longer expects either kindness or ill treatment from the opposite sex. A certain yellowish pallor, something melancholy about the nose, a pinched smile, falling cheeks: Marco's a perfect example. The priest, I tell you, the priest."

He got up to go, adding: "Between ourselves, I prefer that in her to the odalisque."

In the weeks that followed, I made a special point of not neglecting Marco. She was losing weight very fast indeed. It is difficult to hold on to someone who is melting away, it would be truer to say consuming herself. She moved house, that is to say, she packed her trunk and took it off to another little furnished flat. I saw her often, and never once did she mention Lieutenant Trallard. Then I saw her less often and the coolness was far more on her side than on mine. She seemed to be making a strange endeavor to turn herself into a shriveled little old lady. Time passed . . .

"But, Masson, what's happened to Marco? It's ages since . . . Have *you* any news of Marco?"

"Yes," said Masson.

"And you haven't told me anything!"

"You haven't asked me anything."

"Quick, where is she?"

"Almost every day at the Nationale. She's translated an extraordinary series of articles about the Ubangi from English into French. As the manuscript is a little short to make a book, she's making it longer at the publisher's request, and she's documenting herself at the library."

"So she's taken up her old life again," I said thoughtfully. "Exactly as it was before Lieutenant Trallard . . ."

"Oh, no," said Masson. "There's a tremendous change in her existence!"

"What change? Really, one positively has to drag things out of you!"

"Nowadays," said Masson, "Marco gets paid two sous a line."

[*Translated by Antonia White*]

The Photographer's Wife

❦

When the woman they called "the photographer's wife" decided to put an end to her days, she set about realizing her project with much sincerity and painstaking care. But, having no experience whatever of poisons, thank heaven, she failed. At which the inhabitants of the entire building rejoiced, and so did I, though I did not live in the neighborhood.

Madame Armand—of the Armand Studio, Art Photography and Enlargements—lived on the same landing as a pearl stringer and it was rare for me not to meet the amiable "photographer's wife" when I went up to visit Mademoiselle Devoidy. For, in those far-off days, I had, like everyone else, a pearl necklace. As all women wanted to wear them, there were pearls to suit all women and all purses. What bridegroom would have dared to omit a "string" from his wedding presents to his bride? The craze started at baptism, with the christening gift of a row of pearls no bigger than grains of rice. No fashion, since, has ever been so tyrannical. From a thousand francs upward you could buy a "real" necklace. Mine had cost five thousand francs, that is to say, it did not attract attention. But its living luster and its gay Orient were a proof of its excellent health and mine. When I sold it, during the Great War, it was certainly not for an idle whim.

I used not to wait to have its silk thread renewed till it was really necessary. Having it restrung was an excuse for me to visit Mademoiselle Devoidy, who came from my part of the country, a few villages away. From being a saleswoman in a branch of The Store of a Thousand Necklaces, where everything was sham, she had gone on to being a stringer of real pearls. This unmarried woman of about forty had kept, as I had, the accent of our native parts, and delighted me furthermore by a restrained sense of humor which, from the heights of a punctilious honesty, made fun of a great many people and things.

When I went up to see her, I used to exchange greetings with the photographer's wife, who was often standing outside her wide-open door, opposite Mademoiselle Devoidy's closed one. The photographer's furniture trespassed onto the landing, beginning with a "pedestal" dating back to the infancy of the craft, a camera stand of carved, beautifully grained walnut, itself a tripod. Its bulk and its solid immobility made me think of those massive wooden winepress screws that used to appear, at about the same period, in "artistic" flats, supporting some graceful statuette. A gothic chair kept it company and served as an accessory in photographs of First Communicants. The little wicker kennel and its stuffed Pomeranian, the pair of shrimping nets dear to children in sailor suits, completed the store of accessories banished from the studio.

An incurable smell of painted canvas dominated this top landing. Yet the painting of a reversible canvas background, in monochrome gray, certainly did not date from yesterday. One side of it represented a balustrade on the verge of an English park; the other, a small sea, bounded in the distance by a hazy port, whose horizon dipped slightly to the right. As the front door was frequently left open, it was against this stormy background and this slanting sea that I used to see the photographer's wife encamped. From her air of vague expectancy I presumed that she had come out there to breathe the coolness of the top landing or to watch for some customer coming up the stairs. I found out later that I was wrong. I would go into her opposite neighbor's and Mademoiselle Devoidy would offer me one of her dry, pleasant hands; infallible hands, incapable of hurrying or trembling, that never dropped a pearl or a reel or a needle, that gummed the point of a strand of silk by passing it, with one sure twist of the fingers, through a half-moon of virgin wax, then aimed the stiffened thread at the eye of a needle finer than any sewing needle.

What I saw most clearly of Mademoiselle Devoidy was her bust, caught in the circle of light from her lamp, her coral necklace on her starched white collar, her discreetly mocking smile. As to her freckled, rather flat face, it merely served as a frame and a foil for her piercing brown, gold-spangled eyes that needed neither spectacles nor magnifying glass and could count the tiny "seed pearls" used for making those skeins and twists that are known as "bayadères" and are as dull as white bead trimming.

Mademoiselle Devoidy, living in cramped quarters, worked in the front room and slept in the back one, next door to the kitchen. A double door, at the entrance, made a minute hall. When a visitor knocked or rang, Mademoiselle Devoidy would call out, without getting up: "Come in! The key turns to the left!"

Did I feel the beginnings of a friendship with this fellow native of my own province? I most certainly liked her professionable table, covered with green baize, with a raised edge like a billiard table, and scored with parallel troughs along which her fingers ranged and graded the pearls with the help of delicate tweezers, worthy to touch the most precious matter: pearls and the wings of dead butterflies.

I also had a friendly feeling for the details and peculiarities of a craft that demanded two years' apprenticeship, a special manual dexterity, and a slightly contemptuous attitude toward jewels. The mania for pearls, which lasted a long time, allowed the expert stringer to work in her own home and do as much as she chose. When Mademoiselle Devoidy told me, suppressing a yawn: "So-and-so brought me *masses* last night, I had to compose till two o'clock in the morning," my imagination swelled these "masses" to fairy-tale size and elevated the verb "compose" to the rank of creative labor.

In the afternoon, and on dark mornings in winter, an electric bulb, set in a metal convolvulus, was switched on above the table. Its strong light swept away all the shadows on the workbench on which Mademoiselle Devoidy allowed nothing to stand; no little vase with a rose in it, no pin tray or ornament in which a stray pearl might hide. Even the scissors seemed to make themselves perfectly flat. Apart from this precaution, which kept the table in a permanent state of pearl-decked nudity, I never saw Mademoiselle Devoidy show the faintest sign of wariness. Chokers and necklaces lay dismembered on the table like stakes not worth picking up.

"You're not in a great hurry? I'll clear a little place for you. Amuse yourself with what's lying about while I rethread you. So it refuses to get any fatter, this string? You'll have to put it in the hen coop. Ah, you'll never know your way about."

All the time Mademoiselle Devoidy was teasing, her smile was busy reminding me of our common origin, a village ringed with woods, the autumn rain dripping on the piles of apples on the edge of the fields, waiting to be taken to the cider press . . . Meanwhile, I did, indeed, amuse myself with what was lying about on the table. Sometimes there were huge American necklaces, ostentatious and impersonal; Cécile Sorel's pearls mingled with Polaire's choker, thirty-seven famous pearls. There were jewelers' necklaces, milky and brand-new, not yet warmed into life by long contact with women's skin. Here and there, a diamond, mounted in a clasp, emitted rainbow sparks. A dog collar, a fourteen-row choker, stiffened with vertical bars of brilliants, spoke of wrinkled dewlaps, an old woman's sinewy neck, perhaps of scrofula . . .

Has that curious craft changed? Does it still fling heaps of treasures, defenseless fortunes into the laps of poor and incorruptible women?

When the day was drawing to a close, Madame Armand some-times came and sat at the green baize table. Out of discretion, she re-frained from handling the necklaces over which her bird-like gaze wan-dered with glittering indifference.

"Well, so your day's work's over, Madame Armand?" Mademoiselle Devoidy would say.

"Oh, me . . . mine doesn't have to be fitted into the day like my husband's. My dinner to warm up, the studio to tidy, little things here and there . . . it's easily done."

Rigid when she was standing, Madame Armand was no less rigid seated. Her bust, tightly encased in a red-and-black tartan bodice with braided frogs, visible between the stiff half-open flaps of a jacket, made me think of a little cupboard. She had something of the fascination of a wooden ship's figurehead. At the same time she suggested the well-mannered efficiency of a good cashier and various other sterling virtues.

"And Monsieur Armand, what nice thing's he up to at this moment?"

"He's still working. He's still on his last Saturday's wedding. You see, he has to do everything in a little business like ours. That wedding procession on Saturday is giving him a lot of trouble, but it means quite a good profit. The couple in one picture, a group of the bridesmaids, the whole procession in four different poses, goodness knows what all. I can't help him as much as I'd like to."

The photographer's wife turned to me as if to apologize. As soon as she spoke, all the various stiff and starchy phenomena of the close-fitting bodice, the jacket, the imitation gardenia pinned in her button-hole melted in the warmth of a pleasant voice with hardly any modula-tions in it, a voice made to recount local gossip at great length.

"My husband gets tired, because he's starting this exophthalmic goiter, I call it his exo for short. The year's been too bad for us to take on an assistant cameraman. The tiresome thing is, I haven't got a steady hand, I break things. A pot of glue here, a developing tank there, and bang, there goes a frame on the floor. You can see a mile off what a loss that means at the end of a day."

She stretched out a hand toward me that was, indeed, shaking.

"Nerves," she said. "So I stick to my own little domain, I do all the housework. In one way it seems to be good for my nerves, but . . ."

She frequently paused on a "but," after which came a sigh, and when I asked Mademoiselle Devoidy whether this "but" and this sigh hid some melancholy story, my fellow countrywoman retorted: "What an idea! She's a woman who tight-laces to give herself a slim waist so she has to fight every minute to get her breath."

Madame Armand, who had regular features, remained faithful to the high military collar and the tight, curled fringe because she had been told she looked like Queen Alexandra, only saucier. Saucier, I cannot honestly say. Darker, definitely. Heads of blue-black hair accompanied by white skin and a straight little nose abound in Paris and are usually of pure Parisian origin with no trace of Mediterranean blood. Madame Armand had as many lashes as a Spanish woman and a bird's eyes, I mean black eyes rich with a luster that never varied. The neighborhood paid her a laconic and adequate tribute by murmuring, as she passed, the words "handsome brunette." On this point, Mademoiselle Devoidy's opinion allowed itself one reservation.

"Handsome brunette's the word . . . Especially ten years ago."

"Have you known Madame Armand ten years?"

"No, because she and little old Big Eyes only moved into this place three years ago. I've been in the house much longer than they have. But I can very well imagine Madame Armand ten years ago. You can see she's a woman who's devouring herself."

"Devouring herself? That's a strong expression. You're not exaggerating?"

An offended look, the color of spangled iron ore, passed under the lamp and met my eyes in the shadow.

"Anyone may be mistaken. Madame Armand may be mistaken too. Just fancy, she's got it into her head that she leads a sedentary life. So every evening, either before dinner or after, she goes out on foot to take the air."

"It's a good healthy habit, don't you think?"

Mademoiselle Devoidy, as she pinched her lips, made the little colorless hairs of mustache at the corners of her mouth converge—just as diving seals do when they close their nostrils to the water.

"You know what I think of healthy habits. Now that the photographer's wife has got a bee in her bonnet that she has breathless fits if she doesn't go out, the next thing will be she'll be found on the stairs one day, dead of suffocation."

"You very seldom go out, Mademoiselle Devoidy?"

"Never, you might say."

"And you don't feel any worse for it?"

"You can see for yourself. But I don't stop other people from doing what they fancy."

She darted her malicious gaze, directed at an invisible Madame Armand, toward the closed door. And I thought of the tart, ill-natured remarks the women herding the cattle in my native countryside exchange over the hedges as they slap the blood-swollen flies under the heifers' sensitive bellies.

Mademoiselle Devoidy bent her head over the threading of some very tiny pearls; at the edge of her forehead, between the cheek and the ear, the chestnut hair ended in vigorous down, silver, like her little mustache. All the features of this Parisian recluse spoke to me of downy willows, ripe hazelnuts, the sandy bottom of springs, and silky husks. She aimed the point of her needle, pinched between the thumb and forefinger that rested on the table, at the almost invisible holes in the small, insipidly white pearls that she spitted in fives, then slipped on to the silk thread.

A familiar fist banged at the door.

"That'll be Tigri-Cohen. I recognize his knock. The key's in the door, Monsieur Tigri!"

The ill-favored face of Tigri-Cohen entered the little arena of light. His ugliness was now gay and ironical, now sad and imploring, like that of certain overintelligent monkeys who have equal reason to cherish the gifts of man and to shiver with fear at them. I have always thought that Tigri-Cohen took tremendous pains to appear crafty, reckless, and unscrupulous. He adopted, perhaps out of guilelessness, the style and manner of a moneylender who charged exorbitant rates. As I knew him, he was always ready to part with twenty francs or even a "big flimsy," so much so that he died poor, in the arms of his unsuspected honesty.

I had known him in the wings and dressing rooms of music halls, where Tigri-Cohen spent most of his evenings. The little variety actresses used to climb on his shoulders like tame parakeets and leave wet-white all over this black man. They knew his pockets were full of small jewels, flawed pearls and gems just good enough to make into hatpins. He excited his little friends' admiration by showing them badly colored stones with beautiful names, peridots, chalcedonies, chrysoprases, and pretentious zircons. Hail-fellow-well-met with all the girls, Tigri-Cohen would sell a few of his glittering pebbles between ten p.m. and midnight. But to the rich stars, he presented himself mainly in the role of buyer.

His taste for beautiful pearls always seemed to me more sensual than commercial. I shall never forget the state of excitement I saw him in one day when, going into his shop, I found him alone with a small, unremarkable, expressionless little man who drew out of his shabby waistcoat a sky-blue silk handkerchief and, out of the handkerchief, a single pearl.

"So you've still got it?" asked Tigri.

"Yes," said the little man. "Not for long, though."

It was an unpierced pearl, round, big as a fine cherry, and, like a cherry, it seemed not to receive the cold light shed from the even-number side of the rue Lafayette but to emit a steady, veiled radiance from within. Tigri contemplated it without saying a word and the little chap kept silent.

"It's . . . it's . . ." began Tigri-Cohen.

He searched in vain for words to praise it, then shrugged his shoulders.

"Can I have it a moment?" I asked.

I held it in the hollow of my palm, this marvelous, warm virgin, with its mystery of tremulous colors, its indefinable pink that picked up a snowy blue, then exchanged it for a fleeting mauve.

Before giving back the glorious pearl, Tigri sighed. Then the little man extinguished the soft rays in the blue handkerchief, thrust the whole, carelessly, into a pocket, and went away.

"It's . . ." repeated Tigri . . . "It's the color of love."

"To whom does it belong?"

"To whom? To whom? Think I know? To black chaps in India! To an oyster-bed company! To savages, to people with no faith and no feelings, to . . ."

"How much is it worth?"

He gave me a look of contempt.

"How much? A pearl like that, in the dawn of its life, that's still going about in its little blue satin chemise at the bottom of a broker's pocket? How much? Like a kilo of plums, eh? 'That'll be three francs, Madame. Here you are, Madame. Thank you, Madame.' Ah! to hear anyone ask *that* . . ."

Every muscle of his ugly, passionate mime's face was working, that face that was always overloaded with too much expression, too much laughter, too much sadness. That evening, in Devoidy's room, I remember he was dripping with rain and seemed not to notice it. He was exploring his pockets with a mechanical gesture, pockets that were secret hoards of necklaces of colored stones, cabochon rings, little bags in which diamonds slept in tissue paper. He flung some ropes of pearls on the green baize.

"There, Devoidy, my love, do me that for tomorrow. And that one. Don't you think it's hideous? If you pulled out the pigeon's feather stuffed in the middle of that nut, you could thread it on a cable. Anyway, change the stuffing."

From force of habit, he bent over my necklace, with one eye screwed up.

"The fourth one from the middle, I'll buy that. No? Just as you like. Goodbye, my pets. Tonight I'm going to the dress rehearsal of the Folies-Bergère."

"Should be a fine evening for business," said Mademoiselle Devoidy politely.

"That shows you don't know a thing about it. Tonight my good ladies will be thinking of nothing but their parts, their costumes, the audience's reaction, and going off into faints behind a flat. See you soon, pets."

Other visitors, especially female ones, passed through the boltless door into the narrow circle of harsh light. I stared at them with the avid curiosity I have always felt for people I run no risk of seeing again. Richly dressed women thrust out hands filled with precious white grain into the glare of the lamp. Or else, with a proud, languid gesture acquired from constantly wearing pearls, they undid the clasps of their necklaces.

Among others, my memory retains the picture of a woman all silvered with chinchilla. She came in very agitated and she was such a sturdy daughter of the people under all her luxury that she was a joy to the eye. She plumped herself down rudely on the straw-seated stool and commanded: "Don't unstring the whole row. Just get me out that one, on the side, near the middle, yes, that beauty there."

Mademoiselle Devoidy, who did not like despots, calmly and unhurriedly cut the two silk knots and pushed the free pearl toward her client. The beautiful woman grabbed it and studied it from very close up. Under the lamp, I could have counted her long, fluttering eyelashes, which were stuck together with mascara. She held out the pearl to the stringer.

"You, what's *your* idea about this here pearl?"

"I know nothing about pearls," said Mademoiselle Devoidy impassively.

"Sure you're not joking?"

The beautiful woman pointed to the table, with evident irony. Then her face changed; she seized a little lump of cast iron under which Mademoiselle Devoidy kept a set of ready-threaded needles and brought it down hard on the pearl, which crushed into tiny fragments. I exclaimed "Oh!" in spite of myself. Mademoiselle Devoidy permitted herself no other movement than to clutch an unfinished string and some scattered pearls close against her with her sure hands.

The customer contemplated her work without saying a word. Finally, she burst into vehement tears. She kept noisily sobbing: "The swine, the swine," and, at the same time, carefully collecting the black from her lashes on a corner of her handkerchief. Then she stuffed her necklace, amputated of one pearl, into her handbag, asked for "a little bit of tissue paper," stowed every single fragment of the sham pearl into it, and stood up. Before she left the room, she made a point of affirming loudly. "That's not the last of this business, not by a long shot." Then she carried away into the outside air the unpleasant whiff of a brand-new, very fashionable scent: synthetic lily-of-the-valley.

"Is that the first time you've seen a thing like that happen, Mademoiselle Devoidy?"

Mademoiselle Devoidy was scrupulously tidying up her workbench with her careful hands, unshaking as usual.

"No, the second," she said. "With this difference, that the first time, the pearl resisted. It was real. So was the rest of the necklace."

"And what did the lady say?"

"It wasn't a lady, it was a gentleman. He said: 'Ah! the bitch!' "

"Why?"

"The necklace was his wife's. She'd made her husband believe it cost fifteen francs. Yes. Oh, you know, when it comes to pearls, it's very seldom there isn't some shady story behind them."

She touched her little coral necklace with two fingers. I was amazed to catch this slightly sneering skeptic making a gesture to avert ill luck, and to see the cloud of superstition pass over her stubborn brow.

"So you wouldn't care to wear pearls?"

She raised one shoulder slantwise, torn between her commercial prudence and the desire not to lie.

"I don't know. One doesn't know one's own self. Down there, at Coulanges, there was a chap who couldn't have been more of an anarchist, he frightened everyone out of their wits. And then he inherited a little house with a garden and a round dovecote and a pigsty. If you were to see the anarchist now! There's quite a change."

Almost at once, she recovered her restrained laugh, her pleasantly rebellious expression, and her way of approving without being sycophantic and criticizing without being rude.

One night when I had lingered late with her, she caught me yawning, and I apologized by saying: "I've got one of those hungers. I don't take tea and I had hardly any lunch, there was red meat—I can't eat underdone meat."

"Neither can I," said my fellow countrywoman. "In our part of the world, as you well know, they say raw meat is for cats and the English. But if you can be patient for five minutes, a mille-feuilles will be wafted here to you, without my leaving my chair. What do you bet?"

"A pound of chocolate creams."

"Pig who backs out of it!" said Mademoiselle Devoidy, holding out her dry palm quite flat to me. I slapped it and said, "Done!"

"Mademoiselle Devoidy, how is it that your flat never smells of fried whiting or onions or stew? Have you got a secret?"

She indicated yes by fluttering her eyelids.

"Can I know?"

An accustomed hand knocked three times on the front door.

"There you are, here it comes, your mille-feuilles. And my secret's revealed. Come in, Madame Armand, come in!"

Nevertheless, she fastened my little middle-class necklace at the back of my neck. Loaded with a basket, Madame Armand did not at once offer me her chronically trembling fingers and she spoke very hurriedly.

"Mind now, mind now, don't jostle me, I've got something breakable. Today's chef's special is *bœuf à la bourguignonne* and I brought you a lovely bit of lettuce. As to mille-feuilles, nothing doing! It's iced Genoese cakes."

Mademoiselle Devoidy made a comic grimace at me and attempted to unburden her obliging neighbor. But the latter exclaimed: "I'll carry it all into the kitchen for you!" and ran toward the dark room at the back. Quickly as she had crossed the lighted zone, I had caught sight of her face and so had Mademoiselle Devoidy.

"I must fly, I must fly, I've got some milk on the gas ring," Madame Armand cried out, in tomboyish tones.

She crossed the front room again at a run and pulled the door closed behind her. Mademoiselle Devoidy went out into the kitchen and came back with two Genoese cakes, with pink icing, on a plate adorned with a flaming bomb and the inscription *Fire Brigade Alarm*.

"As sure as eggs is eggs," she said, with a thoughtful air, "the photographer's wife has been crying. And she hasn't any milk on her gas ring."

"Domestic scene?"

She shook her head.

"Poor little old Big Eyes! He's not capable of it. Neither is she, for that matter. My, you've gone through that cake quickly. Would you like the other one? She's rather put me off my food, Monsieur Armand's good lady, with that face all gone to pieces."

"Everything will be all right tomorrow," I said absentmindedly.

In exchange for that flat remark, I received a brief, trenchant glance.

"Oh, of *course* it will, won't it? And anyway, if it isn't all right, *you* don't care a fig."

"What's all this? You think I ought to be more passionately concerned over the Armand family's troubles?"

"The Armand family isn't asking you for anything. And neither am I. It would most certainly be the first time anyone had heard *me* asking anyone for anything . . ."

Mademoiselle Devoidy had lowered her voice in the effort to control her irritation. We were, I imagine, utterly ridiculous. It was this cloud of anger, rising suddenly between two hot-blooded women, that fixed the details of an absurd, unexpected scene in my memory. I had the good sense to put an end to it at once by laying my hand on her shoulder.

"Now, now. Don't let's make ourselves out blacker than we are! You know quite well that if I can be any use to this good lady . . . Are you frightened about her?"

Mademoiselle Devoidy flushed under her freckles and covered the top of her face with one hand, with a simple and romantic gesture.

"Now, you're being too nice. Don't be too nice to me. When anyone's too nice to me, I don't know what I'm doing, I boil over like a soup."

She uncovered her beautiful moist spangled eyes and pushed the straw-seated stool toward me.

"One minute, you've surely got a minute? That's rain you hear; wait till the rain's over."

She sat down opposite me in her working place and vigorously rubbed her eyes with the back of her forefinger.

"Get this well into your head first—Madame Armand isn't a tittle-tattle or a woman who goes in for confidences. But she lives very near, right on my doorstep. This place is just a little two-bit block of flats, the old-fashioned kind. Two rooms on the right, two rooms on the left, little businesses that can be done in one room at home. People who live so very near you, it isn't so much that you hear them, anyway they don't make any noise, but I'm conscious of them. Especially of the fact that Madame Armand spends so much time out on the landing. In places like this, if anything's not going right, the neighbors are very soon aware of it, at least I am."

She lowered her voice and compressed her lips; her little mustache hairs glistened. She pricked her green table with the point of a needle as if she were cabalistically counting her words.

"When the photographer's wife goes out shopping for herself or for me, you can always see the concierge or the flower seller under the archway or the woman in the little *bistro*, coming out, one or other of them, to see where she's going. Where is she going? Why, she's going to the dairy or to buy hot rolls or to the hairdresser, just like anyone else! So then the nosy parkers take their noses inside again, anything but pleased, as if they'd been promised something and not given it. And the next time, they start all over again. But when it's me who goes out or Madame Gâteroy downstairs or her daughter, people don't stop and stare after us as if they expected something extraordinary was going to happen."

"Madame Armand has a . . . a rather individual appearance," I risked suggesting. "Perhaps she does somewhat overdo the tartan, too."

Mademoiselle Devoidy shook her head and seemed to despair of making herself understood. It was getting late; from top to bottom of the building, doors were slamming one by one, on every floor chairs were being drawn up around a table and a soup tureen; I took my leave. The door of the photographic studio, unwontedly shut, turned the camera pedestal and the crossed shrimping nets under the gas jet into an important piece of decoration. On the ground floor, the concierge raised her curtain to watch me going: I had never stayed so late.

The warm night was foggy around the gas lamps and the unusual hour gave me that small, yet somehow rewarding pang I used to experience in the old days when I came away from stage performances that had begun when the sun was at its zenith and finished when it was dark.

Do those transient figures who featured in long-past periods of my life deserve to live again in a handful of pages as I here compel them to? They were important enough for me to keep them secret, at least during the time I was involved with them. For example, my husband, at home, did not know of the existence of Mademoiselle Devoidy or of my familiarity with Tigri-Cohen. The same was true of Monsieur Armand's wife and of a certain sewing woman, expert at repairing worn quilts and making multicolored silk rags into patchwork pram covers. Did I like her for her needlework that disdained both fashion and the sewing machine or was it for her second profession? At six o'clock in the afternoon, she abandoned her hexagonal pieces of silk and went off to the Gaîté-Lyrique, where she sang a part in *Les Mousquetaires au couvent.*

For a long time, in the inner compartment of my handbag, between the leather and the lining, I kept a fifty-centime "synthetic" pearl I had once lost in Tigri-Cohen's shop. He had found it, and before returning it to me, he had amused himself by studding my initials on it in little diamonds. But at home, I never mentioned either the charming mascot or Tigri himself, for the husband I was married to then had formed such a rigid, foursquare idea of the jeweler, such a conventional notion of a "dealer," that I could neither have pleaded the cause of the latter nor rectified the error of the former.

Was I genuinely attached to the little needlewoman? Did I feel real affection for the misunderstood Tigri-Cohen? I do not know. The instinct to deceive has not played a very large part in my different lives. It was essential to me, as it is to many women, to escape from the opinions of certain people, which I knew to be subject to error and apt to be proclaimed dogmatically in a tone of feigned indulgence. Treatment of this sort drives us women to avoid the simple truth, as if it were a dull, monotonous tune, to take pleasure in half lies, half suppressions, half escapes from reality.

When the opportunity came, I made my way once more to the narrow-fronted house over whose brow the open blue pane of the photographic studio window slanted like a visor.

As soon as I entered the hall of the block of flats, a cleaner's deliveryman in a black apron and a woman carrying bread in a long wicker *cistera* barred my way. The first, without being asked, obligingly informed me: "It's nothing, just a chimney on fire." At the same moment, a "runner" from a fashion house came dashing down the stairs, banging her yellow box against all the banisters, and yapping: "She's as white as a sheet! She hasn't an hour to live!"

Her scream magically attracted a dozen passers-by who crowded around her, pressing her close on all sides. Desire to escape, slight nausea, and idle curiosity struggled within me, but in the end they gave way to a strange resignation. I knew perfectly well—already out of breath before I had begun to run—I knew perfectly well that I should not stop until I reached the top landing. Which of them was it? The photographer's wife or Mademoiselle Devoidy? Mentally, I ruled out the latter, as if no peril could ever endanger her mocking wisdom or the sureness of those hands, soft as silky wood shavings, or scatter the milky constellations of precious, tiny moons she pursued on the green baize table and impaled with such deadly aim.

All the while I was breathlessly climbing the stories, I was fighting to reassure myself. An accident? Why shouldn't it have happened to the knitting women on the fourth floor or the bookbinding couple? The steamy November afternoon preserved the full strength of the smells of cabbage and gas and of the hot, excited human beings who were showing me the way.

The unexpected sound of sobbing is demoralizing. Easy as it is to imitate, that retching, hiccuping noise remains crudely impressive. While I was being secretly crushed to death between the banisters and a telegraph boy who had pushed up too fast, we heard convulsive male sobs and the commentators on the staircase fell silent, avidly. The noise lasted only a moment, it was extinguished behind a door that someone up there had slammed again. Without having ever heard the man whom Mademoiselle Devoidy nicknamed little old Big Eyes weep, I knew, beyond a shadow of a doubt, that it was he who was sobbing.

At last I reached the top floor, crammed with strangers between its two closed doors. One of them opened again and I heard the biting voice of Mademoiselle Devoidy.

"Ladies and gentlemen, where are you going like that? It doesn't make sense. If you want to have your photographs taken, it's too late. Why no, don't worry, there hasn't been any accident. A lady has sprained her ankle, they've put a crepe bandage on it, and that's the beginning and end of the story."

A murmur of disappointment and a little laughter ran through the crowd flocking up the stairs. But it struck me that, in the harsh light, Mademoiselle Devoidy looked extremely ill. She proffered a few more words designed to discourage the invaders and went back into her flat.

"Well, if that's all . . ." said the telegraph boy.

To make up his lost time, he jostled a cellarman in a green baize apron and a few dim women and disappeared by leaps and bounds, and at last, I was able to sit down on the gothic chair reserved for First Communicants. As soon as I was alone, Mademoiselle Devoidy reappeared.

"Come in, I saw you all right. I couldn't make signs to you in front of everyone. Do you mind? I wouldn't be sorry to sit down for a moment."

As if there was no refuge except in her regular, everyday haunt, she collapsed into the chair she worked in.

"Ah, that's better!"

She smiled at me with a happy look.

"She's brought it all up, so we needn't worry anymore."

"All what?"

"What she'd taken. Some stuff to kill herself. Some disgusting filth or other."

"But why did she do it?"

"There you go, asking why! You always have to have three dozen reasons, don't you? She'd left a letter for little old Big Eyes."

"A letter? Whatever did she confess?"

By degrees Mademoiselle Devoidy was recovering her composure, and her easy, mocking way of treating me.

"You've got to know everything, haven't you? As to confessing, she confessed all. She confessed: 'My darling Geo, don't scold me. Forgive me for leaving you. In death, as in life, I remain your faithful Georgina.' By the side of that, there was another scrap of paper that said: 'Everything is paid except the washerwoman who had no change on Wednesday.' It happened about quarter past two, twenty past two . . ."

She broke off and stood up.

"Wait, there's some coffee left."

"If it's for me, don't bother."

"I want some myself," she said.

The panacea of the people appeared with the sacred vessels of its cult, its blue-marbled enamel jug, its two cups adorned with a red-and-gold key pattern, and its twisted glass sugar bowl. The smell of chicory faithfully escorted it, eloquent of ritual anxieties, of deathbed vigils and difficult labors and whispered palavers, of a drug within reach of all.

"Well, as I was saying," Mademoiselle Devoidy went on, "about two or a quarter past, someone knocked at my door. It was my little old Big Eyes, looking ever so embarrassed and saying: 'You haven't happened to see my wife going downstairs?' —'No,' I says, 'but she might have gone down without my seeing her.' 'Yes,' he says to me. 'I ought to have been out myself by now, but, just as I was on the point of leaving, I broke a bottle of hyposulphite. You can see the state my hands are in.' —'That was bad luck,' I says to him. 'Yes,' he says to me, 'I need a duster, the dusters are in our bedroom, in the cupboard behind the bed.' —'If that's all,' I says, 'I'll go and get you one, don't touch anything.' 'It isn't all,' he says to me. 'What's worrying me is that the bedroom's locked and it never is locked.' I stared at him, I don't know what came into my head, but I got up, nearly pushing him over, and off I went and knocked at their bedroom door. He kept saying: 'Why, whatever's the matter with you? Whatever's the matter with you?' I answered him tit for tat: 'Well, what about you? You haven't taken a look at yourself.' He stayed standing there with his hands spread out, all covered with hyposulphite. I come back in here, I snatch up the hatchet I chop up my firewood with. I swear to you the hinges and the lock bust right off at the same blow. They're no better than matchwood, these doors."

She drank a few mouthfuls of tepid coffee.

"I'll get a safety chain put on mine," she went on. "Now that I've seen what a fragile thing a door is."

I was waiting for her to continue her story, but she was toying absently with the little metal shovel that gathered up the seed pearls on the cloth and seemed to have nothing more to say.

"And then, Mademoiselle Devoidy?"

"Then what?"

"She . . . Madame Armand . . . Was she in the room?"

"Of course she was. On her bed. Actually in her bed. Wearing silk stockings and smart shoes, black satin ones, embroidered with a little jet motif. That was what struck me all of a heap, those shoes and those stockings. It struck me so much that, while I was filling a hot-water bottle, I said to her husband, 'Whatever was she up to, going to bed in her shoes and stockings?' He was sobbing as he explained to me: 'It's because of her corns and her crooked third toe. She didn't want anyone to see her bare feet, not even me. She used to go to bed in little socks, she's so dainty in all her ways.'"

Mademoiselle Devoidy yawned, stretched, and began to laugh.

"Ah! You've got to admit a man's a proper muff in circumstances like that. *Him!* The only thing *he* could think of doing was crying and keeping on saying: 'My darling . . . My darling . . .' Lucky I acted quickly," she added proudly. "Excuse details, it makes me feel queasy. Oh, she's saved all right! But Dr. Camescasse, who lives at number 11, won't let her have anything but a little milk and soda water till further orders. Madame Armand swallowed enough poison to kill a regiment, apparently that's what saved her. Little old Big Eyes is on sentry duty at her bedside. But I'm just going to run in and have a look at her. Shall we be seeing you again soon? Bring her a little bunch of violets, it'll be more cheerful than if you'd had to take one to her in the Montparnasse cemetery."

I was already on the pavement when, too late, a question crossed my mind: Why had Madame Armand wanted to die? At the same moment, I realized that Mademoiselle Devoidy had omitted to tell me.

During the following days, I thought of the photographer's wife and her abortive suicide; this naturally led me to thinking about death and, unnaturally for me, about my own. Suppose I were to die in a tram? Suppose I were to die while having dinner in a restaurant? Appalling possibilities, but so highly unlikely that I soon abandoned them. We women seldom die outside our own homes; as soon as pain puts a handful of blazing straw under our bellies, we behave like frightened horses and find enough strength to run for shelter. After three days, I lost the taste for choosing the pleasantest mode of departing. All the same, country funerals are charming, especially in June, because of the flowers. But roses so soon become overblown in hot weather . . . I had reached this point when a note from Madame Armand—admirable spelling and a ravishing curly handwriting like lacework—reminded me of my "kind promise" and invited me to "tea."

On the top landing, I ran into an elderly married couple who were leaving the photographer's studio, arm in arm, all got up in braided jacket, four-in-hand tie, and stiff black silk. Little old Big Eyes was showing them out and I scanned his heavy eyelids for traces of his passionate tears. He greeted me with a joyful nod that implied mutual understanding.

"The ladies are in the bedroom. Madame Armand is still suffering from slight general fatigue, she thought you would be kind enough to excuse her receiving you so informally."

He guided me through the studio, had a courteous word for my bunch of violets—"the Parma ones look so distinguished"—and left me on the threshold of the unknown room.

On this narrow planet, we have only the choice between two unknown worlds. One of them tempts us—ah! what a dream, to live in that!—the other stifles us at the first breath. In the matter of furnishing, I find a certain absence of ugliness far worse than ugliness. Without containing any monstrosity, the total effect of the room where Madame Armand was enjoying her convalescence made me lower my eyes and I should not take the smallest pleasure in describing it.

She was resting, with her feet up, on the made-up bed, the same bed she had untucked to die in. Her eagerness to welcome me would have made her rise, had not Mademoiselle Devoidy restrained her, with the firm hand of a guardian angel. November was mild only out-of-doors. Madame Armand was keeping herself warm under a little red-and-black coverlet, crocheted in what is called Tunisian stitch. I am not fond of Tunisian stitch. But Madame Armand looked well, her cheeks were less parched and her eyes more brilliant than ever. The vivacity of her movements displaced the coverlet, and revealed two slim feet shod in black satin, embroidered—just as Mademoiselle Devoidy had described them to me—with a motif in jet beads.

"Madame Armand, a little less restlessness, please," gravely ordered the guardian angel.

"But I'm not ill!" protested Madame Armand. "I'm coddling myself, that's all. My little Exo's paying a woman to come in and do the housework for me in the morning, Mademoiselle Devoidy's made us a lemon sponge cake, and you bring me some magnificent violets! A life of idle luxury! You will taste some of my raspberry and gooseberry jelly with the sponge cake, won't you? It's the last of last year's pots, and without boasting . . . This year I made a mess of them, and the plums in brandy too. It's a year when I've made a mess of everything."

She smiled, as if making some subtle allusion. The unvarying glitter of her black eyes still reminded me of some bird or other; but now the bird was tranquil and refreshed. At what dark spring had it slaked its thirst?

"In that affair, however many were killed and wounded, nobody's dead," concluded Mademoiselle Devoidy.

I greeted the sentence that came straight out of our native province with a knowing wink and I swallowed, one on top of the other, a cup of very black tea and a glass of sweet wine that tasted of licorice: what must be, must be. I felt ill at ease. One does not so quickly acquire the knack of conjuring up, in the straightforward light of afternoon, such a very recent suicide. True, it had been transformed into a purging, but it had been planned to prevent any return.

I tried to adapt myself to the tone of the other two by saying playfully: "Who would believe that charming woman we see before us is the very same one who was so unreasonable the other day?"

The charming woman finished her wedge of lemon sponge before miming a little confusion and answering, doubtfully and coquettishly: "So unreasonable . . . so unreasonable . . . there's a lot could be said about that."

Mademoiselle Devoidy cut her off short. She seemed to me to have acquired a military authority from her first act of lifesaving.

"Now, now! You're not going to start all over again, are you?"

"Start again? Oh! Never!"

I applauded the spontaneity of that cry. Madame Armand raised her right hand for an oath.

"I swear it! The only thing I absolutely deny is what Dr. Camescasse said to me: 'In fact, you swallowed a poison during an attack of neurasthenia.' That infuriated me. For two pins I'd have answered him back: 'If you're so certain, there's no point in asking me a hundred questions. I know perfectly well in my own mind that I didn't commit suicide out of neurasthenia!' "

"Tsk, tsk," rebuked Mademoiselle Devoidy. "How long is it since I've seen for myself you were in a bad way? Madame Colette here can certify that I've mentioned it to her. As to neurasthenia, of course it was neurasthenia; there's nothing to be ashamed of in that."

The crochet coverlet was flung aside, the cup and saucer narrowly escaped following suit.

"No, it wasn't! I think I might be allowed to have my own little opinion on the subject! I'm the person concerned, aren't I?"

"I do take your opinion into account, Madame Armand. But it can't be compared with the opinion of a man of science like Dr. Camescasse!"

They were exchanging their retorts over my head, so tensely that I slightly ducked my chin. It was the first time I had heard a would-be suicide arguing her case in my presence as if standing up for her lawful rights. Like so many saviors, heavenly or earthly, the angel tended to overdo her part. Her spangled eye lit up with a spark that was anything but angelic, while the color of the rescued one kindled under her too-white powder.

I have never turned up my nose at a heated argument between cronies. A lively taste for street scenes keeps me hovering on the outskirts of quarrels vented in the open air which I find good occasions for enriching my vocabulary. I hoped, as I sat at Madame Armand's bedside, that the dialogue between the two women would blaze up with that virulence that characterizes feminine misunderstandings. But incomprehensible death, that teaches the living nothing; the memory of a nauseous poison; the rigorous devotion that tended its victim with a rod of iron; all this was too present, too massive, too oppressive to be replaced by a healthy slanging match. What was I doing, in this home timidly ruled by little old Big Eyes? What would remain to me of his wife, whom death had failed to ravish, beyond a stale, insipid mystery? As to Mademoiselle Devoidy, that perfect example of the dry, incorruptible spinster, I realized that I could no longer fancy she was anything of an enigma and that the attraction of the void cannot last forever.

Sorrow, fear, physical pain, excessive heat, and excessive cold, I can still guarantee to stand up to all these with decent courage. But I abdicate in the face of boredom, which turns me into a wretched and, if needs be, ferocious creature. Its approach, its capricious presence that affects the muscles of the jaw, dances in the pit of the stomach, sings a monotonous refrain that one's feet beat time to; I do not merely dread these manifestations, I fly from them. What was wrong in my eyes about these two women, who, from being gratitude and devotion incarnate, were now putting up barriers between them, was that they did not proceed to adopt the classic attitudes. There was no accompaniment of scurrilous laughter, of insults as blinding as pepper, of fists dug well into the ribs. They did not even awaken minute old grievances, kept alive and kicking by long stewing over and brooding on. Nevertheless, I did hear dangerous exchanges and words such as "neurotic . . . ingratitude . . . meddlesome Matty . . . poking your nose in . . ." I think it was on this last insult that Mademoiselle Devoidy rose to her feet, flung us a curt, bitter, ceremonious goodbye, and left the room.

Somewhat belatedly, I displayed suitable agitation.

"Well, really! But it's not serious. What childishness! Who'd have expected . . ."

Madame Armand merely gave a faint shrug that seemed to say "Forget it!" As the daylight was going fast, she stretched out her arm and switched on the bedside lamp which wore a crinoline of salmon-pink silk. At once the depressing character of the room changed and I did not hide my pleasure, for the lampshade, elaborately ruched and pretentious as it was, filtered an enchanting rosy light, like the lining of a seashell. Madame Armand smiled.

"I think we're both of us pleased," she said.

She saw I was about to mention the disagreeable incident again and stopped me.

"Forget it, Madame, these little tiffs—the less one thinks about them the better. Either they sort themselves out of their own accord, or else they don't, and that's even better. Have another drop of wine. Yes, yes, do have some more, it's pure unadulterated stuff."

She leaped from her couch, deftly pulling down her dress. In those days, women did not let themselves slide off a sofa or out of a car revealing a wide margin of bare thigh as they do nowadays with such cold and barbarous indifference.

"You're not overtaxing your strength, Madame Armand?"

She was walking to and fro on her jet-and-satin-shod feet, those feet that had been modest even in death. She poured out the pseudo-port, pulled an awning over the ceiling skylight, displaying a briskness that was not without grace, as if she had grown lighter. A likable woman, in fact, whose thirty-six years had left few traces. A woman who had wanted to die.

She switched on a second pink lamp. The room, extraordinary by its very ordinariness, exuded the false cheerfulness of well-kept hotel bedrooms.

My hostess came and picked up the chair abandoned by Mademoiselle Devoidy and planted it firmly beside me.

"No, Madame, I won't allow people to believe that I killed myself out of neurasthenia."

"But," I said, "I've never thought . . . Nothing gave me any reason to believe . . ."

I was surprised to hear Madame Armand refer to her failed attempt as an accomplished fact. Her eyes were frankly presented to me, wide open and looking straight into mine, but their extreme brightness and blackness revealed hardly anything. Her small, smooth, sensible forehead, under the curled fringe, really did look as if it had never harbored the regrettable disorder called neurasthenia between the two fine eyebrows. Before she sat down, she straightened the violets in the vase with her unsure hands; I saw their stalks tremble between her fingers. "Nerves, you know." Hands that were too clumsy even to measure out an effective dose of poison.

"Madame," she said, "I must tell you first of all that I have always had a very trivial life."

Such a prelude threatened me with a long recital. Nevertheless, I stayed where I was.

It is easy to relate what is of no importance. My memory has not failed to register the idle words and the mild absurdities of these two opposite neighbors and I have tried to reproduce them faithfully. But beginning with the words: "I have always had a very trivial life . . ." I feel absolved from the tiresome meticulousness imposed on a writer, such as carefully noting the overmany reiterations of "in one way" and "what poor creatures we are" that rose like bubbles to the surface of Madame Armand's story. Though they helped her to tell it, it is for me to remove them. It is my duty as a writer to abridge our conversation and also to suppress my own unimportant contribution to it.

"A very trivial life. I married such a good man. A man as perfect and hardworking and devoted as all that really oughtn't to exist. Now could you imagine anything unexpected happening to a man as perfect as that? And we didn't have a child. To tell you the honest truth, I don't think I minded much.

"Once, a young man in the neighborhood . . . Oh, no, it's not what you're expecting. A young man who had the cheek to accost me on the staircase, because it was dark there. Handsome, I have to admit he was handsome. Naturally, he promised me the moon and the stars. He told me: 'I'm not going to take you under false pretenses. With me, you'll see life in the raw. You can reckon I'm quite as likely to make you die of misery as of joy. Things will go my way, not yours.' And so on, and so on. One day he said to me: 'Let me have a look at your little wrist.' I wouldn't give it to him, he grabbed hold of it and twisted it. For more than ten days I couldn't use my hand and it was my little Exo who did it up for me. At night, after he'd put a clean crepe bandage on my wrist—I'd told him I'd had a fall—he would stare for a long time at that bandaged wrist. I was ashamed. I felt like a dog who's come home with a collar no one's ever seen it wearing and they say to it: 'But where on earth did you get a collar like that?' That shows the least evil-minded people can be sharp in their way.

"With this young man, it was all over before it began. Do you know what I couldn't abide? It was this gentleman I'd never spoken three words to daring to call me 'tu.' He just sprang up before my feet as if he'd risen out of the earth. Well, he vanished back into it again.

"Since then? Why, nothing. Nothing worth mentioning. There's nothing to surprise you in that. Plenty of women, and not the ugliest ones either, would be in my state if they didn't lend a helping hand. You mustn't believe men throw themselves on women like cannibals. Certainly not, Madame. It's women who spread that idea about. Men are much too anxious not to have their peace upset. But lots of women can't stand a man behaving decently. I know what I'm talking about.

"Personally, I'm not the kind that thinks much about men. It's not my temperament. In one way, it might have been better for me if I had thought of them. Instead of that, whatever do you think came into my head one morning when I was cutting up some breast of veal? I said to myself: 'I did breast of veal with green peas only last Saturday, all very nice, but one mustn't overdo it, a week goes by so fast. It's eleven already, my husband's got a christening group coming to pose at half past one, I must get my washing up done before the clients arrive, my husband doesn't like to hear me through the wall rattling crockery or poking the stove when clients are in the studio . . . And after that I must go out, there's that cleaner who still hasn't finished taking the shine off my husband's black suit, I'll have to have a sharp word with her. If I get back to do my ironing before dark, I'll be lucky; never mind, I'll damp my net window curtains down again and I'll iron them tomorrow, sooner than scorch them today. After that, I've nothing to do but the dinner to get ready and two or three odds and ends to see to and it'll be finished.'

"And instead of adding, as I often did: 'Finished . . . And none too soon,' I went on: 'Finished? How d'you mean, finished? Is that all? Is that the whole of my day, today, yesterday, tomorrow?' That night, when I was in bed, I was still going over and over all my idiotic thoughts. The next day, I felt better and I had to make some jam and pickle some gherkins, so you can imagine I sent Mademoiselle Devoidy out to do the shopping—it was well and truly her turn—so as to give all my time to hulling my strawberries and rubbing my gherkins in salt. I was deep in my work, when suddenly it came over me again: 'The events of my life, so today's jam-making day? Be careful about the copper preserving pan, it's got a rounded bottom, if it tips over on the hole of the cooking range, what a catastrophe! And I haven't got enough glass jam jars, I'll have to borrow the two jars Madame Gâteroy uses for her potted goose if she can spare them. And when I've finished my jam, what will come along in the way of a sensational event?' At last you can see the picture.

"It wasn't five o'clock by the time my jam was done. Done and very badly done. The worst failure I'd ever had, all the sugar burned to caramel. Luckily, the strawberries cost next to nothing. And there, off I went again: 'Tomorrow, let's see, tomorrow . . . Tomorrow we've got that lady who comes to mount the proofs on fiberboard.' Fiberboard was a novelty imitation felt that made a lovely background for sports photos. But it needed a special knack and special kind of glue. So once a week this lady used to come and I used to keep her to lunch, it made a change for me. We didn't lose by it, she made good use of her time and it was better for her than running around to the little eating house. I added something special in the way of a sweet, or something good from the pork butcher's.

"But this day I'm telling you about, I felt that everything was all one and the same to me, or rather, that nothing satisfied me. And the following days . . . I pass them over in silence.

"What did you say? Oh, no! Oh, you're quite wrong, I didn't

despise my occupations; on the contrary. I've never put my mind to them so much. Nothing went amiss. Except that I found the time long and at the same time I kept looking about for something I could do to fill it up. Reading? Yes. You're certainly right. Reading makes a good distraction. But I've got such a twisted character that everything I tried to read seemed to me . . . a little thin, sort of poor. Always this mania for something big. When I'd done my housework and finished the day's jobs, I used to go out and take a few breaths on the landing—as if I'd be able to see farther from there. But landing or no landing, I'd had enough and more than enough.

"Pardon? Ah! you've put your finger right on the trouble. Enough of what, precisely? Such a happy woman, as Madame Gâteroy used to say when she talked about me. Such a happy woman, why exactly, that's what I would have been if, here and there, in my trivial little life, I'd had something great. What do I call great? But I've no idea, Madame, because I've never had it! If I'd had it even once, I guarantee I'd have realized straightaway, without a shadow of doubt, that it *was* great!"

She rose from her chair, sat down on the bed, rested her elbows on her knees, and propped up her chin. Like that, she was facing me directly. With a wrinkle incised between her eyebrows and one eye nervously screwed up, she did not appear uglier to me; on the contrary.

"What queer things presentiments are, Madame! Not mine, I'm talking of my husband's. Just about that time, he said to me point-blank: 'If you like, in July we'll go off for a month to Yport, as we did two years ago, that'll do you good.' Yport? Yes, it's not bad, mainly a family holiday place, but quite a lot of Paris celebrities go there. Fancy, when we were there before, we saw Guirand de Scevola, the painter who's become so famous, every single day. He was painting the sea in anger, from nature, with the legs of his easel in the foam of the waves. It was a real sight. Everyone used to stare at him. Naturally, I said to my little Exo: 'You're choosing a nice time to go and squander what little money we have at the seaside!' —'When it is a question of you,' he answered, 'nothing else counts.' That day and many days after, I absolutely swore to myself never to do anything to hurt a man like that. Anyway, it wasn't going to Yport that would have brought something great into my life. Unless saving a child who was drowning . . . But I can't swim.

"Little by little, I admit I made myself very unhappy. In the end, what did I go and imagine? I went and imagined that this thing life couldn't do for me, I'd find it in death. I told myself that when death is approaching, not too fast, not too violently, you must have sublime moments, that your thoughts would be lofty, that you'd leave behind everything that's petty, everything that cramps you, nights of bad sleep, bodily miseries. Ah! what a wonderful compensation I invented for myself! I pinned all my hopes on those last moments, you see.

"Oh! But yes indeed, Madame, I did think of my husband! For days and days, for nights and nights. And about his unhappiness. Do me the honor of believing that I weighed it all up and envisaged this, that, and the other before setting out on the road. But once I had set out, I was already far on my way."

Madame Armand looked down at her hands, which she had clasped, and gave an unexpected smile.

"Madame, people very seldom die because they've lost someone. I believe they die more often because they haven't had someone. But you think that, by killing myself, I was cruelly deserting my husband? Well, if the worse came to the worst, my beloved Geo could always have followed me, if it had been too much for him to bear . . . Give me credit for this, before I set out on my way, I worked everything out to the smallest detail. It may seem nothing, but I had all sorts of complications. One thinks it's ever so simple, just to lie down on one's bed, swallow some horrible thing or other, and goodbye! Just to procure this drug, goodness knows what trouble I had and what fibs I had to tell! I had to make up my mind on the spur of the moment one day when I got the chance . . . there'd been an accident to the red light in the darkroom, which meant my husband had to go out immediately after lunch. For two pins I'd have chucked the whole thing. But I recovered my nerve, I was sustained by my idea, by the thought of this . . . this kind of . . ."

I risked suggesting a word which Madame Armand pounced on eagerly.

"Yes, Madame, apotheosis! That's exactly it, apotheosis! That particular day I was uneasy, I kept wondering what other hitch might still occur. Well, the morning slipped by as easy as slipping a letter in the mailbox. Instead of lunch, I took some herb tea. The embroidered sheets on the bed, all the housework properly done, the letter to my husband sealed up, my husband in a hurry to go out. I called him back to give him his lightweight overcoat and I thought he'd gone when really he was still there, he'd broken the bottle of hyposulphite, you remember?

"I think I'm alone at last, I lock the door, and I get myself settled. Yes, here, but inside the bed, the embroidered pillows behind my back, everything all fresh and clean. Right! I'd hardly lain down when I remembered the washerwoman. I get up. I scribble a word on a slip of paper, and I lie down again. First of all, I swallowed a pill to stop stomach spasms, and I waited ten minutes, as I'd been told to do. And then I swallowed the drug, all at one go. And believe me"—Madame Armand twisted her mouth a little—"it was anything but delicious.

"And then? And then I wait. No, not for death, but for what I'd promised myself before it. It was as if I were on a quay, waiting to embark. No, no, I wasn't in pain but I could feel myself getting old. The last straw was that my feet—I'd got my shoes on—were getting hot at the bottom of the bed and hurt like fury wherever I'd got a bad place. Even worse than that, I imagine I hear the doorbell ring! I think: 'It's happened on purpose, I'll never get through.' I sit up and try and remember if someone's made an appointment for a sitting. I listen hard. But I think it was the buzzings in my ears beginning. I lie down again and I say a little prayer, though I'm not particularly religious: 'My God, in your infinite goodness, take pity on an unhappy and guilty soul . . .' Impossible to remember the rest, on my word. But that might have been enough, mightn't it?

"And I went on waiting. I was waiting for my reward, my great arrival of beautiful thoughts, a great pair of wings to carry me away, to sweep me right away from being myself anymore. My head was going round and round, I thought I saw great circles all around me. For a second it was like when you dream you're falling from the top of a tower, but that was all. Nothing else, would you believe it, but all my everyday thoughts and fidgets, including that very day's? For example, I kept worrying like anything that my little Exo would only have cold meat and salad and warmed-up soup when he came in that night. At the same time, I thought: 'Even that will be too much, he'll be so upset over my death, it'll put him off his food. Everyone in the house will be so kind to him. My God, take pity on an unhappy and guilty soul . . .' I'd never have believed that, when I was dying, it would be my feet that I suffered from most.

"The buzzings and the circles went on going round and round me, but I still kept on waiting. I waited lying down, as good as gold." She slid toward the middle of the bed, resumed the attitude and the stillness of her postponed death, and closed her eyes so that I could see nothing of them but the feathery black line of the lashes.

"I didn't lose my head, I listened to all the noises, I went over everything that I had forgotten, everything I had left in a muddle on the other side, I meant the side I was leaving. I reproached myself for those evening walks I used to take without bothering whether my husband might be bored all alone, when his day's work was over. Trifles, petty little things, uninteresting thoughts that floated on the top of the buzzings and the circles. I remember vaguely that I wanted to put my hands over my face and cry and that I couldn't, it was as if I hadn't any arms, I said to myself: 'This is the end. How sad it is that I haven't had what I wanted in life even in my death.'

"Yes, I think that's all, Madame. A terrible icy cold came and cut off the thread of my thoughts and yet I'm not sure even of that. What I am sure of is that never, never again will I commit suicide. I know now that suicide can't be the slightest use to me, I'm staying here. But without wanting to offend Mademoiselle Devoidy, you can see for yourself that I'm in my right mind and that a neurotic woman and myself are two utterly different things."

With a jerk, Madame Armand sat up. Her story had left her with a feverish flush that animated her pale skin. Our conversation ended in "Goodbye, see you soon!" as if we were on a station platform, and after exclamations about the "shocking lateness" we parted for a very long time. She held the door of the flat open behind me, so that the light in the studio should illuminate the landing for me. I left the photographer's wife in her doorway, slender and solitary, but not wavering. I am sure she did not stumble a second time. Whenever I think of her, I always see her shored up by those scruples she modestly called fidgets and sustained by the sheer force of humble, everyday feminine greatness; that unrecognized greatness she had misnamed "a very trivial life."

[*Translated by Antonia White*]

Bella-Vista

❦

PREFACE

No real place served as model for Bella-Vista, a small Provençale inn, which I painted to resemble twenty imitation farmhouses planted on a notch on the Mediterranean, draped, in one season, with plumbago, passion flower, and those convolvulus, bluer than the day, whose teeming avidity I measured against pink walls. Bella-Vista is any chimera of those who, leaving the heart of a dense and exhausting city, demand daily sun, undisturbed good weather, and constant heat. Until I found out for myself that good weather is another chimera and another kind of exhaustion, the region around St.-Tropez gave me all I asked for in the way of daily splendor. I was only just discovering it at the time I was writing "Bella-Vista." With no domain of my own on its shore, I clung to this or that auberge, some Gulf hotel; I didn't realize that the little port into which the dog, the cock, and the saint sailed had, strangely enough, but one access road, a single entrance, like a lobster pot. So that, fifteen years later, I was still moored to this little peninsula jutting out into the sea. At twilight it appears suspended there, the color of lilacs, looking like new steel beneath the full moon; dawn makes all the walls that face east blush briefly with a powdery pink, whereas, before sunrise, the thick vineyard is but a crimped blackness.

There, or thereabouts, is where my knowledge of Provence ends. In fifteen years I moved very little. From St.-Tropez to Fréjus, from Pampelonne to Thoronet, from a rosé wine to a golden wine, from ailloli to pissaladière, from one dawn to one night snowy with stars . . . it is enough to remember enough to be thankful for . . . The prudent weariness of age keeps me from running any risk of forgetting that a sovereign blue color weighs down on the imaginary rooftops of Bella-

Vista, or that the west wind rises fresh toward noon, or that sleep, in the breezy shade, is conducive to dreaming and speaks, to the trusting sleeper, of motionless ships and islands free from danger.

[*Translated by Matthew Ward*]

⟡

It is absurd to suppose that periods empty of love are blank pages in a woman's life. The truth is just the reverse. What remains to be said about a passionate love affair? It can be told in three lines. He loved me, I loved *Him*. His presence obliterated all other presences. We were happy. Then *He* stopped loving me and I suffered.

Frankly, the rest is eloquence or mere verbiage. When a love affair is over, there comes a lull during which one is once more aware of friends and passers-by, of things constantly happening as they do in a vivid, crowded dream. Once again, one is conscious of normal feelings such as fear, gaiety, and boredom; once again time exists and one registers its flight. When I was younger, I did not realize the importance of these "blank pages." The anecdotes with which they furnished me—those impassioned, misguided, simple, or inscrutable human beings who plucked me by the sleeve, made me their witness for a moment, and then let me go—provided more "romantic" subjects than my private personal drama. I shall not finish my task as a writer without attempting, as I want to do here, to draw them out of the shadows to which the shameless necessity of speaking of love in my own name has consigned them.

A house, even a very small house, does not make itself habitable or adopt us in the week which follows the signing of the agreement. As a wise man of few words who makes sandals at St.-Tropez once said: "It takes as much work and thought to make sandals for someone aged six as to make them for someone aged forty."

Thirteen years ago when I bought a small vineyard beside the sea in the South of France with its plumy pines, its mimosas and its little house, I regarded them with the prompt business-like eye of a camper. "I'll unpack my two suitcases; I'll put the bathtub and the portable shower in a corner, the Breton table and its armchair under the window, the divan-bed and its mosquito net in the dark room. I'll sleep *there* and I'll work *there* and I'll wash *there*. By tomorrow, everything will be ready." For the dining room, I could choose between the shade of the mulberry and that of the centuries-old spindle trees.

Having the necessities—that is to say shade, sun, roses, sea, a well, and a vine—I had a healthy contempt for such luxuries as electricity, a kitchen stove, and a pump. More prudent influences seduced me from leaving the little Provençal house in its primitive perfection. I gave in to them and listened to the convincing builder whom I went to see in his own home.

He was smiling. In his garden an all-the-year-round mimosa and purple wallflowers set off to advantage the various objects for sale: concrete benches, upended balusters arranged like skittles, drain pipes, and perforated bricks, the lot under the guardianship of a very pretty bulldog in turquoise Vallauris ware.

"You know how things are here," said the builder. "If you need your villa by July or August, you'll have to come and bully the workman on his own ground now and then."

I remember that I kept blinking my eyelids, which were hurt by the chalky glare of March. The sky was patterned with great white clouds and the mistral was shaking all the doors in their frames. It was cold under the table but a sunbeam, which fell on the estimate covered with red figures and black dots and blue pencil ticks, burned the back of my hand. I caught myself thinking that warm rain is very agreeable in spring in the Ile-de-France and that a heated, draft-proof flat in Paris, staked out with lamps under parchment hats, has an unrivaled charm.

The Midi triumphed. I had indeed just been having attack after attack of bronchitis and the words "warm climate . . . rest . . . open air . . ." became the accomplices of the smiling builder. I decided therefore to try to find a haven of rest, some way away from the port to which I have since become so deeply attached, from which I could sally forth from time to time to "bully the workmen." This would give me an excuse to escape from the most exhausting of all pleasures, conversation.

Thanks to a decorative painter who takes his holidays alone and makes himself unrecognizable, in the manner of Greta Garbo, by wearing sunglasses and sleeveless tennis shirts, I learned that a certain inn, crowded with odd people in the summer but peaceful for the rest of the year, would take me under its roof. I call it Bella-Vista because there are as many Bella-Vistas and Vista-Bellas in France as there are Montignys. You will not find it on the Mediterranean coast; it has lost its proprietresses and nearly all its charms. It has even lost its old name, which I shall not reveal.

Consequently, at the end of March, I packed a good pound of periwinkle-blue paper in a suitcase. I also put in my heavy wool slacks, my four pullovers, some woolen scarves, and my tartan-lined mackintosh

—all the necessary equipment, in short, for winter sports or an expedition to the Pole. My previous stays in the Midi, during a lecture tour at the end of one winter, called up memories of Cannes blind with hail and Marseilles and Toulon as white and gritty as cuttlefish bones under the January mistral. They also evoked bright blue and pale green landscapes, followed by grim recollections of leeches and injections of camphorated oil.

These discouraging images accompanied me almost to the "hostelry" I call Bella-Vista. Concerning Bella-Vista I shall give only certain inoffensive details and draw posthumous portraits such as those of its two proprietresses of whom one, the younger, is dead. Supposing the other to be alive, heaven knows on what work, and in what place of seclusion, those agile fingers and piercing eyes are now employed.

Thirteen years ago, the two of them stood in the doorway of Bella-Vista. One expertly seized my smooth-haired griffon by the loose skin of her neck and back, deposited her on the ground, and said to her: "Hello, dear little yellow dog. I'm sure you is thirsty."

The other held out her firm hand, with its big ring, to help me out of the car and greeted me by name: "A quarter of an hour later, Madame Colette, and you'd have missed it."

"Missed what?"

"The *bourride*. They wouldn't have left you a mouthful. I know them. Madame Ruby, when you can take your mind for one moment off that dog."

Her charming accent took one straight back to the Place Blanche. She had acquired the red, uneven sunburn peculiar to high-colored blondes. Her dyed hair showed grayish at the roots; there was spontaneous laughter in her bright blue eyes and her teeth were still splendid. Her tailored white linen dress glistened from repeated ironing. A striking person, in fact; one of those who make an instant, detailed physical impression. Before I had even spoken to her, I already knew by heart the pleasant shape of her hands baked by the sun and much cooking, her gold signet ring, her small wide-nostriled nose, her piercing glance which plunged straight into one's own eyes, and the good smell of laundered linen, thyme, and garlic which almost drowned her Paris scent.

"Madame Suzanne," retorted her American partner, "you is lost in Madame Colette's opinion if you is nicer to her than to her little yellow dog."

Having made this statement, Madame Ruby announced lunch by ringing a little copper bell whose angry voice quite unhinged my griffon bitch. Instead of obeying the bell, I remained standing in the courtyard, a square which, like a stage set, lacked one side. Perched on a modest eminence, Bella-Vista prudently turned its back to the sea and offered its façade and its two wings to the kindly winds, contenting itself with a restricted view. From its paved terrace I discovered in turn the forest, some sheltered fields, and a dark blue fragment of the Mediterranean wedged between two slopes of hills.

"You isn't any other luggage?"

"The suitcase, my dressing case, the carry-all, the rug. That's all, Madame Ruby."

At the sound of her name, she gave me a familiar smile. Then she called a dark-haired servant girl and showed her my luggage.

"Room 10!"

But though room 10, on the first floor, looked out on the sea, it refused me my favorite southwest aspect. So I chose instead a room on the ground floor which opened directly onto the terrace courtyard. It was opposite the garage and not far from the aviary of parakeets.

"Here you is more noisy," objected Madame Ruby. "The garage . . ."

"It's empty, thank heaven."

"Quite right. Our car sleeps outdoors. It's more convenient than going in, coming out, going in, coming out. So, you likes number 4 better?"

"I do like it better."

"O.K. Here's the bath, here's the light, here's the bell, here's the cupboards"—she swept up my dog and threw her deftly onto the flowered counterpane—"and here's yellow dog!"

The bitch laughed with pleasure while Madame Ruby, enchanted with the effect she had produced, pivoted on her rubber soles. I watched her cross the courtyard and thought that, from head to foot, she was exactly as she had been described to me. She was scandalous, but one liked her at first sight. She was mannish without being awkward, her boy's hips and square shoulders were trimly encased in blue frieze and white linen; there was a rose in the lapel of her jacket. Her head was round and could not have been more beautifully modeled under the smooth cap of red hair. It had lost its golden glint and showed white in places and she wore it plastered to her skull with severe, provocative coquetry. There was something definitely attractive about her wide gray eyes, her unassuming nose, her big mouth with its big, seemingly indestructible teeth, and her skin, which was freckled over the cheekbones. Forty-five perhaps? More like fifty. The neck in the open cellular shirt was thickening and the loose skin and prominent veins on the back of the strong hands revealed that she might well be even more than fifty.

Undoubtedly I cannot draw Madame Ruby as well as I heard Madame Suzanne describe her later in a moment of irritation.

"You look like an English curate! You're the living image of a Boche got up as a sportsman! You're the living image of a vicious governess! Oh, I know you were an American schoolteacher! But I'd no more have trusted you with my little sister's education than my little brother's!"

On the day of my arrival, I still knew very little about the two friends who ran Bella-Vista. A sense of well-being, unforeseen rather than anticipated, descended on me and kept me standing there with my arms crossed on the windowsill of room 4. I submitted myself passively to the reverberations of the yellow walls and blue shutters; I forgot my exacting griffon bitch, my own hunger, and the meal now in progress. In that odd state of convalescence which follows a tiring night journey, my eyes wandered slowly around the courtyard. They came to rest on the rosebush under my window, idly following every sway of its branches. "Roses already! And white arum lilies. The wisteria's beginning to come out. And all those black-and-yellow pansies."

A long dog, lying stretched out in the courtyard, had wagged its tail as Madame Ruby passed. A white pigeon had come and pecked at the toes of her white shoes . . . From the aviary came a gentle, muffled screeching: the soft, monotonous language of the green parakeets. And I was glad that my unknown room behind me was filled with the smell of lavender, dry bunches of which were hung on the bed rail and in the cupboard.

The duty of having to examine them poisons one's pleasure in new places. I dreaded the dining room as if I were a traveler contemplating the panorama of an unknown town and thinking: "What a nuisance that I'll have to visit two museums, the cathedral, and the docks." For nothing will give the traveler as much pleasure as that warm rampart or that little cemetery or those old dikes covered with grass and ivy . . . and the stillness.

"Come along, Pati."

The griffon followed me with dignity because I had only said her name once. She was called Pati when it was necessary for us both to be on our best behavior. When it was time for her walk, she was Pati-Pati-Pati, or as many more Patis as one had breath to add. Thus we had adapted her name to all the essential circumstances of our life. In the same way, when Madame Ruby spoke French, she contented herself with the single auxiliary verb "to be" which stood for all the others: "You is all you want? . . . You is no more luggage?" and so on. As I crossed the courtyard, I had already assigned Madame Ruby to that category of active, rather limited people who easily learn the nouns and adjectives of a foreign language but jib at verbs and their conjugation.

The prostrate dog half hitched himself up for Pati's benefit. She pretended to ignore his existence, and by degrees, he collapsed again: first his shoulders; then his neck, which was too thin; lastly his mongrel greyhound's head, which was too large. A brisk, rather chilly breeze was blowing wallflower petals over the sand but I was grateful to feel the bite of the sun on my shoulder. Over the wall, an invisible garden wafted the scent which demoralizes the bravest, the smell of orange trees in flower.

In the dining room, which was far from monumental but low-ceilinged and carefully shaded, a dozen small scattered tables with coarse Basque linen cloths reassured my unsociable disposition. There was no butter in shells, no headwaiter in greenish-black tails and none of those meager vases containing one marguerite, one tired anemone, and one spray of mimosa. But there was a big square of ice-cool butter and on the folded napkin lay a rose from the climbing rose tree: a single rose whose lips were a little harsh from the mistral and the salt; a rose I was free to pin to my sweater or to eat as an hors-d'œuvre. I directed a smile toward the presiding goddesses, but the smile missed its target. Madame Ruby, alone at a table, was hurrying through her meal and only Madame Suzanne's bust was visible. Every time the kitchen hatch opened, her golden hair and her hot face appeared in its frame against a background of shining saucepans and gridirons. Pati and I had the famous *bourride*, velvet-smooth and generously laced with garlic; a large helping of roast pork stuffed with sage and served with applesauce and potatoes; cheese, stewed pears flavored with vanilla, and a small carafe of the local *vin rosé*. I foresaw that three weeks of such food would repair the ravages of two attacks of bronchitis. When the coffee was poured out—it was quite ordinary coffee but admirably hot—Madame Ruby came over and vainly offered me her cigarette lighter.

"You is not a smoker? O.K."

She showed her tact by going off at once to her duties and not prolonging the conversation. As she moved away, I admired her rhythmic, swaying walk.

My griffon bitch sat opposite me in the depths of a knitted woolen hood I had presented to her. For correct deportment and silence at table, she could have given points to an English child. The restraint was not entirely disinterested. She knew that the perfection of her behavior would not only win her general approval but more concrete tributes of esteem such as lumps of sugar soaked in coffee and morsels of cake. To this end she gave a tremendous display of engaging head turnings, expressive glances, false modesty, affected gravity, and all the terrier airs and graces. A kind of military salute invented by herself—the front paw raised to the level of the ear—which one might call the

C in alt of her gamut of tricks, provoked laughter and delighted exclamations. I have to admit that she occasionally overdid this playing to the gallery.

I have written elsewhere of this tiny bitch, a sporting dog in miniature with a deep chest, cropped ears like little horns, and the soundest of health and intelligence. Like certain dogs with round skulls—bulldogs, griffons, and Pekinese—she "worked" on her own. She learned words by the dozen and was always observant and on the alert. She registered sounds and never failed to attribute the right meaning to them. She possessed a "rule of the road" which varied according to whether we were traveling by train or by car. Brought up in Belgium in the company of horses, she passionately followed everything that wore iron shoes for the pleasure of running behind them and she knew how to avoid being kicked.

She was artful; a born liar and pretender. Once, in Brittany, I saw her give a splendid imitation of a poor, brave, suffering little dog with its cheek all swollen from a wasp sting. But two could play at that game and I gave her a slap which made her spit out her swelling. It was a ball of dried donkey's dung which she had stowed away in her cheek so as to bring it home and enjoy it at leisure.

Glutted with food and less overcome with fatigue than I was, Pati sat up straight on the other side of the table and took an inventory of the people and things about us. There was a lady and her daughter, who appeared to be the same age: the daughter was already decrepit and the mother still looked young. There were two boys on their Easter holidays who asked for more bread at every course, and finally, there was a solitary resident, sitting not far from us, who seemed to me quite unremarkable though he riveted Pati's attention. Twice, when he was speaking to the dark-haired maid, she puffed out her lips to snarl something offensive and then thought better of it.

I did not scold myself for sitting on there, with the remains of my coffee cooling in my cup, glancing now at the swaying rosebush, now at the yellow walls and the copies of English prints. I stared at the sunlit courtyard, then at something else, then at nothing at all. When I drift like that, completely slack, it is a sign not that I am bored but that all my forces are silently coalescing and that I am floating like a seed on the wind. It is a sign that, out of wisps and stray threads and scattered straws, I am fashioning for myself just one more fragment of a kind of youth. "Suppose I go and sleep? . . . Suppose I go and look at the sea? . . . Suppose I send a telegram to Paris? . . . Suppose I telephone to the builder?"

The resident who had not the luck to please my dog said something to the dark-haired girl as he got up. She answered: "In a moment, Monsieur Daste." He passed close by my table, gave a vague apologetic bow, and said something like "Huisipisi" to my dog in a jocular way. At this she put up her hackles till she looked like a bottle brush and tried to bite his hand.

"Pati! Are you crazy? She's not bad-tempered," I said to Monsieur Daste. "Just rather conventional. She doesn't know you."

"Yes, yes, she knows me all right. She knows me all right," muttered Monsieur Daste.

He bent toward the dog and threatened her teasingly with his forefinger. Pati showed that she did not much relish being treated like a fractious child. I held her back while Monsieur Daste moved away, laughing under his breath. Now that I looked at him more attentively, I saw that he was a rather short, nimble man who gave a general impression of a grayness: gray suit, gray hair, and a grayish tinge in his small-featured face. I had already noticed his tapering forefinger and its polished nail. The dog growled something that was obviously insulting.

"Look here," I told her. "You've got to get used to the idea that you're not in your own village of Auteuil. Here there are dogs, birds, possibly hens, rabbits, and even cats. You've got to accept them. Now, let's take a turn."

At that moment Madame Suzanne came and sat down to her well-earned meal.

"Well? How was the lunch?" she called to me from her distant table.

"Perfect, Madame Suzanne. I could do with one meal like that every day—but only one! Now we're going to take a turn around the house to walk it off a little."

"What about a siesta?"

"Everything in its own good time. I'm never sleepy the first day."

Her plump person had the effect of making me talk in proverbs and maxims and all the facile clichés of "popular" wisdom.

"Will the fine weather hold, Madame Suzanne?"

She powdered her face, ran a moistened finger over her eyebrows, and made her table napkin crack like a whip as she unfolded it.

"There's a bit of east wind. Here it rains if there isn't a touch of wind."

She made a face as she emptied the hard-boiled-egg salad out of the hors-d'œuvres dish onto her plate.

"As to the *bourride*, I'll have to do without, as usual. I don't care— I licked out the bowl I made the sauce in."

Her laugh irradiated her face. Looking at her I thought that, before thin females became the fashion, it was the fair-haired Madame Suzannes with their high color and high breasts who were the beautiful women.

"You take a hand in the kitchen every day, Madame Suzanne?"

"Oh, I like it, you know. In Paris I kept a little restaurant. You never came and ate my chicken with rice on a Saturday night in the rue Lepic? I'll make one for you. But what a bloody hell of a place—excuse my language—this part of France is for provisions."

"What about the early vegetables?"

"Early vegetables! Don't make me laugh. Everything's later here than it is in Brittany. Some little lettuces you can hardly see . . . a few beans. The artichokes are hardly beginning. No tomatoes before June except the Spanish and Italian ones. In winter, except for their rotten oranges, almonds, raisins, nuts, and figs are all we get in the way of fruit. As to new-laid eggs, you've got to fight for them. And when it comes to fish! . . . The weekly boarders in hotels are the luckiest. At least they pay a fixed price and know where they are."

She laughed and rubbed her hands together; those hands which had been tried and proven by every sort and kind of work.

"I love the kitchen stove. I'm not like Madame Ruby. Lucie!" she called toward the hatch. "Bring me the pork and a little of the pears! Madame Ruby," she went on, with ironic respect, "cooking's not *her* affair. Oh dear, no! Nor is managing things and doing the accounts. Oh dear, no!"

She dropped the mockery and emphasized the respect.

"No, her affair is *chic*, manners and so on. Furnishing a room, arranging a table, receiving a guest—she's a born genius at all that. I admit it and I appreciate it. I really do appreciate it. But . . ."

An angry little spark animated Madame Suzanne's blue eyes.

"But I can't stand seeing her wandering all over the kitchen, lifting up the saucepan lids and throwing her weight about. 'Madame Suzanne, do you know you is made coffee like dishwater this morning? Lucie, you is not forgotten to fill the ice trays in the refrigerator?' No, that's really *too* much!"

She imitated to perfection her friend's voice and her peculiar grammar. Flushed with an apparently childish jealousy and irritation, she seemed not to mind in the least revealing or underlining what people call the "strange intimacy" which bound her to her partner. She changed her tone as she saw Lucie approaching. Lucie had a succulent, foolish mouth and a great mass of turbulent black hair which curled at the nape of her neck.

"Madame Colette, I'm making a special *crème caramel* tonight for Monsieur Daste. I'll make a little extra if you'd like it. Monsieur Daste only likes sweet things and red meat."

"And who is Monsieur Daste?"

"A very nice man . . . I believe what I see. It's the best way, don't you think? He's all on his own, for one thing. So he's almost certainly a bachelor. Have you seen him, by the way?"

"Only a glimpse."

"He's a man who plays bridge and poker. And he's awfully well educated, you know."

"Is this an insidious proposal of marriage, Madame Suzanne?"

She got up and slapped me on the shoulder.

"Ah, anyone can see you're artistic. You still talk the way artistic people do. I'm going up to have half an hour's nap. You see *I* get up every morning at half past five."

"You've hardly eaten anything, Madame Suzanne."

"It'll make me slimmer."

She frowned, yawned, and then lifted one of the coarse red net curtains.

"Where's that Ruby run off to now? Will you excuse me, Madame Colette? If I'm not everywhere at once . . ."

She left me planted there and I invited my dog to come for a walk around the hotel. A sharp wind enveloped us as soon as we set foot on the terrace but the sun was still on the little flight of steps leading up to my french window and on the aviary of parakeets. The birds were billing and cooing in couples and playing hide-and-seek in their still empty birchbark nests. At the foot of the aviary, a white rabbit was sunning himself. He did not run away and gave my griffon such a warlike glance with his red eye that she went some way off and relieved herself to keep herself in countenance.

Beyond the walls of the courtyard, the wind was having everything its own way. Pati flattened her ears and I should have gone back to my room if, quite close, shut in between two hillocks of forest, I had not caught sight of the Mediterranean.

At that time I had only a rudimentary acquaintance with the Mediterranean. Compared to the low tides of Brittany and that damp, pungent air, this bluest and saltiest of seas, so decorative and so unchangeable, meant little to me. But merely sniffing it from afar made the griffon's snub nose turn moist and there was nothing for it but to follow Pati to the foot of a little scarp covered with evergreens. There was no beach; only some flat rocks between which seaweed, with spreading branches like a peacock's tail, waved gently just below the surface of the water.

The valorous griffon wet her paws, tested the water, approved of it, sneezed several times, and began to hunt for her Breton crabs. But no waves provide less game than those which wash the southern coast and she had to restrict herself to the pleasure of exploring. She ran from tamarisk to lentiscus, from agave to myrtle, till she came on a man sitting under some low branches. As she growled insultingly at him, I guessed that it must be Monsieur Daste. He was laughing at her, wagging his forefinger, and saying: "Huisipisi"—doing everything, in fact, calculated to offend a very small, arrogant dog who was eager for admiring attention.

When I had called her back, Monsieur Daste made an apologetic gesture for not standing up and silently pointed to a treetop. I jerked my chin up questioningly.

"Wood pigeons," he said. "I think they're going to build their nest there. And there's another pair at the end of the kitchen garden at Bella-Vista."

"You're not thinking of shooting them, are you?"

He threw up his hands in protest.

"Shooting? Me? Good Lord! You'll never see *me* carrying a gun. But I watch them. I listen to them."

He shut his eyes amorously like a music fiend at a concert. I took advantage of this to have a good look at him. He was neither ugly nor deformed; only rather mediocre. He seemed to have been made to attract as little attention as possible. His hair was thick and white and was as plentifully and evenly sprinkled among brown as in a roan horse's hide. His features were decidedly small; he had a stingy face which looked all the more stingy when the long eyelids were closed. If I observed Monsieur Daste more carefully than he deserved, it was because I am always terrified, when chance throws me among unknown people, of discovering some monstrosity in them. I search them to the core with a sharp, distasteful eye as one does a dressing-table drawer in a hotel bedroom. No old dressings? No hairpins, no broken buttons, no crumbs of tobacco? Then I breathe again and don't give it another thought.

In the pitiless light of two in the afternoon, Monsieur Daste, medium-sized, clean, and slightly desiccated, showed no visible signs of lupus or eczema. I could hardly hold it against him that he wore a soft white shirt and a neat tie instead of a pullover. I became affable.

"Pati, say how d'you do to Monsieur Daste."

I lifted the dog by her superfluous skin—nature provides the thoroughbred griffon with enough skin to clothe about a dog and a half—and held her over my arm for Monsieur Daste to appreciate the little squashed muzzle, the blackish-brown mask, and the beautiful prominent gold-flecked eyes. Pati did not try to bite Monsieur Daste, but I was surprised to feel her stiffen slightly.

"Pati, give your paw to Monsieur Daste."

She obeyed, but with her eyes elsewhere. She held out a limp, expressionless paw which Monsieur Daste shook in a sophisticated way.

"Are you in this part of the world for some time, Madame?"

As he had a pleasant voice, I gave Monsieur Daste some brief scraps of information.

"We wretched bureaucrats," he rejoined, "have the choice between three weeks' holiday at Easter or three in July. I need warmth. Bella-Vista is sheltered from the cold winds. But I find the very bright light distressing."

"Madame Suzanne is making you a *crème caramel* for tonight. You see what a lot of things I know already!"

Monsieur Daste closed his eyes.

"Madame Suzanne has all the virtues—even though appearances might lead one to suppose just the opposite."

"Really?"

"I can't help laughing," said Monsieur Daste. "Even if Madame Suzanne practices virtue, she hasn't any respect for it."

I thought he was going to run down our hostesses. I waited for the "They're impossible" I had heard *ad nauseam* in Paris to put an end to our conversation. But he merely raised his small hand like a preacher and remarked: "What are appearances, Madame, what are appearances?"

His chestnut-colored eyes stared thoughtfully at the empty sea, over which the shadows of the white clouds skimmed in dark green patches. I sat down on the dried seaweed that had been torn from the sea and piled up in heaps by the last gales of the equinox and my dog nestled quietly against my skirt. The sulphurous smell of the seaweed, the broken shells, the feeble waves which rose and fell without advancing or retreating gave me a sudden terrible longing for Brittany. I longed for its tides, for the great rollers off St.-Malo which rush in from the ocean, imprisoning constellations of starfish and jellyfish and hermit crabs in the heart of each greenish wave. I longed for the swift incoming tide with its plumes of spray; the tide which revived the thirsty mussels and the little rock oysters and reopened the cups of the sea anemones. The Mediterranean is not the sea.

A sharp gesture from Monsieur Daste distracted me from my homesickness.

"What is it?"

"Bird," said Monsieur Daste laconically.

"What bird?"

"I . . . I don't know. I didn't have time to make it out. But it was a big bird."

"And where are your wood pigeons?"

"My wood pigeons? Not *mine*, alas," he said regretfully.

He pointed to the little wood behind us.

"They were over there. They'll come back. So shall I. That slate-blue, that delicate fawn of their feathers when they spread them out in flight like a fan . . . Coo . . . croo-oo-oo . . . Coo . . . croo-oo-oo," he cooed, puffing out his chest and half closing his eyes.

"You are a poet, Monsieur Daste."

He opened his eyes, surprised.

"A poet . . ." he repeated. "Yes . . . a poet. That's exactly what I am, Madame. I must be, if *you* say so."

A few moments later Monsieur Daste left me, with obvious tact, on the pretext of "some letters to write." He set off in the direction of Bella-Vista with the short, light step of a good walker. Before he went, he did not omit to stick out his forefinger at Pati and to hiss "Huisipisi" at her. But she seemed to expect this teasing and did not utter a sound.

The two of us wandered alone along a beaten track which ran beside the sea at the edge of the forest which was thick with pines, lentiscus, and cork oaks. While I was scratching my fingers trying to pick some long-thorned broom and blue salvia and limp-petaled rock roses for my room, I was suddenly overcome with irresistible sleepiness. The sunshine became a burden and we hurried back up the green scarp.

Three beautiful old mulberry trees, long since tamed and cut into umbrella shapes, did not yet hide the back side of Bella-Vista. Mulberry leaves grow fast but they take a long time to pierce the seamed bark. The trees and the façade looked to me crabbed and harsh; there is a certain time in the afternoon when everything seems repellent to me. All that I longed to do was to shut myself away as soon as possible and the dog felt the same.

Already I no longer liked my room, although it was predominantly pink and red. Where could I plug in a lamp to light the table where I meant to work? I rang for the dark-haired Lucie, who brought me a bunch of white pinks which smelled slightly of creosote. She did not fix anything but went off to find Madame Ruby in person. The American winked one of her gray eyes, summed up the situation, and disappeared. When she returned, she was carrying a lamp with a green china shade, some cord, and a collection of tools. She sat sideways on the edge of the table and set to work with the utmost expertise, her cigarette stuck in the corner of her mouth. I watched her large, deft hands, her brisk, efficient movements, and the beautiful shape of her head, hardly spoiled by the thickening nape, under the faded red hair.

"Madame Ruby, you must be amazingly good with your hands."

She winked at me through the smoke.

"Have you traveled a lot?"

"All over the place . . . Excuse my cigarette."

She jumped down and tested the switch of the lamp.

"There. Is light for you to work?"

"Perfect! Bravo, the electrician!"

"The electrician's an old jack-of-all-trades. Will you sign one of your books for me?"

"Whenever you like. For . . . ?"

"For Miss Ruby Cooney. C . . . double o-n-e-y. Thank you."

I would gladly have stopped her going but I dared not display my curiosity. She rolled up her little tool kit, swept a few iron filings off the table with her hand, and went out, raising two fingers to the level of her ear with the careless ease of a mechanic.

Sleep is good at any time but not waking. A late March twilight, a hotel bedroom that I had forgotten while I slept, two gaping suitcases still unpacked. "Suppose I went away?" . . . The noise a bent finger makes rapping three times on a thin door is neither pleasant nor reassuring.

"Come in!"

But it was only a telegram: a few secret, affectionate words in the code a tender friendship had invented. Everything was all right. There was nothing to worry about. Pati was tearing up the blue telegram; the suitcases would only take a quarter of an hour to unpack; the water was hot; the bath filled quite quickly.

I took into the dining room one of those stout notebooks in which we mean to write down what positively must not be put off or forgotten. I meant to start "bullying the workmen" the very next day. Lucie ladled me out a large bowl of fish soup with spaghetti floating in it and inquired whether I had anything against "eggs . . . you know, dropped in the dish and the cheese put on top" and half a guinea fowl before the *crème caramel*.

By the end of dinner, all I had entered in the new notebook was "Buy a folding rule." But I had done honor to the excellent meal. My dog, stimulated by it, sparkled with gaiety. She smiled at Madame Ruby, alone at her table at the far end of the room, and pretended to ignore the presence of Monsieur Daste. Either the young mother or the old daughter was coughing behind me. The two athletic boys were overcome by the weariness which rewarded their energetic effort. "Just think," Lucie confided to me, "they've walked right around the headland. Twenty miles, they've done!" From where I sat, I could smell the eau de Cologne of which they both reeked. Planning to shorten my stay, I wrote in the big notebook: "Buy a small notebook."

"You is seen the drawing room, Madame Colette?"

"Not yet, Madame Ruby. But tonight, I have to admit that . . ."

"You'd like Lucie to bring you a hot drink in the drawing room?"

I gave in, especially as Madame Ruby was already holding my dear little yellow dog under her arm and Pati was surreptitiously licking her ear, hoping I did not notice. The drawing room looked out on the sea and contained an upright piano, cane furniture, and comfortable imitations of English armchairs. Remembering that my room was almost next door, I eyed the piano apprehensively. Madame Ruby winked.

"You likes music?"

Her quick deft hands lifted the lid of the piano, opened its front, and disclosed bottles and cocktail shakers.

"My idea. I did it all by myself. Gutted the piano like a chicken. You likes some drink? No?"

She poured herself out a glass of brandy and swallowed it carelessly, as if in a hurry. Lucie brought me one of those *tisanes* which will never convince me that they deserve their reputation for being soothing or digestive.

"Where is Madame Suzanne?" Madame Ruby asked Lucie in a restrained voice.

"Madame Suzanne is finishing the *boef à la mode* for tomorrow. She's just straining out the juice."

"O.K. Leave the tray. And give me an ashtray. You is too much bits of hair on your neck, my girl!"

Her big, energetic hand brushed the black bush of hair which frizzed on Lucie's nape. The girl trembled, nearly knocked over my full cup, and hurried out of the room.

Far from avoiding my look, Madame Ruby's own took on a victorious malice which drew attention to Lucie's distress so indiscreetly that, for the moment, I ceased to find the boyish woman sympathetic. I am eccentric enough to be repelled when love, whether abnormal or normal, imposes itself on the onlooker's attention or imagination. Madame Ruby was wise enough not to insist further and went over to the two worn-out boys to ask them if they wanted a liqueur. Her manly ease must have terrified them, for they beat a hasty retreat after having asked whether they could do "a spot of canoeing" the next day.

"Canoe? . . . I told them: 'We is not a Suicides' Club here!' "

She lifted the net curtain from the black windowpane. But in the darkness, only the bark of the mulberry trees and their sparse, luminously green new leaves showed in the beam of light from the room.

"By the way, Madame Ruby . . . When you're shopping tomorrow, will you go to Sixte's and get us some more breakfast cups? The same kind, the red-and-white ones."

Madame Suzanne was behind us, still hot from coping with the dinner and the *boeuf à la mode*, but neat, dressed in white linen, freshly powdered, and smelling almost too good. I found her pleasing from head to foot. She felt my cordiality and returned me smile for smile.

"Are you having a good rest, Madame Colette? I'm almost invisible, you know. Tomorrow I shan't have quite so much to do: my beef stew is in the cellar and the noodle paste's in a cool place, wrapped up in a cloth. Madame Ruby, you must bring me back twelve cups and saucers; that clumsy fool of a Lucie has brought off a double again. For an idiot, there's no one to touch that girl! Now, *you* . . . have you been at the brandy? Not more than one glass, I hope."

As she spoke, she searched Madame Ruby's face. But the latter kept her head slightly downcast and her gray eyes half closed to avoid the accusing glance. Suddenly the suspicious one gave up and sat down heavily.

"You're just an old soak . . . Oh, my legs!"

"You is needing rest," suggested Madame Ruby.

"Easy enough to say. My best kitchen maid's coming back tomorrow," explained Madame Suzanne. "After tomorrow I'm a lady of leisure."

She yawned and stretched.

"At this time of night, I've no thought beyond my bath and my bed. Madame Ruby, will you try and shut the rabbit in? The parakeets are all behind the screen and covered up. Are you taking Slough in with you? Oh, and then tomorrow morning, while I think of it . . ."

"Yes, yes, yes, yes!" broke in Madame Ruby, almost beside herself. "Go to bed."

"Really, who do you think you're talking to?"

Madame Suzanne wished us good night with offended dignity. I let the little dog out in the courtyard for a minute while Madame Ruby whistled in vain for Baptiste the rabbit. The night was murmurous and warmer than the day. Three or four lighted windows, the clouded sky patched here and there with stars, the cry of some night bird over this unfamiliar place made my throat tighten with anguish. It was an anguish without depth; a longing to weep which I could master as soon as I felt it rise. I was glad of it because it proved that I could still savor the special taste of loneliness.

The next morning, there was a fine drizzle. Under her folded blanket, Pati lay awake and motionless. Her wide-open eyes said, "I know it's raining. There's nothing to hurry for." Through my open window I could feel the dampness, which I find friendly, and I could hear the soft chatter of the parakeets. Their aviary was luxuriously mounted on wheels and had been placed under the shelter of the tiled roof.

Promptly renouncing the idea of "bullying" the workmen who, forty miles away, were digging my soil, painting my wall, and installing my septic tank, I rang for my coffee and slipped on my dressing gown.

Out in the courtyard, Madame Ruby, wearing a mackintosh, gloves, and a little white cap, was loading hampers and empty bottles into her car. She was agile, without an ounce of superfluous flesh. The beautiful, ambiguous rhythm of her movements and the sexless strength which directed them inclined me to excuse her gesture of the night before. Could I have admitted that a man might desire Miss Cooney? Would I have thought it decent for Miss Cooney to fall in love with a man?

The half-bred greyhound took its place beside her. Just as the rough, battered old car was starting up, Monsieur Daste ran up in his dressing gown and gave Madame Ruby his letters to post. When she had gone, he crossed the courtyard cautiously, wrinkling up his nose under the rain. He lost one of his slippers and shook his bare foot in a comic, old-maidish way. Lucie, who had just come in behind my back, saw me laughing.

"Monsieur Daste doesn't like the rain, does he, Lucie?"

"No, he simply can't stand it. Good morning, Madame. When it's raining, he stays indoors. He plays *belote* with those two ladies and he always wins. Will Madame have her breakfast in bed or at the table?"

"I'd rather have it at the table."

She pushed my books and papers to one side and arranged the coffeepot and its satellites. She was very gentle and very concentrated as she slowly and carefully performed these duties. Her skin was smooth and amber-colored, and her eyelashes, like her hair, thick and curling. She seemed to be rather timid. By the side of the big cup she laid a rain-wet rose.

"What a pretty rose! Thank you, Lucie."

"It's not me, it's Madame Ruby."

She blushed fierily, not daring to raise her eyes. I pitied her secretly for being the victim of a disturbance which she must find surprising and vaguely painful.

The flying, almost invisible rain, so much more springlike than yesterday's parched sunshine, beckoned me outdoors. My loyal dog was willing to admit that this fine, powdery rain not only did not wet one but made smells more exciting and was propitious to sneezing.

Under the eaves, Monsieur Daste was taking a chilly little walk. Shivering slightly, he was walking thirty paces to and fro without putting a foot outside the narrow dry strip.

"It's raining!" he shouted at me as if I were deaf.

"But so little . . ."

I stopped close behind him to admire the sheltered parakeets with their tiny, thoughtful foreheads and their wide-set eyes. To my great surprise, they had all fallen silent.

"Are they as frightened of rain as all that?"

"No," said Monsieur Daste. "It's because I'm here. You don't believe me?"

He went closer to the cage. Some of the parakeets flew away and pressed themselves against the bars.

"Whatever have you done to them?"

"Nothing."

He was laughing all over his face and enjoying my astonishment.

"*Nothing?*"

"Absolutely nothing. That's just what's so interesting."

"Then you must go away."

"Not till it stops raining. Look at that one on the lowest perch."

He slid his manicured forefinger between two bars of the aviary and there was a great fluttering of wings inside.

"Which? There are three all alike."

"Alike to you, perhaps. But not to me. I can pick it out at once. It's the most cowardly one."

One of the parakeets—I think it was the one he was pointing at—gave a scream. Almost involuntarily, I hit Monsieur Daste on the arm and he stepped back, shaking his hand. He was astonished, but decided to laugh.

"You've only got to leave those parakeets in peace," I said angrily. "Stop tormenting them."

His gaze wandered from the birds to me and back again. I could read nothing in that pleasant neutral face, as far removed from ugliness as it was from beauty, but unresentful surprise and a gaiety that I found extremely ill timed.

"I'm not tormenting them," he protested. "But they know me."

"So does the dog," I thought, seeing Pati's hackles stiffen all along her back. The idea that I might have to spend three weeks in the company of a maniac, possibly an enemy of all animals, profoundly depressed me. At that very moment, Monsieur Daste produced his "huisipisi" for Pati's benefit. She attacked him with all her might and he fled with a comic agility, his hands in his pockets and his shoulders hunched up. I stood perfectly still while she chased him around me. But the chase turned into a game and when Monsieur Daste stopped, out of breath, the dog counted the truce as a victory. She insisted on my congratulating her and looked graciously on her adversary.

During the following days she accepted that irritating "huisipisi" as the signal for a game. But she growled when Monsieur Daste pointed at her or teased her with that tapering, aggressive, minatory forefinger. Comfortably wedged on my forearm with her chest expanded and her eyes bulging, she sniffed the soft dampness with delight.

"She looks like an owl," said Monsieur Daste dreamily.

"Do you frighten owls too?"

To protest his innocence more effectively, Monsieur Daste drew his white, naked hands out of his pockets.

"Good heavens, no, Madame! They interest me . . . certainly they interest me. But . . . I keep away. I must admit I keep well away from them."

He hunched his shoulders up to his ears and scrutinized the sky, where a diffused yellow glow and pale blue patches that promised fine weather were beginning to appear between the clouds. I went off to explore with my dog.

The well-being that rewards me when I exchange my town flat for a hotel does not last very long. Not only do the obligation to work and my usual everyday worries soon take the edge off it but I know all too well the dangers of hotel life. Unless that drifting, irresponsible existence is either completely carefree or organized according to a strict timetable, it always tends to become demoralizing. The main reason for this is that people who really mean nothing to us acquire an artificial importance. At Bella-Vista I had no choice except between the seclusion of a convalescent and the sociability of a passenger on a liner. Naturally, I chose the sociability. I was all the more inclined for it after my first visit to the little house I had bought. I returned from it so disillusioned about landed property that I went and confided my disappointment to Madame Suzanne. I made no secret of the fact that I would be only too glad to sell my bit of land again. She listened earnestly and asked me detailed questions.

"How many square yards did you say you had?"

"Square yards? It comes to five acres. Very nearly."

"But come, that's quite a decent size! What's wrong with it, then?"

"Oh, everything! You should see the state it's in!"

"How many rooms?"

"Five, if you count the kitchen."

"Count it. It sounds more impressive. And you've got the sea?"

"It's practically *in* it."

She pushed away her account book and rubbed her polished nails on her palm.

"In your place, I'd . . . But I'm not in your place."

"Do say what you were going to say, Madame Suzanne."

"*I* should see it as a place where people could stop off. An exclusive little snack bar, a snug little dance floor under the pines. With your name, why, my dear, it's a gold mine!"

"Madame Suzanne, it's not gold I'm wanting. What I want is a little house and some peace."

"You're talking like a child. As if one could have any peace without money! I know what I'm talking about. So it's not getting on as fast as you think it should, your cottage?"

"I can't quite make out. The builders play bowls in the alley under the trees. And they've made a charming little camping ground by the well. Open-air fire, fish soup . . . grilled sausages, bottles of *vin rosé* too: they offered me a glass."

Madame Suzanne was so amused that she flung herself back in her chair and slapped her thighs.

"Madame Ruby! Come and listen to this!"

Her partner came over to us, with a napkin over one hand and the middle finger of the other capped with a thimble. For the first time, I saw her occupied in a thoroughly feminine way and wearing round spectacles with transparent frames. She went on gravely embroidering drawn threadwork while Madame Suzanne went over "the misfortunes of Madame Colette."

"You look like a boy sewing, Madame Ruby!"

As if offended, Madame Suzanne took the napkin from her friend's hands and held it under my nose.

"It's true that embroidering suits her about as well as sticking a feather in her behind. But look at the work itself! Isn't it exquisite?"

I admired the tiny regular lattices and Madame Suzanne ordered tea for the three of us. An intermittent mistral was blowing. It would be silent for some moments, then give a great shriek and send columns of white sand whirling across the courtyard, half burying the anemones and the pansies. Then it would crouch behind the wall, waiting to spring again.

During this first week, I had not enjoyed one entire warm spring day. We had not had one single day of that real spring weather which soothes one's body and blessedly relaxes one's brain. The departure of the two boys, followed by that of the lady in black and her withered daughter, gave the partners plenty of free time. My only idea was to get away, yet, against my will, I was growing used to the place. That mysterious attraction of what we do not like is always dangerous. It is fatally easy to go on staying in a place which has no soul, provided that every morning offers us the chance to escape.

I knew the timetable of the buses which passed along the main road, three miles away, and which would have put me down at a station. But my daily mail quenched my thirst for Paris. Every afternoon at tea-time, I left my work, which was sticking badly, and joined "those women" in a little room off the drawing room which they called their boudoir. I would hear the light step of Monsieur Daste on the wooden staircase as he came down eager for tea and one of his favorite delicacies. This consisted of two deliciously light pieces of flaky pastry sandwiched together with cheese or jam and served piping hot. After dinner I made a fourth at poker or *belote* and reproached myself for doing so. There is always something suspect about things which are as easy as all that.

My griffon bitch, at least, was happy. She was enjoying all the pleasures of a concierge's dog. In the evenings, she left her nest in the woolen hood to sit on Madame Ruby's lap. She noted and listed these new patterns of behavior, keeping her ears open for gossip and her nose alert for smells. She continued to react against Monsieur Daste, but as a wary, intelligent dog rather than as his born enemy.

"Madame Suzanne, what does one do in this part of the world to make workmen get on with the job?"

She shrugged her shoulders. "Offer them a bonus. I know I wouldn't offer one."

"Isn't you better give your camping builders a kick in the pants?" suggested Madame Ruby.

She jabbed the air with her needle.

"Tsk, tsk!" said Madame Suzanne reprovingly. "Pour us out some tea and don't be naughty. Drink it hot, Madame Colette. I heard you coughing again this morning when I was getting up at six."

"Did I make as much noise as all that?"

"No, but we're next door. And your hanging cupboard is in a recess so that it juts out right at the back of our . . ."

She stopped short and blushed as violently as an awkward child.

"Our apartment," Madame Ruby suggested lamely.

"That's right. Our apartment."

She put down her cup and threw her arm around Madame Ruby's shoulders with an indescribable look—a look from which all constraint had vanished.

"Don't worry, my poor old darling. When you've said a thing, you've said it. Ten years of friendship—that's nothing to be ashamed of. It's a long-term agreement."

The tweed-jacketed embroidress gave her an understanding glance over her spectacles.

"Of course, I wouldn't talk of such things in front of old Daddy Daste . . . He'll be back soon, won't he?"

"He wasn't at lunch today," I observed.

I was promptly ashamed of having noticed his absence. Petty observations, petty kindnesses, petty pieces of spite—indications, all of them, that my awareness was becoming sharper, yet deteriorating too. One begins by noticing the absence of a Monsieur Daste and soon one descends to "The lady at table 6 took three helpings of French beans . . ." Horrors, petty horrors.

"No," said Madame Suzanne. "He went off early to fetch his car from Nice."

"I didn't know Monsieur Daste had a car."

"Good gracious, yes," said Madame Ruby. "He came here by car and by accident. The car in the ditch and Daddy Daste slightly stunned, with a nest beside him."

"Yes, a nest. I expect the shock is made the nest fall off a tree."

"Wasn't it a scream?" said Madame Suzanne. "A nest! Can't you just see it!"

"Do you like Monsieur Daste, Madame Suzanne?"

She half closed her blue eyes and blew smoke from her painted mouth and her nostrils.

"I like him very much in one way. He's a good client. Tidy, pleasant, and all that. But in another way, I can't stand him. Yet I've not a word to say against him."

"A nest . . ." I said again.

"Ah, that strikes you, doesn't it? There were even three young ones lying dead around the nest."

"Young ones? What kind of bird?"

She shrugged her plump shoulders.

"I haven't any idea. He got off with some bruises and he's been here ever since. It's fifteen days now, isn't it, Ruby?"

"Two weeks," answered Madame Ruby managerially. "He paid his second the day before yesterday."

"And what's Monsieur Daste's job in life?"

Neither of the two friends answered immediately and their silence forced me to notice their uncertainty.

"Well," said Madame Suzanne. "He's the head of a department in the Ministry of the Interior."

She leaned forward with her elbows on her knees and her eyes fastened on mine as if she expected me to protest.

"Does that seem very unlikely, Madame Suzanne?"

"No! Oh, no! But I did not know that civil servants were usually so good at climbing. You should just see how that man can climb. *Really* climb."

The two friends turned simultaneously toward the window, which was darkening to blue as the night came in.

"What do you mean, really climb?"

"Up a tree," said Madame Ruby. "We is not seen him go up, we is seen him coming down. Backward, a tiny step at a time, like this."

With her hands she mimed an acrobatic descent down a mast on a knotted rope.

"A tall tree in the wood, over toward the sea. One evening before you arrived. One of those days when it was so hot, so lovely you is no idea."

"No," I said sarcastically. "I certainly haven't any idea. For over a week I've been disgusted with your weather. I suppose Monsieur Daste was trying to dazzle you with his agility?"

"Just imagine!" cried Madame Suzanne. "He didn't even see us. We were under the tamarisks."

She blushed again. I liked that violent way she had of blushing.

"Madame Suzanne," said Madame Ruby phlegmatically, "you is telling your story all upside down."

"No, I'm not! Madame Colette will understand me, all right! We were sitting side by side and I had my arm around Ruby, like that. We felt rather close to each other, both in the same mood and not spied on all the time as we are in this hole."

She cast a furious glance in the direction of the kitchen.

"After all, it's worth something, a good moment like that! There's no need to talk or to kiss each other like schoolgirls. Is what I'm saying so very absurd?"

She gave her companion a look which was a sudden affirmation of loyal love. I answered no with a movement of my head.

"Well, there we were," she went on. "Then I heard a noise in a tree, too much noise for it to be a cat. I was frightened. I'm brave, really, you know, but I always start by being frightened. Ruby made a sign to me not to move, so I don't move. Then I hear someone's shoe soles scraping and then *poof!* from the ground. And then we see Daddy Daste rubbing his hands and dusting the knees of his trousers and going off up to Bella-Vista. What do you think of that?"

"Funny," I said mechanically.

"Very funny indeed, I think," she said. But she did not laugh.

She poured herself a second cup of tea and lit another cigarette. Madame Ruby, sitting very upright, went on embroidering with agile fingers. For the first time, I noticed that, away from their usual occupations, the two friends did not seem happy or even peaceful. Without going back on the instant liking I had felt for the American, I was beginning to think that Madame Suzanne was the more interesting and more worth studying of the two. I was struck, not only by her fierce, indiscreet jealousy which flared up on the least provocation, but by a kind of protective vigilance, by the way she made herself a buffer between Ruby and all risks, between Ruby and all worries. She gave her all the easy jobs which a subordinate could have done, sending her to the station or to the shops. With perfect physical dignity, Madame Ruby drove the car, unloaded the hampers of eggs and vegetables, cut the roses, cleaned out the parakeets' cage, and offered her lighter to the guests. Then she would cross her sinewy legs in their thick woolen stockings and bury herself in an English or American magazine. Madame Suzanne did not read. Occasionally she would pick up a local paper from a table, saying: "Let's have a look at the *Messenger*," and, five minutes later, drop it again. I was beginning to appreciate her modes of relaxing, so typical of an illiterate woman. She had such an active, intelligent way of doing nothing, of looking about her, of letting her cigarette go out. A really idle person never lets a cigarette go out.

Madame Ruby also dealt with the letters and, when necessary, typed in three languages. But Madame Suzanne said that she "inspired" them and Madame Ruby, nodding her beautiful faded chestnut head, agreed. Teatime cleared Madame Suzanne's head and she would communicate her decisions in my presence. Whether from trustfulness or vanity, she did not mind thus letting me know that her eccentric summer clients did not mind what they paid and demanded privacy even more than comfort. They planned their stays at Bella-Vista a long time ahead.

"Madame Ruby," said Madame Suzanne suddenly, as if in response to a sudden outburst of the mistral, "I hope to goodness you haven't shut the gate onto the road? Otherwise Daddy Daste won't see it and he'll crash into it with his car."

"I asked Paulius to light the little arc lamp at half past six."

"Good. Now, Madame Ruby, we'll have to think about answering those two August clients of ours. They want their usual two rooms. But do remember the Princess and her masseur also want rooms in August. Our two Boche hussies, and the Princess, and Fernande and her gigolo —that's a whole set that's not on speaking terms. But they know each other . . . they've known each other for ages . . . and they can't stand one another. So, Madame Ruby, first of all you're to write to the Princess."

She explained at considerable length, knitting her penciled eyebrows. She addressed Ruby as "Madame" and used the intimate "*tu*" with a bourgeois, marital ceremoniousness. As she spoke, she kept looking at her friend just as an anxious nurse might scrutinize the complicated little ears, the eyelids, and the nostrils of an immensely well-looked-after child. She would smooth down a silvery lock on her forehead, straighten her tie, flatten her collar, or pick a stray white thread off her jacket.

The expression on her face—it was tired and making no attempt just then to hide its tiredness—seemed to me very far from any "perverted" fussing. I use the word "perverted" in its usual modern sense. She saw that I was watching her and gave me a frank, warm smile which softened the blue eyes that often looked so hard.

"It's no news to you," she said, "that our clientele's rather special. After all, it was Grenigue who gave you our address. At Christmas and Easter, you won't find a soul. But come back in July and you'll have any amount of copy. You realize that, with only ten rooms in all, we have to put up prices a bit; our real season only lasts three months. I'll tell you something that'll make you laugh. Last summer, what do you think arrived? A little old couple, husband and wife, at least a hundred and sixty between them. Two tiny little things with an old manservant crumbling to bits, who asked if they could inspect the rooms, as if we were a palace! I said to them—as nicely as possible—'There's some mistake. You see this is a rather special kind of inn.' They didn't want to go. But I insisted, I tried to find words to make myself understood, old-fashioned words, you know. I said, 'It's a bit naughty-naughty, so to speak. People come here and sow their wild oats, as it were. You can't stay here.' Do you know what she answered, that little old grandmother? 'And who told you, Madame, that we don't want to sow some wild oats too?' They went away, of course. But she had me there, all right! Madame Ruby, do you know what the time is? Time you gave that embroidery a rest. I can't hear a sound in the dining room and the courtyard's not lit up. Whatever's the staff thinking about?"

"I'll go and ask Lucie," said Madame Ruby, promptly getting to her feet.

"No," shouted Madame Suzanne. "I must go and see to the dinner. You don't suppose the leg of mutton's anxiously waiting for *you*, do you?"

She was trembling with sudden rage. Her lips were quivering with desire to burst out into a furious tirade. To stop herself, she made a rush to the door. As she did so, there was the sound of a motor engine and the headlights of a car swept the courtyard.

"Daddy Daste," announced Madame Suzanne.

"Why isn't that man switched off his headlights to come in? He might at least do that."

Pati, suddenly woken up, flung herself at the french window, from etiquette rather than from hostility. The dry breath of the mistral entered along with Monsieur Daste. He was rubbing his hands, and his impersonal face at last bore an individual accent. This was a small newly-made wound, triangular in shape, under his right eye.

"Hello, Monsieur Daste! You is wounded? Pebble? A branch? An attack? Is the car damaged?"

"Good evening, ladies," said Monsieur Daste politely. "No, no, nothing wrong with the car. She's going splendidly. This," he put his hand to his cheek, "isn't worth bothering about."

"All the same, I'm going to give you some peroxide," said Madame Suzanne, who had come up to him and was examining the deeply incised little wound at close range. "Don't cover it up, then it'll dry quicker. A nail? A bit of flying flint?"

"No," said Monsieur Daste. "Just a . . . bird."

"What, *another* one?" said Madame Ruby.

Madame Suzanne turned to her friend with a reproving look.

"What do you mean, another one? There's nothing so very astonishing about it."

"Quite so. Nothing so very astonishing," agreed Monsieur Daste.

"It's full of night birds around here."

"Full," said Monsieur Daste.

"The headlights dazzle them and they dash themselves against the windshield."

"Exactly," concluded Monsieur Daste. "I'm delighted to be back at Bella-Vista again. That Corniche road at night! To think that there are people who actually drive on it for pleasure! I shall do justice to the dinner, Madame Suzanne!"

Nevertheless we noticed at dinner that Monsieur Daste ate nothing but the sweet. I noticed this mainly because Madame Ruby kept up a stream of encouragement from her table.

"Hello, Monsieur Daste! Is good for you to keep your strength up!"

"But I assure you I don't feel in the least weak," Monsieur Daste kept politely assuring her.

In fact, his abstinence had endowed him with the bright flush of satiety. He was drinking water with a slightly inebriated expression.

Madame Ruby raised her large hand sententiously.

"Leg of mutton *Bretonne* is very good against birds, Monsieur Daste!"

I remember it was that evening that we played our first game of poker. My three partners loved cards. In order to play better, they retired into the depths of themselves, leaving their faces unconsciously exposed. Studying them amused me more than the game. In any case, I play poker extremely badly and was scolded more than once. I was amused to note that Monsieur Daste only "opened" when forced to and then only with obvious reluctance, but good cards gave him spasms of nervous yawns which he managed to suppress by expanding his nostrils. His little wound had been washed and around it a bruised area was already turning purple, showing how violent the impact had been.

Madame Ruby played a tough game, compressing her full lips, and asking for cards and raising the bid by signs. I was astonished to see her handling the cards with agile but brutal fingers, using a thumb which was much thicker than I had realized. As to Madame Suzanne, she seemed set in her tracks like a bloodhound. She showed not the slightest emotion, pulled each card out slowly before declaring with an air of detachment: "Good for me!"

The smoke accumulated in horizontal layers and between two rounds I reproached myself for the inertia which kept me sitting there. "Perhaps I'm still not quite well," I told myself with a kind of hopefulness.

Suddenly the mistral stopped blowing and the silence fell on us so brutally that it awakened the sleeping griffon. She emerged from her knitted hood and asked clearly, with her eyes and her pricked ears, what time it was.

"Huisipisi, huisipisi!" said Monsieur Daste maliciously.

She stared at him, sniffed the air about his person, and put her two front paws on the table. From there, by stretching her thick little neck, she could just reach Monsieur Daste's hands.

"How she loves me!" said Monsieur Daste. "Huisipisi . . ."

The dog seemed to be searching for a particular spot and to find it just under the edge of Monsieur Daste's cuff. She smelled it with her knowing black nostrils, then she tasted it with her tongue.

"She's tickling me! Madame Suzanne, you pray too long to the goddess of luck while you're shuffling the cards. On with the game!"

"Monsieur Daste, why do you always say 'huisipisi' to my dog? Is it a magic password?"

He fluttered his little hands about his face.

"The breeze," he said. "The wind in the fir trees. Wings . . . Huisipisi . . . Things that fly . . . Even things that skim over the ground in a very . . . very *silky* way. Rats."

"Boo!" cried Madame Suzanne. "I've a horror of mice. So, imagine, a *rat*! On with the game yourself, Monsieur Daste. Madame Colette, don't forget the kitty. I believe you're thinking more about your next novel than our little poker game."

In this she was wrong. Alone in this equivocal guest house, during the pause before the harvest of its summer debauch, I was aware of a complex and familiar mental state. In that state a peculiar pleasure blunts the sharp edge of my longing for my friends, my home, and my real life. Yet is there anyone who is not deluded about the setting of their "real" life? Was I not breathing here and now, among these three strangers, what I call the very oxygen of travel? My thoughts could wander as lazily as they pleased; I was free of any burden of love; I was immersed in that holiday emptiness in which morning brings a lighthearted intoxication and evening a compulsion to waste one's time and to suffer. Everything you love strips you of part of yourself: the Madame Suzannes rob you of nothing. Answering the few careless questions they ask takes nothing out of you. "How many pages do you do a day? All those letters you get every day and all those ones you write, don't you have to cudgel your brains over them? You don't happen to know an authoress who lives all the year round at Nice—a tall woman with pince-nez?" The Madame Suzannes don't catechize you; they tell you about themselves. Sometimes, of course, they keep aggressively silent about some great secret which is always rising to their lips and being stifled. But a secret is exacting and deafens us with its clamor.

In many ways, I found Bella-Vista satisfying. It revived old habits from my solitary days: the itch for the arrival of the postman, my curiosity about passers-by who leave no permanent trace. I felt sympathetic toward the discredited pair of friends. At Bella-Vista I ate admirably and worked atrociously. Moreover, I was putting on weight there.

"Four last rounds," announced Madame Suzanne. "Monsieur Daste, you open for the last time. Afterward, I'll stand you a bottle of champagne. I think that ought to wake Madame Ruby up. There hasn't been a sound from her all the evening."

Her blue eyes shot a glance of fierce reproach at her impassive friend.

"You is usually hear me play poker at the top of my voice?"

Madame Suzanne did not answer and, as soon as the last round was over, went off to get the champagne. While she was going down to the cellar, Madame Ruby stood up, stretched her arms and her firm shoulders till the joints cracked. Then she opened the door between the dining room and the boudoir, listened in the direction of the kitchen, and came back again. She seemed absentminded, preoccupied by some care which made her full mouth look ugly and dulled the large gray eyes under the eyebrows which were paler than her forehead. That evening, the ambiguity of all her features, always disturbing, seemed almost repellent. She was biting the inside of her cheek but forced herself to stop gnawing it when her friend returned, out of breath, with a bottle of *brut* under each arm.

"This is really old," announced Madame Suzanne. "Some remains of the '06. You don't think I pour *that* down the gullets of the summer visitors. It's not iced but the cellar's cool. I don't know if you agree with me that it's nice to have a wine now and then that doesn't make a block of ice in your stomach. Madame Ruby, where are there some pliers? These bottles are wired in the old-fashioned way."

"I'll call Lucie," suggested the American.

Madame Suzanne looked at her almost furiously.

"For God's sake, can't you give Lucie a little peace? For one thing, she's gone to bed. For another, you'll certainly find some sort of pliers in the office."

We drank each other's health. Madame Ruby magically gulped down a large glass in one swallow, throwing her head back in a way which proved how much drinking was a habit with her. Madame Suzanne mimicked the toasts with which drinkers in the Midi raise their glasses: "To your very good!" "Much appreciated! Likewise!" Monsieur Daste closed his eyes like a cat afraid of splashing itself when it laps. Sitting opposite me in the depths of one of the English armchairs, he drank the perfect old champagne, whose bubbles gave out a faint scent of roses as they burst, in tiny sips. The bruise which was now clearly visible around the little triangular wound on his cheek made him seem, for some reason, likable, less definitely human. I like a fox terrier to have a round spot by its eye and a tortoiseshell cat to show an orange crescent or a black patch on its temple. A large mole or freckle on our cheek, a neat well-placed scar, one eye that is slightly larger than the other: all such things mark us out from the general human anonymity.

Madame Suzanne inclined the neck of the second bottle over our goblets and drew our attention to the mushroom-shaped cork, which had acquired the texture of hard wood with age.

"Two bottles among four of us. Quite an orgy! But we'll see better than that in this house this summer."

"We can see it here and now, if you like," said Madame Ruby promptly, pushing her empty glass toward the bottle.

Madame Suzanne gave her friend a warning look.

"Moderation in all things, Madame Ruby. Would you be an angel and go and find that fool of a Slough? And shut the rabbit up, if you can! Have you covered up the parakeets?"

Through the light buzzing of the wine in my ears, I listened to those ritual phrases, not unlike "counting-out rhymes." I know by experience how their sound, their fatal recurrence can be like longed-for dew or a faint, neutral blessing. I know, too, that they can also fall like a branding iron on a place already seared.

But that night I was all benevolence. Pati, who was also getting fatter at Bella-Vista, waddled peacefully into the courtyard and I listened gratefully to Madame Ruby's voice outside announcing that it was going to be fine.

As I stood up, my spectacles and my room key slipped off my knees. As they fell, Monsieur Daste's hand reached out and caught them with such a swift, perfectly timed movement that I hardly had time to see his gesture. "Ah," I thought. "So he's not quite human, this climber."

We all separated without further words like people who have the sense not to prolong the pleasures of a superficial gaiety and cordiality to the point of imprudence. Still under the spell of my optimism, I complimented Monsieur Daste on the appearance of his little wound. I did not tell him that it brought out the character, at once intelligent and uninteresting, of his face. He seemed enchanted. He bridled and passed one hand coquettishly over his ear to smooth his hair.

Lucie did not have to wake me the next morning. When she came in with the tray and the rose, I was already dressed and standing at my open french window, contemplating the fine weather.

Thirteen years ago, I did not know what spring or summer in the Midi could be. I knew nothing of that irruption, that victorious invasion of a season of serenity, of that enduring pact between warmth, color, and scent. That morning I took to longing for the sea salt on my hands and lips and to thinking of my patch of land where my picnicking work-men were drinking *vin rosé* and eating salami.

"Lucie, what beautiful weather!"

"The proper weather for the season. About time too. It's kept us waiting long enough."

As she arranged my breakfast and the daily rose on the table, the dark-haired maid answered me absently. I looked at her and saw that she was pale. Her pallor and a certain troubled look made her more attractive. She had put a little rouge on her beautiful mouth.

"Hello, Madame Colette!"

I answered Madame Ruby, who, dressed all in blue, with a narrow tight-fitting shirt and a beret pulled over one ear, was loading up her hampers.

My dog rushed at her, gave her her military salute, and danced around her.

"You is not want to come with me?"

"I'd love to."

"While I do my shopping, you gives good advice to your pioneers."

"Excellent idea!"

"You say the mason: 'Dear friend.' You say the man who does the roof: 'My boy.' You say the little painter: 'Where is you get made the smart white blouse what suits you so well?' You turn on the charm! Perhaps that works."

"Ah, you know how to talk to men, Madame Ruby! Hold Pati. Just let me get a pullover and I'll be with you."

I went into the bathroom for a moment. When I returned, Lucie and Madame Ruby, one standing perfectly still in my room and the other stationed in the courtyard, were looking at each other across the intervening space. The maid did not turn away quickly enough to conceal from me that her eyes were full of fear, gentleness, and tears.

Madame Ruby drove us, fast and well, through the sparse forest, still russet from the annual fires. Between two tracts of pineland were carefully cultivated allotments now green with young beans and marrows, and fenced-off tracts of wild quince with great pink flowers. The much-prized garlic and onion lifted their spears from the light, powdery earth and the growing vines were stretching out their first tendrils. The blue air was now chill but kindly, now full of new and subtle warmth. The blue air of the Estérels rushed to meet us, and moistened the dog's nose. Along the lane which ran into the main road, I could put out my hand as we drove and touch the leaves of the almond trees and the fruit already set and downy.

"The spring is born tonight," said Madame Ruby softly.

Up till then, we had only exchanged a few commonplaces and these last words, spoken in such a low, troubled voice that they were almost inaudible, came as a surprise. They did not demand an answer and I made none. My strange companion sat impassive at the wheel, her chin high and her little beret over one eye. I threw a glance at her firm profile, so unlike a Frenchwoman's, and noted again the coarse ruddy texture of her skin. The back of her neck, emerging from her pullover, looked as strong as a coal heaver's. With a terrible blast of her horn, she swept the sprawling, dusty dogs off the road, to Pati's intense delight, and kept up a stream of blasphemy in English against the heedless cart drivers. "The spring is born tonight." Imprisoned behind the same ambiguous exterior, a brazen, angular female and a collegian in love with a servant girl were both claiming the right to live and to love. Very likely each hated the other.

It seemed a long time before we came to the coast and drove along the edge of the sea where a few bathers were shrieking with cold as they splashed about. We passed through sham villages; pink, silent, and empty, idly blossoming with no one to admire. At last Madame Ruby put me down in front of my future dwelling. She gave a whistle of ironic commiseration and refused to get out of the car. Raising her forefinger to the level of her pale, bushy eyebrow, she said: "I come and fetch you in three-quarters of an hour. You thinks it is enough for your whole house to be finished?"

She indicated the rampart of hollow bricks, the crater of slaked lime, and the mound of sifted sand which defended my gates, and left me to my fate.

But when she returned, I no longer wanted to leave the place. Instead of the workmen, who were missing one and all, I had found white arum lilies, red roses, a hundred little tulips with pointed cups, purple irises, and pittosporums whose scent paralyzes the will. Leaning over the edge of the well, I had listened to the musical noise of drops that filtered through the broken bricks falling into the water below, while Pati rested after her first encounter with a hedgehog. The interior of the house bore not the slightest resemblance to anything which had charmed me about it at first. But in the little pine wood, the bright drops of liquid resin were guttering in the wind, those drops that congeal almost as soon as they are formed, and tarnish before they fall to the ground. I had treated the mimosa, which flowers all the year round, with scant respect. Feeling like a rich person, I flung my bundle of flowers into the car, on top of the hampers of early artichokes, broad beans, and French beans with which the back seat was loaded.

"Not a soul?" asked Madame Ruby.

"Not a soul! Such luck! It was delightful."

"We used to say that at Bella-Vista too, in the beginning. 'Such luck! Not a soul!' And now . . ."

She raised that clerical chin of hers and started up the car.

"And now we is a little blasé. A little old, both of us."

"It's very beautiful, a friendship that grows old gracefully. Don't you agree?"

"Nobody loves what is old," she said harshly. "Everyone loves what is beautiful, what is young—dangerous. Everyone loves the spring."

On the way back, she did not speak again except to the dog. In any case, I should have been incapable of listening intelligently. I was conscious only of the noonday sun drugging me with light well-being and overwhelming drowsiness. I sat with my eyes closed, aware only of the resonance of a voice which, though nasal, was never shrill and whose deep pitch was as pleasant as the lowest notes of a clarinet. Madame Ruby drove fast, pointing out objects of vituperation to Pati, such as small donkeys, chickens, and other dogs. The griffon responded enthusiastically to all these suggestions, even though they were expressed in English spoken with an American twang.

"O.K.," approved Madame Ruby. "Good for you to learn English. Holiday task. Look to the left, enormous, enormous goose! Wah!"

"Wah!" repeated the little dog, standing up, quite beside herself with excitement, with her front paws against the windshield.

Of the few days that followed, I remember only the glorious weather. The weather spread an indulgent blue and gold and purple haze over my work and my worries, over the letters which arrived from Paris, over the full-blown idleness of the workmen, whom I found singing and playing "she loves me, she loves me not" with daisy petals when I revisited my little house. Fine weather, day and night, induced in me an Oriental rebelliousness against the accustomed hours of sleep. I was wide awake at midnight and overwhelmed with the imperative need of a siesta in the afternoon. Laziness, like work, demands to be comfortably organized. Mine sleeps during the day, muses at night, wakes at dawn, and closes the shutters against the unsympathetic light of the hours after lunch. On dark nights and under the first quarter of a slender, rosy moon, the nightingales all burst out together, for there is never a first nightingale.

On this subject, Monsieur Daste made various poetic remarks which did not affect me in the least. For I never bothered less about Monsieur Daste than I did during that week of fine weather. I saw hardly anything even of my hostesses. Their importance faded under the dazzling impact of the season. I did however observe a little poker incident between Madame Ruby and Monsieur Daste one evening. It was a very brief incident, mimed rather than spoken, and in the course of it I had a vision of Madame Ruby flushing the color of copper and clutching the edge of the green table with both hands. At that, Monsieur Daste gathered himself together in a most peculiar way. He seemed to shrink till he became very small and very compact, and as he thrust his lowered brow forward, he gave the impression of drawing back his shoulders behind his head. It was an attitude that blended ill with his prim face and that hair which was neither old nor young. Madame Suzanne promptly laid her hand on her friend's well-groomed head.

"Now, now, my pet! Now, now . . ." she said without raising her voice.

With one accord, the two adversaries resumed a friendly tone and the game went on. As I was not interested in the cause of their quarrel, I made no inquiries. Perhaps Monsieur Daste had cheated. Or perhaps Madame Ruby. Or possibly both of them. I only thought to myself that, had it come to a fight, I should not have backed Monsieur Daste to win.

It was that night, if I am not mistaken, that I was awakened by a great tumult among the parakeets. As it was silenced almost at once, I did not get up. The next morning, very early, I saw Madame Ruby, trim as usual in white and blue, her rose in her lapel, standing near the aviary. Her back was turned to me and she was attentively studying some object she was holding in her cupped hand. Then she slipped whatever it was into her pocket. I pulled on a dressing gown and opened my french window.

"Madame Ruby, did you hear the parakeets in the night?"

She smiled at me, nodded from the distance, and came up the little steps to shake hands with me.

"Slept well?"

"Not badly. But did you hear, about two in the morning . . ."

She drew out of her pocket a dead parakeet. It was soft and the eye showed bluish between two borders of gray skin.

"What! They're capable of killing each other?"

"So we must suppose," said Madame Ruby, without looking up. "Poor little bird!"

She blew on the cold feathers which parted about a torn, bloodless wound. The dog wanted to be in on the affair and sniffed the bird with that mixture of bewilderment and eroticism which the sight and smell of death so often excites in the living.

"Not so keen, not so keen, little yellow dog. You begins smell, smell and then you eats. And then ever after, you eats."

She went off with the bird in her pocket. Then she changed her mind and came back.

"Please, it's better to say nothing to Madame Suzanne. Nor Monsieur Daste. Madame Suzanne is super . . . superstitious. And Monsieur Daste is . . ."

Her prominent eyes, gray as agates, sought mine.

"He is . . . sensitive. It's better to say nothing."

"I agree."

She gave me that little salute with her forefinger and I did not see her again till luncheon.

In addition to its usual guests, Bella-Vista was receiving a family from Lausanne: three couples of hiking campers. Their rucksacks, their little tents and battery of aluminum cooking utensils, their red faces and bare knees seemed like the emblems of some inoffensive faith.

Lucie went to and fro between the tables, carrying the chervil omelette, the brains fried in batter, and the ragoût of beef. Her face was thickly powdered and she was languid and absentminded.

Their meal over, the campers spread out a map. With managerial discretion, Madame Suzanne signed to us to come and take our coffee in the "boudoir." There was an expression of faint repugnance on her heated face. She gave off her strong perfume which blended ill with that of the ragoût, and she cooled the fire of her complexion with the help of a vast powder puff which never left the pocket of her white blouse.

"Pooh!" she sighed as she fell into a chair. "My goodness, how they fell on the stew, those Switzers! You'll eat God knows what tonight: I haven't a thing left. Those people give me the creeps. So I'm going to treat myself to a little cigar. Where are they off to already, Madame Ruby?"

With a thrust of her chin, Madame Ruby indicated the direction of the sea.

"Over there. Somewhere that isn't got a name, provided it's at least thirty miles away."

"And they sleep on the hard ground. And they drink nothing but water. And it's for idiots like that that our wonderful age invented the railway and the motorcar and the *airplane*! I ask you! As for me sleeping on the ground, the mere idea of ants . . ."

She bit off the end of her little Havana and rolled it carefully between her fingers. Madame Ruby never smoked anything but cigarettes.

"Come, come!" said Monsieur Daste. "Don't speak ill of camping. You must be used to many forms of camping, Madame Ruby? And I'm sure you looked much more chic in plus-fours and a woolen shirt and hobnailed shoes than those three Swiss females. Come along now, admit it."

She threw him an ironic glance and displayed her large teeth.

"All right, I admit it," she said. "What about you, Monsieur Daste? Camping? Nights under the open stars? Dangerous encounters? You is a slyboots, Monsieur Daste! Don't deny it!"

Monsieur Daste was flattered. He lowered his chin till it touched his tie, passed his hand over his ear to smooth the hair on his temple, and coquettishly swallowed a mouthful of brandy, which went the wrong way. He was convulsed with choking coughs and only regained his breath under the kindly hammering of Madame Suzanne's hand on his shoulder blades. I must record that, with his face flushed and his streaming eyes bloodshot, Monsieur Daste was unrecognizable.

"Thank you," he said when he could breathe again. "You've saved my life, Madame Suzanne. I can't imagine what could have got stuck in my thoat."

"A feather, perhaps," said Madame Ruby.

Monsieur Daste turned his head toward her with an almost imperceptible movement and then became stock-still. Madame Suzanne, who was sucking her cigar, became agitated and said shrilly: "A feather? Whatever will she think of next? A *feather*! You're not ill, are you,

Ruby? Now *me*," she went on hurriedly, "you'd never believe what *I* swallowed when I was a kid. A watch spring! But a *huge* watch spring, a positive metal snake, my dears, as long as *that*! I've swallowed a lot of other things since those days, bigger ones too, if you count insults."

She laughed, not only with her mouth but with her eyes, and gave a great yawn.

"My children, I doubt very much whether you'll see me again before five o'clock. Madame Ruby, will you look after the Swissies? They're taking sandwiches with them tonight so that they can have dinner on a nice cool carpet of pine needles which'll stick into their behinds."

"Right," said Madame Ruby. "Lucie is made the sandwiches?"

"No, Marguerite. Go and make sure she packs them in greaseproof paper. I've put it all down on their bill."

Suddenly she extinguished the laugh in her blue eyes and scanned her friend's face closely. "I've sent Lucie to her room. She's not feeling well."

Having said that, she left the room, jerking her shoulders as she did so. The back of her neck suggested a proud determination which I was the only one to notice. Monsieur Daste, shrunken and tense, had still not moved. Madame Ruby paid not the slightest attention either to Monsieur Daste or to myself before she, too, went out.

It was from that moment that I realized I was no longer enjoying myself at Bella-Vista. The saffron walls and the blue shutters, the Basque roof, the plastered Norman beams, and the Provençal tiles all suddenly seemed to me false and pretentious. A certain troubled atmosphere and the menace and hostility it breeds can only interest me if I am personally involved in it. It was not that I repented of feeling a rather pendulum-like sympathy with my hostesses which inclined now to Suzanne, now to Ruby. But, selfishly, I would have preferred them happy, serene in their old, faithful, reprehensible love that should have been spiced only with childish quarrels. The fact remained that I did not see them happy. And as to faithfulness, the yielding gentleness of a dark-haired servant girl gave me matter for thought—and disapproval.

When I ran into Lucie, when she brought me my "rose" breakfast about half past seven, I found myself feeling as severe toward Madame Ruby as if she had been Philemon deceiving Baucis.

I began to suspect "Daddy" Daste, that climber who had been so ill rewarded for his bird watching. I began to suspect his mysterious government employment, his scar adorned with black sticking plaster, and even what I called his malicious good temper. A conversation with

Madame Ruby might have taught me more about Monsieur Daste and possibly explained the obvious antipathy he inspired in her. But Madame Ruby made no attempt to have any private talk with me.

I remember that, about that very time, the weather changed again. During the twilight of a long April day, the southeast wind began to blow in short gusts, bringing with it a heat which mounted from the soil as from an oven full of burning bread. All four of us were playing bowls. Madame Suzanne kept shaking her white linen sleeves to "air herself" as she sighed: "If it weren't that I want to slim down!"

Bowls is a good game, like all games capable of revealing some trait of character in the expert player. Much to my surprise, Monsieur Daste was "shooter." Before launching his wood, he held it hidden almost behind his back. The arm, the small manicured hand, and the wood rose together and the heavy nailed ball fell on his adversary's with a resounding crack which sent Monsieur Daste into ecstasy.

"On his skull! Bang on top of his skull!" he cried.

Madame Suzanne, the "shooter" of the other side, rated about the same as I did as "marker" for Monsieur Daste's. Sometimes I "mark" very well, sometimes like a complete duffer. Madame Ruby "marked" to perfection, rolling her wood as softly as a ball of wool to within a hairbreadth of the jack. Disdaining our heavy woods, Pati snapped and spat out again innumerable insects which had been driven inland by the approach of a solid wall of purple clouds which was advancing toward us from the sea.

"My children, I can feel the storm coming. The roots of my hair are hurting me!" wailed Madame Suzanne.

At the first flash which broke into twigs of incandescent pink as it ran down the sky into the flat sea, Madame Suzanne gave a great "Ha!" and covered her eyes.

A warm gust played all around the courtyard, rolling faded flowers, straws, and leaves into wreaths and spirals, and the swallows circled in the air in the same direction. Warm heavy drops splayed on my hands. Madame Ruby ran to the garage, taking great strides, pulled on a black oilskin, and returned to her friend, who had not stirred. White as chalk, her hands over her eyes, the sturdy Suzanne collapsed, weak and tottering, on the shoulder of Madame Ruby, who looked like a dripping lifeboatman.

The strange couple and I ran toward our twin little flights of steps. Having shut Madame Suzanne in her room, Madame Ruby rushed to the rescue of other shipwrecked creatures, such as the bloodthirsty rabbit and the stupid greyhound. She wheeled the aviary into the garage, shouted orders to the two invisible kitchen maids and to Lucie, who stood in a doorway, her loosened hair hanging in a cloud around her pale face. She closed all the banging doors and brought in the cushions from the garden chairs.

From my window, I watched the hurly-burly which the American woman directed with a slightly theatrical calm. Nestled against my arm, my excited dog followed all that was going on while she waited for the battle of the elements. She shone in exceptional circumstances; particularly in great storms which she boldly defied where a bulldog would have panted with fear and done his best to die flattened out under an armchair. A minute dog with a great brain, Pati welcomed tempests on land or sea like a joyous stormy petrel.

Behind me, the violet darkness of the sky, magnificently rent by each flash, was stealing into my red-and-pink room. Some small, hollow-sounding thunder which echoed back from the hills decided to accompany the lightning flashes, and a crushing curtain of rain, which dropped suddenly from the sky, made me hastily shut my window.

It was almost time for the real night to close in. But the passing night of the storm had taken the place of dusk and I sat down, sullen and unwilling, to my work. I had begun it without inclination and continued it in a desultory way without being decided enough to abandon it altogether. The dog, becoming virtuously quiet as soon as she saw me busy with papers, gnawed her claws and listened to the thunder and the rain. I think that both she and I longed with all our hearts for Paris, for our friends there, for the reassuring mutter of a city.

The rain, which had fallen from a moderate-sized cloud which the wind had not had time to shred, stopped suddenly. My ear, made alert by the startling silence, caught the sound of voices on the other side of the partition. I could hear a high voice and a lower one, then the sound of tearful recriminations. "Extraordinary!" I thought. "The fat Madame Suzanne getting herself in such a state because of a storm!"

She did not appear at dinner.

"Madame Suzanne isn't feeling well?" I asked Madame Ruby.

"Her nerves. You is no idea how nervous she is."

"The first storm of the season affects the nerves," said Monsieur Daste, whose opinion no one had asked. "This one is the first . . . but not the last," he added, pointing to wavering flashes on the horizon.

I began to think impatiently of my approaching departure. Bella-Vista could no longer assuage my increasing restlessness and my sense of foreboding. I took my dog out into the courtyard before her usual time. Like a child with new shoes, she deliberately splashed through the puddles of rain which reflected a few stars. I had to scold her to get her away from a frog which she doubtless wanted to bring home and add to her collections in Paris: collections of mammoth bones, ancient biscuits, punctured balls, and sulphur lozenges. Monsieur Daste undermined my authority and egged Pati on with innumerable "huisipisis." The night had stayed warm and its scents made me languid. What tropics exhale more breaths of orange blossom, resin, rain-soaked carnations, and wild peppermint than a spring night in Provence?

After reading in bed, I switched off my lamp rather late and got up to open the door and window so as to let in as much as possible of the meager coolness and the overabundant scent. Standing in the dark room, I remembered that I had not heard Monsieur Daste come in. For the first time, I found something unpleasant in the thought of Monsieur Daste's small, agile feet walking, on a moonless night, not far from my open and accessible window. I know from experience how easily a fixed idea of a terror can take concrete shape and I invariably take pains to crush their first, faint intimations. Various mnemonic tricks and musical rhymes served to lull me into a dream in which printed letters danced before me, and I was asleep when the french window which led into my hostesses' room was clicked open.

I sat up in bed and heard, from the other side, a deep chest inhaling and exhaling the air. In the silence which foreboded other storms, I was also aware of the slither of two bare feet on my neighbors' stone steps.

"You makes me die of heat with your nerves," said Madame Ruby in a muffled voice. "The storm's over."

The rectangle of my open window was suddenly lit up. I realized that Madame Suzanne had turned on the ceiling light in her room.

"Idiot! I'm naked," whispered Ruby furiously.

The light was promptly switched off.

"Too late. Daste's right opposite, in the courtyard."

I heard a stifled exclamation and the thump of two heavy feet landing on the wooden floor. Madame Suzanne went over to her friend.

"Where d'you say he is?"

"Over by the garage."

"It's quite a long way off."

"Not for him. In any case, it is telling him nothing he doesn't know."

"Oh, don't . . . oh, don't."

"Don't get upset, darling. There, there . . ."

"My pet . . . oh, my pet!"

"Shut up so I can listen. He's opening the door of the garage."

They went silent for a long moment. Then Madame Suzanne whispered vehemently: "Get it well into your head that if they separate us, if they come here to . . ."

Madame Ruby's light whistle ordered her to be quiet. The dog had growled and I gently closed my hand over her muzzle.

"Suppose I shoot?" said the voice of Madame Ruby.

"Are you quite mad?"

This startling interchange was followed by a scuffle of bare feet. I imagined that Madame Suzanne was dragging her friend back into the room.

"Really, Richard, you must be mad. Aren't we in a bad enough mess as it is? Isn't it enough for you to have got Lucie in the family way without wanting to put a bullet through Daste into the bargain? You couldn't control yourself just for once, could you? No, of course not. You men are all the same. Come on, now. No more nonsense. Come indoors, and for heaven's sake, stay there."

The french window shut and there was complete silence.

I made no further attempt to sleep. My astonishment was soon over. Had Madame Suzanne's cry of revelation really given me a genuine surprise? What excited my interest and moved me profoundly was the thought of Madame Suzanne's vigilance, the discreet and devoted cynicism she interposed between the disguised, suspected "Madame" Ruby and the malevolent little Daste.

If the idle looker-on in me exclaimed delightedly, "What a story!" my honorable side wanted me to keep the story to myself. I have done so for a very long time.

Toward three in the morning, the wind changed and a fresh storm attacked Bella-Vista. It was accompanied by continuous thunder and slanting rain. In the moment or two it took to gather up my strewn, sopping papers, my nightdress was soaked and clung to my body. The dog followed all my movements, holding herself ready for any contingency. "Have we got to swim? Have we got to run away?" I set her an example of immovable patience and made her a cave out of a scarf. In the shelter of this she played at shipwrecks and desert islands and even at earthquakes.

Now against a background of total darkness, now against a screen lit up with lightning flashes and driving rain, I reconstructed the neighboring couple, the man and the woman. Two normal people, undoubtedly with the police on their track, lay side by side in the next room, awaiting their fate.

Perhaps the woman's head rested on the man's shoulder while they exchanged anxious speculations. In imagination I saw again the back of "Madame" Ruby's neck, that thumb, that roughened cheek, that large, well-shaved upper lip. Then I dwelt again on Madame Suzanne and wished good luck to that heroic woman; so jealous and so protective; so terrified, yet ready to face anything.

Daybreak brought a gray drizzle on the heels of the tornado and sleep overtook me at last. No hand knocked on my door or laid my breakfast tray with its customary rose on my table. The unwonted silence awakened me and I rang for Lucie. It was Marguerite who came.

"Where is Lucie?"

"I don't know, Madame. But won't I do instead?"

Under the impalpable rain, the courtyard and climbing roses torn from their trellis had the aspect of October. "The train, the first train! I won't stay another twenty-four hours!"

In the wide-open garage, I caught sight of the white linen overall and the dyed gold hair of Madame Suzanne and I went out to join her. She was sitting on an upturned pail and candidly let me see her ravaged face. It was the face of an unhappy middle-aged wife, the eyes small and swollen and the cheeks scoured with recent tears.

"Look," she said. "A nice sight, isn't it?"

At her feet lay the nineteen parakeets, dead. Assassinated would be a better word for the frenzy with which they had been destroyed. They had been torn and almost pulped in a peculiarly revolting way. The dog sniffed at the birds from a distance and planted herself at my heels.

"Monsieur Daste's car isn't in the garage any longer?"

Madame Suzanne's little swollen eyes met my own.

"Nor is *he* in the house," she said. "Gone. After doing that, it's hardly surprising."

With her foot, she pushed away a headless parakeet.

"If you're sure he did it, why don't you complain to the police? In your place, I should certainly lodge a complaint."

"Yes. But you're not in my place."

She put a hand on my shoulder.

"Ah, my dear, lodge a complaint! You don't know what you're talking about. Besides," she added, "he'd paid his bill for the week. He doesn't owe us a farthing."

"Is he a madman?"

"I'd like to believe so. I must go and find Paulius and get him to bury all this. Was there something you wanted?"

"Nothing special. As I told you already, I'm leaving. Tomorrow. Or even today unless that's quite impossible."

"Just as you like," she said indifferently. "Today, if you'd rather. Because tomorrow . . ."

"You're expecting someone to arrive tomorrow?"

She ran her tongue over her dry, unpainted lips.

"Someone to arrive? I wonder. If anyone could tell me what's going to happen tomorrow."

She got up as heavily as an old woman.

"I'll go and tell Madame Ruby to see about your seat in the train. Marguerite will help you with your packing."

"Or Lucie. She knows where I keep all my things."

The unhappy, tear-washed elderly woman reared herself up straight. Flushed and sparkling with anger, she looked suddenly young again.

"Terribly sorry. Lucie's not there. Lucie's through!"

"She's leaving you?"

"Leaving *me*? Considering I've thrown *her* out, the slut! There are . . . interesting conditions that I find very far from interesting! Really, the things one has to put up with in this world!"

She went off down the muddy path, her white skirt held up in both hands. I did not linger to consider the scattered wreckage at my feet, the work of the civilized monster masquerading in human shape, the creature who lusted to kill birds.

Madame Suzanne did everything possible to satisfy my keen and slightly cowardly desire to leave Bella-Vista that very day. She did not forget Pati's ticket and insisted on accompanying me to the train. Dressed in tight-fitting black, she sat beside me on the back seat, and all through the drive, she preserved a stiffness which was equally suitable to a well-to-do businesswoman or a proud creature going to the scaffold. In front of us was Madame Ruby's erect, T-shaped torso and her handsome head with its rakishly tilted beret.

At the station, I managed to persuade Madame Suzanne to stay in the car. My last sight of her was behind the windows misted with fine rain. It was Madame Ruby who carried my heaviest suitcase, bought me papers, and settled me in my carriage with the greatest possible friendliness.

But I received these attentions somewhat ungraciously. I had an unjust feeling which refused to admit that this easy assurance quite caught the manner of a masculine female, adept at making women blush under her searching glances. I was on the verge of reproaching myself for ever having been taken in by this tough fellow whose walk, whose whole appearance was that of an old Irish sergeant who had dressed himself up as a woman for a joke on St. Patrick's Day.

[*Translated by Antonia White*]

April

❧❦❧

"Count again," ordered Vinca. "That makes nine. You made a mistake."

Phil sighed, and then raised his lustrous eyebrows in weariness.

"The two Viénots, Maria and her brother, La Folle and her little dog . . ."

Vinca chewed on her pencil anxiously, turning her blue eyes up toward the denser blue of a spring storm which was raining down a soft and ephemeral snow of plum blossoms and hazelnut-tree caterpillars, blown down from an invisible garden in Auteuil.

"Will the dog follow along?"

"No, he doesn't follow. She puts him in a strawberry basket attached to the handlebars, nestled in a Basque beret and slipped into the sleeve of an old sweater. He loves it."

"Well, it's fine with me . . . We said six, including us, the three Lapins-Géants-des-Flandres, nine. That's all."

"Worse than a wedding," said Phil scornfully.

"The hard-boiled eggs, the pâté, the roast beef, and the ham . . ."

". . . Thirteen," said Philippe. "Miscount."

Vinca burst out laughing, once again behaving like the fifteen-year-old girl she was, and Phil deigned to smile. He dark, she blond and rosy, they looked vaguely alike from having lived near one another since they were born and having loved one another in the aggressive way of adolescents.

"Viénot Henri says he's bringing some Calvados and some . . . kümmel."

Phil raised his head from the back of the wicker chair.

"Oh, yeah? Viénot Henri can do whatever he wants. We're not touching any liquor, if you don't mind! Viénot Henri has the manners of a boor!"

Vinca blushed and did not reply. With Philippe, she would accept authority and rebelled only when teased. She raised her generous face toward him, the face of a blossoming young girl with glowing cheeks. She had glistening, decidedly blue eyes, straight blond hair, and between her slightly chapped lips, teeth that were strong, white, and rounded at the edges.

"You know, Phil, I have a rack on my bike. I can take whatever might get in your way."

"Nothing'll get in my way," said Phil roguishly. "Nothing except our caravan, all the others . . . I'd like for us to go by car, you and me . . ."

"Yes, but since we don't have a car, Phil . . ."

He felt ashamed of himself, as he did whenever Vinca accepted her situation as a young girl without means and without money, taught to ride a bike as well as do the laundry, adept at beating and folding an omelette, at shampooing her little sister Lisette's hair and ironing her father's pants. Tall for her age, long-legged and lanky, she was nonetheless exactly like a woman and often anxious.

"Phil, does your mother know about the roast beef? Tell her she should only get enough for six, meat is so overpriced . . ."

She broke off to listen to the pearly rippling of a hailstorm and Phil snickered, pointing to the low sky.

"A week from today . . ." said Vinca hopefully.

And already her eyes were the color of clear blue skies.

And so it was that the weather did in fact change.

The next day, around the church in Auteuil, Palm Sunday gave forth its odor of tomcat and flowers. Vinca opened the window facing the street, one of the last village streets left in Auteuil, to watch for Philippe and his parents, who were coming for lunch. She leaned out to wonder at the spent lilacs and the mahonia with leaves the color of reddish iron, squeezed in between the gate and the front of the house.

"When we're married, this is where I'll wait for Philippe . . ."

She belonged to that sweet, tenacious, hardy race, oblivious to progress, with no desire either to change or to perish.

Nine bicycles passed through the gate of the park of St.-Cloud in the early-morning sun of Holy Saturday. Pedaling hard up the wide road leading toward Marnes, the nine bicyclists registered without a word the complete image of the motorists who passed them by, and pricked up their ears to the muffled *putt-putt-putt* of the new motor-cycles. None of them was satisfied with his lot, or his age, and none had any burning desire to exchange secrets with the others. Only Philippe and Vinca the Periwinkle shared a past as old as their own sixteen years, rich in tender fraternity and silence.

Most of the nine bicyclists were the children of poor, small-scale Parisian business, cut off from costly pleasures, accustomed to curbing and nourishing their longings in secret. All they lacked was a little simplicity in their way of being poor. So one of the boys, upon reaching Marnes, deliberately tore a hole in the elbow of his threadbare pullover, made one of his socks fall down around his ankle, and gathered magpie feathers, which he stuck in his hair. But his ragamuffin getup did not make anyone laugh. La Folle with the big eyes sped through Marnes, letting out her war cry, and was first to arrive at the woods of Fausses-Reposes, where her tiny dog decided to make a hygienic stop. Out of courtesy, her eight companions dismounted and stood off to the side of the road, in a clearing where the peacefulness of the morning retook possession of the woods with the steady, strong murmuring of the breeze and the birds and the little leaves. Philippe stroked the satiny trunk of a wild-cherry tree; looking up, he saw that the tree bore all its flowers in full bloom. Whenever he felt happy, he appealed, with words and gestures, to Vinca. She tilted back her head to gaze up at the tree and her blue eyes filled with splendor. Nothing more was needed for them to feel bound to each other and withdrawn into that secret place where their tenderness regained its strength and self-awareness.

Back on the road, they took over the lead, wheel to wheel. The steep hill, leading out of Versailles, seemed long to them. The boys stripped; one took off his sweater, one the jacket of his ready-made plus fours. All of them already had wind-whipped cheeks, red eyes, and the happy expression of comforted children with tear-stained faces. They did not even glance at the romantic pond at Voisins-Bretonneux, but at long intervals they shouted out startling truths about temperature, perspiration, and speed. The bitter northwest wind and the biting April sun made them shout out without thinking from time to time, and from the top of its strawberry basket the tiny little dog would respond.

"Peach trees in bloom! . . . Wild daffodils! I saw some daffodils! I'm stopping!" yelped Maria, dark and curly-haired.

"Quiet!" ordered her twin brother, curly-haired and dark. "We can get them on the way back."

"There won't be any left for us! I'm stopping!"

She jumped to the ground, twisted her ankle, and screamed. One of the Viénots yelled out a nasty remark, sharply picked up on by the twin, and La Folle, turning back so as not to miss out on any of the altercation, blocked a car from getting by.

Philippe lost his patience, any desire to wait for his comrades; and the sound of their voices, their choice of insults, made the blood rise in his cheeks.

"C'mon," he said to Vinca. "They'll catch up soon enough. Because of all this it's already eleven-thirty."

The two set off again, relieved, enjoying their solitude and their reawakened good mood. Spring still bathed in the translucent yellow which precedes the universal green. The yellow primroses in the meadows, the honeyed catkins of the willows, the leaves of the poplars which are born pink and golden, enchanted Vinca and Phil only from the moment they felt themselves alone. On the thorny blackthorn hedges, the belated flowering held up round pearls white as hail.

Before passing though Dampierre, the two friends slackened their pace at the Seventeen Turns.

"I only count fourteen," said Vinca at the bottom of the hill.

"What a child you are," said Phil indulgently.

But he too had counted, and he could not keep from breaking into a fit of laughter, which brought tears to his eyes. Winded, sweating, his forehead hot beneath his hair, and his ears cold, he breathed in large gulps, prey to a somewhat exhausted, drained, and contented sense of well-being, as if he had just thrown up some indigestible food.

"Ah!" he sighed as he got off his bike, "that's better . . ."

Under the noonday sun, they climbed the last hill before Les Vaux, between the sparse woods starred with wild anemones.

"Come on, Vinca, let's take a rest."

She was already following him, guiding her bicycle onto a narrow path between low oaks and delicately leaved birch trees.

"Listen . . ." said Vinca. "That's a cuckoo. When the cuckoo sings, it means the wild violets have lost their fragrance."

Philippe had stopped short, his shoulder against Vinca's shoulder. Closer than the two notes of the cuckoo he could hear Vinca breathing. Her eyes, raised toward the tops of the copse, were sparkling with a blue which he believed he had discovered, flecked with slate, speckled with mauve . . . She held her red cracked lips half open, and Philippe suddenly shivered, imagining the coldness of the strong, beautiful teeth.

"Come on, Vinca . . ."

"Where?"

"There . . . over there . . ."

He pointed to a spot that was unfamiliar to him, off the path, a place he imagined as mossy, or blanketed with white sand, or grassy like a June meadow. He came upon it as in a dream. White with sand, green with finely spiked forest grass, mossy at the foot of a beech tree, and frighteningly narrow . . . At the same moment, he nearly stumbled over what he had neither imagined nor seen: a couple, lying spent and motionless on the ground, who did not move under their gaze. The outstretched woman merely closed her eyes and pressed closer to the man.

Turning his bike around, Philippe almost knocked Vinca down. She stumbled and did not say a word.

"Go on, turn around, we made a mistake," he said in a loud, forced voice.

He pushed her inconsiderately toward the road. "Move it, go on, move it! You have lead in your legs today?"

He wished she had not seen the couple lying there. He wanted her, having seen them, to run away, embarrassed and revolted.

"Move, little girl, move . . ."

"It's a bramble, Phil . . . It's caught in my spokes . . ."

He did not help her, and left her to pull free from the fierce old brambles herself, giving her a hard look. She did not ask him for either help or an explanation, and once back on the road she was content to lick her stinging hand.

"Back it up, Vinca . . . Your wheel's sticking out . . . a little farther and that maniac would have mowed you down."

"Yes . . ."

"Twelve-twenty! . . . If they're not here in two minutes, we're leaving."

"Whatever you say . . ."

"You have to say one thing for her, she does what she's told," he thought. "What if, back there in the woods, I'd told her to . . ."

From down in the little valley came shouts and the shrill barking of the little dog. Philippe raised his arms and called back, "Hey, up here!" in a loud voice. When the main body of riders reached the rise, he jumped onto his bicycle and, with a kind of thankfulness, mingled in among his companions.

[Translated by Matthew Ward]

EU Food Law

Protecting Consumers and Health in a Common Market

Caoimhín MacMaoláin

·H A R T·
PUBLISHING

OXFORD – PORTLAND OREGON

2007

Published in North America (US and Canada) by
Hart Publishing
c/o International Specialized Book Services
920 NE 58th Avenue, Suite 300
Portland, OR 97213-3786
USA
Tel: +1 503 287 3093 or toll-free: (1) 800 944 6190
Fax: +1 503 280 8832
E-mail: orders@isbs.com
Website: www.isbs.com
© Caoimhín MacMaoláin 2007

Hart Publishing, 16C Worcester Place, OX1 2JW
Telephone: +44 (0)1865 517530 Fax: +44 (0)1865 510710
E-mail: mail@hartpub.co.uk
Website: http://www.hartpub.co.uk

British Library Cataloguing in Publication Data
Data Available

ISBN-13: 978-1-84113-498-7 (paperback)
ISBN-10: 1-84113-498-8 (paperback)

Typeset by Hope Services, Abingdon
Printed and bound in Great Britain by
TJ International Ltd, Padstow, Cornwall

In memory of Gaye

Acknowledgements

There are several people who assisted in the preparation and publication of this book. I am very grateful to all of them. I would like to thank Professor John Usher, Ms Barbara Powell and Mr Patrick Overy of Exeter University; Professor Damian Chalmers, London School of Economics; Professor Hilary Delaney, Professor Gerry Whyte and Dr Eoin O'Dell of Trinity College, Dublin; Professor Gerrit Betlem, Southampton University; Dr Alan Dignam, Queen Mary, University of London; and Dr Adam McAuley, Dublin City University – who first suggested this topic as a research area. I am particularly grateful to Dr David Tomkin for meticulously reading through drafts and proofs and making numerous suggestions. His influence and expertise have greatly improved this book. My wife Síofra, my children Rían, Cathal and Donncha, and my parents Mícheal and Josephine, have all been most supportive and encouraging throughout. I would like to thank all at Hart Publishing for making the authorship process so enjoyable. Inevitably no text can be error-free, and any errors or omissions that remain are solely attributable to the author who invites comments and suggestions, and can be contacted by email at macmaolc@tcd.ie.

Contents

Acknowledgements   vii
Table of Cases   xv
Table of Legislation   xxi

1 Regulating the Food Industry   1

   1.1 INTRODUCTION   1
   1.2 HISTORICAL DEVELOPMENT OF FOOD LAW   2
   1.3 IMPORTANCE OF THE FOOD SECTOR IN THE EU   5
      1.3.1 Chocolate Debate   7
      1.3.2 Ensuring Compliance with EU Food Law 10
   1.4 SCOPE OF THE BOOK   11

2 Free Movement of Food in the EU   17

   2.1 INTRODUCTION   17
   2.2 MEASURES EQUIVALENT TO QUANTITATIVE RESTRICTIONS
       ON THE FREE MOVEMENT OF FOOD   19
      2.2.1 *Dassonville* and Directive 1970/50   20
      2.2.2 Indistinctly Applicable Rules   22
      2.2.3 Post-*Cassis* Free Movement of Food   23
      2.2.4 National Quality Requirements   29
      2.2.5 Different Products, Same Name   34
      2.2.6 Substantial Difference between Food Products 41
      2.2.7 Protecting Human Health under Article 30 EC 45
      2.2.8 National Authorisation Procedures   49
      2.2.9 Common Agricultural Policy Justification 56
   2.3 TAXES AND DUTIES ON THE MOVEMENT OF FOOD   57
      2.3.1 Internal Taxation on Imported Foodstuffs 57
      2.3.2 Measures Equivalent to Customs Duties on Intra-Community
          Food Trade   60
   2.4 CONCLUSION   64

3 Harmonising Food Standards in the EU: Labelling, Naming and Quality
  Preservation   67

   3.1 INTRODUCTION   67
   3.2 COMPLETING THE INTERNAL MARKET: COMMUNITY
       LEGISLATION ON FOODSTUFFS   68

3.2.1	Public Health Protection	71
3.2.2	Consumer Protection	72
3.2.3	Fair Trading	73
3.3	COMMUNICATION ON FREE MOVEMENT OF FOODSTUFFS WITHIN THE COMMUNITY	74
3.4	FOOD LABELLING	77
3.4.1	Framework Food Labelling Legislation	78
3.4.2	Labelling Language	80
3.4.3	Listing Ingredients	83
	Quantitative Ingredient Declarations	87
3.4.4	Net Quantity	87
3.4.5	Date of Minimum Durability	89
3.5	FOOD NAMES	90
3.5.1	Recipe Laws	93
	Chocolate and Cocoa	94
	Coffee and Chicory	96
	Fruit Juices	97
	Honey	99
	Jams	101
3.5.2	Protected Geographical Indications and Designations of Origin	102
	Regulation 510/2006	103
	Regulation 510/2006 and Existing National Laws	107
	Nature of Generic Food Names: The Feta Cheese Cases	108
	Certificates of Specific Character: Regulation 509/2006	117
	Protection for Geographical Names under Regulation 510/2006	119
	Compatibility of Protecting Names with Article 28 EC	121
3.6	FOOD QUALITY	122
3.6.1	Foodstuff Specific Quality Legislation	123
	Natural Mineral Water	123
	Milk and Milk Products	126
	Spreadable Fats	127
	Minced Meat	129
3.7	CONCLUSION	130
4	***International Influences on EU Food Law***	**133**
4.1	INTRODUCTION	133
4.2	GLOBAL FREE TRADE: INTERNATIONAL RULES ON FREE MOVEMENT OF FOOD	134
4.2.1	WTO Agreements and EU Food Law	135
	Agreement on Trade-Related Aspects of Intellectual Property Rights	135

Agreement on the Application of Sanitary and Phytosanitary
    Measures 138
    Agreement on Technical Barriers to Trade 142
    Agreement on Agriculture 144
  4.2.2 **Dispute Settlement at the World Trade Organization** 145
  4.2.3 **Effect of WTO Rules on EU Food Law** 149
4.3 FAO/WHO CODEX ALIMENTARIUS 151
  4.3.1 **Historical Development of the Codex Alimentarius** 151
  4.3.2 **Operation of the Codex Alimentarius Commission** 152
  4.3.3 **Codex Alimentarius Standards** 155
    Codex Alimentarius Code of Ethics 156
    Codex Alimentarius Food Labelling Standards 158
    Nutrition Labelling and Dietary Claims 162
    Organic Production and Labelling Requirements 167
    Foodstuff Specific Codex Alimentarius Standards 170
  4.3.4 **Relationship between the Codex Alimentarius and EU**
    Food Law 171
4.4 CONCLUSION 172

5 *Food Safety in the EU* 175

5.1 INTRODUCTION 175
5.2 DEVISING A NEW FOOD SAFETY POLICY FOR THE EU:
  THE BSE CRISIS 175
  5.2.1 **Impact of Food Crises on EU Food Law and Policy:**
    White Paper on Food Safety 179
    Regulatory Aspects of the White Paper 181
    Animal Health and Welfare 182
    Emergency Measures 183
    Controls over the Operation of EU Legislation 184
  5.2.2 **The European Food Safety Authority** 185
    Regulation 178/2002 on the General Principles of Food
    Law 187
    Structure of EFSA 189
    EFSA and Scientific Opinions 191
    Rapid Alert System, Crisis Management and Emergencies 192
5.3 USING THE PRECAUTIONARY PRINCIPLE TO PROTECT
  HUMAN HEALTH 195
  5.3.1 **Evidence Requirements** 198
  5.3.2 **Legislature and Scientific Committees** 201
5.4 COMMUNITY FOOD SAFETY LEGISLATION 203
  5.4.1 **Materials Coming into Contact with Foodstuffs** 203
  5.4.2 **Contaminants in Food** 205
  5.4.3 **Irradiated Foods** 206

5.4.4 Hygienic Production Methods   207
    Transportation Rules   209
5.5 FOOD ADDITIVES   210
  5.5.1 Additive Use Rules and Free Movement   211
  5.5.2 Directive 1989/107   215
  5.5.3 Sweetener, Colour and Flavour Use   217
5.6 CONCLUSION   219

6 *Nutrition Law and Policy in the EU*   221

6.1 INTRODUCTION   221
6.2 COMMUNITY LEGISLATION ON NUTRITION   225
  6.2.1 Nutrition Labelling   225
  6.2.2 Nutrition and Health Claims   226
    Background to the Regulation on Nutrition and Health
    Claims   226
    Key Provisions of Nutrition and Health Claims Legislation 228
    Authorisation Procedure   230
  6.2.3 Food Supplements   232
6.3 NUTRITION POLICY AND FREE MOVEMENT   234
  6.3.1 Nutrition Policy in the Member States   234
    UK White Paper on Public Health   234
    Folic Acid Fortification   235
    Determining Member State Autonomy on Health Protection
    Measures   237
  6.3.2 EU Nutrition Policy   237
6.4 CONCLUSION   239

7 *Contemporary Considerations for EU Food Law*   241

7.1 INTRODUCTION   241
7.2 INNOVATION IN FOOD PRODUCTION: GENETIC
    MODIFICATION   241
  7.2.1 GMO Regulatory Framework   243
    Novel Foods Regulation   244
    Deliberate Release Directive   246
    Genetically Modified Food and Feed Regulation 247
    Labelling and Traceability Regulation   250
    Challenging the GMO Regulatory Framework: Labelling
    Difficulties   251
7.3 ALTERING CONSUMER PREFERENCES: THE DEMAND FOR
    ORGANIC FOOD   254
  7.3.1 Organic Production Rules   255
  7.3.2 Organic Livestock Production   256
  7.3.3 Genetic Modification and Organic Food   260

**7.3.4 Coexistence of Genetically Modified Crops with Conventional
and Organic Farming**   262
7.3.5 Future Regulation of Organic Production   263
7.4 ETHICAL FOOD PRODUCTION   264
7.4.1 Animal Welfare Standards   265
7.4.2 Community Legislation on the Protection of Calves and Pigs 265
**7.4.3 Health, Welfare and Consumer Protection: Production and
Marketing of Poultry and Eggs**   266
Welfare Standards and Consumer Protection   267
Hygiene Standards for Egg Production   271
Poultry Production   273
7.5 CONCLUSION   274

Index   279

Table of Cases

EUROPEAN COURT OF JUSTICE AND COURT OF FIRST INSTANCE

7/1968, *Commission v Italy* (art exports) [1968] ECR 423 60
24/1968, *Commission v Italy* (statistical levy) [1969] ECR 193 60
2/1969 and 3/1969, *Sociaal Fonds voor de Diamantarbeiders v SA Ch Brachfeld & Sons* [1969] ECR 211 60
84/1971, *SpA Marimex v Ministero delle Finanze* [1972] ECR 89.....................60
8/1974, *Procureur du Roi v Benoît and Gustave Dassonville* [1974] ECR 837...20–4, 42
12/1974, *Commission v Germany* (sekt) [1975] ECR 181 ....31, 113, 121–2
4/1975, *Rewe-Zentralfinanz eGmbH v Landwirtschaftskammer* [1975] ECR 843...63
87/1975, *Conceria Daniele Bresciani v Amministrazione Italiana delle Finanze* [1976] ECR 129..18, 60–61, 64
104/1975, *De Peijper (Centrafarm)* [1976] ECR 613 46
Case 46/1976, *Bauhuis v Netherlands* [1977] ECR 5 ....18, 60, 61
120/1978, *Rewe-Zentral AG v Bundesmonopolverwaltung für Branntwein* (cassis) [1979] ECR 649 ....4, 17, 22–9, 32, 33, 35, 40–41, 45, 67–8, 70, 75, 95, 102, 116, 119, 130–1
168/1978, *Commission v France* (spirit tax) [1980] ECR 347 58
170/1978, *Commission v UK* (wine and beer tax) [1983] ECR 2265...18, 34, 58, 118
88/1979, *Criminal proceedings against Siegfried Grunert* [1980] ECR 1827 213
788/1979, *Criminal proceedings against Gilli and Andres* [1980] ECR 2071...5,17, 23–4
27/1980, *Criminal proceedings against Anton Adriaan Fietje* [1980] ECR 3839 ....5, 17, 24, 28, 36, 39, 42, 116
53/1980, *Officier van Justitie v Koninklijke Kaasfabriek Eyssen BV* [1981] ECR 409...48, 212
193/1980, *Commission v Italy* (vinegar) [1981] ECR 3019..................................5, 17, 26–7, 31, 35, 92
249/1981, *Commission v Ireland* (Buy Irish Campaign) [1982] ECR 4005..........29
261/1981, *Walter Rau Lebensmittelwerke v De Smedt PVBA* [1982] ECR 3961..28, 33
286/1981, *Criminal proceedings against Oosthoens Uitgeversmaatschappij BV* [1982] ECR 4575...25
94/1982, *Criminal proceedings against De Kikvorsch Groothandel-Import-Export BV* [1983] ECR 947 271

174/1982, *Criminal proceedings against Sandoz BV* [1983]
ECR 2445 ....47, 51, 53, 239, 271
222/1982, *Apple and Pear Development Council v KJ Lewis Ltd and
others* [1983] ECR 4083 29
227/1982, *Criminal proceedings against Leendert van Bennekom* [1983]
ECR 3883...50
237/1982, *Jongeneel Kaas BV and others v Netherlands and other* [1984]
ECR 483...29–30
314/1982, *Commission v Belgium* (imported poultry meat) [1984]
ECR 1543..18, 61, 64
16/1983, *Criminal proceedings against Karl Prantl* [1984]
ECR 1299..28, 31, 122
96/1984, *Vereniging Slachtpluimvee-Export eV v Rewe-Zentral-
Aktiengesellschaft* [1985] ECR 1157..89
176/1984, *Commission v Greece* (beer) [1987] ECR 1193 52
178/1984, *Commission v Germany* (bier) [1987]
ECR 1227 ....3, 4, 17, 33–4, 35, 47–8, 55, 75, 91, 92, 116, 118, 239
182/1984, *Criminal proceedings against Miro BV* [1985] ECR 3731..........30–33, 92
216/1984, *Commission v France* (milk substitutes) [1988]
ECR 793......................................5, 17, 36–8, 39, 46, 48–9, 56, 126, 239
247/1984, *Criminal proceedings against Léon Motte* [1985]
ECR 3887..47, 211, 213–14
304/1984, *Criminal proceedings against Claude Muller* [1986]
ECR 1511..47, 211, 214–15
184/1985, *Commission v Italy* (banana consumption tax) [1987] ECR 2013.......59
193/1985, *Cooperativa Co-frutta Srl v Amministrazione delle finanze
dello Stato* [1987] ECR 2085 59
261/1985, *Commission v UK* (milk and cream) [1988] ECR 547 46
355/1985, *Driancourt v Cognet* [1986] ECR 3231.....................................25
407/1985, *Glocken GmbH and Kritzinger v USL Centro-Sud and Provincia
autonoma di Bolzano* [1988] ECR 4233 ....35, 49, 56, 91, 92, 115
76/1986, *Commission v Germany* (milk substitutes) [1989]
ECR 1021...17, 38–9, 56, 126
90/1986, *Criminal proceedings against Zoni* [1988]
ECR 4285...35–6, 40, 49, 91, 92, 115, 116
98/1986, *Criminal proceedings against Arthur Mathot* [1987] ECR 809...........5, 25
286/1986, *Ministère public v Gérard Deserbais* [1988]
ECR 4907...5, 17, 41–4, 91, 92, 172
18/1987, *Commission v Germany* [1988] ECR 5427.....................................61–3
274/1987, *Commission v Germany* (meat products) [1989]
ECR 229..5, 17, 45–6, 56, 239
298/1987, *Proceedings for compulsory reconstruction against Smanor SA*
[1988] ECR 4489 ....5, 17, 27–9, 41–4, 79-80, 91, 92, 171–2
C-67/1988, *Commission v Italy* (sesame oil) [1990] ECR I-4285 32

C-362/1988, *GB-INNO-BM v Confédération du commerce Luxembourgeois* [1990] ECR I-667...............115, 271
C-95/1989, *Commission v Italy* (added nitrate) [1992] ECR I-4545.................211
C-196/1989, *Criminal proceedings against Enzo Nespoli and Giuseppe Crippa* [1990] ECR I-3647...............39–41, 43, 116
C-238/1989, *Pall Corp v Dahlhausen & Co* [1990] ECR I-4827.................115, 271
C-369/1989, *Piageme and others v BVBA Peeters* [1991] ECR I-2971...............80–81
C-42/1990 *Criminal proceedings against Jean-Claude Bellon* [1990] ECR I-4863...............211, 212–13
C-47/1990, *Établissements Delhaize frères et Compagnie Le Lion SA v Promalvin SA and AGE Bodegas Unidas SA* [1992] ECR I-3669.................8, 107
C-344/1990, *Commission v France* (cheese nitrate) [1992] ECR I-4719...............50, 51, 52, 76
C-355/1990, *Commission v Spain* (conservation of wild birds) [1993] ECR I-4221...............200
C-3/1991, *Exportur SA v LOR SA and Confiserie du Tech SA* [1992] ECR I-5529...............107, 120, 121
C-126/1991, *Schutzverband gegen Unwesen in der Wirtschaft eV v Yves Rocher* [1993] ECR I-2361...............115, 271
C-212/1991, *Angelopharm GmbH v Freie Hansestadt Hamburg* [1994] ECR I-171...............202
Joined Cases C-267/1991 and C-268/1991, *Criminal proceedings against Keck and Mithouard* [1993] ECR I-6097...............20, 86
C-285/1992, *Criminal Proceedings against Coöperatieve Zuivelindustrie 'Twee Provinciën' WA* [1993] ECR I-6045...............80
C-315/1992, *Verband Sozialer Wettbewerb eV v Clinique Laboratoires SNC et Estée Lauder Cosmetics GmbH* [1994] ECR I-317...............115, 271
C-17/1993, *Criminal proceedings against Van der Veldt* [1994] ECR I-3537...............239
Joined Cases C-69/1993 and C-258/1993, *Punto casa SpA v Sindaco del Comune di Capena et Comune di Capena and Promozioni Polivalenti Venete Soc coop arl (PPV) v Sindaco del Comune di Torri di Quartesolo and Comune di Torri di Quartesolo* [1994] ECR I-2355...............20
C-144/1993, *Pfanni Werke Otto Eckart KG v Landeshauptstadt München* [1994] ECR I-4605...............84–5
C-156/1993, *European Parliament v Commission* [1995] ECR I-2019........260–261
Joined Cases C-427/1993 and C-436/1993, *Bristol Myers Squibb v Paranova* [1996] E.C.R. I-3457.................8
C-456/1993, *Zentrale zur Bekämpfung unlauteren Wettbewerbs eV v Privatkellerei Franz Wilhelm Langguth Erben GmbH & Co KG* [1995] ECR I-1737...............115, 271
C-470/1993, *Verein gegen Unwesen in Handel und Gewerbe Köln eV v Mars GmbH* [1995] ECR I-1923...............115, 271

C-51/1994, *Commission v Germany* (sauces and pastries) [1995]
ECR I-3599...48, 86
C-85/1994, *Piageme and others v Peeters NV* [1995] ECR I-2955 81–2
C-313/1994, *Graffione SNC v Ditta Fransa* [1996] ECR I-6039 271
Joined cases C-321/1994, C-322/1994, C-323/1994 and C-324/1994,
    *Criminal proceedings against Jacques Pistre, Michèle Barthes, Yves
    Milhau and Didier Oberti* [1997] ECR I-2343....................................25, 107
Joined cases C-34/1995, C-35/1995 and C-36/1995 *Konsumentombudsmannen
    (KO) v De Agostini (Svenska) Förlag AB and TV-Shop i Sverige AB* [1997]
    ECR I-3843...20
C-317/1995, *Canadane Cheese Trading AMBA and Adelfi G. Kouri
    Anonymos Emoriki Kai Viomichaniki Etaireia v Hellenic Republic*
    [1997] ECR I-4681...44, 91–3, 118
C-358/1995, *Tommaso Morellato v Unità sanitaria locale (USL) n. 11 di
    Pordenone* [1997] ECR I-1431..50
C-368/1995, *Vereinigte Familiapress Zeitungsverlags- und vertriebs GmbH v
    Heinrich Bauer Verlag* [1997] ECR I-3689..20
C-388/1995, *Belgium v Spain* [2000] ECR 3123 106–7
C-17/1996, *Badische Erfrischungs-Getränke & Co KG v Land Baden-
    Württemberg* [1997] ECR I-4617 125
C-18/1996, *United Kingdom v Commission* (BSE) [1998]
    ECR I-2265...196, 197, 199
C-157/1996, *The Queen v National Farmers' Union and others*
    [1998] ECR I-2211 ....52, 54, 196, 197, 199
C-184/1996, *Commission v France* (foie gras) [1998] ECR I-6197 ....25, 42, 44
T-199/1996, *Laboratoires pharmaceutiques Bergaderm SA and Jean-Jacques
    Groupil v Commission* [1998] ECR II-2805 199
C-210/1996, *Gut Springenheide GmbH and Rudolf Tusky v Oberkreisdirektor
    des Kreises Steinfurt – Amt für Lebensmittelüberwachung* [1998]
    ECR I-4657..115, 270–71
Joined Cases C-289/1996, C-293/1996 and C-299/1996, *Denmark,
    Germany and France v Commission* [1999] ECR I-1541 ....26, 29, 109–16
C-385/1996, *Criminal proceedings against Hermann Josef Goerres*
    [1998] ECR I-4431..82
C-77/1997, *Österreichische Unilever GmbH v Smithkline Beecham
    Markenartikel GmbH* [1999] ECR I-431...50
C-87/1997, *Consorzio per la tutela del formaggio Gorgonzola v Käserei
    Champignon Hofmeister GmbH & Co KG and Eduard Bracharz
    GmbH* [1999] ECR I-1301..119–20
T-109/1997, *Molkerei Grobbraunshain GmbH and Bene Nahrungsmittel
    GmbH v Commission* [1998] ECR II-3533...113
Joined cases C-129/1997 and C-130/1997, *Criminal proceedings against
    Yvon Chiciak and Fromagerie Chiciak and Jean-Pierre Fol* [1998]
    ECR I-3315...120–21

C-383/1997, *Criminal proceedings against Arnoldus van der Laan*
[1999] ECR I-731 39–40
C-312/1998, *Schutzverband gegen Unwesen in der Wirtschaft eV v Warsteiner
Brauerei Haus Cramer GmbH & C. KG* [2000] ECR I-9187 108
C-366/1998, *Criminal proceedings against Yannick Geffroy and Casino France
SNC* [2000] ECR I-6579 82–3
C-448/1998, *Criminal proceedings against Jean-Pierre Guimont* [2000]
ECR I-10663 ....25, 117
C-465/1998, *Verein gegen Unwesen in Handel und Gewerbe Köln eV v
Adolf Darbo AG* [2000] ECR I-2297 ....11, 271
T-13/1999, *Pfizer Animal Health SA v Council* [2002]
ECR II-3305 ....196, 198–203
T-70/1999, *Alpharma Inc v Council* [2002] ECR II-3495...................................198
C-269/1999, *Kühne and others* [2001] ECR I-9517...110
T-114/1999, *CSR PAMPRYL v Commission* [1999] ECR II-3331 105
C-12/2000, *Commission v Spain* (chocolate) [2003] ECR I-459 9
C-14/2000, *Commission v Italy* (chocolate) [2003] ECR I-513 9
C-24/2000, *Commission v France* (fortified foods – 'Red Bull') [2004]
ECR I-1277 ....50, 51, 52–5, 64, 76, 239
C-123/2000, *Criminal proceedings against Christina Bellamy and English
Shop Wholesale SA* [2001] ECR I-2795..46–7, 239
C-221/2000, *Commission v Austria* (health claims) [2003]
ECR I-1007 ....50, 227, 230
Joined cases C-421/2000, C-426/2000 and C-16/2001, *Renate Sterbenz
and Paul Dieter Haug* [2003] ECR I-1065 ....11, 271
C-95/2001, *Criminal proceedings against Greenham and Abel* [2004]
ECR I-1333..50–52, 55
C-108/2001, *Consorzio del Prosciutto di Parma and Salumificio S Rita
SpA v Asda Stores Ltd and Hygrade Foods Ltd* [2003] ECR I-5121 120
C-192/2001, *Commission v Denmark* (enriched foodstuffs) [2003]
ECR I-9693 ....51, 52, 53, 54, 64
C-236/2001, *Monsanto Agricoltura Italia SpA and Others v Presidenza del
Consiglio dei Ministri and Others* [2003] ECR I-8105 52
C-420/2001, *Commission v Italy* (caffeine energy drinks) [2003]
ECR I-6445 ....50, 54
C-14/2002, *ATRAL SA v Belgium* [2003] ECR I-4431 50
C-41/2002 *Commission v Netherlands* (fortified foods) [2004] ECR I-11375 17
C-239/2002, *Douwe Egberts NV v Westrom Pharma NV and Christophe
Souranis* [2004] ECR I-7007...11, 271
C-270/2002, *Commission v Italy* (sports supplements) [2004] ECR I-1559.........50
Joined Cases C-465/2002 and C-466/2002, *Germany and Denmark v
Commission,* [2005] ECR I-9115....................................26, 34, 112–16, 117
C-366/2004, *Georg Schwarz v Bürgermeister der Landeshauptstadt
Salzburg,* [2005] ECR I-10139..55

UNITED KINGDOM

*Thoburn v Sunderland City Council; Hunt v London Borough of Hackney;
Harman and Dove v Cornwall County Council; Collins v London
Borough of Sutton* [2002] EWHC 195; [2003] QB 151 88

Table of Legislation

EUROPEAN UNION

EC Treaty

Article 6 197–8
Article 25 ....18, 57–64
Article 28 ....5, 9, 12–13, 15, 17–56, 64-5, 68, 69, 71,
72, 73, 74–7, 92, 118, 121–2, 211–12, 214, 237, 240
Article 29...5, 15, 68, 121, 211
Article 30..5, 13, 15, 21, 40–41, 45–55, 65, 68, 71,
121, 122, 212–13, 214, 215, 233, 241, 277
Article 37 ....183, 260
Article 90 ....17–18, 57–59
Article 94 68
Article 95 ....68, 197–198
Article 151 65
Article 152...21, 65, 197–8, 201, 241, 277
Article 153...21, 65, 241, 277
Article 174 196–7
Article 202 183
Article 211 201
Article 230 26,109,198
Article 251 ....226–7, 240

Regulations

Regulation (EEC) No 2772/1975 of the Council of 29 October 1975 on
marketing standards for eggs [1975] OJ L 282/56 267
Council Regulation (EEC) No 1898/1987 of 2 July 1987 on the protection
of the designations used in marketing of milk and milk products
[1987] OJ L 182/36 ....37–9, 126
Council Regulation (EEC) No 2658/1987 of 23 July 1987 on the tariff
and statistical nomenclature and on the Common Customs Tariff
[1987] OJ L 256/1 ....34, 111, 114
Council Regulation (EEC) No 1576/1989 of 29 May 1989 laying down
general rules on the definition, description and presentation of spirit
drinks [1989] OJ L 160/1 30

Council Regulation (EEC) No 1906/1990 on certain marketing standards
for poultry [1990] OJ L 173/1 273
Council Regulation (EEC) No 1907/1990 of 26 June 1990 on certain
marketing standards for eggs [1990] OJ L 173/5 ....267–70, 276
Commission Regulation (EEC) No 1274/91 of 15 May 1991 introducing
detailed rules for implementing Regulation (EEC) No 1907/90 on
certain marketing standards for eggs [1991] OJ L 121/11 268
Commission Regulation (EEC) No 1538/1991 of 5 June 1991 introducing
detailed rules for implementing Regulation (EEC) No 1906/1990 on
certain marketing standards for poultry [1991] OJ L 143/11......................273–4
Council Regulation (EEC) No 2092/1991 of 24 June 1991 on organic
production of agricultural products and indications referring thereto
on agricultural products and foodstuffs [1991] OJ L 198/1 ....5, 255–61, 269
Commission Regulation (EEC) No 1535/1992 of 15 June 1992 amending
Annexes I and III of Council Regulation (EEC) No 2092/1991 on organic
production of agricultural products and indications referring thereto
on agricultural products and foodstuffs [1992] OJ L 162/15 255
Council Regulation (EEC) No 2081/1992 of 14 July 1992 on the protection
of geographical indications and designations of origin for agricultural
products and foodstuffs [1992] OJ L 208/1 ....34, 91, 93, 102–8,
110, 117, 137–8, 150
Council Regulation (EEC) No 2082/1992 of 14 July 1992 on certificates
of specific character for agricultural products and foodstuffs [1992]
OJ L 208/9 117
Commission Regulation (EEC) No 207/1993 of 29 January 1993 defining
the content of Annex VI to Regulation (EEC) No 2092/1991 on organic
production of agricultural products and indications referring thereto on
agricultural products and foodstuffs and laying down detailed rules for
implementing the provisions of Article 5 (4) thereto [1993] OJ L 25/5........260
Council Regulation (EEC) No 315/1993 of 8 February 1993 laying down
Community procedures for contaminants in food [1993] OJ L 37/1 205–6
Council Regulation (EC) No 2991/1994 of 5 December 1994 laying down
standards for spreadable fats [1994] OJ L 316/2.......................................127–9
Council Regulation (EC) No 1935/1995 of 22 June 1995 amending Regulation
(EEC) No 2092/1991 on organic production of agricultural products
and indications referring thereto on agricultural products and foodstuffs
[1995] OJ L 186/1 ....255, 264
Commission Regulation (EC) No 1107/1996 of 12 June 1996 on the
registration of geographical indications and designations of origin
under the procedure laid down in Article 17 of Council Regulation
(EEC) No 2081/1992 [1996] OJ L 148/1..109, 119, 120
Commission Regulation (EC) No 2400/1996 of 17 December 1996 on the
entry of certain names in the Register of protected designations of
origin and protected geographical indications provided for in Council

Regulation (EEC) No 2081/1992 on the protection of geographical
indications and designations of origin for agricultural products and
foodstuffs [1996] OJ L 327/11 106
European Parliament and Council Regulation (EC) No 258/1997 of
27 January 1997 concerning novel foods and novel food ingredients
[1997] OJ L 43/1 ....244–5, 252
Commission Regulation (EC) No 577/1997 of 1 April 1997 laying down
certain detailed rules for the application of Council Regulation (EC)
No 2991/1994 laying down standards for spreadable fats and of Council
Regulation (EEC) No 1898/1987 on the protection of designations used
in the marketing of milk and milk products [1997] OJ L 87/3 127–9
Commission Regulation (EC) No 1813/1997 of 19 September 1997 concerning
the compulsory indication on the labelling of certain foodstuffs produced
from genetically modified organisms of particulars other than those
provided for in Directive 1979/112/EEC [1997] OJ L 257/7 252
Commission Regulation (EC) No 2181/1997 of 3 November 1997 amending
Regulation (EC) No 577/1997 laying down certain detailed rules for the
application of Council Regulation (EC) No 2991/1994 laying down
standards for spreadable fats and of Council Regulation (EEC)
No 1898/1987 on the protection of designations used in the marketing
of milk and milk products. [1997] OJ L 299/1 129
Commission Regulation (EC) No 623/1998 of 19 March 1998 amending
Regulation (EC) No 577/1997 laying down certain detailed rules for the
application of Council Regulation (EC) No 2991/1994 laying down
standards for spreadable fats and of Council Regulation (EEC)
No 1898/1987 on the protection of designations used in the marketing
of milk and milk products [1998] OJ L 85/3 128
Council Regulation (EC) No 1139/1998 of 26 May 1998 concerning the
compulsory indication on the labelling of certain foodstuffs produced
from genetically modified organisms of particulars other than those
provided for in Directive 1979/112/EEC [1998] OJ L 159/4 252–3
Council Regulation (EC) No. 2821/1998 of December 17 1998 amending,
as regards withdrawal of the authorisation of certain antibiotics,
Directive 1970/524 concerning additives in feedingstuffs [1998]
OJ L 351/4 ....198–9, 202
Commission Regulation (EC) No 38/1999 of 8 January 1999 supplementing
the Annex to Regulation (EC) No 2400/1996 of 17 December 1996 on the
entry of certain names in the 'Register of protected designations of origin
and protected geographical indications' provided for in Council
Regulation (EEC) No 2081/1992 on the protection of geographical
indications and designations of origin for agricultural products and
foodstuffs [1999] OJ L 5/62 106
Commission regulation (EC) No 590/1999 of 18 March 1999 supplementing the
Annex to Regulation (EC) No 1107/1996 on the registration of geographical

indications and designations of origin under the procedure laid down in
Article 17 of Regulation (EEC) No 2081/1992 [1999] OJ L 74/8 110
Commission Regulation (EC) No 872/1999 of 27 April 1999 supplementing
the Annex to Regulation (EC) No 2400/1996 of 17 December 1996 on the
entry of certain names in the 'Register of protected designations of origin
and protected geographical indications' provided for in Council Regulation
(EEC) No 2081/1992 on the protection of geographical indications and
designations of origin for agricultural products and foodstuffs [1999]
OJ L 110/4 106
Commission Regulation (EC) No 1070/1999 of 25 May 1999 amending the
Annex to Regulation (EC) No 1107/1996 on the registration of geographical
indications and designations of origin under the procedure laid down
in Article 17 of Council Regulation (EEC) No 2081/1992 [1999]
OJ L 130/18 111
Council Regulation (EC) No 1804/1999 of 19 July 1999 supplementing
Regulation (EEC) No 2092/1991 on organic production of agricultural
products and indications referring thereto on agricultural products
and foodstuffs to include livestock production [1999]
OJ L 222/1..222, 256, 261, 264
Commission Regulation (EC) No 49/2000 of 10 January 2000 amending
Council Regulation (EC) No 1139/1998 concerning the compulsory
indication on the labelling of certain foodstuffs produced from
genetically modified organisms of particulars other than those provided
for in Council Directive 1979/112/EEC [2000] OJ L 6/13............................253
Commission Regulation (EC) No 50/2000 of 10 January 2000 on the
labelling of foodstuffs and food ingredients containing additives and
flavourings that have been genetically modified or have been produced
from genetically modified organisms [2000] OJ L 6/15 253
Regulation (EC) No 1980/2000 of the European Parliament and of the
Council of 17 July 2000 on a revised Community eco-label award
scheme [2000] OJ L 237/1 235
Commission Regulation (EC) No 2446/2000 of 6 November 2000
supplementing the Annex to Regulation (EC) No 2400/1996 of 17 December
1996 on the entry of certain names in the 'Register of protected designations
of origin and protected geographical indications' provided for in Council
Regulation (EEC) No 2081/1992 on the protection of geographical
indications and designations of origin for agricultural products and
foodstuffs [2000] OJ L 281/12..106
Council Regulation (EC) No 2826/2000 of 19 December 2000 on
information and promotion actions for agricultural products on the
internal market [2000] OJ L 382/2 276
Council Regulation (EC) No 5/2001 of 19 December 2000 amending
Regulation (EEC) No 1907/1990 on certain marketing standards for eggs
[2001] OJ L 2/1 267

Commission Regulation (EC) No 466/2001 of 8 March 2001 setting maximum
levels for certain contaminants in foodstuffs [2001] OJ L 77/1 205
Commission Regulation (EC) No 1651/2001 of 14 August 2001 amending
Regulation (EEC) No 1274/1991 introducing detailed rules for
implementing Council Regulation (EEC) No 1907/1990 on certain
marketing standards for eggs [2001] OJ L 220/5 268
Commission Regulation (EC) No 2491/2001 of 19 December 2001 amending
Council Regulation (EEC) No 2092/91 on organic production of
agricultural products and indications referring thereto on agricultural
products and foodstuffs [2002] OJ L 337/9...256
Commission Regulation (EC) No 94/2002 of 18 January 2002 laying down
detailed rules for applying Council regulation (EC) No 2826/2000 on
information and promotion actions for agricultural products on the
internal market [2002] OJ L 17/20 276
Regulation (EC) No 178/2002 of the European Parliament and of the Council
of 28 January 2002 laying down the general principles and requirements
of food law, establishing the European Food Safety Authority and laying
down procedures in matters of food safety [2002]
OJ L 31/1 ....11, 185, 187-95, 203, 208, 231, 247, 249
Commission Regulation (EC) No 1321/2002 of 22 July 2002 amending
Regulation (EEC) No 1538/1991 introducing detailed rules for
implementing Council Regulation (EEC) No 1906/1990 on certain
marketing standards for poultrymeat [2002] OJ L 194/17.........................273–4
Commission Regulation (EC) No 1829/2002 of 14 October 2002 amending
the Annex to Regulation (EC) No 1107/1996 with regard to the name
'feta' [2002] OJ L 277/10 ....26, 111, 112, 117
Regulation (EC) No 1829/2003 of the European Parliament and of the
Council of 22 September 2003 on genetically modified food and
feed [2003] OJ L 268/1...243, 244, 247–50, 251
Regulation (EC) No 1830/2003 on the European Parliament and of the
Council of 22 September 2003 concerning the traceability and labelling
of genetically modified organisms and the traceability of food and feed
products produced from genetically modified organisms and amending
Directive 2001/18/EC [2003] OJ L 268/24................................243, 244, 250–51
Regulation (EC) No 2160/2003 of the European Parliament and of the
Council of 17 November 2003 on the control of salmonella and other
specific food-borne zoonotic agents [2003] OJ L 325/1 274
Commission Regulation (EC) No 2295/2003 of 23 December 2003
introducing detailed rules for implementing Council Regulation (EEC)
No 1907/1990 on certain marketing standards for eggs [2003]
OJ L 340/16 267–9
Commission Regulation (EC) No 185/2004 of 2 February 2004 amending
Regulation (EC) No 94/2002 laying down detailed rules for applying
Council Regulation (EC) No 2826/2000 on information and promotion

actions for agricultural products on the internal market [2004]
OJ L 29/4 276
Regulation (EC) No 852/2004 of the European Parliament and of the
Council of 29 April 2004 on the hygiene of foodstuffs [2004]
OJ L 139/1 ....207–9, 221
Regulation (EC) No 853/2004 of the European Parliament and of the
Council of 29 April 2004 laying down specific hygiene rules for food
of animal origin [2004] OJ L 139/55...209
Regulation (EC) No 854/2004 of the European Parliament and of the
Council of 29 April 2004 laying down specific rules for the organisation
of official controls on products of animal origin intended for human
consumption [2004] OJ L 139/206..209
Regulation (EC) No 882/2004 of the European Parliament and of the
Council of 29 April 2004 on official controls performed to ensure the
verification of compliance with feed and food law, animal health and
animal welfare rules [2004] OJ L 165/1..10–11, 185
Commission Regulation (EC) No 1515/2004 of 26 August 2004
amending Regulation (EC) No 2295/2003 introducing detailed rules
for implementing Council Regulation (EEC) No 1907/1990 on certain
marketing standards for eggs [2004] OJ L 278/7 268
Council Regulation (EC) No 509/2006 of 20 March 2006 on agricultural
products and foodstuffs as traditional specialities guaranteed [2006]
OJ L 93/1 117–19
Council Regulation (EC) No 510/2006 of 20 March 2006 on the protection
of geographical indications and designations of origin for agricultural
products and foodstuffs [2006] OJ L 93/12.............................5, 34, 93, 102–16,
                                                                                        117, 119–22, 138, 150
Commission Regulation (EC) No 699/2006 of 5 May 2006 amending
Annex I to Council Regulation (EEC) No 2092/1991 as regards conditions
of access for poultry to open-air runs [2006] OJ L 121/36.....................264, 274
Commission Regulation (EC) No 780/2006 of 24 May 2006 amending
Annex VI to Council Regulation (EEC) No 2092/1991 on organic
production of agricultural products and indications referring thereto
on agricultural products and foodstuffs [2006] OJ L 137/9 255

Directives

Council Directive 1964/54/EEC of 5 November 1963 on the approximation
of the laws of the Member States concerning the preservatives authorised
for use in foodstuffs intended for human consumption. [1964] OJ 12/161.
English Special Edition Series I, Chapter 1963-1964, p.99....................4, 211–12
Council Directive 1964/432/EEC of 26 June 1964 on animal health
problems affecting intra-Community trade in bovine animals and

swine. [1964] OJ L 121/1977; English Special Edition Series I,
Chapter 1963-1964, p.164 61
Council Directive 1964/433/EEC of 26 June 1964 on health problems
affecting intra-community trade in fresh meat. [1964] OJ P 121/2012.
English Special Edition Series I, Chapter 1963-1964, p.185 129–30
Council Directive 1966/402/EEC of 14 June 1966 on the marketing of
cereal seed. [1966] OJ 125/2309. English Special Edition Series I,
Chapter 1965-1966, p.143 4
Commission Directive 1970/50/EEC of 22 December 1969 based on the
provisions of Article 33(7), on the abolition of measures which have
an effect equivalent to quantitative restrictions on imports and are not
covered by other provisions adopted in pursuance of the EEC Treaty.
[1970] OJ L 13/29. [1970] OJ English Special Edition Series I,
Chapter 1970(1), p.17 19–22
Council Directive 1970/357/EEC of 13 July 1970 on the approximation
of the laws of the Member States concerning the antioxidants authorised
for use in foodstuffs intended for human consumption [1970]
OJ L 157/31 213
Council Directive 1970/524 of 23 November 1970 concerning additives
in feedingstuffs [1970] OJ L 270/1 202
Council Directive 1971/118/EEC of 15 February 1971 on health problems
affecting trade in fresh poultrymeat. [1971] OJ L 55/23; [1971] English
Special Edition Series I, Chapter 1971(1), p.106 61
Council Directive 1973/241/EEC of 24 July 1973 on the approximation
of the laws of the Member States relating to cocoa and chocolate products
intended for human consumption [1973] OJ L 228/23 ....4, 7–10, 70, 93, 94
Council Directive 1974/329/EEC of 18 June 1974 on the approximation
of the laws of the Member States relating to emulsifiers, stabilisers,
thickeners and gelling agents for use in foodstuffs [1974] O J L 189/1 214–15
Council Directive 1974/409/EEC of 22 July 1974 on the harmonisation
of the laws of the Member States relating to honey [1974]
OJ L 221/10 ....4, 70, 93, 99, 100
Council Directive 1975/726/EEC of 17 November 1975 on the
approximation of the laws of the Member States concerning fruit
juices and certain similar products [1975] OJ L 311/40 ....93, 97
Council Directive 1976/211/EEC of 20 January 1976 on the approximation
of the laws of the Member States relating to the making-up by weight or
by volume of certain prepackaged products [1976] OJ L 46/1 88–9
Council Directive 1976/893/EEC of 23 November 1976 on the approximation
of the laws of the Member States relating to materials and articles
intended to come into contact with foodstuffs [1976] OJ L 340/19 203
Council Directive 1977/436/EEC of 27 June 1977 on the approximation
of the laws of the Member States relating to coffee extracts and chicory
extracts [1977] OJ L 172/20 ....93, 96

Council Directive 1979/112/EEC of 18 December 1978 on the approximation
of the laws of the Member States relating to the labelling, presentation
and advertising of foodstuffs for sale to the ultimate consumer
[1979] OJ L 33/1..35, 42, 72, 78–9, 90, 253, 270
Council Directive 1979/693/EEC of 24 July 1979 on the approximation of
the laws of the Member States relating to fruit jams, jellies and
marmalades and chestnut purée [1979] OJ L 205/5 ....4, 93, 102
Council Directive 1976/893/EEC of 23 November 1976 on the approximation
of the laws of the Member States relating to materials and articles intended
to come into contact with foodstuffs [1976] OJ L 340/19...............................203
Council Directive 1980/181/EEC of 20 December 1979 on the approximation
of the laws of the Member States relating to units of measurement and
on the repeal of Directive 1971/354/EEC [1980] OJ L 39/40 87–8
Council Directive 1980/777/EEC of 15 July 1980 on the approximation of
the laws of the Member States relating to the exploitation and marketing
of natural mineral waters [1980] OJ L 229/1 123–6
Council Directive 1981/389/EEC of 12 May 1981 establishing measures
necessary for the implementation of Directive 1977/489/EEC on the
protection of animals during international transport [1981]
OJ L 150/1 62
Council Directive 1982/711/EEC of 18 October 1982 laying down the basic
rules necessary for testing migration of the constituents of plastic materials
and articles intended to come into contact with foodstuffs [1982]
OJ L 297/26 204
Council Directive 1983/189/EEC of 28 March 1983 laying down a procedure
for the provision of information in the field of technical standards and
regulations [1983] OJ L 109/8..69
Council Directive 1984/450/EEC of 10 September 1984 relating to the
approximation of the laws, regulations and administrative provisions
of the Member States concerning misleading advertising [1984]
OJ L 250/17 ....123, 228, 270
Council Directive 1984/500/EEC of 15 October 1984 on the approximation
of the laws of the Member States relating to ceramic articles intended
to come into contact with foodstuffs [1984] OJ L 277/12...............................204
Council Directive 1988/344/EEC of 13 June 1988 on the approximation
of the laws of the Member States on extraction solvents used in the
production of foodstuffs and food ingredients, hexane may be used
in the production of cocoa butter [1988] OJ L 157/28............................95, 96–7
Council Directive 1988/388/EEC of 22 June 1988 on the approximation
of the laws of the Member States relating to flavourings for use in
foodstuffs and to source materials for their production [1988]
OJ L 184/61 ....218, 244
Council Directive 1989/107/EEC of 21 December 1988 on the approximation
of the laws of the Member States concerning food additives authorised

for use in foodstuffs intended for human consumption [1989]
OJ L 40/27 ....5, 215–16, 217, 244
Council Directive 1989/109/EEC of 21 December 1988 on the approximation
of the laws of the Member States relating to materials and articles
intended to come into contact with foodstuffs [1989] OJ L 40/38 203–5
Council Directive 1989/344/EEC of 3 May 1989 amending, for the ninth time,
Directive 1973/241/EEC on the approximation of the laws of the Member
States relating to cocoa and chocolate products intended for human
consumption [1989] OJ L 142/19 8
Council Directive 1989/437/EEC of 20 June 1989 on hygiene and health
problems affecting the production and the placing on the market of egg
products [1989] OJ L 212/87 271–3
Council Directive 1989/617/EEC of 27 November 1989 amending Directive
1980/181/EEC on the approximation of the laws of the Member States
relating to units of measurement [1989] OJ L 357/28 88
Council Directive 1990/219/EEC of 23 April 1990 on the contained use of
genetically modified micro-organisms [1990] OJ L 117/1 ....243–4, 251
Council Directive 1990/220/EEC on the deliberate release into the
environment of genetically modified organisms [1990]
OJ L 117/15 ....243–4, 246–7, 251, 254, 260
Council Directive 1990/496/EEC of 24 September 1990 on nutrition
labelling for foodstuffs [1990] OJ L 276/40 ....73, 97–8, 225-6, 228–9, 233
Council Directive 1991/629/EEC of 19 November 1991 laying down
minimum standards for the protection of calves [1991]
OJ L 340/28 ....259, 265–6
Council Directive 1991/630/EEC of 19 November 1991 laying down
minimum standards for the protection of pigs [1991]
OJ L 340/33 ....259, 266, 267
Council Directive 1992/115/EEC of 17 December 1992 amending for
the first time Directive 88/344/EEC on the approximation of the laws
of the Member States on extraction solvents used in the production of
foodstuffs and food ingredients [1992] OJ L 409/31 97
Commission Directive 1993/10/EEC of 15 March 1993 relating to materials
and articles made of regenerated cellulose film intended to come into
contact with foodstuffs [1993] OJ L 93/27 204
Council Directive 1993/43/EEC of 14 June 1993 on the hygiene of foodstuffs
[1993] OJ L 175/1 209–10
Council Directive 1993/77/EEC of 21 September 1993 relating to fruit
juices and certain similar products [1993] OJ L 244/23 97
Council Directive 1993/99/EEC of 29 October 1993 on the subject of
additional measures concerning the official control of foodstuffs
[1993] OJ L 290/14 206
European Parliament and Council Directive 1994/35/EC of 30 June 1994
on sweeteners for use in foodstuffs [1994] OJ L 237/3....................................217

European Parliament and Council Directive 1994/36/EC of 30 June 1994
on colours for use in foodstuffs [1994] OJ L 237/13 217
Council Directive 1994/65/EC of 14 December 1994 laying down the requirements for the production and placing on the market of minced meat
and meat preparations [1994] OJ L 368/10...129–30
European Parliament and Council Directive 1995/2/EC of 20 February 1995
on food additives other than colours and sweeteners [1995] OJ L 61/95.......218
Commission Directive 1996/3/Euratom, ECSC, EC of 26 January 1996
granting a derogation from certain provisions of Council Directive
1993/43/EEC on the hygiene of foodstuffs as regards the transport of
bulk liquid oils and fats by sea [1996] OJ L 21/42 210
Directive 1997/4/EC of the European Parliament and of the Council of 27
January 1997 amending Directive 1979/112/EEC on the approximation
of the laws of the Member States relating to the labelling, presentation
and advertising of foodstuffs [1997] OJ L 43/21...97
Commission Directive 1997/35/EC of 18 June 1997 adapting to technical
progress for the second time Council Directive 1990/220/EEC on the
deliberate release into the environment of genetically modified organisms
[1997] OJ L 169/72 251
Commission Directive 1998/28/EC of 29 April 1998 granting a derogation
from certain provisions of Directive 1993/43/EEC on the hygiene of
foodstuffs as regards the transport by sea of bulk raw sugar [1998]
OJ L 140/10 209–10
Directive 1998/34/EC of the European Parliament and of the Council of
22 June 1998 laying down a procedure for the provision of information
in the field of technical standards and regulations [1998] OJ L 204/37 236
Council Directive 1998/58/EC of 20 July 1998 concerning the protection of
animals kept for farming purposes [1998] OJ L 221/23 267
Directive 1999/2/EC of the European Parliament and of the Council of
22 February 1999 on the approximation of the laws of the Member States
concerning foods and food ingredients treated with ionising radiation
[1999] OJ L 6/16 ....91, 206–7
Directive 1999/3/EC of the European Parliament and of the Council of
22 February 1999 on the establishment of a Community list of foods
and food ingredients treated with ionising radiation [1999] OJ L 66/24 207
Directive 1999/4/EC of the European Parliament and of the Council of
22 February 1999 relating to coffee extracts and chicory extracts
[1999] OJ L 66/26 96–7
Council Directive 1999/74/EC of 19 July 1999 laying down minimum
standards for the protection of laying hens [1999] OJ L 203/53.............267, 268
Directive 1999/103/EC of the European Parliament and of the Council of
24 January 2000 amending Council Directive 1980/181/EEC on the
approximation of the laws of the member States relating to units of
measurement [2000] OJ L 34/17..103

Directive 2000/13/EC of the European Parliament and of the Council of
20 March 2000 on the approximation of the laws of the Member States
relating to the labelling, presentation and advertising of foodstuffs
[2000] OJ L 109/29....................5, 35, 72, 78–90, 97, 123, 131, 221, 227, 232, 245
Directive 2000/36/EC of the European Parliament and of the Council of
23 June 2000 relating to cocoa and chocolate products intended for
human consumption [2000] OJ L 197/19...4, 7-10, 94–6
Directive 2001/18/EC of the European Parliament and of the Council of
12 March 2001 on the deliberate release into the environment of
genetically modified organisms and replacing Council Directive
1990/220/EEC [2001] OJ L 106/1.....................5, 242, 244, 246–7, 249, 251, 254
Commission Directive 2001/22/EC of 8 March 2001 laying down the
sampling methods and the methods of analysis for the official control
of the levels of lead, cadmium, mercury and 3-MCPD in foodstuffs
[2001] OJ L 77/14 206
Council Directive 2001/110/EC of 20 December 2001 relating to honey
[2002] OJ L 10/47 ....4, 99–101
Council Directive 2001/112/EC of 20 December 2001 relating to fruit
juices and certain similar products intended for human consumption
[2002] OJ L 10/58 97–8
Council Directive 2001/113/EC of 20 December 2001 relating to fruit jams,
jellies and marmalades and sweetened chestnut purée intended for
human consumption [2002] OJ L 10/67 ....4, 101–2
Directive 2002/46/EC of the European Parliament and of the Council of
10 June 2002 on the approximation of the laws of the Member States
relating to food supplements [2002] OJ L 183/51 232–3
Commission Directive 2003/40/EC of 16 May 2003 establishing the list,
concentration limits and labelling requirements for the constituents
of natural mineral waters and the conditions for using ozone-enriched
air for the treatment of natural mineral waters and spring waters
[2003] OJ L 126/34 125–6

Decisions

Commission Decision 1993/53/EEC of 21 December 1992 setting up a
scientific committee for designations of origin, geographical indications
and certificates of specific character [1993] OJ L 13/16 109
Commission Decision 1994/474/EC of 27 July 1994 concerning certain
protection measures relating to bovine spongiform encephalopathy and
repealing Decisions 1989/469/EEC and 1990/200/EEC [1994]
OJ L 194/96 179
Commission Decision 1996/281/EC of 3 April 1996 concerning the placing
on the market of genetically modified soya beans (Glycine max L.) with

increased tolerance to the herbicide glyphosate, pursuant to Council
Directive 1990/220/EEC [1996] OJ L 107/10 252
Commission Decision 1997/98/EC of 23 January 1997 concerning the placing
on the market of genetically modified maize with the combined modification
for insecticidal properties conferred by the Bt-endotoxin gene and increased
tolerance to the herbicide glufosinate ammonium pursuant to Council
Directive 1990/220/EEC [1997] OJ L 31/69 252
Commission Decision 1997/579 setting up scientific committees in the field
of consumer health and food safety [1997] OJ L 237/18..................................202
Commission Decision 1998/613/EC of 21 October 1998 concerning a draft
Decree of the Republic of Austria on the identification of genetically
modified additives and flavourings used as food ingredients [1998]
OJ L 291/35 253
Council Decision 1999/468/EC of 28 June 1999 laying down the procedures
for the exercise of implementing powers conferred on the Commission
[1999] OJ L 184/23 ....184, 193–4, 231, 233

Recommendations

Commission Recommendation 1980/1089/EEC of 11 November 1980
addressed to the Member States concerning tests relating to the safety
evaluation of food additives [1980] OJ L 320/36 214
Commission Recommendation 2003/556/EC of 23 July 2003 on guidelines
for the development of national strategies and best practices to ensure the
coexistence of genetically modified crops with conventional and organic
farming [2003] OJ L 189/36 262

INTERNATIONAL

General Agreement on Tariffs and Trade, 1947 and 1994............................133, 139
Agreement Establishing the World Trade Organisation 134, 135, 146
WTO Agreement on Sanitary and Phytosanitary
Measures..14, 15, 133, 134, 138–42, 150
WTO Agreement on Technical Barriers to Trade.............14, 133, 135, 142–4, 151
WTO Agreement on Trade-Related Aspects of Intellectual Property
Rights...14, 133, 134–8
WTO Agreement on Agriculture 133, 135, 144–5
WTO Agreement on Subsidies and Countervailing Measures...........................135

Codex Alimentarius recommended International Code of Practice,
General principles of Food Hygiene 1/1969; revised 2003 ....156, 208

Codex Alimentarius General Guidelines on Claims, Codex Guidelines
1/1979; revised 1991 ....158, 164, 166, 227
Codex Alimentarius Code of Ethics for International Trade in Food,
1979; revised 1985...156–8
Codex Alimentarius Standard for Honey, Codex Standard 12/1981;
revised 1987 and 2001 101
Codex Alimentarius Standard for Cocoa Butter, Codex Standard
86/1981; revised 2001 170–71
Codex Alimentarius Standard for Chocolate, Codex Standard 87/1981;
revised 2003..158, 170
Codex Alimentarius Standard for Cocoa Powders (Cocoas) and Dry
Mixtures of Cocoa and Sugars, Codex Standard 105/1981; revised 2001 171
Codex Alimentarius Standard for the Labelling of Prepackaged Foods,
Codex Standard 1/1985; revised 1991 and 2005 ....156, 158–62, 168
Codex Alimentarius Guidelines on Nutrition Labelling, Codex
Guidelines 2/1985; revised 1993 and 2003 ....156, 158, 162–7
Codex Alimentarius Standard for the Labelling of and Claims for Prepackaged
Foods for Special Dietary Use, Codex Standard 146/1985 164
Codex Alimentarius Standard for Cocoa Butter Confectionery,
Codex Standard 147/1985 171
Codex Alimentarius General Principles for the Addition of Essential
Nutrients to Foods, Codex Guidelines 9/1987; revised 1991 166
Codex Alimentarius Standard for the Labelling of and Claims for Foods
for Special Medical Purposes, Codex Standard 180/1991 165
Codex Alimentarius Principles for Food Import and Export Certification
and Inspection, Codex Guidelines 20/1995...170
Codex Alimentarius Guidelines for Use of Nutrition and Health Claims,
Codex Guidelines 23/1997; revised 2004...158, 227, 229
Codex Alimentarius Guidelines for the Production, Processing, Labelling
and Marketing of Organically Produced Foods, Codex Guidelines
32/1999; revised 2001 and 2004 ....158, 167–70
Codex Alimentarius Guidelines on the Judgement of Equivalence of
Sanitary Measures Associated with Food Inspection and Certification
Systems, Codex Guidelines 53/2003 63
Codex Alimentarius Standard for Canned Bamboo Shoots, Codex Standard
241/2003 151
Codex Alimentarius Standard for Fermented Milks, Codex Standard
243/2003 ....42, 171–2
Codex Alimentarius Standard for Oranges, Codex Standard 245/2004 151
Codex Alimentarius Standard for Fruit Juices and Nectars, Codex
Standard 247/2005..151
Codex Alimentarius Advisory Specifications for Food Additives,
12/2006 218

Paris Convention for the Protection of Industrial Property 1883-1967
  (Stockholm Act)..136
International Convention on the Use of Appellations of Origin and
  Denominations of Cheeses 1951 (Stresa Convention) 119
International Plant Protection Convention 1951 139
Vienna Convention on Ozone Depleting Substances 1985...............................196
Convention on Biological Diversity Cartagena Protocol on
  Biosafety 2000 246–7

International Dairy Agreement 1980..135
International Bovine Meat Agreement 1980 135
International Cocoa Agreement 2001...9–10

UNITED KINGDOM

Assize of Bread and Ale 1266..3
Adulteration of Tea and Coffee Act 1724 3
Adulteration of Tea Act 1730 3
Adulteration of Tea Act 1776 3
Bread Act 1822 3
Corn, Peas, Beans or Parsnips and Cocoa Act 1822..3
Bread Act 1836 3
Adulteration of Food or Drink Act 1860 3
Food and Drugs (Adulteration) Act 1928 3

Specified Bovine Offal Order 1995, SI 1928/1995...178
Specified Bovine Offal (Amendment) Order 1995, SI 3246/1995......................178

1

Regulating the Food Industry

1.1 INTRODUCTION

FOOD SAFETY IS an issue of major concern throughout Europe. Much of this anxiety results from a series of well publicised recent health scares. From the mid-1980s onwards, listeria in cheese, salmonella in eggs and chocolate, bovine spongiform encephalopathy in beef, genetically modified vegetables and soya, the use of hormones in meat production, toxins, foot and mouth, avian influenza and e-coli have all, at one time or another, given rise to particular cause for concern. It has become clear, in the aftermath of many of these alarms, that the law is generally ill equipped to respond to new crises as and when they arise, often resulting in legally questionable emergency measures being taken.

In addition to these safety issues, other important matters relating to the production and marketing of food have also surfaced in recent years. For example, the promotion of free movement for goods throughout the 25 Member States of the European Union (EU) has been coupled with concerns about depreciating food quality levels, brought about by the high degree of protection accorded to the principle of mutual recognition. This requires that once a food product is lawfully marketable in any one Member State it must, subject to limited exceptions, be lawfully marketable in all. Furthermore, where the Community has set harmonised standards for generic foodstuffs, these have tended to be set at the lowest common level.[1] Traditional, locally and regionally produced products that have sustained communities for generations now come under threat from mass produced and nutritionally inferior substitutes, manufactured from poor quality ingredients by different methods of production. The resulting products, though qualitatively inferior, are legally marketable under the same food name. It is often very difficult for either national governments or the EU institutions to take action to counteract this without contravening current Community law and policy.

The structure of the law and policy of the European Union directly favours certain practices which devalue the quality of food. Manufacturers and producers are agile and adept at putting pressure on local and European politicians to maintain outdated and unsustainable systems of production preventing improvements in food quality. Producers are even financially rewarded for the non-production

---

[1] For further discussion on how harmonising rules can be used to protect consumers see S Weatherill, *EU Consumer Law and Policy* (Cheltenham, Edward Elgar, 2005).

of goods. Though the common market is based upon the concept of the free movement of goods and services within the EU, the other side of the same coin is to effectively ban the importation of goods from outside the Member States, even where these goods are of equal or superior quality or cheaper in price. This effectively deprives consumers of choice. It is no surprise that the resulting food production system is no longer acceptable, since not only does it result in decreased efficiency of production, lower quality of goods and increased wastage of food; it also has an injurious effect on the economic growth of countries outside the Union, that younger electorates no longer consider politically acceptable.

Globalised rules on technical barriers to trade, sanitary and phytosanitary measures and trade-related aspects of intellectual property rights all have the potential to render EU food laws contrary to international commitments. Measures introduced to protect human health or the environment must be scientifically justifiable to be capable of withstanding World Trade Organization (WTO) scrutiny. This can bring EU legislators into direct conflict with consumer groups who seek to minimise the negative impacts of the ever-increasing use of technology and innovation in food production.

Animal welfare, human nutrition and human rights considerations also have an important, yet much underused, role to play in shaping EU food law. In particular, the Community legislator has tended to overlook the need to ensure that the food that is produced and consumed continues to serve its primary function of providing nutrition and sustenance. Politicians have allowed the fundamental Community principle of the free movement of goods to underlie all key harmonising provisions in this area at the expense of health and consumer protection. Emphasis on safety in the aftermath of the 'food scares' has also resulted in the quality and nutritional value of food receiving less attention in new legislative initiatives. It is here contended that the future of EU food law lies not with the preoccupation with ensuring that food is safe, or at least that the possibility of 'unsafe' food entering the chain is minimised. Instead, attention now needs to be shifted onto a group of key factors, including production efficiency, nutritional value, quality levels, ethical considerations, consumer protection and human health protection which, when combined, should result in the creation of a more unified and simplified body of rules that leaves more autonomy with the individual Member State in deciding what the consumer should be encouraged to eat, and what the consumer should probably be protected from.

1.2 HISTORICAL DEVELOPMENT OF FOOD LAW

The need for laws regulating the production and marketing of food has long been obvious. This is evidenced from some of the earliest historical writings which indicate the existence of codifying rules designed to protect consumers from dishonest practice in the sale of food.[2] Assyrian tablets described the methods to

---

[2] See FAO and WHO, 'Origins of the Codex Alimentarius' in *Understanding the Codex Alimentarius* (1999), ISBN 92-5-104248-9.

be used to determine the correct weights and measures for grain; Egyptian scrolls prescribed the labelling to be applied to certain foodstuffs; in ancient Athens, beer and wine were inspected for purity and soundness; the Romans had a highly organised state food control system to protect consumers from fraud or poor produce.[3] Ancient Irish laws (Bechbretha) legislated for, *inter alia*, the resolving of disputes over the ownership of fruit that fell on a neighbour's land. If a tree growing on A's land drops fruit onto that of B, this is to be divided between A and B for three years. In year four, it all goes to B. The cycle restarts in year five.[4] In Europe during the middle ages individual countries passed laws concerning the quality and safety of eggs, sausages, cheese, beer, wine and bread.[5] The famous German beer-purity laws (Biersteuergesetz) were introduced in 1516.[6] In France, systemised wine quality classification laws (Appelation d'Origine Controlée) were first introduced in 1935.

In the United Kingdom, laws relating to food developed from the medieval guilds, which sought to maintain the purity of the commodities in which their members dealt, resulting in, for example, the Assize of Bread and Ale 1266.[7] Early statutes tended to deal with specific foodstuffs rather than general principles of food law. These included the Adulteration of Tea and Coffee Act 1724, the Adulteration of Tea Act 1730, which prohibited the use of sloe leaves, liquorice leaves and already used tea leaves in tea, the Adulteration of Tea Act 1776, the Bread Acts 1822 and 1836, and the Corn, Peas, Beans or Parsnips and Cocoa Act 1822, which established a licensing system for the sale of these foodstuffs. Most of this legislation tended to be introduced for three main reasons: to protect human health; to promote fair trade; and to protect State revenues gained from trade in pure forms of the foodstuffs.

The first UK Act of Parliament to deal with the sale of food more generally was the Adulteration of Food or Drink Act 1860, which made it an offence to knowingly sell food containing any injurious ingredient or which was adulterated in any way.[8] More ad hoc legislation was introduced later, dealing with the composition and labelling of margarine, milk, butter, dairy products, preservative use and the labelling of imported meat.[9] Existing food laws were later consolidated in the Food and Drugs (Adulteration) Act 1928.

During the second half of the 19th century, more general food laws began to appear throughout Europe, establishing more formalised food control systems

---

[3] *Ibid.*

[4] F Kelly, *A Guide to Early Irish Law* (Dublin, Dublin Institute for Advanced Studies, 1988).

[5] FAO and WHO, *Understanding the Codex Alimentarius*, note 2 above.

[6] These rules, which had persisted for nearly 500 years, were the subject of examination for compatibility with EU rules on the free movement of goods in Case 178/1984, *Commission v Germany* (bier) [1987] ECR 1227. See Chapter 2 below.

[7] 51 Hen 3 Stat 1.

[8] Article 1. The Act also contained provisions on food analysis (Arts 3, 4 and 5) and rights of appeal (Arts 6, 7 and 9), and established a legal definition of 'food and drink' for the first time (Art 14) as including 'not only all alimentary substances, whether solids or liquids, but also all eatables or drinkables whatsoever not being medical drugs or articles usually taken or sold as medicines'.

[9] For further details, see *Halsbury's Laws of Englanwd* 4th edn (London, LexisNexis, 2000).

and compliance monitoring procedures. Around the same time, food chemistry and science brought about changes to the manner in which food was to be produced. Methods were devised to establish the purity of food. Harmful industrial chemicals were often used to disguise the true colour or nature of food. Science could now provide the methods and processes by which these, and other, practices could be readily identified and to enable distinctions to be made between safe and unsafe food.

The preponderance of food laws in the Member States comes directly from the EU since their accession to the EC Treaties. Food Laws come either in the form of new requirements introduced by way of regulation or directive, or by way of alterations that must be made to domestic law following decisions of the Community courts. The EU institutions commenced their harmonisation programme for food laws at a very early stage in the development of the Community legal order. Initial examples of this activity through legislative means can be seen in Council Directive 1964/54 on preservative use,[10] Council Directive 1966/402 on the marketing of cereal seed, which sought to ensure that the quality of seeds used in cereal production were of a set minimum quality standard,[11] and the original 'recipe laws'. The 'recipe laws' set common compositional and production method requirements for, amongst others, chocolate,[12] honey,[13] and jams and marmalades.[14] Initial case law on the free movement of goods was also to have a substantial impact on the food laws of the individual Member States. Cases such as *Cassis*[15] and *Commission v Germany*[16] were to lead to an alteration in domestic customary practices and rules for the production and marketing of food and drink, often nullifying the effectiveness of national laws that had remained relatively unchanged for centuries. It was also clear, from subsequent decisions of the European Court of Justice, that the legal principles developed from these initial judgments would extend to all national rules relating to food and drink that were deemed to be a restriction on trade within the Community in any way, subject to

---

[10] Council Directive 1964/54/EEC of 5 November 1963 on the approximation of the laws of the Member States concerning the preservatives authorised for use in foodstuffs intended for human consumption. [1964] OJ 12/161. English Special Edition Series I, Chapter 1963–4, p 99.

[11] Council Directive 1966/402/EEC of 14 June 1966 on the marketing of cereal seed. [1966] OJ 125/2309. English Special Edition Series I, Chapter 1965–6, p 143.

[12] Council Directive 1973/241/EEC of 24 July 1973 on the approximation of the laws of the Member States relating to cocoa and chocolate products intended for human consumption. [1973] OJ L 228/23. Now replaced by Directive 2000/36/EC of the European Parliament and of the Council of 23 June 2000 relating to cocoa and chocolate products intended for human consumption. [2000] OJ L 197/19.

[13] Council Directive 1974/409/EEC of 22 July 1974 on the harmonisation of the laws of the Member States relating to honey. [1974] OJ L 221/10. Now replaced by Council Directive 2001/110/EC of 20 December 2001 relating to honey. [2002] OJ L 10/47.

[14] Council Directive 1979/693/EEC of 24 July 1979 on the approximation of the laws of the Member States relating to fruit jams, jellies and marmalades and chestnut purée. [1979] OJ L 205/5. Now replaced by Council Directive 2001/113/EC of 20 December 2001 relating to fruit jams, jellies and marmalades and sweetened chestnut purée intended for human consumption. [2002] OJ L 10/67.

[15] Case 120/1978, *Rewe-Zentral AG v Bundesmonopolverwaltung für Branntwein* [1979] ECR 649.

[16] Case 178/1984, *Commission v Germany* (bier) [1987] ECR 1227.

some, albeit very limited, exceptions.[17] The manner in which the Court began to interpret the EC Treaty, in particular Articles 28 to 30 thereof,[18] according to the Commission, removed much of the need to introduce further harmonising measures, such as those set out in the earlier recipe laws.[19] However, secondary Community legislation would still be required for many aspects of the food production and marketing process. This body of legislation now extends to cover matters such as food labelling,[20] additive use,[21] protected geographical food names,[22] organic food production,[23] the deliberate release of genetically modified organisms,[24] and, probably, nutrition and health claims.[25] As new technologies are applied to the production of food, new laws are required to control their use, and to appease consumers' uncertainty about their safety. It is generally the EU that is best placed to respond to these new requirements, given that any law that it introduces will generally become national law in all Member States simultaneously, removing the potential for anti-competitive and unfair trading practices to persist within one of the most lucrative, and probably the most important, of all the markets in the Union. At least that is the intention.

1.3 IMPORTANCE OF THE FOOD SECTOR IN THE EU

Food is of major importance to the European economy. Prior to the 2004 round of enlargement, the food and drink industry was estimated to be worth €600 billion annually, accounting for 15 per cent of total manufacturing output, involving the employment of over 2.6 million people.[26] The European Union is the world's

---

[17] See, for example, Case 788/1979, *Criminal proceedings against Gilli and Andres* [1980] ECR 2071; Case 27/1980, *Criminal proceedings against Anton Adriaan Fietje* [1980] ECR 3839; Case 193/1980, *Commission v Italy* (vinegar) [1981] ECR 3019; Case 298/1987, *Proceedings for compulsory reconstruction against Smanor SA* [1988] ECR 4489; Case 286/1986, *Ministère public v Gérard Deserbais* [1988] ECR 4907; Case 274/1987, *Commission v Germany* (meat products) [1989] ECR 229; Case 76/1986, *Commission v Germany* (milk substitutes) [1989] ECR 1021; Case 216/1984, *Commission v France* (milk substitutes) [1988] ECR 793.

[18] Formerly Arts 30–36 EC.

[19] Communication on the free movement of foodstuffs within the Community. [1989] OJ C 271/3.

[20] Directive 2000/13/EC of the European Parliament and of the Council of 20 March 2000 on the approximation of the laws of the Member States relating to the labelling, presentation and advertising of foodstuffs. [2000] OJ L 109/29.

[21] Council Directive 1989/107/EEC of 21 December 1988 on the approximation of the laws of the Member States concerning food additives authorised for use in foodstuffs intended for human consumption. [1989] OJ L 40/27.

[22] Council Regulation (EC) No 510/2006 of 20 March 2006 on the protection of geographical indications and designations of origin for agricultural products and foodstuffs. [2006] OJ L 93/12.

[23] Council Regulation (EEC) No 2092/1991 of 24 June 1991 on organic production of agricultural products and indications referring thereto on agricultural products and foodstuffs. [1991] OJ L 198/1.

[24] Directive 2001/18/EC of the European Parliament and of the Council of 12 March 2001 on the deliberate release into the environment of genetically modified organisms and replacing Council Directive 1990/220/EEC. [2001] OJ L 106/1.

[25] Proposal for a Regulation of the European Parliament and of the Council on nutrition and health claims made on foods. COM (2003) 424.

[26] Figures taken from Chapter 1 of the European Commission White Paper on Food Safety. COM (1999) 719.

largest producer of food and drink products. In addition to this, agriculture was worth €220 billion per year, including €50 billion in exports to third countries, providing 7.5 million full-time jobs. More recent figures suggest that turnover in the food and drinks industry, post-enlargement to 25 Member States, had risen to €799 billion, involving the employment of 4.1 million people. Meat processing alone accounts for €161 billion turnover in the EU, €31 billion of which is profit. In fact, meat processing has become an even more lucrative industry in recent years, despite the identified decline in consumer confidence levels after the BSE (Bovine Spongiform Encephalopathy), foot and mouth and avian flu scares. Annual turnover in the dairy sector in the EU stands at €117 billion, €18 billion of which is profit. Beverages turnover is €118 billion, generating €31 billion profit in 2005.[27] Total exports of food and drink from the EU in 2003 were worth €44.5 billion, with imports from third countries into the Community standing at €38.7 billion, leaving a trade surplus in the EU for food and drink of nearly €6 billion, with the United States being the main export destination for European Union foodstuffs. Of the top 10 food exporters in the world, seven (France, Netherlands, Germany, Belgium, Spain, UK and Italy) are EU Member States, all of which are currently larger exporters of food than China.[28] Overall, the food and drinks industry is the largest manufacturing sector in the EU, accounting for almost 15 per cent of the sector.

Trade in food is a major political issue. EU Member States seek to preserve the customary method of manufacture for their traditional and national foodstuffs. National laws often reflect the preferences of consumers in each of the Member States. This, however, tends to fall foul of Community law obligations in one of two ways. Either these national rules inhibit the free movement of food in the Community by making it more difficult for producers in other Member States manufacturing the same or similar products to gain access to the domestic market of the host State contrary to Article 28 EC prohibiting quantitative restrictions on trade or measures of equivalent effect. Alternatively, no Member State can maintain national laws that are out of line with the harmonised EU standard introduced by way of secondary Community legislation. In relation to the former, Member States can plead various justifications for the existence of these trade-inhibiting rules before the Community Courts. This is discussed in more detail in Chapter 2. On the latter, much political wrangling may surround the common standard that is to be, or which has been, adopted. Each Member State, or group of Member States, seeks to have the approximated compositional requirement and/or method of production as close to its existing standard as possible. The obvious advantage of this is that the less domestic producers have to modify their own method of production, the more the harmonised Community standard approximates to their existing practices. An example of the duration and intensity of the debate that can surround the introduction of these standardised Community rules was most famously seen in relation to the chocolate directive.

---

[27] USDA Foreign Agricultural Service GAIN Report E35067, *The EU's Food and Drink Industry 2005.*
[28] WTO, *International Trade Statistics*, ISBN 9287012202.

1.3.1 Chocolate Debate

The original directive setting out the compositional requirements entitling producers to use one of the variety of legal names available for different types of
chocolate was finally replaced after much expense and debate in 2000.[29]
'Chocolate' was defined in Annex I to the original chocolate directive as:

> The product obtained from cocoa nib, cocoa mass, cocoa powder or fat-reduced cocoa
> powder and sucrose with or without added cocoa butter, having ... a minimum total dry
> cocoa solids content of 35%—at least 14% of dry non-fat cocoa solids and 18% of cocoa
> butter.

It is similarly, if slightly more simply, defined in the 2000 directive.[30] The original
directive also set out the compositional requirements for legitimate use of the legal
names 'plain chocolate', 'milk chocolate', and 'milk chocolate with high milk content'.[31] Whilst chocolate had to contain a minimum of 35 per cent cocoa, milk
chocolate with high milk content was only required to contain 20 per cent cocoa.
The United Kingdom and Ireland, along with Denmark, were about to become
Member States of what was then called the European Economic Community.
Chocolate produced in the United Kingdom and Ireland was traditionally manufactured using 20 per cent cocoa solids and 20 per cent milk solids. Under the
terms of the directive this chocolate would have to be marketed as 'milk chocolate
with high milk content' in the other Member States. There milk chocolate tended
to contain a minimum of 25 per cent cocoa and 14 per cent milk. Derogation was
granted to the United Kingdom and Ireland from having to use this designation,
claimed to be a consumer repellent, in their own territory, where it could be
marketed as 'chocolate'.[32]

A further difficulty existed in that British chocolate tended to be made with vegetable fats in place of cocoa butter. Many States, particularly France and Belgium,
objected strongly to any derogation allowing a chocolate-type product containing
vegetable fats to be legally marketable on the continent as 'chocolate'. It was felt
that only the chocolate-type product that contained no fats other than cocoa butter should be legitimately marketable as 'chocolate'. Eight Member States had
objected to the marketing of British and Irish chocolate on their territory where it
contained vegetable fat: Belgium, France, Italy, Spain, Luxembourg, Germany,
Greece and the Netherlands. Much political argument followed. It became apparent that the continuance of any prohibition on the sale of British chocolate on the

---

[29] Directive 2000/36/EC of the European Parliament and of the Council of 23 June 2000 relating to
cocoa and chocolate products intended for human consumption. [2000] OJ L 197/19. The original
Chocolate Directive was Council Directive 1973/241/EEC of 24 July 1973 on the approximation of the
laws of the Member States relating to cocoa and chocolate products intended for human consumption.
[1973] OJ L 228/23.

[30] Annex I to Directive 2000/36, *ibid.*

[31] Annex I to Directive 1973/241, note 29 above.

[32] Article 3(1) of Directive 1973/241, note 29 above.

continent under that designation could have serious consequences, both economic and political, for the free movement of goods. More specifically, it became clear that chocolate products containing fat other than cocoa butter, lawfully manufactured in a Member State, had to be permitted to circulate freely within the Community under the original sales name, provided that the products were labelled to indicate that they contained vegetable fat. The case law of the Court of Justice indicated that directives, such as that at issue here, had to be interpreted in the light of the rules of the EC Treaty, in particular those on the free movement of goods.[33] As a consequence, British and Irish chocolate containing 20 per cent cocoa and up to five per cent vegetable fat would have to be legally marketable in all the Member States as 'chocolate'. This applied even in those Member States where chocolate usually contains a minimum of 35 per cent cocoa and no fats other than cocoa butter. Some Member States continued to contravene EU law by continuing to prohibit the importation of chocolate containing vegetable fat. Italy, for example, refused to allow chocolate with a low cocoa content and containing vegetable fat to be sold there unless marketed as 'surrogate chocolate'.

A compromise deal was finally agreed upon by the Council and endorsed by the Parliament in March 2000.[34] All 15 Member States, as there then were, would have to agree to allow British and Irish chocolate to be marketed on their territories, but it had to be clearly labelled as 'family milk chocolate' where it had a high milk content.[35] Reaching this compromise was difficult. It had been complicated further by the fact that many side issues had been introduced to the debate, ranging from taste and quality to the protection of farmers in cocoa-dependent economies. Chocolate products which contain fats other than cocoa butter may now be marketed in all the Member States, provided that their labelling is supplemented by a 'conspicuous and clearly legible statement' that it 'contains vegetable fats in addition to cocoa butter'; this statement to appear in the same field of vision as the list of ingredients, clearly separated from that list.[36] Belgium had contested that this information should be compulsorily placed in a prominent position on the front of the label, but the European Parliament rejected this.

---

[33] Case C-47/1990, *Delhaize v Promalvin* [1992] ECR I-3669 and Joined Cases C-427/1993 and C-436/1993, *Bristol Myers Squibb v Paranova* [1996] ECR I-3457.

[34] Directive 1973/241 had been amended nine times since it was adopted, although many of the amending directives dealt with issues of minor significance only. The last of these amending directives to be introduced was Council Directive 1989/344/EEC of 3 May 1989 amending, for the ninth time, Directive 1973/241/EEC on the approximation of the laws of the Member States relating to cocoa and chocolate products intended for human consumption. [1989] OJ L 142. This 1989 directive added to Art 14(2) of Directive 1973/241/EEC authorisation for the marketing under the name 'chocolate familiar a la taza' and 'chocolate a la taza' of chocolate containing flours and/or starches and intended for consumption with milk after cooking.

[35] Annex I to Directive 2000/36/EC, note 29 above. It had been suggested at one stage in the debate that British and Irish chocolate should be labelled as 'vegelate' given the tendency to use vegetable fats.

[36] Article 2(2). Those vegetable fats which may be added to chocolate include illipe, palm-oil, sal, shea, kokum gurgi and mango kernel. In addition to this, coconut oil may be added to chocolate used for the manufacture of ice cream and similar frozen products. Annex II to Directive 2000/36/EC, note 29 above.

One of the new chocolate directive's main effects is that it permits producers to use cheaper raw materials, considered to be of lower quality than cocoa and cocoa butter, as cocoa substitutes. Almost 30 years of political wrangling ensued about the damaging effects that European Community laws on chocolate could have for both the free movement of goods and the quality of chocolate. It appeared to end in compromise, but the debate continued. It culminated in the Commission taking action against two Member States who persisted in prohibiting the marketing of chocolate from some Member States.

In the cases of *Commission v Spain*[37] and *Commission v Italy*,[38] the Court ruled that the two respondent Members States were in breach of their Community obligations by continuing to prohibit the marketing of products containing vegetable fats other than cocoa butter under the name 'chocolate'. It will be remembered that products containing such fats had to be labelled in these States as 'chocolate substitutes'. Such a policy was, according to the Commission, contrary to EC Treaty provisions designed to ensure the free movement of goods, in particular Article 28. The Member States, on the other hand, contended that their domestic legislation was necessary to protect consumers from inferior quality products. The Court found that the requirement imposed by the Member States on producers of chocolate using vegetable fats other than cocoa butter to alter their sales name to 'chocolate substitute' could compel traders to incur additional packaging costs while also altering consumers' perceptions of products labelled in such a manner. The Court did accept that consumer protection was a legitimate exception to Article 28 EC, but stated that additional labelling indicating that the product was different to that which consumers would normally expect to be marketed by that name was more appropriate than a complete prohibition on the use of the name 'chocolate'.

It has also been claimed that the chocolate directive will inflict serious social and economic damage on cocoa producing countries.[39] It permits the use of significantly smaller amounts of cocoa than most European consumers have become accustomed to, and allows such products to contain fats other than cocoa butter. It is possible that the amended directive is at variance with commitments undertaken by the EU Member States under the International Cocoa Agreements, in particular the undertaking to encourage increased cocoa consumption. The International Cocoa Agreement 2001,[40] to which the European Union is a contracting State, clearly states that for the creation of a sustainable cocoa economy members are required to give:

> due consideration to the sustainable management of cocoa resources in order to provide fair economic returns to all stakeholders in the cocoa economy, bearing in mind the principles and objectives of sustainable development contained in Agenda 21, adopted

---

[37] Case C-12/2000, *Commission v Spain* (chocolate) [2003] ECR I-459.
[38] Case C-14/2000, *Commission v Italy* (chocolate) [2003] ECR I-513.
[39] See, for example, Parliamentary question P-2286/1999. [2000] OJ C 303 E.
[40] International Cocoa Agreement 2001 arising out of the United Nations Cocoa Conference, Geneva, 26 February–2 March 2001.

by the United Nations Conference on Environment and Development (UNCED) of 14 June 1992.[41]

Members must also:

recognise that the use of [cocoa] substitutes may have negative effects on the expansion of cocoa consumption and the development of a sustainable cocoa economy.[42]

The EU is vital to the cocoa economy. Of the top eight importers of cocoa in the world, seven are Member States, the only exception in this list being the United States of America, the world's largest importer of cocoa. Germany and the Netherlands combined account for over one quarter of total world imports of cocoa, the Member States combined accounting for well over half.[43]

The 30 years of debate and political wrangling that have surrounded the labelling of chocolate, and which in some ways continue to surround it, is indicative of the range of sensitivities and agendas that are all being pushed during the attempts to reach agreement on a common Community standard for food products. This makes compromise very difficult to reach. This is more so in an ever-expanding European Union of 25 or more Member States, with 25 plus sets of customs, traditions and domestic industries to be protected. There are also international obligations to be taken into account when drafting Community rules on the production and marketing of food. The EU has signed up to global agreements such as that on cocoa, or even more importantly, and with additional legal binds, the WTO Agreements. Other highly politicised food law-related issues have also arisen in recent years. The most notable of these is the posturing that surrounded the measures to be introduced when British cattle were found to be infected with BSE, a matter dealt with in more detail in Chapter 5 below.

1.3.2 Ensuring Compliance with EU Food Law

Regulation 882/2004 requires Member States to maintain systems of control which ensure that food law standards are met.[44] It states that food and animal feed should be safe and wholesome and that Community legislation 'comprises a set of rules to ensure that this objective is attained'.[45] This is debated throughout this book. The regulation defines 'feed law' as being:

the laws, regulations and administrative provisions governing feed in general and feed safety in particular, whether at Community or national level; it covers all stages of production, processing and distribution of feed and the use of feed.[46]

---

[41] Article 39(1).

[42] Article 38(1).

[43] Figures taken from Annex B to the International Cocoa Agreement 2001, note 40 above.

[44] Regulation (EC) No 882/2004 of the European Parliament and of the Council of 29 April 2004 on official controls performed to ensure the verification of compliance with feed and food law, animal health and animal welfare rules. [2004] OJ L 165/1.

[45] Preamble to Regulation 882/2004.

[46] Article 2.

The regulation does not define 'food law'. It is, however, defined in Regulation 178/2002 as:

> the laws, regulations and administrative provisions governing food in general, and food safety in particular, whether at Community or national level; it covers any stage of production, processing and distribution of food, and also of feed produced for, or fed to, food-producing animals.[47]

For the purposes of this book, 'EU food law' includes all directives, regulations and decisions of the Community institutions and Community courts relating to the production and marketing of food and drink for human consumption. The 'average consumer' has been defined by the Court of Justice as being 'reasonably well informed and reasonably observant and circumspect',[48] a phrase which will recur throughout this work.[49]

Regulation 882/2004 sets a series of obligations on the Member States to ensure that official controls are carried out on a regular basis,[50] 'official control' being:

> any form of control that the competent authority or the Community performs for the verification of compliance with feed and food law, animal health and animal welfare rules.[51]

Competent authorities are:

> the central authority of a Member State competent for the organisation of official controls or any other authority to which that competence has been conferred.[52]

Member States determine who their competent authority will be.[53]

1.4 SCOPE OF THE BOOK

Food and the laws that regulate its production and marketing at European Union level are surrounded by a series of sensitivities and national agendas that complicate and frustrate the role of the Community institutions in their efforts to create a single market for food. It is unsurprising that Member States adopt this defensive position when the ramifications of the decisions that are made by these institutions can prove problematic for those who seek to preserve high food quality levels, good nutritional values or the preservation of traditional and customary practices. The far-reaching effects of free movement principles, in particular the

---

[47] Article 3 thereof.
[48] See, for example, Case C-239/2002, *Douwe Egberts NV v Westrom Pharma NV and Christophe Souranis* [2004] ECR I-7007, para 46; Joined Cases C-421/2000, C-426/2000 and C-16/2001, *Renate Sterbenz and Paul Dieter Haug* [2003] ECR I-1065, para 43; and Case C-465/1998, *Verein gegen Unwesen in Handel und Gewerbe Köln eV v Adolf Darbo AG* [2000] ECR I-2297, para 20.
[49] See further S Weatherill, 'Consumer Policy' in P Craig and G de Búrca, *The Evolution of EU Law* (Oxford, OUP, 1999), pp 699–702.
[50] Article 3 thereof.
[51] Article 2 of Regulation 882/2004.
[52] *Ibid.*
[53] Article 4.

principle of mutual recognition of existing standards in each of the Member States, means that when the Community standardises, it must do so at the lowest common level, or at least very near to it. If Member State A insists that chocolate contain no cocoa butter, then Member States B, C and D are unlikely to be allowed to maintain their domestic provisions stipulating minimum cocoa butter levels in chocolate. If Member State E wants to prohibit or restrict the sale of foods that have a low protein and high saturated fat content, they are unlikely to be allowed to do so where Member States F, G and H have no similar provision. Consumer protection and the preservation of human health are clearly less of a priority in the EU food law harmonisation programme than the promotion of the free movement of goods and completion of the internal market. The result, as will be demonstrated throughout this book, is two sorts of situation. First, the decisions of the Court, and the subsequent conclusions drawn that harmonising standards are no longer required given the development of the mutual recognition principle, have led to a frustration and contravention of the key Treaty provisions on free movement for food. These breaches have been incurred not, as might be expected, by the Member States, but instead by the Community institutions themselves who are failing to adhere to legitimate exceptions to free movement—defining the general principle too expansively, and the exceptions to this principle far too narrowly. This has detrimental consequences for consumers in relation to their level of choice and for Member States who seek to promote healthy habits amongst their populace. Second, although the institutions have modified their behaviour somewhat in relation to human health protection in the aftermath of the BSE crisis, exceptions to the general rule on free movement and an over-emphasis on food safety, coupled with Member States' lack of autonomy in decision-making on food-related matters, has provoked a more far-reaching 'crisis' within the Member States—obesity. Given the manner in which EU food law has developed thus far, these Member States are now relatively impotent when it comes to taking any meaningful action to counter obesity.

Such themes are discussed in detail throughout this book. The main principles that direct EU rules on the production and marketing of food are the free movement of goods, the protection of consumers, and the preservation of human health. International obligations also present a lesser concern for the EU legislator. Through an examination of free movement case law, harmonising legislation and food safety policy, it is demonstrated that the prioritisation of free movement as the main factor in the devising, interpretation and implementation of EU food law creates a series of negative consequences for the other two main concerns. It is only through modification of this approach that these serious deficiencies can be addressed.

The book commences with a detailed examination of EU rules on the free movement of food. Through an assessment of the case law on Article 28 EC, prohibiting quantitative restrictions and measures of equivalent effect, Chapter 2 shows how the Court allows certain mandatory requirements such as consumer protection and fair trading to enable Member States to deviate from these obligations in some circumstances. Article 30 EC provides Member States with the opportunity to implement measures that inhibit free movement where this is deemed necessary to protect human health. However, both operate in very limited circumstances, rendering them relatively ineffective in safeguarding Member States' attempts to protect the health of their populace. The panacea of additional labelling disclosures, presented perennially by the Court to counter Member State representations that their contested measures or actions are proportionate and justifiable, are contradictory and over-simplistic. A reassessment is required in order to accommodate these legitimate exceptions to the general rule on free movement for food, and to protect consumers and producers from unfair trading practices.

Chapter 3 examines the body of existing secondary Community legislation that is used to harmonise standards on food production and marketing in each of the Member States. In particular, it assesses the rules on food labelling, the naming of foods and the preservation of food quality. After noting how the Commission arrived at its controversial decision to cease developing harmonised vertical standards for food (those applying to specific foodstuffs only), our attention turns to the key components of the food label, as prescribed by the horizontal (applying to some aspect of the production and/or marketing of all foodstuffs) framework food labelling directive. Most aspects of this legislation are relatively straightforward, although there is still some confusion regarding the language in which labelling must appear. The name by which a foodstuff may be labelled when it moves from one Member State to another also continues to cause debate. This is primarily because each Member State has its own unique production standards in place. A Member State seeking to preserve the quality of foodstuffs traditionally produced domestically will generally be prevented from doing so due to the free movement principle. To counter depreciating food quality standards, and to preserve to some degree the divergence of foodstuffs produced within the EU, the Council has had to respond. Accordingly, it has introduced rules on food naming where there is some link between the characteristics of the product and its traditional place of production. Recent developments in the case law in this area have raised doubts about the suitability of this legislation in many situations in which it is currently applied. Redefining the limits of, and strengthening the distinctions between, the different categories of food name could remove many of the difficulties that have arisen, attributable to the manner in which the free movement of food agenda has been pursued. If successful, such a strategy would facilitate the proper protection of consumers, fair trading and the promotion of human health.

The extent to which the rules governing international trade can impact on EU food laws is examined in Chapter 4. Here it is noted that the two key organisational structures have the potential to shape Community food law and policy. These are the World Trade Organization (WTO) and the Codex Alimentarius Commission, which operates under the auspices of the United Nations (UN) Food and Agriculture Organisation (FAO) and the World Health Organization (WHO). Several of the WTO Agreements can influence the manner in which the EU devises, interprets and implements its own rules on the production and marketing of food. For example, the existence of the Agreement on Sanitary and Phytosanitary Measures (SPS Agreement) means that the EU must undertake a scientifically sound risk assessment prior to the application of any rules that are designed to protect human health, animal health or the environment. The Agreement on Technical Barriers to Trade (TBT Agreement) obliges the EU to set its own technical standards for food in a manner that appropriately mirrors existing international standards, or those of other WTO members. The Agreement on Trade-Related Aspects of Intellectual Property Rights (TRIPs) requires that schemes designed to protect European food products with local or regional characteristics be made available to producers in third countries as well. All this means that the EU legislator must look beyond the European agenda when creating new, or applying existing, food laws. The primary reference point for assessing conformity of EU rules with international standards is the Codex Alimentarius Commission.

Food safety has been pushed to the top of the EU food law agenda in recent years. The main reason for this is the furore surrounding the BSE crisis that occurred in the 1990s. The EU has had to show itself more than willing to act to safeguard human health in its aftermath. The European Food Safety Authority (EFSA) has been created to co-ordinate efforts to minimise the likelihood of other crises. Safeguard measures, notification procedures, prescribed hygienic practices and other official controls have been introduced to supplement and support the work of the Authority and the relevant Community scientific committees. However, these labours are frustrated by a failure to recognise that Member States are often best placed to act to ensure that the food that enters their marketplace is safe and wholesome. These transnational rules are based on the unsatisfactory premise that action taken at national level in this regard is contrary to Community law on the free movement of goods. While there is acceptance that precautionary measures may be introduced where evidence exists supporting such action, the circumstances in which this principle may be invoked remain unclear and ill defined.

Too much emphasis has been placed on food safety in recent years, and too little on maximising its nutritional value. Chapter 6 highlights how the preoccupation with avoiding 'food crises' has led to insufficient action being taken to counter increasing rates of nutrition-related problems such as obesity. Most of these food crises have affected relatively few people when compared to the devastating consequences for human health that come from being either undernourished or, as tends to be the case now, overfed and obese, contributing to high levels of heart disease, cancers and strokes. EU law in this area does not extend far beyond labelling matters. Studies suggest that consumers do not really understand nutrition labelling, and generally do not read it. Member States have sought to instigate their own initiatives in this regard. However, their efforts have been frustrated by EU rules on the free movement of food. As a consequence, instead of being able to introduce a compulsory system of labelling, informing consumers in clear terms about how beneficial or detrimental a particular foodstuff may be to their health, mutual recognition limits the range of permissible options to voluntary codes of conduct. Proposed new rules on nutrition claims made for food will remove, or at least reduce, the possibility of those marketing a product making certain claims about the health benefits to be gained from consuming their food where there are also health detriments. This does not resolve the key issue here, which is the fact that Articles 28 to 30 EC and the related case law make it almost impossible for Member States to introduce measures designed to protect human health unless the foodstuff in question poses a precipitate danger to health, as opposed to merely eroding it in the longer term.

New technologies or novel ways of producing food bring new difficulties for the EU lawmaker. For example, the introduction of genetically modified organisms (gmos) into the European marketplace created a plethora of problems. Consumer groups lobbied for the complete prohibition of gmos, spurred into action by disputed scientific studies which demonstrated that genetically modified food could have detrimental consequences for the intestines of rats. Rules introduced before this controversy had to be changed on numerous occasions to close loopholes and satisfy the new demands of more conscientious consumers. Ultimately, an unofficial moratorium on the approval or use of new gmos was introduced. This went some way to satisfying the concerns raised within the EU. However, it also alerted the EU's trading partners to the fact that this was possibly in contravention of international trade law obligations, resulting in an investigation into the circumstances surrounding the introduction of this ban and its compatibility, in particular, with the WTO Agreement on Sanitary and Phytosanitary Measures.

At the other end of the spectrum, organic foods and those derived from free-range animals have brought their own difficulties. Given that these types of food tend to attract a higher price on the market, these terms are open to manipulation by those who seek to gain the advantage of using them whilst paying scant attention to the criteria such goods must satisfy before any labelling claims about their ethical production can legitimately be made. This leaves the consumer in a precarious position. He or she may be paying more for a product bearing a description which does not reflect the method of its production.

Generally, this book examines existing EU food laws in order to demonstrate how free movement of food obligations leave the consumer exposed to deception, the producer to unfair trading practices, and human health to the detrimental consequences of an uncoordinated food law structure that fails to adhere to Treaty obligations and Court-made exceptions to the mutual recognition principle. It suggests a three-pronged alternative approach to EU food law and policy: reconsideration of the decision taken by the Commission to cease harmonising food standards for all products; relaxation of the over-regulation of all aspects of the food production process and a resultant move towards more simple common standards; and, instead of concentrating on food safety, emphasising that food should be of high quality and beneficial to health.

2

Free Movement of Food in the EU

2.1 INTRODUCTION

EUROPEAN UNION RULES on the free movement of goods impact on
the food industry in many ways. The most obvious of these is the Article 28
EC prohibition on quantitative restrictions on imports and all national
measures of equivalent effect. In particular, the decision of the Court of Justice in
Cassis,[1] and the subsequent related case law,[2] established the principle that once a
foodstuff is lawfully marketable in one Member State it must be lawfully marketable in all. This is so even where the importing State can demonstrate seemingly
legitimate objections to the sale of a product on their territory. These might
include concerns about public health, fair trading or consumer protection. The
fact that two products differ in composition and/or method of production cannot
generally be used by a Member State to justify national rules that require that these
different products carry different names or descriptions on their labels.[3] Similarly,
Member States cannot prevent the marketing of foodstuffs that have a lower than
usual nutritional value, or that endanger health in some way, even if they try to do
so to preserve the health of their people, so long as the sale of those foodstuffs is
not hindered elsewhere in the Community.[4] Arguing that the nutritional needs
and/or consumer preferences of a Member State justify the existence of trade-
inhibiting national rules is not generally considered acceptable.[5]

The second key Treaty provision that is used to maximise the free movement of
food is Article 90 EC. It prohibits the direct or indirect imposition in national markets of higher taxes on imported goods than on those produced domestically. This
applies to comparisons between both the same and similar food products—those

---

[1] Case 120/1978, *Rewe-Zentral AG v Bundesmonopolverwaltung für Branntwein* [1979] ECR 649.
[2] For example: Case 788/1979, *Criminal proceedings against Gilli and Andres* [1980] ECR 2071; Case
27/1980, *Criminal proceedings against Anton Adriaan Fietje* [1980] ECR 3839; Case 193/1980,
Commission v Italy (vinegar) [1981] ECR 3019.
[3] For example: Case 298/1987, *Proceedings for compulsory reconstruction against Smanor SA* [1988]
ECR 4489; Case 286/1986, *Ministère public v Gérard Deserbais* [1988] ECR 4907.
[4] See, for example, Case 274/1987, *Commission v Germany* (meat products) [1989] ECR 229; Case
76/1986, *Commission v Germany* (milk substitutes) [1989] ECR 1021; Case 216/1984, *Commission v
France* (milk substitutes) [1988] ECR 793.
[5] See, in particular, Case 178/1984, *Commission v Germany* (bier) [1987] ECR 1227; Case 274/1987
Commission v Germany (meat products) [1989] ECR 229; Case C-41/2002 *Commission v Netherlands*
(fortified foods).

that may be deemed to be in at least partial competition in the same market may be compared for Article 90 EC purposes. The Court of Justice has assisted in maximising the positive effects of this by defining 'markets' expansively. This has reduced the possibilities for Member States to indirectly protect their own goods from similar type imports.[6] This could have presented benefits for the domestic consumer and the Community producer alike, but the actual effects remain limited, stifled by the political sensitivities of EU interference with national taxation regimes. As a consequence, the potential profits that could arise from full application of Article 90 EC are far outweighed by the negative effects of Article 28 EC for the protection of consumers. The full benefits of overall free movement policy are, as yet, unfulfilled.

Third, the Article 25 EC prohibition on charging customs duties and charges of equivalent effect presents a difficulty for a national authority that seeks to reduce health risks from imported foodstuffs. Court interpretation of this ban has established that expenses incurred by an importing Member State in inspecting the safety of goods entering their territory may not be passed on to the exporter,[7] subject to some well-defined exceptions.[8] Such an authority consequently faces a dilemma: inspect, and absorb the costs, or avoid incurring these costs by relying on inspections, if there have been any, that have taken place in the exporting State. This Court-created predicament is seemingly at odds with the Community emphasis on creating and maintaining the safest possible system for the distribution of foodstuffs.[9]

Finally, it should be noted at this stage that, despite the preponderance of case law and academic literature pertaining to Articles 25, 28 and 90 EC, it is in fact the much-overlooked European Community harmonisation programme that has the potential to cause the greatest upheaval for the food industry, and for its producers, consumers and the Member States alike. It is often the minutiae of secondary legislation rather than the sweeping and all-encompassing Treaty-enshrined principles that engenders controversy about how the Community behaves in relation to food. Hygiene rules, labelling laws and compositional requirements can all have a significant economic impact on the producer and, consequently, the consumer as well. Consider, for example, the new rules on health and nutrition claims.[10] While obliging producers to substantiate claims of this nature is a welcome move, there can be no doubt about the potentially devastating outcome of this for small businesses, which now have to invest large proportions of their available resources into producing the required scientific demonstration to legitimise statements made regarding the beneficial properties of their goods. Similarly, European

---

[6] Case 170/1978, *Commission v UK* (wine and beer tax) [1983] ECR 2265.

[7] Case 87/1975, *Conceria Daniele Bresciani v Amministrazione Italiana delle Finanze* [1976] ECR 129; Case 314/1982, *Commission v Belgium* (imported poultry meat) [1984] ECR 1543.

[8] See, in particular, Case 46/1976, *Bauhuis v Netherlands* [1977] ECR 5.

[9] In particular that arising out of the Commission White Paper on Food Safety. COM (1999) 719.

[10] Proposal for a Regulation of the European Parliament and of the Council on nutrition and health claims made on foods. COM (2003) 424. Discussed in more detail in Chapter 6 below.

Union rules on hygienic food production render the production of traditional local foodstuffs, such as certain types of cheese, difficult or impossible. By setting strict generic requirements, applicable to the multinational oligopolist and the small-scale producer alike, many EU rules on production methods have rendered it near impossible for foodstuffs that have been produced using traditional methods for supply to local markets to continue legally.[11] Such drastic consequences arise from measures often taken in the name of human health protection. Their effect has been to terminate the production of foodstuffs that have been produced and consumed for generations with no obvious ill effects on anybody's health. It is a combination of the disproportionate and inflexible nature of the EU institutions' responses to so-called 'food crises', along with the tendency to promote free movement above all other considerations, that has the potential to destroy the rich culinary diversity of the Member States. Intensive farming methods have contributed to many of these 'emergencies'. Consumer confidence in the safety and wholesomeness of food will be best restored by reverting to local production through non-intensive methods.[12] This requires proper EU institutional support, and it can only happen when there is acceptance that the citizens of Europe share some similarities but are also hugely different in many ways—with differing tastes, preferences and needs. It must be recognised that the same 'average consumer' does not exist in 25 different States. The harmonisation of habits, tastes and nutritional requirements will never come about, despite the best efforts of the Community institutions to achieve this in the quest for absolute free movement. In the meantime, and until this realisation is accepted, food quality, safety and nutritional value will continue to suffer as a result.

2.2 MEASURES EQUIVALENT TO QUANTITATIVE RESTRICTIONS ON THE FREE MOVEMENT OF FOOD

Article 28 EC (formerly Article 30 EC) sets out the general obligation on Member States to ensure that 'quantitative restrictions on imports and all measures having equivalent effect shall . . . be prohibited between Member States'. This wide-ranging responsibility received further elaboration and clarification in Commission Directive 1970/50.[13] The preamble to the directive states that the abolition of measures equivalent to quantitative restrictions on imports is necessary as otherwise

---

[11] For further discussion see D Chalmers, 'Food for Thought: Reconciling European Risks and Traditional Ways of Life' (2003) 66 *Modern Law Review* 532, in particular 544–7.

[12] For further discussion on the effects on food quality, human health and the environment of modern methods of food production see P Singer and J Mason, *The Way We Eat: Why Our Food Choices Matter* (Emmaus, PA, Rodale, 2006); J Humphrys, *The Great Food Gamble* (Philadelphia, PA, Coronet Books, 2001).

[13] Commission Directive 1970/50/EEC of 22 December 1969 based on the provisions of Article 33(7), on the abolition of measures which have an effect equivalent to quantitative restrictions on imports and are not covered by other provisions adopted in pursuance of the EEC Treaty. [1970] OJ L 13/29; [1970] English Special Edition Series I, Chapter 1970(1), p 17. It has been stated of Article 28 EC that it 'is striking for its brevity'. See S Weatherill and P Beaumont, *EC Law* 3rd edn (Harmondsworth, Penguin Books, 1999).

the customs union would not be possible. To facilitate this, the ambit of the directive covers measures that obstruct the importation of products from other Member States in any way, either by preventing their importation completely or by hindering their access to the market by insisting that certain conditions be fulfilled beforehand.[14] This has come to mean that: (i) any measure that makes it more inconvenient for the seller to market their product in the territory of a Member State other than their own, which cannot be justified under one of the exceptions to this rule (rule of reason or mandatory requirement, dealt with in detail throughout this chapter), or which is not a 'selling arrangement' as defined by the Court of Justice in *Keck* and later clarified by its related case law;[15] or (ii) any similar measure which makes it more difficult for the seller to market their product in their own State, especially if other markets in the EU are more readily accessible, is considered to be an unlawful measure. Directive 1970/50 does state that, in particular, requirements subjecting imported products to a condition with which domestic products were not also obliged to comply, or with which they could comply more readily, are regarded as being measures equivalent to quantitative restrictions on imports.[16] This now, however, also clearly includes marketing conditions (subject of course to exceptions) which domestic producers have to comply with, which they may not face when marketing the same product elsewhere in the Union.

The most important aspect of the directive is that it sets out a list of those measures which, unless justifiable, are likely to constitute an unlawful restriction on the free movement of goods. Out of a list of 19 such examples, only three had, and continue to have, any real impact on the case law and legislation supporting the free movement of food, and arguably of goods in general. These are: (i) compositional requirements and product specifications; (ii) product names not related to origin; and (iii) controls, other than those inherent in the customs clearance procedure, which are more strict than those applied to domestic products where this is not necessary to ensure equivalent protection.[17]

2.2.1 Dassonville and Directive 1970/50

Some of the most significant case law in the Article 28 EC jurisprudence relates specifically to the free movement of foodstuffs. *Dassonville*, which concerned

---

[14] Article 2(1).

[15] Joined Cases C-267/1991 and C-268/1991, *Criminal proceedings against Keck and Mithouard* [1993] ECR I–6097, as further clarified in particular by Joined Cases C-69/1993 and C-258/1993, *Punto casa SpA v Sindaco del Comune di Capena et Comune di Capena and Promozioni Polivalenti Venete Soc coop arl (PPV) v Sindaco del Comune di Torri di Quartesolo and Comune di Torri di Quartesolo* [1994] ECR I-2355; Case C-368/1995, *Vereinigte Familiapress Zeitungsverlags- und vertriebs GmbH v Heinrich Bauer Verlag* [1997] ECR I-3689; Joined Cases C-34/1995, C-35/1995 and C-36/1995, *Konsumentombudsmannen (KO) v De Agostini (Svenska) Förlag AB and TV-Shop i Sverige AB* [1997] ECR I-3843.

[16] Article 2(2).

[17] Article 2(3)(j), (s) and (r).

Belgian rules on the importation of whisky that was not accompanied by appropriate documentation certifying that the consignment was of Scottish origin, set out the formula by which the existence of measures equivalent to quantitative restrictions would be tested in the future.[18] It was stated that 'all trading rules enacted by Member States which are capable of hindering, directly or indirectly, actually or potentially, intra-Community trade are to be considered as measures having an effect equivalent to quantitative restrictions'.[19] Using this formula, the Court held that an importer of Scottish whisky from Scotland to France and then into Belgium was faced with an additional burden that the importer directly from Scotland into Belgium did not face, namely that it would be more difficult for the indirect importer to obtain a certificate of authenticity. This constituted a measure equivalent to a quantitative restriction on imports. The Court had already abandoned the terms, and importance, of Directive 1970/50.

There are three points to note about this decision which signal the direction that the preponderance of Article 28 EC case law has tended to follow ever since. First, it is made clear that national rules that prohibit intra-Community trade are to be treated as being either arbitrary discrimination or a disguised restriction on such trade, unless it can be demonstrated otherwise. The burden of proof on the Member State in this regard has always been very high, and in most cases almost impossible to satisfy. Second, the protection of consumers, and therefore also of scrupulous producers, was, and has remained, of little significance in Article 28 EC case law. The protection and promotion of the free movement of goods has always been of paramount importance. This has made it possible for the Community institutions generally to refrain from introducing harmonising provisions that could be used to improve consumer protection. This is because Article 28 EC, given its wide-ranging influence, can instead be used to render non-justifiable (and it must be remembered that this is a very difficult justification to make) national rules that impede free movement contrary to the terms of the Treaty. Potentially countering arguments that could be made under other areas of Treaty competence, most notably here Article 152 EC (formerly Article 129 EC) on the protection of human health and Article 153 EC (formerly Article 129a EC) on the protection of consumers, have thus remained relatively unexplored before the Court. Arguments based on Article 30 EC (formerly Article 36 EC), which provides a series of exceptions to Article 28 EC, such as public health protection, animal protection and the preservation of industrial and commercial property rights, have of course been presented on numerous occasions. However, such pleadings have had relatively little success. Third, it was demonstrated that Directive 1970/50 would not be used to provide exceptions to the promotion of free movement, the Court preferring to rely on the ambiguous terms of Article 28 EC and its own far-reaching formula on trading rules that inhibit intra-Community trade. The directive, however, makes two points clear. Importation

---

[18] Case 8/1974, *Procureur du Roi v Benoît and Gustave Dassonville* [1974] ECR 837.
[19] *Ibid*, para 5.

controls inherent in the customs clearance procedure are allowable, thus including the presentation of documentary evidence supporting any claims as to origin. In particular, this is necessary for a product that has regional characteristics attached to the name under which it is marketed. It should be noted here that names relating to origin are specifically removed from possible prohibitions on Member State action set out in the directive, especially if this is a key factor in any consumer purchasing determination based on quality and/or taste and/or any other individual preference. The Court in *Dassonville* stated that:

> In the absence of a Community system guaranteeing for consumers the authenticity of a product's designation of origin, if a Member State takes measures to prevent unfair practices in this connection, it is however subject to the condition that these measures should be reasonable and that the means of proof required should not act as a hindrance to trade between Member States.[20]

It is difficult to see how the national authorities could implement a system designed to prevent fraudulent practice, which is clearly allowable under the terms of the directive, where they are prevented from requiring that documentary evidence as to the origin of a product be produced. No effective Community system of guaranteeing authenticity has since been introduced to offer clarification on this matter.

2.2.2 Indistinctly Applicable Rules

Whilst *Dassonville* signalled the intent of the Court to abandon that which had been agreed to be Community law on the free movement of goods, and develop a new jurisprudence based on the promotion of free movement, regardless of the limits placed on this by secondary legislation, this was taken a stage further by *Cassis*, which has proved to be the most influential single decision affecting the free movement of food.[21] By holding that if a product is lawfully produced and/or marketed in one Member State it must be lawfully marketable in all Member States, the Court initiated a system of mutual recognition. Each Member State would now have to presume, unless it could prove otherwise, that the procedures in each Member State are appropriately thorough to protect consumers, either in relation to their health and general well-being, or in relation to the potential that they will be deceived into purchasing a foodstuff believing it to be one type of product when it is in fact another. The weak argument of the German authorities in *Cassis*, who claimed that the ban on marketing fruit liqueurs with a low alcohol content was necessary for the protection of human health and the protection of consumers from unfair commercial practices, did not help in this instance.[22] It is,

---

[20] Case 8/1974, *Procureur du Roi v Benoît and Gustave Dassonville* [1974] ECR 837, para 6.

[21] Case 120/1978, *Rewe-Zentral AG v Bundesmonopolverwaltung für Branntwein* [1979] ECR 649.

[22] See further S Weatherill, *EU Consumer Law and Policy* (Cheltenham, Edward Elgar, 2005), pp 57–59.

however, in relation to one of the valid claims in *Cassis* that the Court's ruling has been most influential. By ruling against the national rules in this case the Court effectively created a system whereby national standards must always be reduced to the lowest level acceptable in any one of the Member States in order to comply with the interpretation of Article 28 EC. If even one Member State has no standards set in domestic law for the production and/or marketing of a particular product then no other Member State can have any such standard either. The Court responded by stating that the 'simple matter' of ensuring that the consumer receives appropriate information on the food label would always be sufficient to ensure their protection from unfair commercial practices.[23] It did not state whether this would also be sufficient to enable consumers to protect their health.

2.2.3 Post-*Cassis* Free Movement of Food

The Court followed up on its decision in *Cassis* by determining that a prohibition imposed by a Member State on the importation or marketing of apple vinegar containing acetic acid not derived from wine was contrary to Article 28 EC.[24] It also added further strength to two points, which are fast becoming well-established facts. First, the *Dassonville* formula was to be consistently followed. Second, it was made explicit, even more so than in *Cassis*, that equal burden rules that are necessary to protect public health, ensure the fairness of commercial transactions or defend consumer interests can, where the Member State is able to satisfy the Court that their national measures are both necessary and proportionate, constitute exceptions to Article 28 EC. This renders seemingly anti-free movement national rules compliant with Community law.[25] In this instance, both human health and consumer protection arguments were rejected. This was because, in the opinion of the Court, apple vinegar contains no injurious substances. The receptacles containing the vinegar were clearly labelled. Thus there was no possibility of the consumer confusing this product with wine vinegar.

    Cassis and *Gilli and Andres* make it clear that unjustifiable national compositional requirements inhibiting trade in foodstuffs contravene Community law. Later cases extend this to prohibitions based on breaches of national rules regulating the external features of food products, such as their labelling or packaging. In *Fietje*, for example, the Court held that a national provision prohibiting the sale of alcoholic drinks not described in a manner prescribed by domestic law, thereby making it necessary for the labels on similar products imported from other Member States to have their labels altered, is a measure equivalent to a quantitative restriction on imports, provided that the details on the original label adequately inform the consumer about the nature of the product. Again, importation

---

[23] *Cassis*, note 21 above, para 13.
[24] Case 788/1979, *Criminal proceedings against Gilli and Andres* [1980] ECR 2071.
[25] *Ibid*, para 6.

was not banned, but the lawful marketing of imported products was made more difficult. However, the Court also stated that national rules that prescribe the use of a description that is necessary to inform the purchaser about the nature of the product, and to enable distinctions from other products with which it might be confused to be drawn, may well be necessary in order to provide consumers with effective protection. It may even be permissible to extend such an obligation to imported products also. This is so, even where this requires the alteration of some external aspect of the product, such as the label. It was not stated as to whether this could also be extended to include internal aspects of the foodstuff setting, for example, a minimum alcohol content requirement or a stipulation that certain ingredients be used in prescribed quantities. To apply such rules to national products only would create the absurd situation whereby the domestic producer has to produce or label their product in a specific way. The importer from another Member State could either market an identical product under a different name or, worse still, market a different product under the same name.

It was later established that this, combined with *Dassonville*, also includes any obligation that the external features of an imported foodstuff, such as labelling, be altered in any way where this cannot be similarly justified. In *Fietje* the Court held that the extension by a Member State of a national provision prohibiting the sale of alcoholic drinks that are not described in a manner prescribed by domestic law, thereby making it necessary for the labels on similar products imported from other Member States to have their labels altered, is a measure equivalent to a quantitative restriction on imports, provided that the details on the original label adequately inform the consumer about the nature of the product.[26] Again, importation was not banned, but the lawful marketing of imported products was made more difficult. However, the Court also stated that national compositional rules for specific foodstuffs that prescribe the use of a description that is necessary to inform the purchaser about the nature of the product, and to enable distinctions from other products with which it might be confused to be drawn, may well be necessary in order to provide consumers with effective protection. It may even be permissible to extend such an obligation to imported products too. This is so even where some external aspect of the product must be altered, such as the label. It was not stated whether this could also be extended to include internal aspects of the foodstuff, for example setting a minimum alcohol content requirement or a stipulation that certain ingredients be used in prescribed quantities. To apply such rules only to national products would create an absurd situation whereby the domestic producer has to produce or label their product in a specific way. The importer from another Member State could either market an identical product under a different name or, worse still, market a different product under the same name.

One problem that the early post-*Cassis* case law created was that Article 28 EC could only be used in situations involving some intra-Community aspect. It only

---

[26] Case 27/1980, *Criminal proceedings against Anton Adriaan Fietje* [1980] ECR 3839.

applied where products moved from one Member State to another. This, again, could put the domestic producer at a disadvantage. Only external parties would be able to challenge national rules, no matter how much these rules might inhibit the activities of the national producer. Rules could only be challenged where a producer from another Member State, or an importer into the host State, felt that they were being prevented from operating in some way, even where all those operating in the marketplace were faced with the exact same marketing requirements. This persisted despite the fact that the producer in the Member State with the more stringent requirements would then have to compete when exporting with those who produced under more flexible rules. This would mean that, in order to be competitive, the producer in State A would have to alter its product, possibly by reducing the quality of the ingredients used, in order to level the playing field with those in State B. To some extent, this situation has improved. At least there is now recognition that a wholly domestic situation may, at some stage in the future, also include an intra-Community element if a producer from another Member State wishes to market their product in the host State whose domestic rules are under review. The Court will now examine such instances under Article 28 EC, even where there is no inter-State free movement question to be answered at the time, but only where the national rules at issue have the potential to impede market access to non-national producers in some way.[27] Article 28 EC cannot be used, for example, by domestic producers against their own Member State in situations where the national rules at issue discriminate against them to the advantage of importers from other Member States.[28] In *Mathot*, for example, criminal proceedings were brought against an operator in Belgium for marketing butter there in a package that did not bear the name and address of the processor. This contravened Belgian law.[29] But there was no similar obligation placed on butter imported from other Member States—had UK or Irish butter been marketed there, the label would not have to list the producer's name and address. It was asked whether this requirement was compatible with Article 28 EC. The Court stated that the object of this provision of the Treaty was to eliminate obstacles to the importation of goods and not to ensure that goods of national origin enjoy the same treatment as imported goods. Consequently, it was held that even where there is clear discrimination against domestically-produced goods, such a difference in treatment, given that it in no way restricts the importation, or prejudices the marketing, of imported butter, does not give rise to an infringement of Article 28 EC.

---

[27] Joined Cases C-321/1994, C-322/1994, C-323/1994 and C-324/1994, *Criminal proceedings against Pistre and others* [1997] ECR I-2343, paras 44 and 45; Case C-184/1996, *Commission v France* (foie gras) [1998] ECR I-6197, para 17; Case C-448/1998, *Criminal proceedings against Jean-Pierre Guimont* [2000] ECR I-10663, para 17.

[28] See, for example, Case 286/1981, *Criminal proceedings against Oosthoens Uitgeversmaatschappij BV* [1982] ECR 4575, para 9; Case 355/1985, *Driancourt v Cognet* [1986] ECR 3231, para 10.

[29] Case 98/1986, *Criminal proceedings against Arthur Mathot* [1987] ECR 809.

The free movement of vinegar was again the subject of attention in *Commission v Italy*.[30] Here, Italy contended that vinegar should be the subject of harmonising standards before national rules prohibiting the marketing of non-wine based vinegar could be examined by the Court under Article 28 EC. This was rejected. It was stated that ensuring the free movement of goods could not be made subject to the condition that laws should first be approximated. While it was recognised that such harmonising standards could help to promote free movement of goods, this could not be considered a necessary condition for the application of such a fundamental principle of Community law.[31] The fact that there are no common rules, in particular through harmonising directives, on the production and marketing of specific goods would not be sufficient to put these goods beyond the scope of the Article 28 EC prohibition. What is particularly interesting about the decision here is that the Court stated that the effects of the Italian rules prohibiting the importation of non-wine vinegar were protective in nature, even if applied to domestic and imported products alike. This was because, by closing its borders to all other types of vinegar, the Italian rules favoured a typically national product.[32]

The situation above has the following implication. Take a particular variety of a product. Assume that this has traditionally been favoured in a Member State, and in several, perhaps many, others. Where other varieties of the same product are produced in even a handful of other States, the importing State must not have in place any measures that prevent the marketing of that other variety in their territory, or which make such marketing any more difficult than it is for these outside producers to market their product in their own States. This adds a new dimension to the argument put forward by Germany in *Cassis* about the standards in all Member States having to conform with the lowest level in the Community in order to comply with Article 28 EC. Here, if all Member States bar a few (or possibly even just one) favour a particular type of product produced in a particular way, they may not, under Community law as it has developed, have in place any provisions that prevent this other variety from being marketed freely and under the same name in their territory. Just such an example was seen in relation to feta cheese, whereby the well-established method of production was left exposed to competition from a product manufactured using different ingredients and a different method of manufacture but marketed under the same sales name.[33] While this may not necessarily be important in the Member State where the traditional

---

[30] Case 193/1980, *Commission v Italy* (vinegar) [1981] ECR 3019.
[31] *Ibid*, para 17.
[32] *Ibid*, para 20.
[33] Joined Cases C-289/1996, C-293/1996 and C-299/1996, *Denmark, Germany and France v Commission* [1999] ECR I-1541. The decision made here has since been superseded by the introduction of Commission Regulation (EC) No 1829/2002 of 14 October 2002 amending the Annex to Regulation (EC) No 1107/1996 with regard to the name 'feta', [2002] OJ L 277/10, which re-registered 'feta' as a protected geographical food name. An application to annul this regulation under the Article 230 EC procedure was rejected by the Court in October 2005: Joined Cases C-465/2002 and C-466/2002, *Germany and Denmark v Commission* [2005] ECR I-9115. Discussed in more detail in Chapter 3 below.

variety originated, or for that matter in the Member States where the new variant is produced, as consumers will tend to continue to favour their own national variety, it does lead to detrimental consequences in the other Member States which do not produce feta cheese. If, for example, Denmark produces 'feta' using pasteurised milk from cows and a high speed filtration and production method, and it is consequently cheap to produce, but Greek producers continue to use sheep and/or goat milk and traditional slow production processes, and it is consequently more expensive to produce, it is clear who has the competitive edge in those Member States which produce neither variety. This situation becomes even more exaggerated where consumers in the importing Member State are exposed to a foodstuff for the first time and remain uneducated about the composition of the traditional variety and, in particular, the differences between the varieties of foodstuff that may all be marketed under the same name.

The Court in *Commission v Italy* again rejected any justification based on the need to protect consumers. It found that less restrictive measures, such as clear labelling, could be used to prevent any potential confusion arising. Italy had claimed that their consumers consider all vinegar (aceto) to be wine-vinegar. Their consumers might thus be misled if other products were marketed using this name. The Court found that 'vinegar' was, in fact, a generic term. It would not be compatible with the objectives of the common market, and in particular the fundamental principle of the free movement of goods, if national legislation were to restrict the use of a generic term to one national variety alone to the detriment of other varieties produced in other Member States.[34] It was accepted that Italian consumers might have become accustomed to the use of the term 'aceto' to describe wine-vinegar only. Consequently, it was accepted that the concerns of the Italian Government to protect consumers in this regard might, in fact, be justified. However, it was held that such protection could be provided by other means, such as labels describing the nature of the product sold, provided that any such requirement applied to all varieties, including wine-vinegar, to enable the consumer to make their choice in full knowledge of the facts, and guaranteeing transparency in trading by providing an indication of the raw material used to make the product.[35] This is a more flexible approach than the Court was ultimately to adopt. Consider the feta situation. When Greece permitted Danish feta to be sold on their territory, but insisted that it be labelled as 'white cheese in brine made from pasteurised cows milk in Denmark' they were prevented from providing the consumer with just such a level of information as that advocated in *Commission v Italy*. Similarly, the French authorities were prevented from insisting that deep-frozen yoghurt be labelled 'deep-frozen fermented milk' when this too would have provided the consumer with that 'indication of the raw material used to make the product'.[36] Despite differences in production methods and/or composition, both were

---

[34] Case 193/1980, *Commission v Italy* (vinegar) [1981] ECR 3019, para 26.
[35] *Ibid*, para 27.
[36] Case 298/1987, *Proceedings for compulsory reconstruction against Smanor SA* [1988] ECR 4489.

allowed to trade under the name of the established 'generic' brand from which they both differed.

Other external features of foodstuffs have been tested for compatibility with Article 28 EC, including the shape of packaging in which the product is sold. It has been held, for example, that by requiring that margarine be marketed in cone-shaped tubs, so that consumers could clearly distinguish it from butter, Belgium was acting contrary to Article 28 EC.[37] What is particularly interesting about the reasoning in this case is that, unlike in most other Article 28 EC examinations, the Court did assess the available economic evidence supporting the assertion that the national rules at issue constituted a measure equivalent to a quantitative restriction on imports by accepting that, despite margarine prices being appreciably higher in Belgium than in other Member States, and therefore offering a more lucrative marketplace for producers from other Member States where prices were not so high, there was practically no margarine of foreign origin to be found on the Belgian market. This illustrated that, by obliging producers from other Member States to alter the shape of their packaging prior to importation into Belgium, the national rules at issue had created an obstacle to trade (although a more holistic examination may also have assessed the markets of other Member States to see whether there were large quantities of imported margarine available there). It was accepted, in principle at least, that legislation designed to prevent consumer confusion about what was butter and what was margarine was justifiable. However, by prohibiting the marketing of margarine lawfully manufactured and marketed in another Member State, the Belgian rules considerably exceeded the requirements of the objective pursued. Most importantly, consumers could be protected just as effectively in other, less trade-restrictive ways, in particular by proper labelling. In similar circumstances, in *Prantl*, the Court held that national rules prohibiting the use of 'bocksbeutel' bottles (of characteristic bulbous shape) for wines imported from Italy into Germany were contrary to Article 28 EC.[38] The rules were unjustifiable on public policy and industrial and commercial property protection grounds as the bottles were lawfully used for local products in another Member State.

Inconsistencies abound. An examination of the Court-developed principles on ensuring compliance with Article 28 EC at this stage identifies three key points. First, Member States may not have measures in place that force an importer to alter the name of the foodstuff on the label. Instead, measures could be introduced that force the importer to alter the description on the label.[39] Second, national rules that force packaging to be altered are disproportionate to the aim pursued.[40] Instead, measures should be introduced to force the importer to alter their label.[41]

[37] Case 261/1981, *Walter Rau Lebensmittelwerke v De Smedt PVBA* [1982] ECR 3961.
[38] Case 16/1983, *Criminal proceedings against Karl Prantl* [1984] ECR 1299.
[39] Case 27/1980, *Criminal proceedings against Anton Adriaan Fietje* [1980] ECR 3839.
[40] Case 261/1981, *Walter Rau Lebensmittelwerke v De Smedt PVBA* [1982] ECR 3961.
[41] *Ibid*, para 17.

Third, where Member States have attempted to oblige importers to alter their labels they have been prevented from doing so.[42]

2.2.4 National Quality Requirements

The preceding case law on the free movement of food seemed, temporarily at least, to be thrown into some doubt after the decision handed down in *Kaas*.[43] At issue here were Dutch rules designed to preserve the quality of agricultural and fishery products and, more specifically, those relating to the quality of cheese. The legislation set out a list of the types of cheese that could be lawfully produced in the Netherlands. This included traditional Dutch varieties such as gouda and edam, as well as varieties traditional to other States, such as cheddar (UK) and feta (Greece). Precise production requirements were set for each variety of cheese. Products not conforming to these standards could not be lawfully produced in the Netherlands. Products from other Member States that did not meet the minimum quality standards could still be marketed in the Netherlands. It was asked whether the Netherlands was prohibited by Article 28 EC from having in place, on a unilateral basis, rules concerning the quality of cheese, such as those at issue. The case centred around the question of whether these rules, given that they were designed to improve the quality of domestic production and thereby increase the sale of such products, were capable of placing imports at a disadvantage and therefore constituted a measure having an effect equivalent to a quantitative restriction. It was held that Article 28 EC does not prevent a Member State from adopting domestic rules which do not set standards for imported products but have as their purpose the improvement of the quality of domestic production so as to make it more attractive to consumers. The rules at issue here were distinguished from other, similar domestic measures which may be contrary to Article 28 EC, such as publicity campaigns designed to promote domestic products,[44] or those which advise consumers to purchase domestic products solely by reason of their national origin.[45] It is here contended that this distinction is not so clear-cut.

The decision in *Kaas* differs from the generally accepted reasoning of the Court on Article 28 EC matters. Domestically produced cheese that carries a quality certification stamp has a clear marketing advantage over an imported cheese that does not carry this mark. There are two reasons for this. First, the consumer is informed that the cheese has met minimum quality guarantees. Second, the consumer is informed that the cheese has been produced within the Member State. Consumers tend to favour domestically produced goods over imported ones—for a variety of

---

[42] See, for example, Case 298/1987, *Proceedings for compulsory reconstruction against Smanor SA* [1988] ECR 4489; Joined Cases C-289/1996, C-293/1996 and C-299/1996, *Denmark, Germany and France v Commission* [1999] ECR I-1541.

[43] Case 237/1982, *Jongeneel Kaas BV and others v Netherlands and other* [1984] ECR 483.

[44] Case 249/1981, *Commission v Ireland* (Buy Irish campaign) [1982] ECR 4005.

[45] Case 222/1982, *Apple and Pear Development Council v KJ Lewis Ltd and others* [1983] ECR 4083.

reasons.[46] A scheme such as that at issue here may thus have a far more restrictive effect on intra-Community trade than may, for example, a national rule obliging a producer to market margarine in cone-shaped tubs. By placing such an obligation on imported margarine the Member State makes the product look similar to the domestically produced variety. Were importers to continue to market their margarine in differently shaped tubs it would immediately draw the consumer's attention to the fact that the good in question is imported. Similarly, here the consumer is automatically informed that cheese has not been produced in accordance with national minimum quality requirements and that it is foreign, thereby reducing the possibility of the average consumer purchasing it.

Despite the decision in *Kaas*, national rules that seek to preserve the quality of products tend to be deemed contrary to Article 28 EC obligations in practically all circumstances, even where the sale of imported goods that meet these standards remains uninhibited by the Member States. In *Miro*, for example, Dutch rules restricting the use of the sales name 'jenever' to a type of drink meeting domestic national requirements including, in particular, the requirement that it have an alcohol content of at least 35 per cent, came under the scrutiny of the Court.[47] A retailer was prosecuted for selling imported Belgian 'jenever' with an alcohol content of only 30 per cent. At the time, the Commission had proposed a regulation laying down general rules on the definition, description and presentation of alcoholic spirits, including jenever, for which it had set a minimum alcohol content of 30 per cent.[48] The Council had not yet taken any decision on this proposal, however. The national court had found that, given the decision in *Cassis*, coupled with the fact that the label made it clear that the product was in fact Belgian jenever, there was no mandatory requirement of consumer protection that would justify banning the sale of the imported product in the Netherlands. However, it was noted that this would then place the Dutch jenever producer at a disadvantage. They would remain subject to additional excise duty and value added tax given that their variant of the product would have to contain at least five per cent more alcohol than the imported variety. The Dutch and German governments claimed that the national rules were justified by mandatory requirements for con-

---

[46] For further discussion see K Philp and L Brown, 'Does Consumer Ethnocentrism Impact on Australian Food Buying Behaviour?' (2003) *Journal of New Business Ideas and Trends* 21, where it is accepted that as globalisation intensifies, consumers' perceptions of foreign products, and hence the country of origin effect also intensifies. See also SM Peris, K Newman, E Bigne and B Chansarkar, 'Aspects of Anglo-Spanish Perceptions and Product Preferences Arising from "Country-of-Origin" image' (1993) 12 *International Journal of Advertising* 131; S-T Hong and RS Wyer, 'Effects of Country-of-Origin and Product-Attribute Information on Product Evaluation: An Information Processing Perspective' 16 (1989) *Journal of Consumer Research* 175.

[47] Case 182/1984, *Criminal proceedings against Miro BV* [1985] ECR 3731.

[48] Proposal for a Council regulation (EEC) laying down general rules on the definition, description and presentation of spirituous beverages and of vermouths and other wines of fresh grapes flavoured with plants or other aromatic substances. COM (1982) 328. [1982] OJ C 189/7. This proposal became Council Regulation (EEC) No 1576/1989 of 29 May 1989 laying down general rules on the definition, description and presentation of spirit drinks. [1989] OJ L 160/1. Jenever was later specifically removed from the scope of Article 3 of the Regulation, which set minimum alcohol contents for other classifications of spirituous beverages, such as whiskey (40%), rum (37.5%) and gin (also 37.5%).

sumer protection as labelling measures are insufficient to eliminate the risk that the consumer may confuse the traditional beverage with another product having a lower alcohol content. This would be particularly so where they are unaware that the traditional variety should contain 35 per cent alcohol. Such measures, it was contended, are completely ineffective where the beverage is sold in hotels and restaurants. Germany also suggested that the question of the validity of the Dutch restriction on the use of the name 'jenever' should be determined by reference to the commercial view prevailing in the country concerned and, given that the national authorities are in the best position to judge on this matter, it should be for those authorities, and not the Court of Justice, to reach any decision in this regard. This argument was rejected. The Court found that the national court had itself accepted that the labelling disclosures on the product were sufficient to inform the consumer about the nature of the difference between the two varieties of jenever. As a consequence, it was only deemed necessary to ascertain whether the need to ensure fair trading could be used to justify the Dutch rules.

The Netherlands put forward the argument, and they were supported by Italy in this regard, that an alcohol content of 35 per cent is one of the inherent characteristics of this traditional national product. Without a ban on using the traditional name for a product not having the traditional qualities, it would be impossible to maintain its quality. A situation would be created whereby even beverages with an alcohol content as low as 15 per cent would have to be accepted as 'jenever'. Producers should therefore, it was claimed, be prevented from using the good reputation of a world-famous product to the advantage of the different and cheaper product. The Court, however, referring to *Commission v Germany*[49] and *Commission v Italy*,[50] stated that it was not compatible with Article 28 EC for national legislation to be allowed to restrict the use of a generic term to one national variety alone to the detriment of other varieties by compelling producers of other varieties in other Member States to use sales names which are either unfamiliar or less esteemed by the consumer. It was recognised that setting compositional requirements could, of course, lead to standardisation and, consequently, provide more transparency in trading. However, following its earlier determinations on the matter, the Court found that in a common market, fair trading interests are to be examined in the context of the fair and traditional practices of all Member States.[51] It could not therefore be regarded as an essential requirement of fair trading that national rules fixing minimum alcohol content be complied with by products of the same kind imported from another Member State if they are lawfully and traditionally manufactured and marketed under the same name in the Member State of origin and the purchaser is provided with the proper information.

---

[49] Case 12/1974, *Commission v Germany* (sekt) [1975] ECR 181.
[50] Case 193/1980, *Commission v Italy* (vinegar) [1981] ECR 3019.
[51] Case 16/1983, *Criminal proceedings against Karl Prantl* [1984] ECR 1299.

The Court summarised its position by stating:

> If in such circumstances the free movement of imported goods were to be subject to the
> condition that there should first exist Community rules, the fundamental principle of a
> unified market and its corollary, the free movement of goods would be rendered mean-
> ingless.[52]

The fact that the imported product may have a price advantage as a result of the application of national taxes and duties proportional to the alcohol content was deemed irrelevant here.[53] The Court stated that these are part of the objective conditions of competition. Every trader may freely take advantage of these, provided that purchasers are given information so that they are free to make their choice on the basis of the quality and price of the products.[54]

The Court essentially states in *Miro* that the mutual recognition principle developed in *Cassis* is not only here to stay but it leaves producers with the following choice. Maintain quality standards and compete with lower priced competitors who are selling lower quality products, or reduce the quality of your own products to meet this new element of competition accordingly. There is also recognition by the Court here that harmonisation of Member States' rules on compositional requirements is no longer necessary given the efficacy of Article 28 EC and related case law in ensuring the free movement of foodstuffs.[55] This reasoning persists despite the Court's own recognition in *Miro* that setting standardised compositional requirements could provide more transparency in trading, leading to fairer trading amongst producers, whilst clearing up any confusion that could be created amongst consumers.

The Court will also refuse to accept the necessity of national rules designed to maintain the quality of food where the Member State imposing them fails to provide that these standards are being properly upheld. In *Commission v Italy*, for example, it was asked whether certain national rules contravened Article 28 EC.[56] These rules required that edible vegetable oils imported from other Member States, other than olive oil, should not be marketed unless colour-reactive sesame oil was added. Italy claimed that this obligation was necessary to prevent fraudulent practices intended to deceive consumers, in particular in the olive oil sector. A lack of effective controls on either domestic production or imports to check that sesame oil had been added, and the fact that the national measures were unlikely to achieve the aim pursued effectively, led the Court to declare this provision contrary to Article 28 EC.

What is also clear from the Court's Article 28 EC jurisprudence on the legality of national quality standards is that it is irrelevant whether or not the Member State actually prohibits the sale of a food lawfully marketed elsewhere in the

---

[52]   Case 182/1984, *Criminal proceedings against Miro BV* [1985] ECR 3731, para 25.
[53]   *Ibid*, para 26.
[54]   *Ibid*.
[55]   Discussed further in Chapter 3 below.
[56]   Case C-67/1988, *Commission v Italy* (sesame oil) [1990] ECR I-4285.

Community. All that is required to make the rule examinable for compatibility with the Treaty is that it obliges the importer who does not meet the national standards to market their product using a different name. This has already been demonstrated in *Miro*. In *Commission v Germany*, the Court made it clear that its intention was to ensure, as far as possible, that no domestic rules inhibiting the lawful marketing of products from other Member States would be safe from its now sprawling Article 28 EC jurisprudence.[57] Here, the national rules at issue were the sacrosanct German beer purity laws (Biersteuergesetz). These rules set method of manufacture and compositional requirements that had to be adhered to by both domestic producers and those from other Member States in order for them to lawfully market their products as 'bier' in Germany. 'Bier' could only contain malted barley and some other malts (artificially germinated cereals other than, amongst others, rice and maize), hops, yeast and water. Beverages not meeting these requirements could still be marketed, but only under a different name. German law also prohibited the marketing of 'bier' containing unauthorised additives, for health protection reasons. This latter aspect of the judgment will be dealt with later in this chapter.

The Commission objected to the German rules. It was claimed that they precluded the importation into Germany of many beers that were lawfully manufactured in other Member States. The Commission did not believe that such a prohibition could be justified on grounds of either consumer protection or safeguarding public health. Germany disagreed. It claimed that if only those ingredients that were listed in its domestic rules were used in manufacturing beer, there would be no need to use additives. The Commission accepted that in the absence of Community harmonisation, Member States could lay down rules such as those at issue. Its primary complaint was, however, that these rules could not be used to limit the use of a generic name to those products that conformed to these standards, such rules going beyond that which was necessary to protect the German consumer who could be informed about any differences between products marketed under the same name on the labelling. Citing *Cassis*[58] and *Rau*,[59] the Court noted that such rules may be necessary to protect consumers or human health, but, most importantly, that any such rules must be proportionate and that where a Member State can choose between various measures to attain the same objective, it should choose the means that is least restrictive on the free movement of goods. There was clearly an obstacle to trade. It just had to be ascertained whether this could be justified.

The argument that the German rules were necessary to protect consumers who associated the designation 'bier' only with the beverage manufactured solely from the ingredients specified was rejected. It was held that consumer conceptions are likely to evolve over the course of time within a Member State. The common market, it was stated, would play a major contributory role in that development.

---

[57] Case 178/1984, *Commission v Germany* (bier) [1987] ECR 1227.
[58] Case 120/1978, *Rewe-Zentral AG v Bundesmonopolverwaltung für Branntwein* [1979] ECR 649.
[59] Case 261/1981, *Walter Rau Lebensmittelwerke v De Smedt PVBA* [1982] ECR 3961.

The German rules, it was claimed, were thus preventing this evolutionary process from taking place. In support of this, *Commission v UK* was cited.[60] There it was stated that the legislation of a Member State must not 'crystallise given consumer habits so as to consolidate an advantage acquired by national industries concerned to comply with them'. Secondly, the designation 'bier' was used generically in other Member States where rice or maize was permitted to be added to the beverage, and it was this definition that was used in the common customs tariff (heading no 22.03).[61] Providing consumers with information about the ingredients used and method of manufacture employed, as the German bier designation did, was seen to be a legitimate labelling function. However, the Court determined that this goal could be better satisfied by measures that were less restrictive on free movement. In particular, this could be achieved by the compulsory affixing of suitable labels identifying the nature of the product sold.[62] The Court stated that where there are clear indications of the raw materials used, the consumer can make his or her choice in full knowledge of the facts. This will guarantee transparency in trading. Such a system of mandatory consumer information could not entail negative assessments for beers not complying with the German rules. In saying so, this was perhaps to admit that the German rules led to the production of a superior product and certainly a product which German consumers found more desirable. The problem that this information might be more difficult to transmit to those purchasing draft beers was seen to be surmountable. Information could be placed on either the casks or the beer taps. However, such a presumption by the Court is clearly questionable. Generally consumers of beer do not inspect the casks to read the labels before consuming the drink.

As the case law of the Court of Justice on Article 28 EC has developed, it has become clear that where a Member State attempts to apply national legislation that prohibits two different products being marketed under the same sales name, it will generally be prevented from doing so.

2.2.5 Different Products, Same Name

In similar circumstances to those that led to the nullification of the German beer purity laws,[63] Italian requirements that pasta be made using only durum wheat

---

[60] Case 170/1978, *Commission v UK* (wine and beer tax) [1980] ECR 417.

[61] Council Regulation (EEC) No 2658/1987 of 23 July 1987 on the tariff and statistical nomenclature and on the Common Customs Tariff. [1987] OJ L 256/1. Combined nomenclature definitions were also scrutinised in Joined Cases C-465/2002 and C-466/2002, *Germany and Denmark v Commission* [2005] ECR I-9115, where it was argued that CN Code 0406 9031 clearly classified 'feta' cheese as a generic food product. However, it was stated that this system of classification applied to customs matters only and was not relevant to any assessment of industrial property rights and could not therefore be used in any examination of how the product should be defined for protected designation of origin purposes under the terms of Regulation 2081/1992 (since replaced by Regulation 510/2006). Discussed in more detail in Chapter 3 below.

[62] Case 178/1984, *Commission v Germany* (bier) [1987] ECR 1227, para 35.

[63] Case 178/1984, *Commission v Germany* (bier) [1987] ECR 1227.

were challenged in *Zoni*.[64] Here, an Italian wholesaler imported pasta from Germany. The pasta in question was made from a combination of common wheat and durum wheat. Domestic law in Italy prohibited the sale of both domestically-produced and imported dry pasta made using such a mixture. The use of common wheat was permitted for the small-scale manufacture of fresh pasta, either for immediate consumption or exclusively for export. Italy contended that the domestic rules were designed to guarantee the quality of pasta and to promote the growing of durum wheat. Producers of this crop have scarce alternative markets for their product in the Community other than the pasta market. They have no real possibility of changing over to other crops in the Mezzogiorno regions in which they are established. The *Dassonville* formula was readily satisfied: this was clearly a measure equivalent to a quantitative restriction. The decision in *Cassis*, however, created the possibility of justification based upon one of the mandatory requirement exceptions. The consumer protection argument was dismissed, in particular on the basis of the findings in *Commission v Germany*.[65] The Court found that labelling would offer a more proportionate solution to the aim pursued. The framework food labelling directive made it possible for Italy to reserve the description 'pasta made from durum wheatmeal' for products made exclusively from this ingredient.[66] The possibility of confusion or deception where pasta is served in restaurants could, it was claimed, be avoided by establishing a system of informing the consumer about the nature of the pasta being offered. Italy offered counter-arguments that were rejected. Italian consumers associate the sales name 'pasta' with products made exclusively from durum wheat, hence the requirement to maintain domestic rules. The name 'pasta' is a generic one. Italian legislation allowed, in some circumstances, products not made from a combination of wheat types to be called pasta, for example, pasta for export. The fair trading argument was rejected on the basis that, although pasta made exclusively from durum wheat was more expensive to produce than that containing common

[64] Case 90/1986, *Criminal proceedings against Zoni* [1988] ECR 4285. See also Case 407/1985, *Glocken GmbH and Kritzinger v USL Centro-Sud and Provincia autonoma di Bolzano* [1988] ECR 4233.
[65] Case 178/1984, *Commission v Germany* (bier) [1987] ECR 1227. Also cited here, Case 193/1980, *Commission v Italy* (vinegar) [1981] ECR 3019.
[66] Case 90/1986, *Criminal proceedings against Zoni* [1988] ECR 4285, para 17. While no specific reference is made here by the Court to a particular provision of Directive 1979/112, presumably it is referring to Article 5(1) thereof which provided: 'The name under which a foodstuff is sold shall be the name laid down by whatever laws, regulations or administrative provisions apply to the foodstuff in question or, in the absence of any such name, the name customary in the Member State where the product is sold to the ultimate consumer, or a description of the foodstuff and, if necessary, of its use, that is sufficiently precise to inform the purchaser of its true nature and to enable it to be distinguished from products with which it could be confused.' However, the new framework food labelling directive, Directive 2000/13, adds a new Article 5(1)(b) which provides that: 'The use in the Member State of marketing of the sales name under which the product is legally manufactured and marketed in the Member State of production shall also be allowed.' Therefore, it is debatable as to whether the assertion made here by the Court about Italy being permitted to prescribe the use of a specific sales name for pasta where it is lawfully marketed using that name elsewhere in the Community is now in doubt. Considering *Cassis*, and related case law discussed previously in this chapter, it is highly probable that this would never actually have been allowed in the first instance given the apparent absence of any 'substantial difference' between the products concerned.

wheat, Italy could, as stated previously, reserve the use of the sales description 'pasta made from durum wheatmeal' to products made exclusively from this ingredient, enabling Italian consumers to express their preference for the product to which they had become accustomed and guaranteeing that the difference in price would be justified by an appreciable difference in quality. This would now oblige the national producer to alter their label, while the importer could continue to market their product using the original sales name. Finally, the producer protection argument, which Italy claimed could lead to grave social and environmental consequences, was dismissed on the basis that Italian producers could still be required to adhere to the domestic requirements and that export markets largely favour durum wheat pasta, even where also exposed to competition from the less expensive mixed wheat variety. The Italian rules were held to be contrary to Article 28 EC, not being justifiable under any of the Court-developed mandatory requirement provisions.

The compatibility of national rules prohibiting the marketing of milk substitutes with the terms of Article 28 EC was first examined in *Commission v France*.[67] Here, the respondent Member State argued that the measures were necessary for both consumer protection and health preservation reasons. Applying its previous case law on the matter, the Court reiterated that Member States may not invoke public interest or mandatory requirement grounds to justify a measure restricting imports unless the same objective could not be achieved by another measure that was less restrictive on the free movement of goods.

France put forward three consumer protection arguments: (i) the difficulties in informing consumers that what they were purchasing was in fact a substitute product; (ii) consumers may be confused as to the characteristics of the product; and (iii) cheaper substitutes will gradually supplant the original variety, ultimately limiting consumer choice. Once again, the Court answered the first argument with the labelling information panacea, in this case where it listed details of the nature, the ingredients and the characteristics of the product on offer. This information could also, it was claimed, be provided, in principle at least, in catering establishments. While it was accepted that there may be some difficulties in providing consumers with full and detailed information where milk substitutes are used in catering, it was also noted that this level of information is not given about the other ingredients used in foodstuffs and meals provided by catering establishments. There was no reason to have more strict requirements in place for milk substitutes than for other foods.[68]

The Court accepted that some national measures designed to ensure clear labelling may be adopted without infringing free movement rules.[69] The stated position, therefore, was that Community law does not preclude a national measure that seeks to secure accurate consumer information and thereby assists in

---

[67] Case 216/1984, *Commission v France* (milk substitutes) [1988] ECR 793.
[68] *Ibid*, para 10.
[69] See also, in particular, Case 27/1980, *Criminal proceedings against Anton Adriaan Fietje* [1980] ECR 3839.

avoiding any confusion about the nature of a product. However, the measures adopted in this case were seen to go beyond this, given that they put a prohibition in place. They were not proportionate to the stated aim pursued.

As to the risk of milk products becoming supplanted by lower priced substitutes, the Court stated that a Member State may not plead a mandatory requirement, such as consumer protection, in order to shield a product from the effects of price competition, on the pretext of economic difficulties brought about by the elimination of barriers to intra-Community trade.[70] Choice, it was stated, would not become restricted. Instead, it was only through the marketing of products like substitute milk that consumers would be presented with a genuine choice between whiteners and real milk products. The prohibition was thus found to be unnecessary for consumer protection purposes. Whether this really presents a proper choice for the consumer is questionable. Where catering or processed foodstuff production establishments are concerned, the consumer does not actually have a choice. The alternative version has already been used in production and is then contained in the finished product. It is also highly unlikely that consumers in catering establishments will ever be informed of this substitution.

Perhaps most controversially, however, the French argument that Regulation 1898/1987 could be used to support the legitimacy of their domestic measures was also not accepted because that legislation provides that only those national regulations that comply with the general provisions of the EC Treaty could be maintained.[71] These national regulations did not, given that which had been stated previously by the Court, satisfy this requirement as they were contrary to Article 28 EC. Article 5 of the regulation actually states that:

> Member States may, until the end of the fifth period of application of Article 5c of Regulation (EEC) No 804/68 and in compliance with the general provisions of the Treaty, maintain their national regulations which restrict the manufacture and marketing in their territory of products not fulfilling the conditions referred to in Article 2 of this Regulation.

It does not state, nor is it stated anywhere else in the regulation, that this is confined to national measures that comply with all aspects, or even the general provisions, of the Treaty. The regulation was actually designed to promote milk consumption; to protect milk and milk products in the interests of Community producers and consumers; to ensure appropriate labelling to prevent the consumer from being misled; to define milk and milk products; to avoid any confusion on the part of the consumer between milk products and other food products, including those consisting partly of milk components; to establish conditions of competition between milk products and competing products in the field of product designation, labelling and advertising which avoid any distortion, and to protect the consumer in this regard; given that milk products have a higher

---

[70] Case 216/1984, *Commission v France* (milk substitutes) [1988] ECR 793, para 12.

[71] Article 5 of Council Regulation (EEC) No 1898/1987 of 2 July 1987 on the protection of designations used in marketing of milk and milk products. [1987] OJ L 182/36.

production cost than substitutes, to safeguard agricultural producer incomes; and to enable Member States having already taken national measures to curb the manufacture and marketing of these substitute products on their territory to maintain their regulations, in compliance with the general rules of the Treaty.[72] The preamble to the regulation does specify the need for compliance of existing national rules, such as those at issue here, with the Treaty. However, if this aspect of the preamble could be used by the Court to declare the French rules incompatible with the Treaty, then it needed also to be ascertained whether the other declarations made in this part of the regulation could have been used to support the French ban. Were such an assessment to have been made, then it could clearly have been identified that the French rules were in compliance with Community law and policy, even if contrary to Article 28 EC. Certainly, it would have made justification of the national rules under Article 30 EC more readily acceptable. To adopt any other approach would render Regulation 1898/1987 virtually meaningless.

The Court was faced with an examination based on a similar set of circumstances in *Commission v Germany*.[73] Again German law prohibited the marketing of milk substitutes. Germany suggested that this prohibition was confined to imitations of milk, which could be confused with real milk, and not milk substitutes as such. The mandatory requirement justification put forward, that this was necessary to protect consumers, was also rejected here. One additional defence put forward by Germany was that the nature of the rules at issue, which only sought to prohibit the marketing of those products that could reasonably be confused with real milk, clearly identified that their aim was to protect consumers from being misled. The prohibition could not thus be said to have a trade restricting intention. It was also claimed that the rules at issue were proportionate as no other measure would be sufficient to protect consumers in this way. This was not accepted. Adequate labelling would suffice. The Court also noted that even where these drinks were sold in vending machines or catering establishments, consumers could also be provided with full and detailed information on the nature of the products. This is, however, unlikely to happen. While it was noted that some difficulties may arise here, this was a problem that applied to all foodstuffs provided in such a way and that there was no particular reason why a higher level of information should be required to be supplied to consumers where milk substitutes were involved. Again, such reasoning is questionable. It is perfectly reasonable that extra information should be provided to consumers when purchasing products that are different from that which they would normally expect. This is especially so where the products involved are different but are marketed using the same name and where there is a clear possibility of confusion or deception in some circumstances, such as where the products are sold in catering establishments or by vending machine. The Court's own case law makes provision for this. Its entire

---

[72]   Preamble to Council Regulation (EEC) No 1898/1987. For discussion of the role of agriculture in the EC Treaty more generally see JA McMahon, *Law of the Common Agricultural Policy* (Harlow, Longman, 2000).

[73]   Case 76/1986, *Commission v Germany* (milk substitutes) [1989] ECR 1021.

free movement of food jurisprudence is based on the presumption that providing additional labelling information to consumers should counter almost all Member State contentions that their national rules that inhibit free movement in some way are justifiable. It was accepted, following *Fietje*,[74] that reasonable national measures that are necessary in order to ensure that products are accurately described do not themselves infringe Article 28 EC. However, the measures at issue here were found to go beyond this, again failing the test of proportionality to the aim pursued. As in *Commission v France*, the Regulation 1898/1987 argument was also here rejected.[75] It was stated that the national measures, although appearing to satisfy Article 5 in conjunction with Article 2 thereof, could not be maintained as they were contrary to Article 28 EC, and thereby did not satisfy the terms of the regulation.

In the milk substitute cases, the Member States sought to justify national rules that prohibited the sale of foodstuffs using the generic name of a product from which the foodstuff in question differed significantly. These cases can be distinguished from those where the national rules under examination prohibit the use of a generic name, even where the two 'different' foods concerned are almost identical.

In *Nespoli and Crippa*,[76] for example, it was questioned whether Italian national rules specifying the minimum fat content of cheese were compatible with Article 28 EC. The minimum fat content for the type of cheese in question was set by the national rules at 45 per cent. The two defendants in the domestic legal action were charged with the importation and marketing for sale respectively of a French cheese containing only 30 per cent fat. It was sold in its original French wrapping, being labelled as 'fromage demi-gras' (semi-fat cheese). A label had also been attached bearing the Italian words 'prodotto caseario' (cheese product).

The effect of the domestic law was to prevent cheese lawfully produced and marketed in one Member State from being lawfully marketed in another under the same generic name: 'cheese'. Italy contended that the rules were designed to protect consumers as their legitimate expectations would not be satisfied if they were offered as cheeses products which, in view of the differences between the national rules, exhibited very different characteristics and were thus different products. This was rejected. The use of adequate labelling would suffice in order to provide proper information on the actual fat content to enable consumers to make their choice with full knowledge of the facts.

Similarly, in *van der Laan* it was held that national rules that prohibited the marketing as 'meat product' a foodstuff that contained only 70 per cent meat was contrary to Article 28 EC.[77] The Member State had contested that given the low level of meat actually contained in the product, it was so markedly different from other cured meat with a 100 per cent actual meat content that labelling disclosures

---

[74] Case 27/1980, *Criminal proceedings against Anton Adriaan Fietje* [1980] ECR 3839, para 11.

[75] Case 216/1984, *Commission v France* (milk substitutes) [1988] ECR 793.

[76] Case C-196/1989, *Criminal proceedings against Enzo Nespoli and Giuseppe Crippa* [1990] ECR I-3647.

[77] Case C-383/1997, *Criminal proceedings against Arnoldus van der Laan* [1999] ECR I-731.

would not suffice to indicate the real level of difference between the product types. This argument was rejected, the Court finding that consumer protection grounds could not be successfully invoked here to justify this restriction on the free movement of food. Consumers would, it was claimed, be sufficiently protected by descriptive labelling and the information available in the list of ingredients.

A comparison of the decisions in the milk substitutes cases to that in *Nespoli and Crippa* on the fat content of cheese highlights a problem with the prevailing remedy that the Court offers to deal with the fact that Member States have different compositional requirements for the same food products. In the milk substitutes cases, a significant difference existed between the prohibited product and foodstuffs normally marketed using that name. The Italian rules on the fat content of cheese prohibited the marketing of products not meeting the required standard even as 'cheese substitutes', despite the fact that both products contained a significant fat content, and both could be considered as being cheese, one full-fat, the other reduced-fat. This would be similar to the milk substitutes cases examining, not whether a substitute product should be allowed to use the universally recognised generic name, but instead testing national rules that prohibited the sale of semi-skimmed or low-fat milk as such. In other words, preventing such products from using the word 'milk' in their sales name. The Court, however, directed in both situations that the national rules were contrary to Community law. Labelling disclosures of difference between products would be the more proportionate response.

This is disputed here. Two levels of difference between products are examined. One level of difference, that in the milk substitutes cases, is substantial. The other level of difference, that between full-fat and reduced-fat cheese, is relatively inconsequential. Levels of difference require different treatment by the Court. The two sets of rules under examination impact differently on consumer protection. The French and German rules on milk substitutes prevent consumers from being deceived into purchasing a product that is quite unlike real milk. The Italian rules on fat content levels in cheese prohibited low-fat cheese from being called cheese, even though it is admittedly a kind of cheese. It could be noted here that the circumstances under examination in *Nespoli and Crippa* are not that dissimilar to those in *Cassis*. There is, however, one key difference. The cheese was labelled as 'semi-fat cheese' or 'cheese product'. In *Cassis*, the liqueur bore no such description. It was not labelled as 'low alcohol liqueur'. If it were, it could be argued that this instantly brings this 'inconsequential difference' to the consumer's attention. For such inconsequential differences, Member States should, of course, be allowed to allow the product to be marketed on their territory using the more descriptive form of labelling, such as that which the Court appears to be advocating in *Zoni*. For any 'substantial difference' further investigation into the degree of difference between products is required in order to ascertain whether a Member State prohibiting the use of the name of the food normally known by that name should be permissible. An outright prohibition on the sale of the foodstuff, unless justifiable under Article 30 EC, should never be allowed. A realigned interpretation of

Community law would, however, permit Member States to prescribe the use of an alternative name in such circumstances.

There is one further difference to note between the national rules prohibiting the sale of milk substitutes and those stipulating the minimum fat content for cheese. For virtually everybody low-fat cheese is a better dietetic choice than full-fat cheese. But milk substitutes could be considered nutritionally or dietetically superior to milk itself for very few people. The latter has the potential to impact positively on human health; the former negatively.

It has become clear since the decision of the Court in *Cassis* that once a product is lawfully marketable in one Member State, it must be lawfully marketable in all—this is the principle of mutual recognition. Essentially, this principle obliges all Member States to concede that the standards set for the production and marketing of foodstuffs in all other Member States, for all food products lawfully marketable there, are of an acceptable level. This is clearly not the case. As a consequence, Member States become obliged to allow the lawful marketing of a variety of foodstuffs, perhaps composed of entirely different ingredients leading to the creation of an entirely different product, using the same food name. This is even the case for the Member State where a foodstuff has been produced by a traditional method and using traditional ingredients for generations, such as pasta or 'bier'. Such food names are deemed to be generic. Given the manner in which the case law of the Court of Justice has developed on this matter, all such food names may be used by any producer in any Member State producing something that resembles the original variety. Fat content may be reduced below minimum standards, ingredients may be altered, traditionally alcoholic drinks need not contain alcohol and powdered substitute varieties can be marketed in a manner that conceals this from the consumer, who is likely to believe that they are purchasing something else altogether.

The Court has made one concession here. It will, albeit in very limited and ill-defined circumstances, allow Member States to introduce measures to prevent the marketing of 'substantially different' products using the same food name, generic or otherwise. Just how limited and ill-defined this level of difference has come to be is examined in more detail below.

2.2.6 Substantial Difference between Food Products

Two of the most important Court determinations on the circumstances in which a mandatory requirement exception to the free movement of food may be successfully invoked were those delivered in *Smanor*[78] and *Deserbais*.[79] In *Smanor*, French rules prohibited the deep-freezing of yoghurt, prescribing that after coagulation, the only processes or treatment to which the product could be subjected

---

[78] Case 298/1987, *Proceedings for compulsory reconstruction against Smanor SA* [1988] ECR 4489.
[79] Case 286/1986, *Ministère public v Gérard Deserbais* [1988] ECR 4907.

were refrigeration and stirring. Minimum quantities of live bacteria were also set (100 million per gram). Smanor, a French company, had been marketing deep-frozen yoghurt in France. The national authorities wished to prohibit the marketing of their products unless sold as 'deep-frozen fermented milk'.

The validity of the French rules was tested under both Article 28 EC and the framework food labelling legislation.[80] The French authorities contended that Article 28 EC did not apply to the facts of the case: this was a French company operating in France contesting French rules, and there was therefore no intra-Community trade element. This was rejected. The Court, for the first time where the free movement of food was concerned, found that while this was the case, it could not be ruled out that products such as those at issue may, at some stage in the future, be imported into France and thus be subject to the French legislation.[81] Article 28 EC thus applied to a wholly internal situation.[82]

The contested rules were caught within the definition of a measure equivalent to a quantitative restriction as set by the Court in *Dassonville*, and presented a similar form of trade impediment to those that were reviewed by the Court in *Fietje*.[83] The Court accepted that the sales name 'deep-frozen fermented milk' was less familiar to consumers than 'deep-frozen yoghurt'. The rules at issue were examined to see whether they could be justified on consumer protection grounds. It is of course legitimate for a Member State to ensure that consumers are properly informed about the products that are offered to them, enabling them to choose on the basis of that information.[84] Consumers could, however, make such a choice where the goods are labelled adequately, with the compulsory inclusion of the description 'deep-frozen' to show the treatment that the product has undergone.[85] This position would only alter if, having undergone the deep-freezing treatment, the yoghurt no longer had the characteristics which the consumer expects when buying this product. Using Codex Alimentarius standards,[86] and an assessment of several Member States' regulations, the Court identified that the characteristic feature of yoghurt is the presence of abundant quantities of live bacteria. As a consequence, the Court found that the national rules appeared disproportionate in relation to the objective of consumer protection when the characteristics of the deep-frozen variety were not 'substantially different' to fresh yoghurts, particularly as regards the quantity of bacteria. When appropriate labelling was attached

---

[80] Then Council Directive 1979/112/EEC of 18 December 1978 on the approximation of the laws of the Member States relating to the labelling, presentation and advertising of foodstuffs for sale to the ultimate consumer. [1979] OJ L 33/1. Discussed in more detail in Chapter 3 below.

[81] Case 298/1987, *Smanor*, note 79 above, para 8.

[82] It has also been argued that national rules cannot be examined under Article 28 EC where very little of the foodstuff type that is subject to these rules is produced in other Member States. This has, of course, been firmly rejected by the Court. See Case C-184/1996, *Commission v France* (foie gras) [1998] ECR I-6197, paras 14–17.

[83] Case 27/1980, *Criminal proceedings against Anton Adriaan Fietje* [1980] ECR 3839.

[84] Case 216/1984, *Commission v France* (milk substitutes) [1988] ECR 793.

[85] Case 298/1987, *Proceedings for compulsory reconstruction against Smanor SA* [1988] ECR 4489, para 19.

[86] Now Codex Standard for Fermented Milks, Codex Standard 243/2003.

to the product, consumers would be properly informed. It would, however, be for the national court to determine, in the light of the information available to it, whether the difference between deep-frozen yoghurt and the product meeting the national rules relating to fresh yoghurt was sufficient to require a different sales name.[87] The Court thus opened up the possibility that Member State rules restricting the free movement of food may actually be compatible with Article 28 EC where there is a 'substantial difference' between the imported product (or domestically produced as in *Smanor*) and the variety generally known by that sales name, which is subject to national compositional rules.

Two months later, in *Deserbais*, the Court made a similar assessment on whether French rules were compatible with Article 28 EC.[88] These rules prohibited the marketing of German edam cheese with a fat content that fell below the level required by domestic law. The French rules were adopted on the basis of the standard for edam set down in the Stresa Convention, which stipulated that it must have a minimum fat content of 40 per cent. The German edam at issue had a 34.3 per cent fat content. Although finding that the French rules were incompatible with Article 28 EC, the Court did again here find that, in some circumstances, where there is a substantial difference in composition or production method from products generally known by that name in the Community, such that they could not be regarded as being the same product, then an exception to Article 28 EC may exist. Peculiarly, the Court in *Nespoli and Crippa* never referred to *Deserbais*, decided over two years earlier, in its judgment. This despite the two cases being bases upon largely similar facts.

The Court also found that the standards set by the Stresa Convention and the Codex Alimentarius, both of which laid down a minimum of 40 per cent fat content for edam cheese, could not be relied upon to prove that the difference between the products at issue here was substantial. It was stated that these standards are in fact only designed to provide guidance, not to enable Member States to introduce prohibitions where these are not met.[89]

In a 1991 communication the Commission examined the *Smanor* and *Deserbais* judgments and proposed criteria for identifying the characteristics of a product that may make it unsuitable for selling under a generic name in the State of destination.[90] Any test must be carried out on the subjective basis of consumer expectations and the objective bases of Codex Alimentarius definitions, the rules and regulations of the Member States and the composition or method of manufacture of the products. In the Commission's opinion, only a substantial difference in one of those respects from national products would permit the importing State to prevent the imported product being marketed under the generic name. However, the Commission failed to lay down the degree of difference required to render this substantial, nor did it state any order of priority for consideration of the criteria.

---

[87] Case 298/1987, *Smanor*, note 86 above, para 24.
[88] Case 286/86, *Ministère public v Gérard Deserbais* [1988] ECR 4907.
[89] The relationship between the FAO/WHO Codex Alimentarius and EU food law is discussed in more detail in Chapter 4 below.

In *Canadane*, when examining whether there was a 'substantial difference' between two forms of cheese made in different ways and with different ingredients, the Advocate General, in his Opinion, accepted that this possible exception to the mutual recognition of generic names was not clearly demarcated in these two judgments.[91] The criteria determining substantial difference between national products and those imported goods that were likely to mislead consumers had not, he stated, been properly defined.[92] The *Smanor* judgment mentioned consumer expectations in the importing State, the provisions of the FAO/WHO Codex Alimentarius and the national law of the importing State. In *Deserbais* only the method of production and composition of the product were referred to. Furthermore, it was noted, no order of priority was laid down for the criteria and, if applied to a particular product in different orders, could produce conflicting conclusions. Nor was any indication given as to the degree of difference that must exist between the imported and national products for this difference to be considered so substantial that additional labelling will not suffice.

In *Commission v France* (foie gras), it was claimed that French national rules introduced in 1993 on preparations using foie gras as a base were contrary to Article 28 EC as they did not put in place any mutual recognition provision for similar products coming from other Member States.[93] France had argued that the rules were necessary in order to enable consumers to identify the true nature of the products that they were purchasing. Rejecting this contention with the usual labelling panacea, the Court did recognise the possible effects of its earlier decision in *Deserbais* here. Substantial difference in composition or production method between products could entitle the Member State to oblige that an alternative description be used on imported varieties. However, this was qualified with the further condition that this test of difference level would not be satisfied merely by the fact that this alternative variety did not wholly conform to the requirements laid down in domestic rules.

While the Court has introduced the possibility that a 'substantial difference' between products may enable Member States to prohibit the sale of the variety which their consumers are not accustomed to, this test of difference remains unclear and, in any case, is a very difficult one to satisfy. Even where such difference may exist, it will always be near impossible for a Member State to justify the introduction of a prohibition on the sale of a product lawfully marketed in another Member State for consumer protection purposes. It is only where substantiated claims about the serious detrimental health effects of a foodstuff can be made that any such action may be tolerated.

[90] Commission interpretative communication on the names under which food products are sold. [1991] OJ C 270/2.

[91] Opinion of Advocate General Ruiz-Jarabo Colomer in Case C-317/1995, *Canadane Cheese Trading AMBA and Adelfi G Kouri Anonymos Emoriki Kai Viomichaniki Etaireia v Hellenic Republic* [1997] ECR I-4681. The case never proceeded to full Court determination.

[92] For further discussion see C Lister, 'The Naming of Foods: The European Community's Rules for Non-Brand Food Product Names' [1993] *European Law Review* 179.

[93] Case C-184/1996, *Commission v France* (foie gras) [1998] ECR I-6197.

2.2.7 Protecting Human Health under Article 30 EC

It is quite clear from the wording of Article 30 EC that those who drafted the Treaty envisaged that exceptions to Article 28 EC would not only be necessary in some circumstances, but could even be vital to ensuring the health of humans, animals or plants. They had probably not expected that the remit of Article 28 EC would spiral out of control in the manner in which it has. More importantly than that, it was presumably not anticipated that the Court of Justice would limit the real effect of the Article 30 EC exceptions in such a manner as to render their existence almost meaningless. It has been made far too difficult for Member States to argue that a national measure escapes the Article 28 EC prohibition as it is necessary for human health preservation. The Court has created a very narrow set of circumstances in which Article 30 EC can be successfully invoked. The case law illustrates that while the Community courts have allowed their own institutions to act on a precautionary basis where uncertainty over the safety of a foodstuff exists, it has always been much more reluctant to allow the Member States to act in such a manner, although recent developments, probably in light of the post-BSE atmosphere of panic, indicates a slight shift in favour of Member State autonomy in this regard.

Article 30 EC states:

> The provisions of Articles 28 and 29 shall not preclude prohibitions or restrictions on imports, exports or goods in transit justified on grounds of public morality, public policy or public security; the protection of health and life of humans, animals or plants; the protection of national treasures possessing artistic, historic or archaeological value; or the protection of industrial and commercial property. Such prohibitions or restrictions shall not, however, constitute a means of arbitrary discrimination or a disguised restriction on trade between Member States.

Right through from the earliest founding case law, such as the decision in *Cassis*, to the challenging of German beer purity rules and those on using substitutes for milk, the Court has persistently rejected Member States' pleas that their national rules are necessary for the protection of human health. While this was not surprising in *Cassis*, where the argument put forward by the Member State in this regard was weak, it is unfortunate that the Court has refused to consider the improvement of health as a legitimate Article 30 EC claim—once it has been established that the measure is not a disguised restriction on trade—such as those made in both the beer and the milk substitute cases. It was never intended that the Article 30 EC exception to the prohibition on measures equivalent to quantitative restrictions on imports would relate to dangers to human health only. The preservation and improvement of health is of at least equal importance.

A clear example of the manner in which the Community courts will not permit the Member States to protect the health of their people was seen in *Commission v Germany*, where the Court examined whether Article 28 EC was breached by a ban on the marketing of some meat products.[94] German rules prohibited the marketing

[94] Case 274/1987, *Commission v Germany* (meat products) [1989] ECR 229.

of 'meat products' where these contained ingredients other than pure meat, subject to some exceptions. There was no dispute as to the restrictive effect that the rules had on Community trade. Germany contended, however, that the rules were necessary in the interests of public health protection, justifiable under Article 30 EC, and mandatory requirements relating to consumer protection, fair trading and the common agricultural policy. The rules were applicable without distinction to national and imported products.

The Court proceeded to examine the protection of public health justification available under Article 30 EC for national rules that act contrary to Article 28 EC. It was first pointed out that the Article 30 EC exception could only be used where it was necessary for the protection of human life and health, and only if that objective could not be achieved by measures less restrictive on intra-Community trade.[95] Germany argued that the measures in question were necessary to ensure that humans received a sufficient intake of essential nutrients from the food they consume, in this case proteins in meat. The Court used two German reports of 1980 and 1984 to repudiate the necessity of the German measures in achieving such an aim as they demonstrated that even where protein intakes were lower than the recommended level, in particular amongst young people, these levels posed no threat to human health. The reports had also expressed concern about increased meat consumption, in particular stating that additional intake of purine, cholesterol and saturated fatty acids from these foodstuffs could be harmful to human health. Finally, Germany argued that vegetable proteins have a lower nutritional value than animal proteins. Here that Court responded by stating that a Member State could not invoke public health grounds in order to prohibit the importation of a product by arguing that its nutritional value is lower than another product available on the market.[96] The fact that an imported product has a lower nutritional value does not mean that it poses any real threat to human health. The contested prohibition could not thus be justified on any grounds relating to the protection of human health within the meaning of Article 30 EC.

The Member State was seeking to ensure that its consumers receive a satisfactory level of nutrients, in this case protein, from the food that they eat. The Court found that this was not a legitimate use of Article 30 EC. This aspect of the Treaty could not be used to improve human health. It was rather designed to prevent threats to human health from specific and determinable ill effects, usually due to either contamination or disease. A further example of this approach to human health protection is seen in *Bellamy*, where it was held that national rules prohibiting the marketing of bread with a high salt content was contrary to Article 28 EC.[97] Despite concerns about the detrimental effects on human health of a high intake of salt in diets, the rules were not justifiable under the terms of Article 30

---

[95] See Case 104/1975, *De Peijper* [1976] ECR 613; Case 261/1985, *Commission v UK* (milk and cream) [1988] ECR 547.

[96] See also Case 216/1984, *Commission v France* (milk substitutes) [1988] ECR 793.

[97] Case C-123/2000, *Criminal proceedings against Christina Bellamy and English Shop Wholesale SA* [2001] ECR I-2795.

EC as the products in question were lawfully manufactured and marketed in another Member State.[98]

In the *Commission v Germany* beer purity case the national rules on additive usage in beer production presented a slightly more complex problem for the Court than the compositional requirements case.[99] It had previously been held that where there are scientific uncertainties about adverse health effects, it is for the Member States, in the absence of harmonisation, to decide what degree of health protection to provide, taking appropriate account of the free movement of goods.[100] Community law does not preclude Member States adopting legislation whereby the use of additives is subject to prior authorisation.[101] However, it was found here that the application to imported products of a prohibition on the use of additives that are authorised in the Member State of production but prohibited in the Member State of importation is permissible only insofar as it complies with the requirements of Article 30 EC. Previous case law indicated that such prohibitions had to be restricted to that which is absolutely necessary to secure the protection of public health.[102] This could not be the case where the scientific evaluations indicate that the additive in question does not present a risk to public health and meets a real need, especially a technical one.[103] The German rules excluded the use of all additives authorised in the other Member States. They also prevented importers from accessing a procedure whereby they could obtain authorisation for the use of a specific additive in the manufacture of beer. This was required by Community law, particularly the principle of proportionality.[104] The German scientific evidence offered referred to the risks inherent in the ingestion of additives in general. Given that beer was consumed in such large quantities in Germany, it was felt necessary to prohibit the use of additives in its production to reduce consumers' overall consumption of additives in their diet. It was also claimed that there was no technological need to use additives in beer.

Both arguments were again rejected. The first was thrown out for obvious reasons: it was, superficially at least, a weak point of contention, especially when considering that some of the additives prohibited were permitted to be present in other types of food and drink. The second was rejected because the Court found

---

[98] The health benefits of reducing salt intake in the diet are disputed. For further discussion on the potential detrimental effects of a high salt diet on human health, in particular increased risk of strokes and heart attacks, see FJ He and GA MacGregor, 'Effect of Modest Salt Reduction on Blood Pressure: A Meta-analysis of Randomized Trials. Implications for Public Health' (2002) 16 *Journal of Human Hypertension* 761; MH Alderman, 'Salt, Blood Pressure and Human Health' (2000) 36 *Hypertension* 890. For an alternative view, although based on less rigorous research, see NA Graudal *et al*, 'Effects of Sodium Restriction on Blood Pressure, Renin, Aldosterone, Catecholamines, Cholesterols and Triglyceride' (1998) 279 *Journal of the American Medical Association* 1383.

[99] Case 178/1984, *Commission v Germany* (bier) [1987] ECR 1227.

[100] See, in particular, Case 174/1982, *Criminal proceedings against Sandoz BV* [1983] ECR 2445.

[101] *Ibid*; Case 247/1984, *Criminal proceedings against Léon Motte* [1985] ECR 3887; Case 304/84, *Criminal proceedings against Claude Muller* [1986] ECR 1511.

[102] *Ibid.*

[103] *Ibid* and Case 178/1984, *Commission v Germany* (bier) [1987] ECR 1227, para 44.

[104] Case 304/1984, *Criminal proceedings against Claude Muller* [1986] ECR 1511.

that the concept of technological need was to be assessed in light of the raw materials utilised, bearing in mind the assessment made by the authorities of the Member State where the imported beer was produced and marketed, and the available scientific data. The fact that German production methods clearly demonstrated that additives need not be used in the manufacture of beer was seen as irrelevant, as this did not prove that the additives could not serve a technological function. What then would be the case for beers produced using only the permitted raw materials but still containing additives? This question was not answered, despite the fact that the German method of beer manufacture was such as not to require additive use. The German rules on the use of additives in the manufacture of beer were, however, also held to be contrary to Community rules on the free movement of goods, being disproportionate to the aim pursued and not justifiable under the terms of Article 30 EC.

The decision on the invocation of Article 30 EC in the German beer purity case clearly demonstrates the stance that the Court has adopted in relation to the use of additives in food. While additives are discussed in more detail in Chapter 5 below, what can be noted here is that 'technological need' does not mean that the product cannot be satisfactorily manufactured without use of the additive, as it might suggest. Technological need also includes making a product last longer (although not necessarily significantly longer), planting the taste of an ingredient into a foodstuff that it does not possess, or making a food product look as though it contains an ingredient it does not contain.[105] Using ingredients that deceive the consumer into believing that they are buying something that they are not is considered by the Court to be a 'technological need'.[106]

As we have seen, in *Commission v France* the respondent Member State submitted two arguments to support its assertion that a prohibition on the marketing of milk substitutes was necessary for health preservation reasons. These were: (i) decreased nutritional value; and (ii) the harmful effects of consuming milk substitutes. Both were rejected. The nutritional value argument was rejected on the grounds that a Member State may not invoke public health grounds in order to prohibit the importation of a product by arguing that its nutritional content is lower, or that its fat content is higher, than another product already available on the market in question—the mere fact that the imported product possesses these characteristics not in itself substantiating any claim that there is a danger posed to human health.[107] This rejection was supported by the fact that there were other products available on the French market which also had a lower nutritional value or which were composed of the same fats as milk substitutes yet there was no ban on the marketing of these products. This assertion, of course, fails to take account

---

[105] Case C-51/1994, *Commission v Germany* (sauces and pastries) [1995] ECR I-3599.

[106] The Court will allow Member States to ban the use of additives in some circumstances, even where their use is allowed in other Member States: Case 53/1980, *Officier van Justitie v Koninklijke Kaasfabriek Eyssen BV* [1981] ECR 409. This is discussed in more detail in Chapter 5 below. For further discussion on this see also Weatherill, note 22 above, p 43.

[107] Case 216/1984, *Commission v France* (milk substitutes) [1988] ECR 793, para 15.

of the fact that milk is a nutritional product, being a rich source of calcium, while these other foodstuffs to which the Court refers are not necessarily consumed for their nutritional value. Other aspects of the health protection argument were finally quashed when the Court accepted the Commission's argument that milk products themselves also pose risks to people suffering from certain diseases and that there was scientific disagreement as to the actual and potential dangers to human health posed by the consumption of animal and vegetable fats. Again, labelling would be sufficient to inform the consumer as to the nature of the product, enabling them to make any decision on consumption for themselves.

In *Zoni*, the Article 30 EC argument presented was immediately rejected, Italy being unable to offer any evidence that the pasta type prohibited by national law could be harmful to human health, despite claims that pasta containing wheat often contained chemical additives and colourants to alter its organoleptic properties to make it appear more like durum wheat pasta.[108]

The case law of the Court of Justice makes it clear that Article 30 EC cannot be used by Member States to justify national measures designed to improve the standard of their inhabitants' health, in particular through improving the nutritional content of food. National measures that inhibit the free movement of goods may only be justified on health protection grounds where there is a clear danger posed through, for example, contamination or severe adverse reaction to ingredients or a particular combination of ingredients. However, the Court has also been reluctant to accept arguments based on this approach where there is not sufficient scientific evidence to support prohibitive national measures that inhibit the free movement of food in some way. This is now central to much EU food law. Essentially, the Community and the Member States do now have licence to act where they believe that there is a danger posed to human health by a particular foodstuff in some circumstances. Assessing the nature and type or level of evidence that is required to support any such measures is key to ascertaining the limits within which those who wish to may act.

2.2.8 National Authorisation Procedures

One aspect of national law that has come under increased court scrutiny in recent years has been the application of national authorisation procedures for the marketing of foodstuffs. It is this body of case law that has indicated the potential willingness of the Court to allow, in some circumstances, national rules designed to protect human health to stand. However, it should also be noted that this relates only to potential dangers posed. Health preservation remains firmly outside the scope of the Article 30 EC exception.

---

[108] Case 90/1985, *Criminal proceedings against Zoni* [1988] ECR 4285. See also Case 407/1985, *Glocken GmbH and Kritzinger v USL Centro-Sud and Provincia autonoma di Bolzano* [1988] ECR 4233.

In *Commission v Italy*, for example, the Court examined the compatibility of national rules, which required that sports foodstuffs be authorised for use prior to marketing, and that the manufacturer pay resultant administrative costs to the national authorities, with Article 28 EC.[109] The Commission was alerted by a British manufacturer of such foods, in particular energy bars and hydrating drinks, who had experienced difficulty marketing their products in Italy. The respondent State argued that the national authorisation procedure at issue was necessary to protect human health and was therefore justifiable under the terms of Article 30 EC. The Court accepted that, in principle, the national rules were not contrary to Community law, once certain conditions could be satisfied.[110] Such rules would, however, have to be justifiable under the terms of Article 30 EC or one of the *Cassis* and subsequent case law mandatory requirements.

According to the case law, it would be for the national authorities to demonstrate that their rules are necessary in order to meet one of the Article 30 EC public protection derogations. In particular, it would have to be demonstrated that the marketing of the products in question poses a serious risk to public health and that the rules are in conformity with the principle of proportionality.[111] The Court found that these elements were not demonstrated here. In particular, Italy had failed, according to the Court, to explain on what scientific data or medical reports its decision was based, and it had not provided even general information on the nature of the alleged risks, despite requests from the Commission for such information. Furthermore, it was not made clear what the link was between the procedure in question and the alleged risk to public health. Nor were reasons given as to why this method of protection rather than another was chosen, which would have evidenced proportionality to the aims pursued. The Court also accepted that other, more proportionate measures could instead have been used to achieve the same objective, such as providing notification to the relevant authority, together with transmission of a model of the labelling and, if necessary, evidence of the accuracy of the factual data appearing on this label.[112] The Italian procedure was thus contrary to Article 28 EC and not justifiable by the terms of Article 30 EC.

In *Greenham and Abel* the Court examined French legislation which prohibited the sale of foodstuffs containing non-authorised chemical products.[113] The defendants were prosecuted before the national courts for selling foodstuffs containing added co-enzyme Q10, which was not authorised for human consumption

[109] Case C-270/2002, *Commission v Italy* (sports supplements) [2004] ECR I-1559.

[110] See also Case C-344/1990, *Commission v France* (cheese nitrate) [1992] ECR I-4719, para 8; Case C-24/2000, *Commission v France* (fortified foods-'Red Bull') [2004] ECR I-1277, paras 25–27.

[111] Case 227/1982, *Criminal proceedings against Leendert van Bennekom* [1983] ECR 3883, para 40; Case C-358/1995, *Tommaso Morellato v Unità sanitaria locale (USL) n 11 di Pordenone* [1997] ECR I-1431, para 14; Case C-14/2002, *ATRAL SA v Belgium* [2003] ECR I-4431, para 67; Case C-420/2001, *Commission v Italy* (caffeine energy drinks) [2003] ECR I-6445, para 30.

[112] Case C-77/1997, *Österreichische Unilever GmbH v Smithkline Beecham Markenartikel GmbH* [1999] ECR I-431, para 35; Case C-221/2000, *Commission v Austria* (health claims) [2003] ECR I-1007, paras 49 and 52.

[113] Case C-95/2001, *Criminal proceedings against Greenham and Abel* [2004] ECR I-1333.

by the relevant French procedures. The product (juice) also contained vitamins in quantities exceeding recommended daily allowances and safety limits. The defendants argued that the foodstuffs in question were already lawfully marketed in other Member States. The Court was asked whether Articles 28 EC and 30 EC were to be interpreted as prohibiting a Member State from preventing the free movement and marketing of a food supplement lawfully sold in another Member State, in this case due to the fact that the products had not received domestic marketing authorisation.

The Court found that national authorisation procedures could be justified if certain conditions were met. These were: (i) that the rules make provision for a procedure enabling economic operators to have a nutrient included on the national list of authorised substances, this procedure being readily accessible and capable of being completed within a reasonable period of time, and if leading to a refusal, the decision must be open to challenge before the courts;[114] and (ii) that an application to include a nutrient on the national list of authorised substances may be refused by the competent national authorities only if the substance concerned poses a genuine risk to human health.[115] It is for the Member States, in the absence of harmonisation and where there is uncertainty in the scientific research, to decide on the level of protection of human health they wish to ensure and whether to require prior authorisation for the marketing of foodstuffs, taking into account the requirements of the free movement of goods.[116] That discretion is to be particularly wide where scientific uncertainty persists as regards the use of certain nutrients which are not as a general rule harmful in themselves but which may have harmful effects if taken in excess.[117] However, the Court found here that in exercising this discretion in relation to the protection of public health in such circumstances, the Member States must comply with the principle of proportionality. They must exercise their discretion by choosing only such rules as are actually necessary and proportionate to meet the objective pursued. They must not have been able to achieve the aim by imposing less restrictive measures.[118] The national authorities must substantiate any measures adopted that they seek to justify under the terms of Article 30 EC. Such a justification must be based on a case-by-case consideration, taking account of national nutritional habits and international scientific research.[119] Such research should demonstrate that the rules in question were necessary to give effective protection to human health. A detailed risk assessment is thus required to justify any prohibitive national

---

[114] Case C-344/1990, *Commission v France* (cheese nitrate) [1992] ECR I-4719, para 9; Case C-24/2000, *Commission v France* (fortified foods-'Red Bull') [2004] ECR I-1277, para 26.

[115] Case C-192/2001, *Commission v Denmark* (enriched foodstuffs) [2003] ECR I-9693, para 46.

[116] *Ibid*, para 42.

[117] *Ibid*, para 43. See also Case 174/1982, *Criminal proceedings against Sandoz BV* [1983] ECR 2445, para 17.

[118] Case C-95/2001, *Criminal proceedings against Greenham and Abel* [2004] ECR I-1333, para 39; also Case C-192/2001, *Commission v Denmark* (enriched foodstuffs) [2003] ECR I-9693, para 45; Case 174/1982, *Criminal proceedings against Sandoz BV* [1983] ECR 2445, para 18.

[119] Case C-95/2001, *Criminal proceedings against Greenham and Abel* [2004] ECR I-1333, para 40.

measure. The Court found that a decision to prohibit the marketing of a fortified foodstuff, which was described as being 'the most restrictive obstacle to trade in products lawfully manufactured and marketed in other Member States', could thus only be adopted where the alleged risk to public health is sufficiently established on the basis of the latest scientific data available at the time of adopting the contested measure.[120] Where there is still uncertainty as to the level or nature of the potential risk posed, the Member State may, in accordance with the precautionary principle, take protective measures without having to wait until the existence and/or gravity of those risks are fully demonstrated.[121] The assessment must not be based on purely hypothetical considerations.[122] It is for the national court to determine whether the legal and factual circumstances demonstrate that any prohibition, such as that under examination here, satisfies the requirements of Community law in order for such a restriction on the free movement of goods to be justified. Any such national measures must first satisfy the requirements that they are accessible and have an appeals mechanism, and that decisions must follow a detailed and reliable risk assessment.[123]

In *Commission v France*,[124] national rules on the marketing of food supplements and fortified foods which prohibited the sale of such products unless they had received prior authorisation, were examined for compatibility with Article 28 EC. There were three issues here to which the Commission objected. First, it was claimed that the national rules made no provision for mutual recognition of foodstuffs lawfully manufactured or marketed in other Member States to which unauthorised nutrients had been added. Second, the lack of a simplified authorisation procedure was contrary to Community law. Third, there was no justification for refusing to include the unauthorised nutrients at issue on the positive list on public health protection grounds, as had been contended.

It was not disputed that the French legislation constituted a measure of equivalent effect to a quantitative restriction on imports. It was not in principle contrary to Community law either, provided that certain conditions could be satisfied, these being the existence of a readily accessible authorisation procedure, the potential to appeal any refusal to grant authorisation and that refusals only occur where strictly necessary to protect human health.[125] The accessibility requirement can be satisfied if the procedure is expressly provided for in a measure of general application which is binding on the national authorities.[126] The Member State had itself recognised in a reply to a reasoned opinion of the Commission that the

---

[120] Case C-95/2001, *Criminal proceedings against Greenham and Abel* [2004] ECR I-1333, para 42.

[121] Case C-157/1996, *The Queen v National Farmers' Union and others* [1998] ECR I-2211, para 63.

[122] Case C-236/2001, *Monsanto Agricoltura Italia SpA and Others v Presidenza del Consiglio dei Ministri and Others* [2003] ECR I-8105; Case C-192/2001, *Commission v Denmark* (enriched foodstuffs) [2003] ECR I-9693, para 49.

[123] Case C-95/2001, *Criminal proceedings against Greenham and Abel* [2004] ECR I-1333, para 50.

[124] Case C-24/2000, *Commission v France* (fortified foods-'Red Bull') [2004] ECR I-1277.

[125] Case C-344/1990, *Commission v France* (cheese nitrate) [1992] ECR I-4719, paras 8 and 9; Case C-192/2001, *Commission v Denmark* (enriched foodstuffs) [2003] ECR I-9693, paras 44 and 46.

[126] Paragraph 37. See also Case 176/1984, *Commission v Greece* (beer) [1987] ECR 1193, para 41.

national legislation required clarification in this regard. In order to satisfy this, national legislation should specify the information that is to be included on the application and describe the procedure for investigating such an application. The national procedure must also be capable of being completed within a reasonable time. The Commission claimed here that the applicable provisions did not fix any time limit for this. However, key to the findings here was the fact that the application for authorisation to market the drink 'Red Bull' had been lodged with the national authorities seven months before there was any acknowledgement of its receipt. More than two years had passed before the applicant was notified of the decision to reject the application. This, and other similar examples, led the Court to determine that such applications were not being dealt with within a reasonable period of time. Nor were the applications being considered by a procedure that was sufficiently transparent as regards the possibility of challenging a refusal to authorise before the courts. The complaint about the absence of a simplified application procedure was thus considered to be well-founded on the evidence presented.

The third complaint, it will be remembered, was that there were no valid public health protection grounds for justifying the refusal to include certain nutrients on the authorised list. The Court reiterated that it is for the Member States, in the absence of harmonisation, and where there is uncertainty in the current state of scientific research, to decide on the level of human health protection that they wish to ensure, and whether to require prior authorisation for the marketing of foodstuffs, taking into account the free movement of goods within the Community.[127] The discretion allowable here is to be particularly wide where it can be demonstrated that there is still uncertainty in the current state of scientific research as to certain substances, such as vitamins, which are not generally harmful in themselves but may have harmful effects if taken in excess.[128] However, in exercising this discretion, the Member States must adhere to the principle of proportionality, confining any national measures taken in this regard to those which are necessary to safeguard public health or to satisfy mandatory requirements, such as consumer protection.[129] Furthermore, it was stated that since Article 30 EC provides for an exception to the free movement of goods, which must be construed restrictively, it is for the national authorities which invoke it to show in each case that, in the light of national nutritional habits and the results of international scientific research, their rules are necessary to give effective protection. In particular, they must show that the marketing of the products in question poses a real risk to public health.[130] A prohibition on the marketing of foodstuffs to which nutrients have been added must therefore be based on a detailed risk assessment by the

---

[127] Case 174/1982, *Criminal proceedings against Sandoz BV* [1983] ECR 2445, para 16; Case C-192/2001, *Commission v Denmark* (enriched foodstuffs) [2003] ECR I-9693, para 42.
[128] Paragraph 50. See also *Sandoz, ibid,* para 17; *Commission v Denmark, ibid,* para 43.
[129] Paragraph 52. See also *Sandoz, ibid,* para 18; *Commission v Denmark, ibid,* para 45.
[130] Paragraph 53. See also *Commission v Denmark, ibid,* para 46.

Member State invoking Article 30 EC.[131] This assessment must demonstrate that the risk is sufficiently well established by the latest scientific assessments. Where the assessments demonstrate scientific uncertainty, the Member State may invoke the necessary protective measures without having to wait for the existence or gravity of those risks to be fully demonstrated.[132]

France argued that consumers may be encouraged to consume numerous vitamin-enriched foods, augmenting their normal intake from a varied diet, stating that the French population, for the most part, obtains a sufficient intake of most vitamins from their normal diet. There was therefore no nutritional need for nutrients to be added to the foodstuffs concerned. The Court accepted that where there is scientific uncertainty, the criterion of nutritional need of the population of a Member State can play a role in the risk assessment of these fortified foods.[133] However, it was also stated that the absence of such a need cannot by itself justify a total prohibition on the basis of Article 30 EC.[134] Given that the decision to prohibit was based on this reasoning, the Court found that the assessment was not sufficiently detailed to satisfy the exceptions to Article 28 EC available under Community law, both Article 30 EC and the related case law. Lack of nutritional benefit is not sufficient to justify a prohibition, on the basis of Article 30 EC, on marketing foodstuffs lawfully manufactured and/or marketed in other Member States. Establishing the fact that some people might suffer digestive problems if they exceed a maximum recommended vitamin intake does not constitute a sufficiently detailed assessment.[135]

The Court did, however, accept the French argument about the energy drink 'Red Bull'. France could of course, in the absence of harmonisation, decide how best to protect its population. It would, however, have to show that the prohibition on marketing energy drinks containing caffeine exceeding a certain limit was both necessary and proportionate for this purpose.[136] The Scientific Committee on Human Nutrition had already stated that there were negative effects in having certain nutrients such as taurine (sulphur containing amino-acid) and glucurunolactone (a naturally occurring chemical compound produced by the metabolisation of glucose) in drinks. In such circumstances, the Court stated, it would be for the Commission to demonstrate why the French Government's argument based on that assessment would not suffice to justify the refusal to authorise the sale of these energy drinks. The Court concluded that the Commission had not demonstrated this and therefore the complaint about the

---

[131] Paragraph 54. This could potentially mean that if the risk assessment justifies the measure then similar measures should be taken throughout the EU on the basis of the precautionary principle. This is discussed in more detail in Chapter 5 below.

[132] Paragraph 56. See also Case C-157/1996, *The Queen v National Farmers' Union and others* [1998] ECR I-2211, para 63.

[133] Paragraph 59.

[134] Paragraph 60. See also Case C-192/2001, *Commission v Denmark* (enriched foodstuffs) [2003] ECR I-9693, para 54.

[135] Paragraph 65.

[136] Paragraph 69. See also Case C-420/2001, *Commission v Italy* (caffeine energy drinks) [2003] ECR I-6445, paras 30 and 31.

prohibition on marketing energy drinks with a high caffeine content and added taurine and glucurunolactone should be rejected.

Finally, on the issue of consumer protection, the Court found that appropriate labelling, informing consumers about the nature, ingredients and characteristics of fortified foodstuffs, could enable consumers who risk excessive consumption of a nutrient added to those products to decide for themselves whether or not to take them.[137]

The recent case law on the compatibility of national authorisation procedures with Article 28 EC raises a number of interesting points about the direction EU food law is taking in this area. Primarily, it is quite clear that Member States may have such procedures in place. Their existence can be justified by Article 30 EC, provided that they can be considered to be 'accessible, independent and transparent'. Decisions must be open to appeal by aggrieved applicants. Allowing such procedures to exist indicates a notable softening in the Court's willingness to accept Member States' justifications for continuing to impose measures equivalent to quantitative restrictions on intra-Community trade.[138] National authorisation procedures inhibit trade by adding expense to the marketing process, and by increasing the length of time it takes to get the foodstuff onto the marketplace. Despite this, they are allowable once they do not overly inhibit market access.

Compare this, for example, with the decision made on the German beer purity rules. Here, the Member State clearly demonstrated that the use of additives in the production of beer was not necessary. Additive use presents a danger to human health.[139] The Member State did not prohibit their use, only the marketing of beverages containing additives as 'bier'. Article 30 EC justifications put forward were rejected. Now, following the decisions in *Greenham and Abel* and *Commission v France* (Red Bull), the presentation of some evidence that adding nutrients to food may present a danger suffices to justify the measure that is equivalent to a quantitative restriction under Article 30 EC. This measure may even be an outright prohibition on marketing—not previously allowable by the Court in such circumstances. Formerly, a clear danger arising out of contamination or disease had to exist before any national trade-inhibiting measure could be justified by the Article 30 EC exception. What has brought about this change in the Court's handling of Article 30 EC claims? It is suggested that there is greater acceptance by all the Community institutions since the BSE crisis that the protection of human health must be placed at the top of the food law agenda to both regain and retain consumers' confidence. This is discussed in more detail in Chapter 5.

---

[137] Paragraph 75.

[138] Similarly, acceptance of Article 30 EC justifications have also been apparent more recently in *Schwarz*, where Austrian rules prohibiting the sale of unwrapped sweets from vending machines were deemed justifiable on public health grounds. Case C-366/2004, *Georg Schwarz v Bürgermeister der Landeshauptstadt Salzburg* [2005] ECR I-10139.

[139] See, for example, JP Groten *et al*, 'An analysis of the possibility for health implications of joint actions and interactions between food additives' (2000) 31 *Regulatory Toxicology and Pharmacology* 77; and DO Carpenter, K Arcaro and DC Spink, 'Understanding the Human Health Effects of Chemical Mixtures' (2002) 110 *Environmental Health Perspectives* 25.

2.2.9 Common Agricultural Policy Justification

Finally, another justification for the existence of national rules acting contrary to Article 28 EC that has been put forward by Member States, with equally limited success, is that the measure in question helps to promote the aims and objectives of the Common Agricultural Policy. In *Commission v Germany* it was contended that the contested ban on the importation of certain meat products was necessary to meet the requirements of the Common Agricultural Policy, particularly the aim of stabilising the market pursued by the common organisations of the markets in beef, veal and pig-meat.[140] This argument was not accepted, the Court finding, as it had done previously,[141] that once the Community has established a common market organisation in a particular sector, Member States must refrain from taking any unilateral measure, even if that measure is likely to support the common policy. It was stated that it was also clear from these judgments that, even if they support a common Community policy, such measures must not conflict with one of the fundamental principles of the Treaty, in this case the free movement of goods, unless they are justified by reasons that are recognised by Community law. This was not found to be the case here.

Similarly, in *Commission v France* the assertion that a national prohibition on the sale of milk substitutes was consonant with the aims pursued by the Common Agricultural Policy was not accepted by the Court because national measures such as those at issue could not act contrary to the fundamental principle of the free movement of goods in any circumstances, unless justified by reasons recognised by Community law.[142]

In *Commission v Germany* the Court,[143] citing *Commission v France*[144] and *Centro-Sud*,[145] reiterated that once the Community has established a common market organisation in a particular sector, the Member States must refrain from taking any unilateral measure that consequently falls within the competence of the Community. It was for the Community and not the Member State to seek a solution to any problem in the context of the Common Agricultural Policy. Even where supporting a common Community policy, national measures may not conflict with one of the fundamental principles of the Community unless justifiable by reasons organised by Community law.[146]

[140] Case 274/1987, *Commission v Germany* (meat products) [1989] ECR 229.
[141] Case 216/1984, *Commission v France* (milk substitutes) [1988] ECR 793; Case 407/1985, *Glocken GmbH and Kritzinger v USL Centro-Sud and Provincia autonoma di Bolzano* [1988] ECR 4233.
[142] Case 216/1984, *Commission v France* (milk substitutes) [1988] ECR 793.
[143] Case 76/1986, *Commission v Germany* (milk substitutes) [1989] ECR 1021.
[144] Case 216/1984, note 143 above, paras 18 and 19.
[145] Case 407/1985, *Glocken GmbH and Kritzinger v USL Centro-Sud and Provincia autonoma di Bolzano* [1988] ECR 4233, para 26.
[146] Case 76/1986, *Commission v Germany* (milk substitutes) [1989] ECR 1021, para 20.

2.3 TAXES AND DUTIES ON THE MOVEMENT OF FOOD

As we have seen, Article 28 EC seeks to promote the free movement of goods by limiting the circumstances in which Member States will be permitted to have domestic consumer protection or human health protection rules in place. In the remaining part of this chapter we show that Article 25 EC, on customs duties and measures of equivalent effect, and Article 90 EC, on internal taxation that discriminates in favour of domestically produced goods in some way, seek to promote the free movement of goods by ensuring, primarily, that imports are fully able to compete on price. By illegitimising charges for border checks being passed on to importers, Article 25 EC removes an additional cost of importation. By prescribing that similar amounts of tax be charged on similar products, Article 90 EC effectively removes the last remaining possibility of Member States protecting domestic production in an indirect or disguised manner.

2.3.1 Internal Taxation on Imported Foodstuffs

Article 90 EC (ex 95) states:

> No Member State shall impose, directly or indirectly, on the products of other Member States any internal taxation of any kind in excess of that imposed directly or indirectly on similar domestic products.
>
> Furthermore, no Member State shall impose on the products of other Member States any internal taxation of such a nature as to afford indirect protection to other products.

In relation to the free movement of food, this has come to mean that national taxation systems levying a lower rate of tax on foods produced in their territory in abundance, and a higher rate on foods produced widely, contravene the Treaty. The most obvious examples of such discriminatory taxation regimes are those where imported alcoholic drinks are taxed at a higher rate than those produced domestically, for example charging a high rate of tax on wine which is not widely produced in the State of taxation, as opposed to charging a relatively low rate of tax on beer which is produced throughout the same State.

In any Article 90 EC case, the first issue that must be examined is whether the products on which the different rates of tax are charged are in competition with each other, because, of course, Member States are perfectly entitled to charge different rates of tax on different types of products that are not interchangeable with each other. The process of determining whether apparently different types of goods are competing in the same market is not always clear-cut. For example, while wine and beer both form part of the market in alcoholic beverages, it is not so easy to establish that they share enough of the same characteristics to be deemed interchangeable with each other when it comes to consumer preferences. In other words, would the consumer with a preference for wine be willing to purchase beer instead, if it were more competitively priced? Similarly, bananas and apples may both be fruit, but for Article 90 EC to be applicable it must first be ascertained whether those who tend to consume the soft banana that comes in its own wrapping would also be keen on hard apples that require washing prior to consumption.

In *Commission v France* a national taxation system that charged the same purchase tax on cereal-based spirits (whiskey) as fruit-based spirits (brandy) but charged a manufacturing tax on the former only was examined for compatibility with Article 90 EC.[147] There was no significant production of cereal-based spirits in France. After establishing that the two categories of spirit shared sufficient common features, most notably the occasions on which they are likely to be consumed, the Court determined that they were in at least partial competition with each other. The fact that the two types of spirit were deemed interchangeable, coupled with the fact that domestically produced spirits were more likely to come within the more favourable tax category than imported spirits, meant that the tax system applied by France here was incompatible with Article 90 EC. The fact that another domestic product, aniseed spirits, also fell within the disadvantaged category did not mean that the system was not protective in nature. Nor was this disproved by the evidence presented to the Court illustrating that the market share of whiskey had increased in spite of the tax disadvantage that it suffered.

Similarly, wine and beer have been deemed to be in competition with each other for the purpose of Article 90 EC examination.[148] The Court has considered that the two beverages are capable of meeting identical needs. It was accepted that beer was in competition with wines that have an alcohol content of nine per cent, based on the fact that these are the most accessible to the public, being the lightest and cheapest varieties. Given that wine was subjected to a much higher rate of tax than beer in the United Kingdom, that Member State was deemed to have in place a system of taxation which subjected wine imported from other Member States to an additional tax burden so as to afford protection to domestic beer production contrary to Article 90 EC.

It is not always clear whether an unfair charge imposed by a Member State on an imported food product may fall within the type prohibited by Article 25 EC on the one hand or Article 90 EC on the other. The consequences of this can be very important when determining what the fate is to be when such a charge is found to be contrary to either Treaty prohibition. As discussed below, Article 25 EC contains an absolute prohibition. Any such charges, no matter how small, are contrary to the Treaty. The practice of imposing such charges must cease. However, a system of taxation that favours a domestic food product over an import with which it is interchangeable may continue, even where found to be contrary to Article 90 EC. The taxation need not stop, it just has to be modified to remove the effect which has been adjudged to be protective.

---

[147] Case 168/1978, *Commission v France* (spirit tax) [1980] ECR 347.
[148] Case 170/1978, *Commission v UK* (wine and beer tax) [1983] ECR 2265.

In *Co-frutta* it had to be determined whether an Italian tax on banana consumption was caught by the prohibition set down in Article 25 EC or Article 90 EC.[149] While Italy did produce some bananas, home-produced bananas constituted a very small proportion of the total tonnage consumed there (150 tonnes out of 357,500 in 1985). However, similar taxes were charged on other tropical foodstuffs sold in Italy, such as coffee and cocoa, as well as on other products including spirits, beer, sugar and margarine. The Court found that the essential feature of a charge having an effect equivalent to a customs duty that distinguishes it from an internal tax is the fact that the former is borne solely by an imported product. The latter is borne by both imported and domestic products. However, it had also been recognised that where a charge is borne by a product imported from another Member State and there is no identical or similar domestic product available, then this charge will be considered to be internal taxation within the meaning of Article 90 EC if it relates to a general system of internal taxation applied systematically to categories of products, irrespective of the origin of those products. This tax at issue here was deemed to form part of such a general domestic system.

Once it had been established that it was Article 90 EC that was applicable here and not Article 25 EC, the Court had to ascertain whether the charge was designed to protect other fruit on the national market, in particular that typically grown in Italy. This was tested on the basis of organoleptic qualities, water content and satisfaction of consumer needs. The Court found here, as it did in *Commission v Italy*,[150] that bananas offer an alternative choice to consumers as fruit. Table fruit typically produced in Italy included apples, pears, peaches, plums, apricots, cherries, oranges and mandarins. These were all differentiated from bananas. Points of difference included the higher water content of pears and other fruit typically grown in Italy, which were seen to possess thirst-quenching properties that bananas do not possess. They were not 'similar products'. However, while this determined that Article 90(1) EC did not apply, the question of whether Article 90(2) EC, on 'other products', was relevant here would have to be tested. Bananas were found to be in at least partial competition with these other fruits due to the interchangeability level of the fruits concerned. While consumers may not choose an apple when they really want a banana, they may choose the banana on occasions if it is competitively priced, and if they are not thirsty. The national taxation system was indirectly protecting domestically grown fruit from competition from other fruits grown elsewhere due to the higher taxation levels imposed on fruits that were not widely produced domestically. The Italian charge was a form of taxation. It was also contrary to Article 90 EC.

---

[149] Case 193/1985, *Cooperativa Co-frutta Srl v Amministrazione delle finanze dello Stato* [1987] ECR 2085.
[150] Case 184/1985, *Commission v Italy* (banana consumption tax) [1987] ECR 2013.

2.3.2   Measures Equivalent to Customs Duties on Intra-Community Food Trade

The primary way in which Article 25 EC can impact upon the free movement of food in the EU is in those situations where a Member State imposes a charge for an inspection carried out at its border. Article 25 EC (ex 12) states that:

> Customs duties on imports and exports and charges having equivalent effect shall be prohibited between Member States. This prohibition shall also apply to customs duties of a fiscal nature.

The Court has made it clear that it is the effect, and not the purpose, of a customs duty, or a charge of equivalent effect to a duty, that is important when assessing whether or not such a levy contravenes Community law.[151] Essentially, any additional charge imposed on either the exportation or importation of goods between Member States, no matter how small, or how it is imposed, is prohibited. This includes payment for a service conducted by a Member State, such as, in some circumstances, an inspection to check that food is safe to eat. It is only where a Member State imposes a charge for an inspection that is mandatory under Community law that the Court will accept that it does not contravene Article 25 EC.[152]

The issue of whether veterinary inspection charges imposed on imports were equivalent to customs duties, even where domestic products and producers were subject to a similar charge, was examined in *Bresciani*.[153] It had already been held that pecuniary charges imposed for reasons of public health examination of products when they cross from one Member State into another were regarded as charges having an effect equivalent to customs duties.[154] In *Bresciani* it was made clear that any pecuniary charge, however small, imposed on goods by reason of the fact that they cross a frontier constitutes an obstacle to the free movement of these goods. Further to this, it was stated that it was of no importance in this regard that the charge imposed was proportionate to the expense of a public health inspection carried out on the goods. An inspection carried out for this purpose was not seen to be a service rendered to the importer which could be lawfully charged to them. The costs of these inspections would have to be met by the Member State. Taxpayers within those Member States were benefiting from the free movement of goods. Costs incurred in the operation of this single market should therefore be borne by the public purse. The fact that domestic production was subject to similar charges for slaughterhouse inspections was not to be taken into account either, unless those charges were applied according to the same criteria and at the same stage of production as those faced by the imported product. It was held that no

---

[151]   See, for example, Case 7/1968, *Commission v Italy* (art exports) [1968] ECR 423; Cases 2/1969 and 3/1969, *Sociaal Fonds voor de Diamantarbeiders v SA Ch Brachfeld & Sons* [1969] ECR 211; for charges of equivalent effect more specifically, see Case 24/1968, *Commission v Italy* (statistical levy) [1969] ECR 193.

[152]   Case 46/1976, *Bauhuis v The Netherlands* [1977] ECR 5.

[153]   Case 87/1975, *Conceria Daniele Bresciani v Amministrazione Italiana delle Finanze* [1976] ECR 129.

[154]   Case 84/1971, *SpA Marimex v Ministero delle Finanze* [1972] ECR 89.

matter what the name or method of applying a charge was, it was to be considered to be a charge having equivalent effect to a customs duty when it was imposed unilaterally on goods imported from another Member State at the point of crossing a frontier, and therefore that its imposition would be contrary to Community law.

Charges imposed for inspecting imported poultry meat were examined for compatibility with Article 25 EC in *Commission v Belgium*.[155] Here, Belgian national law prescribed that all poultry meat intended for human consumption must undergo a health check. This check consisted of inspections, both ante- and post-mortem, at Belgian abattoirs, as well as checks at the meat processing plants and during distribution. Imported poultry meat was inspected either at the customs office or at the final destination of the goods, as well as those stages at which domestic meat would also have been examined. Belgium had contended that Directive 1971/118 allowed a Member State to prohibit the marketing of imported poultry meat if it was found to be unfit for human consumption and that this therefore provided that a fee may be charged for any inspection designed to ascertain the fitness of the meat for such consumption.[156] This was rejected. The provision of the directive that was relied upon did not oblige the Member State to carry out any inspection, it merely permitted it.[157] The directive could not be relied upon to justify the charge, which was of equivalent effect to a customs duty, as the inspection was not necessary in order to apply the terms of the directive.

In *Bauhuis* a cattle dealer sought a refund for fees paid for veterinary and public health inspections carried out by Dutch administrative authorities prior to the export of live animals to other Member States.[158] Directive 1964/432 prescribed that such checks take place, provision having to be made for the issuing of a health certificate to accompany the animals to their destination.[159] The fact that these inspections were prescribed by the Council through Community law meant that they could not be regarded as unilateral measures which hinder trade; they were rather operations intended to promote the free movement of goods, in particular by rendering ineffective the obstacles to this free movement which might be created by the measures for veterinary and public health inspections adopted pursuant to Article 30 EC. Fees charged to cover the costs of an inspection that is prescribed by a Community provision do not constitute 'a charge having an effect equivalent to a customs duty on exports', provided that the charge does not exceed the actual cost of the inspection. This decision was later reaffirmed in *Commission v Germany*, where charges were passed on for inspections carried out on live

---

[155] Case 314/1982, *Commission v Belgium* (imported poultry meat) [1984] ECR 1543.

[156] Council Directive 1971/118/EEC of 15 February 1971 on health problems affecting trade in fresh poultrymeat. [1971] OJ L 55/23; English Special Edition Series I, Chapter 1971(1), p 106.

[157] Article 9(1) thereof states: '... a Member State may prohibit the marketing in its territory of fresh poultrymeat coming from another Member State if at the time of the health inspection carried out in the country of destination it is found that ... such meat is unfit for human consumption.'

[158] Case 46/1976, *Bauhuis v Netherlands* [1977] ECR 5.

[159] Council Directive 1964/432/EEC of 26 June 1964 on animal health problems affecting intra-Community trade in bovine animals and swine. [1964] OJ L 121/1977; English Special Edition Series I, Chapter 1963–4, p 164.

animals during transit to ensure that minimum Community standards on animal welfare were being met.[160] The Court summarised the exception to Article 25 EC, stating that such fees may not be classified as charges having an effect equivalent to a customs duty if the following conditions are satisfied: (i) they do not exceed the actual cost of the inspections in connection with which they are charged; (ii) the inspections in question are obligatory and uniform for all products concerned in the Community; (iii) they are prescribed by Community law in the general interest of the Community; and (iv) they promote the free movement of goods, in particular by neutralising obstacles which could arise from unilateral measures of inspection adopted in accordance with Article 30 EC. These conditions were deemed to be satisfied by the contested fee in this case.

Overall, the Article 25 EC case law clearly demonstrates that Member States may not impose a charge on imported food coming from elsewhere within the Union to cover the costs of inspecting these products, unless that type of inspection is obligatory and has been specifically prescribed by Community law. This is contrary to general Community policy in this area for two reasons. First, the limited exceptions to the rule in Article 25 EC on imposing charges for inspections that the importing Member State deems necessary for human health protection purposes is at odds with the acceptance by the Court in more recent Article 30 EC case law that similar charges may be passed on by the relevant authorities in importing States that require that foodstuffs be subject to a rigorous authorisation procedure prior to their lawful marketing there. Second, in post-BSE Europe, the institutions, and in particular the Commission, have sought to both initiate their own, and support the Member States', programmes designed to guarantee that only food that is safe is marketed. By obliging Member States to absorb the costs of carrying out inspections on imported food and livestock themselves, even where Community law has recognised that there is a potential danger posed by disease or contamination, as Article 25 EC does, these States are faced with a dilemma. They must either accept this financial burden, or assume that safety inspections carried out in the exporting State meet the required standard. This latter option must be further qualified by an acceptance that the exporting State has been willing to absorb these costs themselves as Article 25 EC also applies to charges of equivalent effect to customs duties on exports.

The jurisprudence of the Court on Article 25 EC is very clear. Exceptions to the primary prohibition on this type of behaviour by Member States are limited and well-defined. These rules, and the Court clarifications based upon them, have been long established in Community law. The key cases here all date from the late 1960s to the early 1980s. The rules have become so well established that they are no longer subject to constant challenge, unlike the Articles 28–30 EC jurisprudence which is evolving. One of the key reasons for this is that many of the inspections

---

[160] Case 18/1987, *Commission v Germany* [1988] ECR 8427. The standards were set down in Article 2(1) of Council Directive 1981/389/EEC of 12 May 1981 establishing measures necessary for the implementation of Directive 1977/489/EEC on the protection of animals during international transport. [1981] OJ L 150/1.

now undertaken by Member States are covered by Community legislation. These fall outside the scope of the definition of a measure equivalent to a customs duty as clarified by the Court in *Commission v Germany*. However, for those inspections that the Member State deems necessary that are not covered by any such legislation the dilemma remains. It becomes acute when 'food crises' arise, prior to any emergency or other measures being adopted to deal with the situation. It is possible that in such circumstances, the Member States may be able to act on a precautionary basis, but this is likely to extend to conducting the inspections themselves rather than to covering the passing on of costs incurred to the importer as well.[161] It is further subject to the requirement that sufficient evidence exists to demonstrate that the risk posed to human or animal health is real and potentially serious.

Several key points emerge from an examination of the Article 25 EC case law as it relates to the free movement of food. The decisions of the Court here receive relatively little attention now, primarily because the case law is so well settled at this stage. Article 25 EC contains an absolute prohibition, with exceptions to the general rule a rarity. Clear principles derive from a rule of this nature. Charges of equivalent effect to customs duties may not be passed from the Member State to the importer or exporter unless they are to cover the costs of an inspection specifically prescribed by Community law. However, it is possible that the case law in this area will soon receive more attention, for two connected reasons. The first relates to the new direction that EU food law and policy has taken in the aftermath of the BSE crisis. The emphasis is now firmly on preventing unsafe food from entering the supply chain. This enables Member States to take precautionary action where they suspect, but cannot necessarily verify, that a food source may be unsafe. These precautionary measures include inspections of imported food. The Member State is faced with a dilemma. It can either accept that the safety standards in the suspected Member State are of an acceptable level, thus dispensing with the requirement for any additional inspection.[162] Alternatively, the importing Member State can require an additional inspection of the food, paying for this inspection itself. This latter option presents a disincentive to inspect, leaving suspected threats to food safety unexamined. This is entirely at odds with present Community policy designed to ensure that only the safest of food makes it onto the market. It also fails to support Member States and Community institutions in their efforts to protect human health. That is the general reason.

The more specific grounds for stating that Article 25 EC jurisprudence may now require re-examination is that the body of recent cases on the compatibility of

---

[161] Inspections carried out by Member States on imported foodstuffs only, and not on domestically produced goods, remain subject to the prohibition set out in Article 28 EC where no reasonable Article 30 EC justification exists. See Case 4/1975, *Rewe-Zentralfinanze GmbH v Landwirtschaftskammer* [1975] ECR 843.

[162] Guidelines for testing the equivalence of sanitary measures do exist at international level. See Codex Alimentarius Guidelines on the Judgment of Equivalence of Sanitary Measures Associated with Food Inspection and Certification Systems. Codex Guidelines 53/2003.

national authorisation procedures with Article 28 EC suggests this. The decisions of the Court here state that these procedures must be accessible and necessary. They do not determine that the charges imposed on an application for authorisation have to be borne by the importing Member State. As with the impermissible charges of equivalent effect to a customs duty, these authorisation costs are not part of a system specifically prescribed by Community law. Presumably, the Member State has the procedure in place because it believes that there may be a risk to human health—just as the Member State that insists on inspecting imported poultry meat believes that such a risk exists. There is no real reason why, where the Member State can demonstrate that the inspection is necessary, or alternatively its lack of a protective element, charges for inspections for health protection purposes should not also be passed on to the importer. The only justification offered for preventing this from happening thus far has been that if the citizens of Member States benefit from the free movement of goods generally, then the costs of inspections should be covered by the importing State's general revenues that it takes from these same citizens. Nobody benefits from the free movement of what could be dangerous food.[163] It is difficult to see how in the light of this new policy direction, coupled with the increased acceptance of the precautionary principle, decisions such as *Bresciani* and particularly *Commission v Belgium*, where the introduction of secondary legislation demonstrated that a potential danger had been recognised at Community level, can remain unchallenged when compared to the acceptance of the additional costs being imposed on importers who must comply with a national authorisation procedure before marketing their product, as was the case in both *Commission v Denmark* and *Commission v France*.

At present, therefore, Article 25 EC does not allow Member States to pass on the costs of inspecting imported food. There is an exception: where this is specifically prescribed by Community law. Where the Community has introduced legislation facilitating the possibility of conducting inspections, recognising that a potential danger to human health exists, Member States may not pass costs in relation to this on to the importer. It is now difficult to reconcile this position with the more general Community position of ensuring that food is as safe as possible, as adopted post-BSE crisis, and culminating in the publication of the White Paper on Food Safety, and ultimately leading to the establishment of the European Food Safety Authority.

2.4 CONCLUSION

The case law of the European Court of Justice makes it clear that a Member State will be in breach of its Treaty obligations where measures that restrict the free movement of food in some way are adopted to protect consumers, to support fair trade, or to promote human health. The only exception to this is where the offending State can adequately demonstrate that it could not have chosen a less

---

[163] Assuming there is no dishonesty involved.

restrictive alternative measure to achieve the same aim. Since the decision in *Cassis*, once a foodstuff is lawfully marketable in one Member State it must be lawfully marketable in all. While this obviously facilitates free movement, the limited way in which the exceptions to this mutual recognition rule have been applied runs counter to other provisions of the EC Treaty, most notably Article 30 EC, but also potentially Article 151 EC on promoting national and regional diversity, Article 152 EC on protecting human health and Article 153 EC on safeguarding consumer interests.[164] While the Court has been more ready to accept health protection justifications based upon Article 30 EC in recent years, exceptions to the fundamental principle of free movement for goods continue to be interpreted in an overly restrictive manner.

In general, the only measure that Member States may be allowed to adopt to protect consumers or human health is to require that products display more explicit information on their labelling. This is less restrictive of intra-Community trade than a prohibition on the use of a particular food name, for example. However, as has been demonstrated here, this does not present a solution in many circumstances where a Member State seeks to provide protection from deceptive practices or unsafe food. By creating a panacea such as this, the Court has failed to distinguish between the different sets of circumstances that are presented before it. Allowing two bottles of liqueur with roughly the same level of alcohol content to be marketed using the same name may be acceptable where the label brings this to the attention of the consumer, but allowing an alcohol-free version to use the same name is a different matter altogether. In addition to this, requiring that the labelling be altered to indicate a difference that exists between an imported product and one generally known by that name in the host State is also contrary to Article 28 EC in many situations. It is on the basis of the reasoning in these cases that the Commission subsequently decided to cease setting harmonised compositional standards for individual foodstuffs. A limited re-introduction of this programme is now required to address the many deficiencies and inconsistencies that exist within the Article 28 EC case law, as have been identified in this chapter. This is discussed further in Chapters 3 and 7 below.

---

[164] For further discussion see C MacMaoláin, 'Free Movement of Foodstuffs, Quality Requirements and Consumer Protection: Have the Court and the Commission Both Got It Wrong?' (2001) 26 *European Law Review* 413.

3

Harmonising Food Standards in the EU: Labelling, Naming and Quality Preservation

3.1 INTRODUCTION

A S WITH MANY other aspects of the development of Community law, the Courts, through their intervention in the integration process, increased the pace in creating the single market for foodstuffs.[1] The Court of Justice's expansive interpretation of the rule on measures equivalent to quantitative restrictions, and its restrictive interpretation of the exceptions, removed the immediate need for legislative intervention facilitating free movement.

However, some harmonising legislation had already been introduced prior to the decision in *Cassis*.[2] A piecemeal and discordant set of standards, primarily directives, had been drafted to set common rules for the production and marketing of food in the Community. This legislation was both vertical (applying to specific foodstuffs only) and horizontal (applying to all foodstuffs) in nature. The vertical legislation consisted primarily of a series of directives setting compositional requirements for some foods, such as chocolate and honey. The horizontal legislation included standardised rules for all foodstuffs, such as those setting out how the weight or volume of a product was first to be determined and then labelled. One thing was very clear from the body of legislation that was devised, if it can be called a body: it would never have the desired effect of creating a single market for foodstuffs. The various pieces of secondary legislation were largely unrelated to each other, dealing with diverse, usually very specific, aspects of the food production process. However, it is here contended that developing a variation on this system in a more co-ordinated manner may now be the best way of resolving the difficulties relating to quality maintenance and consumer protection that have developed post-*Cassis*, as discussed in Chapter 2 above. What is now required is an amalgamation of the Court-developed principles stemming from its

---

[1] See also A Arnull, *The European Union and its Court of Justice* 2nd edn (Oxford, OUP, 2006); LN Brown and T Kennedy, *The Court of Justice of the European Communities* 5th edn (London, Sweet & Maxwell, 2000).

[2] Case 120/1978, *Rewe-Zentral AG v Bundesmonopolverwaltung für Branntwein* [1979] ECR 649.

Articles 28–30 EC case law with a set of clear, vertical and horizontal, directives and regulations, setting minimum standards for the production and marketing of food throughout the Union.

This chapter commences by illustrating how the Community institutions arrived at the conclusion that setting harmonised food standards was no longer necessary in the post-*Cassis* era. It will be shown that such an approach is overly simplistic and threatens the quality and diversity of foodstuffs available in the EU. The legislation that has been brought into existence in attempts to equalise the national rules of the 25 Member States is then assessed. In particular, Community legislators have introduced harmonising measures that set minimum standards for the protection of consumers by devising some general rules on food labelling. Arising out of this, and following on from inherent problems that can be created for consumers by invoking the mutual recognition principle, rules have also been developed on the use of specific, in particular geographical, food names. This system is primarily designed to preserve the high quality of these foodstuffs. It is here claimed, following a detailed examination of these rules and the related case law, that the system for protecting geographical food names has not had the desired effect. As a consequence, it is demonstrated how further recourse to, and utilisation of, an already existing Community mechanism for protecting the reputation of food products—namely the use of character certificates—should now take place in order to properly preserve the quality and diversity of foodstuffs available in the Member States. The chapter concludes by outlining some of the vertical measures that have been introduced to harmonise standards for specific food products. It is then argued that the increased use of similar legislative initiatives could help to remedy some of the difficulties identified.

3.2 COMPLETING THE INTERNAL MARKET: COMMUNITY LEGISLATION ON FOODSTUFFS

The Commission produced a communication in 1985, as a follow-up to its White Paper on completing the internal market,[3] setting out its strategy for the creation of a single market in the foodstuffs sector.[4] The White Paper suggested that the recommended strategy for achieving this aim by the completion date of 1992 was to move away from reliance on traditional methods of harmonisation and towards combining the principles of mutual recognition of national regulations and standards based on Articles 28 to 30 EC with a more efficient mechanism for the harmonisation of laws based, in particular, on Articles 94 EC (ex 100) and 95 EC (ex 100a).[5] It was stated in the Communication that two significant advances in

---

[3] Commission White Paper on completing the internal market. COM (85) 310.

[4] Communication from the Commission to the Council and to the European Parliament on the completion of the internal market: Community legislation on foodstuffs. COM (85) 603.

[5] Ex Articles 100 and 100a. The White Paper stated that two communications would be required to clarify how the Community should best proceed on both the harmonisation and mutual recognition issues (ss 71 and 156). The first of these to be introduced was the 1985 Communication on the completion of the internal market in the foodstuffs sector. COM (85) 603 final. The second, on the free

Community law could assist in this process. The first was to extend the provisions of Directive 1983/189, which obliges Member States to notify the Commission in advance of draft technical regulations and standards, to the foodstuffs sector.[6] The second was to extend the scope of the Council Resolution on a new approach to technical harmonisation and standards, which was designed to simplify and speed up the decision-making process for opening up the internal market, to the food-stuffs sector.[7] It was recognised that this latter option would require more careful planning given the nature of the food sector, in particular due to the sensitivity of public opinion in this field, the detailed nature of many national laws and the almost complete lack of standards defining the composition of products. In order to implement this strategy, the Commission would be required to make a clear distinction between those matters that still required legislative action, and those that did not. A new distinction would have to be made between subjects that would require the legislative powers of the Council and those that were within the Commission's competence. The Communication noted that the existing system of decision-making in the Council led to a series of impasses that were blocking progress in the development of Community food legislation. A clear example of this could be seen in relation to the negotiations on the alteration of the composi-tional rules for chocolate.[8] Unless this changed, disputes on the basis of Article 28 EC would require regular recourse to the Courts. Given the unsatisfactory position that this would create, in particular for an already overburdened Court system and overstretched Commission, it was suggested that many matters that required unanimous Council approval could instead be switched to the simplified and qualified majority Standing Committee on Foodstuffs procedure. Responsibility for the basic rules of Community food law would remain with the Council. This would be appropriate given the Council's relative success in obtaining agreement on framework horizontal legislative measures when compared to the slim possibility of obtaining agreement on more specific matters, such as the approval of new additives that were considered by the scientific committees to be safe enough to be included on the Community positive lists for such substances. The Commission would be responsible for overseeing the implementation of the leg-islative measures adopted by the Council. The Standing Committee for Foodstuffs procedure would ensure close co-operation between the Member States and the Commission. In all circumstances, however, where a potential public health prob-lem existed, the Scientific Committee for Food would have to be consulted. Other measures that would have to be taken to remove all obstructions to the advance-ment of Community food legislation included the following: derogations for

---

movement of foodstuffs within the Community, which was due to be published in 1987, appeared in 1989. [1989] OJ C 271/3.

[6] Council Directive 1983/189/EEC of 28 March 1983 laying down a procedure for the provision of information in the field of technical standards and regulations. [1983] OJ L 109/8.

[7] Council Resolution on the new approach to technical harmonisation and standards. [1985] OJ C 136/1.

[8] As discussed in Chapter 1 above.

Member States from Community legislation of general application, such as the framework directive on food labelling, would need to be eliminated.

The Communication noted the acceptance of the principle that technical barriers to trade in foodstuffs resulting from mandatory national provisions could be eliminated only by adopting a Community provision of the same nature. The harmonisation programme that was adopted in 1969, and later updated in 1973, was based on that approach. This programme had suggested that there were 50 sectors relating to food which required Community legislation. By 1985, directives had been adopted in only 14 of these sectors, with proposals outstanding in a further six. Those already supported by harmonising legislation included labelling, preservative use, antioxidant use and foods for particular nutritional uses. There were proposals outstanding for sampling and analysis methods, the use of flavourings, the use of extraction solvents, chemically modified starches, frozen foods, and baby foods. Measures were also being prepared to control the use of irradiation techniques and inspection measures. Hence good progress had been made in relation to the introduction of horizontal measures of general application (such as labelling or additive use), but this was not the case for vertical restraints, which related to specific foodstuffs. There were several recipe laws, setting compositional requirements for products such as chocolate, honey and fruit juice, but this list had not been expanded.[9] It had in fact remained relatively unaltered since the mid-1970s. This suggested to the Commission that the Member States appeared to be able to agree on the general principles of food legislation, but they found it difficult to reconcile their differences regarding requirements for the composition of individual foodstuffs. It was claimed in the Communication that the legislative approach previously followed was based on the assumption that all specific requirements in national legislation on foodstuffs met an essential public need. The Communication called for a revision to this approach, which should be based on a distinction between matters which by their nature must continue to be the subject of legislation and matters which do not need to be regulated. The principles developed by the Court of Justice in *Cassis* and its subsequent case law would now enable the Community to define a system of food legislation that contained only provisions that could be justified as being necessary to satisfy essential requirements in the general interest. Measures would have to conform strictly to the principle of proportionality. As a consequence, any future Community legislation on foodstuffs would have to be limited to provisions justified by (i) the need to protect public health; (ii) the need to provide consumers with information and protection in matters other than health; (iii) the need to ensure fair trading; or (iv) the need to provide for the necessary public controls.

---

[9] Under what have become known as the 'recipe laws', authorisation to use certain product names was a reward for compositional correctness. These rules assumed special importance within the European Union due to frantic efforts to establish a set of standard harmonised rules throughout the common market. Examples of the recipe laws include Directive 1973/241/EEC, [1973] OJ L 228/23, on the approximation of the laws of the Member States relating to cocoa and chocolate products intended for human consumption, and Directive 1974/409/EEC, [1974] OJ L 221/10, on the harmonisation of the laws of the Member States relating to honey. These are examined in more detail later in this chapter.

This serves to illustrate precisely what was developing, and continues to develop, as regards how the Community institutions view the purpose of Community law. Essentially, Article 28 EC could be invoked if any national measure was not strictly necessary, and it would be for the Community Courts to determine necessity. As a general rule, it might be difficult to prove that any legislation not introduced by the Community was 'necessary'. However, this then raises further questions about the role of the Community in determining which national rules are to be deemed necessary. If the Member State introduces rules to protect human health, for example, these are likely to be found contrary to Article 28 EC if they inhibit the free movement of food in any way. However, if on one of those rare occasions where the Court does find that a mandatory requirement or Article 30 EC exception can be successfully pleaded by the Member State, then the Community institutions should likewise be compelled to introduce similar measures in order to afford the same protection to human health or consumers throughout the Union.

The Communication then turned to examine each of the three key exceptions to the prohibition on measures equivalent to quantitative restrictions in turn, assessing whether harmonising legislation would still be required in each case.

3.2.1 Public Health Protection

The Communication recognised that the need to protect human health is reflected in the national laws of all the Member States. Consequently, the Council recognised that the objectives being pursued by the various Member States to protect the health of their people are equally valid, even where different techniques are used to achieve them.[10] As a result, the national regulations and inspection systems, despite their differences, attempt to achieve the same objectives and should therefore normally be afforded recognition in all Member States. As discussed in detail in Chapter 2, trade in a product lawfully manufactured and marketed in one Member State may only be hindered by the other Member States if doing so is necessary to satisfy mandatory requirements and to serve a purpose in the general interest. However, it was recognised that the application of this principle, despite enabling the Community and the Member States to remove unjustified barriers to trade, did have certain shortcomings that would need to be overcome. The lack of a clear position, necessitating frequent recourse to the Courts to determine, on a case-by-case basis, whether a barrier is unjustified or excessive, creates uncertainty for national administrations and for industry. The Communication was therefore to serve as a guide for public authorities on their obligations and for Community citizens as to their rights. In addition, in some circumstances situations would arise where common standards would have to be introduced to promote industry,

---

[10] Council Resolution of 7 May 1985 on a new approach to technical harmonization and standards. [1985] OJ C 136/1.

to protect consumers or to encourage competitiveness. These would still require the introduction of harmonising Community measures. Official inspection, which is designed to ensure compliance with health protection rules, must, according to the Communication, by its very nature be a matter for legislation. Official control could not itself be contrary to Article 28 EC, it being necessary to ensure that foodstuffs can move freely within the Community. Official control of foodstuffs is thus a necessary part of ensuring their smooth import and export into and out of the inspecting Member State.

3.2.2 Consumer Protection

The Communication noted that there were two possible ways to facilitate consumer interests in EU food law. The first was to develop detailed regulations on the composition and manufacture of each foodstuff. This, in other words, would be to expand the use of recipe laws. The second was to work on the basis that, provided that the purchaser was given adequate information regarding the nature and composition of foodstuffs, it would not be necessary to define these elements in law unless necessary for the protection of human health. The Communication made it clear that the Community must commit itself to the second approach, for a number of reasons. These included the fact that it would not be possible, or desirable, to confine in a legislative straitjacket the culinary riches of the Member States; that legislative rigidity concerning product composition prevents the development of new products and is therefore an obstacle to innovation and commercial flexibility; and that the tastes and preferences of consumers should not be a matter for regulation.

Key to ensuring that this favoured option was fully supported by an adequate legislative framework, the Communication elaborated on the future of food labelling rules in the Community. The rejection of furthering the use of recipe laws would require a well-developed and clear system of labelling, presentation and advertising. Rules would be devised to protect producers from unfair competition and consumers from misleading practices. Directive 1979/112 would need to be supplemented to achieve this.[11] National exceptions left to the discretion of Member States would need to be replaced by uniform rules, in particular in relation to the use of additive specification in the list of ingredients and date marking. Furthermore, additions and exceptions to general rules which are needed for specific foods, but which are not applicable to all foodstuffs, would need to be drawn up at Community level where no detailed vertical directive exists on quality requirements for those specific foods. Other additions identified as being required,

---

[11] Council Directive 1979/112/EEC of 18 December 1978 on the approximation of the laws of the Member States relating to the labelling, presentation and advertising of foodstuffs for sale to the ultimate consumer. [1979] OJ L 33/1. This has now been replaced by Directive 2000/13/EC of the European Parliament and of the Council of 20 March 2000 on the approximation of the laws of the Member States relating to the labelling, presentation and advertising of foodstuffs. [2000] OJ L 109/29.

and which have since been implemented, included the introduction of rules on nutrition labelling.[12]

The Communication stated that, given the repeated findings of the Court that Member States could not prohibit the sale of a product not conforming with its own domestic compositional rules, though lawfully manufactured and marketed in accordance with its own national requirements, the Community no longer needed to introduce compositional rules in its legislation. It was recognised that this could be criticised as resulting in legal uncertainty. It was not always clear as to whether a Member State may make an exception to mutual recognition in respect of products imported from other Member States. The only essential requirement that could possibly justify the refusal to accept a food lawfully produced in another Member State is the need to protect consumers against misleading practices and producers against unfair competition. It was stated that existing Community labelling provisions, together with those to be drawn up on additive listing and nutrition labelling, would be sufficient to provide adequate information and avoid confusion. This, it was claimed, would eliminate legal uncertainty.

The second potential criticism was that a lack of Community compositional rules would lead to a reduction in quality, as the most liberal national rules would now become general practice. The Communication dissented from this view. It stated merely that there was no evidence available to support this, without making any further elaboration. It added that the Commission would be initiating discussions with those responsible for national food legislation to determine whether and how the Community should encourage industry to adopt an active quality approach for foodstuffs. This could then result in the development of a Community system for the mutual recognition of labels or other quality marks and for the relevant checks and certification to be examined. In particular, this would be necessary because in order to ensure the proper functioning of a system of mutual recognition based on Article 28 EC, there must be accompanying administrative co-operation with all interested parties, including the relevant authorities in the Member States, and representatives from agriculture, industry, labour, commerce and the consumer body. While the Community has established a system for certifying products of quality or character, it is demonstrated later in this chapter how this process remains under-used throughout the EU, and is relatively ineffective in achieving its stated aim.

3.2.3 Fair Trading

The Communication stated that once a food was not harmful to health, consumers were adequately and correctly informed and not misled, and producers were protected against unfair competition, then fair trading would, in principle, be ensured.

---

[12] Council Directive 1990/496/EEC of 24 September 1990 on nutrition labelling for foodstuffs, [1990] OJ L 276/40 which is discussed in more detail in Chapter 6 below.

3.3 COMMUNICATION ON THE FREE MOVEMENT OF FOODSTUFFS WITHIN THE COMMUNITY

The Communication on the completion of the internal market in the foodstuffs sector identified that some matters required Council legislative action, while others were a concern for the Commission. The Commission would monitor the application of Article 28 EC in the Member States, and the initiation of judicial proceedings where necessary. Member States would, however, still be entitled to keep domestic rules that contravened Article 28 EC in place, provided that these rules were justifiable as being necessary for the protection of human health or necessary to satisfy mandatory requirements, including consumer protection and fair trading. These areas would also be the only ones that would require Community legislation. All other situations could be dealt with by the mutual recognition principle. As a consequence, and in particular to clarify what would constitute a legitimate derogation from this principle, the Commission issued a communication in 1989 on the free movement of food in the post-*Cassis* era.[13]

This Communication opened by emphasising the importance of the foodstuffs sector. It is one of only a few which have a direct bearing on every individual in the Union. It recognised that clarification on the free movement of food would be required imminently as levels of trade were increasing and, consequently, consumers were now confronted by an ever-greater diversity of foodstuffs on the market, some of which they would not necessarily be familiar with. The Communication set out the Commission's strategy to cope with any difficulties that this might cause. This strategy was to adopt harmonised rules at Community level, applicable to all foodstuffs marketed in the Community, with the principle of mutual recognition of national regulations and standards for matters not requiring the adoption of Community legislative measures.

On the issue of legislation, the Communication stated that the Commission was proposing the adoption of harmonised rules at Community level only for matters relating to public health, the protection of consumers, environmental protection and the fairness of commercial transactions. These would, generally speaking, be horizontal measures covering aspects such as additive use, pesticide residues, materials and articles in contact with foodstuffs, certain manufacturing and treatment processes, and the labelling, presentation and advertising of foodstuffs. Official inspection measures would be regularly supplemented and updated. However, Community measures would also be introduced to cover the implementation of other Community policies, such as standards governing composition or the definition of organic production. The Commission would also promote a policy of product quality at Community level. To achieve this, the Commission would provide for a Community framework for prescribing approval procedures and mutual recognition of quality labels, and for claims concerning recognition of quality

---

[13] Communication on the free movement of foodstuffs within the Community. [1989] OJ C 271/3.

products, and claims concerning products of characteristic or traditional origin or manufacture. Integral to all this would be improving the accuracy of descriptions of foodstuffs, particularly as regards the standard of claims made in their labelling.

The position in 1989 can be summarised thus. It was recognised that where no Community harmonised rules existed, Member States could set their own standards for the production of food, including those on the manufacture, composition, packaging and presentation of foodstuffs. They would, however, be required to allow onto their territory foodstuffs lawfully produced and marketed in other Member States. The importation of these products, in the absence of harmonised rules, could only be restricted where (i) the national measure could be demonstrated to be necessary in order to satisfy mandatory requirements relating to public health protection, the protection of consumers, the fairness of commercial transactions or the protection of the environment; (ii) the measure was proportionate to the objective; and (iii) the measure chosen was the means of achieving that objective which least hindered trade. The Communication recognised that these principles, which arose out of the judgment of the Court of Justice in *Cassis*, had been further developed in subsequent case law, in particular the decision in *Commission v Germany*.[14] As a result of this latter decision, and the principles arising therefrom, it was deemed that the basis now existed for resolving most of the problems that were likely to arise in relation to the free movement of foodstuffs, in particular those relating to the name under which imported foodstuffs were sold and the use of additives. As regards food names, the importer could now choose either to keep the name under which the product was lawfully marketed in the Member State of manufacture, or to adopt the trade description under which similar products were marketed in the importing Member State. It was also suggested that there was no reason why the product should not bear both trade descriptions simultaneously, provided that this did not confuse the consumer. The only circumstances where this choice could be lawfully restricted would be where the product differed in terms of its composition or manufacture from goods generally known under the same name in the Community, so that the product would not fall under either description. Where the imported product did not possess certain characteristics deemed to be essential in the importing Member State for the use of the specific trade description, it would be the responsibility of the importer to ensure that the labelling of the product provided the consumer with the proper information about the nature and characteristics of the product to enable it to be distinguished from products with which it might be confused. The only circumstances where the marketing of an imported foodstuff could be restricted by the application of national consumer protection measures would be where the labelling of the product itself would be liable to create confusion as to the nature, characteristics or origin of the product and where this could not be avoided by measures that were less of a hindrance to free trade.

---

[14] Case 178/1984, *Commission v Germany* (bier) [1987] ECR 1227.

What is particularly interesting about the Communication is that it gave clarification on the mutual recognition of the use of additives in foodstuffs. It stated that the importation of a foodstuff containing an additive permitted in the Member State of manufacture, but prohibited in the importing Member State, must be authorised if the additive does not present a danger to human health, taking into account the findings of international scientific research and eating habits in the importing Member State, and if the use of the additive meets a genuine need, in particular of a technological or economic nature. Whilst the relevant case law had alluded to such a position, it had never been quite so explicit as this. To this end, the Member States would have to ensure that they institute an authorisation procedure that would be easily accessible to traders and could be concluded within a reasonable period of time, specifically stated as being no more than 90 days. Under this procedure, it would be for the national authorities in the Member States to demonstrate that the refusal to grant authorisation is justified on grounds relating to the protection of public health. Furthermore, it must be open to traders to challenge an unjustified failure to grant authorisation before national courts.[15]

The Communication stated that the key aspiration of Community food legislation is to ensure a high level of human health protection and that the consumer is accurately and adequately informed as to the nature, characteristics and, where appropriate, origin of foodstuffs placed on the market. Any aspects of the free movement of foodstuffs not covered by Community legislation would be provided for by the case law of the Court of Justice. It was stated that:

> The completion of an internal market in this sector, accompanied by an active promotion of product quality, should also ensure consumer access to the great variety of the Community's agri-food production by offering the producers the advantages and outlets of a large market.

The Communication also set out what the Commission intends to be the key features of the Community food law framework, including:

(i) protecting consumers against misleading practices, and consequently ensuring fair trading, by providing a set of horizontal rules that will ensure that they are correctly and precisely informed of the nature and characteristics of products and, in some cases, the provision of vertical legislation as considered necessary for the implementation of other Community policies, for example setting compositional requirements (although only in very limited circumstances), production methods or defining organic foodstuffs; and

(ii) following on from its Communication 'The future of rural society', the promotion of product quality standards in order to protect agricultural and food products that are known for their high quality level (pasta from durum wheat, cheese types) or which are geographical in nature (protected designations of

---

[15] For further detail on this see, in particular, Case C-344/1990, *Commission v France* (cheese nitrate) [1992] ECR I-4719, para 9; Case C-24/2000, *Commission v France* (fortified foods-'Red Bull') [2004] ECR I-1277, para 26.

origin (pdo) and protected geographical indications (pgi)), as well as ensuring that modes of production, such as 'free range' or 'traditional' become or remain the demesne of genuine cases.[16]

Where no Community rules exist, Articles 28 to 30 EC apply. The most important and influential of those rules that have been developed are the horizontal standards on food labelling. Primarily it is the existence of this legislation, coupled with the decision in *Cassis*, that has led to, and has justified, the policy of not harmonising food standards throughout the Community—facilitating free movement without common standards.

3.4 FOOD LABELLING

Given that consumers have, particularly since the latter decades of the 20th century, become increasingly concerned about the constituents of their food,[17] it is not surprising that the area of EU food law that, in general, leads to the most contention is food labelling. There are several reasons for this. Primarily there appears to be a belief, often a well-founded one, that food producers' main concern is the maximisation of profit, and that in their efforts to achieve this, undesirable practices will occur. This can include replacing natural colours and flavours with artificial ones, adding ingredients that have undergone certain processes or that have been produced in a particular way, for example ionisation or genetic modification, or making claims about a product's origin, health benefits or quality level that are untrue or exaggerated. More recently there have also been increasing calls for fat content levels, nutritional values and the presence of potentially harmful substances, such as trans-fats or monosodium glutamate, to be disclosed. Consumer groups seek clearer labelling information.[18] Producers want to maximise the area on the packaging that they can use for the advertising of their product. Legislators must try, where possible, to appease both interests. This is a difficult task, complicated by the fact that those drafting legislation are faced with a clear paradox. Overburdening the producer with legislative requirements reduces efficiency and consequently stifles economic progress, but it also reduces the clarity of the labelling information presented to the consumer. Neither party is thus best served by this approach. Indeed, many studies have shown that despite constant calls for more information, doubt has been expressed as to whether

[16] Commission Communication on the future of rural society. COM (88) 501.

[17] See, for example, MS Brewer and CJ Prestat, 'Consumer Attitudes toward Food Safety Issues' (2002) 22 *Journal of Food Safety* 67; Rodolfo M Nayga, 'Sociodemographic Influences on Consumer Concern for Food Safety: The Case of Irradiation, Antibiotics, Hormones, and Pesticides' (1996) 18 *Review of Agricultural Economics* 467; M Wandel, 'Understanding Consumer Concern about Food-related Health Risks' (1994) 96 *British Food Journal* 35.

[18] See, for example, A Shine, S O'Reilly and K O'Sullivan, 'Consumer Use of Nutrition Labels' (1997) 99 *British Food Journal* 290.

consumers actually read or even comprehend many labelling disclosures.[19] Too much information can cause consumers to make even more disorientated decisions than those made when there is less information to hand.[20]

Food labelling was one of the earliest, and continues to be one of the more comprehensively, covered areas of EU food law. This completeness derives mostly from the clarity of rules rather than any large mass of requirements. Food labelling was the subject of a well-drafted framework directive as early as 1979.[21] This legislation was replaced in 2000,[22] the new rules being simply a necessary modernisation, consolidation and minor modification of the original.

3.4.1 Framework Food Labelling Legislation

Directive 1979/112 was one of the earliest drafted pieces of horizontal Community food legislation, encompassing all food and food products rather than specific foodstuffs, as had been the case with the earlier 'recipe laws'. It was recognised that the primary consideration for any rules on the labelling of foodstuffs should be the need to inform and protect the consumer.[23] As a consequence, a list of specific labelling requirements was established that would have to appear on all foodstuffs intended for sale to the ultimate consumer, with some minor exceptions. It was intended that the directive would establish the framework around which supplementary measures could be adopted to deal with specific, both horizontal and vertical, circumstances.

---

[19] Successive studies have demonstrated that many consumers remain unable and/or unwilling to understand much of the information that is presented to them on food labels. See, for example, E Einsiedel, 'Consumers and GM Food Labels: Providing Information or Sowing Confusion' (2000) 3 *Journal of Agrobiotechnology Management and Economics* 231; L Levy, RE Patterson, AR Kristal and SS Li, 'How Well do Consumers Understand Percentage Daily Value on Food Labels?' (1999) 14 *American Journal of Health Promotion* 126; DJ Reid and SM Hendricks, 'Consumer Understanding and Use of Fat and Cholesterol Information on Food Labels' (1994) 85 *Canadian Journal of Public Health* 334; W Mueller, 'Who Reads the Label?' (1991) 28 *American Demographics* 36. For further data and discussion on European consumers' interest in, and comprehension of, labelling see 'European Consumers' Attitudes on Product Labelling' published by the European Commission in May 2005, available at http://ec.europa.eu/consumers/topics/product_labelling_en.htm.

[20] See, for example, JC Kozup, S Burton and EH Creyer, 'The Provision of Trans Fat Information and its Interaction with Consumer Knowledge' (2006) 40 *Journal of Consumer Affairs* 163; KR France and PF Bone, 'Policy Makers' Paradigms and Evidence from Consumer Interpretations of Dietary Supplement Labels' (2005) 39 *Journal of Consumer Affairs* 27; and S Burton and JC Andrews, 'Age, Product Nutrition, and Label Format Effects on Consumer Perceptions and Product Evaluations' (1996) 30 *Journal of Consumer Affairs* 68.

[21] Council Directive 1979/112/EEC of 18 December 1978 on the approximation of the laws of the Member States relating to the labelling, presentation and advertising of foodstuffs for sale to the ultimate consumer. [1979] OJ L 33/1.

[22] Directive 2000/13/EC of the European Parliament and of the Council of 20 March 2000 on the approximation of the laws of the Member States relating to the labelling, presentation and advertising of foodstuffs. [2000] OJ L 109/29.

[23] Preamble to Council Directive 1979/112/EEC.

'Labelling' was defined in the directive as being:

any words, particulars, trade marks, brand name, pictorial matter or symbol relating to a foodstuff and placed on any packaging, document, notice, label, ring or collar accompanying or referring to such foodstuff.[24]

It was stated that the labelling must not:

be such as could mislead the purchaser . . . particularly as to the characteristics of the foodstuff . . . its nature, identity, properties, composition, quantity, durability, origin or provenance, method of manufacture or production.[25]

The directive set out a series of indications that must, unless specified elsewhere, be compulsorily presented on all foodstuffs. These included: the name under which the product is sold, the list of ingredients, the net quantity of prepackaged foodstuffs, the date of minimum durability, any special storage conditions or conditions of use, and the name or business name and address of the manufacturer or packager or of a seller established within the Community.[26] In addition to this, particulars relating to the place of origin must be detailed where failure to give such particulars might mislead the consumer as to the true origin of the foodstuff and instructions for use must be supplied where it would be impossible for the consumer to make appropriate use of the foodstuff in the absence of such information.[27]

Directive 1979/112 was later replaced by Directive 2000/13.[28] This directive strays little from the requirements of the original framework food labelling directive, but it does include some important additions. Provision is made for the inclusion on the label of details relating to quantitative ingredient declarations, the 'use-by' date for highly perishable foodstuffs, and the alcoholic strength by volume of beverages containing more than 1.2 per cent by volume of alcohol.[29] All compulsory labels must be easily visible, clearly legible and indelible.[30] They should not be in any way hidden, obscured or interrupted by any other written or pictorial matter.[31]

'Labelling' continues to be defined as it was in Directive 1979/112. It was noted by the Court in *Smanor* that labelling includes any words, particulars and other information relating to a foodstuff that is specifically designed to inform the consumer about the characteristics of the product in question, in particular those relating to its nature, identity, properties, composition, quantity, durability,

---

[24] Article 1(3).
[25] Article 2(1).
[26] Article 3(1).
[27] *Ibid.*
[28] Directive 2000/13/EC of the European Parliament and of the Council of 20 March 2000 on the approximation of the laws of the Member States relating to the labelling, presentation and advertising of foodstuffs. [2000] OJ L 109/29.
[29] Article 3(1).
[30] Article 13(2).
[31] *Ibid.*

origin, and method of manufacture or production.[32] Labelling must thus be intended to specifically inform the consumer in some meaningful way, in order to come within the scope of Directive 2000/13. Despite this broad definition, not all marks on food packaging are labelling. In *Twee Provinciën*, for example, a Dutch national cheese mark consisting of a serial number and a combination of letters indicating, *inter alia*, the region of production and the cheese type did not fall within this definition, and was thus not labelling for the purposes of the directive. This was primarily due to the fact that it was a serial number containing letters that identified the region of production and was not a clear statement about the origin of the product.[33] Its primary function was to assist public authorities in the Netherlands in their verification processes designed to ensure that the cheese was produced in accordance with the relevant rules, not to inform consumers.

Member States may not forbid trade in foodstuffs which comply with the rules laid down in the directive by the application of non-harmonised national provisions governing the labelling and presentation of certain foodstuffs or of foodstuffs in general.[34] Some derogation from this may be allowed to protect public health, prevent fraud or to protect industrial and commercial property rights, or in relation to indications of provenance, registered designations of origin or the prevention of unfair competition.[35]

3.4.2 Labelling Language

Under the terms of the framework food labelling legislation,[36] and the case law of the Court of Justice, food labelling is to appear in a language that is easily understood by the consumer, unless other measures have been taken to ensure that the purchaser is informed. The issue of labelling language first came before the Court in *Piageme v Peeters*.[37] There it was found that the framework labelling legislation precluded national law from requiring the exclusive use of a specific language for the labelling of foodstuffs. The legislation permitted the use of another language easily understood by purchasers, or ensuring that the purchaser was informed by other measures. The applicant, a mineral water producers' association, brought an action against the respondent, a company established in the Flemish-speaking region of Belgium, claiming that the respondent had contravened the framework food labelling directive by selling mineral water in bottles whose labels were only in French or German. It was claimed that the directive required that labelling should appear in a language that is easily understood by the purchaser rather than

---

[32] Case 298/1987, *Proceedings for compulsory reconstruction against Smanor SA* [1988] ECR 4489, para 30.
[33] Case C-285/1992, *Criminal Proceedings against Coöperatieve Zuivelindustrie 'Twee Provinciën' WA* [1993] ECR I-6045.
[34] Article 18(1).
[35] Article 18(2).
[36] Article 16 thereof.
[37] Case C-369/1989, *Piageme and others v BVBA Peeters* [1991] ECR I-2971.

in any specific language. The transposing Belgian legislation stated that the language to be used should be that of the linguistic region where the foodstuff was being offered for sale. While the Court accepted that the language of a region was that which was most likely to be the one that would be 'easily understood', such an interpretation of the provisions of the framework food labelling legislation would fail to take account of the true aims of the directive, in particular facilitating the free movement of goods. To require that a specific language be used was determined to be a measure equivalent to a quantitative restriction on imports and consequently contrary to Article 28 EC, as well as to the aims of the directive.

In *Piageme v Peeters (No 2)* it was questioned whether 'other measures . . . taken to ensure that the purchaser is informed' was restricted to particulars on the label of a product and, if not so restricted, it could also include the entire context in which a product was offered for sale, provided that the information required by the framework food labelling legislation was given in full, and in a manner that could be easily understood by the consumer.[38] The Court noted that the aim of the legislation was to ensure that the consumer was given easy access to the compulsory particulars specified in the directive. It was necessary that these particulars should be available to the consumer both at the time of purchasing and at the time of actual consumption. This was seen to be particularly true in relation to the date of minimum durability and any special storage conditions or conditions of use of the product. The Court noted that the ultimate consumer is not necessarily the purchaser of the foodstuff. It stated that consumer protection could not be adequately ensured by measures other than labelling such as, for example, information supplied at the point of sale or as part of a wide-ranging advertising campaign. All the compulsory particulars specified in the framework food labelling directive must thus appear on the labelling in a language easily understood by purchasers, or by other measures such as designs, symbols or pictograms. It would be for the national court to determine in each individual case whether that which appears on the labelling gives consumers full information as to the compulsory particulars specified in the directive. It is also for the national court to determine in each individual case whether the compulsory particulars given in a language other than the language mainly used in the Member State or region concerned can be easily understood by consumers in that State or region. When determining whether a language used or particulars given are sufficient to inform the consumer, various factors may be relevant, though not necessarily decisive. Examples include the possible similarity of words in different languages, the widespread knowledge amongst the population concerned of more than one language, or the existence of special circumstances, such as a wide-ranging advertising campaign or widespread distribution of the product. Member States should always refrain from laying down requirements more detailed than those already contained in the directive.[39]

---

[38] Case C-85/1994, *Piageme and others v Peeters NV* [1995] ECR I-2955.
[39] Article 17 of Directive 2000/13.

In *Goerres*, proceedings were brought against the respondent for offering for sale in his shop in Germany various foodstuffs, including orange soda, corn flakes and pasta sauce with olives and capers, that were not labelled in German.[40] The foodstuffs were labelled in French, Italian or English. The rules transposing the food labelling directive into German law did clearly state that while German should be used on food labelling, the compulsory particulars could be given in another language, if the provision of information to the consumer was not adversely affected in any way by this. The respondent lodged an objection to the penalty served upon him (a DM2,000 fine), claiming that use of a particular language could not be imposed under the terms of the directive. The decisive factor was the intelligibility of the labelling and that given that the products in question were well known to the public, the use of labelling in a foreign language did not adversely affect the information imparted to the consumer. He further stated that he had placed in his shop, adjacent to the products in question, supplementary signs giving the required information in German.

It was noted by the Court that following its decision in *Piageme (No 2)* that it was for national courts to assess, in the light of all the circumstances in each individual case, the ease with which information supplied in a language other than that of the place of sale could be understood. The Court added that it had to be borne in mind that the required particulars could be satisfactorily indicated other than by words, for example by designs, symbols or pictograms. It thus had to be determined whether placing a supplementary sign in a shop, adjacent to the product in question, containing the prescribed particulars in a language which could be easily understood, was sufficient to ensure that the consumer was informed. The Court decided that it was not. The key aim of the directive—to inform and protect consumers—would not be attained if they did not always have access to the compulsory particulars specified in the directive, not only at the time of purchase but also at the time of consumption.

The issue of labelling language was once more the subject of the Court's deliberations in *Geffroy*.[41] Here, an inspection carried out at the premises of one of the co-respondents revealed that the labelling on certain drinks, namely bottles of cola, cider and ginger ale, was not in French, save for the indications of volume and, in the case of the ginger ale, the alcohol content. It was contested that the cola, the labelling of which was in English, was a well known product that could not be confused with any other by consumers. It was also claimed that the suppliers of the cider and ginger ale had made a mistake by failing to provide the adhesive stickers in French to be attached to the bottles, as they had been requested to do. The rules transposing the framework food labelling directive into French law stated that all the labelling particulars required must be written in French. The respondent claimed that these French provisions were in fact incompatible with the terms of

---

[40] Case C-385/1996, *Criminal proceedings against Hermann Josef Goerres* [1998] ECR I-4431.

[41] Case C-366/1998, *Criminal proceedings against Yannick Geffroy and Casino France SNC* [2000] ECR I-6579.

the directive, in particular in that they required the use of a specific language for the labelling of foodstuffs. Following its earlier case law on the matter, and the perceived aims of the directive, the Court agreed, finding that Article 28 EC and the terms of the directive precluded a national provision from requiring the use of a specific language for the labelling of foodstuffs, without allowing for the possibility of another language easily understood by purchasers to be used or for the purchaser to be informed by other means.

Finally on the issue of labelling language, the directive states that Member States are to prohibit the sale of foodstuffs that do not carry labelling in a language that can be easily understood by consumers likely to purchase or consume those foodstuffs.[42]

3.4.3 Listing Ingredients

Under the terms of Directive 2000/13, the ingredients of a food product must be listed in all cases, bar a few exceptions.[43] Those foodstuffs that need not include a list of ingredients on the labelling include: fresh fruit and vegetables, including potatoes, which have not been peeled, cut or similarly treated; carbonated water, the description of which indicates that it has been carbonated; fermentation vinegars derived exclusively from a single basic product, provided that no other ingredient has been added; cheese, butter and fermented milk and cream, provided that no ingredient has been added other than lactic products, enzymes and micro-organism cultures essential to manufacture, or the salt needed for the manufacture of cheese other than fresh cheese and processed cheese; and products comprising a single ingredient where the trade name is identical to the ingredient name, or the trade name enables the nature of the ingredient to be clearly identified.[44]

'Ingredients' are defined as:

> any substance, including additives, used in the manufacture or preparation of a foodstuff and still present in the finished product, even if in altered form. Where an ingredient of the foodstuff is itself the product of several ingredients, the latter shall be regarded as ingredients of the foodstuff in question.[45]

A compound ingredient may be included in the list of ingredients under its own designation, where this has been laid down by law or established by custom, in terms of its overall weight, provided that this is immediately followed by a list of its ingredients. This list is not required, however, where the compound ingredient constitutes less than 25 per cent of the finished product. This exemption does not extend to additives. Likewise, a list of ingredients is not required for a compound ingredient where this ingredient is a foodstuff for which a list of ingredients is not

---

[42] Article 16(1) of Directive 2000/13.
[43] Article 6(1).
[44] Article 6(2).
[45] Article 6(4)(b).

required under the terms of the directive.[46] The following are not regarded as ingredients for the purposes of the legislation: the constituents of an ingredient which have been temporarily separated during the manufacturing process and later reintroduced but not in excess of their original proportions; additives whose presence in a given foodstuff is solely due to the fact that they were contained in one or more ingredients of that foodstuff, provided that they serve no technological function in the finished product or provided that they are used as processing aids; and substances used in the quantities strictly necessary as solvents or media for additives or flavouring.[47]

Decisions may be taken in individual cases at Community level to ascertain whether the additives used are among those which EU law specifies may be omitted from the list of ingredients.[48] Just what qualifies as an exemption from the ingredients list has previously aroused some level of controversy. In *Pfanni Werke*, for example, the applicant, a manufacturer of dehydrated potato products, was adding diphosphate E450a to the ingredient 'potato puree flakes' in order to counteract grey discolouration of the flakes caused by enzymes during the production process.[49] Objections had been raised about the fact that this additive was not subsequently included in the list of ingredients. It was claimed that its use affected the colour of the finished product and that it should therefore be regarded as an ingredient under the terms of the framework labelling legislation; it served a technological function in the finished product. The applicant had been informed that if it continued to omit this additive from the list of ingredients, then a formal prohibition order would be made and a fine imposed. The applicant responded by initiating an action against the relevant authorities, claiming that the additive actually served no technological function in the finished product. It was added to the potato pulp to prevent it from changing colour. The preparation of the pulp was only one stage in the manufacturing process of the ingredient 'potato puree flakes'. After the subsequent dehydration of that pulp the colour of the potato flakes in the finished product could no longer be affected, because the enzymes in the potato cells were neutralised through heating. The claim was that diphosphate E450a should not thus be required to be listed by the applicant.

During the course of the proceedings, it was submitted to the Court that any additive which directly or indirectly influences the characteristics of the finished product must be included in the list of ingredients. This is especially so, given that the aim of the framework food labelling directive is to prevent consumers from being misled by the labelling of foodstuffs and to inform them as fully as possible about the product's composition. This was not accepted by the Court. It held that although the directive was based on the need to inform and protect the consumer by, *inter alia*, compelling producers to state a list of ingredients on the labelling, that obligation was subject to various derogations, including one relating to the

---

[46] Article 6(8).
[47] Article 6(4)(c).
[48] Article 6(4)(d).
[49] Case C-144/1993, *Pfanni Werke Otto Eckart KG v Landeshauptstadt München* [1994] ECR I-4605.

technological function of additives in the finished product. Consumers are to be provided with effective information which can be easily understood. In the opinion of the Court this did not mean an exhaustive list of the ingredients used in the manufacturing process. It was accepted that the additive at issue no longer served a technological function in the finished product given that the risk of the potato pulp acquiring a grey discolouration no longer existed after the heating and dehydration process, because the enzymes that could be discoloured had already been neutralised by the heating and dehydration process.

The list of ingredients must include all the ingredients of the foodstuff, in descending order of weight, as recorded at the time of their use in the manufacture of the product. It must be preceded by a suitable heading that includes the word 'ingredients'.[50] Where the ingredients include a mixture of fruit or vegetables, or spices or herbs, where none significantly predominates in proportion by weight, those ingredients may be listed in any order, provided that the list of ingredients is accompanied by an expression such as 'in variable proportion'.[51]

Some ingredients, belonging to specified categories, may, where they are the constituents of another foodstuff, be designated by the name of the relevant category only.[52] Examples include all types of cheese, where the cheese or mixture of cheeses constitutes an ingredient of another foodstuff and provided that the name and presentation of the product does not refer to a specific type of cheese. This may appear in the ingredients listing simply as 'cheese'. Similarly too, all species of fish, where the fish constitutes an ingredient of another foodstuff and provided that the name and presentation of the product does not refer to a specific species of fish, may be listed simply as 'fish'. Similarly, all herbs or spices not exceeding two per cent by weight of the foodstuff may be listed as either 'herbs' or 'spices' respectively.[53] Colours, preservatives, flavour enhancers, sweeteners, antioxidants, emulsifiers, thickeners, gelling agents, stabilisers, acidity regulators, anti-caking agents, raising agents, anti-foaming agents, glazing agents, flour treatment agents, firming agents, humectants, bulking agents and propellant gases must all appear in the list of ingredients using the name of the category, followed by the specific name or EC number.[54] If an ingredient belongs to more than one of these categories then the category appropriate to the principal function in the circumstances must be indicated.[55] Where starch or modified starch is present in a product, its appearance in the ingredients listing must always be complemented by the indication of its specific vegetable origin when that ingredient may contain gluten.[56]

[50] Article 6(5).
[51] Article 6(5).
[52] Article 6(6).
[53] Annex I to Directive 2000/13/EC of the European Parliament and of the Council of 20 March 2000 on the approximation of the laws of the Member States relating to the labelling, presentation and advertising of foodstuffs. [2000] OJ L 109/29.
[54] Article 6(6).
[55] *Ibid.*
[56] *Ibid.*

Member States may not exceed the requirements set out in the framework labelling legislation in respect of the listing of ingredients. In *Commission v Germany*, for example, it was questioned whether national rules on this were contrary to free movement principles. These required that béarnaise sauce and hollandaise sauce made with vegetable fats, and certain pastry products containing the additive E160F, should carry a trade description with an additional statement indicating that the substances in question had been used. This was so even where those substances had already been included in the list of ingredients referred to in Article 6 of the directive.[57] It had been claimed that the national measures were necessary for the protection of consumers. It was contended that consumers often buy foodstuffs without undertaking a scrupulous examination of the product, their choice instead being determined by 'reference criteria' such as the trade description and the additional information accompanying it. Consequently it was claimed that, in the case of the sauces at issue, were there no requirement to display the statement in dispute, the consumer could be led to buy those products in the belief that they had in fact been produced according to the traditional German recipe, with eggs and butter rather than vegetable fat. The same, it was claimed, held true of the incorporation of the additive E160F in biscuits and pastry products. The presence of E160F creates an intense yellow colouring, potentially misleading the consumer into believing that a large amount of egg yolk has been used in production. The additional labelling requirements were, however, here found to be unjustified on the grounds of consumer protection. It was held that in certain cases prescribed additional statements may be allowed, but it was the opinion of the Court in this instance that consumers whose purchasing decisions depend on the composition of the product will first read the list of ingredients. It was accepted that on some occasions consumers may be misled, but that this risk was minimal and insufficient to justify the hindrance to the free movement of goods that the national rules at issue created.

It was also contended that the following fair trading issue should be examined. The use of ingredients such as vegetable fats, which are less expensive than eggs or butter, enabled the manufacturer of imported products to enjoy a position of considerable competitive advantage. Given that consumers do not sufficiently distinguish between the various methods of manufacture when making purchasing decisions, that advantage was claimed by the German Government to be unacceptable. The Court did not agree. Citing *Keck and Mithouard*, the Court noted that compositional requirements could not be used to impede free movement, even where the rules are applied without distinction.[58] The fair trading argument was rejected on the same grounds as the consumer protection argument. Conscientious consumers would read the list of ingredients and thus be informed of any difference in product quality.

---

[57] Case C-51/1994, *Commission v Germany* (sauces and pastries) [1995] ECR I-3599.
[58] Joined Cases C-267/1991 and C-268/1991, *Criminal proceedings against Bernard Keck and Daniel Mithouard* [1991] ECR I-6097.

Quantitative Ingredient Declarations

It is in relation to quantitative ingredient declarations that the 2000 directive departs most from the 1979 framework labelling directive where the listing of ingredients is concerned. The directive states that:

> The quantity of an ingredient or category of ingredients used in the manufacture or preparation of a foodstuff shall be stated . . . where the ingredient or category of ingredients concerned appears in the name under which the foodstuff is sold or is usually associated with that name by the consumer [or] is emphasised on the labelling in words, pictures or graphics [or] is essential to characterise a foodstuff and to distinguish it from products with which it might be confused because of its name or appearance . . .[59]

The quantity indicated should be expressed as a percentage, and should correspond to the quantity of the ingredient(s) at the time of use,[60] and should appear either in or immediately next to the name under which the foodstuff is sold or in the list of ingredients.[61]

This is a significant alteration to the original framework food labelling directive. It provides consumers with a transparent mechanism for establishing the quantity of a particular ingredient present in a product. Say, for example, two cartons of cranberry juice sit beside each other on the shelf in a supermarket. One sells for €1.30 per litre; the other for €1.50 per litre. Both are called 'Cranberry juice drink'. Both display a picture of fresh cranberries on the label. Following the introduction of the requirement that the quantity of cranberries must now be stated, and given that the actual name of the product incorporates the word 'cranberry' which is emphasised by a picture on the label, the consumer can now readily identify the actual cranberry content by examining the list of ingredients. It transpires that the €1.30 per litre product contains 15 per cent cranberries; the €1.50 per litre product contains 20 per cent cranberries. The purchaser can now make a fully informed decision as to which product to purchase by weighing up the difference in price against the difference in actual cranberry content.

3.4.4 Net Quantity

The net quantity of prepackaged foodstuffs must be indicated on the labelling of products coming within the scope of Directive 2000/13, in units of volume in the case of liquids, and in units of mass in the case of other products, using the litre, centilitre, millilitre, kilogram, or gram as appropriate.[62] Similarly, all other foodstuffs sold anywhere in the EU must also be weighed or measured according to the

---

[59] Article 7.
[60] Article 7(4).
[61] Article 7(5).
[62] Article 8(1).

metric system.[63] This requirement has caused difficulties in some Member States, in particular in the United Kingdom, where the so-called 'metric martyrs' hit the headlines following their refusal to depart from the imperial measurement system.[64]

Under the terms of the directive, where a prepackaged foodstuff consists of two or more individual prepackaged items containing the same quantity of the same product, the net quantity must be indicated by specifying the net quantity contained in each individual package and the total number of packages. This indication is not, however, compulsory where the total number of individual packages can be clearly seen and easily counted from the outside and where at least one indication of the net quantity contained in each individual package can be clearly seen from the outside.[65] Where a foodstuff is normally sold by number, Member States need not require indication of the net quantity, provided that the number of items can clearly be seen and easily counted from the outside or, if not, is clearly indicated on the labelling.[66] Where a solid foodstuff is sold in a liquid medium, such as water, brine, vinegar or fruit or vegetable juice, the drained net weight of the foodstuff must be indicated on the labelling.[67] No indication of net quantity is required for the marketing of foodstuffs which are subject to considerable losses in their volume or mass and which are sold by number or weighed in the presence of the purchaser, or where the net quantity is less than 5 g or 5 ml.[68] This provision does not apply to herbs or spices.[69]

Council Directive 1976/211 sets out supplementary requirements on the statement of the weight or volume on the labels of prepackaged food.[70] A product is deemed to be prepackaged when:

---

[63] Council Directive 1980/181/EEC of 20 December 1979 on the approximation of the laws of the Member States relating to units of measurement and on the repeal of Directive 1971/354/EEC. [1980] OJ L 39/40. Amended by Council Directive 1989/617/EEC of 27 November 1989 amending Directive 1980/181/EEC on the approximation of the laws of the Member States relating to units of measurement, [1989] OJ L 357/28 and Directive 1999/103/EC of the European Parliament and of the Council of 24 January 2000 amending Council Directive 1980/181/EEC on the approximation of the laws of the Member States relating to units of measurement, [2000] OJ L 34/17.

[64] *Thoburn v Sunderland City Council; Hunt v London Borough of Hackney; Harman and Dove v Cornwall County Council; Collins v London Borough of Sutton* [2002] EWHC 195; [2003] QB 151. For further discussion see S Boyron, 'In the Name of European Law: The Metric Martyrs Case' (2002) 27 *European Law Review* 771. Interestingly, an exemption granted to the UK and Ireland to continue using pints as the unit of measurement for alcoholic drinks in pubs has led to difficulties for the operators of continental themed bars, who wish to use the metric system to serve their drinks in 500 ml glasses.

[65] Article 8(2)(c).

[66] Article 8(3).

[67] Article 8(4).

[68] Article 8(5).

[69] *Ibid.*

[70] Council Directive 1976/211/EEC of 20 January 1976 on the approximation of the laws of the Member States relating to the making-up by weight or by volume of certain prepackaged products. [1976] OJ L 46/1.

it is placed in a package of whatever nature without the purchaser being present and the quantity of the product contained in the package has a predetermined value and cannot be altered without the package either being opened or undergoing a perceptible modification.[71]

Once a prepackaged product complies with the terms of the directive it may place the 'e' symbol on the packaging to indicate this compliance.[72] This symbol must be placed in the same field of vision as the indication of the weight or volume of the product.[73] Producers are entitled to affix the 'e' symbol to their products without having been specifically authorised to do so by the national authorities, provided that the checking procedures employed have been recognised by the national weights and measures authorities.[74]

3.4.5 Date of Minimum Durability

The date of minimum durability of a foodstuff is 'the date until which the foodstuff retains its specific properties when properly stored'.[75] The date stated must be preceded by the words 'best before' when the date includes an indication of the day and 'best before end' in other cases,[76] accompanied by either the date itself or a reference to where the date is given on the labelling.[77] If necessary, the particulars given should be followed by a description of the storage conditions which must be observed if the product is to remain safely edible for the specified period.[78] The date must consist of the day, month and year, in uncoded chronological form. However, in the case of foodstuffs which will not keep for more than three months an indication of the day and the month will suffice; for those foodstuffs which will keep for more than three months but not more that 18 months an indication of the month and the year will suffice; and for those foodstuffs which will keep for more than 18 months an indication of the year will suffice.[79]

Subject to other Community provisions, an indication of the durability date is not required for: fresh fruit and vegetables, including potatoes, which have not been peeled, cut or similarly treated; wines, liqueur wines, sparkling wines, aromatised wines and similar products obtained from fruits other than grapes;

---

[71] Article 2(2).

[72] Article 3(1).

[73] Annex I to Council Directive 1976/211/EEC of 20 January 1976 on the approximation of the laws of the Member States relating to the making-up by weight or by volume of certain prepackaged products. [1976] OJ L 46/1.

[74] Case 96/1984, *Vereniging Slachtpluimvee-Export eV v Rewe-Zentral-Aktiengesellschaft* [1985] ECR 1157.

[75] Article 9(1) of Directive 2000/13/EC of the European Parliament and of the Council of 20 March 2000 on the approximation of the laws of the Member States relating to the labelling, presentation and advertising of foodstuffs. [2000] OJ L 109/29.

[76] Article 9(2).

[77] Article 9(3).

[78] *Ibid.*

[79] Article 9(4).

beverages containing 10 per cent or more alcohol by volume; soft drinks, fruit juices, fruit nectars and alcoholic beverages in individual containers of more than five litres, intended for supply to mass caterers; bakers' or pastry cooks' wares which, given the nature of their content, are normally consumed within 24 hours of their manufacture; vinegar; cooking salt; solid sugar; confectionery products consisting almost solely of flavoured and/or coloured sugars; chewing gum and similar chewing products; and individual portions of ice-cream.[80]

Foodstuffs that are highly perishable, and are therefore likely to constitute an immediate danger to human health after a short period of time, must, instead of the date of minimum durability, display the 'use by' date.[81] Again, the date is to be preceded by the words 'use by', accompanied by either the date itself or a reference to where the date is stated on the label.[82] These particulars must again be followed by a description of the storage conditions that need to be observed to keep the product in prime condition.[83] The date stated must consist of the day, the month, and as we have seen in the circumstances outlined previously, the year, in that order and in uncoded form in all cases.[84] Any instructions that are given on the labelling of a foodstuff should always be stated in such a way that best enables the consumer to use the foodstuff appropriately.[85]

3.5 FOOD NAMES

The original framework food labelling directive stated:

> The name under which a foodstuff is sold shall be the name laid down by whatever laws, regulations or administrative provisions apply to the foodstuff in question or, in the absence of any such name, the name customary in the Member State where the product is sold to the ultimate consumer, or a description of the foodstuff and, if necessary, of its use, that is sufficiently precise to inform the purchaser of its true nature and to enable it to be distinguished from products with which it could be confused.[86]

Thus, for a foodstuff to be named legitimately under the terms of the directive it had to be a legal name, a customary name or a descriptive name. These categories of food name remain under Directive 2000/13. It is this aspect of the food label that has generated, and that continues to generate, the most debate in the years since the inception of the directive. As discussed in Chapter 2, much of the Article 28 EC case law, for example, is concerned with food naming.

In a departure from the 1979 directive, the sales name under which the product is lawfully manufactured and marketed in the Member State of production is allowed, in addition to legal, customary and descriptive names. However, where

---

[80] Article 9(5).
[81] Article 10(1).
[82] Article 10(2).
[83] *Ibid.*
[84] Article 10(3).
[85] Article 11(1).
[86] Article 5(1).

this could create confusion amongst consumers in the Member State of marketing, the sales name must be accompanied by other descriptive information which is to appear in proximity to the sales name.[87] In some circumstances the name used in the Member State of production may not be used in the Member State of marketing where this could cause confusion amongst consumers.[88] It must be noted, however, that no trade mark, brand name or fancy name may be substituted for the name under which the product is usually sold.[89] The name under which the product is sold must include particulars relating to the physical condition of the foodstuff or the specific treatment that it has undergone, for example powdered, freeze-dried, deep-frozen, concentrated or smoked, where the omission of these particulars could lead to confusion.[90] If ionising radiation has been used, this must be stated.[91]

The various types of food name that can be used in accordance with Community law have been further clarified by the Court. In *Canadane*, for example, the Advocate General in his Opinion categorised the various types of food name used in the Community.[92] He stated that 'Community names' are those which are regulated by Community secondary law and define the characteristics and method of production of the product for the entire Community. These 'euro-foods', as he called them, such as honey and chocolate, can be marketed without restriction in all Member States and do not give rise to problems in relation to intra-Community trade.

Second, 'generic names' are common names used to designate agricultural or food products. They form part of the general cultural and gastronomic stock and may, in principle, be used by any producer. It was noted that the Court's case law had not at that stage defined 'generic name', but that examples of food names that had been found to be generic included yoghurt,[93] pasta,[94] beer[95] and edam cheese.[96] The Advocate General also noted how, in many cases, Member States

---

[87] Article 5(1)(b).

[88] Article 5(1)(c).

[89] Article 5(2) of Directive 2000/13/EC of the European Parliament and of the Council of 20 March 2000 on the approximation of the laws of the Member States relating to the labelling, presentation and advertising of foodstuffs. [2000] OJ L 109.

[90] Article 5(3).

[91] *Ibid.* Also, Directive 1999/2/EC of the European Parliament and of the Council of 22 February 1999 on the approximation of the laws of the Member States concerning foods and food ingredients treated with ionising radiation. [1999] OJ L 6/16.

[92] Opinion of Advocate General Ruiz-Jarabo Colomer in Case C-317/1995, *Canadane Cheese Trading AMBA and Adelfi G Kouri Anonymos Emoriki Kai Viomichaniki Etaireia v Hellenic Republic* [1997] ECR I-4681. The case never proceeded to full Court determination due to subsequent withdrawal.

[93] Case 298/1987, *Proceedings for compulsory reconstruction against Smanor SA* [1988] ECR 4489.

[94] Case 407/1985, *Glocken and another v USL Centro Sud and another* [1988] ECR 4233; Case 90/1986, *Criminal proceedings against Zoni* [1988] ECR 4285.

[95] Case 178/1984, *Commission v Germany* (bier) [1987] ECR 1227.

[96] Case 286/1986, *Ministère Public v Gérard Deserbais* [1988] ECR 4907. Criteria that can be applied to determine whether or not a food name is generic are now set out in Article 3(1) of Council Regulation (EC) No 510/2006 of 20 March 2006 on the protection of geographical indications and designations of origin for agricultural products and foodstuffs [2006] OJ L 93/12.

adopted national measures requiring certain conditions of production for the use of a generic name. If those requirements were similar in the Member States, imported products may use the generic name in the importing State with no resultant obstacles to intra-Community trade. However, the production conditions normally differ from one State to another, consequently creating a free movement problem. When such a difficulty had come before the Court in the past, the importing State was deemed to be acting contrary to Article 28 EC. Any national measure reserving the use of a generic name to products manufactured in compliance with the laws of one Member State, preventing similar products manufactured in compliance with the laws of another Member State from using the same generic name, was incompatible with free movement rules.

Any national measure restricting the use of a generic name to a national variety to the detriment of varieties imported from other Member States where they are lawfully produced and marketed was incompatible with the fundamental principle of the free movement of goods.[97] The case law of the Court showed that there were possible justifications to restrictions on such imports, in particular the protection of consumers and fair trading, and, to a lesser extent, the protection of public health. It was noted, however, that the Court considers that the importing State can adequately protect its consumers and ensure fair trading by requiring that the labelling of the imported product show all its characteristics, this labelling requirement being a less restrictive alternative that takes more account of the principle of proportionality than a prohibition on imports or the obligation to market the product under a invented name. It had already been determined that bier[98] and pasta,[99] produced in Member States other than Germany and Italy respectively, were sufficiently similar, despite differences in composition, for adequate labelling to avoid the risk of confusion amongst consumers and to permit them to be sold under the generic names 'bier' and 'pasta'. However, in *Deserbais*,[100] and to a greater extent in *Smanor*,[101] the Court envisaged as an exception to the general rule of mutual recognition of generic sales descriptions subject to adequate labelling, the possibility that the State of destination might prevent the sale in its territory of a product imported from another Member State under a generic name if its characteristics were substantially different from those of national products marketed under the same name.[102]

Third, the Advocate General went on to define what he termed 'geographical' names. He noted that many food names derive from the location in which they are traditionally produced. The Advocate General stated that geographical names were those 'used to designate food products which allude to their origin from a

[97] Case 193/1980, *Commission v Italy* (vinegar) [1981] ECR 3019; Case 182/1984, *Criminal proceedings against Miro BV* [1985] ECR 3731.
[98] Case 178/1984, *Commission v Germany* (bier) [1987] ECR 1227.
[99] Case 407/1985, *Glocken and another v USL Centro Sud and another* [1988] ECR 4233; Case 90/1986, *Criminal proceedings against Zoni* [1988] ECR 4285.
[100] Case 286/1986, *Ministère public v Gérard Deserbais* [1988] ECR 4907.
[101] Case 298/1987, *Proceedings for compulsory reconstruction against Smanor SA* [1988] ECR 4489.
[102] As discussed in Chapter 2 above.

particular geographical area'. He found that these names had the following characteristics: they guarantee the geographical origin of the product and indicate that the product possesses certain characteristics arising from that geographical origin; they are proof of the quality of the product; they impart a good reputation to products amongst consumers; and the legal protection of geographical names safeguards producers' interests against unfair competition and consumers against information that may mislead them.

It was noted how sales descriptions that contain place-names cannot always be considered to be geographical in nature. A name embodying a place-name may also be generic, or it may have become so over the course of time, and thus can no longer be considered as being geographical and therefore may not enjoy the legal protection afforded to such names under Community law, either as a protected geographical indication or as a protected designation of origin. The definition of 'designation of origin' originally set down in Regulation 2081/1992 was seen to be very similar to that laid down by the case law of the Court, but the new type of name created by this legislation, the 'geographical indication', did not appear in the case law.[103]

3.5.1 Recipe Laws

The earliest European Community food laws tended to be vertical in nature, dealing with specific foodstuffs only. In general, these 'recipe laws' limited the use of the legal name to those foodstuffs that possessed certain prescribed characteristics, sometimes in set quantities. Directives were introduced setting out a series of requirements for the production and marketing of chocolate and cocoa,[104] coffee and chicory,[105] fruit juices,[106] honey,[107] and jams, jellies and marmalades and chestnut purée.[108] Most of these original directives have since, primarily due to a multitude of amendments, been simplified and replaced.

---

[103] Council Regulation (EEC) No 2081/1992 of 14 July 1992 on the protection of geographical indications and designations of origin for agricultural products and foodstuffs. [1992] OJ L 208/1. This has now been replaced by Council Regulation (EC) No 510/2006 of 20 March 2006 on the protection of geographical indications and designations of origin for agricultural products and foodstuffs. [2006] OJ L 93/12.

[104] Council Directive 1973/241/EEC of 24 July 1973 on the approximation of the laws of the Member States relating to cocoa and chocolate products intended for human consumption. [1973] OJ L 228/23.

[105] Council Directive 1977/436/EEC of 27 June 1977 on the approximation of the laws of the Member States relating to coffee extracts and chicory extracts. [1977] OJ L 172/20.

[106] Council Directive 1975/726/EEC of 17 November 1975 on the approximation of the laws of the Member States concerning fruit juices and certain similar products. [1975] OJ L 311/40.

[107] Council Directive 1974/409/EEC of 22 July 1974 on the harmonisation of the laws of the Member States relating to honey. [1974] OJ L 221/10.

[108] Council Directive 1979/693/EEC of 24 July 1979 on the approximation of the laws of the Member States relating to fruit jams, jellies and marmalades and chestnut purée. [1979] OJ L 205/5.

Chocolate and Cocoa

The original directive setting out the compositional requirements for use of the variety of legal names associated with chocolate was finally replaced after much expense and debate in 2000.[109] 'Chocolate' was defined in Annex I to the 1973 directive as:

> the product obtained from cocoa nib, cocoa mass, cocoa powder or fat-reduced cocoa powder and sucrose with or without added cocoa butter, having . . . a minimum total dry cocoa solids content of 35%—at least 14% of dry non-fat cocoa solids and 18% of cocoa butter.

It is similarly, if slightly more simply, defined in the 2000 directive.[110] The 1973 directive also set out the compositional requirements for the legitimate use of the legal names 'plain chocolate', 'milk chocolate', and 'milk chocolate with high milk content'.[111] While chocolate had to contain a minimum of 35 per cent cocoa, milk chocolate with high milk content was only required to contain 20 per cent cocoa. As noted in Chapter 1, this led to a 30 year debate over what should be marketable as chocolate in the EU given the differences in cocoa content and the presence of vegetable fats in place of cocoa butter.

In an opinion delivered by the Economic and Social Committee on the simplification of the vertical directives on food arising out of the Edinburgh Summit in 1992, it was noted that of all the proposed Council reforms in relation to the series of directives under scrutiny, the most controversial was that dealing with the issue of vegetable fat in chocolate.[112] The resolution of the milk chocolate problem was deemed to be of major significance given that milk chocolate had come to account for up to 85 to 90 per cent of all chocolate sales in the Community.[113] The Economic and Social Committee noted that the extension of ingredient labelling to chocolate could assist in dealing with the present problem. If non-cocoa butter vegetable fats had been used in the production of the chocolate, this would feature in any ingredients listing. A further separate declaration about this use was thus deemed to be unnecessary in achieving the aim pursued. The separate declaration does now form part of the amended legislation.

---

[109] Directive 2000/36/EC of the European Parliament and of the Council of 23 June 2000 relating to cocoa and chocolate products intended for human consumption. [2000] OJ L 197/19.

[110] Annex I to Directive 2000/36/EC.

[111] Annex I to Directive 1973/241/EEC.

[112] Opinion of the Economic and Social Committee on the simplification of the vertical directives on food: Proposal for a European Parliament and Council directive relation to cocoa and chocolate products intended for human consumption, Proposal for a Council directive relating to certain sugars intended for human consumption, Proposal for a Council directive relating to honey, Proposal for a Council directive relating to fruit juices and certain similar products intended for human consumption, Proposal for a Council directive relating to certain partly or wholly dehydrated preserved milk for human consumption, Proposal for a European and Council directive relating to coffee extracts and chicory extracts, Proposal for a Council directive relating to fruit jams, jellies and marmalades and chestnut purée intended for human consumption. [1997] OJ C 56/20.

[113] Opinion of the Economic and Social Committee on the simplification of the vertical directives on food. [1997] OJ C 56/20.

There is also a health issue attached to the use of vegetable fats in chocolate. It is not solely a quality matter. Some of the vegetable fat varieties permitted for use under the terms of the directive, such as palm oil, are primarily used in the production of soap and candles and their consumption by humans is not advised.[114] The 1973 directive had clearly stated that its terms did not affect any provision of the national laws of the Member States that prohibited the addition of vegetable fats other than cocoa butter to chocolate.[115] As a consequence, eight Member States had prohibited the addition of vegetable fats other than cocoa butter to chocolate, in the light of their concerns over the effects that such an addition may have on both quality and safety.[116] When questioned about the validity of the scientific evidence upon which the new rules set out in the 2000 directive were based, rules that finally and absolutely removed this freedom to prohibit, the Commission stated that the primary responsibility for food safety had to remain with the producers. The role of the competent authorities in the Member States was effectively limited to vetting the extent to which manufacturers comply with their responsibilities through the operation of national monitoring and inspection systems. It is worth noting that the Commission itself has not always been entirely confident about the accuracy with which levels of vegetable fats in chocolate can be detected. In the late 1990s, analysis methods dated from the early 1980s and where five per cent vegetable fats had been used in chocolate production, these methods gave results ranging from three to seven per cent. The degree of accuracy could also be affected by the type of vegetable fat used and by other ingredients that had been added. The use of certain types of vegetable fats, it was noted, resulted in greater or lesser accuracy depending on the type of fat used, and analysis was rendered more difficult where the chocolate had been mixed with other ingredients, for example hazelnuts, which already contain fats.

The difficulties that arose in the efforts to find a suitable compromise on the chocolate labelling question illustrate one very good reason why the Community institutions have proved willing to accept the Commission's position that following the decision of the Court of Justice in *Cassis*, harmonising vertical food standards are no longer necessary or desirable.[117] Some generic foodstuffs, like chocolate, are produced in substantially different ways in different Member States. Harmonising rules present a difficulty here. If no legislation is introduced to standardise what may be lawfully marketable in all Member States then the mutual recognition principle applies—the single minimum standard from amongst those of all Member States must now be the maximum standard allowable for all. If, however, harmonising legislation is introduced, then the standard to be set

---

[114] Those vegetable fats which may be added to chocolate include illipe, palm-oil, sal, shea, kokum gurgi and mango kernel. In addition to this coconut oil may be added to chocolate used for the manufacture of ice cream and similar frozen products. Annex II to Directive 2000/36/EC.

[115] Article 14(2).

[116] Under the terms of Council Directive 1988/344/EEC of 13 June 1988 on the approximation of the laws of the Member States on extraction solvents used in the production of foodstuffs and food ingredients, hexane may be used in the production of cocoa butter. [1988] OJ L 157/28.

[117] Communication on the free movement of foodstuffs within the Community. [1989] OJ C 271/3.

becomes the subject of debate, with each Member State seeking to have its rules used as a model for the new Community-wide standard for all. For a contentious foodstuff, such as chocolate, this can lead to a 30 year impasse, with Member States taking their own action on the matter in the interim. This consequently frustrates the free movement of this product.

At present, Community compositional standards, or 'recipe laws', exist for only a handful of food products. There is no obvious reason why rules have been set for chocolate, coffee, honey, fruit juice and jams, other than the fact that secondary legislation had been introduced for these products prior to the delivery of the judgment in *Cassis*. The decision was taken to cease the legislative harmonisation programme soon after this.

Coffee and Chicory

As part of the continuing process simplifying Community rules relating to the production and composition of certain specific foodstuffs, arising out of the Edinburgh Summit of the Council in 1992, a new directive was introduced in 1999 setting out the requirements for the production and marketing of coffee and chicory extracts.[118] This new directive replaced the original 1977 coffee legislation.[119] 'Instant coffee' is defined in the directive as being:

> the concentrated product obtained by extraction from roasted coffee beans using only water as the medium of extraction and excluding any process of hydrolysis involving the addition of an acid or a base. Apart from those insoluble substances which it is technically impossible to remove, and insoluble oils derived from coffee, coffee extract must contain only the soluble and aromatic constituents of coffee.[120]

The framework directive on food labelling is to apply to those products coming within the scope of the coffee legislation.[121] The labelling must include the term 'decaffeinated' where the caffeine content does not exceed 0.3 per cent by weight of the coffee-based dry matter.[122] This information must be displayed within the same field of vision as the sales description.[123] Those extraction solvents which may be used in the decaffeination of coffee, and for which conditions of use are specified, are set out in a 1988 directive.[124] They include methyl acetate (also used in paint removers), ethylmethylketone (which, when mixed with hexane—a

---

[118] Directive 1999/4/EC of the European Parliament and of the Council of 22 February 1999 relating to coffee extracts and chicory extracts. [1999] OJ L 66/26.

[119] Council Directive 1977/436/EEC of 27 June 1977 on the approximation of the laws of the Member States relating to coffee extracts and chicory extracts. [1977] OJ L 172/20.

[120] Annex to Directive 1999/4/EC of the European Parliament and of the Council of 22 February 1999 relating to coffee extracts and chicory extracts. [1999] OJ L 66/26.

[121] Article 2(a).

[122] Article 2(b).

[123] *Ibid.*

[124] Council Directive 1988/344/EEC of 13 June 1988 on the approximation of the laws of the Member States on extraction solvents used in the production of foodstuffs and food ingredients. [1988] OJ L 157/28.

petroleum product used in the production of chocolate—may induce neurotic effects) and dichloromethane (also used in pesticide products and a recognised carcinogen).[125] The original legislation included a requirement that '[o]nly raw materials which are sound, genuine and of merchantable quality may be used in the manufacture of [coffee]'.[126] There is no similar provision in the 1999 directive.

Fruit Juices

Having already been replaced in 1993,[127] the original legislation on fruit juices[128] was again subject to further simplification and consolidation in 2001.[129] On this occasion there was no parliamentary involvement in the legislative process. The new legislation was designed to codify and clarify further the original and subsequent related legislative provisions, a task that had already commenced with the introduction of the 1993 directive.[130] In particular, this new legislation was to account for two things. First, the introduction of the new quantitative ingredient declaration legislation,[131] codified in the framework labelling legislation,[132] should be used to compel the producer to clearly indicate when a product is a mixture of fruit juice and fruit juice from concentrate. The list of ingredients must bear the names of both the fruit juices and the fruit juices from concentrate used.[133] Where a product is a mixture of fruit juice and concentrate the labelling must sate that it is 'made with concentrate(s)' or 'partially made with concentrate(s)' as appropriate.[134] Second, account should be taken of the nutrition labelling legislation[135] as the addition of vitamins to products coming within the

---

[125] Annex to Council Directive 1988/344/EEC of 13 June 1988 on the approximation of the laws of the Member States on extraction solvents used in the production of foodstuffs and food ingredients. [1988] OJ L 157/28. Council Directive 1992/115/EEC of 17 December 1992 amending for the first time Directive 88/344/EEC on the approximation of the laws of the Member States on extraction solvents used in the production of foodstuffs and food ingredients, [1992] OJ L 409/31, now prohibits the combined use of hexane and ethylmethylketone.

[126] Article 3(1).

[127] Council Directive 1993/77/EEC of 21 September 1993 relating to fruit juices and certain similar products. [1993] OJ L 244/23.

[128] Council Directive 1975/726/EEC of 17 November 1975 on the approximation of the laws of the Member States concerning fruit juices and certain similar products. [1975] OJ L 311/40.

[129] Council Directive 2001/112/EC of 20 December 2001 relating to fruit juices and certain similar products intended for human consumption. [2002] OJ L 10/58.

[130] Preamble 5 to Directive 2001/112/EC.

[131] Directive 1997/4/EC of the European Parliament and of the Council of 27 January 1997 amending Directive 1979/112/EEC on the approximation of the laws of the Member States relating to the labelling, presentation and advertising of foodstuffs. [1997] OJ L 43/21.

[132] Directive 2000/13/EC of the European Parliament and of the Council of 20 March 2000 on the approximation of the laws of the Member States relating to the labelling, presentation and advertising of foodstuffs. [2000] OJ L 109/29.

[133] Preamble 7 to Council Directive 2001/112/EC of 20 December 2001 relating to fruit juices and certain similar products intended for human consumption. [2002] OJ L 10/58.

[134] Article 3(6).

[135] Council Directive 1990/496/EEC of 24 September 1990 on nutrition labelling for foodstuffs. [1990] OJ L 276/40.

scope of the directive is permitted in some Member States.[136] For fruit nectars, which are '[t]he . . . product obtained by adding water and sugars to [fruit juice, concentrated or otherwise]',[137] the labelling must indicate the minimum content of fruit juice, fruit purée or any mixture of those ingredients by the declaration 'fruit content: . . . % minimum'[138] located in the same field of vision as the product name.

'Fruit juice' is defined in the legislation as being '[t]he . . . product obtained from fruit which is sound and ripe, fresh or preserved by chilling . . . having the characteristic colour, flavour and taste typical of the juice of the fruit from which it comes'.[139] The fruit juice directive does authorise Member States to permit the addition of vitamins and minerals to fruit juice.[140] Where a juice is made from only one kind of fruit then the name of the single fruit used is to be substituted in the product name for the word 'fruit'.[141] Thus a 'fruit juice' as defined in the directive that contains no fruit other than oranges is to be called 'orange juice'. For products manufactured from two or more fruits, except in some circumstances where lemon juice has been used, the product name must be supplemented by a list of the fruits used, in descending order of the volume of fruit juices or purées included.[142] Where three or more fruits have been used, the indication of the fruit types may be replaced by the words 'several fruits' or a similar wording, or by a statement of the number of fruits used.[143] Where the juice has been sweetened by the addition of sugars, the sales name must include the word 'sweetened' or 'with added sugar', followed by an indication of the maximum quantity of sugar added.[144] Tomato juice does not come within the scope of the directive as it is not deemed to be a fruit.[145]

The fruit juice directive presents a clear example of reason two as to why the Community institutions may not wish to embark upon a comprehensive harmonisation programme for food standards. Considering the manner in which Community law evolves, each time a new horizontal legislative initiative is introduced, such as that on quantitative ingredient declarations, the related affected vertical legislation, such as the fruit juice directive, must also be altered to reflect this. These amendments add to an already piecemeal body of rules, complicating matters further for producers who must now look in several places to discover what the current rules may be. This difficulty is not helped by a poor track record of consolidation exercises for such legislation.

---

[136] Preamble 8 to Council Directive 2001/112/EC of 20 December 2001 relating to fruit juices and certain similar products intended for human consumption. [2002] OJ L 10/58.

[137] Annex I to Directive 2001/112.

[138] Article 3(7).

[139] Annex I to Directive 2001/112.

[140] Article 2.

[141] Article 3(2).

[142] Article 3(3).

[143] *Ibid.*

[144] Article 3(4).

[145] Annex II to Council Directive 2001/112/EC of 20 December 2001 relating to fruit juices and certain similar products intended for human consumption. [2002] OJ L 10/58.

Honey

In 2001 a new directive[146] was introduced to replace the original legislation regulating the production of honey.[147] This legislation offers a rare example of a 'recipe law' that was not amended at any stage between its introduction and eventual repeal and replacement 27 years later. The sales name 'honey' can only be used where the product is:

> the natural sweet substance produced by Apis mellifera bees from the nectar of plants or from secretions of living parts of plants or excretions of plant-sucking insects on the living parts of plants, which the bees collect, transform by combining with specific substances of their own, deposit, dehydrate, store and leave in honeycombs to ripen and mature.[148]

The directive breaks down the simple definition of honey further into different honey types. The main types of honey are: blossom honey or nectar honey, which is the honey obtained from the nectar of plants; honeydew honey, which is that obtained mainly from excretions of plant-sucking insects on the living part of plants or secretions of living parts of plants; comb honey, which is the honey stored by bees in the cells of freshly built broodless combs or thin comb foundation sheets made solely of beeswax and sold in sealed whole combs or sections of such combs; chunk honey or cut comb in honey, which contains one or more pieces of comb honey; drained honey, which is obtained by draining decapped broodless combs; extracted honey, which is obtained by centrifuging decapped broodless combs; pressed honey, which is obtained by pressing broodless combs with or without the application of moderate heat not exceeding 45°C; and filtered honey, which is obtained by removing foreign inorganic matter in such a way as to result in the significant removal of pollen.[149] In addition to these types of honey, the directive also stipulates the designation 'baker's honey' for that which is suitable for industrial uses, or as an ingredient in other foodstuffs which are then processed and may have a foreign taste or odour, or have begun to ferment or have fermented, or have been overheated.[150] The name 'honey' may only be used where the product meets the compositional requirements set out in the Directive.[151] This

[146] Council Directive 2001/110/EC of 20 December 2001 relating to honey. [2002] OJ L 10/47.
[147] Council Directive 1974/409/EC of 22 July 1974 on the harmonisation of the laws of the Member States relating to honey. [1974] OJ L 221/10.
[148] Annex I to Council Directive 2001/110/EC of 20 December 2001 relating to honey. [2002] OJ L 10/47. The definition of 'honey' under Directive 1974/409/EEC, which was almost identical to that in the 2001 legislation, was set out in the actual text of the directive itself, Art 1(1). This is a common feature of this new wave of directives introduced since the late 1990s to replace the original 'recipe laws'. Definitions previously set out in the main body of the legislation have now been removed to the Annex to it.
[149] Annex I to Council Directive 2001/110/EC of 20 December 2001 relating to honey. [2002] OJ L 10/47.
[150] Annex I to Council Directive 2001/110/EC of 20 December 2001 relating to honey. [2002] OJ L 10/47.
[151] Article 2(1).

also applies, where honey is described as being of a certain kind or type.[152] However, these names may be replaced by the simple product name 'honey', except in the case of filtered honey, comb honey, chunk honey or cut comb in honey and, obviously, baker's honey.[153] In the case of baker's honey the words 'intended for cooking only' must appear on the product label in close proximity to the product name.[154] Where baker's honey has been used as an ingredient in a compound foodstuff, the term 'honey' may be used in the product name of the compound food instead of the term 'baker's honey'. However, the list of ingredients must state that baker's honey has in fact been used.[155]

The country or countries of origin, where the honey has been harvested, must also be stated on the label. However, if the honey originates in more than one Member State or third country then that indication may be replaced with either 'blend of EC honeys', 'blend of non-EC honeys', or 'blend of EC and non-EC honeys' as appropriate.[156]

Specific compositional criteria for honey are also set out in the directive. It is stated that honey: consists essentially of different sugars, predominantly fructose and glucose as well as other substances such as organic acids, enzymes and solid particles derived from honey collection; varies in colour from nearly colourless to dark brown; can be fluid, viscous or partly or entirely crystallised in consistency; has a varied flavour and aroma but should be derived from the plant origin; should not have added to it any food ingredient, including food additives, nor any other additions other than honey; should not have removed from it any pollen or constituent particular to honey except where this is unavoidable in the removal of foreign inorganic or organic matter; should be free from organic or inorganic matters foreign to its composition; and with the exception of baker's honey, should not have any foreign tastes or odours, nor have begun to ferment, nor have an artificially changed acidity nor have been heated in such a way that the natural enzymes have been either destroyed or significantly inactivated.[157] The quantities of, *inter alia*, sugar, including fructose, glucose and sucrose, and moisture content are also specified.[158]

The 1974 honey directive failed to set out any substantive monitoring procedure to ensure compliance with its terms. The 2001 directive also fails to do this. It simply states that methods may be adopted by the Commission, assisted by the Standing Committee on Foodstuffs, to permit verification of compliance of honey with the provisions of the legislation.[159] Until the adoption of such methods Member States are, wherever possible, to use internationally recognised validated

[152] Article 2(2).
[153] *Ibid.*
[154] *Ibid.*
[155] Article 2(3).
[156] Article 2(4).
[157] Annex II to Council Directive 2001/110/EC of 20 December 2001 relating to honey. [2002] OJ L 10/47.
[158] *Ibid.*
[159] Article 7(1).

methods, such as those approved by the Codex Alimentarius, to verify compliance with the terms of the honey directive.[160]

The provisions of the honey directive clearly demonstrate another of the inherent difficulties that exist when the Community attempts to set harmonised food standards—compliance. In an international legal system like the EU, the Member States have to take responsibility for this through the implementation of national measures, ensuring, for example, that only those products that possess the key characteristics of the product in question may be labelled accordingly. The Commission also has a role to play here, albeit a necessarily lesser one. This does not have to be a problem in itself, as the directive does give guidance to the Member States in this regard. They are to follow internationally recognised methods for verification. The Codex Standard for Honey sets common guidelines for methods of sampling and analysis to establish compliance with compositional standards.[161] This includes details of how moisture, sugar and other solid content is to be verified. Origin claims are not accounted for in these standards. Directive 2001/110 does state that the country of origin, or countries or regions where there is a blend, must be given. However, nowhere in the legislation is it stated that the percentage quantity of each variety contained in the blend must be clearly labelled. This means, for example, that a product can be labelled 'Irish Honey', or even 'Pure Irish Honey', if it is actually a blend of Irish and non-EU honeys, harvested in any number of countries. While it must state elsewhere on the label that the product is a blend of Irish and non-EU honeys, the actual content of the product harvested in Ireland could be as little as one per cent. It is 'pure' simply because it is 100 per cent honey, not because it is 100 per cent Irish.

Where specific food standards like this have been introduced at both EU and international levels, sufficient attention should be paid to inconsistencies such as that outlined above to ensure that consumers are protected and that fair trading is facilitated. The inclusion of specific provision in this regard in the Community secondary legislation, or an extension of the quantitative ingredient declaration system to labelling disclosures such as this, could assist here. This would oblige information to be given as to the proportions of the product originating in different regions where there is a blend of ingredients, and where a specific place of origin claim is made on the label. Essentially, the EU standards exist in order to maintain a degree of harmonisation with global standards where these exist, rather than to create any meaningful level of consumer protection provision or to ensure that trade in these foodstuffs remains fair. This is examined in more detail in Chapter 4.

Jams

One final example of a recipe law that was introduced and later updated is that regulating the production and marketing of fruit jams, jellies, marmalades and

---

[160] Article 4.
[161] Codex Standard 12/1981; revised 1987 and 2001.

sweetened chestnut purée.[162] The new fruit jams directive, which was introduced to replace the original rules,[163] was part of the continuing process of simplifying and improving the accessibility of Community food rules, in particular to account for the many alterations that had taken place since the introduction of the earlier directive relating to colourings, sweeteners and other additives.[164] As with the other recipe laws, the directive defines its subject and all permissible variations of it, sets out the compositional requirements for each, and specifies a set of labelling requirements for products marketed under its terms.

The few EU 'recipe laws' that do exist have proved to be problematic, controversial and, in many ways, unable to satisfy the purposes for which they were introduced. Despite this, it is here contended that expanding this system of rules, creating more specific standards for some of the more contentious foodstuffs, such as those that have been the subject of Court examination, as discussed in Chapter 2, could now appease many of the criticisms levelled at the jurisprudence of the Court in Article 28 EC related case law. In particular, this could address aspects of the difficulties arising out of the *Cassis* inspired 'race to the bottom' where quality standards and the nutritional value of food are concerned.

One major legislative initiative that has been introduced to counter claims about how the decisions of the Court of Justice contribute to an overall reduction in food quality and safety standards has been the creation of a scheme designed to protect the reputation and characteristics of geographical foodstuffs.

3.5.2 Protected Geographical Indications and Designations of Origin

Originally, EU legislation containing provisions for the protection of geographical indications and designations of origin was contained in Regulation 2081/1992.[165] In March 2006 a new Council Regulation was introduced, which substantially repeals and re-enacts the same provisions, but which introduces new stipulations facilitating third countries that wish to avail themselves of the protections afforded.[166] These new stipulations were introduced as a consequence of the recommendations of the Dispute Settlement Body of the WTO.[167]

It is necessary to refer here to the motives behind the introduction of the original legislation. Primarily, it was felt that devising a scheme such as this could

---

[162] Council Directive 2001/113/EC of 20 December 2001 relating to fruit jams, jellies and marmalades and sweetened chestnut purée intended for human consumption. [2002] OJ L 10/67.

[163] Council Directive 1979/693/EEC of 24 July 1979 on the approximation of the laws of the Member States relating to fruit jams, jellies and marmalades and chestnut purée. [1979] OJ L 205/5.

[164] Preamble 4 to Council Directive 2001/113/EC of 20 December 2001 relating to fruit jams, jellies and marmalades and sweetened chestnut purée intended for human consumption. [2002] OJ L 10/67.

[165] Council Regulation (EEC) No 2081/1992 of 14 July 1992 on the protection of geographical indications and designations of origin for agricultural products and foodstuffs. [1992] OJ L 208/1.

[166] Council Regulation (EC) No 510/2006 of 20 March 2006 on the protection of geographical indications and designations of origin for agricultural products and foodstuffs. [2006] OJ L 93/12.

[167] WTO DS 174 and DS 290, *EC—Trademarks and Geographical Indications.*

help to satisfy the interests of the increasing number of consumers who were becoming more interested in food quality levels. A scheme designed to protect eligible foodstuffs could be used to distinguish those products that possess certain unique characteristics due to their region and/or method of production. It was also felt that the promotion of products having certain characteristics pertaining to their method and region of production could be of considerable benefit to rural economies, in particular those of less-favoured or remote areas, by improving the incomes of farmers and by retaining the rural population in these areas.[168] Member States had already begun to introduce 'registered designations of origin', which had proved successful with producers—who secured higher incomes in return for improved quality, and with consumers—who could purchase high quality products with guarantees as to their method of production and origin. Ultimately, however, it was the diversity in the national practices for implementing registered designations of origin and geographical indications that led to the introduction of the regulation, designed to harmonise the disparate registration processes and to regain Community control.

Regulation 510/2006

Regulation 510/2006, which does not apply to wines or spirits,[169] lays down rules for registration as a protected geographical food name. A designation of origin is:

> the name of a region, a specific place or, in exceptional cases, a country, used to describe an agricultural product or a foodstuff originating in that region, specific place or country, and the quality or characteristics of which are essentially or exclusively due to a particular geographical environment with its inherent natural and human factors, and the production, processing and preparation of which take place in the defined geographical area.[170]

A geographical indication is:

> the name of a region, a specific place or, in exceptional cases, a country, used to describe an agricultural product or foodstuff originating in that region, specific place or country, and which possesses a specific quality, reputation or other characteristics attributable to that geographical origin and the production and/or processing and/or preparation of which take place in the defined geographical area.[171]

Food names that have become generic may not be registered as either protected designations of origin or protected geographical indications.[172] A name is deemed to have become generic for the purposes of the regulation where, although it relates to the place or the region where the agricultural product or foodstuff was originally produced or marketed, it has become the common name for that

---

[168] Preamble 3-6 to Regulation 2081/1992.
[169] Article 1(1) of Regulation 510/2006.
[170] Article 2(1)(a).
[171] Article 2(1)(b).
[172] Article 3(1).

agricultural product or foodstuff.[173] In order to establish whether a name has become generic, account is to be taken of all factors, in particular the existing situation in the Member State in which the name originates and in areas of consumption, the existing situation in other Member States, and the relevant national or Community laws.[174]

To be eligible to use a protected designation of origin or a protected geographical indication, an agricultural product or foodstuff must comply with the criteria for a registered specification.[175] This specification should include the name of the agricultural product or foodstuff, including designation of origin or the geographical indication; a description of the agricultural product or foodstuff including the raw materials, if appropriate, and principal physical, chemical, microbiological and/or organoleptic characteristics of the product or the foodstuff; the definition of the geographical area; evidence that the agricultural product or foodstuff originates in the geographical area; a description of the method of obtaining the agricultural product or foodstuff and, if appropriate, the authentic and unvarying local methods; the details bearing out the link with the geographical environment or the geographical origin, whichever is applicable; details of the inspection structures ensuring that agricultural product and foodstuffs bearing a protected name meet the requirement laid down in the specifications; the specific labelling details relating to the protected geographical indication or protected designation of origin, whichever is applicable, or the equivalent traditional national indications; and any requirements laid down by Community and/or national provisions.[176]

Only a group or, subject to certain conditions, a natural or legal person is entitled to apply for registration under the regulation.[177] A 'group' is deemed to be any association of producers and/or processors working with the same agricultural product or foodstuff.[178] It may only apply for registration in respect of agricultural products or foodstuffs that it produces or obtains.[179] The application for registration must include all the details of the product specification[180] and should be sent to the authority in the Member State in which the geographical area is located.[181] The Member State checks that the application is justified and forwards it to the Commission.[182] If the Commission concludes that the name qualifies for protection, it publishes details of this in the Official Journal.[183] Member States or third countries may object to the registration proposed within six months of the date of

---

[173] Article 3(1).
[174] *Ibid.*
[175] Article 4(1).
[176] Article 4(2).
[177] Article 5(1).
[178] *Ibid.*
[179] Article 5(2).
[180] Article 5(3).
[181] Article 5(4).
[182] Article 5(5).
[183] Article 6(2).

publication.[184] If there are no admissible objections raised the name is entered in a register kept by the Commission.[185] Where an objection is deemed admissible, the Commission requests that the Member States concerned seek agreement on the matter among themselves.[186] If no agreement is reached, it is then up to the Commission to make a decision.[187] An objection will only be deemed admissible where the objecting Member State can show non-compliance with the terms of the regulation, that the proposed registration would jeopardise the existence of an entirely or partly identical name or trade mark or the existence of products which are legally on the market, or that the name applied for is generic.[188]

Names successfully registered are protected against any commercial use by products not covered by the registration insofar as those products are comparable to the products registered under that name or insofar as using the name exploits the reputation of the protected name; any misuse, imitation or evocation, even if the true origin of the product is indicated or if the protected name is translated or accompanied by an expression such as 'style', 'type', 'method', 'as produced in', 'imitation' or similar term; any other false or misleading indication as to the provenance, origin, nature or essential qualities of the product, on the packaging, advertising material or documents relating to the product concerned, and the packing of the product in a container liable to convey a false impression as to its origin; or any other practice liable to mislead the public as to the true origin of the product.[189] Where a registered name contains the name of an agricultural product or foodstuff that is considered generic, the use of that generic name on other foodstuffs is not prohibited.[190] Protected names may not become generic.[191]

What was previously Article 12 of Regulation 2081/1992 has been removed from Regulation 510/2006. It provided that the system for registering geographical indications and designations of origin could also be applied to agricultural products or foodstuffs from third countries, provided that the third country was able to satisfy the terms of the regulation, in particular those in relation to inspection arrangements, and that the third country concerned was prepared to provide protection equivalent to that available in the Community to corresponding

---

[184] Article 7(1). Previously, there was no procedure expressly afforded to individuals to object to the registration of a protected geographical indication or a protected designation of origin under the terms of Regulation 2081/1992. The Court of First Instance had stated that the fact that an applicant controlled a large part of the market for which a protected designation has been registered, was not in itself enough to differentiate it from any other trader affected by the contested legislation. Further, the fact that an applicant had sent a duly substantiated statement to the competent authority of the Member State in which it was established, objecting to the registration of the name in question, an objection that was not forwarded to the Commission, was not sufficient to establish the admissibility of an individual objection. Case T-114/1999, *CSR PAMPRYL v Commission* [1999] ECR II-3331. The position has now been rectified by the terms of Articles 7(2) and (3) of Regulation 510/2006.

[185] Article 7(4).
[186] Article 7(5).
[187] *Ibid.*
[188] Article 7(3).
[189] Article 13(1).
[190] *Ibid.*
[191] Article 13(2).

agricultural products or foodstuffs coming from the Community.[192] This requirement of reciprocity was central to the dispute at WTO level. While this is discussed in more detail in Chapter 4 below, it should be noted here that this ultimately led to the EU being forced to alter its rules in order to increase the level of access to applicants from third countries.[193]

Regulations are constantly being introduced to add names to the Register of protected designations of origin and protected geographical indications. Examples include presunto de barrancos and berenjena de almango,[194] rocamadour,[195] exmoor blue cheese,[196] and timoleague brown pudding, limone di sorrento, chianti classico and cidre breton.[197]

In *Belgium v Spain* the Court discussed just how important protected designations of origin are.[198] It was stated that Community legislation displays a general tendency to enhance the quality of products within the framework of the Common Agricultural Policy, in order to promote the reputation of those products through, *inter alia*, the use of designations of origin which enjoy special protection. That general tendency had become apparent in the quality wines sector. It had also emerged in relation to other agricultural products, in respect of which the Council had adopted Regulation 2081/1992. The eighth recital in the preamble to that regulation made it clear that the latter was to apply without prejudice to existing Community legislation on wines and spirits, which provides for a higher level of protection. Designations of origin fall within the scope of industrial and commercial property rights. The applicable rules are, it was noted, designed to protect those entitled to use them against improper use of those designations by third parties seeking to profit from the reputation which they have acquired. They are intended to guarantee that the product bearing them comes from a specified

---

[192] Article 12(1).

[193] See Proposal for a Council regulation on the protection of geographical indications and designations of origin for agricultural products and foodstuffs. COM (2005) 698.

[194] Commission Regulation (EC) No 2400/1996 of 17 December 1996 on the entry of certain names in the Register of protected designations of origin and protected geographical indications provided for in Council Regulation (EEC) No 2081/1992 on the protection of geographical indications and designations of origin for agricultural products and foodstuffs. [1996] OJ L 327/11.

[195] Commission Regulation (EC) No 38/1999 of 8 January 1999 supplementing the Annex to Regulation (EC) No 2400/1996 of 17 December 1996 on the entry of certain names in the 'Register of protected designations of origin and protected geographical indications' provided for in Council Regulation (EEC) No 2081/1992 on the protection of geographical indications and designations of origin for agricultural products and foodstuffs. [1999] OJ L 5/62.

[196] Commission Regulation (EC) No 872/1999 of 27 April 1999 supplementing the Annex to Regulation (EC) No 2400/1996 of 17 December 1996 on the entry of certain names in the 'Register of protected designations of origin and protected geographical indications' provided for in Council Regulation (EEC) No 2081/1992 on the protection of geographical indications and designations of origin for agricultural products and foodstuffs. [1999] OJ L 110/4.

[197] Commission Regulation (EC) No 2446/2000 of 6 November 2000 supplementing the Annex to Regulation (EC) No 2400/1996 of 17 December 1996 on the entry of certain names in the 'Register of protected designations of origin and protected geographical indications' provided for in Council Regulation (EEC) No 2081/1992 on the protection of geographical indications and designations of origin for agricultural products and foodstuffs. [2000] OJ L 281/12.

[198] Case C-388/1995, *Belgium v Spain* [2000] ECR 3123.

geographical area and displays certain particular characteristics.[199] They may enjoy a high reputation amongst consumers and constitute for producers who fulfil the conditions for using them an essential means of attracting custom.[200] The Court accepted that the reputation of designations of origin depends on their image in the minds of consumers. That image in turn depends essentially on particular characteristics and more generally on the quality of the product. It is on the latter, ultimately, that the product's reputation is based.

It is, however, in relation to those products and foodstuffs that have not been registered as protected designations of origin or protected geographical indications that most controversy has arisen. In particular, there has been much debate over foodstuffs that have been deemed to be generic and thus are prohibited from benefiting from the protected status and the consequent advantages of successful registration.

Regulation 510/2006 and Existing National Laws

Regulation 510/2006 does not encroach in any way on existing national laws on the use of geographical food names that are not registered under the procedure set out therein and/or which fall outside the scope of the regulation. In *Pistre*, for example, proceedings were brought against the defendants for using labels liable to mislead consumers as to the qualities or provenance of products.[201] The defendants were all French nationals who manufactured and marketed cured food. They were prosecuted for having marketed cooked meat products using a label bearing the description 'mountain', which they had not been authorised to make in relation to those products under French law. It was questioned whether the introduction of Regulation 2081/1992 had precluded the application of this national legislation, which appeared to be more restrictive than the domestic rules given that the Community Regulation restricted indications of provenance to products originating in a defined region. The French rules only required that the term 'mountain' be restricted to upland areas and areas with slopes of a certain degree of steepness and included significant derogations from the requirement that production processes be local by allowing, in particular, the main raw material of the product to come from outside the geographical area or by allowing the product to be manufactured partly outside that area. The defendants submitted that the conditions to which use of the description 'mountain' was subject were too loose and too flexible for that description to be regarded as a geographical indication within the meaning of the regulation. They submitted that the term was simply informative, wholly descriptive, generic and undefined. The French

---

[199] See also Case C-47/1990, *Établissements Delhaize frères et Compagnie Le Lion SA v Promalvin SA and AGE Bodegas Unidas SA* [1992] ECR I-3669.

[200] See, to that effect, in relation to indications of provenance, Case C-3/1991, *Exportur SA v LOR SA and Confiserie du Tech SA* [1992] ECR I-5529, para 28.

[201] Joined Cases C-321/1994, C-322/1994, C-323/1994 and C-324/1994, *Criminal proceedings against Jacques Pistre, Michèle Barthes, Yves Milhau and Didier Oberti* [1997] ECR I-2343.

Government contested that the description 'mountain' was a quality description, designed to promote products from mountain areas and to guarantee that certain requirements had been complied with. The Commission concurred. The Court stated that it was clear from the terms of the regulation that the protection of designations of origin and of geographical indications presupposes registration, which itself requires that there be a direct link between the quality of the product and its specific geographical origin. The Court ultimately found that the description 'mountain' was too remote from the substantive subject matter of the regulation for it to preclude the maintenance of the domestic French legislation.

In *Warsteiner*, proceedings were brought against the respondent to prevent them from using the name 'Warsteiner' on the labels of bottles of beer which it brewed 40 kilometres from the town of Warstein.[202] Domestic German legislation specifically prohibited the use of geographical indications that enjoy a particular reputation from being used unfairly to exploit this reputation. The Court was asked during the course of these proceedings whether the regulation prevented the application of a national provision prohibiting the misleading use of a simple geographical designation of source, one where there was no link between the characteristics of the product and its geographical provenance. The Court noted that it was expressly stated in the regulation that its scope was limited to designations where a link does exist between the characteristics of a foodstuff and its geographical origin. Citing the decision in *Pistre*, it was stated that the regulation does not prevent the application of domestic rules such as those at issue in this case. Regulation 2081/1992 was intended to ensure the uniform protection within the Community of the geographical indications which it covers. Regulation 510/2006 achieves the same effect. The original regulation introduced a requirement of Community registration so that these products could enjoy protection in every Member State. The national protection that a Member State confers on geographical designations which do not meet the conditions for registration are governed by the national law of that Member State and are confined to the territory of that Member State. In view of this it was held that the regulation in no way prevented the application of national legislation prohibiting the use of a geographical indication of source where there was no link between the characteristics of the products and its geographical provenance.

Nature of Generic Food Names: The Feta Cheese Cases

Controversy surrounding the eligibility of feta for protection as a designation of origin centred on three key issues.[203] First, whether or not the name feta, given

---

[202] Case C-312/1998, *Schutzverband gegen Unwesen in der Wirtschaft eV v Warsteiner Brauerei Haus Cramer GmbH & Co KG* [2000] ECR I-9187.

[203] The events outlined here are also discussed in C MacMaoláin, 'Eligibility Criteria for Protected Geographical Food Names' (2006) 31 *European Law Review* 576. However, the discussion here also includes an assessment of how the status of products like feta cheese could be altered from protected geographical names to products of specific character in the interest of transparency, legal certainty, commercial fairness and free movement.

that it derives from an Italian and not a Greek word, and given that it contains no geographical place-name, may be registered as a Greek protected geographical name. Second, whether the geographical area that Greece submitted in its registration application was either too large (extending to almost the entire country) or too indistinct as a single region, possessing only a loosely based set of unifying climatic conditions or environmental factors, factors that were arguably shared equally with other areas where feta was produced, both within and outside of Greece. And third, and most importantly and controversially, whether the name feta had, over the course of time, become generic, and was therefore, under the terms of the registration procedure criteria, ineligible for protection as a designation of origin. In particular, decisions of the Court of Justice on this third contention focused on the extent to which the Commission had properly applied the criteria for the assessment of the generic nature of a food name, as set out in the regulation and the early case law on the matter.

The issue of whether the sales name 'feta' had become generic first came before the Court in *Denmark, Germany and France v Commission*.[204] The three applicant Member States brought actions under Article 230 EC for the annulment of Regulation 1107/1996 insofar as it registered feta as a protected designation of origin.[205] The Court noted how in the explanatory memorandum to the proposal for a decision on the registering of feta as a protected designation of origin the Commission had indicated that, in view of all the information received, it was necessary to act with extreme caution in determining whether the name feta had become generic and therefore to gather convincing evidence to back up any decision to be taken. To that end, in April 1994 the Commission arranged for a Eurobarometer poll of nationals from all the Member States. The results of the study showed that on average, one in five citizens of the European Union had seen or heard the name feta, the majority of those who recognised the name associated it with Greek cheese, and three-quarters stated that it evoked a country or region with which the product has a connection. The Commission concluded from these results that the name had not become generic but that it continued to connote Greek origin for most of those who were familiar with it. In addition to this, the Scientific Committee for Designations of Origin, Geographical Indications and Certificates of Specific Character, as established by Commission Decision 1993/53,[206] whose members are qualified experts with legal or agricultural backgrounds, and particularly with knowledge of intellectual property rights, also

[204] Joined Cases C-289/1996, C-293/1996 and C-299/1996, *Denmark, Germany and France v Commission* [1999] ECR I-1541.

[205] Commission Regulation (EC) No 1107/1996 of 12 June 1996 on the registration of geographical indications and designations of origin under the procedure laid down in Article 17 of Council Regulation (EEC) No 2081/1992. [1996] OJ L 148/1. For discussion of recent developments on the Article 230 EC procedure see JA Usher, 'Direct and Individual Concern: An Effective Remedy or a Conventional Solution?' (2003) 28 *European Law Review* 575; and Chapter 10 of D Chalmers, C Hadjiemmanuil, G Monti and A Tomkins, *European Union Law* (Cambridge, CUP, 2006).

[206] Commission Decision of 21 December 1992 setting up a scientific committee for designations of origin, geographical indications and certificates of specific character. [1993] OJ L 13/16.

expressed the view that the name feta met the conditions for registration as a protected name, unanimously finding that it was not generic.

The three applicant States alleged infringement of the geographical names regulation. These contentions were based upon the fact that the name feta did not meet the conditions for registration as a protected designation of origin since the product did not originate in a region or a specific place and did not display any quality or characteristics which were essentially or exclusively due to the geographical environment, with its inherent natural and human factors, of the region or place in which it originated. They also submitted that the name was generic, thus precluding its possible registration, that it was derived from an Italian word and that it had never been reserved solely for cheese produced in Greece. This was disputed, the claim being that feta had been produced in Greece since ancient times and that the name had been used there since the 17th century when Greece was under Venetian influence.

The Court made it clear here that any argument relating to the fact that the name did not relate to the place where the product that it designated originated was not, even if correct, applicable to the case. It is clear from the provisions of the regulation that registration as a protected designation of origin is still possible even where the name of the product does not emanate from a specific place-name.[207] The examination here was thus restricted to an assessment of the generic, or otherwise, nature of the name feta and, in particular, whether the Commission had applied the correct procedures when determining whether that food name had become generic.

As noted earlier, under the terms of the regulation, three main factors must be considered to establish whether a food name has become generic. These are: the existing situation in the Member State where the name originates and in areas of consumption; the existing situation in other Member States; and the relevant national or Community laws.[208] Here, the Court considered that the Commission, in its pre-Regulation 1107/1996 deliberations, had minimised the importance to be attached to the situation existing in the Member States other than the State of origin, as is required. The Court thus concluded that the Commission had not taken account of the fact that the name feta had been used for a considerable time in Member States other than Greece, stressing that when determining whether a name is to be registered, account must be taken of the existence of products which have been legally marketed under that name in other Member States.[209] As a

---

[207] Article 2(3) of Regulation 2081/1992. This is now contained in Article 2(2) of Regulation 510/2006.

[208] Article 3(1).

[209] Similarly, an application, partially based on procedural grounds, for the annulment of Regulation 590/1999, [1999] OJ L 74, insofar as it registered the designation 'spreewälder gurken' as a protected geographical indication was examined in Case C-269/1999, *Kühne* [2001] ECR I-9517. The Court here found that their assessment had not revealed any matter of such a nature as to affect the validity of the Regulation. In coming to this conclusion the Court investigated whether there had been compliance with the registration process, including whether or not applications had been made in time, whether there had been any amendments to the original application, and whether it mattered that not all the ingredients of the foodstuff came from the Spreewald area.

consequence, it was determined that Regulation 1107/1996 was to be annulled to the extent to which it registered the name feta as a protected designation of origin. This deletion was later validated through the adoption of Regulation 1070/1999.[210] While the Court had stopped just short of declaring that feta was definitely generic in nature, the reasoning that it put forward to annul Regulation 1107/1996 to the extent to which it registered the name as a protected designation of origin, clearly indicates that it believed that the Commission's failure to consider the use of the name in other Member States as a determining factor in deciding whether the name had in fact become generic was likely to have influenced the outcome of those deliberations to the extent that had it been considered then feta would almost certainly have been declared a generic name. According to the Advocate General here, feta was definitely to be considered a generic name.[211]

Despite the findings of the Court of Justice in *Denmark, Germany and France v Commission*, the Commission later introduced Regulation 1829/2002, itself amending the Annex to Regulation 1107/1996, to reinstate feta on the register of protected designations of origin.[212] In October 1999, the Commission conducted new research in each of the Member States on the geographical connotations of the name 'feta'. The data gathered by this exercise demonstrated that in 12 of the then 15 Member States the production of feta was not governed by specific rules laying down precise definitions of quality, production methods or, where applicable, geographical areas of production. In Greece, however, production practices for feta cheese had been codified in increasingly specific terms since 1935. Legislation on the quality specifications to be complied with in producing feta cheese had existed in Denmark since 1963 and had been in force in the Netherlands between 1981 and 1998. A definition also appeared in the combined nomenclature.[213] The production of feta was non-existent in one Member State, Luxembourg, and had been sporadic in nine others. However, production of feta cheese was found to be substantial in four Member States. Greece had been producing it since ancient times, Denmark since the 1930s, France since 1931 and Germany since 1972. Greece was found to account for about 73 per cent of feta consumption in the Community. In addition to these statistics, the Scientific Committee for Designations of Origin, Geographical Indications and Certificates of Specific Character noted how consumers were being sold two products with different compositions and organoleptic properties, but using the same

---

[210] Commission Regulation (EC) No 1070/1999 of 25 May 1999 amending the Annex to Regulation (EC) No 1107/1996 on the registration of geographical indications and designations of origin under the procedure laid down in Article 17 of Council Regulation (EEC) No 2081/1992. [1999] OJ L 130. Article 1(1) of Regulation 1070/1999 states that '[t]he name feta is deleted from the register of protected designations of origin and geographical indications'. Article 1(3) provides that the name feta is to remain protected at national level until such time as a decision is taken in this regard.

[211] Opinion of Mr Advocate General La Pergola delivered on 15 September 1998 on Joined Cases C-289/1996, C-293/1996 and C-299/1996, *Denmark, Germany and France v Commission* [1999] ECR I-1541.

[212] Commission Regulation (EC) No 1829/2002 of 14 October 2002 amending the Annex to Regulation (EC) No 1107/1996 with regard to the name feta. [2002] OJ L 277/10.

[213] Council Regulation (EEC) No 2658/1987 of 23 July 1987 on the tariff and statistical nomenclature and on the Common Customs Tariff. [1987] OJ L 256/1.

sales name. Traditional feta was made with sheep's and/or goat's milk using a slow filtration process. The second type was made from cow's milk using a fast filtration process, known as 'ultrafiltration'. Labels for feta not originating in Greece had made direct or indirect references to Greece, implying that the term was not being used as a common name without any geographical significance. It concluded unanimously that the designation was non-generic for several reasons. First, production and consumption are heavily concentrated in Greece. The products produced in other Member States, in particular Denmark, Germany and France, were primarily produced from cow's milk, using different technology and were exported in large quantities to non-member countries. The original Greek product was dominant on the Community market. Second, there was no specific legislation or rules for the production and marketing of feta in most Member States. Only Greece and Denmark had any such legislation. These rules differed significantly, in particular in relation to the ingredients used and the method of production. Finally, Denmark had offered no satisfactory evidence to support its assertion that the name feta had become generic, with the result that it was permissible to use the name alongside the name of the country of production—in other words, to market a product called 'Danish Feta'.

Following the advisory opinion of the Scientific Committee and the data presented in its survey of consumer perceptions in the Member States, the Commission was now of the view that the overall analysis of the legal, historical, cultural, political, social, economic, scientific and technical information led to the conclusion that none of the criteria required by what is now Regulation 510/2006 to show that a name is generic had been met, and that consequently the name 'feta' had not become 'the name of an agricultural product or a foodstuff which, although it relates to the place or the region where the product or foodstuff was originally produced or marketed, has become the common name'.[214] The application by Greece to have feta registered as a protected designation of origin could proceed. Feta was thus re-registered as a protected designation of origin by Regulation 1829/2002.[215]

The annulment of this regulation was then sought by the applicants in *Germany and Denmark v Commission*, who claimed that the name 'feta' did not meet the criteria necessary for protection as a protected designation of origin set out in the regulation given that it was not a geographical designation at all and that it did not owe its quality and characteristics essentially or exclusively to any geographical environment.[216] It was accepted by all the parties to the case that the name was derived from Italian and only entered into use in Greek in the 17th century. It was also accepted that the name was not one of a region, place or country and could not therefore be registered as a protected designation of origin under Article 2(2) of the regulation. It could therefore only possibly be registered under Article 2(3)

---

[214] Article 3(1) of Regulation 510/2006.
[215] Article 1 of Regulation 1829/2002. Article 1(2) of the Regulation reinserted feta into part A of the Annex to Regulation 1107/1996.
[216] Joined Cases C-462/2002 and C-466/2002, *Germany and Denmark v Commission* [2005] ECR I-9115.

of the regulation, which extends the definition of designation of origin to traditional or non-geographical names which possess qualities or characteristics that are due to the environment in which they are produced. This geographical environment can, of course, under the terms of the regulation, be an entire country, provided that the defined area possesses specific natural and human factors which are capable of giving a foodstuff its specific characteristics. The area must present homogeneous natural factors which distinguish it from the areas adjoining it.[217]

Greek national law defining feta did not extend the areas of production to the entire Greek territory. Crete, for example, was not included in the area covered by the protected designation of origin specification. The Court of Justice, in examining whether or not this geographical area was legitimate for the purposes of the regulation, assessed the factors that had been taken into account by the Greek authorities in determining the environmental features that led to the production of a foodstuff with specific characteristics. The domestic legislation referred to the fact that feta must be produced from 'the milk . . . from breeds of ewes and goats raised using traditional methods and adapted to the region of manufacture of the feta and the flora of that region must be the basis of their feed'.[218] The key features uniting and distinguishing the region of production were the mountainous nature of the terrain, the climate and the vegetation. These factors were seen by the Court to indicate that the area did have homogeneous characteristics distinguishing it from the adjoining areas. The areas of Greece excluded from the defined area of production did not possess the same natural features. The geographical area set out in the national legislation protecting feta as a designation of origin was thus found to have been determined in an acceptable manner.[219]

The applicants also submitted that the quality and characteristics of feta were not essentially or exclusively due to a particular geographical environment, as required by the regulation. However, the Court noted that the preamble to the contested regulation did refer to a series of factors, such as sunshine levels, temperature changes, transhumance practice, extensive grazing and vegetation types, all of which indicated that the characteristics of the cheese were due primarily to the characteristics of its region or production, finding that the applicants had failed to demonstrate that the Commission's assessment here was unfounded. The plea alleging infringement of Article 2 of the regulation was thus dismissed by the Court.

On the second issue, of whether or not the name had become generic, Denmark claimed, and they were not contested on this point, that cheese produced from cow's milk by non-traditional methods (such as 'ultrafiltration', which is a much

---

[217] See Case 12/1974, *Commission v Germany* (sekt) [1975] ECR 181, para 8.

[218] Article 2(1)(e) of Greek Ministerial Order No 313025/1994.

[219] The Court of First Instance has noted that defining too extensive a geographical area may, in theory at least, cause a reduction in the real value of a designation of origin which was previously restricted to a smaller geographical area, and possibly affect the specific rights of the undertakings in the smaller geographical area which use that designation. Case T-109/1997, *Molkerei Grobbraunshain GmbH and Bene Nahrungsmittel GmbH v Commission* [1998] ECR II-3533.

faster process that the traditional Greek slow filtration method) had been imported into, and produced in, Greece until relatively recently as feta. The Court accepted that if this were to persist, it would be sufficient to render feta a generic sales name. However, it was noted that Greek national law had now codified all rules on the production and marketing of feta cheese and, as a result, such practices could no longer take place. The Court noted that it had held in *Denmark, Germany and France v Commission* that the fact that a product has been lawfully marketed under a name in some Member States may constitute a factor which must be taken into account in assessing whether that name has become generic within the meaning of the regulation. The Commission noted the levels of production of feta in Member States other than Greece in the preamble to the contested regulation and that a feta variant had been produced in some of these Member States since the 1930s. However, it was also noted that feta production remained, by and large, concentrated in Greece. Similarly, feta was consumed primarily in Greece. Evidence was also presented to the Court that demonstrated that in Member States other than Greece, feta was commonly marketed with labels referring to Greek cultural traditions. The Court inferred from this that consumers in those Member States therefore perceived feta as a Greek cheese, even where it had been produced in other Member States. These factors combined indicated to the Court that the name feta was not a generic food name.

On examination of the status of existing legislation in the Member States, the third key factor in any determination of the generic status of a food name, the Court noted that Denmark and Greece were the only Member States to have legislation specifically relating to feta in place. The Danish legislation itself did not refer to 'feta' but instead to 'Danish feta', displaying to the Court that the original name had retained a Greek connotation. In addition to this, a convention between Austria and Greece of 1972 reserved the name feta in Austria exclusively for Greek products. It was also therefore found, on the basis of this assessment, that the existing national legislation of the Member States indicated that the name feta was not a generic name but related specifically to a Greek product.

Finally, on the issue of relevant Community legislation, the Court noted that the name was used without further specification as to the Member State of origin in the combined customs nomenclature.[220] However, it was stated that this system of classification applied to customs matters only and was not relevant to any assessment of industrial property rights and could not therefore be used in any examination of how the product should be defined for protected designation of origin purposes. It was also noted that the Commission had previously stated, in response to a parliamentary question, that 'feta describes a type of cheese and is not a designation of origin'.[221] However, this was also seen as unpersuasive here

---

[220]   CN Code 0406 9031 describes feta for the purposes of the Common Customs Tariff as being a cheese made from sheep's milk in brine. Chapter 4 in Part II of Annex I to Council Regulation (EEC) No 2658/1987 of 23 July 1987 on the tariff and statistical nomenclature and on the Common Customs Tariff. [1987] OJ L 256/1.

[221]   Question No 13/1985, [1985] OJ C 248/13.

due to the fact that there was no Community system for the protection of designations of origin and geographical indications in operation at the time.

It was deemed to follow from all this, contrary to previous determinations on the matter, that 'feta' had not become a generic name. The Court thus found that the Commission could lawfully decide that the term had not become generic within the meaning of the regulation. Its validity could not therefore be successfully challenged on the point that the Commission had acted outside the powers conferred upon it by the terms of the regulation by registering for protected status a food name that was, or that had become, generic.

The decision of the Court in *Germany and Denmark v Commission* raises a number of issues about the manner in which applications for recognition as a protected designation of origin may now be assessed. Specifically, the Court appears to have narrowed the definition of 'generic food name', so essential to any Regulation 510/2006 assessment. It is evident from the submissions made in the three feta cases that the production of this foodstuff, or at least a variant of it, has taken place in many states, both within and outside the EU, for many years. This is uncontested. These varieties of cheese have been consistently marketed as 'feta'.

For a long period, the Greek authorities took no action to prevent this practice. Indeed, even many Greek producers, despite the existence of domestic rules providing otherwise, have marketed variants of feta produced in non-traditional ways, using non-traditional ingredients. This seemingly lackadaisical application of domestic Greek law enabled other forms of feta to gain a foothold in the market, to the extent that the proportion of overall consumption of the traditional Greek product has fallen significantly in the Community since 1981.

Despite the existence, and relative success of these other products, the Court has here determined that feta is so strongly, and distinguishably, associated with particular regions in Greece, that it should now be reaccorded protection under the terms of the Regulation. This legislation presents a derogation from one of the fundamental principles of Community law – the free movement of goods. As has been stated on numerous occasions, all such derogations should be limited to situations where an exceptional case can be made for them. This is not the case here.

Consider, for example, the case of pasta (and possibly other generic geographical food names such as cheddar, emmenthal and edam), long considered a generic food name by the Court.[222] There can be little doubt that most European consumers would, if asked, consider this foodstuff to be of Italian origin, remembering that the average consumer is considered to be reasonably well-informed, observant and circumspect.[223] Italian domestic laws on the production and marketing of pasta were

[222] Case 90/1986, *Criminal proceedings against Zoni* [1988] ECR 4285. See also Case 407/1985, *Glocken GmbH and Kritzinger v USL Centro-Sud and Provincia autonoma di Bolzano* [1988] ECR 4233.
[223] See, for example, Case C-362/1988, *GB-INNO-BM* [1990] ECR I-667; Case C-238/1989, *Pall* [1990] ECR I-4827; Case C-126/1991, *Yves Rocher* [1993] ECR I-2361; Case C-315/1992, *Verband Sozialer Wettbewerb* [1994] ECR I-317; Case C-456/1993, *Langguth* [1995] ECR I-1737; Case C-470/1993, *Mars* [1995] ECR I-1923; Case C-210/1996, *Gut Springenheide GmbH and Rudolf Tusky v Oberkreisdirektor des Kreises Steinfurt – Amt für Lebensmittelüberwachung* [1998] ECR I-4657.

in force until declared incompatible with Article 28 EC, and were not deemed to be justifiable on the basis of any consumer protection mandatory requirement or protection of health argument based on Article 30 EC.[224]

In addition to this, the Italian rules on pasta production placed far less of a restriction on the free movement of goods than the recognition of feta as a protected designation of origin does. Pasta could still be lawfully produced in any Member State and be marketed in Italy as pasta—it just had to have been made exclusively from durum wheat. Now feta, even though lawfully produced and marketed in many Member States for many years, often before the Community even came into existence, can only be marketed as such if produced in a defined geographical area, using exclusively local raw materials, of only one Member State—Greece.

This creates a difficulty for the Court-created panacea of additional labelling disclosures that has been presented to remedy the preponderance of Article 28 EC difficulties arising where a Member State has set its own 'recipe laws' for the production and marketing of a particular foodstuff, in circumstances such as those presented here.[225] Narrowing the interpretation of what constitutes a generic food name opens up the possibility of other foodstuffs, previously held or presumed to be generic, gaining protected status under the terms of the regulation, limiting the possibility that those products will be lawfully produced in other Member States. Given the criteria set by the regulation for testing the generic nature of a traditional foodstuff, coupled with the flexible application of these by the Court in *Germany and Denmark v Commission*, it is now perfectly conceivable that a similar assessment of the generic or otherwise nature of a food name such as 'pasta' should arrive at the conclusion that this may also now be rendered a geographical name, consequently throwing the well-established jurisprudence of the Court on much of its Article 28 EC case law into doubt.

It is not here suggested that the registration system set out in the regulation is without merit. On the contrary, just such a system is required to ensure the maintenance of the reputation and quality of traditional local food products in the post-*Cassis* era.[226] However, it is contended that an alternative, and much underused, Community mechanism already in existence could be utilised to great effect in circumstances such as those here presented. Where serious doubts about the generic nature of a foodstuff exist, registration for a certificate of character under the Regulation 509/2006 procedure could, and probably should, be sought instead, reserving use of the PDO/PGI system for those foodstuffs that clearly meet the eligibility criteria set out in Regulation 510/2006.[227]

---

[224] Case 90/1986, *Criminal proceedings against Zoni* [1988] ECR 4285.

[225] Obvious examples of relevant case law here include: Case 27/1980, *Criminal proceedings against Anton Adriaan Fietje* [1980] ECR 3839; Case C-196/1989, *Criminal proceedings against Enzo Nespoli and Giuseppe Crippa* [1990] ECR I-3647; Case 90/1986, *Criminal proceedings against Zoni* [1988] ECR 4285; Case 178/1984, *Commission v Germany* (bier) [1987] ECR 1227.

[226] Case 120/1978, *Rewe-Zentral AG v Bundesmonopolverwaltung für Branntwein* [1979] ECR 649.

[227] Council Regulation (EC) No 509/2006 of 20 March 2006 on agricultural products and foodstuffs as traditional specialities guaranteed. [2006] OJ L 93/1.

Certificates of Specific Character: Regulation 509/2006

There have always been serious doubts over the geographical nature of the food name 'feta'. The Court has been indecisive, changing its position on several occasions, as outlined above. The Commission has also altered its opinion, first claiming that the name was generic, stopping just short of initiating full Court proceedings against Greece for acting contrary to its Article 28 EC obligations, and then later backing calls for a declaration that feta was actually a geographical name. To attempt to prove this, it embarked upon a comprehensive assessment to determine consumer perceptions about the geographical connotations of the name.

Despite this, at no stage did the Court in *Germany and Denmark v Commission*, or the Commission in its initial deliberations prior to the introduction of Regulation 1829/2002, assess whether the registration of feta as a traditional speciality guarantee under the terms of Regulation 509/2006, given the obvious non-geographical nature of the name of the product, would have been a more appropriate response in the circumstances. The regulation enables agricultural products and foodstuffs to obtain a certificate of specific character. Again, certain methods of production, compositional requirements and defined characteristics can all form part of the protected product specification.[228] However, production need not be limited to a single defined region. The registered food name may only be used by those who comply with the registered product specification.[229] These producers can operate in any Member State or third country, provided a designated inspection authority in that State is notified of this.[230]

Use of the certificate of character as an alternative to the protected designation of origin provides a solution to the present problem, for several reasons. Primarily, substantial doubts about the non-generic nature of feta exist. The three-point test in Regulation 510/2006 for establishing whether a food name is generic is not easily satisfied by feta cheese. Feta made from cow's milk and feta produced in other Member States was available on the Greek market and was widely available in other Member States. In addition to this, other Member States did have national laws in place that permitted the marketing of non-Greek, non-traditional feta. There was no mention in existing Community legislation, such as the combined nomenclature, that feta had to be produced in Greece. The Commission, the Court of Justice and an Advocate General had all previously found that feta was a

---

[228] Article 6(2).

[229] Article 12(1).

[230] Article 16. The possibility of registering geographical cheese types under this system was recognised by Advocate General Saggio in his Opinion on Case C-448/1998, *Criminal proceedings against Jean-Pierre Guimont* [2000] ECR I-10663. In paragraph 10 thereof it was noted that '[t]he Community system does not provide any specific protection for the designation emmenthal; it is not a protected designation of origin within the meaning of Council Regulation (EEC) No 2081/1992 of 14 July 1992 on the protection of geographical indications and designations of origin for agricultural products and foodstuffs, and neither has any certificate of specific character been issued for it under Council Regulation (EEC) No 2082/1992 of 14 July 1992 on certificates of specific character for agricultural products and foodstuffs' [1992] OJL 208/9. Mozzarella has been registered as a traditional speciality guarantee (TSG) under what was the Regulation 2082/1992 procedure.

generic name. Feta is not even a Greek name. As a result, feta should not be able to be registered as a PDO. However, it is a product that clearly has identifiable and generally distinctive qualities. Names such as this, which do possess specific characteristics but which have also been lawfully produced and marketed in several Member States for several decades, with the non-traditional variety gaining a substantial share of the market, could instead be registered as traditional speciality guarantees. This enables production by traditional methods to continue, possibly using specific traditional ingredients, but in all Member States. The quality and characteristics of the product that led to the development of its popularity in the first place are preserved, but Community policy on free movement for goods is also protected. Were 'feta' to be registered as a traditional speciality guarantee, as opposed to a protected designation of origin, then a range of products, such as 'Greek feta', 'Danish feta' and even 'Irish feta' could appear on the marketplace. The 'reasonably well-informed, observant and circumspect' consumer could then distinguish between these clearly labelled, quality-maintained, but different products and choose according to personal preference.

The Court of Justice has previously stated in its Article 28 EC determinations that national laws must not be used in a common market to crystallise consumer habits in any way.[231] Prior to the registration of feta as a protected designation of origin, this common market and the free movement of goods that it facilitates, had led to the liberalising of trade in feta cheese to the extent that Greece had seen its share of feta production in the Community fall by nearly a quarter between 1981 and 2002. Non-registration of feta as a PDO was, in relation to the free movement of goods more generally, clearly having the desired effect. More operators had found uninhibited additional markets for their products in other Member States. Consumers were presented with additional choice. However, the Court's recently-found willingness to accept the imposition of national and Community rules that are seemingly at odds with free movement policy now poses a threat to this. As a result of the ready acceptance of the debateable Commission assertion that feta is suitable for registration as a protected designation of origin, the production and marketing of a product lawfully produced and marketed in several Member States, even prior to the foundation of the Community, must now cease from 2007 onwards. Danish, German, French, and all other kinds of feta can be marketed no more. These products will now have to be remarketed throughout the Union under a different name, possibly even as 'white cheese in brine made in Denmark/Germany/France/Another from pasteurised cow's milk', as the Greek authorities sought to impose on the applicants in *Canadane*. This now creates an additional impediment to free movement that the preponderance of Article 28 EC case law has sought to eradicate.

Use of the traditional speciality guarantee registration system, available for food products in a position such as this, under the terms of the Certificates of Specific

---

[231] See, for example, Case 170/1978, *Commission v UK* (wine and beer tax) [1980] ECR 417 and Case 178/1984, *Commission v Germany* (bier) [1987] ECR 1227.

Character Regulation, presents a possible remedy here, maintaining quality standards on the one hand, whilst simultaneously facilitating the free movement of goods on the other. This would also help to counter much of the legitimate criticism that has been levelled in the past at the decision taken by the Commission, following the judgment delivered in *Cassis*, that harmonised Community compositional standards need no longer be set for food products.[232] In post-BSE Europe, where justifications for impediments to free movement created by both the Community institutions and the Member States are more readily accepted, previous over-reliance on this policy must now be reconsidered.

Protection for Geographical Names under Regulation 510/2006

It is not just in relation to feta cheese that a level of protection has been granted in excess of that which would appear to be reasonable in the circumstances, especially considering existing Community rules on the free movement of food. In *Gorgonzola*, for example, proceedings were brought by the applicants for an order to prohibit the marketing in Austria of a blue cheese under the designation 'cambozola' and requiring cancellation of the 'Cambozola' trade mark.[233] Regulation 1107/1996 established gorgonzola as a protected designation of origin.[234] Under the terms of Regulation 510/2006, registered names are protected against any direct or indirect commercial use by products not covered by the registration, in particular where this is liable to mislead the public as to the true origin of the product, even where the actual origin is indicated.[235] The Court was asked here whether it was compatible with Community law for national measures to prohibit the distribution of blue cheese under the name cambozola, even where the packaging of the product in question indicated its true origin.

Gorgonzola had previously been protected under the 1951 Stresa Convention for the use of designations of origin and names of cheeses.[236] The case law of the Court clearly states that such international agreements are not in contravention of the Treaty provisions on the free movement of goods, provided that the protected

---

[232] Communication from the Commission to the Council and to the European Parliament on the completion of the internal market: Community legislation on foodstuffs. COM (85) 603 final. For criticism of this position see, in particular, O Brouwer, 'Free movement of foodstuffs and quality requirements: has the Commission got it wrong?' (1988) 25 *Common Market Law Review* 237.

[233] Case C-87/1997, *Consorzio per la tutela del formaggio Gorgonzola v Käserei Champignon Hofmeister GmbH & Co KG and Eduard Bracharz GmbH* [1999] ECR I-1301.

[234] Commission Regulation (EC) No 1107/1996 of 12 June 1996 on the registration of geographical indications and designations of origin under the procedure laid down in Article 17 of Council Regulation (EEC) No 2081/1992. [1996] OJ L 148/1.

[235] Article 13(1).

[236] The Stresa Convention 1951, or to give it its proper title the International Convention on the Use of Appellations of Origin and Denominations of Cheeses, was an international agreement on the use of designations of origin for cheese. The signatory countries, mostly now EU Member States (Austria, Denmark, France, Netherlands, Sweden, Norway, Switzerland), committed themselves to prohibiting the use of false designations of origin on their territory and to take all necessary measures to ensure the application of the Convention.

names have not become generic in the country of origin.[237] It was thus for the Court to decide whether the protection provided for the registered name gorgonzola had been breached by the use of the name cambozola, and in particular whether this name gave rise to an infringement of the regulation where it sets out to prevent any evocation of protected foodstuffs.

'Evocation' covers situations where the term used to designate a product incorporates part of a protected designation, so that when the consumer is confronted with the name of the product, the image triggered in his mind is that of the product whose designation is protected. The Court stated that since the product at issue was a soft blue cheese that was not dissimilar in appearance to gorgonzola, it would seem reasonable to conclude that a protected name is evoked where the term used to designate that product ends in the same two syllables, with the result that the phonetic and visual similarity between the two terms is obvious. As a consequence the Court found that the principle of the free movement of goods does not prevent Member States from taking measures designed to ensure the protection of registered designations of origin. Use of a name such as cambozola may be deemed to evoke the protected designation of origin gorgonzola, irrespective of the fact that the packaging indicated the true origin of the product.

The rules on protected geographical food names can also be breached by slicing or packaging the food outside its traditional region of production. In *Consorzio del Prosciutto di Parma v Asda and Hygrade Foods*, it was found that parma ham, although produced in Italy, could not be labelled 'genuine Italian parma ham' unless each stage of the production process, including slicing and packaging, took place in the region of production.[238] Parma ham is registered as a protected designation of origin.[239] The product specification for parma ham specifically refers to the slicing and packaging of the product in the region of production.

It should also be noted that it is only the specific food name that is registered which is protected under the terms of the regulation. In *Chiciak, Chiciak and Fol* criminal proceedings were brought against the defendants for marketing cheese using a protected designation of origin, époisses de bourgogne, in breach of the applicable national rules.[240] The defendants did not deny that that the products manufactured by them failed to comply with the French protection provisions. They submitted, however, that they were legally entitled to use the name for their cheese on the ground that the French provisions were contrary to the regulation, claiming that the regulation reserves to the Commission the exclusive power to grant protection for designations of origin and prohibits the Member States from

---

[237] Case C-3/1991, *Exportur SA v LOR SA and Confiserie du Tech SA* [1992] ECR I-5529.

[238] Case C-108/2001, *Consorzio del Prosciutto di Parma and Salumificio S Rita SpA v Asda Stores Ltd and Hygrade Foods Ltd* [2003] ECR I-5121.

[239] Commission Regulation (EC) No 1107/1996 of 12 June 1996 on the registration of geographical indications and designations of origin under the procedure laid down in Article 17 of Council Regulation (EEC) No 2081/1992. [1996] OJ L 148/1.

[240] Joined Cases C-129/1997 and C-130/1997, *Criminal proceedings against Yvon Chiciak and Fromagerie Chiciak and Jean-Pierre Fol* [1998] ECR I-3315.

legislating in that field. They also pointed out that they used only the name époisses, and not the full protected name époisses de bourgogne.

Under the terms of Regulation 2081/1992, Member States could submit a list of those products that they wished to be afforded protected status.[241] The French Government had submitted the name époisses de bourgogne and it was added to the list of protected designations of origin. However, after the name had been registered, the domestic rules regarding use of the protected name were altered to the extent that the name époisses, and not the full protected name époisses de bourgogne, was referred to throughout the amending decree. The Court stated that any alteration of an element of the product specification, such as the name of the product, could only be procured within the framework of the Community arrangements and procedures laid down by the regulation, not domestically. It was held that a Member State may not adopt provisions of national law to alter a designation of origin for which it had requested registration in accordance with the regulation. It was also found that each of the constituent parts of a compound designation of origin, such as that at issue here, are not necessarily protected, this being an issue for determination by national courts. The French Government and the Commission argued unsuccessfully that if it was only the entire name that had been protected, full protection could not be guaranteed.

Compatibility of Protecting Names with Article 28 EC

In *Exportur,* proceedings were brought against the respondents to prevent them from using the names 'Alicante' and 'Jijona', which are the names of Spanish towns, for confectionery produced in France.[242] The Convention between the French Republic and the Spanish State of 27 June 1973 on the protection of designations of origin, indications of provenance and names of certain products provided that the names at issue were reserved exclusively for Spanish products or goods. Relying on this Convention, the applicants tried unsuccessfully to obtain interim relief, and subsequently an injunction, prohibiting the French undertakings from using the Spanish names in question. The applicants appealed.

During the course of the appeal proceedings the Court was asked whether the provisions of the Franco-Spanish Convention protecting designations or indications of origin or provenance were in contravention of Articles 28 and 29 of the EC Treaty and, if they were, whether they could be authorised under Article 30 of the EC Treaty. The respondents claimed that there was no significant difference between the confectionery (tourons) produced in France and that in Spain, that the qualities and characteristics of the tourons were unrelated to their geographical origin and thus that the Franco-Spanish Convention was incompatible with Community law insofar as it was inhibiting the free movement of goods, relying on the judgment in *Commission v Germany.*[243] As discussed in Chapter 2 above,

---

[241] Article 17.
[242] Case C-3/1991, *Exportur SA v LOR SA and Confiserie du Tech SA* [1992] ECR I-5529.
[243] Case 12/1974, *Commission v Germany* (sekt) [1975] ECR 181.

that judgment established that a Member State cannot, without infringing the provisions of Article 28 EC, use a legislative measure to reserve food names for domestic products by requiring that other Member States undertake to use names unknown to, or less highly regarded by, the public. By reason of its discriminatory nature, such legislation could not be covered by the derogation provided for in Article 30 EC.

The applicants, referring to the decision in *Prantl*,[244] contested that the protection of geographical names was only justifiable if it did not adversely affect fair and traditional use by third parties. The application of the Franco-Spanish Convention could not thus prevent them from using the names 'turrón de jijona' and 'turrón de alicante' since this use had been longstanding, consistent and fair. This argument was rejected. The Court had concluded in *Prantl* that an exclusive right to use a type of bottle, granted by national legislation in a Member State, could not be used as a bar to the importation of wines originating in another Member State and put in bottles of the same or similar shape in accordance with a fair and traditional practice observed in that Member State. This was seen by the Court in *Exportur* as relating to a different situation altogether, relating to problems attached to the reconciliation of the use of an indirect indication of national provenance with the concurrent use of an indirect indication of foreign provenance. It raises a general problem about the protection of geographical food names in one Member State, where the place from which the food name derives is actually located in another Member State.

The respondents further maintained that the names 'turrón de jijona' and 'turrón de alicante' were generic names of types of products and were no longer indicative of a particular geographical provenance, claiming that the Convention could not prohibit the use in France of a Spanish name that had become generic in France. The Court disagreed, finding that where the protection afforded by a State to names indicating regions or places in its territory was justified under Article 30 EC, in this case in relation to industrial and commercial property rights, this protection could be legitimately extended to the territory of another Member State, assuming that the names in question had not acquired generic status in the country of origin.

3.6 FOOD QUALITY

Setting prerequisites for the use of a food name is one method that the Community has at its disposal to maintain the quality of food in the post-*Cassis* era. Another way is to set very general minimum requirements for the production and marketing of the most ubiquitous of non-legally-named foodstuffs, such as water, milk and meat. This can help to satisfy two of the key concerns of the EU when it comes to the sale of safe and wholesome food. The European Commission claims that there are two aspects to food quality. One is that foodstuffs should be

---

[244] Case 16/1983, *Criminal proceedings against Karl Prantl* [1984] ECR 1299.

free of harmful or undesirable substances, such as microbes, chemicals or other such substances used in the production process. The other is that foodstuffs should satisfy consumers' expectations in terms of taste, or other subjective criteria.[245] It also claims that the European Union's approach to ensuring food quality reflects these two considerations. This is debatable.

In addition to the 'recipe laws' and the rules on protected geographical names, there are other pieces of Community legislation dealing specifically with the quality of foodstuffs, setting the standards that have to be complied with before a foodstuff can be lawfully marketed under a specific designation. There is often a sizeable overlap between the areas of food labelling and quality. The majority of issues raised in this section on food quality are, to all intents and purposes, really labelling issues, in particular relating to the use of a food name. It is the level of control that is maintained over the use of a name that can often determine its quality. In reality, it is very difficult for legislators to control quality in any other way, and often even this possibility is not available as the food name may already be so generic that no meaningful control over composition can be introduced without the introduction of new recipe laws. Where no legislation relating to a specific foodstuff can be introduced, the consumer may still be afforded some level of protection under the framework food labelling directive,[246] or the misleading advertising directive,[247] but, considering previous case law on the matter, this will often not be the case.

3.6.1 Foodstuff Specific Quality Legislation

Natural Mineral Water

Directive 1980/777 sets out the requirements for marketing natural mineral water.[248] The directive covers waters extracted from the ground of a Member State that come within the scope of the definition of natural mineral water set out therein.[249] 'Natural mineral water' is defined as microbiologically wholesome water:

> originating in an underground water table or deposit and emerging from a spring tapped at one or more natural or bore exits. Natural mineral water can be clearly distinguished from ordinary drinking water: (a) by its nature, which is characterised by its mineral

---

[245] European Commission Directorate General for Education and Culture, 'Healthy Food for Europe's Citizens: The European Union and Food Quality' (2000), ISBN 92-828-8238-1.

[246] Directive 2000/13/EC of the European Parliament and of the Council of 20 March 2000 on the approximation of the laws of the Member States relating to the labelling, presentation and advertising of foodstuffs. [2000] OJ L 109/29.

[247] Council Directive 1984/450/EEC of 10 September 1984 relating to the approximation of the laws, regulations and administrative provisions of the Member States concerning misleading advertising. [1984] OJ L 250/17.

[248] Council Directive 1980/777/EEC of 15 July 1980 on the approximation of the laws of the Member States relating to the exploitation and marketing of natural mineral waters. [1980] OJ L 229/1.

[249] Article 1(1).

content, trace elements or other constituents and, where appropriate, by certain effects; and (b) by its original state, both characteristics having been preserved intact because of the underground origin of such water, which has been protected from all risk of pollution.[250]

The directive also covers waters extracted from the ground of a third country, imported into the Community and recognised as natural mineral waters by the responsible authority of a Member State.[251] Only those waters that meet the definition set out may be marketed as natural mineral waters.[252] It is up to the individual Member States to ensure that this happens.[253] Where appropriate, water should be described as either 'natural mineral water', 'naturally carbonated mineral water', 'natural mineral water fortified with gas from the spring', or 'carbonated natural mineral water',[254] which has had carbon dioxide of an origin other than the water table or deposit from which the water comes added to it.[255]

Labels on natural mineral water should also detail information on the analytical composition, giving its characteristic constituents and the place where the spring is exploited, provided this is not misleading in any way,[256] and the name of the spring.[257] Member States cannot demand that the country of origin be indicated where the natural mineral water comes from a spring in the Community.[258] Marketing natural mineral waters from the same spring under more than one trade description is prohibited.[259] Where the label or advertising of a natural mineral water includes a trade description different from the name of the spring or the place of its exploitation, this place-name or the name of the spring must be indicated in letters larger than those used for the trade description.[260] Drinking water that does not come within the scope of the definitions set out in the directive can never be labelled as 'mineral water' or any other designation where this may be liable to cause confusion with natural mineral water.[261] 'Natural mineral water' properly called can never, through its labelling, suggest a characteristic which the water does not possess, in particular as regards its origin, the date of the authorisation to exploit it, the results of analyses or any other similar references to guarantees of authenticity.[262] All indications attributing to a natural mineral water properties relating to the prevention, treatment or cure of human illness are prohibited unless specifically permitted.[263]

---

[250] Annex I Directive 1980/777.
[251] Article 1(2).
[252] Article 2.
[253] *Ibid.*
[254] Article 7(1).
[255] Annex I to Directive 1980/777.
[256] Article 8.
[257] Article 7(2).
[258] Article 7(3).
[259] Article 8(2).
[260] Article 8(3).
[261] Article 9(1).
[262] *Ibid.*
[263] Article 9(2).

A series of requirements for natural mineral water are also detailed, relating to, *inter alia*, the addition or removal of carbon dioxide,[264] disinfecting treatments,[265] and substances which should not be present in the water, such as parasites, pathogenic micro-organisms and coliforms.[266] Containers used for packaging natural mineral waters should be fitted with closures that are designed to avoid any possibility of adulteration or contamination.[267]

In *Badische* it was questioned whether the designation 'natural mineral water' can only be used, under the terms of the directive, if the product possesses properties that are favourable to human health.[268] The proceedings arose after the respondent refused to recognise water from one of the applicant's springs as natural mineral water because it did not contain specified levels of essential substances in accordance with domestic German provisions. Analysis of the water in question showed that it contained very little sodium and did not therefore satisfy the domestic German requirements on minimum levels of essential substances.

The Court noted that the main definition of natural mineral water set out in the directive makes no reference to 'properties favourable to health'. The Commission had proposed that use of the designation 'natural mineral water' should be dependent on the product possessing properties beneficial to health, but this was omitted from Directive 1980/777. The Annex to the directive merely states that the characteristics of natural mineral water 'may give . . . properties favourable to health'. The Court noted that 'properties favourable to health' is not a term that is defined anywhere in the directive. This was interpreted as indicating that possessing properties favourable to health is merely a possible effect of the water's characteristics, in particular if it contains a high mineral content, rather than being a defining characteristic. It was thus concluded that if the Council had wished to make the possession of properties favourable to health a compulsory characteristic of natural mineral water then the directive, which is drafted in precise and detailed terms, would have laid down rules in that respect. Member States were thus deemed to be precluded from making the recognition of water as natural mineral water dependent on its possessing properties favourable to health.

Directive 2003/40 sets out the limits and labelling requirements for the constituents of mineral waters.[269] Under the terms of the directive natural mineral waters that contain more than 1.5 mg/l have to bear a clear label stating this and pointing out that such products are not suitable for children under seven years of age.[270] Ozone-enriched air can only be used where this treatment can be justified

---

[264] Article 4(1).

[265] Article 4(2).

[266] Article 5.

[267] Article 6.

[268] Case C-17/1996, *Badische Erfrischungs-Getränke & Co KG v Land Baden-Württemberg* [1997] ECR I-4617.

[269] Commission Directive 2003/40/EC of 16 May 2003 establishing the list, concentration limits and labelling requirements for the constituents of natural mineral waters and the conditions for using ozone-enriched air for the treatment of natural mineral waters and spring waters. [2003] OJ L 126/34.

[270] Article 4.

and does not alter the essential constituents of the water.[271] This treatment must be clearly stated on the label.[272] The directive also sets maximum limits for the quantity of certain constituents, such as arsenic, cadmium, lead and mercury, that may be present in natural mineral water,[273] and the methods for analysing these constituents.[274]

Milk and Milk Products

The sales name 'milk' is defined in Regulation 1898/1987 as 'the normal mammary secretion obtained from one or more milkings without either addition thereto or extraction therefrom'.[275] The term 'milk' may, however, also be used where the product has been treated without altering its composition.[276] Milk may be used in association with a word or words to designate the type, grade, origin and/or intended use of the milk, or to describe the physical treatment or any modification in composition to which it has been subjected, provided that the modification is restricted to an addition and/or withdrawal of natural milk constituents.[277]

'Milk products' are defined in the regulation as:

> products derived exclusively from milk, on the understanding that substances necessary for their manufacture may be added provided that those substances are not used for the purpose of replacing, in whole or in part, any milk constituent.[278]

Examples of products falling into this category include cream, butter, buttermilk, cheese, whey and yoghurt.[279] The origin of milk and milk products must be stated if it is not bovine.[280]

The implementation of Regulation 1898/1987 into the domestic law of the individual Member States was not a straightforward procedure. The main difficulty arose because individual Member States had, prior to the introduction of the regulation, provisions in place in their domestic systems prohibiting the marketing of milk substitutes and milk product substitutes. This was particularly evident in *Commission v France*[281] and *Commission v Germany*,[282] as discussed in Chapter 2 above.

---

[271]   Article 5.
[272]   Article 6.
[273]   Annex I.
[274]   Annex II.
[275]   Article 2(1) of Council Regulation (EEC) No 1898/1987 of 2 July 1987 on the protection of the designations used in marketing of milk and milk products. [1987] OJ L 182/36.
[276]   Article 2(1).
[277]   Article 2(1).
[278]   Article 2(2).
[279]   Annex to Council Regulation (EEC) No 1898/1987 of 2 July 1987 on the protection of the designations used in marketing of milk and milk products. [1987] OJ L 182/36.
[280]   Article 2(4).
[281]   Case 216/1984, *Commission v France* (milk substitutes) [1988] ECR 793.
[282]   Case 76/1986, *Commission v Germany* (milk substitutes) [1989] ECR 1021.

Spreadable Fats

Regulation 2991/1994 sets Community standards for the production and market-ing of spreadable fats.[283] A series of sales descriptions are set out in the regulation pertaining to the different types of spreadable fats coming within the scope of the regulation.[284] 'Butter' is defined as:

> The product with a milk-fat content of not less than 80 per cent but less than 90 per cent, a maximum water content of 16 per cent and a maximum dry non-fat milk-material content of two per cent.[285]

Margarine is:

> The product obtained from vegetable and/or animal fats with a fat content of not less than 80 per cent but less than 90 per cent.[286]

Variations on both of these definitions are also set out in the regulation, including that for half-fat butter, half-fat margarine and half-fat blend. The regulation applies to products which remain solid at a temperature of 20°C and which are suitable for use as spreads.[287] Again, only those products complying with the terms of the regulation can use the sales descriptions set out therein.[288] Concentrated butter and margarine with a fat content of 90 per cent or more are excluded from this aspect of the regulation, as are those products the nature of which is clear from traditional usage and/or when the designation clearly describes a characteristic quality of the product.[289] Products covered by this derogation include brandy but-ter, sherry butter or rum butter, which are sweetened alcoholic products with a minimum milk-fat content of 34 per cent, and buttercream, which is a sweetened product with a minimum milk-fat content of 22.5 per cent.[290]

Labelling information additional to that prescribed by the framework food labelling directive is also required under the terms of the regulation. This includes details of the specific sales description, the total percentage of fat content by weight at the time of production, the vegetable, milk or other animal fat content in decreasing order of weighted importance as a percentage by total weight at the time of production, and the percentage salt content, which must appear in a 'par-ticularly legible manner' in the list of ingredients.[291] The sales description may be used together with one or more terms to define the plant and/or animal species

[283] Council Regulation (EC) No 2991/1994 of 5 December 1994 laying down standards for spread-able fats. [1994] OJ L 316/2.
[284] Annex to Regulation 2991/1994.
[285] *Ibid.*
[286] *Ibid.*
[287] Article 1(2).
[288] Article 2(2).
[289] *Ibid.*
[290] Article 1(1) of Commission Regulation (EC) No 577/1997 of 1 April 1997 laying down certain detailed rules for the application of Council Regulation (EC) No 2991/1994 laying down standards for spreadable fats and of Council Regulation (EEC) No 1898/1987 on the protection of designations used in the marketing of milk and milk products. [1997] OJ L 87/3.
[291] Article 3(1).

from which the product originates, the intended use of the product and the method of production,[292] on condition that this does not contravene other Community provisions, such as those set out in Regulation 510/2006 on the protection of geographical indications and designations of origin, or Regulation 509/2006 on character certificates. The term 'vegetable' may be used together with the sales description provided that the product contains only fat of vegetable origin, with a tolerance of two per cent of the fat content for animal fats.[293] All this information must be easy to understand and marked in a conspicuous place in such a way as to be easily visible, clearly legible and indelible.[294]

The term 'traditional' may be used together with the name 'butter' where the product is obtained directly from milk or cream.[295] The cream must have been obtained from milk.[296] The term 'reduced-fat' may be used for products with a fat content of more than 41 per cent, but not more than 62 per cent.[297] The terms 'low-fat' or 'light' may be used for products with a fat content of 41 per cent or less.[298]

Regulation 577/1997 adds further detail to the framework set out in Regulation 2991/1994.[299] The designation 'butter' is extended to include composite products of which an essential part is actually butter, provided that the end product contains at least 75 per cent milk fat and has been manufactured solely from butter, within the meaning of Regulation 2991/1994, and the other added ingredients mentioned in the description.[300] Under the terms of Regulation 623/1998,[301] composite products containing less than 75 per cent but at least 62 per cent milk fat may use the designation 'butter' if the product designation includes the term 'butter preparation' and an indication of the milk fat content, and, if the other added ingredients contain fat, the total fat content.[302] In order to verify the

[292] Article 3(3).
[293] Article 3(4).
[294] Article 3(5).
[295] Article 4.
[296] *Ibid.*
[297] Article 5(2).
[298] *Ibid.*
[299] Commission Regulation (EC) No 577/1997 of 1 April 1997 laying down certain detailed rules for the application of Council Regulation (EC) No 2991/1994 laying down standards for spreadable fats and of Council Regulation (EEC) No 1898/1987 on the protection of designations used in the marketing of milk and milk products. [1997] OJ L 87/3.
[300] Article 3 of Regulation 577/1997 as amended by Article 1(1) of Commission Regulation (EC) No 623/1998 of 19 March 1998 amending Regulation (EC) No 577/1997 laying down certain detailed rules for the application of Council Regulation (EC) No 2991/1994 laying down standards for spreadable fats and of Council Regulation (EEC) No 1898/1987 on the protection of designations used in the marketing of milk and milk products. [1998] OJ L 85/3.
[301] Commission Regulation (EC) No 623/1998 of 19 March 1998 amending Regulation (EC) No 577/1997 laying down certain detailed rules for the application of Council Regulation (EC) No 2991/1994 laying down standards for spreadable fats and of Council Regulation (EEC) No 1898/1987 on the protection of designations used in the marketing of milk and milk products. [1998] OJ L 85/3.
[302] Article 3 of Regulation 577/1997 as amended by Article 1(1) of Regulation 623/1998.

declared fat content of spreadable fats five samples are to be taken randomly from the batch, to be checked and analysed.[303]

Minced Meat

Directive 1994/65 sets out the requirements for the production and marketing of minced meat and meat preparations.[304] The protection of public health was deemed to be a major factor in the introduction of the legislation, particularly considering the potential risk presented where the meats concerned are eaten when undercooked.[305] The directive sets requirements on the quality of minced meat and meat preparations, in particular by prohibiting the use of meat that does not meet standards relating to freshness, and by prohibiting the use of certain parts of slaughtered animals, certain types of animals, and those which have failed a health inspection, in minced meat. The directive does not apply to meat preparations and minced meat which is produced in retail shops or in premises adjacent to sales points with a view to sale there directly to the final consumer. These operations are to remain subject to the health checks required by national rules governing supervision of the retail trade.[306]

Minced meat is defined as 'meat which has been minced into fragments or passed through a spinal-screw mincer'.[307] Meat preparations are:

> meat . . . which has had foodstuffs, seasonings or additives added to it or which has undergone a treatment insufficient to modify the internal cellular structure of the meat and thus to cause the characteristics of the fresh meat to disappear.[308]

Seasonings, for the purposes of the directive, are 'salt intended for human consumption, mustard, spices and aromatic spice extracts, aromatic herbs and aromatic extracts thereof'.[309]

The only animals that are permitted to be used in the production of minced meat are bovine animals, pigs, sheep and goats.[310] Minced meat must have been prepared from striated muscle, except heart muscle,[311] which meets the requirements of Directive 1964/433[312] relating to, *inter alia*, freshness, place of

---

[303] Article 2(3) of Regulation (EC) No 2181/1997 of 3 November 1997 amending Regulation (EC) No 577/1997 laying down certain detailed rules for the application of Council Regulation (EC) No 2991/1994 laying down standards for spreadable fats and of Council Regulation (EEC) No 1898/1987 on the protection of designations used in the marketing of milk and milk products. [1997] OJ L 299/1.

[304] Council Directive 1994/65/EC of 14 December 1994 laying down the requirements for the production and placing on the market of minced meat and meat preparations. [1994] OJ L 368/10.

[305] Preamble to Directive 1994/65.

[306] Article 1(2).

[307] Article 2(2).

[308] *Ibid.*

[309] *Ibid.*

[310] Article 3(1).

[311] *Ibid.*

[312] Council Directive 1964/433/EEC of 26 June 1964 on health problems affecting intra-Community trade in fresh meat. [1964] OJ P 121/2012. English Special Edition, Series I, Chapter 1963–4, p 185.

slaughter, inspection, hygiene and transport.[313] All meat should be examined before being minced or cut up, with the soiled and suspect parts being removed and condemned before the meat is minced.[314] Minced meat may not be obtained from scrap cuttings, scrap trimmings or mechanically recovered meat. In particular, it may not be prepared from meat deemed to be unfit for human consumption under the terms of Directive 1964/433,[315] or from meat from the following parts of bovine animals, pigs, sheep or goats: muscles from the head, with the exception of the masseters, and the non-muscular part of the linea alba, the carpus and tarsus region and bone scrapings. The muscles of the diaphragm, after removal of the serosa, and of the masseters may be used only after an investigation for cysticercosis has been carried out. The fresh meat must not contain any bone fragments.[316]

3.7 CONCLUSION

It is arguable that the two most important decisions ever made by the EU institutions regarding food were that of the Court on mutual recognition and that of the Commission on ceasing to develop harmonised standards. The former facilitates free movement by ensuring that once a foodstuff is lawfully marketable in one Member State it must be lawfully marketable in all. The latter, however, has the potential to frustrate free movement. Member States continue to introduce national laws that deviate from the rules imposed in other Member States in order to protect consumers and/or human health. This would not be necessary if the harmonisation programme had not been dispensed with. Harmonisation gives Member States the opportunity to negotiate towards a common, acceptable standard; mutual recognition does not. Member States are compelled to accept the rules of other Member States, rules that they have had absolutely no input into. Where they are unwilling to accept the standards of others, they introduce or maintain their own, often resulting in a prohibition on the marketing of products coming from other States whose domestic rules are not similar. Ironically, it was because of the acceptance of mutual recognition and future reliance on the principles developed in the decision in *Cassis* that it was later felt that it was possible to dispense with the harmonisation programme for the composition of food products.

While it is contended here that a form of standardisation for some foodstuffs could assist both free movement and food quality levels, the few vertical directives that do exist for specific foodstuffs are not particularly good examples of how any such legislative programme could best proceed. However, existing shortcomings have been identified here. There are perhaps three reasons arising out of this examination, other than a blinkered acceptance that the decision in *Cassis* presents a panacea for all free movement difficulties, which explain why the Community institutions may be reluctant to embark upon legislative intervention. These three

[313] Article 3 of Directive 1964/433.
[314] Annex I to Directive 1994/65.
[315] Article 5 of Directive 1964/433.
[316] Annex I to Directive 1994/65.

reasons are: the difficulty of getting 25 Member States to reach an acceptable compromise standard, the chocolate saga offering a clear example of this; the difficulties involved in ensuring compliance with this common standard, especially where clear monitoring procedures are not set out in the legislation, as is the case with the common Community standard for honey; and finally the interaction that is required between these vertical directives and existing horizontal legislation. Each time a new horizontal legislative initiative is introduced, such as that on quantitative ingredient declarations, the related affected vertical legislation, such as the fruit juice directive, must also be altered to reflect this, adding to an already dissonant body of rules.

While the reasons why the institutions may not wish to legislate for specific foodstuffs are obvious, the key efforts that have been made to minimise some of the negative aspects of free movement policy for the quality and diversity of foodstuffs have failed to achieve their proper potential. Take the Community system for protecting geographical food names. The often erratic and arbitrary manner in which decisions are made on eligibility for protection and/or protection levels has left us with an unclear set of criteria to be used in assessing whether or not a food name may be registered as a protected geographical indication or designation of origin. An alternative mechanism, that relating to foodstuffs of specific character, remains under-used. This despite the fact that it appears that some of the more contentiously registered food names satisfy the criteria for this type of protection more readily.

There are aspects of the Community's harmonisation programme that have been successful. The framework food labelling legislation presents us with a clear set of principles and rules that can be easily applied throughout the EU. While there has been some confusion over the language that labelling must appear in, for the most part the instructions relating to information that must be present on food labels are simple and clear. The directive works because of this simplicity. When applying a standard throughout a club of 25 States, each with their own tastes, preferences and interests to protect, it is only through harmonising at a general level that legislative intervention can prove a success. More than any other, it is this trait that should be carried through to any further standardisation programme that may be developed to counter those negative aspects of free movement policy that continue to blight EU food law.

4

International Influences on EU Food Law

4.1 INTRODUCTION

T HE INTERACTION BETWEEN the regulation of international trade and EU food law has increased significantly in recent years. In particular, since the inception of the World Trade Organization (WTO) in 1995, its agreements have been used to challenge the introduction or continuance of a number of EU rules or actions, most significantly those on the production and marketing of genetically modified organisms and protected designations of origin. Community legislators must now account for these international trading rules in the drafting of new legislation, or be open to challenge from other members before the WTO Dispute Settlement Body (DSB).[1]

Several of the WTO Agreements can impact upon EU food law, each of which will be considered in turn below. In addition to the General Agreement on Tariffs and Trade (GATT), the most significant of these are the Agreement on Trade Related Aspects of Intellectual Property Rights (TRIPs), the Agreement on Technical Barriers to Trade (TBT), the Agreement on the Application of Sanitary and Phytosanitary Measures (SPS) and the Agreement on Agriculture. Essentially, where any aspect of EU food law, be it a piece of legislation, a decision of the Court of Justice or the development of a Community policy, is deemed to be contrary to an aspect of one or more of these Agreements, another WTO member can initiate the dispute resolution mechanism. Given the way in which the WTO has developed thus far, it is most likely to be the United States of America that brings such a challenge, as was the case when the EU introduced a de facto moratorium on the marketing of genetically modified food. There are two reasons for this. First, the European Union offers a lucrative marketplace for American producers, where, given the level of exposure to American popular culture, there is already a degree of familiarity with their products amongst European consumers. Second, the production and marketing of food in the United States is answerable to a very different regulatory regime than that applied in the EU. The American Food and Drug Administration (FDA) tends to be far more liberal as regards the level of evidence

---

[1] See also C Barnard, *The Substantive Law of the EU: The Four Freedoms* (Oxford, OUP, 2004), pp 30–33; JHH Weiler (ed), *The EU, the WTO and NAFTA: Towards a Common Law of International Trade* (Oxford, OUP, 2000); and, more generally, TC Hartley, *European Union Law in a Global Context* (Cambridge, CUP, 2004).

of safety or security required to be presented prior to granting authorisation for the marketing of a new product. As a consequence, where European Union rules subject producers to more rigorous tests, or go further still and prohibit the sale of a foodstuff for precautionary reasons, this lucrative and familiar marketplace is inaccessible to others who have not been subject to the same procedure or whose products do not satisfy the standards set in the EU. In particular, where a prohibition is introduced, recourse to the DSB of the WTO may be the only option available to those whose products can be freely marketed elsewhere within the global trading system.

4.2 GLOBAL FREE TRADE: INTERNATIONAL RULES ON THE FREE MOVEMENT OF FOOD

Currently, the main external threat to the way in which the European Union regulates its food industry is the application of the WTO Agreements, challenging any new or existing EU rules. The WTO is essentially a negotiating forum. Everything it does is a result of negotiations between the members. The Uruguay Round of negotiations of the General Agreement on Tariffs and Trade, which took place from 1986-1994, ultimately resulted in the establishment of the WTO. Key to the WTO global trading system are the WTO Agreements, which can create difficulties for the European Union when it tries to implement a highly regimented regulatory regime on more controversial aspects of the food sector. For the purposes of this book, the two key Agreements that need to be examined most closely are the Agreement on the Application of Sanitary and Phytosanitary Measures and the Agreement on Trade Related Aspects of Intellectual Property Rights. The SPS Agreement sets the parameters within which members of the WTO must operate when introducing rules that inhibit free trade in any way for purposes designed to protect human health, animal health, plant health or the environment. It requires a certain level of scientific evidence supporting the member's claim that a measure is necessary because a failure to introduce it would expose animals, plants, humans or the environment to risk. Key to ascertaining when a member has operated within these limits is an assessment of the suitability of any evidence presented supporting such action. It is this that arouses most controversy in relation to disputes, or potential disputes, under the terms of the SPS Agreement. This is discussed in more detail below.

The TRIPs Agreement raises a number of issues in relation to the manner in which the European Union may protect the identity and character of many of its foodstuffs when trading with other WTO members. In particular, those elements that set rules on the protection of geographical food names need to be examined in detail here. Many foodstuffs that are European in origin, and which owe their geographical name to this fact, have been produced and marketed in other countries for decades. Examples include champagne, which is a generic name for sparkling wine in some parts of the world, but a protected name in the EU entitling only those producers in the Champagne region who produce their beverage in a particular way to use it, or parma ham, which may be freely marketed as such in Canada, despite the pig from which it was produced having never set trotter in Italy. This has obvious detrimental consequences for the producer of the original version of the product who may be protected in the EU but is not accorded protection elsewhere. Not only that, but where the producer of Canadian parma ham is operating under a trademark awarded by his own State, the Italian producer is unable to legally market his product in Canada under that name.

Resolving any of these issues within the WTO system, given the nature of international trade law, and international law more generally, is not an easy task. It requires compromise amongst members who primarily seek to advance their own interests. In order to understand this more fully, a brief examination of the relevant Agreements and the mechanism for resolving international trade disputes is required. The discussion will then turn to a more detailed examination of the two key issues identified here as case studies demonstrating the difficulties that can exist where EU food law and the regulation of international trade interact.

4.2.1 WTO Agreements and EU Food Law

The Agreement Establishing the WTO concludes with a series of annexes which contain the other international trade agreements and the detailed rules and procedures governing the operation of the Organization. Annex 1A contains the multilateral agreements on trade in goods, such as the Agreement on Agriculture, the Agreement on Technical Barriers to Trade and the Agreement on Subsidies and Countervailing Measures. Annex 1B contains the General Agreement on Trade in Services and Annex 1C contains the Agreement on Trade Related Aspects of Intellectual Property Rights. Annex 2 sets out the Understanding on Rules and Procedures Governing the Settlement of Disputes. Annex 3 details the Trade Policy Review Mechanism. Finally, Annex 4 contains the plurilateral trade agreements, such as the International Dairy Agreement and the International Bovine Meat Agreement.

Agreement on Trade Related Aspects of Intellectual Property Rights

The TRIPs Agreement is designed to promote effective and adequate protection of intellectual property rights, but also to ensure that, as far as possible, these and other measures and procedures do not themselves become barriers to legitimate international trade. Included in the scope of intellectual property rights covered by the terms of the TRIPs Agreement are copyright,[2] trademarks,[3] industrial designs,[4]

---

[2] Part II, Section 1, Arts 9–14.
[3] Part II, Section 2, Arts 15–21.
[4] Part II, Section 4, Arts 25–26.

patents,[5] topographies of integrated circuits,[6] and, most importantly for the purposes of this book, geographical indications.[7]

For the purposes of the TRIPs Agreement, geographical indications are indications which identify a particular product as originating in the territory of a member, or a region or locality in that territory, where a given quality, reputation or other characteristic of that product is essentially attributable to its geographical origin.[8] Members are to provide the legal means for interested parties to prevent the use of (a) any means in the designation or presentation of a good that indicates or suggests that the good in question originates in a geographical area other than the true place of origin in a manner which misleads the public as to the geographical origin of the good; and (b) any use which constitutes an act of unfair competition within the meaning of Article 10 of the Paris Convention (Stockholm Act 1967).[9] If their legislation permits, or if requested by an interested party, members are to refuse or invalidate the registration of trademarks that contain or consist of a geographical indication with respect to goods not originating in their territory if the use of the trademark is likely to mislead the public as to the true place of origin.[10]

The TRIPs Agreement sets out additional protection for geographical indications for wines and spirits. It states that each member is to provide the legal means for interested parties to prevent the use of a geographical indication identifying either wines or spirits that do not originate in the place indicated by the geographical indication, even where the true origin of the goods is indicated or the geographical indication is used in translation or accompanied by expressions such as 'kind', 'type', 'style' or 'imitation'.[11] Registration of a trademark for wines or spirits which contain or consist of a geographical indication is to be refused or invalidated by a member if their legislation permits, or if requested by an interested party, where such wines or spirits are not of this origin.[12] In the case of homonymous geographical indications for wines, protection is afforded to each indication, each member determining the practical conditions under which the homonymous indications in question are to be differentiated from each other, taking into account the need to ensure equitable treatment of the producers concerned and that consumers are not misled.[13] In order to facilitate the protection of

---

[5] Part II, Section 5, Arts 27–34.

[6] Part II, Section 6, Arts 35–38.

[7] Part II, Section 3, Arts 22–24.

[8] Article 22.1.

[9] The Paris Convention for the Protection of Industrial Property was concluded in 1883, and has been revised several times since then. As of 12 February 1998, 145 States were party to the Convention. The Convention is administered by the World Intellectual Property Organization (WIPO). The Convention applies to industrial property rights, including patents, trademarks, industrial designs, utility models, trade names, indications of source, appellations of origin, and the repression of unfair competition. In respect of Parts II, III and IV of the TRIPs Agreement, WTO members are obliged to comply with Articles 1 through 12, and 19, of the latest act of the Convention, the Stockholm Act of 1967.

[10] Article 22.3.

[11] Article 23.1.

[12] Article 23.2.

[13] *Ibid.*

geographical indications for wines, negotiations are to be undertaken in the Council for TRIPs concerning the establishment of a multilateral system of notification and registration of geographical indications for wines eligible for protection in those members participating in the system.[14]

There are some exceptions to the protection of geographical indications by the TRIPs rules. For example, members are not required to prevent the continued use of a particular geographical indication of another member identifying wines or spirits by any of its nationals who have used that indication in a continuous manner with regard to the same goods in the territory of that member for at least 10 years preceding 15 April 1994, or in good faith before 15 April 1994.[15] Where a trademark has been applied for or registered in good faith by a member before the date of application of the TRIPs Agreement, or before the geographical indication became protected in its country of origin, any measures adopted to implement the section of the TRIPs Agreement on protected geographical indications do not prejudice eligibility for or the validity of the registration of a trademark, or the right to use a trademark, on the basis that this trademark is identical with, or similar to, a geographical indication.[16] In addition, a member is not required to apply the TRIPs provisions in respect of geographical indications of another member where the relevant indication is identical to the term that is customary in common language as the common name for such goods in the territory of that member. Similarly, members are not required to apply the TRIPs provisions on geographical indications of another member with respect to vine products for which the relevant indication is identical to the customary name of a grape variety existing in the territory of that member at the date of entry into force of the WTO Agreement.[17] There is no obligation on any member to protect geographical indications which are not, or which cease to be, protected in their country of origin or which have fallen into disuse in that country.[18] However, members must be willing to enter into negotiations aimed at increasing the protection of individual geographical indications and these exceptions should not be used by members as a reason for refusing to conduct such negotiations or to conclude any bilateral or multilateral agreements, nor should any member use the exceptions to diminish the protection of geographical indications that existed in that member immediately prior to the entry into force of the WTO Agreement.[19]

The EU system for registering protected designations of origin and protected geographical indications had been found by the Dispute Settlement Body of the WTO to be contrary to the TRIPs Agreement. In the *EC—Trademarks and Geographical Indications* dispute, complaints were brought by both the United States and Australia, who claimed that Regulation 2081/1992 limited the access of

---

[14] Article 23.4.
[15] *Ibid.*
[16] Article 24.5.
[17] Article 24.6.
[18] Article 24.9.
[19] Article 24.1 and 24.3.

nationals of other WTO members to the registration procedure and protections available, contrary to TRIPs Articles 2 (intellectual property conventions), 3 (national treatment), 4 (most-favoured nation treatment), 16 (trademark rights), 22 (protection of geographical indications), 24 (international geographical indications), 63 (transparency) and 65 (transitional arrangements).[20] After the failure of the consultation process, the establishment of a panel was requested. Its report, which was circulated to members in March 2005, found that Regulation 2081/1992, as amended, did not provide the required level of national treatment to other WTO members' trademark rights holders and products because: (i) registration of a geographical indication from a country outside the EU was contingent upon the government of that country adopting a system of similar protection equivalent to that established by the regulation and offering reciprocal protection to registered European geographical indications; and (ii) the Regulation 2081/1992 procedures required that applications and objections from other WTO members were to be examined and transmitted by the governments of those members, and required those governments to operate systems of product inspection similar to those carried out in the EU Member States.[21] As a result, foreign nationals were not guaranteed access to the Regulation 2081/1992 procedure, unlike EU nationals. This reciprocity requirement was contrary to WTO obligations arising out of the TRIPs Agreement, in particular Article 3(1) thereof.

As a direct result of the decision in this dispute, a proposal was introduced for a new amending protected geographical names regulation in December 2005.[22] As discussed in Chapter 3, amendments made to Regulation 2081/1992 primarily concern the issue of registering geographical products from third countries that are members of the WTO. The offending provisions of the original regulation are deleted, and the reciprocity and equivalence requirements are removed. This new regulation came into effect in March 2006.[23]

Agreement on the Application of Sanitary and Phytosanitary Measures

The SPS Agreement applies to all such measures that may, directly or indirectly, affect international trade. Sanitary or phytosanitary measures are defined in the Agreement as being any measure that is applied:

> to protect animal or plant life or health within the territory of the Member from risks arising from the entry, establishment or spread of pests, diseases, disease-carrying organisms or disease-causing organisms; to protect human or animal life or health within the territory of the member from risks arising from additives, contaminants, toxins or disease-causing organisms in foods, beverages or feedstuffs; to protect human life or health

[20] WTO DS 174 and DS 290, *EC—Trademarks and Geographical Indications.*
[21] Article 12 of Regulation 2081/1992.
[22] Proposal for a Council regulation on the protection of geographical indications and designations of origin for agricultural products and foodstuffs. COM (2005) 698.
[23] Council Regulation (EEC) No 510/2006 of 20 March 2006 on the protection of geographical indications and designations of origin for agricultural products and foodstuffs. [2006] OJ L 93/12.

within the territory of the Member from risks arising from diseases carried by animals, plants or products thereof, or from the entry, establishment or spread of pests; or to prevent or limit other damage within the territory of the Member from the entry, establishment or spread of pests.[24]

The term 'measures' covers all relevant laws, decrees, regulations, requirements and procedures including, *inter alia*, end-product criteria; processes and production methods; testing, inspection, certification and approval procedures; quarantine treatments including relevant requirements associated with the transportation of animals or plants, or with the materials necessary for their survival during transportation; provisions on relevant statistical methods, sampling procedures and methods of risk assessment; and packaging and labelling requirements directly related to food safety.[25]

Members do have the right to take sanitary and phytosanitary measures that are necessary for the protection of human, animal or plant life or health, provided that these measures are not inconsistent with other aspects of the SPS Agreement. These measures can only be applied to the extent that they are necessary, and provided that they are based on scientific principles and are not maintained without sufficient scientific evidence to support them. They may not arbitrarily or unjustifiably discriminate between members, nor should they be applied in a manner that constitutes a disguised restriction on international trade.[26] Where possible, and preferably, any measures adopted should be based on international standards, guidelines or recommendations where they exist, such as those of the FAO/WHO Codex Alimentarius Commission. Where measures do conform to these international standards they are to be considered as being consistent with the SPS Agreement and the GATT. Measures that result in a higher level of sanitary or phytosanitary protection than that which would be achieved by the application of the relevant international standards are allowed, but only where there is scientific justification for this. Members are to play a full part in the development of international standards in this area, in particular those of the Codex Alimentarius Commission, the International Office of Epizootics and the organisations operating within the framework of the Plant Protection Convention. The Committee on Sanitary and Phytosanitary Measures is to monitor the international harmonisation process and co-ordinate efforts in this regard with the relevant international organisations.[27]

Members should accept the sanitary or phytosanitary measures of other members as being equivalent to their own, even where these measures differ from their own or from those of other members trading in the same product, if the exporting member can objectively demonstrate to the importing member that its own measures achieve the same level and type of protection as theirs. Reasonable access

---

[24] Annex A to the SPS Agreement.
[25] *Ibid.*
[26] Article 2.
[27] Article 3.

should therefore be given to the importing member to assess the efficacy of the exporter's measures in this regard. Where possible, this should be brought a stage further by the development between members of bilateral or multilateral agreements on the recognition of equivalence of sanitary or phytosanitary measures.[28]

Most importantly, for a member's sanitary or phytosanitary measures to stand up to international scrutiny, or for them to be objectively justifiable to those with whom they trade in the affected products, members must ensure that any such measures taken are based on an appropriate assessment of the risks to human, animal or plant life or health, taking into account the risk assessment techniques developed by the relevant international organisations. In the assessment of risk members are to take account of the available scientific evidence; the relevant processes and production methods; the relevant inspection, sampling and testing methods; the prevalence of specific diseases or pests; the existence of pest or disease free areas; the relevant ecological and environmental conditions; and quarantine or other treatment. In assessing the risk to animal or plant life or health and in determining the measure to be applied for achieving the appropriate level of sanitary or phytosanitary protection from such risk, members are to take account of the relevant economic factors, including the potential damage in terms of loss of production or sales in the event of the entry, establishment or spread of a pest or disease; the costs of control or eradication of a pest or disease in the importing member; and the relative cost-effectiveness of alternative approaches to limiting risks. In making such decisions on the appropriate level of protection, regard should always be had to the objective of minimising negative trade effects. In order to ensure that there is consistency in the application of sanitary or phytosanitary measures amongst members, efforts should be made to avoid arbitrary or unjustifiable distinctions in the levels of protection considered appropriate in different situations if these distinctions result in discrimination or a disguised restriction on international trade. To further this aim of harmonisation and certainty in the taking of such measures, members are to co-operate with the Committee on Sanitary and Phytosanitary Measures in order to develop relevant guidelines on this. In developing such guidelines, the Committee is to take account of all relevant factors, including the exceptional character of human health risks to which people voluntarily expose themselves. When establishing or maintaining sanitary or phytosanitary measures, members are to ensure that these are not more restrictive on trade than that which is required to achieve the appropriate level of protection, taking into account both technical and economic feasibility. A measure is not deemed to be more trade restrictive than that required unless there is another measure, reasonably available, also taking into account technical and economic feasibility, that achieves the appropriate level of protection and which is significantly less restrictive to trade. Where there is insufficient scientific evidence to support a measure, a member may provisionally adopt the measure on the basis of the available pertinent information, including information from the relevant international organisations. In such circumstances, members must seek to obtain the

[28] Article 4.

additional information necessary for a more objective assessment of the risk posed and review the measure accordingly within a reasonable period of time. Where a member believes that a measure introduced by another member is constraining, or has the potential to constrain, its exports, and the measure is not based on the relevant international standards, guidelines or recommendations, or where these standards, guidelines or recommendations do not exist, an explanation of the reasons for the measure may be requested and, where such a request is made, must be provided.[29]

Members must ensure that their sanitary or phytosanitary measures are adapted to the characteristics of the area—whether a country, part of a country, or all or parts of several countries—in which the product originates and for where the product is destined. In assessing these sanitary and phytosanitary characteristics, members are to take account of the level of specific diseases or pests, the existence of eradication or control programmes, and appropriate criteria or guidelines which may be developed by the relevant international organisations. Exporting members who claim that their territories are pest- or disease-free areas must provide evidence of this.[30] Again, in preparing and applying sanitary and phytosanitary measures, members are to take account of the needs of developing country members, in particular the least-developed countries. For example, longer time frames for compliance and certain exceptions should be allowed where possible.[31] The Agreement also establishes a Committee on Sanitary and Phytosanitary Measures to provide a forum for regular consultations, to improve international harmonisation of measures, and to encourage the use of international standards, guidelines or recommendations where appropriate.[32]

The potential for the SPS Agreement to impact upon EU food law and policy is clearly evident from the dispute that has arisen over the implementation of the genetically modified organisms moratorium. Complaints have been brought by the United States, Canada and Argentina, claiming that the actions of the EU in suspending the approval of biotech products has restricted international trade in food.[33] It is also alleged that individual EU Member States have maintained national marketing and import bans on biotech products, even where their use has already been approved by Community law. At the time of going to press, the dispute panel were considering whether this action/inaction by the Community was contrary to Articles 2 (basic rights and obligations), 5 (assessment of risk and determination of the appropriate level of sanitary or phytosanitary protection), 7 (transparency) and 8 (control, inspection and approval procedures), as well as Annex B (transparency of sanitary and phytosanitary regulations) and Annex C (control, inspection and approval procedures) of the SPS Agreement.[34] The panel

---

[29] Article 5.
[30] Article 6.
[31] Article 10.
[32] Article 12.
[33] WTO DS291, DS292 and DS293, *EC—Approval and Marketing of Biotech Products*.
[34] The Panel Report was circulated to WTO Members on 29 September 2006. The Report had not yet been adopted by the Dispute Settlement Body on 31 October 2006.

is also examining whether the moratorium and Member State actions are contrary to aspects of the Agreement on Agriculture,[35] and the Agreement on Technical Barriers to Trade.[36] A decision on this has been delayed on several occasions, the request for consultations originally being made in May 2003, and the panel established in March 2004. After a series of delays, it was estimated that a final report would be presented by June 2005, then October 2005, then December 2005, then March 2006, then September 2006.

Agreement on Technical Barriers to Trade

All products traded between members, including agricultural products, are subject to the provisions of the TBT Agreement.[37] Under the terms of the Agreement, members are to refrain from preparing, adopting or applying technical regulations that create unnecessary obstacles to international trade. Technical regulations must therefore be no more trade-restrictive than necessary to fulfil a legitimate objective. The legitimate objectives listed in the Agreement include national security requirements, prevention of deceptive practices, protection of human health or animal or plant life or health, and protection of the environment. In assessing such risks, members are to consider the available technical and scientific information, related processing technology and the intended end-uses of products.[38] Technical regulations are defined in the Agreement as a:

> document which lays down product characteristics or their related processes and production methods . . . with which compliance is mandatory. It may also include or deal exclusively with terminology, symbols, packaging, marking or labelling requirements as they apply to a product, process of production method.[39]

Technical regulations should not be maintained if the circumstances or objectives giving rise to their adoption no longer exist or if the changed circumstances or objectives can be addressed in a less trade-restrictive manner.[40] Where technical regulations are required and relevant international standards exist, or their completion is imminent, members are to use these standards as a basis for their technical regulations, except when the use of such standards would be ineffective or inappropriate for the fulfilment of the legitimate objectives pursued, for example because of fundamental climatic or geographical factors or technological problems.[41] Members must also play a full part in harmonising technical regulations at the international level by assisting the appropriate international standardising bodies.[42] Any member preparing, adopting or applying a technical regulation

---

[35] Article 4 (market access).
[36] Articles 2 (preparation, adoption and application of technical regulations by central government bodies) and 5 (procedures for assessment of conformity by central government bodies).
[37] Article 1.3.
[38] Article 2.2.
[39] Annex 1 to the TBT Agreement.
[40] Article 2.3.
[41] Article 2.4.
[42] Article 2.6.

which may have a significant effect on the trade of other members must, when requested by another member, explain the justification for that technical regulation. Where a technical regulation is introduced for one of the legitimate objectives listed and is in accordance with the relevant international standards, it is presumed that it does not create any unnecessary obstacle to international trade.[43] Members must, as far as possible, accept the technical regulations of other members, even where they differ from their own, provided that they are satisfied that these regulations adequately fulfil the same objectives as their own.[44] In particular, members must provide differential and more favourable treatment to developing country members on TBT matters. This includes recognising that developing country members should not be expected to use international standards as a basis for their technical regulations or standards which are not appropriate to their development, financial and trade needs.[45]

Members must ensure that their central government standardising bodies accept and comply with the Code of Good Practice for the Preparation, Adoption and Application of Standards, set out in Annex 3 to the TBT Agreement. They are to take the necessary reasonable measures as may be available to them to ensure that local government and non-governmental standardising bodies within their territories, as well as regional standardising bodies (bodies whose membership is open only to some WTO members: see Annex 1 to the TBT Agreement) of which they or one or more bodies within their territory are members, accept and comply with the Code of Good Practice.[46] In addition, members are not to take measures that have the effect of requiring or encouraging such standardising bodies to act in a manner inconsistent with the Code. The obligations of members with respect to the compliance of standardising bodies with the provisions of the Code of Good Practice apply irrespective of whether or not a standardising body has accepted the Code.[47]

Under the terms of the Code of Good Practice for the Preparation, Adoption and Application of Standards, standardising bodies must accept many of the principles of the TBT Agreement that also apply to individual members. For example, there is to be recognition of international standards, such as those of the Codex Alimentarius; standardising bodies are not to introduce standards that create unnecessary obstacles to international trade; and standardising bodies are to contribute to the preparation of harmonised international standards. However, there are additional responsibilities placed on standardising bodies. For example, they are to avoid duplication of, or overlap with, the work of other standardising

---

[43] Article 2.5.
[44] Article 2.7.
[45] Article 12.
[46] The procedures for the assessment of conformity by central government bodies, local government bodies and non-governmental bodies with the terms of the TBT Agreement are set out in Articles 5 to 9 thereof. Requirements relating to the availability of information about technical regulations, standards and conformity assessment procedures are set out in Articles 10 and 11 of the TBT Agreement.
[47] Article 4.1.

bodies in the national territory or with the work of relevant international or regional standardising bodies. Standardising bodies should also, under the terms of the Code, specify standards that are based upon product requirements in terms of performance, rather than design or descriptive characteristics.

The TBT Agreement also establishes a committee on technical barriers to trade. It is composed of a representative of each member and meets as necessary, but at least once a year, for the purpose of affording members the opportunity of consulting on any matters relating to the operation of the TBT Agreement. The Committee may establish working parties as appropriate to carry out further tasks or investigations.[48] Where a dispute arises over the application of the TBT Agreement, a dispute panel may, either on its own initiative or at the request of one of the parties to the dispute, establish a technical expert group to assist in questions of a technical nature that may arise which require detailed consideration by experts.[49] These groups are under the authority of the panel, which determines their terms of reference and detailed working procedures on a case-by-case basis.[50]

Agreement on Agriculture

The WTO Agreement on Agriculture aims to liberalise international trade in the agricultural sector, in particular by easing access to all member markets. The Agreement attempts to achieve this by prohibiting impeding measures, such as quantitative import restrictions, minimum import prices, voluntary export restraints and discretionary import licensing.[51] This is to be done by converting existing measures into ordinary customs duties.

The Agreement also sets out a series of commitments to be undertaken by members regarding import and export subsidy levels. Members are to undertake to reduce these subsidies by agreed amounts. However, it is in relation to the enforcement and monitoring of this that the Agreement falls short. There is no effective procedure in place. The Agreement does provide that the implementation of commitments is to be reviewed by a Committee on Agriculture.[52] However, the evidence suggests that members do not adhere to this in a manner that is conducive to achieving the stated aim of subsidy reduction. This is due to two factors. First, not all members submit the required information to the Committee regarding how they have met their agreed commitments, and second, the information that is submitted tends to be presented in a manner that is both confusing and misleading, making it difficult to establish whether set subsidy reduction targets have been met.[53]

---

[48]   Article 13.
[49]   Article 14.
[50]   Annex 2 to the TBT Agreement.
[51]   Article 4.2.
[52]   Article 18.
[53]   See B O'Connor, 'A Note on the Need for More Clarity in the World Trade Organization Agreement on Agriculture' (2003) 37 *Journal of World Trade* 839.

The second key shortcoming of the Agreement on Agriculture relates to the so-called 'peace clause', inserted into the Agreement after stalemate was reached during negotiations. This clause requests that members exercise due restraint when considering bringing a matter before the DSB.[54] Essentially it is a plea to members not to bring any such action, in particular in relation to domestic support measures and export subsidies, unless absolutely necessary. In fact, some such actions are expressly ruled out by this.

Overall, the Agreement on Agriculture fails to achieve its key aim, the liberalisation of trade in agricultural products. This is not to say that it is devoid of potential, however. For this to be realised, particularly the issue of domestic support and export subsidies, a more rigid monitoring and enforcement mechanism is required to ensure that the commitments undertaken are implemented. It would also be necessary to re-negotiate the 'peace clause' in a manner that further facilitates the possibility of resolving disputes relating to trade in agriculture.

4.2.2 Dispute Settlement at the World Trade Organization

The system of dispute settlement set out in the GATT differed in many ways from that established for the WTO after the Uruguay Round negotiations. The mechanism set out in GATT Articles XXII and XXIII were primarily designed to appraise the practices of the contracting parties rather than to cast judgment on their actions. States were to give 'sympathetic consideration' to complaints that they were acting contrary to the terms of the Agreement. Initially there was not even a formal specific procedure for dealing with these complaints. However, from the early 1950s onwards, panels were established to investigate possible breaches of GATT rules, although their findings did not result in orders being given to states to alter their behaviour where they were found to be acting contrary to their international trade regulation obligations. Suggestions were made as to how compatibility with the terms of the GATT could be increased. Aspects of this customary procedure were later codified during the Tokyo Round negotiations in 1979, resulting in the drafting of an Understanding Regarding Notification, Consultation, Dispute Settlement and Surveillance, including an 'Agreed Description of the Customary Practice of the GATT in the Field of Dispute Settlement' as an Annex.[55] The development of a codified system of dispute settlement had led to an increase in the use of the complaints procedure. However, this had also led to an increase in blocking the adoption of panel reports by the losing contracting party. It was identified, prior to the Uruguay Round, that the dispute settlement procedure would need to be improved and strengthened to counter this. The WTO Dispute Settlement Understanding (DSU) was thus developed to address the issue.

---

[54] Article 13.

[55] For further discussion and analysis see AF Lowenfeld, *International Economic Law* (Oxford, OUP, 2002), pp 135–50 and RE Hudec, 'GATT Dispute Settlement after the Tokyo Round: An Unfinished Business' (1980) 13 *Cornell International Law Journal* 145.

Annex 2 to the WTO Agreement, the Understanding on Rules and Procedures Governing the Settlement of Disputes, details the manner in which disputes may be both heard and resolved at WTO level. The WTO's dispute settlement system is described in the Understanding as 'a central element in providing security and predictability to the multilateral trading system'.[56] The manner in which this mechanism has developed since its initial inception under the GATT would suggest that it has, by and large, been successful in this regard. The prompt settlement of situations in which a member considers that any benefits accruing to it directly or indirectly are being impaired by measures taken by another member is clearly recognised as being essential to the effective functioning of the WTO and the maintenance of a proper balance between the rights and obligations of members.[57] A solution that is mutually acceptable to the parties to a dispute and consistent with the covered agreements is preferred. In the absence of a mutually agreed solution, the first objective of the dispute settlement mechanism is to secure the withdrawal of the measures concerned if they are found to be inconsistent with the provisions of any of the covered agreements. The provision of compensation should only be resorted to if the immediate withdrawal of the measure is impracticable and as a temporary measure pending the withdrawal of the inconsistent measure. As a very last resort, the Understanding provides the claimant member with the possibility of suspending the application of concessions or other obligations under the covered agreements to the infringing party, subject to authorisation of any such measures by the DSB.[58]

The dispute settlement process commences with a member making a complaint against another member which it feels to be in contravention of one or more of the covered agreements. The covered agreements are listed in Appendix 1 to the Understanding and include the Agreement Establishing the WTO and the multilateral and plurilateral agreements on trade in goods. Consultation then takes place, during which members should attempt to find a satisfactory resolution to the matter. If consultation fails to settle the dispute within 60 days after the date of receipt of the request for consultation, the complaining party may request the establishment of a panel. This may also take place before the expiry of the 60 day period if the parties agree. This period is reduced to 20 days where the dispute relates to perishable goods.[59] Conciliation and mediation procedures may be requested at any time by any party to a dispute in an attempt to resolve the matter. All parties to the dispute must agree to the use of these procedures. Once the procedures terminate, the complaining party may proceed with a request for the establishment of a panel. If the parties to a dispute agree, these procedures may also continue while the panel process proceeds.[60]

---

[56] Article 3.2.
[57] Article 3.3.
[58] Article 3.7.
[59] Article 4.
[60] Article 5.

Where the formation of a panel is requested and/or agreed by the parties to a dispute, it is to be established at the DSB meeting following the meeting at which the request first appeared as an item on the DSB agenda. Any request to establish a DSB must be made in writing, indicating whether consultations were held and identifying the specific measures at issue, providing a brief summary of the legal basis of the complaint.[61] Panels are to be composed of well-qualified governmental and/or non-governmental individuals, including, *inter alia*, persons who have served on or presented a case to a panel or who have taught or published on international trade law or policy. They are to be independent and they cannot be citizens of members whose governments are parties to the dispute, unless the parties to the dispute agree otherwise. There are generally to be three panellists, but in some circumstances there may be five. Objections to proposed nominations to the panel may be raised by any party to the dispute: such an objection must be based on a compelling reason. When a dispute is between a developing country member and a developed country member the panel should include, where the developing member requests this, at least one panellist from a developing country member.[62] Whenever feasible, a single panel may be established to examine more than one complaint on the same matter.[63] Any member who has a substantial interest in a matter before a panel and having notified this interest to the DSB must be heard by and be permitted to make written submissions to the panel.[64]

The function of the panels is to assist the DSB in discharging its responsibilities under the Understanding and the covered agreements. Accordingly, a panel should make an objective assessment of the facts of the case and the applicability of and conformity with the relevant covered agreements, and to make such further findings as will assist the DSB in making the recommendations or in delivering the rulings provided for in these agreements. In order to achieve this, panels must meet regularly with the parties to the dispute to give them adequate opportunity to develop a mutually satisfactory solution.[65] Panels have the right to seek information and technical advice from any individual or body that it deems appropriate.[66] All panel deliberations are confidential.[67]

Following the consideration of submissions and arguments, the panel is to issue the descriptive sections of its draft report to the parties to the dispute. The parties are then invited to submit their comments on this in writing. The panel issues an interim report to the parties, including details of its overall findings and conclusions. Requests may be made to review the report at this stage, before it is circulated to all members. If no comments are received, the interim report is considered to be the final report and it is circulated to all members.[68] The reports are then to

---

[61] Article 6.
[62] Article 8.
[63] Article 9.
[64] Article 10.
[65] Article 11.
[66] Article 13.
[67] Article 14.
[68] Article 15.

be adopted by the DSB, unless it is decided otherwise or a party to the dispute formally notifies the DSB that it is appealing the decision. It may, of course, be adopted if any such appeal is unsuccessful.[69] The standing Appellate Body is composed of seven persons, three of whom sit in any one case, serving in rotation. Only parties to a dispute, and not third parties, may appeal a panel report, although third parties who have notified the DSB of their substantial interest in the matter under review may make written submissions to, and be given an opportunity to be heard by, the Appellate Body. Appeals are limited to issues of law covered in the panel report and legal interpretations developed by the panel. The proceedings of the Appellate Body are confidential and their reports are drafted without the presence of the parties to the dispute and in the light of the information provided in the statements. The Appellate Body may uphold, modify or reverse the legal findings and conclusions of the dispute panel. Appellate Body reports are to be adopted by the DSB and unconditionally accepted by the parties to the dispute unless the DSB decides otherwise.[70] Where a panel or the Appellate Body concludes that a measure is inconsistent with a covered agreement, it recommends that the member concerned bring the measure into conformity with that agreement. In addition to its recommendations, the panel or the Appellate Body may suggest ways in which the member concerned could implement the recommendations. Neither the panel nor the Appellate Body can add to or diminish the rights and obligations provided in the covered agreements.[71]

Prompt compliance with recommendations or rulings of the DSB are seen to be essential in order to ensure the effective resolution of disputes. Particular attention is to be paid in this regard to matters affecting the interests of developing country members. The member that is the subject of the ruling is to inform the DSB of its intentions in respect of the implementation of the recommendations made within 30 days of the adoption of the report. Longer periods of compliance may be permitted in some circumstances.[72]

Where the rulings or recommendations are not implemented within a reasonable period of time, compensation and the suspension of concessions or other obligations may be used as temporary measures to deal with the matter. However, full implementation of a recommendation is always preferred. The payment of compensation is voluntary. Where no deal on compensation is reached, the party that invoked the dispute settlement procedure may request authorisation from the DSB to suspend the application of concessions to the member concerned. Several principles should be followed by the complaining party when considering what concessions to suspend. The general principle is that concessions should be suspended in the same sector as that in which the panel or Appellate Body has found a violation. If this is not practicable, or will not be effective, then concessions may be suspended in other sectors dealt with under the Agreement that has been

---

[69] Article 16.
[70] Article 17.
[71] Article 19.
[72] Article 21.

violated. If this is neither practicable nor effective, and the circumstances are serious enough, then concessions that are covered by another agreement may be suspended. The level of the suspension of concessions authorised by the DSB should be equivalent to the level of violation of the Agreement. The suspension of concessions is a temporary measure and it can only be applied until the inconsistent measure has been removed, or until the member that is obliged to implement the recommendations or rulings provides a solution to the impasse, or until some form of mutually satisfactory solution is reached between the parties to the dispute.[73]

The Understanding includes a series of measures designed to make the dispute settlement procedure more attractive, and compliance with recommendations and/or rulings more feasible, for least-developed country members. Those disputes that involve a least-developed country member must give particular consideration to the position of such complainants or respondents. For example, members are to exercise due restraint in raising matters under the dispute settlement procedure. Complaining parties are also to exercise due restraint in asking for compensation or seeking authorisation to suspend the application of concessions pursuant to these procedures. Where a satisfactory solution is not found in the course of the consultation stage of the dispute settlement process, either the Director-General of the WTO or the Chair of the DSB is, when requested by a least-developed country member, to offer conciliation and mediation with a view to assisting the parties to settle the dispute before a request for a panel is made.[74]

Arbitration may be used as an alternative means of dispute settlement in some circumstances. Resort to arbitration is subject to the mutual agreement of the parties, which must also agree the procedures to be followed in their case. Other members, who are notified of arbitration in advance of the actual commencement of the process, may become party to the proceedings where the other parties agree. All parties to the proceeding must agree to abide by the arbitration award.[75]

4.2.3 Effect of WTO Rules on EU Food Law

There can be little doubt about the fact that EU food law must now, where possible, conform to the Community's WTO obligations. The actual impact of this should not, however, be overstated. The difficulties that arise in other areas of international law also arise in international trade regulation. Key to the proper functioning of any such international system of rules is compliance. Member self-interest, delays in proceedings and lack of effective remedy continue to reduce the potential of the WTO dispute settlement mechanism for resolving international disagreements over non-compliance that impedes global trade in food. However,

---

[73] Article 22.
[74] Article 24.
[75] Article 25.

there are also clearly circumstances in which WTO rules can affect the nature of EU food laws—ultimately obliging the Community to alter its legislation or behaviour in some way.

Take, for example, the well-established system for the protection of geographical food names, as originally set out in Regulation 2081/1992.[76] Here, a lack of effective access for applicants from third countries to the EU registration system for these foodstuffs led to findings that this legislation would have to be changed. An emphasis on prompt compliance with the findings of panel reports means that these alterations must be effected quickly. In such circumstances, the dispute resolution process can be judged a success. Compare this to the endless rounds of delay in making a decision on the EU moratorium on the approval and use of genetically modified organisms. Such procrastination minimises the impact of a ruling when it ultimately arrives. The facts here centre on actions that were initiated in the late 1990s, but the dispute panel report will not appear until at least late 2006. Nearly a decade will have passed between the trade-inhibiting actions of the EU and any finding in relation to the incompatibility of this action with WTO rules and obligations.[77] By then, the moratorium will have been lifted. Public concern over the use of genetic modification techniques in food production that led to the moratorium and individual Member State action has already died down. The EU has not suffered as a result of its actions and no effective remedy, such as the suspension of trade concessions or fines, can be imposed.

We note two final points at this stage regarding the interaction between international trade regulation and EU food law. First, increased use of the precautionary principle by the EU institutions, in other words the taking of trade-restrictive actions where a possibility of risk to human health or the environment is reasonably suspected, is likely to increase accusations that such actions are in direct conflict with WTO rules, in particular those set out in the SPS Agreement. This will definitely be the case until more transparent criteria are devised to establish when sufficient evidence that supports any such behaviour exists. This is discussed in more detail in Chapter 5. Second, the WTO negotiations and Agreements are only part of a package of international trade-related rules that affect EU food law. The well-established principles and standards of the FAO/WHO Codex Alimentarius Commission have consistently been used to shape EU food legislation and Court of Justice determinations. These have been influencing the nature of EU food law in a persuasive manner since both the corpus of EU rules and the Codex itself began to develop in the 1960s.

---

[76] These provisions are now contained in Council Regulation 510/2006 of 20 March 2006 on the protection of geographical indications and designations of origin for agricultural products and foodstuffs. [2006] OJ L 93/12.

[77] As noted earlier, the Panel Report circulated on 29 September 2006 had not yet been adopted by the Dispute Settlement Body on 31 October 2006. However, it is noted here that the Report did find that the EU, by applying the moratorium, had acted contrary to its SPS obligations, in particular Article 8 (Control, Inspection and Approval Procedures) thereof. It was also found that the national marketing and import bans imposed by individual EU Member States were inconsistent with the essential risk assessment criteria set out in Articles 2.2. and 5.1. of the SPS Agreement.

4.3 FAO/WHO CODEX ALIMENTARIUS

The Codex Alimentarius (food code) is the seminal global reference point for food standards. UN Resolution 39/248 stipulates that the Codex should be taken into account and, where possible, transposed by States into their domestic laws on food standards. The importance and relevance of the Codex has increased significantly since the formation of regional trade areas, such as the EU, and since the inception of the WTO. Both the SPS Agreement and the TBT Agreement encourage harmonised international food standards. Both have chosen the standards, guidelines and recommendations established by the Codex Alimentarius Commission. The SPS Agreement adopts Codex standards for food additives, veterinary drug and pesticide residues, contaminants, methods of analysis and sampling, and codes and guidelines on hygienic practice. Article 2 of the TBT Agreement states that members of the WTO are to use international standards, such as those of the Codex Alimentarius, where they exist, as a basis for their own technical regulations.[78] This is also the case in situations where no such standards exist but their completion is imminent.[79] As a consequence, Codex standards have become the benchmark for European Union decisions and measures on international trade in food, forming the basis for the specific requirements of many Community regulations and directives. They have also been adopted by the North American Free Trade Agreement (NAFTA), the Southern Common Market (MERCOSUR), and the Asia-Pacific Economic Co-operation Council (APEC).

4.3.1 Historical Development of the Codex Alimentarius

The idea behind the FAO/WHO Codex Alimentarius came from a system of food codes used in the Austro-Hungarian Empire between 1897 and 1911. This system established a collection of standards and product descriptions for a wide variety of foods. It was known as the Codex Alimentarius Austriacus. Although it lacked true legal force, this system was used extensively as a reference resource by courts to determine the typical standards for or identity of a particular foodstuff. The FAO/WHO Codex Alimentarius, which takes its name from the Austrian code, was initiated in 1961. Among the first foodstuffs to be standardised by the code in 1966 were cheddar, edam and gouda, followed by emmenthal in 1967, and cottage cheese and saint paulin in 1968. Among the more recent foodstuffs to be standardised through the Codex are fruit juices (2005),[80] oranges (2004),[81] and canned bamboo shoots (2003).[82] The two main purposes behind the formulation of a global food

---

[78] Article 2.4 of the TBT Agreement. The Codex Alimentarius is not specifically mentioned but it is clear that it is this type of international harmonised standard to which the TBT Agreement alludes.
[79] Article 2.4 of the TBT Agreement.
[80] Codex Standard 247/2005.
[81] Codex Standard 245/2004.
[82] Codex Standard 241/2003.

standards code are food security and consumer protection.[83] However, the remit of the Codex Alimentarius Commission has evolved with the development of the Codex itself. The Codex now covers standards relating to food composition, codes of hygiene and technological practice, evaluation and limitation of the use of pesticides, guidelines on contaminants, and the evaluation of additives and veterinary drugs. Among some of the standards set by the Codex are those on the analysis of contaminants and pesticides, maximum levels for toxins in milk, cadmium in cereals and lead in foodstuffs, the collection, processing and marketing of natural mineral waters and the transportation of food in bulk. The Codex also sets an international numbering system for additives.

Codex standards may be fully accepted, accepted with minor deviations, or accepted by 'free distribution' by the member countries. The FAO and the WHO provide assistance to developing countries to ensure that they have the technical and administrative infrastructure in place to enable them to adopt Codex standards. Such assistance includes convening expert meetings to advise the Codex Alimentarius Commission on relevant issues, conducting workshops and training courses, strengthening analysis and inspection capabilities, and assisting in the establishment of food control agencies.

The other key accomplishment of the Codex is that food hazards and the importance of quality in food have been put in the spotlight. Through its work, the Codex Alimentarius Commission generates scientific studies and convenes expert committees, such as the Expert Committee on Food Additives and the Expert Committee on Pesticide Residues, and consultations, such as those on risk assessment and food safety (1995), biotechnology and food safety (1996), and the role of government agencies in assessing HACCP (the application of hygienic practices in food production) (1998). The Codex Commission is a useful forum for the exchange of ideas and information relating to the need for, and the identification of, best practice in the production and marketing of food globally. It has also prompted action to be taken within individual States that may otherwise have failed to act on many of the key issues. In particular, through the expansion and development of the Codex, many States have recognised the need for domestic food agencies to be created to oversee the implementation of these best practices, or at the very least, an acceptable version of them.

4.3.2 Operation of the Codex Alimentarius Commission

Both the eleventh session of the Conference of the FAO in 1961 and the sixteenth World Health Assembly in 1963 passed resolutions to establish the Codex

---

[83] Food security is deemed to exist when 'all people, at all times, have physical and economic access to sufficient, safe and nutritious food to meet their dietary needs and food preferences for an active and healthy life'. World Food Summit, Rome, November 1996. For further discussion see K Mechlem, 'Food Security and the Right to Food in the Discourse of the United Nations' in F Snyder (ed), *International Food Security and Global Legal Pluralism* (Brussels, Bruylant, 2004).

Alimentarius Commission and adopted statutes and rules of procedure for the Commission. The statutes provide the legal basis for the work of the Commission. Article 1 states the purpose of the Commission, and sets out its terms of reference and objectives. It states that the Commission is:

> responsible for making proposals to, and shall be consulted by, the Directors-General of the FAO and the WHO on all matters pertaining to the implementation of the Joint FAO/WHO Food Standards Programme, the purpose of which is:

(a) protecting the health of consumers and ensuring fair practices in the food trade;
(b) promoting co-ordination of all food standards work undertaken by international governmental and non-governmental organisations;
(c) determining priorities and initiating and guiding the preparation of draft standards through and with the aid of appropriate organisations;
(d) finalising standards elaborated under (c) above and, after acceptance by governments, publishing them in a Codex Alimentarius either as regional or world wide standards, together with international standards already finalised by other bodies under (b) above, wherever this is practicable;
(e) amending published standards, after appropriate survey in the light of developments.

Article 2 defines eligibility for membership of the Commission, which is open to all member nations and associate members of the FAO and WHO. There are currently 173 members of the Codex Commission.

The Rules of Procedure of the Codex Alimentarius Commission state the conditions for membership of the Commission, and provide for the appointment of Commission officers, including the chair, three vice-chairs, regional co-ordinators and a secretary, setting out the responsibilities of each; the establishment of an executive committee to meet between Commission sessions and to act on behalf of the Commission as its executive; the frequency and operation of Commission sessions; the nature of agendas for Commission sessions; voting procedures; the role of observers; preparation of Commission records and reports; the establishment of subsidiary bodies; the procedures to be adopted in the elaboration of standards; budget allocation; and the languages to be used by the Commission. The Commission meets every two years, alternating between the FAO headquarters in Rome and WHO's headquarters in Geneva. National delegations at plenary meetings are generally led by government-appointed officials, who may be accompanied by representatives from industry and consumer organisations, and academics. International governmental and non-governmental organisations may also attend as observers. While their opinions may be heard at the meetings, they are not allowed to partake in the final decisions, which must be made exclusively by the member governments. Contact with the member governments is meant to be continuous. In order to facilitate this dialogue many members have set up Codex contact points and national Codex committees to co-ordinate and report on national activities.

The Codex Alimentarius procedural manual sets out the process by which standards are prepared. First, a proposal for a standard to be developed is submitted by a national government or a subsidiary committee of the Commission. Then, either the Commission or the Executive Committee decides that the proposed standard should be developed, and creates a subsidiary body under the Formal Criteria for the Establishment of Work Priorities and for the Establishment of Subsidiary Bodies, which is to be responsible for steering the standard through its development. A proposed draft standard is formalised by the Commission secretariat and circulated to the member governments for comment. These comments are considered by the subsidiary body that has been made responsible for the development of the proposed draft standard. This body may then present the text to the Commission as a draft standard. If the Commission decides to adopt the draft standard, it is sent to member governments a number of times (usually between five and eight times) in a step procedure. If the parties are satisfied, the draft becomes a Codex standard and part of the Codex Alimentarius. The established format for a Codex standard includes information relating to the name of the standard; description, essential composition and quality factors defining the minimum standard for the food; food additives (as only those accepted by the FAO and WHO may be used); contaminant details; hygiene, weights and measures details; labelling, in accordance with the Codex General Standard for the Labelling of Prepackaged Foods; and methods of analysis and sampling.

Codex standards are both horizontal (applying to all foodstuffs) and vertical (applying to specific foodstuffs) in nature. Horizontal standards are set for food labelling, food additives, contaminants in food, methods of analysis and sampling, food hygiene, nutrition and foods for special dietary uses, food import and export inspection and certification systems, residues of veterinary drugs in food, and pesticide residues in food. The complete Codex is set out in volumes on: general requirements and food hygiene; pesticide residues in foods; residues of veterinary drugs in food; foods for special dietary uses (including those for babies and children); processed and quick-frozen fruits and vegetables; fresh fruit and vegetables; fruit juices; cereals, pulses (legumes) and derived products and vegetable proteins; fats and oils and related products; fish and fishery products; meat and meat products, soup and broths; sugars, cocoa products, chocolate and miscellaneous products; milk and milk products; and methods of analysis and sampling. These individual volumes are structured in sections, each dealing with individual aspects of the subject area. For example, volume 1A on general requirements is divided into eight sections on general principles, definitions, code of international trade ethics, food labelling, food additives, contaminants, irradiated foods, and food inspection and certification systems.

Under its Rules of Procedure, the Codex Commission is empowered to establish two kinds of subsidiary body: Codex Committees, which prepare draft standards for submission to the Commission; and Co-ordinating Committees, through which regions or groups of countries co-ordinate food standard activities in their region, including the development of regional standards. The Codex Committees may be either general subject committees or individual commodity committees. The general subject committees deal with horizontal issues. There are existing committees on general principles, food labelling, methods of analysis and sampling, food hygiene, pesticide residues, food additives and contaminants, import/export inspection and certification systems, nutrition and foods for special dietary uses, and veterinary drug residues. Generally, these committees are hosted by a member country, which is extensively responsible for the maintenance and administration costs of the committee and for providing its chair. Host states include France (general principles), Canada (labelling), Hungary (analysis and sampling), the United States of America (hygiene and veterinary drugs), The Netherlands (pesticides and additives and contaminants), Germany (nutrition) and Australia (inspection and certification systems). These general subject committees develop all-embracing concepts and principles applying to foods in general and specific foods or groups of foods; endorse or review relevant provisions in Codex commodity standards; and, on the basis of expert scientific advice, develop major recommendations pertaining to consumer health and safety.

The commodity committees are responsible for developing standards for specific foods or classes of food, their work being vertical in nature. Again, these committees are hosted by member countries who meet much of the administrative cost of their operation. There are committees on fats and oils; sugars (both hosted by the United Kingdom); fish and fishery products (Norway); milk and milk products; meat hygiene (both New Zealand); fresh fruit and vegetables (Mexico); cocoa and chocolate; natural mineral waters; soups and broths (all by Switzerland); processed fruits and vegetables; cereals, pulses and legumes (both by the United States of America); vegetable proteins (Canada); and processed meat and poultry products (Denmark). The Commodity Committees convene as necessary. They go into recess or are abolished once the Commission feels that their work is complete. New committees may be established on an ad hoc basis to cover specific needs and develop new standards as necessary.

The co-ordinating committees have no standing host country. Meetings are hosted by countries of a region, usually a continent or combination of continents, on an ad hoc basis and in agreement with the Codex Commission. There are co-ordinating committees for Africa, Asia, Europe, South America and the Caribbean, and North America and the Southwest Pacific. The reports of the co-ordinating committees, which must reflect regional interests, are submitted to the Codex Commission.

4.3.3 Codex Alimentarius Standards

Article 1 of the FAO/WHO Codex statutes states that one of the main priorities is the protection of the health of consumers and the maintenance of fair trade practices in the food trade. Other United Nations bodies also recognise the importance of consumer protection. In 1985 a UN General Assembly resolution gave rise to the drafting of Guidelines for Consumer Protection, published in 1986. These guidelines identify food as one of three priority areas that are of essential concern to the health of consumers. The document specifically identifies the Codex as the reference point for these consumer protection-related issues with regard to food. Two important international FAO/WHO conferences were held in the 1990s on food and nutrition. In 1991 the Conference on Food Standards, Chemicals in Food and Food Trade, held in co-operation with GATT, recommended continuing and strengthened consumer participation in food-related decision-making at both national and international levels. The 1992 International Conference on Nutrition recommended that consumers be protected through improved quality and safety and outlined measures designed to accomplish this. The FAO/WHO also held an expert consultation on the Integration of Consumer Interests in Food Control in 1993.

The Codex standards clearly, by their very nature, offer consumers a level of protection by specifying minimum quality levels for foodstuffs. In addition to this, the Codex also sets general horizontal standards which have a direct bearing on consumer protection levels. For example, there is a General Standard for the Labelling of Prepackaged Foods, and there are the Codex General Guidelines on Claims and Codex Guidelines on Nutrition Labelling. Other general standards have a role to play in protecting the consumer too, such as those for food hygiene, food additives, contaminants and toxins in food and irradiated foods. Other, more specific standards have been set relating to consumer health protection, such as the Levels for Radionuclides in Foods Following Accidental Nuclear Contamination for Use in International Trade.

The Codex also sets out a series of codes of practice, such as the Recommended International Code of Practice—General Principles of Food Hygiene and the Recommended International Code of Practice for Control of the Use of Veterinary Drugs. There are also a number of codes of technological practice which are designed to ensure that the processing, transportation and storage of foods produced to Codex standards are such that the end product that consumers receive attains the expected quality level. Such codes exist for infant foods, the transportation of fresh fruit and vegetables and the storage and transportation of edible oils and fats.

The work of the Codex Alimentarius Commission is not limited to the removal of barriers to international trade. It also supports and encourages food traders to adopt voluntary ethical practices to promote fair trade. The Commission has published the Code of Ethics for International Trade in Food to aid this endeavour.

Codex Alimentarius Code of Ethics

The Codex Alimentarius Commission adopted the Code of Ethics for International Trade in Food at its thirteenth session in December 1979. The Code was later amended by the sixteenth session of the Commission in July 1985. The Commission recognised that adequate, safe, sound and wholesome food is vital to achieving acceptable standards of living. The right to such a standard, particularly in relation to the health and well-being of the individual, is proclaimed in the United Nations Universal Declaration of Human Rights.

Food is also vital to international trade. Food quality is influenced primarily by prevailing commercial practices, food legislation and control measures. Given that consumers spend such a significant portion of their income on food, it is important that unfair trade practices should be minimised and that the safety and whole-someness of food should be maximised. The Commission felt it necessary to act due to underdeveloped food legislation and control infrastructures in many states, leaving them vulnerable to unethical trading practices and consequently exposed to poor quality and unsafe food imports. The Codex Alimentarius Commission was, it was claimed, particularly well placed to draft a code on this issue, given that its principal objectives include the protection of consumer health and ensuring fair practices in international trade in food, facilitating such trade through the har-monisation of standards and practice in food production. Its role, and that of the Code of Ethics, would be to assist individual members in establishing or strength-ening their food legislation and food control infrastructures and, where necessary, to take advantage of the work of international organisations competent to advise and provide assistance in such matters, such as the Codex Alimentarius Commission itself. The hope was that the Code would help to establish an interna-tionally agreed norm and a framework for the realisation of effective international co-operation on those ethical aspects of trade covered by it. In particular, the Code seeks to establish standards of ethical conduct for all those engaged in international trade in food or responsible for regulating it and thereby to protect the health of the consumer and promote fair trade practices.[84] In order to achieve this, those engaged in international trade in food would have to commit themselves morally to the code and voluntarily undertake to support its implementation.

The Code states that international trade in food should be conducted on the principle that all consumers are entitled to safe and wholesome food and to pro-tection from unfair trade practices.[85] Therefore, no food should be traded inter-nationally which contains any substance in an amount that renders it poisonous or otherwise harmful to human health; consists in whole or in part of any filthy, putrid, rotten, decomposed or diseased substance or foreign matter, or is other-wise unfit for human consumption; is adulterated; is labelled or presented in a manner that is false, misleading or deceptive; or is sold, prepared, packaged, stored or transported for sale under unsanitary conditions.[86]

The Code also sets out a series of specific requirements on individual aspects of the production and marketing of food in international trade.[87] It states that appro-priate standards should be established and enforced, taking into account that uniform consumer protection and the orderly marketing of food can be better achieved through the acceptance of food standards elaborated by the Codex Alimentarius Commission or the adaptation of national standards to such inter-national recommendations. In addition to this, food should be subject at all times

---

[84] Article 1. The Code also applies, *mutatis mutandis*, to concessional food and food aid. Article 2.1.
[85] Article 4.1.
[86] Article 4.2.
[87] Article 5.

to sound hygienic practices; it should be accompanied by accurate and adequate descriptive labelling information; it should contain only Codex Alimentarius approved additives; pesticide residues and contaminants should be limited to the maximum Codex recommendations; all food should be free from micro-organisms and parasites in harmful amounts; irradiated food should be produced and controlled in accordance with the provisions and standards of the Codex Alimentarius Commission; food for infants and children and other vulnerable groups should be in accordance with Codex standards; no claims should be made about any food, particularly processed food, with minimal nutritive value which implies that the food can make a valuable contribution to the diet; and any information concerning the nutritional value of food should not mislead the public.

The implementation of the Ethics Code is deemed to be a matter for govern-ments, who should provide adequate food legislation and food control infra-structures, including certification and inspection systems and other legal or administrative procedures as necessary.[88] It is recognised that, in some emergency situations, such as famines, it may not be possible or desirable to apply certain pro-visions of the Code. However, in such circumstances, due regard should still be had to the basic principles of the safety of food and other provisions of the Code as may be applicable under those circumstances.[89]

Codex Alimentarius Food Labelling Standards

The Codex Ethics Code sets appropriate food labelling information as one of the primary mechanisms to be used in efforts to ensure that internationally traded food is both safe and wholesome and that the consumer is protected. By obliging the producer to state the composition of a product clearly on an accompanying label there is less potential for consumer deception. Codex standards have thus been devised for labelling requirements generally,[90] foods for special dietary uses,[91] and individual generic food products, such as chocolate and butter.[92] Guidelines have been set for nutrition labelling,[93] the production and labelling of organic foods,[94] and claims made on food labelling.[95] It is hoped that through the international adoption of these harmonised standards consumers will be pro-tected to the best possible level throughout the trading world.

---

[88] Article 7.
[89] Article 8.
[90] Codex Standard 1/1985. Revised 1991 and 2005.
[91] Codex Standard 146/1985.
[92] Codex Standard 87/1981. Revised 2003.
[93] Codex Guidelines 2/1985. Revised 1993 and 2003.
[94] Codex Guidelines 32/1999. Revised 2001 and 2004.
[95] General Guidelines on Claims, Codex Guidelines 1/1979, revised 1991; Guidelines for Use of Nutrition and Health Claims, Codex Guidelines 23/1997, revised 2004.

The Codex General Standard for the Labelling of Prepackaged Foods applies to all prepackaged foods, including those for catering purposes.[96] Prepackaged food must not be described or presented on any labelling in a manner that is false, misleading or deceptive or which is likely to create an erroneous impression regarding its character in any respect, including suggesting that the product is in fact another with which it might be confused, or in such a manner that may lead the consumer to suppose that the food is connected with any other such product.[97] The Codex Food Labelling Standard sets out those aspects of information that must appear on all prepackaged foods. These include:

(i) Food Name
The Codex states the purpose of the food name is to indicate the true nature of the food. It should normally be specific and not generic. It may also be a Codex legal name, that is, one that has been established for a food in a Codex standard. In other cases the name prescribed by national legislation is to be used. In the absence of any such name, either a common or usual name must be used which exists by common usage as an appropriate descriptive term and which is neither misleading nor confusing to consumers. Brand names and trade marks may only be used if they accompany a Codex legal, national legal or customary name. The label should also contain, in close proximity to the name of the food, additional words or phrases as necessary to avoid misleading or confusing the consumer about the true nature and/or physical condition of the product, detailing, for example, any treatment the foodstuff has undergone, such as reconstitution, drying, concentrating or smoking.[98]

(ii) List of Ingredients
A list of ingredients must appear on all prepackaged food, with the exception of single ingredient foods. The list is to be preceded by an appropriate title which includes the word 'ingredient'. Ingredients are to be listed in descending order of weight at the time of manufacture of the food. Where an ingredient is the product of two or more ingredients, this may be declared in its compound form, provided that it is immediately accompanied by a list, in brackets, of its ingredients in descending order of proportion. Where a compound ingredient, for which a name has been established in a Codex standard or in national legislation, constitutes less than five per cent of the food, the ingredients, other than food additives which serve a technological function in the finished product, need not be declared. Foods and ingredients which are known to cause hypersensitivity should always be declared. These include cereals containing gluten, eggs, fish, peanuts, soybeans and milk. The presence in any food or ingredient obtained through biotechnology of an allergen transferred from any of these foods must be declared. Where it is not possible to provide adequate information in this regard, the food containing the

---

[96] Article 1 thereof.
[97] Article 3.
[98] Article 4.1.

allergen should not be marketed at all. Added water should also be declared in the list of ingredients, except where it forms part of another ingredient used in a compound food, such as broth or brine. Water that evaporates in the course of manufacture need not be declared. Where a food is to be reconstituted by the addition of water, the ingredients may be listed in order of their proportion in the reconstituted product, provided that this is made clear on the label. Class names are also set for groups of ingredients that may all be labelled under the same generic name. For example, all refined oils other than olive oil may simply be listed in the ingredients listing as 'oil', provided that this is preceded by the term 'vegetable' or 'animal' as appropriate, and further qualified by the term 'hydrogenated' or 'partially hydrogenated' where applicable. Similarly, refined fats may all be labelled 'fat' if preceded by the term 'animal' or 'vegetable' where appropriate, just as all types of cheese or a mixture of cheeses may be labelled 'cheese', provided that the labelling and presentation of the food does not refer to a specific type of cheese, and all 'poultrymeat' may simply be listed in the ingredients as such, provided that the labelling does not refer to a specific type of poultry. However, pork fat, lard and beef fat must always be clearly labelled as such. Class titles are also available for use in the ingredients listing for food additives. The class title, such as emulsifier, acidity regulator, colour, sweetener or flavour enhancer, is to be used together with the specific name or recognised numerical identification as required by national legislation. The expression 'flavours' may be qualified by terms such as 'natural' or 'artificial' as appropriate. Food additives that do not perform a technological function in the finished product are exempt from declaration in the list of ingredients.[99]

Where the labelling of a food places special emphasis on the presence of one or more valuable or characterising ingredients, or where the description of the food has the same effect, the ingoing percentage of the ingredient at the time of manufacture should be declared. Similarly, where the labelling of a food places special emphasis on the low content of one or more ingredients, the percentage of the ingredient in the final product should be declared. However, a reference in the name of a food to a particular ingredient will not of itself constitute the placing of special emphasis, and a reference in the labelling of a food to an ingredient used in a small quantity and only as a flavouring will not of itself constitute the placing of special emphasis.[100]

(iii) Net Contents

The net contents are to be declared in the metric system ('Système International d'Unités' units). These net contents are to be declared for liquid foods by volume, for solid foods by weight, and for semi-solid or viscous foods by either weight or volume. Any food carried in a liquid medium, such as water, vinegar or fruit juice for fruit products, must state the drained net weight of the food.[101] The name and

[99] Article 4.2.
[100] Article 5.1.
[101] Article 4.3.

net contents of the food should appear in a prominent position and in the same field of vision.[102]

(iv) Other Details

The name and address of the manufacturer, packer, distributor, importer, exporter or vendor should appear on the labelling.[103] Similarly, the country of origin of the food should be declared where its omission would mislead or deceive the consumer. Where a food undergoes processing in a second country which changes its nature, the country in which this processing occurs is to be considered the country of origin for labelling purposes.[104] Instructions for use, including reconstitution where applicable, should be included on the label as necessary to ensure the correct utilisation of the food.[105] The lot number should also be marked.[106]

The date of minimum durability should be declared. This should consist at least of the day and the month for products with a minimum durability of not more than three months or the month and the year for products with a minimum durability of more than three months. The date should be declared as 'best before . . .' where the date is indicated and 'best before end . . .' in other cases. A date of minimum durability is not required for fresh fruits and vegetables; wines, liqueur wines, sparkling wines and aromatised wines; beverages containing more than 10 per cent by volume of alcohol; bakers' wares which are normally consumed within 24 hours of their manufacture; vinegar; salt; solid sugars; confectionery products consisting of flavoured and/or coloured sugars; and chewing gum. In addition to the date of minimum durability, any special conditions for the storage of the food should be declared on the label if the validity of the date on the label depends on this.[107]

The label of a food which has been treated with ionising radiation should carry a written statement indicating this in close proximity to the name of the food. The use of the international food irradiation symbol is optional. When it is used, it too must appear in close proximity to the name of the food. When an irradiated product is used as an ingredient in another food, this is to be declared in the list of ingredients.[108] Any information or pictorial device may be displayed on food labelling provided that it is not in conflict with the mandatory standards of the Codex labelling standard. If grade designations are used, they must be readily understandable and must not be misleading or deceptive in any way.[109] All mandatory labelling must be clear, prominent, indelible and readily legible by the consumer. On language, all the Codex standard states is that if the language used on the original label is not acceptable to the consumer for whom it is intended, a

---

[102] Article 8.1.4.
[103] Article 4.4.
[104] Article 4.5.
[105] Article 4.8.
[106] Article 4.6.
[107] Article 4.7.
[108] Article 5.2.
[109] Article 7.

supplementary label containing the mandatory information in the required language may be used instead of relabelling. The supplementary label should fully and accurately reflect the information given in the original label.[110]

Nutrition Labelling and Dietary Claims

The Codex Guidelines on Nutrition Labelling are designed to ensure that consumers are provided with information that enables them to make an informed choice, based on accurate information. In particular, this must be done by conveying truthful details about the nutrients in food, encouraging the use of sound nutrition principles in the formulation of foods which benefit public health, and providing the opportunity to include supplementary nutrition information on the label. Nutrition labelling should not deliberately imply that a food which carries such labelling necessarily has any nutritional advantage over a food which is not so labelled.

The Guidelines recommend procedures for the nutrition labelling of foods. Nutrition labelling consists of two components: nutrient declarations and supplementary nutrition information. A nutrient declaration is a standardised statement or listing of the nutrient content of a food.[111] Nutrition claims are deemed to include any representation which states, suggests or implies that a food has particular nutritional properties including, but not limited to, its energy value and content of protein, fat and carbohydrates, as well as the content of vitamins and minerals.[112] Nutrient declarations should be mandatory for foods in relation to which nutrition claims are made. Nutrient declarations should be voluntary for all other foods.[113] Nutrition labelling should include information on energy values; protein, carbohydrate and fat levels; any other nutrients for which a nutrition claim is made, such as fibre; and any other nutrient considered to be relevant for maintaining a good nutritional status as required by national legislation. Vitamins and minerals may also be listed, but only when present in significant amounts (usually at least five per cent of the established recommended daily intake).[114] Guidelines are also set in relation to how this information should be presented; for example, information on energy should be expressed in kJ and kcal per 100 g or per 100 ml or per package if the package contains a single portion or 'carbohydrate . . .g, of which sugars . . .g', where the total carbohydrate value and type of carbohydrate is declared.[115]

Supplementary nutrition information may also appear on the labelling. It should be optional and should only be given in addition to, and not in place of, the nutrient declaration, except in countries where the target population has a high

---

[110] Article 8.
[111] Article 2.3.
[112] Article 2.4.
[113] Article 3.1.
[114] Article 3.2.
[115] Article 3.4.

illiteracy rate and/or comparatively little knowledge of nutritional values. In such situations, food group symbols or other pictorial or colour presentations may be used without the nutrient declaration. Supplementary nutrition information on labels should be accompanied by consumer education programmes to increase consumers' understanding and use of the information.[116]

There are also separate Codex guidelines on the use of nutrition and health claims.[117] Nutrition claims are defined as being:

> any representation which states, suggests or implies that a food has particular nutritional properties including but not limited to the energy value and to the content of protein, fat and carbohydrates, as well as the content of vitamins and minerals.[118]

Simply mentioning substances in the list of ingredients, nutrients as a mandatory part of nutrition labelling or quantitative or qualitative declarations of certain nutrients or ingredients on the label as required by national legislation are not nutrition claims.[119] Several additional requirements relating to nutrition labelling are set out in the Guidelines. First, where a food is by its nature low in or free from the nutrient that is the subject of the claim, the term describing the level of the nutrient should not immediately precede the name of the food but the name of the nutrient should also appear, for example 'a low-fat food' or 'a fat-free food'.[120] This really just offers a clarification of how such products should be labelled rather than offering any sort of consumer protection provision. Second, comparative claims that compare the nutrient levels and/or energy values of two or more foods, such as 'reduced sodium', 'fewer calories' or 'increased fibre', are permitted, provided that the foods being compared are different versions of the same food or similar foods and the foods being compared are clearly identified. The amount of difference in the energy value or nutrient content should be stated. Any such claim should be based on a relative difference of at least 25 per cent in the energy value or nutrient content. Use of the word 'light' should follow the same criteria as for 'reduced' and should include an indication of the characteristics that make the food light.[121] Claims relating to the function of a nutrient in the body are permitted by the Guidelines, subject to certain conditions. These pre-requirements include that only those essential nutrients for which a Nutrient Reference Value (NRV) has been established in the Codex Guidelines on Nutrition Labelling or those nutrients which are mentioned in officially recognised dietary guidelines of the national authority having jurisdiction, should be the subject of a nutrient function claim. In addition, the food in respect of which the claim is made should be a significant source of this nutrient in the diet. The nutrient function claim should

---

[116] Article 4.

[117] Guidelines for Use of Nutrition and Health Claims, Codex Guidelines 23/1997, revised 2004. These guidelines originally dealt with nutrition claims only. Health claims were added to the guidelines in the 2004 revision. This is discussed in more detail in Chapter 6 below.

[118] Article 2.1.

[119] *Ibid.*

[120] Article 5.2.

[121] Article 6.

be based on scientific consensus. No such claim should ever imply or include any statement to the effect that the nutrient would afford a cure or treatment for or protection from disease.[122] Claims that relate to dietary guidelines or 'healthy diets' are only permitted in set circumstances. For example, such claims may only be made where they relate to the pattern of eating contained in dietary guidelines officially recognised by the appropriate national authority. However, foods should not be described as 'healthy', or be represented in a manner that implies that it in and of itself will impart health. Foods may only be described as forming part of a 'healthy diet' where the label carries a statement relating the food to the pattern of eating described in recognised dietary guidelines.[123]

The Codex General Standard for the Labelling of and Claims for Prepackaged Foods for Special Dietary Uses also applies to all products that are directly offered to consumers or are supplied for catering purposes.[124] Foods for special dietary uses are those specially processed or formulated to satisfy particular dietary requirements due to a particular physical or physiological condition and/or specific diseases and disorders, and which are presented as such, including foods for infants and young children. Foods coming within such a category must not be described or presented in a manner that is false, misleading or deceptive or that is likely to create an erroneous impression regarding their character in any respect,[125] examples of such claims being set out in the Codex General Guidelines on Claims.[126] Nothing in the labelling and advertising of foods to which this applies may imply that advice from a qualified person is not needed.[127]

The label of all prepackaged foods for special dietary uses should bear several specified pieces of information in addition to those items that must appear under the terms of the General Standard on labelling. In addition to the name of the food, the designation 'special dietary' or 'special dietetic' or an appropriate equivalent term may be used in conjunction with the name, the characterising essential feature to be stated in appropriate descriptive terms in close proximity to the name of the food. Nutrition labelling information must appear, including the amount of energy, protein, carbohydrate and fat per 100 g, 100 ml or portion as appropriate. However, information must also be given as to the total quantity of those specific nutrients or other components which provide the characterising essential feature for the special dietary use for which the food is intended per 100 g, 100 ml or portion. Finally, as one other alteration to the manner of labelling prescribed by the general Codex standard, storage instructions for opened packages of food for special dietary uses should be included on the label if necessary to ensure that the opened product maintains its wholesomeness and nutritive value. A warning

---

[122] Article 7.
[123] Article 8.
[124] Codex Standard for the Labelling of and Claims for Prepackaged Foods for Special Dietary Use, Codex Standard 146/1985.
[125] Article 3.1.
[126] Codex Guidelines 1/1979. Revised 1991.
[127] Article 3.2.

should be included on the label if the food is not capable of being stored after opening.[128] All other aspects of the labelling of these products that are covered by the general labelling standard should be as stated in the general labelling standard.

There are additional labelling requirements for foods covered by the special dietary standard that are not covered in any way by the general labelling standard. For example, a food that has not been modified but which is suitable for use in a particular dietary regimen because of its natural composition may not be designated as 'special dietary' or any other equivalent term. However, such food may bear a statement on the label that by its nature it possesses the essential distinguishing characteristic, provided that this statement does not mislead the consumer.[129] The same exemptions from the terms of this standard apply as for the general labelling standard.[130]

The Codex Standard for the Labelling of and Claims for Foods for Special Medical Uses covers those foods which are for special dietary uses and which are specially processed or formulated or presented for the dietary management of patients only to be used under medical supervision.[131] These foods are intended for the exclusive or partial feeding of patients with limited or impaired capacity to take, digest, absorb or metabolise ordinary foodstuffs or certain nutrients, or who have other special medically-determined nutrient requirements, whose dietary management cannot be achieved only by modification of the normal diet, by other foods for special dietary uses, or by a combination of the two.[132] The formulation of any foods for special medical purposes should be based on sound medical and nutritional principles. Their use must be demonstrated by scientific evidence, to be safe and beneficial in meeting the nutritional requirements of the persons for whom they are intended. Any labels or advertising of these types of foods should always provide sufficient information as to the nature and purpose of the food, as well as detailed instructions and precautions for their use. The advertising of these products to the general public should be prohibited.

Foods for special medical purposes should be labelled in accordance with the Codex General Standard for the Labelling of and Claims for Prepackaged Foods for Special Dietary Uses, except that some aspects, such as those relating to nutrition labelling, quantitative labelling and exemptions, do not apply to medical foods. They are replaced with specific requirements for these aspects of the medical food label. Additionally, a prominent statement 'use under medical supervision' should appear on the label in bold letters, separate from other information.[133] There should also be a warning of the hazards that may result following consumption of the food by individuals who do not have the disease,

---

[128] Article 4.
[129] Article 5.
[130] Article 6.
[131] Codex Standard 180/1991.
[132] Article 2.
[133] Article 4.4.

disorder or medical condition for which the product is intended.[134] A complete statement concerning use of the food, adequate precautions and known side effects should also be included on the labelling.[135] This information may be provided separately from the packaging.

The Codex General Guidelines on Claims apply to all foods, irrespective of whether or not the food concerned is covered by an individual Codex standard.[136] The principle upon which the Guidelines are based is that no food should be described or presented in a manner that is false, misleading or deceptive or is likely to create an erroneous impression regarding its character in any respect. The person marketing the food should be able to justify the claims made. A claim is defined as being:

> any representation which states, suggests or implies that a food has particular characteristics relating to its origin, nutritional properties, nature, production, processing, composition or any other quality.[137]

Claims which it is suggested should be prohibited by the Guidelines include those stating that a food is an adequate source of all essential nutrients, except where these claims are allowable by a Codex standard or where appropriate authorities have accepted the product to be such a source; those implying that a balanced diet or ordinary foods cannot supply adequate amounts of all nutrients; claims that cannot be substantiated; those on the suitability of a food for use in the prevention, alleviation, treatment or cure of a disease, disorder, or particular physiological condition unless they are in accordance with the provisions of the Codex standards or guidelines for foods for special dietary uses or, in the absence of such a standard, they are permitted under the laws of the country in which the food is distributed; and claims that could give rise to doubt about the safety of similar food or which could arouse or exploit fear in the consumer.[138]

The Guidelines also set out examples of the types of claim that could be considered misleading. In particular, it states that meaningless claims include incomplete comparatives and superlatives and claims about good hygienic practice, such as 'wholesome' or 'healthy'.[139] Some claims are expressly permitted by the Guidelines. These include claims that a food has obtained an enhanced or special nutritive value by means of the addition of nutrients, such as vitamins, minerals and amino acids. However, such claims are only permissible where the addition has been made on the basis of nutritional considerations according to the Codex General Principles for the Addition of Essential Nutrients to Foods.[140] Terms such as 'natural', 'pure', 'home made', 'organically grown' and 'biologically grown' may

---

[134]   Article 4.4.3.
[135]   Article 4.5.2.
[136]   Codex Guidelines 1/1979. Revised 1991.
[137]   Article 2.
[138]   Article 3.
[139]   Article 4.
[140]   Codex Guidelines 9/1987. Revised 1991.

only be made if they are used in accordance with national regulations. Claims about religious or ritual preparation, such as 'halal' and 'kosher', may only be made where the food conforms to the requirements of the relevant religious or ritual authorities. Claims that a food has special characteristics may be made even where all such foods have the same characteristics, provided that this fact is made clear on the label. Claims highlighting the absence or non-addition of particular substances to food may also be made, provided that such claims are not misleading. Finally, claims which highlight the absence or non-addition of one or more nutrients should be regarded as nutrition claims and should therefore be accompanied by nutrient declarations in accordance with the Codex Guidelines on Nutrition Labelling.[141]

Organic Production and Labelling Requirements

The foreword to the Codex Guidelines for the Production, Processing, Labelling and Marketing of Organically Produced Goods defines its aim as the protection of consumers from deception and fraud in the marketplace and unsubstantiated product claims; to protect producers of organic produce from misrepresentation of other agricultural produce as being organic; to ensure that all stages of production, preparation, storage, transportation and marketing are subject to inspection and comply with the Codex Organic Guidelines; to harmonise provisions for the production, certification, identification and labelling of organically grown produce; to provide international guidelines for organic food control systems in order to facilitate recognition of national systems as equivalent for the purposes of import; and to maintain and enhance organic agricultural systems in each country so as to contribute to local and global preservation.[142] The Guidelines recognise the importance of harmonising organic standards at international level. It is stated that these guidelines are to be considered a first step in global harmonisation of standards for organic food. As yet, there is limited experience in the development and implementation of such international requirements. Moreover, regional differences on organic production methods persist. The Guidelines were thus claimed to be merely useful in assisting countries to develop national regimes regulating the production, marketing and labelling of organic foods. It was recognised that they would need regular improvement and updating in order to take into account technical progress and experiences of implementation. The Guidelines are not in any way to prejudice the implementation of more restrictive arrangements. More detailed rules may therefore be introduced by member countries in order to maintain credibility amongst consumers and to prevent fraudulent practices.

A product is regarded by the Guidelines as bearing indications referring to organic production methods where, in the labelling or claims, including

---

[141] Article 5.
[142] Codex Guidelines 32/1999. Revised 2001 and 2004.

advertising material or commercial documents, the product, or its ingredients, is described using words such as 'organic', 'biodynamic', 'ecological', or words of similar intent which suggest to the purchaser that the product or its ingredients has been obtained by organic production methods.[143] Materials and products produced from genetically modified organisms are deemed incompatible with the principles of organic food production and are not accepted under the guidelines.[144] More specifically, genetically modified preparations of micro-organisms and enzymes used in food processing are not permitted as an ingredient of non-agricultural origin.[145]

Foods should only refer to organic production methods if they derive from an organic farm system employing management practices that seek to nurture ecosystems which achieve sustainable productivity and provide weed, pest and disease control through a diverse mix of mutually dependent life forms, recycling plant and animal residues, crop selection and rotation, water management, tillage and cultivation. Soil fertility, for example, should be maintained and enhanced by a system which optimises the biological activity and physical and mineral nature of the soil as the means to provide a balanced nutrient supply for plant and animal life as well as to conserve soil resources, while pest and disease management should be attained by means of encouraging a balanced host/predator relationship, augmentation of beneficial insect populations, biological and cultural control, and mechanical removal of pests and affected plant parts. Production should be sustainable, with the recycling of plant nutrients constituting an essential part of the fertilisation strategy. The basis for organic livestock husbandry should be the development of a harmonious relationship between land, plants and livestock, and respect for the physiological and behavioural needs of livestock. This must be achieved through a combination of providing good quality organically grown feedstuffs, appropriate stocking rates, livestock husbandry systems appropriate to behavioural needs, and animal management practices, that minimise stress and seek to promote animal health and welfare, prevent disease and avoid the use of chemical allopathic veterinary drugs, including antibiotics.[146]

Organic products should be labelled in accordance with the Codex General Standard for the Labelling of Prepackaged Foods.[147] Any such labelling claims may refer to organic production methods only where the product has been produced in accordance with the Codex Organic Guidelines and has been subject to its inspection measures.[148] In order to satisfy this requirement, all ingredients of agricultural origin must have been produced in accordance with these guidelines. However, by way of derogation, some ingredients of agricultural origin not

---

[143] Article 1.1.
[144] Article 1.5.
[145] Article 3 of the Guidelines does permit the addition of specified ingredients of non-agricultural origin to organic food. The positive list of such ingredients is set out in Annex 2, Table 3.
[146] Article 2.1.
[147] Codex Standard 1/1985. Revised 1991 and 2005.
[148] Article 3.2.

satisfying these requirements may be used, up to a maximum level of five per cent of the total ingredients, excluding salt and water, in the final product and where these ingredients of agricultural origin are not available, or are not available in sufficient quantity, in their organic state. The product should not contain any ingredient of non-agricultural origin not permitted in Annex 2 to the Guidelines.[149] No organic food, nor its ingredients, may be subjected to ionising treatment.[150] Member countries may consider enabling organic production labelling to be used where the product contains a minimum of 70 per cent organic ingredients.[151]

The rules on the production and preparation of organic foods set out in the Codex Guidelines require that the production requirements of Annex 1 should be satisfied. Substances listed in Annex 2 may be used, provided that the corresponding use is not prohibited in general agriculture and/or food production. Conditions on the use of these substances may be set by organic certification bodies. Annex 1 sets out the principles of organic production. It states that for plants and plant products, soil fertility should be maintained or increased by either the cultivation of legumes, green manures or deep-rooting plants in an appropriate multi-annual rotation programme or the incorporation in the soil of organic material produced in accordance with the Guidelines. For example, by-products from livestock farming, such as farmyard manure, may be used if they come from livestock holdings producing in accordance with the Guidelines. Similarly pests, diseases and weeds should only be controlled by, *inter alia*, appropriate rotation programmes, protecting natural enemies of pests by providing favourable habitats such as hedges and nesting sites or the grazing of animals.

Organic livestock management should aim to utilise natural breeding methods, minimise stress, prevent disease, progressively eliminate the use of allopathic veterinary drugs (including antibiotics), reduce the amount of animal feed containing products of animal origin, and maintain animal health and welfare. The use of chemical allopathic veterinary drugs or antibiotics for preventative treatments is prohibited. The transportation and slaughter of livestock should be managed in a calm and gentle way, avoiding or minimising stress and/or suffering. Herbivores must have access to organic pasture and all other animals to open air runs. The only exceptions to this are where indicated by the animals' physiological state, inclement weather conditions or the state of the land. Livestock may not be transferred between organic and non-organic units. However, where livestock from a non-organic source is introduced to organic land, and products therefrom are to be sold as organic, such livestock must be reared according to the guidelines for set compliance periods. For example, cows used for meat production must have been reared on organic land for a minimum of 12 months and at least three-quarters of their life. In relation to poultry this must be for their entire life, but for eggs it is a minimum of six weeks. All poultry must be reared in open-range conditions and

---

[149] Articles 3.3 and 3.4.
[150] Article 3.3.e.
[151] Article 3.6.

have free access to open-air runs whenever the weather permits. All mammals must have access to pasture or an open-air exercise area, which they must be able to use whenever conditions permit. All mammal housing must contain a comfortable, clean and dry rest area of sufficient size, with ample dry bedding strewn with litter material. All livestock systems should source animals' diet from organic feed containing suitable amounts of roughage, cereals and milk as appropriate. They must also have ample access to fresh water.

Inspection and certification systems may be used to verify the labelling of, and claims for, organically produced foods.[152] Development of these systems is to take account of the Codex Principles for Food Import and Export Inspection and Certification.[153] These inspection and certification systems should comprise at least the application of the measures and other precautions set out in Annex 3. For example, it must be ensured that organic production takes place in a unit where the land parcels, production areas, farm buildings and storage facilities for crops and livestock are clearly separate from those of any other unit which does not produce organically. Written and/or documentary accounts should be kept which enable inspection officials to trace the origin, nature and quantities of all raw materials used and of all agricultural products sold. Livestock should be identified individually, or for small mammals or poultry by herd or flock. Operators should maintain detailed records of breeding, disease management, treatments and medicines administered, feed provided and the source of the feedstuffs and transportation, slaughter and/or sales. There should be a full physical inspection of the production unit at least once a year.

Foodstuff Specific Codex Alimentarius Standards

The Codex Standard for Chocolate sets out the minimum quantity of cocoa solids for chocolate at 35 per cent.[154] Milk chocolate must contain a minimum of 25 per cent cocoa solids and milk chocolate with high milk content a minimum of 20 per cent.[155] All chocolate products must carry a declaration of the cocoa solids content in close proximity to the name.[156] The Codex Standard for Composite and Filled Chocolate sets minimum standards for products described in the Chocolate Standard to which organoleptic property modifying ingredients have been added. This Codex Standard also applies to products consisting of chocolate with a distinct filling of something other than chocolate.[157] The Codex Standard for Cocoa Butter,[158] as an ingredient in the manufacture of chocolate and chocolate products defines this as the fat obtained from cocoa beans with a maximum of 1.75 per cent

---

[152] Article 6.
[153] Codex Guideline 20/1995.
[154] Codex Standard 87/1981. Revised 2003.
[155] Article 3.
[156] Article 7.3.1.
[157] Codex Standard 142/1983.
[158] Codex Standard 86/1981. Revised 2001.

free fatty acid content and 0.7 per cent unsaponifiable matter.[159] The Codex Standard for Cocoa Butter Confectionery covers the product obtained by an adequate process of manufacture from cocoa butter, milk solids and sugars.[160] Cocoa butter must constitute a minimum of 20 per cent of such products, sugar accounting for no more than 55 per cent.[161] These products are to be labelled 'Cocoa Butter Confectionery', or 'White Chocolate' where permitted by national law.[162] Finally, there are also standards set by the Codex Standard for Cocoa Powders (Cocoas) and Dry Mixtures of Cocoa and Sugars, which legislates for these products where they are intended for direct consumption.[163] These are the products obtained from cocoa cake transformed into powder.[164]

4.3.4 Relationship between the Codex Alimentarius and EU Food Law

The work and individual standards of the Codex Alimentarius Commission impact upon EU food law in a variety of ways. Community legislation on the production and marketing of food has been consistently modelled on, and aligned with, Codex standards. The most explicit example of this can be seen in the devising of new rules on the use of nutrition and health claims. As discussed in more detail in Chapter 6 below, the proposal for a regulation on this makes it quite clear that as a result of the existence of Codex criteria for such claims, and the recognition therein that any such declarations would now require proper scientific validation and qualification prior to use, it is now necessary to devise Community rules in alignment with these international standards. This is generally a two-way process, with many Codex standards also taking their initiative from harmonised Community legislation.

The case law of the Court of Justice makes specific reference to Codex Alimentarius standards when determining whether the national laws of Member States on the naming and labelling of food are necessary and/or proportionate to the aim pursued. In particular, the Court will look at the international guidelines when assessing whether there is any 'substantial difference' between the composition of the product that a Member State seeks to prohibit from being marketed using a particular food name and products generally known by that name. Codex standards can be very persuasive in such Court determinations. For example, in *Smanor* the Court looked at the Codex standard for yoghurt in order to identify the key constituents of that food type.[165] If the product that was prohibited by the national authorities in this case from using the generic name 'yoghurt' was found to differ significantly on

---

[159] Article 2.1.
[160] Codex Standard 147/1985.
[161] Article 3.1.
[162] Article 7.1.
[163] Codex Standard 105/1981. Revised 2001.
[164] Article 2.1.
[165] Case 298/1987, *Proceedings for compulsory reconstruction against Smanor SA* [1988] ECR 4489, para 22.

this key constituent from that which was set out in the Codex standard,[166] then this could be key to enabling the Member State to demonstrate that there was in fact a 'significant difference' between the products, potentially enabling it to deviate from its Article 28 EC obligations in the name of consumer protection—a defence so rarely available to the Member States in such circumstances.

It was contended in *Deserbais* that consumer protection and fair trading require that international agreements concerning the use of the name of a particular product be observed. Consequently each Member State could make the right to use a name such as 'edam' subject to compliance with the requirements laid down by the Stresa Convention and the Codex Alimentarius, both of which lay down a minimum fat content of 40 per cent for that type of cheese. The Court, however, found here that the Codex Alimentarius rules are in fact intended to provide guidance on defining the characteristics of foodstuffs. The mere fact that a product does not wholly conform to the standard laid down should not be sufficient in itself to justify a Member State from prohibiting its sale there.[167] The Stresa Convention was not seen to be relevant here either as it was signed prior to the Treaty of Rome and only four Member States were party to it at the time. It was thus found that, provided that the rights of third countries are not involved, a Member State cannot rely on the provisions of a pre-existing convention like Stresa in order to justify restrictions on the marketing of products lawfully produced and marketed in another Member State.

Finally, the important role of Codex Alimentarius standards in international trade regulation should also be noted here. If the WTO Agreements make specific reference to the Codex, and these same WTO rules can influence the shape and direction of EU food legislation, then this recognition at international level can also therefore indirectly affect EU food law. It must, where appropriate, comply with Codex standards in order to ensure, as far as possible, that related EU standards conform to the Community's international obligations. In addition, other WTO members and regional trading blocs, such as NAFTA, recognise the international standards set out in the Codex. Adherence to the principles and requirements set out therein therefore assists in facilitating trade in food between the EU and these other countries.

4.4 CONCLUSION

While both the terms of the WTO Agreements and the Codex Alimentarius standards have an effect on EU food law, these are persuasive, not determinative. The

---

[166] Now, Codex Standard for Fermented Milks, Codex Standard 243/2003.

[167] Codex Standard for Fermented Milks, Codex Standard 243/2003, para 15. The Stresa Convention was not seen to be relevant here either as it was signed prior to the Treaty of Rome. Only four Member States were party to it at the time. It was thus found that, provided that the rights of third countries were not involved, a Member State could not rely on the provisions of a pre-existing convention like Stresa in order to justify restrictions on the marketing of products coming from another Member State where they were lawfully produced and marketed.

primary way of demonstrating compliance with WTO rules is to conform to other recognised international standards, such as those of the Codex. The EU has traditionally based much of its food legislation and case law decision-making on these standards in any case. Even where EU standards were adopted prior to the introduction of similar Codex standards, these tended to follow the Community's rules. They are always at least, in both situations, of persuasive authority. This minimises the potential for international trade disputes over the content of EU food law. While there have been instances where the EU has been accused of breaching its obligations in this regard, most notably in relation to genetically modified organisms and protected geographical food names, so long as the EU continues to base much of its food law on existing international standards and practices, and enables those from third countries to access its authorisation procedures where applicable, global trading rules will have little impact upon EU food law.

5

Food Safety in the EU

5.1 INTRODUCTION

SINCE THE 1990s there has been a succession of highly publicised scares about potentially lethal contaminations of food, such as avian flu in chickens, salmonella in eggs, mad cow disease in beef and dioxins in many foodstuffs. As a result, the institutions of the European Union have been forced to take action on the issue of food safety, and indeed to introduce legislative measures designed to convince the media, consumers and the electorate that they have moved to successfully solve them. This was the political effect of media scares. But the approaches that were taken did not take into account the clear distinction which this work highlights: that between the gravity of the effects of the occasional food contamination episode on the one hand, and the consequences of the obesity pandemic, attributable to the chronically bad diet of so many citizens. Avian flu, salmonella, mad cow disease and dioxins combined have never killed as many people in a year as die daily within the EU from obesity and its sequelae. The EU legislated for 'scares' affecting some, ignoring the approaching health pandemic that would affect many more.

It is primarily due to the level of negative publicity that tends to surround these food safety concerns that the EU institutions have now devised a detailed set of rules designed to ensure that food produced within the Union is safe to eat. This has led ultimately to the establishment of a unique type of bureaucratic administrative body, the European Food Safety Authority (EFSA), which now assists in the development of EU food safety law and policy.[1]

5.2 DEVISING A NEW FOOD SAFETY POLICY FOR THE EU: THE BSE CRISIS

Much of the current food safety policy of the European Union has evolved directly from the crisis that arose out of Bovine Spongiform Encephalopathy (BSE) infections in cattle, particularly in the United Kingdom, of the late 20th century. Individual cattle were probably first infected by BSE in the UK as early as the 1970s.[2] The Pathology Department of the Central Veterinary Laboratory (CVL) of

---

[1] See also Chapter 4 of M Lee, *EU Environmental Law: Challenges, Change and Decision-making* (Oxford, Hart Publishing, 2005).

[2] 'The BSE Inquiry: The Report', ISBN 0105569860. See also K Vincent, 'Mad Cows and Eurocrats—Community Responses to the BSE Crisis' (2004) 10 *European Law Journal* 499.

the UK State Veterinary Service (SVS) first investigated the death of a cow in September 1985, but the nature of the disease that had caused its death was masked by other factors and was thus not registered at the time. A question remains as to why it took so long for the true picture to emerge. The Pathology Department considered two further cases of BSE at the end of 1986 and identified these as being likely to be a Transmissible Spongiform Encephalopathy (TSE) in cattle. By the end of 1987 it had been concluded that the cause of the reported cases of BSE was the consumption of meat and bone meal which was made from animal carcasses and incorporated into animal feed. An inquiry into the BSE crisis was announced in the UK Parliament on 22 December 1997, and set up on 12 January 1998. Its function was to establish and review the history of the emergence and identification of BSE and actions taken in response to it. The BSE Inquiry found that the disease probably originated from a novel source early in the 1970s, possibly in a cow or other animal that developed the disease as a consequence of a gene mutation, but that the true origin of the disease will probably never be known with full certainty.

One of the main difficulties with a disease like BSE is that it has a very long incubation period. This makes it difficult to immediately assess whether it is transmissible to humans. Initially, it was thought that the risk of transmission of BSE to humans was remote and that 'it was most unlikely that BSE would have any implications for human health'.[3] This assessment of risk was made on the basis that BSE was probably derived from scrapie and could thus be expected to behave like scrapie. Scrapie had not been transmitted to humans in over 200 years and so BSE was not likely to be transmitted in this manner either. This report continued to be cited in the following years as constituting a scientific appraisal that the risks posed by BSE to humans were remote and that no precautionary measures were needed other than those recommended by this Southwood Working Party. The BSE Inquiry found that despite increasing knowledge over the years, the public was not informed of any change in the perceived likelihood that BSE might be transmissible to humans. They were repeatedly reassured that it was safe to eat beef. Yet again, one might reasonably ask why this happened.

By the end of 1989, 10,091 cases of BSE had been confirmed in the UK. On 1 March 1990 the EU restricted exports of live cattle to those aged under six months. On 10 May 1990 it was announced that a siamese cat had died of spongiform encephalopathy, resulting in a rash of media comment, speculating that the cat had caught BSE and that humans might be next. Exporting animal feed containing Specified Bovine Offal (SBO—those tissues in cattle considered most likely to be infective) to other EU Member States was prohibited. Its use as such was also banned in the UK, as little as one gram of infective material being enough to infect cattle to which it has been fed. Some education authorities began to ban beef altogether from school meals. On 8 June 1990 the EU Council of Ministers agreed that

[3] Report of the working party on Bovine Spongiform Encephalopathy (Southwood Report) (London, Department of Health/MAFF, 1989).

bone-in beef exported from the UK could only come from holdings where BSE had not been confirmed in the previous two years. By the end of 1990 the number of confirmed cases of BSE in cattle had risen to 24,396. An Expert Group on Animal Feedingstuffs was established by the UK Ministry for Agriculture (then MAFF) on 6 February 1991. It reported on 15 June 1992 that the steps taken to date to prevent BSE being transmitted to animals in feed were satisfactory and adequate. In particular, the Group considered whether the practice of feeding animal protein to animals should be discontinued. It decided that there was no scientific justification for such a step. Figures later demonstrated that the feed ban had resulted in a steady year-on-year reduction in the number of new infections. However, on 27 July 1994 the European Commission decided that existing restrictions on the export of UK beef should be replaced with two new measures. One was a ban on the export of beef-in bone except from cattle which had not been on holdings where BSE had been confirmed in the previous six years. The other measure affected beef from cattle which had been on such a holding within that time. This could not be exported unless it was deboned with adherent tissues removed. In December 1994 the Commission amended this decision to exempt from these measures beef from cattle born after 1 January 1992. Subsequently in July 1995 this exemption was replaced with one that exempted beef from cattle less than 30 months of age at slaughter. These decisions will be examined in more detail later in this chapter.

During 1995 a number of events served to increase public anxiety that it might be possible to contract CJD as a consequence of eating beef. Cases of CJD were reported in farmers whose herds had had BSE, and in several young people, which raised particular alarm because up until then the disease had almost invariably affected older victims. The safety of beef offal was questioned by scientists. In March 1996 it was announced in the UK Parliament by the Secretary of State for Health that 10 people had contracted a new variant of the invariably fatal Creutzfeldt-Jakob disease (vCJD), and that it was probable that they had caught BSE. By September 2000 over 80 cases had been reported. This outbreak of BSE, and its transmission to humans, had been almost exclusively a United Kingdom disaster. Only four other vCJD victims had been diagnosed elsewhere in the EU by the time of the publication of the BSE inquiry report in October 2000, two confirmed and one probable case in France and one confirmed case in Ireland. Over 170,000 cattle had been diagnosed with BSE in the UK at that stage, compared with fewer than 1,500 elsewhere.

One of the key problems with controlling the spread of an infection like BSE that has its source in beef cattle, is that merely not eating beef may not offer sufficient protection to the consumer. Products derived from beef enter the food chain in a variety of ways. Tallow, the fat that is extracted by the rendering process, and gelatine, derived from the skin and bone of cattle, are used in a wide variety of foodstuffs. Bovine fluids and tissues are also used in medicinal and cosmetic products. Another difficulty, identified by the Inquiry, was that the existing primary legislation, which was all that UK government departments could work with when the outbreak of BSE became apparent, was not ideally suited to addressing the problems of BSE, in particular because the statutory powers relied upon to adopt measures had been enacted to deal with known hazards. It was several more years before it became established that there was a known hazard to human health and the extent of the risk that was posed. New secondary legislation could, it was noted, be introduced—but this required clearance, consultation and time under existing legislative processes. Pursuing a policy of deregulation, enforcing rules with a light touch, had also contributed to the magnitude of the outbreak.

The UK BSE Inquiry found that a number of lessons could be learned from the outbreak and subsequent response to a disease like this. The fact that the origin of the epidemic remained unknown did, however, make it difficult to answer many other questions raised. In particular, it was found that an effective system of animal disease surveillance is a prerequisite to the effective control of such diseases. Also, where animal or public health is at stake, resort should be had to the best sources of scientific advice, wherever it is to be found, without delay. Where precautionary measures are introduced, such as the ban on ruminant feed, rigorous thought must be given to every aspect of its operation with a view to ensuring that it is watertight and is properly implemented and enforced. Reliance on a trade association or other similar bodies to communicate the importance of a precautionary measure is not, it was stated, always appropriate. Much was also offered on the use of advisory committees in such situations, such as ensuring that the reasoning behind any advice given is provided, that the nature and extent of any uncertainty should be clearly identified and that the advice of committees should normally be made public. In particular, it was noted that during the BSE crisis much advice and the communication of potential risks tended to be played down in order to avoid provoking any irrational public scare.

The BSE Inquiry highlighted the possibility that in circumstances such as those at issue in this crisis, Member States may be constrained in terms of the protective measures they can take if the Community has already introduced legislation specifying what action may be taken in such circumstances. Specifically, it was noted that once definitive measures for a relevant outbreak of disease had been adopted by the European Commission, individual Member States were no longer entitled to adopt unilateral measures to deal with the risks posed by the disease. Take the Specified Bovine Offal (Amendment) Order 1995, for example.[4] This order was introduced to amend the Specified Bovine Offal Order 1995,[5] creating a new series of restrictions on the use of the vertebral column of bovine animals, and a new registration requirement for premises where meat is recovered by mechanical means. It also extended the restriction on exports from Britain to other Member States to include mechanically recovered beef intended for human consumption. The original order had been introduced to give effect to Decision 1994/474, which had

---

[4] UK Statutory Instrument No 3246/1995.
[5] UK Statutory Instrument No 1928/1995.

established protection measures to counter the spread, and effects, of BSE.[6] This decision prohibited the export from the UK to other Member States of all live cattle over six months old, as well as those of any age which were the offspring of cows in which BSE was either suspected or confirmed.[7] The export of fresh beef on the bone was only permitted where it came from cattle from holdings on which no case of BSE had been confirmed in the previous six years.[8] In addition to this, measures were introduced limiting the sale of offal, such as brain, spinal cord, spleen, tonsils and intestines to that taken from cattle aged less than six months at slaughter.

The fact that measures being adopted at EU level may remove the power from Member States to adopt their own measures to deal with a crisis such as this could render the Specified Bovine Offal (Amendment) Order 1995 unlawful. This means that where a Member State has acted in a prompt manner in order to deal with the problem as soon as possible after it is identified, the measure enacted is open to challenge as being incompatible with Community law. This will continue to be the case until the Community itself has acted, and even then only if it adopts the same safety measures as the Member State.

5.2.1 Impact of Food Crises on EU Food Law and Policy: White Paper on Food Safety

The Commission White Paper on Food Safety, which was published in 2000, was an attempt to clarify and direct future Community policy on the safe production and distribution of food.[9] Its initiation was prompted to a large extent by the preceding BSE crises. The key initiative to come out of the White Paper has been the establishment of EFSA (although it was originally named more simply in the White Paper as the European Food Authority). Other issues dealt with in the 52-page document include controls over, and new methods of, devising food safety legislation, more general food safety controls, aspects of regulation relating to, *inter alia*, animal feed, animal health and welfare, food hygiene, contaminants and residues, packaging and irradiation, the provision of consumer information, and defining the role to be played by the European Commission in international food safety negotiations and developments.

The White Paper commences by setting out, in very general terms, the European Union's policy on food safety. It states that it must be built around high food safety standards that serve to protect and promote the health of the consumer. The importance of food law and policy is noted in the Paper's recognition

---

[6] Commission Decision 1994/474/EC of 27 July 1994 concerning certain protection measures relating to bovine spongiform encephalopathy and repealing Decisions 1989/469/EEC and 1990/200/EEC. [1994] OJ L 194/96.

[7] Article 1(1) of Decision 1994/474.

[8] Article 4(1) of Decision 1994/474.

[9] Commission White Paper on Food Safety. COM (1999) 719.

that the production and consumption of food is central to any society and has economic, social and, in many cases, environmental consequences for all. Although health protection must, it is claimed, always take priority, these other issues should also be taken into account in the development of food policy. Environmental policy is, given that the state and quality of the environment may affect different stages of the food chain, to play an important role in ensuring safe food for the consumer.

According to the White Paper, consumers should be offered a wide range of high quality, safe products coming from all Member States. This is recognised as being the essential role of the internal market. Every link in the food production chain must be as strong as the others if the health of consumers is to be adequately protected. This principle is to apply to food produced both within and outside the EU. It is stated that any food safety policy requires the assessment and monitoring of the risks to consumer health associated with raw materials, farming practices and food processing activities, requiring effective regulatory action to manage this risk, and it requires the establishment and operation of control systems to monitor and enforce the operation of these regulations. The White Paper also summarises the position of the Community in the devising and enforcement of food safety policy and law by stating that there must be a comprehensive and integrated approach to food safety, demanding that all aspects of food safety are addressed at European Union level, and European Union legislation is applied in an efficient way in all Member States in line with the principle of subsidiarity, but that enforcement should above all remain a primarily national, regional and local responsibility, each Member State having a duty towards not only its own citizens but all Union citizens and those of third countries as well.

The White Paper recognises that food safety needs to be organised in a more co-ordinated and integrated way to deliver a high level of public health and consumer protection in accordance with the requirements of the EC Treaty, requiring the full collaboration and co-operation of all parties. Public confidence needs to be re-established, as do food science, food controls and food law. One method of achieving this is through modernising existing EU food legislation to make it more coherent, understandable and flexible, and to promote better enforcement of that legislation, providing better transparency for consumers, as was recommended by the conclusions of the Helsinki European Council in December 1999.

The Commission outlined its determination to improve controls over the safety of food by prioritising the actions set out in the White Paper, imposing upon itself a three year timetable for the taking of appropriate action. Those proposals considered to be the most important were to be put forward by the Commission by the end of 2000, allowing for the creation of a coherent and up-to-date body of food law, to be supported by the envisaged European Food Safety Authority, by the end of 2002.

The guiding principle underlying the White Paper is that food safety policy is to be based on a comprehensive and integrated approach. This means that throughout the food chain, at all stages of the production process, there is to be adherence to what are described as 'the pillars of food safety', namely scientific advice, data collection and analysis, regulatory and control aspects and consumer information. The role of all stakeholders in the food chain, from feed manufacturers and farmers through to consumers, are to be clearly defined to ensure the systematic and consistent implementation of food safety policy. Traceability of feed and food and their ingredients, transparency in food policy, a structured risk analysis process, use of the precautionary principle, environmental considerations, animal welfare, sustainability, quality and clear communication of production and processing information are all deemed to be essential to ensuring that Community food safety policy achieves the desired aims.

Regulatory Aspects of the White Paper

The White Paper recognised that the Community had created a broad body of legislation, covering aspects of primary production of agricultural products and the industrial production of processed food. The legislation, which had evolved over the past 30 years, was seen to be based on a blend of scientific, societal, political and economic forces, in particular within the context of creating the internal market. It was also recognised, however, that no overall coherence had guided this development, resulting in the need to develop and devise the Green Paper on the general principles of food law in the European Union, which identified the need for a major review of European food legislation.[10] The principal problem was recognised as being attributable, not to a lack of legal instruments, but to the broad disparity in the means available to respond to situations in specific sectors, or the multiplicity of actions which need to be triggered in situations where a problem involves more than one sector of the broad regulatory framework. A new legal framework was thus proposed.

Central to the devising of any such replacing framework is the creation of a coherent and transparent set of food safety rules. This would be initiated in the first instance by the Commission making a series of proposals laying down the principles that would ensure a coherent approach and fixing the principles, obligations and definitions applicable to this field, following the lines established by the Commission Green Paper and subsequent consultation on its content. Any new legislation would only be introduced following a detailed consultation process with interested parties, and its content would have to be clear, understandable and simple for all operators to put into effect. The proper implementation of such legislation would be ensured by close co-operation with the competent authorities at the appropriate levels in the Member States to ensure proper and consistent compliance and enforcement. The future proposals were also set the task of providing a general framework for those areas of food law not covered by harmonised rules but where the functioning of the internal market is to be ensured by mutual recognition, as developed by the Community Courts in their *Cassis* jurisprudence. As a

---

[10] Green Paper on the general principles of food law in the European Union. COM (1997) 176 final.

consequence, Member States would only be allowed to restrict the marketing on their territory of products lawfully marketed in another Member State where this could be justified by a legitimate interest, such as the protection of public health, and where any such measures taken adhered to the principle of proportionality.

There was to be a 'stable to table' or 'farm to fork' approach taken, with regulatory control exercised at all stages of production. The White Paper therefore proposed the establishment of a new legal framework for the production and use of animal feed. It was recognised that, although legislation cannot cover all potential incidents affecting the food and feed chain, it can set up appropriate requirements and controls enabling problems to be detected early and fast corrective action to be taken. Specifically, the materials that may be used in animal feed production, including animal by-products, thus need to be clearly defined. The creation of a positive list of those substances that may be used was seen to be desirable, but it was also thought that devising such a list would be a complex and time-consuming task. However, there would be scope for expanding the negative list of those substances that may not be used in food production. It was stated in the White Paper that the Commission was committed to producing a positive list in the medium term. Legislation would be proposed to exclude fallen animals or cadavers and condemned material from the food chain. Then, the only material allowed to be used in animal feed would be that deemed fit for human consumption. The Commission was also committed to pursuing the prohibition or phasing-out of antibiotics used as growth promoters in animal feed depending on their potential use in human and veterinary medicine as part of the broader strategy designed to control and contain antibiotic resistance. Overall, the feed manufacturing industry was to become subject to the same rigorous requirements and controls as the food producing sector. In order to achieve this, legislation would be introduced to ensure that feed producing plants obtain official approval and be subject to official controls at national and Community levels. A rapid alert system, similar to that proposed for the food sector, would be integrated into the feed sector.

Animal Health and Welfare

The White Paper did make proposals specifically designed to promote the health and welfare of animals, but only insofar as this concerned food safety. It was recognised that most of the legislation relating to animal disease, in particular Bovine Spongiform Encephalopathy (BSE) and Transmissible Spongiform Encephalopathies (TSE), has been in the form of safeguard measures taken on an ad hoc basis. The adoption of these measures did not, by definition, involve all the Community institutions, nor do such measures provide for a fully consistent approach. The White Paper claimed that the Commission has addressed this problem by putting forward to the Parliament and the Council a comprehensive proposal based on Article 152 EC covering all measures to control BSE and TSE. Ad hoc emergency measures would continue to be used in the interim. The main measures proposed included surveillance and testing of risk categories, updating feed bans and, most importantly, embargoes put in place in light of scientific advice. Little else about animal welfare is stated in the White Paper. What there is, centres on the need for such issues to be integrated more fully with regard to food policy—in particular, the impact on the quality and safety of products of animal origin intended for human consumption need to be reflected in legislation.

Emergency Measures

The Commission recognised in the White Paper that there were insufficient safeguard measures in place to facilitate an adequate response to identified risks to consumer health. It was noted that no legal instrument existed that would enable the Commission to adopt a safeguard measure on its own initiative, either for feed or for a processed food of non-animal origin originating from one of the Member States. It was thus proposed that a single emergency measure procedure applicable to all types of food and feed, whatever the geographical origin, be introduced to remove any existing disparities and close remaining loopholes. A comprehensive legislative proposal would be required to fulfil this aspiration.

In addition to this, the White Paper recognised the need to simplify the decision-making process in order to ensure better efficacy and transparency and to speed up response times. Community food legislation can be introduced by one of several available Treaty procedures: Article 95 EC in the case of measures for the completion or the functioning of the internal market; Article 152 EC for measures in the veterinary and phytosanitary fields which have as their direct objective the protection of public health; Article 153 EC relating to consumer protection; and Article 37 EC relating to, predominantly, agriculture. Measures are adopted, depending on the applicable legal basis, either by the Council in co-decision with the Parliament following a proposal from the Commission (Article 251 EC) or after consultation of the Parliament following a proposal by the Commission.[11] Article 202 EC provides that in the instruments that it adopts, the Council shall confer on the Commission powers for the implementation of the rules which the Council lays down, save in specific cases where it may reserve the right to exercise directly implementing powers itself. This transfer of competence would normally allow the Commission to rapidly transform the scientific advice that it receives by amending the appropriate legislation or adopting appropriate decisions. In some cases, however, in particular with food additives, implementing powers have not yet been conferred on the Commission. Hence, updating lists of positive substances can take several years from receipt by the Commission of scientific advice. Where such powers have been conferred on the Commission, for example in relation to flavourings, contaminants, pesticide residues, materials in contact with food, diet foods, irradiated foods or quick-frozen foods, the decision-making

---

[11] For further discussion see A Dashwood, 'Community Legislative Procedures in the Era of the Treaty on European Union' (1994) 19 *European Law Review* 343; for further discussion see D Chalmers, C Hadjiemmanuil, G Monti and A Tomkins, *European Union Law* (Cambridge, CUP, 2006), pp 149–55.

process for transforming scientific advice into legislation or decisions was deemed unsatisfactory because the procedures in place were cumbersome and disparate, involved the use of different committees and different modalities, and were inhibited by a shortage of resources. As a consequence, it was recognised in the White Paper that all the procedures for the adoption and implementation of Community food legislation and its adaptation to technical and scientific progress required review. In particular, calls were made for the streamlining and reduction in the number of committees dealing with delegated legislation and the adoption of individual decisions, any new procedures to be in conformity with the Decision on comitology,[12] involving better co-ordination to ensure that food safety issues are addressed as a continuum from 'farm to fork' through the application of a single regulatory procedure for the adoption of individual decisions, and an emergency procedure for all urgent matters of food safety.[13] This could be better achieved, according to the White Paper, if clear and strict deadlines were fixed for the Commission to prepare an amendment or decision, for the Standing Committee to reach an opinion and for the Commission to finalise an amendment or decision, coupled with greater transparency at all stages of the regulatory process, supported by information and communication technologies which should be used extensively to automate the production and tracking of amendments and decisions and to accelerate their circulation between all the parties involved.

Controls over the Operation of EU Legislation

Responsibility for safe food production is shared among operators, who must ensure that they comply with legislative provisions and minimise risk on their own initiative; national authorities, who must oversee compliance with food safety standards by establishing control systems to ensure that Community rules are respected and enforced; and the European Commission, which, through the Food and Veterinary Office (FVO), carries out a programme of audits and inspections. The White Paper stated that the preceding food safety crises highlighted deficiencies in national systems of control, primarily due to a lack of harmonised Community approach to the design and development of national control systems. As a consequence, it was recognised that there was a clear need for a Community framework of national control systems to raise food safety standards across the European Union, with the operation of these systems to remain a national responsibility. This proposed framework would have three core elements, including the devising of operational criteria at Community level which national authorities would be expected to meet, forming the key reference points against which the competent authorities would be audited by the FVO; the development of

---

[12] Council Decision 1999/468/EC of 28 June 1999 laying down the procedures for the exercise of implementing powers conferred on the Commission. [1999] OJ L 184/23. For further discussion see Chalmers *et al, ibid*, pp 159–67.

[13] Several names are used for this approach to food regulation, including 'farm to table', 'stable to table', 'farm to fork' and 'seed to silo'.

Community control guidelines promoting coherent national strategies and identifying risk-based priorities and the most effective control procedures; and enhanced administrative co-operation in the development and operation of control systems involving a reinforced Community dimension to the exchange of best practice between national authorities, promoting mutual assistance between the Member States by integrating and completing the existing legal framework.

The White Paper on Food Safety clearly outlines the direction that EU food law should take in the future. A number of initiatives have been developed at Community level in its aftermath to achieve the aims set out therein. The Paper claims from the outset that the protection of human health must always take priority. While there is clearly a health protection element in much of the new legislation, the manner in which Community law on free movement has developed means that this remains the primary priority of the corpus of EU food laws. The White Paper calls for better enforcement of EU food law. This has since been the focus of a clear and consolidated regulation on verifying compliance with food law and animal welfare rules.[14] It was also proposed that EU legislation should be made clearer, more coherent and more flexible, leading to better transparency for consumers. This has led to public consultations on how food labelling can be improved.[15] It has also resulted in the introduction of new legislation, such as that on nutrition and health claims.[16] However, as will be discussed in Chapter 6 below, lobbying during the legislative process has significantly reduced the potential for positive impact that this legislation could have had on health promotion. Finally, the increased role for scientists in the introduction of food laws has seen two major developments to the manner in which such rules are now devised. First, the scientific committee structure has been streamlined, leading to the establishment of the Standing Committee on the Food Chain and Animal Health.[17] Second, it has led to the establishment of EFSA, which now plays a central role in assessing risks attached to the production and marketing of food.

5.2.2 The European Food Safety Authority

The White Paper envisaged that a European Food Safety Authority would be central to the devising and implementation of EU food safety policy. This is now operational. The Paper states that the Authority is to be independent and is to have

[14] Regulation (EC) No 882/2004 of the European Parliament and of the Council of 29 April 2004 on official controls performed to ensure the verification of compliance with feed and food law, animal health and animal welfare rules. [2004] OJ L 165/1.

[15] DG SANCO Consultative Document on 'Labelling: Competitiveness, Consumer Information and Better Regulation for the EU', February 2006.

[16] Proposal for a Regulation of the European Parliament and of the Council on nutrition and health claims made on foods. COM (2003) 424.

[17] Article 58 of Regulation (EC) No 178/2002 of the European Parliament and of the Council of 28 January 2002 laying down the general principles and requirements of food law, establishing EFSA and laying down procedures in matters of food safety. [2002] OJ L 31/1.

particular responsibility for two key areas underpinning more general Community food safety policy: risk assessment and communication on food safety issues. These are two of the three components of risk analysis. The other component—risk management—is thus to remain outside the remit of the Authority, leaving this task to the politicians and bureaucrats in the Parliament, Council and Commission. It was claimed in the White Paper that the inclusion of risk management in the mandate of the Authority would raise three concerns. First, the transfer of regulatory powers to an independent Authority could lead to a dilution of democratic accountability. Second, control must remain central to the Commission's risk management process to enable it to act most effectively on the consumer's behalf, most notably in providing that recommendations for action are implemented. This is to ensure that this institution remains in control of the responsibilities with which it is charged under the Treaties. Third, an authority with regulatory power could not be created under the existing institutional arrangements. To do so would require modification of the EC Treaty. So, what would be the advantage of a European Food Safety Authority were its role limited to that already undertaken by the existing individual scientific committees and the Commission? The White Paper claimed that the responsibilities of the Authority in preparing and providing scientific advice, collecting and analysing information to facilitate decision-making at institutional level, and the monitoring and surveillance of developments relating to food safety would all add a new dimension to already existing centralised processes and procedures, that it was hoped would assist in eliminating, or at least reducing, the risk of another crisis of BSE's magnitude. In order to achieve this, the Authority was to be based on 'the highest levels of independence, of scientific excellence and of transparency in its operations' and it 'should be in a position rapidly to establish itself as the authoritative point of reference for consumers, the food industry, Member State authorities and on the wider world stage'.[18] It was also set the ambitious aspiration of being:

> ideally placed to develop the flexible, rapid, response that the new challenges require [providing] a single, highly visible, point of contact for all concerned [acting] not only as a point of scientific excellence, but also [to] be available to consumers to provide advice and guidance on important food safety developments [undertaking] information actions with a view to ensuring that consumers can make informed choices, and are better informed on food safety issues.[19]

In order to achieve this, it was envisaged in the White Paper that the Authority would work in close co-operation with national scientific agencies and institutions in charge of food safety, creating a network of scientific contacts throughout Europe and elsewhere, with the Authority at its centre. The Community institutions, in particular the Commission, must support the Authority, ensuring that it

---

[18] White Paper on Food Safety, section 35.
[19] *Ibid*, section 36.

is properly resourced and staffed and, perhaps most importantly, taking full account of the opinions generated by the Authority.

The White Paper on Food Safety initially set three general tasks for EFSA: the provision of scientific advice and information for the Commission on all matters having a direct or indirect impact on consumer health and safety arising from the consumption of food, the work already undertaken by the scientific committees to be a core part of this process; information gathering and analysis, in particular through taking a proactive role in developing and operating food safety monitoring and surveillance programmes; and communicating directly and openly with consumers on food issues to give the Authority a high profile, so that it ultimately becomes the automatic first port of call when scientific information on food safety and nutritional issues is sought or problems have been identified. These three general tasks are designed to facilitate EFSA in carrying out the more specific responsibilities relating to crisis reaction and national and international networking with the national scientific agencies and institutions in charge of food safety.

According to the White Paper, the three key elements that are to underpin all activities of EFSA and the scientific committees, and that are to be used as criteria by the Community institutions when determining the nature and admissibility of scientific advice to decision-making, are 'independence, excellence and transparency'. This is essential to re-establish consumer confidence in the food industry. The three criteria are to be satisfied by all scientific research that is used to direct legislative or judicial action. These benchmarks are not clearly defined in the White Paper. They remain subjective and abstract in their application. However, it is stated that the Authority must act 'independently of outside pressures' and that it must be 'representative and accountable', the impartiality of the Authority's work in this regard to be assessed by the Commission. Key to ensuring this independence is the selection of the head of the Authority. Excellence is to be ensured primarily by 'the identification and recruitment of the highest calibre of personnel'. Transparency:

> involves not only the rapid, open presentation of the findings and recommendations of the Authority, but also implies that the processes followed in reaching them are as open as possible, in order to respond to the fundamental right of access of citizens as laid down in the Treaty [requiring] clear procedures, publicly available, governing the operation of the Authority.[20]

Regulation 178/2002 on the General Principles of Food Law

EFSA was established, following the proposals put forward in the White Paper on Food Safety, by Regulation 178/2002.[21] The preamble to the regulation states that the scientific and technical basis of Community legislation relating to the safety of

---

[20] *Ibid*, section 43.
[21] Regulation (EC) No 178/2002 of the European Parliament and of the Council of 28 January 2002 laying down the general principles and requirements of food law, establishing EFSA and laying down procedures in matters of food safety. [2002] OJ L 31/1.

food and feed should contribute to the achievement of a high level of health protection within the Community. To facilitate this, the Community should have access to high-quality, independent and efficient scientific and technical support. The establishment of a European Food Safety Authority would reinforce the system of scientific and technical support already in place, a system that, it was recognised, was no longer able to respond to the increasing demands placed upon it. Pursuant to the general principles of food law, also set out in the regulation, the Authority should take on the role of an independent scientific point of reference in risk assessment and, in so doing, assist in the smooth functioning of the internal market. It would carry out this role by giving opinions on contentious scientific issues, thereby enabling the Community institutions and the Member States to take informed risk management decisions necessary to ensure food and feed safety, whilst also helping to avoid the fragmentation of the internal market through the adoption of unjustified or unnecessary obstacles to free movement. Whilst the Authority is to be an independent source of advice, information and risk communication to ensure consumer confidence, the Preamble to the regulation also states that in order to promote coherence between the risk assessment, risk management and risk communication functions, the link between risk assessors and risk managers should be strengthened.

The terms of reference set for the Authority initially appear to be both broad in scope and ambitious in aspiration. It is to provide a comprehensive scientific view of the safety and other aspects of the food and feed supply chains, including animal health and welfare and plant health, and it is to provide scientific advice and support on human nutrition in relation to Community legislation and health programmes. However, it is stated that the Authority is to focus on food safety issues and, as such, its mission in relation to animal health, animal welfare and plant health issues that are not linked to the safety of the food supply chain is to be, or at least should be, limited to the provision of scientific opinions.

Chapter III of Regulation 178/2002 sets out the provisions governing the establishment and functioning of EFSA. The mission statement setting the aims for the Authority includes: providing scientific advice and technical support for the Community's legislation and policies in all fields which have a direct or indirect impact on food and feed safety; providing independent information on all matters within these fields and communicating on risks; contributing to a high level of protection of human life and health, taking account of animal health and welfare, plant health and the environment, in the context of the operation of the internal market; collecting and analysing data to enable food and feed risks to be monitored; providing scientific advice and technical support on human nutrition in relation to Community legislation and assisting on nutritional issues within the framework of the Community health programmes; providing scientific opinions on other matters relating to animal health and welfare and plant health and on products other than food and feed relating to genetically modified organisms; providing a point of reference based on independence, information quality and transparency; co-operating with similar authorities in the Member States; and co-operating with the Commission and the Member States to promote the effective coherence between risk assessment, risk management and risk communication.[22]

The tasks set for the Authority that will enable it to carry out its mission include: providing the Community institutions and the Member States with the best possible scientific opinions in all cases provided for by Community legislation and on any question within its mission; promoting and co-ordinating the development of uniform risk assessment methodologies in the fields falling within its mission; providing scientific and technical support to the Commission in the areas within its mission and, when so requested, in the interpretation and consideration of risk assessment opinions; commissioning scientific studies necessary for the accomplishment of its mission; searching for, collecting, collating, analysing and summarising scientific and technical data in the fields within its mission; undertaking action to identify and characterise emerging risks, in the fields within its mission; establishing a system of networks of organisations operating in the fields within its mission and being responsible for their operation; providing scientific and technical assistance, when requested to do so by the Commission, in the crisis management procedures implemented by the Commission with regard to the safety of food and feed; providing scientific and technical assistance, when requested to do so by the Commission, with a view to improving co-operation between the Community, applicant countries, international organisations and third countries, in the fields within its mission; ensuring that the public and interested parties receive rapid, reliable, objective and comprehensive information in the fields within its mission; expressing independently its own conclusions and orientations on matters within its mission; and undertaking any other task assigned to it by the Commission within its mission.[23] These tasks generally reflect the original aspirations set out for the Authority in the White Paper on Food Safety.[24]

Structure of EFSA

EFSA, which has legal personality,[25] consists of a management board, an executive director and his staff, an advisory forum, and a scientific committee and scientific panels.[26] The management board comprises 14 members appointed by the Council in consultation with the European Parliament, from a list drawn up by the Commission, as well as a representative of the Commission. Four of the 14 are from organisations representing consumers and other interests in the food chain. Each member's term of office is four years and may be renewed once. Decisions are taken on a majority basis, one of the members being elected chair by the others

---

[22] Article 22.

[23] Article 23.

[24] For further discussion on the status of EFSA see K Kanska, 'Wolves in the Clothing of Sheep? The Case of the European Food Safety Authority' (2004) 29 *European Law Review* 711.

[25] Article 46.

[26] Article 24.

for a two-year period, meetings taking place when requested by the chair or by at least one third of the members. One of the key functions of the management board is to ensure that the Authority carries out its mission and performs the tasks assigned to it. They also adopt the Authority's programme of work for the coming year, as well as a revisable multi-annual programme, on an annual basis. The executive director takes part in meetings of the management board, but does not have voting rights.[27]

The executive director is appointed by the management board from a list proposed by the Commission following an open competition. The executive director is the legal representative of the Authority and is responsible for the day-to-day administration of the Authority; drawing up proposals for the Authority's work programmes; implementing the work programmes and decisions adopted by the management board; ensuring the provision of the appropriate scientific, technical and administrative support for the scientific committee and the scientific panels; ensuring that the Authority carries out its tasks in accordance with the requirements of its users, in particular with regard to the adequacy of the services provided and the time taken; preparing the statement of revenue and expenditure and executing the Authority's budget; developing and maintaining contact with the European Parliament; and ensuring regular dialogue with its relevant committees.[28]

The advisory forum is composed of representatives from competent bodies in the Member States which undertake tasks similar to those of the Authority itself, on the basis of one representative per Member State. Members of the advisory forum may not be members of the management board. The forum is to advise the Director, in particular on the drawing up of proposals for the Authority's work programme. A system of co-operation between the competent bodies and the Authority is envisaged in the regulation. Another function of the forum is to ensure that, where possible, this happens, in particular to ensure that duplication is avoided between the Authority's scientific studies and those of the Authorities in the Member States and to maximise the possibility of identifying emerging risks. The forum meets at least four times a year, either at the invitation of the chair (the executive director of EFSA) or at the request of at least one third of its members. Representatives of both the Commission and the European Parliament may participate in the work of the advisory forum, usually at the invitation of the executive director.[29]

The scientific committees and scientific panels are responsible for providing the scientific opinions of the Authority, each within their own spheres of competence. Where subjects do not fall within the competence of any of the established scientific panels, the scientific committee is to set up working groups to establish scientific opinions. The scientific committee is composed of the chairs of the individual panels and six independent scientific experts who do not belong to any of

---

[27] Article 25.
[28] Article 26.
[29] Article 27.

the panels. The panels themselves are composed of independent scientific experts. Under the terms of the regulation, panels are to be formed on: food additives, flavourings, processed aids and materials coming into contact with food; additives and products or substances used in animal feed; plant health, plant protection products and their residues; genetically modified organisms; dietetic products, nutrition and allergies; biological hazards; contaminants in the food chain; and animal health and welfare. Representatives of the Commission may be present at meetings of the scientific committee, the scientific panels and their working groups, but only to clarify information. They may not influence decisions at these meetings in any way.[30]

EFSA and Scientific Opinions

EFSA issues scientific opinions either at the request of the Commission, or where Community legislation makes provision for the Authority to be consulted. It may also deliver such opinions on its own initiative on matters falling within its remit or at the request of the European Parliament or a Member State.[31] Where EFSA identifies that there may be divergence between its own scientific opinion and that of others, it is to contact the bodies involved in order to ensure that all relevant scientific information is shared and to identify potentially contentious scientific issues. Where a substantive divergence is identified and the body in question is a Community agency or one of the Commission's scientific committees, that Authority and the body concerned are to co-operate with a view to either resolving the divergence or presenting a joint document to the Commission, a document that is also to be made public, clarifying the contentious scientific issues and identifying the relevant uncertainties in the data. Where the diverging body is a Member State body, the Authority and the Member State body must co-operate in a similar manner.[32]

EFSA is to be informed not only by commissioning scientific studies but also by collecting relevant data that may assist in the early identification of potential risks to human health. For example, it is to collect, collate, analyse and summarise relevant scientific and technical data, in the fields within its mission, in particular on: food consumption and the exposure of individuals to risks related to the consumption of food; incidence and prevalence of biological risk; contaminants in food and feed; and residues.[33] Where the Authority has information which leads it to suspect that there is an emerging serious risk, it is to request additional information from the Member States, other Community agencies and the Commission. The Authority is then to assess all the information at its disposal to identify the extent, if any, of the risk. This information is then forwarded to the

---

[30] Article 28.
[31] Article 29.
[32] Article 30.
[33] Article 33.

European Parliament, the Commission and the Member States.[34] To assist in this, and other EFSA processes, the Authority is to promote the networking of European organisations operating within the field in order to facilitate a scientific co-operation framework by the co-ordination of activities, the exchange of information, the development and implementation of joint projects and the exchange of expertise and best practices within the field. This process commences with the drawing up of a list of the competent organisations designated by the Member States which could assist the Authority, either individually or in networks.[35]

Independence and transparency in decision-making are central to the operations of EFSA. All acts must be in the public interest, free from any external influence.[36] The independence of these activities must be clear to all, therefore the minutes of scientific committee and panel meetings, their decisions (including those of dissenters), the information on which these decisions are based, declarations of the interests of members, the results of studies, annual reports and requests made of EFSA that were refused, such as those from the European Parliament, the Commission or the Member States, and the reasons for any such refusal, are all to be made public without unnecessary delay. Similarly, meetings of the management board are, in general, to be held in public, and in some circumstances consumer representatives or other interested parties may be invited to observe proceedings.[37] Some information which the Authority receives, in particular where this has been requested and justified, is to be kept confidential.[38] However, the conclusions of the scientific opinions delivered by the Authority relating to foreseeable health effects are never to be kept confidential for any reason.[39] In fact, the Authority is to ensure that the public and any interested parties are to be given objective, reliable and easily accessible information, in particular with regard to the results of its work.[40] There is also to be wide access to Authority documents, and those which it possesses.[41]

Rapid Alert System, Crisis Management and Emergencies

In addition to establishing EFSA, Regulation 178/2002 codifies the Community rapid alert system, which is designed to enable it to react to food crises and emergencies. The system involves EFSA, the Commission and the Member States, who all designate a contact point, which is to be a member of this rapid alert network. Where a member of the network has any information relating to the existence of a serious direct or indirect risk to human health deriving from food or feed, this

[34] Article 34.
[35] Article 36.
[36] Article 37.
[37] Article 38.
[38] Article 39.
[39] *Ibid.*
[40] Article 40.
[41] Article 41.

information is to be immediately notified to the Commission under the rapid alert system. The Commission is then to transmit this information immediately to the members of the network. EFSA can then supplement this notification with any scientific or technical information that will facilitate rapid, appropriate risk management action by the Member States.[42]

Under the rapid alert system the Member States must immediately notify the Commission when they adopt a measure which is aimed at restricting the placing on the market or forcing the withdrawal from the market or the recall of food or feed in order to protect human health and requiring rapid action. Similarly, such notification must be made when any recommendation or agreement with professional operators which is aimed, on a voluntary or obligatory basis, at preventing, limiting or imposing specific conditions on the placing on the market or the eventual use of food or feed on account of a serious risk to human health requiring rapid action or any rejection, relating to a direct or indirect risk to human health, of a batch, container or cargo of food or feed by a competent authority at a border post within the European Union. Any such notification is to be accompanied by a detailed explanation of the reasons for the action taken. This information, and any supplementary data, is then passed on by the Commission to the entire network and to a third country where relevant. The Member States must in turn inform the Commission of any action that they take on the basis of this information. Participation in the rapid alert system may also be opened up to applicant countries, third countries and international organisations, in accordance with agreements between the Community and these organisations or States, and, for the former, where there is some form of reciprocal agreement.[43] Information that is available to the members of the network relating to a risk to human health posed by food and feed is, generally, to be made available to the public, including details of product identification, the nature of the risk and the measures taken.[44]

Where it is evident that food or feed originating in the Community or imported from a third country is likely to constitute a serious risk to human health, animal health or the environment, and that this risk cannot be contained satisfactorily by measures taken by the Member States concerned, then the Commission, either on its own initiative or at the request of a Member State, can adopt one of several emergency measures, the measure adopted being dependent on the gravity of the situation. These measures include, for food or feed of Community origin: suspending the placing on the market or use of the food or feed in question; laying down special conditions for use of the food or feed; or any other appropriate measure. For feed or food from a third country: suspending the importation of the food or feed from the, or part of the, country concerned or the third country of transit where applicable; laying down special conditions for the food or feed; or any other appropriate interim measure. The chosen measure is to be taken under

---

[42] Article 50.
[43] *Ibid.*
[44] Article 52.

the procedure set out in Article 5 of Decision 1999/468.[45] However, in some emergencies the Commission may provisionally adopt these measures after consultation with the Member States concerned for up to 10 working days, after which time they must be confirmed, amended, revoked or extended.[46] Where a Member State informs the Commission of the need to take emergency measures and the Commission does not act, the Member State may adopt interim protective measures, provided that it informs the other Member States and the Commission of any decision taken in this regard.[47] The Commission then has 10 days to put the matter to the Standing Committee on the Food Chain and Animal Health under the Decision 1999/468 procedure,[48] with a view to the extension, amendment or abrogation of the national interim protective measures.[49] The Member State may maintain these interim measures until any Community measures have been adopted.[50] Where any Member State is of the opinion that a measure taken by another Member State is incompatible with any of the terms of the regulation or is likely to affect the functioning of the internal market, it is to refer the matter to the Commission, which is then to meet with the Member States concerned in an attempt to reach agreement on the matter, with, where necessary, the help of the Authority.[51]

In addition to the procedures and processes put in place for taking emergency measures, the regulation also stipulates that the Commission, EFSA and the Member States are to devise a general plan for food and feed safety crisis management.[52] This general plan is to specify those situations where the risks posed are unlikely to be prevented, eliminated or reduced by the emergency measures system. It is also to specify the practical procedures necessary to manage a crisis, including the principles of transparency to be applied and a communication strategy.[53] Provision is made for the Commission to identify additional potential serious risks.[54] In an identified crisis, the Commission is to set up a crisis unit, which is to be assisted by EFSA if necessary.[55] This unit is responsible for collecting and evaluating all relevant information and identifying the options available to minimise the risk, and communicating details of this, and any measures to be taken, to the public.[56] They may be assisted in this regard by any public or private person whose expertise can assist in managing the crisis effectively.[57]

---

[45] Article 53(1) in conjunction with Article 58(2) of Regulation 178/2002. Comitology Decision reference: Council Decision 1999/468/EC of 28 June 1999 laying down the procedures for the exercise of implementing powers conferred on the Commission. [1999] OJ L 184/23.

[46] Article 53(2).

[47] Article 54(1).

[48] Articles 7 and 8 thereof. See Article 58 of Regulation 178/2002.

[49] Article 54(2).

[50] Article 54(3).

[51] Article 60.

[52] Article 55.

[53] Article 55(2).

[54] Article 56(1).

[55] Article 56(2).

[56] Article 57(3).

[57] Article 57(2).

The White Paper on Food Safety and its key outcome, the establishment of EFSA, have put in place a detailed set of procedures for dealing with those circumstances where a potential food crisis needs to be averted. The development of this risk management system should certainly assist in consolidating efforts and furthering co-operation between the Authority, the Member States and the Commission. However, two key problems persist. First, Member States remain limited in the action that they can take at national level where a domestic food crisis occurs. The manner in which the case law on Articles 28 to 30 EC has developed effectively leaves any such action open to challenge as to its lawfulness where this inhibits free movement in any way—as was identified to be the case by the inquiry into the outbreak and control of BSE in the UK. Second, all the procedures and processes continue to relate to identifiable and imminent dangers to human health due to contamination or disease. Nutritional content and potential risks that may arise due to the harmful ingredients of a food product, such as sodium, sugar and trans fatty acids, remain firmly outside the remit of EFSA and EU food safety policy more generally.[58] While some specific Community legislation addressing some of these concerns does exist, for example concerning the use of additives in food, we will see below that in line with most of the activities of the Community institutions relating to the production and marketing of food, this exists primarily to promote free movement rather than to ensure that food is of a particular quality level or safe to eat.

5.3 USING THE PRECAUTIONARY PRINCIPLE TO PROTECT HUMAN HEALTH

One of the more influential consequences for food safety arising out of the BSE crisis has been the extension of what is known as the precautionary principle from environmental law into actions taken to protect human health.[59] Essentially, the principle enables the Community institutions to restrict the use of a product or procedure where this could potentially have detrimental consequences for the safety of food where some scientific evidence is presented to support this action. The data must be sufficient, but need not be either undisputed or conclusive.

The use of this principle in environmental law was first formally sanctioned by the London Declaration on the Protection of the North Sea in 1987 and the Bergen Ministerial Declaration on Sustainable Development in 1990.[60] It was accorded

---

[58] The fact that the EU has failed to act on matters such as trans fatty acids makes it easier for Member States to introduce their own measures on this to protect human health, provided they can be justified. This is discussed further in Chapter 6 below.

[59] For further discussion on the use of the precautionary principle in EU law see KH Ladeur, 'The Introduction of the Precautionary Principle into EU Law: A pyrrhic victory for environmental and public health law? Decision-making under conditions of complexity in multi-level political systems' (2003) 40 *Common Market Law Review* 1455; J Cazala, 'Food Safety and the Precautionary Principle: the legitimate moderation of Community courts' (2004) 10 *European Law Journal* 539; and M Lee, *EU Environmental Law: Challenges, Change and Decision-Making* (Oxford, Publishing, 2005).

[60] The initial development of the precautionary principle is generally credited to West German policies of the 1970s. The approach was then used to justify the implementation of various measures to tackle acid rain, global warming and the pollution of the North Sea. For further discussion see

full EC Treaty status in 1993. Article 174(2) EC states that Community policy on the environment:

> shall be based on the precautionary principle and on the [principle] that preventive action should be taken.

The precautionary principle is not itself defined anywhere in the Treaty. It is not specifically defined in any other Community legislation either. Some further guidance on how and when the principle may be used is contained in a Commission communication on the subject.[61] The Communication states that the precautionary principle is to be used within a structured approach to the analysis of risk, which comprises three elements: risk assessment, risk management and risk communication. The principle is usually invoked through the management process, usually resulting in the introduction of measures prohibiting or limiting the use of a suspected product, or procedure. The Communication has been described as being a codification of the law relating to the precautionary principle.[62]

The initial steps taken towards extending the precautionary principle from environmental law into human health protection were taken by the Court of Justice in *UK v Commission*[63] and *Queen v National Farmers' Union*.[64] It was stated in both judgments, which examined the legitimacy of Community measures designed to protect the spread of BSE, that:

> Where there is uncertainty as to the existence or extent of risks to human health, the institutions may take protective measures without having to wait until the reality and seriousness of those risks become fully apparent.[65]

Legislative support for developing the principle in this way was offered by a new interpretation of Article 174(1) EC. It was stated that:

> [the purpose of] Article 130r(1) of the EC Treaty [now Article 174(1) EC] [determines that] Community policy on the environment is to pursue the objective inter alia of protecting human health. Article 130r(2) [now Article 174(2) EC] provides that that policy is to aim at a high level of protection and is to be based in particular on the principles that preventive action should be taken and that environmental protection requirements

A Jordan, 'The Precautionary Principle in the European Union' in T O'Riordan, J Cameron and A Jordan (eds), *Reinterpreting the Precautionary Principle* (London, Cameron May, 2001). The first explicit references to the precautionary principle at international level appeared in the 1985 Vienna Convention on Ozone Depleting Substances and the Declaration of the Second International North Sea Conference on the Protection of the North Sea (the London Declaration). The participants at the North Sea Conference declared that they accepted that 'in order to protect the North Sea from possibly damaging effects of the most dangerous substances, a precautionary approach is necessary, which may require action to control inputs of such substances even before a causal link has been established by absolute clear scientific evidence'. Paragraph VII, London Declaration, 25 November 1987.

[61] Communication from the Commission on the Precautionary Principle, 2 February 2000. COM (2000) 1.

[62] Case T-13/1999, *Pfizer Animal Health SA v Council* [2002] ECR II-3305, para 149.

[63] Case C-18/1996, *United Kingdom v Commission* (BSE) [1998] ECR I-2265.

[64] Case C-157/1996, *Queen v National Farmers' Union* [1998] ECR I-2211.

[65] Case C-18/1996, *UK v Commission*, note 63 above, para 99 and Case C-157/1996, *Queen v National Farmers' Union*, note 64 above, para 63. Both judgments were issued on the same day.

must be integrated into the definition and implementation of other Community policies.[66]

The Court was thus suggesting that there was a connection between Article 174 EC and the protection of human health in areas not directly related to the protection of the environment. This is not the case. The Treaty does state that environmental protection measures should be designed in a manner that protects human health and that environmental protection requirements should be integrated into the definition and implementation of other Community policies. This does not mean that principles of environmental law may be used in areas of Community policy that are not related in any way to the environment, such as food safety. Preventing the contamination of the human food chain with meat from BSE-infected cattle does not come within the scope of Article 174 EC. It is not an environmental protection issue. Article 152 EC, which does state that:

> Community action . . . shall be directed towards improving public health, preventing human illness and diseases, and obviating sources of danger to human health,

could be used to lawfully extent the right to take precautionary action in human health related matters. It should be noted that Article 152 EC did not exist in its current form until after the entry into force of the Treaty of Amsterdam in May 1999, almost a year after the judgments in *UK v Commission* and *Queen v National Farmers' Union* were issued, extending the principle to non-environmental law related matters. Prior to this alteration the treaty merely stated that the function of the Community in this area was:

> to contribute towards ensuring a high level of human health protection by encouraging co-operation between the Member States and, if necessary, lending support to their action.

The Commission has since stated that:

> [although] the only explicit reference to the precautionary principle is to be found in the environment title of the EC Treaty, and more specifically Article 174 . . . one cannot conclude from this that the principle applies only to the environment.

To support this statement the Commission cites Article 6 EC, which provides that:

> Environmental protection requirements must be integrated into the definition and implementation of the Community policies referred to in Article 3, in particular with a view to supporting sustainable development,

as well as Article 95(3) EC, which provides that:

> The Commission, in its proposals . . . concerning health, safety, environmental protection and consumer protection, will take as a base a high level of protection, taking

---

[66] Case C-18/1996, *UK v Commission*, note 63 above, para 100 and Case C-157/1996, *Queen v National Farmers' Union*, note 64 above, para 64.

account in particular of any new development based on scientific facts . . . [T]he European Parliament and the Council will also seek to achieve this objective.[67]

It is here contended that neither Article 6 EC nor Article 95(3) EC supports the advancement of the precautionary principle beyond environmental matters to include food safety. The former refers specifically to the environment. The latter refers only to scientific fact, not supposition. This extension should be allowable under an interpretation of Article 152 EC and not on the existing claimed legal basis.

5.3.1 Evidence Requirements

There must always be a comprehensive scientific evaluation of potential risk prior to invocation of the precautionary principle. This is risk assessment. Scientific evidence must sufficiently demonstrate that there exists a possible risk to human health. Where this is the case, this assessment can be used to instruct and facilitate the taking of action to prevent or minimise this risk. This is risk management. The Commission Communication on the Precautionary Principle states that:

> An assessment of risk should be considered where feasible when deciding whether or not to invoke the precautionary principle [which] requires reliable scientific data and logical reasoning, leading to a conclusion which expresses the possibility of occurrence and the severity of a hazard's impact on [human] health.

The risk management decision is taken by the bureaucrat or politician following consideration of the evidence presented in the risk assessment. Any measure adopted in this way must be proportionate, non-discriminatory, consistent with previous similar decisions and cost effective.[68]

While it is clear that there must be scientific substantiation supporting precautionary action, it is not entirely clear as to the amount or level or consensus on this evidence that must exist for measures enacted to be considered lawful. The most comprehensive assessment of these questions to date was conducted by the Court of First Instance in *Pfizer*.[69] Here, the Court examined the validity of Regulation 2821/1998, which prohibited the use of four, previously approved, antibiotics in animal feed.[70] The applicant, who was the only producer in the world of one of the banned antibiotics listed, sought the annulment of the regulation under the Article 230(4) EC procedure. The regulation had been introduced to counter fears that

---

[67] Communication from the Commission on the Precautionary Principle. COM (2000) 1.

[68] *Ibid.*

[69] Case T-13/1999, *Pfizer v Council*, note 62 above. Judgment was delivered on the same day in Case T-70/1999, *Alpharma Inc v Council* [2002] ECR II-3495, where the applicant was also challenging the validity of Regulation 2821/1998. This application for annulment was also rejected by the Court of First Instance on similar grounds, albeit on slightly different facts.

[70] Council Regulation (EC) No 2821/1998 of December 17 1998 amending, as regards withdrawal of the authorisation of certain antibiotics, Directive 1970/524 concerning additives in feedingstuffs. [1998] OJ L 351/4.

the continued use of these antibiotics in animal feed could make them resistant to the beneficial properties of the medication, and that this resistance could then be transferred to humans via the food chain. This could potentially result in a reduction in the effectiveness of these antibiotics in human medicine.

It was agreed by all parties to the proceedings that at the time of the adoption of the contested regulation neither the reality nor the seriousness of the risk had been scientifically proven. The Council had thus relied upon the precautionary principle as justification for adopting the regulation. The applicant's main argument was that the precautionary principle had been incorrectly applied in this case, in particular due to the fact that the risk assessment, which must be carried out prior to the introduction of any precautionary measures, was incomplete and erroneous. It was thus for the Court to establish what the composition of a risk assessment that is subsequently used to validate employment of the precautionary principle should be, in particular in circumstances such as those under review here, where the assessment ultimately allows the introduction of an outright prohibition on the use of a previously approved product or procedure. In particular, it was necessary to test whether there had been a manifest error or a misuse of power in the introduction of the contested regulation due to either a misapplication of the precautionary principle and/or an illegitimate reinterpretation of the scientific evidence used to support the prohibition introduced.

After a detailed examination of the facts leading to the introduction of the contested regulation, the Court decided that sufficient evidence and information had been available to the Council to justify taking the precautionary measure that it had. The applicant's contention that an improper assessment of the scientific data rendered Regulation 2821/1998 unlawful was rejected. The application to annul was thus dismissed.

It was not in dispute that the precautionary principle was relevant to the circumstances under review in *Pfizer*. Noting the decisions in *UK v Commission* and *Queen v National Farmers' Union*, it was accepted that where there is scientific uncertainty as to the existence or extent of risks to human health the Community institutions may, by reason of the existence of this principle, take protective measures without having to wait until the reality and seriousness of those risks become fully apparent.[71] The applicant, however, contended that the compulsory risk assessment must demonstrate that the risk, although not yet a reality, was nevertheless probable, at least to a very remote degree. Thus the precautionary principle could not, it was claimed, be used to permit the introduction of a measure based upon what was termed a 'zero risk test', the applicant asserting that such an assessment would be inappropriate as it would be impossible to satisfy. To apply such a test would quickly lead to the paralysis of technological development and innovation.

---

[71] See also Case T-199/1996, *Laboratoires pharmaceutiques Bergaderm SA and Jean-Jacques Groupil v Commission* [1998] ECR II-2805.

When questioned at the hearing about the level of verification that should be required in order to justify the withdrawal of the authorisation to use the antibiotics in animal feed, that applicant stated that '[i]t would be proven with the first infection, or with the first proof of colonisation, or the first proof of transfer in a human'. The Court found that this statement was based upon an incorrect interpretation of the precautionary principle as it had developed. It was found that the Community institutions are not required to wait for the adverse effects of a product to materialise before taking action designed to prevent them from occurring in the first place.[72] Thus where the precautionary principle is applied, a risk assessment cannot be required to provide the Community institutions with conclusive scientific evidence of the reality of the risk and the seriousness of the potential adverse effects were that risk to become a reality.

The purpose of a risk assessment is to calculate the degree of probability of a certain product or procedure having adverse effects on human health and the potential seriousness of any such adverse effects. The risk assessment has two components: the ascertainment of the level of risk that is unacceptable, and the scientific assessment of the risks.[73] The level of risk deemed unacceptable is to be determined by the Community institutions on a case by case basis. Several factors must be taken into account when making any such decision, including a general requirement that the political objectives of the EC Treaty are adhered to.[74] More specifically, there must be an assessment of the severity of the impact on human health were the risk to occur, the extent to which there may be possible adverse effects, the reversibility of any adverse effects, and the possibility of delayed effects.[75]

The second component, the scientific assessment of the risk, presents a greater difficulty. The precautionary principle may only be invoked where scientific opinion on the potential risk conflicts. It was the scientific component of the risk assessment that proved the most contentious in *Pfizer*, primarily because the applicant sought justification for the fact that the Community institutions had chosen to accept one body of scientific opinion on the potential risk posed over another, leading directly to the introduction of the contested prohibition. What made this selection even more controversial was the fact that the Commission, and subsequently the Council acting on its advice, had reinterpreted the unambiguous findings of a Community scientific committee to illustrate that the use of the antibiotic produced by the applicant in animal feed presented an imminent danger to human health. They were also both aware that new evidence presented supporting the introduction of the contested regulation was gathered in a process that suffered from 'methodological limitations'.

---

[72] Case T-13/1999, *Pfizer*, para 381.
[73] Case C-355/1990, *Commission v Spain* (conservation of wild birds) [1993] ECR I-4221.
[74] Case T-13/1999, *Pfizer*, para 151.
[75] *Ibid*, para 153.

5.3.2 Legislature and Scientific Committees

Scientific advice is deemed to be 'of the utmost importance at all stages of the drawing up of new legislation and for the execution and management of existing legislation'.[76] The duty imposed on the Community institutions by Article 152 EC means that they must ensure that their decisions are taken in the light of the best scientific information available and that they are based on the most recent results of international research.[77] The applicant in *Pfizer* submitted that the contested regulation was unlawful because of the inadequate nature of scientific data provided by the Danish authorities supporting a ban on the use of antibiotics in animal feed, and because a Scientific Committee for Animal Nutrition (SCAN) report, which had concluded that there was no immediate risk posed, had been reinterpreted and used as evidence to support the introduction of the prohibition, without any further consultation with the scientific committee. The Court noted that the role to be played by a committee of experts, such as SCAN, in the legislative process is restricted to presenting a reasoned analysis of the relevant facts of the case in the light of current knowledge about the subject, in order to provide the institutions with the factual knowledge required to enable them to make an informed decision.[78] The institutions are not bound to follow the Committee's opinion. However, where a Community institution chooses to disregard the opinion of a scientific committee in circumstances such as those at issue in *Pfizer*, it must provide specific reasons for this.[79] This statement of reasons must be of a scientific level equivalent to that of the opinion, being founded upon either a supplementary opinion from the same committee of experts or other evidence, whose probative value is at least commensurate with that of the opinion first presented. Where the Community institution disregards only part of the opinion, it may use those parts that it does not dispute.[80] The institutions may thus disregard the overall conclusions of the scientific committee report, even where they have relied on parts of the analysis. This position is deemed justifiable on grounds of principle relating to the political responsibilities and democratic legitimacy of the Commission. It was stated by the Court of First Instance that the members of SCAN may have scientific legitimacy, but they have neither democratic nor political responsibilities, the Commission's democratic responsibility being based upon Article 211 EC. The Council was deemed to have explained its decision to depart from the SCAN opinion on the ground that it was in the interests of human health protection. Consequently, the Community legislature are not acting in error when they refuse to accept, or when they reinterpret, the findings of their scientific committees. There is no obligation to consult with the scientific committee

---

[76] Commission Communication on Consumer Health and Food Safety. COM (1997) 183.
[77] Case T-13/1999, *Pfizer*, para 158.
[78] *Ibid*, para 197.
[79] *Ibid*, para 199.
[80] *Ibid*.

if new evidence emerges, even where this committee is of the opinion that this data is misleading.[81]

The assertion made by the applicants in *Pfizer* that the Community institutions are compelled to wait for the adverse effects of a product to materialise before taking precautionary action was correctly rejected. If this were not the case, the principle itself would be of little use. However, it is also clear that sufficient, even if contradicted, scientific evidence must be presented to support the introduction of precautionary measures. Where legislation, such as Directive 1970/524 on the use of additives in animal feed, suggests that a scientific committee should be consulted for its judgment as to any potential risk that may be posed by using antibiotics in this way, then this should probably happen.[82] It has also been contended elsewhere that consultation with scientific committees on issues affecting consumer health and safety is preferred, even where the relevant Community legislation is silent on this point.[83] This is necessary to ensure, as far as possible, that any scientific advice resorted to by the Commission is based upon the principles of excellence, independence and transparency, which are explicitly required by Decision 1997/579 establishing these scientific committees.[84] The Commission failed in relation to this on two occasions in the introduction of Regulation 2821/1998. First, the initial unambiguous assessment made by SCAN concluding that there was no immediate risk posed to human health by the continued use of the antibiotic in animal feed was reinterpreted, this reinterpretation forming the basis for justifying the introduction of precautionary measures. Secondly, SCAN was not re-consulted after other, questionable, evidence emerged. Accepting this type of behaviour weakens the precautionary principle. It demonstrates that its application can be arbitrary and uncertain.[85] It bypasses the foundation of any precautionary action—the fact that a sufficiently thorough risk assessment identifying the need for risk management must exist before any such action can take place. Where the Commission lacks the knowledge required to assess this scientific evidence it must consult with the appropriate scientific committee in order to ensure that Community measures taken to protect human health are appropriate to that objective.[86] Any other approach undermines the essential role that sound

[81] Case T-13/1999, *Pfizer*, para 299.

[82] Council Directive 1970/524 of 23 November 1970 concerning additives in feedingstuffs. [1970] OJ L 270/1.

[83] E Vos, 'EU Committees: The Evolution of Unforeseen Institutional Actors in European Product Regulation' in C Joerges and E Vos (eds), *EU Committees: Social Regulation, Law and Politics* (Oxford, Hart Publishing, 1999). See also G de Búrca, 'The Institutional Developments of the EU: A Constitutional Analysis' in P Craig and G de Búrca (eds), *The Evolution of EU Law* (Oxford, OUP, 1999), in particular pp 71–75 thereof.

[84] Commission Decision 1997/579 setting up scientific committees in the field of consumer health and food safety. [1997] OJ L 237/18.

[85] This also increases the risk of precautionary EU measures acting contrary to the WTO Agreement on the Application of Sanitary and Phytosanitary Measures. For further discussion see N Salmon, 'A European Perspective on the Precautionary Principle, Food Safety and the Free Trade Imperative of the WTO' (2002) 27 *European Law Review* 138–55.

[86] Case C-212/1991, *Angelopharm GmbH v Freie Hansestadt Hamburg* [1994] ECR I-171.

science is expected to play at all stages of the legislative process. It effectively limits scientific opinion to the risk assessment stage, leaving risk management to be monopolised by non-expert opinion. This apparent weakening of the position of scientific committees is all the more surprising when one considers the status that is accorded to these bodies through what is know as the 'comitology procedure', whereby the Commission, where provision is created, should be assisted by an advisory committee in the adoption of Community measures.[87] While the Commission is not obliged to follow any advice given, it is required to take 'the utmost account of the opinion delivered'. Regulation 178/2002, which established the regulatory Standing Committee on the Food Chain and Animal Health to replace the Standing Committee on Foodstuffs, the Standing Veterinary Committee and the Standing Committee on Animal Nutrition (as well as taking over certain tasks of the Standing Committee on Plant Health), also provides that the Commission may only adopt implementing measures if it obtains a favourable opinion from the Committee. While the regulation at issue in *Pfizer* was adopted by the Council, the provisions in Regulation 178/2002 do serve to illustrate the strengthened role of these committees in the legislative process.

5.4 COMMUNITY FOOD SAFETY LEGISLATION

The establishment of a European Food Safety Authority, the creation of rapid alert systems and measures to be taken in an emergency and empowering the Community institutions and the Member States to take the initiative in food safety matters on a precautionary basis, is only one aspect of the EU food safety programme. Ensuring not just that the food itself that is safe, but also that the manner in which it is packaged causes no harm, the prevention of contamination and control over processes that the foodstuff undergoes in production must all be dealt with as well.

5.4.1 Materials Coming into Contact with Foodstuffs

The framework legislation controlling materials intended to come into contact with foodstuffs is Directive 1989/109.[88] The key principle underlying the directive is that any material or article intended to come into contact either directly or indirectly with foodstuffs must be sufficiently stable that it does not transfer substances to the foodstuffs in quantities which could endanger human health or

---

[87] Council Decision 1999/468/EC of 28 June 1999 laying down the procedures for the exercise of implementing powers conferred on the Commission. [1999] OJ L 184/23.

[88] Council Directive 1989/109/EEC of 21 December 1988 on the approximation of the laws of the Member States relating to materials and articles intended to come into contact with foodstuffs. [1989] OJ L 40/38. This replaced Council Directive 1976/893/EEC of 23 November 1976 on the approximation of the laws of the Member States relating to materials and articles intended to come into contact with foodstuffs. [1976] OJ L 340/19.

bring about an unacceptable change in the composition of the foodstuffs or a deterioration in their organoleptic properties.[89]

The directive applies to all materials and articles which are intended to be brought into contact with foodstuffs, including water, but not including those covering or coating substances which form part of, and may be consumed with, the foodstuff, such as the substances covering cheese rinds, prepared meat or fruit.[90] Materials must be manufactured in compliance with good practice to ensure that under normal conditions of use there is no transfer of their constituents to foodstuffs in dangerous quantities.[91]

The directive facilitates the introduction of further directives relating to specific materials coming into contact with foodstuffs,[92] such as plastics, ceramics, glass, wood (including cork) and cellulose.[93] Several such specific directives have since been introduced, generally to amend those rules already in existence under similar provisions of the preceding framework directive.[94] These specific directives list those substances that can be used, and the quantities in which they may be used, in the manufacture of the materials that are permitted to come into contact with foodstuffs.[95]

Annex II to Directive 1989/109 sets out a series of general criteria relating to the protection of human health that are to be applied in the assessment and use of those substances that may come into contact with foodstuffs. It is stated that, where appropriate, positive lists of substances should be established for materials and articles intended to come into contact with foodstuffs, the acceptability for inclusion in such a list to be determined by considering both the quantity of the substance which is liable to migrate into foodstuffs and the toxicity of the substance. A substance is only to be included in a positive list where, under normal or foreseeable conditions of use, the substance is not liable to migrate into foodstuffs in a quantity likely to constitute a danger to human health. All substances are to be

---

[89] Preamble 6 to Directive 1989/109.

[90] Article 1(1) and 1(2).

[91] Article 2.

[92] Article 3.

[93] A full list of those materials and articles for which further specific legislative provisions may be introduced is set out in Annex I to Directive 1989/109.

[94] See, for example, Council Directive 1984/500/EEC of 15 October 1984 on the approximation of the laws of the Member States relating to ceramic articles intended to come into contact with foodstuffs, [1984] OJ L 277/12; Council Directive 1982/711/EEC of 18 October 1982 laying down the basic rules necessary for testing migration of the constituents of plastic materials and articles intended to come into contact with foodstuffs, [1982] OJ L 297/26; Commission Directive 1993/10/EEC of 15 March 1993 relating to materials and articles made of regenerated cellulose film intended to come into contact with foodstuffs, [1993] OJ L 93/27.

[95] For example, Annex II in conjunction with Article 2 of Commission Directive 1993/10. Article 3(3) of Directive 1989/109 states that the specific directives may include a list of substances the use of which is authorised to the exclusion of all others (a positive list); purity standards for such substances; special conditions in which these substances may be used; specific limits on the migration of constituents into foodstuffs; detailed rules concerning the analysis of these substances; and, if necessary, provisions aimed at protecting human health against any potential hazards which might arise through contact with the materials.

kept under review and reassessed whenever this is justified by fresh or re-evaluated scientific data.

5.4.2 Contaminants in Food

Regulation 315/1993 establishes the framework for Community procedures relating to contaminants in food.[96] A contaminant is defined as:

> any substance not intentionally added to food as a result of the production, manufacture, processing, preparation, treatment, packing, packaging, transport or holding of such food, or as a result of environmental contamination.[97]

This definition does not cover any extraneous matter, such as insect fragments or animal hairs, that may be present in the foodstuff.[98] Any food containing a contaminant in an amount which is unacceptable from a public health perspective, in particular due to a higher than tolerable toxicological level, is not to be placed on the market.[99] Where a contaminated product is placed on the market, the levels of contamination must be kept to a minimum,[100] the maximum tolerance levels to be set by the Commission assisted by the Standing Committee for Foodstuffs.[101] Member States may restrict the levels of contaminant further than those allowable under Community law in circumstances where, as a result of new information or a reassessment of existing information, they have reason to believe that there is a threat to human health.[102]

Commission Regulation 466/2001 sets a range of maximum acceptable levels for contaminants in foodstuffs.[103] The regulation covers many potentially hazardous contaminants such as: cadmium, which may accumulate in the human body and lead to kidney disfunction, skeletal damage and reproductive deficiencies; lead, which, when absorbed by the body, can induce reduced cognitive development and intellectual performance in children and increased blood pressure and cardiovascular disease in adults; and mercury, which may detrimentally affect the development of the brains of infants and induce neurological changes in adults. The regulation mainly consists of a detailed annex listing maximum levels for certain contaminants in specific foodstuffs and details of the manner in which these foodstuffs are to be tested for the presence of contaminants; for example, the maximum level of lead that is permitted to be present in cows' milk and/or infant

---

[96] Council Regulation (EEC) No 315/1993 of 8 February 1993 laying down Community procedures for contaminants in food. [1993] OJ L 37/1.

[97] Article 1(1).

[98] *Ibid.*

[99] Article 2(1).

[100] Article 2(2).

[101] Article 2(3) and Article 8.

[102] Article 4.

[103] Commission Regulation (EC) No 466/2001 of 8 March 2001 setting maximum levels for certain contaminants in foodstuffs. [2001] OJ L 77/1.

formula is 0.02 mg per kg, the amount present to be tested under the Directive 2001/22 procedure.[104] For cadmium there can be no more than 0.5 mg per kg present in cattle or pig liver and no more than 1 mg per kg in cattle or pig kidney, both to be tested under the Directive 2001/22 procedure. Mercury, which is generally found in fish, may be present up to a level of 0.5 mg per kg for all types, except those specifically listed in the Annex, such as tuna, bass and ray, as these may contain up to 1 mg per kg, again to be tested under the Directive 2001/22 procedure. Under this procedure all sampling is to be carried out by authorised qualified persons as specified by the Member States in laboratories that meet the minimum standards set by Directive 1993/99.[105]

5.4.3 Irradiated Foods

Food may be physically treated with high-energy, ionising radiation to prolong its shelf life and/or to reduce health hazards associated with certain products due to the presence of pathogenic micro-organisms. For example, ionising radiation may, in some circumstances, prevent the germination and sprouting of potatoes, onions and garlic; disinfect grains, dried fruit, vegetables or nuts by killing or sterilising insects with which they are infested; delay the ripening and/or ageing of fruit and vegetables; prolong the shelf life of meat, poultry and seafood and prevent food-borne diseases by reducing the number of viable micro-organisms in them; and reduce the levels of micro-organisms in herbs and spices. Directive 1999/2 recognises that rules relating to the use of ionising radiation for the treatment of foodstuffs should take account primarily of human health requirements,[106] but also—within these limits required for the protection of health—economic and technical needs.[107] Foodstuffs treated with ionising radiation that are intended for the ultimate consumer or mass caterers must be labelled as such, under the terms set out in the framework food labelling directive. Where it is an ingredient that has been treated in this way, then attention must be brought to this fact in the list of ingredients, even if forming only part of a compound ingredient.[108] A foodstuff treated with ionising radiation may not be imported from a third country unless it complies with the conditions set out in the Directive. These conditions include that, where applicable, the foodstuff in question has been treated in a Community-approved irradiation facility, and proper supporting doc-

---

[104] Commission Directive 2001/22/EC of 8 March 2001 laying down the sampling methods and the methods of analysis for the official control of the levels of lead, cadmium, mercury and 3-MCPD in foodstuffs. [2001] OJ L 77/14.

[105] Council Directive 1993/99/EEC of 29 October 1993 on the subject of additional measures concerning the official control of foodstuffs. [1993] OJ L 290/14.

[106] Directive 1999/2/EC of the European Parliament and of the Council of 22 February 1999 on the approximation of the laws of the Member States concerning foods and food ingredients treated with ionising radiation. [1999] OJ L 6/16.

[107] Preamble 6 to Directive 1999/2/EC.

[108] Article 6.

umentation is retained to establish this.[109] Materials used for packaging irradiated foodstuffs must be suitable for this purpose.[110]

Annex I to Directive 1999/2 sets out the conditions for authorising food irradiation. It may only be authorised if there is a reasonable technological need, it presents no hazard to human health, it is of benefit to the consumer and it is not used as a substitute for hygiene and health practices. It may only be used to reduce the incidence of food-borne disease by destroying pathogenic organisms, to reduce spoilage of foodstuffs by slowing decay processes, to reduce loss of foodstuffs by premature ripening, germination or sprouting and to rid foodstuffs of organisms harmful to plants. Directive 1999/3 set a positive list of those foodstuffs that can be treated with maximum ionising radiation doses.[111] The initial list contained only one category of authorised foodstuff—dried aromatic herbs, spices and vegetable seasonings.[112]

EU legislation on materials coming into contact with foodstuffs, contaminant levels and ionising radiation treatment all present a picture of the best interests of human health being served. For the most part, this is the case. Most of these controls, and the methods to be employed in determining whether the set standards are adhered to, are absolutely vital in ensuring that consumer confidence in the safety of food supplied remains high. While it is generally the case that EU food law seeks to keep harmful substances out of foodstuffs, there is always a balance to be struck with the economic needs of producers and in ensuring that supply levels remain high. As a consequence, some dangerous substances may remain in food, provided that they are kept at a tolerable level—that is, there should be no real threat to human health.

5.4.4 Hygienic Production Methods

Standardised rules on the hygienic production and marketing of food are set out in Regulation 852/2004.[113] It is noted in the preamble to the regulation that the protection of human life and health is one of the fundamental objectives of food

---

[109] Article 9(1).

[110] Article 10.

[111] Directive 1999/3/EC of the European Parliament and of the Council of 22 February 1999 on the establishment of a Community list of foods and food ingredients treated with ionising radiation. [1999] OJ L 66/24.

[112] Annex to Directive 1999/3. The Scientific Committee on Food re-examined its 1986 stance on the irradiation of food in 2003, finding that the only technological need for this practice would be the decontamination of spices, dried herbs and vegetable seasonings, that it was still appropriate to specify a maximum dose for the treatment of certain food products by ionising radiation, and that irradiated foodstuffs should continue to be evaluated individually, taking into account the technological need and the safety of the process. Revision of the opinion of the Scientific Committee on Food on the irradiation of food. SCF/CS/NF/IRR/24 final, 24 April 2003.

[113] Regulation (EC) No 852/2004 of the European Parliament and of the Council of 29 April 2004 on the hygiene of foodstuffs. [2004] OJ L 139/1.

law, as laid down in Regulation 178/2002.[114] It is also noted here that the requirements of hygienic production methods set out in EU law should take account of the principles contained in the Codex Alimentarius General Principles of Food Hygiene.[115] 'Food hygiene' is defined in the regulation as:

> the measures and conditions necessary to control hazards and to ensure fitness for human consumption of a foodstuff taking into account its intended use.[116]

The regulation is primarily aimed at food business operators.[117] It is noted that the primary responsibility for food safety rests with them. This responsibility covers all those involved in the production, preparation and sale of food, starting with the primary production of the raw materials.[118]

Food business operators are to ensure that all stages of production, processing and distribution of food under their control satisfy the hygiene requirements set down in the regulation.[119] This is to be ensured primarily through the use of what are known as the 'hazard analysis and critical control points' principles, or HACCP.[120] The HACCP principles consist of: identifying hazards that must be prevented, eliminated or reduced to acceptable levels; identifying the critical control points at the steps at which control is essential to prevent or eliminate a hazard or reduce it to acceptable levels; establishing critical limits at critical control points which separate acceptability from unacceptability for the prevention, elimination or reduction of identified hazards; establishing and implementing effective monitoring procedures at critical control points; establishing corrective actions when monitoring indicates that a critical control point is not under control; establishing procedures that are to be carried out regularly to verify that the measures outlined above are working effectively; and establishing documents and records commensurate with the nature and size of the food business to demonstrate the effective application of the measures outlined above.[121] Evidence of compliance with these procedures must be supplied by food business operators to their national competent authorities.[122] Member States are to encourage the development of national guides to good practice for hygiene and for the application of HACCP principles.[123] Similar Community guides are also to be developed.[124] The Commission is obliged to consult with EFSA on any matter falling

---

[114] Regulation (EC) No 178/2002 of the European Parliament and of the Council of 28 January 2002 laying down the general principles and requirements of food law, establishing EFSA and laying down procedures in matters of food safety. [2002] OJ L 31/1.

[115] Codex Alimentarius recommended International Code of Practice, General Principles of Food Hygiene. CAC/RCP 1/1969. Revised 2003.

[116] Article 2(1).

[117] Article 1(1).

[118] *Ibid.*

[119] Article 3.

[120] Article 5(1).

[121] Article 5(2).

[122] Article 5(4).

[123] Article 7.

[124] Article 9.

within the scope of the hygiene regulation that could have a significant impact on public health.[125]

The real detail on hygienic food production practices is set out in a series of annexes to the regulation. Annex I covers the general hygiene provisions for primary production, including requirements that animals going to slaughter are kept clean, and that staff handling foodstuffs are in good health and report suspected outbreaks of disease to the competent authorities. Annex II sets general hygiene requirements for all food business operators not covered by Annex I. Food premises are to be designed and constructed in a manner that permits adequate cleaning and provides adequate working space for the hygienic performance of all operations. Flush lavatories are to be available for staff, and they should not open directly into rooms in which food is handled. Washbasins are to be made available, suitably located and designated for washing hands. Cleaning agents and disinfectants are not to be stored in areas where food is handled. Additional requirements are set out for movable and temporary food premises, for premises normally used as a private dwelling house but where foods are regularly prepared for sale, and for vending machines. These must all, so far as is reasonably practical, be kept clean and maintained in good repair. In particular, facilities should be made available for the maintenance of personal hygiene, surfaces in contact with food should be in a sound condition and easy to clean, and there should be an adequate supply of clean water.

Two further regulations on hygienic practices in the food sector have been introduced. These are Regulation 853/2004 on foods of animal origin,[126] and Regulation 854/2004 on the organisation of official controls on products of animal origin.[127] The idea behind introducing this body of regulations was to simplify and codify the existing rules set out in framework Directive 1993/43.[128]

Transportation Rules

Directive 1998/28 grants derogations from certain provisions of the hygiene directive for the transportation by sea of bulk raw sugar.[129] The derogation was granted as it was felt that the requirements in the predecessor to Regulation 852/2004, Directive 1993/43,[130] on the transportation of bulk foodstuffs in liquid, granulate or powdered form in receptacles and/or containers/tankers reserved for the

---

[125] Article 15.

[126] Regulation (EC) No 853/2004 of the European Parliament and of the Council of 29 April 2004 laying down specific hygiene rules for food of animal origin. [2004] OJ L 139/55.

[127] Regulation (EC) No 854/2004 of the European Parliament and of the Council of 29 April 2004 laying down specific rules for the organisation of official controls on products of animal origin intended for human consumption. [2004] OJ L 139/206.

[128] Council Directive 1993/43/EEC of 14 June 1993 on the hygiene of foodstuffs. [1993] OJ L 175/1.

[129] Commission Directive 1998/28/EC of 29 April 1998 granting a derogation from certain provisions of Directive 1993/43/EEC on the hygiene of foodstuffs as regards the transport by sea of bulk raw sugar. [1998] OJ L 140/10.

[130] Council Directive 1993/43/EEC of 14 June 1993 on the hygiene of foodstuffs. [1993] OJ L 175/1.

transportation of foodstuffs was not practical and imposed an unduly onerous burden on food businesses when applied to the transportation of raw sugar by sea which is not intended for use as a food nor as a food ingredient without a full and effective refining process.[131] Bulk transportation of raw sugar by sea can thus be done in receptacles and/or containers/tankers that are not exclusively used for the transportation of foodstuffs, provided that prior to loading the receptacle and/or container/tanker is cleaned to remove residues of the previous cargo, and provided that the immediate previous cargo was not a bulk liquid.[132] Similar derogation is allowed for the transportation of bulk liquid oils and fats by sea.[133] It was recognised that the availability of sea-going vessels reserved for the transportation of foodstuffs was insufficient to serve the trade in oils and fats intended for human consumption and that the contamination of liquid oils and fats could be avoided where the tanks used for their transportation are made of readily cleansable materials or where the three previous cargoes are of such a nature that they do not leave contamination and have been effectively cleaned.[134] As a consequence, liquid oils or fats can be transported in tanks that are not exclusively reserved for the transportation of foodstuffs once certain conditions relating to the type of tank used, cleaning and previous cargoes are met.[135] In particular, the three previous cargoes transported in the tank must have been foodstuffs where the oil or fats being transported are not to be processed further.[136] Where there is to be further processing, only the previous cargo must have been a foodstuff or appear on a list of acceptable previous cargoes, listed in the Annex, including glycerine, acetic acid and sodium hydroxide.

5.5 FOOD ADDITIVES

One of the aspects of food production that attracts the most attention amongst consumers is the use of additives. Claims that a foodstuff 'contains no artificial additives' will often be one of the key determining factors for the health-conscious consumer. Additives also present an opportunity for producers who wish to obtain a certain flavour or colour for their product without necessarily incurring the expense, and possibly greater perishability, of more natural ingredients. As a result of the potentially controversial consequences of this aspect of food production, it has become clear that Community rules on additive use must be supported by more than a set of directives drafted in flexible terms. Clear, precise and concise rules on what gets added to food to preserve, thicken or colour it are also required.

---

[131] Preamble to Directive 1998/28.

[132] Article 2.

[133] Commission Directive 1996/3/ EC of 26 January 1996 granting a derogation from certain provisions of Council Directive 1993/43/EEC on the hygiene of foodstuffs as regards the transport of bulk liquid oils and fats by sea. [1996] OJ L 21/42.

[134] Preamble to Directive 1996/3.

[135] Article 2.

[136] *Ibid.*

5.5.1 Additive Use Rules and Free Movement

Member States seeking to preserve the quality of products traditionally made using natural ingredients can give rise to disputes under the terms of Article 28 EC. A series of cases have come before the Court of Justice on the interaction between Community additive legislation and free movement policy. In *Commission v Italy*, for example, the Court examined the compatibility of a national prohibition on the addition of nitrate to cheese with Community rules on additive use and Article 29 EC. Nitrate had been added to cheese for sale on the Italian market in quantities that were within the limits widely accepted in international scientific circles (50 mg per kg).[137] The cheese in question was also lawfully manufactured and marketed in other Member States. Nitrate is added to various types of cheese in the course of their manufacture to help eliminate certain bacteria that make these products swell abnormally. It does, however, also exist naturally in many varieties of cheese, generally acting as a preservative.

Italian law governing certain health aspects of the production and sale of food and drink provided that no chemical additives of any kind whatsoever could be used in the manufacture of foodstuffs and that no foodstuffs containing such additives could be made available for consumption without prior ministerial authorisation. No order pursuant to that law had authorised the use of nitrate in the production of cheese. Nitrate was at the time listed in the Annex to Council Directive 1964/54 as amended, the use of which could be authorised by the Member States.[138]

According to the Commission, the importation of foodstuffs manufactured in another Member State containing an additive included in the Community list had to be authorised provided that it posed no danger to public health and met a particular need. The Court noted that according to its own case law on the matter,[139] rules making the use of an additive subject to authorisation complied with Community law if two conditions were satisfied. First, the rules had to make provision for a procedure that enabled traders to have the additive included on the national list of authorised additives. This procedure had to be one that was readily accessible and capable of being completed within a reasonable period and, if it led to a rejection, that rejection had to be open to challenge before the courts. Second, an application to have an additive included in the list in question could be rejected by the competent authorities only if the additive did not meet any genuine

---

[137] Case C-95/1989, *Commission v Italy* (added nitrate) [1992] ECR I-4545.

[138] Council Directive 1964/54/EEC of 5 November 1963 on the approximation of the laws of the Member States concerning the preservatives authorised for use in foodstuffs intended for human consumption. [1964] OJ P 12/161. English Special Edition Series I, Chapter 1963–4, p 99. Directive 1964/54 was amended on 23 occasions.

[139] Case 247/1984, *Criminal proceedings against Léon Motte* [1985] ECR 3887, para 25; Case 304/1984, *Criminal proceedings against Claude Muller* [1986] ECR 1511, para 26; Case C-42/1990, *Criminal proceedings against Jean-Claude Bellon* [1990] ECR I-4863, paras 16 and 17.

need, in particular a technological need. Even if it did meet such a need it must not present any danger to public health.

The Court noted that it was not sufficient for the purpose of showing that an additive did not meet a genuine need to show that a product could have been manufactured using a different substance. Such an interpretation of the concept of need was seen to be capable of resulting in favouring national production methods over non-national ones, and thus able to constitute a disguised method of restricting trade between Member States. It was noted, however, that the Italian legislation on additives introduced a system comprising a ban, subject to the possibility of authorisation, that applied equally to additives in foodstuffs from Member States where they were lawfully manufactured and marketed and those of domestic origin. There could only be a breach of Article 28 EC if the additive authorisation procedure—compliance with the requirements of readily accessibility, efficiency and offering the possibility of appeal—unjustifiably rejected an application for the inclusion of a substance on the list of authorised additives. The procedure set up by the Italian legislation was not contrary to Community law and, as a result, the Commission's action was dismissed.

The Court will allow Member States to ban the use of additives in some circumstances, even where their use is permitted elsewhere in the Community. In *Eyssen* the Court examined the compatibility with Community law of a prohibition on the addition of nisin to cheese.[140] Here, a Dutch manufacturer, who produced processed cheese for sale on the domestic market and for export to other Member States, was charged with having held in stock for the purpose of sale quantities of processed cheese containing added nisin. The addition of nisin to cheese was not permitted under Dutch law, although its use was permitted in other Member States. In view of this disparity between rules it was found to be indisputable that the prohibition by some Member States on the marketing within their territory of processed cheese containing additional nisin was of such a nature as to affect imports of that product from other Member States where, conversely, the addition of nisin was wholly or partially permitted. The Dutch rules thus constituted a measure having an effect equivalent to a quantitative restriction on imports. However, whilst a hindrance to Community trade was recognised, the prohibition and consequent restrictions on imports were justifiable under Article 30 of the EC Treaty on the ground of protecting human health. The domestic legislation at issue did not constitute a means of arbitrary discrimination, nor was it held to be a disguised restriction on trade between Member States.

In *Bellon*,[141] French rules prohibiting the importation and marketing of pastry to which sorbic acid had been added, from Italy, where its use was permitted, were examined. Sorbic acid use was also permitted in Community law under Directive 1964/54. In France it could only be used in a limited number of specified food-

---

[140] Case 53/1980, *Officier van Justitie v Koninklijke Kaasfabriek Eyssen BV* [1981] ECR 409. For further discussion see S Weatherill, *EU Consumer Law and Policy* (Cheltenham, Edward Elgar, 2005), p 43.
[141] Case C-42/1990, *Criminal proceedings against Jean-Claude Bellon* [1990] ECR I-4863, paras 16 and 17.

stuffs. Since the products concerned were imported from another Member State, here they were lawfully produced and marketed, the application of the French rules was clearly to be regarded as a measure hindering intra-Community trade and thereby constituting, in principle at least, a measure having an effect equivalent to a quantitative restriction on imports. It therefore had to be ascertained whether or not this measure could be justified under Article 30 EC.

The Court noted that any prohibitions on the marketing of products containing additives authorised in the Member State of production, but prohibited in the Member State of importation, had to be restricted to what was actually necessary to secure the protection of public health. It was found that the prohibition was justified on the grounds of public health protection but that, again, a system of approval for products such as those prohibited here must be implemented by Member States enforcing such a prohibition in order to ensure the legitimacy of the prohibition.

In *Grunert*,[142] criminal proceedings were brought against the defendant, the managing director of a company, for having offered for sale and then selling, knowing its intended destination, a product liable to adulterate foodstuffs for human consumption, in this case a preservative containing lactic acid and citric acid. The preservative in question was used in making pork-butcher's meat and was marketed by the company managed by the accused. French law prohibited the addition to foodstuffs of any substance which had not previously been expressly authorised. Neither lactic acid nor citric acid had been so authorised and their use was therefore prohibited in the production of the foodstuff in question. The domestic court did note, however, that Directive 1964/54, and certain other directives,[143] provided an exhaustive list of the preservatives authorised in the Member States and that this list included both lactic acid and citric acid.

The Court was asked whether Member States are bound to authorise all the preservatives which may be used in foodstuffs that are listed in the additives directives, or whether they must merely prohibit the use of all those substances that are not included in those lists. The Court held that the directives require that Member States do not authorise the use in foodstuffs of preservatives or antioxidants which are not included in the lists annexed to the directives, but also that the Member States' freedom to prohibit or to authorise the use of such substances must not have the effect of totally excluding the use in foodstuffs of any of the preservatives that are included in the lists, or of preventing all marketing of such a substance.

In *Motte*,[144] it was questioned whether a prohibition on the use of indigotin and cochineal, a red colourant, in the preparation of non-smoked fish roe was contrary to Community law. Criminal proceedings had been brought against the defendant for importing substances into Belgium that breached this prohibition, from

---

[142] Case 88/1979, *Criminal proceedings against Siegfried Grunert* [1980] ECR 1827.
[143] In particular, Council Directive 1970/357/EEC of 13 July 1970 on the approximation of the laws of the Member States concerning the antioxidants authorised for use in foodstuffs intended for human consumption. [1970] OJ L 157/31.
[144] Case 247/1984, *Criminal proceedings against Léon Motte* [1985] ECR 1329.

Germany, where they were authorised. The use of these colourants was authorised in Belgium for a number of other food types. National law prescribed that the addition of these colourants to specific foodstuffs required prior authorisation, such authorisation to appear in a positive list.

It is clear that a national rule such as that at issue in this case is capable of contravening Article 28 EC given that the products imported are from another Member State where they are lawfully marketed. At the time of the case, only a small degree of harmonisation of the rules relating to the use of colourants in foodstuffs had been achieved. In the absence of harmonisation it is for the Member States to decide the extent to which national rules can be used to protect human health under Article 30 EC, but always taking account of Article 28 EC. The Court noted here that for those purposes Member States must take into account the results of international scientific research and, in particular, the work of the Community's Scientific Committee for Food, the opinions of which do not have binding force. It was also noted that when examining whether an additive may be used in the preparation of a foodstuff the degree of harmfulness of this use is not to be the only consideration; the necessity of adding it to the foodstuff in question is also relevant. This need must be technological or economic, or as far as colouring or flavouring is concerned, organoleptic or psychological.[145] It was thus held that Community law at the time did not preclude national provisions that required that the use of colourants, such as in this case, be entered on a national list drawn up after referral to a committee of experts. However, in applying such provisions to products imported from another Member State where they are lawfully marketed the national authorities must authorise the colouring of the foodstuff if it corresponds to a real need.

In *Muller*,[146] it was questioned whether Directive 1974/329[147] prevented a Member State from prohibiting the use of one of the substances listed in the Annex to the directive.[148] Citing *Motte*, the Court noted that the existence of harmonising directives did not exclude the operation of Article 28 of the EC Treaty and that it is only when Community rules make provision for the full harmonisation of all the measures needed to ensure the protection of health and institute Community procedures to monitor compliance therewith that recourse to Article 30 EC ceases to be justified. Consequently, when prohibitions on the use of additives specifically listed in Community legislation are applied to products imported from other Member States, Treaty provisions, namely Article 28 EC *et seq*, must be observed. It was thus held that Directive 1974/329 did not prevent a Member State from

---

[145] Commission Recommendation 1980/1089/EEC of 11 November 1980 addressed to the Member States concerning tests relating to the safety evaluation of food additives. [1980] OJ L 320/36.

[146] Case 304/1984, *Criminal proceedings against Claude Muller* [1986] ECR 1511.

[147] Council Directive 1974/329/EEC of 18 June 1974 on the approximation of the laws of the Member States relating to emulsifiers, stabilisers, thickeners and gelling agents for use in foodstuffs. [1974] OJ L 189/1.

[148] Article 2(1) of Directive 1974/329 states that 'Member States shall authorise the use as emulsifiers, stabilisers, thickeners and gelling agents in foodstuffs intended for human consumption, of only those substances listed in Annex I and where appropriate, only under the conditions specified therein'.

prohibiting the use of one of the additives listed in the Annex, provided that free movement requirements were properly observed. The marketing of foodstuffs containing such substances must, however, be authorised, under a procedure easily accessible to manufacturers and traders, if the addition of the substance in question meets a genuine need and presents no danger to public health. It is for the national authorities to show in each case why domestic rules might be necessary to give effective protection to human health, or any of the other interests referred to in Article 30 of the EC Treaty.

5.5.2 Directive 1989/107

In order to reduce the potential for impediments to the free movement of goods, such as those in evidence in the preceding body of case law, harmonisation of the national rules was brought about by Directive 1989/107, which sets out Community-wide requirements for the use of additives in foodstuffs.[149] The directive covers all additives, including colours, preservatives, antioxidants, emulsifiers, thickeners, gelling agents, stabilisers and flavour enhancers,[150] which are used or which are intended to be used as ingredients during the manufacture or preparation of foodstuffs and which are still present in the final product, even if in altered form.[151] Food additives are defined as being:

> any substance not normally consumed as a food in itself and not normally used as a characteristic ingredient of food whether or not it has nutritive value, the intentional addition of which to food for a technological purpose in the manufacture, processing, preparation, treatment, packaging, transport or storage of such food results, or may be reasonably expected to result, in it or its by-products becoming directly or indirectly a component of such foods.[152]

The directive does not apply to processing aids, flavourings or substances added to foodstuffs as nutrients, for example minerals or vitamins.[153] In order for a food additive to be legally usable in the manufacture or preparation of foodstuffs it must be specifically listed as being usable and must only be used under the conditions specified,[154] and in certain permitted foodstuffs.[155] Additives can be added to or removed from the list of those permitted to be used depending on the circumstances if they either fulfil the requirements of the directive[156] or if new

---

[149] Council Directive 1989/107/EEC of 21 December 1988 on the approximation of the laws of the Member States concerning food additives authorised for use in foodstuffs intended for human consumption. [1989] OJ L 40/27.

[150] Annex I to Directive 1989/107.

[151] Article 1(1).

[152] Article 1(2).

[153] Article 1(3). The addition of vitamins and minerals to foodstuffs is now dealt with in new legislative proposals. See Proposal for a Regulation of the European Parliament and of the Council on the addition of vitamins and minerals and of certain other substances to foods. COM (2003) 671.

[154] Article 2(1).

[155] Article 3(2)(b).

[156] Article 5.

information shows that a previously approved additive is or may actually be dangerous to human health.[157] The Scientific Committee for Food (now transferred to EFSA) must be consulted where the use of an additive may affect public health.[158] Once approved, the Member States may not prohibit, or obstruct in any way, the marketing of food additives, food or food ingredients on grounds relating to food additives.[159]

The directive sets out a series of general criteria for the use of food additives.[160] Food additives can only be approved if there can be demonstrated to be a reasonable technological need for their use and that purpose cannot be achieved by other means that are economically and technologically practicable. Additives may only be used where they present no known hazard to the health of the consumer at the level of use proposed and if their use does not mislead the consumer in any way. The use of food additives may be considered only where there is evidence that the proposed use of the additive would have demonstrable advantages of benefit to the consumer. The use of additives should serve one or more of specified purposes and only where these purposes cannot be achieved by other means which are economically and technologically practicable and do not present a hazard to the health of the consumer. These specified purposes include the preservation of the nutritional quality of the food, the provision of necessary ingredients or conditions for foods manufactured for groups of consumers having special dietary needs, the enhancement of food quality or organoleptic properties provided that this does not alter the nature or quality of the food to the extent that it might deceive the consumer, and the provision of aids to manufacturing, processing, preparation, treatment, packing, transportation or storage of food provided that the additive is not used to disguise the effects of the use of faulty raw materials or of undesirable, including unhygienic, practices or techniques during the course of any of these activities. Food additives are to be kept under continuous observation and re-evaluated whenever necessary to take account of changing conditions of use and any new scientific information. Any approval for the use of a food additive must specify the foodstuffs to which the additive may be added and the conditions under which it may be added. Additive use must always be limited to the lowest level of use necessary to achieve the desired effect, taking into account any acceptable daily intake, or equivalent assessment, established for the food additive in question and the probable daily intake of that additive from all sources.

---

[157] Article 4.
[158] Article 6.
[159] Article 12(2).
[160] Annex II to Council Directive 1989/107/EEC of 21 December 1988 on the approximation of the laws of the Member States concerning food additives authorised for use in foodstuffs intended for human consumption. [1989] OJ L 40.

5.5.3 Sweetener, Colour and Flavour Use

In addition to the general legislation on additive use, there are also separate rules for the use of sweeteners[161] and colours in foodstuffs.[162] Directive 1994/35 lists those sweeteners which may be placed on the market for sale to the ultimate consumer or which may be used in the manufacture of foodstuffs.[163] Sweeteners may not be used in foods for infants or young children unless specifically provided for.[164] Directive 1994/36 sets similar requirements for the use of colours in foodstuffs. 'Colours' are defined as:

> substances which add or restore colour in a food, and include natural constituents of foodstuffs and natural sources which are normally not consumed as foodstuffs as such and not normally used as characteristic ingredients of food.[165]

Some substances, which are primarily added to the foodstuff for flavouring purposes, are not considered to be colours for the purposes of the directive, including paprika, turmeric and saffron, neither are colours that are used for the colouring of the inedible external parts of foodstuffs, such as cheese coatings and sausage casings.[166] Only those substances listed in the directive are permitted to be used as colours in foodstuffs.[167] Specific conditions for use are also set out in some circumstances.[168] There is also specific provision in the directive for the launch of a campaign designed to inform consumers about the evaluation and authorisation procedures for permitted colours and the meaning of the 'E' number system.[169]

All Community legislation on food additives is based on the principle that only those additives that are explicitly authorised may be used. The use of food additives must always be labelled on the packaging of food products by their category, such as antioxidant, preservative or colour, with either their name or E-number.[170] The official source for these numbers is the body of additive legislation with amendments where the additives are listed with their names and E numbers, normally in the Annex to the legislation.[171] The numbering system is being adapted for international use by the Codex Alimentarius Commission, which is

---

[161] European Parliament and Council Directive 1994/35/EC of 30 June 1994 on sweeteners for use in foodstuffs. [1994] OJ L 237/3

[162] European Parliament and Council Directive 1994/36/EC of 30 June 1994 on colours for use in foodstuffs. [1994] OJ L 237/13

[163] Article 2(1). Those sweeteners that may be used are set out in the Annex to Directive 1994/35.

[164] Article 2(3).

[165] Article 1(2).

[166] Article 1(3).

[167] Article 2(1). Substances permitted to be used as colours are listed in Annex I to Directive 1994/36.

[168] Article 2. These substances are listed in Annex II, III, IV, and V to Directive 1994/36.

[169] Article 8 of Council Directive 1989/107/EEC of 21 December 1988 on the approximation of the laws of the Member States concerning food additives authorised for use in foodstuffs intended for human consumption. [1989] OJ L 40/27.

[170] *Ibid.*

[171] See, for example, Annex V to European Parliament and Council Directive 1994/36/EC of 30 June 1994 on colours for use in foodstuffs. [1994] OJ L 237/13.

developing a system that largely uses the same numbers but without the 'E', used to indicate EU approval.[172]

Additional requirements have been created for food additives other than colours and sweeteners by Directive 1995/2,[173] including preservatives, anti-oxidants, acidity regulators, anti-caking agents and flavour enhancers. Only those substances specifically listed in the directive are permitted to be used for their stated purposes in the manufacture of foodstuffs,[174] with separate additional requirements for foods for infants and young children.[175]

The use of flavourings in foodstuffs, which are not covered by the additive legislation, are controlled by Directive 1988/388.[176] Again, the differences between the national laws of the Member States relating to flavourings, which were deemed to be hindering the free movement of foodstuffs and creating unequal competition conditions, were cited as one of the primary reasons for the adoption of this harmonising legislation.[177] 'Flavourings' are defined in the directive as 'flavouring substances, flavouring preparations, process flavourings, smoke flavourings or mixtures thereof'.[178] Flavouring substances are:

> a defined chemical substance with flavouring properties which is obtained by appropriate [physical or chemical] processes . . . from material of vegetable or animal origin either in the raw state or after processing for human consumption by traditional food-preparation processes [or] by chemical synthesis [which] is not chemically identical to a substance naturally present in material of vegetable or animal origin.[179]

A flavouring preparation is:

> a product, other than [flavouring substances] whether concentrated or not, with flavouring properties, which is obtained by appropriate physical processes (including distillation and solvent extraction) or by enzymatic or microbiological processes from material of vegetable or animal origin, either in the raw state or after processing for human consumption by traditional food-preparation processes (including drying, torrefaction and fermentation).[180]

The word 'natural', or any other word having substantially the same meaning, may only be used for flavourings in which the flavouring component contains exclusively flavouring preparations.[181] They are produced from material of vegetable or animal origin.

[172] List of Codex Advisory Specifications for Food Additives. CAC/MISC 6/2001.

[173] European Parliament and Council Directive No 1995/2/EC of 20 February 1995 on food additives other than colours and sweeteners. [1995] OJ L 6195.

[174] Article 2(1).

[175] Article 2(3)(b). Those products covered by the Directive that are permitted for use in the manufacture of foodstuffs are listed in the Annex to European Parliament and Council Directive No 1995/2/EC of 20 February 1995 on food additives other than colours and sweeteners. [1995] OJ L 61.

[176] Council Directive 1988/388/EEC of 22 June 1988 on the approximation of the laws of the Member States relating to flavourings for use in foodstuffs and to source materials for their production. [1988] OJ L 184/61.

[177] Preamble to Directive 1988/388.

[178] Article 1(2).

[179] *Ibid.*

[180] *Ibid.*

[181] Article 9(2).

Member States are to take all measures necessary to ensure that flavourings do not contain any element or substance in a toxicologically dangerous quantity, that the use of flavourings does not result in the presence in foodstuffs of undesirable substances listed in the directive, and that the use of flavourings and other food ingredients with flavouring properties does not result in the presence of certain substances in quantities greater than those specified in the legislation.[182] Procedures for ensuring that the use of flavourings does not harm human health are set out in the directive.[183] The directive applies to flavourings intended for use in foodstuffs imported into the Community but does not apply to those destined for export outside the Community.[184]

5.6 CONCLUSION

The BSE crisis marked a watershed in the development of EU food law. The aims of devising and implementing rules on the production and marketing of food have been prioritised once more. The emphasis is now firmly on safety. This has resulted in the unprecedented creation of a food safety authority, which must be consulted on a broad range of policy matters, from labelling to crisis management. Existing measures, such as those on the hygienic production and marketing of food, have been reassessed, simplified and consolidated in an attempt to make them more user friendly, and ultimately to improve compliance rates.

The single most profound change to the manner in which EU food law now operates is that the institutions are empowered, due to acceptance of the precautionary principle, to pre-empt and act upon any dangers that may exist in the food supply chain. Once supported by a level of scientific evidence justifying their action, the use of certain products or procedures may be suspended where there is cause for concern about their safety. Member States, through use of the safeguard clauses that are inserted into much of the Community's secondary legislation, may also act contrary to free movement rules where they have reason to suspect that there may be an imminent danger to human health.[185] This new-found flexibility should go some way to protecting consumers from unsafe food making it onto the market. While this liberal (and initially erroneous) interpretation of Treaty provisions is a welcome development, Member States do however remain paralysed as regards the extent to which they can intervene domestically in order to counter the fact that diets are becoming increasingly dangerous throughout the EU, resulting in very serious health concerns for a large proportion of its citizens.

---

[182] Article 4. The substances and quantities referred to are listed in Annex I and Annex II to Directive 1988/388.

[183] Articles 6, 7 and 8.

[184] Article 11.

[185] For further discussion on the availability of these safeguard clauses to the Member States see G Berends and I Carreño, 'Safeguards in Food Law—Ensuring Food Scares are Scarce' (2005) 30 *European Law Review* 386.

6

Nutrition Law and Policy in the EU

6.1 INTRODUCTION

THE PREPONDERANCE OF the body of food law that has been initiated and developed by the Community institutions, in particular the Court and the Commission, has focused on two main areas: food safety and free movement. This could be extended to include health protection and consumer protection. However, we have seen in previous chapters that these two concerns fall well down the rankings in the Community's order of priorities. In particular, it has become clear that Member States lack autonomy in the introduction of national measures that could be used to promote health or consumer protection, despite the existence of Article 30 EC and the development of the mandatory requirement exception by the Court of Justice. This makes it very difficult for the Member States to introduce their own health promotion measures where these may inhibit free movement in any way.

Given the manner in which EU food law has developed, Member States have become over-reliant on the Community as the principal source of new food laws. This, of course, should not necessarily present a problem in itself. However, potential difficulties do arise when the Community is also unwilling to take the necessary measures that could assist the Member States in ensuring, as far as possible, that society is well-fed and, most importantly, well-nourished. The Commission has to date failed to oblige in this regard. By focusing its energies on safety and free movement, the issue of the nutritional value of food consumed in the European Union has always been of secondary priority.

European Community food law could be described as being safe and comfortable, and often not that useful. There are rules to determine the hand-washing facilities that must be available in areas where food is prepared.[1] There are rules in place determining that prepackaged foodstuffs must display a best before or use by date.[2] There are rules specifying the minimum age at which animals can be

---

[1] Annex II to Regulation (EC) No 852/2004 of the European Parliament and of the Council of 29 April 2004 on the hygiene of foodstuffs. [2004] OJ L 139/1.

[2] Articles 3(1) and 10 of Directive 2000/13/EC of the European Parliament and of the Council of 20 March 2000 on the approximation of the laws of the Member States relating to the labelling, presentation and advertising of foodstuffs. [2000] OJ L 109/29.

slaughtered in order to be considered 'organic'.[3] However, there are no controls in place to ensure that the person preparing food *does* wash his or her hands. There are no controls over the producer's choice of 'best before'. There are no controls that can reasonably prevent the slaughtered animal being carved up on the same surface as meat already cooked, maybe by the same, unsterilised, knife.

The claims made here about the negligent focus of European food law on the 'wrong issues' is exemplified by the Commission document *Healthy Food for Europe's Citizens: The European Union and Food Quality*.[4] One might expect that a document so titled would contain information and discussion about Community efforts to increase the nutritional value of food, to maintain food quality levels, and to reduce intakes of salt, sugar and unnecessary fat, especially amongst the young and the vulnerable. Not so. Instead, *Healthy Food for Europe's Citizens* commences by outlining why food safety and quality levels are a concern, stating that 'consumers are demanding the highest possible standards from farmers, food companies and retailers'. This is simply untrue. It may be correct to say that some consumers have reverted to purchasing some of their food from local, possibly reliable, and traceable sources. The vast majority do not do so. They continue to overload their supermarket trolleys with products from untraceable sources, made from poor quality ingredients and which may contain meat from a processing plant that does not maintain minimum hygiene standards, or which has not been reared to acceptable animal welfare standards. Some are oblivious to this. Some are apathetic. If food tastes fine, and most importantly if it is cheap, then the majority of consumers are not particularly interested in 'demanding the highest possible standards from farmers, food companies and retailers'. Such an assertion can only be said to be true if 'the highest possible standards' means that consumers insist upon food that has not gone off, or tastes as if it has not gone off. It does not extend to insisting that juice for children does not make them hyperactive, nor that the ingredients in crisps contribute to making them overweight and improperly nourished.

The EU institutions, and many of the Member States, have incorrectly defined both 'food quality' and 'food safety', rendering them, to a large extent, meaningless terms. While it is noted that 'addressing consumers' safety concerns and quality expectations is a major responsibility for the European Union', this is something that has never been seen through properly. It is stated that 'over the last 40 years, the EU has developed a comprehensive set of rules, standards and monitoring practices to guarantee that the food we eat is as safe and appetising as possible'.[5] It is here contended that EU food law has actually led to a depreciation in the nutritional value of food, or at the very least removed the possibilities for Member States to ensure that food marketed on their territory is of the highest

---

[3] Annex to Council Regulation (EC) No 1804/1999 of 19 July 1999 supplementing Regulation (EEC) No 2092/1991 on organic production of agricultural products and indications referring thereto on agricultural products and foodstuffs to include livestock production. [1999] OJ L 222/1.
[4] European Commission Directorate General for Education and Culture (2000) ISBN 92-828-8238-1.
[5] *Ibid.*

nutritional standard, quite aside from the fact that the rules described are reactive rather than proactive in nature. However, where it is said here that the terms 'food safety' and 'food quality' have not been properly defined, this is primarily due to the fact that nutritional value has remained for the most part outside the factors that are taken into account in determining what qualifies as safe or high quality food. The European Union needs to refocus these definitions to include nutrition, not as a possible by-product of safety and/or quality initiatives, but as an integral part of any determination on just what constitutes safe or quality food in order to ensure that the majority of consumers are protected not only from unscrupulous business practice, but also, and perhaps more importantly, from themselves.

The Commission, through both its documentation and its actions, has combined food safety and food quality into one overarching category of concern. It is also deemed to be the primary function of Community food law and policy to ensure that food products are of a high quality and that they are safe. But what do these terms really mean?

It is clear that the Commission is of the opinion that by ensuring safety it provides quality, and vice-versa. It is not in dispute that there is some overlap between the two issues, but they are more clearly distinguishable than has been presumed to date. The EU intervenes in the food production process in several ways to ensure safety and quality—the much heralded 'farm to factory to fork' approach. The Common Agricultural Policy is the chief mechanism that can be used to maintain or increase food quality levels. The Commission claims that by reducing price support levels farmers are given a greater incentive to produce higher quality foodstuffs in order to secure a higher price on the market. While there is some evidence to suggest an increase in consumer demand for higher quality agricultural products, this generally obtains only amongst the more affluent sections of society. In addition to this, pressure exerted by supermarkets leads to reduced prices being paid to the farmer, who is already without the previous high levels of price support. For his business to survive, something has to give. The competitive farmer placed in such a position can respond in one of two ways. Either their agricultural practices have to become more intensive to reduce unit costs, or quality has to be compromised to reduce overall costs, consequently compromising both quality and safety.

There is little dispute about the fact that the very public scares over the safety of food in the 1990s pushed the issue to the top of consumers' list of priorities.[6] Responses to such scares will always be at their most intense in the immediate aftermath of any such crisis. Soon after, when the media has shifted its focus to a different story, consumers may claim that safety remains their key concern, but in reality price, and to a lesser extent taste, will be the main determinants in any purchasing choice. This takes the pressure off the legislator, which can be left to establish a crisis response process. It is highly questionable whether any legislative

---

[6] See, for example, Eurobarometer 238 on Risk Issues, February 2006.

initiatives taken in this regard can ever achieve the full desired effect. Complementary to this will be a series of legislative measures designed to minimise the potential for such a scare to occur again. This will generally be the body of legislation that existed at the time of the outbreak of the previous scare, or a modified version of it. From the 1970s onwards, the European Community has introduced measures contributing to this body of rules on matters such as veterinary controls, pesticide use and the spread of pathogens. The Commission sees this as one of two aspects of ensuring food quality, the other being satisfaction of consumer expectations of subjective criteria, such as taste. It is here accepted that food quality does indeed have two aspects to it, but the first one is not related to veterinary controls, pesticide use and the spread of pathogens—these are all specifically food safety issues. The first element of quality is actually nutritional value, yet this is not adequately recognised at Community level. To summarise, quality relates to nutritional value and subjective criteria, such as taste, appearance and smell; the organoleptic properties. Food safety concerns harmful effects on human health. This can be distinguished from nutritional value because the intake of a portion of non-nutritious food will not have any medium- to long-term effect on human health as such, but the consumption of an unsafe food due to, for example, the presence of a pathogen or harmful substance, has the potential to damage health, possibly even to kill. As a consequence of this misinterpretation of the extent to which the Community is responsible for the protection of human health through the consumption of safe or quality food, the issue of nutrition has become sidelined, when in fact it should be the key component of any food quality programme.

Nutrition and physical activity are key determinants for the prevalence of obesity, which continues to rise in the EU among children and adults. Despite this, the Community remains unwilling to intervene. European Union food laws actually make it easier to market a food product that is high in fat, sugar or salt as being of nutritional value than a food with added vitamins and/or minerals that is low in unnecessary fat, sugar or added salt. Attempts to at least partially alter this have been made with the proposal for authorising nutritional and health claims. However, as demonstrated below, the procedure used to turn this proposal into a regulation has led to one of the key factors protecting consumers from non-nutritious food being altered to the extent that such claims will now be capable of being made on the labelling of 'unhealthy' foodstuffs.

While the issue of nutrition specifically did not come within the ambit of the White Paper on Food Safety, it was recognised therein that the future direction of European Community food law should, among other things, aim at ensuring the intake of essential nutrients while limiting intake of other elements in order to avoid adverse health effects, including anti-nutritional effects. Nutritional information should thus be made clear and accessible to the consumer. Measures would be taken to establish the conditions for making claims such as 'low sodium' or 'gluten free'. It was also proposed that two directives would be introduced, on food supplements and fortified foods. An overall comprehensive and coherent nutritional policy was to be devised.

It is this policy and the results it has achieved that is assessed below through an examination of existing nutrition labelling rules, new legislation on nutrition and health claims, food supplements controls and, perhaps most importantly, the manner in which EU food law prevents Member States from introducing their own legislative initiatives to help combat nutrition-related health issues—in particular rising rates of obesity.

6.2 COMMUNITY LEGISLATION ON NUTRITION

6.2.1 Nutrition Labelling

Directive 1990/496 lays down Community requirements for nutrition labelling on foodstuffs.[7] 'Nutrition labelling', for the purposes of the directive, means any information appearing on the labelling relating to energy values and nutrients such as protein, carbohydrates, fat, fibre, sodium and certain vitamins and minerals.[8] Nutrition labelling is only compulsory where there is a nutrition claim on the labelling, in the presentation or in the advertising of the food.[9] In all other cases, the placing of nutrition labelling information on the foodstuff is optional.[10] A 'nutrition claim' is defined as:

> any representation and any advertising message which states, suggests or implies has particular nutrition properties due to the energy (calorific value) it [either] provides, provides at a reduced or increased rate or does not provide and/or due to the nutrients it [either] contains, contains in reduced or increased proportions or does not contain.[11]

Nutrition labelling must appear in one of two set forms. It should either detail the energy value and the amounts of protein, carbohydrate and fat present in the foodstuff, or it may display this information and additional details relating to the amounts of sugars, saturates, fibre and sodium contained in the product.[12] Nutrition labelling may also include the amounts of one or more of starch, polyols, monounsaturates, polyunsaturates, cholesterol or any of the minerals or vitamins listed in the Annex to the directive (such as Vitamins A, C, D and E and minerals calcium, phosphorus, iron and zinc), if present in significant amounts (usually 15% of the recommended daily allowance per 100 g or 100 ml or per single portion).[13] The directive also sets out the requirements for how all this information is to be displayed on the label, for example, the manner in which the energy value is to be calculated and then declared.[14] All the nutrition information

---

[7] Council Directive 1990/496/EEC of 24 September 1990 on nutrition labelling for foodstuffs. [1990] OJ L 276/40.

[8] Article 1(4)(a).

[9] Article 2(2).

[10] Article 2(1).

[11] Article 1(4)(b).

[12] Article 4(1).

[13] Article 4(3).

[14] Articles 5 and 6.

covered by the terms of the directive is to be presented together in one place, in legible and indelible characters in a conspicuous place, in a language easily understood by purchasers, and in tabular form, unless space on the label does not allow. In such circumstances, the information may appear in linear form.[15] Member States may not lay down requirements that are more detailed than those contained in the directive.[16]

6.2.2 Nutrition and Health Claims

One of the most interesting, complex and widely debated legislative initiatives to come from the Commission in recent years is the proposal for a new regulation on nutrition and health claims. An examination of this regulation illustrates three key points about the nature of EU food law more generally. First, it is quite clear that increasing attention has been paid to consumer concerns and protection in recent years. This has already been demonstrated in Chapter 2 in relation to the manner in which the Court of Justice now more readily accepts, in some circumstances, Member States' justifications for the maintenance of national laws that are seemingly at odds with Community free movement rules. The regulation on nutrition and health claims presents another example of this. Some producers make unclear and unsubstantiated claims about the beneficial properties of their products. Now, in light of refocused attention on regaining consumer confidence in the food sector, any such claims made in the future will have to be verified prior to marketing. Second, while this new approach to consumer and health matters is a welcome development, albeit one that required a series of food safety crises prior to its initiation, the promotion of the free movement of food throughout the internal market remains the number one priority of the EU legislator. It was only when a threat to the uninhibited movement of foodstuffs bearing health claims surfaced that the proposal to introduce this regulation appeared. Finally, despite the intentions of those responsible for drafting this new legislation, the legislative process— here the Article 251 EC procedure involving full parliamentary consultation—has led to one of the most important aspects of the regulation being altered to such a degree that the original plan to prevent unhealthy foodstuffs from bearing nutrition or health claims has been overruled. Now, as a result of the amendments that have taken place during this procedure, foods that are high, even very high, in substances that may have detrimental effects on human health can bear claims that they are, in fact, healthy.

Background to the Regulation on Nutrition and Health Claims

The proposal for a regulation on nutrition and health claims was first introduced in July 2003, and was accepted by all parties to the Article 251 EC procedure in

---

[15] Article 7(1) and (2).
[16] Article 7(3).

May 2006.[17] It followed the decision of the Court in *Austria v Commission*, where it was held that the terms of the framework food labelling directive prohibited all health claims relating to human diseases.[18] Article 2(1)(b) of Directive 2000/13 provides:

> The labelling and methods used must not . . . attribute to any foodstuff the property of preventing, treating or curing a human disease, or refer to such properties.

When examining whether Austrian national law prohibiting claims made in respect of foods that referred to the prevention, relief or cure of illnesses was compatible with Articles 28–30 EC, the Court stated:

> Article 2(1)(b) of Directive 79/112 [now Directive 2000/13] only allows the Member States to prohibit statements relating to diseases. It leaves room, however, for health-related information on the labelling of foodstuffs, subject to compliance with the other conditions laid down by that directive, in particular the condition that such information must not mislead the purchaser.[19]

The Commission's proposal for a regulation on nutrition and health claims noted how technological innovation in the food sector would make it possible for foods to possess health benefits, in particular disease prevention, in the future. The interpretation of the framework food labelling directive by the Court in *Commission v Austria* would prevent these new foodstuffs from being marketed effectively, making claims that consumers would want to know about and which they would not be misled by. It was therefore deemed necessary to make it possible for such claims to be made, provided they were supported by scientific verification that such beneficial properties could be gained from consuming the products concerned. In addition to this, fears about the consequences for free movement due to fact that some Member States had adopted their own legislation on these types of claims added to the sense of necessity for bringing in new Community-wide legislation in this area.

The impetus to develop EU rules on nutrition and health claims was furthered by the fact that similar guidelines had already come into existence at international level. As noted in Chapter 4, it can be important to keep EU rules similar to international standards in order to minimise the possibility of disputes arising in the WTO. As noted earlier, Codex Alimentarius guidelines exist for claims generally,[20] and for nutrition and health claims more specifically.[21] Initially, the latter dealt with nutrition claims only. Guidelines for health claims were added in the 2004 review. The definitions and general principles of the Codex guidelines are almost identical to the new EU standards. However, the EU regulation goes into far more

---

[17] Proposal for a Regulation of the European Parliament and of the Council on nutrition and health claims made on foods. COM (2003) 424.

[18] Case C-221/2000, *Commission v Austria* (health claims) [2003] ECR I-1007.

[19] Paragraph 16.

[20] Codex General Guidelines on Claims. Codex Guidelines 1/1979. Revised 1991.

[21] Codex Guidelines for Use of Nutrition and Health Claims. Codex Guidelines 23/1997. Revised 2004.

detail on what can constitute a legitimate claim and, in particular, the types of procedure involved in substantiating claims made.

Key Provisions of Nutrition and Health Claims Legislation

Any claim that is made that does not comply with the terms of the regulation is deemed to be misleading advertising within the meaning of Directive 1984/450.[22] Nutrition claims are defined as being:

> any claim which states, suggests or implies that a food has particular nutritional properties due to: (a) the energy (calorific value) it provides, provides at a reduced or increased rate, or does not provide and/or (b) the nutrients or other substances it contains, contains in reduced or increased proportions, or does not contain.

Essentially, therefore, a nutrition claim is any representation that a foodstuff has increased or reduced energy levels or increased or reduced nutrient levels. A representation is not limited to the labelling of the product. It can include any 'pictorial, graphic or symbolic representation, which states, suggests or implies that a food has particular characteristics', thus including the label, packaging, advertising and manner in which the product is displayed for sale. Nutrients include protein, carbohydrate, fat, fibre, sodium, vitamins and minerals as listed in the Annex to Directive 1990/496.[23] Health claims are defined as being:

> any claim that states, suggests or implies that a relationship exists between a food category, a food or one of its constituents and health.

Finally, reduction of disease risk claims are:

> any health claim that states, suggests or implies that the consumption of a food category, a food or one of its constituents significantly reduces a risk factor in the development of a human disease.

No nutrition and health claims made can be false or misleading in any way. They may not raise any doubts about the safety and/or nutritional adequacy of other foods. Most importantly, no claim should ever state or imply that it is untrue that a balanced and varied diet does not provide appropriate quantities of nutrients.

The most controversial aspect of the regulation is that it provides for the establishment by the Commission of what are called 'nutrient profiles' which must be adhered to before a nutrition or health claim can be legitimately made. These profiles establish maximum levels for fats, including saturated fatty acids and trans fatty acids, sugars and salt that can be present in any foodstuff where a nutrition or health claim is made. The profiles are to be based on scientific knowledge about diet, nutrition and their relationship to health, and, in particular, on the role of nutrients and other substances with a nutritional or physiological effect on

---

[22] Council Directive 1984/450/EEC of 10 September 1984 relating to the approximation of the laws, regulations and administrative provisions of the Member States concerning misleading advertising. [1984] OJ L 250/17.

[23] Council Directive 1990/496/EEC of 24 September 1990 on nutrition labelling for foodstuffs. [1990] OJ L 276/40.

chronic diseases. Profiling is to take place after consultation with the European Food Safety Authority (EFSA) and interested parties, in particular food business operators and consumer groups. The original proposal for the regulation stipulated that no aspect of these profiles could be exceeded if a nutritional or health claim was to be legitimately made. However, during the legislative process, Parliament insisted that this be amended. As a result, producers may breach one element of this profile and still make a nutrition or health claim. This essentially means that a foodstuff may carry such a claim even where the product in question is high (or even very high) in fats, sugars or salt. Alcoholic drinks must not carry health claims, or nutrition claims, except where these refer to the fact that the product contains a reduced alcohol or calorific content.

Generally, nutrition and health claims can only be made if the presence, absence or reduced content of the substance in respect of which the claim is made has been shown to have a beneficial nutritional or physiological effect, as established by accepted scientific data. The substance for which the claim is made must be in a form that can be used properly by the body. These claims can only be made where the 'average consumer' as defined by EU law can be expected to understand the beneficial effects expressed. Central to the regulation is the fact that in future all health and nutrition claims will only be capable of being made where there is clear scientific evidence supporting the fact that the food possesses beneficial properties. All products carrying such claims must also bear information on the labelling relating to energy, protein, carbohydrate and fat levels. For health claims, the level of information to be provided is that as set out in Group 2 of Article 4(1) of the nutrition labelling directive, namely details of the energy value and protein, carbohydrate, sugar, fat, saturate, fibre and sodium levels. Full details of the quantity of any substance that relates to the nutrition or health claim must also be disclosed where it is not automatically provided by the general nutrition labelling requirement. Examples of the type of nutrition claims that may be used, and the criteria that must be satisfied for this use to be legitimate, are set out in the Annex to the regulation. They are practically identical to those set out in the Codex Alimentarius Guidelines for Use of Nutrition and Health Claims. These include: low fat, which may only be made where the product contains no more than 3 g of fat per 100 g or 1.5 g of fat per 100 ml; fat free, which may only be used where the product contains no more than 0.5 g of fat per 100 g or 100 ml—claims expressed as 'X% fat-free' are now prohibited; sugar free, which may only be used where the product contains no more than 0.5 g of sugar per 100 g or 100 ml; low sodium/salt, which may only be used where the product contains no more than 0.12 g of sodium per 100 g or 100 ml; source of fibre, which may only be made where the product contains at least 3 g of fibre per 100 g of 1.5 g of fibre per 100 kcal; and natural source of vitamins and/or minerals, which may only be made where the product contains a significant amount of the vitamin or mineral listed, usually at least 15% of the recommended daily allowance, as set out in the Annex to Directive 1990/496.[24]

---

[24] *Ibid.*

Twenty-four such categories of nutrition claims are set out in similar terms in the Annex. The regulation will also apply to trademarks. Existing brand names suggesting health benefits, such as weight loss, that do not satisfy the terms of the regulation will not be permitted for use within 15 years of its entry into operation. Existing nutrition claims may continue to be made for two years, and health claims for three years, even where they do not comply with the regulation's requirements.

A series of additional requirements for health claims are set out in the regulation. These include the fact that there must be a statement on the product indicating the importance of a balanced diet and a healthy lifestyle. The quantity of the food and pattern of consumption required to obtain the benefits promoted must also be stated, as should warnings about possible risks of over-consumption and warnings for those who should avoid consuming the product at all. Implied health claims that make reference to general, non-specific benefits, or which refer to psychological benefits, are not permitted.

The regulation on nutrition and health claims has been criticised for potentially putting small operators to great expense in order to be able to produce the data necessary to substantiate claims that they may wish to make about their food products. This need not be the case. Health claims describing the role of a nutrient in growth, development and normal bodily functions, which are based on generally accepted scientific data and well understood by the average consumer, may be made by all operators if they have been included in the positive list of such claims. Member States must provide the Commission with claims that they want included in this list. The Commission and EFSA will consider such requests. It should also be noted that the types of claim considered by the Court in *Commission v Austria*, namely claims relating to disease, are specifically permitted by the regulation where they are authorised in the same manner as other health claims.

Authorisation Procedure

Authorisation must be granted at EU level before a health claim can be used in the marketing of a food product. Applications are made to EFSA, which must inform the Member States and the Commission of this. The application is to include: the applicant's details; details about the food for which a claim is to be made; copies of studies that have been carried out which demonstrate that the claims being made are verifiable and beneficial—these studies should be independent and peer-reviewed; copies of other scientific studies relevant to the claim; a proposal for the wording, in all Community languages, of the health claim for which authorisation is sought including, where relevant, any specific conditions for use of the food; and a summary of the dossier presented in support of the application. This summary is also to be made available to the public.

Once the application has been received, EFSA must give an opinion on it within three months. Additional information may be requested from the applicant. The key role of the Authority at this stage is to verify that the proposed wording of the health claim is substantiated by the scientific data, that it complies with the criteria laid down in the regulation, for example that a recognisable health benefit must accrue from consuming the product, and that the claim is understandable and meaningful to the average consumer. The Authority forwards its opinion to the Commission, the Member States and the applicant, including a report describing its assessment of the health claim and reasons for arriving at its opinion. The Authority is also obliged, under the terms of Regulation 178/2002, to make its opinion known to the public, who then have 30 days to submit comments.[25]

The Authority does not authorise the use of health claims. It gives an opinion on compliance with the terms of the regulation. The ultimate decision on the use of a health claim rests with the Commission, which takes the opinion of the Authority into account in reaching its decision. The Commission then informs the Standing Committee on the Food Chain and Animal Health, explaining any deviation from the earlier opinion of EFSA where appropriate.[26] The applicant is then informed of the decision taken. This is also published in the Official Journal of the European Union. Granting authorisation does not lessen the civil or criminal liability of food operators in respect of the permitted food in any way.

Authorisations may be modified, at the request of the holder, or suspended or revoked in certain circumstances. EFSA can investigate whether an authorisation to use a health claim continues to meet the conditions required. These investigations can take place on the Authority's own initiative or following a request from a Member State or the Commission. Again, the Authority furnishes the Commission with an opinion. It is the Commission which then decides whether the authorisation previously granted should be modified, suspended or revoked. Where Member States have sufficient grounds for considering that a claim does not comply with the terms of the regulation, or that the level of scientific substantiation provided is insufficient, they may temporarily suspend the use of that claim within their territory. Such a Member State must inform the other Member States and the Commission of this, outlining the reasons for its action. Where this happens, it is up to the Authority to form an opinion on this suspension, which it provides to the Commission, which in turn decides whether this can stand. The suspension may be maintained by the Member State until any such decision has been reached.

Finally, the Commission must establish and maintain a publicly available Community register of nutrition and health claims made in relation to food. This register must include details of both authorised nutrition and health claims and rejected health claims. Member States may require that the manufacturers of products carrying nutrition or health claims notify them prior to placing these

---

[25] Article 38(1) Regulation (EC) No 178/2002 of the European Parliament and of the Council of 28 January 2002 laying down the general principles and requirements of food law, establishing the European Food Safety Authority and laying down procedures in matters of food safety. [2002] OJ L 31/1.

[26] In accordance with the procedure set out in Council Decision 1999/468/EC of 28 June 1999 laying down the procedures for the exercise of implementing powers conferred on the Commission. [1999] OJ L 184/23.

foodstuffs on their domestic market. In such circumstances, a model of the label to be used should be sent to the competent authorities of the Member State in question.

6.2.3 Food Supplements

Scientific evidence makes it clear that a healthy and balanced diet should provide all the nutrients that are necessary to promote human health. Despite this, many people take nutrient supplements to counter dietary deficiencies. Directive 2002/46 lays down Community rules governing the production and marketing of these food supplements.[27] The legislation is necessary for several reasons: obviously there are the usual reasons relating to the internal market, in particular harmonising the different rules of the individual Member States to ensure, as far as possible, the free movement of the goods at issue. In addition to such reasons, it is important to ensure that there is official control over these food supplements because they may pose a danger to human health, in particular if they are taken in excessive amounts. As a consequence, the maximum amount of nutrient that can be present in any supplement must be controlled.[28] Similarly, if a consumer is purchasing these products to supplement nutrient intake from their diet, minimum levels of nutrient must also be set to ensure that the consumer gains the expected benefits.[29] The general labelling provisions of the framework food labelling directive, Directive 2000/13,[30] are applicable to food supplements, but some additional requirements are also set. The labelling, presentation and advertising cannot attribute to food supplements the property of preventing, treating or curing a human disease, or refer to such properties.[31] The labelling must bear information relating to the names of the categories or substances that characterise the product, the portion of the product recommended for daily consumption, a warning not to exceed the stated recommended daily dose, a statement to the effect that food supplements should not be used as a substitute for a varied diet, and a statement to the effect that these products should be stored out of the reach of young children.[32] There must be no statement on the labelling implying in any way that appropriate quantities of nutrients may not be obtained through a balanced and varied diet.[33]

---

[27] Directive 2002/46/EC of the European Parliament and of the Council of 10 June 2002 on the approximation of the laws of the Member States relating to food supplements. [2002] OJ L 183/51.

[28] Article 5(1) and (2).

[29] Article 5(3).

[30] For the purposes of Article 5(1) of Directive 2000/13, products covered by Directive 2002/46 are to be labelled 'food supplement'. Article 6(1) of Directive 2002/46.

[31] Article 6(2) of Directive 2002/46.

[32] Article 6.

[33] Article 7.

'Food supplements' are defined in the directive as being:

foodstuffs the purpose of which is to supplement the normal diet and which are concentrated sources of nutrients or other substances with a nutritional or physiological
effect [marketed in] forms such as capsules, pastilles, tablets, pills and other similar
forms, sachets of powder, ampoules of liquids, drop dispensing bottles, and other similar . . . measured small unit quantities.[34]

Nutrients, for the purposes of the directive, include vitamins and minerals.[35] Only
those vitamins and minerals listed in Annex I to the directive (for example vitamin
C, folic acid, iron) may be used as food supplements.[36] Member States may continue to permit the use of vitamins and minerals not listed in Annex I until the end
of 2009, provided that the substance in question was already in use in this way in
the Community on the date of the entry into force of the directive, and provided
that EFSA has not given an unfavourable opinion on the use of this substance.[37]
Information on vitamins and minerals appearing on the labelling of food supplements should be expressed as a percentage of the reference values mentioned in
the Annex to Directive 1990/496.[38] While Member States may not prohibit or
restrict trade in products that comply with the terms of the directive, provision is
made for resort to Article 30 EC where national rules restrict trade in supplements
that are not regulated under this directive or any acts adopted pursuant to it.[39]

Where a Member State has reason to believe, due to either new information or
a reassessment of existing information, that a food supplement poses a danger to
human health, even though it complies with the terms of the directive, it may temporarily suspend or restrict its use. It must inform the Commission and the
Member States of any action taken in this regard, giving reasons for its decision.
The Commission must then examine this new information, assisted by the
Standing Committee on the Food Chain and Animal Health, and take appropriate
measures on the basis of its findings. Where necessary, the Decision 1999/468 procedure is to be invoked.[40] Any provisions whatsoever that may have an effect on
public health are to be adopted under the terms of this directive after consultation
with EFSA.[41]

---

[34] Article 2(a).
[35] Article 2(b).
[36] Article 4(1).
[37] Article 4(6).
[38] Article 8(3).
[39] Article 11.
[40] Articles 12 and 13.
[41] Article 14.

6.3 NUTRITION POLICY AND FREE MOVEMENT

6.3.1 Nutrition Policy in the Member States

UK White Paper on Public Health

In the light of concern about rising rates of obesity in the UK, a White Paper on Public Health was produced in November 2004.[42] The Paper noted that the promotion of health, communicating information on healthy eating and physical activity were key to meeting this new challenge. Central to achieving this aim would be providing people with the possibility of making informed choices about the food that they eat. Funding campaigns through non-governmental organisations and encouraging industry involvement in providing clear information about healthy eating would be used. In particular, messages relating to health and nutrition would have to be provided in shops and on packaging to ensure that they reach consumers at the time they make purchasing choices. The White Paper noted that consumers had begun to understand the importance of a diet with reduced salt, fat and sugar content. However, they were prevented from making meaningful choices to improve their diet, because the information on labels relating to salt, fat and sugar content was expressed in terms that were difficult to comprehend. As a result, the UK Government had to lobby for changes to current nutrition labelling requirements. It called for their simplification. It also suggested mandatory inclusion of the relevant information on all prepackaged foods. At domestic level, a new system of food labelling was to be devised, by mid-2005, that would 'signpost' fat, salt and sugar levels in order to build on existing nutrition labelling information. The idea was that consumers would be able to identify foodstuffs containing high levels of such substances. The ultimate aim was that by early 2006 a clear, straightforward code system would be in common use, providing obvious information on whether foods were making either a positive or a negative contribution to diet.

The UK Food Standards Agency devised this signpost labelling system in March 2006. Colour-coded information would be provided on the front of food labels indicating levels of fat, saturated fat, sugar and salt. The system would work like traffic lights. Red would indicate a high level of these nutrients. Amber would indicate a medium level, and green a low level. Information would also be provided on the level of nutrients per portion of product. The standards set for the use of each colour followed those set out in the regulation on the use of nutrition and health claims and Codex Alimentarius guidelines. Therefore, in order to be able to use a green shaded area indicating low fat levels, the actual fat content would have to be below 3 g per 100 g or 1.5 g per 100 ml. Medium fat levels were set at between 3 g per 100 g or 1.5 g per 100 ml and 20 g per 100 g or 10 g per 100 ml. High fat

---

[42] UK Public Health White Paper, *Choosing Health: Making Health Choices Easier,* Department of Health, London, 2004.

content, indicated by a red shaded area, was set at over 20 g per 100 g or 10 g per 100 ml. A foodstuff was deemed to be high in salt when actual salt content rises above 1.5 g per 100 g or 100 ml.

There is a major difficulty facing any Member State that devises a scheme using signposting labelling: given the way in which EU rules on free movement have developed, such schemes cannot become compulsory. They must remain voluntary. Member States cannot impose these labelling requirements on producers from other Member States owing to the existence of Article 28 EC, the principle of mutual recognition and the limited scope accorded to Member States on the application of Article 30 EC exceptions. The obvious detriments of this situation are evident in the manner in which the scheme has been applied thus far in the UK. Most major retailers have lent their support to the scheme. However, this support only extends to their own-brand products. It is up to individual producers to follow their lead. In addition to this, each retailer has devised its own variation of the scheme. In July 2006, 14 different signpost label types were identified, none of which were identical to the UK Food Standards Agency model label. Nine of these were developed by the retailers themselves. The other five were devised by major food manufacturers. Some use bar charts to display the colour coded information. Others use pie charts, graphs, logos, lists and symbols. All this meant that, given that the UK is not legally in a position to oblige producers and retailers to adopt a standard form of labelling, as of July 2006, only four months after the introduction of the scheme, the consumer shopping in a UK supermarket could be faced with up to six different types of nutrition signpost labelling. The primary motivation behind the system was to present consumers with clear labelling information on nutrition levels so that they could make informed choices for the benefit of their diet and health.

There is possibly one saving factor in devising a food labelling scheme such as this. The free movement rules that currently scupper the chance of creating a standard label could, in the future, be used to develop a Community-wide nutrition signpost label. If a significant number of Member States were to develop a similar scheme, the Commission might feel compelled to create a harmonised EU label, perhaps something similar to the eco-label.[43] At present, only a handful have such a system in place, such as the UK and Sweden, while several others, for example the Netherlands and Denmark, are considering similar moves.

Folic Acid Fortification

Member States must, of course, take EU free movement rules into consideration when setting national rules on the composition of foodstuffs. As discussed in Chapter 2, the general rule is that any such domestic legislation contravenes Article 28 EC where it inhibits, or has the potential to inhibit, intra-Community

---

[43] Regulation (EC) No 1980/2000 of the European Parliament and of the Council of 17 July 2000 on a revised Community eco-label award scheme. [2000] OJ L 237/1.

food trade. However, in some circumstances Member States may be permitted to introduce such requirements to protect human health. An example of this can be seen in relation to Ireland's proposal to fortify bread with folic acid, with the intention of reducing the number of babies born with neural tube defects, such as spina bifida. Evidence from the USA and Canada suggested that such a policy was effective there. Initially, the Food Safety Authority of Ireland Scientific Committee and Nutrition Sub-Committee recommended the mandatory fortification of flour with folic acid in 2003. The following year, the Irish Government established a National Committee on Folic Acid Fortification, with the Food Safety Authority of Ireland acting as its secretariat, with the aim of reviewing the options that may be available for the fortification of foods in this way.

Research in Ireland demonstrated that a policy of recommending that women of child-bearing age take folic acid supplements was generally ineffective. There were three reasons for this: the high proportion of unplanned pregnancies, inadequate knowledge amongst women about the benefits of taking folic acid, and the cost of purchasing the necessary supplements. Given that 97 per cent of women in Ireland eat bread on a daily basis, it was chosen as the best medium for fortification. Three potential ways of achieving the desired increase in folic acid intake were identified: voluntary addition by producers of breads that would then carry an appropriate health claim on the label, mandatory fortification to ensure that a targeted level of folic acid was present in all breads, and a continuation of the existing policy of health promotion campaigns. A consultative process commenced.

The National Committee on Folic Acid Fortification reported in July 2006 that, following on from the response to calls for consultation, over three quarters of those who expressed an opinion favoured mandatory fortification. It is thus proposed that all bread manufactured or marketed in Ireland, with the exception of some minor bread products, should be fortified with folic acid on a mandatory basis. The Report noted that up to 10 per cent of bread sold in Ireland was imported, primarily from the UK. These products would now, under the proposals, be required to alter their folic acid levels in order to be lawfully marketable in Ireland—seemingly at odds with Community rules on free movement, in particular the decision in *Cassis*. However, rules such as these on mandatory fortification are allowable under EU law where they are justifiable on health protection grounds. The Member State must inform the Commission of any new standards such as this that it sets for food products, advising on the reasons as to why this action is necessary.[44] Proposals for a regulation on the addition of vitamins and minerals to foods make specific provision for Member States to require the mandatory fortification of foods, in particular where dictated by public health considerations that are relevant to the national or regional level.[45] Ireland should

---

[44] Directive 1998/34/EC of the European Parliament and of the Council of 22 June 1998 laying down a procedure for the provision of information in the field of technical standards and regulations. [1998] OJ L 204/37.
[45] Articles 9 and 14 of the Proposal for a Regulation of the European Parliament and of the Council on the addition of vitamins and minerals and of certain other substances to foods. COM (2003) 671.

be able to satisfy a requirement such as this as the data clearly shows that there is a higher than average rate of babies born with neural tube defects in Ireland as compared with other Member States. The evidence presented in support of the mandatory fortification of bread also demonstrated that this approach could greatly assist in preventing the development of such defects by around 70 per cent.

Determining Member State Autonomy in Health Protection Measures

The preceding discussion on UK efforts to combat poor diet and Irish attempts to reduce the number of babies born with neural tube defects illustrates one of the primary deficiencies of EU food law and its interaction with free movement policy. As discussed in detail in Chapter 2, the case law on Article 28 EC makes it quite clear that Member States are not in a position to justify any national measures that restrict intra-Community trade on the ground that it is necessary to improve the nutritional content of food. Claims that it is necessary to protect human health, and therefore capable of justification under the terms of Article 30 EC, are generally dismissed, the Court indicating that these national measures are in fact a disguised restriction on free movement. This results in a situation whereby Member States may only take action where there is an identifiable risk to human health. One example would be the risk that may arise from a folic acid deficiency in pregnant women. However, Member States are precluded from attempting to improve diets in order to counter increasing rates of obesity, which could be achieved by introducing signpost labelling clearly identifying foods harmful to the consumer. In terms of overall human health, the actual impact of chronic consumption of foods causing obesity is much higher than the adverse effects of various food scares. Take Ireland as an example once more. The Report of the National Committee on Folic Acid Food Fortification estimated that each year, between 49 and 93 babies born in Ireland are affected by neural tube defects, one of the highest rates in the EU. Compare this to the facts set out in the launch of a National Taskforce on Obesity in March 2004. There it was stated that obesity accounts for at least 2,500 deaths in Ireland each year, affecting 14 per cent of men and 12 per cent of women, causing diabetes, heart disease, cancer and high blood pressure. Despite this, no legislative action on food labelling or on the compulsory improvement of the nutritional content of food is allowable because of EU rules on the free movement of goods. Such legislation would be contrary to Article 28 EC and its related case law: it would mean that foods lawfully marketed elsewhere in the Community would either be prohibited in Ireland, or would have to be marketed in Ireland with specific labelling, packaging or compositional content. This would be in clear contravention of the principle of mutual recognition.

6.3.2 EU Nutrition Policy

Member States have begun to intervene at the national level to counter increasing obesity rates. As illustrated above, the measures that they can take to implement these policies are limited by EU rules on free movement. However, the EU itself has now embarked upon a programme of measures that could be adopted to assist here. This commenced with the publication of a Green Paper on Promoting Healthy Diets and Physical Activity, in December 2005.[46]

The Paper notes that unhealthy diet, along with a lack of physical activity, are the two main causes of avoidable illness and premature death in the EU. Evidence presented suggests that EU obesity levels have risen by between 10 and 40 per cent over the past 10 years, affecting up to 27 per cent of men and 38 per cent of women.[47] In some Member States, over half the adult population is overweight,[48] rising to over 67 per cent in seven Member States.[49] The number of children affected in the EU is estimated to be rising by over 400,000 a year. One in four children is overweight.[50] The main causes of obesity are recognised as being high intake of energy-dense micronutrient foods and sugar sweetened soft drinks.[51] Dutch studies estimate that excessive intake of trans fatty acids (unsaturated fatty acids produced by partial hydrogenation of vegetable oils) increases the risk of cardiovascular disease by 25 per cent.[52]

Obesity has an economic cost as well. It has been estimated that obesity accounts for at least seven per cent of all health case costs in the EU.[53] This figure probably stands at over 10 per cent in 2006. The UK National Audit Office estimated that obesity in England alone accounted for 18,000,000 sick days from work, 30,000 premature deaths and a cost to the National Health Service in excess of £500 million, in 2001. The wider costs to the economy, including lower productivity and lost output, amount to £2 billion per year.[54] In Ireland, the estimated cost of treating obesity-related illnesses was estimated at €70 million in 2002.[55]

The Green Paper suggests that several courses of action are open to the EU institutions to assist in tackling this epidemic. Practically all involve the provision of advice and encouragement on better diet and lifestyles. These include providing a role for EFSA which, it is stated, 'can make an important contribution to underpinning proposed actions on nutrition . . . with scientific advice and assistance'.[56] It is also stated that consumers should not be misled by advertising for foods with high fat, salt or sugar content. It is suggested that industry self-regulation could be the means of choice here. Improving public knowledge on the relationship

---

[46] Commission Green Paper on Promoting Healthy Diets and Physical Activity: A European Dimension for the Prevention of Overweight, Obesity and Chronic Diseases. COM (2005) 637.

[47] Annex 2 to the Green Paper.

[48] WHO, *European Health Report*, 2002.

[49] Finland, Germany, Greece, Cyprus, Czech Republic, Slovakia and Malta.

[50] International Obesity Task Force, *Childhood Obesity Report*, May 2004.

[51] Annex 2 to the Green Paper.

[52] RIVM Report, *Measuring Dutch Meals: Healthy Diet and Safe Food in the Netherlands*. See also D Mozaffarian *et al*, 'Trans Fatty Acids and Cardiovascular Disease' (2006) 354 *New England Journal of Medicine* 1601.

[53] WHO, *Obesity—Preventing and Managing the Global Epidemic*, 1998 (Technical Report Series No 894).

[54] National Audit Office, *Tackling Obesity in England*, 2001.

[55] Report of the National Taskforce on Obesity, *Obesity—The Policy Challenges*, 2005.

[56] Green Paper, section IV.5.1.

between diet and health, energy intake and output, on diets that lower the risk of chronic diseases, and on healthy choices of food items, is seen to be a prerequisite for the success of any nutrition policy, whether at national or Community level. Therefore 'consistent, coherent, simple and clear messages need to be developed, and disseminated through multiple channels and in forms appropriate to local culture, age and gender'. Children should be 'guided towards healthy behaviours'.

The only references to legislative intervention in the Green Paper are in relation to considering amendments to existing rules on nutrition labelling and on the proposal for a regulation on health and nutrition claims. Key to the proper functioning of this regulation is 'the principle of setting nutrient profiles, in order to prevent foods high in certain nutrients (such as salt, fat, saturated fat and sugars) making claims about their potential nutrition or health benefits'. Finally, it is stated that:

> A coherent and comprehensive approach aimed at making the healthy choices available, affordable and attractive involves taking account of mainstreaming nutrition and physical activity into all relevant policies at local, regional, national and European levels, creating the necessary supporting environments, and developing and applying the appropriate tools for assessing the impact of other policies on nutritional health and physical health.[57]

It is here contended that this 'supporting environment' cannot properly exist given the nature of, and priority accorded to, free movement principles. It is only where the EU has not taken action that the Member States may be able to introduce their own measures to help prevent bad health arising from poor diet.[58] The fact that the Community has not acted, has enabled Denmark to introduce its own rules limiting the amount of trans fatty acids in food. However, the jurisprudence of the Court of Justice indicates that were such national rules to be challenged by an importer into Denmark of food containing a level of trans fatty acids exceeding the permitted level, Danish law would be declared contrary to Article 28 EC. As discussed in Chapter 2, national rules designed to improve the nutritional content of food are not normally deemed justifiable under the terms of Article 30 EC, on health protection grounds.[59]

6.4 CONCLUSION

The most serious health concern relating to food in the European Union is obesity. The first step in tackling this problem is to get consumers to alter their diet.

---

[57] Ibid, section V.8.1.

[58] See, in particular, Case 174/1982, *Criminal proceedings against Sandoz BV* [1983] ECR 2445, para 16; Case 178/1984, *Commission v Germany* (bier) [1987] ECR 1227, paras 28 and 41; Case C-24/2000, *Commission v France* (fortified foods-'Red Bull') [2004] ECR I-1277, para 49.

[59] See, in particular, Case 216/1984, *Commission v France* (milk substitutes) [1988] ECR 793, para 15; Case 274/1987, *Commission v Germany* (meat products) [1989] ECR 229, para 10; Case-17/1993, *Criminal proceedings against Van der Veldt* [1994] ECR I-3537, paras 17–21; Case C-123/2000, *Criminal proceedings against Christina Bellamy and English Shop Wholesale SA* [2001] ECR I-2745, para 12.

However, many appear unwilling to do so. Where Member States want to intervene, in order to assist in behavioural change, they are prevented from doing so by EU law. There is no shortage at national level of initiatives designed to combat dietary excesses and deficiencies. Most revolve around providing information and education, rather than compelling the food industry to ensure that its products are of sufficient nutritional value, or if not, to clarify the position for the consumer. It is only the latter approach that can have any real and lasting impact. The UK system of signpost labelling, for example, has become unworkable and impractical because it cannot be standardised. Efforts to create clarity for consumers consequently create more confusion.[60]

There are two main reasons why Member States cannot be more interventionist when it comes to dealing with a health crisis like obesity. The first is that the manner in which the Article 28 EC jurisprudence on measures equivalent to quantitative restrictions on imports prevents national authorities maintaining laws to compel improvements to the nutritional content of food. This is not deemed to be a legitimate human health-based exception to the general rule on free movement. Second, the fact that nutrition labelling rules already exist at Community level prevents the Member States from obliging producers to adopt any alternative system for providing this type of information. This is still so, despite the fact that the Community nutrition label is only obligatory for foodstuffs where a health or nutrition claim is made. All other products need not carry this data at all. The present method for displaying this information is also deemed to be unclear to the average consumer. The Community institutions have proved unwilling to adopt measures that could assist the Member States in any efforts that they wish to make in this regard. The Commission Green Paper makes reference to the regulation on nutrition and health claims, and in particular how the nutrient profiles will prevent unhealthy foods from making dishonest health claims. Subsequently, through the alterations to the proposal for this legislation via the Article 251 EC procedure, its content has now been altered by the Council and the Parliament. This system of profiling is virtually meaningless given that a product may now be high, even very high, in one of the deadly constituents of food (fat, saturated fat, sugar or salt) and still claim to be of high nutritional value or good for human health. Until Member States are provided with more flexibility to act, or until sufficient and meaningful harmonised standards are introduced at Community level, the obesity crisis, by far the most serious food-related crisis to affect the EU since its inception, affecting infinitely more consumers than BSE ever has, is unlikely to be averted.

---

[60] Recent calls for additional labelling disclosures about trans fatty acid content in food may not therefore present the best method of alerting consumers to their presence in foodstuffs. See R Clarke and S Lewington, 'Trans Fatty Acids and Coronary Heart Disease' (2006) 333 *British Medical Journal* 214. It is not necessarily the information that is disclosed that is important. It may, however, be the manner in which it is disclosed that really affects consumer decision-making. For more on this see JC Kozup *et al*, 'The Provision of Trans Fat Information and its Interaction with Consumer Knowledge' (2006) 40 *Journal of Consumer Affairs* 163 where it is argued that without accompanying consumer education, new labelling regulations on the presence of trans fats may be limited.

7

Contemporary Considerations for EU Food Law

7.1 INTRODUCTION

THE ARGUMENT PRESENTED thus far has contended that the manner in which Community law on the free movement of goods has developed, frustrates the proper protection by Member States of human health and consumers. This situation persists despite the fact that the EC Treaty clearly leaves a large degree of competence to the Member States in these matters. Article 30 EC is designed to enable the Member States to breach free movement rules in order, among other things, to protect human health. Article 152 EC states that Community action on health protection is designed to complement national policies.[1] Article 153 EC enables the Community to contribute to ensuring that consumers are protected by measures which support and supplement the policies of the Member States. The development of the mandatory requirements by the Court in *Cassis* should also assist in this regard.

In addition to the consideration outlined above, EU food law must also respond to changes to the manner in which food is produced and alterations to consumer preferences. Attempts to deal with advancements in these areas at Community level have not always proved successful. Given that consumers in the different Member States are not all likely to want the same things at the same time, and given that there will always be tension between the economic needs of producers and the reluctance of consumers to accept new innovations in the technology and science of producing food, Community law which seeks to standardise rules on these matters across 25 Member States simultaneously will generally prove to be a difficult task.

7.2 INNOVATION IN FOOD PRODUCTION: GENETIC MODIFICATION

Genetically modified organisms (gmos) are, to give them their legal definition, any life form, with the exception of human beings, in which the genetic material has

---

[1] For further discussion on the division of competences under Article 152 EC see T Hervey, 'Community and National Competence in Health after *Tobacco Advertising*' (2001) 38 *Common Market Law Review* 1421.

been altered in a way that does not occur by natural reproduction.[2] There are two distinct, yet related, arguments surrounding the introduction of genetic modification technology. The first relates to environmental concerns. In general terms, environmentalists are anxious about the type of damage that may be caused by alterations to agricultural methods used in genetic modification techniques, such as the potential impact on farmland wildlife of herbicide use associated with genetically modified crops. United Kingdom government-backed farm-scale trials on growing such crops led to mixed evidence on the potential harm of genetic modification techniques. Initial results suggested that growing genetically modified beet and rape was less environmentally friendly than growing their conventional counterparts. In contrast, growing genetically modified herbicide-tolerant maize was better for many groups of wildlife than conventional maize.[3] There were more weeds in and around these maize crops, more butterflies and bees around at certain times of the year, and more weed seeds providing a food source for birds. The most recent studies now suggest that the cultivation of genetically modified herbicide-tolerant sugar beet crops can also clearly benefit the environment in similar ways.[4]

The second key interest regarding the cultivation of genetically modified crops, the one with which this book is primarily concerned, is that their presence in human foodstuffs and animal feed may have detrimental effects on human health. The science supporting such fears remains mixed, although there is an increasing body of evidence suggesting that there is little or no potential harm in consuming

---

[2] Article 2(2) of Directive 2001/18/EC of the European Parliament and of the Council of 12 March 2001 on the deliberate release into the environment of genetically modified organisms and replacing Council Directive 1990/220/EEC. [2001] OJ L 106/1. For further discussion, see also Chapter 9 of M Lee, *EU Environmental Law: Challenges, Change and Decision-Making* (Oxford, Hart Publishing, 2005).

[3] For a scientific evaluation of these findings see DR Brooks *et al*, 'Invertebrate Responses to the Management of Genetically Modified Herbicide-tolerant and Conventional Spring Crops' (2003) 358 *Philosophical Transactions of the Royal Society* 1847; GT Champion *et al*, 'Crop Management and Agronomic Context of the Farm Scale Evaluations of Genetically Modified Herbicide-tolerant Crops' (2003) 358 *Philosophical Transactions of the Royal Society* 1801; AJ Haughton *et al*, 'Invertebrate Responses to the Management of Genetically Modified Herbicide-tolerant and Conventional Spring Crops' (2003) 358 *Philosophical Transactions of the Royal Society* 1863; C Hawes *et al*, 'Responses of Plants and Invertebrate Trophic Groups to Contrasting Herbicide Regimes in the Farm Scale Evaluations of Genetically Modified Herbicide-tolerant Crops' (2003) 358 *Philosophical Transactions of the Royal Society* 1899; MS Heard *et al*, 'Weeds in Fields with Contrasting Conventional and Genetically Modified Herbicide-tolerant Crops' (2003) 358 *Philosophical Transactions of the Royal Society* 1819; DB Roy *et al*, 'Invertebrates and Vegetation of Field Margins Adjacent to Crops Subject to Contrasting Herbicide Regimes in the Farm Scale Evaluations of Genetically Modified Herbicide-tolerant Crops' (2003) 358 *Philosophical Transactions of the Royal Society* 1879. A summary of the scientific evaluations is available in LG Firbank *et al*, 'The Implications of Spring-sown Genetically Modified Herbicide-tolerant Crops for Farmland Biodiversity: A Commentary on the Farm Scale Evaluations of Spring Sown Crops', www.defra.gov.uk/environmant/gm/fse/results/fse-commentary.pdf. The data from these evaluations is available at www.farmscale.org.uk.

[4] MJ May *et al*, 'Management of Genetically Modified Herbicide-tolerant Sugar Beet for Spring and Autumn Environmental Benefit' (2005) 272 *Proceedings of the Royal Society: Biological Sciences* 111. This research demonstrates that the use of the herbicides could increase weed seed production by up to 16 times its normal level as compared to conventional systems, thus providing birds with an abundant autumn food source.

genetically modified food.[5] Despite this, consumer groups, by and large, remain firmly opposed to the presence of genetically altered ingredients in their food-stuffs. This is especially so since 1999, when it was suggested that genetically mod-ified potatoes might be toxic to laboratory rats.[6] The subsequent public outcry led to the introduction of an unofficial moratorium on the growth and importation of genetically modified crops in the European Union, which was not lifted until new regulations were introduced in late 2003.[7] This action has also been the subject of dispute at WTO level.

7.2.1 GMO Regulatory Framework

European Union regulators have sought to appease consumer concerns about the use of genetic modification techniques in food production by introducing legal controls over the placing of these products on the market, and by ensuring that consumers are made fully aware of their presence in food products. The former is managed through notification and authorisation procedures, the latter by the introduction of clear labelling requirements.

The legal framework designed to control the use of genetic modification in food production is now based primarily on four instruments, three regulations and a directive. The first gmo directives were introduced in 1990, setting a framework of rules for their contained use in laboratories and their deliberate release onto the

[5] See, for example, S Roller, 'Genetically Modified Foods: Threat or Opportunity?' (2001) 39 *Food Technology and Biotechnology* 259; R Edwards, 'We Are No Nearer to Knowing if Genetically Modified Food is Safe' (2000) 165 (2228) *New Scientist* 5; L Donaldson and R May, *Health Implications of Genetically Modified Foods* (London, Department of Health, 1999); Institute of Food Science and Technology, *Genetic Modification and Food* (London, IFST, 1999).

[6] SWB Ewen and A Pusztai, 'Effect of Diets Containing Genetically Modified Potatoes Expressing Galanthus Nivalis Lectin on Small Rat Intestine' (1999) 354 *The Lancet* 1353. Eurobarometer surveys demonstrate that there is a high level of concern amongst consumers over the safety of genetically mod-ified food. Almost two thirds of respondents are concerned about the risks associated with genetically modified food (Eurobarometer 1997), nearly three quarters favour clear labelling of genetically modi-fied food (Eurobarometer 1997), and more than half claim that they are willing to pay more for non-genetically modified food (Eurobarometer 2000). Other surveys show similar concerns, for example, a March 1997 survey conducted by the University of Lancaster for Unilever finds 'significant unease about the technology as a whole . . . and much such unease is latent rather than explicit'; an August 1997 survey conducted by Market Measures Ltd for J Sainsbury plc reveals that UK consumers do not favour genetically modified foods because they are 'unnatural'; over half of those aware of genetically engineered food said they would 'probably not' or 'definitely not' buy such food (AgBiotechNet 1997); a March 1998 Gallup poll commissioned by Iceland Foods plc showed that 63 per cent of respondents who were aware of genetically modified food had reservations; a MORI poll indicated a lower degree of distrust of genetically engineered food in Britain where 53 per cent of respondents claimed that they would not eat genetically engineered food, against 63 per cent of Danes, 65 per cent of Italians and Dutch, 77 per cent of French and 78 per cent of Swedes (www.centerfoodsafety.org/facts&issues/polls.htm).

[7] Regulation (EC) No 1829/2003 of the European Parliament and of the Council of 22 September 2003 on genetically modified food and feed. [2003] OJ L 268/1: Regulation (EC) No 1830/2003 of the European Parliament and of the Council of 22 September 2003 concerning the traceability and labelling of genetically modified organisms and the traceability of food and feed products produced from genetically modified organisms and amending Directive 2001/18/EC. [2003] OJ L 268/24.

marketplace.[8] This was followed by a novel foods regulation in 1997,[9] and, after a series of amendments primarily designed to close loopholes that had allowed certain genetically modified foods to escape the key regulatory provisions, a new deliberate directive was introduced in 2001.[10] Deeming this to be an insufficient response to the circumstances that had led to the need to introduce a moratorium, two regulations were devised and brought into force in 2003.[11] Of these, the original contained use directive, the novel foods regulation, the new deliberate release directive and the two new regulations on genetically modified food and feed and on traceability and labelling now form the European Union legal framework for the regulation of genetic modification processes in food production and marketing.

Novel Foods Regulation

Novel foods are those which have not previously been used for human consumption to any significant degree within the Community, generally due to an alteration in their genetic material or molecular structure, including foods and ingredients containing or consisting of, or produced from but not containing, gmos.[12] The regulation does not apply to additives or flavourings already subject to Community legislation,[13] provided that there are corresponding safety standards laid down therein.[14] The primary purpose of the regulation is to ensure that any novel food does not harm or mislead consumers in any way, including ensuring that such foods do not differ from the foods that they are intended to replace to such an extent that the normal consumption of the novel food would be nutritionally disadvantageous for the consumer.[15] This is to be ensured primarily by an application and notification procedure for the placing of novel foods on the market, which should disclose details of the studies and assessment of compliance

---

[8] Council Directive 1990/219/EEC of 23 April 1990 on the contained use of genetically modified micro-organisms. [1990] OJ L 117/1; Council Directive 1990/220/EEC on the deliberate release into the environment of genetically modified organisms. [1990] OJ L 117/15.

[9] European Parliament and Council Regulation (EC) No 258/1997 of 27 January 1997 concerning novel foods and novel food ingredients. [1997] OJ L 43/1.

[10] Directive 2001/18/EC of the European Parliament and of the Council of 12 March 2001 on the deliberate release into the environment of genetically modified organisms and replacing Council Directive 1990/220/EEC. [2001] OJ L 106/1.

[11] Regulation (EC) No 1829/2003 of the European Parliament and of the Council of 22 September 2003 on genetically modified food and feed. [2003] OJ L 268/1; Regulation (EC) No 1830/2003 of the European Parliament and of the Council of 22 September 2003 concerning the traceability and labelling of genetically modified organisms and the traceability of food and feed products produced from genetically modified organisms and amending Directive 2001/18/EC. [2003] OJ L 268/24.

[12] Article 1(2).

[13] Such as Council Directive 1989/107/EEC of 21 December 1988 on the approximation of the laws of the Member States concerning food additives authorised for use in foodstuffs intended for human consumption. [1989] OJ L 40/27; Council Directive 1988/388/EEC of 22 June 1988 on the approximation of the laws of the Member States relating to flavourings for use in foodstuffs and to source materials for their production. [1988] OJ L 184/61.

[14] Article 2(2) of the Novel Foods Regulation.

[15] Article 3(1).

with the safety standards carried out, as set down in the regulation.[16] An additional assessment of adherence may be required in some circumstances.[17] After an initial assessment report is drafted and made available, Member States and the Commission may object to the marketing of the food or ingredient concerned. Objections may also be made regarding the proposed labelling or presentation of the novel food.[18] Where this happens, the Commission is to seek the opinion of the Committee on the Food Chain and Animal Health (formerly the Standing Committee for Foodstuffs) on the measures that it proposes to take to counter any objections. Where the Commission and Committee cannot agree on the proposed measures, the matter is to be referred to the Council to decide what measures to take.[19]

The regulation sets out specific labelling requirements for novel foods, beyond those normally required by Community legislation.[20] These are designed to inform the consumer about any characteristic or food property such as composition or nutritional value which makes a novel food different to similar existing foods.[21] A novel food is deemed to differ from its conventional counterpart where scientific assessment demonstrates that the characteristics of the foodstuff vary to a certain degree from the natural variety. Where this is the case, the labelling is to specify which characteristics have been modified and the method by which those characteristics were modified, indicating clearly the presence in the novel food of this altering material including, where necessary, the presence of a gmo.[22]

Finally, where a Member State has grounds to consider that a novel food may endanger human health, even where it has been introduced in compliance with all relevant procedures, that State may suspend trade in, or prevent use of, the food. This power of suspension or prevention is referred to as the 'safeguard clause'. The Commission must be immediately informed of any such action, and the reasons underlying such a decision should be disclosed. The Commission will then consider these grounds and, along with the Committee on the Food Chain and Animal Health, make a decision on the appropriate measures to be taken in the circumstances.[23]

---

[16] Articles 4, 5, 6 and 7. Fifty-three applications for approval under the terms of Regulation 258/1997 were made between May 1997 and May 2004. Two of these applications were refused. Source: http://ec.europa.eu/food/food/biotechnology/novelfood/index_en.htm.

[17] Article 6(3).

[18] Article 6(4).

[19] Article 13.

[20] In particular, Directive 2000/13/EC of the European Parliament and of the Council of 20 March 2000 on the approximation of the laws of the Member States relating to the labelling, presentation and advertising of foodstuffs. [2000] OJ L 109/29.

[21] Article 8.

[22] Article 8(1).

[23] Article 12.

Deliberate Release Directive

The original deliberate release directive of 1990 presented a very general framework for the regulation of genetically modified food in the European Union.[24] It set out the definition for gmos,[25] specified the circumstances in which they could be used,[26] and established a notification system for their use for research purposes[27] and for their being placed on the market.[28] The primary failing of the directive, as discussed below, was that it failed to set any specific labelling requirements for genetically modified food. It merely stated that where such a product was placed on the market, notification of this was to include information on the proposed labelling, which should contain, at least in summarised form, details of the name of the product and any gmos contained therein, the name of the manufacturer, any conditions of use, and instructions for storage or handling.[29] This was insufficient to satisfy the impending levels of unrest about the use of genetic modification in food production that was to come a few years later.

The new deliberate release directive was introduced in 2001 to address the shortcomings of its predecessor.[30] It is clear from the outset that Directive 2001/18 is largely moulded by a vastly increased consideration for consumer concerns, an input that was largely missing from the provisions of Directive 1990/220. Any measures taken in relation to genetically modified food are now to be based firmly around full use of the precautionary principle, from both an environmental and a human health protection perspective.[31] There is to be closer scrutiny of potential adverse health effects, with Member States and the Commission being compelled to assess any such possible dangers on a case by case basis.[32] There is to be greater enforcement and monitoring of compliance with the provisions of the directive at national level, and the course of action to be taken in the event of non-compliance is made much more explicit.[33] Where a foodstuff makes its way onto the marketplace without first adhering to all the terms of the legislation it is to be immediately withdrawn and consumers, the Commission and the other Member States are to be immediately informed about this.[34] The directive also paved the way

---

[24] Council Directive 1990/220/EEC on the deliberate release into the environment of genetically modified organisms. [1990] OJ L 117/15.

[25] Article 2(2).

[26] Article 15 in conjunction with compliance with Articles 5 to 14 of the Directive.

[27] Articles 5 and 6 and Annex II.

[28] Articles 11 and 12 and Annex II.

[29] Annex III to Directive 1990/220/EEC.

[30] Directive 2001/18/EC of the European Parliament and of the Council of 12 March 2001 on the deliberate release into the environment of genetically modified organisms and replacing Council Directive 1990/220/EEC. [2001] OJ L 106.

[31] Article 4(1). For further discussion on the use of the precautionary approach in genetic modification regulation see ZK Forsman, 'Community Regulation of Genetically Modified Organisms: A Difficult Relationship between Law and Science' (2004) 10 *European Law Journal* 580.

[32] Article 4(3).

[33] Article 4(5).

[34] *Ibid.*

for the implementation of the Cartagena Protocol on Biosafety into Community law.[35]

The compulsory notification procedure is set out in much more detail in Directive 2001/18 than that specified when the procedure was first promulgated in 1990. Information must be submitted regarding the results of any research into the use of the gmo, the environmental risk assessment, conditions of use, continued safety monitoring plans, the proposed packaging of the product, and proposed time limitations for the validity of the consent to run, for up to a maximum of 10 years.[36] Most importantly, the directive makes it quite clear that any proposal for the labelling of genetically modified foods must demonstrate that it will be stated clearly on the label, or on an accompanying document, that 'this product contains genetically modified organisms'.[37] Member States are to ensure that the labelling and packaging of genetically modified foods comply fully with these requirements.[38] The directive specifies that while, in conformity with the general principles of Community law, it is left to the discretion of the Member States to determine what penalties to impose where the national implementing provisions are deemed to have been breached, they are to offer an 'effective, proportionate and dissuasive' remedy.[39] Member States may also temporarily prohibit the sale of a genetically modified food where they have detailed grounds for considering that it may pose a danger to human health.[40] Any such move would have to be supported by a risk assessment meeting the required standards of independence, excellence and transparency.

Genetically Modified Food and Feed Regulation

The general genetically modified food and feed regulation[41] is, according to Article 1, tied to the new general principles of EU food law established by Regulation 178/2002.[42] Primarily, it is to provide the basis for ensuring a high level of protection of human life and health, animal health and welfare, environment and consumer interests in relation to genetically modified food and feed, whilst also ensuring the effective functioning of the internal market. In order to achieve this, the general genetically modified food and feed regulation sets out a detailed authorisation procedure for the use of these products to be applied in each of the Member States. It also contains provisions on labelling requirements, thus

[35] Article 32.
[36] Article 13(2).
[37] Article 13(2)(f).
[38] Article 21(1).
[39] Article 33.
[40] Article 23(1).
[41] Regulation (EC) No 1829/2003 of the European Parliament and of the Council of 22 September 2003 on genetically modified food and feed. [2003] OJ L 268/1.
[42] Regulation (EC) No 178/2002 of the European Parliament and of the Council of 28 January 2002 laying down the general principles and requirements of food law, establishing the European Food Safety Authority and laying down procedures in matters of food safety. [2002] OJ L 31/1.

meaning that the same or similar labelling requirements for genetically modified food are stipulated in three linked pieces of Community secondary legislation. This unnecessary duplication has added to the avoidable complications that already surround European Union genetically modified food labelling requirements. This is discussed in more detail below.

Two distinct forms of authorisation procedure are set by the general genetically modified food and feed regulation, one for food intended for human consumption and one for animal feed. Where a product is likely to be used as both food and feed, then one single application will be considered.[43] Food containing or consisting of, or food produced from, a gmo may only apply for authorisation if it does not have adverse effects on human health, animal health or the environment; if it does not mislead the consumer in any way; and if it does not differ in any way from the food which it is intended to replace to such an extent that its normal consumption would be nutritionally disadvantageous.[44] Obviously enough, under the terms of the regulation, no genetically modified food can be marketed in the EU unless it has received authorisation, following a clear demonstration that the product is safe.[45] This authorisation procedure applies to all products coming within the scope of the regulation. The labelling requirements set out therein, as well as those prescribed by the deliberate release directive and the labelling and traceability regulation, however, only apply to foodstuffs that actually contain or consist of a gmo. Food produced from but not containing a gmo in the finished product is exempt from all the additional labelling requirements set for such products.

The authorisation procedure is as follows. The application is sent to the national competent authority of a Member State, for example the Department for Environment Food and Rural Affairs (DEFRA) in the United Kingdom or the Environmental Protection Agency (EPA) in Ireland. The national authority must acknowledge receipt of the application in writing within 14 days of its receipt. This information is then passed on to the European Food Safety Authority, which in turn informs the other Member States and the Commission about the application and its content. A summary of this dossier is also to be made available to the public. The application itself should include information about the applicant; the name of the food; a detailed description of the method of production; copies of the relevant studies that have been carried out, in particular independent peer-reviewed studies; data and analysis demonstrating that the characteristics of the food are not different from those of its conventional counterpart, having regard to the accepted limits of natural variations of such characteristics; a proposal for the labelling of the food; a reasoned statement that the food does not give rise to ethical or religious concerns; conditions for use and handling; methods for the detection, sampling and identification of the modification processes that the food

---

[43] Article 27.
[44] Article 4(1).
[45] Article 4(2) and (3).

has undergone; samples of the food; proposals for post-market monitoring regarding use of the food for human consumption; and a summary of the dossier in a standardised form. This authorisation procedure applies to all genetically modified food, both that containing or consisting of a gmo and that produced from but not ultimately containing a gmo. Applications for authorisation to use foods containing or consisting of a gmo should also be accompanied by the complete technical dossier supplying the information required by Annexes III and IV to Directive 2001/18, such as information on any previous use of the gmo, proposed packaging and proposed measures to be taken in the event of misuse, and information and conclusions about the environmental risk assessment carried out in accordance with the principles set out in Annex II to Directive 2001/18, as well as a plan for monitoring the effects of the cultivation of the genetically modified food in question on the environment, as prescribed by Annex VII to the deliberate release directive.[46]

The European Food Safety Authority is required to give an opinion on the merits of the application for authorisation, generally within six months of its receipt. Supplementary information may be requested. After a detailed examination of the application, which may involve the Authority calling upon food assessment bodies within the Member States to evaluate the safety of the genetically modified food in question, the opinion is forwarded to the Commission, the Member States and the applicant. This opinion is also to be made available to the public, who in turn have 30 days to submit comments on its content to the Commission.[47]

Within three months of receiving the opinion of the European Food Safety Authority, the Commission is to submit a draft of the decision to be taken in respect of the application to the Standing Committee on the Food Chain and Animal Health.[48] This decision is to be based upon the opinion of the Authority, other relevant provisions of Community law (in particular the free movement of goods and human health, consumer and environmental protection), and any other relevant factors. The Commission must provide a detailed explanation where this decision differs from the opinion of the European Food Safety Authority. The applicant is then to be informed of the outcome, which is also to be published in the Official Journal of the European Union. Authorisations granted are entered into a register, are valid for 10 years, are renewable, and are fully valid throughout the EU.[49] Products already placed on the market under the terms of the original deliberate release directive or the novel foods regulation can continue to be marketed as such.[50]

---

[46] Article 5.
[47] Article 6.
[48] As established by Article 58 of Regulation (EC) No 178/2002.
[49] Article 7. For further discussion on this procedure see E Brosset, 'The Prior Authorisation Procedure Adopted for the Deliberate Release into the Environment of Genetically Modified Organisms: The Complexities of Balancing Community and National Competences' (2004) 10 European Law Journal 555.
[50] Article 8.

A similar authorisation procedure is established for genetically modified animal feed.[51] Labelling requirements are also set out here. Genetically modified animal feed must carry a statement on the labelling indicating this, either as a statement following the name of the feed or in a footnote to the list of feed, printed in a font the same size as text appearing elsewhere on the label. Any characteristics that render the genetically modified feed different from its conventional counterpart must also be disclosed. Where no conventional counterpart exists, information about the nature and characteristics of the feed must appear on the label.[52]

Labelling and Traceability Regulation

The 2003 Labelling and Traceability Regulation both amends aspects of the deliberate release directive labelling regime and introduces a new framework for ensuring that genetically modified foods and ingredients can be traced at all stages of the food production process.[53] The idea behind the introduction of new traceability requirements is to facilitate the withdrawal of products where unforeseen adverse effects on human health, animal health or the environment are established and to ensure the implementation of other precautionary-based risk management measures where necessary.[54] Traceability requirements for food produced from gmos should also assist in ensuring the accuracy of the labelling on such products. The regulation also applies to genetically modified animal feed.[55]

The traceability requirements set out in the regulation for genetically modified food and feed are relatively uncomplicated. It is to be made clear in writing by the operator passing the product on at the initial stage of production, that the product consists of or contains a gmo. This statement is to be accompanied by a 'unique identifier' that has been assigned to the product.[56] The unique identifier is a numeric or alphanumeric code which identifies the gmo and enables specific information pertinent to gmos of that type to be retrieved.[57] This information is then to be passed on to operators at all subsequent stages of the production and marketing process.[58] All operators involved in this food production and marketing chain are to ensure that they retain this information, along with details of those to whom the products were passed, for five years following each transaction.[59]

---

[51] Articles 17–20.

[52] Article 25.

[53] Regulation (EC) No 1830/2003 of the European Parliament and of the Council of 22 September 2003 concerning the traceability and labelling of genetically modified organisms and amending Directive 2001/18/EC. [2003] OJ L 268/24.

[54] Preamble to Regulation 1830/2003.

[55] Article 2(1).

[56] Article 4(1).

[57] Article 3. The Commission, under the terms of Article 8 of the Regulation, is to develop a system for the assignment of unique identifiers to genetically modified organisms, taking account of any relevant developments in international fora, such as the Codex Alimentarius Commission.

[58] Article 4(2).

[59] Article 4(4).

The labelling requirements set out in the regulation clear up some of the unnecessary ambiguity surrounding the stipulations of Articles 13 and 21 of Directive 2001/18. Although the deliberate release directive makes it clear that products consisting of or containing gmos must state that 'this product contains genetically modified organisms' it does so in a circuitous way, prescribing that the required notification should indicate that such labelling should appear, but nowhere does it state explicitly that it must appear on the labelling of such products. Article 6 of the labelling and traceability regulation prescribes that for products consisting of or containing gmos, operators are to ensure that these words appear on the label of prepackaged products. For non-prepackaged products offered for sale to the final consumer this information must appear either on, or in connection with, the display of the product. These provisions on labelling and traceability do not apply to products that contain only a trace of a gmo, below the threshold levels prescribed by the deliberate release directive and the general genetically modified food regulation.[60] Neither do they apply to foods produced from, but not containing, a gmo.

Challenging the GMO Regulatory Framework: Labelling Difficulties

Overall, EU food labelling requirements for genetically modified food are unnecessarily piecemeal and complex. Despite repeated efforts to remedy the situation, it has been this way since the introduction of the original deliberate release directive in 1990.[61] The original deliberate release directive prescribed that prior to the placing of a gmo on the market, either as or in a product, notification of this had to be submitted to the competent authority in the respective Member State.[62] This had to include details of the proposed labelling of the product, which should give, as a minimum, information relating to the name of the product and any gmos contained therein, the manufacturer, conditions of use, measures to be taken in the event of misuse and specific recommendations for storage or handling.[63] The deliberate release directive was later amended, setting labelling requirements for foodstuffs produced using a mixture of genetically modified and non-genetically modified substances.[64] It was now compulsory for the labels on such products to state that there was a possibility that they may contain gmos.[65]

---

[60] Article 4. These threshold levels are set out in Articles 21(2) and 21(3) of Directive 2001/18 and Articles 12, 24 and 47 of Regulation 1829/2003. Regulation 1829/2003 sets this level at 0.5%.

[61] Council Directive 1990/220/EEC on the deliberate release into the environment of genetically modified organisms. [1990] OJ L 117/15. A directive was also introduced at the same time on the conducting of laboratory research into the use of genetically modified micro-organisms. Council Directive 90/219/EEC of 23 April 1990 on the contained use of genetically modified micro-organisms. [1990] OJ L 117/1. While Directive 1990/220 has since been replaced, Directive 1990/219 is still in force.

[62] Article 11(1).

[63] Annex III (B)(5) to Directive 1990/220/EEC.

[64] Commission Directive 1997/35/EC of 18 June 1997 adapting to technical progress for the second time Council Directive 1990/220/EEC on the deliberate release into the environment of genetically modified organisms. [1997] OJ L 169/72.

[65] Annex to Directive 1997/35/EC.

Additional labelling requirements were introduced for novel foods and novel food ingredients in 1997.[66] It soon became apparent, however, that major shortcomings were emerging in the evolving body of genetically modified food labelling legislation. In particular, a new regulation had to be introduced to ensure that the same labelling rules would apply to foods and ingredients placed on the market both prior to and after the entry into force of the novel foods regulation.[67] This was deemed necessary not only to prevent the acquisition of competitive advantages, but also because the original deliberate release directive did not set out any safety grounds upon which products containing either genetically modified soya or genetically modified maize would be brought within the scope of the novel foods regulation and would thus be subject to the additional labelling requirements prescribed by that regulation.[68] Some Member States had introduced their own measures to deal with this failing. Such local action, it was noted, would be liable to impede the free movement of food and thereby adversely affect the proper functioning of the common market.[69]

The regulation introduced to remedy the discrepancy that had enabled products containing genetically modified soya or genetically modified maize to escape the labelling requirements set by the novel foods regulation fell some way short of achieving that aim.[70] The general labelling rules laid down by the regulation did not clarify which soya and maize products would have to be labelled, or how they were to be labelled. Another new regulation, laying down more detailed rules, was thus introduced in 1998 in an attempt to conclusively allay any outstanding concerns regarding the labelling of these foodstuffs.[71] However, under the terms of this new regulation the only products that were required to display a clear statement on the label that they contained genetically modified soya or genetically modified maize were those that were not required to include a list of ingredients

---

[66] European Parliament and Council Regulation (EC) No 258/1997 of 27 January 1997 concerning novel foods and novel food ingredients. [1997] OJ L 43/1.

[67] Commission Regulation (EC) No 1813/1997 of 19 September 1997 concerning the compulsory indication on the labelling of certain foodstuffs produced from genetically modified organisms of particulars other than those provided for in Directive 1979/112/EEC. [1997] OJ L 257/7.

[68] Consent had originally been granted for the placing of these two foodstuffs on the market by Commission Decision 1996/281/EC of 3 April 1996 concerning the placing on the market of genetically modified soya beans (Glycine max L) with increased tolerance to the herbicide glyphosate, pursuant to Council Directive 1990/220/EEC. [1996] OJ L 107/10; Commission Decision 1997/98/EC of 23 January 1997 concerning the placing on the market of genetically modified maize with the combined modification for insecticidal properties conferred by the Bt-endotoxin gene and increased tolerance to the herbicide glufosinate ammonium pursuant to Council Directive 1990/220/EEC. [1997] OJ L 31/69.

[69] Preamble to Commission Regulation (EC) No 1813/1997.

[70] Commission Regulation (EC) No 1813/1997.

[71] Council Regulation (EC) No 1139/1998 of 26 May 1998 concerning the compulsory indication on the labelling of certain foodstuffs produced from genetically modified organisms of particulars other than those provided for in Directive 1979/112/EEC. [1998] OJ L 159/4. The stated aim of Regulation (EC) No 1139/1998 was to require that foodstuffs containing genetically modified soya beans or genetically modified maize would have to be clearly labelled as such. The statement 'produced from genetically modified soya' or 'produced from genetically modified maize', as appropriate, was to appear immediately after the name of the ingredient concerned. Article 2(3)(a).

on the label at all.[72] Under the terms of the framework food labelling directive[73] the following foodstuffs do not have to display a list of ingredients on the label: untreated fresh fruit and vegetables, carbonated water, fermentation vinegars, cheese, butter, fermented milk and cream, and products consisting of a single ingredient.[74] These are products that are highly unlikely to contain either genetically modified soya or genetically modified maize. Products actually containing the genetically modified ingredients only had to state that they contained these ingredients in the listing itself or as a footnote to it, and not in a prominent position on the front of the label as was previously considered necessary.

The shortcomings of the 1998 soya and maize regulation were readily evident. By October of that year, Austria, dissatisfied with the Community provisions, had notified the Commission that it intended to issue a decree requiring that where a foodstuff contained any additives or flavourings produced by genetic engineering, this would have to be clearly indicated on the label. In response, the Commission took action on two fronts. First, it issued a decision requiring Austria to suspend the adoption of its draft decree on the matter.[75] Second, it consulted with the other Member States regarding the Austrian proposal through the Standing Committee on Foodstuffs. It was recognised, as a result of this consultation, that consumers should be informed about the use of additives or flavourings that have been genetically modified in any way. The 1998 soya and maize regulation was later amended to allow foodstuffs containing up to one per cent of ingredients derived from gmos to be marketed without any indication of this on the label, provided that this presence is adventitious.[76] A regulation was also introduced, setting additional labelling requirements for foodstuffs containing genetically modified additives or flavourings.[77] Any foodstuff containing these ingredients must be labelled as such, either in the list of ingredients itself, or as a prominently displayed footnote to this list.[78]

---

[72] Article 2(3)(b) of Regulation 1139/1998.

[73] Council Directive 1979/112/EEC of 18 December 1978 on the approximation of the laws of the Member States relating to the labelling, presentation and advertising of foodstuffs for sale to the ultimate consumer. [1979] OJ L 33/1. This Directive has since been replaced by Directive 2000/13/EC of the European Parliament and of the Council of 20 March 2000 on the approximation of the laws of the Member States relating to the labelling, presentation and advertising of foodstuffs. [2000] OJ L 109/29.

[74] Article 6(2).

[75] Commission Decision 1998/613/EC of 21 October 1998 concerning a draft Decree of the Republic of Austria on the identification of genetically modified additives and flavourings used as food ingredients. [1998] OJ L 291/35.

[76] Commission Regulation (EC) No 49/2000 of 10 January 2000 amending Council Regulation (EC) No 1139/1998 concerning the compulsory indication on the labelling of certain foodstuffs produced from genetically modified organisms of particulars other than those provided for in Council Directive 1979/112/EEC. [2000] OJ L 6/13. It has been suggested that detecting the presence of genetically modified ingredients constituting up to one per cent of the foodstuff can actually, given current testing methods, be very difficult. See P Cohen, 'Telltale Traces: How Reliable are Official Tests for Genetically Modified Food?' (2001) 170 (2286) *New Scientist* 16.

[77] Commission Regulation (EC) No 50/2000 of 10 January 2000 on the labelling of foodstuffs and food ingredients containing additives and flavourings that have been genetically modified or have been produced from genetically modified organisms. [2000] OJ L 6/15.

[78] Article 4(1).

The new deliberate release directive of 2001 prescribes that the statement 'this product contains genetically modified organisms' must appear either on a label or in a document accompanying genetically modified food.[79] This is the key feature of the new deliberate release directive, as far as labelling requirements are concerned. It places a clear obligation on producers to state that a product contains a gmo where this is the case, a requirement that was conspicuous by its omission from the original 1990 deliberate release directive.

The increased use of genetic modification techniques in food production created a difficulty for the EU legislator. Initial regulation was by way of framework directive. As objections to the use of this process became more prevalent, the legislation was found to be insufficient to deal with some of the complexities and sensitivities surrounding health protection, informing consumers and ethical considerations. This was particularly clear in relation to the shortcomings in the rules controlling the labelling of these products. Some types of genetically modified food escaped these requirements due to loopholes in the law, while others did not have to display this information in a prominent position on the label—contrary to increased demands for full disclosure of the techniques used in the production of food. This situation has improved with the introduction of a new regulatory regime for genetically modified foods. The increased use of directly applicable regulations rather than discretionary directives should assist in ameliorating the difficulties presented for free movement by the arbitrary application of the rules by individual Member States. The increased prominence of information on the label, and its more explicit disclosures, should also go some way to protecting consumers who wish to avoid these foodstuffs. However, it remains the case that food containing the meat, eggs or dairy produce from animals fed on a genetically modified diet need not reveal this fact.[80]

7.3 ALTERING CONSUMER PREFERENCES: THE DEMAND FOR ORGANIC FOOD

The various scares, coupled with concerns about the contamination of foodstuffs and an increase in the ethical considerations of consumers when purchasing food, have led to an increased demand for food that has been produced by organic methods. Global sales of organic food stood at €25 billion in 2005. Retail sales of organic produce in the United Kingdom alone exceed £1.6 billion, an increase of 30 per cent on 2004. This included sales of nearly 9,000,000 organically reared birds and two hundred million litres of milk. Nearly two-thirds of all consumers in the UK buy organic foods.[81]

The rules on the production and marketing of organic food in the European

---

[79] Article 4(1).

[80] For further discussion see C MacMaoláin, 'The New Genetically Modified Food Labelling Requirements: Finally a Lasting Solution?' (2003) 28 *European Law Review* 865.

[81] Organic Market Report 2006, published by the Soil Association.

[82] Council Regulation (EEC) No 2092/1991 of 24 June 1991 on organic production of agricultural products and indications referring thereto on agricultural products and foodstuffs. [1991] OJ

Union are set out in Regulation 2092/91 and its many amendments.[82] The regulation covers all products that claim themselves, generally by an indication on the labelling or advertising, to be produced organically, including both unprocessed agricultural animal and crop products and products containing organically produced ingredients.[83] Food product labels may only refer to organic production methods where the product has been produced in accordance with the procedure laid down in the regulation.[84] Under the regulation, products that are not entirely unprocessed may be labelled as organic where at least 95 per cent of the ingredients of agricultural origin contained therein are obtained by organic farming methods.[85] Under an amending regulation, which came into operation in 1995, products may bear indications referring to organic production methods where at least 70 per cent of the ingredients of agricultural origin are, or are derived from, products obtained organically.[86] These foodstuffs may be labelled as being 'X% organically produced'.[87]

7.3.1 Organic Production Rules

Most of the rules for the production of organic food are set out in the Annexes to Regulation 2092/1991. Annex I prescribes that a conversion period leading up to the production of organic food must generally have taken place for at least two years before the crops can be considered as having been organically produced. The fertility of the soil in which the crops are grown can only be increased or maintained by cultivating legumes, green manures or deep-rooting plants as part of a multi-annual rotation programme or by the incorporation of organic material into the soil. Livestock manure may be used if it comes from organically reared animals. Other fertilisers may only be used where these methods do not provide enough nutrients for the soil to grow the organic crops. Pests, diseases and weeds may only be controlled by a combination of permitted measures, such as appropriate rotation programmes, mechanical cultivation procedures, flame weeding, or protecting the

---

L 198/1. Regulation 2092/1991 was first amended by Commission Regulation (EEC) No 1535/1992 of 15 June 1992 amending Annexes I and III of Council Regulation (EEC) No 2092/1991 on organic production of agricultural products and indications referring thereto on agricultural products and foodstuffs. [1992] OJ L 162/15. The Regulation has been amended on 39 further occasions between this and the introduction of Commission Regulation (EC) No 780/2006 of 24 May 2006 amending Annex VI to Council Regulation (EEC) No 2092/1991 on organic production of agricultural products and indications referring thereto on agricultural products and foodstuffs. [2006] OJ L 137/9. As at 21 July 2006, a further nine amendments have been proposed, including a proposal to repeal and replace the Regulation 2092/1991 regime. See Proposal for a Council Regulation on organic production and labelling of organic products. COM (2005) 671.

[83] Article 1(1).
[84] Article 5(1).
[85] Article 5.
[86] Council Regulation (EC) No 1935/1995 of 22 June 1995 amending Regulation (EEC) No 2092/1991 on organic production of agricultural products and indications referring thereto on agricultural products and foodstuffs. [1995] OJ L 186/1.
[87] Article 1.

natural enemies of pests by providing them with nests or hedges. It is only where there is an immediate threat to the crop that recourse may be had to the list of these permitted fertilisers and/or pest controllers listed in Annex II to the regulation.

Annex III to the regulation prescribes that farms producing organic crops must clearly keep cultivation, production and storage locations separate from any parts of the operation not producing organic products.[88] Farmers must maintain written records for inspection which provide details of the origin, nature and quantities of all raw materials bought and the use to which they are put, as well as accounts of all such products sold. Inspections of organic operations, be they farms or factories, must take place on an annual basis. Unannounced inspection visits may also be made. All facilities used for the production of organic food must be made fully accessible to inspectors, as must samples of packaging and labelling used, or any other information deemed necessary for the purposes of the inspection. In particular, organic food must be proved to be transported to other operators, including wholesalers and retailers, in appropriate packaging, containers or vehicles. Similarly, storage must be managed in such a way that any mixing with or contamination by other non-organic products is avoided. Member States are charged with the establishment and operation of inspection systems to ensure that the terms of the regulation are complied with.[89]

7.3.2 Organic Livestock Production

Annex I to Regulation 2092/1991 is amended by Regulation 1804/1999 to include a lengthy section on rules and standards for the production of livestock and livestock products, replacing the single paragraph dedicated to this which appeared in the original organic foods regulation.[90] Originally, the only reference to livestock in the principles of farm-level organic production was to the use of by-products, such as farmyard manure, in the fertilisation of soil, stating that they could be used in accordance with existing national rules or, if none existed, internationally recognised standards. The new Annex I, Part B sets out detailed rules on conversion periods, animal origin, animal feed, veterinary treatment, husbandry management practices, animal welfare and manure use that must be complied with before the description 'organic' can be applied to food products derived from a range of animals, including cows, pigs, sheep, goats, horses, poultry and bees.

The rules relating to organic livestock do not refer only to those animals that are to be slaughtered for meat or those which are kept to provide milk or eggs—they also cover animals kept on farms cultivating organic crops. Livestock not reared in

---

[88] As amended by Commission Regulation (EC) No 2491/2001 of 19 December 2001 amending Council Regulation (EEC) No 2092/91 on organic production of agricultural products and indications referring thereto on agricultural products and foodstuffs. [2002] OJ L 337/9.

[89] Article 9.

[90] Council Regulation (EC) No 1804/1999 of 19 July 1999 Supplementing Regulation No 2092/1991 on organic production of agricultural products and foodstuffs to include livestock production [199] OJ L 222/1.

accordance with these provisions may be present on such farms, but where this is the case they must be kept entirely separate from those areas where organic production takes place.

If livestock is to be sold as an organic product it must first have been reared according to set standards for a minimum of 12 months for horses and cattle used for meat production, six months for pigs and animals used for milk production and 10 weeks for poultry for meat production, provided the birds were brought in before they were three days old, and six weeks for poultry for egg production. Breeds or strains of animal are to be chosen with a view to avoiding specific diseases or health problems that may be associated with some breeds or strains used in intensive production, such as porcine stress syndrome, spontaneous abortion or those which often require caesarean operations due to difficult births. Preference is also to be given to indigenous breeds and strains. Livestock introduced to farms undergoing a process of conversion to organic farming methods must be introduced from organic sources. By way of derogation from this, a maximum of 10 per cent of female adult horses or cattle livestock and 20 per cent of female adult pigs, goats and sheep may be introduced from non-organic sources to supplement the growth or renewal of a herd or flock when organically reared animals are not available. Use of this derogation requires prior authorisation from the competent authority charged with overseeing the implementation of the provisions of the organic food regulations. Non-organic male animals for breeding may be introduced provided that they are subsequently reared and always fed in accordance with the provisions of the regulation.

Under the terms of the new Annex IB, force feeding of livestock is prohibited. Livestock may only be fed on organically produced animal feed. The feeding of young mammals is to be based on natural milk, preferably that of the mother, for a minimum of three months for cattle and horses, 45 days for sheep and goats and 40 days for pigs. Roughage must be added to the daily diet of all organically reared animals at set levels.[91] The feed formula used in the fattening stage for poultry must contain at least 65 per cent cereals. The use of conventional animal feed is to be kept to a minimum and limited to permitted exceptions. However, conventional feed should not be used at all where a sufficient level of similar organic animal feed exists in the EU. Animal feed, feed materials, compound feed, feed additives, processing aids for animal feed and certain products used in animal nutrition must not have been produced using gmos or products derived therefrom. Similarly, antibiotics and growth promoters may not be used in the production of organic livestock.

One of the key principles underlying the rules on the production of organic livestock is that disease should be prevented, rather than cured by the use of veterinary medicines. For example, it is hoped that by carefully selecting generally indigenous

---

[91] For example, at least 60 per cent of the dry matter in daily rations for herbivores is to consist of roughage, fresh or dried fodder, or silage. Roughage, fresh or dried fodder or silage must also be added to the daily ration for pigs and poultry.

breeds, ensuring that they will be comfortable in their environment, adopting animal husbandry practices that encourage resistance to disease, using only high quality feed and ensuring the animals receive regular exercise, and ensuring that density levels are set to avoid overstocking, disease amongst organically reared animals will be reduced. Any animals that do become sick or injured are to be treated immediately in suitable housing, and in isolation if necessary. Where it is deemed necessary to use veterinary medicines these should, where possible, be phyto-therapeutic (eg plant extracts) or homeopathic or products appearing in the positive list set out in the regulation.[92] It is perhaps surprising that the legislation refers to these forms of treatment, given that their effectiveness in treating illness is highly contested.[93] Chemical substances or antibiotics may only be used where other permitted treatments are, or are likely to be, unsuccessful and this is absolutely necessary to avoid causing suffering or distress to the animal. The use of chemically synthesised allopathic veterinary medicinal products or antibiotics for preventive treatment is always prohibited. Where veterinary medicinal products are to be used, the type of product must be recorded together with details of the diagnosis, the dose administered, the method of administration, the duration of the treatment, and the legal withdrawal period. The manufacture of organically produced food from such animals is not permitted until at least 48 hours after the last administration of a veterinary medicinal product. This period may be longer, depending on the type of medicine used.

In principle, the reproduction of organically reared livestock should be based on natural methods. However, artificial insemination is permitted, but other forms of artificial or assisted reproduction, such as embryo transfers, are prohibited. Operations such as attaching elastic bands to the tails of sheep, tail-docking, cutting of teeth, trimming of beaks and dehorning must not be carried out systematically in organic farming. They may only occur where specifically authorised by the competent authority in the Member State for safety reasons, or if necessary to improve the health, welfare or hygiene of the livestock. Castration is permitted to maintain product quality or to preserve traditional production practices. Tethering of livestock is prohibited, unless specifically authorised or where neces-

---

[92] Annex II, Part C, section 3 thereof. For discussion on the usefulness of homeopathic treatments in veterinary medicine see L Hektoen *et al*, 'Comparison of Homeopathy, Placebo and Antibiotic Treatment of Clinical Mastitis in Dairy Cows—Methodological Issues and Results from a Randomised-clinical Trial' (2004) 51 *Journal of Veterinary Medicine* 439; FC Velkers *et al*, 'Isopathic and Pluralist Homeopathic Treatment of Commercial Broilers with Experimentally Induced Colibacillosis' (2005) 78 *Research in Veterinary Science* 77.

[93] The practice of homeopathic medicine was founded by Samuel Hahnemann (1755–1843). Homeopathy is based on the doctrine that diseases can be cured by administering minute doses of drugs which in larger amounts cause the very symptoms it is desired to alleviate. Though large and various claims are made by adherents of this system, and though its evaluation is beyond the scope of this work, there appears to be insufficient scientific evidence to warrant the assumption that all such claims made for this system are valid. For a summary of the scepticism that surrounds the use of homeopathy see P Skrabanek and J McCormick, *Follies and Fallacies in Medicine* 3rd edn (Whithorn, Tarragon Press, 1998), 121–5; L Hektoen, 'Review of the Current Involvement of Homeopathy in Veterinary Practice and Research' (2005) 157 *The Veterinary Record* 224.

sary for safety or welfare reasons. All these practices, where permitted, are to be carried out in a manner that minimises any suffering caused to the animal. Where livestock are reared in groups, the size of the group must depend upon their stage of development and the behavioural needs of the species concerned.

Minimum ages for the slaughter of organic poultry are also set. For example, chickens must be at least 81 days old; peking ducks at least 49 days; and turkeys 140 days. Food derived from animals claimed to be produced organically must be transported in a manner that limits stress, in accordance with other Community or national legislation. Loading and unloading must be carried out without the use of electrical stimulation to coerce the animals. The use of allopathic tranquillisers, prior to and during transportation, is prohibited. Animals are to be treated in a stress-minimising manner in the period leading up to slaughter.

Housing conditions for organic livestock must meet the animals' biological and ethological needs (eg behavioural needs as regards freedom of movement and comfort). The livestock must have easy access to food and water. Insulation, heating and ventilation of the building must ensure that air circulation, dust levels, temperature, relative air humidity and gas concentration levels are kept within limits which are not harmful to the animals. The building must allow plentiful natural ventilation and light to enter. Free-range, open-air exercise areas, or open-air runs must provide sufficient protection against rain, wind, sun and extreme temperatures if necessary, depending on the local weather conditions and the breed concerned. However, housing for livestock is not necessary, under the terms of the regulation, in areas where appropriate climatic conditions enable animals to live outdoors.

The stocking density levels in buildings must ensure the well-being of the animals concerned, taking account of their behavioural needs. As a minimum, there must be enough space for the animals to stand naturally, lie down easily, turn around, groom themselves, assume all natural postures and make all natural movements, such as stretching and wing-flapping. Minimum surface area measurements for this are set in Annex VIII to the regulation. All housing is to be kept clean, to prevent cross-infection and disease. All mammals must have access to pasturage or an open-air exercise area whenever conditions, such as the health of the animals and the weather, allow. However, the final fattening phase of cattle, pigs and sheep for meat production may take place indoors, provided that this period does not exceed one-fifth of their lifetime or a maximum period of three months. At least half of the floor area of such housing must be solid, that is not slatted or of grid construction. Ample dry bedding must be provided. The terms of Directive 1991/629, laying down minimum standards for the protection of calves,[94] and Directive 1991/630, laying down minimum standards for the protection of pigs,[95] must also be complied with.

---

[94] Council Directive 1991/629/EEC of 19 November 1991 laying down minimum standards for the protection of calves. [1991] OJ L 340/28.

[95] Council Directive 1991/630/EEC of 19 November 1991 laying down minimum standards for the protection of pigs. [1991] OJ L 340/33.

Organic poultry must be reared in open-range conditions. They must not be kept in cages. Waterfowl must have access to a stream, pond or lake whenever weather conditions permit. Housing for poultry must meet minimum standards on flooring, cleanliness, perches and exit/entry pop-holes. Poultry houses may not contain more than 4,800 chickens, 3,000 laying hens, 5,200 guinea fowl, 4,000 female or 3,200 male peking ducks or 2,500 geese or turkeys. In the case of laying hens, natural light may be supplemented by artificial light to provide a maximum of 16 hours of light per day, with a continuous rest period without artificial light of at least eight hours. Poultry must have access to open-air runs and feeding and water troughs whenever weather conditions permit and, whenever possible, for at least one-third of their lives. Some derogation from the detail of these provisions is allowed within the Member States until 2010, but only where animal housing was constructed prior to 1999 and had complied with national provisions concerning organic livestock production in force prior to that date, or in the absence of such rules, comply with private standards accepted or recognised by the Member States, such as those of the Soil Association.

7.3.3 Genetic Modification and Organic Food

The organic food regulations did not initially prohibit the use of genetic modification processes in the production of organic food. This was later certified in the decision in *Parliament v Commission*,[96] where the applicant institution brought an action seeking the annulment of a 1993 Commission Regulation, which amended the framework regulation on organic foodstuffs.[97] The Parliament sought the annulment of the contested legislation due to the fact that it included genetically modified micro-organisms in the list of ingredients of non-agricultural origin that may be present in foodstuffs that could be labelled and advertised as organic.[98] It was claimed that the Commission had exceeded its powers, and undermined the objectives of the framework regulation insofar as it related to consumer expectations, the free movement of organic foodstuffs and the balance between agricultural production and protection of the environment. The Parliament also claimed that it should have been consulted on this amendment in accordance with the procedures set down in the Treaty.[99] The Commission maintained that it was not obliged to consult with the Parliament on this issue because the regulation of gmos and micro-organisms was governed by other provisions of Community law, including the original deliberate release directive.[100]

---

[96] Case C-156/1993, *European Parliament v Commission* [1995] ECR I-2019.

[97] Commission Regulation (EEC) No 207/1993 of 29 January 1993 defining the content of Annex VI to Regulation (EEC) No 2092/1991 on organic production of agricultural products and indications referring thereto on agricultural products and foodstuffs and laying down detailed rules for implementing the provisions of Article 5 (4) thereto. [1993] OJ L 25/5.

[98] Annex I to Regulation 207/1993.

[99] Article 37 EC.

[100] Council Directive 1990/220.

The Commission insisted that the contested legislation was designed to ensure that consumers would be protected in the future when genetically modified food would become more commonplace. It also pointed out that the framework organic food regulation did not prohibit the use of either gmos or genetically modified micro-organisms in organic farming, despite the fact that the Parliament had suggested that an amendment be drafted to ensure that this would become the case. The framework regulation did not prevent the addition of genetically altered foods or their ingredients to the lists of authorised ingredients specified therein either. The Commission thus insisted that it was perfectly entitled to act in the contested manner.

The Court of Justice found that the inclusion of genetically modified micro-organisms in the list of permitted non-agricultural constituents was not in contravention of the provisions of the regulation. The Court stated that when the Council adopted the regulation it did not seek to prohibit the use of either gmos or genetically modified micro-organisms in organic farming, despite the proposed amendment suggested by the Parliament. Thus Community rules allowed products containing genetically modified ingredients to be labelled as organic.[101] They also permitted genetic modification processes to be used in the production of organic foodstuffs. It was soon realised that genetic modification techniques were not wholly compatible with the production of organic food. In particular they could lead to a reduction in consumer confidence in the wholesomeness of organic food. Hence it was later decided to remedy this problem by introducing, in a regulation more generally designed to set the standards for organic livestock, a prohibition on the marketing of foods as organic where they have undergone any genetic modification process.[102] Regulation 1804/1999 (the organic farming regulation) amends Article 5(3) of Regulation 2092/1991, adding that the labelling and advertising of food may only refer to organic production where the product has been made without the use of gmos and/or any products derived from such organisms. Regulation 1804/1999 makes it clear that gmos and products derived therefrom includes any substance which is either produced from or produced by gmos, but which does not contain gmos. The 'use of gmos and gmo derivatives' includes their use in foodstuffs, food ingredients (including additives and flavourings), processing aids (including extraction solvents), animal feed, compound feed, feed materials, feed additives, processing aids for animal feed, products used in animal nutrition, plant protection products, veterinary medicinal products, fertilisers, soil conditioners, seeds, vegetative reproductive material, and livestock. Article 13 of Regulation 2092/1991 is also amended. This now provides that

---

[101] Regulation 2092/1991 initially allowed up to five per cent of the constituents of a foodstuff to be genetically modified yet the product could still be labelled as 'organic'. Under the terms of Regulation 1935/1995 up to 30 per cent of the constituents could be genetically modified and the product could still be labelled as being 'X% organically produced'.

[102] Council Regulation (EC) No 1804/1999 of 19 July 1999 supplementing Regulation (EEC) No 2092/1991 on organic production of agricultural products and indications referring thereto on agricultural products and foodstuffs to include livestock production. [1999] OJ L 222/1.

implementation measures must be set according to scientific evidence or technical progress, applying the prohibition on the use of gmos and gmo derivatives with regard, in particular, to a *de minimis* threshold for unavoidable contamination that is not to be exceeded.

7.3.4 Coexistence of Genetically Modified Crops with Conventional and Organic Farming

A Commission Recommendation of 2003 sets out guidelines for the development of national strategies and best practices to ensure the coexistence of genetically modified crops with conventional and organic farming practices.[103] The Preamble to the Recommendation commences with a statement that:

> No form of agriculture, be it conventional, organic or agriculture using genetically modified organisms (GMOs), should be excluded in the European Union.

This, it is claimed, aims primarily at ensuring that the existence of different agricultural production systems will provide a high degree of consumer choice. It will also give farmers a choice between conventional, organic and genetically modified crop production. However, it is recognised that there may be serious economic consequences if genetically modified and non-genetically modified crops are not managed in a manner that helps to avoid admixture between the two. These guidelines were thus developed to establish a set of Community principles for the development of national strategies that, if implemented, could best avoid the contamination of conventional and organic foodstuffs.

The Commission makes it clear from the outset that this recommendation applies to the economic aspects associated with the admixture of genetically modified and non-genetically modified crops only. It does not concern itself here with the environmental or health aspects of the cultivation and marketing of genetically modified food. This is covered in the deliberate release directive of 2001, and now also the general gmo and the labelling and traceability regulations of 2003. The Commission also sees its role in this regard as being limited to the gathering and co-ordination of relevant information, offering advice and issuing guidelines to assist Member States in establishing best practices for coexistence. The way in which advice and guidelines are implemented will need to differ according to particular national or regional conditions. EU farmers work in widely diverse environments. The co-ordination of efforts across Member States is thus best achieved by a broad set of general principles on co-existence. This may be justified on the grounds of the variety that exists across the European Union in terms of farm and field sizes, production systems, crop rotations and cropping patterns, as well as natural conditions. These guidelines, issued in the form of a non-binding recommendation addressed to the Member States, cover the potential for cross-contam-

---

[103] Commission Recommendation 2003/556/EC of 23 July 2003 on guidelines for the development of national strategies and best practices to ensure the coexistence of genetically modified crops with conventional and organic farming. [2003] OJ L 189/36.

ination from agricultural crop production on the farm up to the first point of sale—from 'seed to silo'.

The Recommendation sets out a series of general principles that are to underpin national strategies for best ensuring the peaceful coexistence of genetically modified and conventional and organic crops. All such national strategies are to be based on transparency and stakeholder involvement in decision-making, basing decisions on sound science, building on existing segregation methods and practices, proportionality, differentiation between the different needs of different crop varieties and growing conditions such as climate and farm size, co-operation (especially between farmers), and effective monitoring and evaluation of measures taken. The Recommendation also states that there is no particular policy instrument that can be recommended to best ensure safe coexistence. Voluntary agreements, soft law approaches and legislation all have a role to play in the effective implementation, monitoring, evaluation and control of measures introduced. In devising a national strategy, Member States should take into account the level of coexistence to be achieved (ie single farms, neighbouring farms or farms within the same region but separated by some distance); In order to devise a national strategy, Member States should take into account the level of co-existence to be achieved (i.e. on single farms, on neighbouring farms or on farms within the same region but separated by some distance); the different types of adventitious mixture that can occur (such as pollen transfer between neighbouring fields, the mixing of crops during harvest and post-harvest operations), the transfer of seeds during transport and storage, or seeds remaining in the soil after harvest which produce new plants in successive years, which occurs more frequently in some crops, such as oilseed rape, than in others, such as maize, which is unlikely to survive frost; the labelling threshold values that are set by Community law that prescribe the maximum permitted adventitious levels of genetically modified organisms that may be present in a conventional or organic food without this requiring to be labelled; the types of crops at issue; and lastly the general growing conditions, such as farm size, climate, topography and the activity, behaviour and population size of pollinators.

More specific advice is offered to Member States with regard to how their national strategies can best be devised and implemented. As a minimum, strategies should set guidelines on (i) growing conditions and distances between coexisting genetically modified and other crops; (ii) harvest and post-harvest field treatment; (iii) transportation and storage; (iv) voluntary agreements on farm co-operation; (v) establishment of notification and monitoring schemes, using the feedback obtained from this as a basis for further adjustment and refinement of national strategies; and (vi) keeping of records on management practices, cultivation processes and traceability. Member States should also encourage training courses for farmers on coexistence measures and implement conciliation procedures to solve cases of disagreement between neighbouring farmers concerning the implementation of measures for coexistence.

7.3.5 Future Regulation of Organic Production

Three main difficulties have plagued EU attempts to regulate the production and marketing of organic food. First, the original regulation permitted the presence of genetically modified ingredients in organic food. Second, after a 1995 amendment it also enabled foods containing up to 30 per cent non-organic ingredients to be labelled as being 'organically produced', facilitating the deception of consumers into purchasing a food product not in compliance with generally recognised expectations about what constitutes organic food.[104] Third, there has been a plethora of amendments to the organic foods regulation since its introduction in 1992. More than 40 amending regulations make it difficult for those who wish to produce and/or market organic food to work within the framework. This should be resolved, temporarily at least, by the introduction of a new, consolidating regulation on organic production and the labelling of organic products.[105] The proposal for such a regulation prioritises consumer confidence in organic foods, primarily by reducing the possibility of producers using misleading labelling referring to organic production methods, protection of the environment, and setting high standards for animal welfare. The new regulation should also eradicate the first two difficulties with the original organic foods regulation that were identified above. The use of genetic modification in organic production continues to be prohibited, as it has been since 1999.[106] Labelling products that are up to 30 per cent of non-organic origin as being organically produced is now also to be prohibited. All of this should go some way to making the labelling of organic foodstuffs more reliable. This is subject to the caveat that labelling may continue to be misleading in some circumstances. This became the case for example during the 2006 scare over avian influenza. Rules provided that meat and eggs could be marketed as organic even though the poultry used in their production were kept indoors.[107]

7.4 ETHICAL FOOD PRODUCTION

Consumers are increasingly interested in purchasing food that has been produced in specific ways. As discussed earlier, sales of organic food continue to increase significantly, and ethical concerns regarding the treatment of animals used for food production are similarly prevalent. Community legislation on welfare standards

---

[104] Regulation 1935/1995.

[105] Proposal for a Council Regulation on organic production and labelling of organic products. COM (2005) 671.

[106] Council Regulation (EC) No 1804/1999 of 19 July 1999 supplementing Regulation (EEC) No 2092/1991 on organic production of agricultural products and indications referring thereto on agricultural products and foodstuffs to include livestock production. [1999] OJ L 222/1.

[107] Commission Regulation (EC) No 699/2006 of 5 May 2006 amending Annex I to Council Regulation (EEC) No 2092/1991 as regards conditions of access for poultry to open-air runs. [2006] OJ L 121/36. For further discussion about what this can mean for the welfare standards of supposedly 'free range' and/or 'organic' birds see Chapter 8 of P Singer and J Mason, *The Way We Eat: Why Our Food Choices Matter* (Emmaus, PA, Rodale, 2006).

must thus ensure that where consumers are willing to pay a premium for products produced from animals that have been well treated, this additional cost reflects a real difference between these products and their conventional counterparts.

7.4.1 Animal Welfare Standards

A series of legislative initiatives have been introduced at Community level to ensure that animals used in food production are well treated. In addition to standards relating to the production and subsequent labelling of organic foods, specific directives on the protection of calves, pigs and poultry also exist.

7.4.2 Community Legislation on the Protection of Calves and Pigs

Directive 1991/629 sets minimum standards for the protection of calves.[108] The preamble to the directive makes it quite clear that it was not introduced as a result of any real concerns about animal welfare protection; instead its main purpose was to ensure that differences in required standards of animal care between the Member States did not lead to a distortion in competition. If Member State A sets low standards for animal welfare protection in its national law but Member State B requires that animals reared for food production must be well housed, fed and spend some time outdoors, Member State A is able to produce food at a lower cost, distorting competition between the Member States. The temptation for a Member State to lower its welfare standards may even be encouraged by Community rules on the free movement of goods. If national products are open to competition from products produced elsewhere in the EU at a lower cost, the Member State may now seek to lower its own producers' costs in order to meet this challenge. One of the easiest ways of achieving this is to reduce minimum welfare standards for animals used in food production.

Calves, for the purposes of the directive, are bovine animals up to six months of age.[109] The Directive sets minimum standards for the amount of floor space that each calf should get, with an allowance for the special conditions to be set for those calves that require it on account of their behaviour, the fact that they are pure-bred, or because they are kept with their mothers for suckling.[110] Member States must carry out inspections to ensure that the provisions of the directive are complied with,[111] and these may be supplemented by checks made by veterinary experts from the Commission.[112] This strategy is designed primarily to ensure the

---

[108] Council Directive 1991/629/EEC of 19 November 1991 laying down minimum standards for the protection of calves. [1991] OJ L 340/28.
[109] Article 2.
[110] Article 3.
[111] Article 7.
[112] Article 9.

uniform application of the directive across the Community. As with many of the directives in this area, the detailed rules are set out in the Annex, which provides that materials used to build calf housing must not be capable of being harmful to the animals in any way and must be capable of being thoroughly cleaned and disinfected. Insulation, heating and ventilation of such buildings must be designed to ensure that the calves are not harmed in any way. All automated or mechanical equipment must be inspected at least once daily, and defects must be rectified immediately. Calves must not be kept in permanent darkness—there must be natural or artificial lighting. If artificial lighting is used, it must be maintained for eight consecutive hours per day. Accommodation for calves must be sufficient for them to stand up, lie down, rest and groom without difficulty and they must be able to see other calves. Calf feed must contain suitable quantities of iron and fibre. Calves must not be muzzled, they must be fed at least once per day, and they must have access to a sufficient supply of water when they are over two weeks old. Finally, feeding and watering equipment must be designed, constructed, placed and maintained so that contamination of feed and water is kept to a minimum.

Similar standards are set by Community law on the protection of pigs.[113] The pig protection directive provides for a minimum unobstructed floor space for each pig, depending on its weight.[114] Member States are charged with the responsibility of ensuring that inspections are carried out by the relevant competent authority, checking that the provisions of the directive and its Annex are complied with.[115] They may, on occasions, be accompanied by veterinary experts from the Commission.[116] Animals imported from non-member countries must, as far as welfare standards are concerned, have been reared to a standard at least equivalent to that set out in the pig protection directive.[117] The Annex to the directive sets out a series of requirements relating to the construction of housing for pigs, the provision of lighting to ensure that they are not kept in darkness, daily inspections by farmers to ensure that they are healthy, preventing fighting amongst pigs, and the provision of a healthy diet. Chapter II of the Annex states that castration of pigs should only occur under anaesthetic by a veterinary surgeon and that tail-docking and tooth-clipping may only occur if necessary to prevent injury to other pigs. Tooth-clipping, where it is necessary, must be carried out within seven days of birth.

7.4.3 Health, Welfare and Consumer Protection: Production and Marketing of Poultry and Eggs

Standards relating to the rearing and treatment of animals used for food production are designed not only to improve welfare, but also to protect scrupulous pro-

---

[113] Council Directive 1991/630/EEC of 19 November 1991 laying down minimum standards for the protection of pigs. [1991] OJ L 340/33.
[114] Article 3.
[115] Article 7.
[116] Article 9.
[117] Article 8.

ducers and consumers. Labelling descriptions such as 'free range' and 'organic' should only be used where set minimum standards have been met, guaranteeing that the product is worthy of a premium price.

Welfare Standards and Consumer Protection

Three key pieces of secondary Community legislation determine legitimate use of the marketing description 'free range' as applied to eggs. These are Regulation 1907/1990 on marketing standards for eggs,[118] Directive 1999/74 laying down minimum standards for the protection of laying hens,[119] and Regulation 2295/2003 setting out more detailed rules on the implementation of Community marketing standards for eggs.[120] This body of legislation presents clear rules on the marketing of eggs as 'free range' and the welfare standards that must be applied to laying hens involved in their production.[121] It has not always been, and in many ways continues not to be, so straightforward. Previous rules in this area have exemplified much of that which is also problematic in relation to the marketing and advertising of food more generally in the EU.

The first Community legislation on marketing standards for eggs to appear after free range eggs became popular actually made no reference to the term 'free range'. Instead it dealt primarily with grading classes based on quality and weight.[122] This regulation set three main classes for the marketing of eggs. Class A included all fresh eggs, Class B included all 'second quality or preserved eggs', while those eggs graded as Class C were 'down-graded eggs intended for the food industry'.[123] Such

[118] Council Regulation (EEC) No 1907/1990 of 26 June 1990 on certain marketing standards for eggs. [1990] OJ L 173/5. This Regulation replaced, although not immediately, Regulation (EEC) No 2772/1975 of the Council of 29 October 1975 on marketing standards for eggs. [1975] OJ L 282/56.

[119] Council Directive 1999/74/EC of 19 July 1999 laying down minimum standards for the protection of laying hens. [1999] OJ L 203/53. Whilst Directive 1999/74 does lay down general minimum standards for the protection of laying hens, no standards are set for therein for 'free range' production. Under the terms of the Directive those hens who have the misfortune of spending their lives in 'un-enriched cage systems' must be provided with housing that is at least 40 cm high over 65 per cent of the cage, and not below 35 cm at any point. These cages should also be able to 'support adequately each of the forward facing claws of each foot' on a slope not exceeding 14 per cent (Article 5). The really good news, however, lies in the Annex, where it is stated that 'without prejudice to the provisions of point 19 of the Annex to Directive 98/58/EC, all mutilation (with the exception of beak trimming where deemed necessary) shall be prohibited'. Point 19 of the Annex to Directive 1998/58/EC states: 'Pending the adoption of specific provisions concerning mutilations in accordance with the procedure laid down in Article 5, and without prejudice to Directive 91/630/EEC, relevant national provisions shall apply in accordance with the general rules of the Treaty.' Council Directive 1998/58/EC of 20 July 1998 concerning the protection of animals kept for farming purposes. [1998] OJ 221/23.

[120] Commission Regulation (EC) No 2295/2003 of 23 December 2003 introducing detailed rules for implementing Council Regulation (EEC) No 1907/1990 on certain marketing standards for eggs. [2003] OJ L 340/16.

[121] Community legislators have now recognised the importance of high welfare standards in the successful marketing of eggs. For example, the preamble to Council Regulation 5/2001 states that '[t]he method by which hens are farmed has become one of the major factors for consumers when purchasing eggs'.

[122] Council Regulation (EEC) No 1907/1990 of 26 June 1990 on certain marketing standards for eggs. [1990] OJ L 173/5.

[123] Article 6.

a classification system gives cause for concern, given that practically all eggs of consumable quality fall within Class A, yet those eggs in the lowest quality category may still be used in the production of food. However, a year later, minimum standards for legitimate use of the marketing term 'free range' were introduced in Regulation 1274/1991, which set out, for the first time, more detailed rules on marketing standards for eggs.[124] This regulation provided that eggs marketed as 'free range' must be produced from hens that have continuous daytime access to open-air runs; the ground to which hens have access must be mainly covered with vegetation; the maximum stocking density must not be greater than one hen per 10 metres square; and the interior of the building must satisfy minimum standards on floor covering, perches and cleanliness.[125] This regulation was amended by Regulation 1651/2001,[126] and has now been repealed by Regulation 2295/2003.[127]

Essentially, what resulted was a multitude of legislative measures, with little clarity on the important issues of consumer concern, fair trading and animal welfare and production rules. Regulation 1651/2001 did introduce a new Annex III to Regulation 1274/1991, but it was quite clear from the discordant and piecemeal nature of both the former amending regulation and the body of regulations arising out of Regulation 1907/1990, that by 2001 what was really required was a consolidating act. This new Annex III did categorise egg production methods into standards for free range eggs, barn eggs and eggs from caged hens, but establishing the true definition of any of these required substantial cross-referencing and checking of other pieces of secondary Community legislation, which themselves were subject to regular change and amendment, making clarification of the law difficult. Even now, Community legislation on this matter makes multiple references to criteria set out in already altered legislation. An act of consolidation is still required. Here, however, by sifting through the large body of relevant legal texts that together determine exactly what is meant in Community law by the term 'free range', we can narrow the focus down to the three key pieces of legislation specified at the beginning of this section.[128]

Regulation 2295/2003 sets a series of standards for the production, labelling, traceability and marketing of eggs.[129] The characteristics defining Grade A and B eggs are set,[130] as are the weights that determine whether an egg is considered

---

[124] Commission Regulation (EEC) No 1274/1991 of 15 May 1991 introducing detailed rules for implementing Regulation (EEC) No 1907/1990 on certain marketing standards for eggs. [1991] OJ L 121/11.

[125] Annex II to Regulation 1274/1991.

[126] Commission Regulation (EC) No 1651/2001 of 14 August 2001 amending Regulation (EEC) No 1274/1991 introducing detailed rules for implementing Council Regulation (EEC) No 1907/1990 on certain marketing standards for eggs. [2001] OJ L 220/5.

[127] Article 38.

[128] Namely Regulation 1907/1990, Directive 1999/74 and Regulation 2295/2003.

[129] Regulation 2295/2003 has since been amended by Commission Regulation (EC) No 1515/2004 of 26 August 2004 amending Regulation (EC) No 2295/2003 introducing detailed rules for implementing Council Regulation (EEC) No 1907/1990 on certain marketing standards for eggs. [2004] OJ L 278/7.

[130] Articles 5 and 6.

small, medium, large or extra-large.[131] There is no Grade C classification. There is to be an indication of the date of minimum durability, which should be not more than 28 days after laying.[132] There should also be a 'sell-by' date stated on the label.[133] An indication of the poultry-rearing method employed must also be stated on the label.[134] The different methods that may be employed are set out in Annex III to the regulation. This list includes free range eggs, which must be produced in establishments satisfying the terms of Directive 1999/74. These enable the hens to have continuous daytime access to open-air runs that are mainly covered with vegetation and a set amount of room in which to move freely (one hen per four square metres). Barn eggs are also covered. These must be produced in establishments satisfying Article 4 of Directive 1999/74, which sets minimum standards for eating and drinking facilities for the birds as well as setting requirements on stocking density (no more than nine hens per square metre) and sanitation. Eggs from caged hens must be produced in establishments satisfying Article 5 of Directive 1999/74, including those on minimum cage sizes (550 square cm per hen, and at least 40 cm high over 65 per cent of the cage area). Alternatively, eggs may be labelled as 'organic' where they are produced in accordance with Regulation 2092/1991.[135] All establishments producing eggs, under the terms of Regulation 2295/2003, must be inspected at least once a year.[136] All Grade A eggs must now carry a code designating the producer's distinguishing number and identifying the farming method used.[137] The farming method aspect of this code consists of a number, 0, 1, 2 or 3 representing organic, free-range, barn and cage-reared respectively.

The terms of the body of legislation regulating the production and marketing of eggs may, in some ways, lead to consumers being deceived. For example, Regulation 1907/1990 allows producers to include additional statements on the labelling that are designed to promote sales of their product, provided that they do not mislead the consumer.[138] The most obvious examples are those relating to the production method, such as 'free range', or those relating to their quality. However, under the terms of Regulation 2295/2003 almost all eggs that are marketed to consumers are now Grade A, giving the producers of top-graded eggs no real marketing advantage.

The decision of the Court of Justice in *Springenheide and Tusky* offers a good example of the type of evidence that can be presented in such circumstances to

---

[131] Article 7(1).

[132] Article 9.

[133] Article 11.

[134] Article 13.

[135] Article 13 of Regulation 2295/2003. For discussion on what can constitute 'organic' eggs in the USA see Singer and Mason, n 104 above, Chapter 8.

[136] Article 24.

[137] Article 7 of Regulation 1907/1990 as amended by Council Regulation (EC) No 5/2001 of 19 December 2000 amending Regulation (EEC) No 1907/1990 on certain marketing standards for eggs. [2001] OJ L 2/1.

[138] Article 10(2)(e).

determine whether this additional labelling information has the potential to deceive consumers.[139] The case concerned proceedings brought against a German company which had been marketing its eggs with the description 'six-grain—10 fresh eggs', implying that the hens producing the eggs had been fed on a diet of six varieties of cereal. A slip of paper enclosed in each pack of eggs extolled the beneficial effects of this feed on the quality of the eggs. However, they were ordered to remove this additional labelling and the director of the company was fined by the state authorities, due to the fact that only 60 per cent of the feed given to the hens consisted of the six grain types. This judgment was unsuccessfully appealed before the state administrative court, where it was considered that the description and the pack insert infringed Article 10 of Regulation 1907/1990, as they were likely to mislead a significant proportion of consumers because they implied falsely that the feed given to the hens consisted exclusively of the six cereals indicated. This was appealed on a point of law before the federal administrative court. It was argued that the description and the pack insert actually provided the consumer with vital information and that the appeal court had not been provided with any expert opinion to prove that the purchaser was being misled in any way. During those proceedings, the Court of Justice was asked whether, in assessing whether statements designed to promote sales are likely to mislead the purchaser, the actual expectations of the consumer to whom the statement is addressed should be determined. If so, should this be based on an examination of the expectations of the informed average consumer, or of the casual consumer? How should such consumer groups be identified and what measures should be used to ensure that their expectations have been met? The referring court essentially asked for a definition of the concept of 'consumer' to be used as a standard for determining whether a statement designed to promote sales would be likely to mislead the purchaser.

The Court examined other, more general, existing secondary Community legislation to assist it in ascertaining a Community concept of 'consumer'. In particular, Directive 1979/112 on food labelling[140] and Directive 1984/450 on misleading advertising[141] were scrutinised. The misleading advertising directive prescribes that misleading advertising means any advertising which in any way, including its presentation, deceives or is likely to deceive the persons to whom it is addressed or whom it reaches, and which by reason of its deceptive nature is likely to affect their economic behaviour.[140] In previous cases the Court had considered the presumed expectations of the average consumer, who was deemed to be rea-

[139] Case C-210/1996, *Gut Springenheide GmbH and Rudolf Tusky v Oberkreisdirektor des Kreises Steinfurt—Amt für Lebensmittelüberwachung* [1998] ECR I-4657.

[140] Council Directive 1979/112/EEC of 18 December 1978 on the approximation of the laws of the Member States relating to the labelling, presentation and advertising of foodstuffs for sale to the ultimate consumer. [1979] OJ L 33/1.

[141] Council Directive 1984/450/EEC of 10 September 1984 relating to the approximation of the laws, regulations and administrative provisions of the Member States concerning misleading advertising. [1984] OJ L 250/17.

[142] Article 2(2).

sonably well-informed and reasonably observant and circumspect.[143] It was not thought necessary to order an expert report or to commission a consumer research poll on the matter at issue.[144] It was felt that national courts should be able to assess any misleading effect of a description or statement designed to promote sales on the same basis. However, it was also noted that in cases where the evidence and information before the Court is not sufficient or clear, then it will be for the national court to determine whether the description or statement was misleading on the basis of its own conditions, leaving open the possibility of conducting a consumer survey or seeking expert opinion on the matter.[145] It would thus be for the national court in a case such as this, where no specific Community provision exists, to determine, by whatever means it chooses, whether the percentage of consumers misled by a promotional statement would be sufficiently significant to justify banning its use. Such an assessment must be based on the presumed expectations of reasonably well-informed, observant and circumspect consumers.

Hygiene Standards for Egg Production

Directive 1989/437 lays down hygiene and health requirements concerning the production and the placing on the market of egg products for direct human consumption or for the manufacture of foodstuffs.[146] Egg products are:

> products obtained from eggs, their various components or mixtures thereof, after the removal of the shell and membranes, intended for human consumption; they may be partially supplemented by other foodstuffs or additives; they may be liquid, concentrated, dried, crystallised, frozen, quick-frozen or coagulated.[147]

Member States must ensure that only egg products that meet certain general requirements are produced as foodstuffs or are used in the manufacture of foodstuffs. The products must have been obtained from the eggs of hens, ducks, geese,

---

[143] See, for example, Case C-239/2002, *Douwe Egberts NV v Westrom Pharma NV and Christophe Souranis* [2004] ECR I-7007, para 46; Joined Cases C-421/2000, C-426/2000 and C-16/2001, *Renate Sterbenz and Paul Dieter Haug* [2003] ECR I-1065, para 43; Case C-465/1998, *Verein gegen Unwesen in Handel und Gewerbe Köln eV v Adolf Darbo AG* [2000] ECR I-2297, para 20.

[144] See, for example, Case C-362/1988, *GB-INNO-BM v Confédération du commerce luxembourgeois* [1990] ECR I-667; Case C-238/1989, *Pall Corp v Dahlhausen & Co* [1990] ECR I-4827; Case C-126/1991, *Schutzverband gegen Unwesen in der Wirtschaft eV v Yves Rocher GmbH* [1993] ECR I-2361; Case C-315/1992, *Verband Sozialer Wettbewerb eV v Clinique Laboratoires SNC et Estée Lauder Cosmetics GmbH* [1994] ECR I-317; Case C-456/1993, *Zentrale zur Bekämpfung unlauteren Wettbewerbs eV v Privatkellerei Franz Wilhelm Langguth Erben GmbH & Co KG* [1995] ECR I-1737; Case C-470/1993, *Verein gegen Unwesen in Handel und Gewerbe Köln eV v Mars GmbH* [1995] ECR I-1923.

[145] Case 94/1982, *Criminal proceedings against De Kikvorsch Groothandel-Import-Export BV* [1983] ECR 947; Case C-313/1994, *Graffione SNC v Ditta Fransa* [1996] ECR I-6039; Case C-210/1996, *Gut Springenheide GmbH and Rudolf Tusky v Oberkreisdirektor des Kreises Steinfurt—Amt für Lebensmittelüberwachung* [1998] ECR I-4657.

[146] Council Directive 1989/437/EEC of 20 June 1989 on hygiene and health problems affecting the production and the placing on the market of egg products. [1989] OJ L 212/87.

[147] Article 2(1).

turkeys, guinea fowl or quail, but they may not contain a mixture of eggs of different species. The products must bear an indication of the percentage of egg ingredients they contain when they are partially supplemented by other foodstuffs or additives. They must also have been treated and prepared in an establishment approved under the terms of the directive and in conformity with the hygiene conditions set out therein.[148] Small-scale enterprises, shops and restaurants are excluded from the scope of the directive where their egg products are used for the manufacture of foodstuffs intended for direct sale to the final consumer or which are to be consumed immediately after being prepared.[149]

Staff who treat or handle eggs and egg products must, in particular, wear clean working clothes and headgear, wash and disinfect their hands several times in the course of each working day and whenever they return to their workstation after a break. Smoking, eating, spitting and chewing must all be prohibited in areas where the products are being handled and stored. Animals should not enter establishments where production is taking place. The premises, equipment and instruments used in the production of egg products must be kept clean and in a good state of repair, and if necessary cleaned and disinfected several times during the working day, and they should be used for no purpose other than the processing of egg products.[150]

Member States have various responsibilities under the directive. They must ensure that checks are carried out to detect traces of substances such as pesticides, antibiotics or detergents whose presence in egg products may be dangerous or harmful to human health.[151] They must also draw up lists of approved establishments, each of which should be given an approval number.[152] In order to become an approved establishment, assurances must be given to the effect that the terms of the directive will be complied with.[153] The establishment must have suitable rooms that are large enough for the separate storage of eggs and the finished egg products—with appropriate refrigeration equipment where necessary, there must be facilities for washing and disinfecting eggs, there must be a room for the storage of other foodstuffs and additives, there must be suitable equipment for the hygienic packaging of egg products, and special conditions apply where egg products are to be pasteurised.[154] Member States are obliged to relinquish approval if the conditions for granting it cease to be fulfilled.[155] The directive does recognise that it is the primary responsibility of producers to ensure that egg products meet the health requirements laid down but that the competent authorities of the

---

[148] Article 3.
[149] Article 1.
[150] Annex to Council Directive 1989/437/EEC of 20 June 1989 on hygiene and health problems affecting the production and the placing on the market of egg products. [1989] OJ L 212/87.
[151] Article 5.
[152] Article 6(1).
[153] Article 6(1).
[154] Annex to Council Directive 1989/437/EEC of 20 June 1989 on hygiene and health problems affecting the production and the placing on the market of egg products. [1989] OJ L 212/87.
[155] Article 6.

Member States must, by carrying out checks and inspections, ensure that producers comply with the requirements.[156]

Poultry Production

Regulation 1906/1990 sets out a series of definitions and standards for the grading and marketing condition of poultry meat.[157] Regulation 1538/1991 was later introduced to flesh out the framework set in the poultry meat marketing regulation.[158] It provides a series of additional statements that may appear alongside the sales name, indicating the method by which the poultry was produced, such as 'fed with', 'barn reared' or 'free range'.[159] Use of these terms is further qualified in Annex IV to the regulation, which provides that 'barn reared' poultry must be housed in an area where the stocking rate does not exceed 12 birds (or 25 kg of birds) per square metre of floor space, and that birds must not be slaughtered at less than 56 days for chickens, 70 days for turkeys and 49 days for peking ducks. The term 'free range' may only be used where, during at lest half of their lifetime, the birds have had continuous daytime access to open-air runs in an area of vegetation of not less than one square metre per chicken, two square metres per duck and four square metres per turkey or goose. In addition to this, free-range poultry must be fed on at least 70 per cent cereals during their fattening stage. The term 'traditional free range' may be used where the birds have had continuous daytime access to open-air runs from the age of six weeks for chickens or eight weeks for ducks, geese and turkeys, providing two square metres for each chicken or duck, six square metres per turkey or 10 square metres per goose. The minimum age of slaughter for these birds is 81 days for chickens and 140 days for turkeys (unless they are intended for cutting up, in which case this reduces to 98 days for female turkeys and 126 days for male turkeys)[160] and geese, except for geese intended for foie gras production, which may be slaughtered at 102 days. The phrase 'free range—total freedom' may be used to describe poultry which has been reared in the same manner as traditional free range poultry, but where the run to which they have access is unlimited in size. Regulation 1538/1991 has now been amended to include a provision requiring that geese and ducks used for the production of foie

---

[156] Preamble to Council Directive 1989/437/EEC of 20 June 1989 on hygiene and health problems affecting the production and the placing on the market of egg products. [1989] OJ L 212.

[157] Council Regulation (EEC) No 1906/1990 on certain marketing standards for poultry. [1990] OJ L 173/1.

[158] Commission Regulation (EEC) No 1538/1991 of 5 June 1991 introducing detailed rules for implementing Regulation (EEC) No 1906/1990 on certain marketing standards for poultry. [1991] OJ L 143/11.

[159] Article 10.

[160] As amended by Commission Regulation (EC) No 1321/2002 of 22 July 2002 amending Regulation (EEC) No 1538/1991 introducing detailed rules for implementing Council Regulation (EEC) No 1906/1990 on certain marketing standards for poultrymeat. [2002] OJ L 194/17.

gras may no longer be labelled as 'free range' unless a statement is included which indicates that they have been used for the production of foie gras.[161]

While there are detailed rules at Community level for the production and marketing of poultry and eggs, they do not always satisfy the dual aim of protecting consumers and human health. The ethically aware consumer who wishes to purchase organic or free range meat is conceivably unaware that the animals used in its production may legally have spent a large portion of their lives indoors. In some circumstances, poultry can be labelled as organic even where the bird used to produce it never ventured outdoors, provided that it had access to sufficient quantities of roughage and suitable material in order to meet its ethological needs.[162] Regulations on disease also tend to put free movement first, with consumer protection and human health considerations trailing behind. Measures enacted to control salmonella, for example, make it very difficult for Member States to prohibit the importation of eggs from other Member States where there is a high risk of contamination.[163] Free movement policies dictate the content of EU food law. While other considerations are accounted for, the functioning of the internal market is considered to take priority.[164]

7.5 CONCLUSION

Many food products that are manufactured in the European Union are high quality, wholesome and produced by ethical methods. Equally, many are of poor quality, lacking in nutritional value and produced in a highly questionable manner. Many are safe, many are dangerous. Some arrive at our breakfast bars, office desks and dinner tables containing a mixture of good and bad properties. The EU has played a major role in determining the acceptability of both the positive and negative aspects of food production. The consumer has also had a key part to play in this. Recent history suggests that it is only where consumer unrest surfaces that issues of concern will be addressed. Where such lobbying fails to materialise, matters of huge importance to the health and welfare of humans, animals and the environment are overlooked, or are paid lip-service at best. This has been evident throughout the development of EU food law and policy, and it continues to be the case.

If the issues discussed in this book are examined in general terms, a clear pattern of action and inaction in relation to certain important aspects of the production and marketing of food can be identified. The manner in which rules and

---

[161] Commission Regulation (EC) No 1321/2002 of 22 July 2002 amending Regulation (EEC) No 1538/1991 introducing detailed rules for implementing Council Regulation (EEC) No 1906/1990 on certain marketing standards for poultrymeat. [2002] OJ L 194/17.

[162] Commission Regulation (EC) No 699/2006 of 5 May 2006 amending Annex I to Council Regulation (EEC) No 2092/1991 as regards conditions of access for poultry to open-air runs. [2006] OJ L 121/36.

[163] Regulation (EC) No 2160/2003 of the European Parliament and of the Council of 17 November 2003 on the control of salmonella and other specific food-borne zoonotic agents. [2003] OJ L 325/1.

[164] See also Chapter 5 of I Ward, *A Critical Introduction to European Law* 2nd edn (London, LexisNexis, 2003).

principles on the free movement of food have developed raises a number of issues about the operations of the 'common market'. EU law allows national producers to be discriminated against in their own Member State. Provided that importers are not disadvantaged in any way, there is no contravention of free movement rules. The 'common market' is not a market of equals.

The jurisprudence of the Court of Justice also provides that Member States can not prescribe the use of different food names for different food products, unless there is a 'substantial difference' between them. The test of difference remains arbitrary and unclear. Additional labelling informing the consumer about the nature of the product is a more proportionate response where differences do exist. However, requiring that the labels of imported foods be altered prior to marketing is deemed disproportionate to the aim pursued. Because of this it is assumed that consumers will read labels and ingredient listings, will be aware about the nature of traditional foodstuffs produced throughout the twenty-five Member States, will all have a preference for fully cooked hard-boiled eggs and will understand what the 400 or so 'e' numbers used in additive listings stand for. This type of reasoning has led to justifications that foods containing as little as 70 per cent meat should be labelled as 'meat products', regardless of what the other 30 per cent is made up of, and that substitute versions of products should be marketed as if they are the original version, bearing the same name.

The Court has repeatedly stated that consumer tastes in the different Member States will evolve over time, and that consumer habits should not be crystallised by national laws that inhibit free movement in any way. The common market will create a standardised consumer. This is despite the fact that the evidence suggests that the more food markets are globalised, the more consumers revert to the 'country of origin effect'—preferring domestically produced goods over imported ones.

Of most concern is the fact that EU rules on free movement, despite the existence of an explicit Treaty provision allowing Member States to take action to protect human health, effectively bar Member States from intervening in human habits that are contributing to the obesity crisis. It is only where a clear danger to human health exists, posed by disease or contamination, that Member States may use this exception to justify national measures that impede free movement. Where Community rules exist, such as those on nutrition labelling, Member States cannot take their own interventionist action to protect this 'average consumer' from himself or herself. Conversely, the Member States have more control over the type of measures that they can adopt in the interests of health protection where the EU has failed to introduce related harmonising measures.

The shortcomings of this situation have been recognised by the Community institutions. Nevertheless, the decision has been taken to rely on this jurisprudence to facilitate free movement through the principle of mutual recognition, rather than to develop common food standards, setting minimum compositional requirements across the EU which would increase consumer protection and quality levels, and enhance human health and free movement. It is claimed that the approach advocated here would put food production in a legislative straitjacket. This does not have to be the case. Rather than setting detailed compositional standards for all foodstuffs, a series of simple minimum requirements for the more common generic foodstuffs could be created—similar to the approach advocated in the Commission Communication on Better Regulation.[165] Requiring that meat products contain meat, milk contains milk and alcoholic drinks contain alcohol should not prove overly-inhibitive to food industry innovators.

The European Union is able to address all these shortcomings by modifying some existing rules, and by applying others properly. For example, Regulation 2826/2000 enables the Community to finance, wholly or in part, actions of information and promotion in respect of agricultural and food products and their method of production.[166] This can include public relations work, promotion and advertising which draws attention to intrinsic features and advantages of Community products, in particular the quality and safety of food, specific production methods, nutritional and health value, labelling, high animal welfare standards and respect for the environment.[167] Special provision is also made for raising awareness of Community systems on protected designations of origin and protected geographical indications, organic production and food labelling requirements. In 2002 the Commission introduced more detailed rules for the implementation of this scheme,[168] listing those products that may be subject to the promotion measures, including milk products, quality wines or table wines with a geographical indication and fruit and vegetables, both fresh and processed.[169] Indicative amounts of support that should be made available to finance such campaigns are set at €4 million for protected designations of origin and protected geographical indications and €6 million for each of organic food, milk and milk products, wine and fresh fruit vegetables, with €3 million for processed fruit and vegetables.[170] Support for the promotion of eggs was added to the list in 2004.[171] However, this support was to be aimed at informing consumers how they could decipher the senseless (as far as their worth to consumers is concerned) Community egg code that must appear on all such products since January 2004.[172]

---

[165] Communication from the Commission to the Council and the European Parliament: Better Regulation for Growth and Jobs in the European Union. COM (2005) 97.

[166] Council Regulation (EC) No 2826/2000 of 19 December 2000 on information and promotion actions for agricultural products on the internal market. [2000] OJ L 382/2. Article 1.

[167] Article 2.

[168] Commission Regulation (EC) No 94/2002 of 18 January 2002 laying down detailed rules for applying Council Regulation (EC) No 2826/2000 on information and promotion actions for agricultural products on the internal market. [2002] OJ L 17/20.

[169] *Ibid*, Annex I.

[170] *Ibid*, Annex III.

[171] €3 million of such support for the promotion of eggs for human consumption was set by Commission Regulation (EC) No 185/2004 of 2 February 2004 amending Regulation (EC) No 94/2002 laying down detailed rules for applying Council Regulation (EC) No 2826/2000 on information and promotion actions for agricultural products on the internal market. [2004] OJ L 29/4.

[172] Article 7 of Regulation 1907/1990 as amended by Council Regulation (EC) No 5/2001 of 19 December 2000 amending Regulation (EEC) No 1907/1990 on certain marketing standards for eggs. [2001] OJ L 2/1.

The proper application of, and education about, certification for products of specific character is potentially far more valuable to the EU consumer than the misapplication of the protected geographical indications system ever will be. However, it remains under-used and unheard of by most 'well-informed, observant and circumspect' consumers.

This book has demonstrated that, despite claims to the contrary, consumer protection and human health preservation are not the primary concerns of EU food law. Free movement remains in the top spot. A reconsideration of this approach, enabling full effect to be given to Articles 30, 152 and 153 EC, is now required to preserve the traditional high quality of European foodstuffs, and to address the key safety concerns raised by unwise dietary habits.

Index

Agreement on Agriculture 144–5

BSE crisis 175–95
  beef products 177–8
  impact on EU food law and policy 179–85
  protective measures 178–9
  public anxiety 177
  length of incubation period 176
  origins 175–6
  statistics 176–7
  UK inquiry 177–8
  White Paper on Food Safety. See White Paper
    on Food Safety

Chocolate
  vegetable fat in 94–6
Chocolate debate 7–10
  British chocolate 7–8
  chocolate substitutes 9
  cocoa producing countries, and 9–10
  raw materials 9
Codex Alimentarius 151–72
  accomplishments of 152
  Code of Ethics 156–8
    consumers, and 157
    implementation 158
    purpose of 157
    requirements 157–8
  codes of practice 156
  Commission 152–5
    operation of 152–5
    procedure manual 153–4
    purpose 153
    rules of procedure 153
    subsidiary bodies 154–5
  committees 154–5
  commodity committees 155
  consumer protection, and 172
  co-ordinating committees 155
  Court of Justice case law 171–2
  dietary claims 162–7
    misleading 166–7
  fair trading, and 172
  food labelling standards 158–62
    aims of 158
    date of minimum durability 161
    food name 159
    list of ingredients 159–60
    net contents 160–61
  foodstuff specific standards 170–71

historical development 151–2
horizontal standards 154
importance of 151
nutrition claims 163
nutrition labelling 162–7
  misleading claims 166–7
  procedures 162
  supplementary 162–3
organic production 167–70
  certification systems 170
  inspection systems 170
  labelling requirements 167–70
  livestock management 169–70
  organic farm system 168
  production requirements 169
relationship with EU food law 171–2
relevance of 151
role of standards in international trade
    regulation 172
special dietary uses 164–5
special medical purposes 165–6
standardisation 151–2
standards 155–71
  specification of minimum quality levels 156
vertical standards 154
Common Agricultural Policy 56
  Community, role of 56
  justification for national rules contrary to
    Article 28 56
Communication on free movement of food
    74–7
  importance of foodstuffs sector 74
  key features of Community food law
    framework 76–7
  legislation 74–5
  mutual recognition of use of additives 76
  recognised principles, and 75
  trade descriptions 75
Community food safety legislation 203–10
  contaminants in food 205–06
    minimum acceptable levels 205–6
  hygienic production methods 207–10
    HACCP principles 208–9
    standardised rules 207–8
    transportation rules 209–10
  irradiated foods 206–7
    conditions for authorising 207
  materials coming into contact with foodstuffs
    203–5
    general criteria 204–5

Community legislation on foodstuffs 68–74
   Commission, and 69, 70
   completing the internal market 68–74
   compositional rules 73
   consumer protection 72–3
   Council, and 69
   fair trading 73
   food labelling rules 72–3
   harmonisation programme 70
   public health protection 71–2
   purpose of 71
Consumer lobbying
   effect of 274–5
Contemporary considerations 241–77

Dassonville 20–22
   designation of origin, and 22
   Directive 1970/50, and 21–2
   facts 21
   national rules, and 21
   protection of consumers 21
Date of minimum durability 89–90
   'use by' date 90
Designation of origin 102–22. *See also*
     Geographical indications
   application for registration 104–5
   eligibility 104
   importance of 106–7
   meaning 103
   Regulation 510/2006 107–8
   third countries 105–6

Ensuring compliance with EU food law 10–11
   'feed law' 10–11
   meaning 11
Ethical food production 264–74
   animal welfare standards 265
   calves, protection of 265–6
   eggs 266–73
     additional labelling requirements 269–70
     consumer protection 267–71
     egg products, meaning 271–2
     'free range' 267, 269
     hygiene standards 271–3
     labelling descriptions 266
     legislative measures 268
     marketing standards 267–8
     Regulation 2295/2003 268–9
     secondary legislation 270–71
     welfare standards 267–71
   pigs, protection of 265–6
   poultry production 273–4
     free range 273–4
EU nutrition policy 237–9
   Green Paper 238–9
     legislative intervention 239
     obesity 238–9
     'supporting environment' 239

European Food Safety Authority 185–95
   advisory forum 190
   crisis management 192–5
     crisis unit 194
   emergencies 192–5
     measures 193–4
   establishment 188–9
   executive director 190
   functioning 188–9
   general tasks 187
   independence and transparency in decision-
     making 192
   key elements 187
   management board 189–90
   mission 188–9
   persistent problems 195
   rapid alert system 192–5
     notifications 193
   Regulation 178/2002 187–9
   risk analysis 186
   risk management 186
   scientific committee 190–91
   scientific opinions, and 191–2
   scientific panels 190–91
   structure 189–91
   terms of reference 188

Feta cheese cases 108–19
   certificates of specific character 117–19
   characteristics of feta 113
   conditions for regulation, and 110, 112–13
   Danish feta 114
   Eurobarometer poll 109
   Greek national law 113
   issues 108–9
   manufacturing process 112
   nature of generic food names 108–9
     factors 110–11
     narrowing of definition 115
   production of variants 115
   registration system, and 116
   reinstatement of feta on register 111
   relevant Community legislation 114–15
Food additives 210–19
   banning
     free movement, and 212–15
   citric acid 213
   cochineal 213–14
   colours 217–19
   Directive 1989/107 215–16
     approval 216
     general criteria 216
     observations 216
     scope 215
   flavourings 218–19
   indigotin 213–14
   Italian law 211–12
   lactic acid 213

meaning 215
nisin 212
products imported from another Member
   State 214–15
rules
   free movement, and 211–15
sorbic acid 212–13
sweeteners 217–19
Food labelling 77–90
compulsory indications 79
date of mimimum durability 89–90
   exclusions 89–90
   'use by' date 90
Directive 1979/112 78–9
Directive 2000/13 79–80
framework legislation 78–80
interests in relation to 77–8
labelling, meaning 79–80
language 80–3
   provision of information to consumer 81–3
   ultimate consumer, and 81
   well known product 82
listing ingredients 83–7
   additives 84–5
   categories 85
   compound ingredient 83–4
   exceeding requirements 86
   fair trading, and 86
   form 85
   ingredients, meaning 83
   quantitative ingredient declarations 87
net quantity 87–9
prepackaged food 88–9
two or more individual prepackaged items
   88
Food labelling rules
development of 72–3
Food names 90–112
community names 91
'eurofoods' 91
generic names 91–92
   restrictions of use 92
'geographical' names 92–3
protected geographical indications and
   designations of origin 102–22. *See also*
   Designations of origin; Geographical
   indications
recipe laws. *See* Recipe laws
sales name 90–91
test of difference 275
Food quality 122–30
butter 127–9
   meaning 127
legislation 123–30
margarine 127
   meaning 127
milk 126
   meaning 126

milk products 126
   meaning 126
minced meat 129–30
   meaning 129
natural mineral water 123–6
   constituents 125–6
   labelling 124
   meaning 123–4
   properties favourable to health 125
   requirements 125
spreadable fats 127–8
   labelling information 127
structure of law and policy of European
   Union, and 1–2
Food safety 175–219
BSE crisis 175–95. *See also* BSE crisis
Community legislation. *See* Community food
   safety legislation
emphasis on 14–15
European Food Safety Authority. *See*
   European Food Safety Authority
importance of 1
media scares 175
powers of Community institutions 219
precautionary principle 195–203
   Community institutions 210–3
   environmental law 195–6
   evidence requirements 198–200
   legislative support 196–8
   risk management, and 198–200
   scientific advice 201–3
   scientific assessment of risk 200
   scientific substantiation 198–9
White Paper. *See* White Paper on Food Safety
Free movement of food in the EU 17–65
alteration of labels, and 24
Article 25 18, 57–64
Article 28 17, 19–56
   approximation of laws, and 26
   feta cheese 27
   intra-Community aspect 25–6
   Mathot 25
   principles on ensuring compliance 28–9
   protection of consumers, and 27–8
   shape of packaging 28
   varieties of product 26–7
   wine vinegar 26–7
Article 90 17–18, 57–9
Cassis 17, 22–9
Common Agricultural Policy 56
different products, same name 34–41
   clear labelling 36–7
   consumer protection arguments 36
   human health, and 41
   labelling disclosures 40
   levels of difference 40–41
   lower priced substitutes 37
   meat product 39–40

Free movement of food in the EU (*cont.*):
   different products, same name (*cont.*):
      milk consumption 37–8
      milk substitutes 36–9
      minimum fat content of cheese 39
      mutual recognition 41
      pasta ingredients 34–6
      proportionality 38–9
   effect of 275–7
   harmonisation programme 18–19
   human health protection, and 18–19, 65
   information on labelling 65
   measures equivalent to quantitative
      restrictions 17, 19–56
      Cassis 22–3
      Dassonville 20–22. *See also Dassonville*
   Directive 1970/50 19–20
      examples 20
      French rules on freezing yoghurt 41–3
      indistinctly applicable rules 22–3
   national authorisation procedures
      49–55
      burden of proof 50
      conditions justifying 51–52
      consumer protection 55
      discretion of Member States 51
      foodstuffs containing non-authorised
         chemical products 50–51
      French legislation 52–53
      genuine risk to human health 51
      German beer purity rules 55
      procedure 51–2
      public health grounds 53–4
      risk assessment 51–2, 53–4
      sports foodstuffs 50
      vitamin-enriched foods 54
   national quality requirements 29–34
      alcohol content 30–31
      Dutch cheese 29–30
      German beer quality rules 33–4
      harmonisation, and 32
      jenever 30–31
      Kaas 29–30
      marketing advantage 29–30
      standards properly upheld 32
   new rules on health and nutrition claims
      18–19, 226–32
   obesity crisis, and 275
   post-*Cassis* 23–9
   principles 11–12, 15
   protecting human health under Article 30 EC
      45–9. *See also* protecting human health
      under Article 30 EC
   safeguarding consumer interests, and 65
   substantial difference between food products
      41–4
      consumer expectation 43
      foie gras 44

French rules on deep-freezing of yoghurt
      41–3
      mandatory requirement exception 41–3
      minimum fat content of cheese 43
      mutual recognition of generic names 44
      trade impediment 42
   taxation 57–64
      compatibility with Article 90 57–64
      competitive products 58
      consumer preferences, and 57–8
      different rates of tax 57–8
      inspection of products 60–63
      internal taxation on imported foodstuffs
         57–9
      Italian charge on banana consumption 59
      measures equivalent to customs duties
         60–64
         authorisation costs 63–4
         charges for inspecting imported poultry
            meat 61
         dilemma of Member State 63
         veterinary inspection charges 60–61,
            61–2
      unfair charge 58–9
   unjustifiable national compositional
      requirements 23–4
Fruit juices
   concentrates 97–8
   meaning 98

Genetic modification 241–54
   challenging regulatory framework 251–4
   Deliberate Release Directive 246–7
      compulsory notification procedure 246–7
   environmental concerns 242
   Genetically Modified Food and Feed
      Regulation 247–50
      authorisation procedure 247–50
   genetically modified food 15
   genetically modified organisms, meaning
      241–2
   human health, and 242–3
   Labelling and Traceability Regulation 250–51
      labelling requirements 251
      traceability requirements 250
   labelling difficulties 251–4
      new regulatory regime 254
      soya and maize products 252–3
   legal framework 243–54
   Novel Foods Regulation 244–5
      labelling requirements 245
      safeguard clause 245
   organic food, and. *See* Organic food
   regulatory framework 243–54
Geographical indications 102–22. *See also*
      Designations of origin
   application for registration 104–5
   certificates of specific character 117–19

feta, and 117–18
  national laws, and 118
  compatibility of protecting names with Article
    28 121–2
  eligibility 104
  fair and traditional use by third parties 122
  feta cheese cases. *See* Feta cheese cases
  importance of 106–7
  meaning 103
  pasta 115–16
  protection for geographical names under
    Regulation 510/2006 119–21
  epoisses de bourgogne 120–21
  'evocation' 120
  Gorgonzola 119–20
  parma ham 120
  Regulation 510/2006 107–8
  third countries 105–6
  TRIPs Agreement. *See* TRIPs Agreement

Globalisation
  effect 2, 275

HACCP principles 208–9
Harmonising food standards in the EU
    67–131
  Cassis, before 67–8
  Community legislation on foodstuffs. *See*
    Community legislation on foodstuffs
  Communication on free movement of food.
    See Communication on free movement
    of food
  food labelling 77–90. *See also* Food labelling
  food names 90–122. *See also* Food names
  food quality. *See* Food quality
  free movement, and 130–31
Historical development of food law 2–5
  Adulteration of Food or Drink Act 1860 3
  early UK statutes 3
  early writings 2–3
  EC Treaty, and 5
  nineteenth century 3–4
  recipe laws 4–5
Honey 99–101
  Codex Alimentarius 101
  compositional criteria 100
  country of origin 100
  meaning 99
  monitoring procedure 100
  types 99

Importance of food sector in EU 5–11
  chocolate debate. *See* Chocolate debate
  statistics 5–6
  trade in food as major political issue 6
Ingredients
  listing. *See* Food labelling
  meaning 83

Innovation in food production 241–54. *See also*
  Genetic modification
Instant coffee
  meaning 96
International influences 133–73
  persuasive authority 172–3
  WTO Agreements 133–45. *See also* WTO
    Agreements
International trade
  rules governing 13–14

Jams
  recipe laws 101–2

Labelling
  meaning 79–80

Mutual recognition
  principle of 1, 12

Nutrition labelling 225–6
  meaning 225
Nutrition law and policy 221–40
  authorisation procedure 230–32
    Community register 231–2
    modifications 231
    opinion of EFSA 230–31
  Commission, and 223
  Community legislation 225–33
  EU nutrition policy 237–9. *See also* EU
    nutrition policy
  focus of European food law, and 221–2
  folic acid fortification 235–7
    Ireland 236–7
  food supplements 232–3
    labelling 232
    meaning 233
  forms 225–6
  free movement, and 234–9
  health claims 226–32
  key provisions of nutrition and health claims
    legislation 228–30
    beneficial nutritional or physiological effect
      229
    categories of nutrition claims 230
    nutrition claim, meaning 228
    nutrient profiles 228–9
  Member State autonomy in health protection
    measures 237
  Member States, in 234–7
  obesity, and 224, 239–40
  priorities of consumers, and 223–4
  Regulation on Nutrition and Health Claims
    226–8
    background 226–8
    guidelines at international levels, and
      227
  technological innovation, and 227

Nutrition law and policy (*cont.*):
UK White Paper on Public Health. *See* UK
White Paper on Public Health

Organic food 15, 254–64
demand for 254–64
farm rules 255–6
future regulation of production 263–4
genetic modifications, and 260–63
coexistence 262–3
consumer protection, and 260–61
economic aspects 262
general principles 262–3
national strategies 263
livestock production 256–60
force feeding 257
housing conditions 259
poultry 259–60
prevention of disease 257–8
rearing standards 257
reproduction 258–9
slaughter 259
stocking density levels 259
production rules 255–6
statistics 254

Prepackaged
meaning 88–9
Protecting human health under Article 30 EC
45–9
additives in food 47–8
ban on marketing of meat products 45–6
bread with high salt content 46–7
clear danger 49
exceptions to Article 28 45–9
German beer purity rules 47–8
marketing of milk substitutes 48–9
pasta ingredients 49
proteins in meat 45–6

Quantitative ingredient declarations 87

Recipe laws 93–102
chicory 90–97
chocolate 94–6
cocoa 94–6
coffee 96–7
decaffeinated 96
instant 96
fruit juices 97–8
honey. *See* Honey
jams 101–2

Regulating the food industry 1–15

Secondary legislation 13
SPS Agreement 138–42
'measures' 139

adapted to characteristics of area 141
appropriate assessment of risks 140
decisions on appropriate level of protection
140
international standards, and 139
potential impact on EU food law and policy
141–2
sanitary or phytosanitary measures, meaning
138
scope 138–9

Taxation
free movement of food, and. *See* Free
movement of food in the EU
TBT Agreement 142–4
committee on technical barriers to trade 144
technical regulations 142–4
Code of Good Practice 143–4
international standards, and 142–3
meaning 142
TRIPs Agreement 134–8
aim 135–6
geographical indications 136–8
exceptions 137
wine and spirits 136–7

UK White Paper on Public Health 234–5
signpost labelling system 234–5
voluntary nature of 235

White Paper on Food Safety 179–85
animal health and welfare 182–3
controls over operation of EU legislation
184–5
creation of set of food safety rules 181–2
emergency measures 183–4
EU policy on food safety 179–80
'farm to fork' approach 182
guiding principle 180–81
internal market, role of 180
organization of food safety 180
origin 179
regulatory aspects 181–2
timetable for action 180
World Trade Organization 133–50
dispute settlement 145–9
appeals 148
arbitration 149
complaint 146
covered agreements 146
draft report 147–8
GATT, and 145
panels 147
prompt compliance with recommendations
or rulings 148–9
effect of rules on EU food law 149–50
precautionary principle, and 50
protection of geographical food names 150

negotiating forum, as 134
WTO Agreements 133–45
  Agreement on Agriculture 144–5
    EU food law, and 135–45
    global free trade, and 133–45

SPS Agreement. *See* SPS Agreement
TBT Agreement 142–4. *See also* TBT
  Agreement
TRIPs Agreement 134–8. *See also* TRIPs
  Agreement

Lightning Source UK Ltd.
Milton Keynes UK
UKOW020022250112

185992UK00001B/29/P